Of Love & Dragons

Short Stories

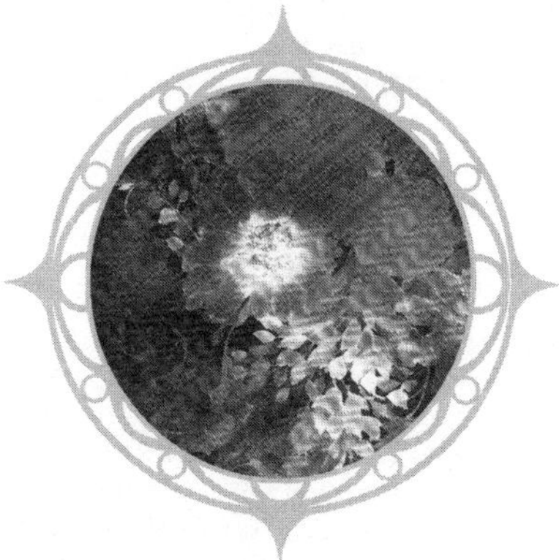

This is a FLAME TREE Book

Special thanks to Tim Leng

FLAME TREE PUBLISHING
6 Melbray Mews, Fulham,
London SW6 3NS, United Kingdom
www.flametreepublishing.com

First published 2026

26 28 30 29 27
1 3 5 7 9 10 8 6 4 2

Hardback ISBN: 978-1-83562-781-5
Special ISBN: 978-1-83562-933-8
ebook ISBN: 978-1-83562-783-9

The cover image is created by Flame Tree Studio from sketches and layered files, new photos and stock images from Shutterstock combined and crafted in Photoshop. No AI, AGI or LLM was used in this process. The cover features specially commissioned artwork © 2025 Xinyue Chen. Shutterstock elements are courtesy of Innoria, Oniks Astarit and Apostrophe. The internal illustrations are © the respective creators – see the back of the book for further information on the artists.

A copy of the CIP data for this book is available from the British Library.

Printed and bound in China

Represented in the EU for product safety and compliance by
Authorised Rep Compliance Ltd, Ground Floor,
71 Lower Baggot Street, Dublin, D02 P593, Ireland.
Contact at www.arccompliance.com

MIX
Paper | Supporting responsible forestry
FSC™ C005748
www.fsc.org

Of Love & Dragons

Short Stories

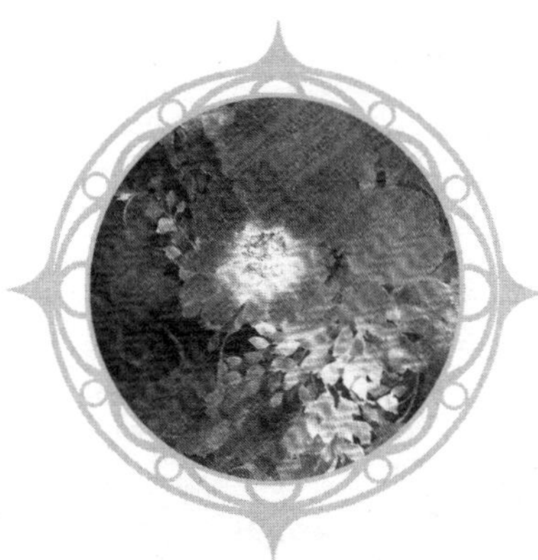

Romantic Fantasy

FLAME TREE
PUBLISHING

Contents

Foreword

Caren Hahn

Move over, Smaug; there's a new kind of dragon story in town.

When *Fourth Wing* by Rebecca Yarros burst onto the book scene in 2023, it dominated the *New York Times* Bestseller chart, spending eighteen weeks in the top spot. The epic fantasy novel written by an established romance author took social media by storm, with related hashtags being viewed over a billion times. Non-fantasy readers gushed on social media, surprised by how much they enjoyed a genre they usually avoided. Many of them wondered, what else had they been missing?

The Queens of Romantic Dragon Fantasy

Long-time fantasy readers know that *Fourth Wing* was hardly the first dragon fantasy series to captivate readers, nor was it the first one penned by a woman. Anne McCaffrey's *Dragonflight* – the first book in her iconic *Dragonriders of Pern* series – was published half a century earlier in 1968, and readers today are still falling in love with Lessa and F'lar's story.

Unlike J.R.R. Tolkien's Smaug, McCaffrey's dragons coexisted with humans, bonding with them as essential companions who exhibited noble traits such as loyalty and cooperation – characteristics which continue to inform dragon fiction today.

My own introduction to dragon fantasy was Robin McKinley's *The Hero and the Crown*, an epic tale featuring a princess who trades her silks for leather and armor in her quest to rid the kingdom of the last of the great dragons. As a ten-year-old devouring Aerin's story, I was inspired by a female warrior who faced insurmountable odds to save her people. I thrilled at the descriptions of the dragon Maur, and lingered over the faint traces of romance, wishing for more.

Of course, McKinley wasn't the only female author writing romantic dragon sagas years before Yarros. Consider the body of work produced by Robin Hobb, Naomi Novik, and Tamora Pierce, and it's clear that Yarros was building off a well-established foundation.

Fourth Wing didn't come out of nowhere. It was the next step in a long evolution of women-driven fantasy that female authors had shaped for decades.

Romantasy Takes Flight

So what made *Fourth Wing* resonate with readers in such a meaningful way?

To understand this, we have to look at the power of merging two of the most popular genres in contemporary fiction – romance and fantasy – to form an entirely new subgenre: romantic fantasy, or romantasy. Amplified by BookTok reader communities, this genre has exploded in popularity and forced everyone in the book industry, from indie authors to major publishing houses, to take notice.

It's not because romance itself is new to fantasy. Fantasy works written by women and men alike have long been infused with romance, but it's typically been limited to subplots threaded through storylines that increase character depth and inform the plot in nuanced ways.

Romantasy, on the other hand, doesn't take the subtle approach. Romantasy unapologetically centers romance, with the plot serving the purposes of the love story rather than the other way around. As a result, romantasy stories are accessible to readers who might otherwise be intimidated by encyclopedic worldbuilding, dense casts of characters, or complex magic systems.

But to highlight only the romantic component misses a crucial aspect of this genre's contribution to today's literary scene. Romantasy began by elevating the female experience in a way that's often missing in traditional fantasy, and has since expanded to include genders and romantic pairings across the spectrum. By focusing on emotion and relationships, these stories transform even the biggest conflicts by making them deeply personal. Indeed, romantasy makes the bold claim that a character's inner world can generate stakes that are as high as any epic battle or world-ending threat.

I can't think of any mythical creature better suited to symbolize this tension than a dragon. In the hands of modern romantasy authors, dragons have left the side of archetypal evil – where they've long been relegated in classical literature – to become something more. Rather than limiting hero status to those who slay the dragon, romantasy readers can now see themselves mastering the beast in a very different way.

Perhaps they're taming the dragon.

Perhaps they're forming a partnership with it that gives them power and status.

Perhaps they are the dragon.

Ally. Pet. Friend.

Lover?

In the hands of a romantasy writer, anything can happen.

When the Familiar Becomes New

Of Love and Dragons is a unique contribution to contemporary romantic dragon fantasy, featuring some of today's most popular tropes presented in unexpected ways. Dragons bonding with humans is a beloved motif, but it manifests a little differently each time. An imprint at birth, a trial to prove worthiness, or a blood bond turned into unwilling nuptials – sometimes the bond strengthens both human and dragon, as in Arda Mori's 'Mercury of the Night

Queen'. Other times, such as in Sarah Hozumi's 'The Name', the bond itself becomes the central conflict.

Most of these stories can be read in ten minutes or less, but the emotional depth lingers far longer. In order to draw the reader in quickly, there's no time wasted warming up the story. Instead, more often than not, we're dropped into the middle of a crisis from the first paragraph.

Consider these opening lines from Abigail Kelly's 'Kingkiller':

In her opinion, Catriona's greatest mistake wasn't murdering a king. It was being foolish enough to love one.

We join Catriona's story mere moments after her royal husband's gruesome death by the very trap he'd lain for her. Despite the shocking entrance, Kelly guides us to quickly find our footing, bringing Catriona's predicament alive in a way that feels relatable and makes us cheer for her success. In this and other stories in the anthology, readers slip into the narrative with little resistance, sinking into the tale until they're swallowed whole.

Fresh voices take readers on adventures that juxtapose the familiar and unfamiliar. Medieval settings abound, but so do jasmine-scented, Eastern-inspired gardens (Kevin Potter's 'Heart of Lightning, Blade of Shadow'). A cursed ship sailing a dying ocean forms the backdrop of Georgina Kamsika's 'We Are Not Them', while J.L. Worrad's 'A Matter of Life and Dragons' imagines an archipelago floating in the clouds where WWII-style aircraft battle with fire-breathing dragons.

Old tales are made new again, such as Damien Mckeating's 'Broken Spell and Shattered Glass', a retelling of Sleeping

Beauty featuring a dragon antagonist. Contrast that with Susan Taitel's whimsical 'Lilt and Luster Spring Newsletter', which uses a framework as uncommon as it is delightful, telling the story through a jeweler's newsletter whose marketing copy hints at a malevolent threat and lost love.

Throughout this anthology, dragons appear as both the hunted and the hunter. They're portrayed as pets, mortal enemies, cunning shapeshifters, and noble warriors. Humans are equally varied, rising up as humble goat farmers destined to save the world (Mia K. Rose's 'Hollow'), or celestial beings incarnated in a mortal life they don't understand (Samara Lo's 'A Thousand Lifetimes Between Us'). Royalty and commoner, warrior and thief, outcast and revolutionary – all have their moment to shine.

As you crack open the pages of this anthology, prepare to be swept away by dying worlds and new beginnings, where love can be a healing balm or a galvanizing force. Each story takes us on a journey to discover romance that defies the odds and inspires courage in the face of ultimate sacrifice. With intersecting themes of identity, duty, and desire, these tales explore the elusive and illuminate the unknown – not just the world of the mythical dragon, but the far more complex motives of the human heart.

The Overlooked Dragon Keeper

Charlotte V. Bond

Annalee looked at the naked sheep in front of her and sighed. "How many times have I told you, Farren? You need to leave some of the fleece on. The dragons need the roughage."

"I'm sorry, Keeper, but…" He shifted uncomfortably. "Well, it's winter soon, and the people on the cliff top villages need—"

"Do you think the Dark Lord of Dragons breeds these sheep to give the peasants wool coats?"

"I…no."

"Why does he breed them?"

"For the dragons."

"Exactly. If you keep taking too much wool from them, you'll have to start feeding the dragons cabbages. Do you remember what it's like to feed a dragon cabbages?"

He shuddered. "Yes, Keeper. I'm sorry. I won't do it again."

"Good." Annalee took the scrawny-looking sheep and led it to the hangar cave, where dragons were housed on the ledges, awaiting their tasks, and the wide floor was used as a launchpad. Fyrne Longtail had been out returning Princess Libera to Sheveral and was ravenous, dancing back and forth in anticipation. The sheep were born and raised adjacent to the dragons so that they got used to the smell and didn't panic or fight in their presence.

"Hang on, hang on," Annalee said to the eager dragon. She put on a thin glove and smeared a small amount of ointment from a pot in her pocket on the sheep's jugular. The sedative worked in seconds. One moment the sheep was awake, then asleep, then hopefully it woke up in sheep paradise. Annalee busied herself with oiling Fyrne's wing feathers as the dragon ate.

The Dark Lord of Dragons could move soundlessly but the scent of him – spices, slightly acrid smoke, and juniper – always let her know when he was behind her. As did the stuttering of her heart.

"The new oil working well?" he asked.

"Yes. Very. Far fewer split feathers."

He ran a hand through his soft brown curls, and Annalee worked hard not to gaze at him. "I had time between crafting a deadly paralytic and refining a wight-summoning spell, so I thought it would be helpful."

Annalee's stomach churned as he stood so close to her that their arms touched and his breath brushed her cheek. At least he was oblivious to the effect he had on her. If she were honest, the moments when he stood too close were the best parts of the day, even if they shouldn't be.

"Another princess gone home?" she asked with a brittle smile.

"Yes. Princess Libera was not suitable."

"How many now?"

Galton's forehead dimpled elegantly as he thought. "Twenty-seven."

Twenty-seven times her heart had sunk as a new captured princess arrived, possibly to become the Dark Lady of Dragons; twenty-seven sighs of relief when she'd been taken home again.

"Your mother doesn't give up, does she? What was wrong this time?" She stashed the oil pot back in the bag over her shoulder.

"She picked her teeth."

"We all have to—"

"While she was eating."

"I see."

Fair.

Fyrne turned her head and nudged Galton's shoulder, nearly sending him flying. He rubbed her nose, wearing a fond smile that he never bestowed on any princesses. He might be known throughout the thirty-five kingdoms as the Dark Lord of Dragons, but really, he was just a magician who lived to explore the possibilities of his craft and whose family had bred dragons for generations. Magic infused his life, and he would just as happily make a potion to turn tears to laughter as he would craft an untraceable assassination spell, but no one ever asked him for the former. He was a good man in his way, but people rarely witnessed that side of him. Except Annalee.

Reaching into his pocket, Galton took out the notebook he always carried. "I shall make a note that the oil was—"

His words were cut off by a bellow as loud as a thunderclap. All the other dragons looked to the entrance and Fyrne gave a little huff of excitement. The sky was momentarily blotted out by the wings of a great blue dragon. With grace, style, and a hint of smugness, Byder the Yellow-Eyed landed. All the dragons bowed their heads while Fyrne trotted over to meet her mate.

Galton groaned. "Oh no. Is that—?"

"Lucky number twenty-eight," Annalee said, anxiety tightening her chest.

Guards were already running to help the woman down, a difficult task since she was paying no attention to dismounting but instead was staring purposefully around the chamber. Her gaze fell upon Galton and, when she'd gained the ground, she strode over and said, "You must be the Dark Lord of Dragons."

Galton bowed. "Indeed."

"I demand to know—" she began haughtily and Galton spoke over her.

"Why you were brought here. Yes, I'm sorry but you see—"

"I demand to know," she said more forcefully, "why you have taken twenty-seven other princesses before me."

Oh dear, Annalee thought. *She's one of those.*

Galton recovered quickly and said, "My dragon makes the choices, not me. I cannot leave my Tower of Magic. Gods know what would happen to the spells if they were not properly tended. If you have a complaint, you must take it up with him."

The princess glanced over her shoulder at the dragon that could easily swallow her whole and was giving her a look that said he'd do just that if he got any lip. "Well, I'm here now," she said dismissively.

"Princess Carrielle," said a mellifluous voice.

Everyone turned to see Lady Theliā Boutroux walking across the cavern in a dress of shimmering aqua green, the hem of which was miraculously free of dragon dung. "How delightful to meet you. I'm so pleased that Byder brought you here."

"Lady Boutroux," Carrielle said, dropping into a deep curtsy. The fear and respect that people held for the Dark Lord was nothing to the terror and awe they felt for his mother. An ex-siren who had married and outlived one of the most powerful men in the kingdom and whose soft, melodious voice could convince almost anyone to anything.

"Let us get you to your room," she said. Three guards hurried over and escorted Carrielle away. Annalee felt a vicious glee at seeing how the dragon dung *did* cling to her skirt.

"Congratulations, Mother, Byder," Galton said, returning to his notebook. "Another hideous offering."

"You can't possibly have taken a dislike so quickly," Theliā said archly.

"I can tell at a glance that that woman has not even heard of Marceau's *Flora, Fauna, and Fantasticals*, and if you gave her a crucible, she'd likely try to serve ridiculously small food in it."

I've read that book. And I know how to use a crucible, was what Annalee did not say, however desperately she wanted to.

"Now, I really must go. I'm at a delicate stage of my levitation incantation."

"We have dragons if we want to fly," Theliā called after her son, but he was already walking away, his gaze on his notebook.

Theliā gave her son a long, considering look then turned to Annalee and announced, "Keeper, you will be joining us for dinner tonight."

"I…what? Why?"

"We are running out of princesses. We cannot keep sending them back. He needs to pick one. And, as much as it irks me to say so, it appears you and he share a kind of honest frankness. He listens to you. So, come to dinner, tell him how advantageous the match will be, and let's get this done."

"What if I don't think it would be advantageous?" Annalee challenged. It pained her enough to watch this parade of potential brides, but to be forced to recommend that obnoxious doxy as her mistress was too much.

Theliā smiled and took a step closer. "I'm sure you agree that the match is in everyone's interest."

The magic hit Annalee's brain like a surge of alcohol, making her dizzy, pliable. But like a surge, it swept over her and away. She folded her arms and glared at Theliā.

"Your siren song doesn't work on me, my lady. Lord Galton gave me drops to put in my ears."

"Did he now?" Rather than annoyance, Theliā's face wore a small smile. "Well, if you won't take my word for it, know it was Byder's idea."

The dragon gave a proud puff of smoke. Annalee would give anything to speak with dragons as Theliā did, rather than just trying to read their body language.

"I know you respect the beasts more than me, so perhaps you'll do it for him."

For all her backchat, Annalee knew she couldn't refuse a direct order from the Lady Theliā, her mistress. "And what will you be serving at this dinner?" she asked haughtily.

Theliā's gaze turned cold. "Roasted impudence with an accompaniment of cheeky bitch." They held eye contact. The posturing was over. Annalee gave a slight nod. "Excellent. I'll have a dress ready for you," Theliā called over her shoulder as she swept away.

Annalee had to resist the urge to pick up a dung ball and throw it at her departing back, to see whether that would leave no mark on the enchanted dress either.

* * *

As promised, an outfit was waiting on Annalee's bed at the

end of her shift, and a bathtub was set by the fire with a whole cart of soaps, shampoos, and scrubs. A note in Theliā's curved handwriting advised: *Use them all.*

"Now who's a cheeky bitch?" Annalee groused, but she knew that the aroma of dragons saturated anyone who dealt with them as much as she did. She dutifully scrubbed and soaped.

The outfit was technically a top and trousers, showing an unexpected sensitivity on Theliā's part (Annalee hadn't worn a dress since she was old enough to undo buttons) but the material was so loose and billowing that they looked almost identical to an ankle-length skirt when she stood still.

Theliā was waiting for her in the corridor leading to the dining room. "Making sure I turned up?" Annalee said archly.

"Oh, no. I have guards for that. I merely wanted to inspect you before we go in. You seem acceptable enough."

Annalee bit back a retort. She'd seen herself in the mirror and she was more than acceptable; she was in the realms of pretty, perhaps even heading towards stunning. She looked nothing like her usual dishevelled self. Still, to comment on her appearance would be playing right into the hands of a woman who descended on a king's court now and then to show off her gowns in full knowledge that less than a moonspan later, the company that made her dresses (which she owned) would be inundated with orders.

As they walked the corridors in silence, a jackdaw flew from its perch on a stag's head and landed on Theliā's shoulder. It cawed in a most put-out manner.

"Is that another lover?" Annalee asked tartly. Theliā was renowned for taking lovers, getting bored of them, then turning them into jackdaws.

"He was a herald, come with a message," Theliā said with a hint of annoyance.

Their footsteps rang on the flagstones. Annalee did not take her eyes from her companion, who glanced at her then admitted, "And an ex-lover. *Ex*-lover. I only turn *ex*-lovers into jackdaws. I'm not wasteful, you know."

"That is certainly something people cannot say about you," Annalee said solemnly.

It was a reckless, stupid thing to say to a woman who was powerful and fickle, but every step closer to that dining room made the anxiety twist even tighter inside her. How could she sit there and try to encourage the man she loved to marry someone else?

This is ridiculous. I can't do it. She can dismiss me or banish me if she wants. Although she can't, because no one is as good with dragons as I am. But being banished would be better than smiling and lying and choking on fine food as I… No. I'm not doing this.

She'd stopped before the dining room doors, ready to turn back, but then Theliā was in front of her. Smiling. With apparent genuineness, which was startling by itself.

"You know I do so *love* our chats, Annalee. I feel like no one sees me as you do. Certainly no one *speaks* to me as you do. Conversations with you are so refreshing. I can just tell you're going to be an asset tonight in helping my son choose his bride. Now, come along, or the roast impudence will get cold."

And the doors were opening, and she was being led (tugged) inside, and it was too late to turn back.

Her agonies were almost wiped away by the look on Galton's face when he saw her. She was used to a companionable smile or a thoughtful frown upon meeting. Never had she seen a look of shock (and was that a little bit of awe? Probably too much to hope for) on his face.

"Well," was all he said, looking her up and down. "Well."

Then Princess Carrielle was there, wearing a silver gown that clung in all the right places. A diamond necklace encircled her delicate throat and a ruby tiara adorned her perfectly coiffed hair. A moment ago, Annalee considered she looked just the part for a grand dinner. Now, she felt she might as well have come in her dragon-feeding leather jerkin and breeches. No one could look anything other than inferior beside such beauty. It was most disheartening.

* * *

Annalee tried to be positive, she really did. When she found that Carrielle would snipe at everything she said, evidently someone who raised herself up by putting others down, Annalee resorted to merely looking like she was listening intently, laughing in what she hoped were the right places, and saying, "Gosh, that's interesting," to even the most vacuous things the princess said. At one point, she beamed at Galton, and his look said: *Really*?

The food was delicious. Crisp toast with smooth pâté; succulent pheasant; vegetables she didn't recognise; and a rainbow platter of sweet confections. But as the evening wore on, Annalee got more and more despondent at the thought that this petty, self-obsessed woman might be her mistress, and her tongue started to run away from her.

It began when Carrielle addressed a subject that had clearly been bothering her. "So, you are a Dark *Lord*, yes?"

"I prefer mage. Dark if you must."

"Yes, but what I mean," said Carrielle, leaning towards him, elbows on the table (nobody should have beautiful elbows, it was just unfair), "is that I need to marry a title. I'm a princess. My family have been rulers of Hevisten for ten generations. A newly acquired title would be fine, so long as it was attached to a man with ambition."

"Oh, if it's a title you're looking for," Annalee said, "then Padhra Kru should be perfectly acceptable to you. And trust me, he wishes to rise as high as he can."

"Oh, really?" Carrielle took a genuine interest in her for the first time all night. "And what is his title?"

"He's—"

"He's not so grand as a lord," Theliā cut in, "and even if his title was acceptable to you," – a glare at Annalee – "the poor man has the largest boil on his neck that you've ever seen."

"Ah," said Carrielle, turning her attention to the strawberry soufflé before her.

That wasn't, of course, what Annalee was going to say. She'd been about to name him as Padhra Kru, Most Vaunted of the Shit Shovellers, a title bestowed on him for being the most arrogant Keeper's assistant. But perhaps it was best she hadn't.

Galton had his head down; she thought she saw a small smile but she must have been mistaken because when he looked up again, his expression was one of polite neutrality.

* * *

"Gods, but that was exhausting," Annalee announced to the empty room.

The castle had so many rooms, she couldn't remember the name of this one, but it was something like the Third Best Drawing Room in the East Wing. Galton, Theliā and Carrielle were all in the Superior White Drawing Room, drinking dessert wine and talking about whatever the ruling classes talked about.

Annalee had excused herself, intending to go to bed in the hope that sleep would obliviate the memories of this evening, if only for a few hours. But Theliā had taken her aside and whispered, "Do not go far in case we need you. And don't give me that look. The servants have been instructed to treat you as a royal guest, so you can order what you like to keep you awake and entertained."

So Annalee had done just that, and now had a glass of best port and a platter of butterscotch tarts next to her, happy in the knowledge that she didn't have to share them or have her delicacies soured by that idiot woman's banal conversation.

As she reached for another tart, her eye fell on a book sitting on the arm of the chair next to her. It was one of Galton's notebooks. Intrigued, she glanced at the door.

He never said it was secret. Just because I've never seen inside and he's never offered to show me doesn't mean I'm not allowed to look. It's right there where any servant or cleaner or guest could look inside it. And I've read The Emotions and Mechanics of Sorcery and Chromancy: Dangers and Safeguards, *so I'd appreciate it more than they ever would.*

Annalee had read those books in an attempt to find something to talk to Galton about. And they had talked about the contents, but Galton's initial excitement at finding a fellow enthusiast soon faded to the humdrum normalcy of conversation.

Satisfied with her logic and unshakeable in her belief that she was owed something in repayment for tonight's misery, Annalee picked up the book and started to read.

It was fascinating. Thanks to her nightly reading and her knowledge of dragons, she understood notes like why bones had to be boiled in rosemary before using and what to do if a dragon made eye contact with you. After she'd worked her way through almost a third of the written notes, digesting each page carefully, she noticed that the pages at the back were dog-eared. Curious, she turned to the last page and stared dumbfounded at the wealth of drawings. A diagram of a dissected nightshade berry; an illustration of a dragon's claw that was twisted and flaking with water rot; symbols to invoke protection from night-hags. And then there was her face. He'd drawn her. She was looking slightly off-centre, and she imagined him sketching her when she was looking at a dragon and talking about their eating habits or a mating flight.

She turned the page. Phases of the moon and their magical significance. A diagram of a summoning candle. Then her again, this time in profile, and another of her with her head tilted up and her eyes closed, as if she was basking in warm sunshine.

Each page had a few more drawings of her until sketches of her took up nearly half of each page.

The smell of spices, smoke, and juniper crept over her before he spoke. "Ah. I see you've found my notebook. You must forgive a mage his idle daydreams."

Annalee shot to her feet then had to grab the arm of the chair to steady herself against a wave of dizziness. "You… drew all of these? Of me?"

"Some from life. Some from memory," he said with an apologetic shrug. The polite neutrality of the dinner table was gone; his expression was shy, his stance awkward.

"I fear you might feel that I've overlooked you at times, both as a companion and a woman. But please know that you occupy my thoughts regularly. With your knowledge of dragons and your surprising grasp of dark magic through self-study, you deserve more praise, greater recognition—"

"Higher wages," she cut in. It was a banal thing to say, but his words were too much praise and she had to break them up before they overwhelmed her. If she got too lightheaded and fell down in a swoon, it would be highly embarrassing and send entirely the wrong message.

"Wages. Yes. Of course. I will see to it in the morning. Only..." He took a step forward, reached out, his hand hovering over hers in a moment of hesitation before he took it. A shiver ran down her spine at being touched so tenderly by him. "I thought, perhaps, there could be other methods of recognition. You see, while pretty dresses and witticisms don't really catch my eye, when I listened to you talk about dragonalia or the arcane arts, I felt as if I'd found a kindred spirit. Over the months, conversing with you, I began to see you in a whole new light, even though I found myself incapable of doing anything about it beyond perhaps finding reasons to visit the hangar more often than was strictly required, and standing a little closer to you than necessary so that our sleeves brushed occasionally. But when you recited Tarquin's *Volatile Runes* at the dinner table, I found myself watching your lips and thinking how much I wanted to kiss you."

In that moment, everything was too much: the fire was too hot on her skin; the feel of the silken top on her shoulders and back was too tight; the grip of his hand on hers was both too hard and not strong enough; the scent of him filled her world.

"Why don't you then?" she asked, her voice hoarse.

"Why don't I what?"

"Kiss me."

His cheeks coloured and he glanced down – that shyness again that she hadn't thought him capable of. "Well, you're not reciting Tarquin."

Annalee took a deep breath. "Those wanting to cast runes for knowledge should be wary that—"

Suddenly he wasn't close to her – he was pressed against her. His hands were in her hair, his lips were on hers, and she forgot all about dragons and princesses and sirens and magic, and lived only in that blissful moment.

* * *

Annalee woke first to euphoric happiness within the arms of the Dark Lord of Dragons, and then the doubt crept in.

I'm just a dragon keeper. He's a lord. And a mage. This means nothing. It was a one-off. Why would he be interested in anything beyond this one night when there's a gods-freaking princess a few doors away? What happened was nice...lovely...wonderful, but I can't think that it changes anything.

When Galton awoke a few minutes later, he smiled, drew her close against him, and made love to her again.

Then things did change. He talked not of marriage but of betrothal. Of Beloved status. Of getting used to each other and this new thing between them in a slow and careful manner. It sounded both wonderful and terrifying.

Later, walking through the castle corridors, Annalee felt a strange sense of detachment, as if she were out of step with reality. Yes, these walls and floors and tapestries and doors were familiar, but they weren't the same as yesterday, surely? Or was it she who had changed? Or had nothing changed and she was just being fanciful? It was so confusing.

"Excuse me, my lady, but can I help you?"

It took Annalee a moment to realise the maid had been addressing her. Maids never addressed her. If they noticed her at all, it was only to frown at her scruffiness or scowl at the boot prints she was leaving on their clean floors.

Oh. I'm still in yesterday's clothes. She's mistaken me for a noble guest or something.

"No, I'm… I'm the dragon keeper."

"Yes, m'lady. I know. They serve breakfast in the Second Smallest Dining Room, but I'm afraid it's all cleared away now. I can bring a tray to your room?"

"No, I, er, have an apple there. I'll just eat that."

"Very good, m'lady."

Utterly confused, Annalee hurried to her chambers and quickly changed. She felt a hundred times better in her normal clothes, and the excited churning in her stomach had settled enough for her to eat the apple too.

Yet by the time she was halfway down the corridor, she slowed and stopped. Galton said he loved her and that he hoped she would one day be the next Dark Lady. But what did that *mean*? What did a Dark Lady *do*? What did a Beloved do? Did she have to start thinking of dresses? Etiquette? Should she stop singing the bawdy ballads she and the other keepers liked to belt out in the hangar and instead sing something…

more refined? Who'd look after the dragons once she was a Lady?

The dragons. There was something solid and familiar. She headed for the hangar and, as she crossed the floor, Fyrne raised her head and gave a little chitter of greeting, fluffing her wings up.

"Late to work, aren't we?" said a voice at her side.

Theliā had appeared from nowhere and fallen into step with her. Annalee's stomach jolted as a new thought occurred to her: they'd have to tell Theliā that Annalee was Galton's Beloved now.

Oh gods. How's that going to go?

"A little. Maybe," Annalee said defiantly. She frowned, doing a head count. "Where's Byder?"

"Oh, he's taken Carrielle back. Frightful woman. I'm so pleased we don't need her anymore."

Annalee looked at her in astonishment. "What do you mean you don't need her anymore?"

"She was never going to be a bride. She was always just a means to an end," Theliā went on, stroking Fyrne's feathers. "It really was Byder's idea. I swear those beasts understand humans better than other humans. I just needed to get the two of you to sit down, to be equals and not surrounded by muck and bones. For all that my son claims clothes and jewels mean nothing, he certainly saw you in a different light in that outfit, didn't he?" Theliā gave her a knowing smile and Annalee felt her cheeks redden.

Well, at least we don't need to tell her if she's already guessed.

"So this was all a set-up then?" Theliã's smug, triumphant smile was answer enough. "Does that mean you approve of me as your son's Beloved?" Annalee asked boldly. "After all, I'm not a princess. Or a duchess. Or any noble at all."

"Such matters are unimportant in true love, don't you think? But if it bothers you, it can be easily settled. Fyrne." Theliã held out her hand, and Fyrne dropped a diadem onto it. She offered it to Annalee, who took it numbly.

"No one will notice an extra princess around. They're so easily created. Fyrne stole this from somewhere, didn't you, pet? No one will miss it."

Fyrne gurgled as Theliã scratched her under the chin. There was a moment of stillness between the three of them.

"I hope," Theliã said, her gaze still on the beast, "that you care for my son's heart as diligently as you care for these dragons. If you don't, then I shall be most displeased."

Annalee let the silence drag out until Theliã turned to her quizzically. "If you think I wouldn't," Annalee said softly, dangerously, "or that threats will alter how I treat people, then you don't know me at all."

Theliã looked at her for a long moment, then shrugged. "Forgive my foolish words. A mother has to say these things, you understand, to potential daughters-in-law. Threats are expected." She flashed a dazzling smile. "Doubly so from sirens. Now, I suggest you carry on, my lady. These dragons need mucking out."

Annalee stared incredulously at her. "Muck out the dragons? But I thought I was a lady now?"

"Oh dear, my dear. And just what did you think a lady did?"

Annalee scuffed the floor with her boot, suddenly abashed. "I don't know. Dresses. Jewels. Singing and stuff."

Theliā stepped forward, wearing a conspiratorial smile. "That's what many people think, but personally, I tend to make up my own ideas. So tell me, Beloved of the Dark Lord of Dragons – what should a Dark Lady spend her days doing?"

Annalee looked around. "Well, I suppose the dragons need mucking out."

Theliā patted her on the arm almost affectionately. "Well then. Get to it."

As the siren walked away, Annalee picked up the shovel and a brush. It occurred to her she could probably be The Dark Lady, Keeper of the Dragons; being one thing did not preclude being the other. And then, if being a dark lady ever proved too much or too confusing for her…well, there were always dragons and they always needed mucking out. It was as good a place to start as any.

Perhaps though, when she became a dark lady, she could ask Theliā for the spell that kept dragon dung off your skirts.

The Princess and the Thief

A.M. Croll

"I thank you with all my heart for your generosity and kindness, and will consider your suit for my hand most carefully," said Princess Amber of Veriton, for the thirty-ninth time that day.

"The pile of presents around her had grown steadily, overspilling from the tables onto the floor and the surrounding chaise-longues. There were fine wines and oils, unfamiliar fruits, delicately crafted sweets in the shapes of castles, or horses, or love hearts. Silk gowns and hair-wraps and corsets, every pattern, weave and weight imaginable. The most common gift was jewellery. Bracelets, earrings, necklaces, inlaid with jewels of all shapes and colours: amethyst from the banks of the great river Tanithel; sapphires from deep within the mines of Regor; pearls from the shallow waters surrounding the Denvi Isles; and, of course, a preponderance of the jewel that was her namesake. The suitors who had gifted her that went immediately on the 'no' list. She didn't want to marry a man who lacked imagination.

She didn't want to marry a man at all. Not right now, and not like this. But the kingdom's crops had failed for three harvests in a row – something about ecological instability, a boom in insect populations, a decrease in average rainfall. Scholars were stumped as to why it was happening, but there was one thing they all agreed on: the country desperately needed money. They'd tried everything else. She was nineteen, more than old enough to marry; she was their final hope. When her father had put it like that, she had to agree. She couldn't let her people starve.

So she spoke the script she'd been given, smiled graciously, allowed her hand to be kissed. She wasn't expecting to find love; she just hoped she could find someone kind.

There was a knock at the door to the Great Hall. Her Aunt Sylvia, chaperone for the day, chosen for her stern and discerning eye, opened it and welcomed the next suitor. The last one of the day, thank the Gods.

He was a handsome man, with his soft brown hair, high cheekbones, twinkling eyes blue as the midday sky. But when he first walked in, Amber hardly noticed him. She was too busy staring at the gift he had brought, dragged in on a cart behind him.

None of the other suitors had brought gifts that *moved.*

"Princess Amber, it is an honour to meet you." He strode to her seat and knelt before her, movements confident, self-assured. She extended her hand, and he planted a kiss on her knuckle. His eyes never left hers. “I am Prince Phylan of Fairmont, the second son of our King Justice, and I am here to seek your hand.”

She smiled, feigning courtesy, but her gaze slid back to the gift he’d brought in behind him. Again, it was rattling side to side. Like something trying to get out.

Phylan caught her gaze and quirked his eyebrow up. “Are you afraid, Princess?”

“Not at all,” Amber replied. “Merely curious.”

“I am a lucky man indeed,” he said, voice velvet smooth, “to have captured your curiosity.” He rose to his feet, stepped back. “Would you like to see it?”

All thought of manners or decorum slipped Amber’s mind. “Yes,” she said, breathless as a child. “Yes, please.”

Phylan cleared his throat, gripped one end of the velvet covering and tugged on it. Amber held back a gasp. The cloth had covered a metal cage, and inside it, nostrils flaring, was a golden-scaled dragon, about the size of a house cat.

“That’s impossible.” Amber stood and walked towards the creature, entranced. In the flickering candlelight, the colour of the scales shifted from one moment to the next, now bright and pale as dawn, now the deep near-brown of polished rosewood, now rich as honey. Its eyes were slits, black as night; its open mouth showed off a set of ferocious teeth.

“Still not scared, my Princess?” Phylan’s voice close to her ear made her jump. She hadn’t noticed him entering her personal space, but now he was in it, she couldn’t avoid him. He smelt pleasant up close. A little like vanilla, a little like smoke.

"How did you catch it?" she asked, trying to keep her voice steady. Dragons roamed wild in the farmlands to the north of Veriton – *wild* being the key word.

"I confess that I am not the first to manage this feat," Phylan replied. "If you know the secret to subduing it, it is not so hard."

"The secret?"

Phylan spoke in a mock whisper. "Saltwater is anathema to them. If you shoot them with a dart coated in it, the fight goes out of them. In fact, they become quite docile."

"So this creature is...docile?" Amber asked, noting how it shifted on its haunches, how its eyes never blinked.

Phylan shrugged. "Docile enough. It will need saltwater infusions twice a day. And if you want, I can have my men file its teeth down for you."

"No," said Amber. The thought of mutilating such a proud-looking creature felt wrong. "I thank you with all my heart for... I just..." She stumbled over the speech she'd practised so many times.

"I'm glad to have pleased you," said Phylan. He took her hand once more, grasped it tight. His voice was low now, speaking words meant only for her. "If you give me the chance, I will devote my whole life to the pursuit of that feeling."

Amber's cheeks flushed. "In three days, I will have my decision," she promised him. She pulled her hand back. The place where they had touched still felt warm.

Once Prince Phylan had left the grand hall, Aunt Sylvia snapped into action, summoning servants to cart away the piles of gifts. A castle soldier stepped forward to pick up the caged dragon. "Where, uh..." He faltered. "Where will we be keeping this?"

Amber looked at the small creature, at its wicked little teeth. "Bring it to my bedchamber," she ordered.

"Princess," protested Sylvia. "Surely it would be better – *safer* – kept in the stables."

Amber used her most imperious voice. "It is a gift for me. And I want it in my bedroom."

* * *

Amber spent the rest of the day ordering servants to deliver food to her room, in an effort to learn what the little dragon liked. It did not like bread, or seeds. It did like dates and other dried fruit, and it really liked the dead mouse one enterprising servant boy managed to catch for it. It picked the mouse up by the tail with its claw, threw it into the air and swallowed it in one enormous gulp.

"I imagine you're quite the hunter in the wild," Amber murmured. The dragon snapped its jaws, as if in agreement. Amber threw it another fig. She was sure it would have liked to eat her, and as much as she wanted to reach through the cage bars to pet it, she kept her limbs clear.

Servants brought up trays of food for her supper and stacked them on her bedside table, since she'd missed the formal dinner with her family. But Amber found she was too tired to be hungry, and fell asleep, curled on the carpet just next to her dragon, lantern on the wall still lit.

She woke in the night with a start, immediately alert. Something was wrong. There was a rattling noise just to her left. Right where the dragon was sleeping.

She leapt to her feet and grabbed the closest object to hand – a butter knife from the dinner she hadn't eaten. "Who goes there?" she demanded, quiet but clear.

The shadows shifted. "Speak," she said again, forcing confidence into her voice.

"My Lady," said a low voice. It wasn't familiar. She clenched the knife tighter.

"Your Highness," she corrected.

"Your Highness," the voice amended. "I – I'll just be leaving now—"

"I think not," she snapped. "Come into the light."

The man obeyed, stepping into the narrow circle of lantern-light. Amber had seen so many different men the day before, they'd all sort of blurred, but she was sure this wasn't one of her suitors. He was a little rougher around the edges, a little rugged, and he wore the dark red tunic that all of the castle servants wore.

"Who are you?" she demanded.

He seemed not to want to answer, but he was clearly unwilling to avoid a direct question. "My name is Laurie, your Highness," he said stiffly.

That, finally, clicked into place. "You're a stable boy, aren't you? What in hell's name are you doing in my bedroom? If I called the guards in right now..."

Laurie jutted his chin forward, defiant. "Then I will have brought my fate upon myself."

Amber lowered her knife at that, just a little. She looked at the stable boy with fresh eyes. "And why would you risk such a fate? Have you been sent to kill me? To kidnap me? Is someone paying you?"

Laurie shook his head. "With all due respect, your Highness, I'm not here for you."

Amber barked out a laugh at the outrageousness of it. "You stand here in the middle of the night in my bedroom, and tell me you're not here for *me*?"

Something clattered, and Amber and Laurie's gazes fell at the same time to the caged dragon. "*Oh*," said Amber. "You're here for him." She rolled her eyes. "Just a common thief, then?"

"It's not theft if I'm returning what was stolen."

Amber frowned. "The dragon was *gifted* to me."

"But it's a living, breathing creature. It's a wonder of the natural world. It shouldn't *belong* to anyone."

"Not a thief," Amber realised. "An...animal lover." She frowned. "I think that's worse."

"Look at it," said Laurie. "Do you think it's happy in a cage? It can't even extend its wings."

Amber looked at the little creature. She'd grown fond of it over the day. She didn't like the thought of it suffering.

But what did a stable boy know about dragon wellbeing? It had seemed content enough when she was feeding it. When Phylan's manservant had arrived to dose it with saltwater, it had barely shuddered. As far as she knew, it would be perfectly happy being pampered for the rest of its life.

"What will you do if I let you go?" she asked.

Laurie tilted his head, narrowed his eyes like a challenge."I suppose I'll come back again tomorrow night and try again."

Amber rose to his challenge. "And will you have a better plan tomorrow?"

"My plan tonight should have worked," he muttered. He gestured towards the soup on the tray her servants had brought her. "If you'd eaten that, you wouldn't have woken up when I came in."

"You poisoned my dinner?"

"Only a mild sedative."

Amber closed her eyes, sucked in a deep breath. Even with that admission, she was pretty sure Laurie hadn't wanted to hurt her. He was annoying, and self-righteous, but not harmful. She walked to the door, and opened it. "Go," she said, quietly. "Before I change my mind."

Laurie didn't argue. He fled the room, and Amber closed the door behind him.

She crouched down next to the cage and looked at the dragon. "Is he right?" she asked it.

The dragon blinked and didn't respond.

* * *

The next day, Amber, her entire family and the royal advisors sat together to narrow down her list of suitors. The gifts they'd brought her weren't the only factor, but they were a big one. They needed to know how much wealth they could expect her husband to commit to their marriage, and therefore to her people. It felt a little like they were deciding who to sell her to, but she pushed that thought aside. Her people needed her, she reminded herself. She saw Aunt Sylvia looking at her with a furrowed brow, and forced a smile.

In the end, they whittled it down to the ten best options. Any of them, according to her father, would be a good match for her. And help buy their kingdom out of famine, was the underlying message.

She was not surprised that Prince Phylan made the list. His lands were rich, and his gift had made quite the impression. All her family, even the disapproving Sylvia, had been in to visit the dragon; as had half the serving staff.

She kept an eye out, but saw no sign of Laurie.

At dinner, she only ate food taken from the communal serving plates, and did not accept the wine poured for her. She doubted Laurie could have afforded to bribe the serving staff, but he did work in the castle. He might have friends in the kitchens. Even the jugs of water on the table seemed suspicious to her, so she didn't drink anything at all, instead visiting the well outside the kitchens to quench her thirst.

She stopped by the kitchen and filched some figs and a rib of lamb for her dragon's dinner. She dropped the food into its cage from above, marvelling at its snapping jaws. Then she found an old skein of embroidery thread and started to play with it, wiggling the loose end just inside the cage and laughing when the dragon swatted at it. She fell asleep, once again curled on the floor, the dragon's breaths as soothing as any lullaby.

When she woke this time, Laurie was actually holding the cage; but the dragon had shifted inside it, and the noise of its claws on the metal bars alerted Amber to the intruder.

"Thief," she said, by way of greeting.

"Not a very good one," he replied. He set the cage down on the floor, defeated. "You didn't have the apple tart for pudding?"

"I was full," she said. Then she paused, and said: "Half my family had the apple tart."

"Then they'll be sleeping very deeply tonight."

Amber shook her head, laughing a little. "Have you *any* morals?"

Laurie's deadpan expression finally cracked. He grinned, eyes crinkling at the edges. Amber sucked in a breath at the way his whole face lit up, and she realised for the first time that he was not an unattractive man.

"I have some morals," he said. "The important ones."

"Name some."

"I don't cheat at cards."

"Good."

"I respect women."

"I'm *sure*."

"I care about animal wellbeing."

Amber's face fell. "Not this again."

"Studies have shown that dragons held in captivity develop all kinds of illnesses. Not to mention the impact of being separated from their social groups..."

"There's almost no proper data on dragon behaviour," Amber countered. She knew this was true because she'd found a book in the castle library on the subject and been horrified at how anecdotal it all was. "We just don't know enough to be certain."

"So you're an expert now?"

"No," said Amber. "But no one is. How do you know what's best for it?"

"I don't know what's best for it," said Laurie. "But I know what isn't good. That prince has it on saltwater, right?" He shuddered. "That stuff is poison to dragons. Even at low doses... Over a long period of time, it won't survive."

Amber swallowed. "I didn't read about that in the books."

"Those of us who care about dragon wellbeing have known it for a long time. Your prince knows it too. He just doesn't give a damn."

"He's not my prince. Not yet."

"He will be?"

"Probably," admitted Amber. She'd ruled out most of the final ten suitors for being too old, or young. Of the remaining few, at least Phylan wasn't boring.

"It's not my place, Princess," said Laurie hesitantly. His gaze was so earnest it hurt to look at him. "But you don't sound too enthused about that."

"You're right," said Amber coldly. "It's not your place."

She'd spoken more harshly than she'd intended to. Laurie's face went very blank, and he made no reply. She hadn't realised how much she enjoyed hearing his voice until it was gone. Even if they were arguing, there was something soothing about it.

"Should I expect you tomorrow night?" she said, voice softer. She took a step forward, a very small one.

Laurie took a step forward too. For a moment, they just stared at each other. Laurie's eyes were dark and wide, brimming with something Amber didn't understand, something wild and dangerous, something with teeth. She broke the connection first, looking down at the floor. She couldn't take him looking at her like that. It would break her.

He walked towards the door. She assumed he wasn't going to respond at all, but at the last moment, he turned and spoke. "I'll be back," he said. And he added: "I was thinking I'd just knock."

* * *

Aunt Sylvia had set up meetings with Amber's four remaining suitors, spread throughout the day. In the morning, she had breakfast with Lord Henry of the Silvered Isles, and decided he had no sense of humour. After that, she went horseback riding with the Emperor Natan of Regor; Laurie saddled her horse, and avoided eye contact. She had lunch with Duke Jaques, heir to the Winterlands, who was so nervous that when he took her hand, his palms were sweating; and finally, she walked the rose gardens with Prince Phylan.

His hair was perfectly curled, his eyes bright in the sun. He held conversation well, asking about her own interests, seeming to actually listen; and more than once, making flirty comments that made her cheeks flush. She liked it, she thought. She liked him – but enough to marry?

"How is your pet coming along?" he asked. "No problems?"

"None at all. It seems happy enough." She paused. "Except when it is given saltwater. I don't think it likes that."

Phylan shrugged. "Dragons are violent creatures by nature. We need to suppress that."

"Do we?" Amber asked.

Phylan smiled, as though he hadn't understood the question.

* * *

Amber returned to her bedchamber, lost in thought. The king would demand her decision the next morning, and she had no idea what she was going to say. Or maybe she did know, and it terrified her. All she knew was that she would not be able to fall asleep that night. So she settled by the dragon's cage and made herself comfortable.

She wasn't foolish enough to push the dragon's boundaries; but it had allowed her to stroke the very end of its tail, where the scales were as small as her fingernails. Their rough surface irritated her hands, but she found she didn't mind. She sank into the pillows she'd laid out, body relaxing. Distantly, she wondered what it would do if she opened the cage. Eat her, probably. And how could she blame it for what was its nature?

When Laurie slipped into her bedroom, it was no shock. She didn't even raise her head.

"Your Highness," he said hesitantly. "Are you alright?" He crouched beside her to look at her. Up close, she noticed the freckles dusting the bridge of his nose. She noticed the curve of his lower lip, the scar just above his chin. There was a story behind that, she was sure. She wanted desperately to know it. Another time. Right now, there were other questions she needed to ask.

She sat up, stretching out her cramped limbs. "When did people first discover the effects of saltwater on dragons?"

Laurie considered this for a moment. "Five years ago? Perhaps a little less. It took a while to catch on, but for the last couple of years it's been common amongst certain groups of nobility."

"And how many dragons are currently in captivity?"

"Dozens, maybe a hundred. Possibly more. My...allies who care about dragon wellbeing—"

"—you should really have a name for yourselves. Like, an acronym—"

"—We keep track as best as we can, but it's not perfect."

Amber hummed. "I was researching what dragons are meant to eat. It occurred to me that feeding this one fruit all the time might not be good for it." She looked at her dragon, and it blinked innocent, beguiling eyes back at her. "It turns out they mainly eat insects. Cicadas, beetles, the like. Did you know that?"

"I did, your Highness."

"So I started to think. If there were fewer dragons in the wild, there'd be far more insects. And the ecological effects would be huge."

Laurie's eyes widened. "You don't mean..."

"The harvests," Amber said. "*That's* why they've been failing. It's our fault. But now we know that, we know how to fix it. We can fix it."

"We could," said Laurie. "But it's mostly nobility who keep dragons. The harvest failures barely touch them. Would they really release their precious pets if we asked, just to save some crops?"

Amber shook her head, grinning. "Trust me, Laurie, I know what nobility are like. I wasn't planning on asking. I was thinking we could take a leaf out of your book. Theft."

Laurie tilted his head. "You keep saying *we*?"

Amber stood now, started to pace the room. "All I ever wanted was to help my people. Maybe it's because I'm a really kind person. Or maybe it's because I have guilt over being, you know, the ruling class. It doesn't matter. But I want to help. And I don't want to get married to a man I don't love. I think..." She looked down at the ground, words catching in her throat. "I think that over a long period of time, I wouldn't survive."

Laurie swallowed. He got to his feet too. "Okay," he said. "So, to be clear, you're not choosing a suitor tomorrow? You want to run away, set your dragon free and then free all other captive dragons from the rich so the ecosystem can right itself?"

"Precisely," said Amber. "Except, there's one more thing I want to do."

"There is?"

Amber nodded. "I want to kiss you."

Laurie stood for a moment in sheer shock. Then he came back to himself, and nodded. Amber smiled, stepped towards him. She cradled his jaw, thumb on the slight raised skin of his scar. His hands fell to her waist, pulling her into him until they were chest to chest; and then he closed the final distance between them. His mouth was so soft and warm, she was certain she might melt. She sighed at the pleasure of it; then gasped at the slight graze of his teeth over her lips.

Below them came a strange noise. They broke apart, startled. The dragon in its cage was watching them intently. And it had…chirped?

"We should probably leave," she said.

"Yes," he replied. "I'm a really terrible thief, but I'm trying to get better."

She grabbed a handful of jewelry and silks, small but expensive things they could sell on the road. Laurie found a cover for the cage, to avoid attracting attention on their journey, then picked it up. Amber tried not to react to how easy he made the weight of it seem.

"You're sure you want to do this?" he asked.

"Certain," she said.

* * *

In the very early hours of the next morning, two figures on horseback stopped at the top of a hill a couple of miles from the castle and dismounted. One of them set down a box on the floor. The other figure bent down and opened the box, and out came a creature: a small, winged dragon. It did a loop over the two people's heads, let out a triumphant cry, then flew out into the sunrise. The figures remounted their horses and continued down the other side of the hill. There, they disappeared beneath the horizon.

The Girl Who Kissed the Sun

Maria D'Antonio-Reich

Moira grabbed Taiyanglong's golden robe and yanked him down as she shushed him. Poor Taiyanglong seemed to lose his sense of awareness when they were together. It was cute and endearing, but they had to be careful.

Taiyanglong wasn't a fully fledged dragon yet, and Moira had been a priestess for only one week.

"Be quiet," she hissed as she shoved him in the brush. His sparkling black eyes finally looked worried.

She pulled her bangs out of her face and peered through the brush. Taiyanglong gathered his rumpled golden robe and joined her, muting his magic.

Hunters roamed nearby. Ike and his new gang. How Ike knew an unfledged dragon lived around here was anyone's guess. She resisted a groan as the three men approached the meadow she and Taiyanglong had recently vacated.

"I thought you said it was here!" shouted Ike, who stood a head taller than his companions.

The mage with him rolled his eyes. "It's a dragon. It probably heard us coming and ran."

The other man silently stared at their hiding spot while the mage spoke.

"Look, I'm sure even you can feel the magic tingling in this place. We can come back prepared with some spelled parchment and blessed ink."

Taiyanglong shook as he fought to conceal his magic, and Moira knew his light would shine whether he wanted it or not. So, she motioned for him to stay hidden and inched her way to the nearby tree. She took a few moments to fix her hair and don a regal, priestly expression on her face before revealing herself. Stepping out on the opposite side of Taiyanglong, she breathed a sigh of relief.

"Oh, it's only you. I came into the forest for meditation and heard some ruckus, so I hid."

Ike sauntered over to her. She did her best not to look disgusted. "There's no need to be frightened, Priestess Moira. No unsavory types around here."

"I suppose you didn't see a dragon?" asked the mage. "It would be young, unfledged."

"No. Perhaps they heard the commotion and ran away. You know how unfledged dragons are."

"Masters of hiding," said Ike. "We can escort you back to the Temple. Oh. I don't think you've met my companions. This is Kieran and that quiet man is Roy. They just arrived from Acostar."

"Wonderful!" lied Moira. "You must tell me everything about the big city."

Hopefully, Taiyanglong would spot this as an opportunity to slip away unnoticed. She let them talk about hunting and dragons, while keeping an extra eye on Kieran. He seemed to know more about magic than the average mage.

* * *

When she finally made it back to the Temple, she slipped into her private chambers and changed into her official garments. The red robe wrapped with the golden sash Taiyanglong gifted her hung over her white pants. She already missed him with his bright smile and easy laughter. He was all warmth and light and as generous with his magic as the sun's rays. A very welcome break from the Temple.

The Temple was divided into public and private spaces. Moira and the other priestesses performed most rituals, blessings, and purifications under the outdoor pavilion's white roof. Inside housed the priestesses' private quarters, a library, and common rooms.

Most of the duties and spells required of her did not come naturally, not like her wind magic. Unfortunately, her duties seldom called for such charms, but she'd like to think she was getting better at being a priestess.

She went out into the open pavilion and performed the harvest blessings for her seaside village while wondering if Taiyanglong made it to safety. It wasn't until an older woman commented on how distracted she seemed that Moira actually focused on the blessings. The rest of the afternoon went by smoothly. She even assisted the High Priestess with their annual Equinox Baptism.

When she made it back to her chambers thoroughly exhausted, she plopped in her chair without looking. She frowned when she sat on a lump.

"Ow!" cried a familiar voice.

She jumped up and spun around. Then she grinned. "Taiyanglong!"

The dragon in question smiled warmly, literally chasing away the chill from the unusually cool autumn air. Magic simply oozed out of him. Even in his human form of shimmering pale skin with black sparkling hair and eyes, he glowed with sunlight.

"I wanted to see you before the day was over." He stood up and walked over to her. With a smile, he kissed her lips. Moira closed her eyes and leaned into him. Kissing Taiyanglong was like kissing a sweet sunbeam, warm and fuzzy.

He wrapped his arms around her and pulled her into the chair with him. "Especially now with these insufferable long nights ahead. I simply can't abide them."

She snorted.

"What's so funny?" he asked.

"If you had it your way we wouldn't even have nights." Moira curled up on him and nuzzled his neck.

"You wound me. I couldn't do that to my sister. Rather, I would make it summer all year long!" He laughed before kissing the top of her head.

"I'm so glad you're here," murmured Moira. "Being a priestess is so hard."

"But rewarding. Did you see how those hunters listened to you back there?" He pulled her close. "Thank you for earlier, but one of these days, I'd like to save you."

Neither one of them wanted to acknowledge it. Taiyanglong, like all dragons, only fledged once he journeyed to the Northern Mountains and listened to the gods. He was supposed to go seven years ago, but that would mean leaving Moira behind. Yet if he continued to stay unfledged, he'd always be hunted.

She closed her eyes. "Maybe I shouldn't be selfish."

"Please don't say that. Let's not talk about sad things." He lifted her chin up. "Besides, Ike and his friends interrupted us."

He kissed her again. She held him and didn't let go.

* * *

That night, she dreamed of simpler times when she ran away from the grueling lessons of the High Priestess to the forest that breathed magic all around her. She was only twelve when Taiyanglong first found her crying in the hollow of a large tree.

* * *

"Why are you crying, human?" asked the strange pale boy. "You look silly."

Moira shot to her feet, glared at him through tears, and held her hand in a spell-casting position. "It's not silly! You take that back!"

"Are you trying to scare me?" With that, he transformed with a burst of sunlight. His long serpentine body radiated so much magic, Moira had to shut her eyes. When she tried to glare at him, she couldn't look away.

His sleek, golden figure illuminated everything under the canopy, as if they stood in a meadow instead of a forest. A single line of black fur that matched his hair ran down his spine, culminating in a furry tuft at the end of his tail. He roared, making her jump back.

Then he grinned. With a flick of his tail and a burst of light, he transformed back into his human form. "See? I'm a real dragon, and once I grow up, no one will be more magical than me!"

"Not even the High Priestess?" she asked. "Or the Yin, the Great Dragon of the Night?"

"Okay, maybe my sister, but definitely not a High Priestess!" The boy pointed at her. "So, why are you crying?"

"Oh, uh, it's nothing."

"Come on! Tell me!" He stomped his feet and pouted.

Envy consumed Moira. It wasn't fair that she had to behave and be polite and respectful all the time. It wasn't fair that she couldn't make one little mistake in the rituals or the High Priestess would whip her. It especially wasn't fair that magic came so easily to this rude boy.

"Fine. Only if you promise to leave me alone." Once he nodded, she continued, "I came out here to practice celestial magic, but it's so hard. Then, I thought I'd practice wind magic, but that's not what the High Priestess wants me to learn!"

He scoffed. "I bet I'm a much better teacher than a stuffy priestess. Celestial magic is easy! I'll show you."

And he did.

* * *

Moira awoke before dawn lying beside Taiyanglong. She rested her head on his bare chest and drew little circles on him, listening to the waves of the North Sea. He didn't stir. He never did before the sun rose. She didn't mind; she could watch him sleep, feel his chest rise and fall beneath her cheek, forever.

She couldn't help but wonder what would've happened if Ike and his companions caught her poor Taiyanglong unawares. Her Taiyanglong at their mercy. They would tame him to control his magic, and from what she understood from the High Priestess, taming a dragon was always violent.

"I'll protect you," she whispered.

Someone tapped at the door. Moira jumped, but Taiyanglong slept soundly. She grabbed the first robe she could find and slipped it on before answering the door.

A woman with hair as white as the moon and skin as dark as night stood in the threshold. Her sparkling white eyes shone as she pointed to the interior of the room. Moira's eyes widened as she bowed to the Great Dragon of the Night, Yin.

The dragon frowned. "I saw some hunters, so I thought I might collect my brother before sunrise."

"He's safe enough with me." Moira pretended that the Great Dragon didn't intimidate her, but those piercing white eyes broke her resolve. "Come in, Lady Yin."

"I won't stay long." The dragon woman stepped inside, celestial energy radiating from her. Usually, her aura emitted gentle flurries like the first snowfall, but somehow, Lady Yin's magic whipped around her like a winter storm. She walked over to the futon where Taiyanglong still lay asleep and effortlessly picked him up, cradling him in her arms.

"Did he say if he was going to listen to the voices of the gods?" asked Lady Yin. "I worry not only for him, but for the balance."

Lady Yin spoke about the balance of the world quite a bit when it came to Taiyanglong's fledging. Whenever Moira asked him about it, he always waved it off. "What's one more year?" he would say.

"Not yet. You told us he wouldn't be the same after he went to the Northern Mountains. He might be there so long that he forgets me." Moira slumped in her chair, glaring at Lady Yin. "Neither one of us wants that."

"I know." Lady Yin walked to the door, still holding Taiyanglong. "That's why I told him to not fall in love with you." With that, the dragons left her alone in the dark.

Moira didn't want to keep Taiyanglong from becoming a fledged dragon, strong and sure like his sister. But she couldn't imagine life without his warm smile either.

She stared at the door wishing she was braver. Braver to fight to be with him or let him go, she didn't know.

* * *

A few weeks later and the nights had already lengthened. With the uncommon bitter cold not letting up, the High Priestess insisted on preparing for the winter solstice, hoping that Lady Yin would attend. It was considered a great fortune for the coming year if one of the great dragons appeared at the festival. Lady Yin hadn't appeared in the last seven years.

The High Priestess threw herself into the preparations this year, so Moira worked herself ragged in running the day-to-day duties of the Temple on her own. Educating the villagers on magic and the gods, performing small purification rituals and blessings, while attending to the needs of the dead for the entire town. With the unusually harsh season, the villagers swarmed the Temple all day, hoping for charms to bring relief from the early winter weather.

Moira tried to avoid thinking about a particular dragon that hadn't fledged yet and thus spent most days contemplating the matter ad nauseum. At least, the priestess duties came more naturally to her now. She'd had plenty of practice this autumn.

Thankfully, Taiyanglong would come by every night with sweets and farfetched stories about places where the day and night were the same length of time all year long. When he came by, Moira could relax and just be Moira, not a priestess. She savored these quiet moments with him.

One day in the last of the autumn weeks, he was late.

When evening crept into night and he still hadn't visited, Moira got worried. Taiyanglong was safe enough at the Temple at night. The priestesses thought of dragons as good omens, but Moira could think of three villagers who did not share that sentiment.

She would just check on him to make sure he didn't get caught in a hunter's trap. Donning her red robe over her tunic, she made for the woods. When it became too dark to see, she summoned a small orb of moonlight in her hand, pushing the fatigue from the day aside.

Only five minutes had passed before she heard Ike and Kieran talking loudly. Soon followed by Taiyanglong's pained roar. Moira raced toward the noise, grimacing as she realized it came from their favorite meadow.

"I told you the spell would work!" Kieran said. "I just needed time."

Ike spoke next. "Well, can you get it to hold still? I might have to break its arm to muzzle it."

Taiyanglong snarled again.

Moira held up her moon orb and shouted, "*Escae Gle*!" Her moonlight encompassed the whole wood. The sight that greeted her shook her to the core.

Three men stood around a golden dragon bound in a net made of spelled parchment and twine. Kieran continued to place more and more spells on the net, scraps of parchment imbued with charms to subdue. Ike and the quiet man hovered over the dragon, sporting bloodied knives.

Her Taiyanglong, covered in blood, thrashed against the net that bound him. Tears sprung to Moira's eyes.

If she'd let him go, he would've fledged and become a dragon too strong to be bound by such spells.

She screamed, letting her rage infuse her magic as the moonlight brightened sharply, winds howling through the trees that surrounded the meadows. The hunters gasped, but Taiyanglong relaxed in her magic. There was no fear when sudden gusts whipped his hair in his eyes. This was her wind.

"Priestess! There's no need, it's not fledged!" said Ike.

"He's not yours to claim!" she shouted over the winds. "I command you to release him!"

"An unfledged dragon is worthless, Priestess," said Kieran. He dropped his spells and held out his hands to stay her wind. "He hasn't listened to the gods, so he's just a bad omen. Might as well put him to some use."

Moira snarled, drawing herself up. The winds buffeted the men, breaking through Kieran's defenses. She was no mere mage. She was a priestess of the North Temple. "You can't have him. Leave now."

The wind howled, throwing them off their feet and into the trees. She ran toward Taiyanglong, ripping the spelled net off him before cradling his head gently in her arms. He purred, sounding like a low growl. "It's okay," she whispered. "I'm here now. I won't let anything bad happen to you." She rested her forehead on his snout so he couldn't see her tears.

Even though he was a rather small dragon, he was still the size of three men and much too big for her to carry. She called on the wind to assist, since he still seemed tired from the blood loss.

The extra spell-casting fatigued her, but she soldiered on. She commanded the wind to help carry him all the way to the docks. While he lay panting on the beach, Moira roused the harbormaster and convinced him to lease her a boat. She paid much more than usual, both as an apology for waking him and to speed up the process.

When she returned to Taiyanglong, he lay unnaturally still, blood oozing from his injuries in the moonlight. Moira bit back a sob and summoned her wind to help her lift up the dragon and settle him in the boat.

The small boat had only one sail and one set of oars, but Moira had the wind on her side. With Taiyanglong mostly squeezed into the boat except for his tail, she summoned her wind again and they sped off for the Northern Mountains, the home of the gods.

"I'll take care of you," she whispered, stroking his snout. He opened up his black eyes just as a tear escaped.

She tried not to cry and rubbed her face. "You just rest. You'll feel much better when the sun rises."

He put one clawed paw on her lap before falling asleep. She finally let herself cry once his breathing evened out. After all, she'd have to be strong for him once they reached the Northern Mountains. Even if he forgot everything, she would remember for the both of them.

* * *

"Look, I caught another one!" he said, holding his hands carefully. "I think we've got enough now."

Moira nodded and opened up the white paper lantern. Instead of a flame, they'd spent the past two days catching fireflies. Moira cheated with her wind magic, but they wanted to be ready for the summer solstice.

"Okay, now, for my spell—"

"I want to do it!" Taiyanglong interrupted. Without waiting for an answer, he spread his fingers, now glowing at the tips. The fireflies inside the dozen or so paper lanterns started changing colors to mimic the Northern Lights. Thankfully, they had already attached their wishes to the lanterns.

Moira watched. After a couple of years of friendship, she was no longer envious, she admired him. Once the fireflies synced with each other, she called a wind to carry the paper lanterns into the sky. The wind kept them steady as Taiyanglong continued to work his magic.

Moira had already attended the festival for the solstice, but his sister had forbidden him to go. Moira didn't want

Taiyanglong to be alone, so she took some snacks, two pieces of spelled parchment, and paper lanterns. They made their own festival.

"Happy Summer Solstice! The best day of the year!" shouted Taiyanglong. He grinned at her, before leaning in for a kiss.

It was their first.

* * *

When the sun rose, Taiyanglong finally resumed his human form. Having never fallen asleep, Moira gave herself a break from the wind magic. She had spotted the stormy clouds ahead and needed to gather her strength.

"Moira?" he asked, sitting up. His soulful black eyes met her brown ones. "Are you okay?"

"Me? You're the one who was attacked! I should be asking you."

"But you're shaking."

Moira looked at her hands quivering in her lap. Funny, she didn't notice. Wordlessly, she pointed to the stormy weather ahead.

"We're going to the Northern Mountains," he said. "The gods and goddesses use storms instead of moats. We should turn around. I'm not strong enough to get us through."

Moira shook her head. "Those hunters wouldn't respect my authority as priestess. I had to use magic to get them away from you. Taiyanglong, I'd rather not see you and know you're free than see you tamed." She didn't cry; she'd run out of tears already in the night.

"Moira..."

She raised her hand, summoning the wind again. They sped toward the storm as she smiled at him. "Just rest. It'll be okay."

At first, the sea shifted gradually. Light rain kissed her face. Then the waves transformed the flatness of the sea into a mountainous landscape, before finally the wind tried to fight her. It was difficult to see or hear anything except the storm as they ventured farther north.

Taiyanglong watched with worried eyes, silent for once.

When the wind slapped her, along with rain and hail the size of her fist, she stood up and gathered every bit of magical strength she possessed. "*Gaeth feth! Gaeth imm fochal!*" Lightning and thunder answered her when she pleaded with the wind. Still, she managed to persuade the wind to push them in the correct direction even as the angry sea tried to cast them from the boat. Moira slipped and fell, scraping her hands and knees, but she still pushed the wind onward.

Taiyanglong, still pale, stood up and uttered one word. "*Grian!*"

Moira didn't notice any difference for a few moments. Then the wind stopped fighting her. The rain softened and the hail disappeared in minutes. Waves the size of hills leveled out slowly, before, unbelievably, the sun broke through the clouds.

He smiled. "I told you I'd save you one day. I know you're technically saving me, but I'm counting this."

Laughter burst out of her before she sagged to the soggy bench, arm still outstretched as she commanded the wind to push them northward. "I guess this counts."

He sat next to her and closed his eyes, but his spell never wavered. "I'm tired," he muttered, keeping her warm with his magic alone.

"Me, too." She never let up her winds, even when she wanted nothing more than to sleep for days.

She didn't know how much time passed before the mountains loomed over them and Taiyanglong released his spell. Even though they approached the home of the gods and no human had ever set foot here, her eyes still drooped, and it took the rest of her strength to make it to shore.

Once she felt the boat crash into land, she finally let go of the wind and passed out.

Moira woke in her own bed. She spent a few moments working out why she was wet and hungry, before she sat up and looked around. Beside her lay an impossibly beautiful clear crystal holding a wisp of magic inside. She stared at it, watching the wisp change colors and textures. A gift from the gods.

"No, no, no!" she whispered. "I didn't get to say goodbye…"

She didn't come out of her room that day. She cried instead.

* * *

Nearly four years later, on the eve of the summer solstice, Moira sat in the empty pavilion of the Temple, preparing blessings and purified water for tomorrow's festival. She tried to keep busy nowadays and did her best not to think about a certain dragon. She pretended that she didn't miss him most days.

Fireflies lit up the Temple gardens and Moira's heart clenched, remembering her first kiss. One of them landed on her spelled parchment as a warm breeze tickled her face. She smiled and invited it onto her hand. Once it crawled on, she carefully lifted her hand and looked up.

And into the black eyes of Taiyanglong.

"Moira," he whispered, smiling. He offered his hand, and she helped herself up. Even more radiant than before, his rich golden skin shone with celestial magic. It spilled out of him and felt more natural than the actual sun.

Tears leaked from her eyes as she laughed. Her heart wanted to burst with happiness.

"I believe we were interrupted," he said. He leaned in and kissed her. It sparked magic more dazzling than the sun's rays but just as gentle as a summer morning. When they broke apart, they simply held each other.

"I know I'll see you at the festival tomorrow, but I was afraid I wouldn't get the chance to say how much I love you." He held her close. "I love you, Moira. I will never forget you."

"I love you, Yang." She smiled. "The Great Dragon of the Day."

"It does have a nice ring to it, doesn't it?"

She laughed. Even though he would soon travel the whole world to ensure the balance of nature and magic, he would always be her sun.

The Last Dragon

Deborah L. Davitt

I'm the last dragon, and I am alone.

Once, we filled the skies. Buried our treasures beneath the ground. But I haven't seen any of my kind in hundreds of years now.

Me? I buried golden scales beneath soft skin; hid my wings within a human shape, and got along as best I could. Sometimes, I'd fall in love for sixty, seventy years. And then I'd get to remember all the reasons I tried *not* to do that.

It always ends in grief.

When I met him, he was learning Japanese, having gone abroad to teach English for two years. The first time we met, at a teahouse in Hokkaido, where I was playing the golden-haired tourist, he asked me if I knew what *koi no yokan* meant.

I did; it's the feeling that, on meeting someone, that you're *fated* to fall in love with them.

I looked down into my tea, and didn't answer.

"You *do* know," he said gently, somehow divining my answer. "It's how I feel right this moment. Like there's nothing I can do to stop it."

"Then you also know that I'll fight it."

He pushed his glasses up, smiling ruefully. "That's why I *won't*."

But he didn't push. He let me walk out the door of the teahouse, into the bitter coldness of a Hokkaido winter, my breath curling up around my face like smoke, away from him. Even though I felt it, too – *koi no yokan*. Much more than love at first sight, more than a mere prediction. It's inevitability.

And I ran from it.

The second time we met was in Norway, on a cruise under the Northern Lights. On seeing him in the crowd, part of me wanted to run again. I wanted to change form into something, someone, that he couldn't possibly recognize. But the greater part of me was curious. Would he even remember the golden-haired tourist he'd met in Japan a decade before?

He did, his face lighting up. "I never even got your name the first time we met," he said, smiling as I joined him at the rail. "I'm sorry. I came on too strong. I feel everything very intensely, and I act on impulse at times."

"It's a failure of the young," I replied, smiling back.

"And you are so very old?" he teased. "You don't look a day older than when I last saw you!"

I make mistakes. That was one of them. Or maybe it was a test out of my subconscious. Though a truer test would have been to disguise myself completely. I don't know. My mind and motivations are as muddled as any human's, sometimes.

This time it was my turn to teach him a word: *forelsket*. The ecstatic, all-consuming sensation of being in love, when everything is new. The sense of being unable to think of anything but your new lover.

But I also knew it couldn't last. It never did. Humans grow old and die, and I'm inevitably left alone again. The word for that? *Onsra*. I learned that one in Nepal, or maybe in Tibet. The knowledge that this love won't last, or that it will be your last love.

But as always at the shining beginning of things, I resolved to make it last. To make each day stretch out perfectly, so I'd have the memory of them when he was gone.

I let my body age alongside his as we traveled the world, learning new things. I hoarded up words, memories, pictures, the way I'd once hoarded up treasures. A light against the long dark that would surely, inevitably come.

When we reached our eighties, he took me for a long and rambling walk in a park one day, and told me, "I have a secret that I've kept from you for many years. And I can't let you go to your grave without knowing it."

"Strangely," I replied, "I, too, have kept something from you that you should know. Which of us should go first?"

I felt no fear that what he was about to reveal would end everything. I did, however, feel trepidation that what I would reveal, would. I had let so many lovers go to their deaths without revealing myself to them before this. But he was… different. He could handle the truth of knowing that I would endure without him. As I had endured so often before.

Under the trees, his form began to change, distort, and reshape itself. Golden scales wrapped themselves around his limbs, and dumbfounded, I allowed myself to do the same.

I am no longer the last dragon, and I will never be alone again.

Shattered Vows

Kit Englard

Moonlight refracted off Suraya's silver glass skin as she stroked the neck of her camel. The light brought out the vibrant colors of the creature's woven halter. A line of animal-hide tents protected her from the strummed chords and thrum of voices in the revelry beyond. The company gathered for an evening of storytelling after a long day's ride, but she took the moment of peace.

Her thoughts were drawn back to her husband, and their first night together six months before. When the doors to the bedchamber had closed and muffled the sounds of wedding revelry. Baran had stood stoic. She'd been breathless. The night had been one of reckless passion, the kind that only came when it was unexpected. It had been stolen kisses and soft caresses that overpowered nerves.

Then he left on an assignment. When he'd returned, the kind, gentle man had been replaced by the emir, leader of the empire's troops. A soldier who never invited her back into his life.

Boots scraped against dirt, and she turned. Baran stood tall. The shadows of the night darkened his complexion of sun-warmed clay. Years of regimented military training had eroded any hint of softness.

He stopped beside her. For a moment they stood in silence as he inspected the camel. "I don't want you to join the company tonight."

She held tight to the resentment threatening to break free. Of course he hadn't come to check on her. Just give orders, like she was one of his soldiers instead of the wife he'd abandoned. "The prince will be expecting me."

"They've been drinking. He's already started asking about you."

She tried to decipher the intent behind his clipped, low voice. He was angry, unsurprising considering the brewing tension between him and the crown prince that had swelled ever since Baran returned. "If he's demanding my presence, then I should go."

A muscle above his eye spasmed. "The bard sang a story about the glass dragons. His Highness was suggesting that they see if the poetic descriptions are real. If you don't go back to our tent right now, he's going to demand that you shift in front of the company and there's nothing I can do to stop him."

Heat crept up the back of her neck. From the corner of her eye, she saw her skin shift from silver to the petal pink of a blush. She hated that her emotions were out on display for anyone who cared to learn how to decipher the color patterns refracted on her crystal-like flesh. "He can't – that's against the laws of my people..." She couldn't even finish the thought. When dragons shifted, they either shredded the clothes they were wearing or had to strip first. She'd be left bare in front of prominent members of the court. "I'm a diplomat."

"He won't care."

Threads of indignation wove through her embarrassment, turning her skin burnt orange. *This isn't for me*, she thought irritably. No, Emir Baran just didn't want it to be known that he let his wife get torn down in public. If word got back to her father, the great emir might as well say his last prayers, because once a glass dragon marked you for death? Nothing would come between them and their target.

She couldn't stop the bitterness from seeping into her tone. "Well, I wouldn't want to be responsible for tarnishing your reputation."

Baran's gaze snapped to hers. For a breathless moment her heart stuttered the way it had on their wedding night. When he'd held her so tenderly and kissed her with lips that promised love. Then the mask of the emir crashed down, leaving her with the impassive face she knew too well. "That's not what I meant."

A burst of menacing laughter rose above the tents, sending a shiver skittering across Suraya's flesh. "Where's the Emira?" the prince called. "I want to see one of these glass dragons for myself!"

"Go!" Baran whispered harshly. "Now."

She grasped the skirt of her dress and sprinted through the gaps in the tents. Each footfall brought the delicate chiming of her skin as vibrations resonated like a crystal singing bowl. She ducked into their tent and huddled in the shadows.

"Ah, Emir Baran," the prince's oily voice was barely audible over the thrum of her own heartbeat. "Where is that gorgeous wife of yours?"

"I ordered her to bed," Baran replied curtly. "This is the first time she's been on an expedition like this. She's exhausted."

The prince barked a laugh. "Dragons don't get tired, if the tales are to be believed. They used to kill entire battalions of human armies."

"Warriors, not princesses. Parness Suraya is the latter."

"She's neither, then. The laws of her people don't apply here. *Emira Suraya* is my subject and will obey when commanded." He snapped his fingers.

She pulled her arms to her chest as footsteps approached. Then a second set in pursuit.

Baran's silhouette cast a shadow on the tent opening, blocking the path of whoever was trying to get inside.

"Stand down, Emir," the prince ordered.

If she didn't do something this was going to escalate. She took a fortifying breath. All her concentration funneled into giving off the air of exhaustion instead of panic as she pushed aside the tent flap. Baran's hands clenched into fists as he glared down one of his men. The young soldier looked terrified to be pitted between his commander and the prince.

"Your Highness," she greeted innocently. "I wasn't expecting company. I would have made myself more presentable."

This feigned flattery caught the crown prince off guard. He blinked at her in drunken confusion.

She took the verbal advantage. "Did you need to discuss the strategy for the trade talks? You'd mentioned on the road that you had come up with a way to force Tengura's hand."

"I – no." He took a step back. "There was, uh, some debate about whether glass dragons are really as beautiful as the stories claim."

Baran's arms flexed.

Suraya put a hand on his shoulder as she came up beside him, willing him to hold his tongue even as her knees trembled. "Tomorrow, if it's your wish, I could entertain the company with some of my illusion magic. That might satisfy the curiosity of the court."

"Yes. That would be acceptable." The prince cleared his throat, the bravado in his voice already crumbling. "Fen, let's get back. Geru was bragging about wine he picked up in the last town. I want to know if it's as good as he claims."

They scurried away and disappeared into the shadows. She pivoted and hurried back into the tent so she could sit on the bed of furs before her legs gave out.

Baran followed her inside, his huge frame looming in the doorway. "That was reckless."

She rubbed her arms, trying to chase away the lingering chill from the encounter. "It was better than you getting into a fight with him."

"I told you to let me handle it."

"No, you told me to go back to my tent. I did. That didn't work, so I decided it was better to take the risk, so he didn't order your execution!"

"You're being melodramatic."

Anger ignited like a spark to kindling. Burnt orange turned russet. "I saw him lose his temper not three weeks ago and behead a serving woman in front of the entire court!"

A light rain started, pattering against the tent. It swelled until it drowned out the thrumming of blood in her ears.

Baran's expression sharpened. "You didn't tell me that happened."

"You've hardly been home!" Bile burned the back of her throat as she pushed out the gruesome images in her mind. Her father had warned her about the prince's temper. Had made sure Suraya was very aware of the danger she was accepting by agreeing to shuttle back information to the resistance her father was mounting in case the prince ever came into full power. But nothing had prepared her to see the violence firsthand. Unbidden tears welled in her eyes, and she swiped them away with her fingertips. "It doesn't matter. I'm tired. Goodnight." She deliberately turned and pulled out the wooden box of her hair supplies.

From the corner of her eye, she caught a flicker of Baran's stricken expression. Then he settled into resignation. "I have to check in with the night watch. Don't leave the tent. I probably won't be back until after midnight."

A light breeze hit her back as the entrance flapped. She dropped her wooden comb onto the blankets and twined her fingers around the soft furs. Regret took root in her soul, then guilt. No one had forced her to accept the marriage match. Her father had presented it as a potential strategy for having someone on the inside – something her people had been denied since the Fatengal Empire had conquered their land and forced them to assimilate as a province. One of dozens that had been claimed in the last three centuries. The empire wanted the alliance because they could hold her hostage and strengthen their control over her people.

They didn't know she'd already forfeited her life.

She pushed back her hair scarf and unwound her braided bun. Baran wasn't the villain here. He was being used by both his emperor and the Crystal Dragon Dynasty. It wasn't fair to put him in the middle of this, but he was savvy enough to know what these kinds of marriages meant. She pulled the comb through the ends of her hair, working her way up as she undid the braid.

The familiar routine soothed her nerves. She was just tired. Sleep would bring her clarity, and then she could focus on the trade talks instead of her shattered heart.

* * *

Her dreams were full of mirrors and crystals. The inner sanctum of the temple dedicated to the goddess of mercy, truth, and light. A grief-stricken keen echoed against the crystal-boned walls, swelling into harmonic chimes that resonated in her bones.

Someone grabbed her with invisible hands. She screamed as she was yanked forward, and the vision shattered.

"Suraya, get up!" Baran shouted.

Her heart pounded as her eyes flew open. The cry from the dream had morphed into something louder.

Ominous.

Baran gave another sharp tug, forcing her onto her knees. "There's a flood, we have to evacuate up the hill!" Rain streamed down his face from soaked hair. He seized the outer dress she'd cast aside and shoved it into her hands before grabbing her boots.

Terror sank its talons into her chest. She couldn't swim. No glass dragon could, they sank like stones. She pulled the dress over her under-tunic and pants and shoved her feet into her boots. Baran hauled her out the tent. Sheets of rain pelted her face. People shouted. Animals brayed in fear.

They splashed through ankle-deep puddles as Baran pulled her into a run, fingers digging painfully into her wrist. The water rose up to their calves as the rumbling grew louder – closer.

"What is that?" she shouted.

A bolt of lightning streaked out of the sky. A date palm exploded, knocking them back. She lost her footing. Her hand slid from Baran's grip. Pain shot up her shoulder as she slammed against rocks.

The ground shook.

Surging water hit like a boulder. It filled her ears, her nose, her throat. Her glass skin scraped against the riverbed like breaking crystal, every impact a shriek of pain. There was no up or down.

Just darkness.

Pressure wound around her torso. She was dragged backward against solid muscle. Her head broke the surface, and she took a spluttering gasp of air. A log jammed into her chest.

"Grab it!" Baran shouted.

Her fingers scrambled to get hold. He let go of her and reached around to grip the log. His body forced hers up, so they were floating together, feet pointing downstream.

"Just hold on. Do not let go!"

Time slowed to an agonizing crawl. Her arms shook from desperately clinging to the wood. Her fingers slipped. Panic threatened to consume her.

"Baran!" she shrieked.

His feral cry split the air. He twisted and kicked, splashing water as debris pounded against them. A jutting rock ripped the wood from their grasp. He seized her around the chest before she was dragged back under the surface.

They crashed into land. Baran scrambled to get purchase and hauled her out of the water. He held tight as they crawled up the slope. Thorns and sticks snagged at their clothes. Her strength gave out. She collapsed onto the ground, gulping air into her burning lungs.

Baran landed next to her, chest heaving as he rolled onto his back.

The rain slowed, then stopped. She lifted her head. Baran was still. Panic overtook her and she scrambled to his side. She hovered over him, desperately searching for signs of life. The fabric of his tunic shifted as he breathed. Her body folded over his as she tried to draw air into her burning lungs.

He'd exhausted himself. *All to keep me from drowning.* The thought hit her like a donkey kick to the gut. He didn't have to come for her. His priority should have been protecting the crown prince.

Carrying him out of this place in her human form would be impossible. Anxiety wrapped around her throat like a vine as the flood water rose and lapped at her ankles. *We are not dying here.* Before she lost her nerve or gave into the throbbing pain, she ripped off one layer of clothing at a time and tied them to Baran.

She stood naked, shivering and lighting up a small circle around them with her inner luminescence.

Silver magic skittered across her skin. Her head snapped back as her skeleton rearranged. She shrieked as pain exploded in her bones. Glass skin became scales. Her torso elongated and morphed. Strength seeped into her sore muscles. Cracks formed on her back as a pair of translucent wings bloomed. Claws sank into the saturated ground as she landed on all fours. A tinkling chime floated delicately above the rushing river with each move she made.

Carefully, she wedged one of her wings under his shoulders. Then braced herself against the fiery strain in her shoulder as she maneuvered so he slid onto her back.

Pale dawn peaked over the ridge ahead of her. If her people hadn't traded the gift of flight for a blessing from the goddess that gave them magic, she could have flown them out. But they had, so all she could do was begin her slow, agonizing march up the slope away from the raging current.

* * *

"Suraya…"

The deep, rasping voice drew her out of the abyss of sleep. Pebbles pressed into her spine as she blinked awake. An impossibly clear azure sky stretched out in all directions. Her damp outer dress clung directly to her skin.

"Thank the goddess…" Baran muttered as he pressed his forehead to hers.

Her breath caught at the warmth of his touch, foreign yet comforting. An ache of yearning sprouted in her chest. Then came the pain. Every inch of her flesh felt like she'd been scraped and bruised. She pushed herself up, crying out as her arm exploded in agony and her strength gave way.

"Don't move," he whispered as his fingers brushed back her hair. "I think you broke something."

She breathed through clenched teeth as the pain dulled to a throb. "I was fine when I carried you."

"You were probably too panicked to notice. Or shifting made something worse."

"How did you know I did that?"

"Your father made me sit through a lot of lectures from one of your court scholars. As a dragon you're nearly indestructible. But in human shape? You're the opposite. It's the only way you could have carried me."

Her father had told Baran to study her people. And he'd listened. "I didn't know that."

"There was a lot going on." His breath brushed her cheek. "I need to set your arm before we find shelter. Stay still."

His absence left her breathless. In a matter of moments, he'd gathered supplies and used his knife to cut strips from her under-tunic. "What are you doing?"

"I'm going to bind your arm then make a sling. It will keep it immobilized. Does anything else feel broken?"

"No."

"Good." There was another ripping sound. "They'll send out a search party for anyone washed downstream. We just need to hold out until someone comes looking. There's a cave I can see up ahead."

"What if we're too far away?"

He reappeared at her side and set down his supplies. "The plateau we were camped by is still in sight. Neither of us are in a condition to walk the distance without clean water and food, but it's close enough that we're within the typical search range." His relentless calm settled her nerves. She winced as he gently pushed the sleeve of her dress up. He frowned down at cracks that spread like spider silk across her flesh. The crevices gleamed crimson as her blood ran through the grooves. "Can you shatter?"

"Um, no. But shards can flake off..." A pink hue emanated from her flesh. "I'm sorry, it's not the kind of thing you want to hear about me."

"I've seen men split open from the navel." He picked up the torn strip and wound it around her hand, wrist, up her arm.

She swallowed the pain as he pulled it tight, holding her body together by force of will. Then he got the limb secured into a sling held snug against her breast.

"Just hold on, I'll get you to the cave so you can rest."

* * *

She woke to the warmth of a fire kissing her chilled skin and the red light of sunset filtering through the cave. Baran was within arm's reach, his head tipped back against the wall and eyes closed.

Stone scraped against her calf as she tried to move, and the eerie screech of crystal peeling off echoed.

Baran jerked awake, his hand flying to the hilt of his knife. For a moment he looked disoriented. Then his gaze met hers and his eyes cleared of sleep. "What was that?"

"Nothing," she lied through clenched teeth.

He grunted in disbelief as he scrutinized her. His eyes tracked the fresh bloom of blood staining her dress. His muscles tensed. Before she could protest, he'd hiked up her dress so he could inspect the injury.

"Baran!"

"You said nothing else was broken!"

"It's not!"

"You're covered in cracks, Suraya. You look like you'll shatter if a feather hits you!"

The long-held simmering resentment turned her burnt orange. "At least then you'll be rid of me!"

He jerked his head up. "What did you say?"

"I'm not some dewy-eyed princess – you've barely looked at me in ages. You don't have to pretend to care just because we almost died!"

His mouth opened, but no words came.

Exhaustion, fear, and simmering rage leaked out as tears down her cheeks. "You've done your duty, Emir. It was a flash flood. There's not going to be any catastrophic political repercussions for the empire if a foreign dignitary—"

He crushed his lips to hers, silencing her spiral. His hand cradled the back of her head as he jerked back.

She couldn't look away from his wild, panicked eyes. It was an expression she'd never seen on his face. "Baran…what are you doing?"

"I'm sorry." His voice cracked.

Hope flickered defiantly in her soul. The burnt orange refracted on her cracked flesh turned pale yellow.

He brushed her damp cheek with his thumb. "You're not a political pawn to me, Suraya."

More tears spilled. *Don't give into this*, she chastised herself. He was just exhausted. "I know the emperor ordered you to agree to this marriage."

"As your father ordered you."

"I agreed."

"So did I."

She blinked rapidly, trying to clear her vision. "It's not the same."

"No, it's not. Because I'm not a royal hostage. If I didn't agree to marry you, I knew the emperor would hand you off to someone else."

"We barely knew each other before this."

"I'd seen you at court once or twice." He traced the outline of her lip. "You're clever – brilliant, really. I saw you put a few courtiers in their place. If someone else got their hands on you…" His breaths turned shallow. "The prince wanted to marry you."

She gasped. "What?"

"The emperor was against it, but I couldn't take the risk. And even if it wasn't him, I've seen the crown prince weasel his way into other courtiers' marriages. As my wife I thought I could protect you. That's all it was at first."

At first. She held her breath.

He pressed a lingering kiss to her forehead. "If the prince knew how much I loved you…"

"You love me?"

"Since the moment I saw you at the harvest feast last year." He cupped her cheek. "I'm a traitor."

It was hard to follow his meaning when he was barely a breath away. "I don't understand."

"When I was on that mission, after we got married, I found evidence that the crown prince was the one who murdered his older brother and his young wife. A man like that shouldn't be allowed to come to power. If anyone found out that I'm working against the prince…that we were intimate in each other's lives…"

"I accepted the marriage because Father wanted me on the inside." The confession tumbled out before she could think better of it.

His brows furrowed. "You were sent to spy?"

"Against the crown prince." Guilt rolled in like fog. She'd never even thought about the risk to him if they were involved.

A wry smile touched his lips. "A pair of traitors then."

Her resolve crumbled. She didn't care about the risk. All she knew was that she couldn't survive years of this horrible separation. "What if we worked together?"

"You could die."

"So could you." Her heart thrummed in her ears. "Please… I – I love you too. And we can't just walk away—"

"Yes."

She didn't have the strength to quell the rising hope.

He leaned in. His lips grazed hers, softer than the brush of a spring breeze. "I want to work together."

"You swear not to push me away?"

"On my life, Parness Suraya… I swear to be the husband you deserve."

Pressure built in her chest until she thought it would burst with joy. She kissed him. Long, and deep. Their tongues brushed in a dance of released passion.

A shout from outside permeated their sanctuary. Baran jerked back and ran for the cave entrance. His shoulders sagged in relief. "It's the lieutenant." He gave a loud whistle then waved. There was more shouting.

Anxiety turned her radiant light from yellow to storm blue as doubt crept in.

Baran crossed the cave and crouched, taking her hand in his. "I meant what I said, Suraya. We're going to build an empire our children can be proud to grow up in."

Children. Future. He wasn't bluffing or just trying to make her forget how close to shattering she was. The weight of responsibility lightened. She gave a tight smile, but the lavender blooming across her skin gave away the depth of her emotions. For the first time since coming to the imperial court, she had an ally.

One who loved her. Had jumped into a raging torrent so she wouldn't drown and nearly got into a fight with the most dangerous man in the empire on her behalf.

"Fight with me?" he whispered.

Lavender light flooded the cave as she was overwhelmed with affection for him. "Until my dying breath."

The Lindwyrm's Wife

Kay Hanifen

"It is a great honor," they said as they dressed me in silks and jewels.

"It is a great honor," they said as they led me to the bridal bedroom after a quick ceremony performed with a proxy groom.

"It is a great honor," they said as they shut the door, locking it with a click. The room was pitch black, forcing my eyes to slowly adjust as I felt my way to the bed.

My lord husband, the rightful prince of the realm, awaited me in the dark, unfit to be seen by any but his wife. I was his third, all others before me devoured after displeasing him. He had no interest in beauty or intellect or proper womanhood. No one knew what he wanted, but still, he insisted upon a wife.

Not knowing what was expected next, I sat, my heart racing as I listened to the rasp of scales on the stone floor. Prince Lindwyrm had yet to reveal himself, but it was only a matter of time before I became his next meal. And all I wanted was for it to be over and done with. "My lord," I called out to the shadows. "My lord husband."

"A bold little queen," something hissed from the shadows. "I've never had one call to me before."

"I wish to finally see the man I have married."

A soft huff of a laugh, the warm breath sending shivers through me. "A man. Do you truly believe you have married a man?"

"You were born of the king and queen, were you not?"

Another laugh, and the sensation of hot breath from behind, displacing the hair to tickle my ear. "I was. And a crone. One who instructed my mother that if she wanted children, she must eat one of two roses, red or white, but not both. Red would give her a son, white a daughter, and she must choose. But she forgot the rule and ate both. Nine months later, my younger twin brother came out a perfect, squalling human boy, while I, the first-born, was an abomination. So, they left me for dead, abandoned in a collapsed cave and forced to fend for myself. But I am the rightful heir, so when I escaped, I returned for what is owed to me."

"I'm sorry you went through that," I replied, keeping my eyes trained forward. "It sounds truly terrible."

"You…what?" the creature in the dark faltered. "What do you mean?"

"I mean that you have been through something terrible, and it grieves me to hear of it, my lord."

"I don't need your pity," Prince Lindwyrm snapped, making me flinch.

"Not pity, my lord." I forced myself to keep my voice calm and even. Every story I heard whispered that he hated it when his brides acted afraid. It ignited his rage and if I wasn't careful, I would be burned. The thought made me bring my hand up to the rough skin of my cheek. It had been years since the illness, but the nerves still ached. "You might call it understanding. Though my disfigurement is nothing like yours, it is enough that I was locked away until they found a suitable husband in you. No one else would take me."

"It seems we are both unwanted creatures," the prince replied.

I chuckled weakly, though my heart ached. As a princess, my only job was to be married, and when my face was marred by a case of the burning pox, I could not even manage that. "I suppose so. May I be permitted to gaze upon my husband, or are we to sit in the dark for the rest of our marriage?"

"Oh, but I do hate it when my wives scream at the sight of me."

"And I hate it when men curl their lips in disgust whenever they gaze upon my face. If you promise not to do that, I promise not to scream."

Another laugh, and then a burst of flame shot across the room. It landed in the hearth in a remarkable display of control. The light blinded me for a moment, but when my eyes adjusted, I turned to look at the source of the fire. My husband wrapped around this small room, his head sitting right behind me. He was long and thin, with opalescent white scales that shimmered in the firelight. In spite of myself, I gasped. I just couldn't help it.

He flicked his massive eyes – vibrant blue and the size of my fist – to me, his gaze apprehensive. "Well?"

"You're beautiful," I breathed.

His serpentine face fell. "Do not mock me."

"I'm not." Getting to my feet, I carefully approached his armored belly. "May I?"

He huffed, instantly warming the room with his breath. "If you insist."

I ran my hands along the scales of his body, surprised by how smooth and dry they were. I'm not sure why I expected them to be slimy, but it was a nice feeling, like basking in the summer sand. His wings were leathery, and simply fascinating. I wondered if they could carry his massive body.

"You do not fear me?" he asked, breaking the silence. "I have killed two maidens before you."

"The murder is a little frightening," I admitted, not taking my gaze off the way the light bouncing off his scales created little rainbows. "But I have no other prospects, and I am placing my trust in you that you will not murder me."

His size did raise several questions, though. Most notably, how we were supposed to…consummate our marriage. The thought alone made my cheeks burn. I supposed that we would not be producing heirs regardless. Dragon and human biology is simply incompatible.

"To be fair, those maidens had designs of dragon slaying," he said, laying his head down. "The two before had brought knives to their marriage bed. I'm inclined to believe that my mother and father put them up to it. They wished for me out of the way so that their golden child would rule."

"They didn't make me the same offer. They simply had me marry you by proxy and sent me here. Perhaps my parents also wished to be rid of me. If I panicked and you ate me, then the problem of me would be solved. If we found ourselves unexpectedly compatible, then both our parents' problem children would be handled. There was no losing for them." Lying back on the bed, I stretched out on my stomach, propping my chin on my hands the way I would on the nights when my visiting cousins and I slept in the same room. We would stay up talking and giggling until the sky lightened into early dawn.

That was before I took ill with burning pox. Even long after I recovered from the infection, no one wished to be close to me for fear of catching it. I suspect, though, that they simply did not wish to see my hideous face.

"What a pair we are."

I chuckled. "Indeed. Now that we've established that we will neither kill nor eat each other, what should we do?"

"Do?" Prince Lindwyrm tilted his head curiously.

"I'm afraid I am a bit too energized to sleep just yet, and I don't think they would expect us to fulfill our…royal duties, as it were."

He inhaled slightly at that. If he were human, I expect that he would have turned cherry red. "No, I do believe that is out of the question." He paused, a puff of smoke curling from his nostrils. "I–I mean, would you? Want to, I mean. Someday. Logistically, it's well…how would that even work?"

I giggled. There was something so charming about such a giant creature looking as flustered as a schoolboy with his first crush. "I suppose we can get creative if we decide to, but I am in no hurry."

Lindwyrm's relief was palpable. "Neither am I." He sighed. "If only I could be rid of this accursed form."

"What would you want to look like? If you were human, I mean." He remained silent for a long time. Rolling onto my back, I lifted my head. "I'm sorry. Was that a rude question?"

"No, I…" He paused, still thinking. "I simply hadn't thought much about it. I suppose I would want to be small. Short and slight enough to be able to get into tight places, but also soft. Some tissue at my breasts and the curves of my hips. I rather like my blue eyes, so I would like to keep those, and I would like to have golden hair like my brother. But I would wear it longer, so that I can braid it intricately like yours." He reached out with a massive, clawed hand, and gently stroked one of my braids. Perhaps I should have been afraid, but still, I leaned into the touch. No one had willingly touched me in a long time. "I've always been jealous of hair."

I giggled, holding just one of his clawed fingers with both hands. "The person you described sounds a lot like a woman."

"It does?" Lindwyrm hummed thoughtfully. "I suppose that does not matter. It's little more than an idle dream. We cannot change what we are."

"Perhaps." I yawned, suddenly exhausted. "But if you were brought into this world through magic, then, perhaps, magic will be able to change you into who you most wish to be."

A soft rumble, almost like the purr of a cat. Another laugh, perhaps. "Go to sleep, my..." He paused. "Well, this is rather embarrassing. I never learned your name."

"Agnes," I replied with another yawn. "And you? Or should I keep calling you Prince Lindwyrm?"

"I have no other name. No one bothered to give me a real one."

"May I call you Lindy?"

Another rumbling laugh. "You may. Goodnight, Agnes."

"Goodnight, Lindy."

That night, I dreamt of an old crone. Before her grew two roses, one red and one white. She plucked the white flower and peeled away the petals one by one. "One for you, one for the wyrm. One for you, one for the wyrm. All seven layers shed to reveal the truth within."

"Is that how to break the curse?" I asked. "What layers do we shed?"

"You have outer layers that may be taken or removed at will. Seven dresses into nothing. Seven layers of fabric skin."

"But what about Lindy?"

She smiled toothlessly as she revealed the flower's bare stem. Before my eyes, a new bud emerged. "The wyrm will know what must be removed."

I woke to the sound of a door unlocking. Sometime in the night, Lindy had laid his head beside me on the bed, and I curled up against him.

A pair of knights opened the door with a gasp. "Is…is she dead?" one knight whispered to the other.

I raised my head. "I'm still quite alive, thank you. I would appreciate some breakfast, though. If the servants feel unsafe, they can leave it at the door for me."

"Y–yes, your highness," the second knight said. They beat an almost comically hasty retreat.

The bed shook with Lindy's chuckles. "They're the only ones brave enough to come up and bring me meals every day. It seems that you have frightened them more than my teeth or claws."

I rubbed the top of his scaled head. "I suppose they expected to find me in the belly of the beast."

"Luckily, you are far too interesting for that, my lady." He yawned, revealing teeth as thick as my wrist. "I trust that you slept well."

"I did, and I—" I gasped, remembering how I dreamt of the crone who gave him life. "I believe I may have found a way to break the curse."

He lifted his head in surprise. "You what?"

I told him everything I saw in that dream, trying to recall every detail.

"So, if you shed seven dresses, and I shed seven layers of something my true self would be revealed?" Lindy asked once I had finished.

"I think so. It was a dream – only a dream – but it feels right, doesn't it?"

"I suppose it cannot hurt to try. It would be nice to walk among humanity without inspiring terror."

I leaned against him, wrapping my arms around his neck in a facsimile of a hug. "I'll send for my things."

If the expressions on the two knights' faces when they saw me alive were amusing, they were nothing in comparison to those of my mother- and father-in-law when I approached them in the court.

Both sat slack-jawed on the throne as I bowed before them, and I had to bite my cheek to keep myself from laughing out loud at the sight. "Your majesties, I trust that you slept well."

The queen blinked, seeming to come back to herself. "Er, yes. And you? I hope your lord husband pleases you."

"Immensely," I replied. "Lindy is a delight."

"Lindy?" the king asked. "You gave it a name?"

I grinned cheekily. This was far too much fun. "Well, Prince Lindwyrm is a bit of a mouthful, and my lord husband rather likes the name."

He sighed, rubbing his forehead. "Of course it does."

"And you have…consummated the marriage?" The queen looked me up and down in a mixture of confusion and concern. She was likely wondering how it all fit and why I wasn't walking bowlegged through her court.

"Not as such," I replied boldly. If she wanted to bring up such an intimate matter in the middle of her court, then I would happily indulge her. Let them be uncomfortable when their ugly little secrets step into the light. "But I am working on it. This is why I have come here. I would like to request that you send for my dresses. Seven of them, please. I would ask a servant, but they've made themselves scarce."

"Right. Of course. We will send for them immediately. In the meantime, is there anything else we can do for you?" the queen replied.

"Breakfast would be wonderful. That honey cake I had last night was delicious, and I would love another slice. I would also enjoy some books and, perhaps, a loom. I have always needed to keep my hands and mind occupied. Oh, and Lindy would like to request that you no longer send him fully grown rams and bulls. The horns get stuck in his teeth."

The queen nodded. "I will do what I must to ensure that you and your lord husband are comfortable."

I gave them an exaggerated curtsy. "You have my gratitude, your majesties. I will be in my room with my lord husband if you need me." With that, I left once again for the tower where Lindy waited for me.

When I opened the door, he picked up his head. With the shutters closed, the room was still rather dark and stuffy. "May I open the windows?"

He seemed reluctant. "I'm afraid that I have spent so long in the darkness that the light hurts my eyes."

"It's the pain of adjustment," I said. "The only way you'll be able to feel the sun is to go through it, the same as anyone else."

He sighed, smoke billowing from his nose. "Very well. But if I am blinded forever, you will join my other two wives."

Perhaps the idle threat should have frightened me, but instead, I snorted, amused, and went to open the window. "I thank you for your indulgence, my lord."

In the light of day, I realized that Lindy was not nearly as large as I imagined in the darkness. He was big and long enough to wrap around the room, but his body was thin – thin enough to slither in and out of the windows if he kept his wings close to his chest.

"Have you ever flown?" I asked.

"Not often. It's one of the few joys of this form, but with my eyes and the fact that people prefer dragons slain than living, I never had much opportunity."

"Has anyone ever ridden you?" It was an absurd question, one that would lead to an even more absurd request.

"My lady, I thought we agreed to wait until the curse had been lifted for that," he replied, his voice pitched slightly higher in mock offense.

I rolled my eyes. "I meant like a horse."

He chuckled. "Well, then no. In fairness, no one has ever asked."

"Would you be willing to let me ride you? I've always dreamt of flying." When he didn't respond, my cheeks flushed in embarrassment. "Forgive me, I should never have said anything."

"No." He got to his feet and slithered to the window. "I fear I may already be too indulgent towards you, my lady, but I cannot seem to help myself. A short flight for my beloved wife."

Like mounting a horse, I hooked my legs over his neck right behind the wings and hugged him close as he leapt from the window. Then, we were falling, falling, falling…

And at the last second, he unfurled himself, gliding as we skimmed the ground. With a few great beats from his mighty wings, we were airborne again and climbing higher and higher until we were among the clouds. Though it was quite cold, his furnace of a body kept me warm.

I screamed with delight and clung to him as he performed flips and barrel rolls, showing off for me in the sky. Below us, the farmers and townspeople bustled about, looking much like ants collecting food for their colonies. He climbed up to a cloud embankment, and I held out my hand, shivering as I touched the freezing water. It made sense, I suppose, but a part of me always imagined that clouds would have the texture of lamb's wool.

Shivering, I clung to him even harder as the ground slowly came closer and he grabbed onto the tower, climbing like a normal sized lizard through the window. Giggling, I flopped to the ground.

"That was…amazing!" I exclaimed, still short of breath.

"You're freezing." With a breath, he lit the fire in the chimney and curled around me. In seconds, I was surrounded by warmth. Between that and the excitement of the flight, I could have fallen asleep right there.

But night was falling soon, and we had to prepare for the ritual. As soon as I was warm and dry, I collected the six other dresses from the box left just outside our room while we were gone.

With seven layers on and the fireplace burning, I began to sweat in my dresses. I felt heavy and stiff, my body clumsy and wrong.

"Are you well? You look hot," Lindy asked, his voice full of concern.

I could barely breathe in the discomfort of the layers. "Well, I can take off a layer. Then, you take off a layer of…something. The crone said you would know what to do."

Lindy sighed. "I believe so. It will not be pleasant, but I will try."

"Will it hurt?" I brought my hand up to his scaly cheek.

"The pain of transformation is better than the agony of stagnation," he replied. "Now, take off your first dress. You look as though you might faint."

I did as he said. It didn't provide much relief, but I could move a little easier and breathe more freely.

Then Lindy began to scratch at himself, peeling away his skin in great flakes and leaving bloodied scales underneath. When he was done, he was noticeably smaller as he collapsed onto the ground.

"Lindy!" I exclaimed, cradling his head in my lap.

The dragon gave me the closest thing to a smile his mouth could manage. "Take off another dress, my wife. You look ready to melt."

"But—" I began to protest.

He cut me off. "I have suffered worse. As have you. Shed another layer, and let me do the same."

So, I did as a proper wife should, and I obeyed my husband. I removed another layer and helped him pull away his skin. The deeper we went, the more the scales began to resemble flesh. But this seemed to hurt him even more. The bloodier the skin, the more he screamed as we pulled it away.

"We should take a break," I said when we had completed the fourth shedding.

"No," he gritted out. "I fear that if I stop, I'll never start again."

I stroked his cheek. His face was becoming more and more human, but his ice blue eyes remained slitted like a snake's. "If you're sure…"

"I am. Let us finish this."

Three layers left. Then two. Then one.

I suppose I should not have felt shy standing nude before my husband. After all, we were expected to produce an heir, but my cheeks burned as I shrugged off the final dress and dropped it to the floor.

Lindy didn't care much anyway. He was too exhausted, breathing hard and focused on clawing away at his own bloodied flesh, revealing pale skin underneath. I helped, bile rising in my throat with the sound of tearing meat and my husband's screams as he clawed his way out of the flesh that had cocooned him his whole life.

Once the last vestiges of scales were gone, he collapsed onto his hands and knees.

"Lindy?" I asked, not daring to speak above a whisper.

The dragon-turned-human pushed himself up, and I finally saw him in his full glory. Lindy had retained his leathery wings and serpentine eyes, but now was tall and lanky, with long, white hair, breasts, curves, and no member. I remembered the conversation we'd had the previous night, how Lindy had come from the white rose – the girl flower – and expressed a desire to look more like a woman than a man. Suddenly, it all made sense. "My husband?"

"Perhaps husband isn't the right word for me," Lindy replied, her pale lips curling in a broad smile.

"This form pleases you, my lady?" I asked, answering her contagious grin with one of my own.

Her cheeks dusted a lovely pink at that. "Lady?"

"Is that what you prefer, or would you still rather be my lord husband?" I asked.

"My lady wife has a better ring to it," she replied, examining her smooth, alabaster hands. When she looked up at me, her blue eyes shimmered with tears. "This is…perfect. Better than I could ever have imagined." Her face fell. "But would you be pleased to have a wife over a husband?"

Kneeling in front of her, I cupped her cheek in my hands. "I was pleased to have a husband who was a dragon. I will be just as pleased to have a wife who is something new and different and altogether extraordinary."

She threw her arms around me, practically tackling me to the ground with her joy. We laughed, rolling in the sloughed-off skin of her previous form. Then, she pressed a kiss to my lips.

Lindy was warm, like curling up within a hearth without the terror of burning. Her lips tasted of brimstone and when she opened her mouth, I let my tongue explore it. We kissed until we were breathless, and then we kissed some more, until our eyes grew heavy and sleep called to us.

We were both exhausted from the night's ordeal, so I scooped her up and laid her in our marriage bed before curling up beside her. She wrapped her wings around me, tugging me in close.

Tomorrow, we will introduce Princess Lindy, the Dragon Lady, to the court. We will ingratiate her to the king and queen and decide if we should stay or strike out on our own. We will forge our own happily ever after. But for tonight, we will rest in each other's arms.

The Name

Sarah Hozumi

Kiros swooped low along the side of our mountain until his claws scraped against the rocks, sending a shower of weaker pebbles down toward the village below. The way the dust glittered in the air around his iridescent wings reminded me of fireworks, as if announcing our arrival to the unsuspecting in the valley. A few people were already standing stock-still in the middle of the cobblestone roads, pointing up at us. We weren't close enough that I could see anyone's expressions yet, but I wanted to believe they were excited to finally see Kiros in all of his glory.

With a dig of my heels into his sides, he eased up and made a quiet landing near a fountain while stunned villagers came rushing up to see us. I watched fathers pull their children behind them, the old fiercely whispering to anyone close enough probably stories they'd heard about us. My attention went to the fountain with its statue of a man standing tall and proud over a fallen dragon with a sword still in the poor creature's neck. Kiros eyed the fountain, too, and wanted to leave, but I climbed down from his back and stood to face the people. There were maybe thirty now, and silence rippled from the front rows to the back, until only Kiros's breathing could be heard like the faint rumbling of a volcano behind me.

Parting my lips, I breathed in deeply and exhaled a brilliant gust of air that carried my voice like a song before falling on the stunned ears of those who had gathered. The blank stares sent me turning to Kiros for help. Why couldn't they understand my voice alone? Kiros seemed amused, but he stamped a foot in my general direction, and an unknown part of my mind clicked open to offer a flood of a language I had no name for. Its rules, the words, the tones all spread out before me like Kiros had unfurled a sheet out to dry in the wind. I wanted to dance around to finally have words to the noises and vibrato I had spilled into the air for decades, but Kiros was growing impatient, folding his wings and spreading them in increasing agitation. This had to be quick.

"We are..." The two words were stunning wrapped around my voice, and the look of sudden recognition and understanding on the villagers' faces was enough that I felt like crying. Kiros lowered his head before raising it high again in a huff of irritation at my distraction. "We are in search of another like me."

"No one go with her! You'll lose yourself forever to the great beasts." A man covered in more wrinkles than Kiros's wings gave a ferocious glare in my direction, but I took a step closer to him. The more willful villagers would need to be put in their place first.

"Old stories." My voice was truly a marvel now that words walked alongside it. It sounded more beautiful to me, more whole. "We are offering immortality and power, and you elders fear such things. Only one may be chosen, and those bitter at being passed over create stories from that hatred to besmirch our glory."

"What are you?" I pulled my attention from the old man to see who had spoken, but the faces were a wall of curiosity and fear. Kiros didn't care who we even chose as long as they were quiet and obedient to the new dragon. We had to hurry.

"I am called the Ki." I turned toward Kiros and swept my hands in his direction as he flicked his tail restlessly. He hated how long I was taking, but I had to explain or they'd never let anyone come with us. "Dragons like him are formally called the An. Together, we form a bond."

The flurry of questions was nearly too much for my mind, new to the language, to comprehend, but Kiros told me to withstand it.

"Do you really offer immortality?"

"Are you truly powerful?"

"What does the dragon eat?"

"Are you the reason I'm losing sheep every summer?"

"How many of you are there?"

But the old man's voice was the loudest.

"No one trust this woman's words! These beasts always wander from village to village in search of a willing victim. Lured with pretty words of immortality and power, the dragons will ensnare your mind until you forget your own name and care only about serving them and their ways. You'll be no better than a disguise for the creature to use to walk among us, luring more to their will until there are none of us left."

"My name is Aria."

The old man's eyes narrowed while every voice near the appalling fountain died away. There was no mistaking the hatred seething from his entire body, but Kiros sensed there was someone in this village who would work beautifully for the new dragon. It would hatch soon, and it needed someone to latch onto. We were running out of time.

"That's the name that *thing* gave you. I've known handfuls of people all just like you, all called the same. I mean your real name."

Kiros's nostrils flared, smoke wafting into the air at the accusation my name wasn't my own. Of course it was mine. There was nothing before it, and there would be nothing after it.

When I failed to provide a different name, however, the villagers' interest turned to disgust and, for some, fear as they scooped up their children or coaxed their animals away. Kiros watched the crowd thin until only the old man remained, his impatience growing to greater heights.

"You are not welcome here. Never return. Find somewhere else for your vessels."

Spitting on the ground, the man sniffed the air in front of me as if a foul smell had offended his sensibilities, then marched away while barking orders at anyone who could hear him that they were not to talk to us.

I turned to Kiros with a shrug and a silent promise we would try the next village. There surely had to still be time before the hatching. Kiros gave a tiny nod of his magnificent head, the blue scales rippling green and gold in the sunlight. There was time, but not much.

Before I could place my feet in the usual places missing scales to climb back up Kiros, a man I hadn't noticed before was standing near us, his shoulders thrown too far back in a failed attempt at bravery. While Kiros looked into his light blue eyes and saw in them the perfect Ki for the new dragon, I felt something stir within my heart that seemed to shake at a heavy mass covering my mind. It was like chains trembling on the ground, and I turned away.

"Take me."

Unlike the old man, he had only a sprinkling of wrinkles around his fascinating eyes, with a few strands of gray woven along his black hair pulled loosely back in a half braid. The way he carried himself as Kiros lowered his body down to ease the man's climb up his back suggested perhaps a carpenter or the village's designated hunter. Would they mourn his loss?

Kiros blew a ring of smoke around me, and I wondered why I should care what the village thought of what we were doing. We were going to give the man what I had: immortality and endless power. As long as the Ki was bound to the An, both would live forever at the height of strength.

I climbed up Kiros's back and sat in front of the man, who put his arms around me just as Kiros lifted off the ground. There was only the one groove between his shoulder blades to accommodate me, making it completely logical the man would cling to me, but the sudden touch sent a shiver throughout my body that once again knocked at the chains buried in my mind. Kiros did a sudden drop before pulling sharply up into the sky to shake me from such thoughts, and the man only held on tighter. I could feel his frantic breathing on my neck even as the wind ripped through my clothing and hair, and I closed my eyes to revel in the sensation.

Though he was annoyed I had already taken an interest in the latest Ki offering, Kiros softly landed at the entrance to our sprawling caverns carved high into the mountain and pressed his body against the ground so we could easily dismount.

As Kiros went to check on the dragon's progress breaking out of its shell, I drank in the sight of the man with complete abandon. Beautifully built with a face slightly weathered with time, he was breathtaking to behold. The man wandered the mouth of the cavern, his hair shining in the rays of the sunlight as he admired the views of the valley below and wondered at the years I had spent carving our history into the rocks surrounding us. His worn fingers traced the outline of Kiros I had etched into a boulder near where we had landed, and he gave a small laugh.

"What is it?"

His magnificently blue eyes found mine, and my heart began stuttering in my chest, each breath a greater effort than the one before. I had no idea how one look from him could have such confounding effects on me, but I liked it, and I wanted more. With a deep breath, I took a step closer to him, then another. We were nearly touching, but he merely froze, his gaze steady on mine.

"Perhaps I was a fool to follow a beautiful woman like this, seeing how much you clearly love that dragon."

Love?

My hand went to the grooves comprising Kiros in the rock, and I offered a small smile.

"It isn't love. It's an eternal bond."

His hand fell on top of mine on the rock, warmth from his skin seeping into mine despite the chill of the stone.

"And if I am bonded to a dragon like you are, will I forget how lovely you look in the sun's light like this? Will I forget how desperately I want to know more about you? How profoundly you have amazed me in this flash of an instant?" His other hand went to my hair before falling to my neck. Instinct long buried beneath something suffocating my senses sprang to life, and I put my hand on his back and pulled him to me.

"No, I'll make you remember me."

Another laugh, though with a note of sorrow tainting it.

"But I am to forget my own name."

His lips drew nearer to mine, the ice of his eyes completely overwhelming every thought in my mind except to coax him closer.

"Your dragon will give you a new name."

"Please," his lips grazed the surface of mine, and something entirely new screamed into being in my heart that began to crack the chains firmly wrapped around my mind. It demanded more from this man, but it also demanded more from me. "Please call me Nolan. Even if I am to lose that name forever, please call me it so some shred of myself remains that will connect me to you."

Kiros, I knew, wouldn't like it, but the new being threatening to burst through my chest answered, "Of course, Nolan."

Another kiss, deeper this time, and I fought to remember what had been my name before Kiros. What had I been called? It had been something dull, ordinary and entirely worthy of being forsaken. Why was I wasting time trying to remember when Nolan had his hands on my back, gently holding me as his lips parted mine.

No, shouted the new being within my heart. No, it was me. I was worthy of being remembered.

A roar from the tunnels in the cavern made me push Nolan away.

"Kiros says the dragon is nearly hatched."

Nolan seemed to be fighting to breathe beside me, his hands rubbing at his lips as his lovely eyes were wide, staring at the ground before us in what I could only interpret as shock.

"Why...why did I do that? I'm so sorry, I normally don't rush things like that. I've... I've been alone for too long, I think. Seeing you has completely undone me, and I can only apologize."

It irritated me he should apologize for what had freed a being in my heart now fighting to find my name, and I responded to his apology with a fierce kiss that slammed him against the rock bearing Kiros's image. I ran my fingers through his hair with such violence, his braid was undone, allowing his hair to ripple around his shoulders like dark water. Despite the attack, Nolan's hands remained at his sides until I reached down and forced them to touch my back again.

What had been my name?

Another roar, louder this time, made the ground shake. I wanted to ignore it, but Kiros was terrified the dragon would hatch without a human to latch onto. It would mean death for the dragon, having no life on this earth to serve as its anchor. Decades of searching for the egg would have been for nothing. I had to bring Nolan to the cave housing the dragon egg. Now.

I pushed Nolan away, whose eyes were wide once more in apparent disbelief he had so easily given in to kissing me again, and I took hold of his hand.

"This way."

He was quiet as I navigated the dark tunnels twisting through the labyrinth of caves burying us deeper and deeper into the mountain. My mind was splintered between Kiros's commands I bring Nolan, the being still fighting to find my name, the sheer joy it had been simply kissing him, and the great pleasure I felt holding his hand.

"No matter what happens," Nolan said into the growing voice of Kiros, beckoning us forward into the cave beyond, "I know I won't forget you. I'll forget myself before I forget you. And we can have eternity together, if you want that."

"Yes." My voice failed against Kiros's growls of frustration that I was taking too long. "I want that."

Kiros stood behind the dragon egg lying in the middle of the decidedly small cave that would be Nolan's home until the dragon was strong enough to fly, his eyes burning into mine. I had taken far too long, and the tiny dragon had nearly bitten its way through the outer layer of its shell. Nolan had to be the first thing it saw or its life would never be tied to this world.

Frustration at still not finding my name within my own mind mingled with the fear Nolan would entirely lose himself to the new dragon, and I ended up shoving Nolan at the egg. He managed to catch his footing in time to not fall face-first in front of it, but he still landed on his knees, much to Kiros's satisfaction. It was the perfect posture for a human in the presence of a dragon egg.

"Do not take your eyes off the egg."

But what was my name? Kiros shot me a deadly look, and the frantic mental search dimmed as my attention fell on Nolan, who was staring intently at the egg while still on his knees, frozen to the spot. The magic of the egg was already working to ensnare his senses, to destroy any willpower he might have harbored to move his focus off it.

I took a few steps away from the egg, per Kiros's command. He wanted me to move closer to him so that he could hide me behind his wing in case the dragon hatched and happened to see me first by mistake. I began to work my way around the perimeter of the cave, my eyes locked on Nolan as I went. His jaw was slackening, his eyes now half closed as he drank in the sight of the dragon's head pushing its way through the shell. It had all been cut too close. I had wasted precious seconds kissing him, and we could have lost the dragon. There were already too few dragons left.

A loud snap ricocheted off the stone walls as a piece of the dragon's shell broke away. I ran to Kiros's slightly unfolded wing, bent low in the confines of the cave, and gratefully hid behind it. There were more cracking and snapping sounds, and then a beautiful, impossibly helpless chirping sound filled the room, and I knew the thing was done. Nolan the Ki would be bound to the An, who would tell him his name as its first act on this earth.

What had come before Kiros had done the same to me? I fought back to remember so long ago, when I had sat before the egg containing him. There had been the same cracking sounds, the same profound fascination possessing me as it now did Nolan. The entire world had faded away at the sight of Kiros pushing his then-tiny head out into the air, and I had been entirely broken. His eyes had locked on mine, and through that one gaze had come my name and then his, and it was all I knew.

But what had been before? Who had I been before that moment?

Kiros was too wrapped in his adoration for the new dragon to stop my curiosity, and I looked around his wing at the center of the cave. There, I found Nolan with his hand outstretched toward the little dragon of green and silver, who was working its way out of the rest of its shell. Nolan had not yet been named, for Kiros would have announced it for me to know. The dragon was still too new to the earth, its footing less sure than Kiros's had been. An entirely pure, heavenly creature.

And then it was there, that which I had been seeking since first laying eyes on Nolan. My name.

"Safa."

Pushing away Kiros's wings, I broke into a run and tackled Nolan to the ground before the little dragon could finally lock eyes on him. Kiros's roar was terrifying, but I gripped Nolan's hand and forced him to stand.

"Look at me!" I screamed over Kiros's rage, and Nolan's eyes found mine. In the single breath that had escaped my lips while turning to run with Nolan, I had taken in the heartbreaking sight of his clear blue eyes now somehow dulled, as though a film of dust had settled upon them. He was already lost in himself, but I wouldn't let that dragon sink its claws into him as Kiros had done to me.

We ran through the tunnels to the sound of high-pitched cries growing increasingly desperate. I could feel Nolan's legs grow sluggish, but I only pulled at him harder until I was dragging him from the cave.

"No, please let me go back!" We reached the moonlight-soaked mouth of the cavern, sweat dripping off my body from the sheer effort it took to keep Nolan in my arms, but I continued pulling him toward the side of the cliff, to a path leading down its side.

Another pitiful cry echoed to us.

"No," wept Nolan, "please, she'll die without me. I have to go back."

Another pull against his stubborn body, but I noticed his eyes were finding mine more and more the farther we went from the entrance. It was difficult to navigate the path down while keeping my grip on him, but I managed to look at him as often as I could.

"Stay with me."

"Please, please let me go." His voice was a mess of regret and yearning that I knew all too well. The first few years with Kiros's will wrapped around my own had been suffocating, but the pain I had felt whenever he had left me in the caves to go hunt had been far greater.

"Give me your name, and I will."

To this, Nolan stopped moving. He was still half twisted toward the cliff now looming above us, a lone tear streaking down his cheek, but he had stopped on his own. Maybe I had saved him in time.

"My name?"

A terrible, heart-shattering roar broke through the cavern and rang out into the air, sending birds in the valley below flying off in a panic. It wouldn't be long before Kiros, now too full of rage and pain to form words in my mind, would find us. I had to somehow find a place where we might hide. I would have to sleep and shut off my mind to stop Kiros from finding us, and Nolan would need to be in his right mind for that.

"You have a name. What is it?"

I pulled at his hand and spied the shadows of a small cave dipping into the side of the path. It felt beyond foolish to stop there, so close to Kiros's lair, but he would hopefully think we had traveled farther, perhaps down into the valley below. It was a weak, pathetic hope, but it was all I had as I pulled Nolan into the darkness.

The cave offered us no room to stand, and Nolan collapsed in a heap beside me, holding his head in his hands as I imagined he fought just as I had to find himself again. I pushed myself back into the cave until I felt cold rock against my back, then tried to think of nothing at all as Kiros's rage tore through me. It was a betrayal too deep for him to comprehend. He wouldn't kill me, thus severing his own ties to the earth, but Nolan no longer served a purpose.

"My name..." groaned Nolan beside me. I coaxed him to sit closer to me and covered his mouth with my hand.

Kiros gave a great roar again and blasted past the cave without giving it a second glance, but I would need to be asleep by the time his wrath had subsided enough that he could think more clearly.

In sheer desperation, my lips found Nolan's, and it was a brief spark of life that I prayed would awaken his identity, as his first kiss had done to me. He gave a small gasp that made me cover his mouth again, but his hands were at the sides of his head, and he doubled over with a low moan.

Please, I inwardly prayed.

Cries of terror floated up into the air, and raw horror was a shard of ice in my throat I was forced to swallow at the thought the villagers down below were suffering Kiros in my place. I couldn't look, though. I couldn't move.

"My name…"

I pressed my hand more firmly against Nolan's mouth, and I waited. The cries from the villages below became mingled with the sounds of massive structures crashing to the ground, and sparks of light flooded the cave that I knew had to be Kiros. He would raze the entire valley, so lost was he becoming in his pain.

A warm hand touched the one covering Nolan's mouth, and with a start, I dropped my hand to see Nolan calmly looking at me. It was too dark to see if the filth was still in his eyes, but I met his gaze, and I hoped.

"I am Nolan."

Tears flooded my eyes, and I took his hands into mine. He kissed the backs of them with increasing enthusiasm before his lips began to wander up my arms. I wanted to lose myself in such bliss, but I pushed him carefully away as I heard more screams from down below. His head snapped toward the cave's entrance, and the alarm on his face was clear enough even in the shadows.

"Nolan, I need to sleep for a while so Kiros won't find us. Can I…could you please watch over me? When everything has been quiet, when you can go no longer without food, then please wake me up again."

"What happened? My village..."

"I'm sorry. I couldn't bear to see you chained to a dragon like I am. Your village is paying the price for my actions. I'm... sorry."

His shaking hands touched my face, but he kissed my cheek.

"That demon is attacking my village, not you. I will happily watch over you as you sleep, Aria."

"No," my voice was automatic, even as I managed to work myself down into the depths of an empty dream, "Safa."

Before the dream completely took me, I took in Nolan's rich voice crooning, "Safa is such a lovely name," and then shut myself away with the one hope that if I dug deeply enough into nothingness, I could find a way to sever the bond to Kiros.

If it took me the rest of my life, I vowed I would not rest until I had.

A Worthy Oath

Valerie Hunter

The day the king demanded his oath-soldiers bring him the blood of a dragon, Fidelia decided she would be the one to do it.

The king had only been crowned sixteen months ago, succeeding the elderly queen who had reigned since Fidelia had arrived at the kingdom eight years ago. She'd only ever seen the queen once, when she'd finished her training and taken her sworn oath, but the king always seemed to be around, making pronouncements or decrees, or just watching them train. He liked to scoff over the lady soldiers as though they hadn't proven their strength and mettle time and again. Fidelia scorned any other man who underestimated her, but she could hardly scorn her own sovereign, the man her oath belonged to. So she would prove herself, bring him the blood he wanted.

After the king had made his demand, their commander, Makany, brought in the chief physician and several scholars to educate them. The physician, a young man who had been at his post for only a few months, told them about the healing properties of dragon's blood – when mixed with certain plants, it created a poultice that healed all but the most mortal of wounds; when mixed with water and certain herbs, drinking it would alleviate nearly any fever. However, the blood must be taken from a living dragon or it lost all its panacean qualities.

"Should we capture one, then?" asked Makany. "Build a big cage, bleed it whenever there's need?"

"No," the physician said. "Dragons are dangerous and clever, and their captivity wouldn't end well for their captors. Better to badly wound one, collect what blood you can before its death, and find another the next time there's need."

Fidelia thought that sounded shortsighted considering she'd never seen a single dragon. Surely you weren't guaranteed to find one whenever you needed one? But the physician claimed a few jugs of dragon's blood could last a long while.

One of the scholars demonstrated a contraption to siphon a dragon's blood, which punched through their hides like a sharp spigot, and then Demir showed diagrams of dragon anatomy. She and Demir had come from the same village, traveling to the kingdom together to train as oath-soldiers. But Demir had taken a violent fall in his first joust, badly injuring his left arm. The old physician had done wonders in healing him, but he was no longer fit to be an oath-soldier. Still, he had stayed on as a scholar, which Fidelia considered quite a feat for someone from their backwards little village.

After Demir finished, Makany dismissed them to practice their archery, and Fidelia hit target after target. But once they were done and the evening meal was eaten, her time was her own, and she headed straight for Demir in the palace archives.

He looked surprised to see her. They'd been inseparable once, but in the years since his injury, she hadn't seen much of him; her training kept her busy, and in truth she was afraid he wouldn't want to see her, that she was a sad reminder of the oath he'd never gotten to take.

But his smile to her now seemed genuine even if he did look exhausted. "How are you keeping, Fid?"

"Just fine. Yourself?"

"Fine, fine," he said. "Did you need something?"

"Everything you know about dragons."

His thick eyebrows rose. "I thought I already provided that earlier."

"Surely that wasn't *everything*."

Demir had gone unnaturally still. In the flickering lamplight his dark eyes looked cavernous, endless holes that a person could get lost in. "What else do you need to know?"

"Enough to catch a dragon and impress the king."

Demir shuffled through books on the table beside him. "Is he worth impressing?"

"He's the king! I'm an oath-soldier. My loyalty – my life – belongs to him."

"He's not worthy of your life," Demir said quietly, but before she could protest, he pushed some books towards her. "Everything you need to know about dragons."

"Thank you," she said, and got to work.

She spent hours poring over the books, her mind swimming in a soup of mythology, conjecture, and facts.

When the lamp was on the dregs of its oil, Demir returned. "Are you an expert now?"

"Too much nonsense and too many contradictions. As if a dragon could actually be a shape-shifting human! And earlier you said a full moon is the best time to find a dragon, but this book says a new moon. And that other scholar warned about the dangers of dragonfire, but according to these there hasn't been a fire dragon around here for centuries."

"There are many types of dragons, and many different theories. Now that you've seen the vagaries of such research, perhaps you've realized dragons aren't worth pursuing."

"Unless the king realizes that, it doesn't matter what I think."

"It always matters what you think," Demir said, his voice strangely intense.

"Are you all right?" she asked.

"Of course." The reply came so quickly that she knew he didn't mean it.

She caught his wrist, only remembering when she felt the crooked knob of the bone that it was his bad one. She loosened her grip. "What's wrong?"

He shook her off. "Nothing. I just wish…"

"What?" she prompted.

He shook his head. "That we had gone on a different adventure." He gave a small smile, like it was a joke.

When they were children, they'd lived on neighboring farms. Her widowed father's was small; he grew enough for them to eat, and hunted and fished for their meat. Fidelia had to keep the house in order and prepare the meals, but her father's standards for both were quite low. So she spent most mornings helping Demir on his family's property – she shared his work, and he shared stories, spinning tales of the adventures they would go on when they were older. In Demir's stories she wasn't the target of her father's fists, his biggest disappointment. She was a pirate on the high seas, a travelling minstrel, an oath-soldier, a hero.

Demir must have held these stories as dearly as she did. "I'm sorry you're not a soldier," she said gently, "but your work as a scholar is worthy—"

He cut her off. "It's not. And I'm not feeling sorry for myself," he added as she opened her mouth to protest. "I don't think your work is worthy, either."

Who was this bitter fool, and what had he done with her old friend? "Thank you for your assistance," she said tightly, turning to go. "I won't trouble you again."

As she strode away, all Demir said was, "May you find your dragon," in a tone that was impossible to read.

* * *

The full moon was a week away. Makany sent patrols out each night in search of a dragon. Each time they came back empty-handed.

Once the full moon passed, Makany halted the patrols. "We'll try again next month."

As the new moon approached, Fidelia sought permission to go out on her own. "Just as a scout. Maybe I'll stumble upon something useful."

Makany looked doubtful, but he allowed it. Fidelia went out each night with her horse, Mercury, as well as her bow, a quiver of arrows, several empty jugs, and a spigot.

She considered returning to the archives. She hadn't been able to read everything in those few hours, and maybe Demir would be in better spirits, could help her sift through the conflicting information. But she didn't feel like seeing Demir, didn't know how to deal with the person he'd become. She could do this herself; she didn't need him.

Yet each night, as she rode aimlessly and found nothing, she was reminded of their journey here, how Demir told stories to keep her spirits up, how he turned the most mundane moments into adventures.

On the night of the new moon, she went the farthest she'd been, through the forest and to the foot of the mountains beyond. She made camp in the mouth of a cave and scanned the dark sky for any unusual shadows.

She must have nodded off eventually because she awoke to an unfamiliar sound. She scrambled to her feet, trying to orient herself. The sound was glorious, powerful—

The beating of enormous wings.

She squinted through the smother of shadows.

There.

It was still just a shadow, but a moving shadow. She scrambled for her bow, nocked the arrow, shot—

The dragon screamed, a terrible sound that split the night and woke Mercury, who added his own whinnies to the cacophony. She shot twice more – it was impossible to aim at anything other than shadows – and then it was down. She grabbed her jugs and spigot and hurried towards her quarry.

One of the dragon's wings continued to beat, and she stayed well clear of that side. The other wing had an arrow punching through its base. Another arrow protruded from the dragon's side, and a third from his left hind leg.

Fidelia took a moment to get her bearings, even as her brain shouted at her to hurry, to collect as much blood as she could while the dragon was still breathing. Its wings looked massive and its twitching tail was as long as Fidelia, but its body, convulsing against the rocks, was smaller than she'd expected.

Fidelia fumbled for the spigot. The scholar had demonstrated how to insert it into the dragon, a quick, forceful punch, but its hide felt thick and she was hesitant to do it. So instead she yanked the arrow from its side and shoved the spigot into its wound, crying her apologies as the dragon's shrieks worsened.

She filled a jug. When she started on a second, the dragon quieted. Both wings were still now, and the cries it was making were hardly audible. Fidelia thought they were the saddest thing she'd ever heard. The night had become overcast in addition to moonless, and her head felt equally murky. She didn't want it to die, but she needed its blood, needed the glory it would give her.

She left the second jug propped against the spigot – the likelihood of the dragon moving enough to upset it seemed slim – and went to get her lantern. She lit it and returned, trying to assess the situation. Blood still flowed from the spigot, but the whimpering had stopped. Fidelia was certain the dragon must be unconscious, but when she looked at its head, it was looking back at her. Its eyes were dark pools, deep as caverns.

Demir's eyes.

Fidelia blinked. She was being foolish. This dragon wasn't Demir, no matter how similar their eyes were.

And yet that book in the archives had claimed that some dragons were humans who shape-shifted at the new moon.

The second jug overflowed, a jet of crimson spilling over her hand and soaking into the ground. She moved a new jug in automatically. The dragon blinked once, twice, then kept its eyes shut. It was easier now to tell herself they hadn't been like Demir's at all. It had just been a trick of the shadows, a quirk of her tired mind.

Yet she found herself reaching for the dragon's left foreleg, what would have been its wrist if it was human. She probed the thick skin, felt the familiar knob of the crooked bone.

Fidelia yanked the spigot from the dragon's body, ramming her hand against the terrible wound while she looked frantically for something to bandage it with. She shoved her handkerchief in it, then ran back to get her pack. There was an extra shirt in there, as well as an arrow spoon and some powdered yarrow leaves, a coagulant. She removed the other two arrows, powdering and bandaging the wounds, her heart pounding in her throat, part of her still insisting she was being foolish, that the dragon couldn't possibly be Demir.

But she continued to sit there, sprinkling the wounds with more yarrow powder at intervals and keeping one hand on the dragon's crooked wrist, as though it might keep him alive.

When the first hint of dawn colored the horizon, the dragon began to quiver beneath Fidelia's hand. She stared, convinced he must be dying, then stared harder, releasing her grip, as the dragon shivered, convulsed, shrank—

The wings folded in, absorbed, somehow, into the sinews of his back. The tail retracted, the legs lengthened – she could swear she heard the crunch of bones as he spasmed violently, transformed into—

Demir.

By the time the sun was fully up, he lay before her, naked, the wounds on his shoulder, side, and leg bleeding afresh.

She reached for the yarrow powder, rebandaged him. She could feel the pulse beating faintly in his neck, but his skin was ashy, his breathing labored. He'd lost so much blood. He'd lost so much…

She forced herself to move. She used Mercury's blanket to fashion a nest of a bed within the cave, then hurried back and managed to carry Demir there. He didn't make a sound, never moved.

"Why didn't you tell me?" she cried to his prone form, but of course he didn't answer.

She would have to leave him here, go back for supplies and permission to go patrolling for a few days, at least. She couldn't tell anyone, couldn't risk bringing him to a physician. She mounted Mercury, rode as quickly as she could.

She collected supplies first. The oath-soldiers were at breakfast when she arrived, meaning the bunkhouse was empty and she could pillage it for linens and extra yarrow powder. She packed a change of clothes as well, and some for Demir. Then she hurried to the archives, found the books and read the parts about healing with dragon's blood carefully. It didn't say whether such remedies would work on a person who could transform into a dragon himself, but it was worth trying.

She memorized the necessary ingredients, gathering some from the garden and harassing a physician's apprentice for the rest. Finally, once she had everything she might need, she went to see Makany.

"You missed breakfast," he said, looking none too pleased. "And you look exhausted. Go rest so you'll be of use later."

"Later, sir?"

"There's unrest at the southern border. The king wants it dealt with."

"And the dragon?"

"Did you see one?"

"No, but I figured on making a sweep of the western villages—"

He cut her off. "We can get back to this dragon nonsense once we've taken care of the south. Go prepare."

"Yessir." She forced herself to walk at a normal pace, even as her mind raced. The cave where she'd left Demir was nowhere near the southern border. She needed to get back to him quickly if she had any chance of saving him.

So she went to the stables, saddled up Mercury, and left. It was midday by the time she reached the cave. She'd half expected Demir to be gone, for last night to have been some nightmarish hallucination. But he was still there, still human, still poorly. She got a little water down his throat, then went to work making the dragon-blood poultice.

Once she'd packed his wounds with the sludgy mixture, she walked Mercury across the river, back to the road. She secured her sword to his saddle before she let him go. Oath-soldiers always gave in their swords if they were booted out or disgraced or had to retire. If she let Mercury go back alone, Makany would think something had happened to her, but the sword would be her resignation. He might still send someone after her, but she hoped not.

Mercury looked at her as though he understood what she was doing and didn't approve. He refused to go at first, pawing the ground and tossing his head. "I know," she said, "but I have to take care of Demir. You understand."

Maybe he did, because he left then. She watched him go, but she wouldn't let herself cry.

There was no turning back now.

* * *

Days passed in a blur, as she focused on nursing Demir. She changed his bandages and made fresh poultices every few hours, and his wounds showed no signs of putrefaction.

She talked to him, as much for her own sake as his. She'd spent the past eight years surrounded by other soldiers, surrounded by an entire kingdom of people. Silence felt unnatural. It reminded her of her childhood, of trying to make herself small and quiet in the presence of her father so that maybe he would forget she was there.

It had been her idea to leave. She was tired of having to be someone she didn't want to be. One day, in the midst of one of his stories, she interrupted Demir and asked if he wasn't ready for a real adventure.

She thought he'd refuse. He had a family, after all, a sweet mother and a boisterous father and many brothers and sisters. Who would want to leave that? But he said yes like he didn't even have to consider it, like he'd go anywhere she asked.

They'd snuck away in the night. Fidelia was convinced that at any moment a hand would descend upon her shoulder and yank her back. But perhaps her father hadn't considered her worth the bother of going after. Maybe he hadn't even noticed she was gone.

She'd clutched Demir's hand that whole first night, and he'd held on just as tightly, their fingers a knot of promise.

Once they were far away from their village and didn't care who noticed them, he told her a steady stream of adventure stories, how they would become oath-soldiers, saving the kingdom from all nature of threats.

She was pretty sure they had defeated a dragon in one of those stories. And it had taken them a month to reach the kingdom, including a new moon. Surely Demir couldn't have been a dragon then, couldn't have hidden that from her?

Unlike now, when she apparently didn't know him at all.

But she kept talking to him like she did, recounting all his old stories. Anything to keep him here, to remind him of happier times. Anything to keep herself from having to think too deeply about everything she'd done.

He started to get a little color back in his complexion, started to groan a bit and flutter his eyes when she forced water and broth in his mouth. And then, one glorious day, he opened his eyes and really seemed to look at her. "What happened?"

It was lovely to hear his voice, despite its raspy weakness. But how to answer him? "You… I… I shot you." She could hear her own voice shattering. "I'm so sorry – I didn't – I—"

Demir's hand closed around hers and squeezed gently. His eyes had already shut again. She cried quietly while he slept, refusing to shake loose from his grip, which felt like forgiveness.

* * *

The next time Demir woke, he tensed and struggled to sit up. "How close is it to a new moon?"

"Over two weeks," she said, and he relaxed again, though his eyes stayed open.

"You could have told me," she said quietly, uncertain whether it was a conversation either of them were up to.

He closed his eyes, and she thought he'd gone back to sleep until he said, "I wanted to. I almost did, that evening in the archives. But how could I tell you I'd become the monster you wanted to kill?"

She found his hand, squeezed. "You're not a monster. But how did it happen?"

"After the joust, I was hurt bad. More than just my arm. The old physician, Merin, gave me dragon's blood to drink. Didn't mix it with water or herbs. Said it was an experiment, but I think he knew what he was doing. He wanted to turn me, wanted to have a dragon at his disposal.

"He kept me in a big cage in the depths of the archives every new moon. He bled me a cup or two each time. Said it was good for me, kept me docile.

"When the king came into power, he demanded dragon's blood daily. At first it was just a few drops in his wine, but then he wanted spoonfuls mixed in. It kept him fit and strong, he said. The healthiest king in the world.

"Old Merin kept me a secret, even as he provided the king with my blood. I think he liked the power it gave him, the control. But then he died of a sudden apoplexy, and I was the only one who knew my secret.

"I transformed in the forest after that, well away from any people. But the king's blood supply dwindled. He needed more…"

"And I was more than happy to deliver," Fidelia said bitterly.

"You didn't know. And of course oath-soldiers have to obey their sovereign."

"I'm not an oath-soldier anymore."

Demir's eyes flew open. "What do you mean?"

She told him what she'd done.

He shook his head. "You shouldn't have sacrificed your oath. Not for me."

"Of course I should have. You're worth more than any oath."

He fell asleep again shortly after, their hands still intertwined. She hoped he knew she meant it.

* * *

Demir continued to gain strength. Fidelia kept making poultices, but his wounds had all but healed, and though he still slept a lot, he seemed to steadily improve. She snared animals from the woods to make stews, and even hiked into a village a few times to barter for some bread and vegetables.

"Will you go back home?" she dared to ask him one day, when he was nearly better.

"I don't suppose my parents will want me. They were going to indenture me out, before I left. They needed the money."

"That's why you left?" She thought of how easily he'd agreed to her plan. Of course that hadn't been because of her.

"I left because you asked me to. But it certainly gave me a reason not to stay. And I can hardly go back now. They already had too many children; they don't need a broken dragon."

"You're not broken," she said.

"But I am a dragon."

"What's it like?" she asked. "Are you still yourself, when you transform? Can you remember?"

"Somewhat. It hurts, the transformation. It was terrible when Merin kept me in that cage. And I was scared the first time I did it outside. Terrified I would lose myself, do something awful. But I'm still aware of myself. I know to stay where there aren't any people. And flying is wonderful."

"Why didn't you just leave, after Merin died?"

He shrugged. "I'd been thinking about it. But I didn't want to leave you behind. It didn't seem the right ending to our adventure."

She could feel her heart beating tremendously hard, but she forced herself to say, "You should have left me. There's more to life than adventures."

"Never," he said fiercely. "How else would we find the path we're meant to take?" He paused. "What about you? Do you want to return to the kingdom?"

"I gave in my sword, remember?"

He nodded towards the two jugs of dragon's blood – his blood – that remained. "If you went back with that, you'd be a hero."

"No. The king's not worthy of your blood."

"He was never worthy of your oath, either."

She took a deep breath. "I think I want to swear a new oath."

"Oh?"

"To you. If you'll have me."

He frowned. "I'm still a dragon once a month. Is that really what you want to tie yourself to?"

"More than anything," she said without hesitation, taking his hand in hers. "We can have a different adventure this time, one with a better ending."

He kissed her hand, drawing her close. "Infinite adventures," he promised, and she snuggled into the crook of his arm.

We Are Not Them

Georgina Kamsika

The oceans were dying.

The *Stormbringer* cut through dull waters with no gulls, no dolphins, not even the flicker of flying fish. The only sound Kael heard was the creak of her ship's bones and the slow, sick rhythm of her crew's breathing. They were all coughing now, a dry, rattling sound, like gambler's dice in a tin cup. Even the sails had taken on a brittle yellow hue, the fabric crumbling.

Kael noticed the rot a few months ago. First the seabirds disappeared from the skies. Then the water casks turned salty. Then the fish were gone, vanished as if the ocean had emptied.

Then Kael's dreams began. Dreams of a dragon, more benevolent than fearsome, with a broad forehead and pearl-like eyes. His four-toed paws, tipped with claws like carved lapis lazuli, held a woman close. She laughed as she braided his whiskers with silver.

The lover stood thigh-deep in the black tide, her skin the same deep brown as Kael, her hair also long and dark as oil.

The dream woman held out her cupped hands, and in them lay a single pearl, blue as a midsummer sky, cracked down the middle.

"Find her," she mouthed. "Before the last tide falls."

Kael woke each time choking on salt water, her grandmother's dagger in her fist.

* * *

"It's the Dragon's Curse," said Old Man Dohyun, one of her crew who'd sailed these waters before the red-coated invaders had renamed everything. He spat over the rail. The spittle didn't even make it to the water, it hit the burned air and turned to dust. "Hundred years back, a Tidebound dragon loved a woman. Gave her his heart, pearl, and all. But she left him. Now the sea remembers."

Kael watched the horizon for other ships. "The ocean is dying because of a dragon?"

Dohyun grinned, gums like spoiled meat. "Nah, captain. It's dying because of *her* betrayal. S'why the dragon will help you."

"Dragons don't help."

"This one will. You're wearing her face."

* * *

The night Kael first met her rival Sehyuna, the moon was a thief. It stole the colour from the world, left everything bone-white and ink-black; the docks, the ships, her grandmother's dagger in her fist.

Kael slipped through the shadows of Port Veyra looking for her past. She was fourteen, and the *Stormbringer* was not yet hers – still just a mouldering merchant's hulk with sails stained yellow as abandoned wedding dresses.

Kael didn't see the silhouette in the crow's nest. A mistake.

"That's a terrible plan," said a voice above her.

Kael nearly gutted herself. A girl hung upside-down from the rigging, her hair a tangle of dark-honey, her grin brighter than the lanterns bobbing in the harbour. She dropped lightly beside Kael, her limbs loose and agile. She looked about the same age, and just as undomesticated.

"You'll want the aft lock to get to the safe," the girl said, plucking the dagger from Kael's grip. "This one by the galley sticks."

Kael glared. "Give that back."

"Make me."

Falling for the provocation was Kael's next mistake.

They fought. Not the pretty, clashing-steel kind from fairy tales, but the messy, elbow-throwing, biting-if-necessary kind favoured by feral children everywhere. They rolled through tar and fish guts and coconuts until the deck beneath them gave way. They landed in the hold, sprawled on a mountain of smuggled spices, both still gripping the dagger.

Sehyuna picked a cinnamon stick from Kael's hair. "So, partners?"

Kael headbutted her.

The girl laughed as blood dripped down her forehead. Kael would spend years pretending that didn't matter.

Sehyuna passed her the dagger hilt-first. "Next time, aim for the kidneys."

Kael spat blood onto the docks. "Next time," she lied, "I won't miss."

* * *

That mission to investigate Kael's past failed, but Sehyuna became a permanent fixture in her life. Never as a friend, instead a rival who would appear after the hard work to claim half the rewards. Mostly with charm, occasionally with force. Kael resented it every time.

But this mission, to find the dragon, to heal the ocean, had no reward Sehyuna could steal, so Kael slipped past the scoundrel and sailed far to the east of the horizon until her ship fell off the edge of known maps.

Dohyun stared at the listless clouds, the still ocean, and the lifeless sails, carefully navigating them until they arrived above a deep canyon in the seabed. The *Stormbringer* slumped against a reef of coral, rotten boards warping.

"Your dragon is down there, neither dead nor alive, cursed to linger in the depths."

"How do you know all this?" Kael asked as she shed her boots and jacket.

"Tales of your ancestors are legendary," he said, helping her prepare to dive.

"You know more about my family than I do," she muttered. "The dragon knows the truth."

* * *

Kael arrived in the dragon's grave with salt in her hair and a knife between her teeth. She'd heard that a shard of Vārija's heart could grant a wish, if one was brave enough to claim it.

The dive should have killed her. Kael swam past the carcasses of ships that had no business being there. Galleons with glass sails, junks with singing figureheads, her own childhood carrack, half-buried in the silt. But instead of death, the water greeted her like a jilted lover. Cold. Familiar. Unwanted.

Kael swam through the wreckage on the sea bed, her feet kicking up centuries of silt, when something moved. Kael paused to peer into the shadows.

Sehyuna, the thorn in her side, the thief of her winds, floated beside her, grinning around her own knife. Her hair, usually sun-bleached honey brown, streamed dark as kelp in the gloom.

Kael's pulse did something treasonous. She blamed the depth.

"Miss me?"

"I do need bait." Kael flipped her dagger. "But I thought I'd got out unseen."

"And yet." Sehyuna caught Kael's wrist as the current tugged her to where the seafloor dropped into forever.

"I'm with you on this one. I've been dreaming about this place."

"Of my ancestor?"

"No, of mine."

Then a shadow moved. Vārija emerged from the darkness, his skeleton draped in the tattered silk of forgotten sails. Endlessly long, coiled like a river around a mountain, his body moved with the sinuous grace of ocean currents.

"Little thieves," he murmured, his voice the creak of a ship's grave. "You smell of them. You are either very brave or very stupid."

"Historically?" Sehyuna spat out her dagger and caught it. "Both."

"You," said Vārija, the word a riptide. "You dare to come before me."

"My ship is dying," said Kael.

The dragon exhaled. His muzzle was lined with coral-coloured feelers, his breath a mist that smelled of rain and salt. "Yes."

"You're doing it."

"No." He uncoiled, revealing the hollow in his chest where a pearl should glow. "Your ancestor is. The oceans have been dying for centuries."

The water shivered. For a heartbeat, Kael saw her – the woman from her dreams, her hair now kelp, her fingers now bone, pressing against the dragon's ribs from inside. She mouthed something, but Kael did not understand.

"She cut the bond," murmured Vārija. "But some hearts won't stay severed."

Kael understood. "You're drowning each other."

The dragon laughed, and the seafloor trembled. "Clever girl. Lift the curse, and your ship will live. The ocean too."

"How?"

"I will answer any request you have," he said, "if you give me your heart."

Kael's fingers found her grandmother's dagger. "Metaphorically?"

Sehyuna eyed the dragon's talons. "Please say metaphorically."

"Enough." Vārija's voice shook the wreck. "You seek my word? Then prove you're worthy. Relive the betrayal that broke me. Survive, and the heart is yours."

"Fine," Kael said, stepping forward.

"No, it's my dream." Sehyuna pushed her behind.

"You go together," said the dragon. The water shimmered.

* * *

Once, when the moon still sang to the tides, there lived a dragon made of seawater and storm. Vārija, last of the Tidebound, had been beautiful then. His scales caught the sunlight and fractured it into a thousand shifting hues. Gold for his pride, blue for his sorrow, silver for the love he'd foolishly given to a mortal woman. She had worn his heart around her throat, a single luminous pearl on a chain of moonlight, and for a century, the ocean itself had sighed with their contentment.

But mortal hearts are fickle things and their bond could not last. The woman who had Kael's dark eyes stood with a woman that had Sehyuna's face, but not her smirk. The dragon slept nearby, golden and trusting.

"I love you, but I can't leave him," Kael's ancestor said. "We're bound."

"Cut it," Sehyuna's ancestor whispered. "And we can be together."

The woman with Kael's eyes hesitated. She touched the pearl at her throat.

"Do it if you love me. We need to be free."

"Why would they do it?" Kael whispered.

Her ancestor turned, eyes full of tears. "Because love is a cage," she said, "and I wanted the sky."

Sehyuna, who had been unusually quiet, touched Kael's wrist. "I'd pick the cage," she muttered.

Kael stared at her.

Sehyuna flushed. "Metaphorically."

Not-Sehyuna pressed a dagger into Vision-Kael's hand. She cut the pearl from her throat, the chain dripping blood into the dark ocean. She let it go, not even watching as it sank. The pearl disappeared into the hungry dark, and Vārija's fire guttered out.

Kael wanted to scream at her past. Sehyuna's fingers tightened around hers, her usual mirth replaced with something raw. "We are not them."

The vision shattered, the memory fading like squid ink in the tide. One moment, Kael was standing on that ancient shore, watching her ancestor's knife flash in the moonlight. The next, she was back beside the dragon, Sehyuna's fingers locked around her wrist like she thought she might dissolve too.

Vārija loomed above them, clouded eyes unreadable. The dragon's voice slithered through them. "One of you will leave. One will drown with me. Choose."

Kael looked at Sehyuna. At the scar through her eyebrow from the time Kael had thrown a compass at her head. At the way her pulse jumped when she smirked. Her reckless willingness to follow Kael into the abyss.

Kael knew the stories. Knew that dragons always meant their bargains. All she had to do was give up Sehyuna, and the oceans would be healed. But she also remembered her dreams. "Find her," her ancestor had mouthed. "Before the last tide falls."

The ocean held its breath.

Beside Kael, Sehyuna struggled against the currents, her knife useless, her arrogance stripped away. Kael met the Tidebound dragon's gaze. Fear there, but something else, too. Kael reached for Sehyuna's hand and pulled. Her rival startled at the contact, before floating to her side. Kael held her steady against the angry ocean.

The water remembered. It remembered this betrayal, the dousing of the dragon's fire, and the slow unravelling of a bond that should have been eternal.

Kael floated before him, her lungs burning, her heart pounding like a trapped thing. The dragon's voice was the crush of the abyss.

"You are hers. Her blood. Her betrayal. Again." The dragon's laugh, like ships breaking on rocks. "You think defiance moves me?"

"No." Kael held her other hand out to the dragon. "But I think you're lonely."

Vārija hesitated. The water remembered that, too.

Sehyuna, ever the fool, grinned. "And we're exceptionally annoying."

The water trembled. Then warmth. Light. A great, shuddering sigh as centuries of seclusion cracked like old ice. Vārija rose, his tarnished scales starting to glow, his eyes clearing.

"I refuse to bond again. But I will consider not killing you." He coughed a single, glowing pearl into Kael's palm. It melted into her skin. When she breathed, the tides breathed with her.

Vārija shifted, his skeleton forming scales of lapping waves of iridescent blue, shifting from pale aqua to the fathomless navy of the abyss. Antlers grew from his bare skull, made of blue-black coral threaded with veins of gold. And Kael's ancestor, long trapped within his chest, dissipated into the salty ocean depths.

"Then it will be the three of us," Kael said, voice firm and sure.

Sehyuna grinned. "Does this mean we're finally friends?"

Kael rolled her eyes. "It means you're my favourite mistake."

The sea does not forgive. But sometimes, if someone was very stubborn, and very lucky, it forgets.

* * *

The trip back to the *Stormbringer* took hours. Not because the distance was great, but because the ocean kept showing off. A patch of seaweed twisted itself into the shape of their clasped hands. A jellyfish pulsed with light in time to Vārija's heartbeat. Kael's feet left prints that filled with liquid moonlight, and when Sehyuna stepped in them, the glow climbed her ankles like vines.

"Stop that," Kael muttered.

Sehyuna grinned, kicking water at Kael. "Make me."

Kael had heard those words before. On a dock, under a thief's moon, with a knife between them. Her heart thumped.

They reached the reef to see her once majestic ship now in ruins. Kael stared at the remains that held her past, and – she'd once thought – her future. Her crew, led by Dohyun, waited on the partially submerged corals.

"We've still got my ship?" Sehyuna offered. "Though it's probably about dead, too."

"Scraps of dead trees are hardly worthy of my ocean," Vārija said. He reared up, his serpentine body suspended in midair. His wave-scales glimmered like mother-of-pearl, revealing hidden patterns of silver bioluminescence, mimicking the night sky.

"What's he doing?" Sehyuna, never mindful, asked.

Kael, heart full from the gravity of this moment, took Sehyuna's hand, and squeezed it.

Dohyun shuffled forward, feet hanging over the edge of the reef. He nodded to the dragon, then stepped off. The dragon whirled forward, flowed more than flew, his body dissolving into mist as he pulled Dohyun deeper into the ocean. Where Vārija passed, the air filled with the scent of an early morning breeze.

The water around them shimmered, Dohyun shifting, changing, growing. It began with his hands, as if his body forgot its own shape. The skin glistened, pearlescent, then blurred into froth, his fingers unravelling into rivulets of foam. His arms followed, collapsing into the surf that surged against the reef. His legs gave way next, then his torso, his heart a pulsating eddy. Dohyun's face lingered, smiling lips parting in a soundless whisper before scattering into the wind.

Kael moved to stand with her crew, but they barely glanced away from the white-capped breakers. The Dohyun-sea gathered itself inside Vārija's coils, the foam knitting into something new. The waves sculpted prow and keel, with mast and rigging spun from seafoam, sails unfurling as if born from Vārija's breath. A new ship, made of living squalls and foam, riding the waves with Dohyun infusing its very timbers.

"Did your crewmate die to make you a ship?" Sehyuna balked.

"Do you think I would let Kael's ancestors roam my seas without a servant to keep an eye on her? He was me. He is still me." Vārija's ribbon-like whiskers curled like reeds, glowing faintly at the tips with will-o'-the-wisp light. "This way we will always be together."

Kael and her crew climbed on board, examining the water-made ship in awe as Vārija watched. Sehyuna hauled herself onto the deck and collapsed against the rippling mast. Kael slumped beside her, close enough to shove, far enough to pretend she didn't want to. Above them, the sails drifted in the new, fresh, breeze. The air smelled of brine, and dragon, and the ghost of Dohyun's tobacco.

"She was afraid," said Sehyuna suddenly.

Kael tensed. "Who?"

"Your many-greats-grandma. When she cut the bond." Sehyuna pressed against the briny deck. "Her hands shook."

Kael remembered the vision – the woman's white-knuckled grip on the knife, the way her eyes had darted to the dragon's sleeping face. Not the look of a traitor. The look of someone choosing between two fires.

"Yours didn't stop her," Kael said.

Sehyuna's smile was a blade turned inward. "Guess some things skip generations."

A wave hit the hull. The ship crested it. Vārija swam beside them.

Kael reached over and flicked her ear. "You'd have stopped me."

"Damn right." Sehyuna caught her hand. "You'd have whined about it, though."

Kael's pulse jumped as Sehyuna's thumb brushed her knuckles – once, twice – before she let go.

There was a time Kael considered Sehyuna a rival. But the world had changed, and so had she. Before fear could steal her courage, Kael reached out and seized Sehyuna, crushing their bodies close.

Kael kissed Sehyuna. It was nothing like she expected. No fireworks. No choirs of angels. Just salt and desperation and the certain, sinking realisation that she'd trade every ship she'd ever stolen for this. Sehyuna, because she was Sehyuna, grinned against her lips.

Their kiss burned away every unsaid word, every past argument, every fear hidden behind a joke. When Kael finally pulled back, her chest heaving, Sehyuna's eyes were dark.

"Took you long enough," she said.

"I was worth the wait," Kael laughed, breathless, victorious.

And this time, when Kael kissed her again, Sehyuna was ready.

Kingkiller

Abigail Kelly

In her opinion, Catriona's greatest mistake wasn't murdering a king. It was being foolish enough to love one.

Youth was no excuse. Neither was gullibility. She'd known better, and more importantly, she'd been warned. Everyone knew the king's wives never lasted.

One was accused of adultery and sent away in disgrace under the cover of night. Another slipped on the stairs. Two died of fever, and one simply disappeared.

But he'd been sweet to her, so different than she'd imagined a king to be, and her family's estate sat on the edge of disputed land, where raiders crossed regularly. She was clever, but even a quick mind couldn't make soldiers out of thin air or fill her people's bellies when their fields were burned. She was desperate for help and foolish enough to believe she would be different from all the wives who came before her.

And the pitiful truth of it was that she fell in love with him.

If it was arrogance and romance that drove her into the king's arms, it was pure bad luck that put her in his path to begin with. Not for her, she supposed, but for him. It wasn't her body cooling on the flagstones.

Catriona wasn't particularly honed for survival. Her fingers were much more used to the brush of parchment than the cool hilt of a blade, and her silk slippers weren't made to withstand the blood that soaked them as the pool widened at her feet.

But needs must. Catriona stood up from her crouched position on the catacomb floor and wiped her eyes. Tucking her wounded hand against her chest, she bunched her skirt with the other and edged around the puddle partially obscuring the ritual circle on the floor. The stench of iron and magic coated her throat as the king's blood began to sizzle, his body convulsing as the circle consumed all that he was – flesh and soul, rotten as they were.

Her skin crawled as she watched. If she hadn't recognized the symbols on the floor, if she hadn't fought, it would've been her body fed to the Void.

Catriona looked away as the king's handsome face caved in, crunched like a nutshell between a god's unseen teeth. There were many things to do and not much time in which to do them. Gawping at the sight of her husband's eyes popping like frog spawn wouldn't help her escape.

Leaving the way they'd come wasn't an option. A bevy of guards walked the halls of the palace and staff lingered around every corner even when the rest of the world slept. Bile rose in her gullet when she realized they must've known. They must've at least *suspected*. There were too many wives and too many of them around, day and night, for them not to. If she appeared without him, they'd immediately suspect her.

And there was no way she could talk herself out of it when she was covered in the evidence of her crime.

The king's blood had splattered her soft dressing gown, and her slippers were more red than ivory now. The stains looked black in the dim glow of the lanterns strung up on the rough-hewn walls, but they couldn't be mistaken for anything other than what they were.

The only option was to head deeper into the catacombs.

Her reading had taught her plenty about the capital and the palace in particular. It was built atop what had once been a dragon's nest, before the royal family drove out the dragon kings of old. The catacombs were an extension of that system, and if the two were connected, it seemed likely that another route to the surface would exist. No intelligent creature would build a home with only one exit, and dragons were the most cunning of all.

It should've been a warning sign when the king readily agreed to guide her down there. He'd never been keen on indulging her curiosity before then, and to pull her out of bed to do it… A burning feeling took root in her chest as she left the cavernous ritual room, a lantern in hand, and padded into the darkness. Her bloody slippers painted the stones with every step.

Catriona did not enjoy being wrong. She enjoyed being made a fool of even less. To know she was solely responsible for both states was nearly unendurable.

The grinning faces of skulls lined the walls of the tunnels, their longbones stacked like matchsticks behind them and the hollows of their eyes flashing as her lamp swayed in her hand. The city's dead watched her from their nooks, but there was no judgment to be found in their gazes. In her experience, the dead rarely had much to say on the deeds of the living – even the murder of kings.

The scent of damp filled her lungs. However, it couldn't quite dispel the scent of the blood that clung to her as it dried on her chest, face, and hair. In hindsight, going for the king's neck had been expedient, certainly, but messier than she thought it would be. Her anatomy books hadn't prepared her for that.

Her lips thinned as she walked on, deeper and deeper, until the flagstones gave way to smooth rock. The confidence that had pushed her onward instead of back toward the palace withered as her sense of direction vanished. Too late she realized she couldn't find her way back if she tried.

Fighting panic, she paused briefly to kneel in an alcove, her wounds smarting and her exhaustion demanding a rest. Just a short one.

Her fingers drifted over the stone as she caught her breath. It was unlike anything she'd seen before. No tools had crafted the passage she walked and no boots had worn down the stone to the smoothness she felt.

It was *melted*.

The hair on the back of her neck stood on end as she picked up her lamp. She was going in the right direction.

Only the slightest changes in air current kept her from becoming completely disoriented in the warren of ancient dragon tunnels. She followed those currents with grim determination, ignoring the ache in her body and the growing desire to rest. The sun would be rising soon, if it hadn't already, and the king would be missed.

But even her determination couldn't stop the slither of fear that skated down her spine as the tunnels went on and on, sloping downward rather than up. Catriona didn't have time to panic, but it clawed up from the back of her mind all the same, gouging holes in the delicate flesh of her calm.

All that concerned her was the next turn, the next fork in the passage, and the raw animal need to see the sky again.

A dead end loomed ahead of her, one of many she'd encountered. But it was the first she'd seen with what appeared to be bars blocking the passageway beyond.

For a moment, she thought it was a trick of the light. She'd grown used to the spelled lamp creating strange shapes out of shadows, but as she edged closer, she realized her eyes weren't being misled.

The iron bars were as thick as her wrist and stretched from the top of the tunnel to the floor, leaving no gaps above or below. There were hinges on one side, so it was a door of some sort, but she couldn't see any way to open it.

Catriona set her lamp down, her arm aching from the strain of carrying it for so long, and examined the door with wild hope. It had to be a way out. They wouldn't guard it so heavily if not.

She was so preoccupied by figuring out how to open the door that she didn't notice the soft sound of breathing that drifted from the other side. It was only when a low, rumbling laugh echoed off the walls did she realize she wasn't alone.

"A little lamb has wandered into my nest," a bass voice rasped from the shadows. "Are you lost?"

Catriona recoiled. Her slippers slid on the fire-polished floor and went out from under her. She landed hard on her injured hand and stared up in horror at the monstrous shape that coalesced in the flickering lamplight.

At first, all she saw was his eyes.

They gleamed like gold coins in the darkness, lit not by her lamp, but by some internal fire forged in the heart and chaos of the Void. Not human. Not anything she'd ever seen before, with their dagger-shaped pupils.

Catriona's nails scraped the stone as she scrambled backward, atavistic fear overriding even her pathological curiosity.

"Now, now," the beast teased, "don't run so fast, little lamb. I've barely gotten a good look at you." The sound of metal clinking, then the slow drag of bare feet on stone announced his approach. Her breath caught as he stepped into the lamplight.

There were stories of dragons taking the forms of men. Children of the Void could take many shapes, and their magic wasn't bound to the rules humans abided by. And there was no doubt that *this* being was something beyond her understanding.

His skin had the color and shine of polished copper. The light sent ripples of color over corded muscle, hinting at subtle scales and the hard planes of an inhumanly handsome face obscured by a heavy iron muzzle.

Simple drawstring trousers and chains were his only clothing, aside from the device on his face. An instinctive disgust took hold of her at the sight of it. She'd never liked seeing dogs muzzled, but to see a Child of the Void humiliated that way was far worse.

His head tilted as he appraised her there on the ground. "My, you've gotten into some trouble, haven't you?" It was hard to tell in the shadow cast by the bars of his muzzle, but she thought she spied a forked tongue flick out from between his lips. His growl rolled through her like thunder. "The little lamb has been naughty, I think."

"What—" She tried to swallow, but her mouth was too dry for it. "What are you doing down here?"

The foolishness of the question hit her a moment before the dragon's taunting voice did. "Oh, I wandered in and liked it so much I thought I'd stay a spell."

Catriona's face warmed. "I meant *why* are you down here. Are you the king's prisoner?"

"I've been many a king's prisoner," he answered, forked tongue flicking. "Which one do you speak of, little lamb?"

Her stomach churned. Even thinking his name made a spasm of feeling steal her thoughts. Squeezing her injured hand to ground herself, she bit out, "Fennack."

But he told me to call him Fenn.

"Ah, the whelp. I haven't seen him since I nearly bit his hand off when he was a boy." The dragon crouched slowly, his towering body a Void-crafted masterpiece of sensual grace and lethality. Every muscle moved with precision as he bent his knees and rested his forearms on his thighs. The chains between his wrist manacles dangled between them. "I think he was afraid of me. Never bothered to come down to taunt or torture like his forefathers."

Catriona straightened, curiosity nipping. She ignored the fresh blood oozing from her hand when she pressed, "How long have you been a prisoner here?"

The dragon's golden eyes tracked her without blinking. That devilish tongue flicked again. "I've seen three kings sit on my throne. How long has it been since Alvrith met the Void? He was the one who locked my cage."

She balked. "Alvrith the Great died a hundred and fifty years ago."

"Then you've answered your question. Now answer one of mine." A shining copper hand gripped a pockmarked iron bar. His wicked claws gleamed in the lamplight as he leaned in as far as his muzzle would allow. "Whose blood is that?"

She couldn't very well answer that. The dragon wasn't exactly in a position to tell someone what she'd done, but it wasn't worth the risk, either. Instead of giving him the full truth, she said, "Some of it is mine. The rest is – was my husband's."

The dragon's expression took on an unsettling cast of approval. "Did Fennack die badly, little lamb?"

"How—"

"I'd know the stench of Alvrith's line anywhere. His blood was sour with the poison of Voidsick. It's been the same for all his kin. How do you think he managed to keep *me* in a cage, hm?"

"Voidsick?" Her stomach bottomed out. *Of course.*

"To unseat me, Alvrith had to strike a deal with the Void," he explained. "But every deal has its cost, and the Void never forgets. To pay his debt, Alvrith used sacrifices. So did his sons. And so did Fennack. The sickness must have been getting truly dire to make the killing of a wife necessary." There was a pause as the dragon seemed to savor the moment. "That's what happened, isn't it? The whelp thought he could feed you to the Void."

Catriona's throat worked around the hard lump of horror lodged within it. "Yes."

The dragon's voice dropped into a coaxing purr. "Come closer. Let me have a look at the kingkiller."

Kingkiller.

Was that her new title? She'd been a lady just that morning, freshly married to a king. A country girl of piddling noble blood, brought up by a reclusive father who shunned the court, raised high by a chance encounter during Fennack's hunting trip near her family's land. Now she was something altogether different.

Catriona shook herself. "I need to get out of here."

"My kin made these tunnels. Without a nose like mine, you'll never be able to find your way out." His lambent gaze sharpened. "You could release me, lamb. I would help you escape."

"I have no idea how to release you," she protested. "And even if I did, I can't unleash a dragon on my people. You'd destroy the city."

"All that's needed is Alvrith's blood, or one of his line." He nodded toward her bloody nightgown. "Even yours might do, if your marriage was consecrated in blood. As his queen, it's your right to release me on his behalf."

A bitter taste filled her mouth. Catriona looked away from the dragon's probing gaze. "He didn't. We were married in a country temple near my home. And I wasn't queen. He said the coronation should be in the spring, when the weather..."

She trailed off, that burning feeling in her chest returning with a vengeance. Speaking the words aloud, she realized that there was never a chance Fennack intended to make her queen. He'd barely waited a week before he led her down to the catacombs. In fact, she couldn't recall *any* of his wives being crowned.

Stupid, she admonished herself. Her eyes stung – another humiliation, crying in front of a creature like a proud dragon. *It was all there. You think you're so clever. Why didn't you pay attention?*

None of the signs or rumors seemed important when Fennack was murmuring in her ear, or showing up in the manor's drawing room like a humble nobleman looking to court her. All the worried glances from her staff were brushed off. Every strange prickling of unease in her belly was dismissed as nerves.

It was a valuable lesson. One among many she learned that night. Even a clever woman could be manipulated by a motivated man.

And aim for the heart next time. The throat is too messy.

The dragon clicked his tongue. His tone was dark and husky when he whispered, "Foolish whelp. He ought to have put a crown on your head the moment he was able. Maybe then he would've lived longer. I won't make the same mistake."

"I don't care about being queen. I just want to live." She forced herself to stand again. Her legs and feet protested, over-tired after so many hours of walking in thin-soled slippers.

"We want the same thing, then," the dragon replied, rising smoothly. "I've lost a hundred and fifty years of my life. It's in your power to release me, and in mine to save you from Fennack's allies. There's little to lose and much to gain, lamb."

The prospect of facing the tunnels on her own again was bone-chilling, but the guilt of turning a dragon loose on her people was worse. "I can't. You'd raze the city."

He was silent for a beat, the muscles of his jaw working hard enough to move the muzzle. "This is dragon country. I am the rightful king and I'll take what's mine. But…if I must swear to spare as many lives as I can, I will. For you."

Catriona dared to step closer to the bars. "The last man who made promises to me tried to sacrifice me to the Void. I won't make that mistake twice, dragon."

"Aye, that's a clever lamb." The dragon tapped the front of his muzzle against the bars. His bare chest rose and fell with deep, even breaths as they eyed each other from across the divide. He was two heads taller than her at least, but she didn't feel small when he looked down on her. She felt *alive*.

"Gift for gift. Gold for gold. Blood for blood." The dragon's claws skimmed down the bars, deceptively gentle. He couldn't reach through them with his manacles, but she could. The fact that the desire to crossed her mind at all was unnerving. "The last man who made you promises is dead. I'll not make his mistakes, either. I'll bind my vow in blood, never to be undone."

Her heartbeat quickened. "You'd swear to help me escape? And to spare the city?"

"Aye." A smile curved his mouth as his eyelids dropped to half-mast. "And more."

There was no good choice, but there hadn't been one since Fennack walked her down the spiral steps into the catacombs. Killing him hadn't been a fair choice, either. It was simply the only one that kept her alive.

She couldn't bring herself to say the words, so instead she focused on tearing away a piece of her gauzy dressing gown. It was heavy with Fennack's blood and still tacky against her fingers. The dragon went preternaturally still as she held it aloft, meeting his gaze.

"Vow first."

A shuddering breath escaped the muzzle. "Put your hand through the bars, lamb. The bloody one you've been hiding."

She hesitated, but eventually forced herself to do as he commanded. The bars were cool against the sides of her wrist, a stark contrast to the burning heat of his skin as he cradled her hand in his.

"Your name," he grated.

It escaped her in a whisper. "Catriona."

"I, Aedan, vow to honor and serve you. I vow to protect and guide and avenge. I vow my body and my children and my troth."

Gooseflesh prickled her arms. She tried to jerk her hand back, but he didn't release it. "Wait, wait! That's not what I—"

His voice rolled on, and as he spoke, the flesh of his other hand split of its own accord – the Void's unseen knife drawing down the meat of his palm to make a wound matching hers. He pressed their bloody hands together, squeezing tight, and finished, "I vow to put a crown on your head, Catriona Kingkiller, and bind us together until the Void takes what it's owed."

Magic was searing. It burned hotter than any fire. It was the heat of creation, the chaos that birthed the stars and the world and the man who stood before her, giving her his marriage vows. It snaked through her veins in a flash, tying them under the all-seeing eyes of the Void.

Catriona yanked her hand back through the bars to stare at the silver scar on her palm in horror. She'd only been a widow for a few hours. Now she was a dragon's bride.

Furious, she waved her scarred hand at him. "That isn't what I meant!"

"Then you ought to have been clearer." He offered her a toothy smile and tipped his head toward the strange lock on the door. "Now, wife, release me."

"I should leave you here to rot," she spat, fists curling.

"Aye, you should. But you won't."

She stepped up to the bars again, anger stealing what little caution she still possessed. "I killed one husband. I can abandon another."

Aedan held her gaze. "Of that I have no doubt, but you won't."

"Why? You have no idea what I'll do."

"Because you'll do anything to survive, same as I will," he answered without a shred of guilt, "and I'm your best chance."

She despised the fact that he was right. Catriona paced away, her back turned to him, as she ran through her options again and again.

There was no other option.

It took everything in her to turn back around and press the scrap of her dress against the lock. Her gaze stayed firmly averted from his smug face as the bloody cloth sizzled under her hand. She stepped back as the latch clicked, allowing the door to swing open on its own.

He sounded amused when he prompted her, "Now my chains, lamb. Hurry now. Can't waste more time, can we?"

Shooting him a withering glare, she stepped into the cell with her bloody scrap. Walking into a bear's cage would've felt less threatening. Sweat dewed her skin as she approached him, but she kept her shoulders back and chin firm, refusing to show her nerves.

She removed his ankle manacles quickly, following the same procedure as the door, before she rose again.

Deciding his muzzle seemed like a safer choice than his wrists, she bit out, "Lean down."

"As my queen commands," he rumbled, stooping. His body heat radiated through her, seeping past her chilled skin to reach some soft, vulnerable place she didn't want to identify.

Catriona pressed the cloth against the locking mechanism at the back of his head. The muzzle released with a snap and fell to the floor. She jumped at the awful racket it made.

A husky whisper caressed the shell of her ear as claws curled into the front of her dress, holding her steady. "Easy, lamb."

She tensed, head turning, and froze at the sight that greeted her.

A vicious scar carved a path from one ear to the opposite corner of his jaw, bisecting his lips along the way. His teeth were perfectly formed, revealed in a slow, hungry smile, but not human. Several of them were too sharp to be called anything other than fangs.

Her gaze dropped. She fumbled with the manacles on his wrists, her heart beating too fast and too loud in her ears. It wasn't fear that gripped her, exactly, but something close to it. Something bright and hot and twisting like the fire of the Void in her veins. Something she'd never felt when Fennack drew her into his arms.

The manacles released. Aedan made a pleased sound deep in his chest and shook them off. He reached for her, and some mad, curious thing in her breast allowed it.

Large, clawed hands cupped her throat. His thumbs pressed into her jaw, holding her still as he skimmed the pads over the flecks of blood that clung to her skin.

"There now," he murmured, bending his neck to hover his scarred lips over hers. "Shall we fetch that crown?"

On the Wing of a Prayer

Sasha Kielman

There was nothing more sacred than the bond between a dragon and their rider. The paths to reach it, however, were perilous.

One could not merely approach a dragon and ask its favor. Every child in the Realm of Elohan knew that simple rule.

One had to prove oneself worthy of that most sacred of bonds, almost as ancient as both humanity and dragonkind themselves. Such a bond was even more powerful than the bond between humans and the gods, for the gods could not walk upon the land in the way that humans and dragons could. The dragons kept their own gods, of whom they rarely spoke to humans.

"One for the dragons, one for the temple, one for the academy," went an old saying recited to those families blessed with multiple children. Usually, the oldest child in the family was deemed the wisest and strongest and therefore worthy of a dragon.

But not always. Everyone still had to make their own way in the world. Find their path. Find their place, whether it was upon a dragon's back or behind an altar or desk. Accept the fate their deity set out for them.

Liadan knew she belonged behind a desk or an altar, even though she was the eldest in her family. She spoke multiple languages, was an expert in history, literature, and politics. She was no warrior or athlete.

Yet here she was, throwing away her career, to find a dragon.

Those dragons not yet bonded with a human companion could be easy or difficult to find, depending on their temperament or experience. There were older dragons hiding in the mountains, waiting to see if one worthy of them could find them. There were younger dragons roaming the skies above villages, daring the bold to try to claim them.

Most of those humans died.

Liadan had no interest in such a dragon. She also did not want to risk climbing a mountain to find an older dragon she might outlive.

For those not wealthy or powerful enough to be born with a dragon egg in their cradle, finding the right partner seemed a daunting task. Especially for a petite woman with no warrior training.

But Liadan had one advantage over at least most of those searching for their dragon: she knew her dragon's name.

She heard it whispered in her ear in her prayers, echoing in her mind during her dreams, repeated with each heartbeat.

Once she heard her dragon's name, she knew she couldn't wait to regret her decision.

Ruah, I'm coming to find you.

The gods never made things easy. She should be grateful they gave her a piece of the puzzle, a name etched in her heart and soul.

Liadan blinked back tears as she lit a candle at the temple.

Please, let me find her soon, she prayed.

Please let us live a long life together.

Please let us die peacefully. I want to die sleeping under her wing.

That last prayer was the least likely to be answered, but she prayed it anyway. Perhaps her Goddess, in Her mercy and wisdom, would finally grant her prayers.

Her gods-given gift had been silent since Liadan heard Ruah's name. Her gift was a precious one, powerful but fickle. To hear a god's voice inside one's head could be dangerous. Devastating to the mind.

But the same was true of a dragon's.

And the voice Liadan had heard was neither her Goddess's, nor her dragon's, as both were female. No, it wasn't a female voice that Liadan had heard in her prayers, in her heart, and that was the piece of the map she was missing.

Liadan had never been afraid of the gift her Goddess had given her, and she wouldn't be afraid of the journey She laid in front of her. Nor would she be afraid of the bond she would form with her dragon. The bond could be life giving, but also death dealing for the weak, the cruel, the unprincipled. Liadan was none of those things.

Thank you, Mother Goddess. I praise you for the life you have given me. Please protect us both.

Rising from her kneeler, she swallowed and took one last look around her in the chapel. Candles flickered, heads bowed in prayer, priests and acolytes walked by. It was a quiet time for the Church; summer was beginning, and most people with the means were traveling. Those without the means were trying to rest for the winter travails ahead, or prepare for fall journeys. Fall was a more typical time for dragon seeking; the cooler weather not only made traveling more comfortable, it also was said to encourage dragons to come down from the mountains.

Liadan couldn't wait for fall. Her journey needed to begin now that she had saved enough money, memorized maps, and researched. The Goddess provided her dragon's name through her gift for a reason.

Liadan would not fail Her or Ruah. Or the person whose voice she heard, whoever they were.

She left the temple, and then walked to the edge of the city for her next errand.

Liadan had been saving for months to buy the finest horse she could find. She researched the best stables, the breeders who were kind to their horses. She didn't need the horse to be the fastest or the prettiest, but one that could carry her as far as she needed to go to find her dragon. And wouldn't startle and throw her at the sight of said dragon.

After informing an attractive young stablehand that she had an appointment, she walked over to a brown horse that seemed to be set aside from the others. Was it hers? She reached over to stroke its nose, her hand shaking.

"Buttercup is her name," John, the stable owner said, approaching from behind her. He was a kind man, with dark brown skin and a smile that crinkled the corners of his eyes. Liadan knew that other stable owners wouldn't take a woman like her seriously, but he met her gaze as soon as she arrived for her first appointment and offered a handshake, and answered all her questions thoroughly.

"She'll get you where you need to go," John continued as they smiled at each other. "You'll take care of one another, won't you?" He nodded at Liadan then Buttercup in turn.

"She's beautiful," Liadan said. Her voice was soft with nerves – and love.

"Let's see how you do together," John said, untying Buttercup's reins, before offering Liadan a hand up into the saddle.

Liadan pushed the curls that always escaped a braid or a ribbon behind her ears and took a deep breath. If riding a dragon was anything like riding a horse, she knew she would love it. But perhaps never quite get used to it. She and Buttercup did a few loops around the stable yard; she had no problems getting a feel for how to move with Buttercup, and how to use the reins, but sitting in the saddle for hours would definitely be uncomfortable.

Feeling much more confident with a sturdy horse beneath her, Liadan set out on her journey.

* * *

Liadan's first stop in each town or village she visited was the temple. There, in addition to her prayers, she could inquire of the priests or elder villagers praying where good places to stay were, and if they had heard of any dragons in the area.

Her Goddess-given gift was still silent. But Liadan knew she was on the right path nonetheless. Even if it was difficult to be so alone sometimes. When she was offered a room in a grandmother's home, she always accepted the offer, for both the company and knowledge she wouldn't find in an inn. And food prepared with love – she would need all her strength to continue on her journey.

It was not unusual for a woman to be traveling alone in Elohan – it was a large realm, with many different towns and cities – but it was perhaps more unusual for someone so obviously not suited to dragon riding to be searching for a dragon. Just as every child knew the rule about asking a dragon for its favor, most children were dissuaded from dragon hunting from a young age. Liadan certainly had been. A small, quiet child who would rather read than play outside and cried easily was not a predicted dragon dancer.

"Are you sure about this?" one of the grandmothers with whom Liadan stayed asked her before she departed. She met her eyes, accepting a gentle hand squeeze.

"You're well educated. And certainly, you could find a lovely partner and build a family, if you wanted to. Why a dragon?"

Liadan swallowed. She revealed her gift to hardly anyone. She closed her eyes before meeting Grandmother Eva's.

"Did you ever just know that you had to do something, or you would regret it for the rest of your life, Grandmother?"

Grandmother Eva smiled softly and nodded. "Yes, my dear." She cupped Liadan's cheek with her gnarled hand. With her wrinkles and calluses from knitting needles and gardening, it was one of the most beautiful hands Liadan had ever seen. She hoped, as she had prayed, that she could live to be a grandmother with knobbled hands.

But she had to find her dragon first. And then she could worry about finding a partner, if Ruah approved of them. Having a dragonbond, a partner, and a family would be difficult. But it would be worth it.

It was this determination that Liadan felt in her heart, knew in her bones, sang in her soul, that Grandmother Eva could see in Liadan's eyes as they both teared up and hugged.

"Be safe," Grandmother Eva whispered. "I will pray for you, that you find your fate, that your Goddess will guide you. That you find whatever your heart longs for on your journey."

Liadan took her hands in her own as they stepped apart, blinking back tears and nodding. "Thank you, Grandmother," she said. "I will remember you and your family in my prayers each night."

Liadan had never doubted the power of her prayers, or her gift. But as she continued through the Elohan countryside, from village to village, receiving blessings from priests and grandmothers and coming no closer to finding her dragon or the person whose voice gave her Ruah's name, she began to wonder if perhaps she should have waited until she heard further from the voice or her Goddess. Or prepared more. Trained in combat or weaponry or something.

But she was on the journey; she had made her choice. She would make her own fate.

She continued to pray and travel onwards.

* * *

Elohan's rolling hills stretching toward the mountains were famously beautiful. It was the height of summer, and the vibrant greenery was a welcome change from Liadan's life in the city, a reminder of her childhood – and a promise of what she had to look forward to. As the days stretched longer, she found her energy and excitement increasing. She had met so many kind people, even if she hadn't yet found her dragon, and got to explore the world in a way she never thought she would. She was accustomed to exploring the world through book pages, through her own imagination, through factual accounts of what was happening in other places.

As she traveled closer to the mountains, the earth began to tremble with the presence of dragons. On a quiet morning just after sunrise, Liadan heard a dragon calling to another for the first time, and burst into tears at the beauty of it.

But none of the calls she heard resounded in her heart. Those songs were not Ruah's. Nor did she hear the other person's voice in the crowds at the market, or at the summer solstice festival. But she smiled and danced and laughed and drank nonetheless.

And as the sun finally set over the western mountains, Liadan felt her prayers in her heart. She heard Ruah's name in that voice in her heartbeat again.

They had not abandoned her. Her Goddess had not abandoned her.

She had only to keep trusting, to know that her fate was certain, to be herself – joyous and kind, soft and quiet, not a typical dragon dancer.

And she wasn't going to stop until her prayers were answered.

* * *

Liadan never felt beautiful. Her ruddy golden hair and freckles weren't considered the height of beauty, nor did she have much height to speak of. But when she put on her leather vest and knee-high riding boots for flying dragonback, she felt like she could be a queen.

She was ready.

Her dragon was near.

All she had to do was find her.

With her spine straight and a smile on her face, Liadan followed the song in her heart and the prayers on her lips to find her dragon.

The hills were quiet compared to the city where Liadan had built her adult life, and the villages she passed through on her journey. But they were alive with birds and bugs chirping, with the breeze through the trees and grass, and the song of dragons in her heart.

When her travels brought her past any villages where she could get more supplies or find a place to spend the night, Liadan knew she was getting close. There were fewer birds singing overhead closer to the mountains – and to the dragons. She curled up close next to Buttercup at night, pulling blankets over them both despite the warmth during the day. She made sure they stayed close to fresh water.

Her every sense was on alert. She had to force herself to concentrate on her prayers and her breaths so that she wouldn't jump at every sound.

It was a warm golden afternoon about a week after the solstice when Liadan and Buttercup descended a rolling hill into a green valley, and ahead of them, a sight that stopped Liadan's heart and brought tears to her eyes.

She could hardly breathe, but her soul was singing, her innermost self feeling the rightness of what she was experiencing, calm and at peace with the truth of Liadan's fate.

A midsize black female dragon lay curled up on her side, asleep. Her scales shone in the sunlight, glistening silver and purple. Next to her, however, was a much larger, and crueler looking, male dragon, one wing protectively covering the female. His scales were mostly green, tending towards gold and yellow iridescence. They would be awe inspiring when flying together.

Liadan found herself blinking back tears. She felt as though she was intruding, but she could feel the call, the answer to all her prayers.

Ruah. And her mate. Presumably. Who looked much scarier to deal with.

She wasn't going to wake them up, that was for certain. What a rude way to meet someone you wanted to spend the rest of your life with. Liadan smiled, thinking of flying with Ruah for the first time. And hoped that her mate would fly away and let them get to know each other once he and she woke up.

She clambered off Buttercup, patting her down to rest. Then she spread a blanket from her pack across the grass under a tree, sat down, pulled out a book, and settled in to wait.

It was hours later when Liadan was interrupted from her reading, not by the dragons awakening, but by a man approaching up the hill from behind her.

She stood, quickly putting her book back in her pack. She had a knife at her side, though she hadn't needed to use it to defend herself. Not yet, at least.

The man was tall and thin, also dressed for dragon riding, a cloak slung over his arm and a sword at his side.

He approached her and stopped a respectful distance away. "Good afternoon, my lady. I mean you no harm."

Liadan nearly sank to her knees.

His was the voice she had heard.

He gave her Ruah's name through her gift, from the Goddess.

Who was this man?

She forced herself to breathe and find her voice. "Good afternoon, sir." She swallowed. "Have you claimed one of the dragons in the valley below?"

He smiled. "Have you come for the other?"

She met his eyes and nodded, not trusting her voice.

He stepped closer to her and offered his hand. "I'm Tiarnach. My companion sleeps below with his partner. I wish you all the best in your attempt to claim her. But I will have to respect my companion's wishes regarding the situation."

"I'm Liadan," she said, taking his hand. He brought it to his lips. Heat rushed through Liadan, and she once again wanted to fall to her knees. Or to weep. She forced herself to do neither and to continue speaking, by the grace of her Goddess. "I understand. I would expect no less of a bonded dragon dancer. I have been waiting for Ruah for a few months now."

His eyebrows raised. "You know her name already?"

"I heard it in my prayers, in my dreams, in the song of my soul. It's my gods gift."

He had to believe her. He, of all people, the companion to her dragon's mate.

His eyes were wide as he assessed her. "That is quite a gift, Liadan. If your god has deemed you worthy of Ruah, I will certainly look forward to getting to know you better."

"Thank you, Tiarnach, and likewise."

Tiarnach was handsome. Too handsome. His hair was a darker red than hers, verging on auburn, and rather than her messy curls, he had one perfect piece curved towards his eyes.

If she felt unworthy of Ruah, who the Goddess designated for her, she certainly felt unworthy of him. But if their dragons were mates, they would be attached to each other for the rest of their lives. Hopefully as friends, at least.

He was looking down at their dragons below as they started to stir. "My gods gift wasn't useful at all in claiming a dragon. I'm glad you took the risk of trusting me with yours, Liadan."

He turned to her. "I'm a singer. Maybe someday I'll sing something about how we claimed our dragons and met."

"I would be honored to hear you sing about anything. That's a beautiful gift."

"It's certainly more common than being able to hear your god."

They watched the dragons spread their wings and soar into the air, their flight pattern directly upward, twining in a spiral around each other.

She swallowed. "What is your dragon's name?"

He smiled. "Tachat. He loves Ruah."

Her heart skipped a beat. "You both have lovely names. It must have been comforting to know your own name is similar to your dragon's. Are Tachat and Ruah really mates?"

Tiarnach met Liadan's eyes and nodded. "They don't have children yet. They've only been mated for a few years." He paused, and cocked his head, his eyes darting up to Tachat. "Tachat expects you to gain his trust in addition to Ruah's." Tiarnach's eyes twinkled. "But you already gained mine, so that will hopefully make things a bit easier."

Liadan couldn't help but laugh. "I'm grateful to meet you both. And to finally find Ruah. I knew that she was the one, but hardly anyone believed that this was the right path for me."

He nodded. "I can understand. I wasn't destined for dragon riding either. But I managed to impress Tachat somehow. He came to reside outside my village, farther to the north. Lots of people wanted to claim him, but I was the one he allowed on his back. He's defended me against those who aren't keen on normal folk like us claiming dragons. I'm sure Ruah will do the same for you."

Liadan smiled, meeting his eyes. "If Tachat lets her out of his sight."

It was Tiarnach's turn to laugh. "He does. He will. He knows you two will have your own journey together. But that you will always come home to us." His voice trailed off softly at the end of his words, his gaze focused on the now quite distant dragons far above them in the sky.

Liadan hesitated to ask her next question. Breaking the fragile moment of truth they had shared seemed like a thunderbolt presaging a storm. But she would have to know.

The answer to her prayers did not implicate just her fate, and Ruah's. Why had she heard Ruah's name in Tiarnach's voice?

She took a deep breath before she ended the precious moment of silence. "And how do you feel about that? Having to worry about not just yourself and your dragon, but your dragon's mate and her partner?"

Tiarnach blinked, and turned his gaze towards Liadan once more. His eyes were wide and open with honesty as he spoke. "Being a dragon dancer is a lonely journey. We all know that, and accept the risks. War could come to our soil. Cruel, jealous people may try to harm us. But that could happen regardless of our choice to love another for life. And if my choice to bond with Tachat, and his choice to love Ruah brings someone else into our lives, someone who has also made that most profound of choices, and has been found worthy? Of course, I would welcome you into my life, Liadan."

Liadan had never hated the fact that she cried about everything more as she felt the telltale drops on her face. "Thank you, Tiarnach," she managed to say, hoping it conveyed her relief, her conviction. "I would be honored to have you and Tachat and Ruah by my side for the rest of my life." She nodded, and managed to blink away the last of the tears with a soft sniffle.

Tiarnach smiled. "Besides, who could possibly find it difficult to travel with such a kind and lovely lass as yourself?"

Liadan laughed, and she felt overwhelmed with joy. The true joy that could only be a blessing from the Goddess Herself.

* * *

The new family of four traveled across the entirety of Elohan for the rest of the summer. Liadan kissed Buttercup goodbye, selling her in the closest village to a brave young woman with warm brown eyes and long tight braids who would start her dragon hunt after Mabon in the fall. They hugged and promised to keep in touch before Liadan took to the skies with Ruah once more, meeting Tachat and Tiarnach in the next village to the north.

As summer began to turn to fall, the breeze becoming cooler at night and leaves beginning to turn as vibrantly red as Tiarnach's hair, Liadan finally began to feel fully comfortable flying. It was more comfortable than riding a horse; there were no worries about bumpy or poor roads, no constant up and down motion to make her back sore.

And she also found herself growing comfortable when Tiarnach brushed one of her curls behind her ear, or placed his hand on her back as they walked through a market for supplies. Or when he didn't correct people who assumed they were a couple. He was considerate, an obliging travel companion, and handsome, and Liadan would not allow herself to hope for more than his friendship. She had already been blessed by her Goddess with her dragon and the life the four of them were building together.

But with their dragons resting for the night of Mabon, their errands completed – including Liadan sending a letter to her new friend and Buttercup, wishing them well on their journey – Liadan and Tiarnach joined the celebrations in the village where they were staying.

"Blessed Mabon, my lady," he said, handing her a goblet of cider.

"Blessed Mabon, my lord," she said, taking a deep swallow and then passing it back to him. They said the traditional blessing to each other, sharing the sweet cider, before joining the dancing.

Liadan had loved dancing on the solstice, finally feeling confident and free, even though she had been entirely alone. Now, on the equinox, she felt cherished with Tiarnach's arms around her. They were surrounded by people laughing and dancing and drinking, bonfires blazing, tables groaning with the harvest's bounty before the cold and dark would set in.

And when their lips met after they shared another goblet of cider and blessing in the privacy of their room at the inn, Liadan knew that the song in her heart, the answer to her prayers, had been more than just her dragon all along.

A Thousand Lifetimes Between Us

Samara Lo

Xing Yue stared in confusion at the dragon and phoenix bangles weighing down her wrists. For some reason, she was dressed in crimson robes girted by pearls, and a red veil obscured most of her vision. Ten hells. She was in the mortal realms – and a bride at that – but to make matters worse, her immortal skin was missing. Without it, she wouldn't be able to take her dragon form.

Her father, the Jade Emperor of the Celestial Kingdom, must've been furious to mete out this kind of punishment. She couldn't even remember what she'd done.

Focusing, she drew on her magic, but there was only a cultivated *qi* – a sign she'd retained only a drop of her powers. It was still more than the average mortal, but only just. Father was definitely furious.

No matter. She had been in worse scrapes. Father would miss her in a few days and send his guards to fetch her. She'd be home enjoying her immortal peach wine soon enough.

Lifting her veil, she peeked at her surroundings. She was in a palanquin and judging from the trill of reed pipes, this was a wedding procession on the way to her betrothed's home.

"Stop! Thief!" Screams filled the air along with the clash of blades.

The music cut short and the palanquin toppled, flinging Xing Yue out. Her veil slipped off as she hit the ground. Oomph. Mortal or not, this was not a way to treat a bride.

Around her, the procession was in chaos as armed soldiers pursued a masked thief through the city street, upturning vendor carts and forcing people to flee.

The thief's *qi* flowed through his movements, giving him the supernatural ability to fly from rooftops and shatter redwood beams with a palm strike. His *jian* flew around him, controlled by his *qi*, the sword parrying against the soldiers' attacks.

Xing Yue pushed to her feet just as the *jian* deflected towards her. Thankfully, she still retained her martial arts to dodge, but before she could move, the thief landed beside her and yanked her out of harm's way. Her long robes tangled around her legs and she tumbled, latching onto the man for purchase. Pressed against him, she could feel the toned muscles of his arms as he held her in a too-tight embrace.

"What are you doing?" she snapped.

One: it was improper to hold her like this.

Two: she could've managed without him.

She drove her knee into his groin.

He sucked in a satisfyingly pained breath as he dropped.

The soldiers closed in.

Without warning, the thief grabbed her hand. Their gazes met. For a second she was falling into an eclipse, a thousand stars dying in the dark depths. It stirred a deep ache buried inside her, but then the moment was gone as he shoved her – right into the soldiers.

She barreled over two of them before slamming into the ground. A sharp pain ran up her side. That bastard. She scrambled up, but he was gone, the soldiers disappearing after him down a side alley.

"Mistress! This is bad luck! Quickly! Put this back on!" Before she could protest, she was swarmed by handmaidens who threw her veil over her head and forced her into the palanquin.

It didn't take long to get the procession back in order, but judging from the rocky ride and the musicians' uneven tempo, they were rushing.

By the time they arrived, the procession was ruffled and huffing. They were stopped before a large manor with grand wooden gates and twin *qilin* statues seated at the entrance.

"Odd, isn't it?" one of the maids nearby whispered.

"Shouldn't the groom be here?" asked another.

They were right. Traditionally, the groom and his family would be waiting outside to receive his bride, but there was no one.

The manor gates flung open and an older woman in embroidered silk robes stepped out. She had a fierce look in her eyes, like a lioness on a hunt, and carried herself as someone used to being obeyed without question.

"What is the meaning of this?" The woman looked over the palanquin in disgust.

The older of the handmaidens stepped forward.

"Noble Lady Yang, we were delayed by—"

"My question is why you dare to arrive after the auspicious hour."

"But Noble Lady, there's still time. The hour is—"

"Late. Go home. My son will not marry today."

Xing Yue wasn't too bothered by the rejection. She had better things to do with this mortal life, but then a sharp pain ripped at her flesh as if her dragon scales were being pried off one by one. She must've been separated from her celestial skin too long, her body longing to break from her tiny mortal frame and soar through the realms.

A gentle tug drew her attention like the beckoning of a dear old friend. Through the doors of the manor floated a trail of scattered stars as if a galaxy had formed right inside the entryway. It didn't make sense. Why would her dragon skin be here?

"But Noble Lady, the fifth prince's marriage was granted by the Emperor. If you refuse—"

"Then you can explain to the Emperor that you were late." The woman gestured to her maids. "Close the gates!"

"Stop!" Xing Yue climbed out of the palanquin and tore off her veil. Gasps rang around her, the forming crowd looking perfectly scandalised. Clearly her future mother-in-law wanted to make a scene. She, being a filial daughter and all, was happy to oblige. Besides, she had to get into that manor.

"You might not welcome me, but I am here to stay by imperial edict. No one will stand in my way." She shoved past the maids.

Noble Lady Yang held her arm out and blocked the entrance.

"Let's see you try to step one foot in here." *Qi* rippled off her.

Xing Yue smirked. Hidden behind the gracefulness of silk robes lurked danger.

"And you're the one to stop me?" Xing Yue stepped towards the threshold. Noble Lady Yang pushed her back. To anyone else, it would've looked like the clawless pat of a kitten, but there was enough *qi* behind it to blast Xing Yue across the street.

Luckily, she was prepared as she countered with her own *qi*, resulting in a stalemate. They exchanged a combo of strikes, their hands like twin snakes writhing and jabbing as they exchanged inch for inch of ground.

Noble Lady Yang was pleasantly skilled, and Xing Yue found she was enjoying herself, but then a sharp pain pierced her chest. She had to end this – fast. With two fingers, she jabbed Noble Lady Yang's shoulder. The blow would've shattered the woman's arm if Xing Yue didn't rein in her full strength at the last moment. It was still enough to cause Noble Lady Yang to yelp in pain and lose her footing, falling towards the stone corner of the *qilin* statue.

Xing Yue latched onto Noble Lady Yang's arm, stopping what could've been a cracked skull. Noble Lady Yang gaped in surprise, then masked it as she recovered her balance.

"Thank you, *Mother*." Xing Yue bobbed in a quick curtsy. "I believe I can find my way to the bridal chambers from here." She forced each step forward, the pain threatening to overwhelm her. She barely made it into a bed chamber where the starry trail led, before she collapsed.

* * *

Yichen stumbled through the garden courtyard, clutching at his wounded side. The soldiers had been relentless in their pursuit, keen to capture the thief who had stolen the Emperor's sacred moon lantern. The small orb was said to be a treasure fallen from the Celestial Kingdom. If he had been caught, his entire manor would be treated as treasonous traitors. But he had to risk it. For her…

He had almost failed her today. Almost believed he had seen her standing in the city street, draped in an elegant bridal gown, looking like the essence of the world had been captured to form a single ethereal being.

Gazing into her eyes was both damnation and elation, sending him to the ten hells and back to the immortal realms all in one blink.

Yet it couldn't have truly been her no matter how real she had felt in his arms.

He had watched her die. Had yelled her name as her body disintegrated, left to the mercy of the celestial storm that had shattered her soul.

But even if this doppelgänger was a manifestation of his mind – another illusion to torment his broken heart – the thought of anyone harming her awoke the need to protect her. As a soldier's sword bore down on her, he had shoved her away and into another pair of soldiers to cushion her fall. Since the soldiers were after him, he lured them away. It's what had messed up his escape plan and scored him the injury.

He staggered into his chambers and dropped onto a redwood chair before yanking off his outer robes and peeling open his inner shirt. An ugly gash ran across his abdomen. He scoffed. His uncle had been ruthless this time, his soldiers using poison. But at least he had what he needed. He patted his pocket where the moon lantern sat safely. It wouldn't be long now…

A soft rustling from the bed set him on guard. He expected an attack, but heard only a pained moan. Slowly, he edged closer and using the blade of his *jian* parted the translucent curtains.

He froze. A thousand knives carved murder into his flesh as he stared at the bride lying there.

She couldn't be here. She couldn't be real…

He desperately wanted to yank her from the bed and crush her against him. To never let her go. But he stood frozen, afraid a single movement would break the illusion and she would disappear like she always did, leaving only a bitter hollowness.

She whimpered again, a helpless, broken sound, and tears rolled down her face. He wanted to wipe them away; to never let anything or anyone hurt her.

"Xiao Xing," he whispered.

No. It couldn't be true. He turned away, unable to look at her any longer, certain that one more breath and he would relent and sweep her into his embrace – lie and all.

But he couldn't. His Xiao Xing was no more. It's why he needed the moon lantern. It held the last fragment of her soul. The one he had shattered. He had spent lifetimes gathering each sliver, and now, finally, he could make right all he had done wrong.

* * *

Xing Yue woke with tears on her face. She'd been trapped in the nightmare of another person's life – one where she had been imprisoned, icy chains binding her body, carving death into her skin; one where she had watched the man she loved tortured in a lightning storm, each bolt striking like a thousand burning metal brands searing his skin.

Her chest ached as though it had been real, as if at this very moment she lay sprawled on the ground as lightning eviscerated him. But she wasn't there. She was on a large bed of fine silk, surrounded by the rich furnishing of a prince's manor – a prince who looked like the lover in her nightmare;

a prince who now stood over her, barely dressed, toned chest exposed and with *jian* in hand.

Alarmed, she lashed out with a kick. Surprise crossed his sharp features and he managed to dodge her before he doubled over. She leapt off the bed at the same time he caught her arm. Her momentum pulled him off balance. He must've over-compensated with his *qi* to regain his balance since he toppled backwards instead of being pulled by her, dragging her down with him.

She landed on top of him, her hands splayed across his toned chest, her face stopping a short distance from his. Their gazes met, and her need to fight and flee evaporated as she was drawn into the void of his dark eyes, seeing all his hopes and dreams in one blink as she travelled to the essence of his being. There in the deepest, secret core she glimpsed the glimmer of gold. She gasped. Her dragon skin?

"Xiao Xing..." he whispered, anguished, as if afraid she would fade as quickly as his whisper. It tugged at the mirroring abyss inside her. One she wasn't aware existed until she felt his rapid heartbeat beneath her palm. It made her pause instead of pushing away.

Shouts rang from outside the doors.

"You can't go in there!" Noble Lady Yang snapped. "The wedding couple are not for you to disturb."

"The Emperor's sacred relic has been stolen and witnesses have accused the fifth prince."

"How can he be this thief when he is with his bride?"

"Alibi or not, this is an imperial edict. His room will be searched."

"Stop! You dare enter the fifth prince's chambers?"

A ruckus broke out.

Xing Yue looked at the prince.

"It's you…you're the thief from the street." She should've known it the second their gazes met and she had spiraled into him again, but the glimpse of her dragon skin had thrown her. Then it clicked: the sacred relic that had been stolen.

"Give me back my dragon skin!"

"How do you know about—" Before he could finish he convulsed, shuddering beneath her in pain. It was then she noticed the gash in his side that had been hidden by his open shirt. It wasn't enough to bring down a man of his prowess, but then she caught the whiff of blood and something else – more stale and rotten. Poison.

"Hey, keep it together." She couldn't let him die. If he did, he would take her dragon skin with him and it would be lost until he was reborn again. Centuries could pass before she got it back.

The doors burst open and the prince gripped his *jian* that had fallen beside them. He was going to fight in this condition? His resolve was admirable, but she wasn't going to let him risk what was hers.

She pinned his sword arm to the bed and pressed her lips to his.

He stiffened, stunned, but she cared little about propriety when her dragon skin was at stake. She breathed *qi* through his lips, summoning the power hidden in her dragon skin, willing its magic to detoxify the poison.

To her surprise it did more than that, pouring healing energy through him and mending his wound as if he and her dragon were somehow compatible. It didn't make sense. A thief shouldn't have been able to live in her skin. She would've needed to have willingly given—

His arms wrapped around her and he rolled her beneath him, kissing her deeply, desperately, like his very life depended on it. And maybe it did, since she could hear the soldiers rushing in, but then it didn't matter who was where or what was going on as his kiss consumed every thought, and she found herself kissing him back, needing him, wanting nothing more than to taste him or else the world would fall apart. What in ten hells was going on?

She had never desired anyone like this. Perhaps it was her dragon skin and the need to be whole again. It felt as though she'd waited her entire immortal life for this moment. For him.

The prince drew back, dazed. He glanced over his shoulder and coldness filled his gaze. Soldiers stood in the room, looking both stunned and confused, while Noble Lady Yang gaped in equal disbelief. The prince yanked the blanket and threw it over Xing Yue as if to keep her modesty intact.

"If you value your lives, get out," he snarled.

The soldiers muttered apologies and quickly retreated with a slam of the doors.

Xing Yue grabbed the *jian* that the prince had lost his hold on, and held it to his throat.

"My dragon skin. Give it back now, thief."

"Xiao Xing…it's really you…isn't it?" He brushed a hand to her cheek and she was suddenly back in her nightmare, watching him fighting to reach her in vain before everything shattered. She rolled him under her, the blade still against his neck.

A small orb slipped from his pocket. It looked like a large pearl and glowed as if a small star was caught inside. The orb beckoned her the same way her dragon skin did. She picked it up and a thunderbolt shot through her.

Pain tore through every fibre of her being and she dropped the orb. It shattered, the light inside crashing into her like a tsunami. She felt as though she was being unmade and remade again, and then a seal in her mind unlocked, opening like floodgates.

Memories crashed in.

* * *

He stood beneath the tree of immortals, a thousand peaches growing on its powerful limbs, each one glowing like stars. If he took one bite, he could become immortal. It meant he would never die. He could be with Xiao Xing forever.

Reaching for the fruit, he hesitated. She had warned him against touching them. Told him that mortals were forbidden and calamity could fall on him if he were to break this law. As much as he cared about living, it was Xiao Xing's trust that mattered more. She had shown him this place because it was her duty to tend to and protect the tree.

"It's my special place," she'd said as she'd thrown her arms around his neck and stole his breath with a single smile. "And one day it can be yours too."

He should've listened. Should've held tightly to her trust. Yet he was a greedy fool, and as he reached for a fruit, he never knew he would spend lifetimes paying the price.

* * *

"Father! Please! It was a mistake. He didn't mean to take it! He didn't know better!"

Father had stood over her, the Jade Emperor himself, his power making even the sun look like nothing more than the light of a firefly. His celestial guards held her in a kneeling position, her body covered in bruises and cuts after she had fought against them to free the man she loved. The ruckus had summoned her father here.

"Did you not warn him? Did you not promise me that he could be trusted to live in our realm?"

A pained cry came from Yichen, who was bound by enchanted chains to four columns, his clothing in strips as celestial lightning bolts struck his body.

"Please! Stop! Stop!" She couldn't bear it. Couldn't watch another bolt hit him. He was mortal after all. Even with father's blessings – rewards for saving her from the demon clan – the punishment was too much. But still he stood against the torture as she cried for him.

"Father, please! He's mortal. His soul could be destroyed!"

"You know the laws. Not only has he attempted to steal the fruit of immortality, but he has lied to you, pretended to love you in order to claim immortality for himself. As the Emperor I would have him killed just for stealing the fruit, but as a father, deceiving my beloved daughter demands a greater punishment."

"I believe in him. He wasn't lying. This was a mistake."

Her father sighed. "Already I have shown leniency for your sake. If he survives the celestial lashing, he will only be banished from this kingdom."

"But no mortal can survive ninety-nine bolts!" And if he didn't, his soul would be destroyed. This was a punishment designed for immortals, not mortals like Yichen.

"That is up to him."

"No," she sobbed. Why had he been such a fool? Why had he gone against the laws of this kingdom? The dragon inside her warred against reason. She knew Yichen was wrong, but she couldn't bear his torture. Couldn't live if he was banished or his soul shattered.

"Yichen!" Her body shifted into a dragon, white and golden scales glistening, and a mane burning like a thousand suns. The heavens themselves rippled and shook before her divine form. Nearby guards were blasted away by her storm. She tore through the air to reach her beloved.

Yichen dropped to his knees, blood from his weeping wounds pooling around him, his flesh scored and charred all over. She ignored her father's cry and dodged his attempt to stop her as she flew through the barriers.

As soon as she passed through, a bolt of lightning struck and cast her from the sky. She crashed beside Yichen, his blood soaking into her robes as her dragon form faded from the blow of the celestial bolt.

"Xiao Xing, it's okay." Yichen sounded as though his life was being drained with each word. "I deserve this. I should've been content with sharing this lifetime with you…but I was greedy… I wanted eternity by your side… I'm sorry…"

The storm intensified, preparing for the final death blow.

"Hurry… Xiao Xing, get to safety."

"No, no, no." The sky lit up. With a burst of strength Xing Yue shoved up and threw her arms around him.

"Get away!" he yelled, fear and horror stretching out his features, then the bolt hit, engulfing them both. Pain convulsed through her, the celestial bolt dissolving her, breaking her down. She clung onto Yichen and a surge of *qi* shot through him as he screamed her name. His biceps tensed and he yanked on the chains. Fresh blood splattered as the sharp links tore his flesh. Still he didn't stop until it cut through muscle and bone, severing his arm.

She screamed, but free from the chain he leveraged himself and rammed his shoulder into her, knocking her away.

She sprawled, everything turning black, her wounds threatening to overwhelm her senses.

"Live, Xiao Xing, please, you have to live," he begged.

Now that she was no longer sharing the punishment, the charge engulfed him entirely. His face riddled with agony as spears of light tore holes through his flesh. "I'm sorry… every lifetime…it was yours. Only yours." He smiled then, still trying to reassure her with his last breaths.

But she couldn't let this happen. Wouldn't allow it. There was still one way. A single sliver of hope she could give.

He seemed to read it in her expression as the smile disappeared, replaced with horror. "Xiao Xing! Don't!"

"Find me," she whispered.

Summoning all her magic, she tore off her dragon skin and cast it over him, wrapping him in its protective layer, all her power sweeping out of her and into him.

"Xiao Xing!" His cries grew distant as darkness took hold, her unshielded body taking the full impact of the celestial death bolt. She shattered, fragmented, broke again and again, until his name was the last lingering piece of her existence.

* * *

"Xiao Xing… Xiao Xing…"

She was cradled in his arms, tears wetting her face. It took her a moment to realise they were both his and hers.

"Yichen…you found me…"

"I'm sorry it took so long."

He pressed his forehead to hers and via their bond through her dragon skin, she saw the thousands of lifetimes he had lived and died alone, every waking moment spent searching for fragments of her soul. He never forgot her no matter how many times he was reborn; his punishment had been received a thousand times over, every lifetime tormented by that one wrong decision.

It was her father who had woven her back together with the pieces Yichen returned with. Father could've kept her in the immortal realms, leaving the final piece missing – for it was the one shard that contained her memory of Yichen – but perhaps Father had been moved by Yichen's devotion. Perhaps that's why they had been allowed to reunite in this time and place, where the last fragment of her soul awaited.

"What happens now?" she asked.

"I spend every lifetime making up for all the lost moments and—"

She pressed her fingers to his lips.

"You've punished yourself enough. How about we look forward instead, and enjoy every new step we walk together?"

"You're letting me off too easily."

"Well…if you insist on making things up to me, I believe you missed our wedding, my prince."

He smiled and kissed her gently.

"Allow me to rectify that oversight immediately, my bride."

Through Fumbles and Flames

J.I. Locatelli

In theory, Guardchange Day was the perfect time to steal a dragon egg. The trained Queenskeep guards were sent to the front lines of the war against Agravia, while newly trained cadets took their place to guard the Keep. It was a celebration. A party.

A funeral, really, if anyone stopped to think about it.

But that was beside the point.

It should have been the perfect day, but somehow, a guard was still pursuing me through the corridor away from the Hatchery as I tried to escape.

I'd spent weeks mapping the route. Every detail, down to the moment I pulled the egg from its incubation chamber, had been planned. My path through the mountain Keep and the woods beyond. A route using trade carriages to the Eastern Wilds, where I could take Ysaldrian's hatchling to a hidden colony. My entire plan to live our lives free from conscription.

I hadn't planned for the man following me through the hall.

Stone gates slammed shut in front of me, sending gravel flying. I ducked, throwing an elbow over my face to guard my eyes and nose. With a thunderous growl, the other gate slammed shut, blocking the route back into the Hatchery. I caught myself against the gate blocking my path and rested my forehead against it. I hugged the egg to my chest.

"I'll get you out of here, I promise," I whispered to the small dragon inside.

The sounds of celebration outside had been muted by the gate, leaving me in an empty and echoing chamber with my surprise guard. The only light came from torches mounted on the wall every five feet.

The footsteps slowed to a heavy ring of metal on rock, the fireproof chainmail that was standard issue clinking quietly as the guard came into the torchlight in front of me.

I turned to face my captor.

The light caught on his face: dark hair with a slight curl at the edges. Dark eyes with bushy eyebrows that were slightly upturned in confusion. Broad shoulders. The first signs of a beard were on his cheeks, chin and nose, taking away the boyish shape of his jaw. His nose was slightly upturned in a way that made him look like nobility.

It was him.

It couldn't be him.

Gareth couldn't be here.

"You." I clutched the egg tighter to my chest. The heat radiating from the egg was enough to burn my skin despite the blanket and several layers of clothing between us. "What are you doing here?"

"I could ask you the same thing." His hand closed on his sword's hilt as he stalked toward me. He moved out of the firelight then back into it. Flickering in and out of the shadows, just as he'd flickered in and out of my life since we were children.

He didn't have the confident stride of the experienced guards normally found in the Queenskeep; he rattled when he walked. His steps were too heavy. He was a new recruit.

"You're supposed to be at the celebration welcoming you to the Keep." I tilted my chin up. My heart pounded in my chest like I wanted to pound against the gate.

I carefully removed my satchel from my shoulder and put it against the wall, leaving a hand on the egg to make sure it was steady before I faced the guard.

"And you're supposed to be at home in our village, helping with the Festival of the Rising Sun." He stopped less than a foot in front of me, forcing me to look up to meet his gaze. "Not here, trying to steal a dragon egg."

I rested my hand on my short sword, trying to determine if he was a friend or a threat. Throughout our lives, we had been both. If he wasn't going to pretend we were strangers, I wouldn't either.

"Says who?" I pulled my sword, the metal singing against its hilt. "I told everyone I would be a dragon rider someday. I would get in to the Queenskeep—"

—"And I'll never let you kill another dragon again, Queensguard!" I swung my stick at Gareth and he parried it, humoring me as always. We were eight years old. He would take the role of the Queensguard, and I was the noble guardian of the dragons. He lifted his stick and slammed it against mine.

We danced through the forest, laughing and squealing as our sticks clacked together in play-battle. He backed me up to a creek and I hopped onto a fallen log. I parried his attack and backed across the log, feet finding the familiar path over the notches in the wood.

"The war is just and good!" Gareth shouted back at me, then cackled at how little he believed his own character.

"You can't laugh, Gareth," I said. "You're supposed to be the evil guard that wants the war to continue—"

"And you're the secret princess that came to stop it, I know," he laughed. "But I hate this war as much as you."

I swung my stick and he ducked under it. With nowhere to go, the momentum carried me to the side until my feet slipped and I tipped over.

Gareth leaped forward and caught me before I could hit the water, pulling me to his side. I stared up at him for a brief moment, then shoved him off. I sent us both crashing into the water with a mighty splash. The creek was only deep enough to make us dirty and soak our clothes.

"You ruined my daring rescue," Gareth groused.

"You didn't have to hug me like that," I said, glad the water cooled my cheeks.

We dragged ourselves out of the creek and the woods to lay out on the hill outside our village, staring up at the sky.

A dragon swooped overhead, no doubt carrying a member of the Queensguard away. A messenger? A scout? We didn't know, from down here.

We lay in silence for a while, drying in the sun and catching our breath as we watched the dragons come and go, great shadows that had passed over our village for as long as we could remember.

"Cecilia," Gareth said.

"What?" I snapped. I didn't mean to snap, but that tone meant bad news.

"My father was conscripted into the Queensguard." He rolled over on his side, dark curly hair falling into his eyes as he looked me over.

"He should say no." I sat up, still dripping from our jaunt in the creek. "Run away. Refuse. No one ever comes home from the Guard."

"And if they refuse, the Guard hunts them down and hangs their head on a stake outside the Keep," Gareth said.

I knew that, but there had to be another way. There had to be something else we could do. Somewhere we could go.

"Run away to the Eastern Wilds," I said.

"We can't do that," Gareth said. "We're moving into the Keep while he's in training. We're going to live there. We're going next week—"

"No!" I shouted. Gareth was my best friend, and I couldn't think of life without him.

"I wanted to make sure I said goodbye," Gareth said. He brushed my blonde hair back from my face, then flicked my nose. "You'll make more friends if you start spending more time in the village rather than hitting people with sticks in the woods."

"You can't go to the Keep," I argued. "Your father—

"—can't be in the Queensguard." I drew my sword and pointed it at him. "You can't be. I refuse to believe you let them bring you here."

"I didn't let them bring me here," Gareth said. "I followed you. I knew you were going to do something foolish in the Hatchery, Cecilia. You've said the same thing since we were children."

"Is that so? You didn't come here because you've gone back to thinking this war is just and noble?" He hadn't lowered his sword, so I didn't either.

My eyes flicked back to the dragon egg, waiting for me. I needed to get it out of there. I promised Ysaldrian that I'd take care of her egg, and I had every intention of doing so. I hadn't been able to save her from the war, but I'd be burned in the Wastes before I gave up the egg.

"To keep you out of exactly this kind of trouble." Gareth pointed his sword at my satchel. "That's an egg, isn't it?"

"It absolutely is not," I slowly lowered my sword and backed up, putting space between us.

"The penalty for stealing eggs is worse than death," he said. "You're going to get someone killed, if you damage that egg. If there's no dragon for the guard, you're dooming him to death. Return it."

"I'd rather die than give this egg back."

Was he with me or against me? If I refused him, was he going to turn me in? If I gave him the egg, would he turn me in, either way?

Who had come to find me: my lover, or my enemy?

"That was supposed to be a childish fantasy."

"It wasn't." I moved closer to him, dropping my sword to my side. Firelight flickered over the glittering chainmail, making it look like he'd caught fire.

He was the only man that had ever made me feel like I was on fire. Years apart hadn't changed that.

* * *

It had been eight years since I stood on the very same road, bouncing on my toes and waving to Gareth. He'd hung out the back flailing his arms until his mother pulled him inside. I'd stayed until my mother had called me back inside and told me to stop being so foolish about a boy.

But he was coming home today, and I had waited since dawn to meet his carriage.

The village had grown since he'd left. I'd watched the sky all the day before, hoping to catch sight of Gareth's father flying away during Guardchange. The dragons were too high in the sky, but I liked to imagine I had seen him. If Gareth's father had left, it meant that Gareth would finally come home.

I put on my best skirt and tied my unruly blonde hair back into a bow. I'd even borrowed some of the paints Lilia used to make her face prettier.

Gareth and I had spoken through letters since he left, so it wasn't as though we were strangers. At first, they had been childish things, but as he'd grown up he'd told me about the Keep. Their family was treated well. There was always enough food and his father started to believe that the war was necessary. Supposedly, Gareth started to believe it, too.

I didn't believe him.

Someone was screening his letters. To say otherwise would have been treason, so I wrote back in kind. Letters that espoused loyalty to the crown, a belief that dragons and the guard should continue to fight the war that had been going on since I knew what the word war meant.

The sun reached its zenith then drifted down to the horizon, almost setting by the time Gareth's carriage approached. I picked myself off the ground and brushed dirt from my skirts, hoping I hadn't smudged any of the paints on my face.

By the time the carriage arrived, I was fidgeting with anticipation. I followed alongside and waved through the windows as it came to a stop.

Gareth opened the door and he looked…different.

He didn't have the dark laughing eyes he'd left with. The whites had gone red, like he'd been crying. The first signs of stubble and shadow were across his jaw. His curly hair stuck up in every direction like he'd been running his fingers through it the entire time.

He was dressed in the Queensguard uniform.

I stopped in my tracks, pressing my hands together in front of me.

"Cecilia," he said. He wasn't excited to see me.

"Gareth." I kept my own tone measured.

If he didn't want to see me, then I didn't want to see him.

I hadn't missed him at all, over the years.

I hadn't thought of a million speeches I could give him when he returned, or a thousand ways I could fling myself at him to say hello.

"It's been a long day," he said. "Can we speak in the morning?"

I went cold. I took a step back to let him pass.

"Of course," I said. "You traveled a long way and your father—"

"Thank you." Gareth walked past me to his house.

My family and I had made sure that everything was maintained, cleaned, and stocked for their return. He didn't even look back at me. At Gareth's hip was a sword I recognized as his father's.

Gareth's mother stepped out of the carriage and put a hand on my shoulder. "Forgive him, he took his father leaving yesterday poorly. He'll find you in the morning."

Of course. It had been selfish of me to think only of seeing him again. To think he'd be excited to see me when his father had just been sent to a never-ending war.

I smiled and nodded. "I understand. I'll come by in the morning."

I spent the next hour in the woods, hitting trees with a stick and pretending they were the Queen.

In the morning, I knocked on Gareth's door. I didn't bother dressing up or putting my hair in a pretty bow.

He didn't answer.

For a week, I knocked without an answer. His mother sent her apologies and excuses, but I would only tolerate that for so long before I pretended he wasn't there at all.

* * *

"What are you going to do with one egg aside from kill the potential rider and yourself?" Gareth shouted. "I came all this way – and you're leaving again? Are you ignoring me?"

"What are you going to do in a war? Aside from kill yourself and the dragon that bonds to you?" I echoed.

He growled in frustration; it was so familiar and so different. "Queen banish you, Cecilia. Why do you have to be so firehearted about this?"

I wasn't the one who had changed. Once upon a time, he had agreed with me. He had pretended to be the evil Queensguard, stealing away people for the war while I pretended to be a noble vigilante. Somewhere along the line, we had stopped pretending.

"Did you even miss me when I left, or did you come here to stop me?" I asked.

His sword lowered for a moment. I took the chance and pushed forward, pressing my blade to his chest. He parried my attack and we danced across the hard, stone floor that was nothing like the grass of our childhood.

We had both learned to fight with swords and not sticks since then. Both learned to fight with words, sharper even than the swords.

* * *

Four months later, he found me in the woods, picking berries and once again tormenting the trees with my stick. I'd made up my mind by that point. I wouldn't be a girl in a village waiting for him to come back to me. Waiting to be acknowledged. I wouldn't marry a boy that would get conscripted into the Queensguard and be left to raise children by myself.

I was going to get into the Keep and do something to change it.

"I hear you've started learning how to train horses."

I looked up, his voice startling me out of my thoughts. His eyes weren't red, but they were dark and angry.

At me?

I didn't even care.

"Yes," I plucked blackberries from a bush and shoved them into my basket. "I've decided I want to learn how to train creatures. I'm not going to stay in this village while others keep leaving me."

"And where are you going to go?"

"To the Keep," I responded. "To train dragons."

I realized how tall he'd grown when he came closer. As children, we stood at the same height. Eight years later, he hovered a full head taller than me. He stopped a foot away from me, pinning me between the blackberry bush and his body.

"Why would you want to train dragons?" he said.

"So I can train them to fly away from battles," I responded. "So I can do something."

I had seen families torn apart by the war. By conscription. By the Queen's need to expand our lands over Agravia.

How long until Gareth was conscripted?

How long until he came back with dead eyes? Or as a dead body, if he came back at all?

"Stay away from the Keep, Cecilia," he said. "There's nothing there for you."

I set my basket down and took a step closer, challenging him to hold his ground. "Is this because you want to protect me? Or do you want to protect the Keep?"

He looked down at me with familiar and unfamiliar dark eyes. "The only way to end the war is to win it."

"And this is a war that can never be won." I reached up to cradle his cheek. "What did you see, while you were there?"

He leaned into the touch and closed his eyes. Tension slipped out of his body. I wasn't going to tell him that I still planned to leave. He'd left me once. I would leave him, this time.

"The dragons are raised to fight," Gareth said. "I was trained to fight, along with some of the other children that were brought along."

"You don't have to do what you're told," I said.

"And what's the alternative?" He drew back. "Run away with you? To the Eastern Wilds?"

"Yes."

I had lost him while he was away. I had convinced myself the letters he sent were a lie, but he had changed. He believed in the war.

"My father is going to die out there," Gareth said. "If we don't fight, Agravia will destroy everything. There's no choice in the matter. There won't be Eastern Wilds without the Queensguard. There would be no you, no us, nothing to come home to."

He put his hand over mine, pressing it into his cheek before he ran his nose over my fingertips. He pulled my hand to his chest, pressing it there so I could feel his heart pounding beneath his clothing.

"All I could think about, as they told us about the way that Agravia destroys everything in its wake, is coming back to you," he said. His other hand moved to cradle the back of my head. "What would I do if Agravia made it this far in and did something to you?"

His words knocked the fight right out of me. More than his words, it was the pain in his eyes as he looked down at me. Imagining a world where I wasn't somewhere, waiting for him.

I loved him, in that moment.

And I hated him, for making me the person that stayed at home waiting for him.

But we could play pretend again, just like we had done as children. I could pretend I would stay here and wait for him while he went to war in a few years. He could pretend to be his father, leaving to protect a family.

"Then let's forget about it all, for now," I said. "Until you're conscripted. We won't talk about it. We won't discuss the war."

* * *

My sword clashed against his. His fingers loosened and I sent the sword flying. I pushed him back against the wall, panting. The egg waited for me.

"I never stopped thinking about you," he said. He lifted his arms up as he pressed back against the wall. "Not once. Not while I was here and watching my mother say goodbye to my father. Not once in the year I went back to you, at home. And I tried to make you hate me so that we wouldn't replay the past, again and again, with every single goodbye. Not once since you left me a note saying that you'd come to the Keep. I volunteered to follow you here. I never stopped thinking about you."

"Then leave with me," I said. I knew it was a compromising question. I had a sword to his throat and his back to a wall. Did he think I could kill him? I didn't think so.

"And what about when they come for us?" he spoke softly.

"Then we say goodbye then," I said. "We train this dragon to defend us. We hide in the Eastern Wilds. When it flies, we fly across the sea and discover what else there is for us. We don't need to hold loyalty for a land that was never loyal to us."

Gareth's Adam's apple bobbed as he swallowed. "Fine."

* * *

We spent a year pretending there was no war in Agravia, no conscription that would come for him. That I wasn't training horses to train dragons. We spent our nights under the moon, discussing our plans in the village. How we could open up a bakery, if we really wanted to. Never mind I couldn't bake and he didn't have the patience for pastries. We talked about what it would look like for us to build a life here, like everyone had done before us. How we could take care of the village.

We laughed. We swam in the rivers and the lakes. We fell into the same creek twelve more times as he chased me through the woods in a game of hide-the-maiden that ended in kissing and getting lost in one another on the forest floor.

And it was fine, to pretend that there was no war that would consume us, the same way we had once pretended that we could turn the tides of war.

My application to join the Dragon Hatchery was approved.

I left in the night, leaving only a note behind apologizing for not warning him. Two years ago, almost to the day.

* * *

I lowered my sword.

He lowered his hands.

For several heartbeats, we froze. Assessing the threat we posed to one another.

Who was pretending and who was telling the truth this time?

"I know the way out."

"I can open the gates." Gareth stepped away from me.

"Then do it." I sheathed my sword. He pushed a piece of brickwork in the wall that I never would have seen in a thousand years and the walls rumbled as the stone gates opened.

I waited for him to run. To leave me. He watched me warily out of the corner of his eyes, expecting me to do the same.

A quiet squeak came from the egg, and a nose poked out of the shell.

I dashed back to the egg, knowing that its siblings were hatching behind us in the Hatchery. The new cadets would come to bond with their dragons and become official dragon riders soon. They started their journey towards death today.

But not this one. Not Ysaldrian's egg.

I stared into the dragon's reptilian eyes. Its wings were soft and wet from the egg, its tiny claws like needles on my wrists as it pulled itself from the shell. Something wrapped around my heart, like a string connecting me to the small being. I had a second awareness of where every little limb on the dragon was.

Gareth lingered behind me, still as death.

"It's too late now," I said. "She's bonded to me. Are you going to kill me? Or turn me in?"

His silence stretched into an eternity.

The void-black dragon crawled up my arm. They had said Ysaldrian's egg would be a Worldkiller, but children were only what you made them. Hatchlings only became vicious when trained to be so.

I turned to face him. There was no wall at my back. No army at his. It was just me, him, and the dragon.

I thought he was going to try and take the dragon from me, but instead, he wrapped his arms around me and pulled me into his chest, kissing me. Fire sprung in my belly and my chest as I wrapped my arms around his neck, the dragon curling between our shoulders.

We only drew apart when we heard footsteps and voices down the hall in the Hatchery.

"You know the way to the Eastern Wilds?" he asked.

I took his hand. This time, we would leave together.

Broken Spell and Shattered Glass

Damien Mckeating

Elizabeth woke up and said, "Ow."

She grabbed her hand and looked at the point on her finger where the spindle had stabbed her.

There was nothing.

No blood.

No wound.

She realised she was lying down in a bedroom hazy with sunlight and dust. There was glass around her, a coffin of glass that was cracked and etched with spiderwebs, as if the whole thing might shatter over her at the slightest touch.

She cried out in panic, her voice hoarse from decades of sleep. She pushed, lifting the glass case, tipping it to the side, sending it tumbling away from her as she rolled in the other direction.

There was a window. She staggered for it as the coffin hit the ground.

The glass shattered, piercing and loud in the silence. Elizabeth fell, clutched at the windowsill, held herself off the ground despite the screaming of her arms and legs, muscles wasted from a century of sleep.

Her palace…her kingdom…her home…

From the window she saw a forest of thorns. They curled around every wall and battlement, ensnarled the gates, filled the moat, left her a prisoner. An island castle in a bramble lake.

Her strength gave out. She slumped to the floor and stared at the twinkling shards of her glass tomb. With each moment her breathing calmed, her mind returned, and she looked around the room. It had been her room, once.

There was a painting on her nightstand. It was a sketch of herself, drawn by an admirer. She'd always loved how much motion and soul he had captured in a few simple lines. 'To my Eliza,' it said at the bottom in a flowing script.

Eliza… She had always loved that.

Eliza… She remembered her birthday, and the curse, and finding the spindle.

How long had she slept for?

Being kind to herself, giving her body time to wake up, she moved from the room, leaning on the walls, sitting down to bump down the stairwell one step at a time. Finally, breathing heavy and heart beating fast, she emerged into the courtyard.

The dragon turned to stare at her.

The wyrm was silver, its scales glistening like stars in the sunlight. Its powerful back legs were curled up under its winding body, the great leathery wings folded back with the clawed vestiges of hands at their tips resting on the ground.

"Princess," it said, the cold eyes with their vertical pupils fixing on her.

"The spell is broken," she said. "I've woken up." She felt a fire in her voice that even the weight of sleep could not diminish.

"Yes," the dragon agreed.

Eliza steadied herself. The elder dragons were tricksters and liars. It had been placed here to guard her as part of the curse. But now the spell was ending because…

"The witch is dead," Eliza said. "Her magic is unravelling. My prince has killed her," she realised, and broke into a smile. "He'll be coming for me."

"The witch is dead," the dragon agreed.

"He'll kill you," Eliza snarled. "I'll be free."

The dragon, lazy and contemptuous, lowered its head to the floor and closed its eyes. Furious at its dismissal, Eliza forced herself to explore her ravaged and decaying home. Her body ached and screamed at her to stop, to sink to the floor, but she grit her teeth and determined to keep going.

"I have slept long enough," she told the empty halls.

And how long had it been? The stones had been old and strong before she had been cursed, but the magical vines and thorns had torn their way through the walls. As the spell began to fail and the brambles retreated, she saw that her home, her prison, would crumble altogether.

She pictured herself escaping with her prince. Finally free to leave, to live the life that had so far been denied her.

In the kitchen she felt the first flicker of despair. There was no food. Of course there wasn't. It had long since gone to rot and dust, or else been eaten by birds and rodents. The wine in the cellars would be bitter, even if she had the strength for the stairs, which she doubted. The same for the well: she could not imagine hauling up even an empty bucket.

The sun dropped below the battlements, plunging the castle into early gloom. The dragon stretched, sat up, launched itself into the air and with a crack of its wings took off, circling once, and then disappearing over the forest.

Eliza watched it go.

This was her chance. She staggered across the courtyard to the gate. The brambles would have weakened, have splintered and ruined the wood. There would be a gap she could squeeze through. Some way to escape.

She saw immediately it was hopeless. The vines were thick. The wood petrified and unyielding.

She sobbed and finally gave in, sinking to the ground, and letting her weakness consume her. Against the will of her screaming soul, she fell asleep.

"Princess."

The voice woke her.

It was dark and she shivered with cold. She had her back to the wall, the empty courtyard ahead of her. The dragon had not returned.

"Princess," the voice called again from the other side of the gate.

"I'm here," she cried, scrambling to her knees, looking for an opening, anything to let her see the man who was speaking to her.

"You're alive," he sighed.

"Yes," she cried, wiping tears from her eyes. "Please, I'm cold, I'm hungry. I'm so tired."

"It's okay. It's okay. The thorns are thick here. They've torn my clothes and my skin. But there's a small gap, down by the base of the gate. Can you see it? Here."

A piece of red cloth slid through the opening, the fabric catching and ripping on the thorns. Eliza took it and opened it, finding bread, cheese, dried meat, a skin of water. She sobbed, grateful beyond belief, and began to eat and drink.

"Slowly," the man said. "Don't make yourself sick. You've been asleep a long time. Your body has to recover slowly."

"How long?" Eliza asked. "How long was I asleep?"

"A hundred years."

She felt numb. So long? "Who are you?" she asked, spraying breadcrumbs in the privacy of the night.

"Your prince," he said, with a smile in his voice.

"The dragon has gone. You have to get me out."

"I will. Not tonight. Listen, don't lose heart. The dragon will return. The thorns are still too thick to open the gate. As the spell fades I may be able to climb the south wall and reach you."

"You killed the witch," Eliza smiled. She took a sip of water and relished the cool sensation down her dry throat.

"She's dead. The spell will go with her, including the one on the dragon that commanded it to stay. But, it will take time."

"You're here now."

"We'll get you free," he promised. "I need to leave before daylight comes. The dragon mustn't know I'm here. I'll be back tomorrow night. I'll bring more food."

"I wish I could see you," Eliza said. "I wish I could feel you."

"Soon."

She sat long after he was gone, shivering in the night, but rejoicing inside. She had eaten her fill, and still had food and drink left. Her prince was here. The witch was gone. She was going to be saved.

Fearing the dragon might return at any moment she went back to the bedrooms, avoiding the one covered in glass. She hid the food and slept in a bed that was not a coffin.

The next morning the dragon was back in the courtyard.

"You look better, princess," it said.

She glared at her jailer. "The spell that binds you will fade soon; you can fly back to whatever rock you call home."

"Consider, princess, that the spell is the only thing stopping me from burning you and this crumbling edifice into ashes." The dragon spoke offhand, barely opening an eye to look at her.

Eliza felt fury rush through her. The way the beast turned from her, wouldn't even meet her angry stare, made her all the more furious. She was insignificant to it.

She stormed away, her anger lending her a bubbling vitality. The dragon had mentioned her looks and she realised now that she must be in a state. A hundred years asleep. What must her hair be like? The dress she wore was faded with crumbling stitching. Did she even look like a princess?

From one room to another she roamed, searching, looking for the bedrooms and dressing rooms where the dresses and mirrors could be found. The clothes were rags and ruins, eaten by moths and more, and the mirrors… She found none.

Fury became curiosity. She ate a little as she walked, searching methodically now. Her memory of the castle was coming back to her, and she went down its hallways in turn, checking each room as she went.

She found the mirrors in the cellar. They were smashed. Not just broken: smashed. Broken into tiny shards so small they were useless.

Feeling tiredness creeping up on her, she went back to the courtyard in time to see the dragon fly away again. Where did it go? Was it feeding? Had it left her alone every night for a hundred years?

She watched it go, its shadow fading into nothing in the deepening gloom of evening.

The prince had said he would climb the south wall. Eliza hurried to it, finding a window that looked down into a thick, shadowed wall of brambles and thorns. There might be, she thought, a way through. A gap in the twisting branches. If she could find purchase on the wall she could climb down…

Eliza sighed and gave a half-hearted laugh. Her body ached after her day of searching. She had no strength for climbing.

"I will have," she promised herself. She would not stay weak for long.

Grabbing blankets from the bed, she went down to the gate, wrapped herself up, and stared at a darkening sky and awakening stars until she slept.

"Princess," he said, and she jolted awake.

"I'm here."

"I brought more food," he said, sliding the wrapped package through the gap.

Eliza grabbed it and held it to her chest. "Who are you?" she asked.

"No one you know," he laughed cheerfully. "You've been asleep for so long, but everyone knows your story."

"So why have you come for me?"

"They said there was a beautiful princess asleep in a castle. I had to see for myself."

Eliza put a hand to her hair, wondering again what she looked like. What would he think when he finally saw her?

"You're a prince," she said. "Do I know your kingdom?"

"Perhaps not," he replied. "In truth, I'm not very important. I'm a fourth son. No one really knew what to do with me. They tried to get me to take orders and join a monastery. Not for me," he laughed again.

"Why not?"

"I don't want to be trapped in one place," he said.

"No," Eliza said softly.

"That was the part of your story I always felt the most; being trapped, held against your will… No person or beast should live in such a way."

Eliza smiled to herself. She liked the way he spoke. She felt freedom in her heart when he talked. "Tell me about the world," she said.

He told her stories of the new kingdoms, of the old kingdoms, of the wars, the ships on the ocean, the mines, the villages high up in the mountains, down in the valleys, the roaming of the tribes across the plains. He talked until the sky began to grow light.

"You need to sleep," he said. "Get your strength back. It's nearly time, we'll escape soon. Together. Go, quick, before the dragon returns."

The joy in her heart seemed to lift her up, to carry her back into the castle and to bed. In her dreams she rode through landscapes open and free, no dark forests and no thorns and no brooding, crumbling castles of stone.

The next morning she approached the courtyard with caution. Dragons were tricksters, and it was possible the beast would fake still being under the spell's control just to lure her in and devour her.

She found it sleeping again, curled up around itself like the snake that it was.

If not for you, she thought, I could leave with my prince tonight.

The idea took hold in her head, gripping her with its own thorns, growing and twisting until, finally, she saw how it could be done.

With quick and silent steps Eliza crossed the courtyard and made her way up the battlements. The castle had known sieges and warfare in its time, and still had the weaponry to defend itself. There were four ballistae around the walls. One was out of reach, the walls and ramparts around it crumbling away. Another was broken, wrapped in vines and thorns and contorted until the wood snapped. A third looked too beaten to be much use, as if any tension at all would shatter the wood. But the fourth…

Eliza studied it. It was old, of course, and had been beaten by time and the elements. But it was free of the vines and it moved when she put her weight against it.

She tested the handle, feeling the resistance of the winch. It moved a little, but could she manage to wind it?

She found a bolt and slid it into place. She had seen crossbows, and the ballista just seemed like a bigger version. Then she started to turn the winch.

Within a revolution her shoulders and arms were aching. There was a fire down her back. Her heart was raging in her chest, and as she kept turning each breath became a stabbing pain and black dots flashed across her vision.

Still, she turned.

There could be no stopping. If she failed now she doubted she had the strength to try again.

The ballista groaned.

Wood creaked.

Still, she turned.

She sobbed. Her body no longer felt like her own. She moved with the pain, she was the pain. She had slept too long, she was too weak, too small.

With a growl she turned the winch.

Clunk.

She felt the ratchet fall into place.

Wheezing and drenched in sweat, she collapsed onto the battlement next to the weapon. It was done. She was stronger than she thought she was. She lay down, looked at the grey sky, and laughed.

When the dragon took flight tonight, it would be for the last time.

She spent the day resting, eating what little food she had left, and dreaming of living beyond sleep and thorns. Readying the ballista had left her shaking and weak. Hours later her heartbeat was still unsettled, fluttering and skipping. She hoped she wasn't going to be ill; there was no way to know what effect a century of sleep would have on her body.

A scraping of claws and scales roused her. Eliza pulled herself upright and tilted the ballista into position. The dragon was big and the courtyard gave it a confined space to rise up from. She knew where it would be: how could she miss?

Shaking with the strain of holding the siege weapon steady, she felt sweat trickle down her face and back.

Her heart now pounded where it had fluttered.

She felt sick.

She felt weak.

She grit her teeth. Wings beat below her, just out of sight.

It was coming.

It was here.

The dragon rose up and filled the sky in front of her.

Eliza released the bolt.

The tension shot through the ballista and shattered it. The weapon exploded, raining shards of wood and metal in all directions, the bolt turned to splinters. Eliza flew backwards and slammed into stone.

There was darkness…

And she woke up in her bed, the shards of a glass coffin littering the floor around her, sunlight streaming in through the window.

Her body ached. Pain lanced down her side as she rolled over. She tried to stand and pain flared in her hip, sending her falling back onto the bed.

Catching her breath, she tried to remember what had happened. She had no memory of getting back to her bed. Had she crawled? Why had she come here, to the room filled with glass, and not the other room she'd slept in?

She looked down at the cuts and bruises across her arms.

Someone had tended to her wounds, had cleaned them at the very least.

Her prince? Was he here?

Letting joy carry her through pain, Eliza fought against her body and made it down to the courtyard. The dragon lay there.

"Princess," it said.

Eliza stared at it. She studied it. She brought to mind everything she knew about dragons, every story and legend ever told.

Then her strength gave out and she fell to her knees.

In a panic she felt herself moving, and realised the dragon had wrapped its claws around her. It pulled her in close and let her lean against its flank. Its scales were warm, and she felt herself rise and fall with its long, slow breaths.

“Rest,” it said.

“I’ve slept long enough.”

“Too long.”

Eliza let her thoughts gather themselves. It was getting difficult to think. Her body was a distraction of pain, and her mind felt fogged. It reminded her of that feeling of having slept too much, and she almost laughed.

“Dragons are tricksters,” she said. “You’re shapeshifters, too, some say.” When the beast didn’t answer, she plunged on. “When did you break the spell?” she asked.

“Some years ago,” the dragon replied. “We are not easy to chain, and I did not need the witch to be dead to break her magic. Still, it took me longer than I would care to admit.”

Eliza started to cry. She had questions but she already felt the form of their answers. “You pitied me,” she said. “So you stayed. No one came for me.” She sobbed. “No one came.”

“No one came,” the dragon agreed. “But I didn’t pity you. I stayed because I could not leave you here alone. No one should be imprisoned for another’s amusement, no person, no beast.”

She heard the echo in his words. "And you became my prince."

"I didn't think you would trust a dragon," it replied. "I wanted to give you happiness before..."

Eliza sniffled and wiped away her tears. It was still trying to protect her, but she knew what the failing spell meant, what had happened to her when the glass coffin cracked. She understood why the dragon had broken the mirrors.

"Time rushed in when the glass cracked," she said. "I'm a hundred and eighteen years old." No true love's kiss to save her. She gave a bitter laugh. "Am I wrinkled and grey? I imagine not so much. Those things are the rewards of a life. And mine was taken from me."

She settled back against the dragon's scales. She felt heavy and tired, as if the weight of all those unlived years had rushed in all at once.

"I might sleep a while," she said.

"I'll be here," the dragon said.

It had always been there. It remembered the first binding of the spell and the impotent rage that had consumed it. It had wrapped itself around the tower and peered through the window at its fellow prisoner in her glass coffin.

No one came for her.

It remembered the cracks appearing in the glass.

The dragon sighed. It watched her sleep, watched her breathing rise and fall, each breath slower and shallower than the one before. The years caught up with her and she breathed out once more.

The princess was dead.

The dragon scooped her up into its claws and leapt into the air. It turned, sweeping over the castle, and unleashed the fury of its breath. It made four passes, leaving the castle and its thorns an inferno.

With the princess cradled gently, the dragon turned and flew towards the horizon, leaving their prison behind, and taking her somewhere far, far away.

Sparks by the Morwich River

Isabel McKeough

"You're overheating the containment ring!" Elira grimaced as the glyphs on the edge of the summoning circle pulsed red-hot, fizzing and stretching.

Fey jumped aside as a streak of frost warped the cobbled floor. It looked like something raised by an old tree root. She'd probably trip over it mid-spell, ruining yet another attempt to stabilise the trans-elemental rift. "Well, you're freezing the leyline!"

Elira's cheeks flushed, and she blamed it on Fey's excess heat. "Only because you're overheating the containment ring!" She pulled back her ice, magic withering into the Tower's enchanted walls like ants scurrying underground at the sense of an approaching storm. "This isn't working."

Fey just grinned, and it made Elira's cheeks redden again. The river was running dry, and winter had quickly gone from months to weeks away. Crops were wilting, cattle thinning. And Fey didn't seem to care.

"Just breathe," she said, flipping her thick braid over one shoulder. It sparkled copper in the early-morning light blazing through the Tower's single stained-glass window. Stories said the figure depicted in shards of coloured glass was the Tower's creator – a mage whose name was forgotten but whose legacy lived on in the river sustaining all of Morwich. With elemental magic too complex to recreate, they'd pulled water from the surrounding forests and bound it to the Tower, creating a river flowing from its base that still fed the entire town. Or would feed the entire town, once Elira managed to stabilise the trans-elemental rift disrupting it. She glanced towards the source of her strife. Sheltered amidst dusty shelves, alchemical jars, weathered spellbooks and scrap parchment was a cracked celestial globe. Above it, the air shimmered faintly with residual magic, a wild rift that flared every hour on the hour with bright threads of arcane lightning.

"We sync up and channel from both ends," Fey said firmly. "Like we practiced."

Elira resisted the urge to roll her eyes. "We didn't practice. You improvised in the tavern and drew sigils on a napkin." She glanced at the desk where the napkin leaned haphazardly against a half-filled bottle of elder root. "There are almost as many holes in the tissue as there are in this plan."

Fey's deep brown eyes sparkled. They reminded Elira of springtime when sun illuminated freshly tilled earth. "Just humour me."

Elira sighed but closed her eyes. If she focused, she could make out the faint mumblings of old mages' incantations, encased in the Tower's walls in languages long forgotten. She hoped the ancient knowledge would guide her casting. Gods knew she and Fey needed it. She began to summon and felt her spell push against Fey's. It circled Fey's flame, wary of its heat, knowing getting too close would melt it away. Elira pushed her magic forward anyway, using Fey's heat to harden her weaves into glass. She felt cold sweat against her forehead but kept channelling until their spells combined and an invisible weight disappeared from her mind. In the entanglement there was no cold or heat, only equilibrium. Her spell hardened into a sphere around Fey's fire. But instead of sputtering out, Fey's flame grew, warping Elira's sphere outward.

"Fey, stop channelling." Elira fought to keep her sphere intact, to patch any seals and stop oxygen leaking in. She couldn't find any fractures, yet Fey's fire still grew. "Fey, stop!"

"I can't!"

Elira's sphere stretched into the shape of an egg, fire burning so hot within that it shifted from red to blue. Then magic ruptured, and the spell burst before she could safely dispose of it. When she opened her eyes the trans-elemental rift was pulsing with light. Beneath it sat a speckled silver egg the height of Elira's shin.

Her hands shook, teeth chattering from the undisposed magic pulsing through her. "What did you do?"

Fey's cheeks flushed the red of freshly bloomed roses. If Elira's head didn't feel like grain under a millstone, she might have pulled the heat from them. "Nothing!"

"Well, you clearly did something!" Elira rubbed her temples, shocked by the volume of her own voice, and wished for maybe the thousandth time that the Arcane Council had sent more experienced mages to save the river. Or paired her with anyone but Fey. Because them being born on the same day in the same village could have been total coincidence. It didn't mean that their powers were tied. Or that they were destined to prove that dual casting could tame wild magic.

"I'm not the one who ruptured the spell," Fey defended. "My head is fine."

Elira grimaced. "Lucky you." She was about to complain that they were incompatible on every level – that she controlled ice while Fey was all fire, and that ice bore scars where fire obliterated them – when the egg under the magic rift cracked. Inside, curled in a tight ball, lay a baby dragon. It was the size of a young sheepdog, and its sleek, silver scales rippled like silt underfoot as it breathed. Its wings were folded, spindled tail ridged with tiny silver spikes the length of acorn caps. Curled around its head, it made the dragon look like it was hiding in a patch of blackthorn.

"Oh no," Elira muttered at the same time Fey yelled, "Oh yes!"

"You made a dragon," Elira accused.

"We made a dragon," Fey said with a grin.

"Magical side effect," Elira decided, stepping towards the sleeping creature. "Technically irresponsible."

The dragon released a loud snore and flames erupted from its nose. They ignited the velvet rug sitting in heavy folds under the stained-glass window, covering a crack from some long-forgotten arcane incident. Elira spun a spell that doused the flames, head pounding in protest, but the carpet was already tinged black.

"We should name him!" Fey said, stretching a hand towards the dragon. As though sensing the movement, its eyes fluttered open. They were different colours – one the same blue as Elira's, the other the red of Fey's hair. The dragon focused on the two of them and tilted its head. It wobbled to its feet and flexed its wings, nostrils flaring once. Then it bounded onto the scorched rug and leapt, scaled body crashing through the window. Glass gave way in a rain of violet, amber, and green and the dragon tumbled into the sky.

Elira gaped at the hole in the window as Fey bolted for the spiral staircase.

"I am not explaining this to the Arcane Council!" Elira yelled once she found the nerve to follow.

* * *

The dragon flew twirling patterns overhead, scales catching the sun with an otherworldly sheen and reflecting patches of light onto the upper wall of the Tower. It already seemed bigger than it had inside. Fey whistled like she was calling in a dog, two fingers pressed against her tongue in that shrill way Elira had never managed to master, and the dragon turned sharply. It flattened its wings and dove towards them, slicing through the sky like a thrown blade.

Elira grabbed Fey by the arm and yanked her out of the dragon's path. They landed in a heap of robes and limbs. Elira scrambled to get off Fey, and in her haste slipped on the riverbank. She yelped and tumbled back, plunging into the water. Its current pulled her down the hill.

"Elira!" Fey scrambled down the embankment, hands held out in front of her readying to cast. Elira slowed the water herself before Fey had the chance. It wasn't hard with the river's volume so diminished, but it still made her head twinge. She found her footing on the rocky bottom and waded to the shallows, failing to hold back a cough as cold water prickled her throat. She lifted her heavy cloak, sodden with water, and scrambled back over the embankment. "It's fine," she said as Fey reached out a hand. "I'm fine."

"You'll catch a chill." Fey's brows were drawn, voice sharp with concern.

Wind swept surrounding grass into a frenzy, flattening stalks of daffodils and rustling the ivy climbing the Tower. Elira suppressed a shiver as water ran in cold rivulets down her back, pooling in her new boots. Begrudgingly, she stepped closer to Fey who brought a hand to her chest. It was surprisingly gentle, and Elira's heart thudded like it had forgotten its natural rhythm. Fey's fingers were soft, long, and lithe, much like the rest of her. She was all torso really.

Angular limbs and wavy, copper hair. If she learned to stand up straight, she could almost pass as elegant.

Fey muttered a spell under her breath, and Elira didn't bother commenting that a simple heating charm shouldn't require verbal incantation. Warmth bloomed from Fey's fingertips and spread over Elira's chest. It felt like stepping into a sunbeam on a harsh winter morning. The sensation made Elira shiver.

"You're shaking." Fey's voice was unusually soft.

"I'm not."

"You are."

"It's just the wind," Elira insisted, even as her clothes began to steam. The warmth of Fey's magic clung to her skin like breath on glass, and she leaned into it instinctively. She was dry again. She should move away. And yet—

"Gods above," Fey murmured. Elira turned in time to see the dragon careen low over the river. Its tail clipped the old lattice bridge and iron shrieked like a wounded pig. With a lurch, the entire central span caved inward, crumbling into the water. The wreckage sent white foam cresting over the banks.

Fey turned ghostly pale. "That was the Mallorn Crossing. My aunt takes it every weekend to the market."

"It's derelict, was about to be decommissioned," Elira said, more to calm herself than Fey. "We're lucky it wasn't the Merchant's Span."

The dragon spun again, dipping towards a tree, and birds scattered. There were no discernible flocks. Just chaos.

"Why is it flying so low?" Fey asked, her voice rendered quiet by howling wind.

Elira was less concerned about the dragon's height and more about its flight path. "I don't know. But it's headed for the square."

* * *

By the time they reached the stone gate at the edge of the Merchant's Span, the dragon had wreaked havoc. Smoke billowed from where Hadric, a burly meat-merchant, situated his rolling brazier cart every weekend. The whole thing was alight, meat unrecognisable under black char. Hadric grabbed a blanket from the hand-spun fabrics stand across the way to smother the blaze, and dropped it with a howl as the cloth caught too.

"Move!" Elira shouted, thrusting her hands forward. The air shimmered as a gust of wind spiralled out, catching the fire and spinning it away from the stall.

"Too much!" Fey shouted, raising her hand too late.

The wind amplified, spinning embers into a miniature cyclone. It sparked against a stall's awning and flames roared anew.

"Dammit, Fey—"

"I was trying to help!"

Overhead, the dragon shrieked – a jagged sound, like wind shearing through a broken window. Elira twisted the wind into shards and the cyclone dropped like a dying bird, crashing against the cobblestones in a scatter of frozen mist and splintering ice. A local cat screeched, back arching before it vanished beneath Hadric's smoking cart. Elira didn't have time to call out an apology. She felt ready to collapse, but the dragon was already swooping on a field where children were playing skyball. A young girl with pretty braids like Fey's nudged the floating orb towards the 10-point ring as the dragon dove and bumped it with its nose. The children scattered, squealing, and the ball careened into the river. Slick blue spread from where it landed, mist dancing like spirits above the water's surface. Frost glittered on the reeds along the bank.

"Since when did dragons breath ice?" Elira panted.

Before Fey could speak, the dragon screeched sharply and flapped towards the crop fields. Fire burst from its mouth in a jagged line and spread over wheat like ink on wet parchment. Corn crackled as a plume of smoke lifted skyward.

Elira ran forward, projecting water from the closest well as Fey flung a coil of molten earth, probably meant to trap the dragon within a stone ring. Their magic collided midair and exploded in a glittering burst that splintered a nearby scarecrow into smoking straw. Elira felt like she'd been slapped, and she saw Fey reach for her forehead.

The dragon shrieked, wings flaring in a startled beat. It spiralled upward, unsteady, tail scything through a stack of wicker baskets and sending charred shards clattering across the field. A nearby cart, laden with onions, overturned as its axles split from the force of the downdraft. Produce rolled like startled rabbits in every direction.

"What were you thinking?" Elira shouted.

Fey's hands were glowing with another surge of heat. "I had it under control!"

Their voices struck like clanging bells, brittle and discordant, and above the dragon's arc faltered. It banked too sharply, wheeling in a confused spiral. Its tail hit the edge of the agricultural manager's chimney and tore loose a spill of red tiles.

"Fey," Elira said, stepping back, voice tight. She could feel something, not panic or adrenaline or the ache in her head, but a pain deeper in her chest. The dragon's movements weren't random. Its shrieks came seconds after her own. Its flare-ups followed every spike of anger in her heart, every flare of heat from Fey's hands. "It's echoing us."

Fey turned, brow furrowed. "What do you mean?"

"When we're erratic, it's erratic. When we clash, it loses control."

"You think it's…mirroring us?"

"Like a focus crystal," Elira said, heart pounding. "It's not just feeding off our magic, it's feeding off our emotions."

Above, the dragon screeched again but the sound was thinner now, ragged, almost confused. Its wings flared wide as if bracing against some invisible storm. Magic shimmered in the air like static.

"We're feeding it everything," Elira whispered. "Fear. Anger. Regret."

"And it doesn't know what to do with any of it," Fey finished.

They turned to face each other.

"Do you think we can calm it?" Elira asked.

"I think we have to calm *us* first."

Silence hovered and beneath it, something old trembled. Fey drew in a deep breath, the tips of her ears turning red. "At the Academy in our last year, you swapped lab partners."

Elira blinked. "You're mad that I left before you could?"

Fey huffed, crossing her arms. "Why would I leave you?"

"You called me insufferable."

"You *are* insufferable. I can't think around you."

"So why are you upset?"

Fey's ears flushed deeper crimson. "I liked you! And from the way you looked at me across the workbench, I thought you might've liked me too."

The words hung between them like smoke in a blocked chimney. They stood there, a breath apart, while above the dragon wheeled, casting shifting shadows on the grass.

Elira drew in a sharp breath. "I shouldn't have left like I did, but I work perfectly fine alone. Prefer it, actually."

"Think you could have made a dragon all by yourself?"

"Probably not. But since the Arcane Council is going to punish us till the end of time, that might not be a bad thing."

Fey's expression softened. "So, what now?"

Elira reached out. Her fingers trembled in the space between them. "We try holding it together."

Fey took her hand and their magic snapped into place like two tuning forks harmonising. Above them, the dragon stilled. It hovered, wings flared wide. Together they cast a circle of light. It gently closed around the dragon, drawing it downward until it landed by their feet. Elira leaned against the cobbled lip of the field's largest well, legs shaking. Her hand was still clasped in Fey's. "You liked me," she said, a smile threatening.

"Still do," Fey said, very seriously. "Gods help me."

Elira looked at the ice-slicked river, the scorched wheat, the collapsed bridge. "We made a mess."

"Technically the dragon made the mess." Fey's eyes danced dangerously. "I think it was born from our sexual tension."

"Never say that again."

"I think it was born from our—"

Elira kissed Fey before she could finish. When she pulled away Fey was red and speechless. She stared at Elira for a few seconds, lips parted, before grabbing her face and pulling them together, warm and wild. Her mouth was soft and Elira sighed into it. If they hadn't just caught a baby dragon, she might have stayed there forever. She pulled away, and Fey released a small groan.

"We're still no closer to closing the rift. All we've done is waste another day."

"And make a dragon," Fey said. It was flopped over on the floor beside them, completely at peace. "But it's okay. I know how to close the rift."

Elira pressed her forehead to Fey's, and it made her headache dull. "I really don't think the sigils are the solution—"

"We do the spell we tried on day one."

Elira leaned back against the well so she could look Fey in the eye. "Maybe memory isn't your strong suit, but that failed miserably."

"Only because I tampered with the leyline."

"You what?"

Fey's whole face flushed. "I've been altering little things here and there for the last two months. I didn't want our experiment to work, because then we'd have to go back to the Arcane Council and you'd choose never to work with me again."

Elira felt her jaw drop. "You were going to let our entire village starve to spend a few extra weeks with me?"

"I wasn't going to let the whole village starve," Fey defended. "Just a little malnutrition. Some of them could use it."

Elira stared at her, eyes dropping involuntarily to her lips. "That's not better."

"It's slightly better."

"How didn't I notice?"

"Oh, you did." Fey smirked. "Caught me mixing the flux channels, so I used a whisper-knot. Cast it while you were making elixirs. Made you forget about ten minutes of time."

Elira blinked. "I should be furious."

"Are you?"

She didn't answer right away. The dragon was curled around their feet now, its silver chest pulsing gently with breath. She looked at Fey. Fey, with wind-snapped hair falling in uneven lengths across her brow. With a smudge of soot marking her cheek like the scratch of a careless god. With the collar of her cloak crooked from tugging at it in frustration. Her mouth twitched with the threat of a smirk and her eyes, two shades brighter than they ought to be, held just enough guilt to pass for honesty.

"Not yet," Elira said, and she wasn't sure if she meant the fury or the forgiveness, or something else entirely.

* * *

The Tower hummed with stillness. Residual light curled in the space where the trans-elemental rift had previously shimmered. Now sealed, the air held a clean pressure, like the breath of a storm just passed.

Elira had layered the stabilising glyphs herself, each line drawn with a precision that left her fingers trembling. Chalk still clung beneath her nails. Across the room, Fey coaxed the resonance field into sync with the leyline below – shifted back into place now – humming to herself as she adjusted the tuning rings with unnecessary flair. The window was still shattered, but beneath it the Morwich river flowed without mercy, tumbling down the hill and pushing through the pass. Along it, townspeople were pulling out remnants of the Mallorn Crossing. Maybe they could use the wood to build new scarecrows. Elira turned from the window towards the hearth. Their dragon lay curled in front of it, tail twitching every few seconds as if chasing phantom echoes in sleep. Its scales shimmered under the flames like iridescent moonstone.

"Renys," Elira said, brushing chalk from her hands.

Fey glanced over from where she was re-aligning an ambient dispersal coil. "What?"

"That should be his name."

Fey raised an eyebrow. "Like…river menace?"

"Renys as in 'rhyne' – the old word for a boundary stream," Elira said. "A place that divides and connects. He's not chaos, not exactly. He just reflects it."

Renys snorted, sending a warm puff of mist into the air. It danced in the Tower's draft.

"Well, we can't give Renys to the Council," Fey said. "They'll dissect him. Classify him. Turn him into a thesis."

Elira shivered at the thought, and Fey drifted a waft of warm air her way. "We can't exactly hide him in the Tower."

Fey smiled her signature smirk. "Who said anything about hiding?"

* * *

For centuries, storytellers across the lands have spun tales of Renys the river-dragon. A conduit for the life of the Morwich river itself, they say he was born from wild magic and still bears scars from the realm of chaos: one of his eyes is frozen blue from an age-long winter dating back before the stars. His other burns with eternal flame that turns anyone who stares too long to ash. Only ancestors from the village of Morwich know the truth. Renys was born from magic, but not the wild kind. The magic that birthed Renys was frustrated, stubborn, frantic yet tender; the magic of love. And every year when winter's cold breath sweeps across the land and brings salmon to the river, the people of Morwich speak of Elira and Fey, two powerful mages set immortal in their Tower's one stained-glass window, whose love saved the village. And gave them a dragon.

The Spell of Edrium

M. McNamara

Vanessa was flying to her own wedding, and she was planning to kill the groom.

There was just one problem: she got caught in a storm on the way, and now she was taking shelter in a mountain cave while the storm raged above her.

She was stranded and alone.

Until Sandor joined her.

* * *

The day had started uneventfully; nine dragonriders left Castle Kralle that morning, flying east in formation shortly after sunrise. They were heading for the Broken Pass, where the ceremony would take place, a location both majestic and remote.

"Oh, it's going to be so *beautiful*," Faera gushed. She was Vanessa's maid of honour, and spoke nonstop about the wedding, for she was certain that she would meet a handsome youth from the groom's clan and have a wildly romantic time. "I hear a knightcake named Rory is the best man."

"Right... I'm glad at least one of us is excited," Vanessa replied gloomily.

"Of course I'm excited! I'll get to have fun with Rory, while you, poor thing, have to be demure and diplomatic and... *wifely*."

"But I don't want to be demure and diplomatic and wifely," Vanessa objected. "And I don't want to marry Lord Drakenstein!"

Faera bit her lip. "At least he's rich."

"And cruel, and tyrannical! I hear he puts prisoners in a cage overhanging his castle gate...a fresh one every week! And he gropes the serving maids!"

Faera shrugged. "So you get to meet lots of new people."

Vanessa rolled her eyes. "Yes, as queen of the Scarred Clan. The people will hate me, just like they hate him."

"Who cares? So you're an evil monarch. You can make it work! And black looks sooo good on you."

Vanessa sighed. All lighthearted banter aside, she really didn't want to become queen of the Scarred Clan – she wanted to stay with her people, the Kralle Clan. The wedding had been arranged as a union between the two groups, who had been warring for centuries; it was meant as the ultimate peace offering. *You are making a noble sacrifice for your people*, her father had told her many times, *as befits a princess*. And what was *her* happiness, compared to the security of her entire clan for generations to come?

So now it was the big day, and the pass would take several hours to reach on dragonback, and they left at dawn, even though the ceremony wouldn't take place until sunset.

"We need plenty of time to arrange your dress," Faera giggled as she mounted her stickleback.

"I'm not wearing that ridiculous thing," Vanessa retorted. "I will just walk down the aisle in my armour. If Drakenstein wants me as his bride, he should accept me as I am: a warrior. A dragonrider."

"Oh, he wants a dragonrider, all right. A girl to ride *his* dragon," Faera quipped, making a suggestive gesture.

Vanessa blanched. The thought of intimacy with a cruel stranger repulsed her, and she had decided, in her usual pragmatic fashion, to solve the problem – by killing him. *I'll keep my word to my father and marry him, then send my dagger through his heart on our wedding night.*

Granted, it wasn't the best plan, but it was the only one she could come up with, and the only thing that kept her from jumping off the highest tower of Castle Kralle.

* * *

The first hour of the trip passed without incident. The girls were all accomplished riders, and they cruised over the mountains with practiced ease, their different dragons forming a V of various sizes and colours: the sticklebacks were purple with dark stripes, the mosstongues were green, the seascales were a deep, brilliant blue. They all gleamed in the dawn light; even Vanessa's steed, a large Kendrian black named Serafina, seemed to reflect glints of violet and cerulean. Vanessa sighed. It was a perfect day for flying, but she felt no happiness. How could she enjoy herself when her errand was so grim?

It wasn't until they came to the Wizard's Peaks that the weather turned.

This area was always unpredictable; it was haunted by the remnants of a wizard's curse, and subject to weird phenomena: storms and avalanches and flickering infestations. These could manifest at any time, and the dragonriders usually avoided the region; but there was no other way to reach the pass.

"Hold formation!" Vanessa called when they grew close. While the others hovered, she sent her mount down, flying low over the mountaintops; she could see nothing amiss.

"Let's go," she said when she returned. "But stay close and fly fast."

The riders nodded, digging in their heels and following their captain. Serafina twitched and lashed her tail as they entered the region, perhaps detecting invisible currents of magic, or echoes of the wizard's spell. Vanessa held her course, but she felt a tingle in her spine. What, she always wondered, had happened here?

The party had almost reached the other side when the storm took them, a great swirling purple wrath that seemed spawned by the very roots of the mountains. It rose up with a clap of thunder and a blast of frigid air, astonishing in its speed – one moment the sky was clear; the next, they had flown into a maelstrom. Serafina was batted around like a fly in a child's fist; she spun and twisted, and all Vanessa could do was cling on and hope not to strike a cliff. She could see nothing but driving rain and purple mist; then, in a lightning strike, she glimpsed a sheer wall of rock. It reared up before her, a terrible premonition of destruction.

They were about to smash into it.

Vanessa braced herself for impact, but nothing happened. Serafina dipped a wing, and instead of striking the mountainside, they slipped over the top of it. A sudden gust pushed them down, as if the storm, furious at their escape, struck a hammer blow of revenge; then all was quiet.

Vanessa rubbed her hands across her dripping face. She was still flying, but the wind was gone, the rain only a smattering of droplets in the air. Where had they gone? She looked around; there wasn't much light, but she had a sense of vast, open space. She could smell earth and damp, could see a shaft of faint luminescence falling down from above, flickering in the flashes of the tempest.

They were inside the mountain itself.

Vanessa leaned forward and hugged Serafina's neck. "You saved us, girl," she whispered, clutching her steed with gratitude. Her body was trembling; a clap of thunder roared above, and she flinched.

But she had escaped the storm. She was safe. She sat back in her saddle, taking a deep breath. Yes, she was alive; but what about her friends?

For a moment she considered flying back out to search for them; but no, that was madness. There was nothing she could do until the storm passed, so she sent Serafina down to land.

And soon found she was not alone.

* * *

The chamber was huge, and much of it bathed in shadow; Vanessa could only detect hints of jagged walls disappearing into an inky void. She landed near the centre of the space, where the shaft of light fell upon the chamber floor; or at least, where it *would* have fallen, if the sun was not blotted out. Still, she could see well enough to discern that the floor was carpeted in moss and ferns, and would provide a comfortable landing. She dismounted and removed her armour and sodden gambeson, then stretched. A clear pool of water trickled nearby, and she knelt down beside it and closed her eyes, her hands clasped together.

Great dragon above, please protect my friends from the storm.

"Do you pray here often?"

Vanessa's eyes flew open. There before her stood a man, half in shadow; at the sight of him, her heart lurched in fear. Was he some mountain-dwelling ruffian? Her hand moved instinctively to the knife in her boot, and he quickly stepped back.

"Don't worry, princess; I have no evil designs upon you. We're on the same side."

"Are we?" Vanessa stood up, her body tense. "Then prove it."

He stepped forward into the dim light and gestured to his breastplate, which bore the sigil of her father's house. She blinked. "How do I know you didn't kill one of my father's men and take his armour?"

"Ask me a question only a man of the Kralle would know."

"How many rings does my father wear?"

The man nodded at the riddle. "*None on his hand, all in the air – dragon scales his jewels fair.*"

Vanessa hesitated, then decided to trust him. "Very well, I believe you…but what are you doing here?"

"I could ask you the same question."

"Yes, but I asked first."

He smiled. "I am one of your father's scouts – Sandor is my name – and I have been on a secret mission for many weeks. I was on my way back to report to your father when a wild storm took me. I was lucky to land here… I feared for my life."

Vanessa nodded. "As did I." She looked around. "Where is your mount?"

"Over there." Sandor whistled, and a large shape appeared from the darkness – a Kendrian black, like Serafina. Vanessa's eyes widened, for this was a mighty beast. At its appearance, Serafina reared her head, and the two dragons approached each other, sniffing and strutting.

Sandor cleared his throat. "Now it's your turn, princess. Where are *you* going on such a fine day?"

Vanessa sighed. "Well, if you must know, I was on the way to my wedding."

"I see." He regarded her for a moment, his expression unreadable. "And who is the lucky groom?"

"Well…" Vanessa bit her lip. "Lord Drakenstein, actually."

Sandor's eyes widened. "Do you know much about him?"

"I know enough." Vanessa sat down. "Which is why I have vowed to kill him." She ran a hand through her hair and closed her eyes. Suddenly the weight of the whole thing fell upon her, and she groaned.

"A murder plot! Does your father know about this?"

Vanessa laughed. "The wedding? Yes. The murder? No. That was all me."

Sandor whistled. "So, you're going rogue and planning to kill an evil warlord. You've got a lot on your shoulders." He stepped closer. "May I?" he asked, gesturing to the moss beside her.

"By all means."

They were quiet for a moment, sitting beside each other, but not touching. The place was peaceful, the only sound the trickling of water…suddenly Vanessa realised she was thirsty. As if he'd read her mind, Sandor produced a flask and drank from it. "Would you like some?"

She hesitated. "What is it?"

"Just water from the spring here. It is fresh and sweet." He took another swig, then held out the flask.

"Yes, please." Vanessa took a deep drink and sat back. The water did indeed taste sweet, and she could almost feel it trickling through her limbs. She closed her eyes, savouring the feeling. After a minute or two, her worries suddenly didn't seem so dire; her body felt lighter. She even had the strangest feeling that she wasn't a human any longer, but a creature of light and air…and *hunger*.

"Thank you." She handed the flask back to Sandor, and glanced at him, wondering if he was feeling the same euphoria. He was handsome, with shaggy dark hair and rugged features…

Suddenly she realised she was staring, and blushed.

"I don't want to marry Drakenstein," she said, quickly looking away. "But I also don't want to carry out a grisly murder. I just…want to get out of it. I know the whole purpose is to broker a peace, which is more important than my happiness, but I cannot bear the thought!"

Sandor ran his hands along the flask; his fingers were long and graceful, and Vanessa found herself transfixed by them. "That is a noble ideal, but it so happens that I bear intelligence that makes your sacrifice null and void. I have been watching Lord Drakenstein, and I know he means to betray you."

She wrenched her gaze from his fingers. "Really?"

"Yes. I intercepted a secret message: he plans to murder you on your wedding night, then blame it on the Torvent Clan, so that your father will attack them. Then, when both clans are weakened from warfare, Drakenstein will step in and conquer both of you."

"The foul worm!" Vanessa stood up. "So, we should just kill him at the ceremony! My bridal party consists of fine warriors…we could take him out when we arrive!"

Sandor grabbed her hand. "No! You must not be hasty, princess. That will start a war. You need to be clever, to find another way."

Vanessa sat back down. She was relieved by Sandor's news, for it released her from her obligation, but there was something else buoying her spirit; she felt as if a wild potion was taking over her body, as if her limbs were on fire. Her mind danced; suddenly the answer was clear. "There *is* one other way I can get out of the wedding." She brought her eyes to his. "To be considered unsuitable."

"What do you mean?"

Vanessa fiddled with the moss by her feet. "A dragonlord's bride must be a virgin. So, if I was not a virgin, I would be rejected. Cast aside."

"Oh." Sandor went still. Then he leaned close to her and spoke slowly, carefully. "So, I take it you are?"

Vanessa nodded. "For now, anyway. But…we could fix that." Vanessa raised her eyes to his then, uncertain, wavering – waiting for rejection, or mockery – but he just stared at her lips hungrily; his eyes, she thought, flickered like the storm above. He seemed about to lean forward; then some pinprick of alarm pierced his intention, and he put up his hands.

"I'm honoured, but I must decline. If you arrive deflowered, Drakenstein would have my balls on a plate."

Vanessa's eyes glinted. "Oh, come on. Where's your sense of adventure?" She leaned forward, about to kiss him, but Sandor leapt to his feet. With a wild laugh she leapt after him, and they chased each other about the cavern; but both were addled, and instead of two warriors sparring, they looked more like a pair of drunkards wandering down the street.

"Princess... I cannot!" Sandor cried. He was pressed against his dragon now, and Vanessa lunged at him, but he mounted his steed and took off. With a boisterous yell, Vanessa mounted Serafina, and they continued their chase in the air. Around the chamber they went, their dragons circling lazily, for the creatures sensed their riders were engaged in a game.

"What, too chaste to have me?" Vanessa shouted as her steed came alongside his.

"More like too smart! You're mad if you think I'm going to bed you on the way to your wedding!"

"Nothing like a challenge." Vanessa stood up as Sandor's dragon slowed for a moment, and she seized her chance; she leapt onto Sandor's saddle. "I have you now," she grunted, sitting down to face him.

"What are you doing—" Sandor began, but Vanessa broke off his words with a kiss. At first it was just playful – she hadn't felt so alive in weeks, and she wanted to see if she could heat his blood a bit – but then she realised something.

The kiss felt *good*.

"I'm not doing this," he croaked when she pulled back, but his voice was weaker now. She wrapped her legs around him and ran her hands along his jaw.

"I can't *make* you do anything. But I'm going to kiss you again, and see if I can *convince* you to do something."

"No," Sandor said, but he was pleading now, and she cut him off with another kiss. This time their tongues intertwined, and he made a low noise in his throat – a noise she'd never heard before – a noise of pure pleasure. For a moment they were suspended, both in the air and in the kiss, and possibility yawned before them like a dark cavern, like a deep pool of water; and then something broke. Sandor thrust his hand up her tunic – a wandering, greedy hand – and Vanessa guided it to her breast.

She forgot her playfulness; it was swept away by a rush of desire.

"Yes," she said as he rubbed her nipple. A shock coursed through her; she tore her tunic off and tossed it over the dragon's side.

"Are you mad?" he asked, watching it disappear into the void. "You'll never find it again!"

"I don't care." Vanessa stood up and, balancing while the dragon cruised, removed her trousers; these, too, she threw aside.

Sandor gaped at her naked body. "You're so beautiful," he said, his eyes taking her in. "I don't deserve you…you deserve to do this with your groom…"

"What, Drakenstein?" Vanessa laughed. "*You* are the one I want. Now, it's your turn."

Sandor hovered in indecision, his gaze roving her body, and she rolled her eyes.

"Let me help you."

Without waiting another moment, she tore his breastplate off – it made a *clink* when it landed somewhere beneath them – and then his tunic. The sight of Sandor's lean muscled body sent another wave coursing through her, and she kissed his neck, his shoulders, his chest as she undid the lacing on his trousers. Sandor groaned, his whole body pressing against her, and she knew he would offer no more objections. He wanted her; she could feel how much, for there beneath her hands was a rigid spear, and the contour of it made her giddy. The space between her legs throbbed in response; the saddle beneath her was getting wet. She felt like the centre of a flame; she felt like the spirit of a dragon. She grasped his manhood with one hand, then used the other to place his hands between her legs.

"I need you," she whispered, rubbing his hand against her wet folds, and he nodded. He stood up and, somewhat shakily, removed his trousers; first one leg, then the other. Then he sat back down, as naked as she, his hot member resting on her leg.

"We're going to fall off," he whispered.

"We've *already* fallen off."

She kissed him again, their naked flesh pressed together, then she lifted her hips and mounted him. His manhood, she discovered with delight, was as hard as the mountain around them; then it met the barrier of her virginity, and stopped.

He looked into her eyes. "Are you sure?"

"Yes." She ground down upon him then, feeling him break through her, and gasped with pleasure at the contact. Then she began to thrust, moving her hips up and down, feeling him grow even more swollen within her. "Oh, *yes*." She'd never known her body could generate such rapture; she'd never known *anything* could feel this good. As they stroked together, she felt herself working towards the summit of something, as if she was climbing a stairway hewn into this very chamber. A wave began to form, a need she'd never felt rose up.

"Don't stop!" she cried, for she was about to reach the summit; the thought of interruption was unbearable.

"I won't," he groaned. The two naked riders strained together; then the wave crested. Vanessa cried out, throwing her body back, moaning as her body pulsed. A moment later Sandor cried out as well, and she felt his ecstasy erupt within her. Her eyes flew open. The chamber seemed brighter, and she could see a mist of raindrops sparkling in the air; then a shaft of sunlight appeared and spun them into a cloud of rainbows.

* * *

Afterwards they lay side by side on the mossy floor of the chamber, utterly spent.

Sandor spoke first. "What are we going to do now?" he asked, propping himself up on one elbow.

"The first thing *I'm* going to do is have a drink." Vanessa sat up. She felt as contented as a cat by a fireplace, her mind still hazy with pleasure. But as Sandor held out his flask, something occurred to her – some distant voice of reason whispered into her mind.

"Not that water. Could you please get the water in my own pack?"

"As my lady wills." Sandor walked over to Serafina and retrieved Vanessa's bottle; the moment she drank from it, her mind cleared. "Sandor...we've been under a spell."

"I'll say." He leaned in and nuzzled her neck. "One I don't want to break."

"Nor do I, but that's not what I mean. The spring water... it's befuddled our senses." Vanessa held out her bottle. "Here, have a drink."

Sandor took it; once the water passed his lips, he blinked and shook his head. "By the dragon in the sky," he whispered. "I feel like I've woken from a dream." Suddenly he looked sheepish. "A most pleasant dream, though," he added, his eyes admiring her body.

"Yes, but we have more pressing matters. There's something amiss here." Vanessa began to pace, searching for her clothes; there, in a distant pile of moss, she spotted the gleam of a belt buckle. "What do you know about this place?"

"Not much... I didn't even know it existed, until today." Sandor stood up too, on the hunt for his own garments, and that was when they found it: a large flat stone in the centre of the chamber with one word written upon it.

"*Edrium*." Vanessa looked up. "What does that mean?"

"I think...it's the name of the wizard who cursed this area. He was part of our clan, long ago."

"Was he? I need to pay more attention to my history tutor." Vanessa bent down and ran her fingers along it; the stone, she soon realised, was part of a larger piece, a massive slab of rock set into the chamber floor.

A tomb.

"The wizard," she whispered. "He is buried here."

They stared at each other, then back at the tomb, and Vanessa discovered more words carved along the side.

I lie here betrayed, a mage of the Kralle Clan, for the woman I loved was seduced by the ruler of the Scarred Clan, and henceforth they shall be our sworn enemies. But a wizard's heart does not break; instead it gathers in a lovelorn dimension. Mine shall bubble up from the earth, from the heart of this place, and bewitch all who drink from this spring, while above my tomb the tempest of my fury shall rage upon the land. The region shall be cursed forevermore, until love can mend the bonds that were broken.

Vanessa stood up. "So, that answers the question; the water is part of Edrium's spell. And it certainly did bewitch us."

Sandor blushed. "In a most pleasant way, though."

They shared a glance; then suddenly, from far above, a voice called out.

"Vanessa?"

The princess looked up; a winged shape hovered near the entrance – first one, then several. "My friends," she whispered. "They are safe…they are looking for me."

Sandor nodded. "Then I guess it's time for you to go."

"Yes." She grabbed his hands. "But you're coming with me. And I know what we're going to do."

* * *

What happened next can easily be conjured, even if one is not a wizard: Vanessa and Sandor brought a great urn full of spring water to the wedding. Once the guests partook of the libations, each person was overcome by amorous intentions, and lost all awareness of their station and circumstances. The men and women (and various magical creatures) began to pair off; as for Drakenstein, it was only too easy to lure him into a cage, for Vanessa filled it with buxom serving girls who distracted him until he fell into a stupor; the evil warlord only woke up when he was hanging over his own castle gate.

As for poor Edrium – his soul was laid to rest, for broken bonds were indeed mended by love; Rory became the next king, and married Faera, which unified the two clans. The storms subsided; but the spring still bubbled, bringing love to all who drank from it – as Vanessa and Sandor soon determined. They kept returning to the chamber, claiming they were searching for pieces of lost armour, but they never found them. But then, they weren't trying very hard – although they did make many noises of exertion on their visits, as did other lovers who came after them, for the chamber became a secret trysting place.

Even to this day, dragonriders sometimes hear weird cries coming from a mountain cave in the Wizard's Peaks.

Most avoid it, for they think it the haunt of ghosts; but if you ever stumble upon the place, drink deeply from the spring and surrender to Edrium's spell, for love is the most potent magic of all, a wizard's gift to a turbulent world.

Mercury of the Night Queen

Arda Mori

It was the cusp of twilight when Angara, the Night Queen of Tephrain, faced her new dragon in Fort Tehom, her hands still scarred from clinging to her last dragon. Flanked by twelve swordgoblins, the burgundy-red dragon lumbered into the hall on four clawed feet, lifting its head as though appraising its audience – a weary monarch, tattle-ready courtiers, and serving wraiths who glowed green and trailed a scent of plumeria and jasmine.

Angara hid her hands in her cloak. *How small, how unsightly.*

But her beloved Malgo was gone, and she needed a dragon to fend off the white-winged, waxen-eyed Celestids, especially after she'd rejected a truce from their Empress, Tzelibet.

"Udomzu," Angara called to the swordgoblin general beside her, "where did you pluck him from?"

"The jade quarries, Your Highness," Udomzu grunted.

"So he's no wardragon."

"No, Your Highness, but he's the fittest one we have now. "

Angara rubbed her temples. She wasn't in a good position to argue; dragons were scarce enough in the realm, especially if they wanted to avoid being hunted, by Celestids or man alike.

In steely tones she ordered the creature, "Reveal yourself."

The dragon nodded; a gold light engulfed its form. The sight of his bluish-green eyes struck Angara first, then his clear, sun-warmed face, framed by hair as pale as parchment.

He knelt. The Night Queen tilted his chin with a velvet-gloved finger. He was possibly in his early twenties, like her. There was a softness to his lithe figure and his mouth she'd observed only in temple dancers, and yet, his gaze was ice-hard, like a glacier entrapping sunshine.

"What should I call you?"

The man said, "Mercury, Your Highness."

Angara frowned. His looks bore no trace of the grey colour or poison.

She released him. "An unusual name."

"My father told me it was the brightest thing he saw on the night I was born."

"What does your father do?"

"He was an apothecary in the south, the Bellait district. A dragon, like the rest of my family – though he never served in the sky. I intend to change that." Mercury's eyes lit up. "You shall not regret selecting me, Your Highness."

Angara smiled. Something about the man's sudden earnestness irritated her.

"I choose what I regret," she said coldly. "Know that your wings outweigh empty words by a hundredfold. Either way, we shall find out your true worth very soon. At Mount Angrabane."

Chatter erupted around the room. The centuries-old trial of Mount Angrabane was inevitable for every dragon chosen by a Night Queen or King before a monarch could mount them into the battle-sky. A dragon who couldn't survive a volcano could hardly struggle against the Celestids.

One of her wraithguards, an aged, bearded man, leaned towards her.

"If he doesn't meet your expectations, we can find another, like Lord Malgo."

Angara shot him a glare.

"Asoke, you know there is no other like Mal."

Asoke gave her a brief sympathetic look which both reassured and embarrassed her. To their audience he declared aloud, "If Her Highness or the dragon wishes to withdraw their decision, speak now, else be subject to the judgment of Mount Angrabane."

The Night Queen turned to Mercury. But the man remained quiet; if he was afraid, he didn't let it show on his face.

"Asoke, while the Trial of Mount Angrabane awaits, see that the dragon is cleaned, fed and thoroughly trained. Most importantly, let the kingdom know," she said, "the Nightlands shall have its new protector."

In the morning, the news would spread throughout the kingdom – for man and creature alike to feed on, the way wilting flowers greet a sudden downpour. A new dragon meant a new hope.

But at the fort, the air hung with the solemn possibility which awaited the young dragon; one which everyone knew but dared not voice. It was difficult for anyone, even Angara, not to think that, as the new Protector of the Nightlands, Mercury had exchanged his freedom for a golden leash or an early death.

That, if she hadn't chosen Mal as her dragon, he would've still been alive.

* * *

Angara saw her first dead dragon at a herbalist's shop. The wild ones were hunted for their leather, their meat and bone dried and powdered for medicine.

The loyal steeds of her predecessors, the rulers of the Nightlands, the dragons deterred enemies from the kingdom for centuries with their strength and pure flame. Her mother, the late Night Queen, would read to her tales of a time before the Age of Man – the Age of Dragons and the Age of Spirits, when day and night flowed in the same sky, and within its currents, wondrous creatures roamed free.

An era before the Sun and its offspring, the Celestids, envied the wholeness of the earth, and yearned to conquer all life beneath.

"Celestids come in brightness, but only to tempt," her mother had warned. "Defy them, and they may unleash enough light to burn and blind entire kingdoms."

Tzelibet, who had once set her sights on the jade quarries, had descended upon Angara's castle to propose a deal. As always, Angara rejected her terms; she'd heard enough stories of their workhands, man or beast, ripped of their tongues or limbs, or worse, cut and reassembled in the wrong places.

Perhaps, because of this, Malgo was no longer at her side in bed, tangling his coal-black hair with hers, murmuring honeyed lies.

Hastily Angara peeled herself from her bed and trudged to her mirror. Another night of tossing and turning had left her amber eyes reddish and her crimson curls unkempt. She downed the herbal tonic her servants had left her on her dresser.

Was your heart ever so heavy, Mother? What would you have done, in my place?

Asoke once cautioned her – to dwell on the past was poison.

But how could she not, when every shiver of her hands, or one glance at a dragon shrank her heart?

* * *

While the mid-spring erupted with blossoms and plumeria, the Night Queen spent her days in the cool shade of the fort, poring over maps and debating strategies with her generals.

Occasionally, she'd stroll past the soldiers' training grounds, perking at the sound of a roar or flapping wings.

Her dragon.

Not wanting another Protector dead, she'd commanded her swordgoblins to wring Mercury through the toughest regimens possible, whilst the cooks and potioneers prepared succulent spiced meats and herbal brews with nutrition fit for giants. As for the reward that came with a Protector's appointment – decades' worth of gold and jewellery – Angara quickly honored it through her envoys, who raced to Mercury's address.

But they returned, stricken, for his village had been razed to the ground, as it had housed the infamous necromancer, Grintul, whom her soldiers had killed. Mercury's parents were nowhere to be found.

Secretly, the Night Queen ordered the owls, her spies, "The dragon's not telling us something. Find out what it is."

For a time, those were the only ways Angara permitted herself to reach Mercury. If others noticed, they didn't dare speak of it, except for—

"Your Highness," Asoke said to her one evening, as she unbraided her hair. "I've heard you haven't met your dragon as of late."

"Why?" the Night Queen said. "Did he request my presence?"

Asoke cleared his throat. "Becoming the Protector of Tephrain not only requires strength and courage, but also, crucially, his master's presence. Else, he shall be like a hound without its master. Astray."

Angara scoffed.

"If anything, he is a pampered cat, demanding the attention of my finest soldiers and sleeping in silks."

"—Are you worried he will share Lord Malgo's fate, Your Highness?"

As Angara stilled, Asoke added, "That lad – never listened to us. Drove the counsel and handmaidens mad with his antics. But he was a born warrior; one whom you chose. Who knows, in time, your new one might prove himself just as impressive."

Angara folded her arms. "Why do you think so?"

Asoke's face crinkled into a smile. "I suggest you see for yourself."

* * *

Through her whisper-web Angara learned that, on the eve of the Trial of Mount Angrabane, a group of soldiers and servants planned to gather outside the fort, at a glade where acting troupes staged their plays. Whenever she visited the fort as a girl, she'd snuck away at times to watch the actors, dreaming of joining them on stage.

More interestingly, the swordgoblins had invited Mercury. They weren't famed for their fondness of man.

On the dusk of the gathering, the Night Queen swathed herself in ragged drapes and hobbled into the wild gardens, when the merrymakers were halfway through the wild boar and game they'd hunted, carelessly spilling mead, laughter and song at the edges of a raucous bonfire. She sat upon a fallen tree trunk, surveying the scene from beneath a former mummer's graying wig and a wrinkled mask.

Within a circle of soldiers and handmaidens, Mercury was dancing, the bonfire's light casting a gold sheen on his hair and complexion. Though he'd gained some muscle from Udomzu's grueling training, his body swayed fluidly like a ribbon unraveling; even for Angara, it was difficult not to find him beautiful.

She waited until Mercury neared her, in the direction of the mead jug, to call to him.

"Good lad, shall I read your fortune?"

Mercury gave her a sheepish look. "Alas, madam, I don't believe in oracles."

Angara tilted her head.

"You are the new Protector of the Nightlands, are you not? Poor lad – so great is the burden you carry, so far from home." From her pocket she drew a pack of cards. "Perhaps this old lady can pick a grain off the load."

Shrugging, the dragon stooped before her.

"Very well. I have two questions," he said. "First, will I live to see the day after tomorrow?"

With bated breath, Angara drew a card.

"The Lightning Bolt. A great change, upheaval, but above all, lightness and triumph. An optimistic sign," she said, not dishonestly. "You must be nervous."

Mercury laughed.

"Every morning, I wonder if I've made a grave mistake. But to turn back now means betraying my kingdom, and these people who have looked after me, built me up." He glanced at the bonfire, smiling ruefully.

Angara was silent. How foolish she'd been, sitting upon her throne and watching her people like a hawk, pretending to know what shaped their hearts.

"Could I ask my second question?"

Mercury leaned towards her. Angara smelled alcohol on his breath.

"What is it?"

"How does a wanderer such as yourself," Mercury said, "wear oil of saffron and iris?"

Angara froze.

"A generous patron's gift. Does it trouble you?"

Mercury shook his head.

"It reminds me of Her Highness, Angara – her perfume on the day she chose me as her Protector." He sighed. "I fear to disappoint her tomorrow."

The Night Queen's cheeks burned. "I'm certain Her Highness has faith in you."

"—I wish she would've told me herself."

Angara shuddered as their shoulders met. Either Mercury didn't notice, or pretended not to; he breathed deeply against her ear, and whispered, "If you meet Her Highness tonight, could you please tell her that I shall be in my chambers, thinking of her?"

As Angara sat, speechless, the dragon arose, and with a curt bow, returned to the waning fire, leaving the Night Queen in the dredges of her unmaking.

* * *

The vermilion sky poured over the Night Queen like an open wound as she stood atop a stone platform, bordered by an entourage of wraiths, and swordgoblins with their gryphon-pulled carriages and supplies of spears and harpoons in anticipation of Celestids, whose bodies burned when touched by volcanic gas.

For her nerves, Angara had taken care to drink more herbal tonic that morning, and yet, the volcano, her namesake, darkened her heart like an ill omen. The ancient legend of a war god's skeleton slumbering in the mountain did little to ease her.

The wraiths presented Mercury before her like a sacrificial bride. He bowed in deference, his expression demure, knowing. Angara's face warmed as his lips brushed her hand.

The trial was deceptively simple. The dragon would fly to the volcano's crater and retrieve a bone of the war god, which would be reshaped into a piece of jewellery for the Night Queen or King, thus binding monarch and dragon. If fortune favoured the dragon, he'd escape the volcano's vicious streams of flame and gas only with minor burns, or scratches from the fanged, flesh-eating rosebirds.

In a light-burst and a rhythmic beating of drums, the dragon named Mercury tore towards the great mountain, as if for his dear life.

Angara watched him longingly.

Hadn't Mal flown in the same sky a year ago?

Like a hound in a garden of clouds, Malgo had tumbled and danced to a cheering crowd. He'd always craved an audience, so much that Angara never truly knew if her feelings meant anything to him. In their pursuit of victory, she'd ridden him through broken ribs and motion sickness.

It became their forbidden language – bruises in the sky, stolen kisses in dusty corners – until neither knew who truly ruled over the other. As the old saying went, a dragon should never harm its rider, but one can never seek to tame a dragon.

And thus, Angara endured, aching in body and spirit.

"He's coming back!" someone cried.

Angara's heart leapt. From the dark clouds darkening the horizon, her dragon soared – twirling, claws pulling smoke into rings.

But something was wrong. Behind him a shadow arose – horned and white as a spectre, colossal enough to topple a castle in a swoop. And Angara no longer cared if Mercury had collected the god's bone, for the winged beast was twice his size; if she hadn't known better, she would've thought it an incarnation of the war god himself.

With an exasperated yell, Angara wrenched a harpoon from a swordgoblin. Across the crowd her name resounded in ashen waves, but they couldn't stop her from mounting the nearest gryphon and charging into the air.

The wind howled in her ears. How she missed flying!

Above the volcano, the rogue beast circled Mercury like a hawk pursuing a mouse; deftly her dragon evaded its blows and streams of fire-breath, narrowly shielding himself with his own smoke and flame, but soon he, too, would tire and fall prey to its death-bite.

Bracing her harpoon, Angara swerved towards the beast's snout. At the very least, the monster would be distracted, and she and Mercury could fly to safety.

The harpoon had barely slipped from the thrust of her arm when a pain shot down her sides, and she shrieked. Her hands trembled violently.

Why now?

Angara stared blankly at the beast's head surging towards her, her harpoon dangling between its eyes; at the fiery glow emanating from its jaw. A numbness encroaching her body, she rolled into the cloud-strewn abyss below. Her eyes watered; the air reeked of rotten eggs.

Through her tears, Mercury darted around his assailant like a hummingbird upon a flower, spilling yellow fumes over its head. Miraculous, the monster slowed, twisting and clawing, before leaning backwards, limp.

As the beast plunged, the last Angara saw of the world was light, filtered through red wings, before smoke-scorched jaws closed around her.

* * *

Angara woke to the sound of a gushing stream and a clear, indigo ceiling. A half-moon glowed, peaceful as a closed eye. Barricaded by cedar trees, Mercury sat by a campfire a few feet away. Sensing movement, he lifted his milky head and hurried to her side. Angara sat up eagerly, his name perched on her lips, only to scream; a lightning-white pain seized her spine.

She coughed red flecks into her palm, curling her body as Mercury held her by the shoulders.

"Your Highness!"

Angara's whole body was afire. The sounds from her throat were thin, uncontrollable, like a dying soldier's.

"Forgive me, Your Highness."

A strange calmness had overcome the dragon. Angara watched helplessly as he stripped her of her armor and loosened her clothes. With slender fingers resting on her pulse, he pressed an ear to her heartbeat, and quickly withdrew with a wild look.

"Poison," he gasped.

The damned tonic!

Angara cursed her fate. They were in the midst of a wilderness, far from healers or antidotes; even if he could scour the forest for remedies, in her state, she wouldn't survive an hour or two. And with a traitor in her midst, she couldn't risk him using his dragon form yet.

At her belt, Mercury groped for her dagger. Without thinking, she lunged at him, knocking the weapon aside.

"No!"

"There is no other way, Your Highness," Mercury said. "Dragon flesh will stop the damage."

"I can't – it's not right—"

Mercury's eyes flashed.

"Are you condemning me to fail as Protector of the Nightlands, before I'd barely begun?"

Tears beaded Angara's eyes. "I can't let you hurt yourself – for me."

A softness crept into Mercury's face. Wordlessly, he retrieved the blade and returned to the fire, so that, through her fading vision, Angara only glimpsed the gold-tinged outline of his back. The scent of blood and burning flesh stung her nostrils.

Again, Mercury took her in his arms. "Trust me," he said hoarsely.

Angara gripped his sleeves, nodding.

Into her mouth Mercury slipped that piece of himself, smoke-browned and bitter. Stifling an urge to throw up, Angara crushed the flesh with her teeth. Her eyes widened in surprise as its charcoal-like aftertaste melted into the buttery nectar-sweetness she'd read of in old tomes of dark magic. She buried her face in his shirt, afraid he would see her swilling her tongue, dazed with exhaustion and want.

His torso smelled of petrichor and tea leaves – of serene mornings with her father, mother, Asoke and the wraiths in her castle gardens.

When Angara roused, an orange slit behind the treetops signaled the late morning.

A heat blanketed her whole, dense yet pliant, like chainmail. Sometime during the night, Mercury the dragon, though wary of hunters and smugglers, had wrapped his limbs around her as he slept.

Angara stood up, astounded. The pain that had wracked her body had vanished completely, save for a slight numbness in her fingers and feet. As she fumbled with her armor, Mercury appeared behind her, taking charge of her clasps. Angara blushed as his hands tenderly grazed her dress.

"About yesterday, I'm sorry – I wasn't thinking straight," she said.

Mercury paused.

"I thought I'd die before hearing you apologize."

The Night Queen sighed. "We should thank my traitor, for humbling me."

Following the wind and daylight, the two plodded through the woodland, with Angara leaning on Mercury. If they had both perished, the five other vassals of the Nightlands would wage war over Tephrain and its dragons. After which, surely, the Celestids would intervene to 'salvage' the enemy states, under the promise of freedom and unity.

"It's not Tzelibet," Angara mused. "She would've struck Fort Tehom, without waiting."

But Mercury had halted in his steps, his face pale. Before them was a path of crushed trees, slick with blood and chunks of meat, stinking of sulfur.

Carefully they stalked the scent to a large mass; the horned beast's carcass, split into pieces at its haphazardly-stitched seams. Angara inched closer to the beast. In the curdling air, a second scent found her nose – a cloying whiff of jasmine and plumeria.

This possession wasn't achieved by wraith-work alone. Only a masterful necromancer could engineer such a foul beast.

"Mercury, you killed this false-born creature with the volcano's gases," she said. "Yet, you're alive."

The light in Mercury's eyes dimmed. His mouth drew a tight line as he lifted the edges of his shirt to expose his body. And Angara, who always thought herself accustomed to scars, exhaled sharply, for they weren't battle scars.

"There's no poison I haven't – there's a reason why," Mercury began, downcast, "my father's medicines cured almost any ailment."

"I–I didn't mean to."

"Don't worry. It was a long time ago."

Angara grasped his hand. They stood in silence as birdsong pervaded the decay-strewn clearing.

The last known necromancer, Grintul, had died at the hands of her soldiers.

Or had he?

"Mercury," she murmured. "We won't be dead for long."

* * *

In the years before the first Night King reigned, Tephrain bore another name: the Plumeria Kingdom, for its roads teemed with those fragrant, skull-white flowers and its native inhabitants: the wraiths, spirits of men who had died in regret, despair or injustice – or, for the more potent ones, perpetuated sins too great to speak of.

Yet the Night King, seeing virtue in every living creature, assembled the wraiths and after weighing their grievances, took the most remorseful under his wing, where alongside battle-hardened dragons and goblins, they built the cities of the night, basking in the eternity and invincibility that came with not having a corporeal body.

But even wraiths might crave warmth.

Alongside Mercury, Angara bade her time, traveling on horseback from one quaint town to another, until the owls brought her news of her memorial and a kingdom-wide hunt for her dragon, blamed for her death.

When the owls chirped that Asoke had been elected as regent, Angara staggered against a tree; Mercury caught her in time before she fell.

"He was like a grandfather – he held me when I was born."

Mercury was bitter on her behalf. "Maybe the old man's forgotten his own kin."

On a moonless night, when the Queen's memorial lanterns swarmed Fort Tehom like fireflies, Angara and her dragon landed squarely in the courtyard garden, tearing into the paper lamps. Upon her command, all the fort's inhabitants surged into a hall, crackling with fear and awe; even in the olden days, no dead could truly be resurrected to life with their body and mind intact, unless they were—

"Goddess, goddess," cried a swordgoblin.

For once, next to her dragon, Angara relished her court – even more so as Asoke barged into the room, terror reddening his eyes. He pointed a shaking finger at Mercury.

"He's with the Celestids; he meant to kill you at the Trial!"

Angara's eyes narrowed. "He saved me twice."

Asoke watched her disdainfully.

"The boy never told you, did he? That monster which attacked you – a necromancer's. Grintul's evil lives through the demon beside you: his own son, your Protector."

"Your Highness, I meant to tell you."

The young man's voice quivered; it was the first time Angara had seen Mercury afraid, which stunned her as much as Asoke's declaration, and yet she couldn't fault him for his concealment. In her head the image of his dried gashes, burns and pin pricks surfaced.

"Asoke, he saved my life," she said coolly. "I won't say it thrice."

She instructed the wraiths to stand before the dragon, who arched his wings as though to pounce, and blew a stream of flame towards their heads. At most, the wraiths flinched or screamed, like her mountain cat in water, but otherwise, the fire passed through their bodies, painless, heatless.

When Mercury reared his head towards Asoke, the old general fled towards the door. Angara charged towards him, but Udomzu and his swordgoblins hounded him first with spears. When they brought him to Angara on his knees, cuts and bruises marked his Celestid-gifted skin.

"A necromancer died for you. Wraiths will perish for you." Angara rasped, "What did the Celestids promise you that I couldn't provide?"

Asoke laughed weakly.

"Decades under the sun. A world you can't fathom, for yours is a dead land; sooner or later, when their light finds you, as it did me, you will learn the beauty and warmth of a life at the apex, far from the night's savagery."

"If your warmth is the fate of the weaker set aflame," Angara said, "it's a world no more warmer than a grave."

She glanced at Mercury and the rest of the court – the world she was born to defend. She regretted that, in her grief, she'd overlooked the brittleness of their peace. Silently she swore to them, to Mercury, that she couldn't risk anything, or anyone, shattering the order they'd fought for.

By dawn, a troop of axe-bearing swordgoblins quietly hauled Asoke away to a hill, where a single stone slab rested. The former wraith was never seen again.

* * *

When the Night Queen sifted the last of Asoke's influence from her forces, the kingdom sat on the precipice of summer and war. With their wraithen cord to the kingdom's inner workings severed, and her continuously refusing Tzelibet's propositions, sooner or later, the Celestids would seize the land by its throat.

But until then, Angara spent the starlit nights journeying the Nightlands, her dragon and swordgoblins in tow. More than ever, it was imperative that every vassal should ally with her against the Celestids' schemes. And while she succeeded in swaying them with the incidents of the horned beast and Asoke's treachery, inevitably, she grew restless of the road.

It wasn't until her next visit to Fort Tehom, when a drizzle broke over her head, that Angara realized that she hadn't spoken to Mercury, alone, in weeks. She wasn't avoiding him, but she had so much she wanted to tell him; she feared she wouldn't hold back when they met.

But I can't wait.

Thus, by a crafty owl, Angara placed a perfumed lock of her hair atop his bed, and dissolved into hours of courtly meetings.

By midnight, as she pored idly over letters in her bedroom, a tapping on her window jolted her to her senses. She flung the curtains open.

Mercury grinned back at her.

Her heart hammering, Angara pulled him inside by his sleeve.

"Someone will see!"

Mercury yawned. "I was hoping you could help read my fortune, Your Highness."

The Night Queen folded her arms, suddenly aware of the thinness of her silk nightgown. After retrieving her cards, she sat at her chaise longue, where Mercury had draped himself, cat-like.

"Just…call me Angara," she muttered. "So, what do you want to know?"

Mercury smiled. "Angara, I wish to know how Her Highness fares."

The Night Queen laughed, incredulous.

"You don't need the cards for that." She twirled a strand of her hair. "She's well. What else do you wish to know?"

"This."

Mercury grasped her hand, spilling her cards onto the floor. Angara had only a second to register his fingers beneath her chin, before he bent over her and kissed her deeply.

As they parted, the dragon smiled, as though admiring his handiwork.

"You tried me that night, in the forest. It's only fair that I have my turn."

Angara gazed into his eyes – the little aquamarines which held the light of her springtime dreams since he first knelt before her. She folded into his arms, tracing the rise and fall of his chest.

"Go on," she whispered. "My night is yours."

Heart of Lightning, Blade of Shadow

Kevin Potter

The air in the Imperial gardens of Heian-kyō was a carefully constructed lie.

Rain-kissed moss merged with the delicate perfume of night-blooming jasmine, which contrasted with the damp earth and cherry blossoms. Akiko Naishinnō knew the artfully crafted scents, and what they disguised, better than anyone.

She sat atop a silk cushion at the pavilion's edge, her delicate brush poised over a fresh sheet of rice paper.

The perfect, luminous moon shone from the lacquered night sky, frosting the glade. But in the pond, its reflection shattered and reformed with the movements of koi beneath the surface.

The scene's exquisite beauty had no impact on the restless energy thrumming beneath her skin. Something was coming. And only the twin obsidian knives concealed within the voluminous sleeves of her jūnihitoe did anything to calm her nervousness.

"Denka?" one of her attendant nyokan murmured. "The ink will dry."

Akiko offered a serene smile, the accepted response, as she dipped the brush.

Her sharp eyes registered movement and shot toward a dozen black-clad figures as they stepped from the darkness around the perimeter of the garden.

In silence, their blades cut down anyone they passed. Blood flowed amid the echoes of the screams of the dying.

Three of the figures darted toward Akiko while the others fanned out to other targets as the emperor's Konoe Shidan closed in to protect him.

Her nyokan screamed, a chorus of terror that almost shattered Akiko's focus.

Several scattered guards shouted as they moved to intercept the intruders, but none would reach her in time. There were too many attackers moving against too many targets.

She was cut off.

Before the screams of the nyokan concluded, the first assassin launched himself from the pavilion's edge. Akiko's training took over automatically. The serene princess vanished, replaced by the Kage-Tsurugi.

She dropped the calligraphy brush. Without thought her fingers found the grip of the knife on her right arm.

The assassin slashed at her throat but she flowed like water around the attack. Her movements defied the many silken layers of her jūnihitoe.

Recovering with impressive speed, the black-clad man spun with a flourish that almost made her laugh and thrust his blade at her heart.

Rather than sacrifice her fragile knife with a parry, she moved around his strike. She danced past him and with a simple, economical movement thrust her blade into the soft flesh beneath his arm.

He grunted and stumbled back, falling to his knees.

Within an instant, the other two assassins converged at her sides in a coordinated attack.

Akiko bounced between them, her mind a cold point of absolute focus. She moved through the forms Master Jin had drilled into her until they'd become instinct.

Slip around a strike. Riposte. Dodge. Strike back. But none of her strikes landed. Her lack of reach would be her downfall.

A point of sweat formed between her shoulder blades and flowed down her spine as a hard reality hit: she couldn't defeat them both. Not with these tiny knives.

One of the assassins telegraphed a thrust at her belly. Though she saw the trick for what it was, she had no choice but to shift toward the other one to evade the strike.

In that instant, however, the other lunged. His blade thrusted toward the very spot her heart would occupy in an instant.

She had no time to counter it. Unstoppable inertia carried her through the movement. And her obsidian blade would not stop his bronze.

A hoarse cry reverberated in her ears. Although the tone was almost right, she couldn't force herself to believe it was Father.

She said a silent prayer, commending her spirit to the kami.

But the strike never came.

A bronze-hued blur intercepted the assassin's lunge.

Ken. She hadn't met him. Had only seen him a handful of times.

He was leader to a foreign delegation of scholars who arrived the day before.

He moved with impossible, inhuman speed. His hand shot out to catch the assassin's sword-arm by the wrist. The sharp crack of bone resounded and the assassin shrieked.

His blade clattered to the pavilion floor.

Ken didn't pause. Spinning, he struck the third assassin in the throat with a devastating crunch.

The man collapsed. Gasping, he clutched at his ruined throat.

The entire exchange took less than a heartbeat. The remaining palace guards finally arrived, surrounding the injured, disarmed assassins.

The courtyard erupted into chaos as the remaining attackers were surrounded and defeated.

Akiko, though aware it was happening, saw none of the chaos. Her world had narrowed to encompass only the man standing before her. His chest rose and fell with controlled breaths, his molten gold eyes smoldering with a scorching heat.

This was no mere scholar.

The power radiating from him, the speed, the lethal precision. This man was something else entirely. Something she couldn't identify. His eyes looked almost…ancient.

His eyes met hers at last and a connection flared between them. Something sharp and undeniable, a chord of Resonance that struck in the heart of the chaos. It was more than just the shared adrenaline of battle, more than recognition of a kindred warrior. It was…something more. A deep, instinctual acknowledgment of spirit, a powerful, inexplicable pull that seemed to vibrate through the air, to the very core of her being.

She saw a flicker of surprise in his golden eyes, a reflection of the same shock, the same dawning wonder.

What could it mean?

"Denka," he said, his voice a low, resonant rumble that did nothing to conceal the power coiled within. He offered a slight, formal bow, but his eyes never left hers. "Are you unharmed?"

"I am," she managed, her own voice steady despite the frantic hammering of her heart. She slid her obsidian blade into its hidden sheath, the movement fluid, practiced, a secret shared between them now. "Thanks to your…timely intervention, Ken-sama."

His lips curved into a faint smile that didn't quite reach his eyes. "It seems we are both more than we appear, Akiko Naishinnō."

The unspoken truth hung between them, a dangerous, exhilarating secret forged in the heat of battle and sealed by the undeniable Resonance that now hummed between them like a living thing.

With the insurrection's first move foiled, she now had the most powerful, most perilous, and most impossible ally she could have imagined.

The aftermath of the attack was a carefully orchestrated storm of imperial outrage and veiled political maneuvering. Hidetora-sama, his face a mask of shock and concern, was among the first to offer his condolences and his clan's resources to hunt down the 'cowardly dogs' who dared attack the Naishinnō. Akiko accepted his performance with practiced grace, betraying none of her certainty of his complicity.

* * *

The Emperor was shaken.

In a private audience, away from the prying eyes of the court, he looked at Akiko, truly looked at her, perhaps for the first time in years.

"Master Jin has trained you well," he said, his voice heavy with conflicting emotions. "You possess the spirit of your ancestors, the first guardians of this throne." He blinked rapidly, leaving her to wonder if the moisture in his eyes had been her imagination.

"I had hoped you would never need to draw upon that strength. I had hoped for a life of peace for you, a strategic marriage to secure the southern provinces. But that hope seems a luxury we can no longer afford. Hidetora grows too bold. This was a test. The next will be a direct challenge."

"I will not fail you, Father," Akiko replied, her voice quiet but firm.

"I know," he said. "You are Kage-Tsurugi. It is your duty. Your burden. You must root out this conspiracy and bring Hidetora out in the open."

She bowed deeply before taking her leave. She would have to begin immediately.

* * *

Her first move was to seek out the foreign scholar, Ken.

She found him kneeling in the Imperial Library, appropriately surrounded by ancient scrolls, with his bronze-hued head bent in concentration. The air around him seemed to hum with a quiet power that belied his calm demeanor.

"Ken-sama?"

He glanced up. When his golden eyes met hers, the Resonance flared between them again in a silent, powerful current that turned the air in the library thick with possibility.

"Akiko Naishinnō," he breathed, rising to his feet in a single, fluid motion.

They spoke for a time, their words a careful dance of protocol and polite inquiry. But beneath the surface was the silent communion of this unexplainable connection.

He asked insightful questions about court politics, his sharp mind cutting to the heart of each topic.

She, in turn, probed his knowledge of military strategy, of history. In him, she found a depth of understanding that seemed to span centuries.

"You fought with the skill of a trained Mononofu, Ken-sama."

He smiled that faint, unsettling smile again. "In my homeland, scholars are expected to understand the practical applications of their studies. History, after all, is largely the study of conflict."

Plausible, yet not the whole truth.

Just as her identity as Naishinnō was not the whole truth. They were twin secrets, circling like combatants, drawn together by undeniable, yet unexplainable intensity.

Their conversation turned to the insurrection and the charge her father had given her.

"What will you do?"

She took a deep breath. "Ideally, catch Hidetora-sama in his conspiracy. If I can get written proof of what he's doing, that would seal the matter."

He nodded. "And barring that?"

She breathed a soft sigh. "I suppose provoking him into an attack before he's ready to mount an insurrection would do it. Or…or kill him, I suppose."

Ken's brows rose fractionally.

"Yes," she whispered. "I know how that sounds."

"I'll help you," he breathed. "In any way I can."

Her overwhelming relief and joy faded as footsteps sounded from behind her. Heart leaping into her throat, she lowered her eyes and stepped back two paces. If anyone were to see them together, especially without an escort, proper decorum must be maintained.

They spoke of philosophy and history until the footsteps receded.

When they had passed, she glanced again into his eyes and the intensity there was almost overpowering. The look in those ancient, golden eyes made her feel...*seen*.

Not as Naishinnō, but merely Akiko.

She wasn't certain how it happened, but as they spoke they somehow moved closer to one another and before she knew it, her hands were in his. His touch was warm, solid, and sent an electric jolt through her.

After a time of meandering through topics, he began to speak of his past, his words carefully chosen. He spoke of a great sundering, a time of catastrophic failure born from a connection between two disparate beings who reached too far, too fast. He spoke of laws enacted out of fear, of boundaries drawn to prevent a repeat of that tragedy.

"Some connections," he said, his golden eyes shining in the dim candlelight, "are deemed...forbidden. Too dangerous to the established order."

She thought she understood his meaning.

"And do you agree with these laws, Ken-sama?" Her heart thudded almost painfully.

He was silent for a long moment, his gaze distant. "I understand the fear that created them. But fear can become a prison. Sometimes, the greatest risks must be taken for the sake of a truth the established order is too blind to see."

His words were, perhaps, an invitation. Recognizing danger, acknowledging this law, yet choosing to defy it.

For her.

For them, if she understood his meaning.

He looked human. But the essence of some ancient, powerful being flowed through his touch. It created a new harmony that was somehow familiar to her spirit.

He leaned closer, his golden eyes searching hers, asking a silent question. She rose to her toes in answer, closing the small distance between them. Their lips met in a gentle brush like the merging of universes, the sealing of a promise that stretched back into eternity. The acknowledgment of a connection that, once solid, could either save her empire or obliterate it into dust.

She leaned into the embrace for the merest of moments while galaxies exploded inside her body before the click of an opening door sounded and they broke their embrace.

How was she going to explain this to her father?

* * *

Weeks passed as Akiko and her Kage-Tsurugi disrupted supplies Hidetora needed and thwarted assassination attempts against those he could not sway or intimidate.

While feeling confident they were winning this shadow war and that he was growing desperate, Akiko had requested a private audience with Hidetora-sama on the pretext of discussing a potential marriage alliance to quell the political tensions.

She prayed to every kami she could think of that he believed it.

Ken accompanied her as a neutral observer. She prayed Hidetora didn't see through it.

They walked toward the tea house where Hidetora had agreed to meet. The air was thick with the scent of pine and palpable tension. Ken stopped her with a hand on her forearm, his golden eyes serious.

"Akiko," he said in a low rumble. "What happens in there… it will change everything. There will be no turning back."

"I know," she replied, her hand resting on the hilt of the bronze Warabitetō sword concealed beneath her formal robes.

"My true nature," he began. "What I am…"

She shook her head. "I don't need to know. Not yet. Let's worry about surviving this for now. We can figure out the rest if we succeed."

Ken sighed. "It is forbidden for me to interfere so directly—"

She put a finger to his lips. "It doesn't matter," she breathed.

"There will be consequences," he mumbled around her finger.

"And my actions tonight could brand me a murderer in the eyes of the court," she countered softly. "We both walk a path of destruction, Ken."

He reached out, his hand gently cupping her cheek. The warmth of his touch, the intensity of his golden gaze, stole her breath. "Then let us walk it together," he murmured.

He leaned in, his lips meeting hers in a fierce, desperate kiss. A sealing of their pact in the face of imminent death. It was a kiss that tasted of love, of fear, of shared destiny.

The couple turned to the tea house, toward the waiting traitors and the battle that would decide the fate of the empire. That would determine the future of their lives, and their hearts.

They moved as one. A heart of fire walking a path of ash, ready to burn down the old world to save it.

The tea house was an island of serene beauty amidst the rising political storm. Paper lanterns cast a soft, warm glow on polished wood floors and meticulously arranged flower displays. The air smelled of sandalwood incense and fresh-brewed tea.

A perfect picture of courtly grace. The perfect stage for betrayal.

Hidetora-sama and his three most trusted lieutenants knelt on silk cushions, their faces masks of polite deference. Yet their eyes held a predatory gleam.

Akiko's heart sang. They had taken the bait. Hidetora, confident in his imminent victory, saw this only as a final, amusing formality before seizing power.

Akiko performed the formal greetings with flawless etiquette. Every movement graceful, every word precise. The perfect image of the Imperial Princess.

Ken stood silently behind her, easily dismissed.

"Akiko Naishinnō," Hidetora began, his voice smooth as poisoned silk. "I am honored by this unexpected audience. To what do I owe the pleasure?"

Akiko seethed. If she had been here for her stated purpose, she would have been insulted, all face lost.

She forced her voice into the calm, coolness of a practiced nyokan. "I have come to discuss the future of the empire, Hidetora-sama."

Hidetora's smile widened. "Indeed. I share your concerns entirely, Denka. A new path is precisely what is needed." He shifted a finger in a gesture so subtle she almost missed it, and his lieutenants' hands drifted casually toward the hilts of the swords concealed within their robes.

She had to force herself not to smile.

"The path to harmony," Akiko continued, her voice suddenly losing its soft, courtly cadence, "begins with the removal of traitors."

In a single, fluid motion, she rose from her kneeling position and slid the sword at her side from its sheath with a sound like whispering death.

Simultaneously, Ken moved. The unassuming scholar vanished, replaced by a whirlwind of bronze-hued motion. He moved with a speed that defied human perception, his hands striking like lightning, disarming two of Hidetora's lieutenants before they could draw their blades.

Hidetora stared, his face a mask of...*amusement.* What was going on?

Akiko moved to engage Hidetora herself, but seemingly from nowhere a line of armed Mononofu streamed into the tea house. Bronze swords at the ready, they surrounded her and Ken.

It took all Akiko's control not to panic. Not to try to flee. Not to surrender.

Ken flashed her a brief look of grim determination and mouthed the words, "It's alright. We can handle this."

Like magic, her confidence returned and she proceeded to engage the nearest of the several Mononofu between herself and Hidetora.

He was no match for her skills, however. Master Jin had taught her well. She roundly disarmed the man and cracked his skull with the pommel of her sword.

After defeating her second opponent, they stopped doing her the courtesy of fighting one-on-one. Two came at her, one on each side. Her mind flashed to how she'd almost lost to a pair of them at the festival, but she banished it.

From the corner of her eye, she glimpsed Ken soundly defeating three Mononofu at once, moving almost faster than her eyes could track. He was still unarmed, but defeated them without so much as a scratch.

The three he had knocked unconscious before the rest appeared were beginning to come around, however.

She pulled her focus back to her own desperate fight. Her one comfort was that she didn't have a reach disadvantage this time.

The two came at her simultaneously, forcing her to dance around one while parrying the attack of the other. She slid her sword down the length of his blade and, with a graceful twirl of the blade, brought it down on the man's hand, biting into the meat between thumb and first finger. His hand spurted blood and he dropped his sword.

She spun to face the other and found two more at either side of him. Evidently, they were done playing good enough odds to give her a chance.

Her heart sank.

Clearly she had underestimated Hidetora. Not only had he seen through her ruse, he had planned for it with at least one contingency to account for the unknown.

How was she going to escape this?

"Mononofu, please, do you understand what you are doing here? Hidetora is not honorable. He is not a good man. I am your Naishinnō. Surely, you are loyal to your emperor and would not strike down your Naishinnō."

The five Mononofu, almost as one, flashed snide smirks at her. They briefly glanced at one another before bursting into laughter. One made a motion with his hands that was commonly translated as 'money' and they all laughed harder.

Akiko sighed, deflated. So this was what it had come to.

Across the room, she could see Ken fared no better. He was surrounded by more men than she could easily count in the second she could afford to check on him. There were enough of them that not even Ken, with his impossible reflexes, could fend them all off.

Stop holding back, Ken's voice sounded in her head.

What in the name of the kami was that?

Akiko, he said, more forcefully. *There's no time. You are a catalyst for my kind. It is forbidden, but with a true link we can be more together than either could ever be apart. But you have to accept it. You have to choose it. Let it in, and we can be more. We can defeat this rabble.*

Her eyes went wide. She wanted to deny it. She wanted to say she had accepted him, all of him, exactly as he was and without reservation.

But it wasn't quite true.

And while a part of her suspected that if Ken just shed his human form he could end this, that wasn't fair. She didn't even know for sure what he was. And shedding his human form could have disastrous consequences, for all she knew.

The five Mononofu before her offered a new onslaught, forcing her to defend with all her might just to keep them at bay. And only then did she feel the pressure tapping at her mind. She realized then that it had been there for weeks now. Since that first meeting in the library, it had been there, silently asking her to accept all it had to offer. Silently asking her to accept Ken for all that he was.

Cursing herself for a fool, she chose.

She accepted it. Accepted *him*. She opened the floodgates and let it all course through her.

In that moment, the Resonance between them, the deep, powerful hum that had connected them from the start, flared into something more. No longer connection, this was fusion. His immense, ancient power flowed into her. The force of it shocked her even as it bolstered her spirit, sharpened her senses.

In counterpoint, she felt her vibrant, human life force, her Catalyst nature, surge into him, grounding his ancient power, lending it a fierce, immediate focus. Their bond became a weapon, forged in the heart of crisis, its true power yet to be unleashed.

From across the room she felt as much as saw Ken's eyes blazing with the intense, otherworldly light they now shared.

She looked, really looked at him. And he at her. They were no longer a warrior princess and a man who was not a man, but two halves of a single, powerful whole. The ancient power from his essence flashed into her, burning away all the darkness, all the weakness, all the uncertainty.

All that remained was the purity of her soul and the love they shared.

Ken exploded into motion, spinning and striking at his opponents faster than she'd thought possible, even for him, the shining light of his eyes illuminating the room.

She turned to her own opponents, and found them moving slower than she'd imagined possible. She turned her attack on them.

Within mere moments, each of the five lay unconscious before her and she turned her attention to Hidetora.

For all his ambition, he was a politician, not a Mononofu.

And Akiko, fueled by years of secret, relentless training and now the incandescent power of the Resonant bond flowing through her, was a force of nature.

She felt Ken's awareness seamlessly merge with hers, their movements perfectly synchronized without a single word.

He anticipated her lunge, moving to block the final Mononofu who tried to flank her. She felt his strength as a warm, steady current bolstering her own, sharpening her senses, quickening her reflexes. It was like dancing to a song only they could hear.

Her blade became an arc of judgment.

She parried Hidetora's clumsy thrust, spun inside his guard, and brought the flat of her blade down in a hard, precise blow against his sword arm. He cried out, his weapon clattering across the floor. In the same fluid motion, she reversed her grip, the pommel of her sword striking him sharply at the temple.

He collapsed, unconscious but alive.

Although she'd been prepared to do whatever was needful, she was grateful not to have to kill him.

She turned. Ken stood amidst more than a dozen disarmed Mononofu, his expression calm, his golden eyes blazing with a power that was decidedly not human.

In that moment, as the adrenaline of battle receded, leaving only the stark reality of their victory, Akiko felt the full, overwhelming force of her connection with Ken.

She felt his ancient, powerful heart beating in time with her own.

She saw the world through his golden eyes simultaneously with hers. She felt the overwhelming power of his love washing over her, a tide of warmth and energy that left her breathless.

He turned to her, his eyes blazing with that shared light.

His physical form still looked human, yet she saw something more beneath it. In a translucent haze around his human form, she saw a metallic, serpentine shape no larger than his human form yet hinting at tremendous mass.

The form of a dragon!

A magnificent bronze wyrm who, she now realized, had defied his own kind, risked everything he was and everything he might ever be, for her.

Their love, this bond, was the all-important factor. This love that transcended species was the one thing, the one power that Hidetora could never have planned for.

Ken stepped toward her, his hand reaching for hers. The touch was electric, sealing their victory, sealing their destiny.

Of Mutton and Marriage Vows

Mere Rain

Gareth wasn't meant to be here, climbing stony hills in search of a dragon. Sheep-stealing, what the hell, that was barely a crime, much less a quest fit for a knight.

But Gareth wasn't fit for a knight, either, was he? He was a failure. His stomach twisted. He had failed his chief duty – keeping safe his charge, Princess Alanis. She was gone, her absence and the ostracism of his peers leaving him with only grief and guilt for company. This mission was his punishment, and perhaps his execution.

The king surely didn't expect him to defeat a dragon, even one the size of a horse. Gareth had said his goodbyes before leaving the capital.

In another story, a more noble and romantic story, Alanis would have been taken prisoner by the monster, and Gareth would be here to rescue her like Saint George saving Princess

Una. Not that Gareth thought himself any sort of saint; he was well aware of his shortcomings. And he'd never had any hope of marrying the princess, who was meant for a foreign prince.

She hadn't been pleased with the match. Gareth, who was secretly fond of Alanis even though she complained at him quite a lot, hoped she had run away to somewhere safe.

There was no indication that she'd been taken by the dragon, or any other monster. She'd simply vanished from her chamber, no clue left, no cry to alert the guards.

Nor had even the most lurid accounts reported the dragon feasting on human flesh. It took sheep. Once a cow. It hadn't hurt the shepherd boy who had slung a rock at it when it snatched his ewe.

Gareth should have sent that lad's name to the king; he'd probably make a better knight than Gareth.

As he crested the slope, thighs burning from walking in armor, he saw smoke trickling from the cleft ahead.

He drew his sword, took a deep breath, and walked forward.

Almost immediately he found his way blocked by a cow.

It snorted at him with more aggression than he'd expected from a bovine – not that he had much experience with livestock – and stamped its hoof, bellowed and tossed its horned head threateningly.

Maybe Gareth was about to die even more ignominiously than he'd expected. Instead of a tragic ballad he'd be remembered in a comic ditty.

"What's the matter, Daisy?" asked a scratchy voice from behind the cow.

A dark green arm reached out of the gloom, making Gareth stumble back with his heart pounding, and picked up what turned out to be a calf from behind the cow, lifting it and bearing it back into the shadows.

The cow mooed anxiously and hurried after her baby, freeing the passage for a moment before the hairy blockage was replaced by a scaly one.

The dragon reared back on its hind legs, looking over Gareth and fixing him with flashing yellow eyes.

"Good grief," exclaimed the dragon. "Go away!"

It whirled away and rushed down the narrow stone passage.

Gareth, heartbeat still pounding in his ears, followed more slowly.

He passed the cow, which tossed her head and snorted angrily at him, but didn't try to attack. Her calf peered curiously from around her black-and-white chest.

The passage widened into a room-like cave with a sandy floor and diagonal crack in the roof that let in light. There the dragon was huddled over a fire pit, turning a sheep carcass on a spit.

It glared at him. "Do you make a habit of walking into people's homes after they've disinvited you?"

"I...apologize?" No one had told Gareth the dragon could speak, much less demand proper etiquette.

"I'll accept your apology on the condition you leave immediately."

"I can't. The king commanded me not to return until I've, er..."

"Slain me?" The dragon snorted irritably. "Nobles prey on their peasantry like locusts and hunt the forests to scarcity, but Lord forbid a dragon eat a couple of sheep."

"You didn't eat the cow," Gareth observed.

"I didn't realize she was pregnant." The dragon sounded… embarrassed? "I chose the fattest one! But she went into labor while I was carrying her, and I can't very well eat her when she has a *baby*."

"Well, the townsfolk complained to the king, and the king… wanted to be rid of me."

"Oh? Did you offend him? Is he a cruel tyrant?"

"No, he's all right, generally. As kings go. Bossy, of course." Gareth sighed. "I was guarding the princess, but she disappeared."

"It was probably magic. Nothing you could have done."

"Well, the king blames me, so here I am."

"Yes, here you are intruding on my solitude. How are you planning to kill me?"

Gareth's sword was still in his hand. He brandished it unenthusiastically.

Something struck his arm with numbing force and the blade went flying, clattering against stones. The sound set cow and calf bellowing in alarm.

It was the dragon's tail that had hit him, he realized as the long, thin limb lashed back and forth. He hadn't known they moved like that.

The dragon picked up his weapon and stretched, balanced against the wall, and set the sword on a rocky ledge well out of reach.

"Not exactly Lancelot, are you?" it said meanly.

"No," Gareth said.

"Why did you become a knight? You don't seem very martial."

"I'm a younger son. It was this or the priesthood."

"I thought noblemen had more choices."

"No, just more food."

The dragon snorted and sliced off a piece of roast mutton. Its claw went through the tough meat as easily as a knife cut one of the dainty cakes served at court.

The dragon spoke like someone at court.

"Are you Sir Dragon or Dame Dragon?" Gareth asked.

The dragon's yellow-slit eyes flashed at him. "I hardly think that's any of your concern!"

"I beg your pardon!" Gareth apologized hastily, eyeing the dragon's claws. "Er, how shall I address you?"

"Dragon is fine," the dragon huffed. "And I will call you Knight."

Since his sword was gone, Gareth unbuckled his armor, which was uncomfortable, and too hot in the fire-warmed cave, even with the crevice that let the smoke and heat escape. The angle of orange sunlight said it was nearing evening.

The dragon cut another hunk of mutton and handed it to Gareth.

After he had eaten it, the dragon said in a pleased tone, "Now you're a sheep thief, too."

Gareth couldn't think of a rebuttal, so he wrapped himself in his cloak and went to sleep.

* * *

Breakfast was also mutton, cold. It had been nicer warm.

"Do you know how to milk a cow?" the dragon asked.

"I've never even touched a cow before yesterday."

"We don't have a bucket, anyway." The dragon sighed. "I'm getting a bit tired of mutton. I wonder if anyone in the village makes pies?"

"The inn there had lovely honey and walnut buns at breakfast. And sausages."

"Why don't you go back there, then?" grumbled the dragon.

But Gareth didn't. He left the cave for long enough to wash his face in a nearby stream, and drink some water. He went down the slope – it was an easy enough climb without the armor – and wandered the woods until he had collected a few late apples, a bit withered.

He went back up the hill and lay near the stream, eating apples and looking up at the sky and not thinking about anything. It was peaceful.

Eventually the dragon came and helped itself to an apple. "Not making much effort with the slaying, are you?" it asked critically.

"I don't think I'm cut out for it," Gareth said. "I might need a new line of work."

"What skills do you have?"

"I'm good at bowing."

The dragon snorted. "You can read and write, can't you?"

"Of course. This isn't the eighth century."

"You could be a scribe. Or a teacher. Travelling messenger. Troubadour?"

"I can play the lute, but not so well that people would pay to hear me."

"Tutor, maybe. Teach country lords' sons to bow prettily and scribble their names and dance with ladies."

"What makes you think I can dance?" Gareth asked, although he could.

"You seem like the sort to prefer dancing to jousting."

The dragon was right again. "How do you know so much about courtly life, Dragon?"

"I read Malory."

Gareth burst out laughing.

It was oddly pleasant, lying out here in the open, unarmed, beside a dragon. The ground was soft and the sun warm.

He fell asleep, and didn't wake until it began to grow cool and it was time to go inside and eat more mutton.

The next few days passed in much the same manner. Bathing in the stream, scrounging for apples and nuts, chatting with the dragon about history and literature and politics. The dragon was either older or better travelled than Gareth, or had a better tutor. It had been serious about reading Malory and asked questions like, "Who was your favorite witch?" and "If you were a Knight of the Round Table, which would you be?" and "Do you think Gawain just *kissed* the Green Knight?" a speculation which made Gareth blush and splutter.

When they ran out of mutton, the dragon stole a smoked ham and a loaf of bread. Gareth felt a little guilty, but not enough to refuse the food.

On the fourth morning of his visit – Gareth couldn't think what else to call it – they were woken early by a child's voice calling, "Hellooo? Dragon? Sir Knight? Are you alive?" and up the hill came the shepherd boy, followed by his nervous flock and an even more alarmed dog.

"What's wrong, Cluny?" the dragon asked.

"Bandits!" the boy panted. "I was up the ridge, and saw them rushing into town. There are cottages on fire."

Gareth had stopped thinking of the dragon's long fangs and sharp claws, but when it reared up with mantled wings and blazing eyes, he remembered.

The dragon sprang up and snatched Gareth's sword down from the wall. "Get your belt and sheath, knight. Then get on my back. Cluny, stay hidden here."

It rushed out of the cave and Gareth trotted after it, buckling his sword belt as he went.

"Are you sure I'm not too heavy?" Gareth eyed the dragon's slender back nervously.

"You weigh less than a cow, don't you? Hurry."

Gareth flung a leg over the dragon's middle. It was hard and smooth. There wasn't anything to hold onto except by putting his arm around its neck, so he did that and pressed close to its back, closing his eyes and praying as its muscles bunched and it sprang into the air.

After a minute of not falling to his death, he opened his eyes. It had taken him an hour to reach the dragon's lair on foot, but the same distance on dragonback took only a few minutes and they were already close enough to make out figures in night clothes trying to fight dozens of men with clubs and spears. Most of the villagers were armed with brooms or rakes and in one case the paddle of a butter churn.

"Get ready to jump!" The dragon angled toward a hay wain and roared as it dove.

Bandits and villagers alike screamed and scattered.

Gareth let go and rolled off the dragon's back into the hay. The straws blinded him for a moment and he missed the first of the dragon's attacks, but when he struggled to his feet there were men lying still on the ground and the milkmaid with the wooden paddle was sprinting away.

The dragon's flight had taken it into the thick of the fighting, so Gareth left it to batter men aside like rats and ran toward a cluster of invaders who were trying to torch a home while the old woman inside leaned out the window and held them back with a haying fork.

Gareth had never slain a monster or dueled to the death. Those sounded noble in poems. This was just work. Nasty, messy work. He cut down the man with the torch, and sliced off the hand of the one who lunged at him with a scythe, and the last turned and ran.

Gareth saluted the woman with the fork, who raised her tool triumphantly in return, and then ran to help the dragon.

He had thought the bandits were like rats, but a swarm of rats can overwhelm a dog. The dragon was winning, but it was also bleeding in numerous places.

Gareth threw himself into the fray. He struck two men serious but probably not fatal blows before they realized he was there. He swiped at a scar-faced man who dodged. Gareth went off-balance, his swing catching another man with the flat of the blade and knocking him over.

Someone shouted "Gareth!" and then there was a pain in his head and everything went dark.

* * *

When Gareth woke he was in a bed. A quite nice one with clean sheets. His head ached a bit, but he felt otherwise well.

A plump older woman was sitting in a chair by the bedside, mending a shirt. He started to sit up and realized he was naked. No wonder he had recognized that shirt so readily, it was his.

The woman set the shirt aside and rose to peer into his eyes. "How are you feeling then, Sir Gareth? You're lucky that dragon went for the bastard with the club just in time, or he'd have split your poor head clean open. Not seeing double, are you? Good, good. Hungry?"

"Very. Is the dragon hurt?"

"It did have some nasty cuts, but it was well enough to command us to take care of you, and to fly itself away. So I shouldn't worry. Do you think it would care for something? A present, I mean, for helping us? Other than a sheep?"

"A pie." Gareth's mind drifted back to the dragon's culinary complaints. "It would like a pie."

It was already late in the day when Gareth woke, and dusk by the time he had eaten. The innkeeper, who turned out to be the sister of the woman by his bed, urged him to rest the night, so he did. It was pleasant to sleep in a soft bed with a warm blanket, but he found himself missing the sounds of a cow and dragon breathing nearby.

He woke early, had a hearty breakfast with no mutton in it, and was presented with two enormous pies and a loaf of bread, to bring back to the dragon. Cluny the shepherd boy carried the second pie back to the cave, apparently having forgiven the dragon for the lost ewe.

The boy waved cheerfully at the dragon when it poked its head out of the cave, set the pie down, and trekked off toward wherever he had left his flock.

"Head in one piece, I see." The dragon bent to sniff the pie, then carried it inside.

"Yes. How are you?"

"Hardly more than scratched," the dragon dismissed. "I could have handled them all. But thank you for your concern. Lunch?"

The dragon turned to take the second pie from Gareth, and he kissed its snout.

The dragon reared back and stared at him. "What in the world was that, Knight?"

"You called me Gareth yesterday."

"And everyone who calls you Gareth gets kissed, whether they like it or not?"

"I thought it might break the curse… Alanis."

The dragon huffed. "Silly knight. There is no curse. And kissing people without asking is very rude."

Gareth continued to gaze at her, not speaking. Silence had always been the best strategy when his princess was feeling uncooperative.

"It was a wish," she said finally. She lifted her chest up and touched a claw to a small pinkish spot in the center, no bigger than a pea. "Do you remember the necklace with the pink pearl my godmother gave me for my eighteenth birthday?"

"Yes." It was around that time that negotiations for her betrothal had started.

"It was a wish. She's a fairy godmother, you know. She said to think long and hard before I used it, because it only works once."

"And you wished to be a *dragon*?"

Her eyes flashed in a way that reminded him of Alanis' when she was cross.

"I wished to be free to go where I wanted and fierce enough to keep myself safe. And then I changed! I didn't think papa would appreciate finding a dragon in his daughter's bed, so I went out the window and flew away. I was traveling at night so as to avoid attention, but then I stole Daisy and she had the calf, so I had to stay until she felt better. And then you showed up." She looked away. "I'm sorry you got in trouble."

"It's all right. I wasn't much of a knight. I only stayed because..." His cheeks heated.

Dragons probably couldn't blush, but Alanis ducked her head shyly.

"If it was a wish, can you wish yourself back into being human?" he asked.

"But I don't wish to be a princess."

"You never wish to be yourself, Alanis?"

He had never called his princess by her name, when he was her knight.

"Perhaps sometimes," she said quietly. "But I like flying free, too. What if I change back and I can't turn into a dragon again?"

Gareth swallowed. "I have a good horse and a good sword. There's nothing to stop us going anywhere and stealing sheep."

There was a long silence, and then the dark green dragon sank down to a pale girl with auburn hair and no clothes.

Gareth squeaked and spun around. He felt her hands come to rest on his shoulders, and then his cloak was lifted away.

After a minute she said, "You can turn around."

He turned. Familiar princess, if unaccustomedly clad in a cloak wrapped around her like a towel.

The hand she put on his cheek was smooth, and the kiss that followed was soft.

The pink pearl still gleamed below her collarbone. When he touched it, it felt warm and smooth like the dragon's scales.

"I'm not a hero," Gareth said softly. "I don't want to be a knight unless I'm your knight."

She put her hand over his. "And I refuse to be a princess, but I'm willing to be your queen. And your dragon. And your friend."

"The dragon and her knight. Sounds like a good story."

"It's far from over," she said, and kissed him.

Hollow

Mia K. Rose

The pen's wooden latch groaned from the cold, goats bleating softly at her presence. One goat butted her thigh with its horn, impatient. Runa scratched behind their ear. With practiced hands, she loosened bundles of dried seagrass and heather, shaking the feed into the wooden trough.

Even the routine of caring for the goats couldn't distract her from the growing pain and warmth at her left shoulder. The mark, shaped like a curled dragon with wings flared and tail looped around itself, had appeared three days past.

Her grandmother's words churned through her mind, but she'd never took them to heart. She spoke of a time with magic; of powers gifted by the greatest primordial force their world had known: dragons.

But the persistence from her shoulder made her recite them once more:

"If ever the mark appears, you must go. Find the last dragon and awaken. Then magic can restore the dying lands."

Runa never truly believed her grandmother's stories. Yet there she stood, marked, and the pain sharpening the more she ignored it.

"Curse it," she said, gripping her shoulder.

With an affectionate rub against the goat's sides, she returned to her cottage, a modest timber home tucked into the edge of the forest. She added kindling and coaxed a fire to life in the hearth.

On the wall above the mantle hung the axe. A memory of her husband, gone two winters. Taken by an ice storm. Her fingers ran over his name she had carved into the hearthstone. She sometimes spoke it aloud. But not as often as before. He was a hollow in her chest, a silence in their home.

The mark throbbed beneath her tunic.

She wasn't worthy of being chosen for a prophecy. Not with how her body failed to carry a child, or how she now took up the mantle of widow. She finally was in a state of contentment.

"Damn you," she whispered to the fates.

The hearth crackled and sparked.

She stumbled back.

Images danced and materialised within the flames.

A flash of silver mountains. A hollow beneath the stars. A man alone with golden eyes.

The fire quietened, resuming its soft crackles and pops as the wood burned.

She fell to her knees. It was no story. No dream. The prophecy was real. The flames showing her a clue to locating the last dragon.

By morning, she'd packed for the journey. Braided back her long dark hair. She took her husband's axe and strapped it across her back.

She'd leave a note for another to tend to the goats in her absence. But she left without farewell. The warmth from the mark was her only companion.

Runa had never journeyed from their village but recalled the stories her husband told of his travels. Of mountains, rivers, and valleys. Her grandmother once said dragons dwelled in the half-hidden places within the world. The flames may have given her a destination, but the journey was unknown.

Yet she walked. Through snow drifts, over frozen brooks and pine. She headed towards the mountains; ones carved of both ice and rock. Each day marked by the intensifying warmth of the mark, and the abating pain, as if it sensed it grew closer to its destination.

Four days into the journey the weather warmed, the snow thinning. An uneasiness settled over her shoulders, for it was deep winter. Then the dreams began. Dreams of silver wings, golden eyes, a summit towering over all the land.

A week passed until she reached the edge of an ash forest. Silvery peaks towered behind the wall of trees. A deep part within her knew she'd finally arrived at the right place.

Night had arrived and moonlight filtered through the ancient boughs as she stepped beneath them. Her breaths slowed. The air heavy, and quiet. Her fingers itched to reach for the axe, but she stilled her hand.

The mark prickled as if in anticipation. It thrummed like a heartbeat, but not her own.

Runa let instincts guide her through the undergrowth, past gnarled roots and dead leaves. The trees thinned without warning. She stepped into a hollow, blanketed in moss and earth soft underfoot.

Stars spilled through the canopy. A weight settled in her chest. This was the place within the flames. This is where she had to be.

"If you could see me now, Erik," she whispered, touching a hand to the axe.

Nestled against the curve of earth and moss was a man. Curled on his side, his long white-gold hair fanned against the ground. His bronzed chest moved with slow steady breaths. He only wore trousers, and the faint glint of scales caught her eye from his wrists. A shimmer of silver.

She stilled. This was no mortal man, but the last dragon.

He made no signs of waking.

Runa didn't believe it'd be as simple as waking him from this state. No, fates and prophecies didn't do easy.

She edged closer and reached out her hand. Before it brushed his shoulder, his golden eyes opened. His gaze fixed on hers, a deep fire alight within them.

Neither of them moved.

He sat up with fluid grace, his gaze never leaving hers. She took in his broad shoulders, the sinewy length of his long limbs. His head tilted slightly, the long strands of his hair catching light.

"You came," he said, his voice deep and soothing.

"I had no choice," she said, and dropped her eyes from him. "You're the last, aren't you?"

He nodded. "And you carry the mark."

The forest seemed quiet, too quiet. As if it hushed to witness the moment. Or the world around them simply froze.

"I'm Runa," she said.

"Sigurd," he replied. He rose and stretched his muscles. Runa tried to avert her gaze but couldn't help but appreciate his form. Or the lean dip of his waist.

He held his hand out to her.

"What happens now?" she asked, and ignored his hand, choosing to stand on her own.

A bird trilled in the distance. Wind stirred his hair. He closed his eyes and took a deep breath.

"You came all this way, and you don't know?" His eyebrows rose.

She blew out a breath. "Your kind was lost to myth. None speak of it."

He swallowed. "Then…" He rubbed at his chest. "Then your lands must be dying."

"I know little of that." She shrugged. "But my grandmother spoke of you. Of the prophecy."

His eyes found hers. Their fiery gold glow made her a little uneasy. Their intensity almost reaching through for her soul.

"We must travel to the Askr Summit," he said. "There we perform the awakening."

"Then you must lead us there," Runa said.

"We rest the night first."

"Have you not slept enough?" she asked.

He smirked. "Perhaps, but you are mortal."

Runa couldn't argue with that. She didn't want to admit how tired she felt. How worn from the travel. From the stretch of loneliness with none for company. She nodded and followed him out of the hollow, and towards a quiet stream hidden away in the forest. A little cave sat near, and he gathered kindling for a fire.

Runa waited for a display of magic, but he lit it like any ordinary human would. She laid out her bedroll and nestled down within its blanket.

He sat by the fire and looked towards her. "You were brave to come by yourself."

"I had no one else." She turned her gaze to the flames. "But you've been alone far longer than I."

The fire crackling filled the stretching silence.

She closed her eyes, for she knew treading up to the Askr Summit was a sacred undertaking. A trail upon the bones of the earth.

* * *

As they moved through the forest towards the mountain, she watched him closely. Watched how he tilted his head at birdsong, how his fingers brushed over bark. He walked barefoot and bore no signs of needing anything else. They'd follow animal paths and river cuts on their ascent. Runa thought of her goats and hoped they didn't miss her presence too much.

It took them until nightfall to reach the foothills of the mountain. Runa looked to the sky, thankful for the absence of clouds, and for the continued unseasonal weather. She peered over at Sigurd, wondering if that was partly because of the dragon by her side. And his primal magic.

The foothills offered little in the way of shelter, so Runa laid the bedroll near the fire. She sat atop it while Sigurd stretched out across from her, the fire between them.

"Do you miss them?" she asked.

The firelight only showed some of his features, the rest in shadows.

"Every moment. Centuries may have dulled it."

She rested her hand on the axe's handle.

"You don't seem like I imagined a dragon to be."

He gave her a faint smile. "And what did you expect?"

"Scales, teeth…fire." All Runa knew is she didn't expect a man. Someone she could mistake for human. Heat stirred low in her belly as she stared at him.

"This form allowed me to escape the ones who hunted us," he said, and stared into the flames. "I need your help to awaken my dragon once more."

Colour bloomed in her cheeks.

"Do not worry." His voice dropped. "It is simple. Nothing to fear."

"Ceremony is not something I fear," she replied. She wouldn't give voice to what did, though.

* * *

Heat tingled over her face as her breath hitched. They'd only started their ascent and yet Runa didn't know how she'd make it up any further.

Sigurd came back to her side. His feet didn't even bleed from the rough stones they traversed. Her own leather shoes seemed to find the sharpest rocks, though.

"Let me lend you my strength," he said, holding out his hand.

She chewed the inside of her cheek as her eyes flitted between his hand and his eyes.

"You came to help me," he said, "so let me help you."

Runa nodded and laid her hand in his. His hand offered a reassuring warmth. He leveraged his other hand below her elbow as she took another step up.

The wind picked up during their trek, with Sigurd lending quiet strength as Runa laboured with each steep incline. This mountain wasn't built for humans. How she wished Sigurd was a dragon already, for surely this mountain was built for dragons alone.

In such proximity to him, she relished the comforting warmth that he radiated. His skin like a hearth. No wonder he felt no need for more layers of clothing.

As light waned and day gave to night, Sigurd stopped them on a ridge.

Wind howled and Runa pulled the blanket tighter over her shoulders. Her muscles ached. She gazed to the path ahead, jagged and steep.

"What if I don't make it?" she said as he approached.

"You will," he said, lowering himself beside her. "I will not let you fall."

She gave a hollow laugh. "I'm a goat keeper," she said, turning to face him. "I'm not meant to be more."

"I wasn't meant to survive," he said, "but here we both are." He faced her, quiet certainty within his eyes.

Wind, the crackle of fire, the distant cries of birds filled the silence between them.

His hand reached for hers.

"You were born for this," he said.

She looked down at their joined hands. "And if the fates are wrong?"

His thumb brushed the back of her hand. "They can't be."

Her heart hammered. His face was so close to hers. His heat cocooned the space around them.

"I am a means to an end for you," she whispered.

He studied her for a moment. "You are more than my salvation."

She didn't move.

His other hand came up over her face, his fingers sliding over her jaw. His eyes snared hers. The gold deepened. He leaned in.

His warm lips brushed hers. Her eyes closed. She leaned into him. Let him draw her close. His head tilted, deepening the kiss. Heat sparked through her. Her hands found the warmth of his shoulders and spread down to the broad expanse of his back.

Sigurd ran his own hand down her back, pulling her tight against him at her waist. She arched into his chest. Her lips parted, letting his tongue sweep in. A pleased groan rumbled through him. She smiled against his mouth.

They broke apart, breathless. She rested her forehead against his.

Together they laid down, her back pressed flush against his body. The blanket discarded to one side.

* * *

As they neared the summit, shadows moved among the trees. A snap of a twig alerted them. Figures cloaked in leather, seaxes in hand, burst from the woods.

"Run!" shouted Sigurd, turning to face the ambush.

Runa couldn't do that. She drew the axe.

She may never have raised such a weapon against another human before, but she knew how to chop wood with one. Her grip tightened over the handle.

Runa surged forward, swinging in a wide arc that bit into the arm of an attacker. He stumbled back. Another came at her, seax raised high. She barely dodged, the blade grazing her side. She turned and drove her shoulder into him, then buried her axe into his thigh.

Sigurd was a blur of motion. His fists weapons as they cracked bone. He caught one man by the throat and flung him into a tree. Leaves showered down over his collapsed form.

Their attackers were many. As if they'd made their lives upon this mountain, waiting patiently for their prey to arrive.

Runa's breathing turned ragged, her arms trembling under the weight of the axe. She ducked a swipe just in time. Slammed the haft of her axe into the attacker's face. Blood sprayed from his nose as he fell.

Sigurd roared, inhuman, and stilled even Runa for a moment. He struck the ground with his fist, the earth cracking and rippling outward. Two men were thrown off their feet. It wasn't without cost. His body sagged from the effort.

One slipped behind him, plunging a blade right into his side.

Runa screamed.

Sigurd stumbled, golden eyes wide, silvery blood spilling down his ribs. His attacker readied for another strike.

On instinct she lunged, her axe finding the space between the man's collar and jaw. He collapsed as she pulled the axe free.

She dropped beside Sigurd. His jaw clenched as he pressed his hand against the wound.

"We need to move," she said.

Sigurd shook his head. "They will not stop."

She couldn't fight them on her own.

The mark on her shoulder flared to life. It'd been quiet since she encountered Sigurd, but it now thumped through her. An impulse made her press her hand to his over the wound.

"What are you doing?"

"I don't know," she said. "But you can't die."

Golden light engulfed both their hands. A discomforting warmth prickled at her palm. Sigurd's body arched.

Runa blinked. His wound had stopped bleeding. She slowly lifted her hand away.

He looked at her, his face pale. "You channelled it."

"What?" Her mouth dried.

"My magic," he said. "You drew it from me to heal."

More footsteps crunched through the trees. More enemies would be upon them soon.

Sigurd staggered to his feet. Runa stood at his side, axe in hand.

"We fight together," she said.

"No," Sigurd said, voice dark and low. "We end this."

Gold flared from his eyes.

His form unravelled. Silver scales shimmered into place. Vast wings burst from his back as his body stretched into the sky. Horns curled from his brow.

Runa staggered back. Her heart raced.

Sigurd now towered above the trees within his dragon form.

But their enemies were undeterred. Their goal unchanged.

The ground rumbled underfoot as Sigurd took a step forward, his great tail curling around Runa. Flames poured from his dragon jaws, engulfing both men and tree. The heat forced Runa to shield her face. Screams and the scent of burning flesh filled the surrounding air.

When the last of their enemies was ash, and trees smouldered, Sigurd's form shrank again, folding back into the man. He crashed to his knees. Runa rushed to his side. Her eyes widening in surprise at his fully naked body.

Both of their breaths were laboured. Steam wafted from his flesh. Waves of heat still radiating out from his body.

He reached a hand up to her cheek. "We're almost there."

She put her shoulder under his. "Then up you get."

With her help, Sigurd got back to his feet.

The wind had returned, screaming through the stone crags and trees.

When they crested the summit ridge, Runa's steps faltered.

A great stone circle waited there, weathered monoliths arranged in spiralling rings. Runa felt a hum through her very bones as they neared the circle.

"This is where it began," he said, "and where it must be again."

"What must I do?" she asked.

He took hold of her hands and lowered them both to a kneel in the centre of the circle.

"You're my anchor," he said. A hand reached up and cupped her cheek. She leaned into the warmth of his touch. "Through you, I bind myself again to the land."

She swallowed. "Will it hurt?"

He gave a small smile. "No." He leaned forward and pressed a kiss to her forehead.

"Place your hand over my heart," Sigurd said.

She rested her palm where he said, feeling his steady pulse underneath her fingertips.

The monoliths pulsed with light, golden veins webbing over the stone surface.

"Do you trust me?" he asked.

Runa looked into his eyes, and though she'd known him only a few days, deep within it felt like the time had stretched for eternity. She nodded.

His lips pressed lightly down the column of her throat and trailed to the shoulder where the mark lay. Her skin pebbled and her fingers dug into his chest. His fingers pushed away the fabric of her clothes, baring her skin. Without warning, he bit down, teeth puncturing flesh. Blood trickled down and over the mark.

He pulled her closer, her hand never leaving his chest. Her eyes closed as his tongue trailed a line from her wound to the mark, a path of heat chasing after it.

The entire circle erupted in golden light.

Sigurd arched backwards. Flames burst along his limbs, scales sweeping over his skin like armour. Runa kept her hand on his chest. Not willing to be the cause of the awakening failing. The fire didn't burn her, as if recognising her as a friend, not a foe.

The ancient stones pulsed once more before darkening. The wind stilled.

Sigurd pressed his lips against hers. She tasted salt and iron in her mouth.

His warmth receded. He stood, and she watched in awe as the dragon once more took over his form.

His golden eyes looked down at her. He bowed his head.

Runa placed her hand upon his muzzle. "Is it done?"

Sigurd's voice echoed in her mind: *Yes. But now, we begin.*

He lowered his belly to the ground, neck and head bowed low.

If you'll have me.

Runa knew there was no other choice. No path without him.

She climbed up his side and slid into the hollow between his wings. A warmth flowed through her limbs like an invisible tether, as if claiming her a part of him. As he launched into the sky, she gripped one of the ridge spines along his back. The wind bent around them.

Runa looked down at the world below. A world that would come alive again.

She reached and touched the mark on her shoulder.

She said a silent thanks to the fates.

The Heart of Aethermoor

Laura Shenton

Janelle pressed her palm against the crystalline dome of the Grand Aviary, watching the iridescent birds of paradise dance through shafts of golden sunlight. Their feathers caught the light like scattered jewels – emerald, sapphire, and burnished copper – but none shone as brilliantly as the artefact at the aviary's heart.

The Crystal of Aethermoor hung suspended in the centre of the verdant dome, a perfect rose-pink gem the size of a ripened apple. Within its translucent depths pulsed a heart of pure lightning – not the jagged bolts that split storm clouds, but something far more beautiful. The magical heart was a perfect two-dimensional symbol, its edges crackling with bright pink energy that seemed to breathe with its own rhythm.

"Still staring at that old thing?"

Janelle didn't turn at the familiar voice. Prince Deryn's boots clicked against the marble as he approached, his presence both welcome and troubling. Three months had passed since their betrothal was announced, yet she felt no closer to understanding the golden-haired prince who would be her husband.

"It's magnificent," she murmured, watching a bird of paradise with tail feathers like liquid flame settle on a branch near the crystal. "My grandmother used to say it held the first love ever felt in this realm."

Deryn moved beside her, close enough that she caught his scent of cedar and sandalwood. "Romantic nonsense. It's a relic of the old magic, nothing more. When we're wed, I'll have it moved to the treasury where it belongs."

Something cold settled in Janelle's chest. "You can't be serious. It's been here for centuries, sustaining the aviary's magic. Without it..."

"Without it, we'll have one less distraction from practical matters." His hand found her shoulder, possessive rather than gentle. "You'll understand once you're queen. Sentiment is a luxury we can't afford."

Janelle pulled away, anger flaring bright as the crystal's inner heart. "This isn't sentiment, Deryn. This is about preserving something beautiful, something that connects us to..."

A sound like wind chimes mixed with distant thunder interrupted her words. Both turned towards the aviary's entrance, where shadows moved against the light. But these weren't human shadows.

The dragon that emerged from the archway was nothing like the great beasts of legend. No larger than a horse, with scales that shifted between deep violet and midnight blue, it moved with grace. Most striking of all were its eyes – silver as moonlight, ancient and knowing.

"Impossible," Deryn uttered, his hand moving instinctively to his sword. "Dragons haven't been seen in Aethermoor for three hundred years."

The dragon's gaze swept over them both before settling on Janelle. When their eyes met, she felt something stir in her chest – recognition, as if she were seeing an old friend after years apart. The sensation was so strong it left her breathless.

Princess, a voice whispered in her mind, gentle and warm. *I have been waiting.*

"You're…speaking to me?" she whispered.

As I spoke to your grandmother before you, and her grandmother before her. I am Zephyr, last guardian of the old bonds. I have slept long, but the crystal's song has grown weak. It calls for its true keeper.

Deryn stepped forward, steel singing as he drew his blade. "Get behind me, Janelle. Dragon magic is unpredictable."

But Janelle found herself moving towards Zephyr instead, drawn by something deeper than curiosity. "The crystal is dying?"

Not dying. Longing. The dragon's telekinetic voice carried infinite sadness. *It was created from the bond between dragon and rider, love made manifest. Without that connection, it fades.*

"Dragon and rider?" Janelle glanced back at Deryn, whose face had gone pale. "What do you mean?"

Your bloodline carries the old gift, Princess. Your ancestors were not merely rulers – they were bonded to dragons, partners in magic and purpose. The crystal was forged from such a union, a love so pure it transcended death itself.

The revelation shocked Janelle to the core. Her grandmother's stories, dismissed as fairy tales. The strange dreams she'd had since childhood, of flying through storm clouds on wings. The way the crystal seemed to pulse a little differently whenever she drew near.

"This is madness," Deryn snarled, raising his sword. "I won't let you bewitch her with your lies."

I speak only truth. Zephyr's scales rippled with suppressed power. *But truth is often harder to bear than lies.*

"What happened to the dragons?" Janelle asked, ignoring Deryn's warning glare. "Where did they go?"

We were betrayed. A king arose who feared our bond with his people. He convinced them we were threats to be eliminated rather than partners to be cherished. Most of us died. The few who survived went into a deep sleep, waiting for someone worthy of their trust.

Janelle's heart clenched as understanding dawned. "King Theron the Bold. Three hundred years ago. My ancestor."

Yes. And now his descendant offers me another chance at partnership. But the choice must be freely made, with full knowledge of the cost.

"What cost?" But even as she asked, Janelle suspected she knew.

To wake the crystal's full power requires the bond to be renewed. Dragon and rider, joined in purpose and heart. But such magic leaves its mark. You would no longer be fully human, Princess. And you could never bond with another as completely as you would with me.

Deryn's sword trembled in his grip. "She's already promised to me. Our marriage will unite two kingdoms."

A union of convenience, Zephyr observed. *I offer something rare and sacred – a bond of souls.*

Janelle closed her eyes, overwhelmed by the choice before her. Marriage to Deryn meant security, alliance, the continuation of political stability her kingdom needed. But it also meant a lifetime of being diminished, her true nature suppressed in service to 'practical matters'.

The crystal pulsed brighter, its pink lightning heart flickering like a flame in the wind. Around them, the birds of paradise grew agitated, sensing magic in flux.

"What would happen to the crystal if I refuse?" she asked.

It would fade completely within a year. The aviary would wither. The old magic would pass from the world forever.

"And if I accept?"

The crystal would burn bright as a star. Your kingdom would be protected by more than armies and treaties. The balance between realms would be restored. Zephyr's silver eyes held hers steadily. *But you would be changed, as would I. The bond, once forged, cannot be broken.*

Deryn grabbed her arm. "Janelle, don't listen to this creature. Think of your duty, your people…"

"I *am* thinking of them," she said quietly, pulling free. "I'm thinking of what they truly need."

She looked at the crystal again, watching its heart pulse with desperate beauty. In that rhythm, she heard her grandmother's voice telling stories of dragon riders who soared above petty conflicts to see the larger patterns, who served as bridges between the mundane and magical worlds.

The choice is yours, Zephyr said gently. *But choose quickly. The crystal's song grows fainter with each passing moment.*

Janelle stepped forward. "You speak of bonds that cannot be broken. What of love?"

Love is the strongest bond of all. It transcends form, transcends species. The bond between dragon and rider is built upon love – not the possessive hunger that passes for it in your courts, but something deeper. Mutual respect. Complete trust. The willingness to die for another's wellbeing.

Janelle glanced back at Deryn, whose handsome face was twisted with frustration and anger. "And if someone cannot accept this bond?"

Then they were never worthy of your heart to begin with.

The truth of it rang through her, alarming and absolute. Deryn desired her as a prize, a political asset. He had never once asked about her dreams, her fears, her hopes for the future. Their conversations revolved around duty and appearance, never touching the deeper currents of who she truly was.

"You mustn't allow yourself to be foolish, Janelle," Deryn warned. "The alliance between our kingdoms…"

"Will have to be built on something more solid than forced marriage," she finished. "Perhaps that would be better for everyone."

She walked towards Zephyr, each step feeling like destiny. The dragon graciously lowered its head, bringing those silver eyes level with hers.

Are you certain, Princess? The path ahead will not be easy. There will be those who fear what we represent.

"I'm certain," she said. And she was. For the first time in her life, she felt completely, unshakably certain. "Show me how to wake the crystal's heart."

Place your hand upon my snout. Open your mind to mine completely. Let the old magic flow between us.

Janelle reached out with trembling fingers, touching the warm scales of Zephyr's nose. The moment their skin met, the world exploded into sensation.

She felt Zephyr's memories flooding through her – centuries of soaring through cloud-kissed skies, the deep contentment of perfect partnership with riders long dead, the aching loneliness of enforced solitude. In return, her own memories flowed outward – childhood dreams of flight, the suffocating intensity of royal expectations, the yearning for something more meaningful than a marriage built on political convenience.

Power rushed between them like a river breaking its banks. Janelle felt her consciousness expanding, touching realms beyond the physical. She was herself but also more than herself, connected to currents of magic that ran deeper than the earth itself.

The crystal began to sing.

It was a sound beyond hearing, felt in the marrow of her bones. The pink heart at its centre blazed rapidly, its lightning expanding until it filled the entire gem. Light poured from it in waves, washing over the aviary in rose-gold radiance.

The birds of paradise took flight as one, their calls joining the crystal's song in perfect harmony. Plants throughout the dome burst into new bloom, flowers unfurling in fast-forward spirals of colour. The very air seemed to sparkle with released magic.

It is done, Zephyr whispered in her mind, but now the voice felt like part of her own thoughts. *We are bonded, you and I. Partners in magic and purpose.*

Janelle marvelled at how vivid everything appeared. Colours were richer, scents more complex, sounds layered with previously unheard harmonies. She could feel Zephyr's presence in her mind, comforting and constant.

"Magnificent," she said breathily, then gasped as she realised she could also feel the dragon's emotions – contentment, fierce protectiveness, and something that might have been love.

As you feel mine, I feel yours, Zephyr confirmed. *We are two souls sharing one purpose now.*

"This is an abomination," Deryn raged, but his voice seemed to come from far away. "I'll tell the king. I'll have armies…"

"You'll have nothing," Janelle said calmly, turning to face him. "Because you never understood what you were trying to claim."

The prince's face was pale with anger and something that might have been fear. "You're no longer human."

"I'm more human than I've ever been," she replied. "Human enough to choose love over convenience. Human enough to protect something beautiful rather than lock it away. Human enough to forge my own destiny."

She looked at the crystal, now blazing with renewed power, its pink heart pulsing in perfect time with her own. Around them, the aviary had become a paradise reborn, every leaf and flower vibrant with magical energy.

What now? she asked Zephyr.

Now we begin the work we were born for. There are other crystals scattered across the realms, other bonds waiting to be renewed. We'll seek them out, restore the balance that was lost. Not as master and servant, but as equals in partnership. Two hearts beating as one.

Janelle smiled. The future spread before them like an uncharted sky, full of possibility and adventure. She would not be a princess trapped in political necessity, but something far greater – a bridge between worlds, a guardian of love and magic.

Behind her, Deryn stormed from the aviary, his boots echoing loudly against marble. Janelle let him go without a backward glance. Some people could only see prisons where others saw wings.

Ready for our first flight? Zephyr asked.

I've been ready my whole life.

The dragon lowered a wing, and Janelle climbed onto the warm, scaled back as if she'd done it a thousand times. Perhaps, in dreams, she had.

They rose together towards the aviary's crystal dome, which opened like a flower at their approach. Beyond lay the vast blue sky and a world full of sleeping magic, waiting for the touch of bonded hearts to wake it.

As they soared into the sunlight, the Crystal of Aethermoor sang behind them – a song of love renewed, of bonds that could never be broken, and of the magic that bloomed when two souls chose partnership over possession.

The birds of paradise followed them up into the endless sky, their joyous calls echoing across the kingdom and beyond, announcing that the age of dragons had returned – not as conquerors, but as partners in the greatest magic of all.

Love.

Shifting the Scales

Liv Strom

Minares crept through the dragon dung, more thankful for her nose plugs than she'd ever been for anything else. The terrifying creatures had a sense of smell to rival any hound, so this plan had seemed bright when sitting in the pub three days ago.

Kep followed in her track, finally no longer spewing useless facts. Beer goggles, that's what caused this. At least this made even him look worse. Minares had learned her lesson. Don't proposition anyone. And if you do, be very, very specific.

She sensed eyes on her and froze, fingers and knees sinking, bringing her face closer and closer to the muck. Nearby, a fire-breathing terror snorted. Sweat stuck to Minares's chest under the waterproof fabric she'd donned to swim through the swamp surrounding the dragon pens. A shadow moved overhead. Passed.

She continued her crawl. Ruby red flashed in the distance.

"They're just lying there like trash," Kep had insisted, offering a wink and a pint. "Easiest drachme you'll ever make, Min."

Of course, she'd refused. She wasn't stupid, and her own awkward flirting wouldn't make her so. The royal dragons were protected, sacred, and so were the elite riders who bonded them. Bastards all of them, who wouldn't even acknowledge anyone poor enough to reside west of the river. No, Minares wasn't ignorant or stupid, but she was competitive.

"Can't do it?" he'd mocked her. Too small. Too weak. *Too girly.* As if he didn't like those parts.

She'd been drunk then but still refused.

But Kep had smiled – that grin that said to trust him. It was just a tad insecure, one perfect dimple. How could Minares not smile back? The words, "Let's get out of here," crossed her lips before settling into her beer-sloshing mind.

Before she knew it, the bastard'd climbed onto the table and announced that she'd agreed to this adventure to the whole pub. How could she back down after that? Her word and reputation were all she owned in this world.

So now she was in deep shit. Literally. At least, so was Kep, for she'd refused to go alone.

Another eight feet. Another shadow.

She dared to look up. Their goal glittered in the sun. Ruby red scales catching the light, the shape deflated like someone let the air out of one of the serpentine creatures. Still beautiful – and worth ten times its weight in gold.

Kep'd been right in what a waste it was. For the first time since Kep climbed the tavern table to announce an adventure very much not of the bedroom variety, Minares smiled.

Behind her was Kep, the swamp, then the coast where their boat waited. Before her, rose the Eld – an ever-smoking mountain that regularly shook the ground. To the west the jungle would turn into the Eld-Hin Royal Garden. And guards. Damn them, and collaborators for turning on their fellow thieves. There was a good chance someone who'd heard Kep would turn them in.

Minares shuddered.

This could go wrong in too many ways, even without anyone betraying them for a drachma – being roasted, eaten, caught, or just sunk into shit. Nightmares were made out of this day. Time to get it over with.

She waved for Kep to come parallel.

"Second thoughts?" he asked, sounding as cheerful as if they were still at their table, still celebrating a reasonable, sensible break-in.

"Thinking of strangling you," Minares answered.

"With what? Drowning would make more sense." They both looked down and shuddered. "Anyway, we're nearly there, nearly out. It glimmers just ahead, like the rumours said."

"I just want to make sure we're clear. When we get there, I'm in charge. It's a grab-and-go, not a study of forbidden creatures."

"You're the boss."

Minares scoffed. They both knew she wasn't. They were both independent contractors who crossed paths more than once. Kep, the infiltrator and information gatherer,

Minares, the sneaky thief. She couldn't deny they made a good team. She'd just hoped to extend that to the bedroom, or a suitably clean alley, not a suicide mission.

But the time to back down had come and gone. Together, they waited. Shoulders brushing, breaths matching.

When no shadows passed overhead, nothing besides the gnats moved, as she rose to a crouch and dashed across the finally solid ground to reach her goal. Kep followed at a slower, louder pace. For once, he didn't draw her attention. They'd reached their goal.

Like the great reptiles they were, dragons shed their skin when they grew. Usually this happened high up on the mountain, but a guard had talked and the talk had spread, and everyone who listened for such things knew one had done so on the low ground. Only Kep, with Minares in tow, had been mad enough to go for it so far. But there would be others, for there was no lack of desperate and crazy in the imperial city.

The shed red skin was smaller than Minares had thought it would be from how it'd reflected the sun. It was less than a horse, a third of the size of those flying above. Her sweating increased. Heart drummed. Fear soured her mouth as she sucked in her cheeks.

"It's so pretty," her partner in crime said as he stepped up to her side, seemingly completely ignorant of the danger they faced. He'd worn exactly the same expression when he talked to her at the pub. It had never been about her.

Kep rolled excitedly on the balls of his feet. The tight fabric, now wet and sticky, clung to his body in a way that should have been reserved for nighttime, when shadows could hide Minares's blush. Time to get this over with. And a drink. Alone.

Minares lifted a shit-covered glove, reached for the dragon-discards, but even this empty husk she couldn't bring herself to stain.

By securing the glove between her knees, she freed her hand and placed it on the deep red, not like blood but a rose out of a precious gem, warm from the sun.

"What's it like?" Kep whispered.

"Nice."

"*Nice*? That's all you can say? Why did we agree you'd take it?"

"Because I'm the thief."

"And what am I?"

"The lookout," Minares snapped. "Why did you even bring me, unless it's to take the scales?"

Kep grumbled something, but finally turned to watch the sky. Good. They needed to hurry.

Still, Minares couldn't resist stroking the overlapping armor. It was nice. Very nice.

But it was time to get to work. They were exposed to the sky and any guard who might come from the palace.

With her other, still-gloved hand, Minares untied her bag, then used the clean hand to withdraw the small crowbar. She'd leave it behind and fit at least five scales into the bag. One for the informant and boat rental. Two for her and half for Kep. Life-changing.

Enough to buy a commission or an apprenticeship. To disappear and become someone else. To be respectable-adjacent at least.

"You done yet?" Kep asked.

Minares sighed and pushed the curved point under a teardrop-shaped scale the size of her hand.

Put her slight weight against it.

The body shivered.

A whimper rose above the sound of her pounding heart.

Minares flinched back, leaving the crowbar stuck under the scale.

"What was that?" Kep had given up even the pretence of keeping watch.

"It's only a shed skin. I moved it," Minares mumbled as the sound came again, like a kitten calling for its mother.

There was no one behind her. Or above. Only Kep, her, and the dragon skin.

"Min…"

She ignored Kep's insistent tone and gripped the crowbar again.

"Min, I don't think—"

"Don't think. We need to get out of here. What do you think will happen if the guard catches us? Or a dragon?"

"Sure, sure, just—" Kep pointed to the other side of the skin.

Minares walked around to see what had made Kep pale.

There was the feathered tail – vermilion but worn as if exposed to the rain and wind of the last few days. The hind legs. Were shed skins supposed to have claws?

A laugh bubbled up, proving she truly was mad. If she were facing death, she'd rather do it smiling. A smile with dimples had after all brought her here.

The feathered belly should also not have been there, for no scales protected it, so they did not need to change as it grew. Still, the colours travelled like a sunrise across the plumage. Red to pink and orange to yellow along the serpentine neck ending in a horned head. Pale blue eyes met hers.

Neither blinked.

It mewed again. Lifted its head before letting it fall, as if it no longer had the strength.

It was enough for Minares to see the broken arrow in its flank. There must have been blood before the rain washed it away.

"It's a dragon," she said. Kep nodded, for once lost for words. "Someone has shot a dragon."

A very young one, Minares assumed from its size. Even stealing a scale had been blasphemous. *This...*

A shadow passed above.

She threw herself down, yanking Kep along, and pressed them against the dragon's side. There was nowhere else to hide, and it didn't seem dangerous. Not anymore.

Who would have done this? And why was no one helping it?

Because no one is as mad as us, she thought. No one had come here. When they did, it would be too late.

The feathers were soft against her face. Lovely until she stained them with shit. In the sky, the larger dragon flew toward the coast. Minares met Kep's grey eyes. They were wide, the dark lashes framing them making them seem even larger. He mouthed, "*Dragon*."

It was unclear if he meant the injured young one, or the one above. As it didn't matter, she nodded. Mouthing back, "*What now*?"

He shrugged, like this hadn't all been his idea, like he wasn't the information gatherer who'd gotten it all wrong, like she truly was the boss.

A thrill shot through her stupid heart, for he was truly looking at her. Kep was always charming; that was how he made his money. But he didn't usually look at her, smile at her. When he suddenly had, together with the beers, she'd thought something had changed between them. He'd only seen a score.

But now…now he was waiting, and all that energy was focused solely on her. She needed that to continue.

"We can still take the scales and leave," she said, hating herself as soon as the words left her mouth.

Kep nodded slowly. "Right…"

The dragon snorted, as if hearing them. They flinched.

"Or we can…" Her voice trailed off. They were thieves.

"We could walk away, tell someone," Kep finished her sentence.

She bit her lip, knowing her next words were not ones she'd ever uttered before. "We could help."

Kep nodded slowly again. "For no return."

"Right…"

"Right."

Decision made, Minares removed her other glove, and with clean hands brushed the dragon's side.

"Shhh, we'll get the arrow out," she said, and walked up to where she'd seen it, protruding just above the shoulder.

"You'll have to turn," Kep said, stroking its other side. "You really are very nice, little one. My friend here has decided we're going to help, and she's very good at that. Helping. She's here helping me, you see."

As if the dragon understood him, it lifted its head, then its long neck. Minares glimpsed the arrow lodged into the smaller scales next to the neck.

It looked deep, but dragons were tough. Magical. No normal arrow would even breach a scale, that's why they were so valuable. This one must be special. She'd get it out, the rest would be up to the Three-Headed God.

She retrieved the crowbar, wedged it under the dragon's side.

"When I push, you roll to the other side," she said. "It's the only way."

The dragon mewed, as if arguing it would hurt.

"Must be done," Kep said, voice soft. "On three. I'll help."

He counted down, then rolled the dragon as Minares put her weight against the crowbar.

The dragon screamed, its high-pitched voice vibrating through her bones, but it also rolled as the crowbar bent, destroyed. Minares hadn't meant to keep it anyway.

An answering cry of a much larger creature came from Eld's cloud-covered slope.

"Did you hear that?" Kep asked, still stroking the dragon's side.

Minares nodded. "Even if the other dragons left this one for dead, they will come now. Shit."

"Yeah, lots of shit to get through."

Minares gave Kep an irritated stare as she scrambled over the dragon's side, dug into the wound, and gripped the tip of the broken arrow.

The small dragon snapped at her, but Kep kept it back by its feathers.

They should run.

Now.

Instead, she gripped the wooden shaft again and with a shout, tore it out.

It wasn't an arrow at all, but the tip of a javelin, its blade some kind of dark metal covered with symbols. She stuffed it into her pack.

"Incoming!"

A roar shook her. Five dragons filled the sky. There was nothing more they could do. Kep was already running, his hand somehow in hers.

They returned through shit and swamp until, by some miracle, they reached the coast. The grown dragons must have stayed with the young one rather than hunt them. Or perhaps it could tell them they'd helped. *Why* didn't matter so much when the result was that no one was chewing on their marrow.

Bobbing on the perfect azure sea was the boat.

With shaking muscles, they swam out, the water washing away the traces of the day. Kep climbed the railing, his unfairly long limbs enabling him to reach the boat first.

He pulled her into the small skiff and set sail, jumping like an overeager puppy.

"We met a dragon, Min! You saved one. You're a hero. A broke hero, but still, wait until this tale spreads."

His eyes, like a stormy sky, caught hers. Somehow, he was holding her hands again. Damn it. Couldn't the man let go? She snatched them back.

"Why did you even insist on bringing me on this madcap mission?"

His smile wavered. "For the money – you're always saying you need a big score to get out. Why else? You're the one who proposed we leave right away."

"Leave the tavern, yes. Together, yes. Not to steal from dragons."

"But where else would we go?"

"Are you messing with me?" He blinked at her as the wind played with his hair. *Did he not know*? "I was inviting you back to my place, for non-lethal, non-lucrative, purely pleasurable fun."

"You wanted to… I never knew… I–I would, maybe still…"

Minares could have spelled it out, in graphic detail, but sometimes actions speak louder than words. She closed the distance between them on the bouncing skiff, grabbed his neck, and pushed her lips against his. They were warm, soft, and quickly got the idea.

A wave rocked the boat to the side, throwing them together. Neither minded.

When Minares pulled back for air, the dimple was back.

"What were you going to use the money for?" she asked, and lay her head down on his chest.

"I'm saving."

"For what?"

He squirmed when she let the silence stretch until he couldn't take it anymore. "A house, okay. A small one, in the countryside. With flowers."

Minares's image of the stylish man reordered. They'd both wanted the money to get out, but there was no lowland dragon skin. No scales waiting to be claimed. With the baby dragon's mews replaying inside her, she wasn't even sure she could have stolen them anyway. It was too close to graverobbing. Even thieves had lines they didn't cross.

She sighed as another option crossed her mind. A foolish, suicidal kind of adventure.

"What if we could still earn the money?" Minares asked, and prepared to cross a line she'd never thought she would. They'd get new labels – *turncoat, collaborator, scum.* Be up to her neck in a different kind of shit.

"How?"

She pulled the still bloody javelin head from her bag. "The right kind of information finder and thief might be able to find out where this came from. If they trust each other. If they'd be willing to try a longer, mutually beneficial partnership." She caught Kep's lips in a quick kiss. "How do you feel about selling information on dragon killers to the Imperial Throne instead?"

Lilt and Luster Spring Newsletter

Susan Taitel

Welcome back, Glitterbugs! I'm thrilled to announce that Lilt and Luster will soon be reopening for in-person shopping.

What a few years it has been, huh? Between the Goblin strike shutting down our supply line and the Wyvern-pox outbreak forcing us to close the storefront indefinitely, we were beginning to doubt this moment would ever come. If I hadn't personally overseen the warding, I would have sworn our humble little jewelry store was cursed.

Honestly, the only thing keeping us going during these unprecedented times has been the unwavering support from you Glitterbugs. We are deeply grateful that so many of you continued to place orders by troll-post, and we are raring to finally get started on filling them.

Even now, Wendy is training this year's clutch of salamanders in advance of lighting the forge. Meanwhile,

Greg and Freya are testing their tools and arranging their workbenches. I, for one, am eagerly anticipating getting my hands on the next batch of raw gems.

You may have noticed a missing name. It is with mixed emotions that I announce that after fifteen years, my co-founder, partner in crime, the Lilt to my Luster, Eloise, is leaving the shop to get married. While we were all a bit shocked by the suddenness of her departure, we wish nothing but the best for our dear Eloise and her fiancé, the Duke of Nightingales.

El, if you're reading this, you will be sorely missed. You were the first person I met after I stumbled through the rift nearly two decades ago. I doubt I would have made it a day without you. You not only taught me to survive in this strange new reality, you also taught me to find beauty in the unexpected. In this world of wonders, you amazed me every day. Though there's no replacing your level of craftsmanship and unique point of view, I promise to keep our dream business going for both of us. Know that should you choose to return, you will be welcomed back with open arms.

In honor of Eloise's joyous, if unexpected, news, I'm dedicating this newsletter to a certain essential piece of jewelry. That's right, we are talking about the all-important engagement ring!

If you are subscribed, you are probably of the mindset that one can never have enough jewelry, and of course I agree, but consider this. For some, an engagement ring is the only piece of fine jewelry they own. Yet so many people wind up with interchangeable diamond solitaires. Cut, set, and boxed for the masses. From the start, Eloise and I believed that your ring should be as unique and beautiful as your love story. Each Lilt and Luster ring is a singular creation, with an origin to match. Designs for our spring collection are already in development (and they are spectacular), but we still have a few unclaimed treasures in our showroom. Read on to find the perfect ring for your intended.

* * *

The Miner's Delight, artist Greg

A perfect blend of materials and design. The gem is a five-carat obsidian-shaded dragon heartstone (so rare!). Although it appears smoky at first glance, when brought to the light, you can see echoes of the flames that came perilously close to snuffing out the lives of the brave dwarves who discovered its source. But what is a little danger when it results in such a find! (I kid! We take the health and safety of our contractors very seriously. The dwarves were rigorously trained in safely exhuming dragon remains and were generously compensated.)

Before I could make the first cut on this beauty, it had to pass an eighteen-month cooling-off period in our deep-freeze, allowing it to be handled safely while retaining the appearance of fire. I cut the perfect facets to show off its shine and etched runes of binding along the rim. This is one heart that won't crack.

Once my work was finished, I handed it off to Greg, who set it in a braided band made of finely polished rose gold and blown glass. Greg has really outdone himself with this one.

This ring is perfect if your intended's emotions run deep until they explode to the surface.

Call for price. Serious inquiries only.

The Mermaid's Tear, artist Freya

At a diminutive three carats, this gem may not be right if your intended believes that size is the only thing that matters. But if they prioritize sparkle, this stunner packs a heck of a punch. As the name implies, it started life as a tear harvested from a lady of the deep. It was then pressurized into a diamond. With a clarity rating above IF, this gorgeous stone needed little cutting to dazzle to the fullest effect.

Displaying the elegance and delicacy we've come to expect from a Freya piece, this ring is truly special. She chose to surround the diamond with a halo of freshwater pearls and complemented it with a platinum band.

If your intended has an affinity for the sea and a penchant for melancholia, this is the ring you want! (You will get used to the constant knell of the pipes. I did.)

Call for price. Installment plan available.

The Suzanne, artist Dagmar (That's me!)

This piece was made for a special commission that has since fallen through; it is now up for grabs. Inspired by the Leonard Cohen song of the same name. (For those of you who've never visited the other side of the rift, think of him as a bard.) This stone is a bit of a departure for me. As much as I adore the gleam of a crystal, some rings require the rich layers of stone. I created this nine-carat cabochon myself, using our patented flash-fossilization process. The result is created with a blend of crushed oyster shells and owl pellets (featuring bonus mouse bones). To finish it off, I carved a cluster of orange blossoms into the surface.

The copper band should oxidize and develop a colorful patina over time, making a ring that evolves with your intended. This ring is meant for a true Bohemian spirit.

Call to apply. All offers will be considered.

The Cold Iron Special, artist Wendy

Forged out of – you guessed it – iron, this simple ring is not meant for your intended but for you.

Are you unsure of where your intended lives and how you come to visit them night after night? Do you not recall exactly how or when you met? Do they appear as young as the morning and as old as the mountains? When in their presence, do you occasionally forget to breathe until they remind you? After you part ways, do you find you have lost days? Months? Decades? Do you yearn to be with them when they are not around and yearn to escape them when they are?

If you answered yes to any of the above, call us, price waived.

El, call me.

* * *

That's all for this newsletter, Glitterbugs! See you in the summer!

– Dagmar

Draconitis: Acute & Chronic

Nemma Wollenfang

"Ouch!" Svala whipped her hand away from the shrub. A ruby-bright droplet beaded on a fingertip. She sucked the pad to ease the sting.

Please just be from a thorn. Please just be from a thorn. Please just be from a thorn.

"Svala?" At the far side of the gorse, Laars stood shading his eyes, panting and sweat-dappled in only his breeches, all of that flaxen hair in messy knots. He'd been in the process of shearing away the long grass encroaching from the meadow – both of them working to clear the wild vegetation nearest their cottage in the hopes of planting a crop of corn – but he quickly dropped his scythe and loped over to where she stood. Gentle as ever, her husband pried the stinging digit from between her lips to examine it with shrewd eyes.

"Looks rather large for a mere thorn prick. What did…"

A rustle shook the gorse, dislodging thin pointy leaves and a spray of yellow petals. From within, came a rumbling gurgle.

"In there," she whispered.

One of Laars's sun-bronzed arms wound about her waist and drew her back until she was half-shielded behind his impressive height. Then, taking up a discarded pitchfork, he used its iron prongs to carefully part the foliage.

At first, there was nothing obvious. It was hard to see beyond the dense gloom, with the noon sun's glare in their eyes. Then…something stirred. Coils glistened in a stray patch of light – mottled brown scales with a mossy sheen. Serpentine and smooth. Another gargling growl. It had been well-camouflaged beneath so much greenery.

Svala's heart gave a lurch. "Is that…is it an iipsy dragon?" The dry hush barely escaped her lips, little more than a croak.

Laars's huge eyes met hers, matched their flash of panic. If it were, if it had bitten…

Breathing hard, he shifted the pitchfork, angling it to reveal more. The beast was small, no larger than a hound. A hound *pup*, come to that. Must have been why she missed it during her pruning. A spiny fringe crested its back, two membranous wings rustled, unfurling… A tiny face rose, canting to one side. Amber eyes with slit-onyx pupils regarded them with a spark of intelligence, before narrowing. Nostrils flared, spewing a geyser of red-hot flame.

Laars was swift. Tugging Svala from its path with near enough force to wrench her arm from its socket, he set them into a clumsy, stumbling run towards their wattle and daub cottage. Crashing across its threshold, Laars slammed the door – though in a last, fleeting glimpse, Svala caught sight of the gorse bush. What remained of it. The fiery blast had been brutal: incinerating petals, vaporising buds, crumbling leaves and thorns into smoking jet ash. The few remaining branches simmered with a veiny orange glow, like embers in a coal bed.

A numb veil descended over her, making every limb feel rubbery and useless, as if they may collapse beneath her at any moment. She registered Laars's movements in a vague, detached way. Unlike her, he was all action as he shoved furniture in front of the door and snatched her hand to drag her to the kitchen sink. One arm kept her upright, working the pump, while he used the other to dunk her damaged finger under its icy spray.

For all the good it would do.

"To prevent infection we must be swift," he muttered. There was a frantic edge to his voice, sharp as any blade, and it cut through some of Svala's numbness, making it possible to suck in a harsh lungful of air, to straighten her swirling thoughts and speak them.

"I – it looked to be a juvenile. Do you not think? I mean, it was rather small. Iipsies are usually much larger, as big as our cottage! Mayhap, with it being so young, all will be well?"

Iipsy dragons were a parasitoid species. Everyone knew. Using their stingers to implant their eggs in living flesh. It was how they procreated – well, one of the ways. Which was why Laars was working so diligently. There were many unpleasant ways one could pass from the world, and to have dragon larvae bursting from one's abdomen had to be one of the worst.

"Aye. You'll be fine. Just fine." His words were fervent. Stilted. Grasping for hope. He kept on scrubbing; his grip hard, his ministrations bordering on painful.

Gently extracting her hand, Svala cupped his cheek to make his gaze meet hers. Now, secure in their cottage, with heartbeat slowing, a layer of calm settled upon her. She felt remarkably placid. With touch alone, she tried to transfer that to him.

"I moved my hand as soon as I felt the jab," she said. "I hardly think it caught me at all. And besides, the younglings aren't mature enough to lay eggs. Its stinger will have no effect."

"You're right, you're probably right." Laars was breathless, still quaking, but that raw edge of panic in his eyes seemed to dull. The kiss he placed on her brow was firm but gentle.

He drew back with a frown. "*Did* it strike with its stinger? Or with its teeth?"

That it could have pierced her flesh with its teeth was just as worrisome a prospect.

"Its stinger, I'm certain." She held up her hand, displaying the slightly swollen finger. "One puncture wound, see? And not even that deep. Hardly any damage at all."

He gave a firm nod, dragging a hand through his tousled hair. She watched his muscles relax. "I'll fetch some men from the tavern. We'll have that beastie gone before dusk."

Dredging up a smile, and ignoring the trembling of her limbs, Svala began to prepare dinner – fetching onions and dried parsley and that salted ham cured on the hook. "Well, if you're going to be ousting a dragon, dear husband, you'll need a hearty supper," she said.

He laughed. Panic averted. All would be well. She was sure of it.

* * *

All was not well. That became apparent during the dark hours of the night, when Svala awoke clammy and aching. Needles pricked every inch of skin, and waves of heat licked their way up her throat. The fever had come upon her swiftly, as they slept. Laars was the one who nudged her to consciousness; dragging her panting and thrashing from nightmares of flaming gorse.

"You're burning," he said, his timbre rough. "Your very skin is aflame."

In the dim candlelight, he tended to her with a damp cloth that stung like ice – though when she complained he assured her that the water was tepid. It did little good. And when Svala's flesh began to steam, Laars ran from their cottage in only his long-shirt to fetch the apothecary. The writhing delirium pulled Svala under as the door slammed on his back.

"…symptoms of Acute Draconitis are usually much more dramatic, and deadly," an aged voice was saying as she came to – thick and syrupy to her ears. She blinked and a man with a wiry grey beard swam into view. The apothecary. "Spontaneous combustion of the victim. Your wife merely has an…admittedly high…fever. *Have* you found any growths?"

"None," said Laars. "I checked. Her finger, where it caught her, is swollen, though."

Another hand touched hers, its grip fragile and texture papery – sharply prominent amidst the turmoil of her mind. It almost stung. Svala could not focus for long. Laars's face loomed out of the gloom, as blurry and indistinct as the withered soul beside him. The dark-robed man wore a neutral expression, while her husband's brow crumpled with fear.

Growths were bad, Svala remembered that much. They indicated the presence of a dragon egg forming beneath the skin, one which, upon hatching, would incinerate the host in a torrent of explosive flames. That fate befell the Godsman's son last harvest-time.

"It is likely a malady of a different sort then," the apothecary wheezed. "With Acute Draconitis, the growths arise first. Combustion is swift – over in a flash. There is no fever. Such swelling on her finger is natural after injury. That's likely what's caused this pyrexia."

With a sympathetic smile, he left a tincture to ease her pains and departed. Laars helped her to drink it; propping her up with one arm while feeding her with the other. All strength appeared to have abandoned her. Why, she felt weaker than a newborn. The tincture was foul too; tasting of offal and sulphur. It stuck in her throat, rolling slow as sludge and making her gag. But it did its job and by dawn Svala felt much improved. The fever had waned, the fog of her mind had cleared. She even felt strong enough to sit by the cold hearth and take some broth. The relief on Laars's face was so transparent that she released a croaky laugh, huddling in her blankets. He returned her easy smile. "For a moment there, I feared I'd lost you."

"Nay," she said. "You'll be saddled with me for many years yet."

"I'll hold you to that, my love."

There was a witty quip on the tip of Svala's tongue, but when she opened her mouth a tickle caught in her nose. A bad one. She tried to restrain the sneeze, but upon realising it was fruitless, she turned towards the charred logs of the hearth, politely aiming it away. Flames spewed from her nostrils, igniting the wood in a burst of orange and red heat.

* * *

Chronic Draconitis is characterised much differently than the Acute form. In some ways it is much more fearsome. At least, with Acute, one was guaranteed a swift demise.

"Bitten then, not stung," the apothecary concluded upon his return. When Laars asked what treatment he could administer now, the aged fellow shook his head, jowls aquiver, and said, "I'm so sorry," before departing with haste. Chronic Draconitis was a shunned malady.

Over the following week, it slowly progressed. Svala's skin became itchy, discoloured; mottling in patches of reddish purple. The image in her looking glass constantly shifted; the contours of her face grew harder, her hair wilder. Even the hue of her eyes shifted, from the soft moss Laars so loved to the molten amber of banked flame. One eve, she leaned closer, noticing how her pupils had narrowed, slitting like a feline's. Light became intolerable, its brightness hurt, so she sequestered herself in their bedchamber with every drape drawn. Only the glow of the hearth provided any comfort. Scents sharpened, a gnawing craving grew for meat – though whatever she consumed tasted of ash. Teeth like barbed razors punctured through her gums, pushing the old out, and she savaged her food, forgoing the silverware. Svala failed to notice her lack of etiquette until she saw the way Laars stared at her, seated at the far end of their dining table, fork hanging loose, mouth agape. She tried harder after, to recall herself, to hold onto those last shreds of humanity. For his sake if not her own.

That proved more difficult when the scales broke through. Where the skin had been crimson and marbled, itching incessantly even under the scratching of her nails, tiny plates began to emerge from what she peeled back. Hard as adamant, their sharp edges scalloped.

That was when it truly struck her. The sense of inevitability.

There was no stopping the spread of badness through her system. No matter what herbal remedy or pasty ointment Laars plied her with, nor how fervently he prayed to the deities of their ancestors. No god was listening. Slowly but surely, she was becoming lost.

The townsfolk treated her worse than a leper whenever she ventured out; hooded and wrapped against the strongest of the light, and only under cloud-cast skies. They alternated between hissing oaths to the saints behind their hands and crossing the road to be as far from her as possible. You'd think, given her situation, there would have been more sympathy. After all, she was not the first among their number to be ambushed by an iipsy. But they feared the threat she posed, she knew. They feared she may pass her affliction on to them too.

Laars was a troubadour, and a fair one at that. Well-respected, loved by the community. In some ways it was easier to venture out while with him – in some ways it was worse. While they did not harass her as they would have alone, she had to suffer the pitying looks directed his way. *Poor man*, they silently said, *yoked to such a wife*. It was hard to ignore the stares but Svala did her best, smiling as Laars engaged her in conversation and they toured the market, asking which apples she thought were ripest, or which loaf looked least stale.

He seemed to have a new idea about how to cope with the situation, which Svala happily complied with. If they playacted normality, mayhap that would make it so.

"Brother!" A bright voice hailed as they perused a mercer's wares – ignoring how the proprietor flinched away. Svala grimaced as they turned to face its recipient, hiding further beneath her hood. A young blonde woman, with blue eyes a match for Laars's, stood before them. "It is so good to see you out taking the air. You've been absent too long. From the tavern too! Perhaps tonight you could grace us with a ballad."

No greeting for Svala – her, his sister ignored completely. Which was no new thing.

"Well, Svala felt better today," Laars said brightly, "so we ventured out."

The woman's eyes flicked to her then, and in them lay a cinder of revulsion. "Mother says you may move back in with us, Laars," she said, addressing only he.

Of course the old witch did. She'd never forgiven Svala for stealing away her only son.

"Lena," Laars grated, with a tone of long-suffering patience, "Svala is my wife. I'm not about to abandon her in her time of greatest need. And would not even if that were not so."

"I'm right here." Neither of them had forgotten, though both ignored her. A low rumble began in her throat, a wrathful keen. How dearly Svala would like to rip into the callous waif. The ebony-tinted claws that had sprouted in place of nails would certainly do damage.

The sudden notion caught her off guard. Violent musings were most unlike her.

Lena set her arms akimbo – in a remarkable mimic of her mother. "Folks do not expect you to stay with a cursed, Laars. Gracious, no one else would! The town will understand—"

"—What we do is none of the town's business."

"But—"

"—No, Lena!" Laars growled, drawing numerous gazes. "Let it alone."

Svala's eyes fixed on him. That primordial rumble, that dominant posturing, called to the beast awakening within her. In a heartbeat, it recognised an equal.

The moment was shattered by his sister's shrieking voice. "You cannot be serious about remaining with her! She's becoming a monster! A beast! She isn't fit to be around normal—"

"—Leave us be, sister!"

Taking Svala's elbow, Laars led her away. Which was best for all concerned.

When they were far enough from wagging ears, Svala turned to him. "You could, you know. Leave, I mean. I'd understand." The words were hard to speak and she dipped her head to hide the ache of them. Yet for his own sake, he should rejoin his kin. Abandon her.

A blunt finger tipped her chin up. His eyes were sad but determined. "In sickness and in health, eh? I made a vow and I mean to keep to it. You could banish me but I'll not go away."

Sweet as that was, there was a bitter flavour to his pledge. For will alone would not restrain her sickness. It would not save her, whatever they pretended. And there was another part to that promise too: 'Til death do us part. Yet death took many forms.

* * *

Over time, her malady only worsened. More symptoms arose. Bones grated and shifted. Muscles elongated and strengthened. Svala's shape continually changed, growing sleeker, more sinuous. More inhuman. As a weight of despair settled upon her, she found herself no longer fighting so hard, no longer *trying*, but allowing the alterations to consume her one scale at a time. And succumbing to the urges…

Dragons of all species were notorious hoarders. Jewels, silver, gold. Especially gold. Being a small peasant village, gold was a rarity. That by no means curtailed what items were worth hoarding, though. Chipped cups, wolf pelts, mink-lined pelisses, even a finely honed hunting dagger with engraved pommel… All joined a growing pile on their bedchamber floor. The sharpness of Svala's newly honed vision made such prizes easy to spy. She fancied herself more a magpie than a dragon, stealing jewels to line her nest.

With every new change, Svala lost a little more of herself. No longer did she recall the taste of buttermilk, or crave sunlight upon her skin. There was no more need to comfort her distraught husband or feel his strong arms around her, laughter rumbling from his chest as he clutched her in their bed. His lined brow, the tears that seeped free, failed to rouse her withering ash-beaten heart. The fear dissipated from her like fog at dawn.

Little empathy remained – that was the hardest of all to hold onto.

It was wearing on Laars, Svala could tell. Exhaustion plagued him, shadows grew beneath his bloodshot eyes, and a growth of stubble crested his jaw. Still, he remained by her side, always there as she slipped further from reach. When her lengthening tail could no longer be concealed beneath voluminous skirts, he beseeched the apothecary once again, begging on his knees. There was no cure, he'd been told more than once. No tincture had any effect, no Godsman chant could rectify what had been done. There was no hope.

"Svala," he gasped, eyes wild as he clasped her scale-ridden face between his palms, hardly caring how it flayed his soft skin, "you must fight this. *Please*, I cannot lose you!"

His worry was an irritant, foreign and cumbersome, and in a fit of temper she lashed out, driving her newly pointed canines through flesh and sinew into bone. A tang filled her mouth, a gush of spiced iron. But at his yelp…a spark of her former self resurfaced.

This was Laars. *Her* Laars.

Her sweet, gentle, ever-caring husband.

Reeling back, she slammed into the wall, putting as much distance between them as she could. Never had she meant to hurt him. She loved him, she *did*. Yet she had bitten him.

Oh Gods. She had *bitten* him.

As Laars stared at his dripping palm, mouth agape at the bloody crescent, a weight seemed to lift from his shoulders, a calmness settling over him.

"All's well," he said, finally looking up at her. "If you're going, I'll be going with you."

She wanted his arms around her then – that need returned to her in a sudden rush – and with a whimper she slunk into his embrace.

* * *

Laars gave up. When his skin mottled and itched, he smiled. When she hovered over the hoard, he added to it with glee. And when his sneeze led to an eruption of flame that burned a fur rug, he laughed more merrily than she had heard him do in a long count of days.

I'll be going with you, he'd said. Clearly, he meant it.

They shut themselves away from the rest of the village, secluding themselves in their somnolent little cottage. It was hard to say if they were happy, exactly – dragons did not feel such a thing – but if nothing else they were content in their joint deterioration.

That was, until a hammering came upon their door one night.

"Bring her out, Laars!" An irate voice shouted – it sounded like the local Godsman's. "This has gone on long enough. She needs to be dealt with before she spreads her evil!"

"Dealt with?" Laars mumbled, looking to her. His eyes were not slitted, yet, but their cornflower blue now bore distinct striations of amber.

"Bring the monster out!" another voice called, followed by fainter cries of agreement.

How many were out there? Svala's ears twitched, honing to the thumping of hearts, the crackle of flames. At the tang of metal, her nostrils flared. Fifteen, twenty, *more* lay beyond their door, and they had come armed with torches and scythes and other field implements.

At their continued hammering, at their blatant hostility, Svala rumbled a low growl, crouching over their hoard with her serpentine tail swishing, claws digging in. China cracked.

If they wished to fight, she would be more than willing to oblige.

Laars held up a hand to stay her and, taking up the poker, he edged towards the door.

"Godsman Emmon? Is that you?" he called. "What business do you have here?"

"The Gods' business! You harbour a monster. They do not suffer such to exist!"

Fangs bared, Svala unfurled her membranous wings and flapped them in agitation. They had sprouted not two days past – around the same time she had abandoned the use of clothes. Linen was constricting and inhibiting and her scales preferred the caress of air.

Laars frowned, glancing back at her. "My wife is very ill, Godsman."

"If you do not bring her out, we shall be forced to come in and fetch her!"

Other shouts erupted. Calls of "Aye, that's right!" and "Kill the beast!"

Laars moved to the window, using his poker to shift the curtain aside a fraction. A throng of townsfolk milled about beyond, including Laars's sister and mother, their faces contorted with malice. But it was not they who caught

Svala's eyes. Beyond them, down the hill in the town square, something was being constructed. Some kind of pyre.

Svala made a sort of chuff. They were going to what? Burn her alive? Clearly they had not thought this through. Dragon hide was impervious to flame. Why, though? Had she and Laars not secluded themselves away? Had they not made sure they harmed no others?

Laars must have seen it too, for a deep rumble erupted from his own chest at the affront and he bared his teeth – which were only slightly pointed. Except for a few draconic mannerisms he could still pass for an unafflicted human, especially in the gloom. Shadows hid the mottling at his neck well. He could come out of this unscathed. She, however…

Laars eyed her stoically, his face expressionless, but in the depths of his eyes there still lay a kernel of the old him, a spark of longing and dread.

"Go," he grated, his voice like gravel. "Fly now. Take to the skies. I'll hold them off."

Words were no longer possible for Svala but her whine was indicative enough.

I do not wish to leave you.

Dragons may not possess the emotions of humans, but he was her partner. Her mate. That innate, primordial bond sung through every vein. Carved deep into bone.

Laars stepped close, clutching the poker in one hand as he cupped her cheek with the other. The scales no longer abraded his palm, hardened as his skin now was.

"They know nothing of me, remember? I'll hold them back." He placed a kiss upon her snout. "And follow when I can."

There was no more time. The townsfolk took it upon themselves to move things along by battering in the door. Two rams and the panel clattered to the hay-strewn floor. Three men stood on the threshold, brandishing hammers and hoes with mean glints in their eyes. Laars barely had time to turn but Svala was quicker. With a flick of her tail she brushed him aside and released a scream of flames. Scorching, blistering. The men fell with hollers of agony, skin blackened and burning, flesh dripping from their bones like melting wax. Others cried out too, beyond them. Some charged in to take their places with sharpened metal held aloft.

Laars yelled at her to "Go! *GO*!" Frantic arms flapping. So, as smoke choked their tiny cottage, she broke through the wattle of the farthest wall, and in a shower of debris took wing, beating air, flapping for the skies, as below the fire swelled into a conflagration.

The cottage fell swiftly. In a crumble of jet ash, the tinder disintegrated, consumed by powerful licks of red and gold flame. Just like that gorse bush, what felt like so long ago.

As she rose, higher and higher, her eyes caught Laars's form stumbling into the streets.

"I will find you!" he cried out. "I vow I will find you again, Svala!"

And she knew that he would. Laars would track her, up into the mountains, where they could bathe in lava and soar through high clouds, where it was rocky and isolated and no man dared to tread. His promise was ageless, sacrosanct. Something that went beyond any vows made in a Gods' circle. And when he did, they would leave the world of mortal-kind behind.

A Matter of Life and Dragons

J.L. Worrad

Deloria

Only me now…

Deloria's world had fallen silent but for the whirr of her fighter's propellers as they cut through the night. The cockpit glowed a flickering orange from the light of the smoldering engines. She could smell smoke, but the cockpit wasn't filling up with it. She wouldn't choke any time soon. She would roast.

Well. This was it then.

Beyond the cockpit's glass, in the sky's far distance, the lights of Whiteshores and Burtonhead islands twinkled like constellations. The *Belle-Elaise* would never reach them, would splutter out, burn and drop. Maybe someone would see her, should they gaze from their bedroom window. A tiny red comet. Then nothing.

The dragon had burst out of an unprepossessing cloud, tearing Dom's fighter in half then roasting Clive's. Deloria had heard Clive's scream in her headset, poor bastard. She had only gotten away when she had flown into a cloud bank. Hardly skill in that, just dashed luck. The dragon had lost sight of her, but another blast of dark flame had done for the *Belle-Elaise*'s engines and more besides. Deloria had let the old girl down. Now there was nothing to be done.

"Final report," Deloria told herself. She punched the radio and spoke into her flying helmet's mic. "G-for-George, G-for-George, come in, breaker."

She repeated it. More static.

Base Fifty-three receiving, came a young woman's voice. *Status, G-for-George.*

"Flight G attacked, single dragon. Two Windstorms downed, just myself remaining. Engines burning out. Guns inoperable. Incapable of ascent nor descent." Deloria drew breath. "Not going to make it, Base Fifty-three."

The young woman had fallen silent. Deloria felt sorry for her. Hardly an easy call to receive. Poor thing, sat in a radio tower on night shift, probably on Burtonhead, Deloria's old home, much as she had tried to forget it. She knew that sort of girl. She had been one herself.

I'm bringing up your flight's file, G-for-George, the voice said eventually. *Remain calm, pilot. I'll call emergency.*

"There's no point," Deloria snapped. "It's hopeless, Base Fifty-three. I'm calling in to tell you the dragon hasn't pursued.

Just another lone plane hunter. Pass it on that my flight-mates fought well," she lied. "Tell their families."

Of course, G-for-George. What's your serial number?

"G08-927." Deloria rubbed her eyes with gloved fingers. "You know, I should thank you, Base Fifty-three. Good to hear another human voice before the curtain drops."

Deloria... the voice said. She must have read the file. *Deloria Hendlethwaite, is that you?*

Deloria froze. "Elaise?"

Elaise

Elaise loved to wander along the coast, the island's very edge where the blue of the sky above met the blue of the sky below. The summer morning was cloudless and the underside of distant Whiteshores island could be seen, even its famous waterfalls that poured from its edges into the sky beneath, becoming vapor that fell down into eternal blue. Elaise stopped to look and the sun blessed her face. She had come here to throw herself off.

She had been stood there some time, toes peering over the chalky edge, the endless sky below. She could make out another island to her left and far below, though she couldn't recall the name. Her geography was terrible. It mattered not: she wouldn't hit it when she fell. It would rush past her as she fell forever.

"Are you about to do what I think you're about to do?"

Elaise turned her head to the voice beside her, as much as she dared, only to see a young blonde woman with sharp features looking back. She wore a long flowery dress, which meant she had to be at least nineteen, though not much older. Her expression was blank, as if paying for a bus ticket.

"I'm sorry," Elaise replied, "but this is the sort of thing one does alone."

"That's fine. I wasn't planning on leaping with you." The woman nodded. "Name's Deloria."

"Hello Deloria. Elaise. I meant it's the sort of thing that doesn't require a witness."

"Right-o."

"I'm afraid my life's an awful rot, Deloria. A boy left me for my best friend. Valerie Snoad; terrible at hockey, laugh like a donkey's bray."

"Hmm. Have you considered throwing *them* off?"

Elaise hid her snigger by looking into the wind. "And my mother is haughty and judgmental and has every right to be because I've failed all my practice exams. Then there's that hole, that 'Rend' they're calling it, that leads into nowhere, isn't there? The one mentioned on the wireless last Tuesday. So it would seem even mother nature is in a terrible funk. Oh, I don't know, Deloria. While I'm not *committed* to taking a step forward here… I'm certainly weighing the options."

"Careful deliberation." Deloria nodded sagely and for a moment Elaise was concerned Deloria's flapping dress might drag her off in the breeze. "That's the ticket. You want to get it right, after all. Whole lot of time for regret should you leap."

"And longer if I don't." Elaise sighed. "You must remember what it's like, being seventeen, surely?"

"I am seventeen."

A woman had to be nineteen to wear dresses and lipstick and the like. You made the choice. Keep to the world of women, with dresses and home life and childbirth, or take the hard world of men with its suits and technical jobs and punch-ups and right to vote. It was how the Archipelago had released steam on the women's rights question a century ago. Elaise still hadn't made her mind up on the choice and it was yet another reason falling off the island had its charms.

"Oh this?" Deloria said, waving her skirt. "I like wearing them. That's my second reason for coming here: the solitude." She looked Elaise up and down. "Hypothetically speaking…"

"What's your first?"

"You're dithering, Elaise."

"I'm genuinely interested." Elaise was dithering.

Deloria stepped directly behind her. "Look down. Give it a minute." Her breath drummed the words on Elaise's bare neck.

Elaise waited, giddy with something she couldn't understand. Fear, perhaps, of this stranger who could push her off. But no. Not fear. Not quite. For she had the curious feeling she had never been so safe.

A low and quiet hum came. Many hums, like a choir.

"See?" the stranger whispered.

Then they came. Far below Elaise's toes, below the cliff and the island: a flock of airplanes, silhouettes at first until they came out of the island's shadow and flashed silver beneath the sun.

"Windstorm Mark IIIs," Deloria said and Elaise supposed that that was the make. "Top speed o' four-twenty-o, can dive at full power and not lose the wings. Queens of the blue. It's the best of us, isn't it? Flight, I mean. Once, not so long ago, each island floated alone in the sky, but men dared to fly. First with hot air, then propeller and who-bally-knows what's to come hereafter. They reached out to one another, Elaise. And no island in the endless blue had to be alone anymore."

"It's beautiful." The propeller choir sang below Elaise's feet. The hem of Deloria's floral dress danced, curling around Elaise's leg.

"I'll walk you home."

"Actually, Deloria… I'm a little too terrified to move. Funny that, isn't it? I got here well enough but…my legs won't get me back."

A forearm came around her midriff, gripped her tightly and drew her back. The arm went to remove itself but Elaise kept it there with her palm, and the two of them watched the flock of humming silver fly into the wide gold and blue.

Deloria

A pause and everything was the hum of the props again, the glow of fire and the stink of smoke. Deloria went to cut the radio.

Don't you dare cut me off.

Deloria grimaced. "I wasn't, Base Fifty-three."

Remain professional, Flight Lieutenant. There was pain in Elaise's bark and it pained Deloria. *We'll bring you back.*

"The game's up, Elaise."

I'm not who I was, G-for-George. She emphasized the last part, an admonishment for using her name. *I'm a signaleer, first rank. Believe me, Base Fifty-three has brought worse back.*

She had always been victim to hope, Elaise, despite her dramas. Her willful naivety was part of her charm. It was a hope Deloria had no wish to contract.

"Tell mother I said I love her," Deloria said. "My family too. They might even believe it, coming from you."

Stop it! Always so sure of yourself. Well, you're not sure. You're wrong.

"What happened to remaining professional?"

Silence.

Alright, Elaise said after some time. Deloria was relieved to hear it. *We've a plan here.*

"Did you scratch it out just now on a cigarette packet?"

It's been on our books awhile. Theoretical. Sort of. Set course for altitude 09, 1.1069 slash 52,2364.

Deloria checked her maps. "Whiteshores island. Can't land there, I can't ascend. The engines'll blow."

You fly below Whiteshores, G-for-George. Remember the waterfalls? Fly just right and you'll catch the vapors in your engines. Stop the fire, then glide the rest to Burtonhead.

"What? Ridiculous. What clowns have you got down there?"

Tonight? Just the clown you're speaking to.

Deloria drew breath. "This plane can't take a shower. In this state she'll tumble soon as a droplet hits her."

We've done the maths, G-for-George. We—

"You said 'sort of'. 'Sort of theoretical'."

The radio paused, then: *There was one attempt.* She didn't complete the story.

"This is a farce," Deloria muttered.

Shut up! You're going to live, Dee. Live. You hear me? And then I can call you a selfish, weak and arrogant ass and not feel awful doing so. Now do as you're damn well ordered!

The *Belle-Elaise* flew out of the cloud bank. A line of lights twinkled above and to the right: the coast of Whiteshores island. Gently, so as not to turn the engines into infernos, Deloria edged for starboard.

"Orders confirmed, Base Fifty-three."

Understood.

"Funny." Deloria deliberated whether to say what followed. "You were looking out to Whiteshores island. When I first saw you. Funny, life, isn't it? Don't you think?"

The radio was silent awhile. *You can see me now.*

Deloria looked into the night, lower than Whiteshore, toward Burtonhead coast.

"Haven't been home awhile," Deloria said. "They made the golf course into an airfield, didn't they? So that light there, I presume, is the radio tower."

I'll be waiting for you. No sugar, splash of milk, yes?

Deloria's eyes watered. Damn that girl. Now they were both victims of hope.

Elaise

Deloria Hendlethwaite was a strange egg. Home schooled in her village of Bixley-on-Heigh, smug and infuriating and forever uttering strange thoughts. Elaise was simply in awe of her. The last year since they met had been wicked fun, each day an adventure, each month racing by with giddiest delight.

"I'd hoped for a better view," Elaise said.

The two of them watched the rain batter against the windows of the airship's starboard promenade. Behind them, fellow passengers wandered by, making up for the lack of a view by patronizing the shops and bistros the promenade offered.

"I think that's Whiteshores," Deloria said, pointing at a blurry silhouette beyond the glass. "Seen from the other side, as we do when we walk the coast's edge. There's the waterfalls, see?"

"That's just raindrops on the glass," Elaise replied. "I'm so frightfully sorry, dear. I'd meant for you to see all the planes and airships and what-not. The marvels of the air. Not drizzle."

"Nonsense. I'm looking at an airship as we speak." Deloria gestured all about. "And she's a beauty. Top of the line." Her eyes met Elaise's and she smiled. "Besides, have you ever known us not to have fun, hmm? No damp weekend has defeated us yet."

Elaise nodded. "Many have tried. All failed."

They were dressed as one would expect eighteen-year-old women to dress: short skirt over jodhpurs, shirt and cardigan, hair scraped back into buns. Deloria looked a different creature without her long dresses and pin curls. In exile from her true self. Perhaps they both were. Their birthdays – and therefore their choice days – were five months away and only two days apart. Deloria would choose the feminine path, of course, despite her love of things like planes, and so would Elaise. Most women did. It would be a fine time. Choosing dresses, styling each other's hair. They both talked about it. While in Deloria's attic bedroom, she had convinced Elaise to wear one of her dresses, though Elaise was comically too short for it and had stumbled into her while tripping over the hem. Elaise smiled to think of it, stumbling into Deloria's arms like that.

"What *are* you smiling at, Elaise?"

"Oh, nothing..."

Deloria grinned. She stopped and glanced about.

"We're turning." The engines' dual hum had shifted pitch. "Turning back."

Elaise felt it in her stomach, her legs.

People were looking to one another. Their chatter hushed to mutterings.

Overhead, a loudspeaker squealed to life: *Attention all passengers, attention all passengers, we are returning to Burtonhead Aerodrome. Prepare for disembarkation at 11.01 AM. We ask that you remain calm.*

The muttering grew louder.

Deloria was searching the sky beyond the window, her face close to the rain-dappled glass.

Elaise tugged Deloria's wrist. "The radio bar. Come on, before they think to switch it off."

They ran along the promenade, catching looks as they passed, and soon reached the bar, a saloon that played the Islands Service on speakers above a serving hatch. Passengers had already gathered there. Elaise and Deloria were too young to enter but no one said anything when they did. Someone said something about things sighted at the Rend, that hole into nowhere that had emerged at the center of the Archipelago a year back.

Hundreds of them, the wireless said. The voice was some reporter with a New Isles accent. *They were pouring from the Rend, their hides black, as if made from the Rend itself, an endless legion, their wings like night. Flames. I see flames everywhere as we fly over Edmaine Isle. Not a field untouched, not a house. These...dragons...they had no pity on them. No pity...*

"What is this?" Elaise heard herself say.

One is in pursuit of us now. Our plane is faster, keeping ahead. Its body is a...bright shadow, like a silhouette glistening with, with malice. Eyes burning coals. I can hardly look at it. It hurts the eye to look at. It...shouldn't exist.

Every eye in the bar was wide and searching, each mouth open and mute. A palm gripped Elaise's shoulder.

"Let's go," Deloria said. Elaise couldn't move. Deloria grabbed both her shoulders and dragged her out of the place. Del's expression was blank but her eyes studied every passenger they passed.

She knows panic is in the offing, Elaise thought. *She's right.*

They got to their twin cabin and Deloria locked the door behind them. Elaise leaned against the side of her bunk.

"It's over," she muttered. "The whole world's over..." Deloria stared at the door. "Well?"

"I'll believe the world's over when I see it," Deloria said. "No sooner."

"Del—"

"Edmaine Isle is two thousand miles or more. The reporter said they couldn't match his plane's speed. He's probably in a Whitley Monarch or the like. Max speed two hundred and ninety seven miles per hour."

"What are you saying?"

"I'm saying we're safe here and now. Safe, Elaise. Everyone is scared now because it's all so unknown. But we'll get the measure of 'em. First time you take a punch in the guts it seems the end of everything. But after? You toughen. You learn how to hit back."

"Deloria, you've never been in a fight in your life."

"No. But I think that's soon to change for the bally lot of us."

"I've long admired your facility to face harsh facts," Elaise told her, "but I *really* don't need an exhibition of it right now."

Deloria drew a long breath. She turned from the cabin door and embraced Elaise. Held her so tight, so close. Elaise placed her forehead on Deloria's shoulder and fought not to cry.

They kept like that for some time, swaying in silence, then Elaise moved her mouth, tracing it across Deloria's jaw. She drifted higher, to her cheek, so warm and soft. Terrified, she kissed her there. Deloria hesitated, then, lips trembling, her mouth met with Elaise's. A first kiss, then a series, tender and uncertain and mad.

It made no sense. They were both girls, both set on walking the path of women. If Elaise were meaning to choose the masculine path then maybe, yes, but they both enjoyed dresses and eyeshadow and curling their hair. It made no sense. And yet it did. It *did*. So very much, and not even the end of the world could tell them no.

Deloria

Water vapor dappled the canopy. Not rain: spray from the waterfalls ahead carried by the winds. *This won't work*, she told herself.

"Base Fifty-three?"

Receiving.

"You were right. I'm weak. I should have told you I was leaving. I…" The fuselage rattled and her heart jumped. But it was nothing, a change in outside pressure. "I thought if I left without saying goodbye you would hate me. I needed you to hate me."

Why?

"Because you needed it, Base Fifty-three. You'd be free of me quicker. Move on." Deloria looked about. Everything was getting mistier. "Indeed, far better you hate me now, now it's come to this. But I should have faced you. Told you. That was weakness."

The *Belle-Elaise* entered the shadow of Whiteshores island and a darkness entered the cockpit that was more than the night, that Deloria could feel in her stomach.

I wore a dress, the radio said, *the day we were old enough to decide. We decided we would take the path of women, remember? I walked down the street in my dress I'd bought especially and I couldn't wait to get to your house and see you in your dress. But your mother answered. She was proud, in her cold way, you had taken the other path. Proud you were signing up to fight. I had to smile, G-for-George. I had to nod and agree. And, inside, I knew I had been a fool all along.*

The fuselage began to rattle. Water lashing down, the outer edge of the torrent that fell forever.

You never cared for people, Deloria, the radio continued. *Not for me. And not for this silly war either. It's all for your bloody airplanes. You even took a masculine path you hated just so you could be with them.*

Deloria couldn't reply. She was hitting the deluge faster than expected. Ahead she thought she could see a gap between the raging waters, a space where the barrage might allow a tiny plane.

So I don't hate you, Del, much as it might make you glad. I'm happy for you. Happy. I was always the other woman. Your real love you're sat in. And I wish you both the best, by God I wish you the very best right now. I want you to come through. You and that damn alloy bitch, no doubt you've a name for her. You and, and…

Static cut into Deloria's headphones. It seemed part of the torrent all around. She'd misjudged the misty space between the falls: too tight. A wingtip would be hit and the *Belle-Elaise* would roll and that would be it, down, down.

The falling water all around was white with moonlight and movement, the static in her ears pure noise. Last card, she thought, last card. She shifted the control column and the *Belle-Elaise* made a starboard roll, her wingtips vertical, and all Deloria's weight lurched on to her right shoulder. The cockpit rattled and shook, the engines pushing to the point, drowning.

Last card…

Elaise

"*Belle-Elaise…*"

The words blew over her lips. *Belle-Elaise*.

The radio had fallen silent. Only the pitter-patter of rain upon the radio tower's windows remained. Elaise cursed herself and placed the receiver to her mouth.

"G-for-George!" she barked. "Request status report G-for… Deloria! Speak to me!"

Silence, terrible and cruel, stretching each second. Elaise closed her eyes, begged chance and fate and God above for the radio to utter a single word.

Looks like I owe your boffins an apology, Base Fifty-three. The old bird's through. Engines washed.

Elaise almost squeaked. But she wanted to laugh, to…

She controlled herself. "Congratulations, pilot. Now come to me, I mean come to Burtonhead island. If you can't make the strip you'll have to land in a field. I'll send a team."

Should make the strip. Seems I've a spark of life in the engines, so I can more than glide. I'll know better when I come out of this cloud bank and see Burtonhead. Better have that tea for me, eh?

"No sugar," Elaise said. She leaned back in her chair. "Splash of milk. You know, we shall have a lot to talk about. Don't you think?"

Talk? I want to hold you, hold you and never let go. Not ever— A pause. *Apologies, Base Fifty-three. I'm rather elated up here.*

"I want to hold you too, Deloria." She laughed. She could not remember the last time she had laughed but it must have been with Deloria. "I want to walk through fields of bluebells with you, you hear me? You absolute cad, I want to, to kiss you… I want a cottage by the shore when this war is all packed up and gone. I want to grow old with you, Deloria Hendlethwaite, you hear me?"

She could hear the cockpit's interior, the hum of the dying engines, but not her woman. Her love.

"G-for-George, come in G-for-George," she tried.

I can see it, Deloria said.

"You and me?" She couldn't help but grin.

The dragon.

Elaise froze. "What?"

It's ahead of me. I'm flying above it. Deloria had that familiar revulsion in her tone, as all did who set eyes upon those impossible beasts.

"Has it seen you, G-for-George?"

Negative. Bloody thing's making for the coast. It was never hunting planes, it just took an opportunity when it saw us. The voice paused. *Base Fifty-three, I think its heading for you.*

Elaise stretched over the console desk and pulled the red cord that hung from the wall. Sirens went off across the airstrip. She would have to go. Leave the tower to the safety of the bunkers. She sat back in her chair and picked up the receiver.

"Don't get its attention," she said. "You hear me? Decelerate, land in a field."

That's a negative, Base Fifty-three. Deloria's voice was shaved of all feeling. *I've got the jump on it.*

"You've no guns," Elaise said, half whispering as if the dragon might hear, then remembering she would not be heard over the siren's blare. "You said you've no guns."

I'm going in. I'm faster. It won't know what hit it.

Comprehension hit Elaise like a punch.

"No!" She tried reason. "You can't know it's coming for this airstrip. It's not coming for me."

It's coming for someone, Elaise. It always will, unless I settle its hash here and now.

"Del, please."

Listen to me. Listen. There'll be a better world after we win this war. A peaceful world, a just world, the world we should have made long ago, where women can wear what they like and each human soul is his brother's keeper. I know it. I know it because you showed me a heart I never could have imagined. Hearts like yours will make that world, Elaise, not mine. A pause then, just the siren's scream and the hiss of static. *Be brave. I love you.*

The transmission cut.

"No!"

Elaise screamed. She wept amid the lights and sirens. She stumbled to the window and searched the dark heavens above. Through watering eyes she spied a flicker, like a tiny red comet. Then nothing.

Biographies

Charlotte V. Bond – *The Overlooked Dragon Keeper*
(First Publication)
Charlotte is an author of horror and dark fantasy. She is also a freelance editor, ghostwriter, and podcaster, co-hosting the award-winning podcast, Breaking the Glass Slipper. Her micro collection *The Watcher in the Woods* won the British Fantasy Society's award for Best Collection in 2021. Her dragon novellas *The Fireborne Blade* and *The Bloodless Princes* were published by Tordotcom in 2024, and feature a sweet, sapphic romance pitted against death and dragons.

A.M. Croll – *The Princess and the Thief*
(First Publication)
A.M. Croll is a writer from London who loves all things fantasy. They are a former Foyle Young Poet of the Year, and have a degree in Classics. When not writing, they work in a school for autistic teenagers. They are represented by Maddy Belton at Madeleine Milburn Literary Agency, and can be found on Instagram @ amcrollwriter.

Maria D'Antonio-Reich – *The Girl Who Kissed the Sun*
(First Publication)
Maria D'Antonio-Reich is a speculative fiction writer whose works have appeared in the *Spirit of the Wolf* anthology and *Dirty Magick Magazine*. At her day job, she performs ultrasounds for high-risk pregnancies, and when she needs a screen break, she still feels the itch to create. The ensuing sewing and crocheting has resulted in an impressive fabric stash. She lives in New Orleans with her husband and two scruffy mutts. See more at mariadantonioreich.com.

Deborah L. Davitt – *The Last Dragon*
(First Publication)
Deborah L. Davitt was raised in Nevada, but currently lives in Houston, Texas with her husband and son. Her award-winning poetry and prose have appeared in over seventy journals, including *F&SF*, *Asimov's*, *Analog*, and *Lightspeed*. For more about her work, including her poetry collections, *The Gates of Never*, *Bounded by Eternity*, *From Voyages Unreturning*, *Xenoforming*, and *To Love Unquietly*, see deborahldavitt.com.

Kit Englard – *Shattered Vows*
(First Publication)
Kit Englard is a DeafBlind romantic fantasy author whose stories draw on her background in Disability Studies. Her fiction examines how power, agency, and identity shape the lives of disabled characters within fantastical worlds. She is the author of *The Nocturne Cage Trilogy*, a dark fantasy romance of divine magic, forbidden love, and sacred desire. When not writing, she can often be found hiking with her guide dog or vanishing into research rabbit holes.

Caren Hahn – *Foreword*
Caren Hahn is an award-winning fantasy and suspense author best known for the *Hatched* dragon adventure series, and *Owl Creek*, a small town suspense series. She discovered at a young age that the only thing more thrilling than reading fictional adventures was writing them herself, though it took the disruption from a global pandemic before she was driven to share her stories with the world. Caren lives with her family in the Pacific Northwest.

Kay Hanifen – *The Lindwyrm's Wife*
(First Publication)
Kay Hanifen was born on a Friday the 13th and once lived for three months in a haunted castle. So, obviously, she had to become a horror writer. Her work has appeared in over 100 anthologies and magazines. Her first anthology as an editor, *Till the Yule Log Burns Out*, was published in 2024. Her first novel, *The Last Ballard*, debuted in 2025.

When she's not consuming pop culture with the voraciousness of a vampire at a 24-hour blood bank, you can usually find her with her black cats or at kayhanifenauthor.wordpress.com.

Sarah Hozumi – *The Name*
(First Publication)
Sarah Hozumi is a writer who has lived near Tokyo for about sixteen years. To read short stories she's had published, and to read her blog mostly about all things Japan, please visit sarahhozumi.com. You can also follow her on Facebook at sarahjhozumi and Instagram at @author.sarah.hozumi.

Valerie Hunter – *A Worthy Oath*
(First Publication)
Valerie Hunter teaches high school English, and has an MFA in writing for children and young adults from Vermont College of Fine Arts. She writes in an attempt to make sense of the world, and has a penchant for creating awkward and misfit characters. Her stories have appeared in publications including *Beneath Ceaseless Skies*, *Capsule Stories*, *Baubles from Bones*, and *Sonder*, as well as multiple anthologies. She can be found on Instagram @somanystories_solittletime.

Georgina Kamsika – *We Are Not Them*
(First Publication)
Georgina Kamsika writes about monsters and ghosts and aliens. Sometimes the people kiss. Sometimes the monsters do too! Georgina is currently writing an interactive fiction game for Choice of Games, but when the coding gets too much, she finds she must write a short story or two. This is one of them. For more information, find her at kamsika.com and @GKamsika on most socials.

Abigail Kelly – *Kingkiller*
(First Publication)
Abigail Kelly is an author-illustrator of alternate histories, love stories, and women with drive. She's the author of *The New Protectorate Series*, which is heavily inspired by her love of history and science. After nearly a decade as a bookseller in San Francisco's independent bookshops,

she will always love putting books in eager hands and celebrating the city that inspires so many of her stories. See more at abigailkkelly.com.

Sasha Kielman – *On the Wing of a Prayer*
(First Publication)
Sasha Kielman is an attorney in Washington, DC, USA. In addition to her story in this anthology, she has short stories published in the anthologies *Living With Demons*, *Crimson Bones*, *Unleashed: Set Your Monster Free*, *Wickedness & Wonder*, and the forthcoming *Wichelen Vol. 2*. You can find her on BlueSky and Tumblr @SashaKielman.

Samara Lo – *A Thousand Lifetimes Between Us*
(First Publication)
Samara Lo is an author from Sydney, Australia. She was shortlisted for the Penguin Literary Prize 2025 and was recipient of the CreateNSW – Next Steps Writing Grant 24/25. In the past, she has also been awarded the Nan Tien Temple Childrens' Writers and Illustrators Residency, Westwords Emerging Writer's Residency at Varuna House and the Copyright Agency-WestWords Fellowship. Her short fiction includes 'Witch Ash' (*Meniscus Literary Journal*), 'After Me, the Flood' (*Shadows on the Water* by Flame Tree), 'Songs of Yesterday's Tomorrows' (*The Saltbush Review: Issue 3*) and others.

J.I. Locatelli – *Through Fumbles and Flames*
(First Publication)
J.I. Locatelli lives in Miami, Florida with her wife, Natalia, and dog, Antigone. She's fascinated with the actions and interactions of people, which led to a degree in brain and cognitive science and a habit of writing. She wishes she was more of a sunshine-and-beaches person, but prefers a warm cup of tea, thunderstorms and her laptop. Her short fiction can be found in *Elegant Literature* and *Story Street*.

Damien Mckeating – *Broken Spell and Shattered Glass*
(First Publication)
Damien Mckeating was born, and soon after developed a love of fantasy and the supernatural. He has written for radio, comics, and prose collections. His short stories have found homes in a

range of anthologies and he is currently awaiting the publication of his first novel, *Tallulah Belle*. Sometimes he remembers to blog at skeletonbutler.wordpress.com but often he doesn't, because writing stories is more fun than writing blog posts.

Isabel McKeough – *Sparks by the Morwich River*
(First Publication)
Isabel McKeough is a Sydney-based author and a graduate of the Australian Writers' Centre. She has a passion for all things speculative-fiction and loves exploring what it means to be human in unfamiliar contexts. She is currently studying creative writing at the University of Technology, Sydney and has fiction published in *Far Futures Book Four*, *Jacaranda Journal*, *AntipodeanSF*, and *The Miserere Review* among others. Find out more at isabelmckeough.com.au or on Instagram @isabelmckeough.writes.

M. McNamara – *The Spell of Edrium*
(First Publication)
M. McNamara is a Brisbane-based author who dabbles in fantasy, science fiction, and a smidge of horror. She has written three books and many short stories; her work has appeared in *Of Metal and Magic*, *The Pink Hydra*, and the *Murderfish* anthology, among other publications. Her short story 'Welcome to the Fantasy Fair' is also a podcast on *Connor Reads Books*. If you like her work, please visit her website at mmcnamarabooks.com, or on Instagram @m_mcnamara_books.

Arda Mori – *Mercury of the Night Queen*
(First Publication)
Arda Mori is a Malaysian-Chinese writer with an incurable weakness for dark fantasy and horror. Her poetry and stories are featured in magazines including *The Deadlands*, *All Worlds Wayfarer*, *Apparition Lit* and Fifth Wheel Press. She currently lives in Malaysia with a cat; by day, she tackles the dragon that is technology consulting. Find her online at ardamori.wordpress.com.

Kevin Potter – *Heart of Lightning, Blade of Shadow*
(First Publication)
Kevin Potter is an award-winning author who enjoys spending time masquerading as dragons larger than some cities! Although somewhat of a recluse, he loves discussing the three F's (faith, fantasy, and fandom) with readers, especially on Substack. His labour of love is his ongoing epic fantasy series, *Blood of the Dragons*, which resulted from taking seriously the adage, "If you can't find what you want to read, write it." He lives in Oklahoma with his daughter and several animals.

Mere Rain – *Of Mutton and Marriage Vows*
(First Publication)
Mere Rain is an author of speculative fiction and romance, often at the same time. Mere has written several romances that are available from JMS Books, and also short fantasy and science fiction stories that have appeared in periodicals such as *Astral*, *Fix the World*, and *Mad Scientist Journal*. Feel free to reach out on social media and share book recommendations or pet photos!

Mia K. Rose – *Hollow*
(First Publication)
Mia K. Rose lives in the Gold Coast, Australia (Yugambeh Country) with her husband, two children, and two Cavalier King Charles Spaniels. When not writing, you'll find her in a D&D campaign, reading the latest romantasy, adding to her book trophy collection, or on a pilates reformer to assist with her hEDS.

Laura Shenton – *The Heart of Aethermoor*
(First Publication)
Laura Shenton is probably best known for her music non-fiction, particularly *Dance With the Devil: The Cozy Powell Story* (Wymer Publishing) and *Tommy Bolin: In and Out of Deep Purple* (Sonicbond Publishing). Her fiction books are character-driven with a short, punchy narrative that gets straight to the point – typically novellas and novelettes. Genres include gothic, fantasy,

and adventure (mostly, with the occasional diversion). Laura's children's books are simple, accessible, and fun – an excellent choice for youngsters with fertile imaginations who are just beginning their reading journey.

Liv Strom – *Shifting the Scales*
(First Publication)
Liv Strom is a Swedish-Swiss writer with stories in *Apex Magazine*, *Hexagon*, and *Mystery Magazine*, among others. She has been included on Tor.com's Must-Read Speculative Fiction and reviewed on *Locus*. As a writer with aphantasia (she cannot visualize anything), she considers it a magic power to write characters that live on in others' minds. She is the author of *Tales of Bones & Roses*, a fairy-tale-influenced romantasy series. She can be found online at livstromwrites.com and on Instagram as @authorlivstrom.

Susan Taitel – *Lilt and Luster Spring Newsletter*
(Originally Published in *Interstellar Flight Magazine*, 2024)
Susan Taitel was born and grew up in Chicago, Illinois. She now lives in Minnesota and thinks wistfully of the comparatively mild Chicago winters. Her work has appeared in *Nature Futures*, *Cast of Wonders*, and *Baffling Magazine*, among others. She can be found online at susantaitel.com, on Instagram as @susantaitel, and on Bluesky as @susantaitel.bsky.social. If you want to find her in the real world, try checking the nearest craft store.

Nemma Wollenfang – *Draconitis: Acute & Chronic*
(First Publication)
Nemma Wollenfang is an MSc postgraduate and prize-winning writer who lives in Northern England. Over fifty of her short works have been published in various venues, including: Titan Books, Chicken Soup for the Soul and previously with Flame Tree Publishing. Some of her novelettes have featured in Amazon #1 bestselling anthologies, and she is a Speculative Literature Foundation grant winner and a participant of Writers on the Moon. She can be found on Amazon and Facebook.

J.L. Worrad – *A Matter of Life and Dragons*
(First Publication)
J.L. Worrad lives in Leicester, England, and has for almost all his life. He is the author of the fantasy novels *Pennyblade* and *The Keep Within* (Titan Books). In 2011 Worrad attended Clarion, the science fiction writing workshop held at the University of California, and has fond memories of all the hummingbirds. See more at jamesworrad.com.

Illustrations

Key cover art: Xinyue Chen
Xinyue Chen is an illustrator and book artist based in New York, mostly working in traditional media. Since receiving their BFA from the Central Academy of Fine Arts in Beijing and their MFA from the School of Visual Arts in New York, they have provided editorial illustrations, book illustrations and designs for many renowned clients, including the *NY Times*, *Scientific American*, Bloomberg and many more.

Illustration page 7: Taateli
Taateli (@taatelija) is a hobbyist artist from Finland. Her biggest inspirations are historical, romantic and fantasy themes and she excels at both digital art and gouache painting, having held multiple art exhibitions.

Illustration page 14: Faziela Harris
Faziela (@lilium.artistry) is a Cape Town based anime artist and urban fantasy author who spends her time weaving magic into everything she creates.

Illustration page 405: Jeff Kovach
Jeff Kovach is an artist and musician. He spends his time playing the Sitar and contemplating the universe while posting on Reddit. More of his art can be found at ko-fi.com/revx1212.

Illustration page 414: Nemma Wollenfang
Nemma is a prize-winning speculative fiction writer first. Her stories have appeared in several venues, including books by Flame Tree. She can be found on Facebook and Amazon.

Romantic Fantasy

Flame Tree Romantic Fantasy is a captivating blend of our signature Gothic Fantasy collections with the passion and magic of Romantasy. This new series featuring stories selected from open submissions is an exciting addition to Flame Tree's Beyond & Within, Myths, Gods & Immortals, Gothic Fantasy, Classic Stories and Epic Tales Collections, all beautifully presented, perfect as a gift and offering a lifetime of reading pleasure.

OFFICE*US* Atlas

Edited by
Eva Franch i Gilabert
Michael Kubo
Ana Miljački
Ashley Schafer

Lars Müller Publishers
Storefront for Art and Architecture

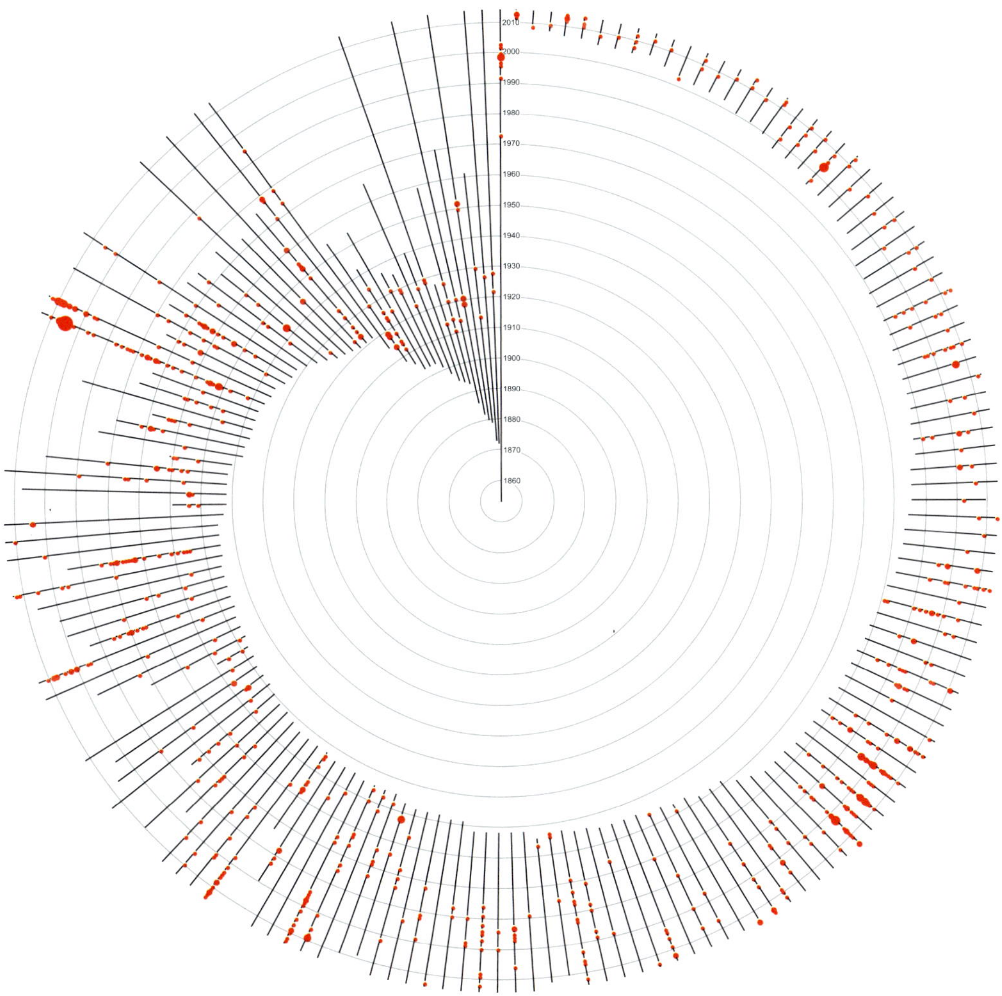

OFFICE *US* Atlas

Atlas is the second book in the series of publications for Office*US*, US Pavilion, 14th International Architecture Exhibition–la Biennale di Venezia

Editors

Eva Franch i Gilabert
Michael Kubo
Ana Miljački
Ashley Schafer

Assitant Editor

Ann Lok Lui

Layout

Sam Ghantous
Jessica Jorge
Patrick Evan Little

Infographics

Gabriel Kozlowski

Copy Editors

Kyle Barker
Abby Bussel
Sarah Hirschman

Image Permissions

Irina Chernyakova

Text Authors

Christianna Bonin [CB]
Irina Chernyakova [IC]
Andrew Colopy [AC]
Nathan Friedman [NF]
Juan Jofre [JJ]
Michael Kubo [MK]
Amanda Reeser Lawrence [ARL]
Ann Lok Lui [AL]
Ana Miljački [AM]
Deepa Ramaswamy [DR]
Jacob Reidel [JR]
Ashley Schafer [AS]
Austin Smith [AWS]
Fred Tang [FT]
Michael Waldrep [MW]
Rixt Woudstra [RW]
Wenfei Xu [WX]

Design

Pentagram: Natasha Jen,
Jeffrey Waldman; Yenwei Liu, Rona Binay,
Giovanni Pamio, Leo Porto

Publisher

Lars Müller Publishers
Zürich, Switzerland
www.lars-mueller-publishers.com

Printing

Passavia, Passau, Germany

Typefaces

Arial and Times New Roman are the typefaces of the Office*US* project. These two typefaces are among the most mundane and readily available on the market, and as such are frequently used for efficiency by US offices. With a few necessary exceptions, all Office*US* deliverables, including this publication, are designed with these two generic typefaces.

The editors thank the following sources for permission to reproduce articles in *Office*US *Atlas*:

L'Architecture d'Aujourd'hui / © L'Architecture d'Aujourd'hui
Architectural Design (AD) / Reproduced with permission from Wiley
Architects' Journal
The Architect's Newspaper
Architectural Record
The Architectural Review
Arts & Architecture / Courtesy and © David Travers
Bauen + Wohnen
Blueprint / Progressive Media International
Harvard Design Magazine
The Los Angeles Times © Ruth Ryon, Reprinted with permission
Oculus / AIA NY Chapter
Mimar / © Concept Media / Aga Khan Trust for Culture / Brian Brace Taylor
RIBA Journal
Saudi Aramco World Magazine
Urban Land / Reprinted with permission from Urban Land, a publication of the Urban Land Institute. © 2007 by the Urban Land Institute

ISBN 978-3-03778-438-9

This publication has been made possible with funding from The Graham Foundation.

OFFICE*US* Atlas

On Office*US*

Occupying the US Pavilion at the 14th International Architecture Biennale in Venice from June 7 through November 23, 2014, Office*US* presented a global history of the architectural office while mapping aspirations for its future. The exhibition contained an archive of nearly one thousand projects produced by US offices abroad between 1914 and 2014—the Office*US* Repository—that located the intersection between the operations of US architecture firms and their international impact over the last century. An office of six partners worked within the Repository over the 25 weeks of the Biennale, in collaboration with global outpost offices and a series of visiting experts, with the mission to look backward and forward simultaneously, submitting historical material to contemporary critique while projecting alternative futures out of it. The chronologically organized project binders of the Repository were punctuated by a series of 25 OfficeUS Issues, outlining weekly investigations and debates based on pressing historical and contemporary questions. The project—both archive and office—served simultaneously as an archaeology of global architectural firms and a critical challenge to them.

The projects compiled and displayed in the Office*US* Repository may have been regarded as singular interventions by their architects, clients, or inhabitants. More often than not, however, the activities of US architecture firms abroad have been analogous to the country's fraught political and economic international involvements, historically in sync with more or less benign forms of imperialism. In order to produce a prehistory of the contemporary global office and influence its future course, Office*US* provided a transversal cut through this body of work. Conceived as an operational, experiential, and historical mirror of past and contemporary concerns, the exhibition provided a platform for projection and critique and a challenge that demanded visitors' sustained attention to the depth of work on display, assembled for the first time as a totality by Office*US*. In order to disallow the simple consumption of prepackaged history often expected of such exhibitions, the organization of the Repository purposely denied any easy classification through political or social clichés, formal discourses, or facile oppositions between supposedly "critical" or "corporate" practices. Instead, it aimed to produce conversations about the ideological, ethical, and aesthetic dimensions of architectural production through new historical grounds and references.

While recasting a number of elements that have together constituted the architectural office—from the drafting desk to the meeting table, the organizational chart, and the materials and project library—Office*US* also rewired relationships between partners, clients, consultants, and critics. The Office*US* Repository, which served as the library for both visitors and the live office, was presented neither as a definitive body of research nor as the final word on this history. With ideas serving in place of clients, and all of their interlocutors acting as potential double agents, the Office*US* Partners examined the contemporary implications of global work through the complex and problematic history presented in the archive.

While the first publication of this project, Office*US Agenda*, provided essays looking backwards from a multiplicity of contemporary voices, Office*US Atlas*, the second in the series of Office*US* books, collects a key press archive of US architectural production abroad and the transformations of the US architectural office over the last hundred years. In highlighting some of the major historical narratives threaded through the century, the book uses the timeline of offices and projects established in the exhibition as its backbone. Office*US Atlas* functions as a map, a seed for future research, and an instigator of further discussions regarding our architectural pasts and futures.

— Eva Franch i Gilabert, Ana Miljački, and Ashley Schafer

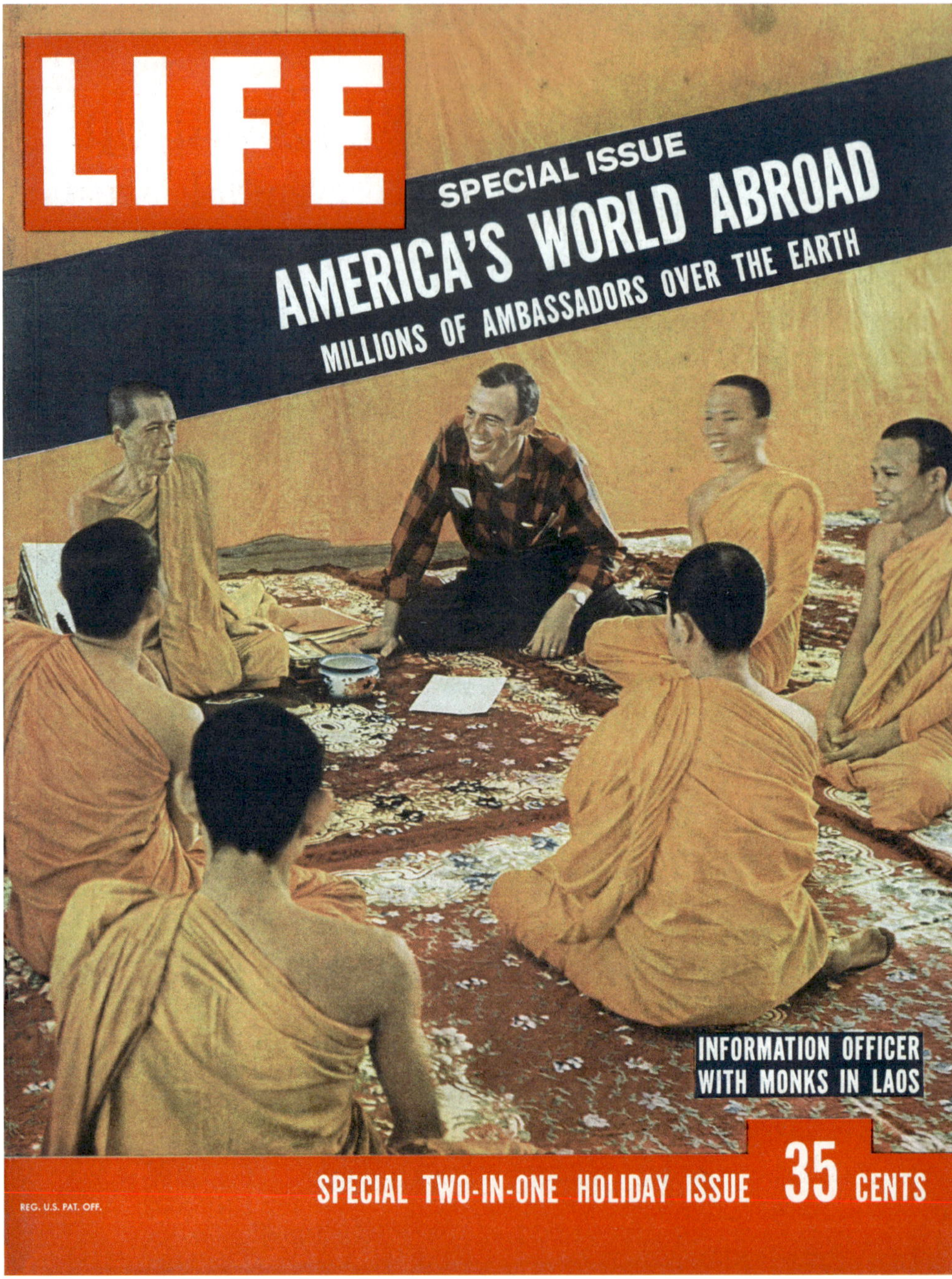

"America's World Abroad," *Life*, December 23, 1957. John Dominis/The LIFE Picture Collection/Getty Images

On Office*US* Atlas

The object in your hands may send signals of authority or comprehensiveness. Despite its encyclopedic dimensions, its aim is rather different: to open doors to further investigation while outlining the curatorial choices at stake in producing the Office*US* Repository for the US Pavilion in Venice. Indeed, Office*US Atlas* presents only a small selection of the immense press archive that was compiled for the Office*US* exhibition as a critical mirror of US architects' global operations since 1914. Though it is by no means the first of its genre, this compilation is unlike any other.

The material included here is best understood as an extension of the exhibition—one that benefits from the physicality and temporality required by the book. This same type of attention span was deliberately demanded by the physical space of Office*US*, but its impossible fulfillment within a short visit to the exhibition was part of the point. The *Atlas* is thus a reduction of the Office*US* Repository in the culinary sense: it is a concentrate made up of the most potent extracts from the immense collection of documents that were gathered around the offices and projects on display in Venice, reorganized in this curatorial book-object in support of specific areas of historical concern.

Whereas the exhibition sought to correlate the personal curiosity and patience of visitors with the depth of experience they would take away and provided resources upon which to mount potential critiques and hopes for the future, the *Atlas* exposes some of the main historical narratives that guided the selection of offices, projects, and documents for the archive itself. From early Beaux Arts-inspired urban plans designed for cities in US territories at the turn of the twentieth century to the emergence of architectural megafirms one hundred years later, these narratives traverse both geography and time, highlighting the instruments and conditions that enabled US architecture firms to work internationally, and how such engagements shaped those practices in return. Throughout this history, the operation of US architects abroad has been aligned with the larger political, economic, and cultural interests of US institutions and actors during a period that was famously dubbed "The American Century" in 1941 by media magnate Henry Luce, founder of *Fortune* and, at the time of his pronouncement, the owner of *Architectural Forum* and chief editor of *Life*.[1]

The twenty sections of this volume frame key historical narratives through which to enter this century of US architectural export. The *Atlas* opens with the professionalization of architectural practice in the United States in the second half of the nineteenth century, and the episodes that follow outline the successive transformations of both offices and their products in response to political, economic, and technological forces. The story of international philanthropy, for example, begins in the early twentieth century in China and Japan, only to be recaptured in different forms in post-independence India and Pakistan. Cold War politics track through a series of interrelated narratives in the postwar period, from the international hotel chains enabled by the Marshall Plan to the US Embassy program and the national pavilions built for trade fairs and world expositions under the guidance of the United States Information Agency. Oil and other global resource flows, the deregulation of markets,

(1) Henry Luce, "The American Century," *Life* (February 17, 1941): 61–65.

"Machine Made America," *The Architectural Review*, May 1957

"America," *Zodiac* 8, 1961

"USA," *Bau* 5/6, 1965

"USA 71," *L'Architecture d'Aujourd'hui*, August-September 1971

the demand for iconicity, building booms, and other contingent forces have been among the historical factors that have drawn US architecture firms into foreign contexts over the last century. Traversing these conditions, the forms of professionalization and expertise required to operate offices and design projects across great distances have led to dramatic fluctuations in the size and scope of US firms and fueled the complexity of their entanglements abroad.

Each of the historical narratives in the *Atlas* is structured around a dossier of evidentiary artifacts, including period articles reproduced with all of the traces of their previous lives in bound library volumes or other archival collections. While few of these publications harbored overtly radical intentions, their status as trade journals marks them as key megaphones for the profession, and, in some cases, channels for official governmental policies.[2] The *Atlas* includes these journal articles as documents that embody the symptoms of the eras that produced them, ranging from *The Brickbuilder* at the turn of the twentieth century to Luce's *Architectural Forum* after World War II to more recent publications like *The Architects Newspaper*, among a rich catalog of sources. The fanfare, criticality, and preoccupations of these articles are among the most telling indicators of the US architecture profession's understanding of its role in the global arena. The exhibition of the Office*US* Repository in Venice included additional material from popular magazines like *Life*, *Time*, and *Fortune*, as well as from newspapers like *The New York Times*—all valuable for their address to a broader audience and for their colorful, propagandistic overtones—and these references are present throughout the *Atlas*, as well as in the bibliography of Repository articles included at the end of this volume.

In addition to this evidentiary material from the architectural press, many of the narratives in the *Atlas* incorporate a singularly illuminating archival document, such as Marion Mahony's exhortation to spread the gospel of democracy in "the Magic of America," excerpts from the presentation folio of SOM's 1946 Creole Petroleum Town in Amuay Bay, Venezuela, advertisements for Hilton Hotels abroad, or W.W. Rostow's memorandum on the controversial *Unfinished Business* exhibition for the US Pavilion at the 1958 Universal and International Exhibition in Brussels. Throughout the book, infographics visualize the geographic and temporal extents of the story in question, as threads extracted from the mass of data compiled in the archive. In the tradition of the historical atlas and its graphic depiction of droughts, migrations, or the rise and fall of empires, the synchronic map view is presented here in a number of instances as both an antidote to the chronological accumulation of projects and firms and a visual aid for discerning historical patterns.

At a time when thematization rules architectural publishing, and when nonlinear thinking is often first nature, the Office*US* Repository relies on chronology for its structure of offices and projects, and this structure has been carried from the exhibition into the book. Like the twenty-five Office*US* Issues tackled in the exhibition, the narratives in the *Atlas* identify thematic threads across this chronology, and readers are invited to make transversal connections between them. Insisting on the historical patterns through which certain sets of ideas, acts, and buildings have been related, the project accounts for the circumstances of history while emphasizing the importance of historicity for architectural thinking.

Rather than providing specific readings of the archive through narrowly defined or linear stories, the Office*US* exhibition provided tools to navigate this

(2) *Architectural Forum*, for example, was purchased in 1932 by Henry Luce and was, as historian Jane Loeffler has argued, a forum for Luce's anticommunist Cold War rhetoric. See Loeffler, *The Architecture of Diplomacy: Building America's Embassies* (New York: Princeton Architectural Press, 1998).

collection in ways that might allow for different connections, histories, and judgments to be made by each visitor. In the context of the Venice Biennale, a venue in which affirmation is often implicit, aesthetic products are celebrated and deemed to be of value to the nations represented, and critique, when present, has been sanctioned to signify "democratic openness," storytelling is easily co-opted, flattened, "pinned," and "liked." The challenge, then, was to present the work in a way that would both problematize the nature of contemporary exhibition consumption and preserve the irreconcilable elements of the hundred-year history of US architects operating in a global context. This led us to imagine how a curated archive might summon judgment and imagination in the contemporary subject, the curious navigator of information, the *Google* searcher, or the indifferent critic whose a priori dismissal is structured by the very nature of their involvement with the effort. The curatorial desire for projective engagements with the archive, including the operation of the Office*US* partners upon it, aligned with the function of the Office*US* Repository as a looking glass of sorts. The partners—and those audience members willing to participate—were invited to perform like the angel of history invoked by Walter Benjamin, modeled after Paul Klee's *Angelus Novus*, moving forward while turned backward to cast its gaze upon the ever-accumulating debris of the past.[3] Readers of the *Atlas* are similarly invited to traverse through the material presented here based on their own interests and judgments. The historical narratives highlighted in this volume constitute an archeology of the present, globalized moment. While some threads are closely connected—as in the recurring narratives that describe the development of US professional practices, and their organization and tools, over the last century and a half—others diverge, implicating entire fields of study in the cautionary tale of US architectural exports.

③ Walter Benjamin, "Theses on the Philosophy of History," in Benjamin, *Selected Writings, Vol. 4: 1938–1940* (Cambridge, MA: Harvard University Press, 2003): 392–393.

In creating a critical mirror of the last century of architectural production, a key precedent for us was a similar (and similarly controversial) case of the curatorial mirror as a form of critique: Arthur Drexler's *Transformations in Modern Architecture*, presented at the Museum of Modern Art in New York in 1979.[4] Constituting a comprehensive survey of 406 international projects built in the previous two decades, *Transformations* sought to lay bare what Drexler described (following the historian Peter Collins) as the "archaeologically unclassifiable" nature of late- and post-modernist architectural production through a curatorial strategy based on a deliberate overload of images, an emphasis on the visual appearance of buildings as seen in photographs rather than through architectural drawings, and an emphasis on formal similarities over architectural uniqueness in the criteria by which projects were selected and juxtaposed. Rejecting the typical expectation of the curator to advocate for, validate, or appraise the work on display, Drexler opted to cast light on the realities of contemporary architectural production, whether positive or negative, through the distancing tactics of multiplication, repetition, and leveling.[5]

④ Arthur Drexler, *Transformations in Modern Architecture* (New York: Museum of Modern Art, 1979).

⑤ Arthur Drexler in interview with Andrew MacNair, "Response: Arthur Drexler on 'Transformations'," *Skyline* (Summer 1979): 6.

Superseding *Transformations* considerably in scope numerically, temporally, and geographically, the exhibition of the Office*US* archive has relied on a related repertoire of critical devices. The offices and projects displayed in Office*US* diverged fundamentally from Drexler's mirror, however, in that the criteria for their selection has been primarily political and historical, rather than formal. Culled from an investigation of over 2,300 projects built by US firms abroad over the last hundred years, the 675 projects included in the Office*US* Repository were chosen for their relevance in illuminating the key

"US Building Abroad," *Architectural Forum*, January 1955

"Design as a Political Force," *Industrial Design*, February 1957

From *Fortune* Magazine, September © 1978, Time Inc. Used under license. Cover image by René Burri/Magnum Photos

"Asia Bound," *Progressive Architecture*, March 1995

historical events, actors, and phenomena without which it would not be possible to tell the stories—the good, the bad, and the ugly—of US offices and their implication in a global context. Reproduced in the *Atlas* in full, this selection of projects does not deny the possibility of reading formal patterns, for example in the symbolic, "tropical" screens that embellished many US embassy buildings in the late 1950s and early 1960s, or the lineage of perfectly idealized urban figures that extends from City Beautiful urban capitals in the early twentieth century to the Middle Eastern Gulf States in the 1970s, the lush extensions of Walt Disney urbanism in the 1990s, and the virgin deserts of Mongolia in the 2000s. Yet their selection prioritizes the fact that architectural production depends on an array of difficult, contingent, messy, and often banal historical circumstances. For this reason, the synchronic, Drexlerian overview of the "bewildering, profuse, overloaded, contradictory" consequences of US architectural production abroad is complemented in the *Atlas* by the construction of diachronic depth, through narratives that overlap and migrate in time.[6]

(6) Ibid.

Each of the 169 architectural firms included in the *Atlas* is presented through a profile page with basic data, modeled on the corresponding covers of the office folders on display in the Office*US* Repository in Venice. Since the earliest of these offices precedes the hundred-year temporal framing that governs the projects in the archive, the historical narratives in the *Atlas* track backward to encompass their establishment and growth. In providing textual description of offices, we have focused on firms established prior to 1985, since many of these offices and their international involvements have fallen out of the historical canon and material on them is difficult to find. For contemporary offices that contributed their own mission statements to the exhibition, whose promotional material is easily found, or whose stories are in too early a stage to begin to be "written," we have included only basic data on their organization and work abroad, along with the bibliography of articles collected in their respective exhibition binders. Likewise, the narratives that arrive to the present moment are open-ended, tentative speculations on possible evolutions of practice to come. If this volume does its work, further investigations will follow, and we might hope that certain trajectories of future practice may even change course as a result. In this sense, the *Atlas* is the beginning of a history that is yet to be fully constructed.

— Ana Miljački and Michael Kubo

Historical Narratives

Gentleman and Architect: 1846
The Formation of Professional Practice in the US

Imperial Beauty: 1893
Planning For Democracy Abroad

The Missionary Challenge:
Philanthropy and Institution-Building After World War I

To Russia With Love:
Reverse-Engineering "American Efficiency"

Flight Paths:
Emigrating European Practices and Pedagogies

Incorporating Architecture:
The Business of Postwar Practice

Marshalling Resources:
The Regulation of the Pax Americana

Intercontinental Comfort:
Little Americas Abroad

The Image of Good Government:
The Foreign Buildings Operations Program

Broadcasting USA:
Soft Power and the United States Information Agency

Nation Buildings:
Post-Colonial Symbols and Infrastructures

Money Matters:
Architectural Competition on the Open Market

Crude Ideals:
Architecture and Oil in the Gulf States

Command Line:
The Computer-Aided Office

Profit Margin:
Signature Developments In Europe and Japan

Getting Defensive:
Security Protocols After the Cold War

Architecture, Engineering, Construction, Operations, Management:
The Rise of The Multinational Office

Dreamworlds:
The Architecture of Conspicuous Consumption

Open For Business:
Developments in Asia

Architectural Playgrounds:
Emerging Practices, Global Platforms

Beyond Mega-:
Sustaining Superlatives

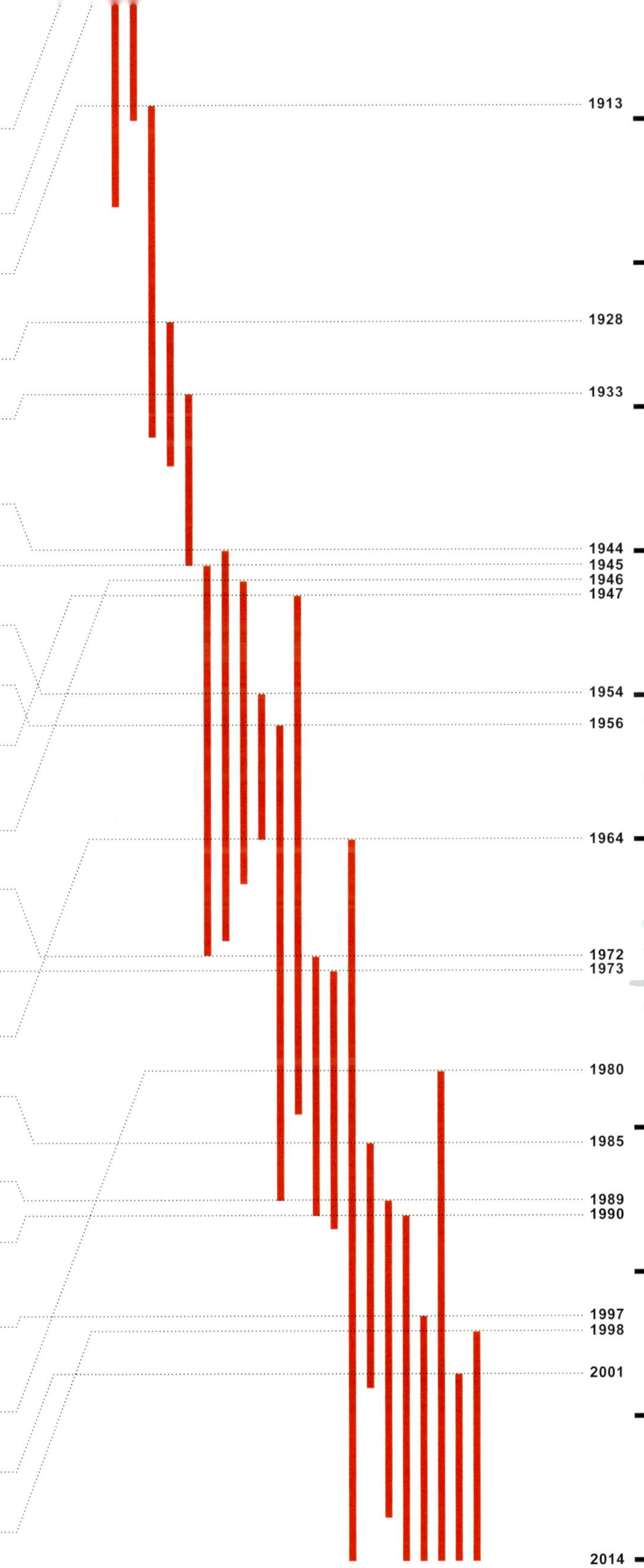

How *Atlas* Works

Historical Narratives

Office*US* Repository

Office*US*: Projects

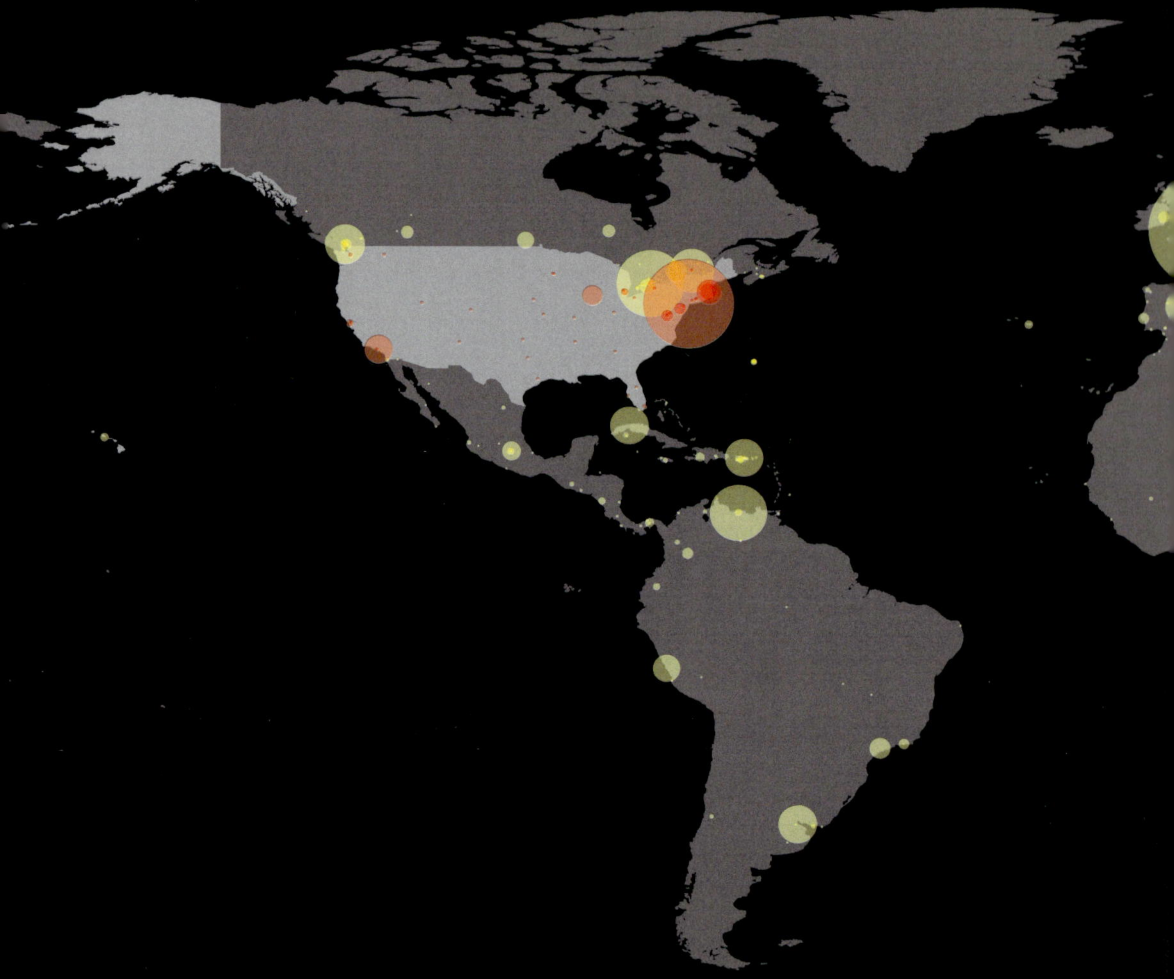

Legend

The circle size indicates the sum of al projects built in a specific location

- **Projects**
  Projects by US architecture offices built abroad, 1914–2014
- **Offices**
  US architecture offices building abroad, 1853–2014

See *Crude Ideals*
See *Nation Buildings*

Office*US*: Firms

1 SmithGroupJJR
2 D. H. Burnham & Company
3 The Austin Company
4 McKim, Mead & White
5 Holabird & Root
6 George A. Fuller Company
7 Cass Gilbert
8 Shepley Bulfinch
9 Helmle & Corbett
10 Frank Lloyd Wright
11 Perkins, Fellows and Hamilton
12 Albert Kahn Associates
13 William Welles Bosworth
14 Delano & Aldrich
15 John Russell Pope
16 Henry Killam Murphy
17 Walter Burley Griffin and Marion Mahony
18 Leo A Daly
19 Epstein
20 Raymond & Rado
21 Schultze & Weaver
22 Paul R. Williams Architects
23 Perry Dean Rogers | Partners Architects
24 Shreve, Lamb & Harmon
25 Richard J. Neutra
26 Harrison & Abramovitz
27 Adrian Wilson Associates
28 William L. Pereira & Associates
29 Payette
30 Edward Durell Stone & Associates
31 Ellerbe Becket
32 Louis I. Kahn
33 Perkins + Will
34 Alfred L. Aydelott Associates
35 Skidmore, Owings & Merrill
36 Marcel Breuer Associates
37 The Office of Mies van der Rohe
38 The Eggers Group
39 Arthur B. Froehlich and Associates
40 Victor Gruen International
41 Eero Saarinen and Associates
42 Morris Lapidus Associates
43 Philip Johnson / Alan Ritchie Architects
44 Ralph Rapson
45 Town Planning Associates
46 NBBJ
47 The Architects Collaborative
48 NELSON H2L2
49 Cannon Design
50 Wimberly Allison Tong & Goo
51 CRSS Inc.
52 Daniel, Mann, Johnson & Mendenhall
53 Joseph Allen Stein and Associates
54 RTKL
55 Vincent G. Kling Associates
56 Bassetti Architects
57 Lathrop Douglass
58 Harry Weese & Associates
59 John M. Johansen
60 Oficina Don Hatch
61 Yamasaki and Associates
62 Edward Larrabee Barnes Associates
63 Hugh Stubbins and Associates
64 ROMA Design Group
65 Eduardo Catalano
66 Paul Rudolph
67 Davis Brody Bond Architects & Planners
68 Sert, Jackson and Associates
69 Integrus
70 John Portman and Associates
71 Sasaki Associates
72 John Hejduk
73 Robert P. Madison International
74 Victor A. Lundy
75 HOK
76 Pei Cobb Freed & Partners Architects
77 Wiliam B. Tabler Architects
78 Brown Daltas and Associates
79 Mitchell/Giurgola Architects
80 Parker Design Group
81 Venturi, Scott Brown and Associates
82 Gunnar Birkerts and Associates
83 Zimmer Gunsul Frasca Architects
84 Tigerman McCurry Architects
85 Cambridge Seven Associates
86 Gehry Partners
87 KMW Architecture
88 Polshek Partnership
89 Richard Meier & Partners Architects
90 Michael Graves & Associates
91 Eisenman Architects
92 Gwathmey Siegel Kaufman Architects
93 Bohlin Cywinski Jackson
94 Gensler
95 Hartman-Cox Architects
96 Kevin Roche John Dinkeloo and Associates
97 Studio Hillier
98 BTA Architects
99 Antoine Predock Architect PC
100 Center for Environmental Structure
101 JAHN
102 Goettsch Partners
103 Robert A.M. Stern Architects
104 SITE
105 Morphosis Architects
106 Machado and Silvetti Associates
107 Kohn Pedersen Fox Associates
108 Steven Holl Architects
109 Gluckman Mayner Architects
110 Arquitectonica
111 Moore Ruble Yudell Architects & Planners
112 Pelli Clarke Pelli Architects
113 Jerde Partnership
114 FXFOWLE Architects
115 Koetter Kim & Associates
116 MACK Architect(s)
117 Safdie Architects
118 Diller Scofidio + Renfro
119 Santos Prescott and Associates
120 Duany Plater-Zyberk and Company
121 Toshiko Mori Architect
122 Populous
123 Rafael Viñoly Architects
124 KieranTimberlake
125 Hodgetts + Fung
126 STUDIOS Architecture
127 Office dA
128 Sorg Architects
129 Tod Williams Billie Tsien Architects
130 RUR Architecture PC
131 Bernard Tschumi Architects
132 Acconci Studio
133 Selldorf Architects
134 Asymptote Architecture
135 LEESER Architecture
136 Preston Scott Cohen
137 Studio Daniel Libeskind
138 WEISS/MANFREDI Architecture/Landscape/Urbanism
139 AECOM
140 KVA matx
141 Stan Allen Architect
142 Louise Braverman, Architect
143 Zago Architecture
144 LOT-EK
145 Michael Maltzan Architecture
146 VJAA
147 Carlos Zapata Studio
148 SHoP
149 Hashim Sarkis Studios
150 Slade Architecture
151 Studio SUMO
152 OBRA Architects
153 L.E.FT
154 SsD
155 Studio Shanghai
156 Utile
157 MOS Architects
158 Wodiczko + Bonder
159 WORKac
160 Höweler + Yoon Architecture
161 over,under
162 REX Architecture
163 Adrian Smith + Gordon Gill Architecture
164 ATOPIA
165 ORG Organization for Permanent Modernity
166 MASS Design Group
167 SO–IL
168 Leong Leong
169 NADAAA

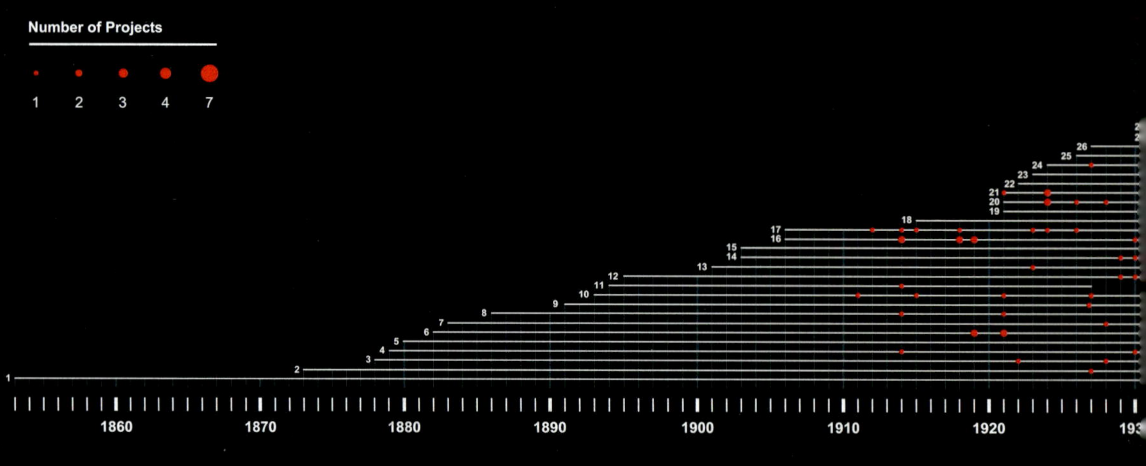

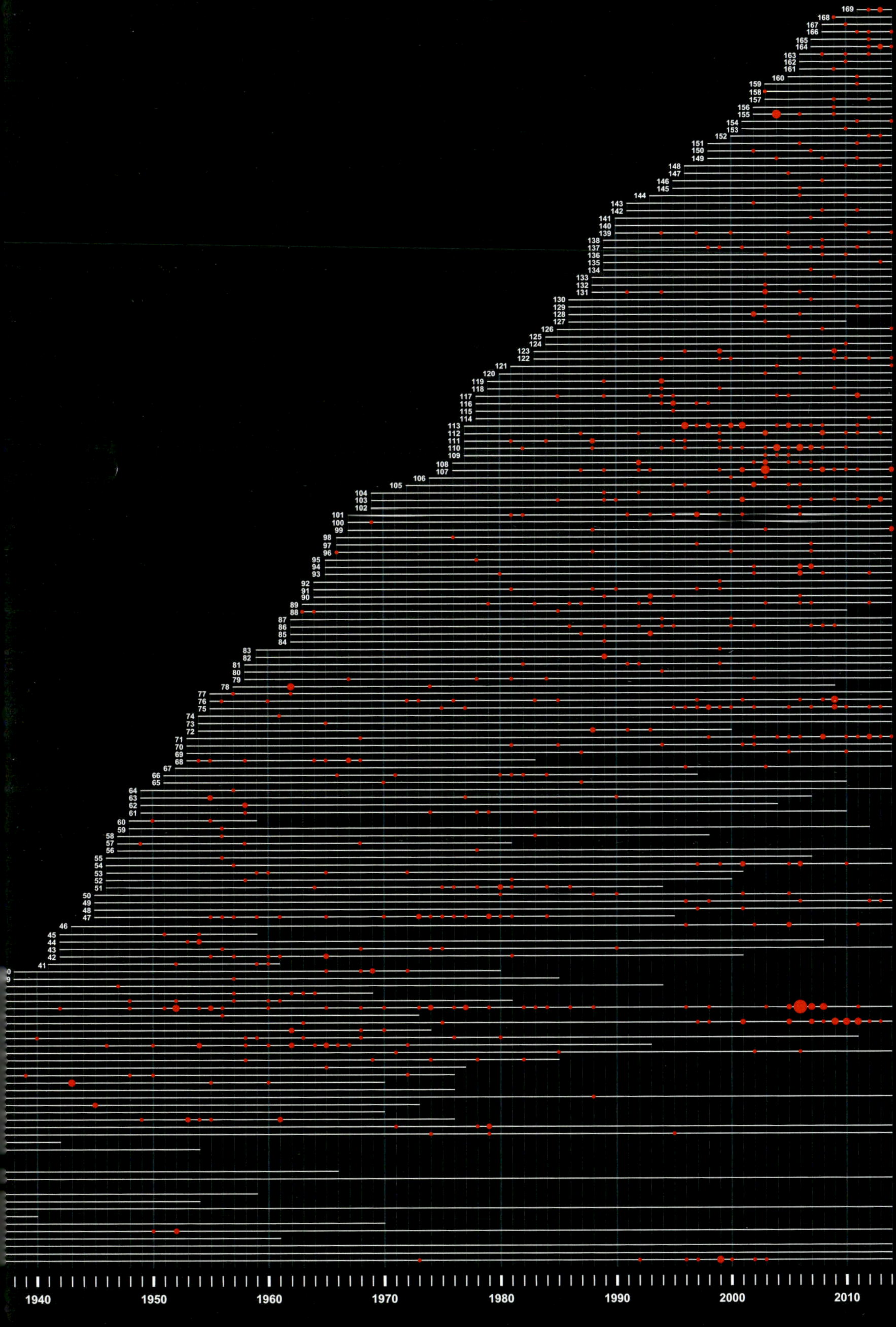

169
168
167
166
165
164
163
162
161
160
159
158
157
156
155
154
153
152
151
150
149
148
147
146
145
144
143
142
141
140
139
138
137
136
135
134
133
132
131
130
129
128
127
126
125
124
123
122
121
120
119
118
117
116
115
114
113
112
111
110
109
108
107
106
105
104
103
102
101
100
99
98
97
96
95
94
93
92
91
90
89
88
87
86
85
84
83
82
81
80
79
78
77
76
75
74
73
72
71
70
69
68
67
66
65
64
63
62
61
60
59
58
57
56
55
54
53
52
51
50
49
48
47
46
45
44
43
42
41
1940
1950
1960
1970
1980
1990
2000
2010

Gentleman and Architect: The Formation of Professional Practice in the US

From its origins in the nineteenth century, the formalization of architectural practice in the US has been marked by the tensions between differing conceptions of architecture as a benevolent profession, a market practice, or a field of cultural production. The inherited British notion of the professional as a gentlemanly practitioner, entrusted to mediate the interests of clients and builders with social obligations in a financially disinterested manner, encountered an established tradition of carpenters and craftsmen hostile to the definition of architecture as a discipline distinct from such trades. The first expatriates who sought to gain an elevated professional status for the architect, like Benjamin Latrobe, encountered resistance as the idea of the professional became increasingly democratized, coming to signify any member of a learned trade.[1]

The increasing organization of dedicated architectural practices and the conscious introduction of European models of practice was initiated by the first Americans to study at the École de Beaux-Arts in Paris, beginning with Richard Morris Hunt in 1846. Upon their return to the US, architects such as Hunt and H.H. Richardson sought to raise the professional and cultural status of the architect by replicating both the structure and the discursive formations of their academic training. Their studios combined the domain of the Beaux-Arts *atelier* (the collegial space in which students worked under the guidance of a master) with the working space of a professional office, at once business practice and learning environment.[2] Along with the German polytechnic, the École also provided a formative pedagogical model for the first schools of architecture in the US, including programs at the Polytechnic College of Pennsylvania (1861), the Massachusetts Institute of Technology (1865), the University of Illinois (1868), and Cornell University (1871).[3]

① See Mary N. Woods, *From Craft to Profession: The Practice of Architecture in Nineteenth-Century America* (Los Angeles: University of California Press); Bernard Michael Boyle, "Architectural Practice in America, 1865–1965—Ideal and Reality," in Spiro Kostof, ed., *The Architect: Chapters in the History of the Profession* (New York: Oxford University Press, 1977): 309–344.

② See Richard Chafee, "The Teaching of Architecture at the École des Beaux-Arts," in Arthur Drexler, ed., *The Architecture of the École des Beaux-Arts* (New York: Museum of Modern Art, 1975): 61–109.

③ Michael J. Lewis, "1860-1920, The Battle between Polytechnic and Beaux-Arts in the American University," in Joan Ockman and Rebecca Williamson, ed., *Architecture School: Three*

1840

1846 Richard Morris Hunt first US student to enroll at the Ecole des Beaux Arts in Paris

1857
- Hunt founds first architecture school in the US (Tenth St Studio Building)
- American Institute of Architects (AIA) established

1861 Polytechnic College of Pennsylvania establishes school of architecture

1866 Massachusetts institute of Technology establishes school of architecture

1876 *American Architect and Building News* established, first US professional journal

Attempts to establish a firm pedagogical foundation for architectural practice were paralleled by the consolidation of new learned societies and professional associations, chief among them the American Institute of Architects (AIA), established in New York in 1857. For the AIA questions concerning the ethics and economics of architectural practice were paramount, including the establishment of standards for architectural fee structures, the registration and licensing of practitioners, and bans on advertising and other competitive practices which were seen to lower the professional stature of the field. Such disciplinary concerns were circulated in parallel through the first architectural journals in the US, particularly the *American Architect and Building News*, established in 1876.

The industrial revolution and the "great merger movement" in US manufacturing which saw the consolidation of the first large corporations after 1895 soon found their parallel in the rise of architectural firms equally organized to meet the demands of a newly industrial society. Louis Sullivan later recalled that among his peers, "The only architect in Chicago to catch the significance of this movement was Daniel Burnham, for in its tendency toward bigness, organization, delegation, and intense commercialism, he sensed the reciprocal workings of his own mind."[4] The body of increasingly large architecture firms at the turn of the century was heavily concentrated in Chicago and New York as poles of industrial and architectural production, led by the offices of McKim, Mead, & White, with 110 employees in 1891, and D.H. Burnham & Company itself, with 180 employees by 1912.[5] Such firms often relied on a division of tasks among partners specialized as architects, engineers, and business managers.

The increasing size and organization of architecture practices was accompanied by new office settings, typically combining open drafting rooms with private offices through which partners could communicate directly. These firms were often concentrated in large buildings designed to house the architects' own offices as well as those of their clients. Steinway Hall (1895) in Chicago, designed by Dwight Heald Perkins, quickly became home to the "Steinway Group" of architects including Frank Lloyd Wright (previously chief architect to Adler & Sullivan), R. C. Spenser, and Myron Hunt.[6] The Architects' Building (1913) in New York, designed by Ewing & Chappell and built by a stock-holding cooperative of architects and engineers, was "home to a large group of T square and triangle men" including McKim, Mead & White, the largest US firm at the end of the nineteenth century.[7] — MK

Centuries of Educating Architects in North America (Cambridge, MA: MIT Press; Washington, D.C.: Association of Collegiate Schools of Architecture, 2012): 66–89.

④ Louis Sullivan, *Autobiography of An Idea* (New York: Dover Publications, 1956): 314.

⑤ Robert Gutman, *Architectural Practice: A Critical View* (New York: Princeton Architectural Press, 1988): 5; Jay Wickersham, "Learning From Burnham: The Origins of Modern Architectural Practice," *Harvard Design Magazine* 32 (Spring/Summer 2000): 22.

⑥ On Steinway Hall, see William R. Hasbrouck, *The Chicago Architectural Club: Prelude to the Modern* (New York: Monacelli Press, 2005): 210-216.

⑦ D. Everett Waid, "The Business Side of An Architect's Office, With A Description of the Architects' Building," *The Brickbuilder*, Vol. 22 (August 1913): 179-181; see subsequent firm profiles in the September, November, and December 1913 issues.

school of architecture

1884 Western Association of Architects (WAA) founded in Chicago to compete with the AIA

1893 World's Columbian Exposition held in Chicago

1894 Society of Beaux Arts Architects (today Van Alen Institute) established

1895–1904 The Great Merger Movement

1897 Charles Follen McKim begins work to establish an American Academy in Rome

1898 Spanish-American War

1914 American Academy in Rome inaugurated

1914–1918 World War I

1920

THE ENGINEERING & BUILDING RECORD

AND THE SANITARY ENGINEER

DEVOTED TO ENGINEERING · ARCHITECTURE · CONSTRUCTION

A JOURNAL for the ARCHITECT · ENGINEER · CONTRACTOR · MECHANIC & MUNICIPAL OFFICER ·

CONDUCTED BY HENRY C. MEYER.

INDEX TO VOLUME XXI.

DECEMBER 7, 1889, TO MAY 31, 1890.

277 PEARL STREET, NEW YORK.

London Office, 92 & 93 Fleet Street.

ARCHITECTURAL ILLUSTRATIONS

GENERAL SUBJECTS.

A

B

NEW ENGLAND WATER-WORKS ASSOCIATION MEETING.

AN adjourned meeting of the New England Water-Works Association was held at Young's Hotel, Boston, January 8, with an attendance of 63. The usual dinner was followed by a business meeting, President Dexter Brackett in the chair, and R. C. P. Coggeshall Secretary.

Mr. W. H. Richards, of New London, Conn., read a paper in which he considered the matter of thickness of cast-iron water pipes and special castings, referring to the new cast-iron water-main, five miles long, recently laid in New London for an increased water-supply. The paper was discussed by Jones, Hawes, Brackett, Darling and Tidd. Mr. Darling thought that cities and towns were much inclined to use too light and small pipe. With the introduction of sprinklers, elevators, fire service pipes, etc., there is a constantly increasing demand in the water-supply. Mr. Tidd believed in large pipes, but thought the pressure should determine the thickness, and pipes were sometimes laid too thick.

Mr. Brackett made some remarks on the recent Boston fire. The total number of engines in use on this occasion was 52, which, with the assistance of the hydrants of two large business concerns in the district, gave a total of about 86 streams of water, yielding approximately 20,000 gallons per minute. He estimated that, exclusive of leaks and waste, there was a total of 24,000,000 gallons of water thrown on this fire. Twenty-five hydrants supplied all the water drawn through 8-inch and 12-inch pipes, fed by the 24-inch main, and there was an ample supply of water, as was shown from the fact that water could be drawn during the fire at the tops of buildings in the water circuit then in use. Referring to the great Boston fire of 1872, Mr. Brackett, stating that there were 21 engines belonging to the city, assisted by 45 from outside, making a total of 66 engines used at that time, said it was a question whether the quantity per minute then thrown was any greater than at the conflagration of November last.

Following Mr. Brackett, Mr. Tidd said that there should be some understanding between the fire and water departments of a city as to the number of streams to be used in any given circuit, illustrating his remarks by referring to the case of a house between two hydrants being completely burned on account of using both hydrants at the same time, whereby the pressure was so reduced as to give two small streams, doing little or no good, in place of one large and effective discharge of water which might have been obtained by using only one of the hydrants. At the Lynn fire, from the cause spoken of, the pressure was reduced from 60 to 23 pounds.

Mr. Winslow, of Waltham, and Mr. Walker, of Manchester, gave some instances of leaks in the water pipe system, consisting of cement-lined iron pipe, in use in these places and a few remarks were made discouraging to the use of such pipe for water-supply purposes.

Mr. Brackett spoke of the importance of carefully discussing the matter of 4-inch fire pipes. It is a question whether the introduction of these pipes will not materially reduce the water pressure, especially by the breaking of such pipes in buildings during a fire. Their introduction on a large scale must cripple any system of water supply. Mr. Harkell, of Lynn, referring to the recent fire there, expressed the same views, and referred to the greatly increasing demands put on the Lynn system by the introduction of the automatic sprinklers, etc.

The following named gentlemen were elected resident active members: Lewis M. Bancroft, Chairman of the Water Commissioners, Reading, Mass.; Walter Hale, C. E., Westfield, Conn., Arthur F. Salmon, member of the Water Board, Lowell, Mass.; F. P. Webster, Superintendent of the Water-Works, Lake Village, N. H.; Philip J. Doherty, member of the Water Board, Boston, Mass.; Charles E. Drake, C. E., New Bedford, Mass.; L. R. Forbes, Assistant Superintendent, Brookline, Mass.

Associate member: Wilmer Reed, Burlington, N. J.

ENGINEERING SOCIETIES.

THE ENGINEERS' CLUB OF KANSAS CITY held its annual meeting December 4, 1889, with President Gunn in the chair, Kenneth Allen, Secretary, and eight members present.

During the year there were held 1 annual meeting, 9 regular meetings, 2 adjourned meetings, 12 executive committee meetings.

Sixteen papers were presented during the year, besides the general discussion of "Sewerage" at the November meeting.

The Committees on Bridge Reform, National Public Works, Transfer of Members and Affiliation of Engineering Societies have done considerable work, but in each case developments are awaited before further action is taken.

The membership report showed 3 honorary, 79 active, 2 associates and 9 associate members.

Officers for 1890 were elected as follows: President, W. H. Breithaupt; Vice-Presidents, J. A. L. Waddell and A. J. Mason; Directors, W. B. Knight and W. Kiersted; Secretary, Kenneth Allen; Treasurer, F. W. Tuttle; Librarian, C. E. Taylor.

THE WORCESTER SOCIETY OF CIVIL ENGINEERS held the regular monthly meeting January 3. Officers were elected for the year as follows: President, J. H. Shedd; Secretary, M. A. Boyden; Treasurer, F. L. Allen. Executive Committee, E. K. Hill, A. W. Woods and W. E. Hassen.

ARCHITECTURAL SOCIETIES.

THE ARCHITECTURAL LEAGUE OF NEW YORK held its regular meeting Monday, January 6. The Metropolitan Opera House was visited in the afternoon, and in the evening there was the usual dinner at Marello's. Prof. Arthur L. Frothingham, of Princeton College, read a paper entitled "Some New Aspects of Mediæval Architecture in Italy" illustrated by the stereopticon. At the business meeting the pasting of candidates for offices—president, vice-president, and three members of the executive committee—was in order, and the name of every member of the League was pasted for each office.

THE NEWARK ARCHITECTURAL SKETCH CLUB organized in December with officers as follows:

President, W. Frank Bowers; Vice-President, J. C. Swinnerton; Secretary, H. A. Hickok, and Treasurer, W. C. Hudson. The Executive Committee are F. S. Sutton, A. E. Hudson, W. G. Smith, L. A. Virtue, and E. K. Taylor, with the officers. It is intended, in addition to the usual monthly competitions, to make a special feature of regular class work through the year. This will consist of courses in constructional work, free-hand drawing, water-color work, plumbing, architectural history, etc. The courses will be under the direction of specialists, who are club members. Applications for membership will be received by the Secretary at 762 Broad Street, Newark, N. J. The club expects to have permanent quarters soon, which will be open every evening to members.

AN OLD COLONIAL BUILDING, DORCHESTER, MASS.

THE ORGANIZATION OF AN ARCHITECT'S OFFICE. No. I.

IT has more than once been intimated by readers of THE ENGINEERING AND BUILDING RECORD, that a description of the organization and methods of work in some leading architectural offices would be of much interest, and in many cases of value, to others in the same profession. Understanding that the office of Messrs. Burnham & Root, of Chicago, afforded an excellent example of careful and successful organization, a representative of this journal, while on a recent visit to that city, called upon those gentlemen, and on making known his errand was courteously accorded every facility for a thorough understanding of the working methods of their office and the principles upon which it is conducted.

In their practice the constructive features of a building are considered of paramount importance, and in accordance with this policy the gentleman in charge of the office is an engineer, a graduate of the Stevens Institute of Technology, and is styled Chief Engineer. This position is filled by John Meiggs Ewen, M. E., (S. I. T. '80). C. L. Strobel, Consulting Engineer of the Keystone Bridge Company, is Consulting Engineer, and W. S. McHarge is employed as Sanitary Engineer, and gives four days in each week to the preparation of drawings and specifications for drainage, sewerage, ventilation, etc. Mr. Root is the chief designer of all architectural features, and he and Mr. Ewen between them practically determine the form and character of all structures.

Mr. Burnham is the head of the office, and controls, in a general way, the working of the entire force, not only in business, but in planning and execution.

The general arrangement of the office, which occupies the southeast corner of the eleventh and highest floor of the Rookery Building, can be learned by an examination of the plan which is herewith published. The bathroom adjacent to the lobby is not merely for luxury, but for refreshment on a hot day or after a journey, in the belief that by its use more and better work can often be done. From the lobby also opens the reception-room, used for consultation with clients and for meetings of building committees, etc. It is suitably furnished, and contains on one side a library of choice architectural books, in which, among other valuable works, may be found a complete set of Piranesi, of which there is believed to be only one other in the country. This library is not for show, but for use, the selections having been made primarily with reference to their suggestiveness to the designer, at whose service they are always placed. Next to this come the private offices of the firm and Mr. Root's studio or draughting room. Beyond this is the superintendent's office, occupied by Chief Engineer Ewen and his immediate assistants, which opens into the main draughting-room. This, under normal conditions, will accommodate eighteen principal draughtsmen and assistants, but has ample floor space for twenty-four or even thirty men on an emergency. As many as sixty have been at work there at once. It is well lighted on both sides, the three windows on the lower side of the cut facing the street and the six on the other side opening into the light well or central court, which is finished with white glazed bricks, and in this highest story especially the light is fully as good as from the outside. The room is 40 by 50 feet. The most noticeable feature of the room is the division of its working space into separate compartments by partitions extending out from either side between the windows. These partitions are about 7 feet high, and serve to partially isolate each draughtsman, or pair of draughtsmen, so as to prevent distraction by their neighbors, and to give each one a house to himself. They also serve to give additional wall space for shelves or hanging, and are convenient for pinning up drawings or other papers that have to be often referred to. The arrangement is found to be helpful, and is generally liked by the men.

Beyond the draughting room again is the coat and wash-room, marked "gymnasium," and generally used for that purpose. It has been equipped by the firm with foils and masks, several pairs of Indian clubs and a set of chest weights, and all the apparatus shows evidence of appreciative use, which has had a very good effect on the health and spirits of those who patronize it. THE ENGINEERING AND BUILDING RECORD on July 28, 1888, took occasion, under the title of "Office Exercise," to note with approval this new departure in architectural practice.

On the other side from the gymnasium is the stock room and storage vault, and between the two is the printing room, which, from its darkened location, was perhaps originally meant for blue printing, but is now used for making the colored hectographs that have become a marked feature of the office.

Previous to the introduction of this process all drawings were traced, separate sets being made for each contractor. This necessitated the employment of a large number of cheap draughtsmen who, besides being a very undesirable addition to the office force, were in the aggregate very expensive, and their work required much oversight to make it at all reliable. In endeavoring to improve this state of things it occurred to Mr. Ewen to utilize the hectograph, which he has most successfully accomplished. A complete set of drawings of each building is made and tinted in aniline colors, from which as many sets as may be needed by the contractors are quickly and cheaply reproduced by the hectograph. The copies are very perfect and of course exact fac-similes of the originals, the figures showing through the tints with much distinctness. The host of cheap draughtsmen has gone, and those who remain are picked men, carefully sifted, ready to respond heartily to any call and well able to do good work at short notice.

To return to the vestibule. The visitor, if a client, is shown to the waiting-room until one of the firm is at liberty to see him. The contractors enter their waiting-room where they transact their business with the bookkeeper, or, if they desire to see one of the superintendents in charge of the various buildings that are being erected, they enter the superintendents' general office adjoining. Beyond this is the superintendents' private office, with a large vault for the storage of their papers. No business is done with contractors except between 11 A. M. and 1 P. M.

Each important building is in charge of a separate superintendent employed by the firm, but paid for by the client. These men are not mere "clerks of works" but trained engineers, able to make their own calculations and meet their own emergencies, if need be, without assistance. This policy was adopted by the firm after serious trouble with a large building due to an incompetent superintendent. Theodore Starrett, for instance, the superintendent of the Rand & McNally Building, now being erected only a block away, was, until that building started, one of the office engineers engaged in designing and construction of just such structures, in which position he has been succeeded by J. H. Dinwiddie.

The clerks' office is placed at the entrance, for convenience of dealing with callers, and is also handy to the offices of the firm and the chief engineer. It, as well as the superintendents' general office and the contractors' waiting room is lighted by a large skylight shown in dotted lines, the clients' waiting room being lighted in a similar way by a smaller one.

The office, as will be noticed, is well provided with vaults, in fact there is a large vault, not shown, which is over the vaults for drawing room and work under contract. In these vaults all drawings in progress are locked up at night, and no paper of record is ever destroyed, but every scrap is filed away after the job is completed for the owners' benefit. It may be noted here that the time of each man on each drawing is carefully kept, and each man signs the drawings for which he is responsible.

When a client or committee wants a building designed either Mr. Burnham or Mr. Root will make the layout, determining the plans and style. Then the preliminary studies are made in Mr. Root's studio, or in the drawing room, under his immediate direction, Mr. Ewen being consulted on all structural points. When the general design and arrangement has been fully determined the work is placed in Mr. Ewen's hands to get up the plans and elevations, on which, when complete, Mr. McHarge lays in the plumbing, heating and ventilating arrangements.

So the work progresses; Mr. Ewen making notes from time to time for the specifications, and when the drawings are finished he takes the whole set into his room, and pinning them on certain roller shades which are arranged around the wall for the purpose, he is able to have all the drawings where they can be seen at a glance, and the specification is then dictated in brief to others who extend it in detail.

When the specifications are printed and the drawings hectographed bids are invited, which, when received, the client or committee decide on the contractor or contractors, the work is let, and the building is begun, and the labors of the superintendent of the building begin.

In the preparation of the drawings, as before stated, everything is subordinated to correct construction, the metal-work, if any, is carefully allowed for from the first, although usually the last thing to be worked out in detail.

In small buildings, such as cheap dwellings, simple indications in rough are furnished by Mr. Burnham or by Mr. Root to draughtsmen in the office, who therefrom carry out the entire work.

The working force in the draughting-room is composed of constructing engineers, of whom there are three; of designers, pure and simple, of whom there are many, and of assistants to the principal men.

There is a clerk who does nothing but act as librarian for the drawings in the vaults and wait on the superintendents.

There is a large force of engineers, who act as superintendents of the firm's local works, and there is another force who have charge of the buildings out of town, from San Francisco to Bar Harbor. All these have an exact system of reporting to the chief engineer, including the periodical sending of photographs, showing the progress of the work. The office-hours are from 8.30 A. M. to 5 P. M. During summer the entire force has Saturday afternoon free. Besides this and the regular holidays, there is a vacation every year for old hands, during which their salaries go on.

REGARDING COMPETITION FOR ROAD-MAKING ESSAYS.

J. V. HAZEN, Hanover, N. H., writes: "I cannot determine from your specifications exactly the scope of the essays on Road Construction and Maintenance. Are they expected to cover or treat of simply suburban and country roads, or those and also city street coverings, as stone, wood, asphalt, and brick pavements? In other words, will you define a little more fully the term 'Roads' as used in this case? I have judged from the number of words allowed that only suburban and country roads are meant."

[Country and suburban roads are intended—not city pavements.]

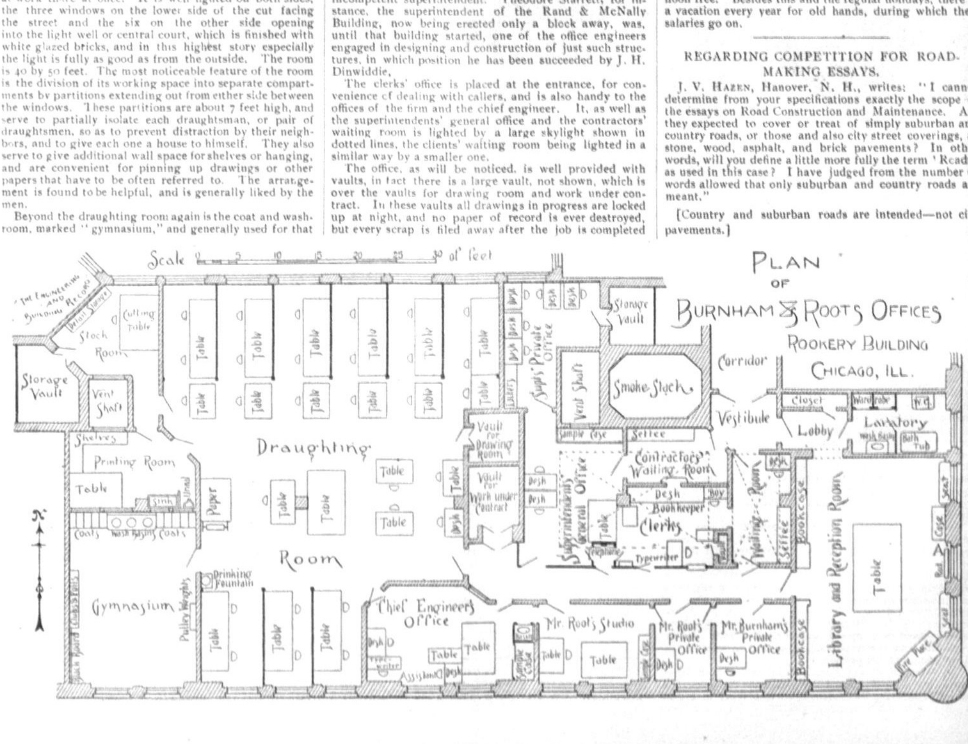

BUILDERS' AND CONTRACTORS' ENGINEERING AND PLANT.

No. LXXXIII.

(Continued from page 56.)

NEW CROTON AQUEDUCT.—METHODS OF LIGHTING.

THE methods employed for lighting the tunnel of the New Croton Aqueduct during its construction were chosen by the different contractors to suit their own ideas as to system, except on that portion of the work where the orders to use improved methods were complied with.

On the Northern Division, where the work was executed by Brown, Howard & Co., kerosene lamps and gasoline torches were generally used. Each torch being provided with fifteen burners, consumed a large amount of oxygen, nearly as much as fifteen men would require, and the smoke from the torches and lamps sometimes became so dense in the headings as to cause a stoppage of the work. When more torches were added to increase the light, the increased amount of oxygygen consumed, and smoke evolved, produced an opposite effect, making the lights so dim that the darkness was almost visible; while the lamp-black emitted by these lamps filled the lungs of all exposed to its influence.

The stationary lamps were constructed of tin, with a flat reservoir to hold the burning fluid, from which a small pipe extended down about two feet and then projected horizontally about ten inches, terminating in the burner. Hat lamps were used by the miners, in which miner's oil was burned with kerosene added to increase the flame. Candles were also occasionally used for hat lights.

These lights were also used by John Brunton & Co. at the beginning of the work below Harlem River, but they were generally replaced by electric lights in December, 1886. As the headings on this portion of the work were advanced only a few hundred feet at that time, the bad effect of the oil lamps was less noticeable.

Electricity was introduced on the Northern Division in 1886, but the lamps placed in the tunnel were very far apart. In the tunnel leading from Shaft 2 the intervals between the lamps varied from 500 to 600 feet. At Shaft 11 there were three lamps in 2,000 feet. In November and December, 1886, the official report showed that seven electric lights were burning in the headings of Shaft 2, and the same at Shaft 3. At Shaft 5, on December 21, three lamps were reported to be in use by the bricklayers, and eight along the tunnel; but this is the only case where so many lamps were used. Two lamps were reported at Shaft 6, and 4 at Shaft 9. The full number of electric lamps given above was not burning all the time, but only at intervals, particularly in the tunnel. Frequent reports were made of from five to seven gasoline torches being used by the bricklayers in one heading.

On the Southern Division, which was built by O'Brien & Clark, electric lights were the rule, and, consequently, the condition of the atmosphere was very much better. The lights were not frequent enough in the tunnel to permit one to travel about freely without the aid of lamps, but all points where work was in progress were well lighted by electricity. On a portion of the work four lamps were burning within 1,000 feet; but in other places they were 500 feet apart. The miners and muckers were provided with the usual hat-lamps, but in some of the headings candles were used altogether for hat-lights, especially at Shafts 16 and 17.

An electric light plant was placed at nearly every shaft. A complete electric lighting plant would have required a steam boiler, an engine, a dynamo, and necessary lamps, but as boilers were provided for operating the compressors and hoisting engines at each shaft, the surplus power was generally sufficient for operating the dynamos. At many of the shafts the dynamos were placed in a room separated from the rest of the plant to guard against accidents.

The best location for the wires in the tunnel was up out of the way near the roof, and secured to the rock or to the arch of the completed conduit. On a portion of the work the wires were placed only a few feet above the floor, where they were liable to cause accidents whenever the insulation became imperfect. The lamps were suspended from the centre of roof or at one side as was most convenient.

The engines used for operating the dynamos were small, usually from 15 to 20 horse-power, and the dynamos were adapted for divided arc lamps. To operate a full sized arc lamp, of 2,000 candle-power, requires about 1 horse-power. The lamps used were of 1,200 candle-power, which did not require more than ¾ of a horse power each. Only one plant supplied more than 15 lights, so that a 15 horse-power engine gave ample power except where there was more than one dynamo at a shaft. At Shaft 30 there was a large dynamo with capacity for 30 lamps, which supplied the current for lighting 6 shafts, from Shaft 27 to 32, inclusive. The conditions here were different from those on any other portion of the line, and unusually favorable for lighting several shafts with a single plant, as these shafts were either located in Tenth Avenue or adjacent to it, permitting the telegraph poles on the avenue to be used for carrying the wires between the shafts, which were only ½ a mile apart or less.

The dynamos and conductors used on the Aqueduct were in use continuously day and night, and were subjected to pretty rough treatment, the wires being carried in wet shafts and tunnels, in process of construction, and having, with the lamps, to be shifted daily to permit blasting.

Lightning arresters, to protect the dynamos, were placed on the main current wire, outside of the stations, except in the Ball system, where the wet poles were expected to supply all the conduction needed.

The lamps used for arc lighting on the Aqueduct differed slightly from the ordinary lamps for street service, but the change was only that necessary to adapt them for rough usage.

The dynamos and lamps used for supplying light in the Aqueduct shafts and tunnels were furnished by the following parties: the Bell Electric-Light Co., New York City; the Thomson-Houston Electric Co., Boston, Mass.; the Schuyler Electric Co., Middletown, Conn.; the United States Electric-Lighting Co., New York City, and the Brush Electric Co., New York City and Cleveland, Ohio.

Power for running the dynamos was supplied by engines of the following makes—viz.: Westinghouse, Payne, Lidgerwood, Greenfield, Sullivan & Ehlers, and the New York Safety Steam Power Co.

MILLS AND MILLS ENGINEERING.*

(Continued from page 69.)

THE speeds of shafts are limited mainly by these considerations:

a. It is desirable to have them fast enough to transmit all the power required with the smallest practicable diameters. Also to have the pulleys which drive the machines as small as may be without having any of them too small—*i. e.*, to get the proper belt speeds with small, quick-running pulleys, which are cheaper and less in the way than larger ones.

b. The speed is limited in the other direction, not only by the condition that none of the pulleys shall be too small, but also by the fact that it is unwise to incur unnecessary friction, etc., by running faster than needful; also by the obvious inconveniences and dangers of running ordinary shafting and pulleys faster than about 500 revolutions per minute.

Much has been said lately, with some show of probability, as to the impending transfer of a large share of our New England manufacturing business and especially in the heavier and coarser lines, to the South and West. Whether this movement is to be more or less rapid and general, it seems that our best policy here is to turn an increasingly large part of our attention to the production of fine and high-priced goods, the business of making which cannot be so easily learned and started by beginners elsewhere.

The principal requisites for this are capital, of which we have plenty; energy, in which we are not deficient; and skill, which is most important of all. We have considerable of this already developed, and perhaps an unrivaled capacity for acquiring more by trying.

This skill is needed not only at the head, but down through the ranks of the operatives. Bad conditions do not develop, attract nor hold good operatives; instead of this they give a procession of indifferent ones; sometimes there are not enough of them to keep all the machinery going, and at other times the pay-rolls are loaded with too many spare ones, in anticipation of such a scarcity.

Some of the good conditions which are profitable to have everywhere, and are especially needful in making fine and high-priced products, are as follows:

1. Good light, temperature and ventilation. In many places some or all of these desiderata are lost or thrown away with scarcely any saving of cost or other advantage, without thought or question.

2. The different departments should be well balanced, so that none may be overstrong and costly for the amount of work required from it.

3. Every shaft should make its appointed number of revolutions, with clock-like regularity, through every second of running time.

All these things depend largely upon the design and construction of the mill, partly also upon the management.

4. The overseers and sub-overseers must do their work well and promptly, so that no machine will wait for attention longer than is positively unavoidable.

5. To make sure that these possibilities are made actualities, that no machines shall wait unnecessarily for power, material or overseer's attention, a live manager is usually needed. In many cases he will find it essential to have a good and minute system of accounts and reports, so that he may keep watch not only of his total weekly products, but also of the details by machines.

6. If these things are well attended to, the principal condition for keeping good operatives will be fulfilled—viz., they will have opportunity and incentive to do full work, and will be able to make good products in large quantities; hence to earn good pay at moderate rates per pound.

This brings us to the end of our story. These are the results for which mills are built; the making of good products in large quantities at moderate cost is the prime condition of success.

DISCUSSION BY MR. JOHN R. FREEMAN.

The percentage of useful effect developed by the Boyden turbine stated in the valuable and interesting paper to which we have just listened, is so very remarkable that it would add much to the interest if Mr. Sawyer would kindly give us the authority for the efficiency of 95 per cent. which he quotes as attained by Mr. Boyden.

Mr. James B. Francis, whose knowledge, skill and experience in these matters is, I think we will all cheerfully grant, not excelled by that of any man living, in his "Rules for Propo tioning Turbines," published in the Lowell Hydraulic Experiments in 1855, and based upon a study of several of Boyden's best works as well as upon his own experiments, assumed 75 per cent. as a fair average value for the efficiency; this being intended, probably, as a conservative estimate which could be relied upon as a result of care in design.

The very greatest efficiency attained in any one experiment upon Mr. Francis' Tremont turbine, built in 1851, and designed in the light of a full knowledge of the details of some of Mr. Boyden's best works, was 79.4 per cent.; this being a test by Mr. Francis where all the conditions for the highest degree of accuracy were fulfilled, and with the computation of water discharged based upon the Francis weir formula as established at a somewhat later date.

The highest turbine efficiency mentioned in the Lowell Hydraulic Experiments is that for Mr. U. A. Boyden's "Appleton Turbines," which, in a test where Mr. Francis was, I understand, responsible for only the computations and not the observations,* developed an efficiency of 88 per cent., and was paid for on this basis. From general descriptions I have inferred that this 88 per cent. wheel was one of Boyden's masterpieces, and contained, I think, substantially all the devices that he ever applied to a turbine for bringing out its utmost percentage of useful effect at full gate, and was built almost regardless of expense. Of this 88 per cent. three per cent. was due to the use of the diffuser, a device not applied to the Tremont turbine.

As this Appleton turbine was built some five or six years previous to the well known weir experiments, I have sometimes wondered if the data for the exact computation of the discharge was not less perfect than for the Tremont, or if perhaps the conditions necessary for great accuracy in weir measurement were not then less perfectly understood. This is a mere notion, however, for I have no information on this point other than the printed statement above referred to, but have thought perhaps this might account for some portion of the 5.6 per cent. superiority of the Appleton over the Tremont after allowing for the diffuser.

The only tests I can recall of a Boyden wheel with which the figures 96 per cent. are in any way connected are those of the Atlantic Mills turbines at Lawrence. These were constructed under a contract giving a generous premium for each one per cent. above 76 which might be obtained, and were designed and built within about a year of the Appleton turbines above mentioned, but did not contain the feature of spiral approach of water, which was considered to add to the efficiency of the Appleton turbine. Thus these wheels also were constructed five years prior to the establishment of a reliable weir formula.

I remember to have heard it said that in the somewhat celebrated lawsuit for compelling payment of the very large premium claimed, Mr. Boyden's lawyers claimed 96 per cent. efficiency, and attempted to prove it by ponderous mathematical deductions, but other evidence was put in tending to show an efficiency of about 86 per cent., and final settlement was made, I believe, on the basis of an efficiency about the same as that for the Appleton turbine already mentioned.

* A paper read by Edward Sawyer, member of the Society, before the Boston Society of Civil Engineers, September 18, 1889, and published in the *Journal of the Association of Engineering Societies*.

* It is not intended to cast the slightest intimation that the observations were taken with any other than a view to give, most impartially, the exact truth. These words happened to be prompted by the same feeling, which is more clearly expressed in the next paragraph—namely, that this was in the very early dawn of extremely accurate measurement of very large currents of water, and that perhaps the conditions surrounding the measurement might have been just enough different from those which attended the standard weir measurements made by Mr. Francis himself a few years later to account for, say, two or three per cent of this very high record.

I have always been taught to feel that Mr Boyden was an earnest and honest investigator, who published very little, and whose clear, deep insight into these hydraulic principles has never been appreciated, except by the very few who were brought into immediate contact with him.

THE BRICKBUILDER

VOLUME XX — DECEMBER 1911 — NUMBER 12

PUBLISHED MONTHLY BY ROGERS & MANSON

85 Water Street - - - Boston, Massachusetts

Entered at the Boston, Mass., Post Office as Second-Class Mail Matter, March 12, 1892.

Subscription price, mailed flat to subscribers in the United States, Insular Possessions and Cuba	$5.00 per year
Single numbers	50 cents
Subscription price, mailed flat to subscribers in Canada	$5.50 per year
To Foreign Countries in the Postal Union	$6.00 per year

SUBSCRIPTIONS PAYABLE IN ADVANCE

For sale by all news dealers in the United States and Canada. Trade supplied by the American News Company and its branches.

ADVERTISING

Advertisers are classified and arranged in the following order :

Advertisements will be printed on cover pages only.

CONTENTS

PLATE ILLUSTRATIONS

FROM WORK BY

BIGELOW & WADSWORTH AND R. CLIPSTON STURGIS; FRANK CHOUTEAU BROWN; COPE & STEWARDSON; ELLICOTT & EMMART; IRA W. HOOVER; HORNBLOWER & MARSHALL; FRANK B. MEADE.

LETTERPRESS

How Architects Work.

D. EVERETT WAID.

I.—OFFICES OF NOTED ARCHITECTS.

A STUDY of what architects do, where they do it, and the means they use, — is intended to be briefly compassed under the title, "How Architects Work."

As an introduction, it may be interesting to many to catch a glimpse by means of plans and photographs of the interiors of the workshops of some of the well-known members of the profession. Each observer will detect for himself the extent to which each workshop shows a tendency as between an artist's studio and a cold business office; as between a dominant serene and well-lighted drafting room and an engineer's vibrant executive headquarters. Each imaginative visitor may speculate for himself as to the influence on the plan of each office due to the personal qualities and taste of each architect, or the volume of his work, or the class of work, if he specializes, or all those factors.

OFFICES OF H. J. HARDENBERGH, 47 W. 34TH STREET, NEW YORK CITY.

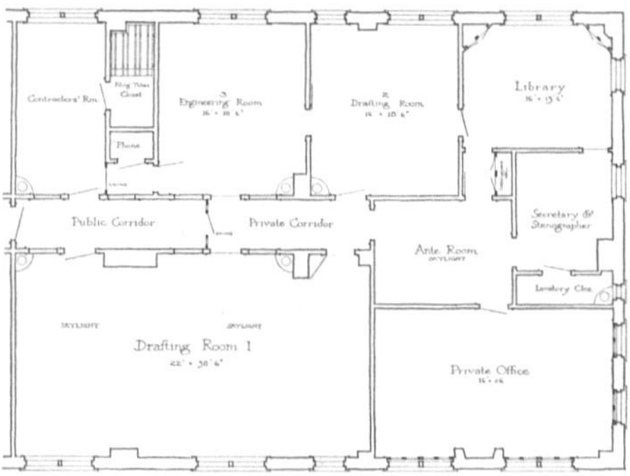

An architect's office in its beginning is a single room with one lone draftsman to give it a name. As soon as he scents a job and material dealers get wind of it and call too numerously, he curtains off an entry and gets a boy to close the door. The drafting room is still the consultation room for the client, and letters and plans and specifications are concocted on the same drawing board. In good time the entry grows to be divided into a business office for stenographer, letter files, and contractors; and the drafting room swells remarkably and suffers successive protoplasmic separations of private office, consultation room, library, specification room, engineer's room, superintendent's room, drawing file room, testing laboratory, photographic room, sample room, etc.

Let us imagine that our first visit to such a development of a real architectural shop is a call upon a great designer of hotels. He is located in a plain office building, and inasmuch as his reception room is nothing more than a piece of the plain public corridor of the building, we are disappointed, and, in fact, are not quite sure that we have arrived. The open door at the left, however (marked on plan "Contractor's Room"), discloses a wide-awake office boy sorting blue-prints to issue to bidders or to file in the very small filing closet, and he takes our card and disappears. Very quickly he returns to conduct us through the "Anteroom" (where first we perceive that we have entered an architect's domain) to the "Private Office." There alone, in a quiet spot, — so silent that not even the hum of New York streets or the distant rumble of elevated trains can be heard, is Mr. Hardenbergh quietly writing specifications. The roll-top desk is made to fit its place and the beautiful Florentine chair revolves as comfortably as the ugliest business chair could possibly do. As we are greeted courteously by this gentle host, and the conversation turns to the table, the mantel, the rug, even the interesting fixtures which he has designed to light the mural paintings, and note the soft color harmony illumined by six plain leaded glass windows, which, at the same time, shut out unpleasant neighbors, we feel that the individuality of the architect must be impressed upon the client who comes here. This is not a domestic room, a room in a palace, nor an office. It is the studio of an architect. The library near at hand is not different from others. Aside from its treasures of books, there is a conference table in the middle of the room and under one window an engraving case, such as one sees in print shops, in which are kept for easy reference some of the fine interior scale drawings which should not be ruined and lost among files of blue-prints. We pass through the suite of simply furnished rooms, note the two drafting rooms with boards all neatly protected with cloth covers (it is Saturday noon and the draftsmen have gone home), and the engineering and specification rooms. Before we end our call we have seen the floor plan of a Titanic new hotel with its admirable scheme of circulation, and then Mr. Hardenbergh refers to that nuisance of an architect's office, the filing of drawings, expresses the preference for flat filing instead of rolls, and mentions as hope deferred the famous file room of Carrère & Hastings.

OUTER OFFICE.

DRAFTING ROOM.

OFFICES OF CASS GILBERT, 11 EAST 24TH STREET, NEW YORK CITY.

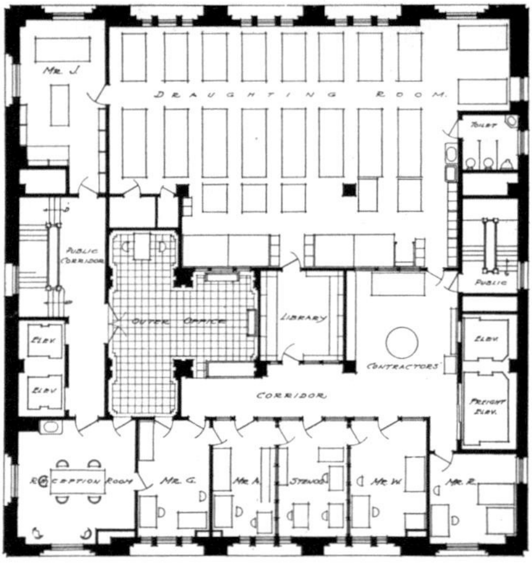

Next we turn our steps to 24th street and enter the T planned outer office of Mr. Cass Gilbert. Here our first impression is unmistakable; we are in an architect's office. Sculpture and rendered drawings of magnificent buildings hold us enthralled while we try to propitiate the guardian who issues blue-prints over the counter at one side. Beyond the "Outer Office" everything seems business-like as we pass through the rooms of "Mr. G.," "Mr. A.," the secretary, and into the executive offices of "Mr W." and "Mr. R." Bidders probably take drawings to their own offices and never see the "Contractor's" room, which is in reality a sample room. The walls are lined with "unit" bookcases whose glass fronts save the necessity of dusting innumerable pieces of hardware, bricks, and marble. This is also the mailing and general utility room. The wealth of the library is easily accessible from either the drafting room or the executive offices. When we enter the drafting room we get a vista of endless drawing boards. Roll-top desks are located on opposite sides of the column, one for the mechanical engineer and one for the specification writer. Immense steel cases stand against the side wall, with drawers six feet long or more, topped with box files of drawings of completed buildings. Each draftsman has a wire wardrobe locker placed as indicated. The room designated on plan "Mr. J." is a small drafting

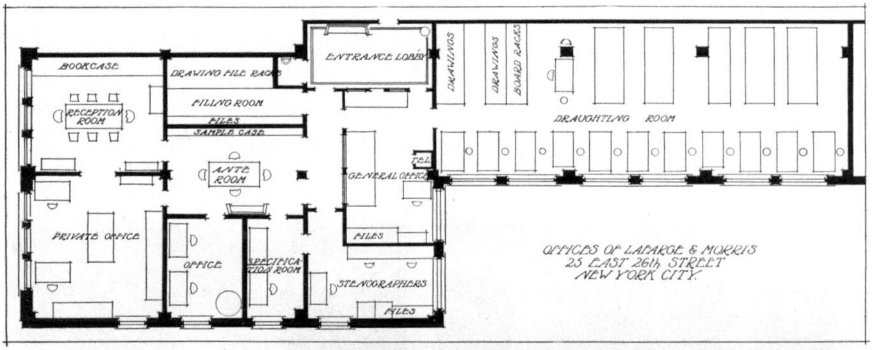

OFFICES OF LAFARGE & MORRIS
25 EAST 26th STREET
NEW YORK CITY

room, a desirable feature in every large office. Business is in progress, a conference is on in the reception room, so we must call again to see that handsome sanctum which opens from Mr. Gilbert's private office and commands a fine view of Madison Square.

Many of the New York architects are to be found around Madison Square. We shall wish to call upon three, all in one building at the north end near Madison Square Garden and the Society for Prevention of Cruelty to Animals. The first of these is the firm who designed the Lion House, the Reptile House, and others in Bronx Park, where is to be found the finest Zoo, not even excepting that at Amsterdam. Heins & La Farge, now La Farge & Morris, have a long narrow drafting room with eastern light. The reception room and library looks out on the Park through south windows. It is simply furnished, but has a reversible table worth going a mile to see. An attractive decorative effect is given by the books, a piece of tapestry, a large example of Japanese carving, and a fine perspective of the Cathedral of St. John the Divine. One passes from the "Anteroom" or from the "Reception Room," into the "Private Office," where both members of the firm have their desks. The very plain "Entrance Lobby" which one sees first on entering this office is floored with richly colored tiles. Opening a glass screen door, the visitor then finds himself in a spacious "Anteroom" with a floor which is a testing out of an almost white composition. The plan suggests clearly the arrangement and furnishing of the convenient and well-lighted office of La Farge & Morris.

If we take elevators to the roof of this same twelve-story building, which was designed by our next victims, Maynicke & Franke, we shall see an example, an exceptional one, of a New York "pent house." Since they

VIEW OF DRAFTING ROOM AND PLAN. OFFICES OF MAYNICKE & FRANKE
25 MADISON SQUARE NORTH, NEW YORK CITY

have all there is of a thirteenth story, we land from the elevators in, not a public corridor, but their own private hall, which is simply decorated with enough perspectives to impress the visitor that he is in an architect's office. The "Hall" is part of the generous "General Office," which is made impressive with an immense color representation of St. Mark's at Venice, hung opposite the fireplace. Before one can reach the hotel-like counter, his approach is detected by the telephone lady and he can quickly learn whether he may see one of the firm.

DRAFTING ROOM.

PRIVATE OFFICE.

OFFICES OF DONN BARBER, 25 EAST 26TH STREET, NEW YORK CITY.

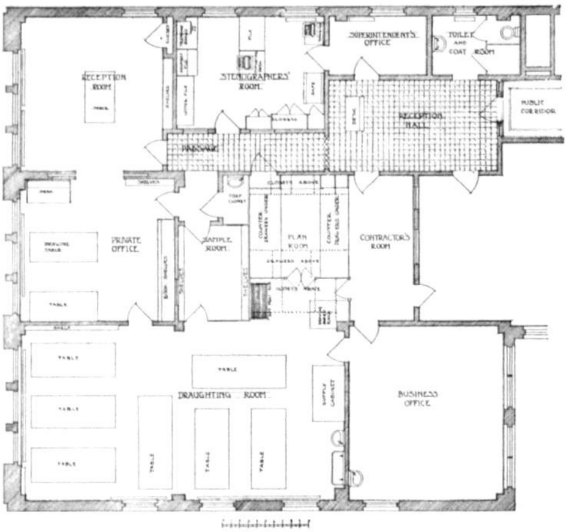

On this occasion, we are ushered into Mr. Franke's room, which has a floor of cork tiles, and walls covered with very white oak wainscot and bookcases. The table covered with rare books, the flat-top desk, and the chairs, are dark mahogany. When we visit Mr. Maynicke's room, we may discover that both partners are expert amateur photographers and can show us some of the marvels of color photography and a model dark room in which they are developed. A new exclamation of surprise is elicited when we go into the drafting room. Here is the Grand Central Terminal of drafting rooms. This pent house, not hampered with a low roof, has a lofty vaulted ceiling and four great bays of windows flooding the room with draftmen's soft northern daylight, which combine to make an exceptionally spacious and well-ventilated and lighted workroom — another worthy architectural studio.

Turning our attention now to a third office in this same building, we call upon Donn Barber. We enter the "Reception Hall," which is treated in tones harmonizing with light oak. It breathes a gentle, refined welcome and makes us know at once that a designer's atelier is somewhere near. There is, however, at the guardian's desk in front of us a smiling, polite, young major domo, who knows that Mr. Barber is out at the present juncture, and who is sure moreover that we could not possibly be interested in an office without Mr. Barber in it. He is quite right, for we believe that the plan tells quite a bit about Mr. Barber. Note how he placed the business end of the office, touching the drafting room at one end, and the reception room at the other, and how the primary designing board is hedged on both sides. The interesting arrangement of the office and relation of its parts are evident on plan. Perhaps we may have some details to consider in a subsequent issue.

THE ARCHITECT'S LIBRARY: J. H. Sellars, in discussing "The Architect's Use of a Library," says that it is doubtful if the old architects understood the history of art as we do to-day. Knowledge of history obtained through our books and photographs impresses upon us the fact that great styles are based on reason and logical construction, and that buildings to be considered great must fulfil their purpose. Wide reading will aid us in the formation of an artistic character and a power of æsthetic reasoning.

The Business Side of an Architect's Office.

WITH A DESCRIPTION OF THE ARCHITECTS' BUILDING, NEW YORK.

BY D. EVERETT WAID.

WE propose to illustrate in this series of articles the offices of a number of noted architects. Plans and photographs will be presented and also descriptions of salient features of each. Architects are invited to write to Mr. D. E. Waid, 1 Madison Avenue, New York, who will be interested to learn of any office devices, methods, or printed forms which they have found valuable in their office management and which might be of general interest to the profession.

ONE Hundred and One Park Avenue, New York City, has been christened "The Architects' Building." It is one of the buildings completed this year which most assuredly has an unique interest to every one in the architectural profession. The attention of the building world has been attracted because it was built as the home of a large group of T square and triangle men; it was designed by them and is owned by them. Already some twenty-five architects and engineers have collected under this one roof. One Hundred and One Park Avenue is theirs, and it will be interesting to follow the method by which the scheme of co-operative offices was handled among so many and in a city where there is so much competition and such great activity in building. The fact that the building has accommodations for general and sub-contractors, decorators, material men, etc., would indicate a greater efficiency in handling the working forces of those who are fortunate enough to be numbered as tenants. One's office boy, with a tracing, can disappear into an elevator and in ten minutes bring back a blueprint hot and dry from an electrically lighted cylinder. Sets of drawings can be most conveniently delivered to contractors, and that contractor, called General, can quietly tap at the door and delicately insinuate that if F. S. details are not ready by such a date, the time of completion of the building will have to be extended. It seems quite ideal to be able to go next door for a criticism, or to borrow a draftsman, or to admire a set of competition drawings.

One Hundred and One Park Avenue is interesting to the architectural profession because here its members can see the offices of several distinguished architects designed by themselves and undoubtedly expressive to a large degree of the taste and character of each. The building is interesting to the building world in general, because here the architects were their own clients and presumably handled the whole enterprise in an ideal way from the architects' point of view — from the purchase of the ground to the solution of the office building problem, and finally, in the letting of contracts and execution of the work.

The real history of the enterprise is quite as interesting as one's fancy could wish. The scheme of co-operative offices for architects had been suggested by Charles Ewing seven years before, and, at that time, with the encouragement of John M. Carrère and others, had almost been realized. Now all signs seemed propitious. Mr. Mead gave strong support to the idea, and, with Ewing & Chappell and La Farge & Morris as the active leaders, it quickly assumed definite form. Mr. Burt L. Fenner, as president, headed a stock company composed of fifteen architects and seven engineers.

After a long search for a site one was finally selected, excellent as to its proximity to a great transportation center, the lot chosen being on the corner of Park Avenue and Fortieth Street, two short blocks from the new Grand Central Terminal. The building obtains a south and west frontage. This we may label surprise number one. In the outcome, however, considering the north court light for those who wish it, the long, sunny, breezy south front is voted altogether fortunate.

The financing scheme having been worked out, several general contractors were called upon for estimates. But they couldn't bring the cost down to fit the finances. Speculative builders have constructed the larger part of New York, and they came to the rescue in this case — surprise number two. A firm of builders who had begun with modest tenements and crowned their success as expert buyers of ground and labor and building materials for great hotels

PARK AVENUE FAÇADE.

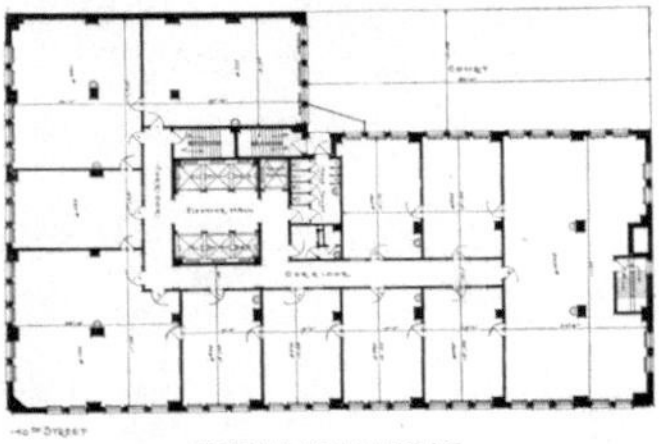

TYPICAL FLOOR PLAN.

THE ARCHITECTS' BUILDING, NEW YORK CITY.
Ewing & Chappell, La Farge & Morris, Associated Architects.

and commercial buildings, agreed to furnish our group of architects with both land and building ready for use. A two million dollar bargain was struck over sketch plans and outline specifications. It was agreed by preliminary contract, June, 1912, that working drawings and specifications were to be developed by a certain date, and then, if minds shouldn't meet in design upon one side against price on the other, either party to the contract could withdraw. The preliminaries proved true and the contract was confirmed July 10, 1912, for the completion of the building May 1, 1913. As a matter of fact, the first tenant moved in April 3, 1913, and the building was *really* completed May 1, 1913 — surprise number three. The builders furnished ground and building and procured a first mortgage cash loan and gave a second purchase money mortgage. The architects paid cash for their stock and thus completed the financial deed which made the property theirs. The amount of stock allotted to each bore no absolute relation to the office space desired by each, although the limit of subscription ranged from three to five dollars per foot. But the largest subscriber had first choice of space, and so on. Each subscriber takes a lease like any other tenant at the average price, $1.75 per square foot. His advantage is expected to accrue in the form of dividends which may cover his capital at the rate of five per cent the first year, and, if all goes well, may reduce his rent one-half later on. A special sinking fund is provided to pay off the second mortgage in ten years and a substantial sum, $20,000, in addition, goes annually into a general sinking fund.

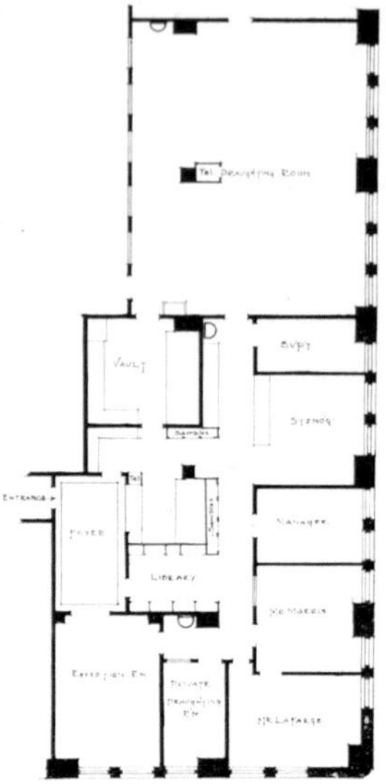

PLAN.
OFFICE OF LA FARGE & MORRIS.

The structure has a basement and sixteen stories, with provision for four additional stories. It complies with the law for "loft" or light manufacturing buildings as to floor loads (one hundred and twenty pounds) and as to exits. The three stairways afford evenly distributed fire-protected exits from each story, and are in fact equal in value to five stairways placed in the ordinary fashion. Other ingenuities of plan also are evident and are accomplished in a simple way which gives flexibility as to subdivision highly commendable both from commercial and fire protection standpoints. The typical stories are 12 feet high in the clear instead of the usual 10 feet, and windows placed close to the ceiling give good light even to the rear of 29-foot rooms. In this connection it may be well for architects to recall that drafting tables 32 inches high are better illuminated under the same daylight conditions than tables 42 inches high.

The frame of the building is steel, carrying all walls story by story and reinforced concrete floor slabs with a span of about five feet. The finished floors are concrete with surfaces hardened by the oxidized iron filings process. Each tenant, however, is likely to have a part, at least, of his floors covered with linoleum or some plastic composition. The regular base is of slate, five inches high, and there is a wide border of slate to support radiators and cover their branches. Window frames and sashes are of hollow sheet steel with no inside trim save plaster jambs and slate stools.

The corridor floors are of terrazzo. This material, objectionable because of the tendency of shedding its feather-edged chips of marble and leaving a pitted surface and because of its future zigzag shrinkage cracks, is yet attractive in appearance. It is laid in panels with mosaic borders on the beam lines. The corridor base is Tennessee marble, eight inches high. The critical visitor should know that the owners fully and regretfully realized that, in economizing on plaster wainscot in corridors and omitting marble, they were incurring an increased maintenance cost.

The material used for the first two stories of the building is limestone. The entire shaft of the building is built of brick. Brick lintels have been used without any embellishment, the only break in the plain surfaces being at the fourteenth floor, where a terra cotta sill course runs around the two street façades. A terra cotta cornice with slight projection crowns the upper stories. The building expresses frankly that it is to be used for offices where maximum light is the chief requirement. The design does not conceal the fact that the framework is steel. The corner piers, however, express a certain amount of strength which adds to the pleasingness of the composition.

RECEPTION ROOM.
OFFICE OF LA FARGE & MORRIS.

DRAFTING ROOM.

PLAN.
OFFICE OF EWING & CHAPPELL.

MR. EWING'S PRIVATE OFFICE.

We illustrate herewith plans and several photographs showing the individual offices of the two firms who promoted and designed the building. The plans show the possibilities of layout where the conditions are absolutely favorable. The architects in each case subdivided the space allotted them, always keeping in mind relative importance of space for drafting room, reception room, library, filing, etc., as to insure efficient administration.

It will be noted that special attention has been given in both the offices shown to the matter of office entrances and the control of these. The operator of the telephone switchboard is in a position to direct all visitors to the proper department, quickly sending clients one way and contractors another and, at the same time, can issue and receive drawings and is the better able to do all the useful things which are expected of that functionary.

Messrs. La Farge & Morris have collected and placed in their reception room several bits of interesting oriental carving, rugs, etc., the rich coloring of which is suggested by our photograph. The walls are covered with burlap painted a dark green. The color scheme in all other portions of the office is in a light cream or buff. Besides the private offices for the members of the firm it will be noted that provision has been made for an office manager and superintendent. A vault large enough to serve as a filing room is a feature of this office. It is accessible from the main office and drafting room.

The lobby and reception rooms of Ewing & Chappell are light gray and white in a simple and pleasing treatment. The panels of the wainscot are nearly white canvas applied to the walls, overlaid with stiles and rails of plain gray wood. The coat room has hangers on metal rods set at right angles to the wall with individual hat pigeon holes above. In the drafting room, a horizontal bar is hung on curtain pulleys and travels from floor to ceiling in hoisting detail drawings for judgment.

One device which Mr. Ewing recommends to his interested visitor is a bunch of blank cards which are kept within reach for a memorandum record of first interviews with clients. These cards are larger than a letter sheet and have printed down the left margin a list of items suggesting questions which always need to be asked at the outset of any commission to give a clear understanding of the problem in hand.

These two offices which we have considered are an interesting study, not because they are larger than those occupied by the average architect, but because being newly planned by their owners after a long experience in building up and organizing a successful professional practice, they represent what has been found to be the most economical and efficient arrangement of the various parts making up the business side of an architect's office.

RECEPTION ROOM.
OFFICE OF EWING & CHAPPELL.

THE BRICKBVILDER

AN ARCHITECTVRAL MONTHLY

VOLVME XXII DECEMBER 1913 NVMBER 12

CONTENTS

PLATE ILLVSTRATIONS

LETTERPRESS

PVBLISHED MONTHLY BY

NEW YORK — ROGERS AND MANSON COMPANY — BOSTON

ARTHVR D. ROGERS, PRESIDENT AND TREASURER — RALPH REINHOLD, VICE-PRESIDENT AND BVSINESS MANAGER — RVSSELL F. WHITEHEAD, SECRETARY AND MANAGING EDITOR

SUBSCRIPTION RATES

For the United States, its insular possessions and Cuba, $5.00 per year

For Canada, $5.50 per year   For Foreign Countries in the Postal Union, $6.00 per year

All copies mailed flat

Trade supplied by the American News Company and its branches

The Business Side of an Architect's Office.

THE OFFICE OF MESSRS. McKIM, MEAD & WHITE.

BY D. EVERETT WAID.

THE office of McKim, Mead & White is a focal point of interest to architects. It is the studio and workshop of the firm whose work overtops that of any architectural office in the history of the country. It is the one office from which has come the greatest volume of architectural design and executed buildings in any age or in any country. The artistic standard of achievement has been so high and the style and quality of design so consistent that they command the respect and admiration of all the profession. Since so great a volume of work must have been the product of several minds and the handiwork of many, the genius and methods of work which could exercise such an unifying influence are naturally of interest to the profession. But Mr. Mead amazes the visitor, who may be thinking merely of the routine machinery of so great a business, by saying: "We never had any system and haven't now — have we, Fenner?"

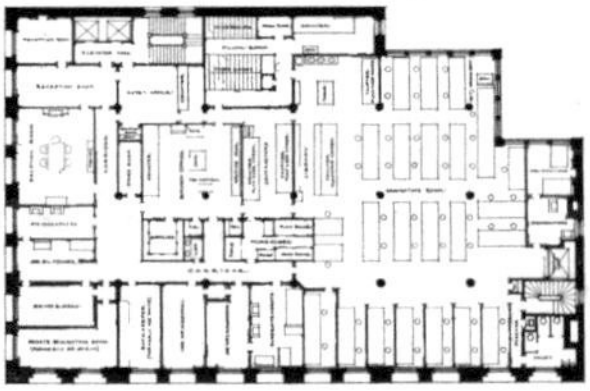

PLAN OF FORMER OFFICE AT 160 FIFTH AVENUE.

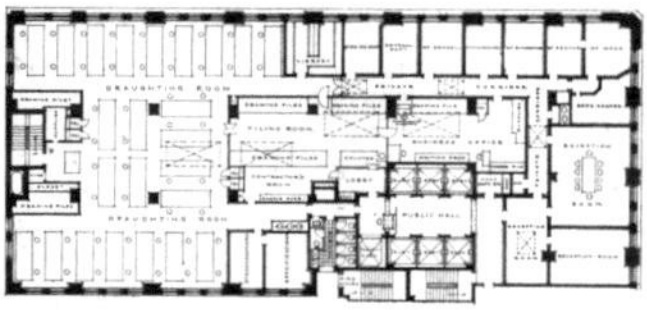

PLAN OF NEW OFFICE IN THE ARCHITECTS' BUILDING.

As a matter of historical interest, we present a plan of the office at 160 Fifth avenue, which was occupied many years and is treasured in the memory of so large a number of the able architects of to-day who look back upon that office as the home of their youthful hopes and training. The plan indicates how the private offices were apportioned while both Mr. McKim and Mr. White were alive. An interesting comparison can be made by the reader between the old office and the new one in the Architects' Building at 101 Park avenue, New York.

The plan of the new office indicates the location of the "Information" desk, where an usher receives a caller as he arrives by the elevators and conducts him at once to any of the three reception rooms or to the lobby of the business office as the case may demand. The general scheme of the plan is quite obvious to an architect who, however, on seeing the office, will be surprised at the real extent of the place and the spaciousness of the "Business Office" and "Filing Room," which are really all one skylighted room. And a busy spot too is that center of the physical activities of the office.

RECEPTION ROOM IN THE OLD OFFICE AT 160 FIFTH AVENUE.

The skilled man at the telephone switchboard can place an outsider in instant communication with a member of the firm or perhaps shield him by switching the inquirer to some assistant qualified to answer the call. There are four telephone booths and a dozen annunciators distributed about the drafting room. A draftsman or any one who happens to be in the drafting room can be called to some booth designated by a miniature light.

The large reception room, however, is the center of interest to the visitor and there is enough of the former office here to make one feel at home immediately. The long mahogany table, the comfortable old fiddleback chairs, and the entire simplicity of the decoration and furnishing of the room offer a lesson in the dignity and comfort of quiet good taste which is in striking contrast with some other offices where elaborate efforts have been made to design fine rooms for the effect on clients. The walls are paneled in oak with a soft grayish finish, the ceiling is tinted, and the floor inside the Istrian marble border and base is covered with a plain rug woven to tone with the oak wainscot.

The series of private offices are decorated to harmonize with the main reception room — the ceilings tinted and the walls covered with "woven paper." Mahogany furniture and soft cork tile floors complete the effect of the sort of plain luxury which is consistent with the term "office," as we ordinarily interpret it.

The curious visitor walks on through the office and notes the fine "working" library invitingly accessible from the drafting room; the drawing files, which are alcoves with sets of drawings of current work bound between wood strips and hung from hooks (see illustration of similar file closets in office of Mr. Magonigle in THE BRICKBUILDER, November, 1913); closets for storage of boards and table tops; a supply

FILING AND CONTRACTORS' ROOM LOOKING TOWARD DRAFTING ROOM.

MARBLE SAMPLES IN DRAFTING ROOM.

room from which even paper is issued from behind lock and key to prevent careless waste.

The drafting room has ceiling and frieze tinted white down to the gray picture mould, and the soft tan colored wall is reflected in the composition floor which resembles linoleum. The big room, for reasons of light, air, cleanliness, and economy of space, is clear of alcoves which were used in the old office. The firm recognizes the fact that an architect's office is a hazardous fire risk and so forbids smoking in the drafting room.

The specification room has an interesting device which in part could be useful in the corner of a small office. On each of three sides of the room there are hung from the ceiling two curtains of strong muslin as large as the side of the room will allow. One is hung some three inches in front of the other, and, being on spring rollers, they can be run up and down at will to display pinned to their surfaces a whole series of drawings. For one large building the lower halves of all six curtains could be used at once. The specification writer can walk around the room with his eyes on the drawings, dictating specifications to his stenographer. The expert who has done the work for McKim, Mead & White for many years has no need for reminders or card forms, though he occasionally follows a specification which he has written previously for a similar building. But he has one convenient memorandum in the form of a single sheet of blank paper, perhaps 24 inches wide, ruled in vertical columns headed by "Mason," "Carpenter," "Structural Steel," "Ornamental Iron," etc., one column for each trade. If he happens to be dictating specifications for mason work, he jots down in any of the other columns special items which need to be covered later in writing the other respective specifications. The single large sheet saves time which we all have wasted turning leaves to place a note aright.

A RECEPTION ROOM.

The specialist in specification writing may spend two or three days first of all in studying a set of drawings and getting instructions in the forms of answers to a series of questions. After dictation, a preliminary typewritten draft of specification is read over by a member of the firm and corrected for the final writing.

The writing of specifications for heating, electrical, and sanitary work is allotted to specialists outside the office. The same remark is true of structural engineering. Both specifications and framing plans are made by engineers in their own offices.

The so-called "filing room" contains under the extensive polished mahogany-birch counter tops steel cabinets of very large drawers in which are kept "flat" tracings, etc. Old drawings are transferred

LARGE RECEPTION ROOM.

to a room in another story of the building big enough to engulf the entire office of the average architect. Here in tubes (though all filing would be flat if started anew) are the accumulations of years, not including thousands of drawings which it was considered could safely be destroyed.

Returning now to the "Business Office," the interviewer is shown the card index, through which can be found the location in the files of all drawings. When new drawings are made, one card 6 inches by 4 inches is provided for each, on which the issue and receipt of all prints of that drawing are entered. This involves a large amount of clerical labor, as one can imagine when he sees a whole drawer full of cards for one building alone such as the New York City Post Office.

Incoming mails are opened by the chief clerk in the business office and letters sent by him to the several members of the firm. This leads us to the method of administration of the office. There is no chief draftsman, and, previous to the time of the Pennsylvania station, the firm never had a general superintendent. Each building on the boards is assigned to one of the five members of the firm. He is responsible for that piece of work throughout. He directs the draftsman in charge of that particular building, visés the working drawings before issue, deals with the client, and receives reports from the draftsman or superintendent who supervises the building. One of the secrets of the success of the firm is perhaps individual responsibility; the draftsman in charge of a particular piece of work is expected to follow it through to the completion of the building, keeping in touch even when there is, as at present, a general superintendent in charge of construction. The responsible draftsman may even conduct correspondence, always sending carbon copies of his letters to the desk of the member of the firm interested.

CORNER OF THE SPECIFICATION ROOM.

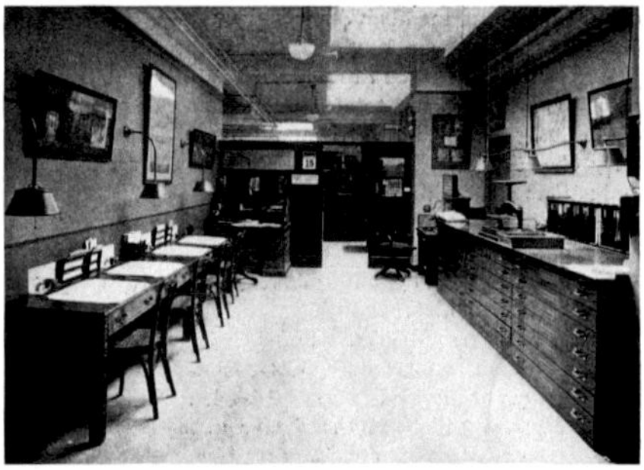

THE BUSINESS OFFICE LOOKING TOWARD FILING AND CONTRACTORS' ROOM.

A RECEPTION ROOM.

That method has certainly been the means of giving an all-round training to many a successful architect who has swarmed as it were from the hive of McKim, Mead & White.

The general superintendent, it may be observed here, spends half his time in the office and half out. He keeps tab on the weekly reports of the several assistant superintendents and also gets verbal reports from them or the clerk of the works on the job, and takes care of extras and changes. This system of supervision is found to work well.

The general superintendent and the expert specification writer have been mentioned. The veteran accountant who is skilled in drawing contracts carries unusual responsibilities in keeping tab on estimates, extras, orders, and certificates, aside from all the office accounts which include a notable system of keeping office costs on each building. One

MAIN DRAFTING ROOM.

other important member of the office staff is an experienced estimator who has had training in a contractor's office. He is engaged in making carefully detailed estimates to arrive at the total cost of prospective buildings while designs are in preliminary stages. He is also kept busy checking up contractor's estimates for extras and deductions on work under construction.

Some stray items of information regarding the practice of the office may be noted thus:

Letters are filed by buildings, by subject, in order of date, in vertical files.

Letter press copy books, one for each building, are kept as a precaution lest carbon copies go astray.

Telegrams are copied in special books.

Contracts provide that the owner may carry fire insurance to the amount of payments made, and the contractor is expected to carry insurance to cover his interest.

Bonds from contractors are seldom required except on public work.

The firm has its own form of agreement for building contracts.

Orders for extras and certificates are in the usual form. A short form order is used for lesser contracts, accepting an estimate, and signed of course by architect and owner.

One excellent form used is a printed application for builders' payments.

The firm does not use printed forms for superintendents' reports, but they have kindly consented to our printing the following excerpt from a routine construction report which indicates their scope and completeness.

PENNSYLVANIA STATION—MONTHLY REPORT.

March 31, 1910.

Messrs. McKim, Mead & White,
160 Fifth avenue, New York.

Dear Sirs: — I transmit herewith my report showing the progress and general condition of the work to date:

WEATHER.

Total number of days in working month	35
,, ,, ,, Sundays and Saturdays (½ days)	7½
,, ,, ,, holidays	0
,, ,, ,, days worked	27½
,, ,, ,, working days to date	713

LABOR.

Exclusive of executive force, the George A. Fuller Company are employing an average of 476 men per working day, classified as follows: 160 masons' helpers, 15 masons, 1 stone setter, 44 carpenters, 87 carpenters' helpers, 1 engineer, 3 carpenters' apprentices, 1 mason's apprentice, 19 ironworkers, 58 painters, 4 electricians, 1 blacksmith, 1 blacksmith's helper, 28 day watchmen, 17 night watchmen, 9 wire lathers, 1 rivet boy, 3 derrickmen, 1 stonecutter, 8 plasterers, 5 helpers, and 9 cement masons.

All contractors combined employed an average of 767 men; total men employed per working day by all contractors average 1,243.

	Estimated Totals.	Received to date.	Set or Used to date.	Set Since last rep.	Per cent finished.
Granite (exterior)	480,200 cu. ft.	480,200	480,200	0	100
,, (misc. and conc.)	60,000 cu. ft.	60,000	60,000	0	100
Marble (exterior)	5,576 cu. ft.	5,576	5,576	0	100
,, (interior)	8,035 cu. ft.	8,035	7,200	370	90
Marble and Slate (misc.)	15,000 cu. ft.	14,850	14,825	25	99
Terrazzo Floors	2,452 sq. ft.	2,452	2,452	0	100
Travertine	71,533 cu. ft.	71,433	71,000	3,300	99

(The estimate of material received and used continues through ornamental iron, cement, painting, glazing, etc., etc., to include every material which has arrived at the works to the date of the report.)

GRANITE.

Exterior, Concourse, and Miscellaneous.

This stonework is completed in accordance with the original contract.

MARBLE.

Exterior.

This work was completed on July 31st, 1909.

Interior.

This work has all been set, except the flooring in the sub-waiting rooms, the setting of which has been started.

Cleaning and pointing of work in this contract is progressing and is about eighty per cent complete.

(The report continues under various headings, "Cut Limestone," "Concrete," "Brick Work," "Cork Flooring," etc., etc., to the extent of ten typewritten pages.)

Appended is a letter from Mr. H. Van Buren Magonigle, with reference to the description of his office, published in our previous issue:

"I have read with interest your article in the November BRICKBUILDER; but there is one correction, rather vital, which I should like to see made in some way. You say 'all expenses directly chargeable to individual work, including specification writing, *and including a salary which the architect allows to himself, are called drafting expenses.*' I do not allow myself a salary — but when I work on any job as a draftsman, I keep my time, and the *hours* so spent go to make up the total drafting-room hours, and affect the 'unit of overhead charges' obtained by dividing the total overhead per month (rent, light, towels, ice, office boy, stenographers, supplies, telephone) by the total of drafting-room hours per month. But no charge for my time as a draftsman is posted against the drafting cost of any job, for I consider my salary to be the profit (if any, alas!) on the work.

"Referring to your comment, 'Inasmuch as there is a great disparity in salaries per hour, a uniform allowance per hour for overhead would appear rather disproportionate'; it is worth while pointing out that a draftsman at $100 per month occupies just as much office space, uses the same amount of light, drinks as much ice-water, uses as many towels, as much paper, as many pencils as a man at $200 per month; and that on the job he is working at there is no greater proportion of office boy's and stenographers' work or telephone service chargeable in the one case than in the other; so that the salary a man gets has no relation whatever to overhead expense.

H. Van Buren Magonigle."

It would be interesting to theorize as to the distribution of overhead charges on work done entirely by high-salaried draftsmen as compared with another piece of work done entirely by low-salaried draftsmen, and then on a third piece of work done by both high- and low-salaried men. How would they figure out in contrast with the usual method of estimating from the year's previous experience that on any job the overhead charge will amount to a fixed percentage of the actual drafting expense charged up to that job?

Expressions of opinion and experience concerning the two methods of calculation will be welcomed by the author.

THE ARCHITECTURAL FORUM

VOLUME XXIX NUMBER 5

CONTENTS for NOVEMBER 1918

PLATE ILLUSTRATIONS

LETTERPRESS

Published Monthly by
ROGERS AND MANSON COMPANY
85 Water Street, Boston, Mass.
Advertising Department, 42 West 39th Street, New York
Yearly Subscription, payable in advance, U.S.A., Insular Possessions and Cuba $5.00
Canada .... $5.50 Foreign Countries in the Postal Union 6.00
Single Copies .... 50 cents All Copies Mailed Flat
Trade Supplied by American News Company and its Branches. Entered as Second Class Matter, March 12, 1892, at the Post Office at Boston, Mass.

The Offices of Albert Kahn, Architect, Detroit, Michigan

By GEORGE C. BALDWIN

THE offices of Albert Kahn, Architect, occupy the entire upper floor of the Marquette Building, a structure originally used as a power building and recently remodeled into a loft building.

The offices were especially designed by Mr. Kahn about two years ago with the idea of affording his organization every advantage and up-to-date facility for taking care of his business interests.

The various departments occupy approximately 14,000 feet of floor space. In addition to the executive and administrative offices, lobby, corridors, vaults, toilets, sample room, girls' rest room, reception and conference rooms and library, there are two large drafting rooms, separate structural and mechanical engineering rooms, designing room, two specification rooms, one for the specification writers and a separate room for the typing and assembling of specifications, chief superintendent's office and field superintendent's room, estimating room for contractors, two filing rooms for contracts, correspondence, etc. The executive offices and conference rooms are arranged along one side of the building, the drafting rooms on the other. The mechanical engineering department is at one extreme corner, the structural engineering department at the opposite corner. The grouping of contractors' space for estimating, the accounting department, and the chief superintendent's office, as well as the office for field superintendents, works out particularly well. It brings these closely related departments into easy communication with one another.

Entrance to the lobby is direct from the public elevators and the position of the telephone room is such that the operator can see at once any one entering the office; there is one entrance from the outer lobby for the use of clients, another at the side for the use of contractors, and a third at the opposite side for the use of the employees who pass through the cloakroom to their respective rooms.

The placing and arrangement of the vault for filing of drawings is very satisfactory. It is conveniently near the drafting and specification rooms where reference to drawings is most often needed. The vault is large and high and so arranged that all drawings are readily accessible by means of a vertical suspension filing system and boxes for the folded, full-sized details. A copy of each specification is kept here in filing cabinets. An attendant is in charge, who

Entrance Lobby

passes out the drawings and keeps a record of their destination. He also sees to their being returned to their proper places.

The corridor running parallel to the large drafting room is arranged for the handling of blueprints, for packing and mailing; this work is thus kept out of the main drafting room.

Filing of correspondence is arranged by trades, and steel fireproof files are used for both current and transfer files. These files are concentrated in one room with a clerk in charge, thereby making it an orderly process to refer to any matter and avoiding the confusion that would be entailed if each department had individual files. The contractors' room is served by a plan room adjacent to the file room, where copies of current plans, specifications and bulletins are on file for use of contractors in taking off quantities and other data.

Interior of Typical Private Office

The offices of the executives are arranged in two groups at either side of the consultation room. The corridor which serves them is floored with composition tile to insure quietness. A very useful adjunct to the offices is a sample room off this corridor and conveniently near all the executive offices. Herein a fairly complete line of building materials is exhibited for office reference and the information of clients.

The several drafting rooms are divided by partitions glazed with clear glass. The private offices are divided by solid partitions.

Each office is equipped with a city telephone, an inter-office telephone and a buzzer. The city telephones are connected with a private switchboard in the information room at the entrance lobby. The inter-office telephone system is independent of the city lines and operates through an automatic switch-board.

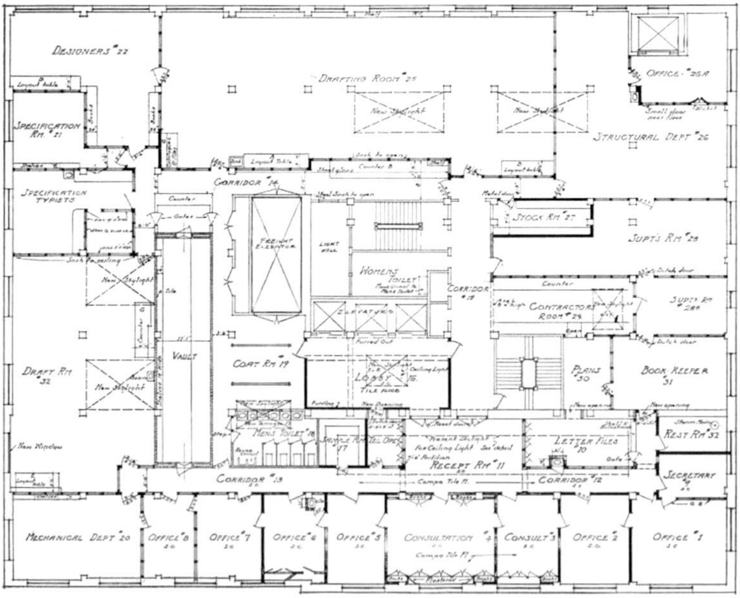

Floor Plan, Offices of Albert Kahn, Architect

The outer lobby is treated with walls in imitation of Caen stone and hung with a number of Piranesi prints and plaster casts. The floor is of composition tile, finished at the walls with a black marble base. The inner lobby as well as the conference rooms are paneled to the ceiling in oak. These rooms have ornamental plaster ceilings. The larger conference room has a number of built-in bookcases, which hold the more important works of Mr. Kahn's library. The bound volumes of architectural magazines and other technical books are kept in the designers' room.

VIEW OF RECEPTION ROOM

VIEW OF LARGE DRAFTING ROOM

OFFICES OF ALBERT KAHN, ARCHITECT, DETROIT, MICH.

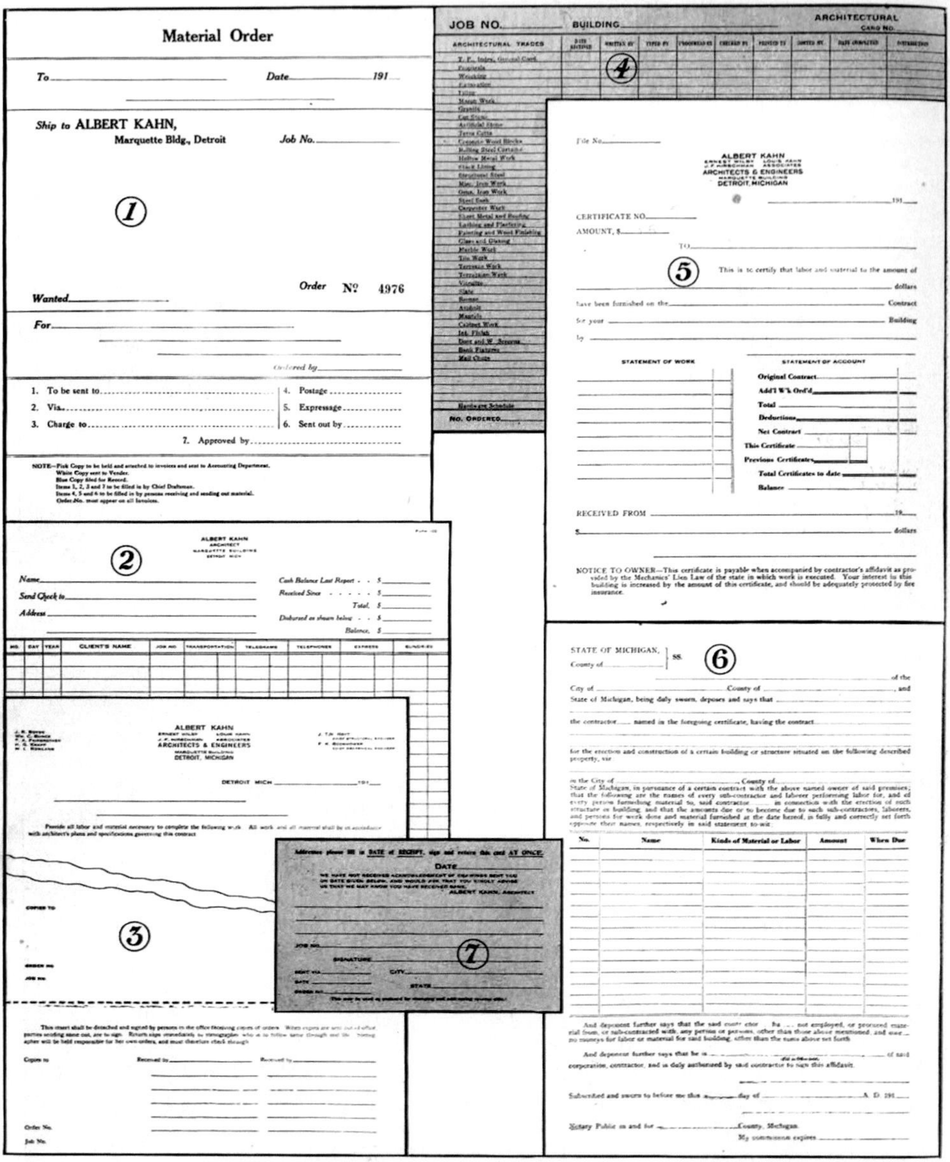

Material Order

To ________ Date ________ 191__

Ship to ALBERT KAHN,
Marquette Bldg., Detroit

Job No. ________

Order № 4976

Wanted ________

For ________

Ordered by ________

1. To be sent to ....
2. Via ....
3. Charge to ....
4. Postage ....
5. Expressage ....
6. Sent out by ....
7. Approved by ....

JOB NO. ________ BUILDING ________ ARCHITECTURAL CARD NO.

ARCHITECTURAL TRADES

No. ORDERED ________

File No. ________

ALBERT KAHN
ARCHITECTS & ENGINEERS
DETROIT, MICHIGAN

CERTIFICATE NO. ________
AMOUNT, $ ________
TO ________

This is to certify that labor and material to the amount of ________ dollars have been furnished on the ________ Contract for your ________ Building by ________

STATEMENT OF WORK

STATEMENT OF ACCOUNT
Original Contract
Add'l W'k Ord'd
Total
Deductions
Net Contract
This Certificate
Previous Certificates
Total Certificates to date
Balance

RECEIVED FROM ________ 19__
$ ________ dollars

NOTICE TO OWNER—This certificate is payable when accompanied by contractor's affidavit as provided by the Mechanics' Lien Law of the state in which work is executed. Your interest in this building is increased by the amount of this certificate, and should be adequately protected by fire insurance.

ALBERT KAHN
ARCHITECT

Name ________
Send Check to ________
Address ________

Cash Balance Last Report $ ________
Received Since $ ________
Total $ ________
Disbursed as shown below $ ________
Balance $ ________

NO.	DAY	YEAR	CLIENT'S NAME	JOB NO.	TRANSPORTATION	TELEGRAMS	TELEPHONES	EXPRESS	SUNDRIES

STATE OF MICHIGAN, } ss.
County of ________

________ of the City of ________ County of ________, and State of Michigan, being duly sworn, deposes and says that ________ the contractor ________ named in the foregoing certificate, having the contract ________ for the erection and construction of a certain building or structure situated on the following described property, viz: ________

No.	Name	Kinds of Material or Labor	Amount	When Due

Subscribed and sworn to before me this ________ day of ________ A. D. 191__

Notary Public in and for ________ County, Michigan.
My commission expires ________

ALBERT KAHN
ARCHITECTS & ENGINEERS
DETROIT, MICHIGAN

DETROIT MICH ________ 191__

DATE ________
ALBERT KAHN, ARCHITECT

JOB NO.
SIGNATURE
CITY
STATE

1 Material Order
2 Expense Account
3 Work Order on Contractors
4 Schedule of Sub-Contracts (Architectural) Reverse of this card has schedule of Mechanical Trades
5 Certificate for Payments
6 Reverse of Payment Certificate
7 "Follow-up" Receipt Card

REPRODUCTION OF FORMS IN USE IN THE OFFICES OF ALBERT KAHN, ARCHITECT

(8)

ALBERT KAHN, ARCHITECT, 58-60 Lafayette Boulevard, Detroit, Mich. — ERNEST WILBY, Associate

_______ 191__

Our records show that Drawings No. _______ on Specifications No. _______ _______ Building sent you on _______ have not been returned to us.

Would you kindly have them sent back at your earliest convenience.

(12)

Addressee please fill in DATE of RECEIPT, sign and return this card AT ONCE.

DATE _______

RECEIVED FROM ALBERT KAHN, ARCHITECT, DETROIT, MICH.

JOB NO. _______

SIGNATURE _______

SENT VIA _______ CITY _______

DATE _______ STATE _______

ORDER NO. _______

(This may be used as postcard by stamping and addressing reverse side.)

(13)

TIME CARD

Name _______

Week Ending _______

Job Number	Fri.	Sat.	Sun.	Mon.	Tues.	Wed.	Thur.	Total	Chg. to	Rate	Amount
TOTAL											

Design. / Drft. / Mech. / Struct. / Spec. / Supt.

(9)

Date _______ Weather _______ Temp. _______

Report on Progress of Building for _______ Job No. _______

CONTRACTOR	No. Men	CONTRACTOR	No. Men

REMARKS—State in full progress of work.

DELINQUENT CONTRACTORS—State in full when notified to be on job, etc.

VERBAL INSTRUCTIONS RECEIVED—Note instructions of owners and others.

VERBAL ORDERS given and to be confirmed.

DRAWINGS REQUIRED.

RECEIVED DRAWINGS — RECEIVED BULLETINS

Supt. _______

Superintendent to hand report to office each night. Keep carbon copy in book on job. Turn in on completion. Under delinquents, mention in advance when contractor and materials should arrive at job according to schedule.

(14)

JOB NO. _______ DRAUGHTING ROOM RECORD CARD NO. _______

Office of ALBERT KAHN, Architect, ERNEST WILBY, Associate, 58-60 Lafayette Ave., Detroit, Mich.

BUILDING _______ LOCATED _______

WORK	Date	By Whom	Form	Referred To	Date	Remarks
EXCAVATION PLANS PRINTED						
SPECS. PRINTED						
STRUCTURAL DRAWINGS PRINTED						
SPECS. PRINTED						
HEATING PLANS PRINTED						
SPECS. PRINTED						
ELEC. WORK PLAN PRINTED						
SPECS. PRINTED						
PLUMBING PLANS PRINTED						
SPECS. PRINTED						
ELEV. PLANS PRINTED						
SPECS. PRINTED						
SPRINKLERS PLAN PRINTED						
SPRINKLER SPECS. PRINTED						

(15)

JOB NO. _______ CONTRACTOR'S PRINTS CARD NO. _______

Office of ALBERT KAHN, Architect, ERNEST WILBY, Associate, Detroit, Mich.

BUILDING _______ LOCATED _______

(16)

JOB NO. _______ RECORD OF DRAWINGS CARD NO. _______

Office of ALBERT KAHN, Architect, ERNEST WILBY, Associate, 58-60 Lafayette Ave., Detroit, Mich.

BUILDING _______ LOCATED _______

Sheet No.	Order No.	Date	Sent To	Date Ack. Rec'd	No. of Copies	Remarks	Sheet No.	Order No.	Date	Sent To	Date Ack. Rec'd	No. of Copies	Remarks

(10)

Week Ending _______

Weekly Report on Progress of Building for _______ Job No. _______

State in full progress and present status of work. Advise of contractors not completing work with dispatch. State how progress of building compares with progress schedule. If behind schedule, state why and possibilities for making up time.

RECEIVED BULLETINS

Supt. _______

Superintendent to hand report to office each week. Keep carbon copy in book on job. Turn in on completion.

(17)

JOB NO. _______ DRAUGHTING ROOM RECORD CARD NO. _______

Office of ALBERT KAHN, Architect, ERNEST WILBY, Associate, 58-60 Lafayette Ave., Detroit, Mich.

BUILDING _______ LOCATED _______

DRAUGHTSMEN IN CHARGE _______ WHEN PROMISED _______

	Date	By Whom	Form	Referred To	Date	Remarks
INFORMATION REC'D						
SKETCHES MADE						
BOOK OPENED						
SURVEY						
WORKING DRAWINGS STARTED						
CONSTRUCTION DESIGNED						
PENCIL DRAWINGS FINISHED						
TRACING STARTED						
PRELIMINARY SET PRINTED						
PLANS CHECKED						
SPECS. STARTED						
SPECS. PRINTED						
PLANS PRINTED—NOT INCLUDING						
STRUCTURAL DRAWINGS						
HEATING, PLUMBING						
WIRING, ELEVATORS						
SPRINKLERS, INTERIOR FINISH						
FIXTURES						
REFERRED TO FRONT OFFICE						
BUILDING PERMIT SECURED						
CONTRACT COPY FILED						
OFFICE COPY MADE						
PLANS REVISED						
GRAPHICAL REPORT MADE						

(11)

Bldg. _______ Job No. _______ Date _______

Work at the above building DEVIATES from the ARCHITECT'S plans or specifications as follows:
(Give detailed description, sketch if possible, and reason for change. This report is to give ALL changes, even though such changes are covered by orders, bulletins or contractor's structural drawings.)

Supt. _______

Authorized by Bulletin No. _______ Order No. _______ or by whom _______

Credit or Addition to Contract _______

(18)

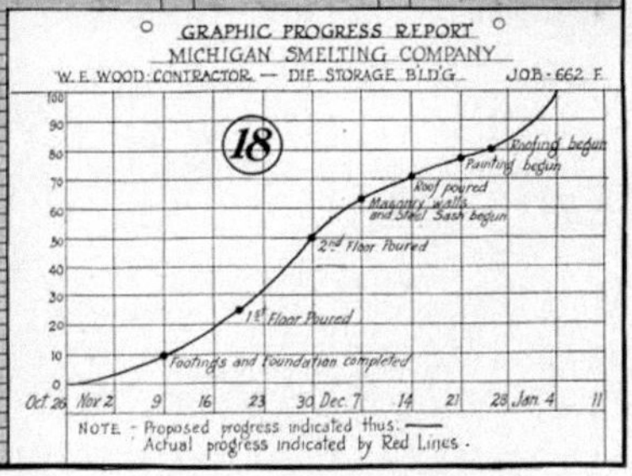

8 "Follow-up" Return Card
9 Superintendents' Daily Report
10 Supts.' Weekly Report (size 7½x10)
11 Superintendents' Report (size 8¼x10¾)
12 Receipt Card
13 Draftsman's Time Card
14 Office Print Record
15 Contractors' Print Record
16 Progress Record of Drawings
17 Office Record of the Commission
18 Graphic Progress Report

REPRODUCTION OF FORMS IN USE IN THE OFFICES OF ALBERT KAHN, ARCHITECT

In Mr. Kahn's practice, particular attention is paid to the business administration of the work. To this end a practical, up-to-date system and a staff of competent accountants are employed.

All departments have graphical progress reports for their work. At the beginning of any work the estimated progress is indicated by a curve in black ink on co-ordinate paper, and the actual progress recorded from day to day in red ink. Any marked divergence in these curves indicates serious delay, and daily inspection of the records enables prompt action to be taken to remove it. The superintendent reports his progress in this way and also by means of daily and weekly reports. Reproduction of the superintendent's progress schedule is shown herewith, others for drafting and specification rooms are similar. Thus a general and detailed supervision of all work is possible from the executive offices.

Examples of the various reports kept for the different items of work are illustrated herewith, also samples of reports and certificates. The general scheme of office procedure is, briefly, inter-office communication for preliminary notification or questions and bulletins for formal notification. The forms for these latter are not reproduced. They are on lightweight paper of standard letter size, green being used for inter-office communication and buff for bulletins. Deviations from plans and specifications as based on contract are formally ordered on official order blanks. These, together with contracts, give the accounting department all necessary information.

It could safely be assumed from the magnitude of work of consistently good character that this office produces, that its working plant would exhibit marks of orderly business arrangement. The brief description noted here, together with the reproductions of office forms in use, prove this thought not to be unfounded. Mr. Kahn's office is particularly successful in combining two ideals that must characterize any successful office. The dignity and art aspect of the architectural profession are fully represented, and to no less a degree is the business structure upon which harmonious professional relations depend recognized.

Interior View of Consultation Room
Offices of Albert Kahn, Architect, Detroit, Michigan

Vandivert Photos

1.

2.

3.

HOLABIRD & ROOT

BACK to the World's Columbian Expositio and earlier go the beginnings of Holabird & Root, front-rank Chicago architectural firm Son of Daniel H. ("Make no little plans") Burnham's partner, whose fame today rests not on the 1893 Fair but on the bleak, utilitarian Monadnock building, John Wellborn Root entered the firm of Holabird & Roche in 1919, eight years later formed a partnership with William Holabird's son John Augur Since then the firm has done an impressive list of sleek, important buildings, notable among which are 333 North Michigan, Chicago Board of Trade, Chicago Daily News, Stevens Hotel (world's largest) Forest Products Laboratory in Madison, Wisconsin, and the North Dakota State Capitol (with De Remer and Kurke), given distinction to a A Century of Progress with its prize-winning Chrysler exposition building, found itself in the midst of depression with a handful of key men who designed slot machines and streamliners for want of anything larger. Today, like other firms throughout the U.S., the office of Holabird & Root is filling out again, and takes time off to pose for its composite picture Included is that handsomest of all pictures: an architect's office (10)—with a client in it With things once again under way, Partners Holabird and Root (upper left) prepare for a busy year, agree that the future looks even more promising.

Helmuth Bartsch (1) is one of the firm's crack designers, graduated from architectural school in Berlin in 1924, has been with the office for eight years. J. Z. Burgee (2), in charge of superintendence and contracts, is now in his fourteenth year with the office Too busy to turn around was H. J. B. Hoskins (3), chief specification writer, formerly of Birmingham, England, Cape Town, South Africa, and, for the past 22 years, Chicago. The gentleman who can draw without taking his coat off (4) is J. C. Sherrick, Illinois graduate, head of the drafting room and (5) is the drafting room of which Mr. Sherrick is head David Werner Carlson (6), designer, not only takes off his coat when he draws, but rolls up his sleeves. (7) might be a quiet corner in a bank; it contains Frank A. Byrne, (mechanical and electrical engineering) and Verne O. McClurg (air conditioning and structural engineering).

4.

5.

6.

7.

8.

9.

Holabird & Root has done its own interior decorating for years; in charge is Johns H. Hopkins **(8)**. For 28 years Richard McP. Cabeen **(9)**, designer, has been with the office; he is an authority on the planning of office buildings, hotels, and theaters. Messrs. Holabird, Root, Cabeen, two clients, and a model **(10)**. Designers Bartsch, Carlson, and Partner Root **(11)**. More oblivious are these two draftsmen in rear elevation.

10.

11.

12.

PRIORITIES MEAN TO BUILDING

REN'S HOME..RECREATION..BUSINESS

INGS..FACTORY..SCHOOL..CLUB..

ING TYPES STUDY ON HOSPITALS

50th ANNIVERSARY YEAR

ARCHITECTURAL record

AUGUST 1941

THE FIRM OF SHREVE, LAMB & HARMON

A first-hand account of how an outstanding office is organized and how it operates. . . . It's the first of several similar stories pesented to give a behind-the-scenes picture of America's architects in action and to report the personnel, policies and procedure that make for success in day-by-day office operation.

By HENRY H. SAYLOR, AIA

All photographs by the author.

ARCHITECTURAL OFFICES are something like the cells of living tissue. Cells double up and split. Where there was one today, two may exist tomorrow. A famous firm of New York City was such a cell. One day it was Carrère and Hastings; the next day it was Carrère & Hastings, Shreve & Lamb; shortly afterward it became two offices instead of one.

It was in 1924 that the inevitable split occurred. Among the more sizable jobs in the office were the Fisk, Macmillan and Standard Oil buildings. Upon the insistence of the clients, these works were completed under a temporary association of Carrère and Hastings and the new firm of Shreve, Lamb and Blake. Theodore Blake subsequently returned to the C. and H. fold, and five years later Arthur Loomis Harmon joined the firm of Shreve & Lamb.

Each of the three partners has achieved distinction as an individual, entirely apart from the firm's outstanding reputation. Each has been elevated to Fellowship in the Institute.

Richmond H. Shreve had been two or three years late in entering Cornell to study architecture, due to his having had to go to work after high school days to earn his tuition expenses. This work was in an architect's office and brought a sense of values that made up for the delay.

After his four-year course Shreve's appetite for graduate study was satisfied through Cornell's offer of an instructor's job. He also prepared illustrations for a textbook on shades and shadows. Even then, time hung heavily on his hands until, at the suggestion of the faculty, Carrère and Hastings made him clerk of the works for a million dollars' worth of buildings they were erecting on the campus. Just how one man could pursue graduate study, instruct freshmen in the graphic arts, and hold down a full-time job of clerk of the works is not clear, but Shreve did it. The Cornell buildings finished, Mr. Carrère asked him to join the New York office. By 1920 he had become a partner.

Mr. Shreve was Chief Architect of the Williamsburg Housing Project, and of the Vladeck Housing Project, each carried out by a group of associated architects. For the New York World's Fair, he served as a member of its Board of Design. He is at present Chairman of the Board of Design of Parkchester, Metropolitan Life's big residential community. His outside activities include the past-presidency of the New York Building Congress and membership on the Advisory Board of Architects of Goucher College, Baltimore, and on the Advisory Council of the College of Architecture of Cornell University. After serving two terms as Regional Director of the New York District, AIA, he was elected President of the Institute last May.

William F. Lamb was graduated from Williams College before he elected to follow architecture. In his first summer after graduation he served as an office boy for the architectural office of Frank Helmle, probably at the foot of his class in earnings—three dollars per week. Two years of the architectural course at Columbia would ordinarily have been considered hopelessly inadequate preparation for the Ecole des Beaux-Arts, but after that short period of training Lamb was admitted to the Paris school as top man among those attempting the entrance examinations.

After four years he was awarded the coveted *Diplome par le Gouvernement Francais*, returned to New York and at once entered the office of Carrère & Hastings. By 1920 he also had become a partner in the firm then styled Carrère & Hastings, Shreve & Lamb.

For three years — 1937-9 — Mr. Lamb was the hub of the World's Fair Board of Design. He coordinated the work of all the outside architects and directed the design activities of the Fair's Board of Design. President Roosevelt made him a member of the national Commission of Fine Arts, a post which he now occupies. For the City of New York he served as a member of the Art Commission. In 1932 Williams College honored him with the degree, Doctor of Science.

Arthur Loomis Harmon was born in Chicago, earned his way through a year of architectural study at the Armour Institute and the Art Institute. The combination did not seem to be giving him the training he sought, so he came to New York and entered the architectural school at Columbia in the fall of 1898. This should have brought him to graduation in 1902, but he beat the gun by a year and went back to his home town. The summers between terms had offered little time in the way of vacation. In one of them Harmon worked as a carpenter on a house that the late Frank Wallis had designed in Montclair.

Back in Chicago, Harmon saw the inside of several offices—Holabird and Roche, D. H. Burnham and Company, Howard Van Doren Shaw, Benjamin Marshall. But the lure of New York beckoned and Mr. Harmon came east in search of a new connection. Walking along the street, he met William Partridge who invited him up to help render the reconstructed L'Enfant plan of Washington in the McKim, Mead & White office. It proved to be a nine-year tenure in that distinguished organization, interrupted only by travel and a look at the architecture abroad. For two

SENIOR PARTNERS: top, Richmond H. Shreve; center, William F. Lamb; bottom, Arthur Loomis Harmon

years he practiced in association with Wallis and Goodwillie, then on his own until he joined Messrs. Shreve and Lamb in 1929.

Mr. Harmon is a past president of the New York Chapter, AIA, and also of the Architectural League of New York. He is a member of the National Academy of Design and the Fine Arts Federation of New York City. In 1925 The League awarded to him its Gold Medal for the Shelton Hotel, and that same monument brought him the Gold Medal of the American Institute of Architects.

So much for the individual backgrounds. In view of these, it is rather surprising to find the office of Shreve, Lamb & Harmon an example of closely welded teamwork. Three such vigorous personalities do not often find it possible to merge their efforts in a comfortable collaboration, year in and year out.

How do the wants and needs of a new client become translated into working documents and a completed structure? Sometimes all three of the partners are in on the first conferences, occasionally only two, but Shreve is pretty sure to be one of them. From this point the development of the design usually becomes the personal responsibility of either Lamb or Harmon until the preliminary drawings are made, a scheme accepted and the work put into the hands of a job captain to be executed. Both Lamb and Harmon refuse to be cheated out of the fun of putting a scheme on paper with their own hands. In the private office of each, drawing-board, T-square and triangles are in front of the principal's seat. Letters, memoranda and other impedimenta may cover them for a while, but the actual tools of design are never put aside.

The office is conducted on the job captain plan, but rather more so than usual. A job captain, having been given the accepted preliminary sketches, not only makes the working drawings, aided by his crew, but writes the specifications and supervises the job. He is the one man who is expected to know all about the job in his care. Having been with it daily and hourly since its inception, he does know it, else he would not be holding the job captain's table. A man out of an architectural school usually serves seven or eight years before he achieves a job captaincy.

In this procedure, specifications take form with the drawings instead of being written afterwards, thus avoiding the inevitable risk of gaps in conformity. Matters of design are subject to the constant supervision of either Mr. Lamb or Mr. Harmon, sometimes of both. Although Mr. Shreve leaves the evolution of a design pretty much in the hands of whichever partner is controlling it, he is likely to step into the batter's box when presentation drawings are about ready for submission to the client. When he does, his criticism is usually aimed from the client's point of view. He will question the workability of the building rather than a detail of esthetics.

A distinctive feature of the Shreve, Lamb & Harmon office is its Operating Committee. Four persons constitute its membership. In effect they are junior partners. Their names appear on the building's directory, on the letterhead and as individual listings in the telephone directory, and in addition to their salaries they participate in the profits. Every Thursday the four lunch together in a private room at a nearby restaurant, discussing ways and means of conducting the office more efficiently, allocating tasks and supervision among themselves, counseling upon "hiring and firing." The extent to which these administrative efforts relieve the three partners from routine and free them for more creative work is one of the conspicuous characteristics of the organization.

Three of the four Operating Committee members pioneered with the young firm of Shreve & Lamb when it stepped out on its own from under the Carrère & Hastings banner: H. F. Vanderbeck, Margaret Livsey and H. R. Dowswell. H. C. Bernhard came out of Cornell, the son of an architect now retired but for many years architectural engineer of James Gamble Rogers' office. Before he had had time to orient himself in the S. L. & H. office Bernhard found himself in charge of the Reynolds Tobacco Company Building, a two-million dollar project in Winston-Salem. Neither he nor the building came out of it any the worse for the shotgun marriage, and Bernhard has been job-captaining ever since. It was about three years ago that he was made a member of the Operating Committee.

Vanderbeck began as an office boy in Carrère & Hastings' office. Today he is a revered master of preliminary drawings. They say he can knock out a set of sketch plans almost before Mr. Lamb or Mr. Harmon finishes explaining to him a tentative *parti*. Another branch of the office practice that inevitably falls to his hand is tenant space—the design or remodeling of leaseholds in office buildings the firm has built. That sort of work, incidentally, is the nearest approach

OPERATING COMMITTEE: left to right, H. F. Vanderbeck, H. R. Dowswell, H. C. Bernhard and Margaret Livsey

to a backlog in the firm's practice. In good times and bad it keeps rolling along.

Miss Livsey was one of Shreve's assistants in the C. & H. office and is, according to him, his "boss." She has added to her jobs that of confidential secretary, the hiring, training and managing of the clerical accounting staffs, and the correlation of all and sundry information and records of the firm's activities. I suspect she knows more of what is going on in the wide orbit of the office than any other single individual, and I am quite sure that she knows enough to pass through to R. H. S., W. F. L. and A. L. H. only what it is good for them to know. An after-hours visitor to the office, awaiting one of the staff, regretted the fact that he had encountered no member of the firm; but he had been much impressed by the activities of "Mrs. Shreve, Lamb & Harmon."

Dowswell has made a national reputation for himself as an all-'round technician and specification writer.

No individual in the S. L. & H. office has a secretary. There is a secretarial pool of highly trained girls —five at present—who work in very close collaboration. Any one of them is subject to call by the partners, associates and job captains. The obvious objection that in this system no one girl becomes familiar with all the names and personal relationships involved seems to have been overcome by unusually close teamwork of the five and their long service together. Correspondence files and library are in charge of a file clerk who is also a trained librarian. Accounting, bookkeeping, telephone and reception work are done by persons expert in each special field rather than by members of the general secretarial pool.

Down the lefthand margin of the draftsman's weekly time sheet are printed the office regulations. Hours are 9 to 5, with the hour between 1 and 2 for lunch. Draftsmen register their arrival and departure at the reception room desk. Extra time and make-up time are recorded on special daily tickets and require the approval of the job captain. Persons employed for six months or more are entitled to half pay for sick time, up to two weeks in any one year. After the first six months of employment, vacation time is earned at the rate of one week for each six months prior to June 1st of any year. The drafting staff is on a five-day week the year round; the clerical staff, a 5½ day week.

Unlike some of the large offices, this one believes in enlisting the services of outside structural and mechanical engineers rather than maintaining its own. Of course, with long-experienced master builders like Dowswell in the place, the office needs no outside help in figuring steel or sizing pipe for the ordinary job, but they usually call in engineers with whom they are constantly collaborating, to do the job more quickly and without the cross-checking the regular staff would feel was needed in this less familiar work.

Several contract forms are used by the office. Those calling for cost plus a fee are drawn after the pattern arising from the firm's experience. For lump-sum contracts, the AIA long or

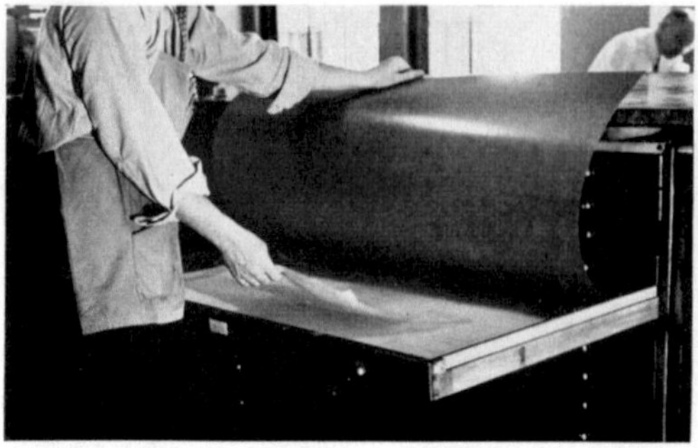

Drawings for active jobs are filed flat

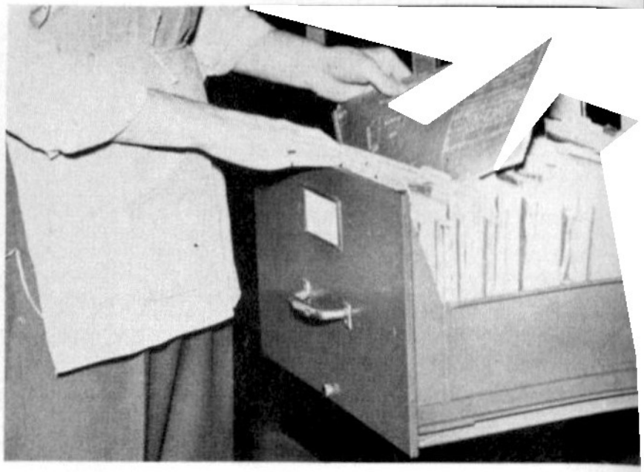

. . . and shop drawings folded to legal size

short forms are used as a general rule.

Change orders are made out in quadruplicate, and must originate in the contractor's office. Each is a proposal of the contractor to do a certain piece of work for a specified sum. The original, when approved by both architect and owner, is sent to the contractor; copies are retained by owner, job captain and auditing department.

Minutes are written covering all meetings of owner's representatives with architects and builders, listing those who attended and setting down the findings agreed upon. Decisions made by the firm, the associates or job captain are invariably put into memorandum form and filed as a documentary history of the job.

The system of numbering drawings is helpful. In addition to the job number, a working drawing will bear a combination of four digits. The first two digits, from left, give the classification as to materials, 20 being reserved for the general plans and elevations. The final two digits become more specific. Thus 2001 is the first floor plan; 2006, the sixth floor plan. Scale details of first floor plan would take the number 2011; full-size details of first floor would be labeled 2021. Numbers below the 2000 are for preliminary drawings in order of production. A number starting with 21 indicates that it is concerned with excavation; if with terra cotta it starts with 34. Each category of construction has its regular number, ranging from 21 through 55. Thus the number of a drawing alone is sufficient to identify its purpose, and the subtitle becomes unnecessary.

Each working drawing bears, along its righthand edge, a table in which is entered each successive revision, if any, and each issue of prints. A glance at this tabular matter on any original will show when prints were issued, to whom, and the package number under which they were sent out. Drawings are kept flat in drawers between pressboard guides while the job is active, then rolled in a large tube, indexed and stored.

Sheet sizes of working drawings are established for each job by the size of plans and elevations at the desired scale with regard for stock widths of linen. Once established, this sheet size is maintained throughout the job. Drawings are made in ink on linen in cases where much blue-printing is anticipated. Government jobs require it in all cases. Full-size details requiring few prints are made in pencil on paper. Minor jobs are occasionally drawn in pencil on linen, or even on paper.

Shop drawings are received in duplicate; one is returned with approval or corrections, one is folded to legal file size and filed under category guides and job number with the drawing file clerk. It is an unwritten rule of the office that each shop drawing submitted is returned with approval or corrections within five days.

Every drawing or print that leaves or arrives at the office is recorded by the clerk in charge of the file. Prints going out are accompanied by a transmittal form typed in triplicate: original with the prints, duplicate to the job captain, triplicate to the drawing clerk's file. This specifies the

Drafting room of the Shreve, Lamb & Harmon organization

rk's desk where all drawings are checked in and out

Photographic records of completed jobs are uniformly bound for reference

drawing by name and number, to whom it is sent, and for what purpose.

The lads who are entrusted with these files usually step up from the office boys, and these are selected with far more than the usual care. Most of them come from the Brooklyn Technical High School's architectural department. To qualify, a boy must have ambition to become an architect, and a conviction that he has a long and hard road of study ahead. The office gladly pays half the cost of night-class schooling he will undertake. Ten or twelve of these boys have put their feet on the ladder; two have gone on up to Cornell; four or five have studied at New York University.

Recalling their own early days and the awesome difficulties of getting a start, the firm established some years ago the Shreve, Lamb & Harmon Fellowship at Cornell. Each year the faculty selects from the senior class in the architectural school a man whose record and personality deserve this recognition. He is welcomed to the office on a year's contract at a salary that will support him comfortably in New York. In that year the organization tries to acquaint him with every branch of the work, including outside supervision. It is an ideal arrangement for the fledgling, giving him every opportunity of finding the particular niche his tastes and capabilities indicate. At the end of the year he will either have shown that there is a place for him in the organization or will seek new fields.

A subject on which I sought information was the march of new products and techniques. How does the office keep abreast of these? Messrs. Dowswell and Bernhard try to see every salesman who calls and hear his story. Catalogues and data sheets that he may leave are filed in the regular AIA file, and it is an extensive one. Advertising matter which arrives by mail is routed by Miss Livsey to Mr. Bernhard who indicates what is to be filed and what destroyed. For the sake of convenient and economical filing space, all hands plead for the standard 8½ x 11 in. size in manufacturers' literature.

New materials and methods that impress Bernhard or Dowswell are shown to S. L. & H. partners for the effect these products may have upon future basic design.

Current magazines are routed to the partners and associates, each marking pages that he wants clipped and filed. These clippings—or sometimes whole issues—are gathered into portfolios covering a wide range of subjects, and stand on the library shelves, accessible to any of the staff. In the office library stands a row of tall portfolios, each a photographic record of an architectural achievement in the firm's less than twenty years of practice.

At the moment the large drafting-room is only sparsely occupied with active boards. On two lower floors, however, are large rooms filled elbow-to-elbow with draftsmen and engineers busy with plans for the Army's Newfoundland Outlying Defense Base. And the name on the doors is "Shreve, Lamb & Harmon, Fay, Spofford & Thorndike, Architect-Engineer." The Newfoundland Base job, like Trinidad and Bermuda, was awarded to the architect-engineer combinations on the basis of cost plus a fixed fee.

NEWLY ELECTED PRESIDENT OF THE AIA

RICHMOND H. SHREVE, with a bent for "order, forethought and system," discusses architectural practice and the trend of a changing professional field.

TWO invitations were important factors in the professional life of R. H. Shreve. The first, extended by John M. Carrère in the course of a warm friendship, invited the young man to leave his instructorship at Cornell and enter the Carrère & Hastings office. The second, offered with some heat by Thomas Hastings, invited Shreve, then a partner in the firm, to leave the office within 24 hours. Shreve accepted the first and declined the second.

While Carrère was debating whether to put the new employee, brought down from Cornell, on the New York Library job, or on a large country house, Shreve roamed the office, seeking what he could devour. The mail seemed a promising tidbit, so he opened and routed it. A new sort of indoor game was soon evolved. Shreve played it with himself as opponent. He would study in advance a

SmithGroupJJR

Headquarters
Detroit, MI

Other Locations
Ann Arbor, MI; Chicago, IL; Dallas, TX; Los Angeles, CA; Madison, WI; Phoenix, AZ; San Francisco, CA; Washington, D.C.; Shanghai, China

Founding and Key Partners
Sheldon Smith, Maxwell Grylls, Theodore Hinchman (founding principals), Minoru Yamasaki, George Hellmuth, Joseph Leinweber

Ezra Stoller, Esto

Currently one of the largest architecture and engineering firms in the world, the office today known as SmithGroupJJR was founded in 1853 by Sheldon Smith. Never formally trained as an architect, Smith opened his office in Sandusky, Ohio, before moving it to Detroit in 1955. The firm continued as a family practice under his son Mortimer L. Smith and grandson Fred L. Smith through the end of the nineteenth century. In 1903, Fred Smith joined two engineers, Henry G. Field and Theodore H. Hinchman, to form Field, Hinchman & Smith. Three years later, H. J. Maxwell Grylls replaced Field and the firm became Smith, Hinchman & Grylls (SH&G), the name under which it practiced for nearly a century.

Growing in concert with the industrial expansion of Detroit in the first decades of the twentieth century, the office quickly became one of the few architecture firms in the city to take on factory commissions. Among the most prolific designers of industrial facilities in Michigan and adjacent Ontario, Canada, SH&G produced factories for Ford, Daisy Manufacturing Company, Olds Motor Works and Olds Gasoline Engine Works, Walker & Sons, and Dodge Brothers, all designed prior to 1905.

From its early years, the practice of SH&G was characterized by vertically integrated departments and a close integration of architecture and engineering across a wide range of industrial, civic, entertainment, medical, research, and residential commissions. Its factory expertise for Detroit manufacturers extended overseas with an assembly plant for General Motors in Antwerp, Belgium (1948–1953). As a major firm in the Detroit area, SH&G launched the careers of a number of architects after World War II. Notable among these were chief designer Minoru Yamasaki and partners George Hellmuth and Joseph Leinweber, who left SH&G in 1949 to found a group practice that would eventually split into Yamasaki & Associates and Hellmuth, Obata + Kassabaum (HOK), two of the largest US firms of the second half of the twentieth century.

Throughout much of its history, SH&G complemented its more well-known commissions with less visible projects for correctional facilities, military bases and hospitals, corporate research centers, and federal buildings. In the 1980s and 1990s, its international factory work grew to include plants for Imperial Oil and DaimlerChrysler in Canada, Caterpillar Engine in Russia, Renault in Brazil, and General Motors, Midwesco, Weyerhaeuser, and American Axle Manufacturing in Mexico. In the 2000s, the firm's projects have included hospitals and research laboratories in India, Algeria, South Korea, and China.

In 2000, Smith, Hinchman & Grylls was renamed SmithGroup. A year later, the office merged with landscape and planning firm JJR, which was founded in Michigan in 1961, to become SmithGroupJJR. — AWS & MK

1873–1970

D.H. Burnham & Company

Headquarters
Chicago, IL

Founding and Key Partners
John Wellborn Root, Daniel H. Burnham (founding principals), Ernest R. Graham, Hubert Burnham, Daniel Burnham Jr., William Peirce Anderson, Edward Mathias Probst, Howard Judson White

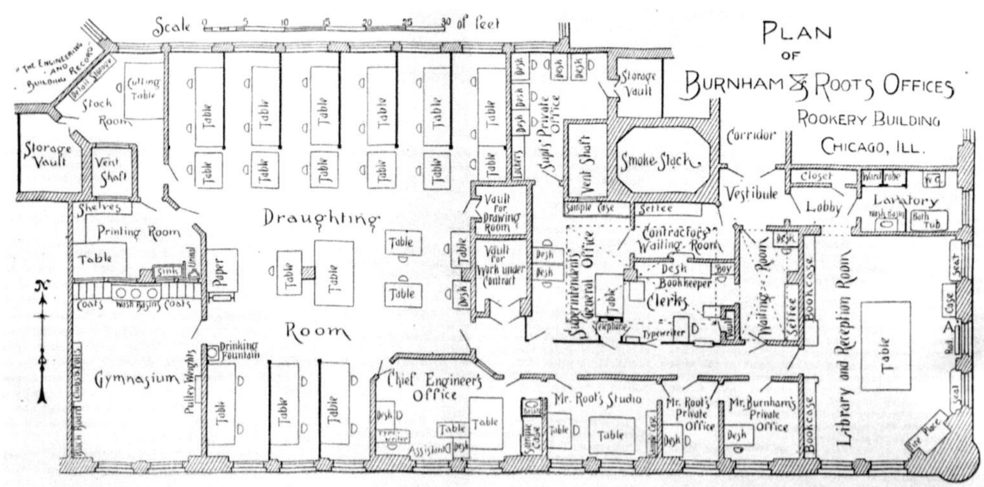

The Engineering & Building Record, January 11, 1890

Cited in any discourse on the emergence of large architectural firms in the United States is the office of D. H. Burnham & Company, the largest private architectural firm of the early twentieth century. The firm's managerial and professional advancements, including Daniel Burnham's involvement in early professional bodies—the Western Association of Architects and the American Institute of Architects—marked a new era in which the architect emerged as a professional operating within a large, organized office. These advances established a context in which projects of great scale and complexity could be realized, such as the iconic Monadnock Building (1891) and Merchandise Mart (1930) in Chicago and the Flatiron Building in New York City (1902).

The firm was established in 1873, when two young architects, Daniel Burnham and John Wellborn Root, ages 26 and 23, respectively, opened Burnham & Root in Chicago. Throughout their collaboration, Burnham served as the business arm and public face of the office, dealing directly with clients and managing the development of the practice, and Root held the role of lead designer. The partners' division of labor proved a successful model. The firm was prolific, designing some two hundred buildings in fewer than twenty years during one particularly active period, and in 1912 eclipsing McKim, Mead & White, the New York office that had previously held the title of largest firm in terms of sheer number of employees.

Occupying office space in buildings of their own design, first in Chicago's Montauk Building (1883) and, later, the Rookery (1888), Burnham & Root organized its employees' desks into areas by specialization—management, administration, drafting, engineering, and construction administration—establishing the strategies of efficiency that allowed the firm to take on large quantities of complex design work. This period of Burnham & Root's success and the following decades were deemed the first Chicago School in architectural history. Together with other Chicago architects the firm both led and benefited from advances in building technology, including a shift from masonry-bearing walls to steel framing as well as early models of the glass curtain wall. These systems would come to symbolize the commercial office building typology—Burnham & Root's bread and butter.

When Root died during the firm's planning of the World's Columbian Exposition, the Chicago's World Fair (1893), Burnham set his gaze on the next phase of the office's development. Hiring new designers to replace Root, including Peirce Anderson in 1900, as well as a construction supervisor, Ernest Graham, to help with the enormous project of realizing the exposition, Burnham put in place a second generation of leaders in the office. Under the name of D.H. Burnham & Co., the office came to focus on large-scale projects and added branches in New York City and San Francisco. Burnham also expanded his practice abroad, travelling to the Philippines during the winter of 1904–1905. Burnham had been hired by the US government to design a master plan for Manila (1905), envisioning the city's growth to 800,000 residents, and a master plan for the city of Baguio as well. Appointed by W. Cameron Forbes, on behalf of the US Philippines Commission, Burnham's master plan represented the complex colonial relationship between the United States and the Philippines, acquired in 1898 at the end of the Spanish-American War. Burnham's largely unbuilt plan for Manila deployed precepts from the City Beautiful Movement and attempted to simultaneously be, in Burnham's words, an "adequate expression of the destiny of the Filipino people."[1]

Despite criticism for his lack of progressive design vision from contemporaries like Louis Sullivan, who questioned Burnham's focus on "bigness, organization, delegation, intense commercialism," Burnham's ability to gauge public taste and to practice across a range of styles allowed the office to grow.[2] After Burnham's death in 1912, the firm was reborn as Graham, Burnham & Co. Once Daniel Burnham's sons left in 1917 to form Burnham Brothers, the firm was renamed Graham Anderson Probst & White, and it operated under that name until 1970 when it was sold to one of its employees, Robert Surman. —AL

① Quoted in Charles Moore, *Daniel H. Burnham, Architect: Planner of Cities* (Boston and New York: Houghton Mifflin Company, 1921): 195.

② Louis Sullivan quoted in Thomas Hines, *Burnham of Chicago: Architect and Planner* (Chicago: The University of Chicago Press, 1979): XXV.

THE AUSTIN COMPANY

1878–

The Austin Company

Headquarters
Cleveland, OH

Other Locations
New York, NY; Philadelphia, PA; Detroit, MI; Pittsburgh, PA; Birmingham, AL; Seattle, WA; St. Louis, MO; Los Angeles, CA; Dallas, TX; Japan; Australia; Canada; Mexico; Belgium; Netherlands; United Kingdom; Irvine, CA; Portage, MI; Atlanta, GA; Leon, Mexico

Founding and Key Partners
Samuel Austin (founding principal), Wilbert J. Austin

Current Partners
Mike Pierce (president)

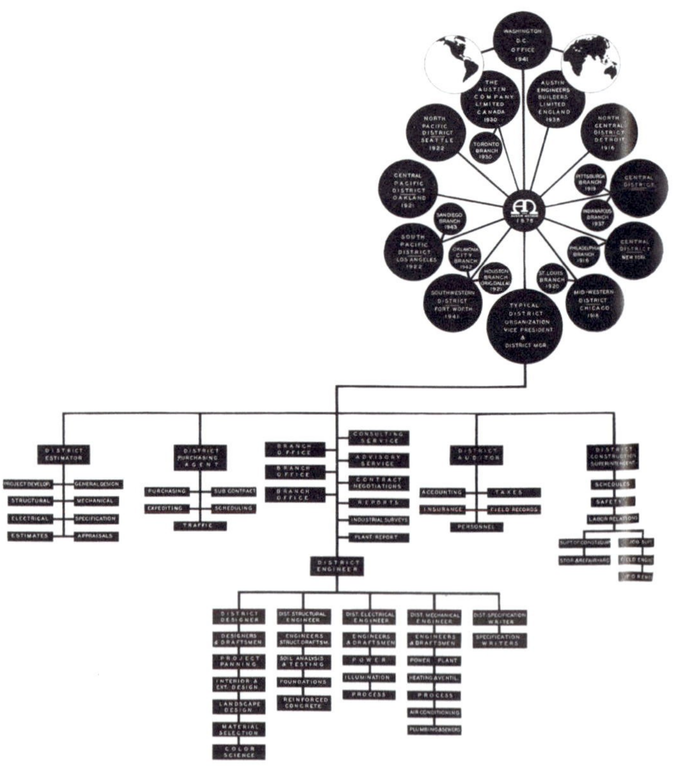

Architectural Forum, January 1945

Standardized, yet variable, building units that are designed, produced, and assembled quickly and economically under the auspices and expertise of a single firm define The Austin Method, a "full-service" industrial building process spearheaded and trademarked by The Austin Company in 1913. Founded in 1878 in Cleveland, Ohio by Samuel Austin, the firm quickly gained prominence and notoriety in the United States and abroad by working under the slogan "undivided responsibility." With hundreds of employees, including builders, contractors, draftsmen, and salesmen, The Austin Company challenged what was then standard practice: maintaining professional divisions between architects, engineers, and contractors, and prioritizing and building for a-la-carte desires rather than average, industry-wide requirements. Instead, the firm promised accelerated planning and construction to their clients, whose industries varied from incandescent lighting to airplanes. One of its brochures boasted that "plans for factories could be drawn and accepted while the excavation was being made."

Like its Iron Belt contemporary Albert Kahn Associates and other architecture firms who saw and reaped the economic benefits of building standardization, The Austin Company profited from the assembly line-based industrialization that would define wartime America. After World War II, the firm advertised extensively in the popular press and elite business glossies alike, promoting itself as the maker of modern and efficient factories of the future. It pledged to give form and space to the new assembly line industries as allegedly forward-thinking as itself. During the latter half of the twentieth century, The Austin Company Standard Factories were built worldwide. With several autonomous offices in each hemisphere, the firm became a major exponent of the prefabricated factory building.

Today a wholly owned subsidiary of the Kajima USA Group, The Austin Company utilizes research-based focus groups to collaborate with outside experts and diversify its own areas of building expertise. From the one-story, saw-toothed, Austin Standard Daylight Building of the 1910s and the windowless, climate-controlled factories of the late 1930s to atomic-war ready shelters of the 1970s, the firm now produces the neutrally clad, acres-wide containers of robotics, catwalks, and computers of present-day industrial complexes and accepts commissions in areas such as television broadcasting and web-based product distribution.
— CB

1879–1961

McKim, Mead & White

Headquarters
New York, NY

Founding Partners
Charles Follen McKim,
William Rutherford Mead,
Stanford White

1961

The Brickbuilder, December 1913

Employing more than 110 designers at the time of the World's Columbian Exposition in 1893, McKim, Mead & White was cited by *Brickbuilder* in 1913 as "the one office from which has come the greatest volume of architectural design and executed buildings in any age or in any country."[1] Though the firm was soon surpassed in scale by the office of Daniel Burnham, at the height of its operation, it served as a model for large architectural offices and nurtured many of the architects who went on to lead those practices. Between 1900 and 1910, McKim, Mead & White's contracts reached a total of over $36 million. The New York City firm produced a total of over 940 projects during its eighty-plus years in business.

McKim, Mead & White opened in 1879 in a country emerging from a recession in the previous decade. The economic upturn offered a range of commissions for the three young architects, Charles Follen McKim, William Rutherford Mead, and Stanford White, whose backgrounds provided access to elite social spheres on the East Coast. The office's work in the following decades ranged from summer houses through casinos to libraries. The firm designed a variety of projects types, diversifying their expertise rather than specializing in a single program. Prior to the deaths of the founding partners, the office was responsible for many of the largest cultural commissions in the United States, including the main buildings of the World's Columbian Exposition in Chicago (1893), the central branch of the Boston Public Library (1895), and the campus for Columbia University in New York (1897). All delivered academic Beaux-Arts composition through American methods of professionalized office production. Yet the office was also distinct in its organizational structure from the large firms that followed it. Despite the many designers employed in the office, the firm did not employ an overall strategy or bureaucratic system for "efficiency," it instead gathered its draftsmen in one large room and its principals in another in its first office space. Throughout its lifespan, the firm designated no chief draftsman or superintendent. Designers aligned themselves with one of the partners and were responsible for all aspect of a project with the help of experts in accounting, specifications writing, and contract documents.

McKim, Mead & White completed a number of high-profile buildings in Canada and Cuba, including the Bank of Montreal Building in Manitoba (1913) and the Hotel Nacional de Cuba in Havana (1930). The firm's influence abroad extended to McKim's interest in fostering the growth of young architects, included his funding of a traveling scholarship in his name. The partners' most enduring legacy abroad remains the founding of the American Academy in Rome, which is housed in a classical building designed by McKim, Mead & White in 1914. McKim had worked to fund the establishment of the American Academy since the late 1880s as a home base for traveling scholars in Europe, including recipients of the McKim scholarship. The program of the Academy was modeled on the Prix de Rome—the pinnacle of the French Beaux Arts training system—reappropriated for American architects abroad.

McKim, Mead & White retained its original name until 1961, long after its founding partners had died. In 1961 in turned into Steinman, Corrigill, Cain and White, to be reborn in its last incarnation, as Walker O. Cain and Associates, in 1971. —AL

(1)
Everett Waid, "The Business Side of An Architect's Office: The Office of Messrs Mckim, Mead and White," *The Brickbuilder*, Volume XXII, Number 12 (December 1913): 267.

1880–

Holabird & Root

Headquarters
Chicago, IL

Founding and Key Partners
William Holabird, Ossian Simmonds (founding principals), Martin Roche, John Holabird, John Wellborn Root Jr., Joseph Burgee

Architectural Forum, April 1937

Holabird & Root was one of the largest US architectural offices in the first half of the twentieth century. Founded as Holabird & Simmonds in 1880 by William Holabird and Ossian Simmonds, the firm had several incarnations (Holabird, Simonds and Roche, Holabird & Roche), throughout which it played a significant role in the transformation of the Chicago skyline. The firm opened its doors in the aftermath of the Great Chicago Fire (1871), a time when new construction techniques were deployed in the redevelopment of the city center. Holabird and Root were early practitioners of the Chicago School style, and the office was among the pioneers of the structural iron and steel in the construction of early skyscrapers. They gained critical acclaim for the design of the Tacoma Building in 1888, the first Chicago building to deploy a true curtain wall, and the Marquette Building in 1895, one of the first skyscrapers with an exclusively steel structure.

The office enjoyed great success through the turn of the twentieth century, with major projects in Chicago as well as throughout the Midwest. The completion of the La Salle Hotel in Chicago in 1909 cemented the firm's reputation as the premier designer of hotels in the country, and led to other major commissions, including the Muehleback Hotel in Kansas City and the Stevens Hotel, now the Hilton, in Chicago. In 1919, John Holabird, son of William Holabird, and John Root Jr. whose father was a famous architect himself John Root of Burnham & Root, became partners at the firm and effectively took control of daily operations. After the death of Martin Roche in 1927, the firm was reorganized and became Holabird & Root.

The Great Depression reduced the scale and scope of the projects in the office and nearly shuttered the firm. However, after World War II, it emerged once again — renamed Holabird, Root & Burgee — as a leader in hotel design. In the 1950s, the office received its first international commissions: all of them hotels in South America. As part of long-term partnership with Intercontinental Hotels, Holabird, Root & Burgee designed the architecturally acclaimed Tamanaco Hotel in Caracas, the Hotel del Lago in Maracaibo, the Tequendama Hotel in Bogota, and the Hotel Copan in Rio de Janeiro. Further commissions followed, but none would garner as much attention from critics as these four projects.

In 1957, the office once again transformed after the departure of Joseph Burgee, returning to its previous moniker, Holabird & Root. Until 1987 two further generations of Holabirds served as partners in the firm, which continues to operate as Holabird & Root today, though no one with that name is involved in it at this point. — JJ

1882–1970

George A. Fuller Company

Headquarters
Chicago, IL

Other Locations
New York, NY; Boston, MA; Philadelphia, PA; Washington, D.C.; Miami, FL; Montreal, Canada; Shanghai, China

Founding and Key Partners
C. E. Clark, George A. Fuller (founding principals), Harry S. Black, Paul Starrett

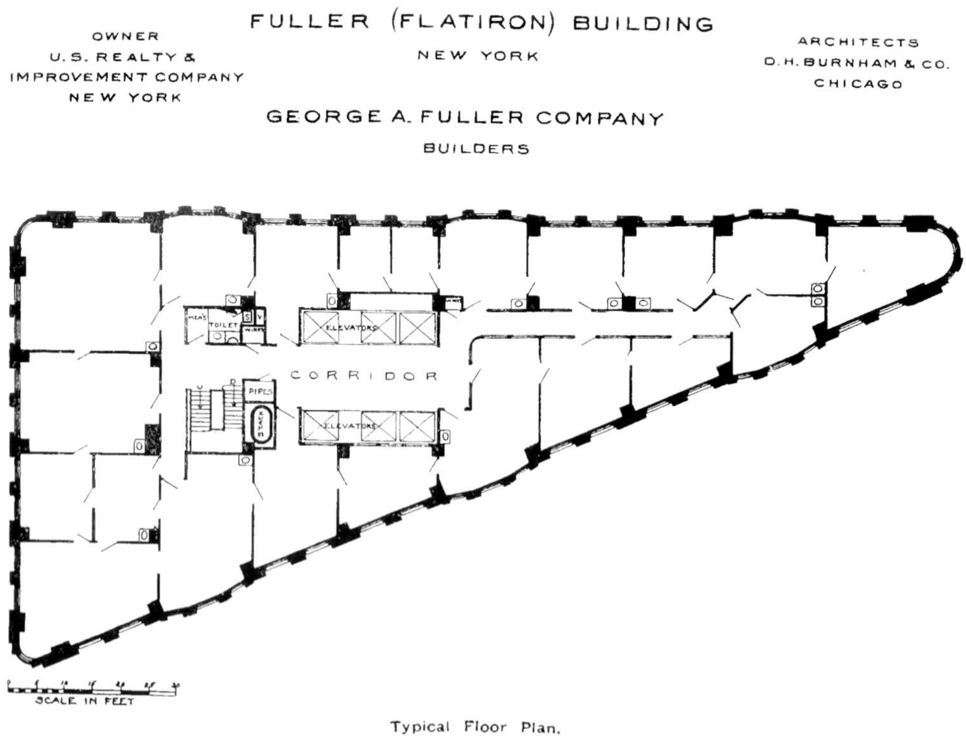

George A. Fuller Company offices in Fuller (Flatiron) Building. *Prominent Buildings Erected by the George A. Fuller Company*, 1910

Founded by George Fuller in 1882 in Chicago, the George A. Fuller Company was one of the most prominent construction companies in the United States by the 1920s. The company expanded quickly in those decades, opening offices in New York, Boston, Philadelphia, Washington DC, and Montreal.

Via these various branches, the company constructed many of the most prominent buildings of the day, including Pennsylvania Station in New York, designed by McKim, Mead & White, and the Flatiron Building, designed by D.H. Burnham & Company—originally called the Fuller Building, as it housed the Fuller company offices in New York. The George A. Fuller Company was one of the first companies to rationalize its construction methods by internalizing subcontracting into specialized in-house departments.

The firm's success was due in part to the Fuller Construction Company of the Orient, a branch of George A. Fuller Company, which introduced reinforced concrete and steel-framed building technologies to Japan after World War I. A delegation of Japanese businessmen who were in the United States to study developments in architecture and city planning, with a particular interest in the skyscraper, asked the two managers of the New York office of the George A. Fuller Company, Paul Starett and William Black, to send a team of engineers to Japan in order to erect "two, and possibly more office buildings on the American model," and thus teach Japanese builders and architects about the construction technologies and organization of US building practices.[1]

The Fuller Construction Company of the Orient constructed several buildings in Japan in the 1920s, including offices for the Nippon Oil Company and the Mail Steamship Company. Building abroad had its complications. Fuller company's chief emissary to Japan Paul Starrett's brother, William Starrett, noted that "[although] it is easy to stand in a Japanese city and visualize a Woolworth Building or a Boston Public Library on any corner, it is a very different matter to construct out there a modern structure, to marshal the leadership and instruct the native labor, to organize where no organizations exists, to translate drawings from shaku and meters to feet and inches, and accurate notations from Japanese to English."[2] Yet Fuller single-handedly transformed the Japanese construction industry. In fact, the George A. Fuller Company was one of many US firms that sought to exploit the potential of foreign markets in the decades between the World Wars, both earning commissions abroad and opening new markets for US manufacturers of building materials through their presence. — RW

① Jeffrey Cody, *Exporting American Architecture, 1870–2000* (London: Routledge, 2003): 74.

② Quoted in Cody, *Exporting American Architecture, 1870–2000*: 76.

1883–1940

1940

Cass Gilbert

Headquarters
New York, NY

Other Locations
St. Paul, MN

Founding Partner
Cass Gilbert

Architectural Record, June 1942

Having received his education at Massachusetts Institute of Technology under the guidance of William Ware, having taken his requisite European tour, and having worked for Stanford White, the youngest and most flamboyant of the McKim, Mead & White partners, Cass Gilbert opened his own office in St. Paul, Minnesota. The year was 1883, and the population of the Twin Cities was about to triple in the following decade, an auspicious moment for a young architect. Gilbert soon formed a partnership with his childhood friend James Knox Taylor, which lasted six years before dissolving. As with many young architects of the period, the World's Columbian Exposition in Chicago (1893) clarified the stylistic path for Gilbert, who would continue to uphold his specific version of classicism after its time had come and gone in the American context.

In 1895, having produced residential work in the Twin City area and often competing against New York architects to get it, Cass Gilbert was selected to design the Minnesota state capitol in St. Paul. The ornate building was finished in 1898, securing an instant national reputation for Gilbert and providing a model of neoclassicism for the post-civil war capitols. A year later, Gilbert moved his practice to New York City, where he remained for the rest of his career. Secured through a competition, his first commission in the city was for the New York City US Custom House (1907). Gilbert received much contemporary praise for it, superseded only by the reaction to Carrère & Hastings's New York Public Library a few years later. This federal commission also cemented his relationship with the Republican administration in Washington, DC. When the United States entered World War I in 1917, Gilbert offered his services to Woodrow Wilson's government without profit. Although his support for the war quickly lessened, his taste for American exceptionalism remained strong. Seen more positively, Gilbert channeled his politics into architecture, and his buildings were in turn read by some as "an ornament of this country" that "help establish a nation, draw people together, and make them love the more their native land."[1]

Gilbert designed many important buildings, including the West Street Building (1907), the New York Life Insurance Company Building (1928), the New York County Lawyers Association Building (1930), and the Federal Courthouse (1936). The Woolworth Building, his stunning "gothic tower" completed in 1913, was the world's tallest building for a decade, inspiring much praise and discussion at the time. Subsequently, he worked on a series of capitol buildings, putting "his great talent in the service of an ideal combining artistic excellence with social improvement, that of the City Beautiful," in Robert Stern's view.[2] Gilbert's only work abroad, the US Embassy in Ottawa, was completed in 1932. His last project was the US Supreme Court Building in Washington DC, completed in 1935, just a few months after Gilbert died. — AM

① Sir Christopher Wren, quoted in Geoffrey Blodgett, "Cass Gilbert, Architect: Conservative at Bay," *Journal of American History*, Volume 71, No. 3 (December 1985): 615.

② Robert Stern, "Introduction," in Barbara S. Christen and Steven Flanders, ed., *Cass Gilbert, Life and Work: Architect of the Public Domain* (New York: W.W Norton & Company, Inc., 2001): 15.

Shepley Bulfinch

Headquarters
Boston, MA

Other Locations
Phoenix, AZ; San Francisco, CA

Successor Firm To
Office of H. H. Richardson (1874–1886)

Founding and Key Partners
George Foster Shepley, Charles Hercules Rutan, Charles Allerton Coolidge, Sr., George C. Shattuck, Henry Richardson Shepley, Francis Vaughn Bulfinch, Joseph Priestly Richardson, Lewis B. Abbott

Current Partners
Carole Wedge (president), Jennifer Aliber, Janette Blackburn, Sidney R Bowen, David Derr, Stephen J Erwin, Joe Herzog, Uma Ramanathan, Peter J Schlosser, Mario Vieira, Angela Watson

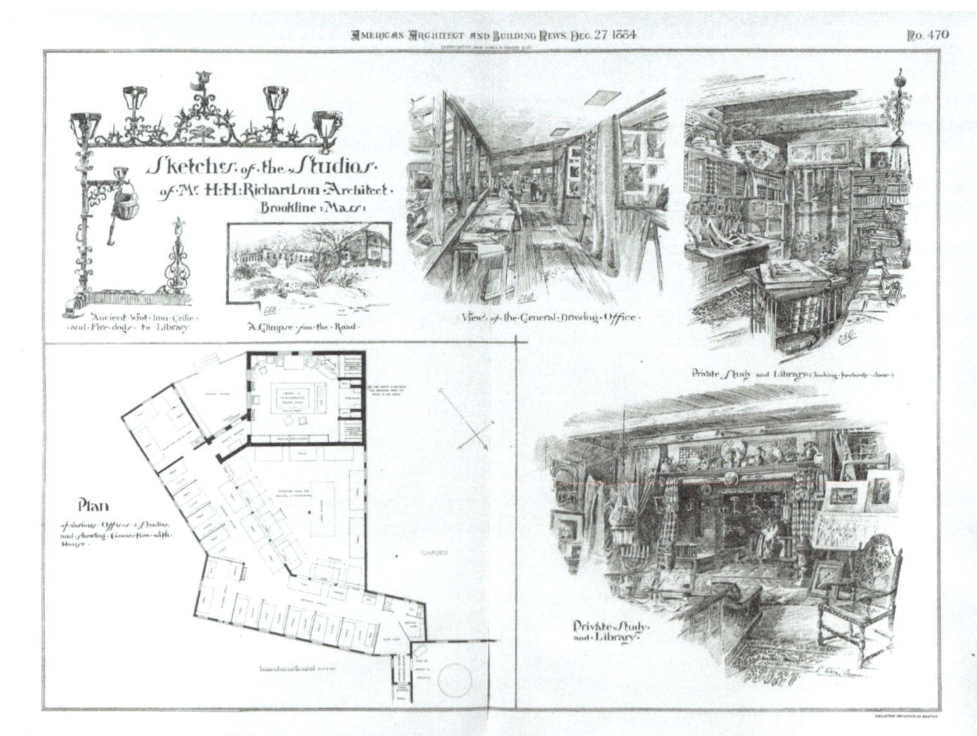

The American Architect and Building News, December 1884

One of the oldest continuously operating architecture firms in the United States, Shepley Bulfinch is a successor to the practice established in 1878 in Boston by Henry Hobson Richardson, the most celebrated American architect of the nineteenth century. Richardson was among the first American students of the École de Beaux-Arts in Paris who sought to replicate the atelier model of their academic training in their professional practices in the United States; his office, attached to his suburban home in Brookline, was known for its collegial atmosphere, centered around a sumptuous, book-filled study in which Richardson entertained colleagues and clients. Following Richardson's untimely death in 1886 at age 47, the practice was taken over by employees George Foster Shepley, Charles Hercules Rutan, and Charles Allerton Coolidge, continuing as Shepley, Rutan & Coolidge. Shepley died in 1903 and, when, staff member George Shattuck was named as partner in 1915 after Rutan's death, the firm became Coolidge & Shattuck.

Major projects from the firm's early years following Richardson's death included the campus plan and buildings for Stanford University (1888–), together with Frederick Law Olmsted, the Art Institute of Chicago (1893), originally built as the World's Congress Auxiliary Building for the World's Columbian Exposition in the same year, and the Harvard University Medical School (1906), one of over 120 commissions completed for the University. The size of the Stanford commission led Coolidge & Shattuck to maintain a temporary office in San Francisco from 1888 to 1891, while the firm's expanding work in Chicago led the firm to establish a second office there from 1892 to 1916, when it became the independent firm of Coolidge & Hodson.

Coolidge & Shattuck's first two international projects, the American College for Girls in Istanbul (1914) and Peking Union Medical College in China (1916–1921), were among numerous examples of Western-style colleges built by US firms abroad in the early decades of the twentieth century. Peking Union Medical College was funded by John D. Rockefeller as part of an expansive program to modernize medical training and practice in China, following the model of medical education programs previously established by the University of Pennsylvania in Canton (1904) and Harvard University in Shanghai. Rockefeller had previously selected Coolidge & Shattuck to design the Rockefeller Institute for Medical Research (1903) in New York, and when Rockefeller purchased land in China from the Missionary Society in 1915, on the site of a former palace near Beijing's Forbidden City, he asked the firm to design the new medical school.

The success of Peking Union Medical College and commissions for medical buildings in the US, including the Boston Lying-In Hospital (1923) and buildings for Massachusetts General Hospital, established Coolidge & Shattuck as experts in hospital facilities. In 1924, the firm was renamed Coolidge, Shepley, Bulfinch & Abbott with the addition of George Foster Shepley's son, Henry Richardson Shepley—named after Shepley's former employer—Lewis B. Abbott, and a civil engineer, Francis Vaughn Bulfinch, as partners. Though Coolidge died in 1936, the firm retained his name until 1952, when it was replaced by that of Joseph Priestley Richardson—H. H. Richardson's grandson—to become Shepley Bulfinch Richardson & Abbott (SBRA). The firm was incorporated in 1972, and the last direct connection to the founding partners ended upon the retirement of Hugh Shepley, George Foster Shepley's grandson, from the company in 1990. In 2000 the firm became Shepley Bulfinch, the name under which it practices today. Still based in Boston, with a staff of 165 employees, the office continues to specialize in medical, academic, civic commissions among an extensive array of projects. — RW & MK

1891–
1954

Helmle & Corbett

Headquarters
New York, NY

Founding and Key Partners
F. Livingston Pell, Harvey Wiley Corbett (founding principals), Frank J. Helmle, Wallace K. Harrison, William MacMurray

1954

Architectural Record, February 1931

The partnership of Helmle & Corbett brought together two prominent New York architects at the midpoint of their careers. Frank J. Helmle, an Ohio native, attended Cooper Union and spent a year in the office of McKim, Mead & White, then the largest architecture firm in the country, prior to starting his independent practice in 1891. He received a range of commissions throughout Brooklyn in the first decade of the twentieth century, including St. Barbara's Church (1903), Prospect Park Boathouse (1905), and Greenpoint Savings Bank (1908). Harvey Wiley Corbett, a graduate of the École de Beaux-Arts in Paris, began his career in 1901 in the New York office of Cass Gilbert before establishing a practice with F. Livingston Pell in 1903, the first of many partnerships over the course of Corbett's career. Pell & Corbett were known for the design of the Municipal Group (1913) in Springfield, Massachusetts, featuring paired City Hall and Auditorium buildings in Greek Revival style, flanking an Italianate 300-foot campanile. By 1912, Corbett had split with Pell and joined together with Helmle to form Helmle & Corbett.

Helmle & Corbett's work in New York was particularly associated with the rise of the skyscraper as a building type in the 1910s and 1920s. Corbett's writings and involvement with civic planning in this period of the city's population growth included proposals for sidewalks to be raised above street level, separating zones for pedestrians and automobiles, and for car parks to be integrated into new tower constructions. After New York became the first city to enact a comprehensive zoning ordinance in 1916, Corbett famously hired delineator Hugh Ferriss to render the building setbacks required by the new law in a series of perspective drawings that dramatically illustrated the formal implications of the ordinance for future skyscrapers. These images, which first appeared in a 1923 issue of Pencil Points as part of an article by Corbett, "Zoning and the Envelope of the Building," later became famous through their publication by Ferriss in *The Metropolis of Tomorrow* (1929).[1]

Helmle & Corbett's thirty-story Bush Terminal International Exhibit Building, or Bush Tower (1916–1918), in New York's Times Square, was among the first structures to demonstrate the formal possibilities for tall, slender towers under the New York Zoning Ordinance of 1916. Designed for Irving T. Bush of the Bush Terminal Company, the owner a complex of shipping, manufacturing, and warehousing facilities in Brooklyn, the building provided commercial and exhibition space in which designers, manufacturers, and buyers could meet under one roof. When the tower was completed, Helmle & Corbett moved their office into its top two floors.

The success of the Bush Tower led to Helmle & Corbett's first international commission, the Bush House in London (1923–1935), through which the Bush Terminal Company sought to bring its business model to Europe following its rapid growth in New York. A central sales building for the company in which both English and US firms were represented, Bush House was the first building in London designed specifically to facilitate direct interaction between wholesale sellers and retail buyers, combining all trade activity into a single location. The central block of the building opened in 1925, with additional wings added between 1928 and 1935. Bush House became home to the foreign language broadcasting services of the British Broadcasting Company (BBC) in 1941, following the bombing of its headquarters during World War II, and the BBC continued to occupy the building for 70 years until moving its facilities in 2012.

Helmle & Corbett's commissions for commercial businesses in the US continued following its buildings for the Bush Terminal Company, including the Pennsylvania Power and Light Building (1926–1928) in Allentown, Pennsylvania. Wallace K. Harrison, a junior partner, was added to the firm's masthead in 1927 prior to Helmle's retirement in 1928. William MacMurray became partner in the same year, and the firm was renamed Corbett, Harrison & MacMurray. Harrison left in 1935 to establish his own practice, and the office continued as Corbett & MacMurray for another six years before Corbett founded his own firm, Harvey Wiley Corbett, Architect, in 1941. — NF & MK

① See Harvey Wiley Corbett, "Zoning and the Envelope of the Building," Pencil Points (April 1923): 14–18; Hugh Ferriss, *The Metropolis of Tomorrow* (New York: Ives Washburn, 1929).

FRANK LLOYD WRIGHT

1893–1959

Frank Lloyd Wright

Headquarters
Oak Park, IL

Other Locations
Spring Green, WI; Scottsdale, AZ

Founding Partner
Frank Lloyd Wright

1959

Ezra Stoller, Esto

"The most widely known architect in America today is Frank Lloyd Wright," wrote Harry Seckel in 1938 in the *North American Review*, "and his reputation is not altogether due to his buildings.... In the case of Frank Lloyd Wright there is an intimate relation between the man's work and the unusual life and personality that have caught the public eye."[1] Even within his lifetime, it was clear that Frank Lloyd Wright's model of success eclipsed the boundaries of his building practice, taking on an almost mythic quality orbiting his personal life and career narrative. Wright carefully crafted his own persona, from sartorial capes and flashy cars to changing his own birthday so as to appear younger, enhancing his image as, in Ada Louise Huxtable's words, a "precocious" and "impressively youthful talent."[2] These small affectations through Wright's marketing of his image as auteur and genius lent themselves to his legend, from his hungry arrival in Chicago to his meteoric rise to Louis Sullivan's right-hand man, to his angry split from Adler & Sullivan—recounted by Wright as the elder architect's anger at his protégé's success in designing private residences during the off-hours. Constantly supplemented by public curiosity about his persona and practice, Wright's work provided the perfect example for Henry-Russell Hitchcock's characterization, in 1947, of the "architecture of genius," a mode of practice he saw as necessary for the most iconic cultural commissions of the time.[3]

Between 1889 and 1909, Wright operated his office out of the Studio, an annex he designed to his home in Oak Park, Illinois. He then left for Europe, where he lived for two years before returning to the United States in 1911, and building his studios in Spring Green, Wisconsin, later named Taliesin East. After it became the site of a shocking personal tragedy—the murder of his mistress and her family by a deranged servant while Wright was completing a project in Chicago—he abandoned Taliesin for nearly a decade, establishing an office in Los Angeles in pursuit of projects in California and Japan. Upon returning from travels to Japan he finally went back to Taliesin. Taliesin West, at the foothills of MacDowell Mountain in Scottsdale, Arizona, was conceived in direct response to the brutal Wisconsin winters that forced Wright's office and the Taliesin Fellowship, established with his wife Olga Lazovich, to relocate during work on his utopian Broadacre City proposal in 1934.

Beyond his influence in the United States, Wright had become well known among a small but influential number of young European architects after the publication in 1910–1911 of the Wasmuth Portfolio, a two-volume folio which was the first monograph of his work. Wright's later work abroad is most often associated with his design of the Imperial Hotel in Tokyo (1915–1923). During his time in Japan, Wright also designed the Jiyu Gakuen School (1921) and several private residences. Historians have speculated on the impact of global architecture on Wright's work—including Japanese design as well as Mayan motifs, which are evident in the development of his textile-block system of construction—and, conversely, Wright's impact on other designers, such as his influence on Czech-born architect Antonin Raymond and his own career in Japan. Wright's last completed design, initially for a house in Maryland, was built posthumously in Ireland in 2007. One of 380 unbuilt projects held by the Frank Lloyd Wright Foundation, it was realized by Wright scholar Marc Coleman.

Wright was a household name in the United States by the midpoint of his career and later acclaimed by consensus as the most significant American architect of the twentieth century. His buildings have become icons in the broadest public sense. Sites of particular reverence include his many house designs in Oak Park, where Wright's practice began; the Robie House in Chicago (1909); the Kaufmann Residence, known as Fallingwater, in Mill Run, Pennsylvania (1936–1939); the Johnson Wax Headquarters in Racine, Wisconsin (1939); and the Guggenheim Museum in New York City (1943–1959), completed posthumously. Wright's influence on architectural pedagogy through the establishment of his Taliesin ateliers, first in Wisconsin (1911) and later in Arizona (1937) continues even today in the education of architects dedicated to perpetuating Wright's design legacy. —AL

① Harry Seckel, "Frank Lloyd Wright," *The North American Review* (September 1938): 48.

② Ada Louise Huxtable, "'Frank Lloyd Wright,' First Chapters," *The New York Times* (October 31, 2004).

③ Henry-Russell Hitchcock, "The Architecture of Bureaucracy and the Architecture of Genius," *The Architectural Review* (January 1947): 3–6.

1894–1927

1927

Perkins, Fellows and Hamilton

Headquarters
Chicago, IL

Founding and Key Partners
Dwight Heald Perkins (founding principal), William K. Fellows, John L. Hamilton, Laurence Edgar Wilkinson

Architectural Record, December 1917

In 1916, the editor of *Western Architect*, Robert C. McLean, considered the work of three Chicago architects who were at the time "engaged upon the most notable works performed by 'foreign' architects in the history of the modern world."[1] The first architect mentioned was Walter Burley Griffin, who was designing a federal capital for Canberra, Australia (1912–1920). The second was Frank Lloyd Wright, who was engaged in the design of the Imperial Hotel in Tokyo (1915–1923). The third Chicagoan was William K. Fellows, of Perkins, Fellows & Hamilton, who was then involved in creating plans for the University of Nanjing (1914–1935), one of the many Christian colleges designed by US architects in China in the early twentieth century.

The original founder of the firm, Dwight H. Perkins, trained as an architect at the Massachusetts Institute of Technology. He opened his office in 1894 with a commission for the Wisconsin Normal School, which he obtained with the assistance of Daniel Burnham. Perkins was involved in designs for the campus plans of the University of Chicago and Northwestern University. During his tenure as the chief architect for the Chicago Board of Education he designed more than forty schools, while running a private practice with John Hamilton at the same time. The pair designed numerous buildings in and around Chicago, including the park buildings for the city's Lincoln Park Zoo. Perkins, Hamilton, and Fellows joined forces in 1911 to establish the practice that bore their names, designing and constructing their own office building at 814 Tower Court, on Chicago's Magnificent Mile. Griffin worked for Perkins, Fellows & Hamilton prior to launching his own practice, while Griffin's wife, architect Marion Mahony, was a cousin of Perkins.

The design of a residence for the McCormick family in Chicago in these years led Perkins, Fellows & Hamilton into the design of a campus for Nanjing University in China, which was partially funded by the McCormicks. Although Perkins never went to China, Fellows spent five months there in 1914. Writing about their efforts, the firm compared itself to other Western architects building in China in these decades, sparing no words about what they saw as the superiority of their approach. "The foreign style has so far developed nothing worthy of imitation," the firm warned in one of its reports. "Foreign architecture as introduced into China through the Treaty ports from Hong Kong and the south has not one feature to redeem its stupidity. Transplanted Gothic, no matter how well it may be executed, looks out of place."[2] In contrast, the firm claimed its university design was an interpretation of Chinese architecture. While the building material included bricks taken from the old walls of a Manchurian city, however, the university program, understood by the architects to mandate strong symmetry and axial vistas, conflicted with traditional Chinese designs. Typological elements that had no precedent in Chinese architecture, such as the chapel and the tower, therefore required reinterpretation by the architects in form and material to harmonize with local examples. — RW

① Robert C. McLean, *Western Architect* (April 1916), cited in "Ricker House Chronicles," January 23, 2014, http://kaiser355.wordpress.com/tag/perkins-fellows-and-hamilton/ (last accessed November 17, 2014).

② Perkins, Fellows & Hamilton, "Report on Building Conditions, University of Nanking" (1914), cited in "Ricker House Chronicles," January 23, 2014, http://kaiser355.wordpress.com/tag/perkins-fellows-and-hamilton/ (last accessed November 17, 2014).

1895–

Albert Kahn Associates

Headquarters
Detroit, MI

Other Locations
Moscow, USSR (1929); Birmingham, AL; São Paulo, Brazil

Founding and Key Partners
Albert Kahn (founding princpal), Louis Kahn, Moritz Kahn, George W. Nettleton, A. B. Trowbridge

Current Partners
Alan Cobb (president and CEO), John Enkermann (COO), Gar Hoplamazian (senior VP), Pete Lynde (principal), Clift Montague (CSO), Chuck Robinson (director of engineering), Robb Sharrow (VP), Ron Simon (CFO), Arthur Britto

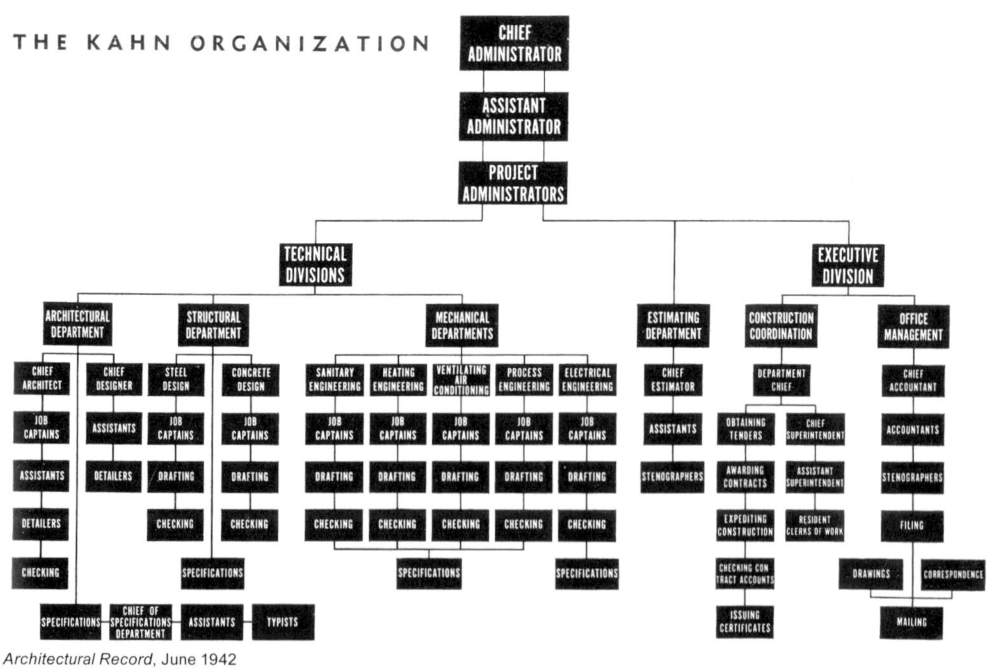

Architectural Record, June 1942

Identified by historian Henry-Russell Hitchcock as "the bureaucratic office par excellence," Albert Kahn Associates rose to prominence in the early twentieth century as the architect of industrial buildings for Ford Motor Company and other Detroit automobile manufacturers, including Packard, Dodge, Chrysler, and General Motors. Assessing the firm's extensive construction of industrial plants during World War II to meet the demands of wartime production, Hitchcock praised "The strength of a firm such as Kahn... [that] depends not on the architectural genius of one man... but in the organizational genius which can establish a fool-proof system of rapid and complete plan production."[1] Achieving extreme speed and quantity through coordinated divisions of specialists working simultaneously across architecture, engineering, and construction rather than in successive phases, the firm's assembly-line organization mirrored the Fordist organization of the factories it produced. Such a system, organized in technical divisions from design to engineering to construction, enabled different sets of design information to "meet on the site with as perfect mutual co-ordination as machine parts come from the various sections of a factory to be joined first into sub-assemblies and then into the finished product on the final assembly line."

While the firm undertook an extensive range of public and private commissions throughout its history, including hospitals, schools, office buildings, libraries, houses, temples, and academic buildings, both Kahn and his office remained associated primarily with factory buildings in the architectural press, coming to epitomize (as later for Hitchcock) the image of the "bureaucratic" or industrial architect. The series of factories with which Albert Kahn Associates became synonymous began in 1903, when the firm designed the first of nine buildings for the Packard Automotive Plant in Detroit. Subsequent designs for Pierce-Arrow Motor Car Company and Ford Motor Company followed, culminating in the massive River Rouge complex of factory buildings for Ford (1917–1928). Images of these buildings were among those circulated most heavily after 1914 by European architects who sought to emulate the efficiency of US building practices as well as the forms of US industrial buildings. Kahn's Highland Park Ford Plant (1908–1910) appeared among the photographs of factories and grain silos compiled by Walter Gropius in the *Jahrbuch des Deutscher Werkbund* (1913); the extensive republication of these images by European architects thereafter included, most famously, their copying and alteration by Le Corbusier in *Vers une Architecture* (1923).

In 1929, Albert Kahn Associates was commissioned to design a massive tractor factory in Stalingrad (today Volgograd) to spearhead the urgent modernization of agriculture and industry in the Soviet Union, a process largely based on the import of US industrial techniques and the production of machinery copied directly from US examples. A year later, Kahn became the consulting architect for all industrial construction in the Soviet Union under the first Five-Year Plan, a vast program of national building that included the formation of a design bureau in Moscow with over 2,000 Soviet workers under the direct authority of expatriate Kahn architects and engineers. By the end of the contract in 1932, the firm was responsible for a substantial portion of the industrial base of the Soviet Union, building over 500 factories across the country including monumental tractor plants in Stalingrad and Chelyabinsk, which were converted to the production of tanks during World War II.

The speed and scale of the Soviet commissions soon benefited Albert Kahn Associates in the US as well. By 1938, the work of Kahn's firm accounted for roughly twenty percent of all industrial buildings in the United States designed by architectural firms. The office grew to over 600 employees by 1942 to support a massive expansion of plant construction for the wartime production of tanks, aircraft, and other military equipment during World War II. Though Kahn died in the same year, the firm continues to operate under his name. —MK

(1)
Henry-Russell Hitchcock, "The Architecture of Bureaucracy and the Architecture of Genius," *The Architectural Review* (January 1947): 3–6.

Imperial Beauty: Planning For Democracy Abroad

The first involvement of US architects in a campaign of properly imperial building abroad came in the wake of the Spanish-American War. Launched by the US in April of 1898 as an intervention following Cuba's achievement of autonomy from the Spanish Empire in the same year, the war was advertised to the American public as a response to both Spanish aggression and civil unrest following Cuban independence, and fomented by the mysterious sinking of the *USS Maine* in Havana harbor. The ten-week long war gave the US possession of Cuba, Guam, Puerto Rico, and the Philippines, its first territorial possessions abroad.

The architect responsible for designing a new federal capital for the Philippines under US control, Daniel H. Burnham, had already laid the foundations for imperial city-building abroad as the director of the World's Columbian Exposition in Chicago in 1893, known as the "White City" for its monumental grandeur and gleaming, white-painted neoclassical buildings. Indebted to earlier Beaux-Arts models, particularly the plan by Pierre Charles L'Enfant for the then new capital city of Washington, D.C. (1791), Burnham first applied the City Beautiful methods ushered in by the Exposition as chairman of the commission to update and enlarge L'Enfant's scheme in 1901. Plans for Cleveland and San Francisco (1903) followed before his appointment in 1904 by close friend W. Cameron Forbes, a commissioner to the Philippines under Secretary of War William H. Taft, to produce plans for a new federal city.

Burnham's plans, for seasonal winter and summer capitals at Manila and Baguio, respectively, were explicitly understood by their commissioners to serve US as well as Filipino interests. His *Report on Proposed Improvements at Manila* (1906) expressed this double purpose, describing the hope that Manila might "become the adequate expression of the destiny of the Filipino people as well as an enduring witness to the efficient services of America in the Philippine Islands."[1] Burnham held to the conviction that such efforts did not constitute

(1) Daniel H. Burnham, "Report on Proposed Improvements at Manila," *Proceedings of the Thirty-Ninth Annual Convention of the American Institute of Architects* (Washington, D.C., 1906): 151.

- **1890**
- **1893** World's Columbian Exposition held in Chicago
- **1898** • January 1 Cuban autonomy from Spain set to begin • U.S.S. Maine warship sinks in Havana harbor from undetermined causes • December 10 Treaty of Paris: US gain colonial authority over Cuba, Puerto Rico, Guam, the Philippine Islands
- **1900** Taft Commission (Second Philippine Commission) established as sole governing body of the Philippine Islands
- **1904** Burnham/Anderson begin master planning for Manila,

1898 Spanish-American War

a form of imperialism as such, but rather a kind of "trusteeship," one that would operate, as historian Thomas Hines has described it, as "a period of tutelage in which the more 'advanced' Americans could help effect a 'progressive civilization' by instruction and example."[2]

The task of building this progressive example would fall to William E. Parsons, the consulting architect for the US colonial government, selected by Burnham to realize the civic buildings projected under his plan. Contemporary articles in the US architectural press sanctioned this civilizing mission, claiming that, because "The Philippines and their people appear to one as being, not exactly primitive, but still rather elemental…It remained for an American architect to establish city plans and buildings of a permanent nature suited to the needs of a tropical country."[3] Parsons's involvement in the Philippines came to an end in 1914, as the consequence of a US "scuttle policy" intended to "wind down the American colonial machinery with a view toward early Philippine independence."[4]

At the same time, a second campaign of federal building was underway in Australia, where an international competition to design a new national capital at Canberra had been won by US architects Walter Burley Griffin and Marion Mahony in 1912. Both were prominent among the Chicago circle of advocates for City Beautiful planning, and both had been directly influenced by Burnham's Plan of Chicago (1909), following his work in the Philippines. Projecting a new capital on a site halfway between Sydney and Melbourne—"a magnificent setting for a city of monumental character"[5]—the couple envisioned a city organized radially around a series of federal, municipal, manufacturing, and residential centers. Though only partially realized over the next two decades, the commission would lead Griffin and Mahony to a quarter-century of living and working as expatriates in Australia and India, ending with Griffin's death in 1938. Looking back after World War II at their professional journey in her unpublished manuscript, "The Magic of America," Mahony reaffirmed the civilizing ambitions of their work abroad, declaring that "The immediate task of Americans is to go out individually to every part of the world—emigrate instead of immigrate the watchword—and break down the bondage of individuals everywhere."[6] — MK

② Thomas S. Hines, "The Imperial Façade: Daniel H. Burnham and American Architectural Planning in the Philippines," *Pacific Historical Review*, Vol. 41, No. 1 (February 1972): 40.

③ A. N. Rebori, "The Work of William E. Parsons in the Philippine Islands," *Architectural Record* (April 1917): 305, 309.

④ Hines, "American Modernism in the Philippines": 325.

⑤ "'Canberra', The New Capital City of Australia," *Architectural Record* (July 1912): 483.

⑥ Marion Mahony Griffin, *The Magic of America*, electronic edition, August 2007: I.16. The Art Institute of Chicago and The New-York Historical Society, October 29, 2008. http://www.artic.edu/magicofamerica/link/moa_1_016.html.

1920

1909 Burnham, Plan of Chicago

1912 Griffin and Mahony win international competition to design Federal Capital at Canberra

1914–1918 World War I

1920

THE MAGIC OF AMERICA

SECTION - I - THE EMPIRIAL BATTLE

Americans have smashed the atom as Jefferson smashed the power of governments by creating a new type, and Jackson smashed the byreaucracy. Their taske today are to construct, and their fields as individuals is the world. What the Gods have given us we are under obligation to share with humanity, with the world. It is for us to free humanity for we alone are free human beings. Only individuals can do this, for the Christ broke up all peoples and races giving the individual spirit, the Ego, the Light, to every man in the world.

Democracy is as important as the smashing of the atom. Unless democracy is applied to humanity as a whole the power released in the atom will become demonic and destroy humanity. Only in America has it been experienced. In democracy the Spirit of the human is released as in Atom smashing the Spirit of Matter is released.

In this physical experiment the 20th century has fulfilled its basic task with the dual law - that of up and down, inside and outside, force and form - where you can't have one without the other. The reality of matter is form and nothing else. The smashing of the atom releases forces, no substances are to be found when form is smashed. The smashing of the atomic form frees the spiritual forces of matter. They are not things that can be weighed and measured except in terms of force.

Thus do the Orient and the Occident meet, through America.

The reason why America won the war and will win the peace is because the strength and power of the individual is recognized and given full play. The first step was to escape from the rest of the world - the ancient eastern world, Eur-Asia - to establish a community organization in which no individual nor group had power over another, a community whose basic principle is Equity. There are many lovely and wonderful people elsewhere in the world but they are helpless. Migration to America frees their spiritual forces. That is the magic of the United States. The founders of the CONGRESSIONAL system smashed the political atom which holds the rest of humanity in bondage.

The immediate task of Americans is to go out individually to every part of the world - emigrate instead of immigrate the watch-word - and break down the bondage of individuals everywhere. It is a difficult but not impossible task. It is the task of path-finders. The following is the story of one such American. He found individuals wherever he went who leaped to help him blaze the way in this battle against the Powers.

THE ARCHITECTVRAL RECORD

AN ILLUSTRATED MONTHLY MAGAZINE OF ARCHITECTURE
AND THE ALLIED ARTS AND CRAFTS.

INDEX-VOLUME XXXII

JULY-DECEMBER

1912

PUBLISHED BY

THE ARCHITECTURAL RECORD CO.

11-15 EAST 24TH ST., NEW YORK

841 MONADNOCK BUILDING, CHICAGO
BESSEMER BUILDING, PITTSBURGH

603 CHESTNUT ST., PHILADELPHIA
114 FEDERAL ST., BOSTON

"CANBERRA", THE NEW CAPITAL CITY OF AUSTRALIA

Walter Burley Griffin, Architect.

IN THE PROJECTED capital city of the Commonwealth of Australia modern theories in city planning are to be applied on a scale heretofore unknown. The commonwealth was organized twelve years ago. At that time provision was made for the creation of a new capital in preference to utilizing for that purpose either of the leading cities of the commonwealth, and, accordingly, a federal district corresponding to our District of Columbia was established in the Yass-Canberra region of New South Wales. In June, 1911, an international competition was announced. The first prize in this competition was won by Walter Burley Griffin, of Chicago, whose plan provides for a city having an area of approximately twenty-five square miles. In the matter of details this plan is necessarily tentative, much being left for future development. But in its essential outlines the city is completely planned, while the arrangement of the federal and other public groups is developed in considerable detail.

The location of the projected capital is about midway between Sidney and Melbourne and seventy-five miles from the east coast of Australia. The site is a valley having a general elevation of two thousand feet above sea level, and is bordered by hills and mountains. Two prominent peaks, Mount Ainslie and Black Mountain, rise abruptly out of the northerly part of the valley. On the southerly edge is a low-lying mountain, Mugga Mugga, and sheltering forested ranges culminating in the distance in the snow-capped peaks of the Murrumbidgee watershed. Scattered over the valley are a number of lesser hills, among which are Kurrajong, Camp Hill, Vernon, Russeell and Shale. A small stream known as the Molonglo River flows through the site from east to west. A determining factor in the plan of the city is the form of the valley, which, as will be noted from the map, is irregular. It is evident that while presenting a number of serious problems this site furnishes a magnificent setting for a city of monumental character.

The city as planned by Mr. Griffin consists of a group of connected functional centers. In an ordinary city a gradation in relative requirements from centers of lines of activity would be sufficient; but in a capital city the problem of distribution of centers in accordance with their relative importance becomes much more complex. The functional centers to be provided for are as follows: Federal, municipal, educational, recreation, manufacturing, market, residential and agricultural.

The central portion of the city is designed with reference to two axes placed at right angles to each other. One, designated as the land axis, extends from the summit of Mount Ainslie through Camp Hill and Kurrajong, and has its distant terminus in the peak of Mount Bimberi, thirty miles to the southwest, it being a fortunate coincidence that the line joining the summits of these two mountain passes through the two lesser hills. The secondary axis, designated as the water axis, extends from the summit of Black Mountain to a prominent point on the shore of the proposed upper lake. These axes lie midway between cardinal and diagonal points of the compass. Since this is recognized as the most favorable orientation with reference to sunlight and shade, the federal and other public groups are located parallel to these axes.

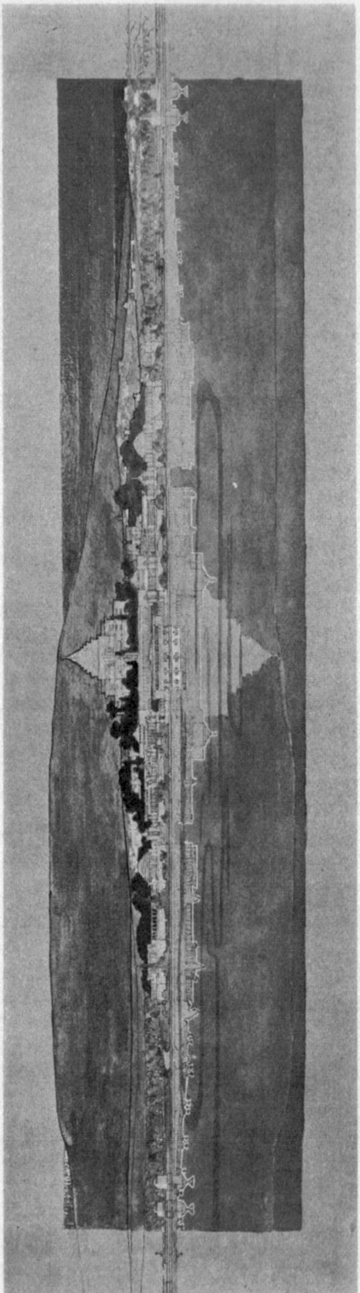

THE AUSTRALIA CAPITAL—"CANBERRA": SOUTHERLY SIDE OF WATER AXIS, SHOWING CENTRAL BASIN, FEDERAL BUILDINGS WITH THEIR TERRACES AND RAMPS. WATER GATE IN CENTER.
WALTER BURLEY GRIFFIN, ARCHITECT.

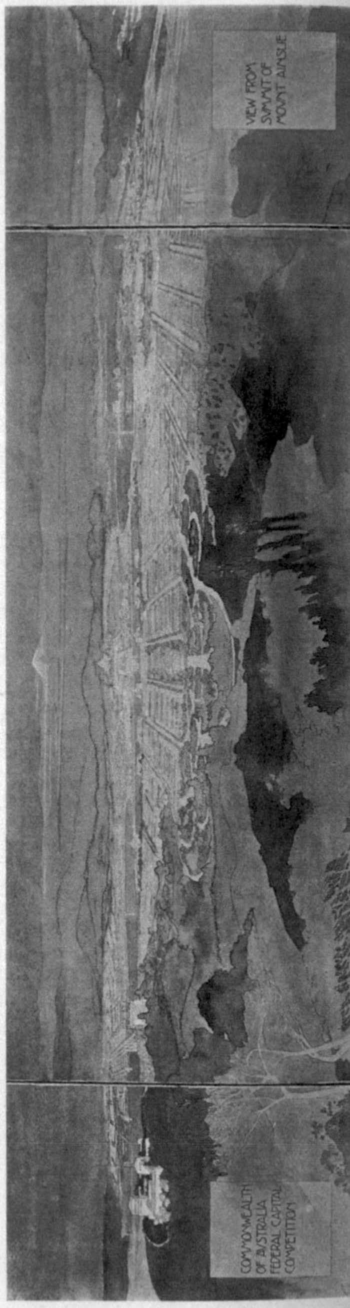

THE AUSTRALIA CAPITAL: PERSPECTIVE VIEW OF THE CITY FROM THE SUMMIT OF MOUNT AINSLIE. MOUNT BIMBERI IN THE DISTANCE.
WALTER BURLEY GRIFFIN, ARCHITECT.

The Molonglo River is utilized for the development of five lagoons, two of which have shore lines determined by the topography, and three of which are architectural in form. These lagoons are designed as the central feature in the architectural setting, and determine the location of the public groups. The fall of the river is slight, and a weir dam of moderate height is sufficient for impounding the water for the four lower lagoons. For forming the upper lake a dam with sluiceways for regulating the flood water is provided. This dam will also serve for carrying the railway across the waterway.

Since the prime object of a federal capital is the housing of various federal activities, the federal group is the one of dominating importance, and is therefore given the central position. A further consideration is that such activities are largely deliberative and require an accessible but quiet location. The center of the federal group is at Kurrajong Hill, on the land axis. From this center radiate one avenue to the north through the Municipal Center and continuing through the Manufacturing Center at the northern limits of the city, and another avenue to the northeast terminating in the Market Center. On the crest of Kurrajong is the administration building, flanked on the east by the premier's residence and on the west by the governor general's residence. In the triangle formed by the two radial avenues and the south shore of the central lagoon is the federal group. The arrangement of the federal group is as follows:

Premier's Residence.
Administration Building.
Governor General's Residence.
Parliament House and Library.
Departmental Buildings.
Prime Minister.
External Affairs.
Defense.
Future.
Attorney General.
Departmental Buildings.
Treasury and Commonwealth Bank.
Home Affairs.
Trade and Customs.
Future.
Postmaster General.
Forum.
Courts of Justice.

The crest of Kurrajong is about one hundred and sixty feet above the general level of the valley. From this hill the ground slopes to Camp Hill, and thence to the lagoon. This feature of the topography has been utilized in a series of terraces, on which the parliament and departmental buildings are located. As will be seen from the above tabulation, this group is developed in sequence of function. The parliament houses are located on the first terrace below the crest of Kurrajong, this terrace being about forty feet above the second terrace. The second terrace contains the departmental buildings. Extending along the land axis through the center of this group is a lagoon, beyond which, continuing on the same level, is the forum. The forum is thirty feet above the lower terrace and has subways for the passage of two driveways. The buildings for the courts of justice have their foundations on the lower terrace, and form at the same time the north frontage of the middle terrace. Stairways between the buildings connect the two levels. The forum terminates in a semi-circular colonnade resting on the arcade of the Water Gate at the south shore of the central lagoon, the two being connected by several tiers of stairways. Driveways wind in and out among the units of the federal group. Connection between driveways on different levels and between driveways and main radial avenues is made by means of ramps.

Across the lagoon from the water gate, recessed into the hill to avoid obstructing the view along the land axis, is the stadium. The zoo, museums, gymnasium and baths are located along the north shore of the lagoon between the radial avenues, the intermediate and adjoining spaces being used as public gardens. North of the public gardens are the theater and opera and several other buildings devoted to public and non-utilitarian uses. Continuing on the land axis north from the stadium is Ainslie Parkway, terminating in Ainslie Park on the lower slopes of the mountain. This entire group, to be used in general by the people as distinct from their representatives and agents, comprises the Recreation Center.

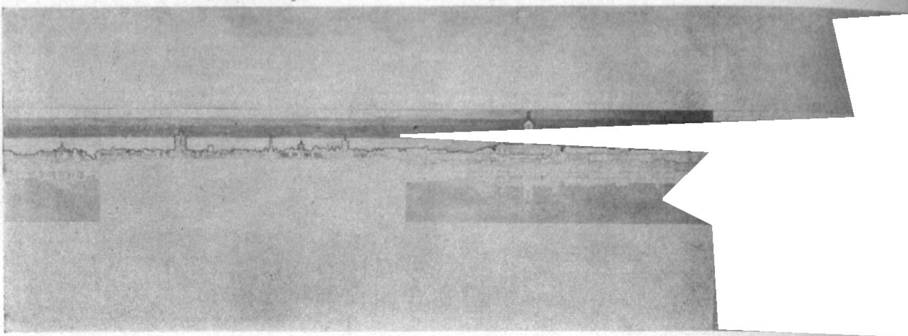

NORTHERLY SIDE OF WATER AXIS.

(Left to right) University and Professional Schools, Municipal Center, Printery and M
Bridge, Public Gardens and Zoo, Museum, etc.

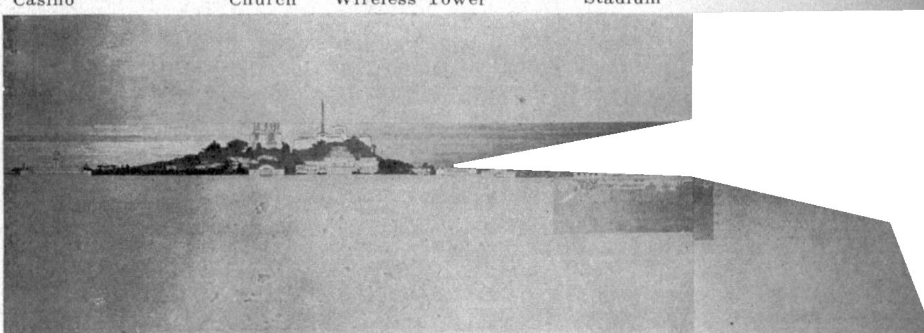

EASTERLY SIDE OF LAND AXIS.

(Left to right) Ainslie Parkway, Casino in Section, Railway, Viaduct, Freight House, way Entrance and Church, Library, Station and Military Headquarters, Opera, Mu of Plastic Arts, Museum of Archaeology, Stadium, Baths. Gymnasium, Central Basi Bridge.

THE AUSTRALIA CAPITAL, "CANBERRA," SECTIONS.

Walter Burley Griffin, Architect.

Church Military, Manufactories, Barracks and Wireless

Railway Station Power Station

NORTHERLY SIDE OF WATER AXIS.—Continued.

Ainslie, Hotel, Bridge, Church, Station, Market, Public and Military, Manufactor-
ntral Power Station, Viaduct, Military Headquarters, Armory, Etc., Lake Ports.

Capitol Mugga-Mugga

EASTERLY SIDE OF LAND AXIS.—Continued.

ater Gate, Courts of Justice, Departmental Buildings on First Terrace, Fountain,
and Ramp, Houses of Parliament on Second Terrace, Plateau with Plaza, Mon-
t and Cataract, Subway for Tramways and Street Traffic, Capitol, Red Hill.

THE AUSTRALIA CAPITAL, "CANBERRA,"—Sections Continued.

Walter Burley Griffin, Architect.

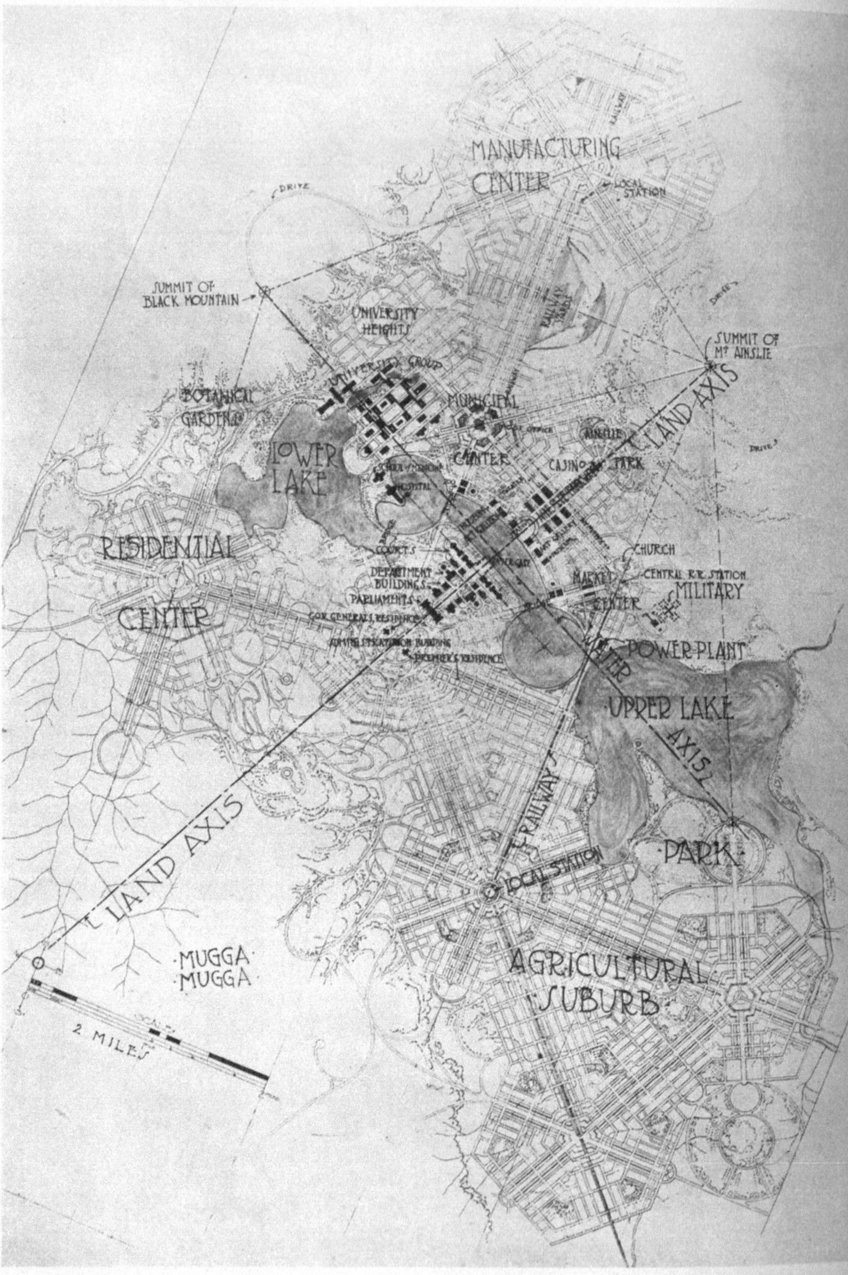

GENERAL PLAN: "CANBERRA," THE NEW CAPITAL CITY OF AUSTRALIA.
Walter Burley Griffin, Architect.

At the Municipal Center are the buildings required for conducting the business of the municipality, while surrounding this center is a district devoted to the administration of financial and industrial affairs, such as banks, stock exchange and office buildings generally.

It is planned to locate the important wholesale and retail establishments around the Market Center. At this center will also be located the central railway station. The streets connecting the Market and Municipal centers will form a shopping district.

West of the Municipal Center is a large group of buildings forming the commonwealth university. These buildings are arranged in logical sequence, and radiate, as nearly as a rectangular group plan will permit, from centers in the order given below:

1. Natural Sciences—Descriptive.
2. Theoretical Sciences—Derivative.
3. Applied Sciences.

The building devoted to each natural science is correlated to the group of buildings devoted to its derivative theoretical sciences, and the same principle is observed in correlating the theoretical and applied sciences. This principle is carried further in locating different sciences adjacent to facilities for illustrating their theory and application. In the application of this principle the school of law is located on the side nearest the Municipal Center, the school of agriculture is adjacent to the botanical gardens, which extend inland from the west shore of the lower lake, while the school of medicine is adjacent to the hospital, which occupies the small peninsula jutting into the west circular lagoon. On the east slope of Black Mountain is a district to be known as University Heights, and to be occupied by residences for the university faculty and dormitories for the students.

The remaining functional centers are, briefly, a residential district west of the Federal Center, and at the southeast limits of the city three centers which, with adjacent territory, comprise the agricultural suburb, a section devoted to truck gardening and allied industries.

The various centers are laid out roughly in polygonal form, both the hexagon and octagon being used. Such an arrangement results in a multiplicity of obtuse street angles within the polygons, and, owing to the relative positions of the different centers, in the intermediate sections as well. With the exception of the main avenues, practically all streets will be discontinuous or will have vistas closed by obtuse angles, a condition furnishing excellent opportunity for informal and picturesque treatment by means of residences, or otherwise. At the same time this plan provides rectangular building plots between points of junction of the different systems thus formed. It was considered desirable to leave certain tracts to be laid out and developed according to individual initiative. For this purpose many of the blocks in the intermediate sections are made of unusual size. These blocks, in whole or as subdivided, are available as sites for institutions of various kinds, horticultural gardens, playgrounds, enclosed residential courts, etc.

The modern tendency in city development is toward long alignments of trade along lines of communication. With the long avenues connecting the centers, as provided in this plan, this tendency is encouraged. The plan is such, however, as to discourage the spread of trade into adjacent territory, since the intermediate streets, owing to discontinuity or change in direction, are ill adapted to use as thoroughfares, and are therefore unattractive as locations for trade. In this way permanently quiet zones are provided, that are suitable for residential purposes, and are at the same time convenient to lines of trade and communication.

Main avenues are planned for a width of two hundred feet. They will be divided by parkways into three separate arteries of travel to provide for fast and slow vehicles and tramways. It is designed so as to locate the tramways in the intermediate sections that any point in the city will be within five blocks of a tramway. The Federal Center is the focus and transfer point of all tramways in the city. Tramways will be laid in the avenue encircling Kurrajong Hill, and connections will be provided to lines on each of the radial avenues. The circular avenue, with its tramways, passes through a subway under the avenue leading from the administration building to the parliament building. The avenue curving along the northerly edge of the public gardens is also provided with a tramway, assuring direct access to the opera, theatre, and public buildings along the north shore of the central lagoon.

In the program of the competition it was stipulated that a railway should pass through the city in a northerly and southerly direction. It was a difficult problem to locate this railway in such a way as to avoid injury to the main avenues in the central part of the city, interference with the waterways, and serious lessening of the general architectural effect. The location selected meets these conditions and appears to be the best available. On this location the gradient is slight and practically uniform. The railway throughout the city will be depressed twelve feet below street level, all streets being carried over the tracks by means of viaducts. The central station is at the Market Center, where the railway passes through a tunnel under the slopes of two hills. A local station will be provided at each of the other centers passed through. The railway yards are located immediately south of the Manufacturing Center. Water supply and sewerage will be developed from plans prepared by the federal government. The water supply will be obtained from the Cotter River, a stream lying some distance south of the projected city, and having an average daily flow of fifty million gallons. The sewerage system has not been definitely worked out. On account of the extreme variation in freshet run-off the separation of sewage and storm water is involved.

As would be expected in view of Mr. Griffin's well known canons of design the buildings of the public groups, if built according to his recommendation will consist of compositions in line and mass, designed with reference to the purposes of the buildings and the requirements of the materials used, and independently of all historical styles. Reinforced concrete is recommended by him as the material best suited to the purpose. A study of the plan reveals remarkable success in utilizing prominent points for aspect and prospect. In this connection it is only necessary to call specific attention to Mount Ainslie and Kurrajong Hill, both visible from all parts of the city, and both commanding the widest possible view of the city and its mountain background.

J. E. M.

VOL. XLI. No. 4 APRIL, 1917 SERIAL NO. 223

THE ARCHITECTVRAL RECORD

CONTENTS

Editor: MICHAEL A. MIKKELSEN. Contributing Editor: HERBERT CROLY

Advertising Manager: AUSTIN L. BLACK

Yearly Subscription—United States $3.00—Foreign $4.00—Single Copies 35 cents

Entered May 22, 1902, as Second Class Matter, at New York, N. Y.

PUBLISHED MONTHLY BY

THE ARCHITECTURAL RECORD COMPANY

115-119 WEST FORTIETH STREET, NEW YORK

F. T. MILLER, Pres. W. D. HADSELL, Vice-Pres. J. W. FRANK, Sec'y-Treas. E. S. DODGE, Vice-Pres.

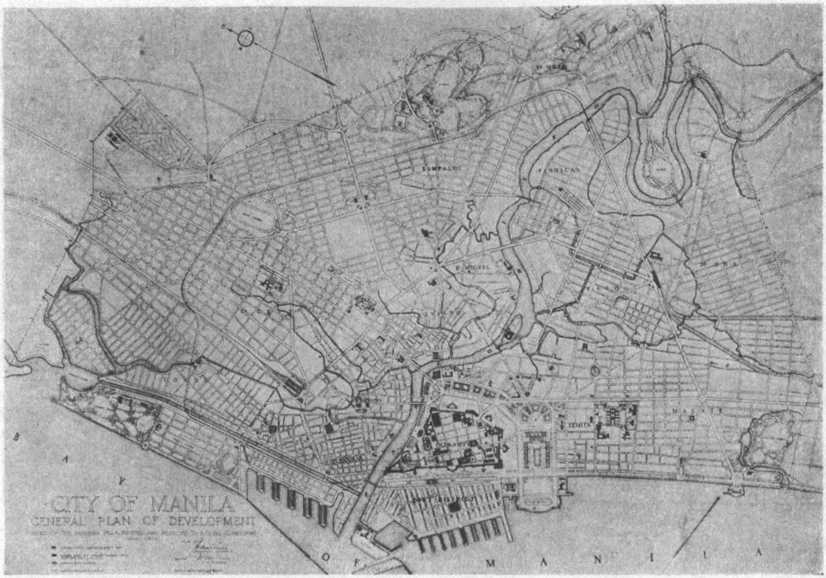

FIG. 1. GENERAL PLAN OF MANILA, WITH IMPORTANT PUBLIC BUILDINGS ERECTED DURING THE PERIOD FROM 1906 TO 1914 INDICATED IN BLACK.

The WORK OF WILLIAM E PARSONS IN THE PHILIPPINE ISLANDS

By A N. REBORI

Part I

UNLIKE other Oriental countries, as Japan, Korea and China, the Philippines have developed no peculiar architectural or art traditions of their own. While the native Filipino has the average instincts for artistic expression in its various phases, yet these have shown up better in adapting the art of other countries than in creating one of their own.

In architecture, Spain has given them sound traditions, and has left monuments of undoubted merit. I should say that Spain has given them the best that is in Spanish art, the principles inherited from Rome itself, rather than the peculiarities of the Spanish Renaissance.

The Philippines and their people appear to one as being, not exactly primitive, but still rather elemental. Perhaps, unconsciously, Mr. Parsons felt that architecture as an expression of the real conditions should be reduced to its simplest elements; and you will find that this impression is given generally by his work, where there is nothing, I think, which would remind you of our modern French or Italian architecture, and certainly not any Americanism. It is evident from the start that the designer, in

FIG. 4. VIEW OF THE PUBLIC PLAYGROUNDS, FORMED FROM THE MOATS SURROUNDING THE WALLED CITY. THE AQUARIUM IS BUILT IN THE BASTION AT THE CENTER.

FIG. 5. CITY AQUARIUM, BUILT IN THE INNER SLOPE OF A BASTION. 1912.

laying out his work, thought it best to begin with the elemental and the universal, and, with this once firmly established, let it develop with whatever peculiar local character it demanded. It remained for an American architect to establish city plans and buildings of a permanent nature suited to the needs and requirements of a tropical country.

The results, after eight years of unprecedented activity, are most gratifying in more ways than one. Not only do they speak of artistic ability born of an understanding that is the outcome of thorough training, but they reflect credit on the men who had the foresight to entrust a capable architect with this work. Moreover they stand as a lasting tribute to the period of our Government's constructive interest in the Philippines, now for some years past relegated to the dusty archives of a former administration.

The credit for the inception of building construction and city planning in a comprehensive way should be given to Mr. Taft. While he was Secretary of War he instructed W. Cameron Forbes, member of the Philippine Commission, to engage competent advice on this subject. He induced the late D. H. Burnham to visit the islands, which he did together with his designer, Pierce Anderson, making general preliminary plans of Manila and Baguio. This was followed by the recommendation that an architect of suitable training and experience be appointed as consulting architect for the Government.

William E. Parsons was recommended and appointed for the job. At the time of his selection he was practicing architecture in New York City, having been but recently diplomated at the Beaux Arts, Paris. With enthusiastic ambition, the best heritage of a thorough French training, he went to Manila in November, 1905, and served until February, 1914, resigning because "there seemed to be no further progress to be made under the scuttle policy of the present administration."

Under the terms of his appointment and of an act of the Philippine Commission, he was given general architectural supervision over the design of all public buildings and parks throughout the islands, including provincial and municipal work as well as insular. Consequently he was charged with interpretation of the preliminary plans prepared by Messrs. Burnham and Anderson for Manila and Baguio.

He received a salary from the Government which paid the cost of plans, etc. Also he was allowed to engage in private practice, and maintained a separate office during most of his years in Manila.

"At the time of my arrival," said Mr. Parsons, "the standard of Government construction was very low. While the islands had an ample supply of splendid hard woods, Oregon pine was found to be cheaper at first cost, and was becoming generally used. The beautiful old tile roofs which had been used by the Spaniards were giving way to glaring galvanized iron.

"I found that in my first interviews regarding building plans, officials were concerned first in obtaining maximum floor space and had little regard for durability. The first step was to induce the Government to discontinue the use of Oregon

FIG. 6. CITY AQUARIUM, MANILA, SHOWING THE FILTER TANKS SCREENED WITH BOUGAINVILLEA.

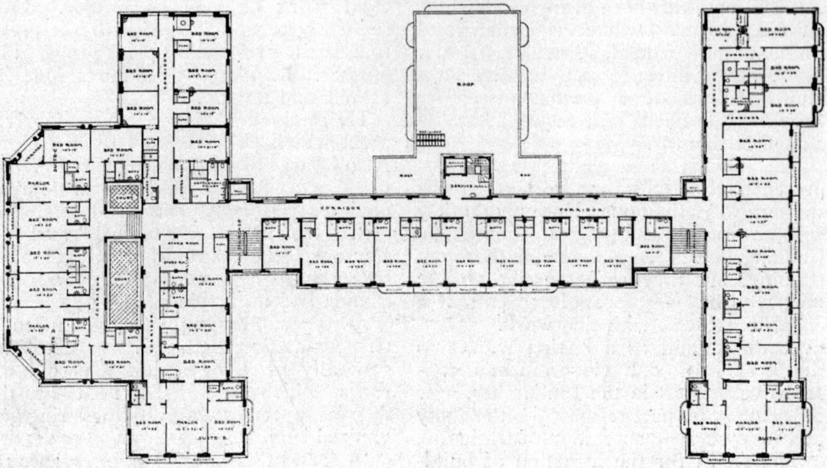

Second Floor Plan.

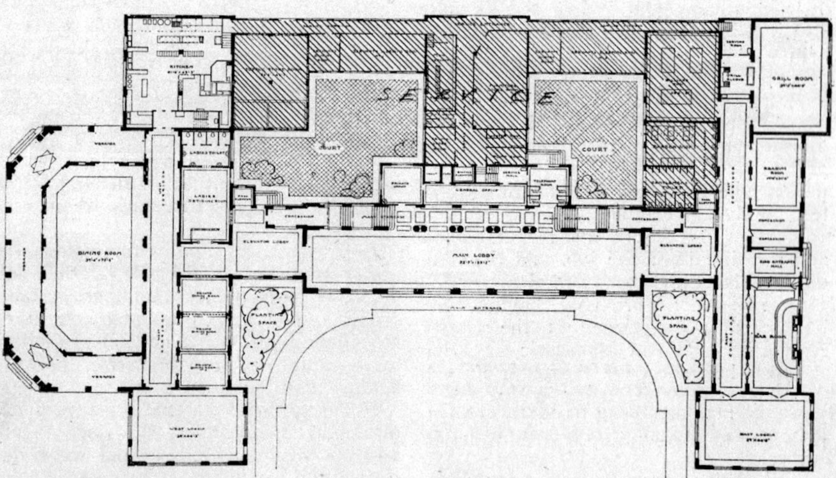

First Floor Plan.

FIG. 8. FLOOR PLANS OF THE MANILA HOTEL.
W. E. Parsons and the Eastern Engineering Company, Associated Architects.

FIG. 9. THE MANILA HOTEL, 1912.
W. E. Parsons and the Eastern Engineering Company, Associated Architects.

pine, which is tempting food for the anay (white ant), and to encourage the development of Philippine hard woods, which nature has prepared to withstand the ravages of the tropical climate better than any imported woods. The next step brought reinforced concrete as the standard form of construction."

It is obvious that this is the proper material for a country having no workable and durable stone for building, where the anay and decay eventually destroy even the hardest timbers, where earthquake shocks are at times severe, and where skilled labor is scarce and unskilled labor cheap.

The adoption of permanent materials by the Government would hardly have been possible, according to Mr. Parsons, without the constant support of Mr. Forbes.

It would be difficult to set a standard for tropical architecture without a realization of tropical conditions. In the real tropics (not as in Italy or Spain, where thick walls and small windows are used to shut out the sun), the maximum of ventilation is considered essential to comfort. Large windows and small wall surfaces are the rule. Windows should extend to the floor and be shaded either by metal canopies or by arcades or colonnades, both from the sun and from the glare of the sky.

Protection from driving rain is necessary also, for ventilation through open windows is required in rainy weather as well as in sunshine.

Low structures, two or three stories in height, are the general rule, as the sites available for public buildings usually are of ample size. The use of elevators is seldom required; a natural prejudice, on account of earthquakes, prevails against high buildings.

From the brief statement I have given of actual conditions as described to me and shown by the illustrated work designed and executed, we can see that the architectural problem as an expression of truth resolved itself into that of finding a treatment of reinforced concrete walls and large shaded window openings. Here is where the designer's skill mani-

FIG. 10. A CORNER OF THE DINING ROOM VERANDA, LOOKING TOWARD MANILA BAY—MANILA HOTEL.

FIG. 11. THE LOBBY—MANILA HOTEL.

FIG. 12. THE PHILIPPINE GENERAL HOSPITAL, AT MANILA, CONSTRUCTED ON THE PAVILION PLAN. 1910.

fests itself in the forceful manner by which the exterior of his buildings are handled and made artistically to functionate to the needs of the plan.

As to reinforced concrete, its successful use depends upon finely proportioned masses and interesting relations of openings to solids, rather than upon moulded decoration or applied color. This reasoning would not apply so well to northern climates as to the tropics, where there is an abundance of luxuriant and colorful foliage to contrast with plain wall surfaces.

It was obviously the intention of Mr. Parsons to treat reinforced concrete as

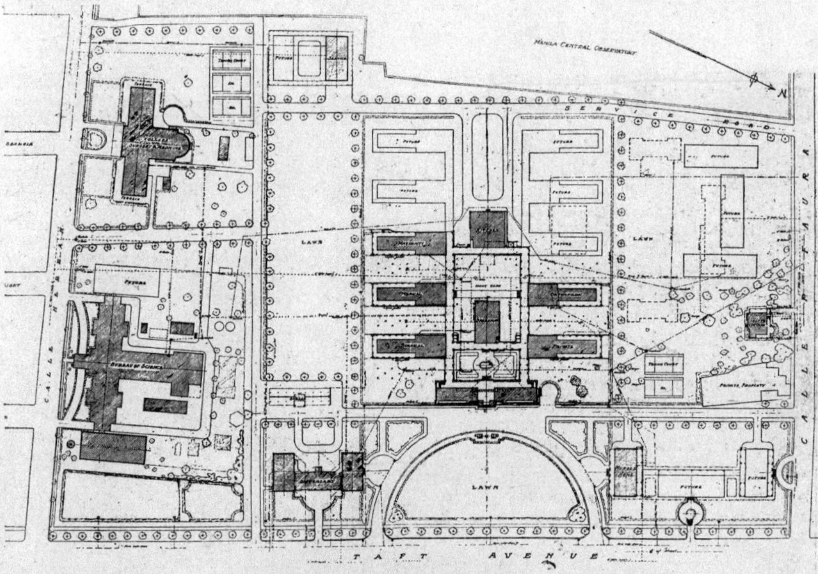

FIG. 13. PLAN OF THE PHILIPPINE GENERAL HOSPITAL, MANILA, SHOWING EXECUTED BUILDINGS, INCLUDING THE COLLEGE OF SURGERY AND MEDICINE (THE BUREAU OF SCIENCE PREVIOUSLY CONSTRUCTED).

FIG. 14. COURTYARD OF THE GENERAL HOSPITAL, SHOWING THE OPEN CORRIDORS.

FIG. 15. ADMINISTRATION PAVILION OF GENERAL HOSPITAL, SHOWING CORRIDORS CONNECTING WITH OTHER PAVILIONS.

a form of masonry and not as a metal. Historical precedent was of little assistance, for that applies mostly to temperate climates and antedates reinforced concrete. However, the architecture developed by the Spaniards, consisting usually of heavy stone walls for the first story and timber construction for the upper story, projecting several feet beyond the lower story, furnished good suggestions, of which the designer took fair advantage.

One of the features of local architecture adopted generally was the use of conchas for window sash in place of glass. The concha is a flat sea shell about four inches in diameter. It is trimmed down to squares, which are set in thin strips of wood. They give a soft pearly light, where clear glass would be intolerable on account of the glare.

A typical example showing the artistic use of these shells is found in the manner the openings of the Manila Hotel are treated. This hotel was constructed on land reclaimed from Manila Bay, facing public parks on two sides and Manila Bay on a third. Note the large exterior window openings carefully arranged and spaced, broad and wide, as they should be in a country where air is essential at all times and shade is required from the direct glare of the sun. All these openings are shaded with canopies giving the strong horizontal lines to the design so typical in tropical architecture. It is always easy to tell the time of day in the tropics by the number of people in the street.

In the plan of this hotel the maximum natural ventilation was sought and admirably achieved. As a result corridors have bedrooms on one side only, affording the best cross ventilation. The original plans had no roof garden, which was added as the building approached completion, causing somewhat of a makeshift in design. In general, both the exterior and the interior of the Manila Hotel are remarkably well handled, and considering the limitations of the material employed in its construction the building is unusually imposing.

The majority of Government buildings designed by Mr. Parsons in the Philippines are located in or near Manila. Pro-

FIG. 16. SUPERINTENDENT'S COTTAGE—GENERAL HOSPITAL, MANILA.

FIG. 20. WOMEN'S DORMITORY OF THE NORMAL SCHOOL, MANILA. 1914.

FIG. 21. COURTYARD—WOMEN'S DORMITORY OF THE NORMAL SCHOOL, MANILA. 1914.

FIG. 22. WOMEN'S DORMITORY OF THE NORMAL SCHOOL, MANILA. PART OF THE COURTYARD.

vincial buildings, schools, public markets and many other types of buildings erected are scattered throughout the islands. A fair idea of the amount of work done can be had by looking over the general plan of Manila, on which the buildings constructed are shown in heavy shaded block form.

The plan of Manila, in general, is based on Burnham's preliminary layout revised to meet actual needs and conditions. The old walled city is now used as a recreation park possessing expansive promenades where the people gather during open air band concerts. One corner of the bastille has been made over into an underground aquarium, which has its trellised entrance showing above the old inclosing walls.

Up to the present time the central capital group remains to be built, and although the designs have been entirely completed, there is but a remote chance of its realization.

During Parsons' stay in the Philippines a part of the general plan of Manila was carried out consistently with the limited municipal resources. Since then its further development has been at a standstill.

Of the many buildings erected, the

FIG. 23. THE SALA—WOMEN'S DORMITORY OF THE NORMAL SCHOOL, MANILA.

FIG. 30. FIRE STATION, JONDO, MANILA. 1913.

Philippines General Hospital, planned on the pavilion scheme to allow for future expansion, is worthy of mention. It was designed to meet tropical conditions by means of pavilions connected on both floors with open arcades. Its exterior treatment is one of extreme simplicity, depending solely on arches for effect and upon the tropical foliage with which the courtyard and grounds are richly planted for contrast against otherwise plain concrete walls. The general type of plan and construction of this group has been followed by U. S. Army surgeons in Panama and other tropical places.

The central educational group for Manila shows to a marked degree the state of development this class of building was carried to in the Philippines. The peculiar angles of the Normal School, an important building of this group, are due to the street lines with which the building lines are parallel. The plan is evident from the exterior which expressed in a direct manner the entrances and stairs, the classrooms and the assembly hall at the apex. Designed in strict accordance with the condition, consistent with the limited appropriation, the structure presents an interesting mass resulting for the most part from the skillful manner in which its unusual angles are handled. What might otherwise be a commonplace design is thus made to possess architectural significance.

Of a more interesting character, the dormitory for girls of the Normal School is a brilliant bit of design harmoniously suited to its surroundings. Here again the building lines are parallel to the streets, affording that opportunity for picturesque composition of which the designer takes full advantage In general conception, this design follows the local domestic architecture developed by the Spaniards, this being particularly noticeable in the projecting upper stories and the continuous window surfaces.

1901–1966

William Welles Bosworth

Headquarters
New York, NY

Other Locations
Paris, France

Founding Partner
William Welles Bosworth

1966

William Welles Bosworth with MIT students, 1889. Courtesy MIT Museum

After earning his architecture degree in 1889, William Welles Bosworth studied drawing with Sir Lawrence Alma-Tadema in London, and then continued his training at the École des Beaux Arts in Paris. Upon his return to the United States, he worked for Frederick Law Olmsted and Shepley, Rutan and Coolidge (today known as Shepley Bulfinch) before establishing an independent practice in New York. Early commissions for industrialist and philanthropist John D. Rockefeller led to major projects for academic and corporate clients, including the design for the campus of the Massachusetts Institute of Technology (MIT), at the time the largest non-governmental structure in the United States. Other clients in this period included Brown University, the American Telephone and Telegraph Company (AT&T), and Western Union. Bosworth also worked as a landscape architect, designing the gardens for Rockefeller's Kykuit Estate at Tarrytown, New York, in 1906.

When Rockefeller traveled to France in 1922 and witnessed the neglect of French cultural sites which had preceded World War I as well as the damage they had sustained during wartime, he enlisted Bosworth as a member of the Comité Franco-Américain Pour la Restauration des Monuments. This involvement marked a shift in Bosworth's practice from the US to France, where he would remain (except for the duration of World War II) for the rest of his life. Subsequent restorations of the Palace of Versailles (1924–1931), the Château de Fontainebleau, and the Cathedral at Reims, all carriedout by Bosworth, registered both the increasing economic and cultural influence of the United States abroad and the central role of Rockefeller in such missionary efforts.

Bosworth's alliance with Rockefeller continued in Egypt where, in 1926, the architect designed a proposed New Egyptian Museum and Research Institute in Cairo, funded by Rockefeller and developed under the guidance of the American Egyptologist James Henry Breasted. Designed in a "neo-pharaonic pastiche of styles", the new museum was intended to replace the existing French-run Museum of Egyptian Antiquities, commonly known as the Egyptian Museum. The project collapsed when, in return for funding the museum, Rockefeller proposed that all proprietary rights to the institution's artifacts be given to the United States, a plan that was strongly opposed by the French and the British — the other colonial powers present the country — as well as by the Egyptian government, which deemed the project a violation "upon the sovereignty of Egypt."[1] — RW

① Nasser Rabbat, "Circling the Square: Nasser Rabbat on Architecture and Revolution in Cairo," *ArtForum* (April 2011): 186–187.

1903–1935

1935

Delano & Aldrich

Headquarters
New York, NY

Founding Partners
William Adams Delano,
Chester Holmes Aldrich

Though William Adams Delano and Chester Holmes Aldrich finished their first architectural degrees at Columbia University's School of Mines and subsequently acquired diplomas from the École des Beaux-Arts in Paris, the architects' paths did not converge until they became colleagues in the office of Carrère & Hastings in the late 1880s. When they met, Aldrich had already been to Paris and was a famed draftsman in the office, and he convinced Delano to travel to France as well. The two young architects formed their own partnership in 1903, starting on drafting tables borrowed from Hastings. Within a year of launching Delano & Aldrich, they had secured a series of illustrious house commissions from the Rockefeller, Stokes, and Winthrop families. Their family, work, and school connections gave them an auspicious launch into a rapidly changing New York City context, in which art and architecture were becoming increasingly important for a population growing in riches and sophistication.

Though they both had experience in Beaux-Arts architecture, and were influenced by their experience at the school in Paris—and Delano had on many occasions articulated the importance of "tradition" as central to his lifelong attitude toward architecture—the partners have most often been identified with a distinctly American form of traditionalism, predicated in part on combining the received stylistic program of the Beaux Arts together with Anglo-American style. Their buildings have been noted equally for the clarity of their parti, the whimsy of their details, and the resolution of their volumes.

The architects lived two blocks apart in New York and only a block away from their studio. Over three hundred employees passed through their small studio on East 38th Street. By the early 1950s Delano & Aldrich's projects numbered over 500. Though they functioned as each other's critics and supporters, the firm was organized based on partners' commissions, and of those 500 projects only about thirty were logged as Aldrich's.

Having built their early reputation as preeminent architects of houses—second homes and urban mansions—from the 1910s to the 1930s, Delano & Aldrich were integral to the transformation of New York's Park Avenue. They built many houses, clubhouses, schools, and apartment buildings in the area, including the Knickerbocker Club, the Colony Club, and the Union Club. Though they designed very few skyscrapers or loft buildings, Delano & Aldrich did produce a thirty-seven-story banking tower for the Brown Brothers & Company on Wall Street, which spawned the commission for a forty-eight-story Carew Tower in Cincinnati. In this period, the firm was also responsible for a series of important university and civic buildings, including the Sterling Chemistry Laboratory (1921–1923) and the Yale Divinity School (1930–1932), Sage Hall at Smith College (1923–1926), a series of buildings on the campuses of the Lawrenceville School in New Jersey and the Hotschkiss School in Connecticut, and importantly, the United States Post Office Department Building and circular plaza in Washington, DC (1928–1935). The firm was also responsible for a series of airport terminals for Pan American Airways. Delano & Aldrich designed the New York Municipal Airport complex at La Guardia Field (1937–1942), of which only the famous Marine Air Terminal still stands.

In 1922, Delano & Aldrich designed the interiors of the Grand Central Art Galleries at Grand Central Terminal in New York for a cooperative of artists established in 1922 by Walter Leighton Clark. Eight years later, the organization commissioned the firm to design the US Pavilion at the Venice Biennale, for which Delano & Aldrich donated their architectural services. The US Pavilion—described in a 1929 dispatch from Venice to *The New York Herald-Tribune* as "an early Colonial style," brick-and-stone building "fronting on the Canal"—was Aldrich's project.[1] The US Embassy in France (originally, the American Government Building) on Place de la Concord in Paris, completed in 1932, was the firm's only other international commission.

Though Aldrich left the firm in 1935 and died in 1940 in Rome, where he had presided over the American Academy. Delano continued to practice under the original firm name until his death in 1960. —AM

(1) Quoted in *The Los Angeles Times* (September 29, 1929): Part III, 18. The Pavilion was owned and operated by the Galleries until 1930, when it was sold to MoMA, only to be re-sold in 1986 to the Guggenheim Museum.

1905–1937

John Russell Pope

Headquarters
New York, NY

1937 Founding and Key Partners
John Russell Pope (founding principal), Otto Reinhold Eggers, Daniel Paul Higgins

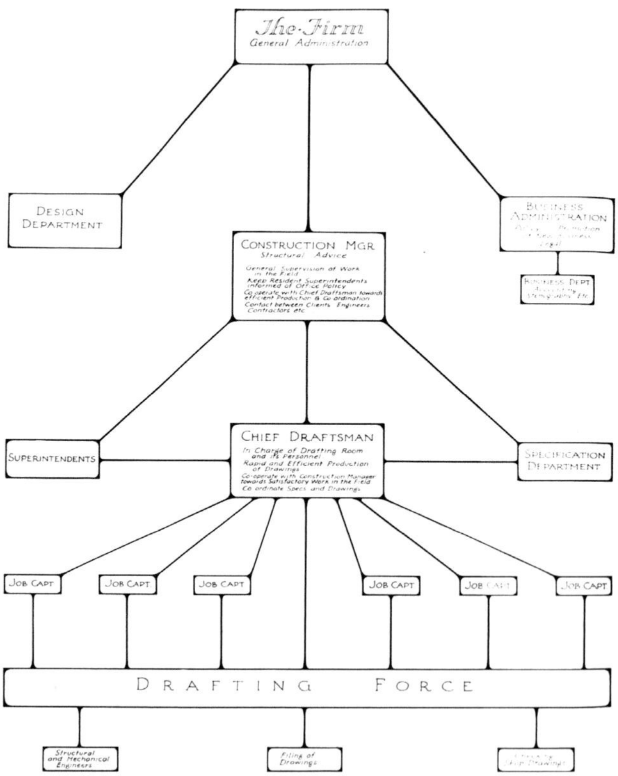

Architectural Record, February 1931

Referred to at the time of his death as "the dean of American architects," John Russell Pope was trained as an architect at Columbia University, where he graduated in 1894.[1] The following year, he won the prestigious McKim Travelling Fellowship and was awarded first prize by the American Academy in Rome. Following eighteen months spent studying the monuments of antiquity and the Renaissance in Rome and Greece, Pope continued his education at the École des Beaux-Arts in Paris. In 1900, he returned to New York and took a position in the office of Bruce Price before establishing his own firm in 1905. When he first opened his office, Pope supplemented his income by teaching at Columbia University with Charles Follen McKim, a mentor throughout his career.

In keeping with his French academic training, Pope shunned commercial commissions in favor of monuments and residential projects in his practice. Sometimes called "the last of the Romans" because of his preference for neoclassical architecture, Pope undertook numerous private commissions for wealthy patrons such as the Vanderbilts, as well as a variety of monumental public buildings and memorials, including the Jefferson Memorial in Washington, D.C. and an extension to the Frick Museum in New York.[2] His international commissions included an extension to the British Museum in London to house the Elgin marbles (1931–1938), the United States Government Offices in London, and the American Battle Monument at Montfaucon, France, inaugurated in 1937.

While Pope accepted the need for stylistic eclecticism in his residential commissions, designing in virtually any style a client requested, he continued to believe in the preeminence of classical form, particularly for his governmental commissions. At the laying of the cornerstone for his National Archives Building in Washington, D.C. in 1933, President Henry Hoover declared that Pope had designed "one of the most beautiful buildings in America, an expression of the American soul."[3] An obituary in the *New York Times* reaffirmed the perceived link between Pope's monumental classicism and the expression of a timeless, national architectural character, hailing his belief in "the rightness and the practicability of perpetuating in America the ideals of an ancient world," embodied in "temples that sit serene in the moil and toil of modern commerce."[4]

Pope's office remained small throughout his career. In 1909, Otto Eggers joined the practice. In the same year, Pope hired Daniel Higgins, who acted as the firm's accountant. Although Eggers and Higgins would become the successor firm to his practice upon his death in 1937, Pope never named the two men as partners during his lifetime, continuing to manage his office in a strictly hierarchical fashion in which he retained veto power over all decisions. — RW

①
"Dean of Architects Dies in New York," *The Boston Globe*, August 28, 1937: 11.

②
Joseph Hudnut, "The Last of the Romans: Comments of the Building of the National Gallery," *Magazine of Art* No. 34 (1941): 169-73.

③
"John Russell Pope, Architect, 63, Dead," *The New York TImes*, August 28, 1937: 15.

④
"John Russell Pope," *The New York TImes*, August 29, 1937: 8.

**1906–
1954**

Henry Killam Murphy

Headquarters
New York, NY

Other Locations
Shanghai, China (1918)

Founding and Key Partners
Henry Killam Murphy (founding principal),
Richard Henry Dana, Jr.

1954

Above. — HENRY KILLAM MURPHY, well-known American architect, is responsible for the design of the Revolutionists' Memorial. He was formerly architectural adviser to the national government in the Nanking City-Planning Bureau during 1929, and has done much to improve that type of architecture which brings West and East into happy combination.

The China Press, April 1, 1934

Henry Killam Murphy was one of many US architects, planners, real estate firms, and construction companies looking for economic opportunity in China after the fall of the Qing Dynasty in 1911. After graduating from Yale, Murphy established his practice in Connecticut in 1906, and was joined by partner Richard Henry Dana Jr. two years later. In 1910, the pair received the commission to design Yale University's campus in China, shifting the firm's primary interest to Asia. Murphy became the planner and architect for numerous Chinese campuses modeled on Western examples, including Yenching University (1919–1926) and Tsinghua University in Beijing, garnering commissions from the national government and various missionary organizations. After ending his partnership with Dana, Murphy moved to China in 1918 to establish an office there.

As an American architect working in China, Murphy sought to develop what historian Jeffrey W. Cody has called an "adaptive" architecture, merging Chinese building traditions with Western technologies.[1] Upon his completion of the Ginling College for Girls in Nanjing (then called Nanking by Westerners), a commissioner of public works for the local province described Murphy's work as the first successful modernization of Chinese architecture by a foreign architect. Murphy's approach was well suited to both Western-style university campuses and to the indigenous church movement launched by missionaries in China in the early 1920s, which sought to develop a "native" form of Christian art and architecture that could accommodate both Western and Chinese traditions.

When Chiang Kai-shek, the head of the ruling Kuomintang (Chinese Nationalist Party), chose the ancient city of Nanjing as the new capital of China in 1927, he asked Murphy to design a modern Chinese capital there. In his plans, Murphy's notions of a traditional Chinese city based on "long vistas" fused with the planning principles of the American City Beautiful movement. While others advocated the demolition of the old city walls and their replacement with a ring road, Murphy believed that "the battered old gray city wall should be maintained at all cost." Journalist Chester Rowell, who interviewed the architect in the late 1920s, reflected on Murphy's approach by comparing his efforts to the work of other US architects designing national capital cities abroad, notably Walter Burley Griffin and Marion Mahony's contemporaneous plans for a federal capital in Australia. He wrote: "At Delhi, in India and at Canberra in Australia, architects are building the great European government edifices in the far corners of the earth. But Murphy's job is to build a Chinese capital out of the ancient city of Nanking, and his dream is to make it Chinese. One of his tasks is to convince the leaders of the new China that this Chinese capital ought to be Chinese. He has nearly done that."[2] —RW

①
Jeffrey W. Cody, *Building in China: Henry K. Murphy's "Adaptive Architecture," 1914-1935* (Hong Kong: The Chinese University Press and Seattle: University of Washington Press, 2001).

②
Cited in Jeffrey W. Cody, *Exporting American Architecture 1870-2000* (London and New York: Routledge, 2003): 118.

1906–1942

Walter Burley Griffin and Marion Mahony

Headquarters
Chicago, IL

Other Locations
1942 Sydney, Australia; Melbourne, Australia;
Sydney, Australia; Lucknow, India

Founding Partners
Walter Burley Griffin, Marion Mahony

Archive Authority of New South Wales

New York State Historical Society

Walter Burley Griffin and Marion Mahony met as young architects working in Frank Lloyd Wright's office at the beginning of the twentieth century. By 1906, Griffin had established an independent practice and the two began working together on projects, notably entering the competion to design a federal capital for Canberra in 1911. Having won the competition in 1912, they relocated their thriving Chicago practice to Australia in 1914 to design the master plan for the nation's new capital city, and established offices in Sydney and Melbourne. Although little known in the United States, they designed over 350 architecture, landscape, and urban design projects.

Mahony graduated from the Massachusetts Institute of Technology in 1894, and returned to her hometown of Chicago where she became the first employee Frank Lloyd Wright hired in his newly established practice; there she also became the first registered woman architect in the United States. In Wright's office, she primarily worked on drawing detailed watercolor renderings that were subsequently reproduced in the German publication of Wright's 1910 Wasmuth Portfolio, which helped establish his career abroad. Mahony would later describe Wright as a person "who originated very little but spent most of his time claiming everything and swiping everything."[1]

Griffin started his career as a draftsman in the office of architect Dwight H. Perkins in Chicago. After passing the licensing exam, he joined Wright's Oak Park Studio and collaborated with Wright on projects such as the Larkin Administration Building. For six months in 1905, while Wright was in Japan working to obtain the Imperial Hotel commission, Griffin and Mahony ran his office in the US.

Mahony and Griffin married in 1911, and while on their honeymoon, they decided to enter the Canberra competition. In the early years, in Chicago they constructed over thirty-five projects, mainly houses in the Midwest, including the J.G. Melson House in Mason City, Iowa.

In her memoir, "The Magic of America," Mahony writes of her life as composed of several struggles. One, which she termed the "Federal Battle," referring to their (failed) struggle to implement the masterplan for the Canberra capital, complicated by World War I, lasted for decades. The "Civic Battle" she describes as the couple's efforts to develop a community in Castlecrag near Sydney in the 1920s, based on ideas of universal democracy, equity, living in harmony with nature, and the esoteric philosophy of theosophy—principles that would define their practice throughout their lives. Mahony details the difficulties they had with US society, particularly its class structure and environmental neglect, as the "Individual Battle."

The Australian economy began to falter even prior to the Great Depression, leaving many of the Mahony-Griffin's projects on the boards. As an entrepreneurial maneuver to keep the firm solvent, they partnered with a longtime client, Nisson Leonard-Kanevskya, an engineer and businessman, to design garbage incinerators. The construction of incinerators was part of the Australian government's infrastructure program designed to both support the country's growing population and to supplantto previous methods of garbage disposal with an environmentally friendlier solution. Between 1929 and 1938, Griffin and Mahony designed thirteen incinerators in collaboration with Leonard-Kanevskya's Reverberatory Incinerator and Engineering Company for sites along the southeastern coast of Australia. The team provided local governments with a complete architectural and engineering package that wrapped industrial function in decorative envelopes that belied the project's pragmatic program.

Following Griffin's death in 1938, Mahony completed the couple's projects then underway in Australia and India before returning to Chicago, where she seemed increasingly absorbed by anthroposophy—a philosophy of spiritual knowledge. Although she lived another twenty-four years, she mostly retreated from public life, spending her time writing and editing "The Magic of America."
—RW & AS

① Marion Mahony Griffin, The Magic Of America: Electronic Edition, The Art Institute of Chicago and the New YorkHistorical Society (August 2007) http://www.artic.edu/magicofamerica/link/moa_4_062.html (last accessed November 17, 2014).

LEO A DALY

1915–

Leo A Daly

Headquarters
Omaha, NE

Other Locations
Abu Dhabi, United Arab Emirates; Atlanta, GA; Austin, TX; Benghazi, Libya; Chicago, IL; College Station, TX; Dallas, TX; Denver, CO; Doha, Qatar; Fort Worth, TX; Honolulu, HI; Houston, TX; Istanbul, Turkey; Las Vegas, NV; Los Angeles, CA; Miami, FL; Minneapolis, MN; Riyadh, Saudi Arabia; Sacramento, CA; San Antonio, TX; San Marcos, TX; Tampa, FL; Tripoli, Libya; Waco, TX; Washington, D.C.; West Palm Beach, CA

Founding and Key Partners
Leo A. Daly (founding principal), Leo A. Daly, Jr., Leo A. Daly III

Current Partners
Leo A. Daly III, Dennis W. Petersen

Leo A Daly

The office of Leo A Daly was founded in 1915 in Omaha, Nebraska, where it continues to be headquartered today. Eponymously named, the firm has been led successively by Leo A. Daly, his son, Leo A. Daly Jr., and currently by the founder's grandson, Leo A. Daly III. The firm's business model has been based on a commitment to expansion through both strategic acquisitions and a willingness to open new branch offices to meet the demands of its clients. According to Daly III, "When a bank comes to you and says, 'We want to build 1,000 offices spread throughout the U.S.,' you need to have offices in those areas."[1] By 1952, the firm had 50 employees, while less than twenty years later, in 1970, it employed 500.

Leo A Daly's international practice began in East Asia in 1966, with the opening of an office in Vietnam, followed by an office in Hong Kong in 1967.[2] The firm practiced heavily in the Middle Eastern Gulf States in the 1970s, as one among the many US firms that grew large through building in the region during the boom in crude oil prices after 1973. The firm opened an office in Tehran in 1975, followed by an office in Riyadh in 1979. Leo A Daly developed a partnership in 1975 with Saudi Consulting House (SCH) to work as a joint venture, SCH/LAD, on projects including the headquarters of the Saudi Arabian National Guard (1974–1980) near Riyadh, commissioned through the US Army Corps of Engineers. The collaboration with SCH extended beyond the traditional affiliation between foreign office and local consultant, as Leo A Daly's office lent their professional expertise through a program "to train Saudi technical staff for the future development plans of the kingdom."[3] Other projects by SCH/LAD in Saudi Arabia in this period include a headquarters for Al-Jubail Petrochemical Company (1979) in Jubail, a company formed by Exxon and the Saudi Arabian Basic Industries Corporation (SABIC); a residential district for Yanbu New Town (1979), a communications and data processing facility for Saudi Arabian Airlines (1979) in Jeddah, and the SABIC Petrochemical Company Headquarters (1979) in Riyadh.

Leo A Daly currently has over 800 employees, and is the 19th largest firm in the US in terms of architectural revenue.[4] The firm operates 31 offices around the world, including those of Lockwood, Andrews and Newnam, Inc. (LAN), based in Texas, which Leo A Daly acquired in 1991. LAN brought the firm a client network throughout Texas and Mexico, expertise in services including infrastructure consulting and public works engineering, and a range of projects including pipelines, wastewater, and transportation systems. Leo A Daly's international practice continues today in East Asia, including the design of Cheung Kong Center (1999) in Hong Kong, designed in collaboration with Cesar Pelli & Associates. The firm's international reach currently includes projects in 87 countries, as well as all 50 states of the US. —AL

(1) Phillip Langdon, "When Bigger Is Better: Lessons from America's Largest Firms," *Architectural Record* (August 1998): 61.

(2) Leo A Daly, "History," http://www.leoadaly.com/company.aspx?wpage=company&loc=History (last accessed October 22, 2014).

(3) "American Designers in Arabia," *Middle East Construction* (Mid-August 1985): 40.

(4) Zachary Edelson, "Top 300 Architecture Firms," *Architectural Record* (August 2014).

Master Plan for Manila
1904–1914

Architect
D. H. Burnham & Company (master plan), William E. Parsons (architect)

Location
Manila, Philippines

Client
Howard Taft, United States Secretary of War; W. Cameron Forbes, Philippine Commission

Master Plan for Baguio
1904–1914

Architect
D. H. Burnham & Company (master plan), William E. Parsons (architect)

Location
Baguio, Philippines

Client
Howard Taft, United States Secretary of War; W. Cameron Forbes, Philippine Commission

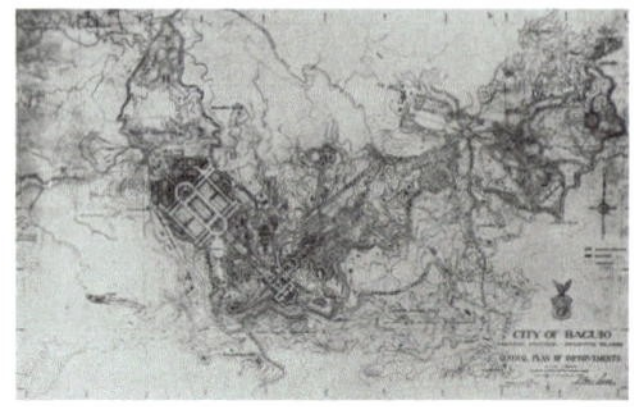

Master Plan for Canberra Federal Capital
1912–1920

Architect
Walter Burley Griffin and Marion Mahony

Location
Canberra, Australia

Client
Parliament of Australia

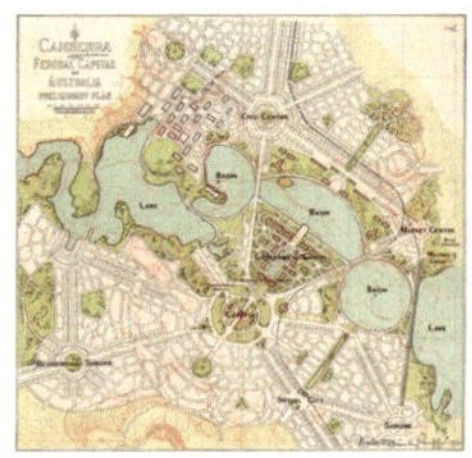

American Academy in Rome
1914

Architect
McKim, Mead & White

Location
Rome, Italy

Client
American Academy in Rome

Leeton Town Centre Plan
1914

Architect
Walter Burley Griffin and Marion Mahony

Location
Leeton, Australia

Client
Leeton Shire Council

Nanjing University
1914–1935

Architect
Perkins, Fellows and Hamilton

Location
Nanjing, China

Client
Nanjing University

1918

Newman College, University of Melbourne
1915–1918

Architect
Walter Burley Griffin and Marion Mahony

Location
Melbourne, Australia

Client
Executive Committee of the Provisional College Council

Imperial Hotel
1915–1923

FRANK LLOYD WRIGHT

Architect
Frank Lloyd Wright

Location
Tokyo, Japan

Client
Imperial Hotel

Peking Union Medical College
1916–1921

Shepley Bulfinch

Architect
Shepley Bulfinch

Location
Beijing, China

Client
Rockefeller Foundation/China Medical Building

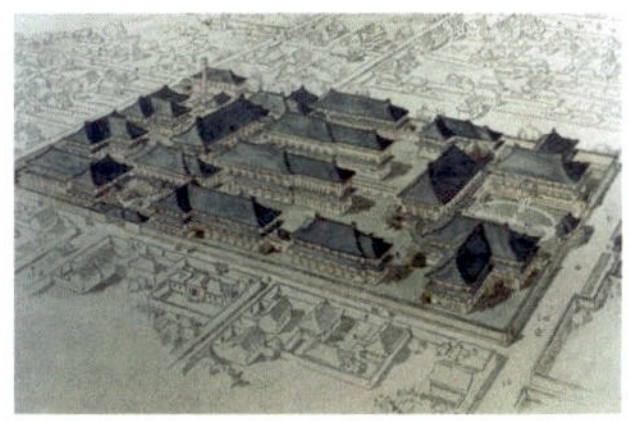

Master Plan for Castlecrag Residential Community
1918–1926

Architect
Walter Burley Griffin and Marion Mahony

Location
Sydney, Australia

Client
Greater Sydney Development Association

The Missionary Challenge: Philanthropy and Institution-Building at the Turn of the Century

In 1937, a quarter-century after the antitrust ruling against Standard Oil which required the world's largest corporation to be splintered into 34 separate entities, the *New York Times* characterized the relationship between its former empire and the Rockefeller Foundation as "the outstanding example of the romance of American business."[1] When Rockefeller first set out to incorporate his philanthropic endeavors in 1910, the public spectacle of the trial against Standard Oil, which controlled 90 percent of the US oil refining business by 1880, was still ongoing.[2] In the same year, Andrew Carnegie established the Carnegie Corporation of New York on the basis of the remaining wealth of the Carnegie Steel Company. As Rockefeller's attempts at federal incorporation failed, he too attempted to operate through the State of New York, which incorporated the Rockefeller Foundation in 1913 for the stated purpose of promoting "the well-being of mankind throughout the world."[3] Carnegie, who had stated his views on the moral obligation of the rich to give away their wealth "wisely" in "The Gospel of Wealth" (1899), gave away up to 90 percent of his wealth during his lifetime by some estimates, sponsoring over 2500 libraries around the world.[4] Upon his death in 1937 at the age of 97, Rockefeller had given away over $500 million through various philanthropic enterprises during his lifetime. Both architecture and US architects played a key role in these efforts.

Upon its incorporation, the Rockefeller Foundation focused on expanding its philanthropic efforts to medical services abroad, forming the International Health Commission in 1913 and the China Medical Board the following year to promote modern medicine in China. Following the examples of medical education programs established by Harvard University in Canton and the University of Pennsylvania in Shanghai, the China Medical Board planned to

① "Financier's Fortune in Oil Amassed in Industrial Era of 'Rugged Individualism,'" *The New York Times* (May 24, 1937): 8.

② Raymond Blaine Fosdick, *The Story of the Rockefeller Foundation* (New Brunswick: Transaction Publishers, 1989).

③ This quote has since become the branding byline of the Foundation. See George F. Vincent, *The Rockefeller Foundation, A Review of its War Work, Public Health Activities and Medical Education Projects in the year 1917* (New York: The Rockefeller Foundation, 1917): 53.

④ Andrew Carnegie, "Wealth," *North American Review*, No. CCCXCI (June 1889).

1890

1899 Andrew Carnegie, "The Gospel of Wealth"

1910 Carnegie Corporation of New York established

1913 Rockefeller Foundation established

1914 American Academy in Rome inaugurated

1918 U.S. President Woodrow Wilson issues The Fourteen Points Statement (policy of open trade, open agreements, democracy and self-determination)

1919 Treaty of Versailles and the establishment of the League of Nations (which would turn into UN in 1945)

1898 Spanish-American War

1914–1918 World War I

found Western-style educational institutions in both Peking and Shanghai. One of these, Peking Union Medical College, became the first major building project sponsored by the Rockefeller Foundation abroad. John D. Rockefeller Jr., at the time chairman of both the board of trustees and the executive board of the Foundation, wrote to his father upon the dedication of the College that its buildings, designed by Coolidge and Shattuck (later Shepley Bulfinch), were "perfectly adapted to the purposes and a great contribution not only to science but to architecture."[5]

Foreign missionaries of various religions and nationalities operated in China in this period according to what historian Jeffrey Cody has described as two different visions of progress.[6] The first, "directed to the bottom of the ledger," was exemplified by Western-styled buildings for the Young Men's Christian Association in nearly every province of China. The second, "more aesthetic and aimed at linking China's past with a scientific future," involved attempts to mediate Western institutional models with "Chinese-style" buildings, as at Peking Union Medical College, Yale-in-China's Hunan campus, or Yenching University (1919–1926), designed by Henry Killam Murphy and "founded, supported, and in large portion administered by American friends."[7]

After World War I the Rockefeller Foundation directly supported the recovery of the European countries hardest hit by the war. Though the Foundation officially expanded its focus to include culture only in 1924, Rockefeller Jr. had already supported the restoration of the Palace of Versailles and other French cultural sites, hiring the Beaux Arts-trained architect William Welles Bosworth as a member of the Comité Franco-Américain Pour la Restauration des Monuments.[8] The Foundation also supported the nascent American Academy in Rome along with other industrialists-turned-philanthropists such as J.P. Morgan and Henry Clay Frick, making a $200,000 donation in 1922 towards securing the institution's endowment.[9]

The Rockefeller Foundation's institution-building after World War I expanded from investment in health, medicine, and the humanities to include research in the social and natural sciences. The trend was paralleled by other major foundations, all infused to some extent by the promise of efficacy through "scientific management."[10] When the Ford Foundation was established in 1936, the philanthropic project outlined by Carnegie at the end of the nineteenth century, of providing "ladders upon which the aspiring can rise," was already assuming the form of systems-oriented, developmental thinking, which would correlate more directly with US foreign and economic policies during the Cold War. — AM

⑤ Letter from John D. Rockefeller Jr. to John D. Rockefeller Sr., quoted in Mary Brown Bullock, *An American Transplant: The Rockefeller Foundation and the Peking Union Medical* (Berkeley: University of California Press, 1980).

⑥ Jeffrey Cody, "Striking A Harmonious Chord: Foreign Missionaries and Chinese-style Buildings, 1911–1949," *Architronic*, Vol. 5, n.3 (1996).

⑦ Samuel L. Chao, "Yenching University Carries on Tradition of Early Founders," *The China Press* (July 4, 1934): 20.

⑧ "Editorial Comment," *The American Architect and The Architectural Review* (August 27, 1924): 181.

⑨ "Rockefeller Gift Aids Rome Academy," *The New York Times* (July 3, 1922); website of the American Academy in Rome, *http://www.aarome.org/about/place/academy* (last accessed October 3, 2014).

⑩ Merle Curti, *American Philanthropy Abroad* (New Brunswick: Transaction, Inc., 1988).

1924 John D. Rockefeller Jr. establishes *La Comité Franco-Americain pour la Restauration des Monuments*; Bosworth appointed architect member

1936 Ford Foundation established

1940 The Office of Inter-American Affairs founded by Nelson Rockefeller

1947 The *International Basic Economy Corporation (IBEC)*, founded by Nelson A. Rockefeller

1939–1945 World War II

1950

Personal Reminiscences of CHARLES·FOLLEN·McKIM

By Glenn Brown

McKim's Way

McKIM'S way, which in my experience led to success, was a most interesting study of personality. There was, in his intercourse with others, an innate diffidence which was flattering, a charming deference which was winning, a fund of knowledge which was convincing, a refinement of taste which was enlightening, a breadth of view which was enlarging, a concentration which was absorbing and a persistence which was successful. Positive in his convictions, sensitive, refined and unerring in his judgment of beauty, persistent in carrying out his ideas, he was unrivalled, in my experience, in winning against opposition.

He entered a discussion by apparently agreeing with his opponent, frequently calling attention to good points not seen by the author, then, bit by bit, a suggestion was made here and there, showing where the scheme or idea might be improved. The suggestions often called for radical changes, and I have yet to see anyone fail gladly to avail himself of the ideas offered, as they were always good. His concentration on the subject in hand was most notable; no side issues or outside problems, no matter how important, were allowed to interfere.

His study of a subject was painstaking and exhaustive, starting with the broad principles and descending to the minutest details. His power of enthusing others through his charming deference and clear ideas was exceptional, whether it was brought to bear on a strenuous President like Roosevelt, a great college President like Eliot or broad statesmen like Elihu Root, an eminent brother artist like Saint Gaudens, a literary enthusiast like Gilder, or a cosmopolitan like Frank Millet. The capacity of exciting enthusiasm and securing co-operation extended through his office to the youngest draftsman. This power made many of his dreams for the advancement of the fine arts and the culture of the people blossom out into realities.

Time and labor were never considered by him or by those enthusiastically working with him; the object in view was the most perfect design or the best method of advancing the fine arts.

McKim's way is well illustrated by the following occurrences which came under my knowledge.

The American Academy in Rome was started by the brilliant group of artists who had charge of the Chicago Exposition in 1893, to give our country a post graduate school of architecture. It was soon after I became secretary of the American Institute of Architects that I became, through McKim, interested in the future of the American Academy. For years he had largely supported the school from his private income, and it was his ambition to secure an endowment and see it firmly established before his death. He felt keenly that a school of this character was the surest step toward advancing the fine arts and adding to the refinement and culture of the public. His first move was to secure an endowment and one of the means he adopted was the noted dinner of the American Institute of Architects, a full account of which has been given in a previous paper. McKim thought a national charter was necessary to give the Academy a recognized dignity among the other foreign schools in Rome, which are all endowed by their governments, while the American school remained only a private affair. To secure the national charter required an act of Congress. To get an act of Congress called for the approval of the Committee on Library. To get the approval of the Committee on Library required Speaker Cannon's approval. Cannon was opposed, he said, because while the bill for a charter did not call for an appropriation, it was only an entering wedge for final government support of the school.

For several years the bill was held up by the Committee of the House. Finally Representative J. T. McCleary from Minnesota was persuaded by Cass Gilbert, whom McKim called to his assistance, and Gilbert's friends from Minnesota, to take an interest in the subject and Cannon allowed a favorable report to be made. I think Cannon felt assured that the measure would be stopped in the House, as a single objection would kill the bill for that session, as the bill must be brought up out of the regular order and during the last days of the session.

Representative J. T. McCleary and Representative Henry Kirke Porter gave us the names of the five Representatives, any one of whom if present would object and thus prevent the passage of the bill. McKim laid his plans to ward off these objections by securing the aid and co-operation of prominent men in the State of the member. I recollect I was delegated to see Secretary Hay, who was a friend of one objector, and secured his assurance of help. Aid was sought from New York, Chicago, St. Louis and Boston for this purpose and all asked responded to the call.

There was one objector from the South, and W. S. Eames got an assurance from a Representative that he would take the member down for a drink just before the bill was called. The bill came up, no objection was raised, due to the carefully laid plans of McKim, and passed the House.

The Senate had already passed the bill, but slight modifications made it necessary for the Senate to again pass upon the measure and it was the last day of the session.

I had been in touch with Senator Newlands and Representatives Porter and McCleary during the days of the campaign, and acting on instructions, I secured a copy and hurried over to the Senate with the modified charter. Senator Newlands immediately brought it before the Senate, by previous arrangement, but here again a single objection would have prevented its passage. Senator Teller, as we knew, had signified his intention to object to all bills of this character. Senator Newlands when it was read went across the Senate chamber and sat by Senator Teller and as he arose to object, Senator Newlands actually pulling him down by the coat tails, asked as a personal favor that Teller allow it to come before the Senate for consideration. The Senator yielded to this personal plea.

The bill passed and was signed by President Roosevelt and the American Academy in Rome received its national charter. McKim felt that we had started the Academy on a firm foundation.

The first home of this school was a rented building, the Villa Aurora; the second was the Villa Mirafiore (without the walls) presented to them through the generosity of Mr. Henry Walters; the third and permanent home, given a short time before McKim's death, is the Villa Aurelia on the summit of the Janiculum Hill in Rome. This Villa within the walls overlooking the historic hills, cathedrals, arches and temples of Rome from the Alban Hills to the Mediterranean, was devised to the Academy by the will of Mrs. Clara J. Heyland, formerly Miss Jessup of Philadelphia, as a memorial to her parents and to assist and encourage education in the fine arts.

This Villa makes real the dream of McKim, which revealed a place where the students would be constantly in the atmosphere and under the influence of Rome and nearby Italy, in daily association with its enlightening antiquities, being adjacent to the Villa Pamfili Doria, not far from Saint Peter's, the Vatican, and the Roman Forum. New buildings are being erected to give the students studios and work rooms, and a fine library, reserving the Villa for the residence of the director and more or less public functions.

Through the zealous and wise conduct of Mr. William R. Mead, who became president after McKim's death, and Frank Millet, appointed director, the

AMERICAN ACADEMY IN ROME. McKIM, MEAD & WHITE, ARCHITECTS.

school is now in a position to fulfill in the highest degree the ideals of Charles Follen McKim, who left his estate, subject to a life annuity to his daughter, to carry forward the education of the bright students in sculpture, painting and architecture, who will by their good work in the future interest, enlighten and lead the public to demand only the best in the fine arts.

McKim's persistent way of searching for and attaining the best results was shown vividly to me in his design for the base of the Sherman Statue in New York. One day he was lunching with me at the Cosmos Club, when he opened the conversation by saying, "I am thankful Saint Gaudens and I have settled on the design of the base for the Sherman Statue. My first idea was a high base something on the order of Colleoni, while Saint Gaudens wanted the figure only a few feet from the ground. We have compromised, making it higher than he first wanted it and lower than my first idea. I have made about fifteen hundred studies for this base and I am thankful that it has been settled."

We had not been at the table half an hour when McKim received a telegram which he opened. A curious expression crept over his face as he read the telegram to me: "Charles, that base is all wrong. Gus." I don't know how many other studies were made before these two men of genius were satisfied, as they finally were, with the result. Just before the Sherman Statue was unveiled I spent three hours with McKim and Saint Gaudens at the statue while they were discussing pro and con the minor details of the tone for bronze in the ornaments on the base to make it harmonize with the gilded statue and red granite base, and the question of leaving the sculptured earth on which the figures stood, as it was cut of red granite, or gilding it to go with the statue.

During the three hours many tints were tried on the bronze band and on the trophies, and each shade carefully considered in its relations to the granite base and to the bronze sculpture. The tints were chosen and the determination reached to gild the sculptured stone earth just in time to have them ready before the unveiling.

It was McKim's way to give of his time and talent to serve the public, as in his constant efforts to maintain the design of the Park Commission Plan when new buildings were erected or new parks planted.

He freely gave of his time and talents on juries for selecting the designs for public buildings and monuments. He was one of the jury which selected the design for the Bureau of American Republics, one of the most satisfactory structures of recent date, and his criticisms and suggestions for modifications and changes were of assistance to the architects, Messrs. Kelsey and Cret.

He was one of the jury in selecting the memorial to Grant which is now being erected at the eastern end of the Mall, and he not only selected a monument that would be suitable for this most important position, but by his advice made it more fitting than it was in the original form.

McKim's way caused him to often try full size models or sections in place, ignoring the criticism of the thoughtless, so as to judge more clearly of their scale and relation to each other. I recollect spending an afternoon with him in the Harvard Club building, New York, when he was experimenting with the beams in the ceiling, trying their depths and distance apart until he had arrived at the solution which he thought best. At the same time several designs for paneling the lower third of the walls, made full size, were put in place and the one most suitable chosen. All acknowledge that this hall is one of our best interiors.

He acted in an advisory capacity in many directions in which, while not adding to his reputation, his good judgment was of great value to the community which sought his advice, as was the case in saving the Confederate State Capitol in Montgomery, Alabama. Additions to this old building, a good example of the Greek revival of about 1820, were contemplated; and some of the officials being sufficiently doubtful of their capacity to undertake these changes, determined to ask McKim's advice or judgment on the proposed additions. I received a letter

FOUNDERS' COURT—AMERICAN ACADEMY IN ROME—McKIM, MEAD & WHITE, ARCHITECTS.

ENTRANCE VESTIBULE—AMERICAN ACADEMY IN ROME. McKIM, MEAD & WHITE, ARCHITECTS.

asking if I would go with him to the hearing on the subject, before the Governor and other State officials, in Montgomery, Alabama. We spent the next day in the drawing room of the Pullman, studying the drawings of the proposed additions, which would have overshadowed the original building and destroyed its dignity and importance. He mapped out the proposed changes in the drawings which he considered would keep them in harmony and subordinate to the old structure. The arguments for the changes were mapped out so the case was well prepared when we met the Governor and his official family the next day. After McKim had given his views, he called upon me as author of the History of the United States Capitol, to give mine, which it goes without saying coincided with his. Advocates of the improper scheme as proposed made their statements and cross questioned McKim and myself. Before the meeting was over we could see that the majority was with us and the Confederate State Capitol was saved.

During our trip McKim said, "If my father knew I was trying to save the Confederate State Capitol where Jefferson Davis took the oath of office and was inaugurated President of the Confederacy, he would turn over in his grave." McKim's father was a clergyman and strong abolitionist.

It was McKim's way to draw to him by his charming, lovable disposition, brilliant mind, sensitive and highly cultivated sense of the beautiful, keen appreciation of the best in literature, music and the fine arts, other spirits who were seeking the best in art, literature, education—such intimates as Richard Watson Gilder, Augustus Saint Gaudens, D. H. Burnham, Frank Millet, John La Farge, Elihu Root, Joseph Choate, Nicholas Murray Butler, Charles Eliot and Theodore Roosevelt. It was to McKim that such men listened and by whom they were swayed and guided in discussions of the fine arts. When one differed with him those who did not know would think he had changed his views, while he was simply working around to it by what appeared to be roundabout paths, but by ways that carried him and his opponents with him to his goal. He never gave up until he gained his end in every instance that came under my observation.

Another factor in the success of McKim's way was his genius as a designer.

I recollect very well as a young man the sad feeling of disappointment, when McKim, Mead and White showed their tendency in design as illustrated by the Boston Public Library and other early work.

I had only a short time before left the Massachusetts Institute of Technology, where just across the street Richardson was completing his great masterpiece, Trinity Church, which enthused me, as it did many others, with the idea that the true expression for American architecture was the Byzantine or Romanesque. Many of us felt that this style, which never reached its highest expression in the old country, was capable of development into a national distinctive style and that it would reach its artistic development in this country through the genius of H. H. Richardson and his students.

When Charles McKim and Stanford White, two of the brilliant men in Richardson's office, showed they were not following in the Byzantine, but were adopting the Italian Renaissance, I was distinctly disappointed, as I thought they were the men to give us a national style developed from the beginning by Richardson.

As the years passed and I saw the effect of Richardson's brilliance and personal genius as it spread over the country and the woeful results produced by the strong men and the weak men in attempts to follow his example, my views changed. It may be safely said that no building, among the thousands erected as Richardsonian or Romanesque, can even approximately be thought a work of art, except those on which Richardson left his personal impress. I began to feel that it was a misfortune that any one tried to follow Richardson, and I am now glad that no one attempts his style. As the years passed I became more and more enthusiastic on the work of McKim, Mead and White, particularly admiring the buildings in which the design was attributed to McKim.

The grasp of big composition, careful proportions, the charmingly refined details, the due consideration of the setting and harmony with surroundings, the treatment of landscape with just the proper formality to enhance the building, all were more perfect and more artistic than had been done in this country before.

Nothing in this country, and I know of nothing better in other countries, illustrate these principles more fully than the approaches and flanking buildings combined with the Columbia Library, New York. Here we have dignity, harmony, good proportion, refined detail, combined with just the proper formal landscape, making one of the great architectural compositions of the world.

I was very much interested some time ago in attending a lecture on modern architecture, where there was a mixed audience of some six hundred people. Views were given of noted foreign buildings, showing their influence on American work. Views were given of the noted buildings in this country. When the view of the Morgan Library, New York, by McKim, Mead and White, was thrown upon the screen, there was a spontaneous burst of applause and this was the only slide among the many good things shown that produced applause.

This showed an appreciation of the beautiful by a mixed American audience that I felt augured good for the future of the fine arts. McKim's influence, in simplicity, harmony, refinement, and landscape, has been one of the greatest factors which, spread through the great men who have graduated from his office on whom his principles have been impressed, has placed architecture in this country in the forefront in modern architecture.

Another factor that led to success in McKim's way was the power of concentration, the faculty of wiping from his mind surroundings, other problems and conditions, and focussing his mind on the problem in hand.

It was this concentration, while innumerable other problems were thrust upon him, but ignored, that proved so successful in his work of restoring the White House, in designing the great plan for the Mall in Washington with its great vistas and monumental memorials and buildings, and in his work for the public through the American Institute of Architects which proved so effective and satisfactory.

McKim's way meant loyalty, through good and evil report, to friends and associates when he had tested and knew the good qualities of a man or the capabilities of the artist. He defended them against malicious attacks and brought forward their good qualities and good works. On many occasions it has been my pleasure to hear him defend men to whom false motives had been attributed; while it was difficult for him to see the evil, he was quick to see the good in a person.

McKim was diffident in expressing himself before a large body of men and his delivery was not impressive, as he often hesitated and apparently missed the proper word. Strange to say that while a stenographic report of his speeches required but little change, many of the ready and fluent talkers had to rewrite their efforts. In his hesitation he found the right word to convey the thought; it was McKim's way to seek, while apparently hesitating, the word best suited to the idea.

McKim's way drew around him a coterie of men, idealists, but practical in presenting, persistent in maintaining and effective in attaining their ideals, among which was the advancement of the nation in the fine arts; they believed appreciation of the beautiful by the people was a long step in the culture of the nation.

EDITORIAL COMMENT

LEARNING THAT WELLES BOSWORTH had been appointed architect member of the committee to administer the fund given by John D. Rockefeller, Jr., for the restoration of monumental buildings in France, we wrote Mr. Bosworth for some authoritative information as to the work of the committee. Mr. Bosworth replied as follows:

"The committee is officially called "La Comité Franco-Americain pour la Restauration des Monuments." The other members are Ambassador Jusserand; the late Premier and man of letters, Gabriel Hanotaux; the one-time ambassador to Russia, M. Paleologue, now president of the 'Amis de Versailles;' and Colonel H. H. Harjes, of the firm of Morgan, Harjes, Paris. We work in collaboration with the 'Direction des Beaux-Arts,' whose directeur is M. Paul Léon.

"After going into all the needs of Reims, Versailles and Fontainebleau, we voted credits at our June meeting to cover the following:

"The cost of the new roof over the nave, choir and the two arms of the transept of the Cathedral at Reims, including lead roofs, gutters, and the erection of the spire, called clocher à l'ange, 40 meters high; ornaments and figures of lead repoussé; interior carillon, and so forth:

"At Fontainebleau, the rebuilding of many of the roofs; the re-establishment of the planting; partial repaving of the courts, with attention to drainage; the putting in condition of many of the apartments, including restoration of paintings, reconditioning woodwork, repairing of tapestries, and so forth:

"At Versailles, the restoration of the little Theatre of Marie Antoinette; rebuilding and reconditioning of the woodwork of the windows and doors throughout the Palace of Versailles, the two Trianons, and the Orangerie; in the Parks and Gardens, the renewing of the hedges and plantations; clearing off the dead branches from the trees and grounds; regravelling the alleys and putting the avenues in commission, including drainage; rebuilding of terraces; reconditioning of the trophies on the balustrades crowning the Palace on the side toward the Gardens, etc; also a thing long desired by the French people, which was voted not long ago afresh, is the removal of the great statues from the Court of Honor, placed there under Louis Philippe.

"There are many minor details involved and much other work is to follow, but these are the principal items in hand at present. The French people have themselves done a great deal on these buildings, and this is merely in supplement of what they have done and are unable to do further because of the strain their Government has been under since the war. I am sure your readers will take satisfaction in having America, who owes so much to the French tradition, come to their relief at this time."

We feel sure that every architect in this country will regard with the greatest satisfaction the fine start that has been made in this important movement and equally gratified to learn that the work will be carried forward by a committee composed of men, who each in his separate field represents the highest efficiency.

* * *

THE CONTRACTOR'S BOND is an important factor in the building industry. Its influence on the business of architecture is not fully appreciated by many members of that profession. There are too many architects who will accept a proposal, which is plainly too low, as a basis of a contract. Often they are urged by the owner to do so. The actuating motive must be the foolish idea that they can get something for nothing. Business transactions which are influenced by such incentives can never eventuate satisfactorily for anyone—not even the architect. The only satisfactory building operation is one from which the contractor makes a reasonable profit.

Unfortunately, some bonding companies have been careless, to say the least, in becoming surety for contractors who were incompetent, dishonest or who had bid too low for the work to be done. Such a course is manifestly unfair to the competent, honest and reliable contractor of whom there are many. The only way to place the business of building construction on a satisfactory basis is to prevent the irresponsible contractor from securing a contract bond.

Steps leading to this end are under way through the joint action of the Associated General Contractors of America and a committee representing the bonding companies. It is difficult to understand why organized architects are not a party to this work. It vitally affects their business and the national, state and local architectural organizations should bestir themselves and become active in the matter. Their co-operation will be welcomed.

MAGAZINE SECTION

PART FOUR
The Churchman Afield

Boston Evening Transcript

SATURDAY, SEPT. [illegible], 1921
Books—Features

Peking Union College, the Harvard Medical School of the Far East

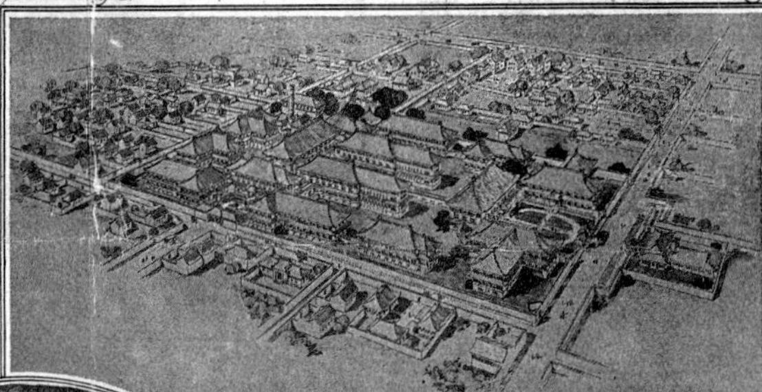

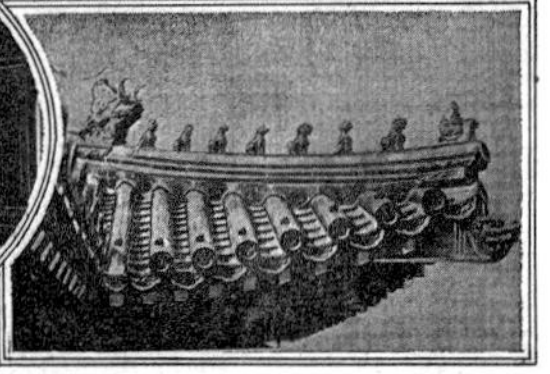

ILLUSTRATIONS

UPPER LEFT—War-wounded Soldiers Receiving Care and Treatment in the College Hospital.

UPPER RIGHT—North Residence Compound, Where Are Grouped the Homes Built for Members of the Faculty.

CENTRE—General View of the College, Illustrating the Chinese Style of Architecture Common to All the Buildings Except the Residences.

LOWER LEFT—The Lobby of the Nurses' Home.

LOWER RIGHT—A Detail from the Roof of One of the College Buildings.

An American Missionary Venture, Endowed by the Rockefeller Foundation, to Be Dedicated Next Week—With the Arms of Modern Science, It Will Wage Relentless War on the Preventable and Easily Curable Diseases Which So Long Have Run Unchecked in China — An Event Full of Significance for the Future Welfare of the Entire Orient.

By GEORGE E. VINCENT
President of the Rockefeller Foundation

PEKING will witness this month an event which may have as much significance for the future welfare of China as the Washington conference on disarmament and the Far East in November. In the week of Sept. 15-22 will be held medical conferences in connection with the dedication exercises of the Peking Union Medical College and Hospital, which the Rockefeller Foundation is building, equipping, and staffing. The plant of the college includes laboratories for anatomy, physiology and chemistry, a pathology building, a 250-bed hospital with provision for about thirty private rooms, a large out-patient department, a hospital administration unit with quarters for resident physicians and internes, a nurses' home, an animal house and plants which will supply water, heat, electric light and power and fuel gas. Thirty-five faculty houses, grouped, with a few exceptions, in two walled areas or compounds, are of brick and concrete with slate roofs and are supplied with every convenience of Western life.

The medical and hospital buildings, which are fireproof, are in harmony with the best traditions of Chinese architecture and symbolize a desire to make the college not something imposed from without but an agency which shall in time become an intimate, organic part of a developing Chinese civilization. The campus of the college, on which fourteen hospital and laboratory buildings have already been erected, was until the latter half of 1917 the site of the palace and garden of a Chinese prince. The great gray bricks which formed the wall enclosing the prince's garden have been cut up and used as the face brick for all the college buildings.

Eaves and porticos are embellished with conventional Chinese decorations in red, blue, green and gold, painted by native artisans. Glazed green roof tiles of the sort used only for imperial palaces and temples in days gone by have been supplied by one of the same factories which has made them for hundreds of years. The very descendants of the tile makers and builders of ancient Chinese edifices have been at work on the new Chinese-American structures.

Like Our Building Methods

The Chinese laborers take kindly to American building methods. The reënforced concrete construction which was employed for the floors was a welcome novelty. The use of wood-working machinery has aroused much interest. The turning out of uniform sash, doors, window frames, etc., was a new idea to a people accustomed to hand work whose nearest synonym for identical is "not so very different."

The interior of the building is equipped with the most modern facilities for elementary and advanced instruction in all major medical sciences and clinical branches. This new school and hospital in Peking will enable the medical missionaries to keep abreast of current discoveries and procedures in medicine, surgery and public health.

Missionary societies incidentally have played a leading part in introducing a knowledge of modern medicine into communities scattered throughout the entire republic. Dispensaries, begun as adjuncts [illegible] evangelistic work, have in many cases [de]veloped into small hospitals, in a few in[st]ances in larger centres into institutions [co]mparable with the average of those in the West. In 1919 the Protestant missions in China supported 317 hospitals. Catholic orders and societies maintain hospitals and dispensaries in large ports, such as Shanghai and Hankow, and in several smaller places.

Students Make Good Progress

The need for Chinese assistants in these missionary hospitals led to the opening of pioneer medical schools, which, through the devotion of teachers, were able to give a preliminary training of practical use in the routine of the hospital. Some of the students of exceptional ability made considerable progress. A few were sent to Western schools to complete their training. Of late, missionary medical education has been concentrated in a few schools.

A Japanese medical school in Moukden, until recently a German-manned school in Shanghai, a British medical school in the University of Hongkong, groups of European and American physicians in the chief treaty ports, hospitals supported by local town councils or voluntary societies in foreign concessions and military and naval hospitals maintained by various foreign governments have had an appreciable educative effect upon Chinese public opinion. The influence of Chinese physicians who have been trained in the medical schools of the United States and of Europe has been significant and of increasing weight.

The Peking Union Medical College has been in process of organization and construction since 1915. This college is an outgrowth of the Union Medical College, which was founded by the joint effort of six British and American missionary societies in 1906, following the disorganization of mission work resulting from the Boxer outbreak. On July 1, 1915, the China Medical Board of the Rockefeller Foundation assumed the full support of the Union Medical College, and in 1917 a provisional charter was secured from the regents of the University of the State of New York.

To Prevent as Well as Cure Disease

China's Medical Problem, Like Our Own, Is Two-Fold—The Story of American Enterprise in the Orient

IT was in 1915 that a special commission sent to China by the Rockefeller Foundation reported that the need of medical relief in China was very great. Many preventable and easily curable diseases have prevailed there almost unchecked, from the earliest days down to present times, while intercourse with foreign countries and modern methods of communication have introduced into regions previously unaffected such terrible scourges as the bubonic plague and have contributed largely to the spread of other dangerous infections.

So also have modern systems of transportation and of industry brought in an entirely new series of accidents and occupational diseases with which Chinese civilization is not yet prepared to cope. It was felt that a special obligation rested upon Western civilization to mitigate this suffering, for part of which it may be held directly responsible.

The foundations work in the Orient is under the direction of the China Medical Board, which has as its primary aim "to aid the agencies which represent Western medicine in China to make steady progress toward higher standards and more efficient service." In fulfilling its purpose to promote modern medical education in the republic the Board recognizes the following essentials:

(1) Pre-medical education.
(2) Undergraduate courses for physicians.
(3) Graduate study for investigators, laboratory workers, teachers and clinical specialists.
(4) Short courses for private practitioners and missionary doctors, both foreign and Chinese.
(5) Medical research, especially with reference to the problems peculiar to the Far East.
(6) Standardized hospitals as training centres for internes, as models for imitation by the Chinese, as headquarters for practising physicians and as a means of popular education.
(7) Organized efforts to diffuse among the Chinese a knowledge of modern medicine and public health.
(8) The fostering of professional ethics through the development of character and idealism.

Open to Both Sexes

The chief agency by which it is hoped to further these aims is, of course, the new Peking Union Medical College, which now has an enrollment approaching one hundred. Women are admitted to both the premedical school and the medical courses on equal terms with men. Chinese are appointed to the teaching staff, which is expected to include steadily increasing numbers of native teachers and investigators. Graduate students are welcomed, and with the opening of the new hospital will be offered excellent opportunities to pursue both laboratory and clinical studies under well-trained and enthusiastic teachers. Special efforts will be made to put the resources of the school and hospital at the service of medical missionaries and other doctors who wish to keep abreast of progress in medicine and surgery, or to undertake specific investigations. Short courses of six weeks or more will be given in the summer, and possible during the Chinese New Year season.

The purchase of books for the library of the college has been another branch of work. Although delayed during the war, it again became possible, during 1919, to negotiate with book dealers in France and Germany. Late in that year arrangements were made for Mr. James F. Ballard, assistant librarian of the Boston Medical Library, to go abroad to secure books and sets of periodicals for the college. A full and adequate scientific library is more important in Peking than it would be for a similar school in the United States, because in China there are no other complete libraries available for the use of the staff. A sum in the neighborhood of $100,000 has thus far been appropriated for the special needs of the Peking Library.

It has been the hope of the trustees that Chinese women nurses may be trained for all nursing work, including that of the men's wards. This is an innovation in China and one upon which progress is being made slowly and cautiously. The purpose is always that candidates should be carefully selected, given a course thorough and ample in scope, under constant supervision, and with the accompaniment of every possible effort to foster a professional spirit and a sense of ethical responsibility.

Moreover, a religious and social department has conducted, with energy and enthusiasm, its work in the hospital and among the students. The department has arranged for religious meetings, addresses by the faculty, and chapel exercises, at which attendance is voluntary. Athletics and competent physical direction are also provided for. Successful efforts have been made to arouse, on the part of the Chinese students, an interest in sports and games.

Pre-Medical Work

Until a sufficient number of secondary or "middle" schools in North China can give satisfactory training in the pre-medical sciences of physics, chemistry and biology, as well as in English and French or German, the Peking Union Medical College will continue to offer this preliminary training. In central and southern China it has been deemed best to assist certain well-established institutions which are offering pre-medical courses, by appropriations toward laboratories, equipment and maintenance. Such aid has been given to two institutions: St. John's University, Shanghai, and Fukien Christian University, Foochow. Appropriations were also made toward the current support of medical schools in Shangtung Christian University, Tsinanfu, and in the Hunan-Yale College, Changsha.

Appropriations are also made to many hospitals conducted under the auspices of missionary societies. In each case the amount given by the China Medical Board was supplemented by mission funds and was used to increase the staff, or to provide additional buildings or equipment. In December, 1919, the board, in the light of five years' experience in coöperating with hospitals, adopted a somewhat revised policy for the future. This includes concentration upon a small number of hospitals of the better type, which by reason of location, staff and equipment are in a position to promote directly the cause of medical education.

Instruction in English

Although the instruction in the Peking Union Medical College is conducted in the English language, the board recognizes the importance of translating standard medical works into Chinese, for use in Chinese medical schools and in missionary schools which teach in the Mandarin. An annual appropriation is made to the publication committee of the China Medical Missionary Association, which supervises translation work.

A further form of assistance to Chinese medical education has been the granting of fellowships and scholarships to Chinese to enable them to study medicine in the United [illegible] who, during their furloughs at home, wish to pursue graduate courses or attend special clinics. When the college in Peking is fully under way the need for the first type of fellowships will largely disappear. To a considerable degree, also, medical missionaries will resort to Peking for opportunities which heretofore they have been able to secure only when at home on leave.

The Need Is Still Acute

The importance to China of all this medical missionary work will be the more easily appreciated if it is remembered that the country has an area of approximately 4,300,000 square miles and a climate ranging from that of the tropics to that of the north temperate zone. The population is reported to be about 400,000,000, about one-sixth of the total for the globe. For this large country, with its dense population, widely varied climate, intense poverty and many diseases, there are very few doctors and still fewer medical institutions.

In the introduction of the theory and practice of modern medicine among the Chinese, Japanese influence has been direct and important. For the most part the Government and provincial medical schools have been staffed by Japanese-trained Chinese, together with considerable numbers of Japanese teachers. A large majority of the native physicians who profess to practice Western medicine have been trained in Japan. Unfortunately, with few exceptions these Chinese medical students have resorted to special schools which are not fully recognized by the Japanese Government. It is even asserted that the tests applied to Chinese graduates have been lenient. The Chinese medical schools and hospitals suffer from lack of well-trained staffs, absence of adequate laboratory and hospital facilities, the intrusion of political and social influences, and the generally disturbed condition of the country. In a few cases there are hospitals under Chinese control which approach the average Western standards.

The central government and provincial governments maintain several medical schools, usually with Japanese trained teachers. The Japanese schools in turn have looked to Germany for their medical inspiration. The various missionary societies of America and Europe have made valuable contributions to medical learning in China. Through hospitals, large and small, through widely scattered dispensaries and through a few medical schools, they are bringing to the door of China the learning of the Western world.

European and American physicians in treaty ports, a British medical school in Hong Kong, a Japanese medical school in Moukden, and various hospitals locally organized and supported have had an educative effect on public opinion. Two organizations, the Chinese National Medical Association and the China Missionary Association, have done much to bring together the various forces for medical progress and to standardize the ethics and methods of the profession. There is still, however, an acute need in China for well-trained native practitioners and for thoroughly equipped and adequately staffed hospitals. [illegible] the Peking Union Medical College hopes [illegible]

Rallying Point for Far East

This Peking centre ought in time to become not only an influence in North China and the republic generally, but a rallying point for medical training and research for the entire Far East. It will maintain constant relations with Europe and North America. From time to time visiting professors from abroad will be in residence. To Peking will restort graduate students of ability and ambition. Practicing physicians and medical missionaries will find it a place of stimulation, refreshment and congenial comradeship. Here, too, there is reason to believe, original contributions will be made to the world's knowledge of disease and its prevention. Already promising beginnings have been reported.

It is one thing to give Chinese men and women a modern medical training; quite another to provide the conditions under which that training can be of larger service to Chinese communities. Unless the native physician can have access to laboratory and operating room, unless he can maintain professional and personal relations with competent and high-minded colleagues, unless he can count upon a certain confidence in Western methods among his fellow countrymen, the chances of permanent and worthy success are slight. Conservatism, faith in native medicine, family demands for quick financial returns, absence of publicly enforced standards, temptation to quackery and compromise, beset the path of the Chinese doctor who undertakes to practice scientific medicine in his native land.

Yenching University Carries On Tradition Of Early Founders

Funds From American Churches And Universities Put School In Forefront Of Education In China: $1,000,000 Endowment Drive Being Pushed

By SAMUEL M. CHAO

Yenching University of Peiping is a Chinese institution established in China for the education of Chinese youth but, it is founded, supported and in large portion administered by American friends. And it is a modern educational institution following American educational principles, modified by local needs. The university, while registered with the Ministry of Education here in China, is also chartered under the regent of the University of the State of New York, thus giving Yenching a legal status like other American universities, graded among, and with its degrees accepted by all the leading American institutions.

The forerunners of Yenching University, the North China College, the Hui Wen University, the Peking Women's College, and the Theological Seminary, were founded by American missions separately some 30 to 60 years ago. Amalgamation of the four was completed in 1917, largely through the effort of Dr. J. Leighton Stuart, well-known American educator, who is now the president of the University, and to whom must be credited with the institution's growth from an improvised shabby plant in town to the present most up-to-date Sino-American educational center.

Plant Costs $4,000,000

The university's palatial buildings and beautiful campus gardens, built on an attractive landscape of some 780 mow under the shadow of the famous Western Hills, alone costed some $4,000,000. The sum, except that of two dormitories and the campus wall, came from America. The annual expenditures, running close to $1,000,000 a year, has 60 per cent remittance from the United States through the University's Board of Trustees in New York. Nearly 15 per cent is met by grants given by the various mission boards, including the Methodist, Presbyterian, Congregational, and London Missions. Only 15 per cent of the sum is raised in China by fees from students and other sources. The remaining portion is met by grants and help from other co-operative organs. Of these, the Rockefeller Foundation has associated itself with the work of the college of natural science. Harvard University with the research school of Chinese studies, Princeton University with the department of political science, the University of Missouri with the department of journalism, and the Welsley College with the women's college. Exchange fellows and other educational facilities are also provided by these co-operative organs aside from financial gifts.

The general administration and teaching, at the same time, have also been helped greatly by American friends. Out of a teaching staff of 111, one fourth are Americans, while the principal executives of the university, the president, the dean of women's college, the dean of the college of natural science, the treasurer, are also U.S. citizens. The Sino-American side is not limited to faculty members alone. Out of the 800 students of the University, 14 are American boys and girls, having a percentage of 1.7, in addition 20 American born Chinese holding U.S. citizenship, studying in Yenching.

Million Drive Begun

Sino-American co-operation in maintaining this famous educational center has taken a further step since the announcement of the Yenching Million-Dollar Endowment Campaign at the beginning of this year. This fund is going to be raised in China, so that the Chinese may enter into a closer partnership, and let Yenching advance into a place of fullest possible usefulness. It is the chief specific objective of the campaign that a capital fund be created, and the income of which be used, as required, to balance an approved annual budget, which, under the present world economic conditions, has proved to be a difficult task.

The announcement of the plans for raising the million-dollar endowment fund for Yenching has been, from the very beginning, greeted with warm response and endorsement from all quarters. Those who already consented to lend their leadership and support of the campaign include some of the most important and outstanding leaders of the country representing various walks of life. Important cultural societies throughout the country have also consented to help. The alumni and student body are solidly behind the movement. The alumni groups in Peiping, Tientsin, Nanking, Shanghai, and other places have generously pledged to contribute both money and service to the campaign. In a systematic way, the students home organized themselves into groups of 10 for solicitation among themselves and their relatives and friends. The faculty members have already subscribed one tenth of the fund.

The campaign has also started solicitations among Chinese friends after hearing pledges from those directly related to the university. A recent Tientsin report stated that the first night there had a pledge of $20,000 from Tientsin leaders. Friends in other cities will also be approached.

Crises Faced

This is how Yenching, an educational institution where the East meets the West, is trying to face its present financial crisis. Its magnificent achievement of Sino-American co-operation in less than a score of years is gravely imperilled by inadequate resources. But the university is confident that friends, new and old, throughout China will help support the institution and thus enter into a fuller co-operation with Yenching's friends in America.

Golden Roofs Of Education At Yenching

This is a bird's-eye-view of the Lang Jun Yuan, northwest corner of Yenching University compound showing the beautiful lake with main plants in the background. Still further back may be seen the famous Western Hills of Peiping. The arrangement of the campus as well as the designs for the buildings here shown was done by the noted American architect, Mr. Henry Killam Murphy who now resides in Shanghai. At right is the famous water tower which Mr. Murphy cleverly worked into a Chinese pagoda. It is located on the east shore of the lake.

Sing Sing Convicts Feel The Depression

ALBANY, New York State.—(Reuter Mail).—Even the convicts in Sing Sing have been unable to escape the financial depression.

During the past year the average wealth of a prisoner dropped from $7.50 to $4.95.

The total bank balance for the convicts, according to Mr. Walter N. Thayer, Commissioner of Corrections, shrank from $18,775 in March, 1933, to $11,775 in March, 1934.

Most of the balance is made up of sums sent to the convicts by their relatives and friends, but some of the prisoners also save their small earnings.

American automotive products shipped to foreign countries increased 17 per cent in 1933 over the preceding year.

The sales volume of automobiles dropped from more than 5,000,000 cars in 1929 to about 1,000,000 cars in 1932.

In 1932 two-thirds of the nation's 60,000,000 tons of merchandise traffic moved by truck.

U.S. Legation Guard In Peiping Lives In Colorful Setting

500 Marines Are Nearly Self - Contained Unit; Hold Big Responsibility

"Perhaps at no place in the world, has the association between the Marine Corps and the Foreign Service of the United States had such a close and friendly relation as here at Peiping," writes Mr. Nelson T. Johnson, U. S. Minister to China.

From its initial start during the perilous days of the Boxer rebellion the American Legation Guard at Peiping has developed into a model military organization and it is no doubt for that reason that the friendliness attributed to it by the American minister is to no small degree due to this fact.

Headed by Colonel Presley Marion Rixey, Jr., one of whose sons is a First Lieutenant in the U. S. Marines in Shanghai, the Legation Guard has a strength of 500 men of which 30 are officers. Every state in the United States is represented. It is almost a community in itself as to its activities and centralization, but this does not mean that the Marines are an anti-gregarious group!

Commandant

Col. Presley M. Rixey Jr.

Many Ask To Stay

When two months ago Brigadier-General Frederic L. Bradman inspected the Legation Guard, he reported that everything was found in perfect order. He found that many of the men, whose tour of duty is two and a half years, usually prefer to stay on for another tour of duty, and many of the officers have stayed in Peiping for several years. Colonel L. M. Gulick, three times Commandant, still lives in Peiping.

To enumerate the activities of the Legation Guard is a rather difficult matter as there are so many of them. Sports occupy the head of the list and there are few varieties in which the Marines do not indulge. There is polo, tennis, golf, bowling, handball, basketball, baseball, swimming, boxing, pool, billiards, and others. The guard has its own swimming pool, polo field, hand-ball courts, tennis courts, bowling alleys, and other facilities. Coming to other activities, one finds that the Marines take a great interest in reading and writing.

The popular novel "Salt Winds and Gobi Dust" was written in part by Captain J. W. Thomason while a member of the guards at Peiping.

Each year they publish their own annual, funds for which are contributed by the marines themselves, and since 1926 have published every other week "The American Legation Guard News." In the barracks is a spacious reading room and a well-stocked library, and in another room is complete equipment for sound-film projection.

Have Own Power Plant

It is of interest to know that the American Legation is entirely independent as to its power and heat requirements. Marines run power-plant, ice-plant, and water-softener, and telephone exchange equipment. The bake-shop turns out enough bread and other products to take care of all the needs of the men. Radio is another important step. "NFC" is always in touch with Radio Cavite and with the American ships in China waters.

Less than 50 men constituted the original Legation Guard in 1900. At that time the Legation was located approximately where the Bank of Indo-China now stands on Legation Street. In the same year the Marines were withdrawn, the 9th U.S. Infantry providing guard until 1905 when the Marines, 100 strong, again were stationed in Peiping. In that year the Legation stood at its present location near Chien Men gate. As there were 10 nations maintaining Legation Guards in Peiping (as compared with five at present), there were the usual "scraps resulting from women and alcohol."

Changes Take Place

From 1905 to 1917 several changes took place in China. There was the Revolution in 1911 and the abdication of the Imperial family. However, the changes had little effect on the activity of the Marines. New buildings were added and the force strengthened from time to time.

The guard was increased to its present size in 1928 when the Nationalist armies moved into North China. Anti-foreign feeling ran high in those days and the various guards at Peiping served as a stabilizing influence until the feeling lessened with the expulsion of communist leaders from the government. Peiping was again excited during the Sino-Japanese hostilities and Peiping was tense until the Tangku Truce.

And now, quietly and efficiently, the American Marines continue to perform their duties of guarding the American Legation in Peiping. Who can tell but that, in view of the approach of ominous circumstances, they will have an important and significant role to play?

Epstein

Headquarters
Chicago, IL

Other Locations
New York, NY; Warsaw, Poland;
Bucharest, Romania

Founding Partner
Abraham Epstein

Current Partners
Mike Damore, Jim Jirsa

Epstein

Epstein began as a firm led by an engineer who employed architects, rather than an office with architects at the helm. Abraham Epstein, a Russian immigrant trained at the University of Illinois, opened A. Epstein, Structural Engineer in Chicago in 1921. The office's first project was for the Central Manufacturing District of Chicago, a client of Epstein's former employer, architect Scott Joy. Throughout the Great Depression, Epstein's office struggled for contracts. Taking advantage of the upswing in construction after World War II, Epstein expanded his services in 1948 to oversee construction work at a time when the American Institute of Architects (AIA) still frowned upon architects engaging directly in the construction trades. Only later did the AIA sanction such "design-build" contracts as a profitable business model. In the 1950s, Epstein's sons, who had joined their father's firm, became "architects by examination" in order to broaden the scope of the office.

The firm, renamed A. Epstein and Sons, turned its gaze overseas in the 1960s, opening offices in Tel Aviv and London, where it offered its expertise in industrial buildings and food processing plants. In the 1970s, after signing a contract with the Polish government to design food plants, A. Epstein and Sons opened an office in Warsaw to designed a meat-processing facility for Polimex Cekop in Ostrada (1971), launching thus a long period of work in Central and Eastern Europe. By the 2000s, the office saw further growth in the region, opening an office in Bucharest in 2005. Epstein International, as the firm is called now, currently employs over 500 designers and operates divisions in architecture, engineering, interiors, and construction. Uncommon for architectural practices, the company is 100 percent employee owned.

Epstein has built up its portfolio by working often for repeat customers and by occupying a key role in the Chicago architectural scene as the architect of record for large-scale projects by firms like The Office of Mies van der Rohe and JAHN. In recent years, projects like the Serta International Center (2009) have received architectural awards, adding design to the firm's areas of expertise alongside technical and managerial delivery. — AL

1921–1976

1921

1976

Raymond & Rado

Headquarters
Tokyo, Japan

Other Locations
New Hope, PA; New York, NY

Founding and Key Partners
Antonin Raymond (founding principal), Noémi Raymond, Leon Whittaker Slack, Arthur Tuttle, Elwyn Seelye, Clyde Place, Ladislav Leland Rado

Antonin Raymond: An Autobiography (Rutland, VT: C.E. Tuttle, 1973). Courtesy Tuttle Publishing

Tracing a professional path that crossed three continents over half a century, the work of Antonin Raymond and his collaborators was defined by their negotiation of the diverse cultural contexts of Japan, Europe, and the United States. Raymond's international practice literally spanned the globe, with offices in New York and Tokyo (sometimes simultaneously) completing over 500 projects in Japan, India, South East Asia, Europe, and the United States.[1]

A Czech national who studied architecture at the Czech Polytechnic Institute in Prague, Raymond immigrated to the United States in 1910. He worked in the office of Cass Gilbert, alongside architect and draftsman Hugh Ferriss, before meeting Noémi Pernessin, a graphic designer whom he married in 1914. Together they moved to Spring Green, Wisconsin, to work for two years as unpaid apprentices for Frank Lloyd Wright.

As Wright sailed for Tokyo in 1917 to oversee construction of the Imperial Hotel, the Raymonds returned to New York, where Antonin received his first independent commission, which was for the Garrick Theater, that same year. The practice was disrupted by Antonin's service as an intelligence officer in Switzerland during World War I. Following his return from the war to New York in 1919, Wright persuaded the couple to return to Japan to supervise construction of the hotel as well as work on the design of its banquet hall, theater,and rooms.

While working for Wright in Japan, Raymond launched the American Architectural and Engineering Company with architect Leon Slack in 1921, with funding assistance from the American Trading Company. In its first year, the firm designed forty modestly budgeted projects in Japan, including a new campus for Tokyo Women's Christian College. Raymond was active in the rebuilding of Tokyo after the Great Kanto Earthquake of 1923 destroyed much of the city, winning the commission to design the US Embassy compound there soon after. He formed another office with Alec Sykes, a British-trained architect, in 1925, but Sykes returned to England two years later, and Raymond renamed the firm Antonin Raymond, Architect.

During the interwar years in Tokyo, many of Raymond's projects were notable for an innovative use of concrete that was especially timely following the earthquake. He built houses and religious and commercial structures, all influenced by European modernism and adapted to the climate and vernacular context of Japan. Significant works during this time include his own home, the Reinanzaka House (1924), Hoshi University (1924), a series of projects for the Rising Sun Petroleum Company (1928–1930), and the Tokyo Golf Club (1932). The US Embassy staff housing commission led to numerous other diplomatic projects, including embassies for Italy, Belgium, France, and the Soviet Union.

In 1937, on the eve of World War II, the Raymonds left the office in the care of their Japanese staff and moved back to New York, where they remained until 1949. Inspired by their time at Taliesin, the couple established the New Hope Studio in Pennsylvania in 1939, which functioned between atelier and school, with twenty apprentices at any one time.

As the United States entered into the war in 1941, Antonin returned to New York, leaving Noémi to run the studio in New Hope, and partnered with a civil, mechanical, and structural engineer, respectively to form the firm Tuttle, Seelye, Place & Raymond. By 1942 the firm had a staff of eighty and a series of US defense contracts, including prefabricated barracks, an airport at Fort Dix, a prototype design for a postwar community airport, and models for prefabricated postwar housing. The partnership dissolved at the end of the war, when Raymond joined with his then-assistant Ladislav Rado to form Raymond & Rado in 1945. Though Raymond & Rado was established in New York, it eventually involved Rado leading work in the States and Raymond directing projects in Japan. Before the geographic and ideological differences between the branches effectively created two independently operated offices in 1955, Raymond & Rado produced their important building for the offices of *Reader's Digest* magazine in Tokyo (1951).

Based solely in Japan after a lifetime of traveling, Raymond went on to build significant religious, educational, commercial and institutional buildings over the next twenty years. — AS & AC

①
Kurt, G.F. Helfrich and William Whitaker (eds.). *Crafting a Modern World: The Architecture and Design of Antonin and Noemi Raymond* (New York: Princeton Architectural Press, 2006).

1921

1921–1970

1970

Schultze & Weaver

Headquarters
New York, NY

Founding and Key Partners
Leonard Schultze, S. Fullerton Weaver (founding principals), Lloyd Morgan

Beaux Arts Ball, New York, New York, 1929. Leonard Schultze, second from left, dressed as Waldorf Astoria Hotel

By the time Leonard Schultze and S. Fullerton Weaver formed their partnership, in 1921, they had both gained substantial experience and contacts, which helped position the firm in the post World War I era. Schultze, the architect among the two, had spent the previous two decades working in the New York office of Warren & Wetmore, while Weaver was a civil engineer and real estate developer. Both were in their forties when they launched their partnership.

During the first decade of their partnership they were involved in producing a variety of projects,from private homes to office buildings, all serving the new population of clients that emerged on the country's wave of economic exuberance and concomitant forms of conspicuous consumption. By far the largest portion of their output attended to that rising elite's leisure time, in the form of hotels and private clubs. By 1931, when the Great Depression forced them to seek other types of projects, Schultze and Weaver had built fourteen hotels, including several of the country's largest and most luxurious, such as the Biltmore in Los Angeles, the Breakers in Palm Beach, and, most importantly, New York City's Waldorf-Astoria.

Lloyd Morgan, a Beaux-Arts graduate and Paris Prize winner, joined the firm in in 1926, becoming a key designer alongside Schultze. The firm's key territories of operation were New York City, where they produced a large number of tall hotels and hotel-apartment buildings and south Florida where both Schultze and Weaver had many real estate connections. The Waldorf-Astoria was Schultze and Weaver's last hotel and their most expensive, largest, most publicized; indeed it remains their most famous building. Boomer-DuPont companies commissioned the hotel as a replacement of the Waldorf-Astoria that was cleared to make room for the Empire State buildings. The old hotel was torn down in 1929 and that year the company announced plans for the new one on an entire block leased from the city between Park and Lexington Avenues, and Forty-ninth and Fiftieth streets. Though Lewis Mumford saw "Modernism, revivalism, eclecticism, and plain gimcrackery," in this 2,200-room, 625-foot-tall hotel, other critics noticed its unmistakable shift away from historical styles.[1] The machine aesthetic of its exterior—attributed to Morgan's design leadership—was contradicted and softened by the luxurious and varied interior designed by the older partners, and which, Schultze proposed, eschewed "anything approaching modernism."

Relatively early in its existence and before Morgan came onto the scene, the firm built its only hotel abroad, the 1924 Hotel Sevilla-Baltimore in Cuba, joining the ranks of hotel architects such as Carrère & Hastings and McKim, Mead & White.

As their hotel commissions dried up they moved onto refurbishing existing hotels with bars, following the repeal of Prohibition, and a number of smaller civic buildings, slowly building up to larger commissions, such as the hospital in White Plains and a board of education building in Brooklyn in 1939. Weaver died in 1939, and the firm was reorganized and renamed Leonard Schultze & Associates, with Morgan and two other architects as Schultze's partners. With the death of Schultze in 1951, and another partner in 1955, the firm became Lloyd Morgan, Architect, and Morgan practiced into the 1960s, though the office never regained its hotel-era preeminence. —AM

①
Lewis Mumford, "The Skyline: Unconscious Architecture," (February 13, 1932) in Robert Wojtowitz (ed.), *Sidewalk Critic: Lewis Mumford's Writing on New York* (New York, NY: Princeton Architectural Press, 1998): 70.

1922–1973

1922

Paul R. Williams Architects

Headquarters
Los Angeles, CA

Other Locations
Bogota, Colombia

Founding and Key Partners
Paul R. Williams (founding principal),
Milton W. Nigg, A. Quincy Jones

1973

Paul Revere Williams, the first African American architect registered with the AIA, opened his practice in Los Angeles in 1922. He was the chief draftsman in John C. Austin's office as well as an active member of the Los Angeles City Planning Commission when he established Paul R. Williams & Associates. A gifted businessman and draftsman, Williams mastered the art of drawing upside down so that his clients, many of whom would be opposed to sitting beside a black man, could see his ideas come to life.[1] He started with a series of small residential commissions before winning the competition for the Monrovia Administrative Group campus that would help catapult his career. His office built several public projects during the 1920s, including the 28th Street YMCA, but it was its residential work that made Williams's office among the most preeminent in Los Angeles. Williams became famous for his vast number of high-end residences, including the homes of many of Hollywood's rich and famous. Frank Sinatra and Lucille Ball were among his clients.

Toward the end of the 1930s, the nature of Williams's commissions changed from nearly exclusively residential to an even split between residential and commercial work. Significant projects of this time include the Music Corporation of America offices, the Beverly Hills Saks Fifth Avenue, and the Arrowhead Springs Hotel. The office continued to operate throughout World War II, while Williams himself also worked as an architect for the US Navy.

As the war drew to an end, the office became heavily involved in several large-scale projects in the US and began to produce buildings overseas. In Bogotá, the office was awarded several significant projects, beginning with two large private residences. In 1945, the firm completed the commissions for the Bogotá Country Club, and, a year later, the Hotel Granada. The Granada, a fourteen-story, three-hundred-plus room hotel, was one of the largest and most important hotels built in Bogotá at the time. Within a few years, the building would be heavily damaged during the El Bogotazo riots, which followed the assassination of presidential candidate Jorge Eliecer Gaitan, in 1948. Later that year, Williams would complete a similar commission for the Hotel Nutibara in Medellín, Colombia.

Throughout the postwar period the office continued to produce significant buildings in and around the Los Angeles region, completing the Beverly Hills Hotel, the Palm Springs Tennis Club, and several dozen residences in 1951 alone. A year later, Williams became the first African American to be named an AIA Fellow. Other accolades and several hundred more projects would follow. The pace and scale of work slowed during the 1960s, and Paul Williams retired and the office closed in 1973. Over the course of its five-decade tenure, the firm of Paul Williams had designed more than 2,500 residences and several hundred other buildings. — JJ

(1)
Karen Hudson, *Paul Williams Architect: A Legacy of Style.* (New York, NY: Rizzoli International Publications Inc.,1993): 14.

1923

Perry Dean Rogers | Partners Architects

Headquarters
Boston, MA

Founding Partners
William Graves Perry, Thomas Mott Shaw, Andrew Hopewell Hepburn

Current Partners
Martha A. Pilgreen, Mark Freeman

Perry Dean Rogers | Partners Architects

The office of Perry Shaw & Hepburn was founded in 1923 in Boston by William Grave Perry, Thomas Mott Shaw and Andrew H. Hepburn. Within the first five years of their partnership, the office became established through their restoration of the city of Colonial Williamsburg to its eightieth century appearance, funded in part by John D. Rockefeller Jr.[1] In parallel to its reconstruction and restoration practice, the firm established itself with a range of New England projects, focusing on educational buildings. These included Longfellow Hall at Radcliffe College (1934) and Aldrich Hall at Harvard Business School (1955). In the 1960s and 1970s, renamed to Perry Shaw Hepburn and Dean and with a second generation of partners, the office furthered its practice through the repeat work from local universities who became their regular clients.

In the 1980s, the firm, operating as Perry Dean Rogers | Partners Architects, expanded the scope of its work, including a project for the US Embassy in Amman, Jordan (1992). The firm received their Amman commission in the aftermath of the 1983 Lebanon embassy bombing, and was thus pressed to prioritize security in the building's design. While adhering to new security measures in its scheme for the building, Perry Dean Rogers deployed its signature use of bright colors. The firm translated the security restrictions, which stipulated a façade less then 15 percent open to the exterior into a motif reminiscent of "Bedouin weavers."[2] Charles Rogers, a partner at the firm, also touted the secure windows as climatically appropriate: "It's so hot, you don't want large openings."[3] True to the common emphasis of the firm's focus on 'context' the US Embassy in Amman included local stone throughout the project. Ultimately despite these nods to regional material and ornament, *Architectural Record* perceived the project as representing a changing face of the US in the world, citing the Amman embassy as "defensive, inward-looking, its message about America ambivalent."[4]

Today, Perry Dean Rogers continues its "design stewardship" by restoring historic buildings throughout New England, including Alvar Aalto's Baker House (2002) at MIT. The office's sensitivity to history and context extends to their signature design process. Dating back to 1974, and developed through interaction with large institutional clients with multiple stakeholders, the "Wall Process" is an "interactive and on-site" strategy that facilitates a conversation between the building's future occupants, and incorporates the critique of the design through post-its on a wall.[5]

The office has also expanded its services to working in association with out-of-town architects. Perry Dean Rogers worked in the role of the associate architect with Diller Scofidio + Renfro on the Institute of Contemporary Art (2005) and on Steven Holl's Simmons Hall (2003) at MIT. Citing the importance of "technical memory," which comes from experienced employees and operating through shifting teams that feature "multiple talents of different ages, the firm has been a leader in staff retention": in 1992, the average tenure of an architect at Perry Dean Rogers was fifteen years.[6] — AL

① Will Molineux, "The Architect of Colonial Williamsburg: William Graves Perry," *Colonial Williamsburg Journal* (Autumn 2004).

② Michael J. Crosbie, *Color and Context: The Architecture of Perry Dean Rogers* (Rockport, MA Washington, DC: AIA Press, 1995): introduction.

③ Charles Rogers, quoted in James S. Russell, "Ambivalent Symbol: United States Embassy Amman, Jordan," *Architectural Record* (May 1993): 68.

④ Russell: 68.

⑤ Perry Dean Rogers & Partners, "Renovation Feasibility Study" (1996), http://mit81.com/baker/content/renovation-feasibility-study (last accessed November 17, 2014).

⑥ Antonio DiMambro, "Perry Dean Rogers & Partners: Progetti Recenti," *Spazio e Societa* (July/September 1992): 24.

1924–
1976

1924

Shreve, Lamb & Harmon

Headquarters
New York, NY

Founding Partners
Richmond H. Shreve, William F. Lamb,
Arthur Loomis Harmon

1976

The Architectural Record, August 1941

A 1941 article in *Architectural Record* on the firm of Shreve, Lamb & Harmon described its establishment via a vivid biological metaphor of cells splitting and multiplying. One day, the magazine reported, a famous New York firm was "Carrère & Hastings; the next day it was Carrère & Hastings, Shreve & Lamb; shortly thereafter it became two offices instead of one."[1] The "inevitable split" and subsequent formation of Richmond Harold Shreve and William Lamb's New York partnership occurred in 1924, and it revolved around two sizable commissions, the Fisk Macmillan and Standard Oil buildings. On the insistence of clients, these were completed under a temporary association of two firms Carrère & Hastings, Shreve, Lamb & Blake. After completion of these buildings Blake returned to the Fold of Carrère & Hastings, and Shreve & Lamb acquired a new third partner, Arthur Loomis Harmon. Harmon also had previous experience working at a large New York office—in his case, McKim, Mead & White. Shreve & Lamb was already on the rise and engaged in its most famous commission, the Empire State Building, when Harmon joined the firm, forming, Shreve, Lamb & Harmon in 1929.

Much has been made of the anecdotal rivalry between the two men responsible for New York's tallest buildings of the day, Walter Chrysler (of Chrysler) and John Jacob Raskob (previously of General Motors). While Chrysler had hired architect Van Allen to design his Chrysler Tower, Raskob had asked Lamb to build the tallest building that would stand up. Their "race to the sky" literally included adding floors at the last minute, with the Chrysler building holding the title for a year until the Art Deco Empire State Building was finished in 1931, remaining New York City's tallest building until 1972. The building launched Shreve, Lamb and Harmon as builders of East Coast skyscrapers, even as the Great Depression hit, though no subsequent building of theirs would be even half as tall as the Empire State.

Shreve, Lamb & Harmon has been described as "an example of closely welded teamwork," despite the vigorous personalities and personal acclaim of the three partners. Their educational paths were somewhat different, with Shreve coming out of Cornell and Lamb and Harmon training at Columbia, after which Lamb earned his Beaux Arts degree in Paris. Their office's teamwork was predicated on Shreve taking on the financial dimension of the firm and its client relations, with Lamb and Harmon both acting as key architects on projects. A decade after they finished the Empire State Building, the office was organized in a sophisticated chain of command from thethree partners on down. Immediately following the partners was the four-member Operating Committee—junior partners—with three of them splitting from Carrère & Hastings together with Shreve and Lamb. Next in line, were the project captains, who were responsible for everything pertaining to a particular project, from developing the drawings to writing specifications and under direct supervision by the firm's designer partners, Lamb and Harmon. The operations of the firm were highly standardized, including set drawing conventions, naming conventions, contracts, and communication and filing procedures.

Shreve, Lamb and Harmon built a series of East Coast skyscrapers, including the R. J. Reynolds Building (1929) in Winston-Salem, North Carolina and 500 Fifth Avenue (1930), 475 Park Avenue South (1969), and 3 Park Avenue (1975), all in New York City. In the early 1940s they were involved in the production of several military bases in Newfoundland, Trinidad, and Bermuda, though their most important building abroad predates World War II: the 150-feet-high YMCA tower (1933) in Jerusalem designed by Harmon. Its façade inscribed with quotes in Arabic, Hebrew, and Aramaic, the landmark tower has been a vibrant center of cultural and athletic life in Jerusalem for decades. —AM

(1)
Henry H. Saylor, "The Firm of Shreve, Lamb & Harmon," *Architectural Record* (August 1941): 73.

1926–1970

1926

1970

Richard J. Neutra

Headquarters
Los Angeles, CA

Founding and Key Partners
Richad J. Neutra (founding principal), Robert Evans Alexander, Dion Neutra

After briefly assisting Frank Lloyd Wright at Taliesin and Holabird & Roche in Chicago, Austrian émigré Richard Neutra moved to California in 1925, planning landscapes for residences designed by fellow expatriate Rudolf Schindler before establishing an independent architectural practice in Los Angeles in 1926. Exploring what he called the "human microclimate," Neutra designed spacious residences with sweeping glass facades, sea-breeze fronts, and complex roof ventilation systems. Built to enhance physical and psychological comfort in Los Angeles' desert climate, the projects — including Lovell Health House (1929), VDL House (1932), the Kaufmann House (1946) — linked spare modernist aesthetics and modular construction techniques with West Coast residential lifestyle. *TIME Magazine* featured Neutra on the cover of a 1949 issue, headlining the article about postwar American domesticity and Neutra's houses with the question: "What will the neighbors think?"[1] Uncertainty about Neutra's residential modernism may have lingered in the article, but by the 1960s, the architect's houses had become synonymous with modern American lifestyle. Architectural photographer Julius Shulman's photographs of Neutra's houses, together with *Arts & Architecture* Magazine's series *Case Study Houses* contributed to their influential role in residential design and discourse at the time. Neutra worked in Los Angeles for most of his career, though his firm built several large-scale public works and housing projects in Puerto Rico and Europe beginning in the late 1940s.

Both fascinated and troubled by the ability of architects, planners, and engineers to shape the environment and human habits, Neutra explored American architectural processes early in his career with the 1927 book *Wie Baut Amerika* (How America Builds). It featured Neutra's Rush City Reformed, an experimental urban design system of schools, small-scale drive-in markets, and housing complexes, all of which encouraged social improvements based on "universal principles." Published in Germany by Julian Hoffmann, a celebrated editor of architectural texts, *How America Builds* disseminated Neutra's views on contemporary design challenges, building materials, infrastructure, and zoning laws in the United States to European and Russian students and professionals. Henry-Russell Hitchcock praised the book and included Neutra's work in the Museum of Modern Arts's seminal 1932 exhibition of modern architecture. With less than a decade of residency in the United States, Neutra became a crucial contributor to architectural modernity in the US.

In 1943, Neutra was commissioned to design prototypes for schools, hospitals, and community centers in Puerto Rico. In the context in which the US was actively attempting to secure its political and economic influence, Neutra's prototypes were responding to the basic need for shelter, while they programmatically encouraged larger social transformations, as well. In 1955 Neutra was commissioned by Foreign Buildings Office to design the US Embassy in Karachi. His climatically mindful, concrete slab building, with an open and glazed ground floor, was turned into a consulate once the capital of Pakistan moved to Islamabad. In his postwar *Survival Through Design* (1954), fearing atomic war and the technologies that could precipitate it, Neutra argued that even the "smallest dose" of design may improve or damage a person and a community's physical and mental capabilities at the level of "brain and nerves."

In the final decades of his practice, Neutra continued to design individual homes as well as larger public commissions, with the close assistance of his son, Dion Neutra. After Neutra's death in 1970, his son took over management of the office. Dion Neutra remains an active spokesperson for the preservation and restoration of his father's projects. — CB

①
"Architect Richard Neutra," *Time Magazine* (August 15, 1949): 58–66.

1927–1976

1927

Harrison & Abramovitz

<u>Headquarters</u>
New York, NY

<u>Founding and Key Partners</u>
Harvey Wiley Corbettt, Wallace K. Harrison, William MacMurray (founding principals), Jacques André Fouilhoux, Max Abramovitz

1976

William Morgan

In the early 1920s Wallace Harrison worked as a draftsman for McKim, Mead & White while attending Harvey Wiley Corbett's atelier in New York City. After studying at the École de Beaux-Arts in Paris, Harrison worked briefly for the New York office of Bertram Goodhue before Corbett invited him to join Helme & Corbett in 1927 as a junior partner. The firm turned into Helmle, Corbett and Harrison until Helmle retired in 1929 and William MacMurray became a partner, forming Corbett, Harrison & MacMurray. The now resolutely modernist firm began its participation in the design of the Rockefeller Center, whose fourteen art-deco buildings took nearly a decade to construct, with the last one opening in 1940. During the Rockefeller Center project, for which Walter Hood was the principal architect until his death in 1934, Harrison formed a life-long friendship with Nelson Rockefeller, who would continue to rely on the architect for all of his major projects. Hood's death precipitated changes in the firm, with Harrison leaving Corbett, Harrison & MacMurray and after a year forming a new office with Hood's former partner André Fouilhoux, Harrison & Fouilhoux.

Harrison & Fouilhoux designed the Rockefeller Apartments before World War II, and were commissioned by Nelson Rockefeller to design the Hotel Avila in Caracas Venezuela (1942), the firm's first project abroad as well as Rockefeller's first foray into South America. At Rockefeller's own initiative, President Roosevelt created the office of the Coordinator of the Inter-American Affairs in 1940 and appointed Rockefeller as its head, who in turn invited Harrison to join him. A year later, having made one of their key apprentices, Max Abramovitz, into a partner in the firm, Harrison took the position of Assistant Coordinator, which turned into Deputy and finally Coordinator before he returned to New York in 1946. While Harrison was in Washington, Abramovitz had joined the Air Force, and just before the end of the war their third partner, Fouilhoux, died on the construction site of an apartment building in Brooklyn. Harrison and Abramovitz reorganized their firm in 1946. Their first commission was for "X City" in New York, on what later became the site of the United Nations complex. Along with John D. Rockefeller's financial support, Nelson Rockefeller and Harrison were key in securing the site for the complex, following which the UN Secretary General, Trygve Lie, appointed Harrison as the director of planning of the UN permanent headquarters. Together Harrison and Lie formed a representative international design board for the project which included Le Corbusier, Oscar Niemeyer, Sven Markelius, Howard Robertson, and others. Harrison's role was to ensure that the board authored the project as a group, while Abramovitz ran the team of draftsmen, designers, and model-makers.

Immediately following the firm's work on the United Nations headquarters the firm produced designs for the US embassies in Havana (1952) and Brazil (1952). Harrison & Abramovitz continued to produce large works throughout the 1950s and 1960s. The firm produced a master plan for the Lincoln Center plaza for which both men contributed building designs as well — Harrison with the Metropolitan Opera House (1966) and Abramovitz with the Philharmonic Hall, now Avery Fisher Hall (1962). Other major projects included the Corning Museum of Glass (1951), the Alcoa Building (1953), and the Time and Life Building (1960).

Over the course of its existence from 1941 to 1976, Harrison & Abramovitz became one of the most influential architectural offices in the United States, with 200 employees at its peak during the building boom of the 1960s. From 1976 until Abramovitz's death other partners joined the firm, from which Harrison retired in 1979. Though some historians have been ambivalent about the firm's influence, others have sided with writer Herbert Warren Kind's proposal that, apart from Frank Lloyd Wright, Harrison was "the person commonly regarded as the most influential figure in present-day building design in this country."[1] More recently, Rem Koolhaas has referred to Harrison as both New York's Hamlet and "Manhattan's last genius of the possible."[2] — AM

①
Herbert Warren Kind, "Architect Wallace Harrison, Part II: The Square that Became a Center," *The New Yorker* (November 27, 1954): 51.

②
Rem Koolhaas, *Delirious New York* (New York: The Monacelli Press, 1994): 285.

Nippon Oil Company Building
1919

Architect
George A. Fuller Company

Location
Tokyo, Japan

Client
Nippon Oil Company

Yenching University
1919–1926

Architect
Henry Killam Murphy

Location
Beijing, China

Client
Yenching University

Jiyu Gakuen School
1921

FRANK LLOYD WRIGHT

Architect
Frank Lloyd Wright

Location
Tokyo, Japan

Client
Jiyu Gakuen Myonichikan

Marunouchi Building
1921–1923

Architect
George A. Fuller Company

Location
Tokyo, Japan

Client
Mitsubishi Banking Company

Hotel Sevilla-Biltmore
1921–1924

Architect
Schultze & Weaver

Location
Havana, Cuba

Client
Bowman-Biltmore Hotels Corporation

Austin Standard Factory
1922

THE AUSTIN COMPANY

Architect
The Austin Company

Location
France, Cuba, Columbia, England, Turkey, Greece, Bulgaria, Jamaica, Panama, Mexico, Puerto Rico, South Africa, Gibraltar, Argentina

Client
Multiple

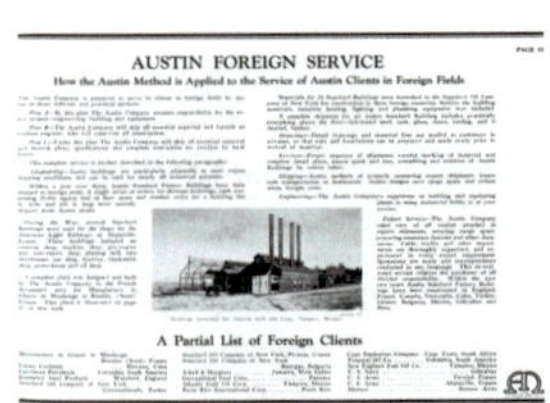
AUSTIN FOREIGN SERVICE

How the Austin Method is Applied to the Service of Austin Clients in Foreign Fields

A Partial List of Foreign Clients

1919

1930

Leonard House Office Building
1923

Architect
Walter Burley Griffin and Marion Mahony

Location
Melbourne, Australia

Client
Nisson Leonard-Kanevsky

Bush House
1923–1935

Architect
Helmle & Corbett

Location
London, UK

Client
Bush Terminal Company

Tokyo Women's Christian College
1924

Architect
Raymond & Rado

Location
Tokyo, Japan

Client
Tokyo Women's Christian College

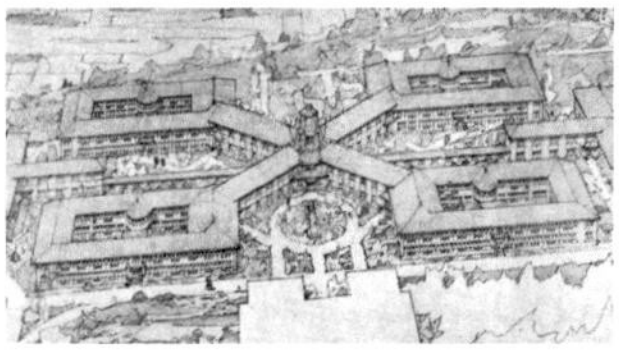

Hoshi University Main Building
1924

Architect
Raymond & Rado

Location
Tokyo, Japan

Client
Hoshi University

Capital Theatre
1924

Architect
Walter Burley Griffin and Marion Mahony

Location
Melbourne, Australia

Client
Phillips Brothers

Restoration of the Palace at Versailles
1924–1931

Architect
William Welles Bosworth

Location
Versailles, France

Client
John D. Rockefeller Jr., La Comité Franco-Americain pour la Restauration des Monuments

8 THE NEW YORK TIMES MAGAZINE, SEPTEMBER 5, 1926

VERSAILLES IS REGAINING OLD SPLENDOR

American Gold Helps To Refurnish Famous Palace of Louis XIV.

US Embassy
1926–1931

Architect
Raymond & Rado

Location
Tokyo, Japan

Client
US Department of State, Foreign Buildings Operations

Incinerators for Reverberatory Incinerator and Engineering Company (REICo)
1926–1938

Architect
Walter Burley Griffin and Marion Mahony

Location
Melbourne (4 locations), Sydney (7 locations), Geelong, Adelaide (2 locations), Newcastle, Canberra

Client
Reverberatory Incinerator and Engineering Company (REICo)

Oriental Park Racetrack
1928

Architect
Schultze & Weaver

Location
Havana, Cuba

Client
Cuba America Jockey Club, Bowman-Biltmore Hotels Corporation

Casino Nacional
1928

Architect
Schultze & Weaver

Location
Havana, Cuba

Client
Bowman-Biltmore Hotels Corporation

Housing and Offices for Rising Sun Petroleum Company
1928–1929

Architect
Raymond & Rado

Location
Yokohama, Japan

Client
Rising Sun Petroleum Company (Shell Oil)

US Embassy
1928–1932

Architect
Cass Gilbert

Location
Ottawa, Canada

Client
US Department of State, Foreign Buildings Operations

Automobile Plant and Industrial City
1928–1931

THE AUSTIN COMPANY

Architect
The Austin Company

Location
Nijni Novgorod [Gorki], USSR

Client
Autostroy

YMCA Jerusalem
1928–1933

Architect
Shreve, Lamb & Harmon

Location
Jerusalem, Palestine

Client
Young Men's Christian Organization, Dr. Archibald Clinton Harte

Stalingrad Tractor and Tank Factory
1929–1930

Kahn

Architect
Albert Kahn Associates

Location
Stalingrad, USSR

Client
Amtorg Trading Corporation

To Russia with Love: Reverse-Engineering "American Efficiency"

Ten years after the October Revolution of 1917, Josef Stalin's first Five-Year Plan introduced the logic of the command economy in the Soviet Union for many decades to come. In opposition to the earlier corrective measures of the New Economic Policy (NEP) under Vladimir Ilyich Lenin, the goals of rapid industrialization involved transforming the vast agrarian economy of the USSR, which Stalin suggested lagged "a hundred years behind" other developed countries, into a true "land of metal."[1] Though Stalin would later link this competitiveness to the ability of the Soviet Union to fight the Axis during World War II, in 1931 his eagerness to "overcome and overtake" was a symptom of his mistrust of the non-Communist world and its intentions towards the USSR, one which had both personal and historical roots.

Rather than looking to Western Europe for technical knowledge after World War I, Stalin idealized the industrial example of the US, to the point of suggesting that it was necessary to combine "American efficiency" together with "Russian revolutionary sweep" in order to produce "the finished type of Leninist worker, the style of Leninism in work."[2] Going further, Stalin defined the American model as "that indomitable force which neither knows nor recognizes obstacles… and without which serious constructive work is not possible." Stalin's position was shared by many in the Soviet Union, to the point that Henry Ford held a mythical status among both the public and the political class. This was the image of Ford not as the ultimate capitalist but rather as a revolutionary, willing to give away cars to his laborers, including factory workers.[3]

Both the mythological and the verifiable capacity of such models thus opened the Soviet gates to both US industrial producers and US architects, as the purveyors of the sought-after "American efficiency." The production targets

① Quoted in Evan Mawdsley, *The Stalin Years: The Soviet Union, 1929–1953* (Manchester: Manchester University Press, 1998): 29.

② Josef V. Stalin, *The Foundations of Leninism* (Peking: Foreign Language Press, 1970): 118–121.

③ Jean-Louis Cohen, *Scenes of the World to Come: European Architecture and the American Challenge, 1893–1960* (Paris: Flammarion, 1995).

④ Jeffrey Cody, *Exporting American Architecture, 1870–2000* (New York, London: Routledge, 2003): 101.

⑤ "Building in One Package," *Architectural Forum* (January 1945): 93–112; *Architectural Forum* (February 1945): 113–128.

1921–1928 New Economic Policy

1928–1933 First Five-Ye

1915

1917 • October Revolution • Albert Kahn designs half-mile long Ford River Rouge Complex in Dearborn, MI

1922 Stalin becomes the General Secretary of the Communist Party of USSR

1924 • V.I. Lenin dies • Soviet agency for the development of trade and industrial cooperation, Amtorg Trading Corporation, established in New York City

1929 US stock market crash, beginning of worldwide recession

1914–1918 World War I

of the first Five-Year Plan included 70,000 trucks and 30,000 cars.[4] The Supreme Industrial Council selected The Austin Company to build the first Soviet automobile plants and the industrial city surrounding them, Nizhny Novgorod. Having developed a full-service model of "Building in One Package" through integrated teams of architects, engineers, and construction experts, The Austin Company was seen as bringing both the right product and the right methods for its delivery to the Soviet Union, training over 40,000 Soviet workers in construction methods.[5] Other US construction and engineering firms made their own forays into Soviet industrialization, producing factories and large-scale infrastructures including the world's biggest dam at the time, Dneprostroi.[6]

The Soviet Union of the first Five-Year Plan provided ample work for US firms starved by the Depression at home. Chief among these firms was Albert Kahn Associates, the key architect of factories for Ford Motor Company and other Detroit manufacturers. Following Kahn's appointment as advisor to Stalin's first and second Five-Year Plans and soon after the incorporation of the firm in the US, Albert Kahn Associates was responsible for designing over 500 industrial buildings across the Soviet Union within a brief period from 1929 to 1932.[7] Kahn's tasks included the establishment of a special design bureau in Moscow, Gosproektstroi, which with some 2,000 workers by 1932 formed the largest design office in the Soviet Union.[8] While The Austin Company offered an integrated relationship between design and construction, it was the assembly-line organization of Albert Kahn Associates and its emphasis on economy and functionality that were perfectly tailored to the demands of Soviet industrialization.

At the time of his involvement with the USSR, puzzled by Soviet requests to over-structure the foundations of the firm's tractor plants in Chelyabinsk and Stalingrad, Kahn already speculated that his clients were secretly planning for the manufacture of heavy military tanks as well.[9] Indeed, the rapid industrialization of the Soviet Union in the 1930s would prove historically crucial during World War II. Working abroad also prepared Albert Kahn Associates and other US architects for "coordinating experienced experts" in the war effort at home.[10] By 1942, at the height of the national mobilization for wartime production, Kahn's firm had the ability to deliver new industrial plants in a mere 3 months each, from drawings to finished building. — AM

⑥
Cody, *Exporting American Architecture*: 101.

⑦
Peggy Deamer, "Office Management," in Eva Franch i Gilabert, Amanda Lawrence, Ana Miljački, Ashley Schafer, ed., *OfficeUS Agenda* (Zurich: Lars Müller, 2014): 52–63. See Sonia Melnikova-Raich, "The Soviet Problem with Two 'Unknowns': How an American Architect and a Soviet Negotiator Jump-Started the Industrialization of Russia," *IA*, Issue 2 (2010): 57-80. Anatole Senkevitch, "Albert Kahn's Great Soviet Venture as Architect of the First Five-Year Plan, 1929-1932," *Dimensions* 10 (1996): 35–49.

⑧
Melnikova-Raich, "The Soviet Problem with Two 'Unknowns'": 62–63.

⑨
Claire Zimmerman, "Albert Kahn's Territories," in *OfficeUS Agenda*: 123.

⑩
"Producer of Production Lines," *Architectural Record* (June 1942): 40.

1933–1938 Second Five-Year Plan

1930 Magnitogorsk competition

1942 Architect Albert Kahn dies

1945

1939–1945 World War II

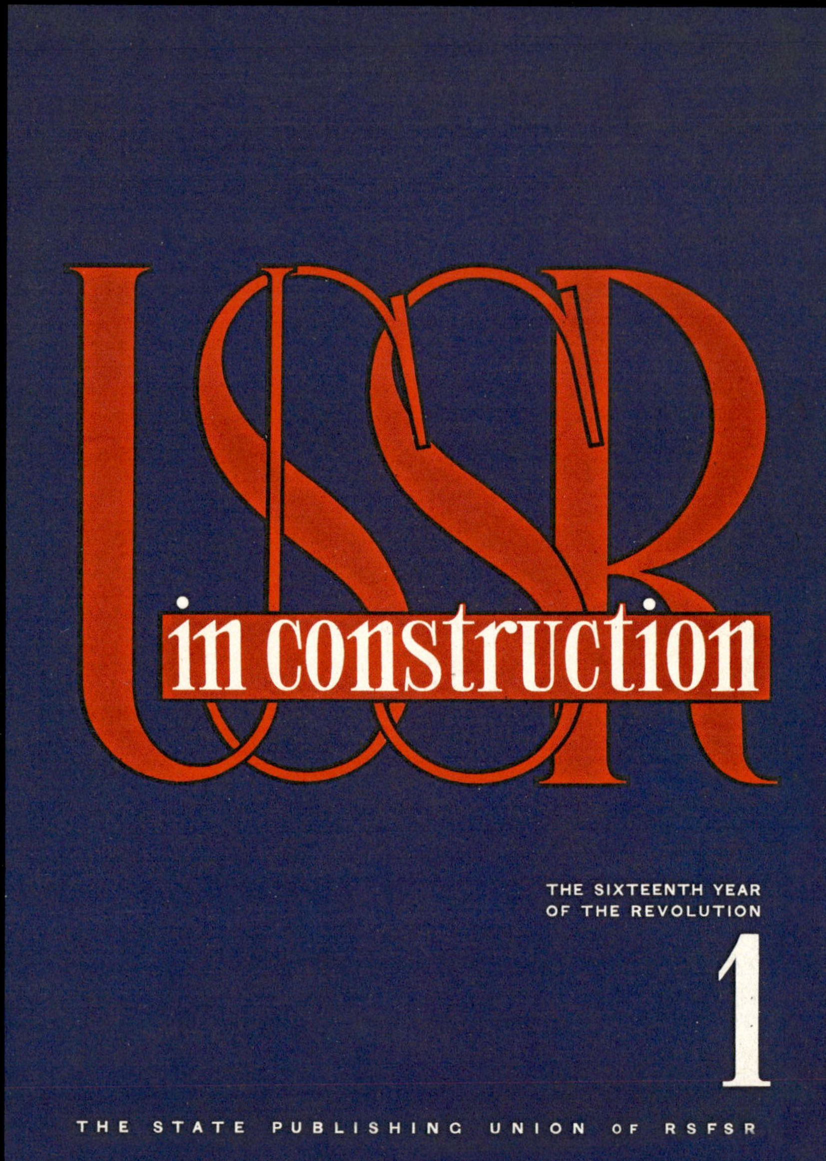
USSR
in construction
THE SIXTEENTH YEAR
OF THE REVOLUTION
1
THE STATE PUBLISHING UNION OF RSFSR

USSR IN CONSTRUCTION

№ 1 • JANUARY • 1933 • A MONTHLY ILLUSTRATED MAGAZINE

The historical decree of the soviet government concerning the creation of a powerful automobile factory with an annual output of 100 000 automobiles, on a two-shift basis, was issued on March 4, 1929. Soviet engineers went to America to study the problem. What did they see there? Soviet engineers saw the greatest automobile plant in the world — Ford's „River-rouge" in Detroit. They had to study the works of the plant with the attention of scrupulous scholars.

A commune was organized in one of the boarding-houses. They were pitiless to themselves in distributing their time. Studies began. They first tackled language and technique. The firmest of engineers decided to work without the aid of translators, in order to force themselves to master the language. They started from the very bottom — from the stamping of springs and „exercises" with steam-hammers. After work, they sat evenings over projects, figures and blue-prints, leaving only four hours for sleep.

There exists an opinion that the Nijni-Novgorod automobile plant is nothing more or less than a diminished copy of Ford's „River-rouge". This is not true. The engineers returned with the intention of imitating the Ford factories. Nevertheless, they immediately dropped the idea: it proved that such factories were insufficient for a socialistic industry. It became necessary to study scores of other factories, each of which opened new technical possibilities to the Soviet engineers. The problem was to „take the cream" of the entire automobile industry of the United States. And while designs for the plant were being made in Detroit, rolls of foundation projects were on their way to Nijni-Novgorod.

The project of the plant grew from day to day. Here it is in its general outlines. And here is the place where it is to be realized. Monastirka village. Windmills. Draw-wells. A grey confusion of wretched wooden lodgings, sheds and gates mournfully stretched alongside the road, on the shores of numerous lakes of mud. What an enormous amount of individual effort has been put into this wooden grotesqueness, into these hen-coops with two tiny rooms and a perron — the owners life-long dream!
An assembly of solitude, a community of petty Robinson Crusoes, whose names are inscribed on sheets of rusty tin nailed to the gates. Weddings, division of property, quarrels over petty what-nots, etc., made up the life of the dwellers...

RECORD

„In execution of the decision of the government of USSR, of May 20,1930, on the 13th anniversary of the Great Proletarian Revolution, in the presence of workers-builders of the plant, workers delegations from Kanavino, Sormovo, Moscow, Dzerjinsk and Balakhna, and representatives of party, trade-union and public organizations of the Nijni-Novgorod region, the first stone of the future gigantic automobile plant has been laid, wherefore this record has been made".
A bare tract. A small wood. Barracks. People, gathered from all ends, and not yet knowing exactly what they are going to do. Seasonal workers arrived from neighboring villages and intending to return as soon as harvest calls them. They are in a collective for the first time. They do not yet comprehend why they came here, and their minds are occupied by the sole thought of earning enough money to straighten matters in their household.

Engineers, not yet acquainted with one another, frightened by the difficult conditions of work in such a dull place, and also dreaming of going away under that or other pretence.
What should be done to rally nine thousand men around one concrete aim? How could energy and a determination to fight be put into them? Articles made their way into the press, comsomols devoted free evenings to discussion, representatives of the central press made their visits more and more frequent — a society was springing up on the site of construction. This was an attack of bolshevism on the plant. Class enemies who wormed their way into the community began to fly out headlong. The new-born society became the organizational center of energy and enthusiasm among the workers.

ЗАВОД
НИЖНИЙ НОВГОРОД 1929г.
СОЦИАЛИ
ПЛАН ВЕЛИКИХ РАБОТ-
ОСТРОИ

Celebrating the opening of the plant.

ON JANUARY 1ST, 1932, THE GIGANTIC AUTOMOBILE PLANT IN THE CITY NAMED AFTER GORKY WAS COMPLETED AND READY TO START PRODUCTION. From that day it began to master and develop its productive process. It was built in 17 months. If one compares this term with American terms, he will immediately see what great advantages our methods of work offer. It should be remembered that it took more than one decade to bring the Ford factories up to their present standard, that there is a difference of 26 years between to-day and the construction oi the first model „T", and that even now, in spite of the fact that he possesses enormous technical resources, a great amount of experience and excellent workmen, Ford is building his factories in Europe at a slower pace than that at which the Molotov plant was built. The extent of work done on the site near the Oka river can be seen from the following figures: in the course of 15 months, 1 600 000 cubic meters of earth was excavated, thirty million bricks were laid, 180 000 cubic meters of concrete was poured, 25 000 tons of metal was erected, 186 000 square meters of glass was set, in addition to which 10 kilometers of pipe-lines and 3 000 kilometers of electric wires were laid underground.

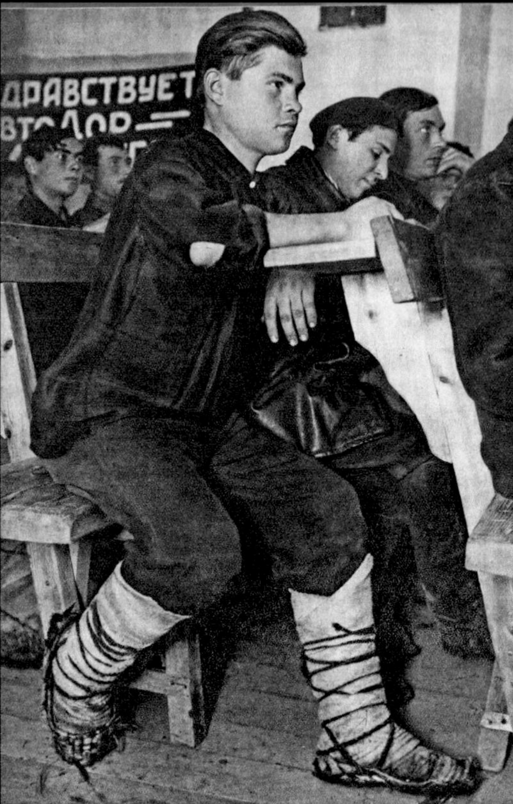

AUTOMOBILIZATION HAS EMBRACEI

Photo by S. Shingarov.

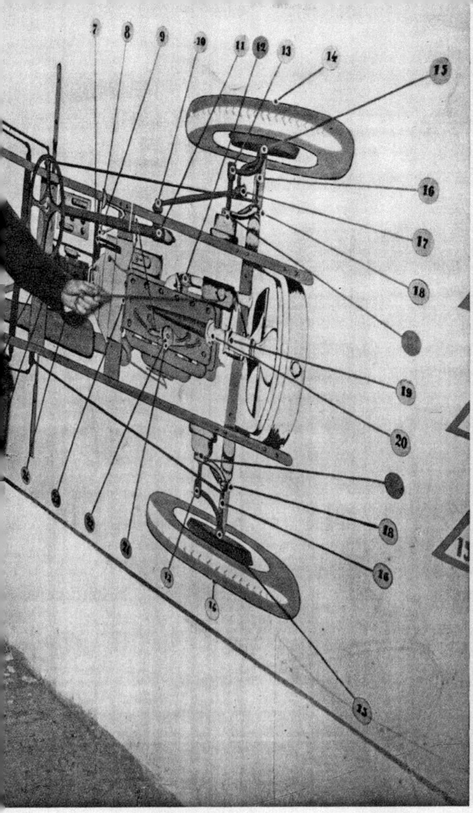

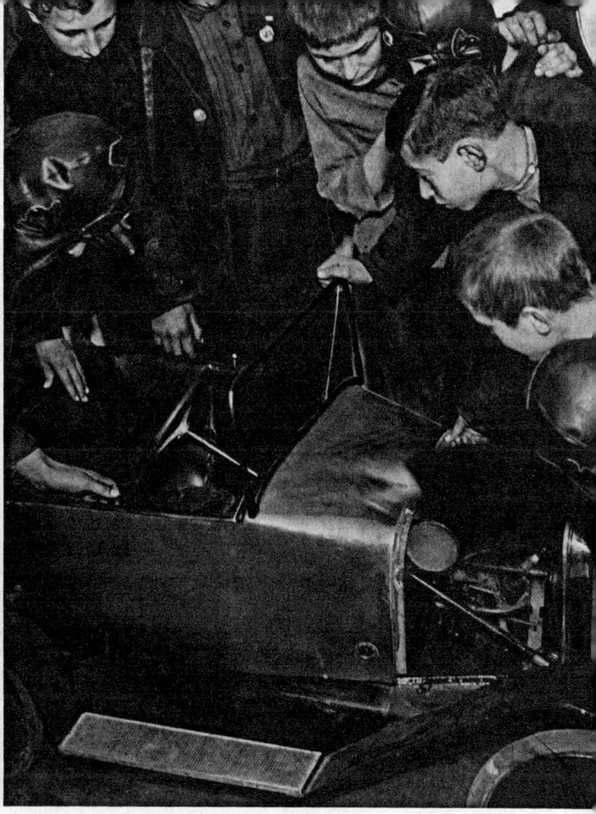

Photo by S. Shingarov.

HE ENTIRE LAND OF SOVIETS

The idea of transferring the USSR from a telega onto an automobile, is being materialized by millions of people.

The „Avtodor" (automobile and road society) has millions of members, and thousands of circles in which the construction of automobiles and tractors is taught. Even in the most remote corners of the Union people are intensely studying the Soviet machine of time — the automobile.

WE HAV

to make automobiles of various typ heavy trucks, army trucks, buses, trucks, etc. Automobile communic has been established in all parts o Soviet Union, and is developing at a pace particularily in those places w railroads cannot be built. Automobile of tremendous importance in agricul It is our aim to have at least one to every tractor.

Our automobile park is yet very s We have only 45 000 cars. Neverthe it differs in quality from the autom parks of other countries: 37 percent trucks. Such a ratio exists nowhere ex maybe, in Holland. In America tr comprise only 13 1/2 percent of all a mobiles. This means that the powe an automobile is utilized more producti in our country than in America. ring the past ten years our autom

EARNED

increased fourfold, but one must in mind that our automobile industry ly three years old. During these three the number of automobiles in the ₹ increased three times.

it will continue to grow still faster. rding to the plan, the total freight ver in 1937 will reach 80 milliard per kilometer, of which 72 percent be transported by automobile. In of this, the second pyatiletka con- lates the production of 115 500 auto- les in 1933 and a proportional increase llowing years bringing the annual iction to 480 000 automobiles by . A greater part of these will be s. The aggregate power of all auto- les in the Soviet Union will reach nillion H. P. by 1937 — hundred prostrois on wheels!

THE ARCHITECTURAL FORUM

…DUSTRIAL BUILDINGS ALBERT KAHN · AUGUST …

Hedrich-Blessing

ALBERT KAHN has written his story in glass and steel in three dimensions around the world. Measured by sheer bulk, this 800,000,000 odd dollars worth of building is impressive. Equally imposing are the names of clients like Ford, Republic Steel, General Motors, and Chrysler. If the story is glamorous, it is also significant. It means that Albert Kahn has established the architect as an important factor in industrial building. It also means that Albert Kahn, perhaps more than any other single individual, has helped create a new industrial architecture.

To reduce this accomplishment to the basis of a formula would be to miss the essential genius of the man. Yet there are certain items to be noted. There is for instance some truth in the statement that Albert Kahn is Albert Kahn, Inc.—and vice versa. He has developed the organization of an architectural office to a pitch of business efficiency seldom excelled even by his clients. He has drilled into his organization the dictum that the client's analysis of the problem is the first move toward its solution. He has systematically endeavored to translate the client's purpose into every successive step in the creation of the building.

This attitude of the business architect is one reason why last year Kahn's volume of work reached total of 19 per cent of all architect-designed U. S. industrial building. But a more important reason is that

The early nineteenth century factory which was standard during the period; its chief disadvantages were short spans and bad illumination. It went out of existence just about the time the Kahn office began its practice. The first modern construction to replace it was reenforced concrete, and later steel. Examples of the firm's early work are shown below.

1908

1910

Manning Bros.

the firm's span of existence covers precisely those four decades in wh the factory changed from a cumbersome mill to a perfectly functior organism in steel, concrete and glass.

In considering this last fact it is as misleading to overlook, as to o rate, the obvious. And obvious it is that here was an almost per combination of the time and the place and the men. In 1903 Det was predestined to spawn factories. That it was incidentally to prod a new architecture may also have been inevitable, but the pro was hastened by the men in the combination—Albert Kahn and clients. To emphasize the clients is not to minimize the archit he consistently puts them first.

Thus all that follows must be told against the background of th men who created the automotive industry. Henry Ford is their epito They possessed extraordinary vision to foresee new possibilities, were willing to back their hunches with perseverance as well as mo When they came to the problem of housing the new industry made great demands upon architecture, literally, if unconsciou forced revolution in design, innovations in engineering, new technic in construction. They were no less exacting on the architect. T wanted to deal with a businessman, they were profoundly suspic of artists; they wanted fast work, no mistakes and flexibility to pro for inevitable changes in production. To all this they added a pr requirement of economy in first cost and maintenance. That th thoroughly materialistic demands have resulted in a series of som the finest modern buildings, esthetically as well as otherwise, is Al Kahn's contribution.

One could argue that industry would have found its new architec without Kahn, or conversely, that Kahn's career would have flouris without this particular inspiration. All that is beside the point. It h pened the way it did. About thirty-five years ago a wealthy Detro one Henry B. Joy, walked into the office of his architect and as him to design a factory. The architect had never designed a fac before, but said he would try. The factory was for the infant Pack Motor Car Company; the architect was Albert Kahn, age 34, twenty-two years of experience behind him, seven of which had b in his own office.

The pattern of the Kahn career parallels that of many of his clie The child brought to America by parents in search of the more ab dant life; poverty and the needs of a large family take him out of sc at the age of eleven; he gets one job by day and another by night. can also add those sentimental embellishments which so enrich story of the self-made man. There was, for instance, the architect charitably fired his office boy because he showed no artistic prom Later, the flattering offer of a job with Louis Sullivan to take Fr Lloyd Wright's place, refused because he was afraid he couldn't hol and a family of ten was dependent on his earnings. Or the winning traveling fellowship which sent him to Europe, where he was so be dered by the profusion of masterpieces that he didn't know what t until Henry Bacon took him in hand. Such tales, to be sure, interesting and revealing. But the important part of the story is here was an energetic and extremely ambitious personality, stro conditioned by a bitter struggle for existence which began much early in life. His driving vitality kept him afloat where so many

2

4 Manning Bros.

5

under; it was the struggle, however, which ultimately determined the direction to be followed by the firm.

To the architect of the early 1900's, trained to think of himself as a kind of high priest of art, the designing of a factory was something beneath his dignity. But Kahn's rigorous training had developed in him a more realistic approach, and when he was given his first factory job he felt no such scruples. Today he recalls the situation at that time with a certain understandable satisfaction: "When I began, the real architects would design only museums, cathedrals, capitols, monuments. The office boy was considered good enough to do factory buildings. I'm still that office boy designing factories, I have no dignity to be impaired."

"That office boy" has been Packard's architect for 35 years, Ford's for 30, Chrysler's since the firm was incorporated in 1926, General Motor's on 127 important structures. One of his favorite remarks, invariably shocking to his colleagues, is "Architecture is 90 per cent business and 10 per cent art." In his rare weak moments he may reduce the figures to 85 and 15.

It was characteristic of Kahn's restless and inquiring mind that his first factory, the Packard building, did not follow the mill construction which was standard at the time. He used a reenforced concrete frame and steel sash, the latter a novel importation from England. It is hard today to realize what courage it took to design in concrete; handbooks were not available, and formulas were virtually non-existent. The Packard job was the first reenforced concrete factory in America, and for the first time an industrialist got a plant in which fenestration was reasonably adequate and production departments were coordinated with an eye to efficiency.

Following the successful completion of this building, others began to come. The automotive industry, with its new mass production techniques, had an inevitable effect on other industries, and Kahn's reputation as the designer of a new type of factory quickly spread. Other commissions included plants for food, textiles, clothing, business machines, cement, and chemicals. By the time America entered the war the office was large enough to take over all of the government's aviation work. In 1929 its output was considerably more than a million dollars worth of work per week.

It was in 1928, however, that the most extraordinary commission ever given an architect came in the door unannounced. In that year a group

7

STALINGRAD U.S.S.R. *Jeffery White*

CHELYABINSK U.S.S.R. *Sovfoto*

KUZNETSK U.S.S.R. *Sovfoto*

of engineers from the USSR came to the Kahn office with an order a $40,000,000 tractor plant, and an outline of a program for additional two billion dollars worth of buildings. About a do: of these factories were done in Detroit; the rest were handled i special office with 1,500 draftsmen in Moscow.

Probably no organization has ever had a more severe test of flexibility, speed, and competence. Not only did the plants have to designed, but machinery had to be selected and ordered, process l outs had to be prepared, and the very tools needed to build the pla had to be ordered here and shipped over. The office in Moscow c sisted of a large percentage of Soviet draftsmen who had apparer never seen a pencil before, and the Kahn representatives not only to run it by day, but hold classes at night. Factories such as the gr Stalingrad tractor plant or the Nijhi-Tagil freight car factory w erected in deserts or virgin forests, and the labor was chiefly peasants who were unfamiliar with any machine more complica than a shovel. For almost three years the Kahn technicians labo with their untrained human material, an impossibly overloaded tra portation system, and inaccessible building sites. Hundreds of pla were designed and equipped.

The Soviet work was, of course, unique in any architect's experier and it points up the amazing capabilities of the Kahn organization. cause such a firm of industrial architects must rely on a large num of small plants rather than an occasional large one, the prime need such an organization is flexibility. It must be able to turn out a h dred small jobs as satisfactorily as a half dozen large ones. And beca mistakes show up on small work, it cannot afford to make them. to the requirements of speed, it must have all its engineers and ot specialists in the office; outside consultants, save in rare instances, not feasible. If Albert Kahn had done nothing more than develop organization to its present pitch his accomplishment would have b considerable.

In addition to factories, the firm has done a large amount of n industrial work, hospitals—where they are rated as specialists—scho banks, clubs, hotels, theaters, and office buildings. This imposed further requirement of versatility as well as flexibility. The princip must be able to go from a power house to a hospital to a country cl and still know what they are doing. This work is not illustra here.

But it might be of some interest to note that, unlike the factor it exhibits the eclectic tendencies which have long been characteri of American architecture. The problem of the non-industrial build obviously, is far less clear cut than that presented by the factory, there has been the temptation to lean on so-called tradition. Thus K will speak of "the re-use of well-tried forms" or state that "evolu is preferable to revolution." Coming from one who has played insignificant part in bringing about an architectural revolution, s statements present a striking contradiction. Perhaps the best expla tion is that Kahn, precisely as his contemporaries in 1900, still divi building into factories and architecture.

But designing shelter for mass production industry nonetheless rem his favorite occupation, and the story of this new industrial architect is still largely the story of Albert Kahn.

ORGANIZATION

In normal times the firm of Albert Kahn, Inc. employs about 400 men and women; among them some 40 secretaries, stenographers, typists and file clerks; about 15 accountants; 80-90 mechanical and electrical engineers; 40-50 field superintendents; some 30 specification writers, estimators, expeditors, etc.; 175 architectural designers and draftsmen. The manner in which its several departments function, and their interrelationship, is shown on the organization chart on the following page.

The outstanding fact about the organization of Albert Kahn, Inc. is its completeness. The departments of the Technical Division design the entire construction, including mechanical work. All departments start work simultaneously instead of working in successive stages, and this, in addition to speeding-up the work of making the drawings, means that plans and specifications for all trades can be submitted for bids at one time, thus enabling the client to determine the cost of the building in its entirety before starting to build. With this procedure, the drawings for a large factory can be completed in a week or ten days' time.

Quite as important as the technical work is that of the Executive Division. This division is responsible for the management of the job in the course of construction. One department obtains competitive bids from contractors, submits them to the client. When the contractor has been selected, another department drafts contracts for submission to the client's attorney for approval. This department also attends to the various types of liability and fire insurance. The principal function of the Executive Division is, however, to supervise the work in course of construction; to expedite those parts of the work which fall behind the construction schedule; to check the contractor's charges for additions, his credits for deductions; and to check the contractor's requisitions for payments and issue payment certificates.

Inasmuch as twenty or thirty buildings may be going through the organization at one time it is apparent that a standardized procedure must be strictly followed, so that the work in its various stages can flow through the office as smoothly as a product flows through a well-designed factory. Not only have Albert Kahn, Inc. brought architecture to industry, they have also brought industry to architecture.

ORGANIZATION

Administrators ALBERT, MORITZ, and LOUIS KAHN

Hedrich-Bless

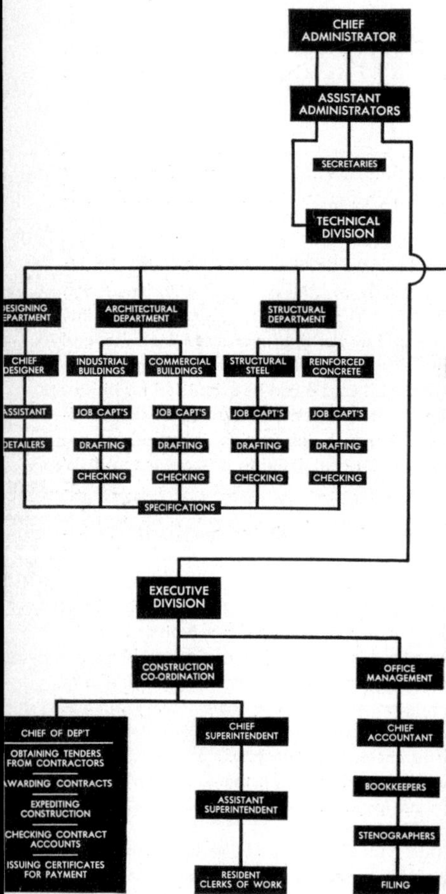

LOUIS KAHN, chief executive, conducts weekly conference of department heads

BUNCE, chief architect, HUBEL, chief designer, ALBERT KAHN

BOOMHOWER, SAULSON, chief mechanical and sanitary engineers

HOYT, chief civil engineer, and MATTE, chief structural engineer

CANFIELD, job coordinator

LEWIS, chief specification writer

FETTES, chief superintendent, and MARSTON, chief expeditor

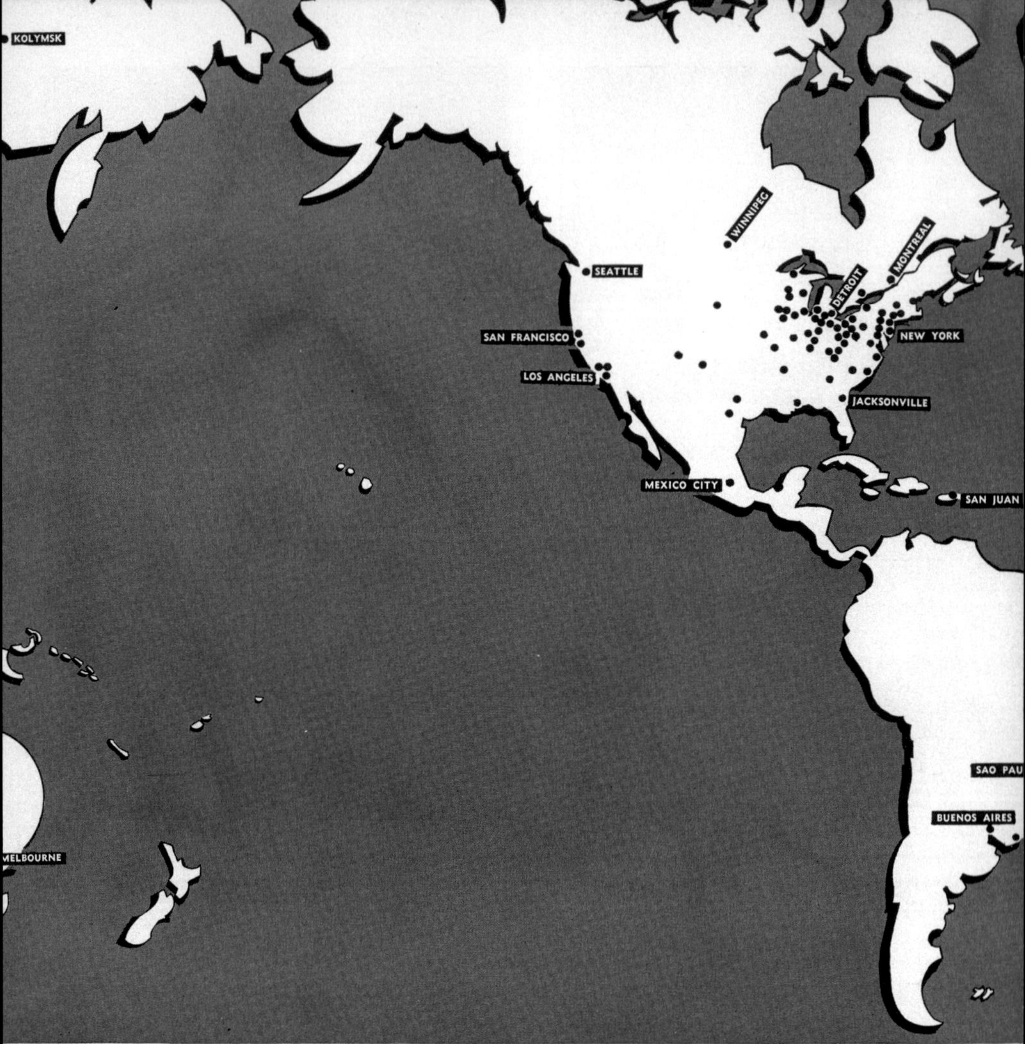

IT is doubtful if there has ever been another firm of architects which could open an atlas and spot buildings their design on all five continents. Certainly there is none which can show an almost solid series of constructio girdling the entire northern hemisphere. Kahn industrial buildings, not including their general work, are locat in 134 U.S. cities. Moving due east one finds their plants in England and Scotland; Oslo and Stockholm have warehouse and grain elevators; in France there are automobile assembly plants and a caterpillar tank facto

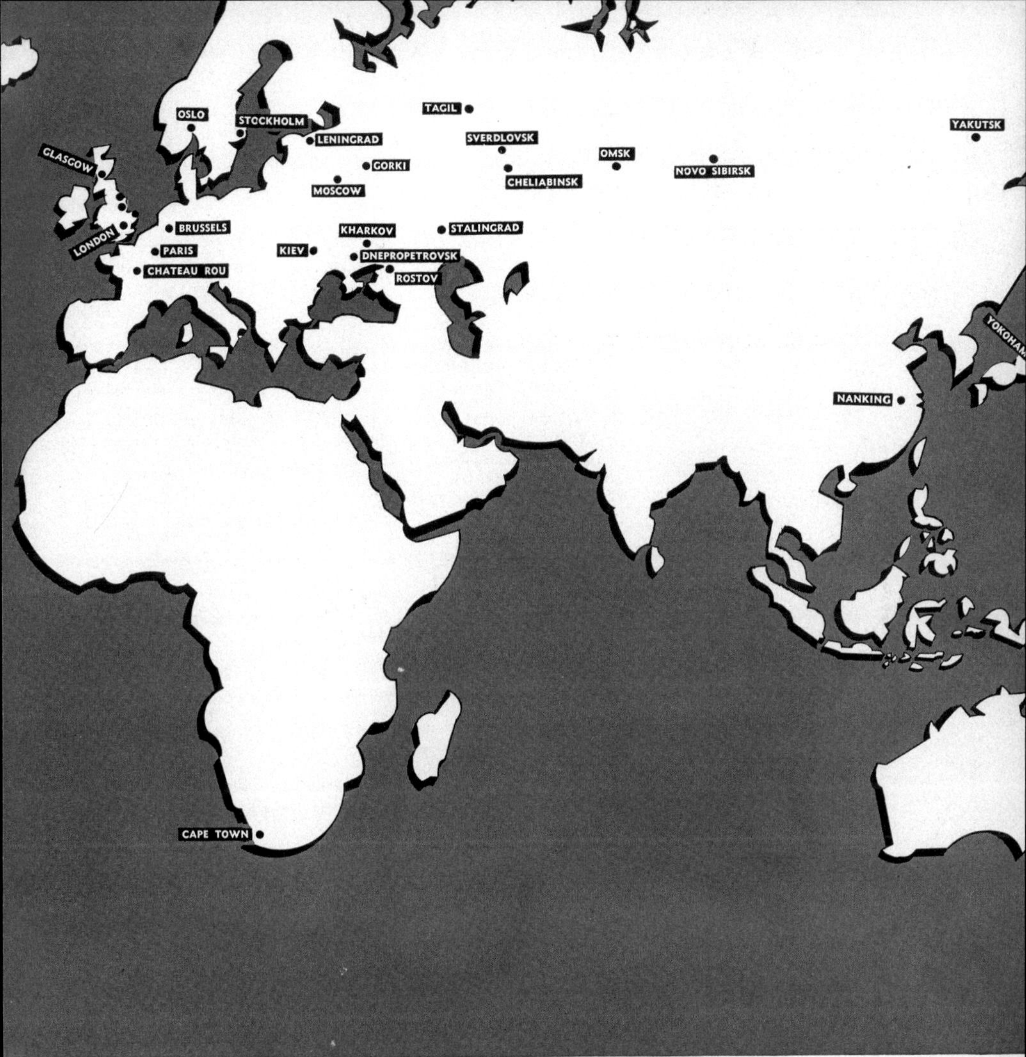

her on there are the scores in European Russia, more in Siberia, and one, at Kolymsk, almost on the borders the Far Eastern Republic. At Nanking there is—or was—an office building for which they were consulting itects, and in Yokohama, a Ford assembly plant. The types are as varied as industry itself: there are airplane nts, warehouses, docks, foundries, creameries, filtration plants, rubber factories, steel plants, silos, distilleries, lters, textile mills—the list could be extended almost indefinitely.

WHAT THE MANUFACTURER WANTS FROM HIS ARCHITE

Manufacturers about to build too often approach the architect with the mistaken notion that his only funct the preparation of construction drawings. Actually, of course, the service rendered by the architect should be more comprehensive. Albert Kahn, Inc. believes that the proper functions of the industrial architect fall two main headings, lists their more important subdivisions as in the outline below.

1. FUNCTIONAL DESIGN.

The purpose of a factory building is to facilitate production. It should hous manufacturing equipment in such a manner as to enable that equipment to function efficiently. To this en general scheme is all important, and should provide:

STRAIGHT-LINE PRODUCTION — Various departments for successive operations located to effect a simple and direct produ flow, so that transportation and handling of materials will be cut to a minimum. There be no crossing or retracing of the production line with consequent congestion.

FLEXIBILITY — A departmental layout sufficiently elastic to permit rearrangement in accordance with ch in production methods, or expansion of departments as production expands without dis izing the existing scheme.

GENEROUS COLUMN SPACING — Interior columns spaced as far apart as economically possible, to allow for free locat machines and cause the least interference with the transportation of materials.

SUITABLE FLOORS AND CEILINGS — Clear ceiling heights adequate for the work performed, and floors strong enough to me loading requirements.

PROPERLY LOCATED UTILITIES — Elevators, stairs, locker and toilet rooms located where they best serve the purpose and c interfere with the flow of production.

GOOD LIGHTING — Adequate natural and artificial illumination, properly distributed and of sufficient int for the tasks performed. Absence of disturbing glare.

ADEQUATE VENTILATION — Air movement sufficient for human needs, and special equipment to meet any problems cr by the manufacturing process.

LOW FIRST- AND UPKEEP-COSTS — Economies resulting from skillful design and the efficient use of materials, reducing initial cost and maintenance expense to the minimum.

2. BUSINESS-LIKE EXECUTION.

Just as important as good design is the provision of adequate ser Especially important are the following service items:

ACCURATE PRELIMINARY ESTIMATES — Before the work is begun, a preliminary cost estimate sufficiently accurate that there w no overrunning of the manufacturer's budget.

SPEED — Because no manufacturer decides to build until the need for new production facilities is a ent and pressing, the work in its entirety—from preliminary design to final completion— be carried out with utmost dispatch.

COMPLETE AND ACCURATE DRAWINGS — Construction drawings and specifications prepared in such detail and with sufficient ca provide a proper basis for competitive bidding by responsible contractors and to elimina minimize extras.

A GOOD CONTRACTOR — The Architect must furnish helpful and qualified advice on the selection of a contracto to do the work expeditiously and well.

ADEQUATE SUPERVISION — All branches of the work must be carefully supervised, during construction, in such a w to expedite the work as much as possible.

Thus factory design imposes a severe responsibility on the architect. The successful completion of the pr depends upon his ability to analyze the problem, to plan the structure properly and practically, to effect e economy, and to give the building external and internal distinction without extravagance.

ARCHITECTURAL RECORD

JUNE 1942

ARCHITECTURE FOR WAR PRODUCTION · · ALBERT KAHN

INDUSTRIAL PLANT EQUIPMENT · · REMODELING IDEAS

Wide World

ALBERT KAHN, ARCHITECT

PRODUCER OF PRODUCTION LINES

IT WAS on Thursday, February 5, 1939, that Albert Kahn received a telephone call from the Glenn L. Martin Company, Baltimore.

"Can you furnish plans quickly enough for us to put up a 440,000 sq. ft. building by May 1?"

That was quite an order: a mammoth aircraft factory building to be ready for use in 84 days. But Kahn was prepared to answer, "Yes." Actually manufacturing began in that building on April 27, just 81 days after the call.

Mr. Kahn did not realize, then, that this request was to set the pattern and the pace for a program of war-impelled plant expansion such as industry had never seen before. Or that this order, one of dozens to come, was setting a pattern and a pace for building designers, which, though previously unheard of, would come to be accepted as the wartime obligation of architects and engineers.

Such miracles of speed in design and construction have not been wrought without greatly expanded planning organizations, and, more significantly, a highly developed coordination of planning procedures. They have required coordination not only within the architectural and engineering organization, but also among designers, contractors, manufacturers, and wartime clients.

Take the case of the Glenn Martin expansion. After receiving the long-distance call from Baltimore, Kahn and members of his organization left Detroit immediately for the East. They arrived at the Martin plant Friday morning, February 6, and set to work immediately, aided by a general plan and details that had been worked out by Martin engineers. The structural steel contract was negotiated at two o'clock Saturday afternoon. Later that same afternoon, the excavation contract was let to a company that agreed to move 83,000 cubic yards of wet clay from the site of the building within an eight-day period. Within the next few days still other important contracts were awarded. And on February 16, the concrete footings for the new building were poured.

On April 23, only 77 days after word had been given to go ahead with the building, the manufacturing area was under roof and well enclosed, and machines were being set in place. Actual manufacturing was started April 27, just 81 days after February 5. So was set not only a building record, but a production record as well, for a million dollars worth of tools had to be ordered and installed as construction work proceeded.

Another case in point is the new $37,000,000 airplane engine plant of the Wright Aeronautical Corporation, which, until the mammoth Ford bomber plant began to take form, encompassed the nation's largest one-story industrial building.

Wright's engineers started work on the plant layout even before it was known where the building would be located. Then, in swift succession, land near Cincinnati was purchased, the architects were called in, sketches were turned out within a matter of a few days and approved. Structural steel drawings were prepared with great rapidity, and the architectural drawings were prepared coincidentally by a large staff of architects and engineers.

Steel bids were taken and contracts let while excavation plans were being completed. Contracts for the architectural trades were awarded while steel work was being fabricated.

The foundations were ready by the time the steel was delivered for erection. Ground was broken October 23, 1940; steel erection began January 3, 1941, and installation of machinery was under way February 15. All major construction had been completed in June, when the first airplane engines rolled off the line two months ahead of schedule. Just 142 days after ground breaking, manufacturing operations were in progress!

Albert Kahn and John Schurman inspect the "Victory Sash," their newly-developed steel-saving factory window (see page 82)

The magic in the formula for such work is the coordination of experienced experts. And coordination gets more important as the personnel is expanded. Normally, the Detroit firm of Albert Kahn Associated Architects and Engineers, Inc. employs approximately 150 men and women—architectural designers and draftsmen, specifications writers, estimators and expediters, field superintendents, mechanical, electrical and ventilation engineers and office workers. Now the organization has expanded until this spring it was employing over 600, and was still increasing. Last year Kahn and his associates designed and supervised the construction of more than three-score buildings for the production of implements of war—armor plate foundries, synthetic rubber plants, airplane plants, naval bases,

In telling how it was all done, Mr. Kahn stresses three elements—organization, teamwork and business management. It is the hard-hitting teamwork of real specialists.

Instead of working in successive stages, all departments of the Kahn firm start their work simultaneously. If under normal conditions the group could turn out complete drawings for a factory in a week or ten days, under the war speed-up it is done almost literally overnight.

In Kahn's own words the building of a war plant goes thus:

"Even before definite commitments are made by the Government, the respective manufacturers have spent night and day on process layouts and the architects and engineers have been called in to prepare tentative schemes for properly housing their equipment.

"With contracts definitely placed, not a moment can be lost. The type of building best suited has been decided upon; so has the floor space required. Often, within less than a week's time, the structural steel drawings must be developed sufficiently to obtain competitive prices ready for placing contracts. Supplying the steel frame, obtaining the necessary material, much of which must come from the mills, and fabricating it are the bottlenecks. We used to have five and six weeks' deliveries. Today 12 weeks' delivery is considered remarkable, and 18 weeks is normal.

"To save time, we must exercise care in employing structural shapes most readily obtainable. Certain sections are practically unavailable. And to speed up deliveries, substitutions must often be made to suit the company's stock piles or rollings of the mills. Standardization, as far as possible, is all-important, and so is simplicity of construction.

"To accomplish the necessary results requires an organization keyed up to the situation, thoroughly experienced so that decisions may be immediate and accurate, and production must be just about machinelike. Defense work means quantity production. The many problems must be handled systematically and all coordinated so that the results desired are turned out with greatest dispatch, as well as accuracy. In attacking these problems, the process is something like this:

"With preliminary sketches approved by the owners, a meeting is held of the men selected to take charge of the architectural work, the structural engineering, the sanitary engineering, the ventilating, the heating, the air cooling, sprinkler work, electrical engineering, power house work-

THE KAHN ORGANIZATION

A thoroughly integrated organization of design specialists, with two divisions and six major departments and more than 600 employees, has made it possible for Albert Kahn to make impressive speed records in the construction of tremendous war production plants

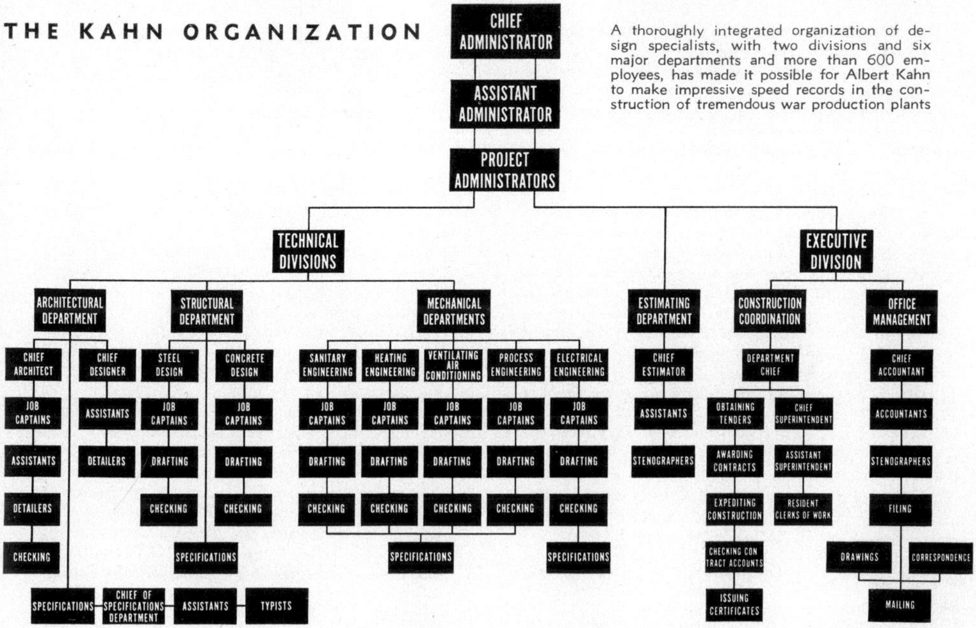

and specification writing. The most important points are taken up and at least tentatively decided upon, each representative taking notes. And the drawings and calculations are started. Frequent other meetings naturally follow, and many additional conferences are required to determine lesser details."

While these several departments of the Technical Division are working simultaneously on planning, other functions are left to the Executive Division. This Division is responsible for the management of the project in the course of construction. One department obtains competitive bids from contractors, then submits them to the owner. When the contractor has been selected, another department drafts contracts for submission to the owner's attorney for approval. This department also takes care of the various types of liability and fire insurance.

There is still another department that coordinates all the work in the field. It acts as liaison office between the contractor and the owner. It obtains from the owner such special requirements as may arise, or as may be modified during building operations, and sees that they are properly incorporated in the work. This department, through weekly reports and diagrammatic schedules, keeps the owner fully informed as to progress of the work. As far as possible, it shoulders the many troublesome details connected with actual construction.

Chief functions of the Executive Division are the supervision of the work which falls behind the construction schedule; the checking of the contractor's charges for additions and his credits for deductions; the checking of the contractor's requisitions for payments and the issuing of payment certificates.

In spite of the high priority ratings that most of Kahn's work receives, his organization has encountered many problems of material shortages and substitutions. Kahn himself speaks with especial emphasis on the need for building code revisions, to permit of substantial savings in construction materials:

"I feel strongly that a National Building Code should be adopted. It would substantially help us in our effort to conserve critical materials, and, at the same time, meet the obligations of the vast war building program that lies ahead. The attempt to set up a National Building Code, sponsored by Herbert Hoover when he was Secretary of Commerce and continued until the days of the depression, was based upon the principle that maximum allowances be permitted skilled designers and not minimum allowances as established in most cities to guard against the unskilled. . . . Those who are highly competent would be encouraged to use their skill to the utmost in planning entirely safe buildings utilizing a minimum of material."

Some of the most interesting experiences of Kahn engineers have to do with shortages of metals normally of relatively minor importance in building, but now critical even in small amounts.

So far, the electrical engineers are feeling the shortages of aluminum and zinc the most. Diversion of vast amounts of aluminum to the aircraft industry has made considerable difference in the planning of industrial electrical systems. For instance, aluminum cases for lighting fixtures are definitely out of the picture. In line with Government stipulations as to materials, plant designers are substituting cases of steel or of iron, with baked-on paint finish. Where once highly-burnished aluminum served for reflectors in lighting fixtures, silvered glass or porcelain-enameled steel is now called upon to do the job.

Next to aluminum, the greatest metal shortage so far as the electrical engineers are concerned is zinc. That, at any rate, is the experience of the Albert Kahn organization. So great is the pinch when it comes to zinc that these designers are now incorporating into plant electrical systems pull-boxes, panel boxes, conduit and outside transformer fences of plain, black painted iron.

Tungsten is another of the critical materials. And tungsten is used as filament material in incandescent lamps. Thus, to conserve the supply of this valuable metal and make it available for other war purposes, the Government is suggesting that fluorescent lights be used in place of incandescents. This suggestion meets with the hearty approval of the Kahn engineers who are planning the lighting systems of war plants. They are specifying fluorescent tubes and fixtures widely, for this type of lighting is more efficient and less expensive to operate than tungsten filament bulbs.

Important plants being built for war production are getting what rubber they need for electrical purposes. However, the Government is suggesting and engineers are using wherever they can certain substitute insulating materials. At least, they are using these substitute materials to the extent that they are commercially available.

For instance, a thermoplastic insulation is suggested for building wire that carries a load of 600 volts or less. Other alternatives along lines of insulation for such wire include varnished cambric (N. E. Code Type V), slow-burning Weatherproof (N. E. Code Type SBW), or Weatherproof (N. E. Code Type W), the last-named installed on insulators only, not less than 10 feet above the floor except where suitably enclosed and protected. The Government points out that synthetic plastic, varnished cambric and slow-burning Weatherproof insulation may be used in the following classes of wiring: (1) Single conductors for installation in raceways or on insulators, (2) non-metallic sheathed cable, and (3) covered neutral cable.

In plumbing, heating, ventilating and air conditioning, due regard is being paid to the existing metal shortages in all respects, according to members of the Albert Kahn organization. For engineers in these categories realize they must give utmost consideration to the business of conserving critical metals and other materials, even though the defense work in which they are engaged receives preferred priority treatment.

Shortages of materials, coupled with the continual demand for speed and more speed in the construction of the country's war production plants, have not made the task of architectural and engineering organizations exactly easy. But, taking their cue from the coordinated production and assembly techniques of the manufacturers whose buildings they are erecting, designers are making records quite as spectacular as the output of fighters and bombers—working on "impossible" schedules and finishing ahead of time.

Typical of Kahn's current war work is this huge military aircraft plant in an eastern city

Hedrich-Blessing

THE ARCHITECTURAL

FORUM

JANUARY 1945

▶ With this article THE FORUM introduces a series of studies of modern building organizations. In future issues the editors will examine other significant examples of modern building practice.

3UILDING IN ONE PACKAGE

s chief exponent, The Austin Company, with $600 million of wartime building behind it, ill challenges professional fetishes with its 40-year-old slogan, "undivided responsibility." he Austin Method: what it is and how it works.

rst to cut across accepted lines of professional and com- ercial responsibility, upset long-established taboos against lvertising and offer complete design, construction and fabri- tion service, The Austin Company is Building's maverick. ıt The Austin Method is more than a new way of getting ıd doing business, more than an expeditious system of nstruction, more than an attractive prospect to harassed dustrialists lost in the maze of involved building proced- es. Almost everyone knows something of the organization hich designs, builds and equips factories, airports and ice buildings from Maine to California, Alaska to South frica; few fully understand its ramifications or know of the vances in building and engineering science which Austin's sources have made possible. Some of its ways of getting isiness would leave the average architect or contractor gasp- g. About two years ago, for example, the Company invited e of the leading manufacturers of television equipment to co- erate with it in the development of designs for a series of pothetical television broadcasting studios.

"At whose expense?" asked the manufacturer, realizing the onths of work and study involved.

"We are willing to match our time and experience with urs and foot the bills connected with our part of the work," e Austin executive replied. "We simply want to prepare rselves for postwar activity in this field, and feel that you ould be willing to contribute your experience and advice help the development of a new industry."

The manufacturer agreed. Followed months of intensive ork and conferences, including visits by Austin engineers existing television studios all over the country. A master ıtion was designed for continuous large-scale network esentations, planned around existing and anticipated oadcasting equipment. It had a turntable stage and dual dience seating areas to minimize equipment costs, a single, ntral control room. After this design—in model form—had en exhibited to potential television broadcasters from coast coast, a revised scheme, more adaptable to the require- ents of the average city, was developed. Also built in work- g model form, the second station had one large studio with two-section sliding stage, and two smaller ones served by common, pivoted platform for broadcasting equipment.

All of this work, including the restudy of the original sign, was carried out without lining up a single client. It s not just a new promotion scheme (although it was a od one); it was an honest effort to anticipate postwar ilding activity in a hitherto unexplored field and to get eliminary research work out of the way to clear the decks actual construction at the earliest possible date.

While there are still professional practitioners who turn pink around the jowls when the name Austin is mentioned, and are likely, if pressed, to launch into tirades against "contractors trying to masquerade as architects," few would deny the soundness of this approach to a new design problem, or the advantages of an organizational set-up which makes such research possible. As a matter of fact, although the professional standards of the American Institute of Architects still forbid participation in construction work, more and more large architectural firms now subscribe to the idea that some relaxation of this rule to permit more direct control over the building process might be advantageous to both architect and client. Especially since the war, former distinctions between purely architectural and purely engineering services have broken down almost entirely. In The Austin Method, as in any arrangement which combines design, specifying and contracting in a single organization, the client loses any advantages to be gained from competitive bidding, and the advice of a disinterested professional. He gains the services of a integrated team of designers, engineers and construction superintendents, a team which The Austin Company has developed, step by step, in pace with modern industry's insatiable need for better working space.

In the 63 years since Samuel Austin, British carpenter, arrived in the United States, the name "Austin" has been the performance bond on some 6,800 industrial and commercial building projects—over 6,000 of them under complete service contracts embracing design, engineering and construction.

In 1904 this carpenter-contractor's craftsmanship and business acumen were merged with the professional abilities of his young engineer son to provide the first all-inclusive design and construction service. Unique in its scope, character and operating methods, this 40 year old partnership of designers, engineers and construction men has handled more than $900 million worth of work under The Austin Method,—over $600 million of this during World War II.

Serving private industry, government agencies and the armed forces through eight district organizations which function independently, except insofar as they draw upon the research and engineering counsel, financial resources and professional manpower available through their national headquarters, Austin's wartime activities have been concentrated in the U. S., Alaska and Canada. Each district has its own staff of designers; structural, mechanical, electrical and process engineers; estimators; purchasing agents and supervisory construction force. The flexibility of the organization enables jobs to be handled in ways most efficient for their type and

AUSTIN PRESIDENT George A. Bryant (standing) confers with the district managers who are Austin's operating heads. In the group (left to right around the table) are: Richard Ellis, acting district manager, Seattle; R. E. Ward, vice president and district manager, Los Angeles; A. F. Plant, vice president and district manager, Detroit; W. R. Engstrom, vice president, Seattle; Mr. Bryant, Charles W. Payne, Jr., district manager, Chicago; H. A. Anderson, district manager, New York; Frank W. Maynard, vice president and district manager, Oakland, Calif.; H. F. Miter, vice president, Cleveland; C. W. Wolfe, acting district manager, Cleveland; and Laurence E. Cooney, vice president and general sales manager, Cleveland.

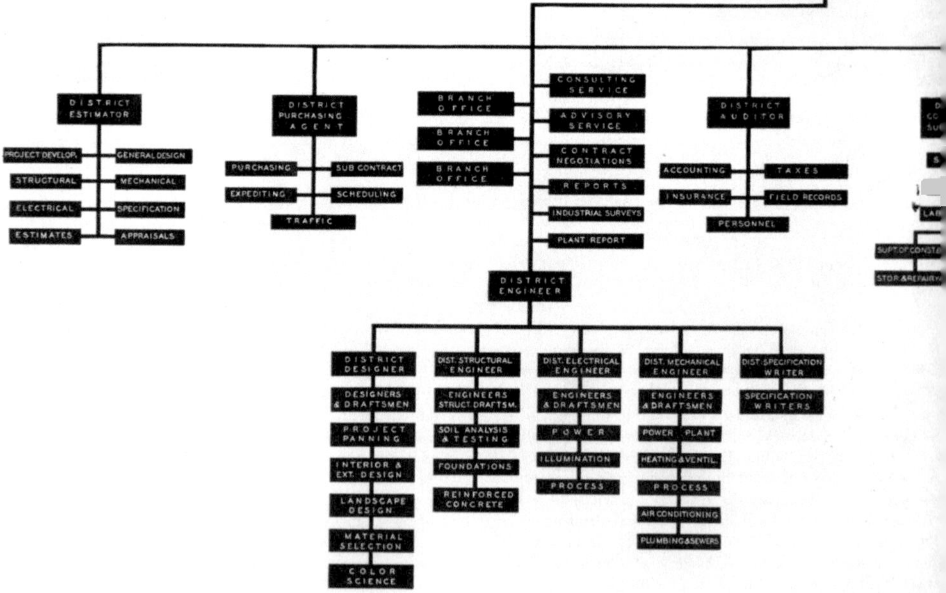

G VICE PRESIDENT H. A. Hallstein, seated, shares president's Vice president W. G. Paton handles personnel and fabrication.

RESIDENT Albert S. Low (center) who handles government con- ss't research director Waidelich and fabricating sup't Burr.

RESIDENT J. K. Gannett (right) who directs engineering and h, with Robert Smith, Jr., designer. Below: drafting room.

special problems. Austin is one of the few building organizations of national scope, and makes much of this advantage. In the case of a large radio studio on the West Coast, built for a firm with headquarters in New York, the basic architectural design was developed by the research department in Cleveland, with the New York office acting as liaison with the owners on the early phases. All of the structural, electrical and mechanical drawings were developed by the Austin district organization on the West Coast, where the owner was represented by the members of his own engineering staff who were constantly available for consultation.

Another interesting case was that of a large food industry having headquarters on the West Coast and for whom Austin designed and built a very large modern plant in the New York metropolitan area. In this instance the first contacts were made with the district organization out West. The contract was finally concluded, however, by the eastern district manager, who went to the Coast for that purpose. The flow chart and general machinery layout, as well as detailed drawings for much of the equipment directly related to the manufacturing process, were worked out on the West Coast, where members of the Austin district organization could readily observe operations in the company's existing plant, and had the benefit of day to day contact with the owner's engineers and operating staff. The actual selection of the site, however, was entrusted to the New York district, which likewise handled all of the architectural and structural drawings. While the owner made a number of trips East during the period of construction, between visits all matters which required their attention were handled through Austin personnel on the West Coast.

It was the planned doubling and redoubling of personnel in these district organizations in advance of mounting war business that enabled Austin in five years to deliver plants worth $200 million to aircraft, aviation and related industries; $100 million worth of airports, air stations and other aviation facilities; plus $200 million worth of chemical, food and process plants; and another $100 million for mining, machinery, and miscellaneous industries. With a peak payroll in 1942, when its employes totaled 49,972, Austin entered 1945 with about 10,000 on its construction payrolls and an operating staff of nearly 1,500 persons, 480 of whom are designers, engineers and draftsmen actively engaged in design, research and development work.

The personality largely responsible for Austin's growth is George A. Bryant. General sales manager of the company from 1918, when its activities became worldwide, until 1930 when he became the company's directing head as general manager and promptly negotiated a $60 million contract for design and construction of a complete industrial city for the Soviet government, Mr. Bryant has been Austin's president since 1940.

The organization he heads is not the only one which offers design, engineering and construction in a single package. Its volume of work is not the largest in the industrial field. But the scope of Austin's activities—in terms of kinds of construction and geographic coverage—is as broad, or broader than any other firm now in existence, while its championship of the integrated-building-organization idea is unique. For this reason, Austin's solutions of typical problems of industrial construction are of interest not only as examples of executed work, but as evidence of what such an organization can accomplish.

Adrian Wilson Associates

1930

Headquarters
Los Angeles, CA

Other Locations
Honolulu, HI; Saigon, Vietnam; Bangkok, Thailand; Seoul, South Korea; Tokyo, Japan; Manila, Philipines; Ankara, Turkey

Founding and Key Partners
Adrian Wilson (founding principal), J. K. Johnston, Patrick Cloud, J.R. Hatch, John Allgair, R.M. Houston, A.R. Stoner, Turhan Turker, H. Lee Higlew, R.J. Dimit

1977

AROUND THE GLOBE—Managers of Adrian Wilson Associates offices show world-wide interests of Los Angeles-based concern. Clockwise, surrounding President Adrian Wilson, center, in dark suit, are J. K. Johnston, F. Patrick Cloud, J. R. Hatch, John Allgair, R. M. Houston, A. R. Stoner and Turhan Turker. In the foreground are H. Lee Higley, left, vice president, and R. J. Dimit, vice president and general manager, Los Angeles.

Los Angeles Times, January 14, 1968

Adrian Wilson served as a private during World War I, in 1918, which overlapped with his studies in Architectural Engineering at Washington University from 1917–1919. Having moved to Los Angeles before finishing school, he completed his studies in a night school in 1926 while working as a draftsman with William Richards. Wilson formed his firs office with a partner, Erie F. Webster & Adrian Wilson in 1930, and six years later, in 1936 he founded his own solo practice. During World War II, Adrian Wilson designed numerous US Naval bases near Los Angeles, including the Roosevelt Naval Base in Long Beach and twelve buildings at the Naval Air Station on Terminal Island.

The firm grew rapidly during the 1940s, evolving into one of the leading large-scale defense, aviation, and governmental master-planning offices. In the 1950s, Wilson paired up with Paul Williams, another renowned Los Angeles architect, their collaboration resulting in the addition of several major buildings to the Los Angeles skyline throughout the 1950s, including the Los Angeles General Hospital (1949–1955) and the Los Angeles Courthouse (1955). The firm also worked together on convention centers in Las Vegas, Honolulu, and Anaheim.

Toward the end of the decade, "especially acclaimed for completing projects in difficult, dangerous environments" Adrian Wilson Associates once again became involved in defense projects with the development of NATO installations in Turkey, where it opened an office in Ankara.[1] This work led to commissions for air-base designs in Vietnam and Thailand during the Vietnam War era. In 1965, Adrian Wilson Associates was awarded a contract to conduct surveys and develop master plans for six US air bases in Vietnam and nine in Thailand. The office also designed the US Embassy in Saigon, and received a US Navy Certificate of Commendation upon its completion. During this period, Adrian Wilson Associates operated offices in Los Angeles, Seoul, Bangkok, Tokyo, Manila, Honolulu, and Ankara, continuing to provide services to the US military overseas in the late 1960s and early 1970s before resuming work on domestic airports and major master-planning projects in the US.

Completing billion dollars worth of projects during its last five years in operation, including "power plants, churches, schools, radar sites, hospitals, underground headquarters for the military, air fields, recreational centers, docks, theaters, submarine shelters, tire plants, roads, gymnasiums, and communication facilities," Adrian Wilson Associates was sold and incorporated into TI Corporation (Ticor), as its subsidiary in 1970.[2] Wilson continued to function as the president and CEO of the subsidiary under Ticor's ownership. In 1976, Howard Needles Tammen & Bergendoff (HTBN) acquired the remnants of the firm from Ticor. — JJ

(1)
David Moore et al, *A Guide to Architecture and Engineering Firms of the Cold War Era* (Department of Defense: Legacy Resource Management Program, Project 09-434): 413.

(2)
Dick Turnpin, "Huge War-Time Contract," *The Los Angeles Times* (January 14, 1968).

1931–1985

William L Pereira & Associates

1931

Headquarters
Los Angeles, CA

Founding and Key Partners
William Leonard Pereira (founding principal), Charles Luckman

1985

© J. Paul Getty Trust. Used with permission. Julius Shulman Photography Archive, Research Library at the Getty Research Institute (2004.R.10)

William L. Pereira and Charles Luckman, friends and graduates of the University of Illinois, each had unusual and successful paths before forming their partnership in Los Angeles in 1950, when both men were 41 years old.

After putting himself through architecture school at the height of the Depression by painting stage sets, Pereira found work in the Chicago firm of Holabird & Root, where his involvement in the production of the Chicago World's Fair prompted him to open his own firm in 1931. He soon became involved in designing theaters for a chain controlled by Paramount, which hired Pereira to design its studios, prompting him to move to Los Angeles in 1938. There he continued his work in scenography in addition to architecture, earning an Oscar in set design for the film *Reap the Wild Wind* (1942), directed by Cecil B De Mille.

Luckman had gone into sales during the Depression, starting as a draftsman in the advertising department of the Colgate-Palmolive-Peet Company. He graduated to manager at the Pepsodent Company, where his marketing techniques were credited with quadrupling profits, before becoming president of Lever Brothers, the owners of Pepsodent, in 1946. Luckman was instrumental in hiring Skidmore, Owings & Merrill to design the firm's headquarters in New York, the iconic Lever House, an endeavor that purportedly reminded him of his love for architecture. He left Lever Brothers to found his own architectural firm, going on to propose the scheme for the Seagram Building in New York that was eventually rejected in favor of a design by Ludwig Mies van der Rohe.

It was at this moment in their careers that the pair formed their partnership, Pereira & Luckman, in Los Angeles in 1950. The firm grew quickly to more than 400 employees and $500 million in projects by 1955, including CBS Television City (1953) and the Los Angeles International Airport (1958). In 1955, the firm designed Hilton's headquarters in Los Angeles, followed by the design of the Berlin Hilton Hotel, which opened in 1958 amid political tensions in the city. Despite their success, the partners' business priorities were incompatible, and the two split in 1959, with Luckman buying out Pereira for $500,000.

Pereira continued on his own, initially as a planner. His third firm, William L Pereira & Associates, built over 250 projects from the 1960s until Pereira's death in 1985, prompting *The Los Angeles Times* to describe Pereira's architecture as dominating "the look of Los Angeles for more than 30 years."[1] His work had a major impact further north too: Pereira's dramatic, 853-foot pyramidal tower for Transamerica in San Francisco (1972) produced a vehement public reaction.

In the early 1970s, in the midst of the boom in oil revenues in the Middle Eastern Gulf States, William L Pereira & Associates became involved in the planning of Qatar and its capital city, Doha. Planning studies led to architectural projects, including the iconic Doha Sheraton (1982), which, completed at the end of the oil boom, sat for over a decade at the end of a largely empty urban center. The firm built heavily in the region in these years, including airports in Tehran and Baghdad, hotels in Kuwait and the United Arab Emirates, and the Imperial Medical Center (1974–1976) in Tehran.

Luckman also opened his own firm in Los Angeles after the split, with satellite offices in New York and Phoenix. While critic Herbert Muschamp later suggested that some of Luckman's work "lacked a firm grasp of the aesthetic dimension" of modernism, his office was responsible for a series of landmark projects in US cities, including Madison Square Garden in New York, the Prudential Center in Boston, and Macy's Plaza in Los Angeles.[2] Luckman retired in 1977, but he continued to be involved in the office, then run by his son, until his death in 1989. The Luckman Partnership continued for some time, and its website currently links to the promise of another successor: Luckman Salas O'Brien, which dates its beginnings to the establishment of Pereira Luckman. — AM

① Michael Seiler, "Pereira, Architect Whose Works Typify L.A., Dies," *The Los Angeles Times* (November 14, 1985).

② Herbert Muschamp, "Charles Luckman, Architect Who Designed Penn Station's Replacement, Dies at 89," *The New York Times* (January 28, 1999).

© J. Paul Getty Trust. Used with permission. Julius Shulman Photography Archive, Research Library at the Getty Research Institute (2004.R.10)

© J. Paul Getty Trust. Used with permission. Julius Shulman Photography Archive, Research Library at the Getty Research Institute (2004.R.10)

PAYETTE

1932–

Payette

Headquarters
Boston, MA

Founding and Key Partners
Frederick Markus, Paul Nocka (founding principals), Thomas M. Payette, John Wilson, Dave Rowan, James H. Collins Jr.

Current Partners
Thomas M. Payette, J. Ian Adamson, Sho-Ping Chin, James H. Collins Jr., Leon W. Drachman, David G. Feth, Roberta F. Haney, Charles S. Klee, George E. Marsh Jr., Robert J. Schaeffner, Kevin B. Sullivan

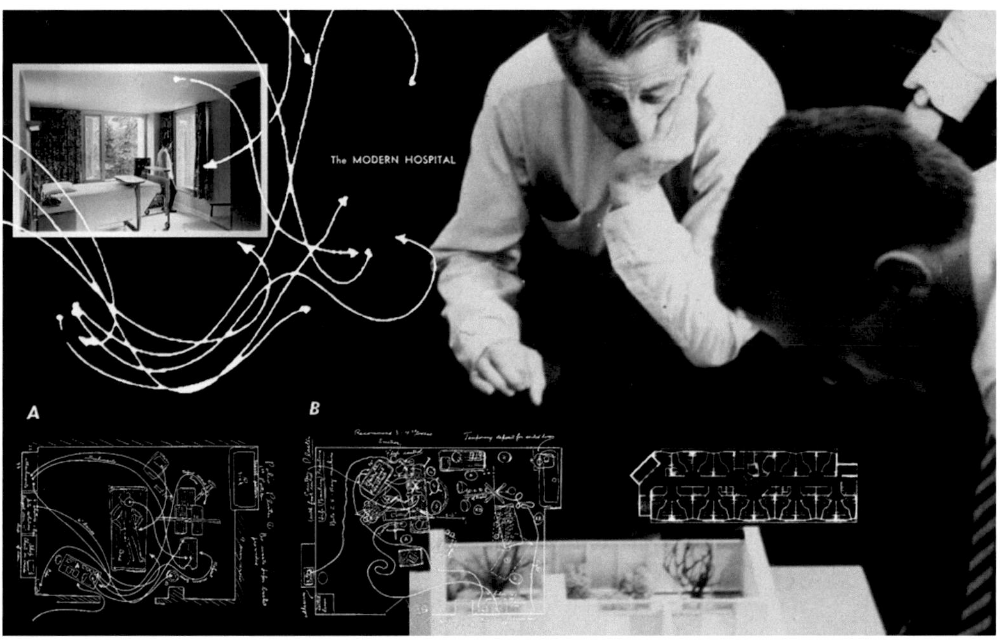

Payette

1932–1993

Edward Durell Stone & Associates

1932 Headquarters
New York, NY

Other Locations
Palo Alto, CA; Los Angeles, CA

Founding and Key Partners
Edward Durell Stone (founding principal), Pete Capone, Gary Vowels, Raymond Gomez, Robert O. Brown, Edward O. Woodrich, Vincent Furno

1993

Pedro E. Guerrero Archives, University of Arkansas Special Collections

Edward Durell Stone began his architectural education at the Boston Architectural Center, while working in the offices of Strickland, Blodgett and Law. He next worked for Coolidge Shepley Bulfinch and Abbott, where Henry Richardson Shepley became an important mentor to Stone. After receiving a scholarship to attend the Harvard Graduate School of Design, where he studied under the Beaux Arts architect Jean Jacque Haffiner, Stone finished two years of studies in one year and in 1926 transferred to the Massachusetts Institute of Technology, where another Beaux Arts-trained professor, Jacque Carlu, had opened the door to modernism.

Stone won the Rotch Scholarship, which funded his travels to Europe and North Africa. Upon returning to the States in 1929, Stone opted to work in New York, where Schultze & Weaver, then designing the Waldorf Astoria hotel, offered him a higher salary than Coolidge Shepley Bulfinch and Abbott had in Boston. After working on the iconic hotel, he joined Corbett, Harrison, and MacMurray, where he worked under Wallace K. Harrison on various aspects of Rockefeller Center and became the lead designer of the Roxy Theater and Radio City Music Hall. Stone went on to collaborate with colleagues he met while working at Corbett, Harrison, and MacMurray on the design of private residences, including houses for department store heir Richard Mandel and industrial designer Norman Bel Geddes. He made important connections to the Rockefeller and Luce families and found an enduring supporter in *Architectural Forum* critic Howard Mayer. Yet Stone struggled until Harrison passed on to him a project for the Museum of Science and Industry, which was to occupy a space at 30 Rockefeller Plaza. The project would help establish Stone's private practice. After receiving his professional license in 1935, Stone opened a small office in Rockefeller Center. Within a year he became part of politically complex machinations involving the design and construction of the new Museum of Modern Art (MoMA) in New York, for which he was credited as the design architect together with Philip Goodwin. Though critics had called the MoMA building "ultra modern" when it opened in 1939, according to Stone's son and biographer, Hicks Stone, by this time Stone had already begun to revise his aesthetic convictions.

During World War II, Stone enlisted in the Army and instigated the creation of its Planning and Design Section in 1944; he was responsible for planning airfields and designing military bases as section chief. Returning from the war, Stone continued to design private residences and received commissions such as hotel El Panama in Panama (1946–1951) that was described by *Life* magazine as "the most original tropical hotel in the Western Hemisphere."[1] He also designed two large hospitals, one in Arkansas and the other in Lima, Peru. The US Embassy in New Delhi, completed in 1959, was Stone's pivotal design in this period. The response to it was so overwhelmingly positive that many other commissions followed, including the US Pavilion for the 1958 Universal and International Exposition in Brussels.

His success put Stone on the covers of both architectural journals and popular magazines like *Time*. The stream of prominent commissions that followed included buildings in the United States as well as abroad. Stone was invited to design a series of monumental institutional buildings for the new nation-state of Pakistan, including the capital complex (National Assembly, Supreme Court, and Presidential Palace), the Institute of Nuclear Science and Technology (1965), and the University of Islamabad (1967). By the mid-1960s Stone's firm had grown to over 200 employees with offices in New York and California, newly organized as a corporation with licensed architects counting as one quarter of the firm.

Though the office garnered important commissions in the following decade, these projects became increasingly controversial, with the Gallery of Modern Art at 2 Columbus Circle in New York (1964) and the John F. Kennedy Center for the Performing Arts (1972) in Washington, DC, producing the most heated public debates. Stone's declining health forced him to retire from the practice in 1974. After his death in 1978, Edward Durell Stone & Associates continued to practice in various forms until 1993. — AM

① "Beehive in the Tropics: Panama's trade winds cool a Windowless and Doorless Hotel," *LIFE* (January 7, 1952): 51.

ELLERBE BECKET

1933–2011

Ellerbe Becket

Headquarters
1933 Los Angeles, CA

Other Locations
Cairo, Egypt; Dallas, TX; Kansas City, MO; San Francisco, CA; Washington, DC; Dubai, United Arab Emirates; Doha, Qatar

Succeeded By
AECOM

Founding and Key Partners
Charles Plummer, Walter Wurdeman, Welton Becket (founding principals, Plummer, Wurdeman and Becket); Franklin Ellerbe (founding principal, Ellerbe and Company), Olin Round, Thomas Ellerbe

2011

© J. Paul Getty Trust. Used with permission. Julius Shulman Photography Archive, Research Library at the Getty Research Institute (2004.R.10)

The West Coast branch of Ellerbe Becket's family tree came to life in Los Angeles when Walter Wurdeman and Welton Becket, classmates at the University of Washington, joined local architect Charles F. Plummer to form Plummer, Wurdeman & Becket in 1933. Initially sustained through small-scale commissions, the firm's early residential work led to the design of 14,000 military housing units after World War II. Following the deaths of Plummer in 1939 and Wurdeman in 1949, the firm was renamed Welton Becket & Associates, a name that remained even after Becket's own passing in 1969.

The design and construction of a Bullocks department store (1947) in Pasadena, California, brought the firm wide recognition and laid the groundwork for decades of large-scale commissions around the world. Working across a wide range of building typologies, Welton Becket & Associates espoused a philosophy they called "total design," which served as the title of a monograph on the firm's work methods published in 1972.[1] The term referred to a scope of comprehensive practice that the book's author, William Dudley Hunt Jr., described as embracing "almost anything that could remotely be called professional architecture," including services in engineering, programming, space studies, survey and analysis, site selection, master planning, zoning assistance, industrial design, furnishing and decorating, graphics, plan checking, and cost control.

From the 1950s onward, the firm was known particularly for its hotel designs for Hilton and Hilton International, beginning with the iconic Beverly Hilton (1955) in Beverly Hills, California. The project, which typified the firm's signature of clean, modern design with luxurious interior detailing, initiated a series of hotel commissions around the globe. These included the Habana Hilton in Cuba (1958), the Nile Hilton in Egypt (1959), and the Manila Hilton (1968) in the Philippines, along with hotels for Intercontinental in Kinshasa and Sheraton in Beijing and Tehran. By the 1960s, Welton Becket & Associates was one of the largest architecture firms in the United States, with some 500 employees.

The beginnings of the firm's Midwestern branch are rooted in the practice founded by Franklin Ellerbe in St. Paul, Minnesota, in 1909. Ellerbe and Company became known for the design of medical facilities and institutional buildings, including numerous commissions for the Mayo Clinic in Minnesota following the firm's design (while practicing as Ellerbe & Round) of the original Mayo building in 1914. Expanded by Thomas Ellerbe after his father's death in 1921, Ellerbe Architects merged with Welton Becket & Associates in 1988 to form Ellerbe Becket. In the next two decades, large-scale international projects by the firm included the World Trade Center complex in Moscow (1976–1980) and the supertall Kingdom Centre in Riyadh (1997–2002), at the time the tallest tower in Saudi Arabia.

In 2009, Ellerbe Becket became one of a growing roster of architecture firms absorbed into the mega-conglomerate AECOM. The firm practiced under its own name as "an AECOM company" until fully transitioning to operations under the AECOM name in 2011. AECOM lists the Kingdom Centre and other Ellerbe Becket buildings among its built projects, though these were completed prior to the firm's acquisition. — AWS & MK

① William Dudley Hunt, *Total Design: Architecture of Welton Becket & Associates* (New York, NY: McGraw Hill, 1972).

1935–
1974

Louis I. Kahn

Headquarters
Philadelphia, PA

1935

Founding and Key Partners
Louis I. Kahn (founding principal),
Anne Tyng

1974

After receiving his bachelor of architecture from the University of Pennsylvania in 1924, where he studied under the Beaux-Arts architect Paul Cret, Kahn went on a European tour in 1928. Upon his return he worked for several offices, including Cret's, before establishing the Architectural Resources Group (ARG), a "salon for young modernists," in 1932.[1] The Depression had stimulated the interest of progressive architects, including the members of the ARG, to address social issues which would eventually align with the concerns and policies of the New Deal.

As some of the first New Deal commissions began to come in, ARG folded and Kahn opened his own office in Philadelphia in 1935. His first engagements were with the City Planning Commission and the Housing Authority in Philadelphia, though these did not result in much built work. Kahn collaborated briefly with George Howe, a convert to modernism with connections to government commissions for wartime housing, on the design of several defense housing complexes before meeting the German immigrant architect Oscar Stonorov, with whom he subsequently shared an office from 1942 to 1947. The Kahn-Stonorov partnership was responsible for 54 projects and two publications, *Why City Planning is Your Responsibility* (1943) and *You and Your Neighborhood* (1944).

In the same period, Kahn began teaching at Yale University, remaining there from 1947 to 1957. Thanks to Howe, who had taken on the deanship at Yale in 1950, Kahn received the commission to design the Yale University Art Gallery (1953). He worked on the project with Anne Tyng, a young Harvard graduate interested in geometry as the generator of architectural form, who had joined Kahn's office in 1945. Kahn and Tyng also produced a series of speculative drawings of Philadelphia in this period.

Kahn began teaching at the University of Pennsylvania in 1955, where he stayed until his death. Though he took visiting positions at other schools, his charismatic presence and influential teaching at Penn led to a following quickly termed "the Philadelphia school."[2]

In 1944, Kahn wrote in an essay on monumentality that architects should embrace the past in order to discover future possibilities. His contribution to the reassessment of how postwar modernism could be endowed with "eternal" values centered on the nature of structure and its architectonic capacities, the need to represent, or instigate, social cohesion, and the impossibility of repeating the past. He warned against discarding the lessons that monumental buildings of another epoch might teach, "for they have the common characteristics of greatness upon which the buildings of our future must, in one sense, or another, rely."[3] Historian Sarah Williams Goldhagen has singled out Kahn's efforts in this period to balance the "practical agenda of situating people with internally manifold phenomena of monumentality and authenticity" as his key contribution to twentieth-century architecture.[4]

Kahn's rising popularity led to numerous commissions from the 1950s onward, including the Jewish Community Center (1954–1959) in Trenton, New Jersey, the Salk Institute for Biological Studies (1959–1965) in La Jolla, California, the Indian Institute of Management in Ahmedabad (1962–1974), India, and the National Assembly Building in Dhaka (1962–1983), Bangladesh.

The National Assembly complex in Dhaka was not yet finished when Kahn suffered a heart attack in May 1974 and was found dead in the men's room at Pennsylvania Station in New York City; his body remained unidentified for two days. The Dhaka project would go on for nearly another decade after Kahn's death. — RW & AM

①
Andrew M. Shanken, "The Uncharted Kahn: The Visuality of Planning and Promotion in the 1930s and 1940s," *The Art Bulletin*, Vol 8, n. 2 (June 2006): 310.

②
Jan C. Rowen, "Wanting To Be: The Philadelphia School," *Progressive Architecture* (April 1961): 131–163.

③
Louis Kahn, "Monumentality," in Paul Zucker, ed., *New Architecture and City Planning* (New York: Philosophical Library, 1944): 577–588.

④
Sarah Williams Golhagen, *Louis Kahn's Situated Modernism* (New Haven, CT: Yale University Press, 2001): 208.

Perkins+Will

Headquarters
Chicago, IL

1935

Other Locations
Atlanta, GA; London, UK; Austin, TX; Dallas, TX; Boston, MA; San Francisco, CA; New York, NY; Vancouver, BC; Washington, D.C.; Los Angeles, CA; Seattle, WA; Minneapolis, MN; Sao Paulo, Brazil; Toronto, Canada; Miami, FL; Shanghai, China; Dubai, United Arab Emirates; Dundas, Canada; Charlotte, NC; Houston, TX; Research Triangle Park, NC; Ottawa, Canada; Honolulu, HI

Founding and Key Partners
Lawrence Bradford Perkins, Edward Todd Wheeler, Phillip Will, Jr. (founding principals), Charles Williams Brubaker, Raymond Charles Ovresat

Perkins+Will, Inc.

Chicago-based Perkins+Will opened in 1935 as the eponymous office of Lawrence Perkins and Phil Will, classmates from Cornell University. They were joined by Edward Todd Wheeler the following year to form Perkins, Wheeler and Will. Perkins served as the face of the firm in procuring projects, while Will deployed his skills as an architectural designer. Perkins's father had been a successful Chicago architect in his own right, leading his own office and working in the office of Burnham & Root on projects such as the iconic Monadnock Building, the tallest load-bearing masonry building in the world at the time. "In architecture I can help you with more than money," Perkins recalls his father telling him. Residential projects sustained the firm until 1939, when the office partnered with Eliel and Eero Saarinen to design the Crow Island School in Winnetka (1940), Illinois. Crow Island served as an apprenticeship for the nascent office, setting the stage for Perkins+Will to grow into an architectural firm known in later years for its expertise in school design.

Though Perkins+Will struggled like its peers during World War II, the office continued to work on school projects, first in the Chicago area and later in New York and New England. In 1945 the partners shifted gears from its previously informal practice model and hired management consultants Booz Allen Hamilton to grow their business. The firm moved into a larger office space, reorganized its management structure, and began to expand deliberately. By 1957, according to *Architectural Forum*, Perkins+Will was known as the "biggest and best known school architects," a success that let the firm turn its gaze to other building types. This included the health care and hospital sector, a task taken on by Wheeler, who had left the firm in 1944 and returned in 1957 with a decade of experience and connections in Chicago health care architecture. By 1960, Perkins+Will had a staff of 150 people, satellite offices in New York and Washington, DC, and a burgeoning international practice launched through collaborations in South America with a Mexican architecture firm. Perkins+Will operated through small design groups under a "studio" model of multidisciplinary teams with a partner at the top of each team. In 1985, then-partner William Brubaker described the success of the firm in strategic terms, saying "We have never been design superstars... The firm kept its focus by not embracing any dogmas or one particular esthetic."[1]

In 1986, Perkins+Will was acquired by the Lebanese conglomerate Dar Al-Handasah to form part of an international network called The Dar Group. Perkins described the merger as a "happy solution" to a financial problem: namely, the debt taken on by the firm in the period after his retirement.[2] Giving The Dar Group access to the US market while providing Perkins+Will with a vastly expanded scope of international practice, the partnership has led to a number of extremely large projects in the Middle East, including Dubai International Airport's Concourse 2 (2009) and the recently completed Princess Nora Bint Abdulrahman University in Riyadh (2006–2011), Saudi Arabia, the largest university for women in the world. Despite these changes, Perkins+Will continues to be headquartered in Chicago under the same name it began with nearly eighty years ago. — AL

① Ronald Litke, "Perkins & Will: The First 50 Years," *Inland Architect* (September/October 1985): 15.

② Betty J. Blum (interviewer), "Oral history of Lawrence Bradford Perkins, F.A.I.A," *Chicago Architects Oral History Project* (Department of Architecture, the Art Institute of Chicago, 2000): 155.

1936–1973

1936

1973

Alfred L. Aydelott & Associates

Headquarters
Memphis, TN

Founding and Key Partners
Alfred L. Aydelott (founding principal), B.I. Brown, Chai-Yi Jen, Maurice Wood, Robert Sawyer

Progressive Architecture, April 1954

In 1949, Alfred Aydelott opened an office in Memphis, Tennessee, following his departure from the partnership that he and Minor Dent had founded in 1936. Aydelott's new firm got its start with the development of a small hospital project in the 1940s and continued to develop its expertise in medical facilities throughout the 1950s. Notable projects of the time include the Bristol Memorial Hospital and the Hospital at Blytheville Air Force Base in Memphis (1959). Along with its work in medical buildings, Aydelott Associates became known as the premier modern design firm in Memphis and produced several significant buildings that shaped the city's skyline. Among those, the Memphis City Hall (1966) remains one of the office's most significant projects.

The firm received its first international commission in 1952, when it was asked to design, in conjunction with Edward Durrell Stone, a massive hospital in Lima, Peru. The project was developed to provide health care facilities to support a local population of seventy-five thousand residents, with more than 800 patient beds and facilities to treat over six hundred out-patients every six hours. At the time of its construction, the hospital was the largest and most modern health-care facility in the country.

In 1956, Aydelott Associates was retained for its second, and final, project overseas by the State Department's Foreign Buildings Operations (FBO) office as part of embassy building program in the 1950s. Aydelott Associates' embassy in Manila, Philippines (1956-1960), was recognized for its sculptural, prefabricated-concrete façade and was prominently featured in several FBO publications.

Aydelott Associates continued to produce significant work in and around Memphis until 1973, when Aydelott relocated to Carmel, California, and the office was dissolved. Upon his death in 2008, Aydelott was referred to as "The Father of Modernism in Memphis."[1] — JJ

(1) Paulo Alcazaren, "The Grill is Gone," *Philippine Star* (January 7, 2012).

SOM

1936–

Skidmore, Owings & Merrill

1936

Headquarters
Chicago, IL; New York, NY

Other Locations
San Francisco, CA; Los Angeles, CA; Washington D.C., London, England; Hong Kong, China; Shanghai, China; Mumbai, India; Abu Dhabi, United Arab Emirates

Founding and Key Partners
Louis Skidmore, Nathaniel Alexander Owings (founding principals), John O. Merrill, William Hartmann, Walter Severinghaus, Gordon Bunshaft, Charles Bassett, Natalie de Blois, Bruce J. Graham, Walter A. Netsch, Myron Goldsmith, Fazlur Khan, David Childs, Adrian Smith

Current Partners
Mustafa Abadan, Stephen Apking, William Baker, Carrie Byles, Leo Chow, Roger Duffy, Philip Enquist, Xuan Fu, T.J. Gottesdiener, Gary Haney, Craig Hartman, Brian Lee, Jeffrey McCarthy, Mark Sarkisian, Gene Schnair, Richard Tomlinson, Anthony Vacchione

Ezra Stoller, Esto

Skidmore, Owings & Merrill (SOM) was founded in 1936 on the Chicago lakefront by two brothers-in-law, Louis Skidmore and Nathaniel Owings; engineer John Merrill joined them in 1939. Emerging in the wartime and postwar era, SOM began with military and government contracts domestically and overseas, including the design of the "Atomic Village" (1942) at Oak Ridge, Tennessee, and the Air Force Academy (1962) in Colorado Springs. Cited historically as the firm that spearheaded the spread of the now-ubiquitous tall office building with a curtain-wall facade, SOM gained acclaim for Lever House (1952), the modernist headquarters for a British soap company in Manhattan. SOM indeed went on to build tall office towers prolifically in the United States and abroad, as well as other large-scale projects such as airports, universities, and corporate headquarters. Responsible for many of the world's tallest buildings, including the Sears (today, Willis) Tower (1973) in Chicago and Burj Khalifa (2010) in Dubai, SOM is acclaimed today for its "supertall" engineering expertise.

Since the firm's emergence, SOM has been the architectural office synonymous with the term "corporate" in its practices. Modeled on many of the same managerial principles of its corporate clients, SOM applied strategies such as decentralization and specialization to its own practice. This included the creation of regional offices, beginning with New York in 1937, which operated largely autonomously under the broad direction of a group of partners in a limited liability model. Crystallizing the firm's reputation for technical expertise, William Hartmann, who became partner in 1951, led the integration of in-house engineering disciplines, resulting in the design of many buildings driven by a structural or heating-cooling concept. Situating the emergence of large-scale practice historically, in 1957, historian Sigfried Giedion positioned "the Experiment of SOM" in a lineage of large Chicago School firms including Adler & Sullivan and Burnham & Root—offices which would spawn more big firms such as JAHN and Goettsch Partners, some of SOM's key competitors today.[1]

Despite its scale, SOM has also represented a unique combination of design authorship and pragmatic acumen, both embodied in the divergent expertise of SOM's founding partners, Skidmore and Owings respectively. Unique among corporate giants, SOM has been shaped by the driving influence of four generations of iconic designers and engineers including Gordon Bunshaft, Bruce Graham, Natalie de Blois, Walter A. Netsch, Myron Goldsmith, Fazlur Khan, David Childs, and Adrian Smith. Speaking to SOM's early status as a "plan factory," in Giedion's words, the office had over 2,000 employees in 1981. In opposition to the production-line model, however, SOM produces work through smaller, interdisciplinary "studio" teams. In 1950, it was the first corporate office to have an exhibition dedicated to its work at the Museum of Modern Art (MoMA) in New York.

The largest US exporter of architecture to date, SOM works prolifically around the globe as well as in the United States. In the firm's early decades, SOM's work abroad focused on housing for the US government and military and for large oil and industrial corporations. Later, during the 1960s and 1970s, SOM began working directly for international clients in the United Kingdom and the Gulf region following oil-boom funded development. Beginning in 1976, SOM turned its attention to China's expanding markets, completing over 150 projects there to date, including plans for new cities, corporate campuses, and supertall buildings. — AL

①
Sigfried Giedion, "The Experiment of S.O.M.," *Bauen + Wohnen* (April 1957): 109–113.

US Pavilion, Giardini della Biennale
1929–1930

Architect
Delano & Aldrich

Location
Venice, Italy

Client
US Department of State

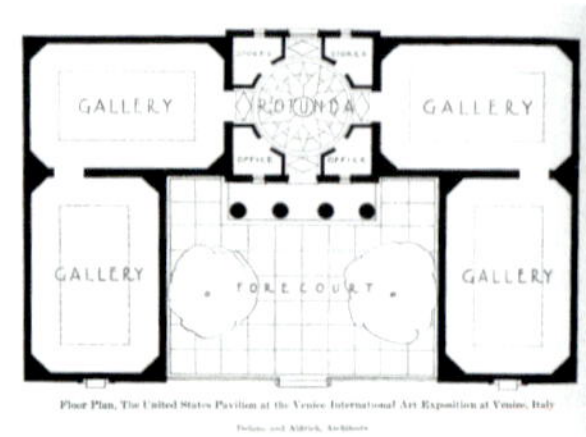

US Embassy
1929–1931

Architect
Delano & Aldrich

Location
Paris, France

Client
US Department of State, Foreign Buildings Operations

Nanjing Revolutionists Memorial
1933

Architect
Henry Killam Murphy

Location
Nanjing, China

Client
Kuomintang

Hotel Nacional de Cuba
1930

Architect
McKim, Mead and White

Location
Havana, Cuba

Client
Bowman-Biltmore Hotels Corporation

Gasoline Stations for Rising Sun Petroleum Company
1930

Architect
Raymond & Rado

Location
Yokohama, Japan

Client
Rising Sun Petroleum Company (Shell Oil)

Tokyo Golf Club
1930

Architect
Raymond & Rado

Location
Asaka, Japan

Client
Tokyo Golf Club

Chelyabinsk Tractor and Tank Factory
1930

Architect
Albert Kahn Associates

Location
Chelyabinsk, USSR

Client
Amtorg Trading Corporation

1929

Elgin Marble Wing, British Museum
1931–1938

Architect
John Russell Pope

Location
London, UK

Client
British Museum

1939

Overseas Chinese Home
1932

Architect
Henry Killam Murphy

Location
Nanjing, China

Client
Kuomintang

NEW HOME FOR OVERSEA VISITORS TO NANKING STANDS AS MONUMENT TO LOVE OF FATHERLAND

Lucknow University Library
1935–1937

Architect
Walter Burley Griffin and Marion Mahony

Location
Lucknow, India

Client
Executive Council of Lucknow University

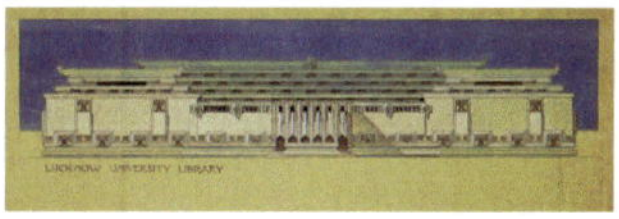

Golconde Dormitory
1935–1942

Architect
Raymond & Rado

Location
Pondicherry, India

Client
Pondicherry Ashram

Avila Hotel
1939–1942

Architect
Harrison & Abramovitz

Location
Caracas, Venezuela

Client
Compañia de Fomento Venezolano, Nelson Rockefeller

Flight Paths: Emigrating European Practices and Pedagogies

The course of architectural practice in the US and its international export after World War II was heavily affected by the paths of the European architects who emigrated in the decade prior to the war. While the victory of the National Socialist Party in Germany after 1932 and the parallel rise of fascism in Spain and Italy were the ultimate causes for this mass movement, European fascination with architectural "Americanism" in architecture and city planning went as far back as the World's Columbian Exposition of 1893.[1]

A mutual interest between young European and US architects in the interwar period paved the way for modernist movements on both sides of the Atlantic. German architects traveled to the US to study its urban and industrial landscapes, inspired particularly by Frederick Taylor's theories of scientific management and the factory models of Henry Ford.[2] Press photographs of US industrial buildings like those compiled by Walter Gropius in the yearbook of the German Werkbund (1913) were superseded by the reportage of Erich Mendelsohn's *Amerika, Bilderbuch eines Architekten* (1926) and insider accounts of US building practices like *Wie Baut America?* (1927) and *Amerika* (1930), written by Austrian émigré Richard Neutra after working for Holabird & Roche and Frank Lloyd Wright before moving to Los Angeles.[3] The ground was prepared in turn for European modernism in the US by proselytizing critics and curators, chief among them Alfred Barr, Henry-Russell Hitchcock, and Philip Johnson at the Museum of Modern Art (MoMA) in New York. *The International Style*, the publication which resulted from their "Modern Architecture: International Exhibition" at MoMA in 1932, quickly became what Sibyl Moholy-Nagy called the "passport that secured the entry of the 'Makers of Modern Architecture' into this country."[4]

① Jean-Louis Cohen, *Scenes of the World to Come: European Architecture and the American Challenge 1893–1960* (Paris: Flammarion, 1995).

② See Ivan Rupnik, "Exporting Space-Time: American Industrial Engineering Tools and European Modernism," in Eva Franch i Gilabert, Amanda Lawrence, Ana Miljački, Ashley Schafer, ed., *OfficeUS Agenda* (Zurich: Lars Müller, 2014): 105–116.

③ See Reyner Banham, *A Concrete Atlantis: U.S. Industrial Building and European Modern Architecture* (Cambridge, MA: MIT Press, 1986); Mark Jarzombek, "The Discourses of a Bourgeois Utopia, 1904–1908, and the Founding of the Werkbund," in François Forster-Hahn, ed., *Imagining Modern German Culture 1889–1910*,

1905

1913 Walter Gropius publishes US industrial buildings in *Jarbuch des Deutscher Werkbund*

1914–1918 World War I

1923 Richard Neutra emigrates from Vienna

1924 Erich Mendelsohn travels to the US

1928 Gropius travels to the US

1932 • *International Style* exhibition at the Museum of Modern Art (MoMA) • National Socialist Party wins German parliamentary elections; Adolf Hitler named Chancellor of the Reich

1933 • Closure of the Bauhaus • Mendelsohn leaves Germany for London

1934 Gropius, Marcel Breuer leave Germany for London

1935 Le Corbusier travels to the US

1936–1939 Spanish Civil War

1937 • Gropius emigrates from London to Cambridge as chair of Harvard Design School • Breuer emigrates from London to Cambridge • Sert leaves Spain for Paris

1939–1945 World

The closure of the Bauhaus by the Nazi government in 1933 formed the first major impetus for the mass departure of European architects over the decade that Moholy-Nagy termed “The Diaspora.” Gropius and Marcel Breuer left for England in 1934 and from there to Cambridge in 1937, practicing together until a contentious split in 1941. Ludwig Mies van der Rohe left last among the Bauhaüsler, arriving in 1937 in Chicago, a city he saw as both open to German immigrants and possessing favorable regulations for licensing foreign architects.[5] Josep Lluís Sert escaped the Spanish Civil War to Paris in 1937, departing for the US in exile following Franco’s victory in 1939. Victor Gruen (née Gruenbaum) fled Austria in 1938 on the eve of World War II, practicing first in New York before moving to Los Angeles.

As immigrants, these architects were aware that only university posts would allow them to obtain permanent residence in the US. Joseph Hudnut, dean of the architecture school at Harvard University, sought a European modernist as chair of the program, choosing Gropius after Mies declined to compete for the position.[6] Mies instead went to the Armour (later Illinois) Institute of Technology, joined by Ludwig Hilberseimer, while Laszlo Moholy-Nagy founded the short-lived New Bauhaus School of Design in Chicago in 1937. The opening of the retrospective exhibition “Bauhaus: 1919–1928” at the Museum of Modern Art in 1938, curated by Barr, placed a definitive stamp on the arrival of the Bauhaüsler en masse to the US.

The absorption of the émigrés into architectural practice in the US proceeded rapidly. Mies, Breuer, and Gropius were received as the major figures among the émigrés after World War II, though the later interpretation of the work of such “masters” within the context of their US offices proved to be problematic. Breuer, for his part, saw the two professional cultures as complementary: “Americans are efficient,” he said, while “Germans are systematic,” a combination he felt to be ideal in adapting to the new context.[7] Significantly, the postwar work of these architects often included commissions in their countries of origin, many of them identified publicly with the personae of the émigrés and their conceptual return. By 1957, a special issue of the *Architectural Review* on “Machine Made America” reflected on the integration of these architects into the mainstream of US practice, including Mies, Gruen, Neutra, and Gropius equally with their colleagues and students among the postwar “Personal Contributions to American Architecture.”[8] — MK

(Washington, D.C.: National Gallery of Art, 1996): 127–145.

④ Sibyl Moholy-Nagy, “The Diaspora,” *Journal of the Society of Architectural Historians* (March 1965): 25.

⑤ Cammie McAtee, “Alien #5044325: Mies’s First Trip to America,” in Phyllis Lambert, ed., *Mies in America* (Montreal and New York: Canadian Centre for Architecture and Whitney Museum of American Art, 2001): 133–185.

⑥ Jill Pearlman, *Inventing American Modernism: Joseph Hudnut, Walter Gropius, and the Bauhaus Legacy at Harvard* (Charlottesville: University of Virginia Press, 2007).

⑦ William H. Jordy, “The Aftermath of the Bauhaus in America: Gropius, Mies, and Breuer,” in Donald Fleming and Bernard Bailyn, ed., *The Intellectual Migration: Europe and America, 1930–1960* (Cambridge, MA: Harvard University Press, 1969): 485–526.

⑧ “Genetrix: Personal Contributions to American Architecture,” *The Architectural Review* (May 1957): 336–386.

1933

1945

1938 • Mies van der Rohe emigrates from Germany to Chicago as director of Armour Institute of Technology architecture school • Victor Gruen emigrates from Vienna to New York • *Bauhaus* 1919–1928 exhibition at MoMA

1939 Sert emigrates from Paris to New York

1941 Mendelsohn emigrates from London

1945 Gropius among founders of The Architects Collaborative

1969 • Gropius dies • Mies van der Rohe dies

1970 Neutra dies

1980 Gruen dies

1981 Breuer dies

1983 Sert dies

1985

1950–1953 Korean War

1962 Cuban Missile Crisis

1950–1975 Vietnam War

Émigrés: Arrival and Projects Abroad

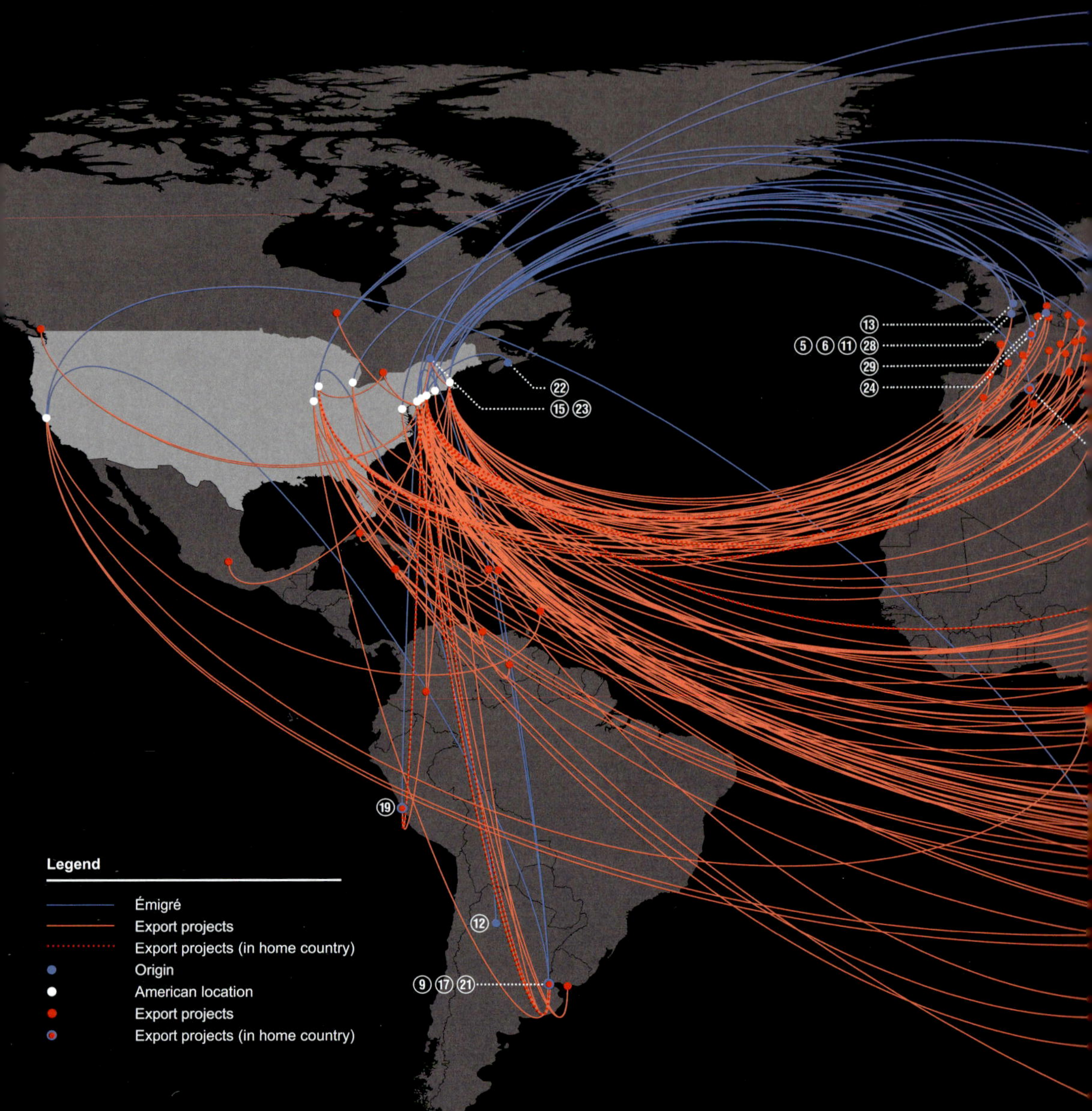

① **Antonin Raymond**
1910: Prague, CZ → New York, NY

② **Richard J. Neutra**
1923: Vienna, AT → Chicago, IL

③ **I.M. Pei**
1935: Shanghai, CN → Cambridge, MA

④ **Mies van der Rohe**
1937: Dessau, DE → Chicago, IL

⑤ **Walter Gropius**
1937: London, GB (DE) → Cambridge, MA

⑥ **Marcel Breuer**
1937: London, GB (HU) → Cambridge, MA

⑦ **Victor Gruen**
1938: Vienna, AT → New York, NY

⑧ **Josep Lluís Sert**
1939: Barcelona, ES → New York, NY

⑨ **Eduardo Catalano**
1941: Buenos Aires, AR → Philadelphia, PA

⑩ **Romaldo Giurgola**
1949: Rome, IT → New York, NY

⑪ **Gunnar Birkerts**
1949: London, GB (LV) → Detroit, MI

⑫ **Cesar Pelli**
1952: San Miguel de Tucaman, AR → Champagne, IL

⑬ **Christopher Alexander**
1958: Cambridge, GB → Cambridge, MA

⑭ **Adele Santos**
1961: Capetown, ZA → San Francisco, CA

⑮ **Moshe Safdie**
1964: Montreal, CA (IL) → Philadelphia, PA

⑯ **Helmut Jahn**
1966: Munich, DE → Chicago, IL

⑰ **Rudolfo Machado / Jorge Silvetti**
1968: Buenos Aires, AR
→ Berkeley, CA

⑱ **Suman Sorg**
1968: New Delhi, IN → Washington, DC

⑲ **Bernardo Fort-Brescia**
1969: Lima, PE → Princeton, NJ

⑳ **Mark Mack**
1973: Judenburg, AT → New York, NY

㉑ **Rafael Viñoly**
1979: Buenos Aires, AR → New York, NY

㉒ **Krzystof Wodiczko**
1983: Nova Scotia, CA (Warsaw, PL)
→ New York, NY

㉓ **Hani Rashid / Lise Anne Couture**
1984: Montreal, CA
→ Bloomfield Hills, MI / New Haven, CT

㉔ **Bernard Tschumi**
1988: Paris, FR → New York, NY

㉕ **Minsuk Cho**
1988: Seoul, KR → New York, NY

㉖ **Ada Tolla / Giuseppe Ligano**
1990: Napoli, IT → New York, NY

㉗ **Ziad Jamaleddine / Makram el Kadi**
1995: Beirut, LB
→ Cambridge, MA / New York, NY

㉘ **David Turnbull**
1996: London, GB → New Haven, CT

㉙ **Alexander d'Hooge**
2005: Leuven, BE → Cambridge, MA

economical, weathertight, comfortable and good-looking buildings; much more than that the average man doesn't ask; indeed if he got that, the status of the architects and specialists who provided it would be very high indeed, but he too often fails to get it because without specialization it cannot nowadays be provided.

The position of the architect with outstanding creative ability (the artist-architect as he has been called here) is rather different. In common with all artists, society doesn't recognize its need of him quite as much as it does of the efficiency experts. His will often be the lonely struggle, aided perhaps by part-time teaching, and punctuated by competitions—until recognition comes. It may take him long to achieve this recognition or it may happen quickly; when he does achieve it, he may be over-valued or under-valued; he may even be valued for the wrong reasons; he may or may not make more money than the specialist; his status may be higher or it may be lower; to him this is, or should be, a matter of relative unconcern. The only thing we do know is that he's very valuable and there will be very few of him in any day and age. There are certain marks which distinguish him, though they sometimes turn out to be camouflage; however, what the public takes to be camouflage often turns out to be the mark of genius. Without him there would be no architecture, and without the lead of some of the greatest of his kind the anonymous architecture that has been the subject of discussion in this article would not have been worthy of consideration as the exciting and important new factor that it is.

PERSONAL CONTRIBUTION

2

ago

Mies van der Rohe **71**
Richard Neutra **65**
William Wurster **61**
William Lescaze **61**
Pietro Belluschi **57**
Louis Kahn **56**
Mario Corbett **55**
Edward Stone **55**
Marcel Breuer **54**
Victor Gruen **53**
Paul Schweikher **53**
Bruce Goff **52**
Philip Johnson **50**
Robert Alexander **49**
Raphael Soriano **49**
Vernon DeMars **49**
Gordon Bunshaft **48**
John Rex **48**
Eero Saarinen **46**
Eliot Noyes **46**

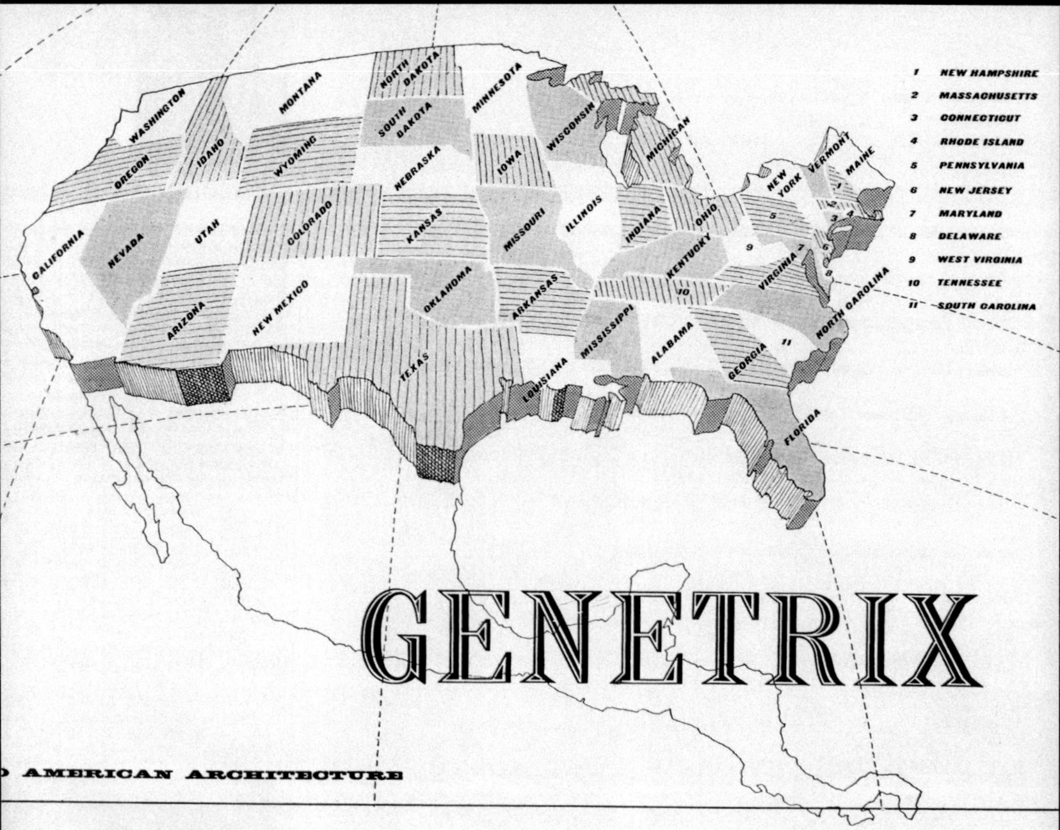

GENETRIX

D AMERICAN ARCHITECTURE

age
46 *Whitney Smith*
45 *Ernest Kump*
45 *Hugh Stubbins*
44 *Minoru Yamasaki*
44 *Carl Koch*
44 *T.A.C. (average age)*
44 *A. Quincy Jones*
42 *Ralph Rapson*
42 *Edward L. Barnes*
41 *Harry Weese*
41 *John Johansen*
40 *I. M. Pei*
39 *King Lui-Wu*
38 *Paul Rudolph*
37 *Roger Lee*
37 *Peter Blake*
36 *Ulrich Franzen*
34 *Reginald C. Knight*
33 *Thornton Ladd*
32 *Pierre Koenig*

The first part of this issue concerned itself with an aspect of architecture which is a collective achievement, many individuals have, of course, contributed to it, but its chief value comes from the fact that as well as being popular, practical and generally applicable it tends to discourage 'personal' expression in favour of raising the architectural quality of a standard product.

The part that follows traces the isolated contributions of the individual, of the men who make a valid contribution to contemporary architecture through a personal vision; it attempts to trace each contribution to its source in a man's background, training, the vicissitudes of his career, his heroes, his outlook and his inner convictions. It is specially designed to give architects outside America a more rounded picture of the American architectural scene. The outsider may be, and often is, aware of the latest news and pictures; he may have attended one of the lectures by architect-visitors to America—a growing phenomenon now that an American grand tour is becoming almost obligatory for the bright young European architect; he is aware of innumerable names, some of them famous and firmly established in his mind; but with many of the younger Americans it is often hard to relate names to buildings; the development of American architecture has been so rapid in recent years and the idiom is becoming so consistent that the picture seen from a distance spreads itself thin and takes on a distressingly two-dimensional appearance. One way to give it depth is to try to bring the personalities behind it to life.

With this in mind, the architects that follow were sent questionnaires designed to 'draw them out'. The answers to these, accompanied by photographs of their newest works (and an occasional reminder of earlier ones), are published in order of seniority (Frank Lloyd Wright's work has been omitted at his own request). The aim is to give those who have not been able to see US architecture in three dimensions, a rounded picture of some of its architects.*

*The field is too vast to pretend that this can be more than an introduction to contemporary American architecture, and an interim one at that; there are parts—Texas, the south-east and the middle-west, for instance, which deserve more detailed attention than we have been able to give them here; and to which we shall return.

71

Chicago, Illinois

Mies van der Rohe, at the age of seventy-one and a long way from his native Aachen, has acquired the standing of a touchstone, the living embodiment of a moral absolute, by which US architecture may expect to be judged, a polarity opposed diametrically to Frank Lloyd Wright. However true it may be that his famous Lake Shore towers are the fulfilment of the dream of a glass skyscraper that had exercised him in Berlin as early as 1919, however true it may be that he is 'always the same Mies,' the fact remains that his coming to America in 1938 marks a real break in his career, and his American architecture is very unlike that which he had earlier done in Europe. The earlier body of work had consisted mostly of small buildings and large projects—except for the Weissenhof-siedlung of 1927, which was an event of International significance—and less and less of either as Germany's intellectual life contracted towards the null-point of 1933, at which null-point it was left to Mies, as its last director, to turn the key on what remained of the Bauhaus—and on what remained of an adventure, a generation, a dead world. The New World offered him the chance to realize his large projects; offered him the necessary patrons, the materials, the techniques, the engineers and collaborators—and the IIT campus, as its buildings were completed one by one over the

The new, Miesian, Chicago School at work—a house in Geneva, Ill., by J. C. Brownson, completed in 1952.

years on his twelve-foot planning grid, revealed to US architects an extreme point in architectural integrity, a right rectangular aesthetic of structure and space and precious little else. This aesthetic, summed up in two basic Miesian sayings, *Wenige ist Mehr* and *Beinahe Nichts* (Less is More, and Almost Nothing) has been called the 'Absence of Architecture,' but on a middle generation of Americans it has reacted as a positive presence, and as Mies has gone on developing it, refining and subtilizing its structural forms and formal structure, a giant ghost has followed it at a safe and not-quite-comprehending distance—the curtain wall industry. For, though Mies's achievement could hardly be more personal, the superficial appearance of the buildings in which that achievement is embodied has

Esplanade Apartments, *left*, adjoining the original Mies blocks at 860 Lake Shore Drive, Chicago, have black-anodized aluminium trim and facings instead of the steel of the earlier scheme. The even more recent Commonwealth Promenade Apartments, of which the first two blocks are seen at *right* and *above*, have natural-anodized aluminium surfaces. The Cullinan Hall extension for the Museum of Fine Arts at Houston, Texas, *below*, has the usual Miesian structure of brick, steel and glass, but a curved plan, which is rare among his recent work.

facilitated the visual acceptance of a repetitive, endless, grid façade, while the work of two architects most ready to admit his influence, Eero Saarinen and Gordon Bunshaft, has effectively bridged the gap between one man's vision and an industrial product.

America could not have nurtured Mies, Europe could not have fulfilled his promise; he has perhaps gained more from and given more to the US than any other emigré outside the realm of atomic physics. He has produced a lyricism of two constituent US psychological facts—unlimited space and unmitigated technology—in a form that is neither provincial nor crude, and can be held up to the rest of the world as an example of a convincing machine-age architecture. The rest of the world has taken note and, wherever architectural thought is on the move, the influence of Mies—*American* Mies—can be felt. Indeed, he ranks with Le Corbusier, Nervi and Candela as one of the fundamental form-givers of the fifties, and of no other American architect can this be said.

Above, the most famous, and the most controversial, of all pieces of Mies detailing, the I-section mullions on the elevations of 860 Lake Shore Drive, including the 'unnecessary' ones on the corner stanchions. *Right*, Crown Hall, the architectural school of IIT: *above right*, end wall; a pure and uninterrupted space-box, completed in 1956, and probably the most Miesian building there will ever be.

65

Los Angeles, California

Richard J. Neutra, almost alone of America's leading architects, has tangled at many points in his career with the great names of the Modern Movement. Born in Vienna in 1892, his early admirations were for Otto Wagner and Adolf Loos. In the early 'twenties he shared an office with Erich Mendelsohn in Berlin, and like Mendelsohn and Rudolph Schindler (another Viennese) he soon crossed the Atlantic and headed for Chicago and there met Sullivan and Wright. Unlike Mendelsohn, who returned to Berlin, he stayed on long enough in Chicago to help nurse Sullivan through his last illness, and then followed the path that Schindler had pioneered to the Pacific Coast. It was a classic education in Modernism, which he was soon passing on through his Academy of Modern Art to such rising talents as H. H. Harris and Gregory Ain. Ever since then, his rigorous and imaginative attitude to technology (which has its roots in the Neutra Family tradition), his thoughtful attitude to the psychology of architectonic form (which has its roots in his readings in the works of Wundt) have gained and maintained for him a solid reputation on both sides of the Atlantic, while the basic attitude which he derives from these interests, and sums up as 'Constructed human environment should be an entity, and not split up by specialists'. Both in his writings and his buildings he has shown a remarkable consistency over the years—works of 1927, like the 'Health-house,' and of 1955, like the Brentwood Gemological Institute, are equally unmistakably Neutra, even though they also bear witness to a careful and pondered architectural development. In spite of this quiet and self-effacing devotion to the problems of his art, he has attained wide public recognition, and deservedly.

Entrance to Richard Neutra's own house and office in Silver Lake Boulevard, Los Angeles, a pioneer experimental building of 1932.

Neutra (cont.) *Opposite page, constructed human environments by Neutra, exemplifying the extremities of his approach to house-design in the Fifties; above, a view-facing extrovert house at Ojai, Cal., below, a courtyard-facing introvert house at Bel Air, Cal. Left, a recent community building by Neutra, a Teenagers' club at Eagle Rock, which shows his continued command of cantilevered forms and precise detailing.*

61

San Francisco, California

Emmons, Wurster, Bernardi

The development and consistency of William Wurster's domestic work are shown by the

Gregory Farmouse, above, an early commission that won a House Beautiful award in 1927, and the Nowell house at Stockton, Cal., centre completed in 1953, but still maintaining the

Bay Region tradition. The Monterey Public Library, below, 1952, is one of a number of community buildings that have come from the office of Wurster Bernardi and Emmons.

William Wilson Wurster was born at Stockton, California, in 1895; it was a town of 30,000 people in the Great Central Valley of the San Joaquin, and Wurster's father would take him on each bank holiday (he worked in a bank) to see some new aspect of it. Starting with a fire station, a foundry, a mill and leading through to the City Hall, County Court House and the offices of the local newspaper, until he got to know how the town worked in all its details. He decided to be an architect at the age of three, guided, he thinks, by his mother, who had been impressed by his question 'How do chimneys stay on roofs?' The motto of the New England side of his family was 'At least learn some one thing well—you can change to something else if a greater opportunity comes.'

During High School he worked in the summer for E. B. Brown, an English architect in Stockton, a gifted, irascible and unbusinesslike man, but it was a good office to be in and the work had character and style.

He went to the University of California in 1913 to study architecture under John Galen Howard; however, health and the first world war broke in and he didn't finish until 1919. At architectural school Wurster remembers himself as a conformist, and the whole group, prior to the 'twenties, missed the 'modern surge', though, even then, façadism made him uneasy.

The first office job after qualification was in San Francisco with an honourable, tight-fisted architect of Scottish descent; he obtained his work as a brother-in-law of the mayor, but his performance was beyond reproach. It was not, however, a gay office. Wurster left to work for Charles Dean in Sacramento on an engineering project; there he learned all the field things fast, designed and built

54

New York City

Marcel Breuer, outstanding product of the Bauhaus's most brilliant period (1920-24) and designer of its most famous artefact (the steel tube chair), was born in Hungary in 1902, and decided to become an architect in 1904. After his Bauhaus training, and a phase when he combined headship of the Bauhaus interiors department with independent design-work outside, he passed by way of the Isokon network (which also handled Gropius and Moholy-Nagy) and collaborations with F. R. S. Yorke in England, to the USA in 1937, to team up with Gropius once more, teaching at Harvard, and partnering him as an architect. He was thus among the spearheaders of full, European modernism in US Academic circles and in New England house-building, and he has left his mark in both fields.

In house-design, however, he has made his deepest impression since the partnership with Gropius was dissolved in 1941, particularly with his 'butterfly' exhibition house for the Museum of Modern Art, which was visited in 1949 by over 70,000 people, and probably did as much as anything to sell split-level sections to the US public. Epoch-making as this may have been in the context of US housing at large, in the context of his own work it was only one of a series of remarkable houses produced by him between 1945 and 1955, houses marked by an extensive, original and authoritative employment of wood and stone. The successes of this period, and the very high quality of the work he put into them, focused attention on him as a house-architect more than anything else, but he had always possessed the abilities and ambitions for larger work, and in the very middle of his house-period he designed a dormitory for Vassar and the Arts Centre for Sarah Lawrence College. Since then projects and work in hand outside the domestic field include schools and college buildings, a factory, a monastery, and two widely-discussed designs done in collaboration with Europeans in Europe, the UNESCO buildings in Paris, with Zehrfuss and Nervi, and the new *de Bijenkorf*, Rotterdam, with Elzas. With both these latter teams he maintains project offices, as well as his own office in New York, where he has three associates and twenty assistants. As might be expected from one of the Bauhaus's star pupils his work is unforcedly personal, but never individualistic, and—as might also be expected of an old Bauhaus student—he has a distinguished roster of collaborators from the other arts.

A large part of Marcel Breuer's recent work has been concerned with educational buildings of a very varied kind: above, a classroom wing and the gable wall of the gymnasium at Litchfield High School,

Conn.; for the Sarah Lawrence College, Bronxville, NY, he designed in 1950 an Arts Centre, left, above, with a dance-studio, right, above, under the rake of the auditorium floor; and for St. John's Abbey,

Collegeville, Minn., a large programme of extensions (AR, July, 1954) of which the monastery wing, above left, has been completed—the abbot's reception room is seen above right. Breuer's post-war

reputation in America stems largely from his work in house-design—the Grieco house, Andover, Mass., with its boarded exterior, wire-braced sun-shade and binuclear planning is typical of his manner in the 'fifties.

Breuer (cont.) *Among the varied commissions that have come Breuer's way in recent years have been the new library block for Hunter College, New York, above, the design-overhaul of the New Haven Railroad—a projected paint-job for Train X is seen below—and the site office for the building work on the new de Bijenkorf store in Rotterdam, below right.*

Left to right: Contini, Baumfeld, Gruen, Van Leeuwen.

Victor Gruen was born in Vienna in 1903. His father was a lawyer, whose interest in the theatre and abilities as a pianist led him to represent many theatres, actors and musicians; he died when Gruen was fifteen and had no influence on his choice of career except to warn him not to become a lawyer and to bequeath him a friend who was an architect and into whose office Gruen went after training in a school of architecture. Parallel with his work in the office he studied at the Academy of Arts under Professor Behrens (passing an entrance examination which had been flunked a few years earlier by Adolf Hitler). Those who had the strongest influence on him at that time were Adolf Loos (whose obituary he wrote for a Viennese newspaper) and Le Corbusier, whose concepts of 'La Ville Radieuse' he wrote about in Austrian magazines. He spent nine years in the office of Melcher and Steiner, and then set up on his own, winning a prize in a housing competition entered with R. L. Baumfeld (one of his present partners in America) and Karl Langer (now practising in Australia). However, economic conditions didn't favour large-scale building projects at that time and work in the office was mostly concerned with decoration and

53

New York City

Victor Gruen's first store-design in the USA was Lederer's, below left, on Fifth Avenue, New York, done just before the War. Although the growth of his firm's reputation has largely depended on its skill in handling store and shopping-centre problems, its output is by no means restricted to such work, and a small office building for medical services in the Los Angeles suburbs is seen below.

industrial design (a store front for the Deutsch Men's Store was published in the ARCHITECTURAL REVIEW in 1938.) A large commission for a department store in Vienna coincided with the arrival of Hitler in Vienna, and after three months, when all seemed lost, Gruen obtained a visa for the USA and in July 1938 left with his family, T-square, drawing board, books and $8.

After a period of struggle which included helping to produce two shows on Broadway, Gruen met by chance a man he had known in Europe, who commissioned him to design a store (see page 349). The firm now has five partners and thirty-two associates, employing in all between 150 and 250 men. There are two production offices, in Los Angeles and Detroit, and four smaller offices, in New York, San Francisco, Minneapolis and Miami. The organization includes structural, mechanical, electric and civil engineers, interior designers, graphic designers and specialists in traffic planning, landscaping and other fields. Gruen believes there is a serious division in American architecture between, on the one hand, an ' austere, formalistic attitude to architecture which subordinates human needs, utility and even the rationale of technique to preconceived and personal, ascetic concepts ' and, on the other, a ' humanistic approach in which forms are derived from a careful study of physiological and psychological human needs and from the logical use of techniques '. He thinks that America is at present facing a fad for structural ingenuities, expressing itself especially in roof forms, resting on four points, three points and two points (he awaits breathlessly the one-point supported shell). He blames this, as do a number of other American architects, on the desire for publicity.

Gruen (cont.) *The most famous of Victor Gruen's shopp centres is still Northland, outside Detroit, and the air-view ab of the centre and its parking lots emphasises the sheer size of problems involved in its design. Subsequent Gruen shopping cen have made even more lavish use of applied arts—below left, is court of Southdale Centre, Minneapolis—but some have been a more intimate scale, as is the Pala, at San Jose, Cal., bel*

Gruen's proposals for A Greater Fort Worth Tomorrow are—consciously—the application of his shopping-centre planning methods to a central area, automobile penetration being restricted to peripheral parking zones, and the rest of the area made over to pedestrian circulation at various levels, below. The resultant urban scene, left, has an aspect that will be familiar to readers of THE ARCHITECTURAL REVIEW, *and its repeated pleas for the creation of pedestrian networks in central area re-developments.*

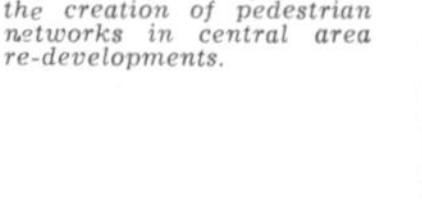

53

Pittsburgh, Pennsylvania

Paul Schweikher was born in 1903 in Denver, Colorado, where his father was President of the Western Institute of Music; he was a pianist and an organist.

Schweikher left Denver at the age of 18 to study painting at the Chicago Art Institute, but switched abruptly to architecture. What decided him was not the example of Sullivan or the presence of Wright (he didn't know of the existence of either until a year after the decision) but the city itself and the impression its vigour in life and building made on a newly arrived far-westerner. This was in the early 'twenties. After I. I. T. Schweikher worked with David Adler, well known then for his skill with 'English Georgian'; in 1927 he left for Yale, graduated in 1929 and then travelled in Europe for a year on a Matcham Fellowship.

In 1930 he returned to Chicago and found a job in the office of Robert Work and Russell Walcott; emphasis was on technical expertise—it was good discipline. After the depression life became a matter of imaginary projects: some were done with Keck of Chicago and Beatty of Wisconsin, and the group held an exhibition in a local Chicago gallery. It coincided with the visit of the International Exhibition of Architecture organized by Henry-Russell Hitchcock and Philip Johnson, and Hitchcock was impressed with their work, though it was too late to incorporate it as a local entry in the International Exhibition; instead they were invited to show at the Museum of Modern Art. The first commission came shortly after, as the outcome—a small music school and house for David Dushkin and his wife, Dorothy (counterparts, Schweikher suggests, to the Dolmetschs). Built around 1933-34, at Winnetka, Illinois, the Dushkins taught music and made instruments in it for many years.

Schweikher considers it was not until the construction of a house for himself in 1938 that he developed an idiom he felt was his own. It was in wood, Douglas fir for the structure and redwood for the cladding on a post and beam system, with pintles and dowels as connectors in place of nails. It led to the use of standard, mill-run lumber, and to an appearance sometimes described as 'stick architecture'.

The office of two assistants was joined by a partner, Ted Lamb, in 1936, and in 1938 by another partner, Winston Elting. It closed during the war, when Lamb was killed, and re-opened after as Schweikher and Elting, with Elting as administrative partner. In 1953 Schweikher went to Yale as chairman of the Department of Architecture and in 1955 to Pittsburgh as head of the Department of Architec-

Paul Schweikher's architecture has developed in a personal manner, which he first felt was truly his own in the house he built at Roselle, Ill., for himself in 1938. There—as is seen in the living-room, left, and master bedroom, right—heavy emphasis was laid on materials and structural methods. The same qualities appear nearly a decade

later in the Upton House, whose cactus garden is seen at left, and patio shelter at right, but raised there to an almost Wrightian pitch, as befits a building near Taliesin West (the house is at Scottsdale, Ariz.) and built by the same contractor. But by 1950 these qualities had begun to develop in another way and the Fine Arts Centre at Maryville,

Tenn., using different materials and housing different functions, tends towards almost Brutalist treatment in the classroom wing, left. Later work in Maryville, however, such as the chapel-theatre group, right, shows a more formal tendency which has been maintained since, even in the exotic Peruvian hill-side site which appears over the page.

Left to right, Sarah Harkness, Jean Fletcher, Robert McMillan, Norman Fletcher, Walter Gropius, John Harkness, Benjamin Thompson, Louis McMillen

TAC, The Architects' Collaborative, is one of the pioneers of group practice, and here one of the partners, Sarah Harkness, contributes an account of the working of the group and its approach to the problems of collective design.

'After ten years The Architects' Collaborative is intact, with the original partners. It was started immediately after World War II, the outcome of several coincidences amongst people who were not even all acquainted with one another, but who had each had a dream in mind of a group practice. Gropius had long before made his experiment in the Bauhaus, where both instructors and students worked collaboratively. Collaborative problems were initiated in the Harvard School of Design under his guidance, and have become a regular part of the curriculum. The Yale members of TAC—Norman Fletcher, Robert McMillan, Louis McMillen and Benjamin Thompson—had talked among themselves about setting up a group practice when they finished school. There was always an idea of making an experiment in living. This later developed into building the communities of Six Moon Hill and Five Fields.

'When the war ended everyone was free at approximately the same time. Gropius asked John Harkness (who incidentally is the only original partner of TAC who was ever a student of Gropius*) to assist him in teaching the Master's class at the Harvard School of Design. It happened that we received a letter from Norman and Jean Fletcher the same day on the subject of how to set up a practice. Putting two and two together we discussed the matter with Gropius, and it was decided within two days to set up a collaborative office in Cambridge. An added push to the establishment of the office was given when the Smith College Dormitories Competition was judged. The Fletchers and Ben Thompson, working in Michigan and Washington, DC, won first place, and John Harkness and I, then in Milton, Mass., came in second. The prize money made the first office funds.

'The first year consisted of very few jobs, but a great deal of discussion. The system of job captains and office meetings was set up. There is a meeting every Thursday noon to discuss either design or business. Meetings are called in between times whenever a subject needs special attention. Every job has to go through a meeting before the design is frozen. The job captain, together with those who have been assisting him, brings drawings, models and pertinent facts and figures to the conference room. A really "hot" design meeting often produces the best architecture. In the end, the changes are those of the job captain himself, because he has the final authority.

'Architects who practice alone have doubts sometimes about a collaborative office, fearing that if they were part of such a group they would lose their individuality. In a collaborative office, however, something is added, rather than subtracted. Creative talents are stimulated by an active environment. Another question that comes up: is it easier or harder to take a risk in a large partnership? I suppose the answer to that depends in good part on the nature of the partners. However, most risks involve backing. Without the resources of a group most risks could not be taken at all. Although collective thinking sometimes puts on the brakes, or adds safety measures, TAC has gone out on a limb on projects that would have been inconceivable for any member alone at this stage of his career.

'So much for "how" TAC works; the most interesting question is "why" it works. Is it, in reality, "Gropius's Architects' Collaborative"? No one is more annoyed by this misconception than Gropius himself. The idea of a Master surrounded by his disciples is absolutely contrary to Gropius's own precepts. Is it then a remarkable coincidence of personalities that happen to click? Actually, the personalities could not be more different. It is such a "bunch of individualists" that one might wonder how they ever happened to come together. They even have different ways of working and different ways of running a job. To some, a pencil is their sword—if they lost their hold on it they would lose control of the design. Others feel that they can guide the design by remote control. I do not think that the success of a collaborative office is dependent on a remarkable combination of particular people. It is a practical system—on the way to becoming more usual.

'If there is anything magic in the whole set-up, I believe a good deal of it may simply be a matter of numbers. The partnership (all of the partners having been trained as architects) is large enough so that it would be almost impossible for one person to dominate it. It is also large enough so that whatever idea one member may have, he will always find a willing ear to listen. If it is a constructive idea, he can always find someone to try it out on; if it is merely a "gripe," he will probably talk himself out. However, the group is small enough so that the partnership can meet round the conference table for informal discussion; small enough so that decisions do not have to be made by vote, but only by the "sense of the meeting." Our meetings have been likened to Quaker meetings in this respect.

'Just as it would be impossible to say exactly why a marriage is successful, one can only make a guess as to why an organization works. Along with diversity there must at the same time be a mutual understanding of starting points and directions. In regard to TAC, a few common denominators come to mind: first is the attitude of "live and let live," which could only be held by strong individualists; second is a social conscience—a building is not considered successful unless it answers the requirements of programme and client relations, as well as design—and finally, Gropius's definitions of Total Architecture, the "reunification of art and science," is taken for granted. Owing largely to Gropius's influence over a long period of years, most architects under forty have come out of school equipped, to the best of their ability and understanding, with aesthetic ideals in tune with the world we live in. Various aesthetic expressions have arisen, and will continue to arise. However, there is always a danger that a particular aesthetic expression will cut loose from its origin, at which point it becomes stylistic. There is also the danger that an architect, or an architectural office, that has had some measure of success will become afraid to try anything different. The aim of TAC is to keep a lively approach to every individual design problem, without forgetting the basic precepts of modern architecture that have been so well expressed by Gropius.'

*Chester Nagel, Associate in TAC, is another.

Above and top, facing page, proposed auditorium building for the Tallahassee, Florida, new civic centre. The roof structure, of tapering concrete barrel vaults, is suspended from a parabolic arch. Below, bird's eye view of the civic centre which is a pedestrian precinct. Planning consultants: Reginald Issacs, William Goodman, Hideo Sasaki.

Below, model and right, facing page, perspective of the new US Athens Embassy. The structure is a steel frame, the outer columns uphold canopied eaves, which shade glass curtain walls. The plan centres round a shaded courtyard garden.

america

Zodiac 8

William H. Jordy

The Place of Mies in American Architecture

When one thinks about it, few cultural phenomena of the postwar years are more astonishing than the contribution of Ludwig Mies van der Rohe to the United States, or the American contribution to his genius.

In 1937, when he arrived in the United States to escape Nazi oppression, who would have expected that a deliberate and austere perfectionist would so spectacularly succeed in the bustling pragmatism of his new environment. Yet when Mies (as his compound surname is commonly abbreviated) reacher the United States at the age of fifty, he had only begun his career. His practice of over thirty years in Europe had resulted in far more projects than realized buildings.

During these three decades he completed just six houses that he cares to remember, two small apartment buildings, a memorial monument, half a dozen exhibition structures and some furniture design — statistically about one realized building every two years! They were, moreover, for the most part rather small commissions which would hardly have been important were it not for their quality and their significance as embodiments of Mies' philosophy of architecture. Only a select group of architects, critics and discriminating clients knew of Mies' European work and, in fact, the first book on his work only appeared after he had been ten years in the United States, when he was nearly sixty.

In his adopted country Mies not only built many times the number of buildings which he had realized in Europe, but his commissions were far larger and more prominent. Moreover, the work of a perfectionist who had appealed to a very restricted audience suddenly became so influential that the Miesian reticulated skeletal building, infilled with glass and panels of various sorts, transformed American cities during the fifties. Overnight it seemed the skyscraper silhouette of brick and stone at the heart of large American cities gave way to highly polished reticulated metal and glass walls reflecting other highly polished reticulated metal and glass walls nearby. In the suburbs and countryside, a comparable style appeared in low, spreading shopping centers, schools and industrial complexes.

From the United States, the style spread throughout the world to become truly international. In this spread, inevitably, some buildings were good; most were mediocre. Some were appropriate for their locations; others were not. Whatever their quality or the appropriateness of their location, buildings with exposed skeletal walls extravagantly glazed came to be described (not always accurately) as « Miesian » or « American » in style. What, in fact, did Mies van der Rohe contribute to modern architecture from the time of his arrival in the United States? How did the American environment make this contribution possible? These are the questions which Mies' phenomenal American career suggests.

When Mies arrived in the United States he went to Chicago, where he eventually headed the architectural school at the Illinois Institute of Technology. His fellow refugee from Nazism, Walter Gropius, went to Harvard at the about the same time. In downtown Chicago, Mies saw for himself the world's first completely developed skyscrapers, hich had been built in the eighties and nineties of the 19th century. In the boldest of these buildings, the skyscraper is stripped to its essence.

And in its essence the skyscraper is a tall elevator building completely supported by its skeletal framing. The generous rectangular intervals created by the supporting frame can be almost completely filled with glass if the architect chooses — and the boldest architects working in Chicago in the eighties and nineties did so choose, in order to coax as much light as possible into the densely packed office buildings.

An easterner visiting Chicago at the time was astonished at the transparency of these buildings. One of the architects informed him how simply the design originated. « I get from my engineer », he said, « a statement of the minimum thickness of the steel post and its enclosure of terra cotta (required to fireproof the frame).

Then I establish the minimum depth of floor beam and the minimum height of the sill from the floor to accomodate what must go between them. These are the data of my design ». The procedure was so simple that the buildings seemed almost to design themselves. « One might think that such a problem would interest no one but an engineer », the French traveler Paul Bourget wrote in his *Outre Mer* of 1895. « Nothing of the kind! The simple power of necessity is to a certain degree a principle of beauty; and these structures so plainly manifest this necessity that you feel a strange emotion in contemplating them. It is the first draft of a new sort of art — an art of democracy made by the masses and for the masses, an art of science, where the invariability of natural laws gives to the most unbridled daring the calmness of geometrical figures ».

These early skyscrapers inevitably appealed to Mies, who has characterized his architectural ideal as « almost nothing ». In coming to Chicago, Mies happened upon the one city in the world which offered so thorough a demonstration of his philosophy of « almost nothing » in buildings so explicitly modern.

It is not that the Miesian skeletal building might have gone unrealized had Mies happened to settle in another American city. But the « bare bones » quality of early Chicago skyscrapers made him instantly aware that the prefabricated metal skeleton was the essence of technologically advanced building in the United States. Some countries possess a tradition of masonry building and the planear wall predominates; other countries, like the United States, possess a tradition of wood and metal building and emphasize the skeletal frame. The American frame, whether of wood or metal, tends to be comprised of highly standardized parts substantially prefabricated in the factory, so as to insure rapid assembly by highly paid American construction workers. Hence, in viewing the « almost nothing » of the early Chicago skyscraper, Mies happened upon a spectacular demonstration of one of the bases of American construction.

Almost nothing: by this motto Mies means that sound achitecture emerges so intimately from its structure as to seem its inevitable consequence. But Mies' « almost nothing » is a trap for the simple-minded. His deprecating phrase conceals the number of esthetic decisions which his spare architecture calls forth. We have only to look closely at the early Chicago skyscrapers in order to observe the crudity of most of them. Frames and windows are often ill proportioned. The terra cotta sheathing is often clumsy in both its profile and its surface ornamentation. The juncture of one member or one material with another is often awkward. There are, to be sure, great buildings among these early Chicago skyscrapers — especially Louis Sullivan's Carson, Pirie, Scott Department Store, which is among the masterpieces of the pioneer phase of modern architecture. The majority, however, are boldly, vitally, courageously gawky.

We could forgive some gawkiness had the boldness been maintained. But the architects of the early Chicago skyscrapers became so uncomfortable about the gawkiness of their buildings that they lost their boldness of approach. To these architects, « almost nothing » was too largely a practical program and too unconscious as an esthetic ideal. The buildings just happened to appear as they did, thanks to technological developments and the clients' desire for speedy and economical construction. Although their designers were proud of what even then wás called the « Chicago style », only Louis Sullivan fully realized what the esthetic possibilities of the style might be. To the rest, « almost nothing » eventually became something to be ashamed of as a provincial production. As East Coast architects imbibed the teachings of the French École des Beaux Arts, which were just beginning to influence American architectural schools at the end of the 19th century, they convinced the midwesterners that their buildings were not architecture at all, just naked construction. Thus, around 1900, the native

Chicago version of « almost nothing » disappeared behind masonry and terra cotta wrappings composed of fragements lifted from Gothic cathedrals and Renaissance palaces. The brash promise of the new vanished in a masquerade of the old.

With Mies, the pragmatic « almost nothing » becomes the self-conscious starting point for an architectural esthetic. He extends his « almost nothing » by his equally famous aphorism « less is more ». In reducing the buildings to its essence, he believes that the designer can concentrate on perfecting this essence, until naked construction becomes architecture. Less becomes more in that the building is objectively experienced as an intensely beautiful « thing in itself », without the interference of any literary, symbolic or sentimental recollections, and so inevitable as seemingly to transcend the uniqueness of the designer's personality. « I don't want to be interesting », Mies has said. « I want to be good ». It is precisely because Mies seeks to universalize the building experience, rather than to smite us with the uniqueness of his genius in the manner of Frank Lloyd Wright or Le Corbusier, that he has become the great grammarian of modern architecture. Like all grammarians, Mies is concerned with basic language and the manner in which language correctly and elegantly goes together.

Correctness *and* elegance: Mies makes the linearism of the steel frame the *visual* as well as the structural basis for his architecture. Hence his architecture consists in bringing the frame to the surface of the wall; in proportioning the frame to both the rectangular window intervals and the rectangular building mass and, finally, in detailing the frame itself from prefabricated parts so that what had been raw becomes beautiful. Each aspect of what at first sight seems a simple problem is fraught with the kind of perplexity for which only a genius with Mies' temperament for patient refinement could find the most compelling solution.

If, in this process of laying bare and refining, Mies makes construction beautiful, he also makes it *symbolic*. To take a specific example: since the actual supporting steel frame of multi-story buildings must be sheathed in a fireproof material, much as the frame of the early skyscrapers had been clad in terra cotta, this structural skeleton is lost to view. Mies makes it visual by attaching purely symbolic flat steel sections outside of the fireproofing. He often intensifies the symbolism by welding a projecting outrigging of I-beams to the exterior wall which rise from the bottom of the building to its cornice.

The I-beam — so-called because its cross section resembles the Roman letter « I » — is, of all steel sections, the most familiar shape in skeletal framing. This detail of the projecting I's, like all of Mies' detailing, serves in three ways: functionally (or structurally), visually and symbolically.

Functionally, the I-beams rising vertically outside the edges of the horizontal floor slabs provide enframement for the windows. Visually, they provide a slightly sculptural element for the otherwise flattish elevations, while animating the wall by seeming to open and close, like louvers, as we move past them. Visually, too, they provide architectural scale, since these rails running the full height of the wall transcend the individual window units, thereby making the building something more than a pile of tiny rectangles.

Symbolically, the I-beams, as the basic shape for skeletal framing, create a modern equivalent for the classical pilasters affixed to Renaissance buildings. Moreover, in being welded to the outside edges of the horizontal floor slabs, so as to create a double plane of crossing verticals over horizontals, each element in the construction appears as a separate entity, literally coming together in order to create the building. Hence not only are the structural *parts* made symbolically visual, but so is the structural *process*.

Were there time, we might examine the other refinements by which Mies makes more of less. We might observe how he uses the entire alphabet of structural steel shapes — the I's, H's, L's, U-shaped channels and flat plates — in order to create modern equivalents for the carved moldings of the past. Now he recesses a steel section below the plane of the wall; now he projects sections like his I-beam outrigging; again he welds a complex of shapes together so as to turn a corner.

Were there time we might also analyze how thick members combine with thin; how brick elegantly collides with steel, and steel with glass. Quite obviously, in designing the building in terms of the pieces which comprise it, and then refining these pieces for eventual assembly, Mies has exerted a profound effect on architectural prefabrication.

Herein lies his immense American, and later worldwide, success. He has taught that architecture may emerge from the discriminating design and use of the prefabricated part produced by the most advanced technology. As a grammarian, Mies expected his language to be used by others. Indeed, the widespread use of his ideas has validated its universal quality. Inevitably, the achievements of his disciples and imitators have ranged the gamut of quality from superb to awful. But this is the fate of any common language.

Mies' language must be judged, first, by looking at those buildings which are closest to Mies in that they both frankly resemble his work and partake in some measure of its quality. Thus, to mention only the familiar vanguard, there is Eero Saarinen's General Motors Technical Center. There are the best of the business buildings by the sizeable firm of Skidmore, Owings and Merrill, as inspired by the leadership of the chief designer in the New York office, Gordon Bunshaft. There are the suburban houses of Philip Johnson, Mies' closest disciple who wrote the first book on his mentor and collaborated with him on the renowned Seagram Building in New York.

In both extending and popularizing Miesian ideas, the buildings of these architects have been quite as influential as Mies' own work in spreading his gospel. But a common language has also to be judged by the results produced by those less competent, and even perhaps by those positively incompetent.

At its lowest common denominator, the Miesian esthetic is reduced to the routine repetition of lines and panels, extended horizontally or heaped vertically until the grid either meets the client's needs or exhausts his pocketbook. Where Mies and his most influential disciples design a *building*, low level « Miesians » (so-called) more or less blindly lift a *system* from manufacturers' catalogues. The subtlety of Mies' proportions and scale disappears. So does the refinement of his profiling of components. His restraint is customarily replaced by billboard gaud and glitter. Vulgar as these routine buildings are, however, Miesian language at least gives them a degree of discipline, precision and relevance to modern technological processes. Since a certain amount of vulgarity is as inevitable in architectural as in verbal language, the controls implicit in the Miesian esthetic tend to mitigate the most virulent tastelessness.

If Miesian language possesses the virtue of discipline, is intensity of discipline purchased at the expense of a wide range of expressiveness? Some say it is, and on two grounds. First, there are those who protest Mies' continous use of rectangular massing in his American work, asserting that he fails to express the function of his buildings in any significant manner. The same boxy container serves as a house, a classroom, a theater, a chapel. Then, there are those who condemn the rationalistic severity of Mies' esthetic for too drastically limiting the emotional range of his buildings — so much so that the experience provided by one of them is identical for all. The first criticism holds that Mies' architecture is too abstract; the secondo that it is too austere. How justified are these complaints?

Ever since his arrival in the United States, Mies has been so intent in developing an esthetic for the building envelope that he has generally slighted the space which it envelopes. His exteriors record interior space only insofar as the interior space is one large room equivalent to the box enclosing it, or insofar as the gridded frame suggests the possibility of compartmentalizing the space inside into repetitive cubicles. If the interior spaces of these ideal enclosures are functional, they are so in the negative sense that a regularly framed space can, like a warehouse, contain almost anything.

Thus such an enormous glass room as Mies' architectural building at the Illinois Institute of Technology in Chicago accomodates whatever happens within it, in the same manner that a trunk holds whatever can be stuffed into it. The handsome proportions of the room are considerably concealed by the random placement of obstacles inside. Aside from the overall proportions of the room, the architect relinquishes all control of interior space. As the critic Arthur Drexler has pointed out, in only two of Mies, enormous boxes — neither of them realized — has he conditioned the interior space in a very positive manner. In one, an enormous box projected for the Library of the Illinois Institute of Technology, a central court somewhat modulates the space. In the other, his project for a convention hall for Chicago is housed in so vast a box that the sheer grandiosity of the space would overwhelm whatever went into it.

If the raw space of these neutral containers is in any way inadequate for its function, elaborate mechanical equipment compensates for the deficiencies of the ideal building. Such equipment has proliferated since World II in the United States as in no other country. Air conditioning corrects excessive hot or cold occasioned by large areas of glass. Tinted panes counteract glare. Luminous ceillings dispell shadow at the centers of very deep buildings. But there are those who ask whether the architect should relegate so much of his traditional concern for the expression of function to machinery buried in the innards of his building.

Of the extremely abstract spaces which mechanical equipment makes viable, it may almost be said that they work *in spite* of the architect. To be sure, vast, mechanized spaces in which anything can happen have the functional advantage of maximum flexibility, and hence they will certainly remain a necessity for much future building. But many architects feel it imperative to reassert their ancient prerogative of molding beautiful spaces around specific activities. Others, admitting the increasing role of mechanical equipment in building, feel equally strongly about giving visual expression to this buried complexity. Future talks in this series will make clear the thinking of some architectural leaders with respect to making the function of the building more vivid in terms of both its space and its machinery.

So much for criticisms of Mies' abstractness. What about his austerity? Some architects are enriching the Miesian esthetic by making it more decorative. By screening and ornamenting his structure in various ways, its austerity is banished. Some are exploring more dramatic kinds of structure: vaults, domes, curved and folded forms instead of Mies, reticulated skeleton. Still others are extending his classicistic approach to the building with rather literal images of classical porticoes, cellas and entablatures, thus re-invoking the Beaux Arts classicistic image from which modern architecture once revolted. That such elaboration of Miesian themes is immensely expanding the design potential available to the modern architect is undeniable. It is equally true that much of this elaboration of Mies represents the superficial appeal of easily understood surface effects, and is therefore less profound than extensions of his esthetic based on the articulation of space and equipment.

Before welcoming this diversely enriched Miesian esthetic, therefore, should we not ask whether the range of experience provided by his buildings is not somewhat wider than it might at first appear? Admittedly, like all geniuses of abnegation, Mies has sought experience through exclusion rather than abundance. In his emphasis on deliberation, discreteness and discrimination, he focuses exclusively on the idealizing art of rationalization within such rigorous limits as always to suggest that he is creating the same building over and over, just as Piet Mondrian's canvases always suggest the same picture. But the fact that Mies makes something new of something which persists with all the absoluteness of a universal prototype is precisely the dramatic element in what is carefully calculated as an undramatic development. The Greek Temple of Poseidon at Paestum becomes the Parthenon. The two temples are the same temple, and yet the ruggedness of the one with respect to the litheness of the other results in two completely different experiences. Just so, with Mies' architecture. His Lake Shore Apartmente and the Seagram Building are exactly the same building creating different experiences.

Relative to one another, the Paestum-like severity of Lake Shore contrasts with the Parthenaic refinement of the Seagram. In the Lake Shore Apartments, vertical blocks are set at right angles to one another across a narrow interval of space in such a manner that their static shapes are always in tension with one another. As we circle the complex, we find that it possesses neither a true « front » nor a true « back ». We always see the narrow side of one block against the broad side of the other in a constantly changing relationship. The I-beam projections from the walls appear to close over the windows seen obliquely and open over those seen head-on, while in moving so as to open those which closed we automatically close those which were open. The Seagram Building, on the other hand, reconciles the Lake Shore paradox of static elements in perpetual disequilibrium. The bronze building rises like a dense, dark cliff behind the absolute void of its entrance plaza. The axis of the plaza culminates in the formal grandeur of the entrance with its two-story stilts each backed by the pylons of the elevator shafts. Where, in the window grid of the Lake Shore Apartments, horizontals constantly challenge the verticals, this tension too is reconciled in the Seagram by the clear affirmation of verticality. In the Lake Shore, then, a perpetual tension; in the Seagram, the reconciliation of tension in climax.

Thus Mies' neoclassicism is only partly apprehended in the manner in which he conceives his architectural vocabulary. He is also profoundly neoclassical in the way in which he squeezes different kinds of experience from his universal image. If his emotional range is narrow, it is its very narrowness which makes his point. He does not turn somersaults to create new experience. A change of material, a shift of proportions, an adjustment in profile, a realignment of his simple masses and — with « almost nothing! » — what was becomes something new, while yet remaining what it was. The Temple of Poseidon at Paestum becomes the Parthenon.

How much with how little! The steel I-beam from the rolling mill becomes a structural, visual and symbolic entity for the creation of beautiful buildings. The same building becomes a different building. If so many architects today owe so much to Mies even in rebelling against him, it is because his « almost nothing » contains the paradoxical plenitude of an elemental demonstration.

William H. Jordy

1

Of all the European architects who have emigrated to America since 1933, Breuer is, perhaps, the one who has most easily, and, I daresay, most naturally shared in the aspirations and limits of American culture. While Gropius has never been able to eliminate a certain tension between his vision of the world and the ideological vacuum of an America unprotected against the threat of tecnocracy, Breuer has not had to force his natural disposition towards problems in the development of society in order to adhere unreservedly to an attitude of confidence in progress, progress understood as the inevitable development of a dynamic and open social situation.
It is this optimism, far from any possibility of compromise in the narrow framework of his profession, which has spared Breuer that formal uncertainty typical of so many architects of his generation; it has permitted him to follow with admirable coherence a line of research embracing the whole gamut of architectonic activity, from industrial design to town-planning. In respect to town-planning, it might be useful to recall here his «Stuyvesant Town» quarter in New York. On re-examination after many years, despite its adherence to a speculative programme in its adhesion to the continuity of the walled city, to the urban aspect of large blocks of flats raised to considerable heights, this quarter is unexpectedly immediate and a realistic contribution to the correct solution of a theme which in recent years, especially in Italian circles, has more and more been taking on a precise ideological content.
Looking to the experience of « Stuyvesant Town » may be useful as a proof of the interest and fertility of Breuer's results even on a plane transcending its own interests. The exceptionally high quality of these products makes it possible for them to have a much greater range of influence and a power of communication not limited by the pragmatical vision which brought them into being.
Breuer undoubtedly gives the best of himself in that part of his production in which there figures the image of the human being studied with exemplary devotion and refinement in his activities and in his physical and psychological reality. The objects that he derives from this careful functional analysis, particularly chairs and houses, which are his favourite themes, are a blend of a certain provisional and discreet air with the brilliance of a severely controlled form living on its reactions with light, atmosphere, sound, and heat,

Paolo Portoghesi

Marcel Breuer

and on its relationships with the environment and the tenant himself.

Breuer's houses all show the unpretentious warmth characteristic of utility objects, and programmatically refuse any kind of exaggerated idiom requiring formal justification and breaking up that legible and comprehensible character of the whole spatial organism which is among the most obvious premisses of Breuer's method.

Once found in the relation between form and function (obviously admitting a psycological range of functions) the motive for establishing a relationship with the user, the architect rids his architectonic text of all superstructure such as might cause a break or interruption in this contact, and tends to lead all formal aspects towards this immediacy of relation.

And Breuer is not much concerned if, as a result of this, the architect's function as a guide is overwhelmed by his desire to further, and therefore, to express a certain style of life. There being little point in distinguishing between the terms «guide» and «serve» in this architect's activity the problem is no longer that of finding a correct distribution of these two modes of creation, but that of seeking a sound direct relation without concerning oneself about anything else.

It is on this plane of adherence to a way of life that Breuer interprets the American vernacular tradition (in Italy we would say « spontaneous »), and the almost folk-like character of some of his details become the fascinating images that have in recent years acquired an international reputation.

Breuer's neatness, naturalness, and facility are the consequence not only of a private call but also of a programme which never idealizes expressive means, the terms of an idiomatic relationship, but uses them with propriety, mistrusting lofty tones, vernacular complexity, the limits imposed on the building by respect for certain laws having nothing to do with the user's visual experience, remaining the sterile object of the technical speculations of the chosen. In other words, Breuer firmly and didactically opposes that « architecture for architects » which is the obvious limit of a whole school of methodology.

Think of the neat rhythm of the Chamberlain house (1940) planned with Gropius, and of its lack of any vernacular compromises. The perfection of the formal result is related to the possibility of endlessly refining the distributional scheme

1. Marcel Breuer.
2. Living room, Gagarin house, Conn.

and derives from the anticipation of the movements and acts which will be carried out in that space.

This and Breuer's successive experiences are so many portraits of commissioners often dynamic and extrovert to whom the architect at times makes suggestions as to the interior, advising a pause for a moment's reflection; but with quiet discretion, without giving the impression of a programme.

The realization of this aesthetic scheme of quiet and open architectonic discourse limited to suggesting possible content, is articulated in a series of highly successful images deeply rooted in time and yet effectively resistant to time: Geller house, Thompson house, Clark house, and Wolfson house - buildings in which it is difficult to detect the development of a definite theme except by concentrating on the continual re-appearance of those values of texture, and grain, of that interpretation of material in which Breuer's rationalistic auto-criticism becomes manifest.

Even when the occasion induces him to experiment with partially blocked volumetrical forms, contradicting his devotion to neo-plasticism understood more as a methodological starting point than as his repertory, he always recovers in his definition of the interior-exterior relationship the same anti-rhetorical resolution, which leads him to reject und undercut all formal schemes, breaking up their intellectualistic rigidity.

A different meaning appears from the study of Breuer's results in the great themes undertaken in recent years. The Unesco building in Paris, the Bijenkorf store in Rotterdam, St. John's Church in Collegeville, Minn., and the American Embassy in the Hague are all buildings which instead of expressing, as the previously mentioned constructions, the certainty of a long-experimented method, seem rather to point to the uncertainty of one who cannot quite adapt the expressive means of his repertory to the new scale of his commitment. It is significant that the crisis of psychological functionalism appears at the point in which adherence to the human parameter can no longer be direct, and a much more precise ideological equipment is required to make a choice.

The Unesco building — which with its concavity in tension repeats the suggestion of a pre-existent town-plan — takes its place onto the Parisian scene with all the power and peremptory character of a new event; but in the delicate and extremely elegant scoring of the façade and in the weak connexion between the various bodies, it reveals the tendency of the author to surrender before the opposing temptations of technological hedonism and longing for the plastic and sculptural prestige of form. This clash resolves itself into neither a quiet balance nor the highly dramatic.

Again, the meeting of architecture, sculpture, and painting, which promised to be the main point of interest in this building, is rather disappointing in the casualness of their association and the frequently evasive use of the method of providing the work of art with a neutral background so as not to interfere with its visual value. Equally disappointing in regard to its exterior is the Bijenkorf store in Rotterdam, which made many regret the passing of the former building by Dudok, even though Gabo's exciting sculpture facing it gains power by its contrast with the enormous blind wall covered with hexagonal plates. This is a defect of scale in which the limpid simplicity, so typical of Breuer, seen in the division is degraded to the point of nearly becoming a monument of the elementary.

A risk also run by he plan for th American Embassy in the Hague in which the architect, developing with unwonted severity his favourite theme of the trapezoid, seems to be aiming at a paradoxical and ironic version of the mannered neo-classicism which has won over so many American architects of his generation.

The frankest and most explicit reaction of Breuer's to a great theme is perhaps to be found in the St. John's Church in Collegeville, Minn., where the analysis of the psychological value of the single elements making up the organism generates a volumetrical articulation of considerable interest. The great lamellar steeple which assumes the function of an element of attraction and invitation, takes on an emblematic value from the simplicity and visual power of the design: it leaves its mark on the memory with the effectiveness of a symbol.

This result should be considered in the light of Breuer's activity as a designer, and indicates how interrelated his experiences are.

There is perhaps a contrast between the plastic and scenographic effectiveness found in the great screen of the steeple and the static character of the church interior, which stems from the rigid application of a structural rule; but on the whole the work shows how the contribution of Breuer, a practicing and deeply commited architect, cannot easily be classified and artificially delimited, and should rather be considered an open critical problem of great importance for the history of these difficult years.

Paolo Portoghesi

1

Fourth in a series of Design Firm Case Studies:

VICTOR GRUEN ASSOCIATES

Architects-city planners who started out in the interiors field and have never left it

Bank of America, Beverly Hills

3 Proposed Syracuse plaza

(On 3, Gruen's collaborators were Ketcham-Miller-Arnold, Gordon Schopfer, Raymond & May. On 4, Gruen Associates collaborated with John Carl Warnecke & Associates and Gardner A. Dailey & Associates.)

4 San Francisco proposals

gordon sommers

5 Rochester Midtown Plaza (detail)

From a door handle to a community

How it happened that an architect who designed interiors went on to plan

As a recognized profession the rehabilitation of old cities and planning of entirely new communities is relatively new—in this country and for that matter anywhere in the world. But it is entirely logical for it to spring up in times like these. The boom in our population and even more spectacular changes in our economy, communications, and way of life have burst the seams of our communities and reduced the usefulness of many of our existing centers to such a point that a process of decay has set in. We must both rebuild and build new, and we cannot do it at the comfortable pace of old but in huge leaps of decision and achievement that represent commitments and investments of frightening scope. We cannot just let things happen. We cannot afford mistakes. Planning is called for.

The firm of Victor Gruen Associates, employing about 200 people in five permanent offices—Los Angeles, New York, San Francisco, Chicago, and Minneapolis—is one of the leading purveyors of planning service, famous for solutions to the problems of downtown rehabilitiation which it has provided for the municipalities of Fort Worth, Detroit, Syracuse, Rochester, and San Francisco—in some cases alone, in other cases in collaboration with local architects. *Architects* of course, since city planners are invariably architects, though city planning necessarily involves industrial planning, geology, population studies, climate studies, landscape architecture, and a host of other vocational specialities. Victor Gruen Associates are officially *architects and engineers,* but the firm also has staffs of landscape architects, of graphic designers, and of interior designers. It uses these staffs to plan cities, city centers and shopping centers, to design and erect individual buildings in or out of these centers, and in some cases to design and execute the interiors of those buildings. That is one of the reasons why this firm of architects and engineers is of some interest to the interiors field. The other reasons are that Victor Gruen, A.I.A., the head of the firm, was active in the interiors field *before* he entered city planning, and that the attitudes and principles indicated in his smaller early works (published in *Interiors*) prevail in the firm's major assignments today, and are immensely influential in department store, supermarket, motel, and restaurant interiors throughout the country.

Gruen's "open Sesame": the shopping center

In spite of their obvious importance, city planners don't often succeed in turning their brain children into tangible and detailed structures—at least not in the short time that city planning has been recognized. Realization of the most ambitious urban schemes requires decades, and we have yet to see the completion of any.

Many an architect has dreamt of vast total designs complete from land and traffic studies to the placement of the last tree, street sign, and building. Very few have seen their dreams come true. Gruen is one of them, and the reason for his practical success is that at some point in his career he applied his interest in the slow-moving field of city planning to the fast-moving department store field. What this required was a stroke of genius—to see that in a country whose population moved on wheels, the community center did not need to be a *residential* cluster, but might well be a *shopping cluster.* He realized that every center worthy of the name—and worthy, also, of dedicated planning and design—must offer cultural and human amenities: visual delights, facilities for recreation and repose, spaces designed for no other purpose but to walk, talk, sit, and play in.

In the past such centers have been conceived only as urban phenomena—village squares, city plazas or malls. Few cities of the old world are without them, but unfortunately the same cannot be said for the vast majority of small and medium-sized American towns. Gruen has succeeded in pointing out that in the automobile age such magnets for gregarious gatherings need not be in towns, and that indeed they might have greater drawing power in dispersed suburban land or even open country. Certainly they could be built at relatively low cost because of lower land values there. Combine such amenities with a full range of small and large stores and plenty of free parking space anywhere on our nation's network of highways and you can be sure that the stores will be well filled.

Realizing these facts, and persuading others of them, provided Gruen not merely with a respected entry to the planning field, but gave him rare practical opportunities to show what he could do. It is however also important that he was able to carry out his all-encompassing ideas with a caliber of design which was high in every detail. Northland Shopping Center near Detroit, Eastland Shopping Center near Detroit, and Southdale Shopping Center near Minneapolis—to name only a few of the twelve major centers completed by the firm—have been pioneer achievements not only from the standpoint of planning but also for their design quality in every aspect from the largest structures to the signs, lighting, landscaping, and the works of art for which Gruen campaigns.

Meantime the firm has achieved a notable record in architectural assignments carried off with distinction, including the Tishman office buildings in Los Angeles, the Wilshire Terrace luxury apartments in Los Angeles (overleaf), Joseph Magnin's, Las Vegas (June 1959 *Interiors*), the City National Bank in Palm Springs (pages 58 and 59 of this issue), the Penn Fruit Supermarket in New Jersey (pages 64 and 65), and The May Company store in Cleveland (pages 60 and 61). In many of these, the Gruen organization has designed and executed the interiors landscaping.

The beginning; the metamorphosis

Obviously such a record requires an efficient organization well supplied with talent — diversified talent. Gruen has been building such an organization for the last fifteen years. But Gruen's history before the founding of the firm reveals that the largeness of outlook, versatility of talent, and flexibility of mind required by an operation of such scale and diversity were shaping an exceptionally varied career for Gruen well before he had a staff.

He was born in Vienna 57 years ago, and trained at Vienna's Technological Institute, Advanced Division of Building and Construction, as well as Vienna's Academy of Fine Arts. He began his career there first in an architectural firm, then on his own, concentrating principally on store fronts and interiors. In 1938, when he arrived in New York penniless and of course without an architectural license, he found it possible to make a living in display, working for Ivel Corporation and on the General Motors Futurama at the *ities; how his organization grew; how it operates in diverse fields*

'ew York World's Fair. Architectural pportunity was still at depression ebb, nd his association, as designer, with Iorris Ketchum Jr., as architect, on ,ederer's small Fifth Avenue handbag tore, was a golden windfall. Still conidered one of Fifth Avenue's most up-)-date establishments, it put both men 1 the forefront of the specialty store eld, enabling Gruen to open his own esign office. Among his clients was a 'omen's wear chain, Grayson's, whose apid growth all over the country was ot impeded by the war. Because many f its units were going up around Los ngeles, Gruen opened a second office iere—a toe hold which has become the urgest of his five offices. He has since ivided his time between Los Angeles nd New York, has homes in both cities. 1 1949, having built up a formidable eputation as an avant-garde designer f small shops, he won his first opporınity in the big store field with Million's, a two-story department store in os Angeles. It was surrounded by a eld that provided not quite enough arking space. Gruen solved the problem y using the store's roof for that purose, working a system of sweeping amps into the imposing concrete buildıg. He also designed the interiors, hich, on re-examination, look as iough they had been done yesterday October 1949 *Interiors*).

he qualities which enabled Greun to ansform himself from a store designer) a regional planner are rare, perhaps nique. The boldness indispensable even or conceiving such a step does not show, ıst that famous traditional Viennese narm (he retains some accent). Only ter does one sense his perceptiveness s an analyst of planning problems, and is outstanding ability to state his case early and forcefully, on the lecture latform, in print, and in decision-makıg conclaves. He is the author of inımerable articles and two books, *How Live with Your Architect*, and, with arry Smith, *Shopping Towns, U.S.A. -The Planning of Shopping Centers* to be reviewed here shortly). His onors include the Gold Medal of the .I.A. Memphis Chapter; Hall of Fame, oston Conference in Distribution; 7 onor and Merit Awards, A.I.A.

mong the firm's shopping centers are herry Hill in Delaware, N.J.; Conejo alley in California; Eastland in Deoit; Maryvale in Phoenix; Northland 1 Detroit; Midtown Plaza in Rochester; South Shore Plaza in Boston; Southdale in Minneapolis.

Among the firm's community planning projects are Coronado in El Paso; Huntington Shores in Huntington Beach, California; Laguna Niguel (on our cover) in California; Marina Del Rey in Los Angeles; Palos Verdes Peninsula. Among urban renewal studies are Charles River Park, Boston; Fort Worth, Fresno; Green Bay, Wisconsin. In urban planning and the shopping center field, the firm is conceded to be a creator of concepts as well as a leading performer.

The quality of the architecture may be suggested in the collection of jobs illustrated on the following pages. In recent years the firm has worked more and more with concrete slab structures of a powerful sculptural quality. As far as interiors are concerned, the firm's established style has neither changed nor dated since the early fifties. It is architectural and strong, sometimes very rich, uses works of commissioned art impressively.

Partners, Associates, and a few others

Rudi L. Baumfeld, Partner in charge of Architecture, is like Gruen a Viennese born in 1903, and trained at the same Technical Institute, also graduating from the Federal Academy of Fine Arts and the Master School for Architecture in Vienna. His own practice in Vienna ranged from a war memorial through large and small residences, factories, and specialty stores. He joined Gruen as chief draftsman in 1943.

Edgardo Contini, Partner in Charge of Engineering, a summa cum laude graduate of the University of Rome's Department of Engineering, has had an award-garnished career in Rome and in the United States, has been with Gruen since 1951.

Karl O. Van Leuven, Jr., Partner in Charge of Development, is a 46-year-old, Missouri-born, University of California and Art Center School (Los Angeles) graduate who started as a Walt Disney artist and joined Gruen in 1941.

Ben Southland, Partner in Charge of Planning, is a 43-year-old registered architect, graduate of the University of Southern California. He joined Gruen in 1948.

Herman Guttman, Partner in Charge of Production, is a 42-year-old Minnesotan with a Bachelor of Architecture from the University there. He joined Gruen in 1945.

1

3

2

4

5

6

7

1 VICTOR GRUEN, A.I.A.,
senior partner
2 RUDI L. BAUMFELD,
partner in charge of architecture
3 HERMAN GUTTMAN,
partner in charge of production
4 EDGARDO CONTINI,
partner in charge of engineering
5 KARL VAN LEUVEN, JR.
partner in charge of development
6 BEN SOUTHLAND
partner in charge of planning
7 OLIVE EMSLIE
associate in charge of interior design, New York office

MBA

1937–1981

Marcel Breuer Associates

Headquarters
New York, NY

1937 Other Locations
Paris, France

Founding and Key Partners
Marcel Breuer (founding principal), Herbert Beckhard, Murray Emslie, Hamilton Smith, Robert F. Gatje, Tician Papachristou

1981

PROCESS:Architecture, September 1982

Hungarian-born architect Marcel Breuer established his own practice in New York City in 1946, following partnerships with F.R.S. Yorke in London, from 1935 to 1937, and Walter Gropius in Cambridge, Massachusetts, from 1937 to 1941. It was Gropius, as chair of the newly established Graduate School of Design at Harvard University, who invited Breuer to teach and practice in the United States in 1937. And it was also Gropius who had earlier lured Breuer to the return to the Bauhaus in Dessau, Germany, where he had been a student from 1921 to 1924, to be master of the joinery workshop as well as the designer of the new building's interiors.

In the immediate postwar years, Breuer's New York office had few commissions. During this time he built his own house in New Canaan, Connecticut, with wood siding and a dramatically cantilevered porch originally tethered by marine cables. Yet soon Breuer's widely publicized, butterfly-roofed *House in the Garden*, which was constructed full scale in the courtyard of the Museum of Modern Art in the summer of 1949, brought him international notoriety and a surge in commissions at home and abroad.

The firm went through a number of changes in the following years. Breuer opened a satellite office in Paris in 1964 to oversee the firm's increasing number of European commissions. In 1964 he took on four partners—Herbert Beckhard, Murray Emslie, Hamilton Smith, and Robert F. Gatje—and changed the firm's name to Marcel Breuer and Associates; a year later Emslie left and was replaced by Tician Papachristou. Unlike Gropius's role among the partners of The Architects Collaborative, Breuer maintained a more hierarchical model in which he directed all major decisions.

Known for robust concrete buildings with bold structural forms and dramatic cantilevers, Breuer's architecture after 1945 became synonymous with an expressive postwar modernism. By the late 1950s his practice was truly global, with realized projects in the United States, Europe, and South America; the 1970s brought commissions in the Near East (unrealized) and Australia. Notable buildings abroad include The UNESCO Headquarters in Paris (1952–1958), his first large-scale public building and the turning point in a shift to more international work; IBM Research Center (1960–1962) in La Gaude, France; and Hotel le Flaine (1961–1976) near Chamonix, France. Significant US projects in this period included the Whitney Museum of American Art (1963–1964) in New York City, with its bold reverse ziggurat façade, and St. John's Abbey Church and University Complex (1954–1968) in Minnesota, though Breuer also maintained a steady stream of single-family residential projects as well.

In poor health, Breuer retired in 1976, and the firm made a subtle name change to Marcel Breuer Associates. He died in New York City in 1981. — ARL

1937–
1969

The Office of Mies van der Rohe

Headquarters
Chicago, IL

1937 Founding and Key Partners
Ludwig Mies van der Rohe (founding principal), Joseph Y. Fujikawa, Bruno Conterato, Dirk Lohan, Gene Summers

1969

Werner Blaser

In 1960, curator Arthur Drexler wrote that German émigré Ludwig Mies van der Rohe was "the architect par excellence of civilization, of law and order, of the great metropolis."[1] Mies' career can be seen as having two acts: the first in Germany during the Weimar period, and the second in Chicago, where his modernist legacy would influence architectural practice for decades to come. Sigfried Giedion and other historians argued for Mies's preeminence among what came to be referred to as the "Second Chicago School," credited with the revival of Chicago architecture following the building lull of the Great Depression and World War II.[2] Influenced by his teachings at IIT and mentored in his office, Mies's protégés—often dressed like their guru in suit and tie, drawing with soft lead, and smoking cigars—went on to lead offices that sought to continue his legacy of structurally expressive, formally minimal, and technically elegant buildings in the United States and abroad.

"Here we shall take our stand," Mies declared at his inaugural speech as director of the Department of Architecture at the Illinois Institute of Technology in 1938. Chicago architects were apparently ready and welcome to Mies's changing ways: William Holabird, of Holabird & Root—a prominent designer of the First Chicago School—was instrumental in drawing Mies to the city, seeking to change the direction of IIT's languishing Beaux-Arts pedagogy.[3] As director, Mies led an extensive campus building program, which culminated in the design of its school of architecture, Crown Hall (1956). In the early years following his emigration from Germany, Mies built significantly, if not prolifically, in the US through projects such as the Farnsworth House (1946–1951), crystallizing and spreading his design methodology through his students and staff in particular.

During this period, Mies's Chicago office, in a loft at 230 East Ohio Street, consisted mostly of young men who had been his students at IIT. Compared to the large corporate firms whose work would be indebted to his own in the coming decades, Mies's office was fairly small in size, and staff positions and hierarchy were never officially stated. Nonetheless, designers like Gene Summers, who rose to become Mies's right-hand man as the architect's mobility decreased in later years, were afforded both opportunities and mentoring. While Summers formalized the professional and managerial operations of the office amid Mies's increasingly frequent absences, it was Mies's own connection to real estate developer Herbert Greenwald that resulted in the high-rise buildings that stand among the firm's crowning achievements.

In 1954, seven years after the first major retrospective of his work at the Museum of Modern Art in New York City (1947), Mies returned to work in the city following his commission to design an office building for the Seagram Company. Several large commissions for urban tower complexes followed in the United States and Canada, including the Toronto Dominion Center (1963–1970), Westmount Square (1964–1968) in Montreal, and the Chicago Federal Center (1974). In the same period the unrealized design of an office building for Bacardi in Cuba led to a more modest building for the company in Mexico City (to which its operations had moved after the Cuban Revolution), as well as to the clear-span structural type that found its fullest realization in the Neue Nationalgalerie (1962–1968), the project that marked Mies's postwar return to building in West Germany.

After Mies' death in 1969, his eponymously named office closed, though successors Joseph Fujikawa, Bruce Conterato, and Dirk Lohan went on to found the firm that eventually became known as Goettsch Partners. — CB

① Arthur Drexler, *Ludwig Mies van der Rohe* (New York: George Braziller, 1960): 9.

② See Sigfried Giedion, *Space, Time and Architecture*, 3rd ed. (Cambridge, MA: Harvard University Press, 1956): 368–393.

③ See Cammie McAtee, "Alien #5044325: Mies's First Trip to America," in Phyllis Lambert, ed., *Mies in America* (Montreal and New York: Canadian Centre for Architecture and Whitney Museum of American Art, 2001): 133–185.

The Eggers Group

Headquarters
New York, NY

1937 Successor Firm To
John Russell Pope (1903–1937)

Founding and Key Partners
Otto Reinhold Eggers, Daniel Paul Higgins (founding principals), Theodore J. Young, George S. Holderness, Bradford N. Clark, Richard M. Pott, R. Jackson Smith, David L. Eggers, Richard F. Higgins

1994

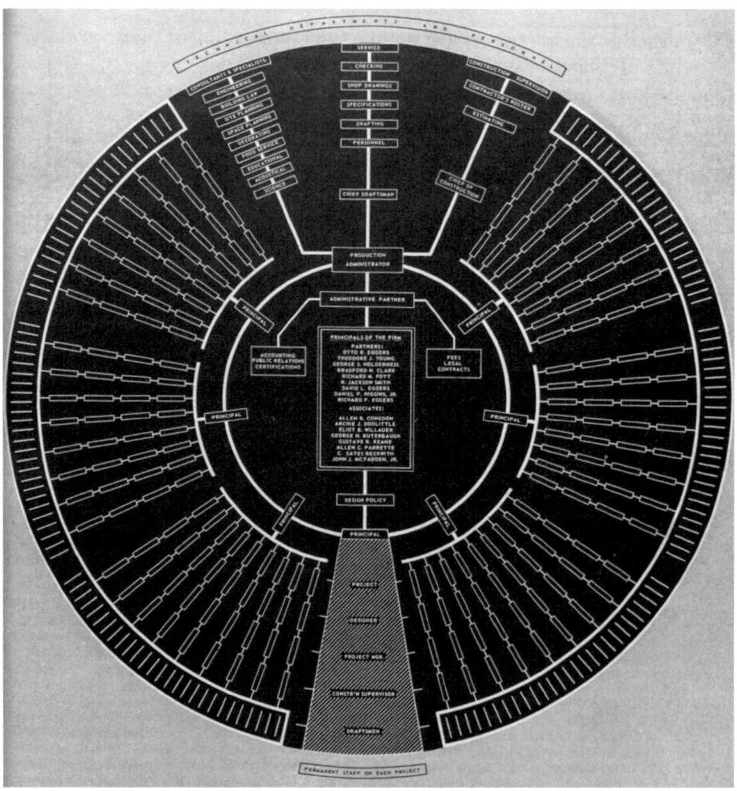

Architectural Record, April 1960

Otto Eggers and Daniel Higgins opened their office in New York in 1937, inheriting the practice and projects of neoclassical architect John Russell Pope upon his death. Both Eggers and Higgins were longtime members of Pope's office and had been instrumental in the firm's design of both the Thomas Jefferson Memorial and the National Gallery of Art in Washington, D.C. After taking over Pope's ongoing projects and renaming the firm Eggers & Higgins, throughout the 1940s, the office continued to build in the neoclassical style for which Pope had been famous. Whereas Pope had kept his office relatively small during his lifetime, Eggers and Higgins now combined this architectural language with an approach to the design of building structures that allowed the firm to expand its scope and grow rapidly. Major projects of this time included the Brooklyn War Memorial, the Vanderbilt Law School Building, and the Indiana University campus.

Although the firm would later gain a reputation for its expertise in athletic facilities, during the 1950s the projects undertaken by the office varied greatly in terms of scale and program. The office worked on interiors, housing, university campuses, federal buildings, public institutions, and memorials. In this period Eggers & Higgins also undertook its only international project, the US Embassy in Ankara (1947–1953). In marked contrast to the modernist designs sought by the Federal Building Operations (FBO) office of the US State Department after 1954, the Ankara embassy was one of the last instances in the 1950s in which the FBO office approved the construction of a Beaux-Arts style building abroad.

In 1953, Eggers & Higgins restructured into a multiple partnership, which allowed principals to specialize in specific building typologies and spurred additional growth. By 1958, the office had completed over one thousand commissions and was the fourth largest architecture firm in the country, with over 250 employees. During the 1960s, the office continued to produce work across the Eastern United States, but the quantity of the firm's commissions declined. Significant projects in this period included the Jacob Javits Federal Building and One Pace Plaza at Pace University in New York and Eigenmann Hall at Indiana University.

In 1970, the office was rebranded as The Eggers Partnership. Soon after, in 1976, the office became a professional corporation and was renamed again as The Eggers Group. The firm continued in operation until 1994, when it was bought and incorporated into the New York office of Hillier Architecture. At the time of its acquisition, The Eggers Group had forty employees. — JJ

1938–1985

Arthur B. Froehlich and Associates

Headquarters
Los Angeles, CA

Other Locations
1938 Philadelphia, PA

Founding Partner
Arthur B. Froehlich

1985

Paul Williams (left) and Arthur B. Froehlich (right). Photographer: Rothschild Photo, Herald Examiner Collection, Los Angeles Public Library

Arthur Froehlich founded his office in Los Angeles in 1938, with the firm's early work consisting of a series of Von's grocery stores and other small residential and commercial projects in the city. Following the completion of the firm's first major project, the Hollywood Park Club racetrack, in the early 1940s. Arthur Froelich & Associates went on to specialize in and build its reputation on the design of racetracks, including Keeneland in Lexington, Kentucky and two of New York State's four principal tracks, Belmont Park in Elmont and Aqueduct in Queens, New York City. In the 1950s, the firm opened a second office in Philadelphia to accommodate its numerous racetrack projects in the eastern United States.

In 1955, the Venezuelan government of Marcos Perez Jimenez approached Arthur Froehlich & Associates to design its national racetrack in the southern suburbs of Caracas. El Hipodromo La Rinconada, as the project would be known, became one of the largest and most expensive racetracks in the world. At a time when Belmont Park, the largest track in the United States, had cost a staggering $32 million dollars, the construction of the Hipodromo more than doubled that budget, totaling some $80 million dollars.[1] The firm continued to produce work both nationally and internationally, including the design and construction of racetracks in Canada, New Zealand, South Africa, Panama, France, and Trinidad and Tobago, but El Hipodromo La Rinconada remains Froehlich's most significant built project.

Beyond its reputation for racetrack projects, Arthur Froehlich & Associates designed numerous other buildings in California in the postwar period, including the Hanna-Barbera Studios (1963) in Los Angeles, the Jack Rose Building (1948) and the remodeling of the US Post Office (1964) in Ventura, and several medical centers in the Los Angeles region. In 1978, Mario Kow became a partner and the firm was renamed Froehlich & Kow. Arthur Froehlich continued to work until his death in 1985, when the office became Froehlich Kow & Gong. Although still in business, Froehlich Kow & Gong no longer produces work abroad. — JJ

① Bill Christine, "Hollywood Park Architect Arthur Froehlich is Dead," *The Los Angeles Times* (October 5, 1985).

VICTOR GRUEN INTERNATIONAL PLANNING AND ARCHITECTURE ENTWURF UND PLANUNG URBANISME ET ARCHITECTURE

1938–1980

Victor Gruen International

Headquarters
Los Angeles, CA

Other Locations
1938 New York, NY; Chicago, IL; Minneapolis, MN; Vienna, Austria; Detroit, MI; Miami, FL; Rochester, NY; Honolulu, HI; San Francisco, CA; Washington DC

Founding and Key Partners
Victor Gruen (founding principal), Cesar Pelli

1980

Victor Gruen Collection, American Heritage Center, University of Wyoming

Associated primarily with the development of the postwar enclosed shopping mall, Victor Gruen—originally Viktor David Grünbaum—began his career in the United States in 1938 after fleeing Nazi-ruled Austria. He joined with designer Elsie Krummeck in 1939 to establish Gruen & Krummeck, designers in New York, where the partners focused on retail storefronts and interiors, much as Gruen had done in Vienna. The commission to design a series of eleven Grayson's stores brought the couple to Los Angeles in 1942, where they married that same year; in the same period, Grünbaum received US citizenship and officially changed his surname. Together, the partners designed their first free-standing department store, for Milliron's (1948) in Los Angeles. Following his divorce from Krummeck in 1951, Gruen formed Victor Gruen Associates.

The completion of the Northland Center (1954) in Detroit and the Southdale Shopping Center (1956) in Edina, Minnesota, the world's first air-conditioned enclosed shopping mall, brought the firm critical acclaim and made Gruen synonymous with the subsequent proliferation of the suburban mall. Victor Gruen Associates designed approximately fifty shopping centers in the United States and abroad before Gruen retired from the Los Angeles office and returned to Europe in 1968. In its nearly two decades of practice, the firm played a profound role in the transformation of the American landscape through its unparalleled expertise in designing the spaces of modern retail. The progenitor of countless facsimiles of this new commercial type, Victor Gruen Associates proposed a radically expanded new role for shopping in the postwar period. In the later phases of Gruen's career the firm deployed the retail model at larger scales, taking on urban renewal projects as well as master plans. What began as an acute understanding of shopping spaces grew into larger planning proposals for Forth Worth, Texas, and other city centers—proposals based on pedestrian retail cores as the key to urban revitalization. Gruen was a conflicted character: an avowed socialist specializing in commercial spaces, yet one who was unafraid to criticize the legitimacy of suburbia, the middle-class, and even the legacy of his own work. His original intention to combat pollution, environmental degradation, and the over-proliferation of cars through consolidated suburban commercial centers largely backfired. In the final act of his career, Gruen spoke out against what he perceived as the misinterpretation of his architectural typology.

Gruen returned to Austria in 1968, leaving the Los Angeles office in the hands of partner and head of design Cesar Pelli, previously director of design at Daniel, Mann, Johnson & Mendenhall (DMJM). In Austria, Gruen established Victor Gruen International, dedicating his work to urban planning that would mitigate the damaging effects of suburban sprawl, caused in part by the autonomous shopping malls that he had helped invent. Victor Gruen International became known for large urban master plans, including the expansion plan for Tehran, Iran (1965–1969), which Gruen began while still in Los Angeles. Yet his firm continued to design shopping centers in Europe, as with the Cap 3000 mall (1968–1970) in Saint Laurent du Var, France and the Printemps shopping center (1968) at La Defense, France. —AWS & MK

1941–1961

Eero Saarinen and Associates

Headquarters
Bloomfield Hills, MI

Other Locations
Hamden, CT

1941

Founding and Key Partners
Eliel Saarinen, Eero Saarinen, J. Robert Swanson (founding principals), Joe Lacy, Kevin Roche, John Dinkeloo

1961

Ezra Stoller, Esto

Eero Saarinen, the son of celebrated Finnish architect Eliel Saarinen, arrived in the United States at the age of thirteen. The family moved to Bloomfield Hills, Michigan, in 1924 following Eliel's commission to design the Cranbrook Academy, an artists' colony and school that he oversaw from 1924 to 1941. Eero joined his father's architectural practice in 1936. Five years later they formed Saarinen Swanson Saarinen with Robert Swanson, husband of Eero's older sister; in 1947 Swanson left the partnership and it became Saarinen Saarinen. That same year Eero submitted under his own name a competition entry to the Jefferson National Expansion Memorial, better known as the St. Louis Gateway Arch; when he won, the award was mistakenly mailed to his father.

After Eliel's death in 1950, Eero established Eero Saarinen & Associates in Bloomfield Hills; by 1960 the firm employed over 100 architects. Critical to the firm's success were a few key partners: John Dinkeloo oversaw the office production and many of the firm's technical accomplishments, Kevin Roche was a key design partner, and Joseph N. Lacy was integral to running the business of the firm.

Heralded as one of the best-known "form-givers" of mid-century American architecture and a member of the so-called "second generation" of modernist architects, Saarinen's work epitomized the shift from the rational, functionalist architectural language of the 1920s and 1930s to a more sculptural, expressive architectural language. Eero Saarinen & Associates was especially known for arched concrete forms, among them the emphatic Gateway Arch (1947–1965), clad in stainless steel, David S. Ingalls Hockey Rink at Yale University (1956–1958), Dulles International Airport (1958–1963) in Washington, DC, and, perhaps most sensationally, the TWA Terminal (1956–1962) at John F. Kennedy Airport (then Idlewild Airport) in New York, with its soaring, vaulted concrete shells. Yet an entirely different architectural language informed the General Motors Technical Center (1948–1956), a series of Miesian, steel-and-glass boxes wrapped in colored glazed bricks. Saarinen's lack of a consistent style and seeming betrayal of the modernist credo "form follows function" led to considerable critical vitriol, notably from eminent architectural critics Vincent Scully and Reyner Banham: the latter infamously derided Saarinen as an "Ad Man" employing "a style for the job."[1]

Nonetheless, major commissions continued unabated. General Motors was just one of the many corporate headquarters Saarinen designed during the 1950s. Other clients included IBM, CBS, Bell Telephone, and John Deere and Company. He was also a critical figure in the US Embassy building program of the 1950s, designing the US Chancellery Buildings in Oslo (1955–1959) and London (1955–1960). In 1957 he was appointed to the Office of Foreign Buildings Operations (FBO) Architectural Advisory Council.

Following Saarinen's untimely death at age 51, in 1961, partners Roche and Dinkeloo completed the projects that were underway in the office; in 1966, together with Lacy, they formed Kevin Roche John Dinkeloo and Associates. — ARL

(1) Reyner Banham, "The Style for the Job," *New Statesman* (February 14, 1964): 261.

1942–2001

Morris Lapidus Associates

Headquarters
Miami, FL

Founding and Key Partners
Morris Lapidus (founding principal),
Deborah Desilets

1942

2001

Ezra Stoller, Esto

Born into the oppressed Jewish community of Odessa, Ukraine, in 1902, architect Morris Lapidus died nearly a century later in sunny Miami Beach, having transformed hotel design and the American vacation along the way. As a young child he moved with his family to New York City, where he learned to speak English, and where he later attended an acting program at New York University. Discovering a love for scenic design, and inspired deeply by the extravagant Hollywood film sets of the time, Lapidus transferred to Columbia University, where he earned an undergraduate architecture degree in 1927.

Unable to find scenographic work on Broadway, Lapidus went to work for Warren & Wetmore, the firm famous for designing New York's Grand Central Terminal and Detroit's Michigan Central Station. After several years learning how to build large-scale projects, including hotels, Lapidus moved to the firm of Ross-Frankel, where he was responsible for a prolific interior architecture practice. Lapidus saw hundreds of his interiors built in the 1930s, and was recognized by *Architectural Forum* in 1936 for three of his bold storefront designs. The journal noted that "some of the best architecture of America today is to be found in store front design," and Lapidus had become among the most respected leaders in that field.[1]

Relocating to Miami Beach in 1942 and establishing his own practice there, Lapidus began receiving major hotel commissions by the end of that decade. By the mid-1950s, the Sans Souci, Eden Roc, Algiers, Seville, and Fontainebleau Hotels lined the narrow strand of Miami Beach along Collins Avenue; their clean modernist lines and sumptuous details formed the district's singular image. Yet while Lapidus would continue to receive occasional accolades for his retail design, his hotels would remain largely unpublished in the major trade journals through the 1950s and 1960s. The largest and most famous of Lapidus's hotels, the Fontainebleau (1954) in Miami—well known for its Hollywood-inspired "stairway to nowhere"—was snubbed by the architectural press. The only contemporary recognition of the "curved and many-windowed" hotel was in a 1955 *LIFE* magazine article entitled "Miami's Costliest."[2]

From his base in Miami Beach, Lapidus took his Floridian opulence to the Caribbean, with major resort projects in Aruba, Puerto Rico, and Jamaica in the 1950s and 1960s. Although the architectural press continued to take little notice, boosterish reports in newspaper travel sections catalogued his blend of "Miami Beach motifs" and "informal" and "colorful" Caribbean atmospheres. With the rise of package travel deals and cheap flights through airlines like Pan Am, American tourists could explore locales beyond Florida in sunny poolside retreats designed by Lapidus.

The designer's reputation seemed on the road to recovery when critic John Margolies organized "Morris Lapidus: Architecture of Joy," an exhibition at the Architectural League in New York in 1970, to honor what he called Lapidus's "active and beleaguered career as the undisputed king of the 'give 'em what they want' school of architecture." In an interview of Lapidus by Margolies, published in *Progressive Architecture* in the same year, Lapidus espoused his belief that "people are looking for illusions," and that through his hotels he sought unapologetically "put them on stage."[3] Before his retirement in 1984, Lapidus designed over 1,200 buildings, including 250 hotels. Yet he was hurt by what he called his "exile" from architecture, reportedly burning many of his early sketches after his retirement and despairing when the interiors of his beloved hotels were altered or destroyed. He returned to practice in 1996 in partnership with Miami architect Deborah Desilets, continuing to work until his death at age 99 in 2001. Lapidus lived long enough to see many of his works earn landmark status before passing away in his flamboyant duplex in the Terrace Towers, a building designed by his firm, amid the luxury of Miami Beach that he had defined. — MW

①
"Stores, New York City and Los Angeles," *Architectural Forum* (October 1936): 316–318.

②
"Miami's Costliest hotel, Fontainebleau," *LIFE* (January 17, 1955): 100–102.

③
John S. Margolies, "Morris Lapidus: 'Now, Once and for All, Know Why I Did It'," *Progressive Architecture* (September 1970): 118–123.

Philip Johnson / Alan Ritchie Architects

Headquarters
New York, NY

Other Locations
1942 Houston, TX

Founding and Key Partners
Philip Johnson (founding principal), John Burgee, Alan Ritchie

Current Principals
Alan Ritchie, Marko Dasigenis

Philip Johnson / Alan Ritchie Architects

Kingmaker, curator, critic, eclectic architect, and *éminence grise* in the American architecture scene, Philip Johnson's career spanned nearly eight decades. Born in 1906 in Cleveland, Ohio, and supported financially throughout his life by returns from stock in the Aluminum Company of America given to him by his father, Johnson graduated from Harvard University in 1927, after studying Greek and pre-Socratic philosophy, though he frequently interrupted his education with trips to Europe, where he became interested in classical architecture.

Shortly after the establishment of the Museum of Modern Art (MoMA) in New York in 1929, Johnson became the first curator of the institution's Department of Architecture. In 1932, Johnson and Henry-Russell Hitchock, his European traveling companion, curated "Modern Architecture: International Exhibition" at MoMA, and edited the resulting publication, *The International Style*, that was primarily responsible for introducing the work of Ludwig Mies van der Rohe, Le Corbusier, Walter Gropius, and other avant-garde European architects to an American audience.[1] Focusing on the aesthetic qualities of European modernist buildings while largely ignoring the theoretical and social concerns of their architects, the exhibition coined the term "International Style" as a rubric under which the divergent strands of modern architecture were presented as a set of consistent stylistic principles.

Johnson's activities prior to and during the early years of World War II were clouded by his open sympathies with Nazism, a decision that continued to follow him for the remainder of his career. Johnson was soon implored in no uncertain terms by family and colleagues to relinquish his political interests, and his next act would lead him from curating into architectural practice, enrolling at the Harvard Graduate School of Design in 1941. His first built work was a house he designed for himself, at 9 Ash Street in Cambridge, Massachusetts, as his thesis project at Harvard. The iconic Glass House (1949), the first of many buildings Johnson designed for his estate in New Canaan, Connecticut over the course of his life, established Johnson's reputation as a practitioner. His curation of the first major retrospective of Mies van der Rohe's work at MoMA in 1947 and his collaboration with Mies on the design of the Seagram Building in New York (1954–1958) established the pattern of Johnson's persona, at once tastemaker and direct participant in the promulgation of movements and architects he admired. Yet Johnson had already begun to explore more decorative and historicizing tendencies in his own work, as indicated by his 1954 Harvard lecture, "The Seven Crutches of Modern Architecture."

From 1961 to 1991, Johnson worked in partnership with John Burgee in New York, undertaking an array of large commissions for corporate and institutional clients. Johnson/Burgee's work went through numerous stylistic iterations, from prismatic glass-and-steel buildings for Pennzoil Place (1976) in Houston, Texas, and the Crystal Cathedral (1981) in Garden Grove, California, to the controversial postmodernism of the AT&T Building (1984) in New York, decorated with a Chippendale-style broken pediment. Johnson summarized both his eclecticism and his cynicism toward working with developers in the conference in 1982 at the University of Virginia School of Architecture, eventually published as *The Charlottesville Tapes*, in which he famously declared, "I am a whore and I am paid very well for building high-rise buildings."[2] Johnson continued to practice—as a partner in Philip Johnson/Alan Ritchie Architects—until shortly before his death in 2005 at the age of 98.
—WX & MK

① Henry-Russell Hitchcock and Philip Johnson, *The International Style: Architecture Since 1922* (New York: Museum of Modern Art, 1932).

② *The Charlottesville Tapes* (New York: Rizzoli International Publications, 1985): 19.

1942–
2008

Ralph Rapson Architects

Headquarters
Minneapolis, MN

Founding and Key Partners
Ralph Rapson (founding principal),
John van der Muelen

1942

2008

Rapson Architects

Ralph Rapson opened his office in 1942, shortly after finishing his studies at the Cranbrook Academy of Art. The office operated in tandem with Rapson's teaching positions and was relocated according to his movements among schools, beginning with the New Bauhaus School of Design (later part of the Illinois Institute of Technology) in Chicago in 1942. From there Rapson and his practice moved to Boston in 1946 to teach at the Massachusetts Institute of Technology, and then to Minneapolis in 1954, where he served as the head of the University of Minnesota School of Architecture for thirty years until 1984. Rapson gained notoriety early in his career for his modernist houses, including the Greenbelt House (1945), his unbuilt entry to the Case Study House program led by *Arts & Architecture* magazine under editor John Entenza. Rapson went on to design some of the first modern embassies for the US State Department, in Copenhagen and Stockholm, before settling into a productive and illustrious career as one of the major architects of the Midwest.

Rapson received a two-year fellowship to study at Cranbrook Academy in 1938. There his fellow students included Harry Weese, Florence Knoll, Charles Eames, Ray Kaiser, and Eero Saarinen, in an immersive design curriculum created by Eliel Saarinen. This group of friends went on to have successful individual careers. Florence Knoll, along with her husband, Hans Knoll, continued working with Rapson and helped launch his career in the 1940s, as a series of rocking chairs by Rapson were produced as part of the *Living Project* series for the Knoll Furniture Company. In 1951, after Knoll was selected to provide furnishings for the US Embassy in Havana, Hans sent word to Rapson that Fritz Larkin, director of the Foreign Buildings Operations (FBO) office of the State Department, was looking for architects to design several embassies. Rapson promptly flew to Washington, D.C. to meet with Larkin and was soon commissioned to design four embassies, in The Hague, Netherlands; Stockholm, Sweden; Copenhagen, Denmark; and Oslo, Norway.

In 1952, Rapson and his new partner, John van der Meulen, moved to Europe to begin selecting sites for the embassies. By 1955, the Stockholm and Copenhagen embassies were built, along with Rapson and der Meulen's design of staff housing for the US embassy in Paris. Hailed at their time for their progressive design, the firm's engagement with the State Department marked a significant moment for the FBO's embassy program, one in which architects were given a substantial role in developing the design and program of its buildings. Rapson and van der Meulen used that freedom to propose an entirely new, modern, and largely transparent model for future embassies. Although many of their designs were never realized, their work set in motion a decade of in which the State Department fostered progressive architecture by US architects abroad.

Rapson returned from Europe to his teaching position at MIT in 1954, but soon relocated to become the head of the School of Architecture at the University of Minnesota. Rapson continued to produce significant buildings in Minnesota, including the Pillsbury House (1963–1964) in Wayzata, and the Guthrie Theater (1963) and the Cedar-Riverside apartment complex (1967–1974), both in Minneapolis. Rapson retired from the University in 1984, but continued to practice until his death in 2008. The office is still in operation and is currently headed by Rapson's son, Thomas (Toby) Rapson. — JJ

1942–1959

Town Planning Associates

Headquarters
New York, NY

Founding Partners
Josep Lluís Sert, Paul Lester Weiner

1942

1959

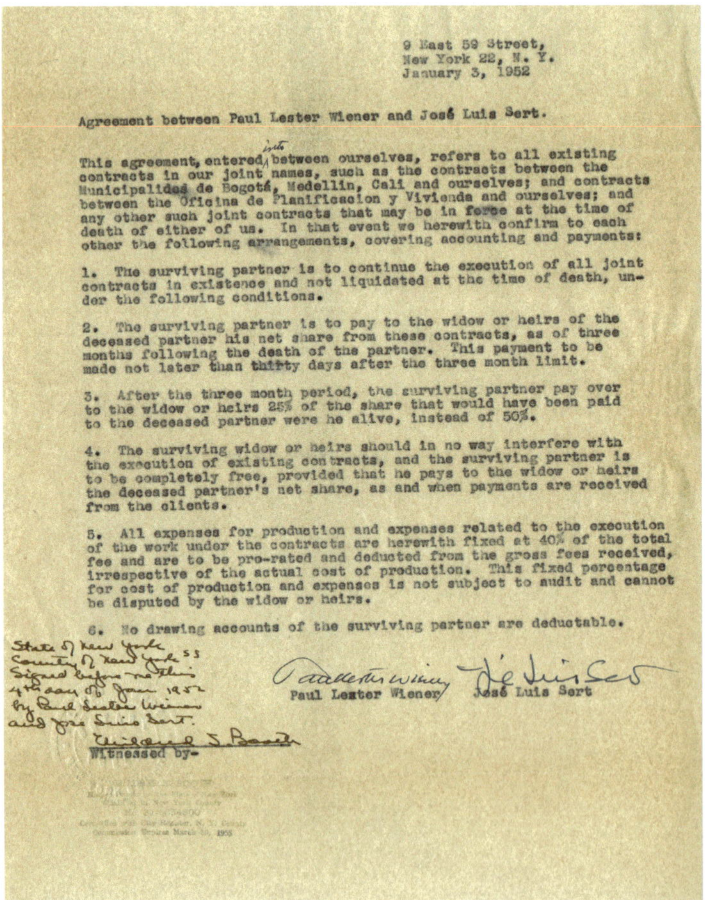

9 East 59 Street,
New York 22, N. Y.
January 3, 1952

Agreement between Paul Lester Wiener and José Luis Sert.

This agreement, entered into between ourselves, refers to all existing contracts in our joint names, such as the contracts between the Municipalides de Bogotá, Medellin, Cali and ourselves; and contracts between the Oficina de Planificacion y Vivienda and ourselves; and any other such joint contracts that may be in force at the time of death of either of us. In that event we herewith confirm to each other the following arrangements, covering accounting and payments:

1. The surviving partner is to continue the execution of all joint contracts in existence and not liquidated at the time of death, under the following conditions.

2. The surviving partner is to pay to the widow or heirs of the deceased partner his net share from these contracts, as of three months following the death of the partner. This payment to be made not later than thirty days after the three month limit.

3. After the three month period, the surviving partner pay over to the widow or heirs 25% of the share that would have been paid to the deceased partner were he alive, instead of 50%.

4. The surviving widow or heirs should in no way interfere with the execution of existing contracts, and the surviving partner is to be completely free, provided that he pays to the widow or heirs the deceased partner's net share, as and when payments are received from the clients.

5. All expenses for production and expenses related to the execution of the work under the contracts are herewith fixed at 40% of the total fee and are to be pro-rated and deducted from the gross fees received, irrespective of the actual cost of production. This fixed percentage for cost of production and expenses is not subject to audit and cannot be disputed by the widow or heirs.

6. No drawing accounts of the surviving partner are deductable.

State of New York
County of New York ss
Signed before me this
4th day of Jan 1952
by Paul Lester Wiener
and José Luis Sert.

Witnessed by-

Paul Lester Wiener   José Luis Sert

The Josep Lluis Sert Collection, Courtesy of the Frances Loeb Library, Harvard University Graduate School of Design

Catalan architect Josep Lluís Sert escaped the Spanish Civil War in 1937, fleeing to Paris after an invitation to work in the atelier of Le Corbusier. He had been the founder of GATCPAC (Grup d'Arquitectes I Tècnics Catalan per al Progrés de l'Arquitectura Contemporània), the Spanish working group of the Congrès International d'Architecture Moderne (CIAM), and had designed the Pavilion of the Spanish Republic at the World's International Exposition in Paris in 1937. Following Francisco Franco's victory in 1939, Sert, prohibited from accepting any architectural position in Spain under the regime, moved to New York to begin his career in the United States in exile.

In 1942, Sert joined architects Paul Lester Wiener and Paul Schulz to form Town Planning Associates (TPA), a consultancy dedicated to realizing the group's CIAM-inspired architectural and urban planning concepts in practice. Wiener, a German émigré who had moved to the US in 1913, had designed the US Government building for the World's International Exposition in Paris of 1937, adjacent to Sert's Pavilion of the Spanish Republic. Sert and Schulz joined Wiener in his office on West 42nd Street in New York. TPA's letterhead designated Wiener as director of design, Schulz as architect, and Sert as town planner within the group.

In its first years of operation, TPA dedicated its attention to architectural and planning needs emerging from World War II, including designs for war industry workers' housing. Sert published his functionalist approach to city planning in 1942 in *Can Our Cities Survive?*, among the publications that first introduced the urban principles of CIAM to the US public.

The bulk of TPA's work in the 1940s and 1950s was in South and Central America, where the firm produced more than ten master plans for cities in Brazil, Peru, Venezuela, Columbia, and Cuba, none ever fully completed. Following a series of successful lectures by Wiener in Brazil in 1942, TPA received its first planning commission in the following year, to design the Cidade dos Motores, a new industrial city near Rio de Janeiro, for the Brazilian Airplane Factory Commission. As Wiener acknowledged years later, these planning efforts began in the context of strategic efforts to forge political and economic ties between the US and South America as part of the "Good Neighbor Policy" under Franklin Delano Roosevelt, intended to counteract Axis influence on the continent during World War II.

In TPA's plans during the war and after, the group struggled to negotiate the interests of its governmental and industrial clients, the expansionist US economic framework which made them possible, local conditions and the examples of regional building types, and the firm's dedication to CIAM principles of town planning. Subsequent commissions included master plans for Chimbote (1946–1948) in Peru and Medellin (1948–1950), Cali (1949–1950), and Bogotá (1949–1953) in Colombia, the latter in collaboration with Le Corbusier; new towns for Ciudad Piar and Puerto Ordaz (1951–1953) in Venezuela for the Orinoco Mining Company, a subsidiary of US Steel; a new neighborhood unit in Maracaibo, Venezuela (1951–1953); and in Havana, Cuba, a master plan for the old city center (1955–1958) and a partially completed residential district, Quinta Palatino (1954–1957), with local architects Arroyo and Menéndez.

Only portions of the firm's extensive planning efforts in South America and Cuba were ever realized. Sert's involvement with Town Planning Associates diminished when he became Dean of the Harvard University Graduate School of Design in 1953, succeeding Joseph Hudnut, and as he began to focus on his independent architectural practice. Six years later, on March 31, 1959, Wiener formally announced the end of TPA. — RW & MK nbbj

1943–

NBBJ

Headquarters
Seattle, WA

Other Locations
Beijing, China; Boston, MA; Columbus, OH; London, UK; Los Angeles, CA; New York, NY; Pune, India; San Francisco, CA;
1943 Shanghai, China

Founding Partners
Floyd Naramore, William Bain, Sr., Clifton Brady, Perry Johanson

World Architecture, 1995

Jai Alai Auditorium
1940

Architect
Wurdeman and Becket

Location
Manila, Philippines

ELLERBE BECKET

Hotel Granada
1941–1946

Architect
Paul R. Williams Architects

Location
Bogota, Colombia

Client
Hotel Granada Corporation
of Bogota

1940

1944

Prototype for Open-Air Schools
1943–1945

Architect
Richard J. Neutra

Location
Puerto Rico (150 locations)

Client
Puerto Rican Committee on
the Design of Public Works
Development

Prototype for Rural Health Centers
1943–1945

Architect
Richard J. Neutra

Location
Puerto Rico (150 locations)

Client
Puerto Rican Committee on
the Design of Public Works
Development

Prototype for District Hospitals
1943–1945

Architect
Richard J. Neutra

Location
Puerto Rico (5 locations)

Client
Puerto Rican Committee on
the Design of Public Works
Development

Hotel Nutibara
1944–1948

Architect
Paul R. Williams Architects

Location
Medellin, Colombia

Client
Hoteles Nutibara

Incorporating Architecture: The Business of Postwar Practice

In the years immediately after World War II, a perceived consensus around the principles of the modern movement in the US was accompanied by the belief that such unity might, for the first time, enable newly collective forms of work that would unite the building disciplines in addressing the complex tasks of postwar construction. Inspired by both big business and the large-scale coordination of prewar federal entities like the Tennessee Valley Authority under the New Deal, *collaboration* became the watchword for a generation of architects schooled in the belief that anonymity, teamwork, and the broadest scale of action were the keys to progressive architectural production. In practice, these interests were reflected in the wave of offices founded immediately after World War II and committed to tackling the demands of an expanding postwar society through the principles of specialization and distributed production. Such developments were accompanied by speculation across the disciplines of architecture, sociology, and business on the coming impact, positive or negative, of the corporation as both business model and institutional form.[1]

Contemporary architectural critics looked back to the largest firms of the early twentieth century in order to comprehend what this new scale of team-based practice might mean for postwar architectural production. Among the earliest attempts, Henry-Russell Hitchcock announced in "The Architecture of Bureaucracy and the Architecture of Genius" (1947) that the major categories of postwar architecture would be distinguished not by style, but by economy of production. Hitchcock predicted that, while the demand for speed and competence in large-scale projects would engender the rise of the bureaucratic design office—those "large-scale architectural organizations…from which personal expression is absent"—a special realm of practice would remain reserved for monumental cultural commissions requiring artistic or creative synthesis, "the world of the architecture of genius." While Frank Lloyd Wright provided the inevitable image of the latter, the former was represented by Albert Kahn Associates, the architect of factories for Ford Motor

① See Michael Kubo, "The Concept of the Architectural Corporation," in Eva Franch i Gilabert, Amanda Lawrence, Ana Miljački, Ashley Schafer, ed., *OfficeUS: Agenda* (Zurich: Lars Müller, 2014): 37–45.

1940

1945 The Architects Collaborative (TAC) first US architecture firm named anonymously as group practice

1946 Peter Drucker, *Concept of the Corporation*

1947 Henry-Russell Hitchcock, "The Architecture of Bureaucracy and the Architecture of Genius" (*Architectural Review*)

1949 "Designers For a Busy World: Mood For Working" (*Newsweek*) article on SOM

1950 *Skidmore, Owings & Merrill, Architects U.S.A.* first exhibition at the Museum of Modern Art on a group firm

1954
• Sigfried Giedion, *Walter Gropius, Work and Teamwork*
• "2-Billion Worth of Design by Conference" (*Business Week*) article on SOM

1957
• Sigfried Giedion, "The Experiment of S.O.M."

1939–1945 World War II

1950–1953 Korean War

Company, which Hitchcock praised for "the organizational genius that can establish a fool-proof system of rapid and complete plan production."[2]

Yet by the time of Hitchcock's article, the assembly-line system embodied by Kahn and Ford was already an anachronistic example for postwar organizations. A year earlier, the sociologist Peter Drucker argued that the progressive firms of the coming economic boom would emulate instead the flexible, decentralized model of General Motors, the largest corporation in the world by the 1950s.[3] Such managerial principles found their closest architectural parallel in the offices of Skidmore, Owings & Merrill (SOM), the firm which became uniquely synonymous with the term "corporate" in the postwar period. SOM's success was based on the development of the "package deal," in which large teams of architects and engineers delivered complex projects from site planning and structural engineering to detailed design, facade systems, interiors, budgeting, and administration. *Fortune* magazine soon extolled SOM's "group design," while *Newsweek* made explicit the firm's affinity with Drucker's managerial paradigm, praising SOM for its "enormous and assiduous activity and production—something like a General Motors of the architectural world."[4] Meanwhile, the belief in team-based practice as a social ethos was represented by firms like The Architects Collaborative (TAC), established in 1945 by eight architects including Walter Gropius, the German émigré identified with the Bauhaus and later with the Harvard Graduate School of Design, or by Caudill, Rowlett, Scott (CRS), founded a year later in College Station, Texas. All of these offices would eventually number among the largest architecture firms in the United States.

By the close of the next decade, critics again turned to earlier examples of large-scale architectural organizations, now in order to describe the scale and success of these and other firms in the postwar years. Sigfried Giedion situated SOM within the lineage of Chicago firms like Burnham & Root that had been among the pioneers of the large-scale architectural organization at the turn of the twentieth century.[5] Responding with a view from outside the United States, Peter Smithson placed SOM's genealogy not with the commercial architects of the Chicago School but rather with the New York office of McKim, Mead & White, among the largest architectural firms at the end of the nineteenth century.[6] — MK

② Henry-Russell Hitchcock, "The Architecture of Bureaucracy and the Architecture of Genius," *The Architectural Review* (January 1947): 3–6.

③ Peter Drucker, *Concept of the Corporation* (New York: The John Day Company, 1946).

④ "The Architects From Skid's Row," *Fortune* (January 1958): 137–140, 210, 212, 215; "Designers For a Busy World: Mood For Working," *Newsweek* (May 4, 1959): 97–100.

⑤ Sigfried Giedion, "The Experiment of SOM," *Bauen + Wohnen* (April 1957): 113–114.

⑥ Peter Smithson, "The fine and the folk: An essay on McKim, Mead and White and the American tradition," *Architectural Design* (August 1965): 394–397.

1945

1972

und Werkform on TAC
• *Machine Made America*, *special issue of Architectural Review* on "Personal Contributions to American Architecture"

1958
"The Architects From Skid's Row, 'Group Design' As Practiced by S.O.M." (*Fortune*)

1959
Special issue of *Bauen + Wohnen* on TAC

1961
• Henry-Russell Hitchcock, "The Rise to World Prominence of American Architecture" (*Zodiac 8: America*)
• Henry-Russell Hitchcock writes introduction to *Architecture of Skidmore, Owings & Merrill*, 1950–1962

1965
• Peter Smithson, "The fine and the folk: An essay on McKim, Mead and White and the American tradition" (*Architectural Design*)
• *America*, special issue of Bau 5/6

1971
• USA '71, special issue of *Architecture d'aujourd'hui*
• William Wayne Caudill (CRS Inc.), *Architecture By Team*

1980

1962 Cuban Missile Crisis

1950–1975 Vietnam War

he Architecture of Bureaucracy & The Architecture of Genius

he architecture of

BUREAUCRACY

&

he architecture of

GENIUS

The re-emergence of team-work in the planning and design of buildings in combination with the improved methods of factory production have resulted in a new architecture of bureaucracy. The procedure of work differs from that which went to produce the gothic building owing more to the development of scientific means for attaining mechanical precision than to any other factor. (Mechanical precision, it has been said, is the only really original contribution of our age to the works of man). But parallel with the development of this architecture, there are still the few individuals working independently to create the architecture of genius—that is, the prototypes that will set the standard in the next stage of bureaucratic development. In the following article Professor Hitchcock gives his reasons for using these terms to describe the two main tendencies in contemporary architecture, and illustrates his argument with examples from Europe and America.

By Henry-Russell Hitchcock

THE early twentieth century, in considering its own cultural phenomena, was much obsessed with time, or more precisely, with pace of development. Many who ere not technically Futurists were all for rushing headlong ito the future, while others, who admitted no antipathy in rinciple to technical or artistic change favoured only a slow nd measured departure from the tried ways of tradition. s regarded architectural developments neither side, perhaps, lly realized the rapidity with which a new way of building as coming into general use regardless of their polemics: e real question was less whether the pace of technical advance ould be forced or held back than how to cope *architecturally* ith developments that had already taken place, in some cases veral generations earlier! But criticism of architecture own almost to the war was frequently and tediously concerned ith whether buildings were "advanced" enough or too advanced."

In the twenties such great innovators of the beginning of e century as Perret and Wright were often castigated ecause their practice did not conform to the particular gours of architectural expression which a younger generation ere establishing. This was the more ironic because so many the positive qualities of the new architecture derived om the work of these older men. It is worth while to mpare such a house as Wright's Millard house in Pasadena, uch criticized in the twenties, with the houses or even the ojects of the same period of the early twenties by Le orbusier, which were thought to have established a more lvanced canon. In a retrospective view more than twenty ears later, it is not the differences but the similarities hich strike one. In both, the living rooms are raised off e ground and carried up two storeys, with the service commodations and bedrooms on two separate floors ehind; in both, the front of the living room opens through ouped doors and windows on to a raised terrace; and both se concrete with reinforcement throughout in a bold and genious way. Indeed, it was Wright, the "old master" s he so hated to be called), whose system of construction, ith the reinforcing rods in channels between precast blocks, as the more novel. Wright was technically free to cast s blocks in any way he wished, so long as he used only a w standard moulds. He had, moreover, been aware ever nce his Unity Church of twenty years before of the grace-ss weathering of concrete, even with an exposed pebble ggregate. Therefore he provided his blocks with modelled rfaces in geometrical patterns, while Le Corbusier used nooth rendered surfaces, out of deference partly to the pposed nature of his type of construction and partly to abstract æstheticism. Those patterns on Wright's blocks ere, and to many still are, anathema. Yet time has, on e whole, justified Wright's use of them, even though when sing concrete blocks in later years he has rarely given them ich elaborate surface patterns. The smooth rendered sur-ces of Le Corbusier's houses—and of many buildings by her architects throughout the world who followed his lead—are too often cracked and stained; so that they cannot be considered technically to represent good workmanship, while expressively they no longer provide the abstract effect originally intended. The Millard house, however, even after many years of relative neglect, has aged gracefully because the shadow patterns of the modelled blocks are so much stronger than any deterioration of their concrete surfaces. Thus the conviction, so generally held in the twenties and even later, that Le Corbusier was more *advanced* than Wright appears in this instance to be rather exaggerated.

As to which is the more romantic, there was and is little to choose between them, though Wright's somewhat nineteenth century romanticism about "Nature" is, paradoxically, perhaps less dated to-day than Le Corbusier's early twentieth century romanticism about the "Machine." There was, and there has continued to be, a marked difference of personal expression. However, Le Corbusier began about fifteen years ago to use rough timber in a house in South America and rubble walls, not only there and for a Riviera house, but even for a house near Paris, while Wright has raised more and more of his houses off the ground on piers and even projected them out into space by cantilevering. The two architects were not influenced each by the other; it was rather that both were exploring parallelly a comparable range of contemporary building possibilities. Though their minds were as different as the minds of two architects could well be and one was nearly a generation younger than the other, their innovations tended to follow similar paths, since each gave his imagination free rein within the range of technical possibilities of the age in a way their earlier doctrinaire writings would not always seem to sanction.

When the superficial appearance of modern architecture was more widely accepted as familiar and even agreeable by the public in the thirties, two sorts of derivative work appeared in increasing quantities. On the one hand there was all the worthy work of the younger men who were following the bold leadership of the first masters of the twenties, and of such older men as underwent a sincere conversion. On the other hand there was the "pseudo-modern," some of it unpretentious if conspicuous commercial work whose designers sought cheap popularity through the strident use of clichés. Quite as much, however, represented merely tongue-in-cheek modification and simplification of traditional stylisms by means of which the conservatives, now beginning to lose their assurance, attempted in practice (as earlier in theory) to compromise the differences between the new and the old architecture. With regard to the first sort of work it was sometimes just perhaps to say that it was "too modern." Both young inexperienced men and more mature converts were utilizing as conventions types of construction, of planning, and of expression which they had not as yet fully mastered technically, nor considered sufficiently subtly in relation to problems of setting and of climate. During a certain stage of adaptation and apprenticeship, a large body of architects got, almost literally, ahead of themselves. In attempting to emulate the startling innovations of the founders of modern architecture they sometimes essayed fan-

1, the cafeteria at Vallejo, California ; William Wilson Wurster, architect. 2, Normart Terrace, Los Angeles ; W. L. Risley and S. R. Gould, architects. 3, Cameron Valley, Virginia. These are typical examples of wartime housing and community building on the west coast of America. 4, the Dodge-Chicago plant ; Albert Kahn Inc., architects. 5, on the facing page, a model of Frank Lloyd Wright's design for a gallery to house the Guggenheim Collection of non-objective art.

1

2

3

4

tastically drastic solutions of structural and planning problems which were already satisfactorily solved in principle and merely required coherent development. Instead of being content to develop the fruits of a particular architectural revolution which had already taken place, they aimed at a sort of permanent revolution, just at the time when the passage of years began to make evident that the revolution of the twenties rather required patient consolidation of its initial gains. On the other hand, the men who attempted superficially to modernize essentially traditional types of construction and composition by scraping off detail and introducing this or that temporarily fashionable new material were quite clearly " not modern enough," since they were in reality not modern at all ; while the commercial work was "too modern" in the worst sense and not modern at all in principle.

It is not too optimistic, on the basis of the building done during the war in America—and I believe also in England—to say that the particular situation which justified a primary critical approach to new buildings in terms of their degree of modernity came to an end with the present decade. Though the lack of certain materials and various other conditions limited and restricted wartime building in many ways, it came about that there was at last only one contemporary way of building. This applied not only to large steel or ferro-concrete factories but also to associated temporary housing or canteens in wood or brick. So at least in the countries which were involved in the war it might appear that both attempts at permanent revolution on the one hand—the sort of building that may properly be considered "too modern"—and on the other hand disguised traditionalism—the sort of building that is " not modern enough "—will not be serious problems for critical consideration in the near future.* (Since both are the products of types of mind which will continue to exist, they will obviously turn up once more, but presumably in a very different, even a reversed, guise than the guise of radicalism and conservatism they wore in the thirties.) I do not know at first hand the wartime work of neutral countries, but judging from photographs it would appear that there had been a similar clarification of the architectural picture in Sweden and Switzerland, where architectural development was in any case already well integrated in the thirties.

The major problem of architecture in the middle of the twentieth century is presumably going to be a problem not of up-to-dateness but of quality. But if the quality of postwar buildings is to be properly considered it is most important that the basic conditions of the times as they control architecture should be appreciated. We must not expect each individual type of prefabricated dwelling to have the striking originality and the subtle qualities of abstract expression of the first modern serial dwellings designed by Le Corbusier and others twenty-five years ago, nor each factory office block to have the richness of form, the elegance of materials and the elaborate interplay of volume of Wright's

* This was written before the announcement of the results of the Crystal Palace competition.

Johnson Wax Administration Building. The major divisi architecture into categories is, I believe, going to be bet what may be called the architecture of bureaucracy and architecture of genius, and of the latter we may presume very little will be built for some years to come. By the a tecture of bureaucracy I do not mean merely such buildi is designed by civil servants, nor even the building whi closely controlled by the regulations of one or more minis although in England there will be little building which i in one or the other of these classes. By bureaucratic a tecture I mean all building that is the product of large architectural organizations, from which personal expre is absent. Indeed the type of bureaucratic architecture *excellence* is not that of government ministries, which ha a matter of fact been on the whole up to now rather f organized, but the production of such an architectural fi Albert Kahn, Inc., in Detroit, where the anonymity i more obvious now that Albert Kahn, the founder, is The strength of a firm such as Kahn, or for that matt a state architectural bureau, depends not on the architec genius of one man (there is sufficient evidence that Kahr a mediocre architect considered as an individual), but in organizational genius which can establish a fool-proof syste rapid and complete plan production. The different se plans for construction, for wiring, for heating, etc., and for design, ought to come down the line and meet on the with as perfect mutual co-ordination as machine parts from the various sections of a factory to be joined first sub-assemblies and then into the finished product on the assembly line. No one mind can master all the prob involved and the only assurance that no amenities wi

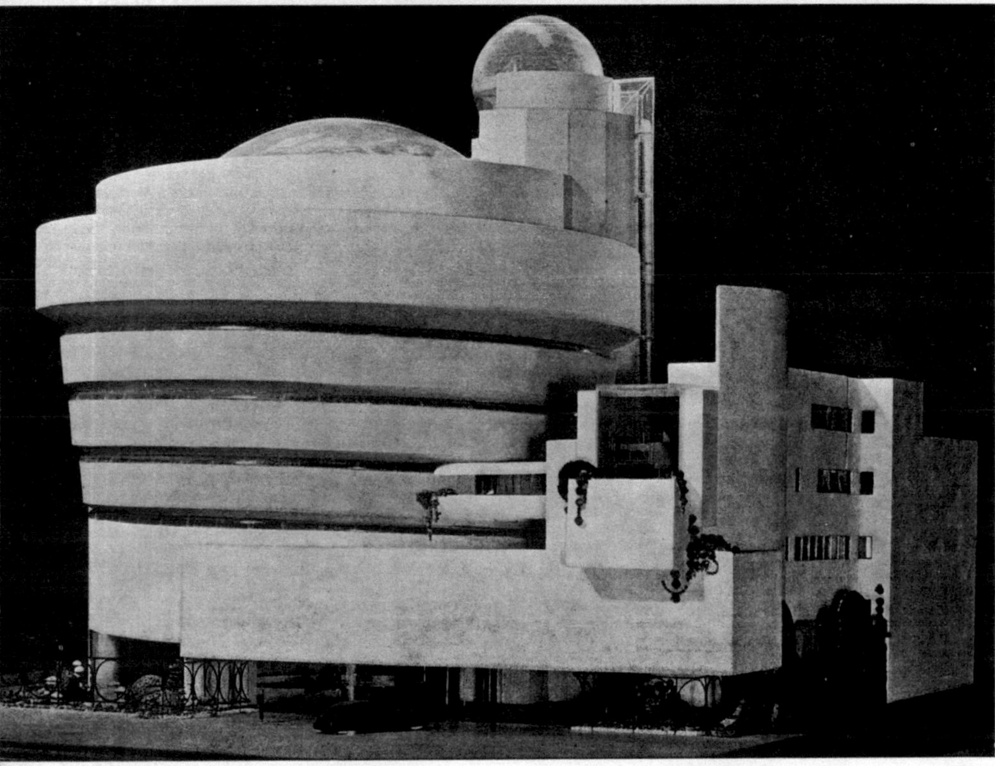

5

otten lies in the intelligence with which the system of production is set up and the skill with which the key ts in the system are filled. Thus Kahn, Inc., have lately ght Roland Wank from another great American archiıral bureaucracy, that of the T.V.A., to be their chief gner. Such methods can produce buildings of high amenity. e perhaps would not consider them architecture in the st sense, since they are necessarily without that overall on of plan and construction into a vehicle of personal exsion which may be considered, as in the Johnson Wax ding, alone to produce a major work of architectural art. e are few if any *trouvailles* in a Kahn plant, such as the ime Dodge-Chicago plant for aircraft engines. There is, ever, in every way a certain rightness, straightforward- , and cleanliness both actual and symbolic, which is the er generalized expression of an efficient workplace. It is er parallel to the quality of a finely designed and skilfully mbled machine, likewise the product of many technical ds rather than of a single mechanical genius.

ty development is another field in which efficient production it theoretically to be undertaken by a bureaucratic archiıral organization. It is because we have no really large- organizations in America in this field (except the T.V.A.) the results are generally inferior to our factories in those ities which only large-scale organizations can provide. s although the *fiat* city of 75,000 built at Oak Ridge for production of the atomic bomb is remarkable in that it ides the necessary plants (by Stone and Webster, of Boston) necessary housing (some decent blocks of flats ; also many onal houses supplied by the T.V.A.) and all the shopping res, parking spaces, schools, community buildings, cinemas, which advanced sociological city planning requires (mostly provided by Skidmore, Owings and Merrill), it might appear that the general layout was the product of no conscious planning at all. The rapidity of construction and the completeness of the facilities provided were extraordinary. Moreover, no single existing architectural organization could possibly have undertaken to carry out all the work in the time demanded, but the absence of an overall city-building organization is very evident in any comparison between a section of Oak Ridge and the Dodge-Chicago plant. Of course there is no comparison possible between the difficulty and complexity of the two operations, since Kahn has been building large aircraft engine plants for many years, and no one ever built a city of 75,000 in the space of a few months.

But public housing, rather than the construction of whole cities, is really the other great field of bureaucratic architecture beside factory building. Alas, there also really serious large-scale organizations have yet to be set up.

The West Coast housing that is illustrated was intentionally both experimental and temporary, and bureaucratic organization will function effectively in the housing field only when the methods become somewhat stabilized—as they were stabilized in rather traditional ways by various English local authorities in the twenties and thirties—and are conceived as permanent or at least 60-year duration projects. There are also economic and perhaps political reasons why housing, while heavily bureaucratized in the usual sense of the word, is not yet in England or America efficiently bureaucratized in the special architectural sense used here.

Bureaucratic architecture can achieve in experienced hands a high level of amenity. But it is ironic that in America we seem to be able to house our machines—or more accurately our people when they are at work—with a surer hand than we house them when they are at home. It is now an old complaint but it is still a sound one. In bureaucratic architecture the problem of quality is to raise housing, schools, and other community facilities to the level of the best new factories. This will come about most surely by the organizational development of the architectural offices which handle the work. A broader and more continuous attack on the problem—perhaps National Housing Corporations with complete architectural staffs—rather than the present piecemeal approach, which has most of the recognized vices and few of the possible virtues of bureaucratic organization, will be needed.

Wright's Modern Gallery for the Solomon R. Guggenheim Foundation, of which the model has been widely illustrated, belongs to an entirely different world—the world of the architecture of genius. As I have used the terms "bureaucrat" and "bureaucratic" without the pejorative connotation which they have for many people, I should hasten to say that I use the word "genius" merely to define the sort of architect who functions as a creative individual rather than as an anonymous member of a team. The term refers to a particular psychological approach and way of working at architecture which may or may not produce masterpieces. The products of the "genius" cannot be assessed from the sum of their particular amenities in the way one might justly compare one factory with another or one housing estate with another on a percentage score-card basis. Their qualities depend on overall impact, just as the qualities of the more intensely expressive types of art such as poetry or painting or music do.

It is easy to query, particularly while the Modern Gallery is still a project, whether this or that feature of plan or construction or detailed expression will be convenient or effective, but it is impossible to judge the building as a whole until it is a whole, just as it would be in the case of a project for a poem or a sketch for a painting. The building itself when completed will be, to use a favourite image of Wright's, an organism not a mechanical assembly of parts. Every element will be so organically interrelated with every other in a single expressive whole that they will cease to have independent existence. The gallery may or may not be going to be successful as a whole, but if it is not, it will be because of some inherent flaw in the essential concept, not because it could be improved by changing this or that part. In other words, the architecture of genius is a kind of artistic gamble which may or may not come off, but rarely just gets by. It would not be sensible to leave the conduct of large-scale operations, such as factories or schools to be built in series or prefabricated housing, thus in the hands of a single architect-gambler, because the community's practical stakes are too high. Indeed a single architect could hardly hope to plan and supervise really large projects without setting up a sort of makeshift pseudo-bureaucratic organization. For this the "genius" is rather unlikely to have either the taste or the special administrative and executive talent.

The world of the mid-twentieth century will need some buildings by architects of genius, for only thus can the necessary monotony and the low level of plastic interest of bureaucratic architecture be balanced and relieved. But where, as in England, large-scale reconstruction is the overwhelming present need, individual monuments of distinction—admittedly economic, if not necessarily cultural, luxuries—must wait. While we wait for them, we must not ask of the vast quantities of building immediately required the qualities which they cannot be expected, given the necessary conditions of their production, to possess. But we must guard against the enticement of ideas and features which promise to give to bureaucratic building something of the special expressive power that can be legitimately provided only by architects of genius working as individuals.* Likewise when opportunities arise to build focal structures, call them "monuments" if you will, the theatres, churches, libraries, municipal buildings and so forth which serve the community as a whole, symbolically as well as actually; their vigour and richness of expression ought to raise them out of the world of amenity into the w of art. If this is to be so, we must make sure that they are left to bureaucrats to design. Unfortunately it is in field of public architecture, to which most of these "mo ments" are likely to belong, that public authority has b most inclined to employ bureaucrats. The best exis private firms of bureaucratic character like Kahn's, b specialists, are little inclined to undertake commissions of order. Among architects in organizations working directl indirectly in the public service there should also be fairly sho a tradition of specialization in housing or in the provisio such things as schools or hospitals, which would equally them to avoid monumental commissions. As most ma architects will be drawn into operations of bureauc character, the designing of types of building unsuited to bur cratic production should be thrown open to competi or commissioned to architects of proved individuality.

The distinction between the character of the operations leading bureaucratic organization like Kahn, Inc., and individual practitioner of established fame like Wrigh real, but can be exaggerated if applied ruthlessly to the w architectural profession. While it would not be wise to h Kahn design your Modern Gallery—though you would do less get a useful structure—or Wright your aircraft pla though you would certainly get an interesting one (eventua —sensitive and well-trained modern architects are ordina capable of working (since they have usually had to do in both ways. But conceptually the two types of work distinct and should not be subjected to the same typ analysis and criticism any more than the same typ analysis and criticism should be applied to a Hawksm church or a Soane art gallery on the one hand and to a Lon square or terrace of their periods on the other. Both s of work require technical mastery of the structural m of the day, both require skilful analysis of purpose and mas of functional planning, both need thorough and consis designing; but only complex individual structures of gen ized symbolic meaning actually fail architecturally when t has been no individual imaginative formulation. Whil the eighteenth century terrace of houses or the twent century factory too intense an imaginative formulation actually lead to pretentious absurdity.

We have in the middle of the twentieth century, after decades and more of development, an established modern of building. We are free to use it now for the satisfac of our enormous practical needs and eventually for the sa faction of our spiritual needs. We need not worry m about "style" or rate of development, but only about qua in the terms appropriate to the method of architectural duction. Where imagination is required in the realm bureaucratic architecture is in site-planning, which may may not be within the province of architects' bureaucratic ganizations. The lack of such imagination is very eviden Oak Ridge, but it is clear no one architectural organiza had overall responsibility there. It may well be, now "planning" is becoming more and more a separate acti from architecture, that architects of broad imaginative capa ought to shift their base of operations to that field. Corbusier for example seems to some extent to be doing thi relation to current French programmes of reconstruction.

The "modern way of town-planning" has still, howeve receive a clear formulation. Its sanctions are still multi even alas! eclectic. Although several of the great mo architects have given us imaginative projects on paper, where, unless perhaps in the new quarters of Amsterd is there an executed modern plan which *combines* bold inn tion with mature assurance in the same way that a buildings did in the twenties when modern architecture manifestly came of age. Let us hope that among the reconstruction projects and the new towns which the few years will see being executed a few really coherent convincing examples will appear. Then we need have fear that the prose of the bureaucrats will be presented t only in garbled and monotonously repeated passages or the poetry of the geniuses, when we are ready to employ th will be provided with no suitable sites.

* The public monuments of Nazidom might serve as a warning. Moreover, England and America have their own horrible examples of twentieth century bureaucratic "monuments."

Building + Home

Skidmore, Owings & Merrill

Chicago, New York, San Francisco, Portland

4 Bauen+Wohnen

Organisation, Bauten, Projekte der größten amerikanischen Architekturfirma

Organisation, réalisations et projets de la plus grande maison d'architecture americaine

The Organisation, the Buildings and the Plans of the Leading American Architectural Firm

Construction + Habitation

Zürich / April **1957**

S. Giedion

Das Experiment S.O.M.

In Chicago fließt das Herzblut der amerikanischen Architektur. Weder in Europa noch in Amerika gab es in den achtziger Jahren des vergangenen Jahrhunderts — zwischen 1883 und 1893 — eine Architektur, die mit dem inneren Nerv der Zeit verwachsen war und neue Probleme neu anzupacken den Mut hatte. Die sog. Schule von Chicago, die in jener Zeit aus dem Nichts, aus dem Prärieboden wuchs, war in der Durchführung ihrer neuen Bauprobleme, den großen Verwaltungs- und Bürobauten, wie sie das Zentrum des Middle-West verlangte, mit diesem Nerv verwandt. Als ich bei meinem ersten Aufenthalt in Harvard in den Weihnachtsferien 1938 nach Chicago fuhr, war ich überwältigt von der Ungebrochenheit des Ausdruckes, den diese Bauten des späten 19. Jahrhunderts ausströmten.

Das Typische an dieser Entwicklung, die ich in »Space, Time and Architecture« (11. Auflage 1956) kurz aufgezeichnet habe, ist, daß die Architekten und Ingenieure wie William Le Baron Jenney, Holabird and Roche, Burnham und Root, Adler und Sullivan, die damals die Führung hatten, nicht tote Firmennamen bedeuteten, vielmehr scharfumrissene Individualitäten.

Mit Ausnahme von ganz wenigen, wie der Monadnock Block von Burnham und Root (1891), kannten wir keine jenseits des Ozeans. Aus der Masse des Ungewerteten versuchte ich einige aus ihrer Anonymität in die Architekturgeschichte einzureihen, wie William Le Baron Jenneys Leiter Building (1889), das völlig unbeachtete Reliance Building von Burnham and Company (1894) und Louis Sullivans Carson, Pirie and Scott Warenhaus, begonnen 1899. Dieses letztere war das einzige, von dem eine vage Vorstellung bestand.

Nach 1893 kam ein langer Schlaf für Chicago. Nur die Wunderblüten der Einfamilienhäuser F. L. Wrights sprangen in den Vororten Chicagos um 1900 auf. Die Bautätigkeit zentrierte sich mehr und mehr nach New York, vollkommen versunken im merkantilen Klassizismus. In New York begann mit dem stets komplizierter werdenden Baubetrieb der Aufstieg der Architektur»fabriken« mit ihren Hunderten von Angestellten. Die scharf ausgeprägten Architektengesichter Chicagos verlieren sich im Wallstreetdunkel. Kommerzialisierung ohne moralischen Hintergrund hat die Herrschaft. Diese Architekturfabriken, die die Architekturgeschichte des vergangenen Jahrhunderts beschließen, zeichneten sich durch solide Bauausführung und konstruktive Erfahrung aus. In den Ordnern (files) befanden sich klassifiziert die Formen der ganzen Architekturgeschichte, die während des 19. Jahrhunderts gesammelt worden waren. Wohlgeordnet und ausgepreßt wie Herbariumspflanzen standen sie fertig zum Gebrauch. Für jeden Anspruch des Klienten fand sich dort die entsprechende Antwort. Parallel dazu wurden Berechnungen für die neuen Stahlkonstruktionen statistisch gesammelt.

Es gelang gelegentlich auch ein großes Stück Architektur, wie — um 1900 — die tonnengewölbte luftige Halle der Great Central Station in New York. Im ganzen aber näherte sich die Architektur immer mehr gut konstruierten Maschinen.

Wohin dies führt, dafür legt das Wallstreetviertel am Südende von Manhattan Zeugnis ab: wie im tropischen Urwald versucht jeder Bau auf Kosten des anderen sich durchzusetzen. Aus den dörflichen Straßen von Neu-Amsterdam werden die Schluchten des Finanzzentrums der Welt. Ebensowenig wie die Architektur als moralischer Begriff können städtebauliche Überlegungen unter diesen Umständen ein Existenzrecht haben.

Und was geschah gleichzeitig im großen Baubetrieb Chicagos? Es war, als ob es nie einen Sullivan oder eine Chicago School gegeben hätte. Was der Loop, das Geschäftsviertel von Chicago, seit dem Ende der Chicago School an Architektur bis zum Erscheinen von Mies van der Rohe am Illinois Institute of Technology produzierte, ist für die Geschichte der Architektur inexistent, wertlos. Alles schwimmt im Routinefahrwasser New Yorks, gleichgültig ob es sich um die Kaugummiarchitektur der Wrighly-Bauten oder um die Kinogotik der Chicago Tribune (1923) handelt, deren Häßlichkeit täglich angeleuchtet wird. Es brauchte, wie Sullivan dies 1893 vorausgesagt hatte, ein halbes Jahrhundert, bis Chicago selbst wieder fähig wurde, auf seine eigene, innere Stimme zu hören.

Lever-House, New York.

Wie und worum gearbeitet wird

Das Unternehmen S.O.M., das sich in weniger als drei Jahrzehnten über die USA und verschiedene Weltteile ausbreitete, ist im Grunde ein Experiment, ein Experiment großen Stils, denn ihm liegt ein bestimmtes Problem zugrunde: Ist es im heutigen Stadium der Entwicklung möglich, mit sauberen architektonischen Mitteln zu arbeiten, ohne daß die Auftraggeber Reißaus nehmen?

Experimente sind stets von zwei Faktoren abhängig: vom Beobachter und vom Beobachteten. Das Beobachtete ist in diesem Fall die Kundschaft. Ist sie derart strukturiert, daß ein Gleichklang zwischen den Wünschen des Auftraggebers und den Geboten der heutigen Architektur entsteht, so wird das Experiment Zukunft haben. In Amerika ist das trotz des scharfen Konkurrenzkampfes leichter als auf europäischem Boden, denn der Klient hat mehr Vertrauen zum Fachmann als in Europa. Er meint nicht auch auf künstlerischem Gebiet alles besser zu verstehen als der beratende Architekt.

Der Experimentator hat seinerseits einen verpflichtenden Anteil am Gelingen des Experiments. Er muß selber die Einsicht und den Mut besitzen, das Experiment kompromißlos durchzuführen. Das ist bei einem Unternehmen, das ungefähr 900 Angestellte umfaßt, durchaus nicht einfach.

Ist es ein Zufall, daß Skidmore, Owings & Merrill während der letzten dreißiger Jahre in Chicago Fuß faßten? Ich glaube nicht. Es ist ebensowenig ein Zufall wie die seltsame Tatsache, daß ein so kompromißloser Avantgardist wie Mies van der Rohe schließlich im größten Stil in den offenen Chicago-Baumarkt eindrang. Es ist der merkwürdige Prärieboden, der architektonischem Wachstum günstig ist, viel günstiger als der Malerei oder der Musik. Es ist heute immer noch ein Eiertanz, Qualität gegen Kundengeschmack den Vorrang zu lassen, und doch besteht der Erfolg des Experiments S.O.M. gerade darin.

Wie wird dies erreicht? Indem anstelle einer Architekturfabrik fast ein Architektenkollektiv tritt, indem individuelle Planung und Gemeinschaftsplanung verbunden wurde. Stilherbarien wurden gegen lebendige Menschen ausgetauscht, von denen jeder sein Maß an künstlerischer Freiheit erhält.

Wie dies im einzelnen geschieht, darüber geben die Beiträge Auskunft: William E. Hartmann, der Leiter des Chicago Office, über die Organisation im ganzen, Paffard Clay über das Zustandekommen eines Entwurfs, Bruce Graham über die letzte Entwicklung der Verwaltungs- und Geschäftshochbauten, Walter Netsch über die Air Force Academy in Colorado Springs, die in die Regionalplanung ausmündet (17500 acres in fünf Tälern).

Das Eingehen auf die Möglichkeiten des einzelnen und auf gegebene lokale Verhältnisse äußert sich bereits in der Organisation. Sie ist regional verschieden. In San Franzisco ist sie anders als in Chicago und in Chicago anders als in New York, obwohl alle dauernd miteinander kommunizieren. In New York ist es Gordon Bunshaft, der die Zügel führt und in allen Bauten sein architektonisches Profil zeigt. Er ist einer jener Architekten, die wissen, wie die moderne Kunst mit der heutigen Architektur zusammenhängt und daß Architektur und Malerei befruchtend einander nötig haben. Man kann sicher sein, ihm in den New Yorker Kunstausstellungen zu begegnen, die kurze Pfeife in dem leicht schief geneigten Gesicht. Als mir die Manufacturers Trust Company-Filiale in der Fifth Avenue gezeigt wurde, da fragte ich, wie es möglich war, daß er im obersten Stockwerk des sog. Pent House in den Räumen des Präsidenten und des Verwaltungsrats Gemälde von Braque, Léger, Mirò, de Chirico — bis zu Steinberg von auffallend guter Qualität aufhängen konnte. Mir kam das nach Erfahrungen, die man etwa in der Schweiz sammeln kann, höchst unwahrscheinlich vor. Bunshaft sagte einfach: »Man hat Vertrauen zu meinem Urteil.«

Ihm dankt New York seinen bis jetzt saubersten Bau, das Lever Brother House (1950) in der Park Avenue. Die bekannte englische Seifenfirma Lever Brother ist darauf eingegangen, einen Teil des kostbaren Terrains zu opfern und in Platzraum für das Publikum zu verwandeln. Dahinter steht die Überzeugung, daß

Warren-Petroleum Corporation in Tulsa, Oklahoma.

ein Bau nur wirklich atmet, wenn er räumlich eine städtebauliche Situation erfüllt. Das bedeutete für New York einen wichtigen Anfang.

Nun steht der Bau der Chase Manhatten Bank an der Pine Street im Wallstreet-Viertel bevor, in dem ähnliches versucht wird: Freier Raum vor den 60 Stockwerken, von denen jedes 30000 Quadratfuß umfaßt.

Das Chicagoer Office leitet William E. Hartmann, wie Bunshaft ein Mann in den vierziger Jahren. Man kennt ihn als Architekt eines Hotels in Cincinnati, wo er, wiederum ein Novum in USA, einem Maler wie Joan Mirò die Ausmalung eines Saales übergab. Sein Büro befindet sich in einem der obersten Stockwerke von 100 W. Monroe Str. Auf der riesigen Marmorplatte seines Schreibtisches liegt kein Brief und kein Löschblatt. Im naheliegenden Zeichensaal sitzen die Entwerfer (Designer) — nicht die Zeichner. Sie bilden den Generalstab — den »braintrust«. Ausschließlich junge Leute. Alle unter 35. Sie sind sorgfältig ausgewählt. Die Firma hält schon an den Hochschulen Ausschau nach dem Tüchtigsten unter dem Nachwuchs. Eine wohltuend scharfe Luft, die durch Selektion erreicht wird, ist in diesem Raum spürbar. Wer nicht taugt, verschwindet raschestens, wer aber taugt, der hat eine Chance zur Entfaltung, zur persönlichen Verwirklichung und — zum Sammeln eigener Erfahrung in ingenieurmäßigen Spitzenleistungen. Man bringt dem Eintretenden zuallererst Vertrauen entgegen, selbst auf die Gefahr hin, daß etwas mißlingen könnte. Er wird verantwortlich von der Planung an bis zur Bauübergabe. Er hat die Unterhandlung mit Unternehmern und Klienten zu führen. Für europäische Gepflogenheiten wäre es kaum denkbar, daß einem jungen Architekten, der niemals zuvor eine Schule baute, am Tag seines Eintritts eine Mittelschule (High School) für eineinhalb Millionen Dollars übergeben würde.

In dem hellen Saal sitzen die jungen Architekten, einzeln oder in Gruppen, um ihre Zeichenbretter oder Modelle. Aus allen Ecken der Windrose hergeweht, arbeitet der Südländer neben dem Nordländer, der Japaner neben dem Mann aus dem Mittelwest. Reibungslos begegnen sich die Erdteile, wie dies auch an den besten Universitäten dieses Landes üblich ist.

Es liegt im Wesen der heutigen Entwicklung, daß die behandelten Probleme die Tendenz haben, über den engumschriebenen Begriff »Architektur« hinauszugreifen. Der ungefähr fünfunddreißigjährige Walter Netsch ist gerade damit beschäftigt, einzelne Baulichkeiten des großen Programms der Air Force Academy mit ihren Schulen, ihrer Stadt und ihren Tälern auszuarbeiten.

Einige Tische weiter ist Bruce Graham mit einigen andern wie dem jungen Engländer Paffard Clay daran, in der Konstruktion eines modernen Bürogebäudes — es handelt sich um den Wolkenkratzer aus rostfreiem Stahl der Inland Steel Corporation — die Tragkonstruktion nach außen zu drücken. Keine Säule beeinträchtigt das Innere, so daß der verfügbare Raum bis zum letzten Zoll frei ausgenützt werden kann. Aus demselben Grund ist der Aufzugsturm als Baukörper für sich behandelt. Auf dem Tisch liegen zwei Vorschläge für die Behandlung der Fassade.Einer davon zeigt die Konstruktionsglieder mit schwarzer Farbe überstrichen, der andere läßt das rostfreie Skelett blank aufsteigen. »Was würden Sie vorziehen?« wurde ich gefragt. »Warum eine schwarze pompe-funèbre-Architektur? Warum nicht lieber das rostfreie Skelett in dem grau-rußigen Chicagoer Loop?« »Aber Mies van der Rohe malt das Skelett seiner Lake Shore Apartments auch schwarz...« Der nun aufsteigende Bau, immerhin seit mehr als einem halben Jahrhundert der erste moderne Wolkenkratzer im Loop, wird nun tatsächlich ein Silberfisch.

Die Atmosphäre in diesem Saal der Jugend erinnert an die Skizze, die F. L. Wright in »Genius and Mobocracy«, dem Buch, das er seinem Meister Louis Sullivan widmete, vom Atelier Adler und Sullivan gibt (p. 47), das sie im damals (1889) neu erbauten Turm des »Auditoriumskomplex« eingerichtet hatten und in dem der zwanzigjährige Wright bereits seinen Raum neben dem von Sullivan »lieber Meister« hatte und alles auf menschlichem Maßstab und menschlichem Kontakt beruhte. Schließlich taucht die Frage auf, was für eine Rolle spielt ein Unternehmen wie S.O.M. in der heutigen Architekturentwicklung? Sind Vorstöße ins Unbekannte möglich wie sie die vorangegangene Generation von Corbusier, Gropius, Mies oder Aalto hinstellten?

Noch ist eine eindeutige Antwort nicht möglich. Die Magie, die Mies van der Rohe mit dem Stahlskelett vollbrachte, liegt den jungen Leuten tief im Blut. Darüber hinaus ist es sein Begriff der Moral im architektonischen Bau, der sie fasziniert.

Veterans' Hospital in Brooklyn, New York.

Wieweit dem Experiment S.O.M. dauerndes Gelingen beschieden ist, hängt auf der einen Seite davon ab, wieweit heute bereits Teamwork den einzelnen Genius ersetzen kann? Noch sind wir weit von der Kathedrale von Chartres, wenn es sich um Zusammenarbeit handelt. Auf der andern Seite, wieweit ist es in einem so großen Unternehmen möglich das Geschäftsinteresse gelegentlich vor Architekturüberlegungen zurückzustellen?

Aber das ist nicht nur eine Frage, die das Experiment S.O.M. allein angeht, es ist eine Schicksalsfrage, die an unsere ganze Zeit gerichtet wird.

S. Giedion

L'Experience S.O.M.

C'est à Chicago que s'épanouit l'essence de l'architecture américaine. Ni en Europe ni en Amérique, il n'a existé au cours des années quatre-vingt du siècle dernier, une architecture qui ait été intimement liée à l'esprit du temps et qui ait eu le courage d'aborder de façon nouvelle des problèmes nouveaux. Ce qu'on a appelé l'école de Chicago, qui est sortie à ce moment du néant, était apparentée à cet esprit dans la solution de ces nouveaux problèmes posés par la construction des grands bâtiments administratifs et commerciaux qu'exigeait le centre du Middle-West. Lorsque je me suis rendu à Chicago à Noël 1938, au cours de mon premier séjour à Harvard, j'ai été saisi par l'impression de force qui se dégageait de ces édifices de la fin du 19ème siècle.

L'élément typique de cette évolution, que j'ai brièvement esquissée dans «Space, Time and Architecture» (Ilème édition 1956), est le fait que les architectes et les ingénieurs tels que William Le Baron Jenney, Holabird et Roche, Burnham et Root, Adler et Sullivan — qui jouaient à ce moment un rôle de premier plan — ne représentaient pas des noms vides de sens, mais bien au contraire des personnalités nettement marquées.

A l'exception de rares bâtiments, comme le Monadnock Block de Burnham et Root (1891), nous ne connaissions aucun édifice de ce genre de ce côté de l'océan. Parmi la masse des bâtiments inconnus, j'ai tenté de sortir quelques-uns de leur anonymat pour les incorporer dans l'histoire de l'architecture, comme par exemple le Leiter Building de William Le Baron Jenney (1889), le Reliance Building de Burnham and Company (1894), ainsi que le grand magasin de Carson, Pirie and Scott, réalisé par Sullivan. Ce dernier était le seul dont on avait une vague idée.

Après 1893, Chicago est entrée dans une longue période de sommeil, qui n'a été troublée que par la floraison des habitations familiales de F. L. Wright dans les faubourgs de la ville aux environs de 1900. L'activité de la construction s'est de plus en plus centrée sur New York, où elle a entièrement sombré dans le classicisme mercantile.

C'est à New York qu'a commencé, avec l'activité toujours plus compliquée dans le domaine de la construction, l'essor de ce qu'on pourrait appeler les «fabriques» d'architecture, avec leurs centaines d'employés. Les fortes personnalités des architectes de Chicago se sont perdues dans les ténèbres de Wall-Street, et la commercialisation, sans arrière-plan moral, a de plus en plus joué un rôle prédominant. Ces «fabriques d'architecture», qui ont mis fin à l'histoire architecturale du siècle dernier, se caractérisaient par une solide exécution des bâtiments et par une bonne expérience de la construction. Dans les fichiers, on pouvait trouver toutes les formes de l'histoire architecturale qui avaient été rassemblées durant le 19ème siècle.

Soigneusement rangées et pressées comme des plantes dans un herbier, elles étaient constamment prêtes à l'emploi, et l'on pouvait y trouver la réponse appropriée à chaque exigence des clients. En même temps, on a réuni sous forme de statistiques les calculs pour les nouvelles constructions métalliques.

Von links nach rechts / De gauche à droite / From left to right: John O. Merrill, Nathanial A. Owings, Louis Skidmore.

Gordon Bunshaft und William Hartmann.

Gruppenarbeit an Modellen für die Air Force Academy.

Travail en groupe aux maquettes de la Air Force Academy.

Members of the Air Force Academy Design Group.

Housing-Oak, Ridge, Tenn.

Cette période a vu aussi la réalisation de quelque grande œuvre architecturale, comme par exemple vers 1900, le vaste hall aéré, en forme de voûte, de la Great Central Station à New York. Mais dans l'ensemble, l'architecture s'est de plus en plus appliquée à la production quasi-mécanique de machines au fonctionnement impeccable.

L'aspect du quartier de Wallstreet, au sud de Manhattan, montre où conduit cette tendance: chaque bâtiment cherche à s'élever au détriment des autres. Les rues villageoises de la Nouvelle-Amsterdam sont devenues les profondes gorges qui caractérisent le centre financier du monde. Dans ces conditions, les considérations urbanistes — pas plus que l'architecture en tant que notion morale — ne peuvent avoir droit à l'existence.

Et que s'est-il passé en même temps dans le domaine de la construction à Chicago? Dans cette ville, l'évolution s'est faite comme s'il n'y avait jamais eu un Sullivan ou une Chicago School. Ce qu'a produit le Loop — quartier des affaires de Chicago — depuis la fin de la dite école jusqu'à l'apparition de Mies van der Rohe à l'Institut de technologie de l'Illinois, a été inexistant et sans valeur pour l'histoire de l'architecture. L'activité de la construction a été en quelque sorte à la remorque de New York, qu'il s'agisse de l'architecture de chewing-gum des bâtiments de Wrighly ou du gothique de cinéma de la Chicago Tribune (1923), dont la laideur s'impose chaque jour à la vue.

Comme Sullivan l'avait prévu en 1893, il a fallu un demisiècle pour que Chicago soit de nouveau capable d'écouter sa propre voix.

Comment et dans quel but travaille-t-on?

L'entreprise S.O.M., qui s'est étendue en moins de trente ans aux USA et dans diverses régions du monde, est en principe une expérience, et même une expérience de grand style, puisqu'elle s'attaque à ce problème très précis: au stade actuel de l'évolution, est-il possible de travailler avec des moyens architecturaux nets et sobres, sans que les commettants ne prennent la fuite?

Les expériences dépendent toujours de deux facteurs: l'observateur et l'observé. Dans le cas particulier, c'est la clientèle qui est l'observé. Si sa structure est de telle nature que l'harmonie soit réalisée entre les vœux du commettant et les exigences de l'architecture actuelle, un grand avenir s'ouvre certainement devant cette éxpérience. En Amérique, la chose est plus facile que sur le continent européen, malgré la forte concurrence, car le client y a davantage confiance qu'en Europe dans les spécialistes. Il ne prétend pas en savoir plus dans le domaine artistique que l'architecte-conseil.

De son côté, l'expérimentateur a un rôle important à jouer dans la réussité de l'expérience. Il doit avoir lui-même la largeur de vues et le courage de mener l'expérience sans compromis, ce qui est loin d'être facile dans une entreprise comptant environ 900 employés. Est-ce l'effet du hasard si Skidmore, Owings & Merril ont pris pied à Chicago au cours des dernières trente années? Je ne le crois pas. C'est autant un hasard que le fait qu'un pionier aussi intransigeant que Mies van der Rohe se soit finalement imposé en grand style sur le marché libre de la construction à Chicago. C'est le cadre étonnant de la prairie qui est favorable au développement de l'architecture, beaucoup plus qu'à celui de la peinture ou de la musique.

Aujourd'hui encore, il est extrêmement délicat de vouloir donner la prédominance à la qualité, contre les goûts de la clientèle, et pourtant c'est précisément là que réside le succès de l'expérience S.O.M.

Comment ce résultat est-il obtenu? Il est réalisé par le fait qu'une fabrique d'architecture est remplacée par une véritable collectivité d'architectes, où l'étude individuelle est intimement liée à l'étude collective. Les systèmes stéréotypés ont été changés contre des hommes pleins de vie, dont chacun jouit d'un haut degré de liberté artistique. Quelques publications donnent une idée de la manière dont ce résultat est réalisé: William E. Hartmann, directeur du bureau de Chicago, sur l'organisation dans son ensemble; Paffard Clay, sur l'élaboration d'un projet; Bruce Graham, sur la dernière évolution de la construction des grands bâtiments administratifs et commerciaux; Walter Netsch, sur l'Académie de la Royal Air Force à Colorado Springs, qui trouve sa conclusion dans l'étude des plans régionaux (17,500 acres dans cinq vallées).

L'étude attentive des possibilités particulières et des conditions locales données s'exprime déjà dans l'organisation. Celle-ci est extrêmement diverse selon les régions. A San Francisco, elle est autre qu'à Chicago, et à Chicago autre qu'à New York, bien qu'elle travaille constamment en harmonie sur le plan commun. A New York, c'est Gordon Bunshaft qui mène la barque et qui réalise ses principes architecturaux dans tous les bâtiments. Il est un de ces architectes qui connaissent les relations entre l'art moderne et l'architecture actuelle, et qui savent à quel point l'architecture et la peinture ont besoin l'une de l'autre. On le rencontre dans toutes les expositions artistiques de New York.

Quand on m'a montré la succursale de la Manufacturers Trust Company, dans la Cinquième Avenue, je me suis demandé comment il avait été possible qu'il ait pu placer à l'étage supérieur de la Pent House, dans les bureaux du président et du conseil d'administration, d'excellents tableaux de Braque, Léger, Miro, de Chirico, et jusqu'à Steinberg. D'après les expériences que l'on peut faire en Suisse, la chose m'a semblée hautement invraisemblable. Mais Bunshaft a simplement déclaré: «On a confiance dans mon jugement.»

New York lui doit la construction la plus sobre qu'elle ait connue jusqu'à présent, à savoir la Lever Brother House (1950), dans la Park Avenue. La célèbre fabrique de savon anglaise a décidé de sacrifier une partie de son précieux terrain et d'en faire un emplacement à l'intention du public. Cette décision est inspirée par la conviction qu'un bâtiment ne respire vraiment que s'il remplit un rôle, sous le rapport de l'espace, dans l'aménagement urbain de la cité. Ceci représente un important début dans une ville comme New York.

On s'attaque maintenant à la construction de la Chase Manhattan Bank, à Pine Street dans le quartier de Wallstreet, où l'on poursuit un but semblable: laisser plus d'espace devant les 60 étages, dont chacun couvre 30,000 pieds carrés (2790 m^2).

Le bureau de Chicago est dirigé par William E. Hartmann, qui est âgé d'une quarantaine d'années, comme Bunshaft. On le connaît comme architecte d'un hôtel de Cincinatti, où il a confié la décoration d'une salle à un peintre tel que Joan Miro, faisant ainsi une nouvelle innovation aux Etats-Unis. Son bureau est aménagé dans l'un des étages supérieurs du N°100 de W. Monroe-Street. Sur l'immense plaque de marbre de sa table de travail, on ne trouve aucune lettre ni aucun buvard. Dans la salle de dessin voisine se tiennent les créateurs de projets (Designers) — et non les dessinateurs. Ils constituent l'état-major général, le «braintrust». Ce sont tous de jeunes gens de moins de 35 ans, très soigneusement sélectionnés. L'entreprise repère déjà les plus capables d'entre eux dans les écoles supérieures. Cette sélection a pour effect de créer une atmosphère saine et salubre, que l'on perçoit très nettement dans cette salle. Celui qui ne réussit pas disparaît rapidement, tandis que celui qui fait l'affaire a une chance de se développer, de faire aboutir ses réalisations personnelles et de récolter ses propres expériences en menant à chef quelque œuvre d'avant-garde. On commence par faire entière confiance au nouveau-venu, même au risque d'enregistrer quelques échecs. Le nouvel arrivant est responsable, du commencement à la fin, de l'étude d'un bâtiment jusqu'à sa remise au commettant; il est chargé de mener les pourparlers avec les entrepreneurs aussi bien qu'avec les clients. En se plaçant du point de vue des habitudes européennes, il est à peine concevable qu'un jeune architecte, qui n'a encore jamais construit une école, puisse se voir confier, le jour de son entrée, la réalisation d'une école supérieure pour une somme d'un million et demi de dollars.

Cette salle claire est le lieu de travail des jeunes architectes, assis isolés ou par groupes devant leurs planches à dessin ou leurs modèles. Ils sont venus de tous les coins du monde, du nord et du sud du pays, du Japon et du Middle-West, et toutes les races se coudoient harmonieusement, comme c'est d'ailleurs le cas dans les meilleures universités de ce pays.

L'évolution actuelle est essentiellement caractérisée par le fait que les problèmes traités ont tendance à sortir du cadre étroit de la notion d'«architecture». Le jeune Walter Netsch, âgé d'environ 35 ans, est précisément occupé à élaborer les grands programmes de l'Air Force Academy, avec ses écoles, sa ville et ses vallées.

Quelques tables plus loin se trouve Bruce Graham en compagnie d'autres collaborateurs, dont le jeune Anglais Paffard Clay, travaillant à la mise au point d'un bâtiment moderne de bureaux — il s'agit du gratte-ciel en acier inoxydable de l'Inland Steel Corporation — où ils cherchent à mettre l'accent de la construction portante vers l'extérieur. Aucune colonne ne gêne l'intérieur de l'édifice, si bien que l'espace disponible peut être utilisé jusqu'au dernier centimètre cube. Pour la même raison, la cage des ascenseurs est considérée comme une partie intégrante de la construction. Sur la table, on peut voir deux projets pour l'exécution de la façade. L'un montre les éléments de construction soulignés en couleur noire, tandis que l'autre laisse apparaître en blanc le squelette inoxydable.

«Que préfèreriez-vous?», m'a-t-on demandé. «Pourquoi une architecture noire genre pompes funèbres? Pourquoi pas plutôt le squelette inoxydable dans le gris de suie du Loop de Chicago?»

«Mais Mies van der Rohe peint aussi en noir le squelette de son appartement de Lake Shore...»

La construction qui est en train de s'élever, tout en étant cependant le premier gratte-ciel moderne du Loop depuis plus d'un demi-siècle, sera effectivement un édifice de ton argenté.

Dans cette salle de la jeunesse, l'atmosphère rappelle l'esquisse que F. L. Wright, dans «Genius and Mobocracy,» ouvrage qu'il a dédié au maître Louis Sullivan, a faite de l'atelier d'Adler et Sullivan (page 47), avaient qu'ils en aménagé 1889 dans la nouvelle tour de l'«Auditorium», où le jeune Wright — qui avait à ce moment 20 ans — avait déjà sa place à côté de son «cher maître» Sullivan, et où tout était fondé sur les contacts humains. Pour conclure, on peut se demander quel rôle une entreprise comme le S.O.M. est appelée à jouer dans l'évolution architecturale actuelle. Des incursions dans l'inconnu comme celles de la génération précédente des Le Corbusier, Gropius, Mies ou Aalto, sont-elles possibles?

On ne peut encore donner à cette question une réponse précise. La magie que Mies van der Rohe a fait naître par son squelette d'acier a fortement impressionné les jeunes, qui sont fascinés en outre par sa notion de morale dans la construction architecturale.

La mesure dans laquelle l'expérience S.O.M. est appelée à une réussite durable dépend, d'un côté, de la question de savoir jusqu'à quel point le travail en équipe peut remplacer aujourd' hui déjà le génie individuel. Or nous sommes encore loin de la cathédrale de Chartres, si l'on parle de travail en commun. D'un autre côté, on peut se demander dans quelle mesure il est possible, dans une entreprise aussi importante, de faire passer les intérêts commerciaux après les considérations architecturales.

C'est là cependant une question qui ne concerne pas uniquement l'expérience S.O.M.; c'est au contraire un problème vital qui est posé à toute notre époque.

S. Giedion

The Experiment of S.O.M.

From Chicago flows the life-blood of American architecture. No architecture either in Europe or elsewhere in America developed so closely in accord with the time or had such courage to tackle new problems as in Chicago, between 1883 and 1893.
The so-called Chicago School grew out on the prairie from nothing in answer to the new problems posed by the large commercial and business buildings demanded by this new hub of the Midwest.
When I first travelled to Chicago, during the Christmas holidays of my first visit to Harvard, I was overwhelmed by the integrity and the aspect of these late nineteenth century buildings. It is characteristic of this development (which I have outlined in Space, Time and Architecture, 11th printing, 1956) that the leading names, such as William Le Baron Jenney, Holabird and Roche, Burnham and Root, Adler and Sullivan, were not just impersonal titles of firms, but highly individual architects and engineers. With very few exceptions, such as the Monadnock Block by Burnham and Root (1891), their buildings were unknown to us on the other side of the ocean. I attempted to single out certain of them, from the general mass of unevaluated structures, and to introduce them into the history of architecture. These included William Le Baron Jenney's Leiter Building (1889), the completely unnoticed Reliance Building of Burnham and Company (1894), and Louis Sullivan's Carson, Pirie, Scott department store (1899), the latter being the only one already vaguely recognized.
After 1893 Chicago went into a deep sleep. Houses by Frank Lloyd Wright grew as if by magic in the environs of Chicago at the beginning of the century, but they stood alone. Building construction turned for inspiration more and more towards New York and became completely submerged in mercantile classicism.
With the increasing complexities of the profession, large architecture factories began to crop up in New York, with hundreds of employees. The clearly articulated features of Chicago's architecture became obscured by the darkness of Wall Street. Commercialism without conscience was the rule of the day. The architecture factories which arose at the end of the nineteenth century were respected for their practical experience and sound knowledge of building. Neatly classified, all the forms of architectural history that had been collected during the nineteenth century were now filed and ready for use. The architectural solution was immediately available for whatever the client requested. Simultaneously, other files in the same office were accumulating analytical data on the latest developments in structural steel.
Occasionally a significant work emerged such as the airy, barrel-vaulted space of the Grand Central Station in New York, around 1900. Construction assumed the appearance of well-made machines.
Wall Street at the southernmost tip of the Manhattan peninsula bears evidence of the consequences of this approach. There each building grows higher at the expense of the next, like an overgrown tropical jungle. The village streets of New Amsterdam became canyons through the financial capital of the world. In the absence of a moral concept, city planning, just as architecture, lacks a basis for existence.
Meanwhile, what was happening in Chicago? There it was just as if Sullivan and the Chicago school had never existed. The building activity of Chicago in the "Loop," the business district, drifted in a stream of clichés from New York. Nothing of any value to the history of architecture was produced between the end of the Chicago School period and the advent of Mies van der Rohe at the Illinois Institute of Technology. There was the movie-gothic of the Tribune Tower and the chewing-gum architecture of the Wrigley Building, the ugliness of which is flood-lit each night. Sullivan's prediction of 1893 proved true. Half a century elapsed before Chicago could stand on its feet again and listen to its own conscience.

Manufacturers Trust Company, New York.

What is the objective and how can it be reached?
S.O.M., which has spread in less than three decades across the U.S., and even into far corners of the world, is still basically an experiment, an experiment on a grand scale. Why? Because it cannot at this stage be predicted if it is possible to employ purely architectural elements without fear of losing the client. An experiment depends on two factors: on the observer and on the object

Talman Bank

under observation. The object under observation in this case is the client. This experiment can only succeed if there is concord between the requirements of the client and the fulfillment of contemporary architecture. This may be somewhat easier in the U.S. despite the tougher competition since the client does not always believe that he knows everything on the artistic level better than the architect he has commissioned. The experimentor has to take the responsibility for the success of the experiment. He must have sufficient foresight and courage to carry the experiment through without compromise,

which is no easy matter in the firm of 900 employees.
It seems hardly an accident that S.O.M. has established itself in Chicago so firmly, at least no more accidental than the strange fact that a man of the avant-garde so unwilling to compromise as Mies van der Rohe was finally able to build for the real-estate market on such a large scale. It seems that the soil of the prairie is far more fertile for the growth of architecture than for either painting or music, but it is still like treading on ice to propose quality in place of the ruling taste, and this is where S.O.M. has succeeded.

How was this accomplished? The architecture factory has been almost replaced. Small groups of architects work together so that both individual design and large-scale planning can coincide within one organization. The herbarium of styles is replaced by living people, each with the responsibilities of artistic freedom. The following articles will show how this has been achieved. W. E. Hartmann explains the organization as a whole, Walter Netsch describes how the Air Force Academy extends into planning over 17,000 acres of five valleys. Bruce Graham outlines the development of the modern office building and Paffard Clay its design method. The potentialities of different individuals and regional characteristics are respected and immediately visible in the result. Work from the Chicago office differs from San Francisco and both differ from New York, although they are in close contact with each other.

1

2

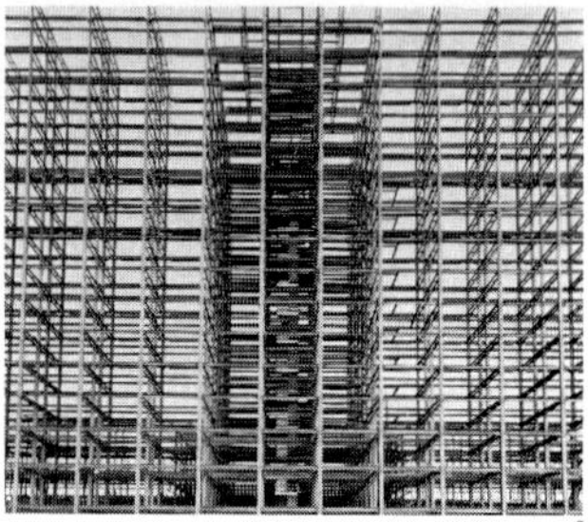

3

1
Auto-City Fords in Dearborn bei Detroit, Mich.
2
Pan American Life Ins., New Orleans.

3
Hamilton Veterans' Hospital in Brooklyn, New York (Stahlgerüst / Squelette d'acier / Steel skeleton).

In New York it is Gordon Bunshaft who holds the reins and his mark is on every design. He is one of those few architects who recognize that modern art and modern architecture are interdependent and benefit from each other. He can be seen at the art exhibitions in New York with his short pipe in his mouth and his head slightly tilted to one side. At the time I was shown around the Manufacturer's Trust on Fifth Avenue, I asked him how they bought such an exceptionally fine collection of paintings for the executive suite and Presidents' room. There were paintings by Braque, Leger, Miro, de Chirico — all the way to Steinberg. Bunshaft's reply was simple: "They trusted my judgment."

New York is indebted to Bunshaft for its most clear-cut building up to 1956 — Lever House on Park Avenue. Lever Brothers, the famous English soap company, agreed to donate the major part of the high rental ground floor so that pedestrians could freely circulate within its court, a demonstration of the conviction that a building can only breathe when it makes a spatial contribution to city planning. This proved to be an important contribution to New York. It is being followed by the sixty-story Chase Manhattan Bank, with a typical floor area of 30,000 square feet which will open the way for a large plaza in the heart of the Wall Street area.

The managing partner of the Chicago Office is William E. Hartmann. Like Bunshaft he is a man in his forties, and he is known for his Terrace Plaza Hotel in Cincinnati, Ohio, where again something new was introduced to the U.S.: The employment of a painter such as Joan Miro to execute a large mural on a curved wall. Hartmann's office in Chicago is in one of the upper floors of 100 West Monroe. The large marble slab which forms his desk top is clean of any scrap of paper and his pen holder is attached behind its supporting leg. The designers are in the adjacent drafting room. They constitute the "brains trust," exclusively young people, all less than thirty-five. One can immediately detect a healthy and alive atmosphere in this room, which is the result of the careful selection of the designers, some of which have been selected even as students from among the most talented in the architectural schools. If the designer is not proficient, he soon disappears from the scene, but if he is an asset he is given every opportunity of personal development and of acquiring experience in most carefully engineered projects. From the very first he is confided in, even at the risk of failure. He follows the project in all its stages from the initial planning through to construction; he is in contact with both the client and the contractor. In European practice it would be hardly conceivable that a young architect who has never yet worked upon a school should be entrusted with a million and a half dollar school project on the day of his arrival. In this brightly day-lit room are young architects at work over their drawing boards or upon their study models who originate from all the corners of the earth, from the north and from the south. There is a Japanese working together with a man from the middle east, and as is common in the best universities, people from all countries work together without any friction.
It is characteristic of current problems that they tend to expand beyond the confines of architecture. Walter Netsch, who is about thirty-five, is currently involved in designing not only the individual academic buildings for the large program for the Air Force Academy, but also the community supported by it, and the entire surrounding terrain.
Nearby, Bruce Graham is at work on the design of a modern office building — a high-rise structure in stainless steel for the Inland Steel Company — studying the expression of columns on the exterior so that every square foot of interior space might be uninterrupted, the service tower being detached for the same reason. There were two proposals on the boards for the exterior cladding. One with the structure painted black and the other the silver of stainless steel.
"Which do you think it should be?" I was asked.
"Why black funeral-parlour architecture? Why not give sooty-grey Chicago a structure in stainless steel?"
"But Mies's apartments on Lake Shore Drive are black."
The cladding is now being erected, the first modern skyscraper office building in the Loop for half a century — and it will be a silver fish.
The atmosphere in this room, full of young people, recalls a description by Frank Lloyd Wright in "Genius and Mobocracy," dedicated to Louis Sullivan. He describes the Adler and Sullivan office, which had just been set up in the newly constructed tower of the Auditorium, where the twenty-five years old Wright had already found his place beside Sullivan, his "lieber Meister," and where everywhere one feels the human scale and human contact.
Finally there remains the question: what is the role that an organization like S. O. M. plays in the development of contemporary architecture? Can it forge ahead into the unexplored as did those of the previous generation — Le Corbusier, Gropius, Aalto, Mies? It is not yet possible to give a clear answer. The magic that Mies instilled into the steel skeleton runs deep in the blood of the younger generation, and still deeper his concept of the moral force in construction. The success of the S. O. M. experiment depends on whether teamwork can supplant the force of individual genius. We are still far from the kind of teamwork that built Chartres Cathedral.
Further, how far is it possible in such a large organization to hold business interests in the background, so that they do not interfere with pure architectural solutions? This is not only a question that concerns the S. O. M. experiment. It is a question that affects the fate of our whole period.

William E. Hartmann

Die Organisation der Firma Skidmore, Owings & Merrill

Gründungsgeschichte

1936 beginnt die Zusammenarbeit von Louis Skidmore und Nathaniel A. Owings in Chicago. 1939 gesellte sich als dritter Architekt John O. Merrill zu ihnen, und die heute als S.O.M. (Skidmore, Owings & Merrill) bekannte Firma wurde gegründet.

Entwicklung

In den darauffolgenden Jahren entwickelte sich die Firma von einer kleinen Architektengruppe mit relativ unbedeutenden Bauaufgaben im Gebiet von Chicago zu einer bedeutenden Organisation von Architekten und Ingenieuren, deren Aufgaben über ganz Nordamerika, ja die halbe Welt verstreut sind und die in vier große, selbständig arbeitende Büros in verschiedenen Gegenden der Vereinigten Staaten gegliedert ist. Das Büro in New York bearbeitet die Projekte im Osten der Vereinigten Staaten, in Europa, im Mittleren Osten und in Südamerika; in San Franzisko wird für die Westküste und den Orient gearbeitet. Das Büro in Portland, Oregon, das ursprünglich in Zusammenarbeit mit Pietro Belluschi entwickelt worden war, baut im nordwestlichen Teil der pazifischen Küste und in Alaska. Das ursprüngliche Büro in Chicago ist das administrative Zentralorgan und bearbeitet Projekte in allen Teilen der Vereinigten Staaten.

Nationale Gliederung

Die Gliederung in Zweigorganisationen nach Landesteilen ergab sich als natürliche Folge aus der Art der Bauaufgaben. Klienten der Firma sind vielfach Industrien und Unternehmungen, die ebenfalls staatenweise gegliedert sind, und schon früh in der Geschichte der Firma erwies es sich, daß diese Kunden am besten in ihren eigenen, ihnen unterstellten Gebieten bedient werden konnten.

Teilhaber

Die Teilhaberschaft von S.O.M. hat sich von den ursprünglichen zwei auf dreizehn Teilhaber erweitert, die hier in der Reihenfolge ihres Beitritts aufgeführt sind:

Louis Skidmore (von der aktiven Teilnahme zurückgetretenes, beratendes Mitglied)
Nathaniel A. Owings
John O. Merrill
William S. Brown
Gordon Bunshaft
Robert W. Cutler
J. Walter Severinghaus
John B. Rodgers
William E. Hartmann
Elliott F. Brown
James W. Hammond
Walter A. Netsch, jr.
Edward J. Mathews

Ein früh eingeführtes Prinzip der Arbeitsaufteilung in S.O.M. ist auch die sogenannte »Tiefenorganisation«. Den eigentlichen Teilhabern sind zwei Gruppen technischen und administrativen leitenden Personals unterstellt, die ebenfalls materiell an den Einnahmen der Firma beteiligt sind: die »Associate Partners« und die »Participating Associates«.

Associate Partners

Die sechzehn Associate Partners sind ausgebildete Architekten, Ingenieure, Städteplaner und Landschaftsarchitekten und sind einzeln für größere Tätigkeitsgebiete der Firma in ihren verschiedenen Zweigstellen oder für besondere Bauaufgaben verantwortlich.

Participating Associates

Den siebenundzwanzig arbeitenden »Participating Associates« sind technische oder administrative Tätigkeitsgebiete unterstellt.

Arbeitsorganisation

Die Organisation der vier Zweigstellen ist sich im wesentlichen ähnlich. Unter der Leitung eines der Teilhaber operieren fünf Arbeitsgruppen:

Durchführung der Projektierung

- Entwurf
  - Festlegung des Programms
  - Gestaltung des Projektes
  - Innenausbau
  - Materialien- und Methodenforschung
- Ausführung (Pläne)
  - Architektonische Detailpläne
  - Ingenieurpläne (Konstruktion, Bauplatzorganisation, Fundamente, Bodenuntersuchungen)
  - Installationen (Elektrizität, Sanitärinstallationen, Materialbehandlung, Heizung, Ventilation und Luftkonditionierung)
  - Kostenberechnungen
- Ausführung (Bauaufsicht)
  - Arbeitsvergebung
  - Bauaufsicht
  - örtliche Bauführung
- Administration
  - Organisation der Büros
  - Archivierung
  - Buchhaltung
  - Nichttechnisches Personal

Innerhalb dieser Grundstruktur besteht ausdrücklich ein großes Maß an nationaler und lokaler Flexibilität. Das Personal, einschließlich der oben erwähnten Teilhabergruppen, gilt als beweglich, so daß Erfahrung und momentane Abkömmlichkeit des einzelnen gegeneinander abgewogen werden können, um so das stärkste mögliche Team zur Lösung jeder Bauaufgabe zusammenzustellen. Dieses Prinzip trägt weitgehend zur Einheitlichkeit innerhalb der Arbeiten der Firma bei.

Architektonische Gestaltung

Von Anfang an wurde der architektonischen Gestaltung besonderes Gewicht beigelegt; in jedem Zweigbüro ist ein Teilhaber für diesen wichtigen Bereich im Aufgabengebiet der Firma verantwortlich. Unter seiner Leitung werden für jedes Projekt die Entwurfsleute (oder Projektarchitekten, wie sie gewöhnlich genannt werden) ausgewählt, die dann von der ersten Festlegung des Programms durch die ganze Entwicklung und Ausführung des Projekts hindurch bis zur letzten Vollendung und Bauübergabe für die architektonische Gestaltung verantwortlich sind. Diese Entwurfsleute arbeiten oft in Gruppen von zwei, drei oder mehr, je nach Größe, Komplexität und Terminsetzung der Aufgabe. Die Einheitlichkeit in der Arbeit des Entwurfteams wächst aus dem gemeinsamen Verständnis und der Achtung aller Mitarbeiter vor den geistigen Grundsätzen, auf denen die Begriffswelt der modernen Architektur, Konstruktion und Mechanik aufgebaut ist.
Dem Entwurfsteam werden Spezialisten für besondere technische Fragen aus den Reihen der Firma selbst oder von außen her zugeteilt. Es besteht eine enge Zusammenarbeit zwischen Entwurfsarchitekt, Elektro-Ingenieur, Bau-Ingenieur und anderen Fachleuten jeden Gebiets, so daß Akustik, Landschaftsgestaltung, Installationen oder Luftkonditionierung als verschiedene Aspekte eines Ganzen aufs engste in das Projekt einbezogen werden.
Im endgültigen Bauwerk, wie es aus dieser Arbeitsweise entsteht, sind alle technischen Aspekte durch den Architekten koordiniert und einer Gesamtkonzeption unterstellt. Dabei ist für S.O.M. die lebenswichtige Funktion der Installationstechniken im modernen Bauen der Vereinigten Staaten eine anerkannte Realität, und die Forschungsarbeit der Firma richtet sich ebensosehr auf dieses Gebiet wie auf Konstruktion, Material und Baumethoden.

William E. Hartmann

L'organisation de la maison Skidmore, Owings & Merrill

Fondation

1936 vit le début de la collaboration entre Louis Skidmore et Nathaniel A. Owings à Chicago. En 1939, l'architecte O. Merrill se joignit à eux; ainsi fut fondée la maison connue aujourd'hui sous S.O.M. (Skidmore, Owings & Merrill).

Développement

Durant les années qui suivirent, ce petit groupe d'architectes, aux constructions relativement insignifiantes dans la région de Chicago, grandit jusqu'à devenir une organisation importante d'architectes et d'ingénieurs dont l'activité s'étend sur toute l'Amérique du Nord et même presque sur le monde entier, et qui se divise en quatre grands bureaux autonomes dans différentes régions des Etats-Unis, l'Europe, le Moyen Orient et l'Amérique du Sud tandis qu'à San Francisco, on travaille pour la Côte Occidentale et pour l'Orient. Le bureau de Portland, Oregon, constitué à l'origine en collaboration avec Pietro Belluschi, construit dans la partie nordouest de la côte du Pacifiques et dans l'Alasca. Le bureau d'origine, à Chicago, est l'organe central d'administration et traite des projets de toutes les parties des Etats-Unis.

Subdivision nationale

La subdivision en organisation partielles pour les différentes régions résulta de la nature même des problèmes posés. Bien souvent, les clients de la maison sont des entreprises divisées, elles aussi, par état. On reconnut très tôt dans l'histoire de la maison que ces clients se seraient le mieux servis dans la région même dont ils sont à la tête.

Associés

De deux personnes à l'origine, le nombre des associés de S.O.M. est passé à treize personnes, énumérées ici selon leur ordre d'entrée dans la société:

Louis Skidmore (retiré de la participation active, membre consultatif)
Nathaniel A. Owings
John O. Merrill
William S. Brown
Gordon Bunshaft
Robert W. Cutler
J. Walter Severinghaus
John B. Rodgers
William E. Hartmann
Elliot F. Brown
James W. Hammond
Walter A. Netsch, jr.
Edward J. Mathews

Un principe de travail, adopté très tôt, fut celui de l'«organisation verticale». Les associés ont sous leurs ordres deux groupes de personnel dirigeant technique et administratif, ayant également part, matériellement, au revenu de l'entreprise. Ce sont les «Associate Partners» et les «Participating Associates».

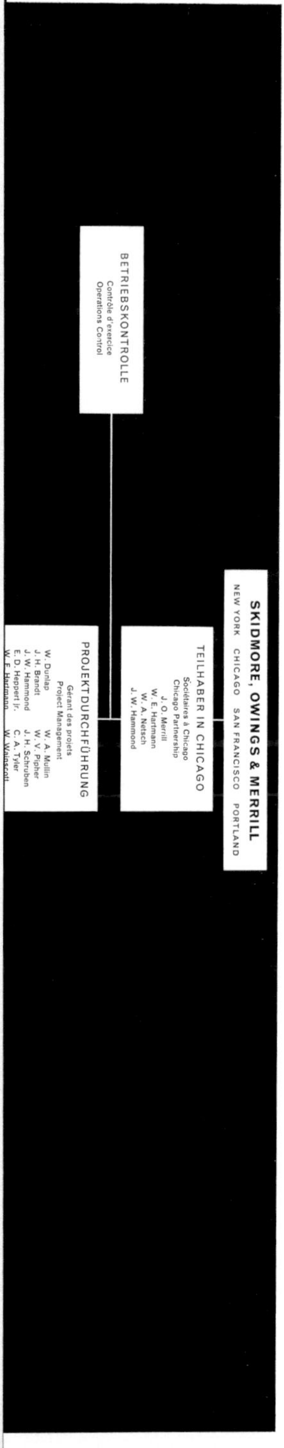

which is no easy matter in the firm c
employees.
It seems hardly an accident that S.O.M
established itself in Chicago so firm
least no more accidental than the st
fact that a man of the avant-garde so unv
to compromise as Mies van der Roh
finally able to build for the real-estate n
on such a large scale. It seems that th
of the prairie is far more fertile for the g
of architecture than for either painti
music, but it is still like treading on
propose quality in place of the ruling
and this is where S.O.M. has succeede

How was this accomplished? The archit
factory has been almost replaced.
groups of architects work together s
both individual design and large-scale
ning can coincide within one organiz
The herbarium of styles is replaced by
people, each with the responsibiliti
artistic freedom. The following article
show how this has been achieved.
Hartmann explains the organization
whole, Walter Netsch describes how th
Force Academy extends into planning
17,000 acres of five valleys. Bruce Gr
outlines the development of the m
office building and Paffard Clay its d
method. The potentialities of different i
duals and regional characteristics are
pected and immediately visible in the r
Work from the Chicago office differs
San Francisco and both differ from New
although they are in close contact with
other.

In New York it is Gordon Bunshaft who
the reins and his mark is on every desig
is one of those few architects who reco
that modern art and modern architectu
interdependent and benefit from each
He can be seen at the art exhibitions in
York with his short pipe in his mouth a
head slightly tilted to one side. At the
was shown around the Manufacturer's
on Fifth Avenue, I asked him how they b
such an exceptionally fine collection of
ings for the executive suite and Presid
room. There were paintings by Braque, L
Miro, de Chirico — all the way to Stein
Bunshaft's reply was simple: "They tr
my judgment."

New York is indebted to Bunshaft for its
clear-cut building up to 1956 — Lever H
on Park Avenue. Lever Brothers, the fa
English soap company, agreed to donat
major part of the high rental ground flo
that pedestrians could freely circulate v
its court, a demonstration of the conv
that a building can only breathe when it n
a spatial contribution to city planning.
proved to be an important contributi
New York. It is being followed by the
story Chase Manhattan Bank, with a t
floor area of 30,000 square feet which will
the way for a large plaza in the heart c
Wall Street area.

The managing partner of the Chicago
is William E. Hartmann. Like Bunshaft h
man in his forties, and he is known f
Terrace Plaza Hotel in Cincinnati, Ohio, v
again something new was introduced t
U. S.: The employment of a painter su
Joan Miro to execute a large mural on a c
wall. Hartmann's office in Chicago is i
of the upper floors of 100 West Monroe
large marble slab which forms his desk
clean of any scrap of paper and his pen h
is attached behind its supporting leg.
designers are in the adjacent drafting r
They constitute the "brains trust," excl

Associate Partners

Les seize Associate Partners sont architectes, ingénieurs, urbanistes ou architectes paysagistes. Ils sont individuellement responsables de parties étendues de l'activité de la maison dans ses différentes succursales ou de problèmes de construction spéciaux.

Participating Associates

Les vingt-sept Participating Associates nationaux ont des tâches techniques ou administratives.

Organisation du travail

L'organisation des quatre succursales est similaire. Cinq groupes de travail opèrent sous la direction d'un des associés:

Direction des projets

Projet
- établissement d'un programme
- façonnement du projet
- architecture intérieure
- étude des matériaux et des méthodes

Exécution (plans)
- plans architectoniques de détail
- plans d'ingénieurs (construction, organisation du chantier, fondations, études du sol)
- installations (électricité, installations sanitaires, chauffage, ventilation et conditionnement d'air)
- devis

Exécution (construction)
- adjudication des travaux
- surveillance de la construction
- direction du chantier

Administration
- organisation des bureaux
- archives
- comptabilité
- personnel non-technique

Cette structure de base est très flexible, à l'échelle nationale aussi bien qu'à l'échelle locale. Le personnel, les groupes d'associés inclus, est considéré comme mobile. En tenant compte de l'expérience et de la disponibilité de chacun, il est ainsi possible de former, pour chaque solution d'un problème de construction, le team le plus fort possible. Ce principe contribue fortement à la continuité dans les travaux de la maison.

Conception architectonique

Depuis le début, on attribua une grande importance à la conception architectonique. Dans chaque succursale, un associé est responsable de ce domaine important dans l'activité de la maison. Sous sa direction, les projeteurs sont choisis pour chaque cas. Ceux-ci sont responsables de la conception architectonique tout le long du développement et de l'exécution du projet depuis l'établissement du programme jusqu'à l'achèvement et la remise de la construction. Ces projeteurs travaillent souvent en groupes de deux, trois ou plus, selon l'envergure, la complexité et le terme du projet. La continuité dans le travail du team de projeteurs résulte de la compréhension et de l'estime commune de tous les collaborateurs pour les principes fondamentaux de l'architecture, la construction et la mécanique moderne.
Le team des projets est soutenu pour les questions techniques particulières par des spécialistes venant de la maison même ou de l'extérieur. Il existe une collaboration étroite entre l'architecte-projeteur, l'ingénieur-électricien, l'ingénieur en bâtiment et les autres spécialistes de tous les domaines, de sorte que l'acoustique aussi bien que la tournure du paysage, que les installations ou que le conditionnement d'air soient assimilés au projet en tant que différents aspects d'un seul tout.
Dans la construction définitive, telle qu'elle résulte de cette façon de travailler, tous les aspects techniques sont coordonnés par l'architecte et subordonnés à une conception globale. S.O.M. reconnaît avant tout l'importance primordiale de la technique des installations dans les immeubles modernes des Etats-Unis; les travaux de recherches de la maison sont donc dirigés autant sur ce domaine que sur la construction, les matériaux ou les méthodes de construction.

William E. Hartmann

S.O.M. Organization

S.O.M. Origin

In 1936, Louis Skidmore and Nathaniel A. Owings established in Chicago, Illinois, a partnership for the practice of architecture. In 1939, John O. Merrill joined the original two, and Skidmore, Owings & Merrill, now widely known as "S.O.M.," was created.

Growth

In the ensuing years, the firm has evolved from a small architectural group working on comparatively small projects in the Chicago area to an architect-engineer organization with four semi-autonomous offices located across the United States, engaged on projects in all parts of North America and elsewhere throughout the world. The office in New York undertakes projects in the Eastern part of the country, in Europe, the Middle East, and South America; and the San Francisco office works on the West Coast and in the Orient. The Portland, Oregon, office (originally developed in association with Pietro Belluschi) operates in the Pacific Northwest and Alaska. The original, Chicago office, the central office from the aspect of administration, handles projects in all sections of the United States.

National Operation

The establishment of offices across the country was a natural development from the type of professional service the firm offers to American commercial and industrial clients. Many of these clients function nationally, and it was obvious early in the firm's history that the highest quality of service could best be given by serving these clients in each area in which they may be operating.

Partnership

Organizationally, S.O.M. is a partnership. From the original two, the partnership has grown to the following thirteen, listed chronologically as they were admitted to the firm:

Louis Skidmore (semi-retired, consultant)
Nathaniel A. Owings
John O. Merrill
William S. Brown
Gordon Bunshaft
Robert W. Cutler
J. Walter Severinghaus
John B. Rodgers
William E. Hartmann
Elliott F. Brown
James W. Hammond
Walter A. Netsch, jr.
Edward J. Mathews

S.O.M. also established as an early principle of its operation, an "organization in depth." Supporting the partnership with a direct interest in the firms' successful performance are two groups of key technical and administrative personnel: Associate Partners and Participating Associates.

Associate Partners

The sixteen Associate Partners are all professionally trained architects, engineers, city planners, or landscape architects. Individuals in this group are responsible for major sections of the firm's activities in respective offices or manage specific projects of various types.

Participating Associates

In addition, there are twenty-seven Participating Associates operating nationally. These comprise individuals with varied technical or administrative responsibilities.

Office Organization

There is a general similarity in the organization of each of the four offices. Under a managing partner, there are five functioning groups:

Project Management

Design
- Programming
- Design of Projects
- Interiors
- Research (Materials and Methods)

Production
- Architectural
- Civil Engineering (Structural, Site, Foundations, Soils)
- Mechanical Engineering (Electrical, Plumping, Process, Heating, Ventilating, and Air Conditioning)
- Estimating

Construction
- Contracts
- Construction Supervision
- Field Offices

Administration
- Office Procedures
- Records
- Accounting
- Non-technical Personnel

Within this basic structure, there is maintained deliberately a wide degree of national and local flexibility. Personnel, including the partnership groups described above, are considered to be fluid so that by balancing experience and availability the strongest possible technical team can be applied to solution of every project. It is this operating principle which contributes greatly to the unity of the firm's production.

Design

From its early origin, S.O.M. has strongly emphasized design; and a Partner in each office is responsible for this important aspect of the firm's activity. Under his guidance, architectural designers (or project architects, as they are usually designated) are selected for each project, with responsibility starting with the first determination of requirements and extending completly through its development and construction, until completion and final use. These designers work frequently in groups of two, three or more, varying with the magnitude, complexity, and time schedule for any particular project. Integration of the work of the design team is achieved through common understanding and respect of its members for basic philosophic principles underlying architectural, structural, and mechanical concepts in modern architecture.
The design team has assigned to it engineering specialists, either from within S.O.M. or from consultants, to assist in solution of technical phases of projects. An intimate relationship is encouraged among the designer, the electrical engineer, the structural engineer, and other specialists in such fields as acoustics, landscaping, process engineering, plumbing or air conditioning.
The final building resulting from this approach reflects all these technical elements, coordinated and integrated in the overall concept by the architect. S.O.M. recognizes the increasingly vital role that the mechanical systems will play in modern buildings in the United States and undertakes research into new developments in this area as well as structures, materials, and construction techniques.

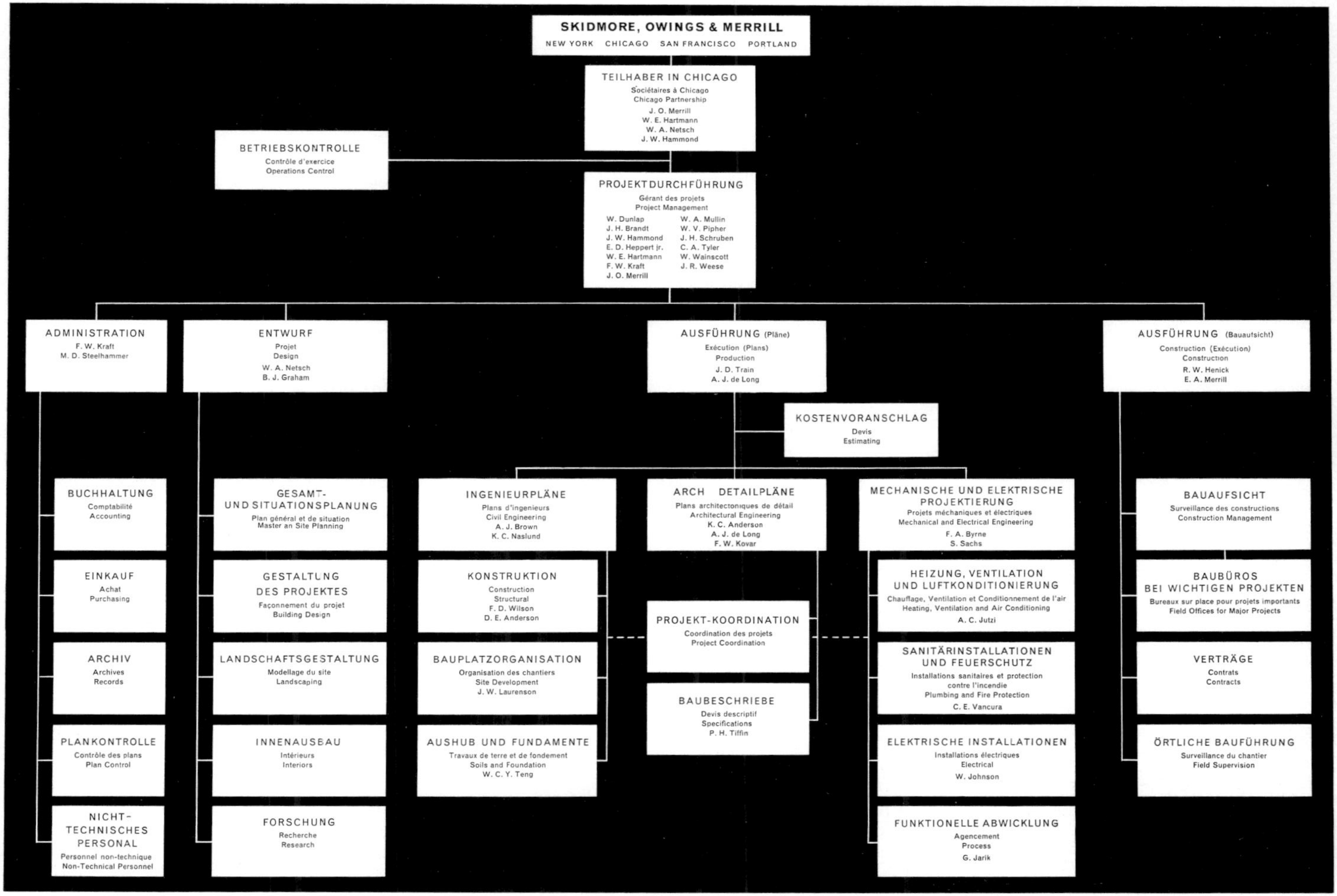

SKIDMORE, OWINGS & MERRILL
NEW YORK CHICAGO SAN FRANCISCO PORTLAND
TEILHABER IN CHICAGO
Sociétaires à Chicago
Chicago Partnership
J. O. Merrill
W. E. Hartmann
W. A. Netsch
J. W. Hammond
BETRIEBSKONTROLLE
Contrôle d'exercice
Operations Control
PROJEKTDURCHFÜHRUNG
Gérant des projets
Project Management
W. Dunlap
J. H. Brandt
J. W. Hammond
E. D. Heppert jr.
W. E. Hartmann
F. W. Kraft
J. O. Merrill
W. A. Mullin
W. V. Pipher
J. H. Schruben
C. A. Tyler
W. Wainscott
J. R. Weese
ADMINISTRATION
F. W. Kraft
M. D. Steelhammer
ENTWURF
Projet
Design
W. A. Netsch
B. J. Graham
AUSFÜHRUNG (Pläne)
Exécution (Plans)
Production
J. D. Train
A. J. de Long
AUSFÜHRUNG (Bauaufsicht)
Construction (Exécution)
Construction
R. W. Henick
E. A. Merrill
KOSTENVORANSCHLAG
Devis
Estimating
BUCHHALTUNG
Comptabilité
Accounting
EINKAUF
Achat
Purchasing
ARCHIV
Archives
Records
PLANKONTROLLE
Contrôle des plans
Plan Control
NICHT-
TECHNISCHES
PERSONAL
Personnel non-technique
Non-Technical Personnel
GESAMT-
UND SITUATIONSPLANUNG
Plan général et de situation
Master an Site Planning
GESTALTUNG
DES PROJEKTES
Façonnement du projet
Building Design
LANDSCHAFTSGESTALTUNG
Modellage du site
Landscaping
INNENAUSBAU
Intérieurs
Interiors
FORSCHUNG
Recherche
Research
INGENIEURPLÄNE
Plans d'ingenieurs
Civil Engineering
A. J. Brown
K. C. Naslund
KONSTRUKTION
Construction
Structural
F. D. Wilson
D. E. Anderson
BAUPLATZORGANISATION
Organisation des chantiers
Site Development
J. W. Laurenson
AUSHUB UND FUNDAMENTE
Travaux de terre et de fondement
Soils and Foundation
W. C. Y. Teng
ARCH DETAILPLÄNE
Plans architectoniques de détail
Architectural Engineering
K. C. Anderson
A. J. de Long
F. W. Kovar
PROJEKT-KOORDINATION
Coordination des projets
Project Coordination
BAUBESCHRIEBE
Devis descriptif
Specifications
P. H. Tiffin
MECHANISCHE UND ELEKTRISCHE
PROJEKTIERUNG
Projets méchaniques et électriques
Mechanical and Electrical Engineering
F. A. Byrne
S. Sachs
HEIZUNG, VENTILATION
UND LUFTKONDITIONIERUNG
Chauffage, Ventilation et Conditionnement de l'air
Heating, Ventilation and Air Conditioning
A. C. Jutzi
SANITÄRINSTALLATIONEN
UND FEUERSCHUTZ
Installations sanitaires et protection
contre l'incendie
Plumbing and Fire Protection
C. E. Vancura
ELEKTRISCHE INSTALLATIONEN
Installations électriques
Electrical
W. Johnson
FUNKTIONELLE ABWICKLUNG
Agencement
Process
G. Jarik
BAUAUFSICHT
Surveillance des constructions
Construction Management
BAUBÜROS
BEI WICHTIGEN PROJEKTEN
Bureaux sur place pour projets importants
Field Offices for Major Projects
VERTRÄGE
Contrats
Contracts
ÖRTLICHE BAUFÜHRUNG
Surveillance du chantier
Field Supervision

RCHITECTURAL RECORD

April 1960

ilding Types Study: Hospitals

ies van der Rohe

o New Office Buildings in San Francisco

uses by Wurster

ll Contents on Page 5

ORGANIZATION FOR EFFICIENT PRACTICE

1.
ggers and Higgins Architects

For some months now, ARCHITECTURAL RECORD has been examining the role of the architect in our time. So far, the major concern has been with the Image of the Architect. In March, a new phase began with the publication of a number of letters from architects; in these, each told about his own approach to the realities of current practice. This month, the new phase continues by means of a study of the methods of organization now being used by one large firm to meet the demands of today. In succeeding months, methods of other firms will be presented.

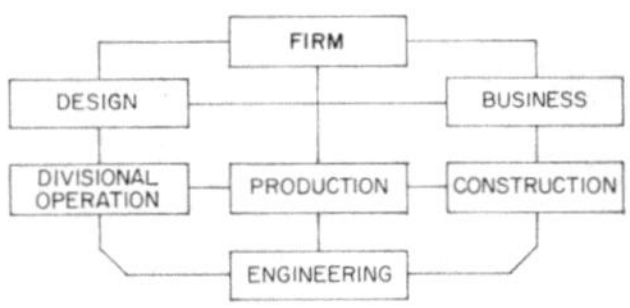

ORGANIZATION CHART

Right, above: Early organization chart developed by the firm. Right, below: Chart in use during the years from 1951 until the current circular chart (page 209) has been developed

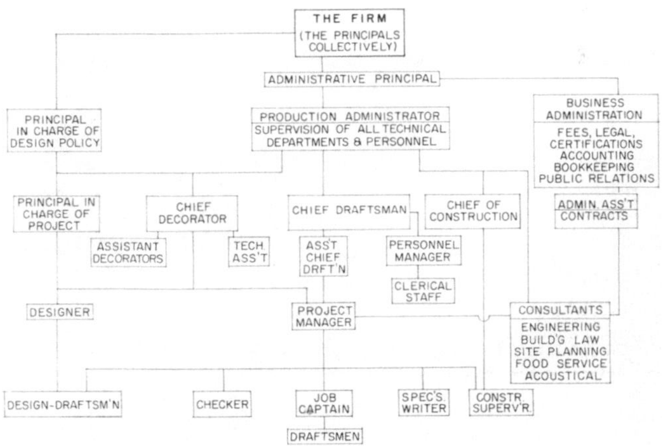

BASIC ORGANIZATION CHART

FOR LINE OF AUTHORITY READ CONNECTED POSITIONS FROM TOP DOWNWARD

Form No. 1

Sunset Sr. High School
Poughkeepsie, N. Y.

November 30, 1959
B. N. Clark: ams

Sunset Sr. High School
Poughkeepsie, N. Y.

PROJECT NO. 59-1081

Partner-in-charge	-	R. Jackson Smith
Description of Project	-	Senior H.S. for 1200 students
Scope of Services	-	Complete

cc: Firm, Business Office, All Principals, Bulletin Boards (4), Reception Desk, Production Administrator, Chief Draftsman, File Dept.

Immediately after commissioning, a form similar to that above is prepared for each project and circulated within the firm. As may be noted, only the most important information is included. Posting on the bulletin boards assures that every employe, regardless of his position, is kept informed. The form below is typical of the continuing index maintained on all projects

Form No. 2

February 15, 1960

ALPHABETICAL INDEX OF PROJECTS

	JOB. NO.
A	
American Office Building, NYC	58-922
American Elementary School, Washington, D.C.	58-965
Athletic Field, Raritan High School	56-755
B	
Baptist Church, Larchmont, N.Y.	56-865
Bayley School, NYC	57-935
Bay Shore Museum, Bay Shore, L.I., N.Y.	58-927
Bright Hospital, NYC	59-1035
Brooksville University Law Bldg.	58-906
Burnside Laboratory, Ithaca, N.Y.	59-1102
C	
Cathedral, Stamford, Conn.	58-983
Cook School, Greenwich, Conn.	60-1282

"The architect must be an astute businessman as well as a sensitive artist." This is the opening sentence on the first page of the Eggers and Higgins brochure. In order to accomplish these goals, the firm has set up methods for efficiently handling its internal affairs. Through organization for the business of architecture, the firm is able to devote more time to its art and science.

In a small office, the principal often assumes all of the responsibility for all jobs. He may retain all of the authority. In a larger office, for example one with two partners, each partner may assume a part of the overall responsibility and authority, yet each may be able to keep himself informed about most of the details of all projects. Decisions are relatively easy since only the two principals are directly cerned in them. This is the position the firm of gers and Higgins was in at the end of World Wa

After the war, the firm experienced a perio rapid growth. In 1953, the principals decided further growth without lowering the standar their services was impossible, unless the firm h sufficient number of principals to offer every c personal attention by a firm member. In order t complish this, Eggers and Higgins changed in year from a dual to a multiple partnership. To the firm has nine partners and eight associate has more than 250 employes and has executed 1000 commissions.

The growth of the firm was inevitably ac panied by organizational and production probl The solution to these problems has been the dev ment of production methods based on workable trols. The status of the firm's organizational th ing before 1951 is indicated in the smaller char the preceding page. David L. Eggers, then chi production developed the larger chart in 1951. A 11 years with the firm as draftsman, designer, ject manager, and construction supervisor, Gus R. Keane was given the job, in 1956, of furthe veloping the production system. He was given thority equal to his responsibility. From stud that time and through continuing re-examina and revision the present system has evolved.

The foundation of the production system is policy formulated by the principals. Authorit delegated by the principals to individuals for ticular jobs. To supplement the general policy descriptions have been prepared. These desig the duties, responsibilities, and authority of all tions in the firm. The key to all of this is the cular Wall Chart.

In the Circular Wall Chart, the major lines o sponsibility and authority are indicated. Rela ships between various functions are defined. As be seen, one principal, Bradford N. Clark, acts a administrative partner. He has direct charge o business affairs of the firm. Through him, policy ters are channeled to the production administr Another principal acts as chief of construc Other principals act as administrative officers projects. To them are assigned the permanent sonnel required for the work. This team is su mented, as necessary, by specialists on the sta from outside the firm as circumstances warr

By the use of the production system, the Cir Chart and other forms, the firm has been ab virtually eliminate overlapping of responsibility authority between individual jobs. There are f misunderstandings. The firm's capacity for work, the availability of personnel and their bilities, and projected future requirements may be accurately determined. Continuing projec sponsibility is centered within small work gr yet specialists are available when needed.

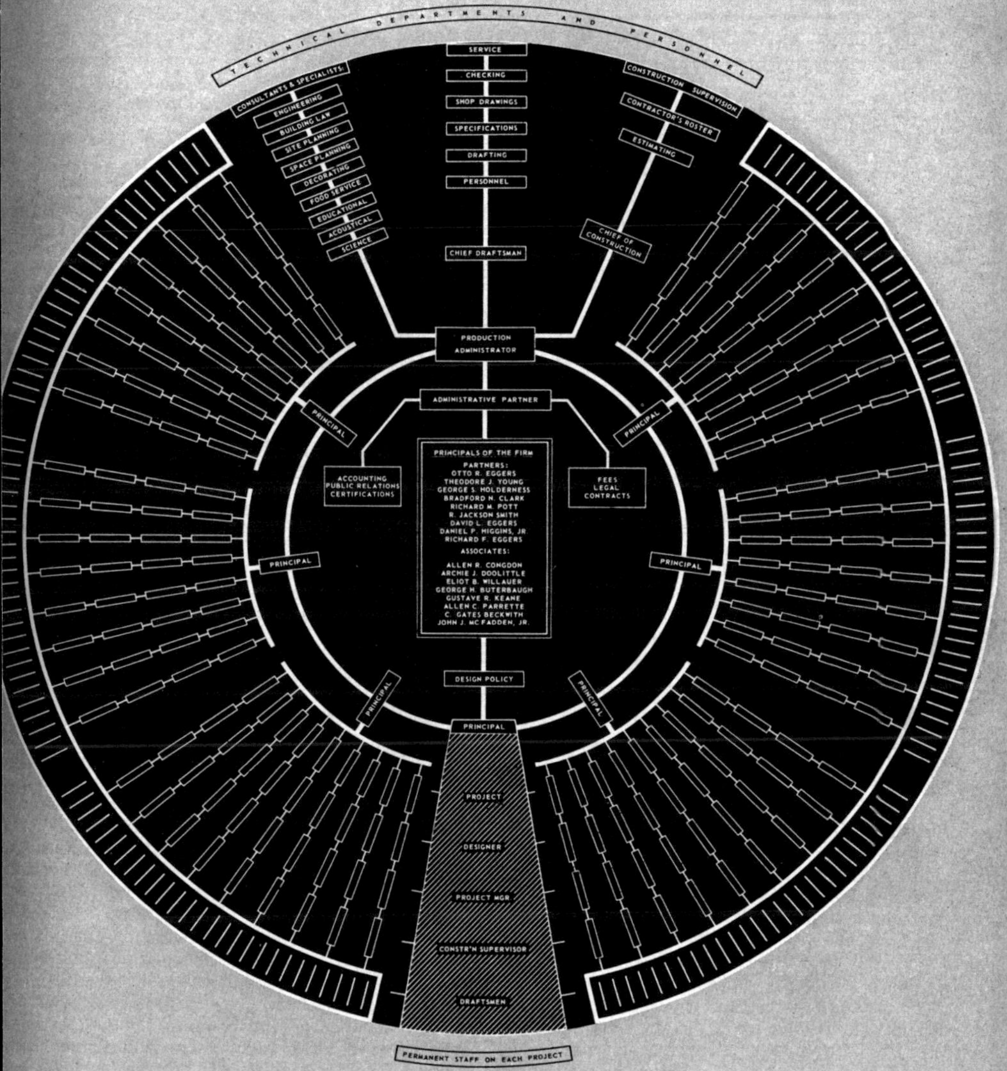

This chart is the heart of the system. In actual use, it is in the form of a large wall chart, equipped with metal card holders. Into these, the names and numbers of projects and of the people working on each, are inserted. The chart is kept current. In general, it works this way: the principals (center) determine policy. Design policy is translated through individual principals (inner ring) in charge of particular projects. These are indicated in the next ring. A designer, project manager, and construction supervisor (their names are on cards in the appropriate rings) are assigned to each job. The outer ring is symbolical only; draftsmen are listed in other records. Production policy, initiated by the principals, is translated through production administrator

EGGERS AND HIGGINS PRODUCTION REPORT — SHEET 28 OF 30 — DATE Jan. 1 -1960

PERS.	DWG.	COMPLETE	PCT.	BID DATE				FIRM	T.J.Y.	
DFTSM. HAVE 3	PRLM.	4-15-58	100	2.1.59	G.C.	A.B.C.-constr. co.		P.M.	DICKENS	Mutual insurance co.
NEED –	WKG.	12.1.58	100	GRND. BRKG. 3.1.59	P.L.	———		ASST.	Land	Home office Bldg.
SPEC. –					H.V.	———		CONST.	Ehrlich	
CHK. –	CONST.	4.15.60	85	DEDICATION 5.1.60 !	EL.	———		STR.	W. & P.	TRENTON, N.J.
								MECH.	S. & H.	

REMARKS Constr. approx. 3 weeks behind schedule due to lathers strike.

JOB Nº	57	932
CONST. COST	$10.235,800 -	AWARD DATE 2.15.59

PERS.	DWG.	COMPLETE	PCT.	BID DATE	G.C.	CBA CONSTR.	FIRM	R.J.S.	
DFTSM. HAVE —	PRLM.	1.12.58	100	7.15.58	P.L.	BSA PLBG.	P.M.	ROMANO	SYOSSET Jr.
NEED —	WKG.	6.1.58	100	GRND. BRKG.	H.V.	XYZ	ASST.	PETRAGLIA	High School
SPEC. —					EL.	MNO ELECTR. CO.	CONST.	O'HARE	SYOSSET N.Y.
CHK. —	CONST.	9.4.59	99	DEDICATION 10.15.59			STR.	H.E.	
							MECH.	CONSA	

REMARKS School fully in operation. Complete except for punch list, terms and guaranties, etc.

SITE: DARLING ASSOCIATES

JOB Nº	57	933
CONST. COST	$4.172,400	AWARD DATE 8.3.58

PERS.	DWG.	COMPLETE	PCT.	BID DATE	G.C.	———	FIRM	D.L.E.	
DFTSM. HAVE 10	PRLM.	8.1.59	100	5.1.60	P.L.	———	P.M.	FRANZ	Gen'l Pharmaceutical
NEED 2	WKG.	3.15.60	82	GRND. BRKG. ———	H.V.	———	ASST.	SATER	New Research Cntr.
SPEC. 2.1.60					EL.	———	CONST.	—	Morristown N.J.
CHK. 1.1.60	CONST.	5.1.61	—	DEDICATION ———			STR.	T. & F.	
							MECH.	J. & B.	

REMARKS ON SCHEDULE ESTIMATOR'S CHECK OF 11.30.59 SHOWED ESTIMATER COSTS 4% BELOW budget. Owner DECIDING on adding 2 story parking garage

JOB Nº	58	982
CONST. COST	$8.500.000	AWARD DATE

THE PRODUCTION ADMINISTRATOR

The roles of the production administrator are many and diverse. He is directly responsible for the coordination of all of the technical or production operations of the firm. In practice, this means that he is the person who schedules production and is responsible for maintaining the schedules. He assigns project managers and other personnel to individual projects.

The production administrator works with department heads to insure smooth communications between various departments. He prepares the production reports on the status of projects and makes estimates of production costs for unusual projects. When a question of the efficiency of production of a particular project arises, the production administrator makes a project analysis and has the responsibility for following through on his recommendations for correction.

Hiring and discharge of technical personnel is the responsibility of the production administrator. He also reviews the performance of personnel semi-annually and makes recommendations for raises and bonuses ordinarily granted at these times.

In addition to his administrative responsibilities directly related to the daily problems of production, the production administrator has important nical duties to perform. He initiates research o materials, methods, and systems. Information c latest developments in building technology ar sembled and distributed to key personnel by h fice. Investigation of material or system failure made and information distributed on metho avoiding recurrences. The production administ initiates the writing of guide specifications an proves them for office use.

Several miscellaneous functions are perform the production administrator. Among these a gotiations with labor unions, consulting engi and other consultants. Other duties include se on A.I.A., B.R.I., and Building Congress tec committees.

The production administrator is charged wi development of new ideas and revision of olde cedures to meet changing demands. These incl cost control system, methods for sub-contracto provals, a system for obtaining approval of agencies for hospital projects, an office manua the like. There is even a file on languages; a count, present employes speak some 30 foreig guages.

DATE: *Jan 1, 1959*

PROJECT MANAGERS & THEIR ASSIGNED PROJECTS

SK. - SKETCH PHASE
W. - WORKING PHASE
C. - CONSTR. PHASE
SH. - SHELVED OR NOT STARTED

PROJ. MGR.	PRIN-CIPAL	PROJ. NO.	PROJECT NAME	PHASE	% OF TIME TO BE SPENT IN NEXT 2 WEEKS	DATE OF COMPL. OF PHASE	REMARKS
Dickens	*TJT*	*56-861*	*Nat'l. Trust Off. Bldg*	*C*	*10*	*10-21-60*	
"	*"*	*57-932*	*Mut. Insur. Home Off.*	*C*	*80*	*4-15-60*	
"	*RJS*	*59-1081*	*Sunset H.S.*	*SK*	*10*	*3-1-60*	
Doutney	*RHP*	*58-983*	*New Cathedral*	*W*	*100*	*3-1-60*	
Franz	*DLE*	*58-982*	*New Research Bldg For General Phar.*	*W*	*90*	*3-15-60*	
"	*GSH*	*59-1097*	*XYZ General Hosp*	*W*	*10*	*4-21-60*	

The Production Report (left) indicates the status of all current projects. Each principal receives a copy of the entire report listing all of the firm's jobs. At monthly intervals, the principals note on their copies the changes in status of their own jobs and return the forms to the production administrator. Changes are then transferred to the master and revised copies are returned to the principals. Current lists of the jobs assigned to project managers (above), designers and supervisors are maintained. A report (right) on schedules, estimates of personnel required, and the like is prepared for each job, soon after it is received, by the principal in charge, and sent to the production administrator

DATE: *8-1-59*

PROJECT NO. *58-982*
EST. CONSTR. COST *8,500,000*
CUBIC CONTENT ______

PROJECT *General Pharmaceutical Co, New Research Center, Morristown N.J.*
FIRM MEMBER *David L. Eggers*
PROJ. MGR. *Karl Franz* CONSTR. SUPER ______
DESIGNER *Paul Campl* RENDERER *Jimenez*
GENERAL DESCRIPTION OF PROJECT *New Research Center (4 buildings on new site centralizing exist. facilities at various locations.) 2 story concrete, S.S. & Stone window walls, Panelled Conference Rooms, Separate power house*

WORK SCHEDULE

	SCHEDULED	ACTUAL		SCHEDULED	ACTUAL
EXTERIOR DESIGN DWGS., START	*2-1-59*	*2-15-59*	COMPLETE	*6-15-59*	*8-1-59*
RENDERING, START	*5-1-59*	*7-1-59*	COMPLETE	*6-22-59*	*7-20-59*
ARCH. INTERIORS, START	*10-1-59*	*9-15-59*	COMPLETE	*3-1-60*	
WORKING DWGS., START	*8-1-59*	*8-1-59*	COMPLETE	*3-15-60*	
SPECIFICATIONS, START	*2-1-60*		COMPLETE	*3-1-60*	
CHECKER STARTS	*1-1-60*		COMPLETE	*3-16-60*	
ADV. FOR BIDS	*3-15-60*		REC. BIDS	*6-1-60*	

NUMBER DRAFTSMEN REQ. (PER MONTH)

Aug. 59	*Sept.*	*Oct.*	*Nov.*	*Dec.*	*Jan. 60*	*Feb.*
3	*5*	*8*	*12*	*12*	*12*	*12*

DRAFTSMEN TO BE ASSIGNED

	DATE		DATE		DATE
1. *Sater*	*8-1-59*	2. *Jones, L.*	*8-1*	3. *Whitman*	*8-1*
4. *Pierce*	*9-1*	5 *Peters*	*9-8*	6. *D'Onofrio*	*10-1*
7. *Heinecke*	*10-1*	8. *Duval*	*10-1*	9. *Jocusco*	*11-1*

CHECKER *Allgaier* *1-2-60* SPEC. WRITER *Fuller* *2-1-60*

	SCHEDULED	ACTUAL		SCHEDULED	ACTUAL
SIGN CONTRACT					
CONSTRUCTION STARTS			COMPLETE	*5-1-61*	
PUNCH LIST STARTS			COMPLETE		
OCCUPY BLDG.					
JOB COMPL. CONTROL SHEET STARTS			COMPLETE		
FINAL PAYMENT MADE					

'HE PRODUCTION SYSTEM

Vhen an individual commission has been received, he first step in putting the production system into peration is the appointment of a principal as overll administrator for the project. He is chosen by the irm on the basis of his knowledge of the building ype and availability. Soon after this, the adminisrative partner issues form no. 1 (top, page 208) givng the broad particulars of the project and its numer. Project is entered in Alphabetical Index (page 208), on Production Report (across page), and on the Circular Wall Chart (page 209). At this stage, little nore is known about the project than its name, locaion, and job number, the general building type, the scope of the services to be performed, and the prinipal in charge.

After analysis of the project and necessary conerences with the client and others, the principal in harge of the project completes an estimate of the production schedule and manpower requirements for he work (above, right). This form contains considerable data on the timing of the project, estimated dates for the completion of various phases and of construction, and personnel information. The form s submitted to the production administrator. The nformation is then transferred to the Production Report and to the Wall Chart. If circumstances require, this form may be revised later to reflect extreme changes.

The Production Report is kept up to date at monthly intervals. Each principal notes on his copy of the form current information on his own jobs. A space is provided for this purpose under each percentage complete block and to the right of the remarks block. Corrected forms are submitted to the production administrator, who then has all information transferred to the master. This is duplicated and a current copy is distributed to all principals and other key personnel. Each of the principal's jobs are color coded to expedite easy identification.

A number of auxiliary forms and charts are used for various specialized purposes. One of these is the project manager work load list (above, left). By means of this list, the production administrator readily keeps track of the assignments of the project managers. Thus, he has a quick and efficient means of determining the appointment of these people to new projects. Similarly, lists are maintained of designers, construction supervisors, and other key personnel.

PROJ. No	PROJECT TITLE	PROJ. MGR.	FIRM	DRAFTSMEN	JAN.	FEB.	MAR.	APR.	MAY	JUNE	JULY	AUG.	SEPT.	OCT.	NOV.	DEC.	COMP DATE	REMARK
932	MUTUAL INSURANCE CO.	Dickens	T.J.Y.	Land, Smith, Strange	3	3	1 / +2	1 / +2	+3	+3								
933	SYOSSET Jr.-Sr. High School	Romano	R.J.S.	Petraglia,	--	+1												
982	GENR'L Pharmaceutical Bldg.	Franz	D.L.E.	Sater, Jones, Whitman, Pierce, Peters, D'Onofrio, Heineke, Duval, Jacuszko, Stueber	12 / -2	12 / -2	12 / -2	8 / +2	8 / +2	6 / +4							5.61	Specs. writer 2
983	CATHEDRAL Stamford	Doutney	R.N.P.	Sberna, Kleld, Jones R., Messo, Proctor, Valdo, Oris, V. Vitorovich, Santo, Fried, Larson, Russo	15 / -3	15 / -3	15 / -3	10 / +2	8 / +4	8 / +4	8 / +4	4 / +8	4 / +8	4 / +8	2 / +10			
1079	NATIONAL News Plant	Hopp	G.H.B.	Gilman, Keiser, Gerde, Cross, Palle, Malmo, Nagle, Venti, Rusk, Nash, Ash, Dumas, Rusher, Dunn, Hanvey,	19 / -4	19 / -4	19 / -4	19 / -4	12 / +3	12 / +3	10 / +5	10 / +5					12.61	
1081	SUNSET High School	Dickens	R.J.S.	Mackie			4 / -3	6 / -5	10 / -9	10 / -9	6 / -5	4 / -3					8.61	Bond issue feb. 20. 196
.... sketch phase ——— working drawing phase ---- constr. phase	CARRIED OVER / TOTAL			AVAILABLE MEN +	0	0	2	6	12	15								Date: Jan.1
				ADD. MEN REQ'D −	9	9	-12	9	9	5								
				AVAILABLE MEN	-9	-9	-10	-3	+3	+10								

All current jobs are listed on the Project Chart shown above. Information is included on the present stage of the work and a projection of the future stages. From this data, scheduling of jobs and controls over their production can be efficiently handled. In addition, the chart indicates present and estimated future personnel requirements and other pertinent information. In practice, the chart operates in this manner: personnel assigned to jobs are listed and job progress is indicated by coded bars. The figures over the bars show draftsmen presently assigned. Figures under the bars indicate the estimated numbers of people who will become surplus (plus signs) or the additional people needed (minus signs) in the various future stages of production. Totals are tabulated at the bottom of the form and carried forward to show the personnel requirements for the entire firm. The form below indicates the organization for a particular project

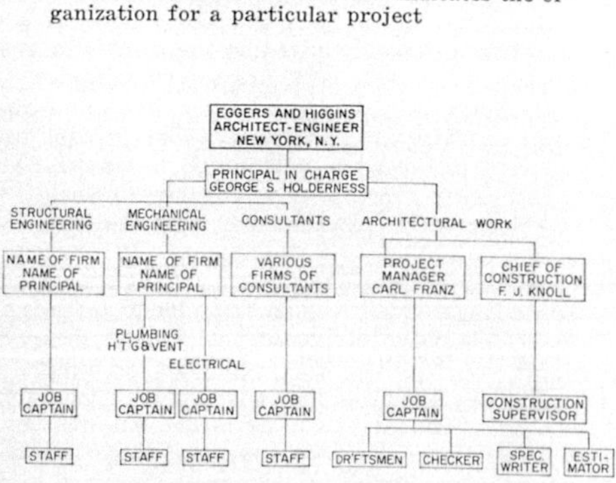

PROJECT ORGANIZATION CHART
FOR XYZ GENERAL HOSPITAL AT ABC, TENNESSEE
PROJECT NO. 59-1097

The Production Report is supplemented by the ject Schedule chart shown above. Together wit Circular Wall Chart, these two forms provid overall picture of the status of individual pro and of the firm as a whole. Their use in conne with the other systems and forms, permits deci to be made concerning such important matters a taking of new commissions, their scheduling, th of present personnel, and the hiring or dismiss employes.

The Project Schedule chart includes inform on the job number, name, and location, the pr manager (he has overall responsibility for th under the principal in charge), the principals' tials, and the names of assigned draftsmen. importantly, it shows by means of bar graphs estimated time of production for various phas the work. As may be seen, these schedules are jected for at least six months ahead of the da preparation of the chart.

The bars are coded to indicate phases of the v Above the bars are penciled figures represer the estimates of total number of draftsmen ne Below the bars are penciled figures representin surplus or additional draftsmen required. In a use, these figures are in red pencil for surplus sonnel, green if more draftsmen are needed. T figures are totaled at the bottom of the sheet. T from all sheets are added on the last page of th of forms. In this way, a picture is obtained of manpower requirements and availability for at six months ahead.

One of the miscellaneous forms used for sp purposes by Eggers and Higgins is the Project ganization Chart (left).

ORGANIZATION FOR EFFICIENT PRACTICE

2.

Daniel, Mann, Johnson, & Mendenhall, Architects & Engineers

niel, Mann, Johnson, & Mendenhall is an architect-
gineer firm. This in itself is descriptive of a somewhat
ader range of capabilities than is usually the case in
st architectural firms. DMJM is even more complex
n the usual A-E firm; it has become an organization
ich operates on a global basis, accomplishing profes-
nal work of a varied and highly complex nature, work
t is far beyond the capabilities of most organizations.
Much of the work of the firm is on buildings of the
al kind—schools, office buildings, institutions—but a
wing percentage of the jobs obtained by the firm are
new fields such as missile and space exploration bases.
se fields are poorly defined even now, and many of
m didn't even exist a few years ago. So involved is the
n in the new types of projects that—to an extent—
firm members have begun to talk in the manner of
clients they serve. It is not unusual to hear a DMJM
tner or employe use a phrase of the research and de-
pment man such as "the state of the art" to describe
level of development or of sophistication in a given
l. Exactly how all of this came about, no one includ-
the firm partners seems to know precisely. Perhaps
best way to take a look at the firm and how it accom-
hes the work it takes on is to examine its background
abilities, and the types of operations in which it is
aged. Perhaps in this way, a key to the firm can be
nd. By examining the "what," possibly the "how" will
me apparent.

Ladera Elementary School, Manhattan Beach, Calif.

Herbert Bruce Cross

Apartment Buildings, Barrington Plaza, Los Angeles

s Missile Launching Pad, USAF Missile Test Center, e Canaveral, Fla. *Official USAF photo*

Rocket Engine Test Stands, Rocketdyne Div., North American Aviation, Inc., Santa Susana, Calif.

Daniel, Mann, Johnson, & Mendenhall

Background

DMJM is, at the present time, a little less than 15 years old. It was founded shortly after World War II, by Phillip J. Daniel and Arthur E. Mann, architects, and S. Kenneth Johnson, architect and engineer. Another architect, Staley A. Moe, and a structural engineer, Irvan F. Mendenhall later joined the firm as partners. Each of the original partners brought a few jobs into the firm with him. During its first three years, DMJM did a number of projects (mostly public schools) and lost money. At this stage, it became apparent that the firm's future health and success depended on making some basic decisions about the goals the partners desired for the firm and how to get there.

The partners subjected the firm and themselves to a severe and searching re-examination, and went through a survey by an outside management consulting firm. The essential decisions were made: 1) to seek out a variety of large, complex work on a world-wide basis, in addition to the building types being done at the time; 2) to do all (or almost all) engineering and other technical work within the firm; 3) to establish a business-like organization, departmentalized with a partner in charge of each department; 4) to grow.

With the basic decisions made, the firm has grown and has gone into the types of work it wanted. This has not been accomplished overnight or without pain, however.

While growing, the firm has developed a distinct philosophy and approach to architecture and related fields, and the capabilities for putting these into practice. As expressed by DMJM, the capabilities might be listed in this manner: 1) adequate financial ability of the firm to handle its commitments; 2) experienced and knowledgeable people within the organization, with the ability to interpret and direct complex programs, perform major technical and management functions for clients, and evaluate and establish technical solutions to the client's problems; 3) ability to meet difficult and changeable production schedules; 4) ability to perform professional work within budgets; 5) flexible and reasonable professional fees. It should be profitable to examine, in some detail, the DMJM approach to these ideals. This should be possible by taking a look at the types of jobs the firm does, the services they offer, their geographical range of operations, the types of people on the staff (and their capabilities), the DMJM organizational setup, and the extra-professional activities of the staff.

Types of Work

Since its founding, DMJM has performed professi services for well over $2 billion of construction. T total represents over 600 commissions. The firm has c a large number of buildings of every usual type. Th include schools, apartment houses, office buildings, in trial buildings of various kinds, hospitals, laborato hotels, public buildings, shopping centers, and the l

In addition, DMJM has done such highly special jobs as Wonder Palace (an integrated convention ce at Anaheim, Calif.), master planning of Mountain P near Los Angeles (includes residential, commercial educational areas), designs for a food store chain, Atc Energy Commission facilities for storage and disposa radioactive waste, Santa Susana, Calif., Hyperion S erage System, Los Angeles, Calif., San Bernadino and Angeles flood control projects, streets, roads, and h ways in California, Maryland, Washington, D. C. and ot locations.

The firm has been responsible for the professional w on numerous military projects, including officers quar and other military housing, complete air bases, harb communications centers, and other types.

Missile and space work has rapidly become a firm cialty. DMJM has performed complete professional s ices, including master planning, for a number of mis launching complexes and test facilities. Work done the firm has included, in addition to the usual serv such things as roads and drainage ditches, high po transmission systems, utility systems, water distribu and sewerage systems, and specialized storage for li oxygen and other materials. For much of this work, programs were incompletely defined because of the m unknowns present. Much out-of-the-ordinary rese and development work was required of DMJM in orde do the work for which they were engaged.

Services of the Firm

In general, DMJM offers complete architectural servi along with all of the related engineering, planning, specialized services required for almost any exis building type. All of the work is accomplished within firm itself, except for the most specialized areas suc satellite tracking equipment or atomic physics. For sultation in these and similar areas, DMJM has made

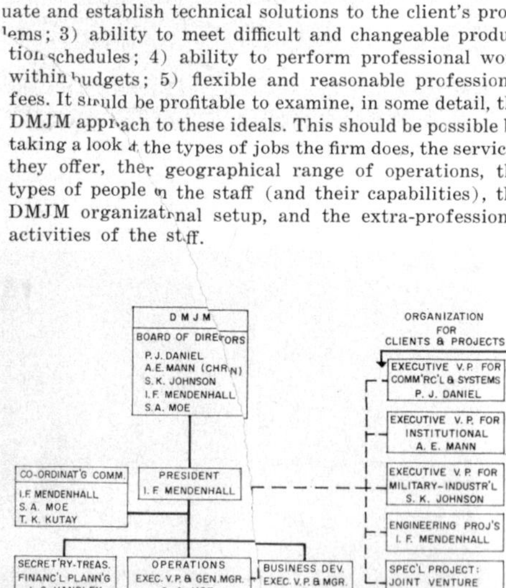

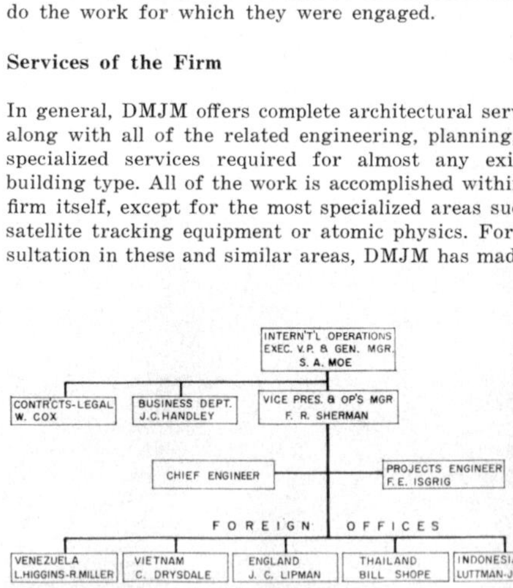

Left: Basic DMJM Firm Organization Chart
Above: Foreign Operations Division Chart

ngements with a number of specialists outside the firm r consultation on a continuing basis.

The firm has become more and more involved in space ojects, missile base design, atomic design, and other ojects of this advanced nature. In order to do work in ese areas, it has become necessary to build up the firm's pabilities in fields less closely related to architecture an the usual engineering specialities. Service are now rformed by the firm in such areas as industrial engiering, statistics, electronics, and the like.

The following is an outline of the types of services w being offered by the firm:

Master Planning
A. Establishment of client's requirements and limitations
B. Evaluation of influencing factors
  1. Location and interrelationship with other facilities
  2. Climate
    a. Rainfall
    b. Temperature
    c. Wind
    d. Humidity
  3. Transportation and accessibility
  4. Zoning and governing codes
  5. Utilities and rates
    a. Water Supply
    b. Gas
    c. Electrical Services
    d. Waste Disposal
  6. Tax and insurance rates
  7. Characteristics of population, labor force
  8. Community support and acceptance
C. Determination of feasibility
  1. Economic evaluation
D. Determination of future expansion
E. Scheduling of construction of urgently needed components
F. Recommendations and counsel

Architectural Planning and Design
A. Analysis of client's requirements
B. Development of concepts
C. Preliminary engineering
  1. Structural
  2. Mechanical
  3. Electrical
  4. Civil
D. Estimates
E. Development of working drawings
  1. Architectural
  2. Engineering
F. Preparation of Specifications
  1. Interior Design
  2. Color coordination
  3. Flow studies
  4. Architectural lighting
  5. Architectural rendering

III. Engineering Planning and Design
A. Planning
  1. Site development
  2. Cost analysis and economic evaluation
  3. Reports
  4. Investigations
B. Design of Complete Facilities for:
  1. Sanitary Sewage Systems
    a. Collection systems, trunks, and outfalls
    b. Treatment plants
    c. Pumping plants
    d. Industrial waste
  2. Flood Control and Drainage Facilities
    a. Hydrology and hydraulic design
    b. Storm drains and appurtenances
    c. Flood control dams, spillways, channels, and storage reservoirs
    d. Water conservation and erosion control, debris and detention basins
  3. Water Works
    a. Transmission lines and distribution systems
    b. Treatment plants
    c. Well development
    d. Storage tanks, reservoirs, and pumping plants
  4. Highway Engineering
    a. Alignment and right of way
    b. Drainage
    c. Bridges
    d. Traffic potential surveys
    e. Foundation and soil analysis
    f. Pavement design
  5. Airfields
    a. Runway configuration
    b. Sound suppression and blast protection
    c. Maintenance and storage facilities
    d. Pavement design
    e. Fueling systems and airfield lighting
    f. Grading and drainage

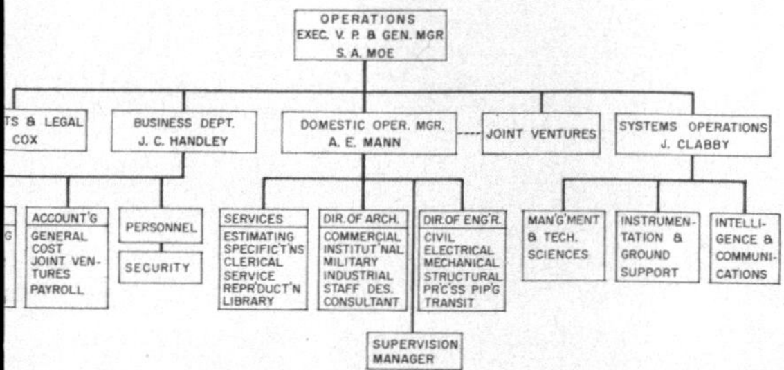

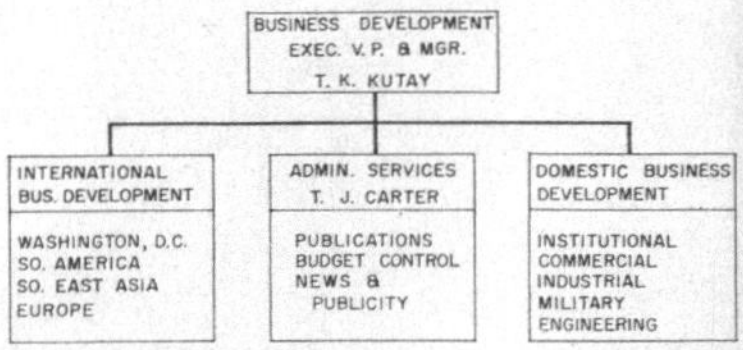

Left: Domestic Operations Division Chart

Above: Business Development Division Chart

6. Miscellaneous Engineering
   a. Marinas and harbors
   b. Missile facilities
   c. Subdivisions
   d. Aerial photography, surveying, mapping
   e. Soils and foundations
   f. Processing and industrial waste

IV. Systems Engineering
  A. Instrumentation Systems
    1. Design of instrumentation systems for:
      a. Environmental test facilitie.
      b. Missile launch and static test facilities
      c. Sound attenuation test and laboratory facilities
      d. Data handling and analysis equipment
  B. Communications Systems
    1. Design analysis of:
      a. Microwave equipment
      b. Weapon system, static test, and launch control communication equipment
      c. Military tactical communications equipment
      d. Traffic control and dispatch equipment
  C. System Integration
    1. Integration of functional requirements of facilities into planning documents and design criteria
  D. Systems Analysis
    1. Analysis of existing or proposed operating systems to determine optimum design criteria to meet total requirements of the proposed complex

V. Construction Management and Supervision
  A. Preparation of documents
  B. Issuing of drawings and specifications
  C. Analysis of bids and making of recommendations
  D. Preparation and execution of contracts
  E. Surveillance of shop drawings
  F. Approval of materials
  G. Preparation of change orders
  H. Provision of resident inspectors and construction supervision personnel
  I. Surveillance of guarantees and as-built drawings
  J. Recommendations and counsel during construction

VI. Process Engineering
  A. Foods
  B. Beverages
  C. Industrial
  D. General Industrial Chemicals
  E. Military

For projects of such extreme size or complexity tha the firm feels it is incapable of handling them ade quately alone, DMJM associates itself with other archi tectural and engineering firms in joint ventures. An ex ample of a project of this type is the Titan missile facil ity project now being handled by DMJM in joint ventur with The Rust Engineering Co., Leo A. Daly Co., Archi tects and Engineers, and Mason & Hanger-Silas Maso Co., Inc., Engineers and Contractors. Under the terms o their contract the joint venture (known as DMJM an Associates) is furnishing all of the architectural, engi neering, and related services for the project other tha actual construction.

The Firm's Staff

The firm employs specialists in a great variety of field An idea of the breadth of the technical staff (in additic to architecture and building engineering people) may b gained from the following partial list of firm personne

Systems Mgrs.	Nuclear Engs.
Systems Engs.	Mechanical Handling Engs
Master Planners	Aerodynamicists
Civil Engineers.	Physicists
Electronics Engs.	Mathematicians
Process Engs.	Statisticians

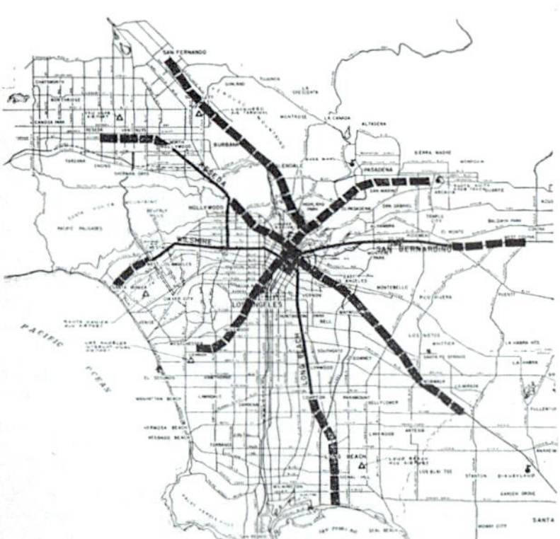

One example of the types of projects DMJM gets involved in, in its expanding architectural role, is this study of mass rapid transit requirements for Los Angeles. This sort of project goes far beyond the "single building" concept so prevalent today in architectural practice. Transportation is probably the most important key to the design of a city. Thus, in a commission such as this, an architectural firm has a chance to establish over-all concepts of planning on a large scale, eventually affecting the lives of all who live, work, or visit in the city

emical Engs.
el Engs.
draulics Engs.
eumatics Engs.
trumentation Engs.
dio Propagation Engs.
fra-Red Engs.
tics Engs.
rasonics Engs.
mputer Engs.
nd Tunnel Engs.
Pipe Line Engs.
Sanitary Engs.
Surveyors
Technical Writers
Airport Systems Engs.
Missile Engs.
Propulsion Engs.
Servo Engs.
Inertial Guidance Engs.
Microwave Engs.
Communications Engs.

ssiles Systems

DMJM became more and more involved in the design missile bases, it became apparent to the firm that it eded to provide itself with capabilities for research and velopment work in the fields of the missiles themselves d the related sciences. Accordingly, the firm bought existing company, Systems Laboratories, Inc. This n performs research, consulting work, and developnt work in aeronautics, nucleonics, missile systems, auatic control and computer systems, physics, chemis-, mathematics and similar fields.

rldwide Operations of the Firm

ile the largest percentage of the DMJM work is in the ited States, the firm does projects on a worldwide is. The foreign offices are extremely flexible. They are up, moved, or modified in accordance with the needs the firm at a particular time. At present, foreign ofs are located in London, Bangkok, Honolulu, Saigon, ris, Guam, Djarkata and Caracas. Each of these has a mary reason for being. The London office is of parılar importance in the administration of the DMJM contract with the U.S. Third Air Force. This work is concerned with architectural and engineering coordination of all of the Third AF bases in England. The Thailand office has, as its major project, a waterwell drilling and exploration program involving some 335 wells to be drilled in an area of 40,000 square miles. This work is for the International Cooperation Administration. The Guam office is handling a large amount of military housing on the island and complete facilities for a 44,000 kilowatt-net power plant. The Caracas office is designing a submarine aqueduct for supplying water to the offshore islands of Margarita and Coche.

Extra-Professional Activities

Growth of the DMJM practice has brought with it an increasing awareness of, and participation in outside activities by the firm members and employes. Increasingly, it has become apparent that the progress of the organization, dependent as it is on efficient service to its clients, is almost equally dependent on the outside activities of the firm. So DMJM gets itself involved (as a firm and individually) in a great number of civic and other peripheral pursuits. Firm members think these activities add stature to themselves as individuals and help the firm. The activities range from membership in such groups as the American Rocket Society, to full sponsorship of a Space Science Exposition for Explorer Scouts, from A.I.A. and other professional organization activities to the establishment of firm lectureships at colleges and the making of a film designed to stimulate young people's interests in science and mathematics. Activities of this sort round out the program DMJM has set for itself. In this way, the firm and its members become more important and integral members of their communities and of society than would be possible within the strict confines of professional practice.

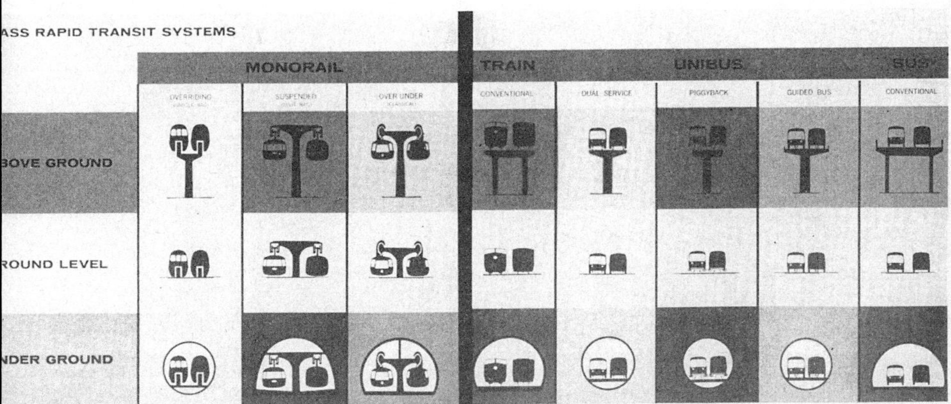

ARCHITECTURAL RECORD

7 July 1960

Full Contents on Page 5

ORGANIZATION FOR EFFICIENT PRACTICE

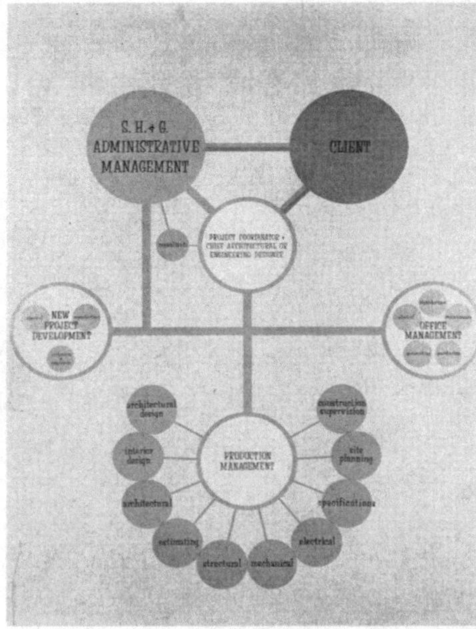

1. Smith, Hinchman and Grylls Organization Chart

3.

Smith, Hinchman and Grylls Associates, Inc. Architects & Engineers

The Smith, Hinchman and Grylls firm, reported on in this issue, is seriously concerned with the currently expanding architectural horizons. It is equally concerned with the development of a philosophy of architecture for today and a philosophy of architectural practice to make the architecture work. Some of the SHG ideas of architectural practice, how the ideas are now being put into effect by the firm, and the obstacles that now prevent full realization of the results of the ideas are examined here

In any investigation of the role of the architect in today's society, it soon becomes necessary to take a long, hard look at the philosophy of architectural practice, in order to place the other important aspects of architecture in the proper perspective. In order to design the best possible buildings, how should the architectural, engineering, and other professional services be organized? How can the architect make the most profitable use of his time and talents? How can he integrate his work with that of the other members of a design group?

For some time now, the RECORD has been concerned with the opportunities and problems of present-day practice. What their clients and the public think of architects and what architects think of themselves have been investigated. The directions in which some firms are now turning in order to do new types of work and offer more complete services have been given consideration and their organization has been discussed.

In this issue, a report is made on the Smith, Hinchman and Grylls patterns of organization. More importantly, perhaps, an attempt is made to explain the SHG attitudes toward architecture and its practice. Though it may sound trite, SHG believes, basically, that architecture is concerned with buildings; to improve architecture, it is indubitably necessary to improve buildings. SHG believes that improvements in buildings—in the scientific, as well as the esthetic, aspects—are needed. Architectural esthetics have a part to play—a large part—but they are not the entire production. Mysticism has no role, unless it is a religious one as in the design of a church, rather than an architectural one.

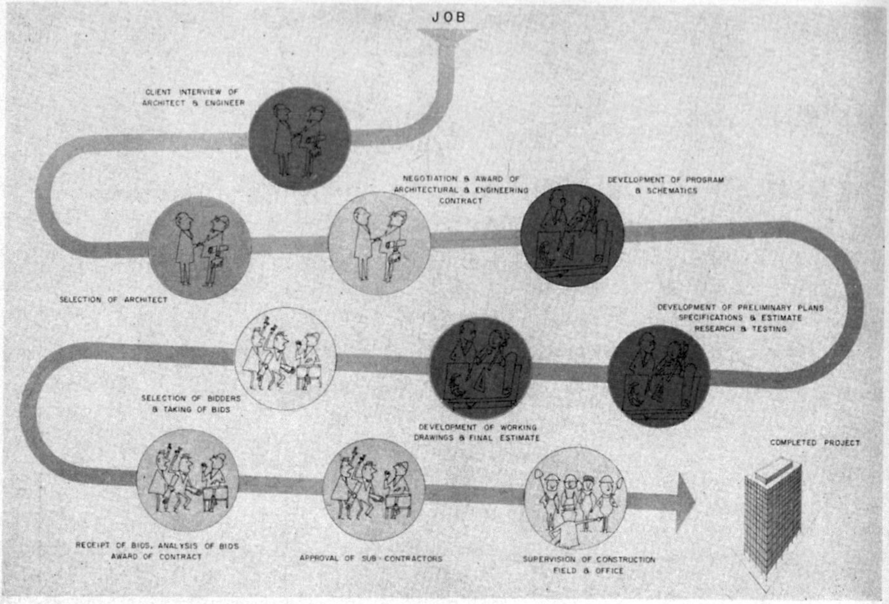

2. Client Chart: Phases of Building Planning

SHG Organization

The Smith, Hinchman and Grylls organization is large; it now employs about 300 people. The firm has a long record of accomplishment and is more than fifty years old. SHG operates nationally and internationally; in addition to the home office, it maintains a Canadian office in Windsor, Ontario and sets up job offices wherever they are needed. The Canadian office is operated as a separate organization incorporated in Canada.

SHG completely occupies a 40,000-ft leased building in Detroit. The four floors of the building, which SHG remodeled to suit its own requirements, are utilized in somewhat the following manner: ground floor—structural engineering division and miscellaneous departments, first floor—architectural division, second floor—mechanical engineering and electrical engineering divisions, third floor—executive and administrative offices, clerical and accounting, and central files.

The organization is set up to do all of the usual architectural and engineering professional services for nearly all types of buildings. In addition, the staff has the experience and capabilities required for many specialized design services. Some of these are design of blast-resistant structures, industrial waste systems, atomic facilities, and a number of other special types.

The chart (1.) on the preceding page gives an indication of how SHG organizes its operations to accomplish the work of the firm. The important relationships between the client, the firm, and various departments within the firm are shown. Each project is assigned to a project coordinator who works closely with the chief designer for the project. The production managen group is composed of an officer of the company and heads of all major departments and is under the di tion of a production manager. This group is the ce around which the production of a project revolves.

Approach to Architectural Practice

Smith, Hinchman and Grylls takes for granted that practice of architecture is concerned, not only with architectural design, but with all of the accompany engineering and planning disciplines necessary for complete design of complex buildings. SHG believes the client's needs in his building are important; also believe that what the client wants in his buil is important. Essentially, the firm is attempting to l all it can about each client's needs and wants, to ana these things by thorough and creative programm schematics, and design (engineering as well as archi tural), and arrive at the best possible preliminary sign. By spending adequate time and effort in the c tive phases to allow for close study of almost all of big problems and their interrelationships, a detailed quite complete set of figures, drawings, prelimi specifications, and so on can be developed. The pre tation can then be made in such a manner that the cl can have no doubt of what is intended, what budg required, how long the remaining professional and struction phases will take. An attempt is made to de solutions or definitions of all of the major design p lems (including budget and technological problems the design phases. In this way, the preparation of

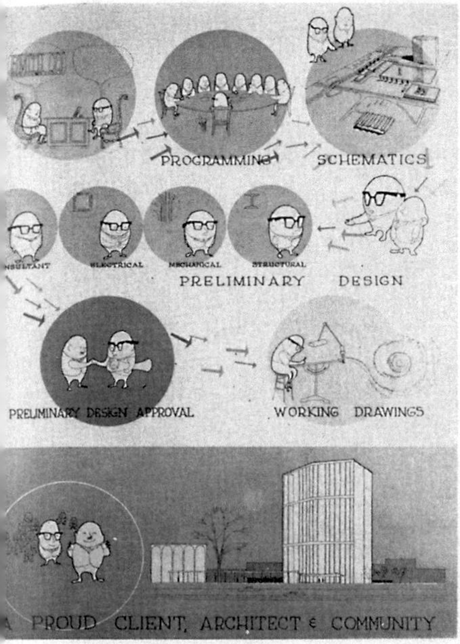

HG Organization of Architectural Services

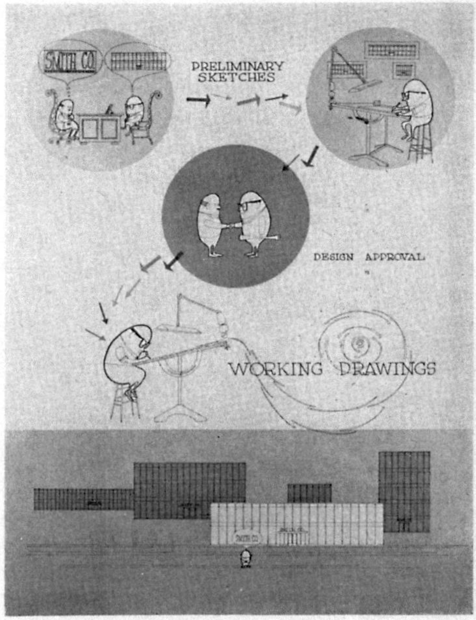

4. More Customary Organization of the Services

:t drawings and specifications can become in reality, ıt so many architects call them, production.

:y allotting more time and effort in the creative first ;es, the architects and engineers, working closely to- ıer, are able to concentrate their activities more ef- :ively on the things they do best, and where they can of most service to their clients, creative problem solv- and design. Through all of this, SHG believes it must l the client by the hand, keeping him informed and olved in the planning processes. Needless to say, all :hese things are ideals, which sometimes cannot be lized in particular projects. But this does not make principles less valid.

: Client

: office tries to begin each project with the basic idea : everything that is feasible will be done by the staff :king on the project to dig into the client's basic prob- ıs. The client is encouraged to go as far into these ic problems as he cares to or is able. The firm feels : its people have got to understand the client's pur- e in the development of the project, his organization, operation, his needs for flexibility and expansion, his ıncial problems. Of equal importance is understand- of the client's philosophies, interests, and cultural ıght. All of these things are interrelated in principal; of the architect's major tasks is to see that they be- ıe interrelated, in the correct ways, in actuality.

ı order to present clearly to clients the processes ough which the design and construction of a building st pass, SHG has prepared charts similar to that shown (2.). Through graphic simplification, in such charts, of the main steps toward the finished building, the firm finds its professional relationships with its clients progress more smoothly and effectively.

Creative Concentration

The SHG organization believes that the professional efforts in the preliminary phases on a project should be somewhat as shown in figure 3. above. After having been engaged by a client, the architect approaches the problem without preconceived notions of what sort of building should result. Thorough programming requires effort and close attention, talented and creative architects and engineers, the client, and, in many instances, highly specialized consultants. Research and programming studies lead to schematic designs in which broad concepts are established. Preliminary design follows. In this stage, as in the ones preceding, the engineers (and consultants) are very much involved in what is going on. After client approval of the preliminary documents, the production of contract documents can go ahead efficiently, leading, if all goes well, to the inevitable happy result. Through all of this, the client has been brought along at a more or less equal pace with this building.

A more common approach to architectural practice in the past might be similar to figure 4. At the beginning, the architect tries to visualize the client's building (it is quite different from that in the client's mind or dreams). The architect then disappears and "designs" the building, reappears to get approval. Then he "draws it up." The final result is blank and anonymous, bearing

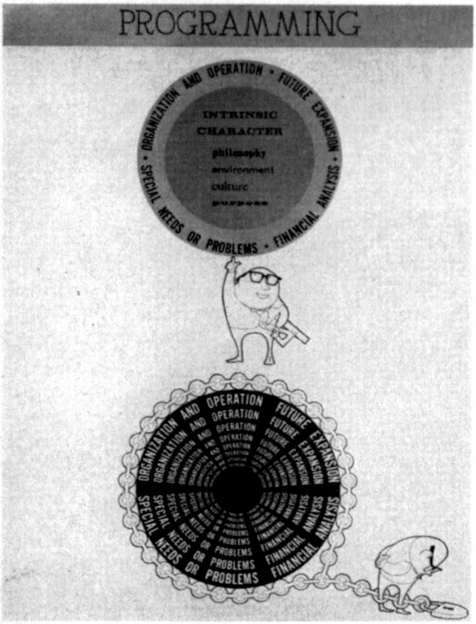

5. Program—A Blend of Ideas and Facts

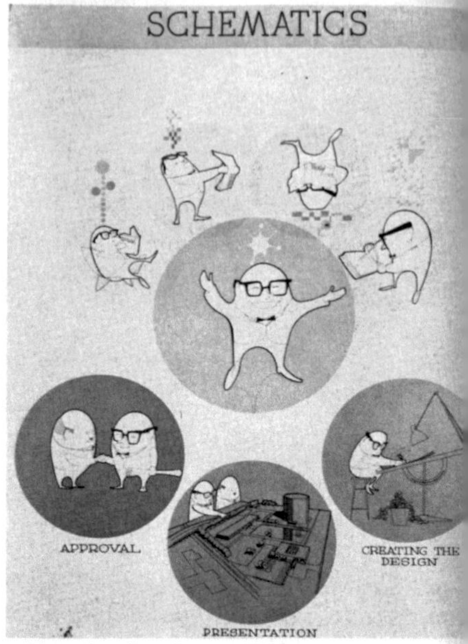

6. Schematics—Free Study and Vision

no resemblance to the client's original picture, but a marked similarity to other similarly conceived buildings.

In order to give the client's problems the sort of concentrated attention needed in the beginning phases of the work, as shown in figure 3., SHG allocates a larger percentage of its total time here and reduces the time spent in production. By developing the more complete preliminaries made possible by closer study over a longer period of time, the firm believes it can furnish its services for the fees it would get under the older scheme.

In the first instance (figure 3.), the architects and engineers are able to spend enough time with the client and with his project to gain some real understanding of both. By the time the broad concepts of the design begin to be defined, each of the individuals involved in the work understand each of the other's viewpoints. Next comes more detailed evaluation, always relating the elements of architectural and engineering design to one another and to the entire project. The basic concepts get exhaustive testing to determine whether they are actually valid. The program and the budget are continuously re-examined. If the concepts stand up and it seems likely that they can be integrated with other aspects still to come, then the work can go on through the preliminary design stage. Further study leads to the final design.

In the second instance (4.), very little of this sort of searching creative activity is possible. The buildings that result from this way of doing things are quite likely to be defective when considered as total architecture with all of the many requirements this implies, though they may be highly acclaimed for some narrower accomplishment. One need only picture a building of gr artistic merit but which is inhabitable, or another w estimable spacial qualities which does not function.

Program, Schematics, and Design

In programming a building (5.), the SHG project ordinator and designer attempt to avoid being trap into the confining chains of preconceived or poo thought out ideas concerning the client's organizat and operation, special requirements, expansion, bud and the like. Instead, an attempt is made to keep de sions on all of these things completely open, and to c sider them freely and thoroughly. In addition, such thi as the environment in which the building will be pla and that to be created within, the intrinsic characte the problems, and real purpose are studied in detail.

The schematics (6.), are, for the SHG firm, a time searching, of deep study and research. An attempt made by the people working on the project to exam all of the basic concepts in detail, and to test and ev uate them. After the design concepts have been est lished and approved by the owner, all of the many s cialists involved work closely together to correlate aspects of the building design and arrive at a carefu conceived final design.

Thorough and prolonged study of a building proj in the programming, schematic, and design phases le to a very complete presentation package (7.). By time the presentation is made, the individuals work on the building have become deeply involved in the pr ect in all of its aspects. The client has been brou

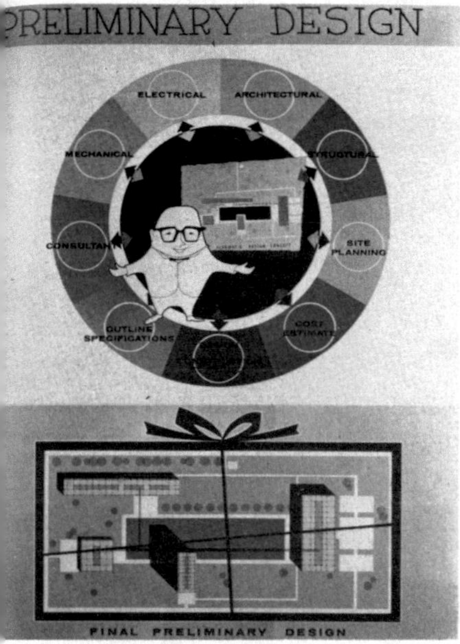

)esign—Interrelating All of the Problems

8. Presentation—Complete Picture of Solutions*

ng with the design, step by step. Major problems have n solved or closely defined. The client's approval may n be based on a quite clear picture of the architec- al and engineering intent.

Presentation

ne idea of the effects of the system may be gained by examination of the preliminary presentation on a par- lar building. For the Consolidated Gas Co. Office lding (done in association with Minoru Yamasaki), presentation to the client at the end of the design ses included the following: 3/16-in. plastic scale del of the building, 71 sheets of drawings, a 41 page iminary specification, a preliminary estimate (giving s in detail, including unit costs on all major items) ked up by two estimates made by contractors, a duction and construction schedule, and a full size kup of two floors of the building. Prior to the pres- ation, some 50 study and detail models had been made ⅛-in. scale schematic model had been presented. The el shown (8.) was used for explanation of certain ails of the building. An indication of the results of this can be gained from an examination of the articles his issue on the architecture and engineering of the solidated Gas Building.

gineers for Architecture

Smith, Hinchman and Grylls organization is deeply cerned about the extreme difficulty of obtaining en- eers who are able to assume large roles in building gn and architects with knowledge and ability in engineering. Members of the firm have spent considerable time and effort in examination of the problem and in attempts to do something about it. Visits by firm members to architectural and engineering schools throughout the country have invariably corroborated the SHG feeling that schools are not developing engineers for architecture. Electrical engineering colleges are training students in electronics, not in lighting, power, power distribution, or wiring. Mechanical engineering colleges are training men for research and work in industry, not for building engineering. Visits with architects over the country showed that most were agreed that the problem exists and something should be done about it. Neither the colleges nor the architects showed much readiness to take action on the problem.

Smith, Hinchman and Grylls has tried to attack the problem by giving college scholarships to enable graduate architects to take further courses in electrical or mechanical engineering. After some time, it was decided that the problem was much more basic than such scholarships could hope to overcome. Firm members have participated in a number of conferences and study sessions on this subject, some sponsored by the A.I.A. The thinking of the firm on the problem now tends toward the necessity for action on the part of the architectural profession and the entire industry. Architects must initiate this and lead the way.

*Office Building, Michigan Consolidated Gas Company, Detroit, Mich., Minoru Yamasaki-Smith, Hinchman & Grylls, Associated Architects & Engineers

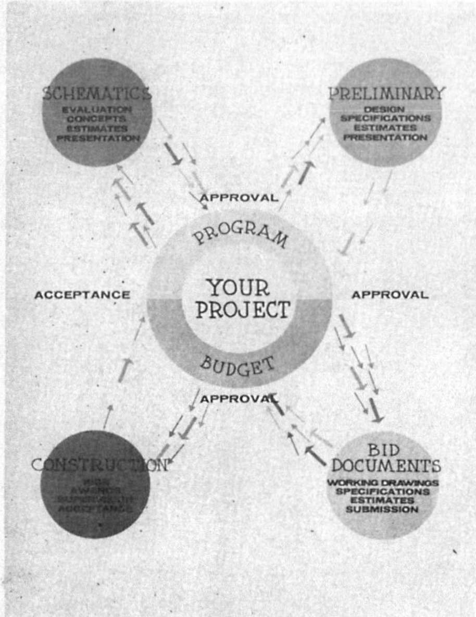

9. Program, Budget Interrelate with All Phases

Charts used as illustrations in this article were prepared by Smith, Hinchman & Grylls for use in studying their organization and procedures and for explanations to clients and others

REQUISITES FOR PRESENT-DAY ARCHITECTURAL PRACTICE *by Robert F. Hastings**

In our firm, we want to do not only good architectural design, but all of the related engineering as it pertains to buildings. In order to accomplish these things well, we believe that we must be able to give our best creative efforts to each project. This requires organization. It requires a concentration of creative effort in the design stages. We do not believe that good building design can be done by committee. So, we take some rather basic steps. For each project, the firm appoints a coordinator who is essentially an administrator. Working with him is a designer, a person who has creative skills.

The project coordinator and designer bring other firm architects, engineers, and consultants into the picture as soon as they can reasonably begin to grasp the problems. Eventually, the lead man of the group, the project coordinator will have available to him our production organization and all of the various specialized departments of the firm. All of the people working on a project get deeply involved in the design as a whole.

In order to practice the art and science of buildings in this manner, we need people who are well-trained in the overall aspects of building design, and who in addition have specialties such as mechanical or electrical engineering, or architectural management or design. We need people with cultural backgrounds, deep interest in buildings, creative attitudes toward building design. In the purely architectural aspects of our practice, we succeed—to a degree—in obtaining this kind of person. But we need engineers of the same sort.

"For several years now, we at SHG have been attempting to find solutions to the shortage of trained, talented, and creative engineers for architecture. It is our belief that the architect has created this problem for himself. If we are to have talented engineers, it will be necessary for the architect to develop more sympathy for and understanding of engineering design. The engineer must be given a reasonable share of the responsibilities for the building design and of the rewards. We must make him a creative member of the design group. In order to accomplish these objectives, it will be necessary to revamp architectural professional organization membership, education, registration, and restudy our objectives in buildings."

Robert F. Hastings

* Executive Vice President & Treasurer, Smith, Hinchman and Grylls Associates, Inc.

ORGANIZATION FOR EFFICIENT PRACTICE

4. Caudill, Rowlett and Scott, Architects-Planners-Engineers

The basic personal relationships in architecture—since it is essentially a profession—are apt to be those between the individual practitioner and his client. Most architects would agree that this is right and proper. But as architectural services become more complex and complete and are performed for buildings far from the home offices of firms, it is increasingly difficult to maintain the traditional relationships with clients, yet expand geographically, offer more complete services, and perform those services better.

After some experimentation during the years, Caudill, Rowlett and Scott has developed a system to answer some of these problems. The firm members call it the "squatters" technique. It consists of sending out a team of CRS specialists, headed by a project architect, to the location of a building commission. These people set up shop on the spot, work closely with the client. Concept drawings and related materials are developed. After client approval of these, the team goes home to complete the preliminaries and contract drawings.

The "squatters" technique is only one CRS answer to the problems of their expanding practice. But it is an important one. Some of the details of the technique are discussed here.

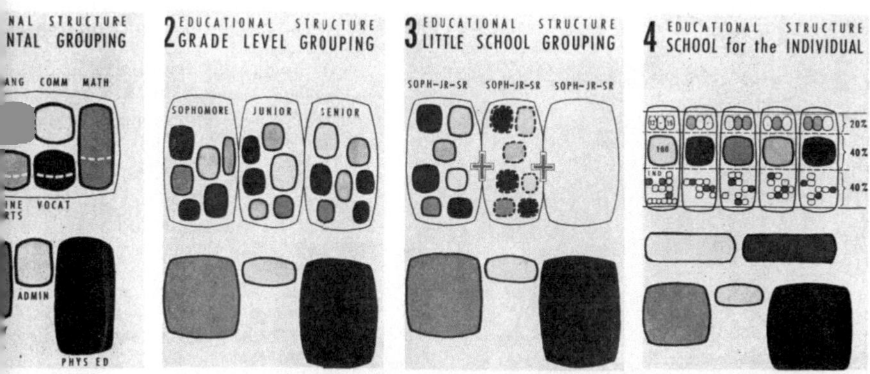

Long Distance Operation By An Architectural Team

by Thomas A. Bullock, Partner,
Caudill, Rowlett and Scott

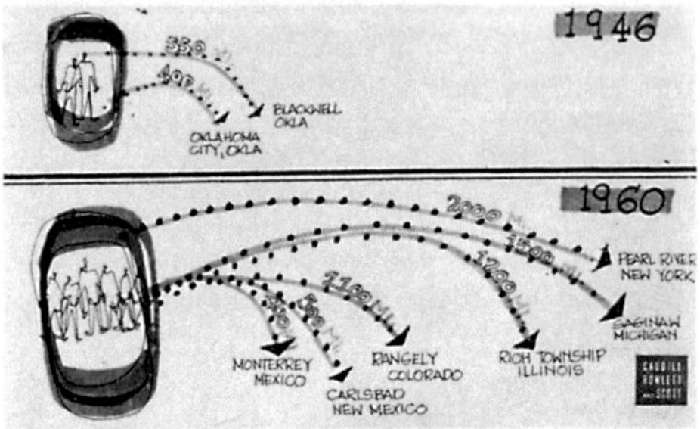

Increasing Range of CRS Operations

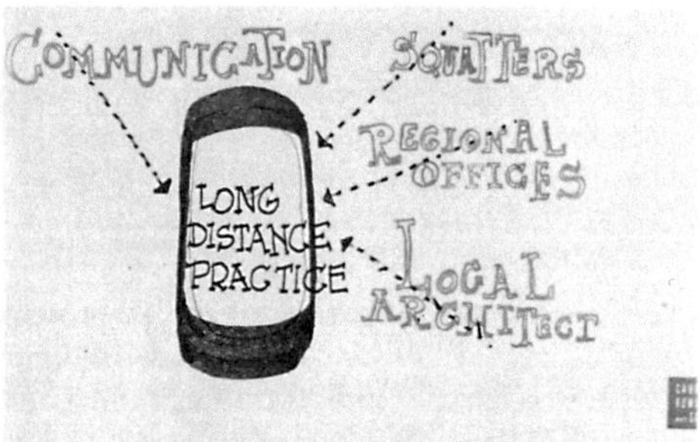

Elements of Long Distance Practice

Evolution of Firm's Team Concept

A KALEIDOSCOPE ORGANIZATION

Caudill, Rowlett, and Scott is a postwar firm fourteen years of its existence, a lot of or tional changes have taken place—changes to needs of clients—changes necessary to surv architect's number one problem of either to work or not enough, while at the same time b a firm for the long term. The name has been c from Caudill-Rowlett, the partnership fro members to seven, and the total staff from eighty. The firm's growth, though it breaks cords, has been (even with the usual ups and consistent organizationally and architec Like a kaleidoscope, the CRS organization h constantly changing. With so many chang question might well be, "What has been con Some tracing back may reveal the answer . .

LONG DISTANCE PRACTICE—— FIRST CRS CONSTANT FACTOR

The firm, located in a small town, got its f opportunity—not within the city limits b miles away. This was a shopping center. second opportunity except that this time, it school 525 miles away from home base. U present time, the trend has continued with p covering seventeen states and two foreign co So the fact that CRS has been willing to g where to have a better opportunity to prac chitecture has been constant.

A long distance practice has its probler know, for we have our local or home based p with which to compare. We don't wish to leading by giving the impression that CRS h a long distance practice. The fact is, we ha and national clients, but we are trying here out the unique and we believe the present or tion is largely the result of our long distanc tice. A basic reason for our great amount o is that CRS specializes in educational archi The firm is called upon by many out-of-town because of this, although some 20 to 25 per our volume (locally and nationally) is in no building types.

There often seems to be a conflict betwe and national practice. CRS believes that it i ble to do both. There simply cannot be an e on professional talent, if our profession is to a major role in the future. Certainly it is m complicated to have a client just down th from the office as opposed to one across the st This may be oversimplification, but it is tr have had to face this problem and have ha vise methods to give equally good service t away client as to another who is located

To eliminate the problems of operating a distances, we have devised the following op techniques:

e-Spot Design—Working in the client's
l has been a method of shortening the
g distance. This CRS technique may well be
Here's how it works: in the beginning stages
ing, a team of architects, city planners, and
's (carefully selected for the specific job in
noves into the location, where the project is
nstructed, for a three to ten day period. The
ends on the size of the job. The designers set
in space near the client's office, in a hotel or
fice of a local professional associate. This is
concentrated night and day endeavor. The
enables the client to look over the shoulder
esigners and see his project grow from the
ketches. It enables CRS to solve the client's
s better by on-the-spot analysis of the site,
ing-architectural problems, and functions re-
y the program. In CRS we refer to this as the
r's technique". We do not attempt to make
preliminary plans, but only the sketches and
terials necessary for concept approval. From
return home for preliminary drawings.

nal Offices—In 1952 we established our first
office in Oklahoma City. We recognized then
e were certain phases of architectural prac-
require close contacts with the client, princi-
programming and supervision. The regional
o plays a major role in CRS new business de-
nt.

unications—We have worked hard through
s to develop clear lines of communication be-
e client and the firm. Very often the differ-
ween good or bad communications will mean
ence between a good or bad building. To help
he distance we have strengthened communi-
o a high degree in the form of programming
research reports, and analysis cards.

Associate Architects—Approximately 40 per
ur work has been in association with other
s. To be perfectly frank, this undoubtedly
ot have occurred if our practice had been
ocal. Still, local associates often have much
hat we cannot, and vice versa.

ONCEPT-SECOND CRS CONSTANT FACTOR

nitely believes in the team concept of prac-
s was more belief than actual practice in
years. Although the original partners prac-
team approach by using consultants and
pecialists, it has only been possible for CRS
e a fully integrated team of specialists with-
ast three years. It takes time, plus a sub-
business volume, to build a team. It simply
re money to operate with a team than with
eaded organization. To us it has been worth
It will continue to be if our architecture
because of it. In a sense we have "talked the game" for years and now we can finally play it. In what league? We wouldn't venture a guess, but we do feel that we have a long way to go to approach really great architecture.

English architect David Medd talks of horizontal and vertical firms. In this sense, CRS would be horizontal because of its broad organizational base. For project participation, we insist on a team of creative specialists working together under strong practical leadership—leadership for stimulation and guidance, not dictation. This does not mean one architect working only with other architects. It means a complete team of specialists—the project architect, the architectural analyst, the designer, the city planner, the cost engineer, the electrical engineer, the mechanical engineer, the structural engineer, as well as the architect—stimulating each other to do a better and more complete job.

What may be unique about our particular team are the facts that:

1. The Client is an Integral Part of our Team—Without the client, our team would be incomplete. We know that when we insist upon bringing in our client as an active member of the team, the building will be better because of it. And when the building is complete, the client (having been involved in the planning process) is going to know how to use it more efficiently.

2. The Local Associate Architect is a Team Member—A CRS association is based more on a merging of talent and assignment of responsibility according to talent than on a strict division of responsibility. CRS believes in association on the basis of—together we can do it better than alone. Otherwise the project will probably suffer by an association. The local architect has much to contribute from his experience and knowledge of his own particular region.

3. The Team Members Are Involved in the Concept Stage—Engineers are brought in at the very beginning of the project instead of at the start of working drawings. This goes for each team specialist. Each is then continuously involved until his phase of the work is completed. The associate architect, whose usual responsibility is supervision only, is included in all phases of the work from programming through final inspection.

1960 Plus—To sum up . . . . To take advantage of opportunity, CRS has had to span distance. In an attempt to do better architecture, CRS has held to the team concept. Where do we go from here? Well, we expect to grow. And as architects, engineers and planners, we do have a long range plan. For the plan to work we believe many operational changes will take place and many new techniques of operation will need to be invented and adopted. But the two constants, *long distance practice* and *team concept* will probably remain major factors in any growth that may take place.

Reproduced here are some of the analysis studies done in Gary, Indiana by a CRS design team for an elementary school to be constructed there. After presentation to the clients for concept approval, the team went home to continue preliminaries

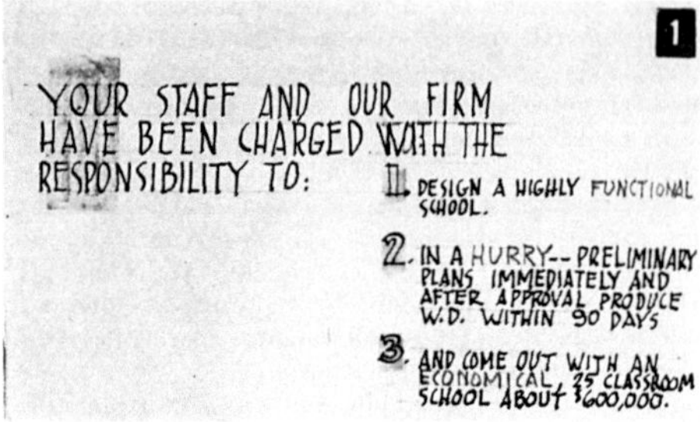

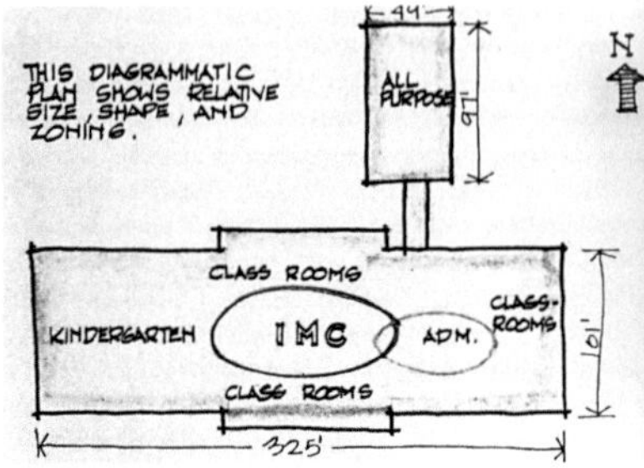

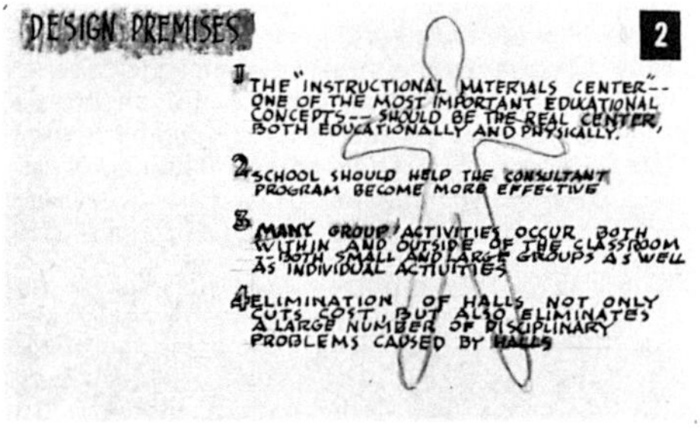

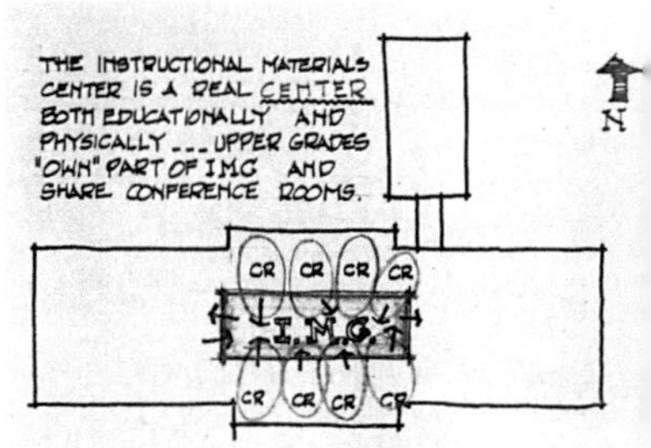

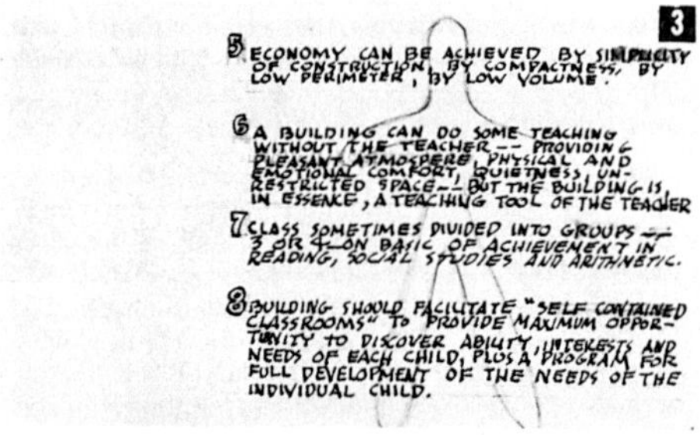

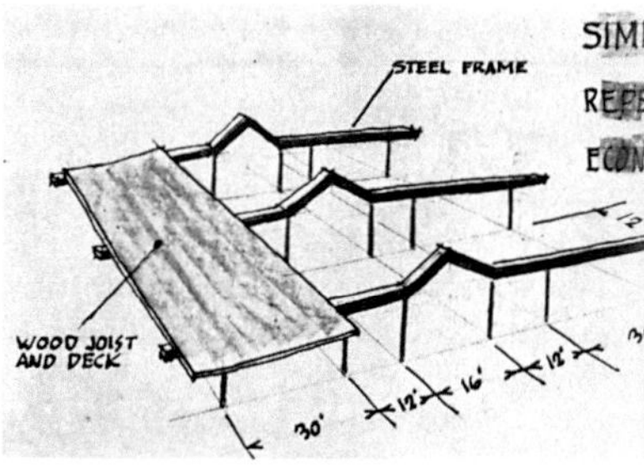

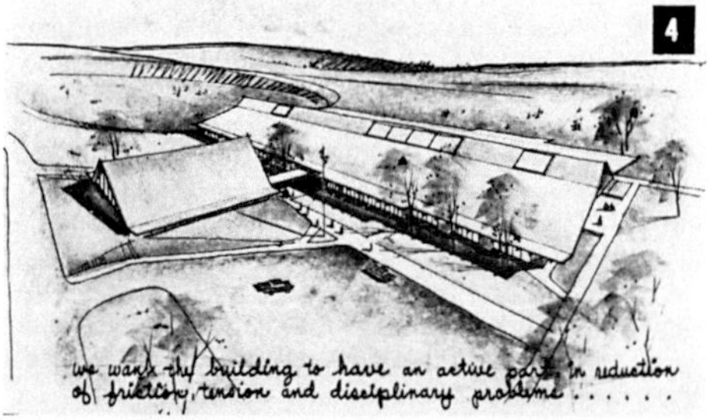

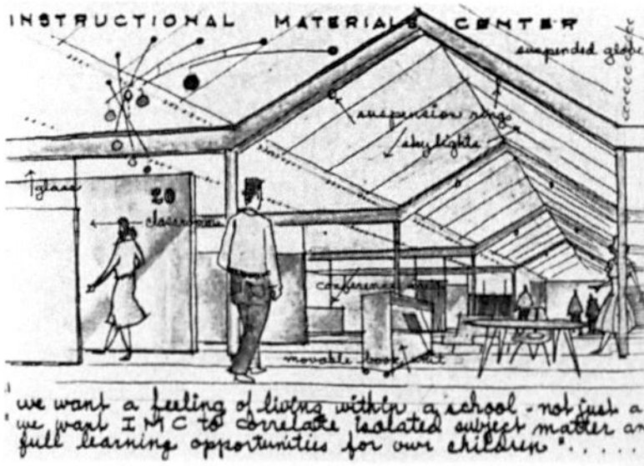

9

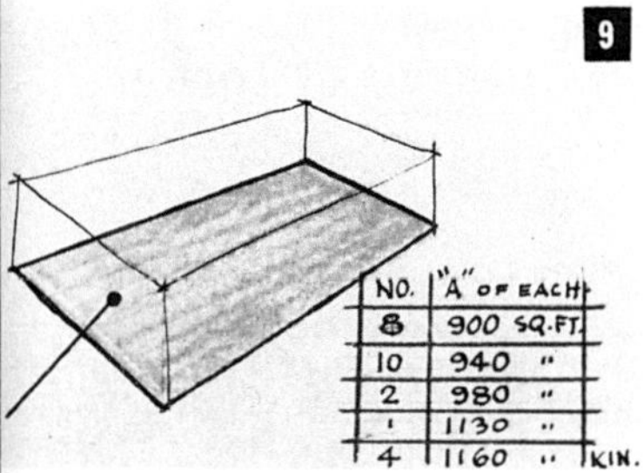

13

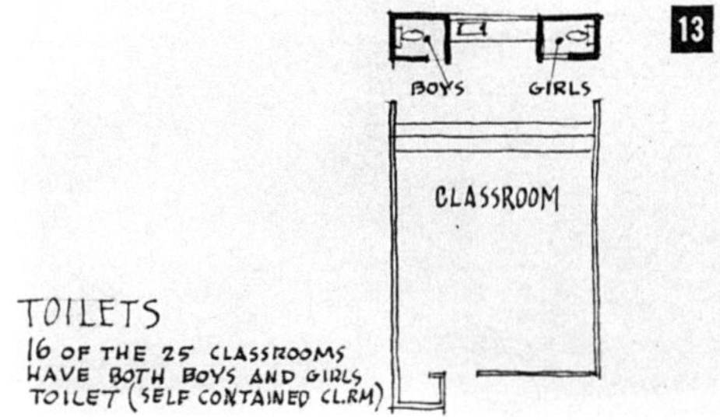

10

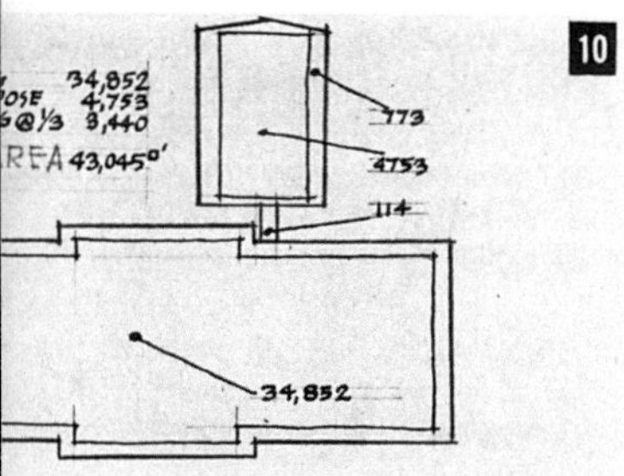

14

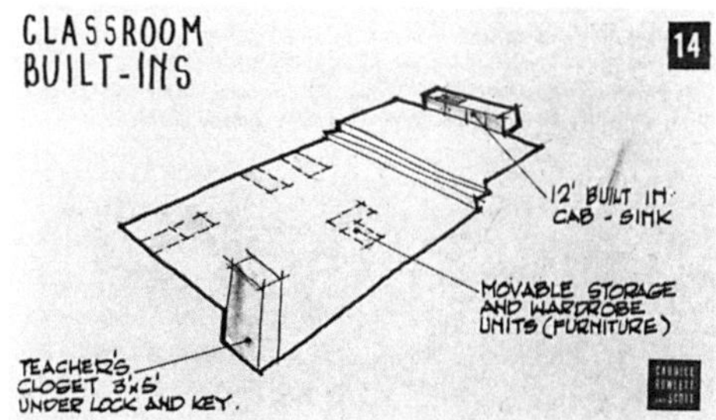

11

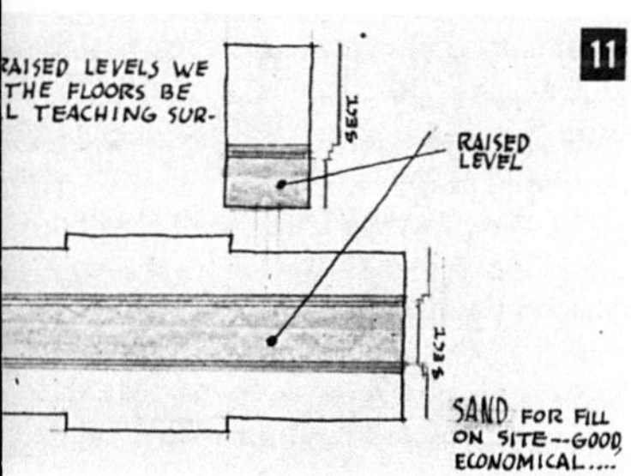

15

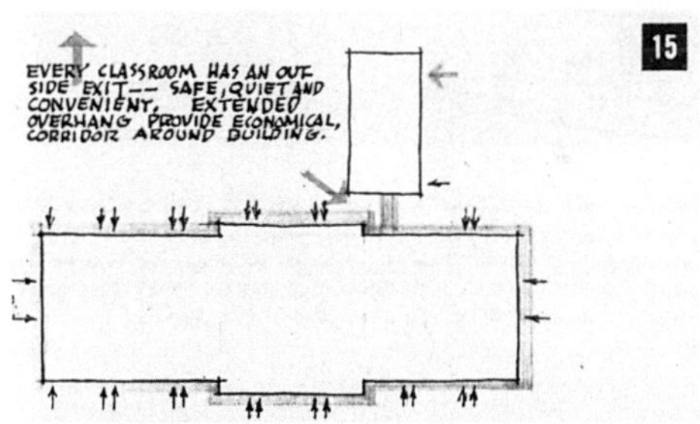

12

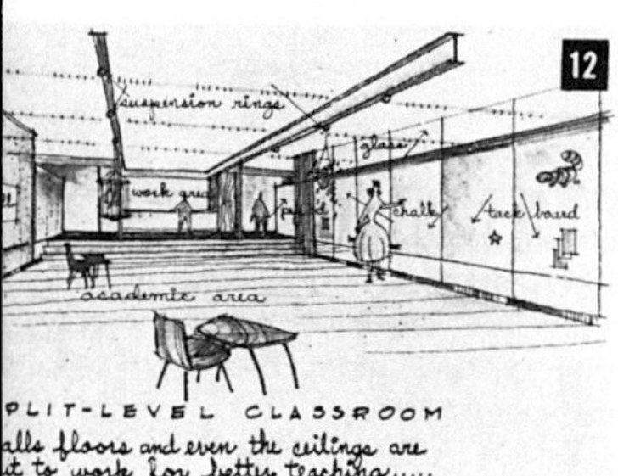

16

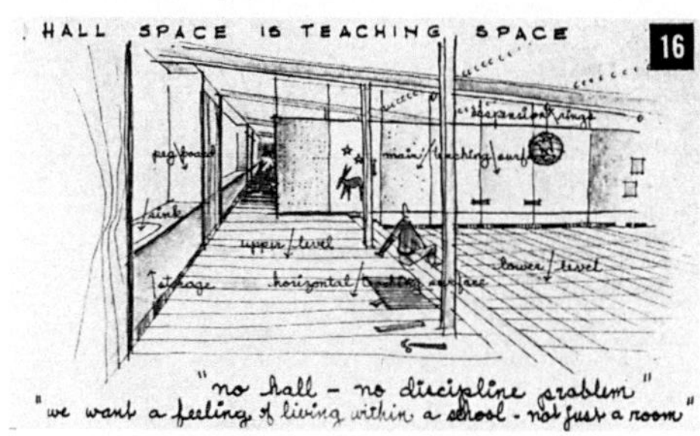

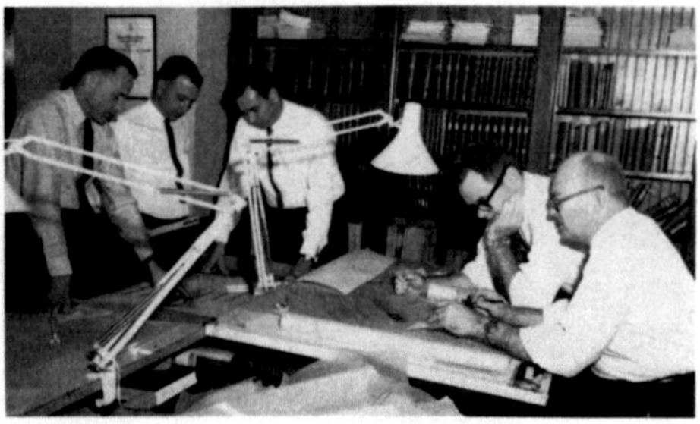

Above: a CRS team works out the conceptual design of a new high school, in the client's backyard. Included on this team are (left to right): Charles Estes, project architect, Joe Thomas, mechanical engineer, Jerry Thornton, production specialist, Bill Caudill, partner-in-charge, Frank Lawyer, designer

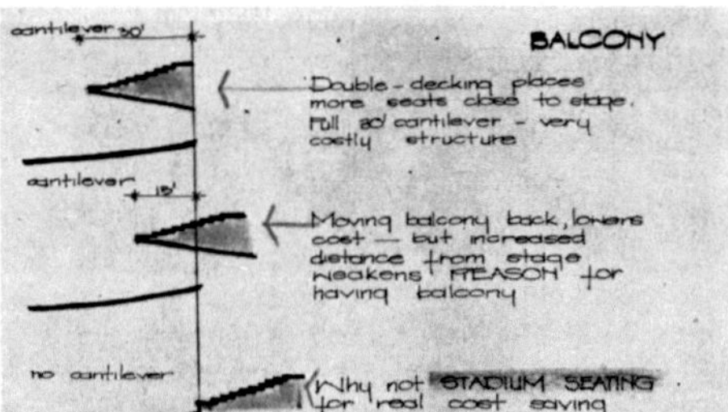

Above and below: two of a set of special analysis cards prepared to show the thinking behind an idea for stadium seating in a school auditorium. The analysis cards shown represent a tentative solution to a particular problem and may be augmented, if necessary, by further and more detailed studies

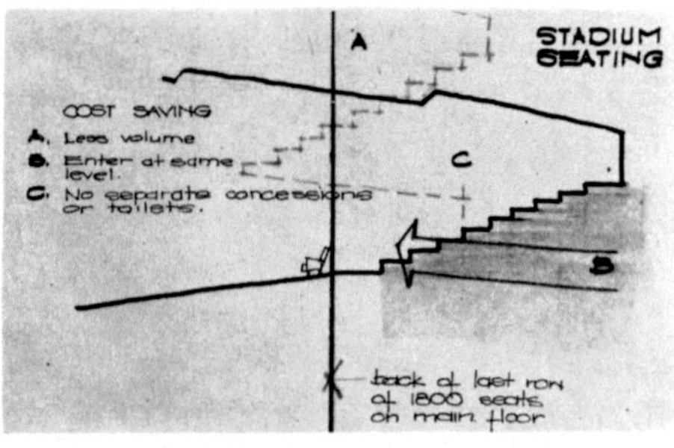

Caudill, Rowlett and Scott: DESIGN GROUP IN ACTION

The basic constants in the story of the grow Caudill, Rowlett and Scott firm have been the ment of the team concept in order to practic distance. By working within these constants, believes it can offer better and more comple tectural services to clients wherever they ma important method used by CRS is what they "squatters" technique, described in these p

The actual events of one "squatters" sess for the elementary school in Gary, Indiana, scribed by Bill Caudill as follows:

"The squatters at Gary, Indiana, lasted, recall it, only three days. The team set up in the Gary Hotel. We had a suite of rooms these was converted into a drafting room, into a conference room where we could work school board and staff. Like all squatters this was a night and day endeavour.

"The school superintendent, the school pl cialist, the supervisors, and various scho members looked over our shoulders and actu ticipated as members of the design team.

"The total package we turned out duri three days included not only the analys shown, but also a set of measured floor plan sections, elevations, and a cost analysis.

"These materials were presented to th board during the evening of the last day we Gary. Since the presentation was made to people, the cards were used in an opaque and blown up on a screen so every one coul performance. I think this is a good techniqu multi-headed client."

The "squatters" technique or some variat could make it possible for many medium-si (or even small ones) to establish long-dista tices. In this way, they might be able to obta and more satisfying commissions than mig wise be possible.

ORGANIZATION FOR EFFICIENT PRACTICE

5.

Hellmuth, Obata and Kassabaum, Inc., Architects

In order to practice the type of whole architecture they feel is necessary in the world of today, Hellmuth, Obata & Kassabaum has instituted a flexible system of checks and controls. Not only does this system operate in the usual quantity areas of practice such as costs, time, and the like, but the firm believes they are enabled, because of the system, to practice a better quality of architecture through quality controls. The HOK systems and philosophies are discussed by the members of the firm in these pages

Mac Mizuki

Priory of St. Louis and St. Mary, St. Louis, Mo.

St. Louis Planetarium, St. Louis, Missouri

Mac Mizuki

Temple Israel Synagogue and School, St. Louis County, Mo.

Obata: HOK Philosophy of Design

The architect today is free as he has never before been free. No longer do the limitations of physical circumstance, of materials and techniques, provide him with a context of discipline within which he can achieve meaning. Today *any* space can be functional, *any* structure is possible. He is also free of national or regional characteristics—a Persian screen (in modern aluminum, to be sure, and gold anodized at that) is accepted as not out of place in Detroit. "The will of the epoch," which Mies has said it is our ultimate task to express, is anybody's guess, and we are all free to guess it as best we can.

Because of this unique freedom, because we can do anything we want to do, because we can meet all of the traditional demands upon architecture in an unlimited variety of ways, we face the problem of meaning in a new way. Meaning for architecture can no longer come from external esthetic theories like 'functionalism,' 'structuralism,' 'Formalism,' 'mannerism' or 'brutalism.' I suggest that meaning, and therefore discipline, must come from *within*. For me the only valid architecture today, the only architecture which can fulfill the demands made upon it as art and as building, and also escape the perils of falling into one 'ism' or another, and hence becoming trivial, is architecture which evolves outward, in a natural and organic process, from the program it sets out to fulfill.

In this approach, the greatest need is to understand the problem. In our work we seek always to penetrate to the essence of the client's problem, and to understand it in all of its individuality. We try to let ourselves be en-

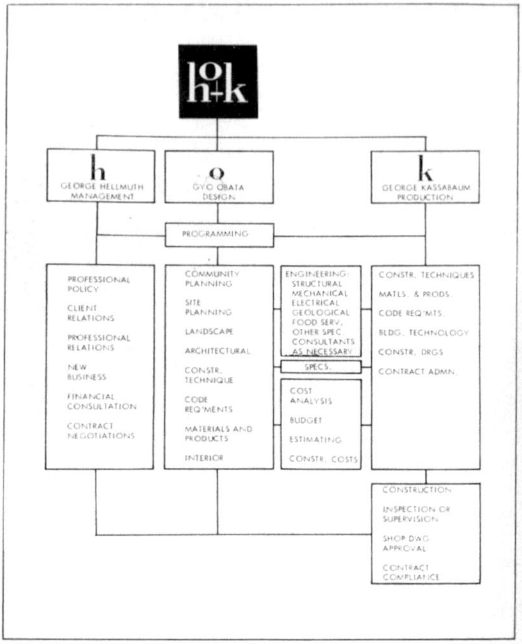

No. 1 Basic Organization Chart

The basic organization of Hellmuth, Obata & Kassabaum, as shown in the chart, is divided into three main departments—management, design, and production. Each of these is directed by a firm principal who has the direct responsibility for his particular sphere of operations. There is considerable interplay between all of the departments, and each principal keeps himself involved in all of the work of the firm insofar as is practical

tirely grasped by, and in turn to grasp, the unique combination of needs, desires, aspirations and attitudes of this particular client and his particular program. When we can do this, then the project will, in a sense, design itself. I say in a sense, because I do not mean by "design itself" that anything mystical or beyond the rational control of the designer is going on, but rather that total understanding and absorption of the problem, when joined with rigorous study and broad experience, reveals to the designer the one right solution to that problem, the single design which for him *is* the design of that project.

This process proceeds by tough minded analysis, experimentation and research, all based on the principle of exploiting the individual characteristics of each project to determine the expression of form and the arrangement of space and mass. Our Priory Church is circular because a monastic church with many monks participating in the service requires a central altar. The central altar is reflected in the tall lantern tower forming the upper tier of arches, while the lower tier of parabolic arches reflects the ring of small side chapels which are an important part of the church.

If the Priory Church design also expresses something of the grace and power of an ancient religion alive and relevant in the terms of the present, this too, follows from the approach to design which I have described. All of the

Art Fillmore

Priory of St. Mary and St. Louis, St. Louis, Mo.

Mac Mizuki

Brith Sholom Kneseth Israel Center, Richmond Heights, Mo.

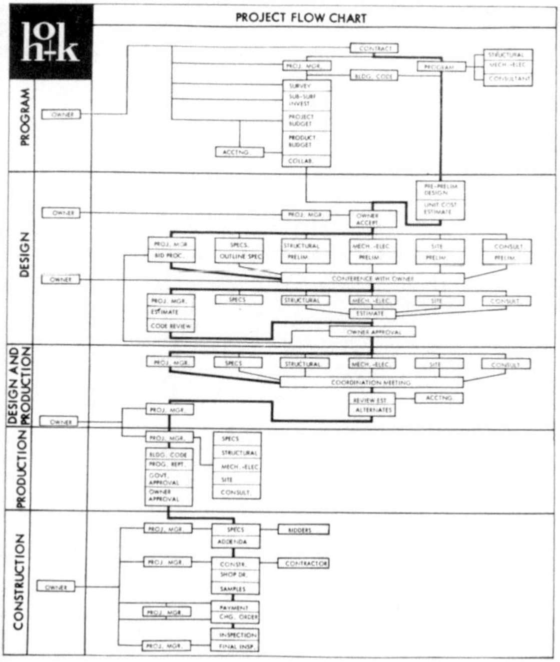

No. 2 Project Flow Chart

This chart indicates the flow of projects through various stages. Another function is the definition of prime responsibility within the firm for different stages. Also shown are the principal points of client contact for consultations and approvals. To insure continuity in projects, most contacts with clients are made by the project managers in charge of individual commissions

projects shown here demonstrate the working of this approach—each is an attempt to express, in each detail as well as in the over-all conception of the design, both the functional requirements and the inner spirit of each building.

In doing this we have not consciously employed any 'style,' but have rather let the style of each project grow from the materials, the structure and the nature of the problem. Freed of the need for a constant search for new forms (for the sake of their newness) we can search for the right form. Freed also from the need for superficial ornamentalism, we can exploit the essentials of each building to give it its own proper form and beauty.

This is, perhaps, the hardest kind of architecture to practice. It's easier to cram a program into a theory of design than it is to help a building be itself. And there is always the question, 'Is it right? *Is* this the one right expression of this project?' If we operate according to an external principle, then the principle will authenticate our work—at least for those who agree with the theory. But with us, there is no external authentication, and hence no absolute (even if only temporarily absolute) certainty. The result is to force us further and further into ourselves and into the heart of each problem, to seek there the only certainty we can know—the certainty of truth as we see it.

Gyo Obata

Burt Wenneker Housing, St. Louis County, Mo.

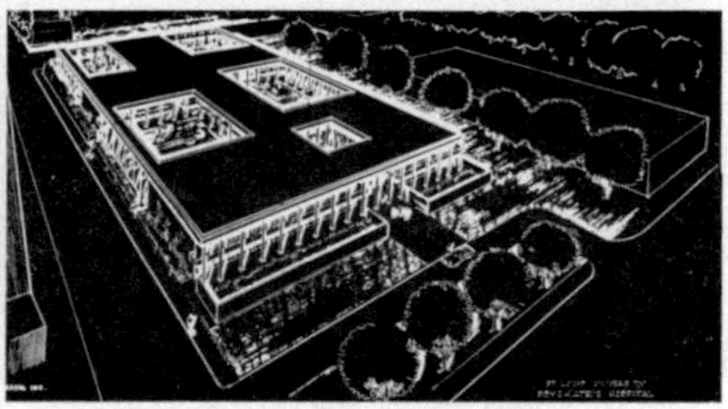

David P. Wohl Health Institute, St. Louis, Mo.

PROJECT BUDGET SHEET (hok)

PROJECT:		
a. Land Acquisition Cost	*	
b. Surveys	3,000.	
c. Soil Borings	2,500.	
d. Construction Cost	1,740,000.	
1. Buildings 1,680,000.		
2. Site 60,000.		
3. Off-site Utilities	-	IN CAFETERIA CONTRACT
e. Planning Fees 4.85 % of (d)	84400.	
f. Consultants	-	IN PLANNING FEES
g. Reproduction of Bid Documents	1,100.	
h. Advertising	500. *	
i. Contingency 5 % of (d)	87,000.	
j. Interest During Construction	45,000.*	
k. Owner's Legal & Administrative Costs	1.500.*	
l. Owner's Supervision 1 % of (d)	17,400.*	
m. Equipment	2,000.	KITCHENETTES
n. Furnishings	144,000.	DRAPERIES, FURNITURE
o.		
p.		
TOTAL PROJECT COST	2,128,400.	

* TO BE CONFIRMED OR ADDED BY OWNER — Approved by: (Owner) (Date)

No. 3 Project Budget Form

PROJECT CHECK LIST (hok)

PRELIMINARY	DATE	REMARK
Contract signed	11-15-57	
Surveys ordered		SURVEYS MADE PRIOR TO OUR CONTRACT
Surveys received		
Test borings ordered	12-12-57	ADD'L DATA 5-58
Test boring data received	1-3-58	
Applicable Building Codes		BOCA + CLAYTON, MO.
Program received	11-22-57	
Preliminaries submitted to Owner	12-23-57	
Preliminary Estimate	12-23-57	
Preliminary approval of Bldg. Commissioner	12-19-57	VERBAL APPROVAL
Owner's Approval on preliminaries rec'd.	1-8-58	
PRODUCTION		
Contracts with Collaborators	11-25-57	
Working Drawings Begun	3-3-58	HHFA APPROVAL REC'D.
Completion Date	5-22-58	
Final Estimate	6-4-58	
Final Approval of Bldg. Commissioner and other Authorities	5-23-58	
Owner's Final Approval	5-23-58	
Drawings and Specs to Bidders	5-26-58	
CONSTRUCTION		
Work order issued	6-17-58	
Occupancy	9-9-59	PARTIAL OCCUPANCY
Certificate of Completion	1-11-60	

No. 4 Project Check List

Kassabaum: How Our Firm Works

Modern times require systematic procedures. This switch from the individualized and rather unsystematic procedures for the practice of architecture in previous times may be attributed to several causes: (a) the expansion of the architect's role from design in a limited sense to everything from programming through construction supervision, (b) new techniques, (c) new materials, (d) more complex needs of more and different types of clients, (e) the modern emphasis on group decisions by clients, which in turn is bound to put greater trust in group decisions made by architects, particularly in materials selection, estimating and other technical areas. It is, in short, no longer fashionable to be vague, and when you have to offer both the services of many people making up you architectural team, plus precision, you must have orderl procedures—system—or you wind up with chaos.

No doubt at this point the reader will ask, 'Yes, bu how *does* your firm work?' One way to answer would b to discuss in detail the Project Flow Chart (page 139 Indeed this is the way a project is handled as it goe through our office. I believe that a better answer to th question (since the Project Flow Chart virtually explair itself) is simply: 'As smoothly and accurately as we ca possibly make it in the light of current conditions.' I d not consciously intend to beg the question with an answe of this sort. The hard fact is that we at HOK do not prac tice architecture by formula, any more than our desig

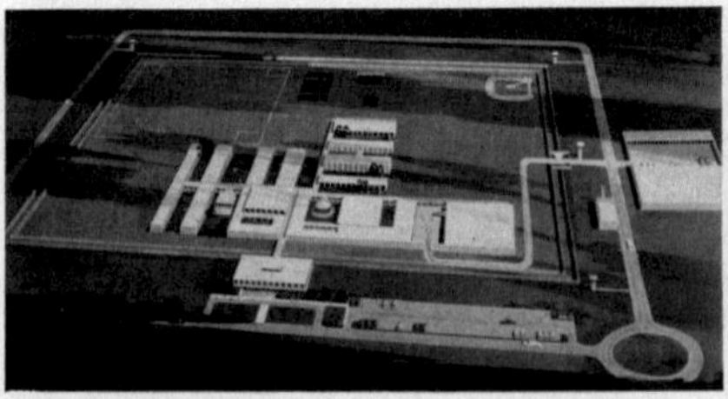

Federal Maximum Security Prison, Marion, Ill.

Alexandre Georg

University of Missouri Men's Dormitories, Columbia, Mo.

[N]o. 3 Project Budget [c]hart—prepared by the [fi]rm before starting pre[li]minaries, to tie down [fi]nancial considerations. [H]OK makes three esti[m]ates for each project, [f]rom sketches, intermedi[a]te drawings, and final [d]ocuments, each based on [a]ccurate quantity surveys [N]o. 4 Project Check List [—]serves as a schedule and [r]ecord of progress. Each [p]roject manager submits [a] revised form at the end [o]f each month. In this [w]ay, controls are possible [o]n individual job progress [a]nd the overall situation [o]n all of the firm jobs [N]o. 5 Production Schedule [—]derived from project [c]heck lists and man-hour [b]udgets. Projected ahead [si]x months, schedule [sh]ows estimated progress [o]f all jobs and man-hour [r]equirements for efficient[ly] handling the expected [w]ork load of the firm

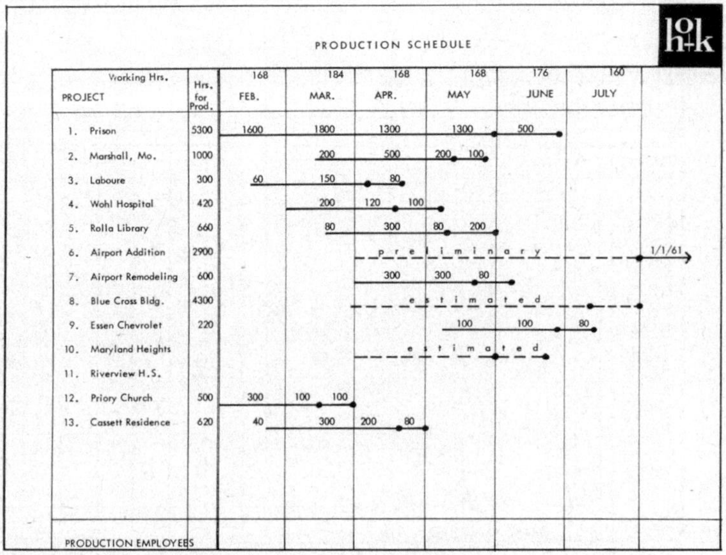

No. 5 Production Schedule

[d]epartment produces design ideas for our architectural [p]rojects by formula.

What I am saying is that our charts, schedules and [c]heck lists exist for the sake of our operations, and the [n]eeds of our clients, not the other way around. In practice, [st]arting with the client's needs and budget, this means [th]at we do not stop with one estimate, and that based on [u]nit cost. We make three estimates of our costs and some[ti]mes more than three, always working closely with the [o]wner to reach an understanding about other costs over [w]hich we have no control. These efforts result in what we [h]ope are quite accurate Project Budgets similar to Chart [N]o. 3 shown on page 140.

We do not have a fixed form for Planning and Procedures Studies (Chart No. 9 on page 144). We make one on almost every project that we consider, but the form (and most assuredly the content) can vary considerably from one project to another.

We frequently adjust our Man Hour Budgets (Chart No. 8 on page 143) as we go along, and particular problems may force periodic revision of our Production Schedules (Chart No. 5, above). Construction Schedules (such as the examples shown as Chart No. 6, page 142) would be most unusual indeed if the actual construction curves intersected the projected construction curves at every point. Even our Project Flow Chart itself has been recently revised to give a better representation of how work flows through the office.

[W]ilson Residence, Ladue, Missouri

Good Samaritan Home for Aged, St. Louis, Mo.; Manske & Dieckmann, Associate Architects

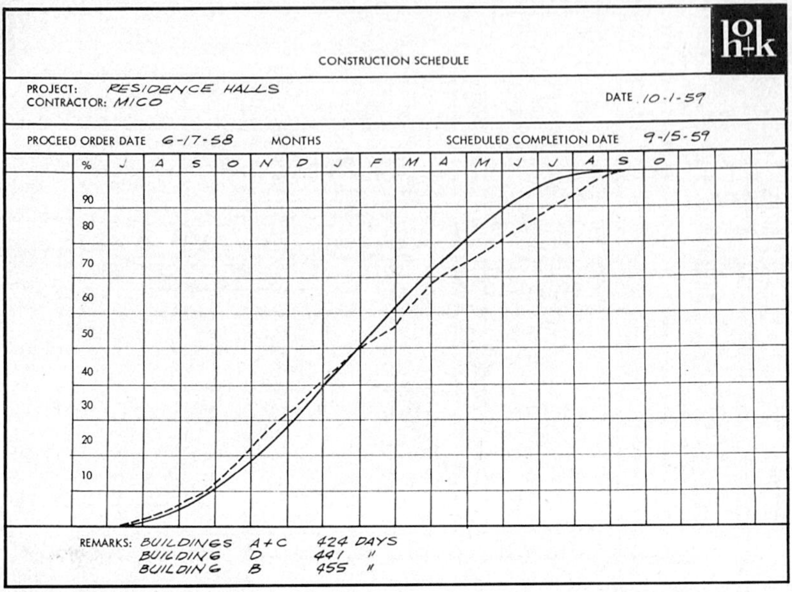

No. 6 Construction Schedule

Our intention in all of this is to serve our clients' total architectural needs, and the goal throughout all this seeming flexibility is to aim ever closer to the bullseye. We use the experience gained from one Planning and Procedures Study to make an even better one next time. We learn from the problems we may have had from one job to try to solve similar problems on the next job, in advance. We change our 'ideal' Construction Schedule curve every time we learn about factors which might alter it. Just as even these paragraphs represent some recent thinking on the question of how our firm operates, so do our procedures themselves represent plenty of hard thinking, before, during and after our work on every project we do in our office.

We simply do not practice architecture at HOK in a rigid and inflexible way, so we are stopped, by our own method, from providing an unshifting picture of our operations. On the other hand, it may be of some help to know that we do alter our procedures to meet specific conditions, and also to learn, from our particular charts, schedules and check lists the procedures which up to this time, have proved quite valuable to us in maintaining the internal controls necessary for the successful practice of architecture in a busy office.

George E. Kassabaum

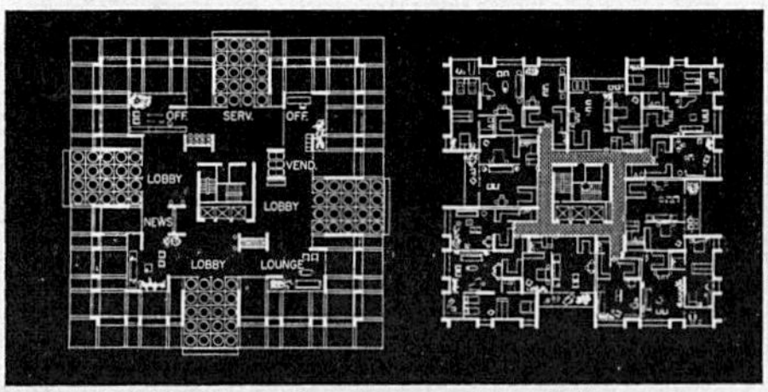

St. Louis Hills Towers Apartments, St. Louis, Mo.

Art Fillmore

Washington University Residence Halls, Clayton, Missouri

hok

PROJECT COST INFORMATION SHEET

PROJECT	RESIDENCE HALLS
NO.	57103a
DATE BID	JUNE 13, 1958
ENR BUILDING COST INDEX	560

DESCRIPTION - 4 BUILDINGS - 2 MENS AND 2 WOMENS
144 STUDENTS PER BLDG. - 576 TOTAL
203.36 FT² ENCLOSED AREA PER STUDENT

AREA 117,140 ENCLOSED (98.1 %)
TOTAL 119,461
VOLUME 1,062,382

	BID	% TOTAL	% GENERAL	$/sq.ft.	$/cu.ft.	$/STUDENT
General	$ 1,332,160.	77.17		11.37	1.25	2313.
Heating	170,840.	9.90	12.82	1.46	.16	296.
Plumbing	131,150.	7.60	9.84	1.12	.12	228.
Electrical	92,000.	5.33	6.91	.79	.09	160.
TOTAL	$1,726,150.(1)	22.83% M-E	29.57%	$14.74	$1.62	$2997.

UNIT COSTS AT TIME OF BID	UNIT COSTS ADJUSTED TO: 5-60 581
$ 14.74 sq.ft. (enclosed)	$ 15.27 sq.ft. (enclosed)
$ 14.45 sq.ft. (total)	$ 14.99 sq.ft. (total)
$ 1.62 cu.ft.	$ 1.68 cu.ft.
$ 2997 / STUDENT	$ 3109 / STUDENT

REMARKS: (1) INCLUDES ADDITIVE ALTERNATES

o. 7 Project Cost Information Form

. 6. Construction Schedule—prepared in advance of con-ruction for each project, showing estimated time of con-ruction as solid line; actual progress is plotted on form broken line as the work progresses during construction. elps architects in controlling time factors and in later an-ysis of deviations from estimates. Aids owner in determin-g when construction funds will be necessary and approxi-ate amounts that will be needed

. 7. Project Cost Information Form—master form, com-eted for each job after its final acceptance, contains com-ete data on major factors of construction costs for jobs

. 8. Man Hour Budget Form—completed in advance for each oject and amended as required as job progresses. This form, gether with final actual production costs within firm helps e architects to control own costs in producing their jobs

MAN HOUR BUDGET

hok

Construction Costs	General	1,390,000.	
	Mech. & Elec.	350,000.	
	Kitchen	-	
	Others	-	
	Total	1,740,000.	
Fee @ 6 %		104,400.	$ 84,400.
Actual Fee	4.85		
	Difference		
	Less 1.15% No Supervision		
	Reduction due to duplication	20,000.	
Collaborator Fees	Mechanical 3.23 % of	338,000.	10,910.
	Structural .485 % of	1,740,000.	8,440.
	Kitchen - % of		
	Other - % of		1,000.
	Total Collaborator Fees		20,350.
Preliminary	a. 15% of Total Fee	104,400.	15,660.
	b. 25% of Reduction	20,000.	5,000.
	c. Less 90% of Prog. Cons.		-
	d. Less 10% of Collab. Fees	20,350.	2,040.
			8,620
	e. Less 15% Profit	8,620.	1.300.
	f. Less Direct Expenses		300.
	g. Less Estimating 40 hrs.		320.
			6,700.
Intermediate			6700/6.25* = 1072MH
	a. 20% of Total Fee	104,400.	20,900.
	b. Less 27% of Reduction	20,000.	5,400.
	c. Less 3% of Prog. Cons.		
	d. Less 23% of Collab. Fees	20,350.	4,700.
			10,800.
	e. Less 15 % Profit	10,800.	1,620.
	f. Less Direct Expenses		400.
	g. Less Estimating 80 hrs.		640.
			8,240.
			8,240/6.00* = 1370 MH
Working Drawings	a. 35% of Total Fee	$ 104,400.	$ 36,540.
	b. Less 48% of Reduction	20,000.	9,600.
	c. Less 7% of Prog. Cons.	-	-
	d. Less 42% of Collab. Fees	20,350.	8,540.
			18,400.
	e. Less 15 % Profit	18,400.	2,750.
	f. Less Direct Expenses		500.
	g. Less Estimating 80 hrs.		640.
			14,510.
	h. Less Specifications (min. 40 hrs. + 10%)	240 @ 6.25*	1.500.
			13,010.
Bidding Period and Constr. Contract Negotiation			13,010/6.00* = 2168 MH
	d. 5% of Total Fee	104,400.	5,220.
	e. Less 15 % Profit	5,220.	800.
	f. Less Expenses		200.
			4,220.
Construction			4220/6.25* = 672MH
	a. 25% of Total Fee	104,400.	26,100.
	b. Amount Allowed for Supervision		-
	c. Less No Supervision		
	d. Less 25% Collab. Fees	20,350.	5,100.
			21,000.
	e. Less 15 % Profit	21,000	3,150.
	f. Less Direct Expenses		400.
	g. Less Salary of Clerk of Works		9,000.
			8,450.
			8450/6.25* = 1352MH

* LABOR + OVERHEAD
MH - MAN HOURS

No. 8 Man Hour Budget Form

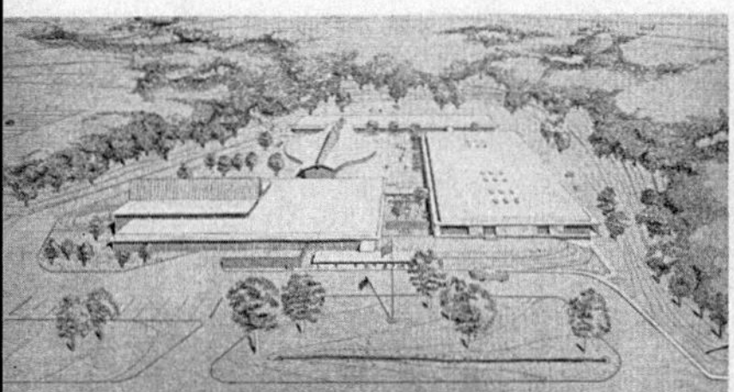

onard Steger Junior High School, Webster Groves, Mo.
udill, Rowlett & Scott, Associate Architects

© Ezra Stoller

Warson Woods Elementary School, Webster Groves, Mo.

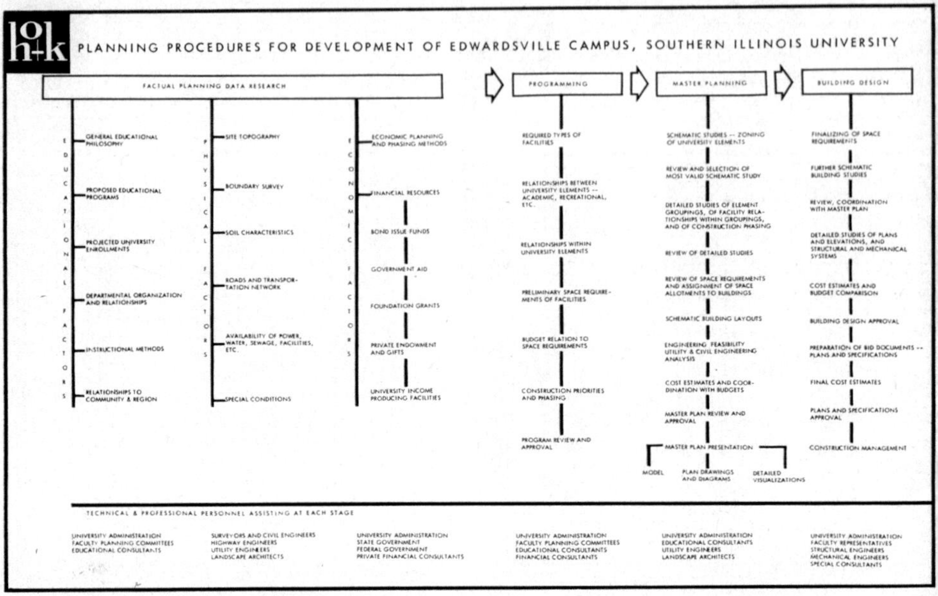

No. 9 Planning Procedure Chart

HOK prepares this type of chart for each project of any complexity, as an aid in controlling its work and explaining it to clients. As George Hellmuth put it, in ARCHITECTURAL RECORD, February, 1960, p. 175, "The purpose of all this is to perfect a thoroughly hardheaded, cost conscious business operation in order to make available the creative abilities of outstanding architects to clients."

Hellmuth: Practice of Architecture

Sixteen years ago I wrote down what I believed then to be some sound principles for building a broad practice. Reviewing the list recently only served to confirm what I had felt about them all along. Here are some of the points:

Specific clients whose interests are national and international have a tendency to have one firm do their work wherever it may be.

After a firm has completed several projects of one type, or for other reasons, it is considered expert. It can successfully compete for that type of business wherever that business may be located.

By effective local associations, other 'trade territories' can be added.

A helpful interest taken in architectural and engineering problems of (the right) people frequently leads to contracts, if not with those people then with others in allied or closely related fields.

An outstanding national reputation would, of course, be most productive, followed up by well directed personal calls by members of the firm.

All past clients of the film should be continuously cultivated.

Unless past clients as well as new prospects see ample evidence of continuing vitality and a progressive tendency, there is always the possibility they will go elsewhere.

Ability to build an effective staff quickly—to man a large project which suddenly goes ahead—is second only in importance to getting the contract.

These points have been valuable both to our firm and to me personally and they are, I believe, just as valid today as they were back in 1944. The trouble with them of course, is that architecture is not practiced by formula. Assembling top talent, exercising crisp operational control following a policy of "consultation unlimited," being ready to expand, showing continuing vitality, these things are not the whole story.

Architecture is not just putting up buildings. It is, in reality, a major part of a broad spectrum. Properly, it should start with programming, not just for one building or group of buildings but for local, state and even national plans. Properly, architects should function down through completion of construction, not in contracting, of course but through the giving of helpful, indeed invaluable, construction supervision.

Many architects presently limit themselves to a narrow band on the spectrum. We at HOK propose to widen our area on that spectrum, for we believe the added strength resulting from such broader participation is central to the solution of architecture's major problem in the days ahead: to secure a place at the council tables where community, state and national planning policy decisions are to be made in the future.

George F. Hellmuth

ROTCH LIBRARY
School of Architecture and Planning
Massachusetts Institute of Technology
ITECTURAL FORUM THE MAGAZINE OF BUILDING APRIL 1963
FORUM
APR 8 1963
LIBRARY

THE NEW SAARINEN OFFICE

BY WALTER McQUADE

Last spring the head of one of the largest U.S. architectural firms telephoned Aline Saarinen to ask her to lunch. When lunchtime arrived, in the opulent surroundings of Manhattan's 21 Club restaurant, it became evident that what he really was hungry for was Eero Saarinen and Associates. He offered to buy the firm outright, saying, winningly, that he could put all that talent to good use, including Mrs. Saarinen's public-relations expertise.

The conversation was never allowed to reach the proposed purchase price; Mrs. Saarinen declined, in behalf of Saarinen's surviving partners, so the money value of the 94 talented people of this organization is not yet clearly established. Yet it can be assumed to be very high. The 94, with very few defections since Saarinen's death, are immensely busy in their headquarters in a Connecticut mansion (above), whose efficient new drafting-room wing (below) contrasts amusingly with the romantic old front. For more details, turn the page.

PHOTOS: JOHN HILL

PHOTOS: JOHN HILL

$125 million in work

The Saarinen office has not lost a single client since the death of Saarinen, and there is now $125 million of work underway. Most telling is the fact that $25 million of that work has come in since Saarinen's death, including such prized commissions as a municipal museum for Oakland, Calif., whose directors went on a nationwide architect-hunt before picking Saarinen Associates, (page 116); a large high school for New Haven (page 115); a department store outside Dallas for Neiman-Marcus (page 118); a brace of college buildings; and—in collaboration with Charles Eames—one of the few exciting buildings so far proposed for the 1964 New York's Fair (the exhibitor being one of the world's corporate connoisseurs of architecture, IBM).

That the Saarinen organization has survived the death of its namesake is thus evident. It will not be the first firm to have done so: McKim, Mead and White, established in 1880, did not change its name until 1960—some 32 years after the death of the last remaining original partner. But the success of successors is difficult to define, and this will be especially true in the case of the Saarinen office, because it has been such a special breed. One of its industrialist clients said recently, "We've felt it has always been an R. and D. kind of operation—not just technical research and development, but also visual ideas—architecture, I guess." Can the same kind of operation survive without the personal touch of Saarinen? The answer is up to three men: Joseph Lacy, John Dinkeloo, and Kevin Roche.

The Administrator

Joe Lacy, the senior partner, is a quiet, stocky man, soundly conservative in appearance, unassuming in manner. He was born 57 years ago in Kansas City, Mo., into a family in the construction business, and by the time he was in high school, he was working summers as an architectural draftsman. Then came the University of Pennsylvania architecture school, followed by drafting jobs in Philadelphia, including several years with Paul Cret.

In 1945 Lacy was associated with another Penn and Cret alumnus, Louis I. Kahn, in the construction of a housing project in Washington, D.C. One day, Eero Saarinen came looking for

an experienced project manager for a big job he and his father had landed. Kahn recommended Lacy generously, and Lacy made the move to Bloomfield Hills, outside Detroit, joining an office called Saarinen, Saarinen & Swanson, which then numbered, he remembers, about 15 people, but was building up for a very big project, which was the General Motors Technical Center. Upon Eliel's death and Robert Swanson's departure into his own practice, the firm was remade in 1951 with Saarinen as principal owner and Lacy as one of two other partners.

Lacy took over general administration, which he continues to handle today. But today he also checks the drawings and closely supervises several projects, including the big John Deere Co. group near Moline, Ill.

The Technologist

Dinkeloo, 45, the other partner, is a dark, good-looking man who sometimes appears sardonic but never is. Instead he is that rare combination: a very practical man who is also an enthusiast. He too started in architecture young, working in the summer of 1939 for Skidmore, Owings and Merrill in Chicago while he was attending the University of Michigan. After graduating in 1942, and spending several informative years with the Seabees in the Pacific, Dinkeloo returned to Chicago and SOM, and, by the time he was 28, was chief of production and coordinator of structural and mechanical work for that office.

It was Harry Weese who took him to the Tavern Club one day in 1950 to meet Saarinen, who commented at once on the unusual name, Dinkeloo. "It's Dutch, originally," said its owner. "Whenever you hit a double vowel, it's Dutch, you'll find."

"Oh?" said the Finnish-born Saarinen. Then he told Dinkeloo he was looking for a buffer between the designers and the engineers on the still-expanding G.M. job. "We made a deal," says Dinkeloo, and he moved enthusiastically to Bloomfield Hills. In 1956 he became the thir ner, with responsibility n for working drawings but very important generativ cialty of the firm: searchi side the usual building i to find industrial process adaptation to constructior as the plastic zippers for th glazing, the mirror glass Labs, etc. Dinkeloo is stil he has just uncovered liquid honing finish fo granite in the CBS buildir

The Designer

The third force in the fu the firm, who is not yet a p will be. Kevin Roche, 4(pleasant, pale-eyed man faint Irish brogue. Born an cated in Ireland, he work Dublin and in London for well Fry, before coming U.S., then spent a semes two at Illinois Institute of nology with Mies van der In 1948 he was working i York for the UN Planning when he met Saarinen shortly thereafter he, too, Bloomfield Hills, working GM Research Center. Roc on very well with Saarinen fast formed great respect designing talent.

Roche is rich with hur well of Celtic mirth which b frequently to the surface, bu anything but a whimsical, my-way Irishman. Instead an intellectual, somewhat drawn. Although poised socially, he frequently has

continued on pa

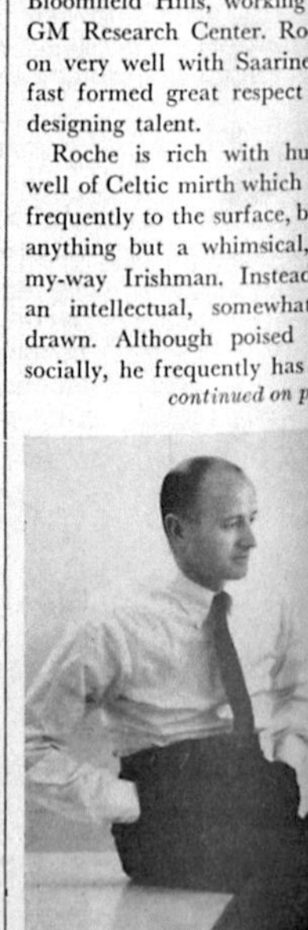

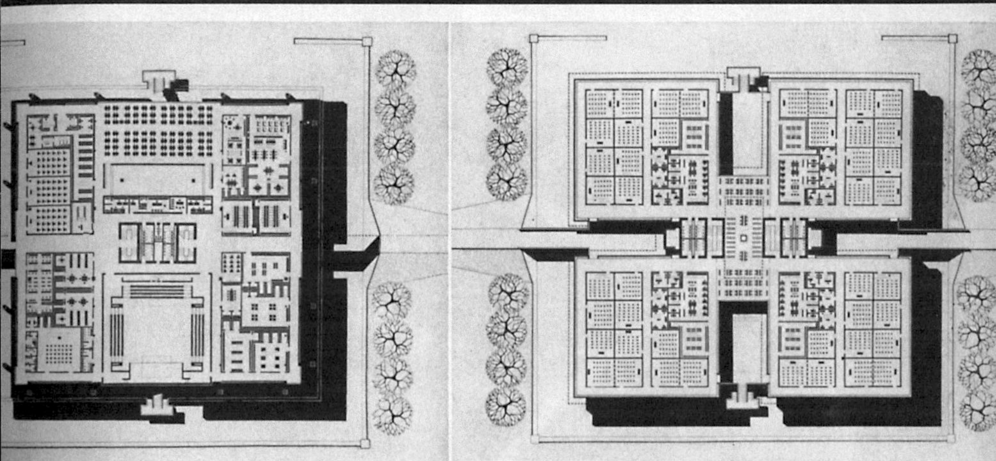

NNECTICUT HIGH SCHOOL

a cramped site in midtown New ven, this strong concrete structure l divide its 1,600 students into r "houses" in the four quad- ts of the top-floor plan (above, right). In each of these houses will be a number of classrooms with relocatable partitions, plus a commons or general purpose room, and office space for the house master. Around all will run galley-like corridors, through which the peripheral classrooms will look outdoors. In the center of this level are a library and the toilets.

Downstairs will be specialized classrooms, such as science laboratories, home-economics rooms, industrial-art workshops, and business education classrooms, administrative offices, cafeteria, and auditorium. A separate building, not shown, will house the gymnasium.

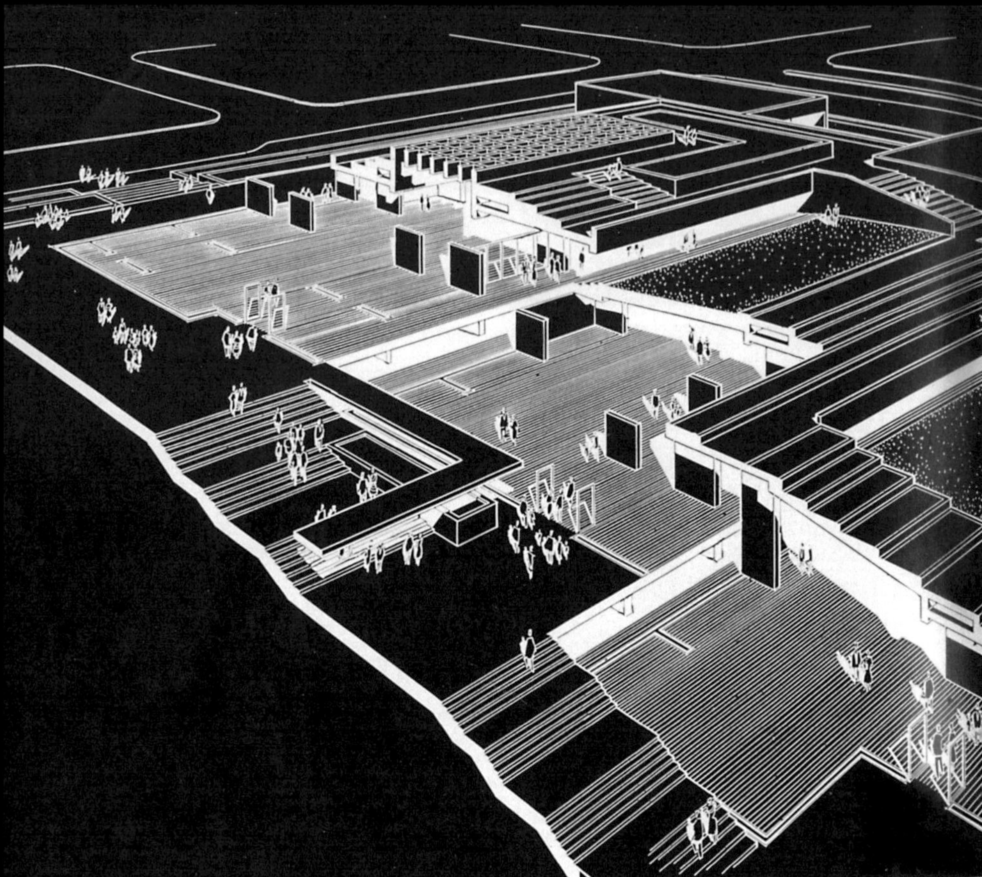

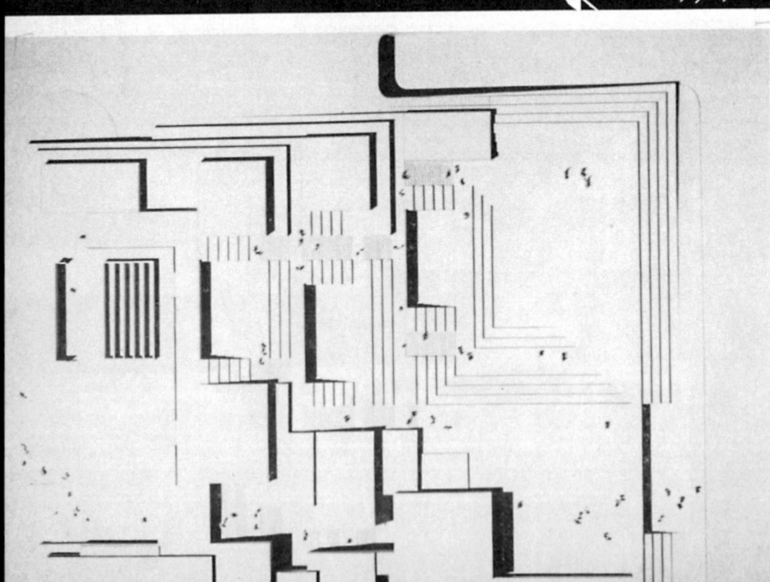

MUSEUM FOR OAKLAN

*Three levels of galleries—one
for natural history, for cul
and for art—together will fo
$6 million regional museum fo
California area. These sets
rooms will face outward on
more levels of gardens and
door displays (see schematic
away drawing above). There
also be a large gallery for tr
ing exhibitions, two auditorium
lectures, and a restaurant. Th
ner buried shelves behind the
leries will be a municipal ga*

*Beyond details, it is as a
plete "surround" that the de
is construed, a pleasantly dive
place to take a walk, indoo
out, while learning someth
perhaps something unexpected
signer Roche believes the m
photographed left, in plan
best reveals the character of
he is after in the way of a s
tural environment in the midd
the California city of which
trude Stein was once able to
"There is no there there."*

of standing around, waiting for someone else to say something *first*. When he speaks it is at a quiet pitch, and quite slowly. The brogue whittles his words into a gently commanding diction, however. Nor are his ideas easy to anticipate, or to ignore.

Several years before Saarinen died, in 1961, he announced that he wanted to make Roche a partner; this could not be done legally, however, until Roche became a registered architect. To do that he had to begin the process of obtaining U.S. citizenship.

Today Roche is still too busy to do either. A bachelor, he literally lives in the old mansion in Hamden, in an upstairs room, frequently working seven days a week in a very time-consuming manner of designing—by means of models and mock-ups. People who know Roche well say he is a more "rationalist" designer than was Saarinen, who had a wide romantic streak. But there are two qualities which the two obviously shared: full devotion to the laboriously detailed programming of any project, in the attempt to distill out the prejudices pulling the designer toward a commonplace solution. The other quality is audacity.

The first new job

Typically, Roche and Dinkeloo won the campaign for the design of the Oakland Museum by urging almost a nonbuilding, a three-level set of bunker-like galleries largely buried to one side in enclosed parking areas for cars, and opening on intricately terraced gardens on another side. It will be a very vernal place, with much man-made boskiness, something of a combination of Copenhagen's Tivoli Gardens and the Villa D'Este outside Rome. "There was this opportunity to make a unique thing," Roche murmurs, "to show that art is not just esoteric but a part of nature and culture. . . . The essence of the thing was to make the gardens come forward. The Renaissance garden was an architectural thing, but there is no longer any such thing today. This is an effort to really tie the museum and the garden together, to combine them. What we're really looking for is just a very nice place to be in for a day."

Charles Eames points out something else about the Oakland job: "Kevin's great worth is the same large view of architecture that Eero took. The office got the Oakland museum as a building to design, then they began to consider the next larger thing, which is what the museum really could and should be, both in terms of the rest of the city physically and as a museum. Kevin said, in effect, 'OK, now wait a minute; let's look at the whole thing.' This is a difference in *kind* from the usual architectural approach."

"But," adds Eames, "it would be a mistake to view the development of the office as a linear thing. What Kevin did for years was backup Eero, a very helpful thing. But now there is a new development. The one-time backup to the main show becomes the main show."

The future

Perhaps fortunately, the busy Roche does have a positive deadline for getting his registration. The present partnership must be dissolved and renamed by 1966, the year in which the Saarinen estate ceases to hold even a minority interest. The estate has three equal beneficiaries: the architect's two children by his first marriage, Susan, 18, and Eric, 20, and his widow, Aline. Mrs. Saarinen is not a partner in the firm, as widely supposed, but is a part-time employee, spending four mornings a week in the office as director of public information, and has been invaluable in continuing the intimate client relations which the Saarinens created. But her other interests are beginning visibly to pull her back into the busy world in which she whirled before marrying the architect—art and publishing. She expects to finish a book about Stanford White soon, and is in demand for TV appearances.

To the visitor to the Hamden hilltop office, the office seems the same quiet studio as ever. Immense working models stand in the big design drafting room with

continued on page 118

DALLAS DEPARTMENT STORE

At one end of a huge new shopping center in the Dallas suburbs, the merchandising lord of the central city, Neiman-Marcus, will take a strong stand. The idea is to construct an indoor "street" through the $2 million building with exhibitions all along the way, and an indoor "public square" for such displays as a yacht or a Maserati—Texas type impulse merchandise. Opening off the indoor avenue will be broader merchandising pastures.

shirt-sleeved young men making adjustments to them. There is no rush, but long, long hours. Saarinen was proud of the fact that he sometimes seemed to be running a finishing school, with a very high turnover in employees; since 1948, some 166 designers and draftsmen have come and gone, besides the people in the office at present. But recently the turnover has not been high.

This may be partly as a result of the strong shake-out in the organization when it moved from Bloomfield Hills to Hamden in 1961. At that point almost 60 per cent of the employees (45 per cent of the architectural force) stayed behind, in Michigan, where a number of them are today working for Minoru Yamasaki. But there are also strong loyalties not only to the firm itself, but to the individual projects: Deere & Co., the CBS Building, the Jefferson Memorial, the repertory theater for Lincoln Center, North Christian Church in Columbus, Ind., Athens airport.

Design orientation of the firm is indicated by the fact that there are about as many men in the design department as in working drawings (about 40 in each).* The average age of the key people is just over 35, and it has been pointed out that Roche himself, at 40, is in somewhat the same situation that Saarinen was at that age, when he was given the opportunity—with the need—to move out from under the shadow of his father, who originally had been awarded the vast GM job.

The main burden not only of design, but of client relations, has fallen on Roche, who, as a result, has travelled more than 100,000 miles in the past year. He has also made presentations to larger groups than was usual with Saarinen. His audiences have been as big as 500, because of the two city jobs the office has acquired, the museum and the school. Roche stays discreetly out of limelight at these presentati putting the design to the fore means of wide-screen projec and other late technical devi In contrast, Saarinen made alr all of his presentations to sma groups of corporate clients, was famous for his very pers al, country-doctor approach. would explain a design carefu calmly, kindly—as if it were very serious medical operation client was facing.

Determining the Method

So far all the new office's signs have been in concrete brick, except for the forest of trees which will support a of the IBM pavilion at World's Fair, but, says Roche, indicates no flagging of their vor for the industrial solution is the job that must determine method, he points out. But h capable of small wistful jokes this score: "I'm worried just a about the technological aspec using all this bearing brick and brick piers. I suppose it wo be preferable to have someth instead that could be flown in helicopter and instantaneously sembled on the site, but it not always be in the cards." obligations of the past practice there in his mind.

Daring is the quality which always identified this office r easily, and Lacy, Dinkeloo, Roche know that to keep t crack staff together, the big spe jobs must be attracted and proached with that special ve It can be said that so far momentum has been lost; Oakland Museum, especi should be one of the most uni designs the office has ever veloped. One thing is certain that old brick mansion on hilltop in Hamden, with its d ble deck of drafting space jecting out to the rear, the li will continue to burn late.

** Among the people who moved with the office from Michigan and carry sp responsibility: in design, Robert Burley, Olav Hammarstrom, Paul Kennon Anthony Lumsden, Cesar Pelli, David Powrie, and Harold Roth; in inter Warren Platner; in graphics, Jill Mitchell; in estimating, Joe Jensen; in spec tions, Dorothy Carlin; in working drawings, Norbert Blum, Allan Dehar, Owen, James Owens, and Victor Zampa; in field supervision, R. Jerome Cham lain, Clarence Mogridge, and Ralph Price; as project managers, Bruce Detr Philip Kinsella, Glenn Schneider, and Edward Saad (whose own private th about double vowels in names is that they are neither Dutch nor Finnish, Arabian).*

JOHN HILL

The fine and the folk

An essay on McKim, Mead and White
and the American tradition

Peter Smithson

The strongest architectural tradition in United States is the tradition of careful det in expensive materials—granite, trave bronze, plate glass and lately in stainless

This tradition can safely be said to have founded by McKim, Mead, and White. monograph on their work* covers the p 1879–1915, and this may be assumed to be high period, although one's own feelin that what one always assumed to be e McKim, Mead, and White, such buildin Selfridges, Bush House and the Rootes building in Piccadilly, were still being fin in the late 1920s.

The present-day architecture of this trad that of Skidmore, Owings and Merrill, is th architecture in the United States that fo architects regard as really American. An with Detroit cars, they admire it withou restraints that would operate against the ad tion of such architecture were it a prod their own culture. It is admired for its unma technological competence.

They are, of course, perfectly aware th underlying planning models are those of th Beaux Arts: banal, overblown, official **6**.

But the expertise that has been brought to can lift the product into the category of th —and this is what fascinates, the hint of 'ar architecture' outside the traditions of E and Japan.

This, of course, one has been able to se recently and is apparent in very few buil and only a breath of it can be felt in the wo the founders of the tradition—McKim, and White.

But there is no doubt that Skidmore, Owing Merrill's Union Carbide **5** and Chase Man Bank buildings **1, 2, 3 & 4** in New York are s made and of such expensive materials th cannot imagine who could have made them arouse the strongest cargo-cult feelin foreigners, and are truly hints of *une archit autre.* Yet the same architects' Conne General Building is a load of nothing (in way one senses really life-diminishing occupants); and the same tradition's L Centre a load of near-wicked nothing (a kind of morally corrosive).†

*Paul Wenzel, Maurice Krakow *A monograph work of McKim, Mead and White,* 1879–1915. Ar tural Book Publishing Co. N.Y. (There seems t biography of this firm. This would make a good for a European's Ph.D. Thesis.)

†One can be definite in one's judgments of thi sort of building for the architectural language f after is a known one, the cribs obvious, the int too familiar.

5

se Manhattan Bank, New York, Marilyn Monroe US Army jeep

3

se Manhattan Bank, New York—1957–61

se Manhattan Bank with the Federal Reserve ding by McKim, Mead and White in the back- nd

n Carbide Corporation, New York—1957–60

Force Academy, by Skidmore, Owings and Merrill, rado Springs—1956–62

tage by Geoff Reeve from photos by Eric Locker and ard Avedon and American Information Services; & 4, P. Smithson; 5, Moss Photo Service; 6, Stewart's

6

8

9

10

The breath of 'another architecture' in the founding firm of the tradition can still be experienced outside the University Club (corner of 54th and 5th Avenue) **8**, and can be seen in the plates of the Madison Square Presbyterian Church **7** in the monograph on their work.

These exteriors are detailed in a way outside of a foreigner's experience of the possible.

In no real Renaissance building was so much trouble taken. That sort of perfection only appeared in buildings as rare as the Parthenon or the Ise Shrine, and they were not so machine-absolute then, as they are, or appear to be, now.

No bollard for us so well made as at the Washington Arch **9**.

The square-section lengths of granite that lie so simple, so expensive, so eloquent, between the pavement and the building at the new Museum of Modern Art are impossible for us, for we are outside that special tradition of concentration on detail which Americans enjoy.

And the lavatories are what we envy most of all. Those luxe vitreous enamelled partitions, the thick-glazed pans, and the flush brush-finished stainless steel towel dispensers. All from catalogues. What a culture that can produce such pleasures for every man! And they really are potentially for most men, as Detroit has shown.

There seems to be a straight line from the frame house to the Pepsi building **10** which comes to Americans without special thought.

Those American architects who are thoughtful about the making of spaces, H. H. Richardson or Louis Kahn, make *our* sort of architecture—and Mies van der Rohe has never left Germany in his head. Mies of course, in his material aspect, has grown out of a parallel tradition to that of McKim, Mead, and White—even his earliest work is made with materials of the finest quality detailed with great care—the marble, travertine, plate glass, and chromed steel of the Barcelona Pavilion; the vast veneered-wood doors and careful brickwork of the Krefeld Houses.

But even with the example of Mies, Skidmore, Owings, and Merrill could not have bridged the gap from McKim, Mead, and White to their present cargo-cult style without Richard Neutra, for Neutra was the first to make the precise glamorous. His houses, as photographed, are so polished, so perfect, as to seem impossible to achieve. As if their builders all wore white gloves and Tabi in the Japanese manner and their owners never had an unguarded moment. They have a kind of de-materialized glamour, almost that of soap-advertisements, that is specially, even uniquely, American.

This American cargo-cult architecture of technology is un-exportable. It is a much lesser thing that is exportable.

What SOM did with the Lever House was of the utmost banality. Without good proportions, meaningless in the town-pattern (routine Emery Roth perversely enough makes more sense), its language illiterate. But it is precisely for these reasons it has become a universal model.

It is not frightening, makes no demands. It hasn't 'made Mies acceptable'—for Mies still has secrets and these frighten. Lever House has no secrets, there is nothing in it which can't be copied by an average team of average architects with a fair amount of money and a fairly developed industry.

A 'Lever House' can give the illusion to a foreign city of having a genuine technological culture. The glamour without the century of one half's effort needed to produce one.*

Soon those same foreign cities that have 'Lever Houses' will have copies of the black anodized aluminium/grey glass people's '900' office towers of New York two years ago, and later be freckled with brown anodized aluminium (or cor-ten)/brown glass poor man's Seagrams that are currently going up there. (We in England have a rash of black ones this year, and brown ones due to arrive in '68–'69.)

For these too are glamorous—desirable often in defiance of climate and situation. Their presence in our cities is intended to be read as a gauge of our nearness to the fountain of technological culture—they are aspects of the cultural reversal.†

But we will build no copies of the Chase Manhattan Bank. It will never be a model, for it is built with unimaginable wealth and resources. Like the Pyramids. And almost equally remote, for it too has its secret. The secret of being quite sure what to do. A secret that has been held in turn by Egypt, by Greece, by Rome, by Spain, by France, by England. By the Dutch, by the Rajputs, and so on—this is the history of the world.

It would seem that it is the identifying characteristic of a technological culture that its key objects—those things in which the discipline of their evolution is most clear and most assured—should appear as a by-product of concentration, not on old-world notions like 'the discipline', but on perfection of process and of detail. This would certainly seem to be so in that the strongest hints of the emergence of 'another architecture' are in multi-storey buildings with a great deal of repetition, where what Americans know most about in their bones—mass-production, process control, etc.—becomes 'the control', rather than any notions of composition, or art.‡

We have had much slighter hints in Europe with the early Hertfordshire schools and from the *école Prouvé*—but their acheivements are so incomplete as to be far from assuring us that we have indeed a technological culture.

American architects almost have it made: if they could only stop worrying about architecture.

*The acceptance of the 'automatic mill' came in the 1790s. See Roger Burlingame's *Machines that built America*. Signet Key Books, 1955.

†Whereas in 1891 McKim, Mead, and White built a cricket club in Germantown, Philadelphia, Pa., and called their elevators 'lifts' on plan (see Houses for Jas J. Goodwin, New York City 1898), we now build 'A.B.C. Bowlings', and are beginning to call our lifts 'elevators'.

‡H. Russell-Hitchcock's introduction to the SOM book seems for him to be quite extraordinarily lacking in insight and objectivity. Its comparison of the achievement of the 'integration of the arts' between SOM on the one hand and Mies van der Rohe and Le Corbusier on the other, is either an impertinence, or else a kind of comic misunderstanding of what art is all about.

7
Madison Square Presbyterian Church—1906
8
University Club, New York—1900
9
Washington Arch, New York—1892
10
Pepsi- Cola Company, 1958–59

TAC

1945–1995

The Architects Collaborative

Headquarters
Cambridge, MA

Other Locations
Rome, Italy; Kuwait City, Kuwait

Founding Partners
John Harkness, Sarah Pillsbury Harkness,
1945 Jean Bodman Fletcher, Norman Fletcher,
Walter Gropius, Robert McMillan,
Louis McMillen, Benjamin Thompson

1995

Ezra Stoller, Esto

Emblematic of the belief in team-based practice as a social ethos after World War II, The Architects Collaborative (TAC) was established in 1945 by seven young architects along with Walter Gropius, the German émigré who led the Bauhaus and, later, the Harvard Graduate School of Design. By the 1970s TAC, founded as an experiment in collective production, had become the largest architectural practice in the United States.

The architects who came together to form TAC with Gropius were linked by a network of overlapping personal and professional connections, formed in a climate of social and architectural optimism at the start of the postwar building boom. Norman Fletcher, Louis McMillen, Robert McMillan, and Benjamin Thompson had been classmates at Yale; John Harkness had worked with Fletcher during the war (both were conscientious objectors) at Skidmore, Owings & Merrill in New York, and with Jean Bodman at Saarinen Swanson Saarinen in Michigan. Sarah Pillsbury and Bodman had both studied at the Cambridge School of Architecture and Landscape Architecture, the first degree-granting graduate school in the United States designed specifically for women. Harkness and Pillsbury had married in 1941, Bodman and Fletcher in 1945.

The firm represented a model of practice distinct from the hierarchy and specialization common to other prominent team-based firms of the postwar decades. Key to the TAC approach was the idea that teams should consist of generalists able to criticize each other as equals, rather than parceling tasks among specialized practitioners according to the managerial principles of efficiency and division of labor. This structure was formalized through a weekly meeting in which the partners, including Gropius, critiqued one another's projects. The firm's work initially paralleled the growth of the baby boom generation in the United States, moving from suburban houses and elementary and secondary schools to universities, hospitals, office buildings, and other institutional and cultural commissions. The eventual consolidation of TAC's offices, which had originally occupied a series of small houses in Cambridge, Massachusetts, into a purpose-built headquarters at 46 Brattle Street in 1966 spurred the development of what came to be known as the "Architects' Corner," so called for the number of fellow architects who built their own buildings on neighboring sites. The firm's headquarters formed the nucleus of a vibrant professional culture of designers gathered around Harvard Square, numbering into the hundreds — many of them working in offices indebted to the collective atmosphere first established by TAC.

TAC's commission for the University of Baghdad in 1957 was among the first examples of what would become a growing involvement in the Middle East by large US firms. It was largely through this work over the next 25 years, first in Iraq and then in Saudi Arabia, Jordan, Kuwait, and the United Arab Emirates, that TAC grew to a peak of some 380 employees by 1980. The sudden collapse of the Souk Al-Manakh stock bubble in the fall of 1982, the economic fallout of the Iran-Iraq War, and the end of the boom in crude oil prices were among the factors that precipitated the slow demise of TAC after 1983, culminating in the firm's bankruptcy in 1995. TAC is survived by firms founded by former principals who were influenced by the collaborative and multidisciplinary ethos of TAC's early years, notably Cambridge Seven Associates, founded in 1962, and Benjamin Thompson and Associates, founded in 1966. — MK

Ezra Stoller, Esto

Ezra Stoller, Esto

NELSON H2L2

1945–

Nelson H2L2

Headquarters
Philadelphia, PA

Other Locations
See data sheet

Successor Firm To
Paul Philippe Cret (1907–1945)

Founding Partners
John Harbeson, William J. H. Hough, William Livingston, Roy Larson

Current Partners
John "Ozzie" Nelson Jr., Tony Manuelli, Jill Hackenmueller, Douglas Steele, Barry Eiswerth, Stacy Chambers, Brad Black, George Athens, Lisa Brinkman, Lynn Osborne, Gary Miciunas, Angel DeElse, Mitchell Cohen, Ann Marie Clay, Claudia Reichert, John Brinjac

1945

John Harberson Collection, Athenaeum of Philadelphia

CANNONDESIGN

1945–

Cannon Design

Headquarters
Buffalo, NY

Other Locations
St. Louis, MO; Washington, D.C.; Springfield, MA; Boston, MA; New York, NY; Toronto, Canada; Houston, TX; Baltimore, MD; Chicago, IL; Vancouver, Canada; Shanghai, China; Mumbai, India

1945

Founding Principal
Will Cannon Sr. (founding principal), Will Cannon Jr., Don Cannon

Current Principals
Paul O. Cannon, Robin V. Cibrano, Stephen Johnson, Bradley Lukanic, Gary R. Miller, Meg Osman, Deborah Sheehan, Michael J. Smith, James M. (Sandy) Stevenson, Kevin L. Sticht, W. Kenneth Wiseman

Cannon Design

Operating fifteen offices worldwide, Cannon Design has emerged as a large firm whose core work hinges on its expertise in healthcare design. Joining the architecture practice begun by their father, Will Cannon, in Niagara Falls, New York in 1916, brothers Will Jr. and Don Cannon established Cannon Corporation in 1945, following the end of World War II. The firm grew steadily through 1975, when it operated three offices in Buffalo, St. Louis, and Washington, D.C. Over the next two decades the firm grew exponentially through the strategic acquisition of numerous smaller offices, which added to Cannon's expertise in areas including sustainability and urban planning, and extended its reach internationally. In 2000, the firm was renamed Cannon Design.

In the 1990s and 2000s, under a second generation of principals, with Gary R. Miller as CEO and Mark R. Mendell as president, Cannon began to look abroad, opening offices in Shanghai and Mumbai. The acquisition of the New Delhi office of Peter Ellis New Cities in 2011 resulted in expanded international urban planning and architecture practice, beginning with Cannon's design for Sports City in India, a comprehensive plan for one million residents designed for local developer Jaypee Group.

Despite its strategic forays into urban planning, science and technology, and educational buildings, the majority of Cannon's research and design has centered on healthcare. The firm has both produced and reflected shifts in the design of hospitals, outpatient facilities, and specialized care projects, including the University of Kansas Hospital Authority (2011) and the Seidman Cancer Center (2011) in Cleveland, Ohio. Today, Cannon's specialized model involves the publication of texts, interviews, and research on trends and developments in healthcare design. The firm's publications include studies of the role of architecture in reducing health-care associated infections (HAIs) and research in "clean design" and how architects can respond to and incorporate clients' expectations through "evidence-based design."

Cannon Design currently operates with a "one firm, multi-office" organization, with a staff of over 1000 employees. Unlike other large corporate offices whose subsidiaries operate under a single masthead, Cannon Design includes practices like Yazdani Studio that operate autonomously to some degree, publishing and marketing under their own names. — AL

WATG

1945–

Wimberly Allison Tong & Goo

Headquarters
Honolulu, HI

Other Locations
Irvine, CA; Los Angeles, CA; New York, NY; Istanbul, Turkey; London, UK; Singapore, Singapore

1945 Founding and Key Partners
George J. Wimberly, Howard L. Cook (founding principals), George Whisenand, Jerry Allison, Greg Tong, Don Goo

Current Partners
Bill Reed, Brad McNamee, Bryan Algeo, Chris Panfil, Chris Singer, Craig Takahata, David Moore, Deborah Rosenblum, Greg VillegasJeremy Heyes, John Goldwyn, Juan de Anda, Kevin Scholl, Lance Walker, Margaret McMahon, Mark Yoshizaki, Mike Chun, Mike Seyle, Monica Cuervo, Muriel Muirden, Nic Jacobs, Nick Carrier, Nicole Hammond, Perry Brown, Peter Priebe, Rachel Johnson, Raj Chandnani, Richard Myers, Rob Day, Robert Payan, Robert Zheng, Roger Gaspar, Ron Van Pelt, Sean Sih-Young Jeon, Sharmila Tanka, Stacy Larsen, Stephen Albert, Tom Fo, Tom Williams

WATG—or Wimberly, Allison, Tong & Goo—has its roots in the chance migration of twenty-four-year-old architect Pete Wimberly to Hawaii in 1940. Raised in Washington and educated at the University of Washington, Wimberly moved to Honolulu to work as a civilian contractor at the Pearl Harbor naval base in 1940. At the end of World War II, and almost fifteen years before the Islands (then a U.S. Territory) would gain statehood, Wimberly joined Howard Cook to form Wimberly and Cook in Honolulu.

The firm immediately engaged in the renovation of one of Hawaii's most historic luxury hotels: the Royal Hawaiian Hotel in Waikiki. Through the 1950s, the firm's work expanded to the continental United States and to Bora Bora and Tahiti, where it produced regionally inflected designs for hotels in the 1960s.

By the seventies, the firm had added new partners and expanded to Asia with its designs for one of the three wings of the luxurious Shangri-La Hotel in Singapore in 1971. Their design for a resort in Malaysia, the Tanjong Jara (1979), was awarded an Aga Khan Award for Architecture in 1983. Citing "such traditional Malay techniques as raising buildings on stilts for flood protection," the Aga Khan commended the project for a genuine sensitivity toward the Islamic architecture of Malaysia. In the 1980s, with the move of its headquarters to California and the assembling of the four partners who would give the firm its contemporary namesake, the firm poised itself to take on larger and larger projects.

The largest projects the firm has completed to date—including the $3 billion Emirates Hotel in Abu Dhabi and projects in South Africa and the Bahamas for hotel magnate Sol Kerzner—strike a markedly different tone from Tanjong Jara. The Atlantis Hotel, on Paradise Island in the Bahamas, draws little from any Bahamian architectural dialect; the massive complex, as described by the firm, was inspired by the "Atlantian [sic] civilization," and boasts one of the world's most expensive hotel suites, at $25,000 a night. Though designed in 1992, near the end of white rule in South Africa, the firm's design of an "ancient royal residence" known as the Palace of the Lost City was constructed as part of a casino development best known as a target of the international anti-Apartheid movement. The Emirates Hotel reportedly has a full-time staff of ten to keep its 1,000 chandeliers clean.

From the Tanjong Jara to the Emirates Hotel, the scale and style of WATG's work has changed over the years, but the firm has remained consistent in many ways too. It has been designing hotels for almost seventy years as an inherently international practice since its postwar beginnings in a US Territory. — MW

1946–1994

CRSS Inc.

Headquarters
Houston, TX

Other Locations
College Station, TX

Succeeded By
HOK

1946 Founding and Key Partners
William Wayne Caudill, John Rowlett, Wallie Scott (founding principals), William Peña, Thomas A. Bullock, Jonathan King

1994

Progressive Architecture, December 1970

After returning from overseas duty during World War II, William Wayne Caudill, a young professor at Texas A&M, and John M. Rowlett, a professor at the University of Texas, established Caudill & Rowlett above a grocery store in Austin, Texas, in 1946. The pair was soon joined by Wallie E. Scott, Jr. and unnamed fourth partner, William Peña, becoming Caudilll, Rowlett, Scott (CRS) in 1948. The office grew primarily through the design of a large number of elementary and secondary schools throughout Oklahoma and Texas during the postwar baby boom of the 1940s and 1950s, characterized by a shared need for openness and flexibility. The partners' expertise in school design had begun with Caudill's thesis project in 1939 as a masters student at the Massachusetts Institute of Technology, in which he proposed a comprehensive school building program for Stillwater, Oklahoma, where he had attended Oklahoma State University as an undergraduate. This expertise was later promoted in publications by Caudill, including *Space for Teaching* (1941) and *Toward Better School Design* (1954).[1]

Through the firm's early school commissions, CRS pioneered methods of pre-design analysis for developing building programs together with clients, later known as the architectural sub-discipline of programming—a process the firm referred to as "problem-seeking"—as well as methods of "fast-track" management for the rapid planning and construction of projects.[2] Major commissions for schools, universities, hospitals, and institutional buildings followed throughout the United States after the 1960s.

In 1964, CRS was asked to assist with site selection for a university of petroleum and minerals in Dhahran, Saudi Arabia, the beginning of three decades of a deep involvement with large-scale construction in the Middle East that would ultimately transform the company. Eventually producing a complete campus plan for the King Fahd University of Petroleum and Minerals (1964–1982), the buildings designed by CRS for the University were built of poured-in-place sandblasted concrete, a composite of local materials and foreign expertise that partner Charles E. Lawrence described as "a Saudi product," despite its reliance on Western protocols of sourcing and assembly. The firm's subsequent commissions for governmental, industrial, and military clients in Saudi Arabia included workers' housing for the Arabian-American Oil Company (1975–1980) in Dhahran, King Abdul Aziz Military City (1976) for the US Army Corp of Engineers, housing for the Ministry of Foreign Affairs (1978) in Riyadh, and office buildings for National Methanol and Saudi Petrochemical Company (1981) in Jubail.

The firm began a program of domestic expansion in 1970, incorporating in Delaware and renaming itself CRS Design Associates (CRSDA) in the same year. In 1971, the firm became the first publicly traded architectural corporation with an initial public offering of stock, subjecting itself to shareholders and paving the way for a series of acquisitions that transformed the company (renamed CRS Group) into a vast global engineering and construction conglomerate over the next decade. In 1983 the firm merged with J. E. Sirrine, a major designer of power plants and a provider of engineering services to pulp and paper, tobacco, and chemical businesses in the southeastern United States, to become CRS Sirrine.

By 1985, CRS Sirrine had grown to become the largest architectural design firm, construction-management company, and interior architecture design firm in the US, with over $20 billion in construction in the Middle East by 1992. Renamed CRSS Inc. in 1989, over the previous decade the firm had expanded its construction business into China, Hong Kong, and South Korea, becoming a major global designer of energy infrastructure, before gradually divesting itself of its less profitable divisions in architecture and design. In 1994 the firm became an independent power-plant business, selling its architecture group (with 220 employees) to Hellmuth, Obata + Kassabaum (HOK) and its engineering and construction management units to Jacobs Engineering. — MK

① William Wayne Caudill, *Space for Teaching* (College Station: Texas A&M Engineering Experiment Station Series, 1941); Caudill, *Toward Better School Design* (New York: F. W. Dodge Corporation, 1954).

② See William Peña, William Wayne Caudill, John Focke, *Problem Seeking: An Architectural Programming Primer* (Boston: Cahners Books International, 1977).

1946–2000

Daniel, Mann, Johnson & Mendenhall

Headquarters
Los Angeles, CA

Other Locations
London, England; Bangkok, Thailand; Honolulu, HI; Saigon, Vietnam; Paris, France; Guam; Jakarta, Indonesia; Caracas, Venezuela; Anchorage, AK

Succeeded By
AECOM

Founding and Key Partners
Philip James Daniel, Arthur Edwin Mann, Kenneth S. Johnson, Irvan F. Mendenhall (founding principals), Cesar Pelli, Anthony J. Lumsden

© J. Paul Getty Trust. Used with permission. Julius Shulman Photography Archive, Research Library at the Getty Research Institute (2004.R.10)

Phillip J. Daniel, Arthur E. Mann, Kenneth S. Johnson, and structural engineer Irvan F. Mendenhall began DMJM, the office that bore their initials, in 1946. From the outset the firm sought to work on large, complex projects at an international scale, offering a full scope of services in architecture, engineering, planning, and consultation. This scale of practice was enabled by a managerial structure of coordinated yet autonomous departments with a partner at the head of each section, a structure that allowed all engineering and technical work to be done in-house.

In its first fifteen years of practice, DMJM received over 600 commissions, beginning with a wave of public school buildings in the years after World War II. The work grew to encompass offices, institutional buildings, city planning, and, later, large-scale waterworks, well drilling, and other urban and environmental infrastructure. DMJM grew large in part through its expertise in military architecture, designing military housing, airbases, harbors, and communication centers in Guam, England, and Thailand. Its domestic military work in this period included missile installations for the Titan I and II missile silos at the Delta Nine complex near Wall, South Dakota, designed in a joint venture of architecture and engineering firms including Leo A Daly. Future commissions included a focus on highly specialized technical domains such as industrial engineering, statistics, and electronics.

Within its building unit, DMJM gained a reputation in architectural circles through the work of designers Cesar Pelli and Anthony J. Lumsden, both of whom left the emerging office of Kevin Roche John Dinkeloo (then completing Eero Saarinen's posthumous projects) to head the firm's design division. Pelli was hired as the first director of design at DMJM in 1964, with Lumsden soon to follow as principal for design. This duo led the group that became known as the "LA Silvers," in reference to its use of slick, hermetic mirror-glass curtain wall systems distinguished by their equivalent treatment of thin horizontal and vertical mullions to produce a homogeneous or "two-way" grid effect. Such systems developed from the expertise gained in Saarinen's office, where Lumsden had been the project designer for Bell Labs in Holmdel, New Jersey, the first mirror-glass curtain wall ever built. The epitome of this aesthetic was the monolithic Pacific Design Center (1975) in Los Angeles, designed by Pelli as design director at Victor Gruen Associates following his years at DMJM, and known as the "Blue Whale" for its large size and shimmering blue cladding.

The acquisition of DMJM in 1984 by Ashland Oil was the first in a series of steps that eventually led to the formation of AECOM, today the largest architectural conglomerate in the world. When Ashland decided to refocus on its core petroleum refining business in 1990, Richard G. Newman, the president of DMJM before its acquisition, initiated a management-led employee buyback program to acquire the remnants of Ashland Technology Corporation, the subsidiary of which he had become president after the merger. The new entity took the name AECOM Technology Corp.—the acronym standing for architecture, engineering, construction, operation, and maintenance, the services offered by the firm—and reestablished itself in Los Angeles, where DMJM had been located. The company then began the wave of acquisitions that would lead to its current status as the largest architecture and engineering firm in existence, with over 45,000 employees around the world, some 1,300 of them architects. Though the firm reorganized its divisions in 2000 and consolidated the use of the AECOM name, DMJM continued to exist as a brand name appended to the work of specific branches within the company. — AWS & MK

1946–2001

Joseph Allen Stein and Associates

Headquarters
New Delhi, India

Other Locations
San Francisco, CA (1946); Kolkata, India (1952); New Delhi, India (1955); Ahmedabad, India (1977)

Founding and Key Partners
1946 Joseph Allen Stein, James Funk (founding principals), Benjamin Polk, Binoy K. Chatterjee, Balkrishna V. Doshi, Jai Rattan Bhalla

2001

Stein, Doshi & Bhalla studio. *Architecture + Urbanism*, July 1997

After studying at the University of Illinois and then under the guidance of Eliel Saarinen at the Cranbrook Academy in Bloomfield Hills, Michigan, Joseph Allen Stein took his first job in the office of Richard Neutra in Los Angeles in 1938. He soon moved to San Francisco to open his own practice. There he was among the young architects identified by historian Lewis Mumford as developing a "Bay Region Style" rooted in the local vernacular, as an important counter to the notion of a homogeneous International Style then occupying the mainstream architectural press in the United States. Within this group, Stein was particularly concerned with producing quality low-cost housing. His wife Margaret became his most important critic and design partner, despite having no formal training in architecture. Stein's major project from this period was the Ladera cooperative housing community near Palo Aalto, designed in collaboration with landscape architect Garret Eckbo.

After participating in the war effort during World War II, Stein joined forces with John Cooper Funk, forming Funk and Stein Architects in 1947. The firm operated as a partnership until 1955, despite the fact that Stein and his family moved to Europe, and subsequently to India, in 1952. Disillusioned by the McCarthy era of Cold War politics in the United States, the Steins relocated to newly independent India where, in Stein's words, "the spirit of Gandhi and Tagore was fresh and bright."[1] Stein fell in love with India and spent the next five decades in Kolkata and New Delhi, adjusting his regional California modernism to engage the political and environmental context of India. His genuine engagement with living and working in the country set him apart from other foreign contributors to India's postwar architecture.

In the role of advisor to the government of West Bengal, Neutra proposed Stein as the head of the new architecture and planning department at the Bengal Engineering College in Kolkata. And Stein began working soon after he arrived in India with Benjamin Polk, a compatriot, on a township in West Bengal. After moving to New Delhi in 1955 he began to receive bigger commissions for cultural and institutional buildings in and around the city. These included the Triveni Kala Sangam arts complex, which he worked on for two decades; the India International Center, completed in 1962 and surrounded by landmark buildings also designed by Stein; and headquarters for international institutions including the Ford Foundation, the United Nations, and the World Wide Fund. Joseph Allen Stein and Associates designed key buildings outside of New Delhi as well, from the American International School (1960–1970) in the hills of Chanakyapuri to factories for Escort, in which Stein adapted local technologies to create a complex roofscape. In 1972 Stein completed the tallest building in East Asia at the time and his only skyscraper, the India Express Tower, in Mumbai's Nariman Port.

In 1977, Stein joined forces with the famous Indian architect Balkrishna Doshi, moving his office to a studio designed by Doshi in Ahmedabad and forming a collaborative practice, Stein, Doshi & Bhalla. Stein's contributions to buildings credited to the firm, like the Gandhi Institute of Labor Studies (1984) on the outskirts of Ahmedabad, seems to have been undermined by the sheer force of Doshi's prominence in the architectural press. Stein remained an active partner in the firm until his retirement in 1995. — AM

① Quoted in A.P. Kanvinde, "Joseph Stein in India," *Journal of Landscape Architecture* (Winter 2001-2002): 11–12.

AN ARCADIS COMPANY

1946–

RTKL

1946

Headquarters
Baltimore, MD

Other Locations
Chicago, IL; Dallas, TX; Los Angeles, CA; Miami, FL; Washington,D.C.; London, UK; Abu Dhabi, UAE; Dubai, UAE; Jeddah, KSA; Beijing, China; Shanghai, China; São Paolo, Brazil

Founding and Key Partners
Archibald Rogers, Francis Taliaferro (founding principals), Charles Lamb, George Kostritsky

Current Senior and Executive Vice Presidents
Todd C. Lundgren, Randall S. Pace, Bradley T. Barker, Lance K. Josal, Norman M. Garden, Timothy R. Twomey, Richard H. Yuan, Wayne W. Barger, Debra D. Cameron, John L. Castorina, Donald R. DeBord Jr., Jeffrey Gunning, Ardeshir Aliandust, Katherine J. Sprague, Daun P. St Amand, Gregory Yager, Jeffrey L. Davenport, Kim S. Heartwell, D R. Henderer, Lance Hosey, Raymond E. Peloquin, Karl W. Stumpf, Sandra V. Whipp

RTKL

With thirteen offices from Baltimore to Beijing, close to one thousand employees, and international revenues in the hundreds of millions of dollars, RTKL is one of the largest and most successful American architecture firms to have ever existed. In the words of a former chief executive, the ultimate intention of the firm has long been to establish themselves as no less than "the premiere design firm in the world."

Archibald Rogers founded the firm in Annapolis, Maryland, in 1946 after practicing as a naval architect during World War II. Within a year, he partnered with Frank Taliaferro, a Marine Corps veteran who had returned from combat in the Pacific to complete his studies in architecture on the GI Bill. The addition of a third partner, former merchant marine sailor Charles Lamb, led to the firm's first commendation from the AIA in 1954—for a project commissioned by Lamb's mother. That same year, working for famed shopping center developer James Rouse, Rogers, Taliaferro, and Lamb designed the first enclosed shopping mall on the East Coast: the Harundale Mall outside of Baltimore (1958).

By the beginning of the 1960s, the firm became embedded in the process of urban renewal in downtown Baltimore; Rogers became acting director of the private business group—led by Rouse—responsible for the dramatic clearance and redevelopment of the city's business core. As the design and construction of the redubbed Charles Center progressed through the 1960s, the firm became RTKL with the addition of George Kostritsky, who had served as lead planner on the project. The landmark public-private development displaced nearly nine thousand jobs in order to build a superblock of office towers and plazas atop a parking structure that represented 47 percent of the assessed value of the development, but the complex, anchored by Mies van der Rohe's One Charles Center marked a symbolic victory for progress in the historic city.

Charles Center was an archetypal example of the concerted responses to the urban crisis in the dated cores of American cities at the time, and its prominence established RTKL as a national authority on large-scale urban projects. Poised to grow, with commissions to redesign the urban cores of a number of midsize American cities, the firm took the then-unusual step of hiring a chief executive to manage the company in 1967. Harold Adams, then 28, would lead RTKL for three decades, as it came to encompass fields such as engineering and interior design, and grew from four dozen employees to nearly six hundred.

By the early1990s, RTKL had opened its first international offices, in London and Tokyo. Ina 1990 interview, Adams characterized international expansion as a way to insulate the firm from cyclical economic slumps at home—working abroad functioned to "design a firm that is as recession-proof as possible," in his words.[1] Through Japan's economic boom of that moment, RTKL earned massive commissions, and when Japanese markets collapsed by 1992, the firm was buffered by its ability to pivot back to work in the United States as well as in other international markets.

Today the firm is "consistently ranked among the world's largest architecture, engineering, and planning firms."[2] — MW

①
Harold Adams, quoted in Michelle Singletary, "Cushioning the Blow: Japanese projects help RTKL weather U.S. slump," *The Baltimore Sun* (October 15, 1990).

②
"RTKL Fact Sheet," http://www.rtkl.com/wp-content/uploads/2013/12/RTKL-Fact-Sheet.pdf (last accessed November 11, 2014).

1946–2007

Vincent G. Kling Associates

Headquarters
Philadelphia, PA

Succeeded By
KlingStubbins (2007)

Founding and Key Partners
Vincent G. Kling (founding principal),
Don Kriebel, Ralph B. Melick,
1946 Fred Lindquist

2007

Contract Interiors, February 1972. Photographer: Jules Schick

After a brief but meaningful tenure at the New York office of Skidmore, Owings & Merrill (SOM), Vincent G. Kling opened his own office in Philadelphia in 1946. Vincent G. Kling Associates got its start with a series of small medical and educational buildings in the late 1940s that garnered awards and propelled it toward increasingly larger commissions. Kling modeled the structure of his firm on SOM's, with studios each led by an architect responsible for supervising teams of designers and draftsmen. This highly efficient structure allowed the firm to expand rapidly, taking on a large and varied range of projects. The office continued to cultivate its expertise in medical and educational buildings throughout the 1950s, but it also received commissions for numerous headquarters for major industrial corporations, including the Radio Corporation of America (RCA) and Monsanto.

The development of Penn Center in Philadelphia, a key undertaking in the city's postwar revitalization efforts, was one of Vincent G. Kling Associates' largest projects from the 1950s onward. At the time of its construction, Penn Center was hailed as a modern centerpiece for the city and an emblem of urban renewal. In later years, urban planners would come to criticize it for its underground pedestrian access and lack of civic spaces. The development included office buildings by Kling Associates at Two Penn Center (1953), Seven Penn Center (The Transportation Building, 1957), Six Penn Center (The IBM Tower, 1965) and Five Penn Center (1970). The firm designed numerous other major landmarks for Philadelphia in these decades, including Lankenau Hospital 1953), the Municipal Services Building (1963), JFK Plaza, known as LOVE Park (1965), Dilworth Plaza (1972), and Centre Square Towers (1973).

Although Kling worked almost exclusively in the United States, in 1956 his firm was approached by the Foreign Buildings Operations (FBO) office of the US State Department to design an embassy in Quito, Ecuador, part of the FBO's efforts in this period to award foreign buildings to leading US architects. Widely praised upon its completion, the embassy in Quito (1956-1960) was featured in several FBO publications.

In the 1970s, Vincent G. Kling Associates continued to expand, the firm was restructured into corporate subdivisions to allow for the integration of engineering and landscape design among its services. In 1973, the office was renamed The Kling-Lindquist Partnership, as Fred Lindquist, the head of the engineering division, became a partner. By that time the firm had become the largest in Philadelphia, with almost 400 employees.[1] Kling retired in 1987, but the office retained his name. In 2007, after four years of working on projects in affiliation with the Boston firm of Hugh Stubbins and Associates, the two offices merged to create KlingStubbins. As a result of the merger, KlingStubbins became one of the ten largest firms in the country, with over 500 employees in six offices. In 2011, the firm was acquired by Jacobs Engineering. — JJ

(1)
Emily Cooperman, "Kling, Vincent George (1916-2013)," American Architects and Buildings database, http://www.philadelphiabuildings.org/pab/app/ar_display.cfm/18734 (last accessed November 22, 2014).

1947–

Bassetti Architects

Headquarters
Seattle, WA

Other Locations
Honolulu, HI, Portland, OR

Founding and Key Partners
Fredrick Bassetti (founding principal),
Jack Morse, John Tatum, Skip Norton,
1947 Richard Metler, Karlis Rekevics

Current Partner
Jack Morse, John Tatum, Skip Norton,
Richard Metler, Karlis Rekevics,
Lorne McConachie

Bassetti Architects

Frederick Forde Bassetti trained at the Harvard Graduate School of Design under Walter Gropius, graduating in 1946, working briefly in the Cambridge, Massachusetts office of Alvar Aalto before returning to his hometown of Seattle in the same year. Following a year of work at Naramore, Bain, Brady, and Johanson (NBBJ), Bassetti partnered with Jack Morse to establish Bassetti & Morse, Architects in 1947. The firm began by designing small residential work in the Pacific Northwest, but expanded quickly, opening a second office in Honolulu as Bassetti, Morse and Tatom, Architects by the end of that year. The firm's projects continued to be mainly residential, including several large apartment buildings, but its portfolio began to shift toward educational and cultural facilities by the end of the decade.

Bassetti, Morse and Tatom, Architects went on to gain notice during the 1950s as one of the leading members of the "Northwest School," advocates for the development of a new regional identity for the architecture of the Pacific Northwest. The office's key projects in this period included the Gamma Rho Apartments (1950–1951) and the University Professional Building (1954) in Seattle, and a series of schools for the Mercer Island School District including the Island Park Elementary School (1957). Bassetti split from Morse and Tatum in 1962 to begin a partnership with Skip Norton, Richard Metler, and Karlis Rekevics. Renamed Bassetti/Norton/Metler/Rekevics the firm continued to expand, becoming one of the largest offices in Seattle by the early 1970s. Later public and institutional commissions in Seattle included the Seattle Aquarium (1971) and the Henry M. Jackson Federal Building (1971–1974), designed together with John Graham & Associates.

In 1977, Bassetti/Norton/Metler/Rekevics was retained to design the US Embassy in Lisbon by the Foreign Buildings Operations (FBO) office of the US State Department. The embassy was the only international project that the office designed under Bassetti. Unlike many of the embassies from the heyday of the FBO building program from 1954 to 1964, the embassy in Lisbon (1977–1983) was part of a new generation of designs for FBO building that were largely dictated by security concerns. Although generally well received upon its completion, the Lisbon embassy and other FBO projects by contemporaries in the 1970s and 1980s marked a turning point in the design priorities of the State Department.

With the retirement of Bassetti, Norton, and Rekevics in 1994, the firm was rebranded Bassetti Associates. Meter retired from practice in 1997. The firm continues to operate in the Seattle region and has opened an additional office in Portland, Oregon. Over the last two decades the firm's work has focused primarily on educational facilities, including the completion of more than twenty-five schools. — JJ

1947–1981

Lathrop Douglass

Headquarters
Greenwich, CT

Other Locations
Paris, France

Founding Partner
Lathrop Douglass

1947

1981

PERHAPS THE BEST IS ACTUALLY THE CHEAPEST

By Lathrop Douglass, Architect

If this really is a new era for office buildings, with improved functional designs and better styling, let it also be a new era as regards costs. And not a penurious era.

In making this special plea for a new type of realism on costs, I am not going to dwell upon the high building costs that have been making headlines. Certainly costs are high, but the *level of costs* does not greatly affect the *comparative costs*. This message deals with relative costs of the buildings and the operations that go on inside them. I think I can show that in the past we have been building offices too cheaply.

It seems reasonable to say that "first costs" fall into three fairly obvious classifications:

1. The cost of space; that is, the structure itself.
2. The cost of "plush," or the advertising value of a handsome show — the marble, the 100-story tower.
3. The cost of such features as partitions, lighting, air conditioning, acoustical treatment, etc., which are all a means of improving the efficiency of the office employees.

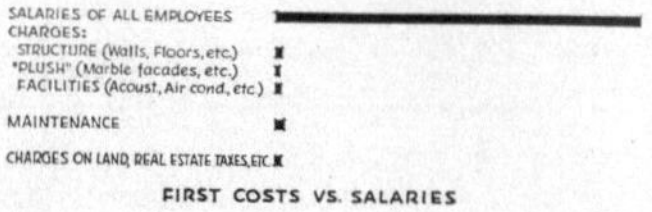

FIRST COSTS VS. SALARIES

To repeat once again, an office building is a means of providing, on a proper site, the most comfortable, efficient, flexible space for housing the activities of employees; whether for one firm or for many. The important and very interesting question is: to what extent do these features affect the employee? Does a man turn out more work in a cool, dehumidified building, a well-lighted building with a private, sound-proofed office for himself? How much more work does he turn out in these surroundings than in a humid, hot, ill-lighted bull pen amidst the clatter of typewriters and the time-wasting gabble of his fellow employees?

During the early part of the war I worked in a room with two other people, no acoustical material, hard floors and ceiling, poor lighting, drafty, no air treatment. When I wasn't wasting time talking to my office mates I was going crazy listening to the racket of their talking to each other. When people came in to see me I was apologetic. In the summer the office had to be closed every so often because the heat made work an impossibility. Yet this was structurally and in appearance one of the best office buildings in New York. I used to try to calculate the average amount of time I lost every day over a long period of time. From all causes combined, the best guess I could make, and of course it was only a guess, was about 20 per cent. I understand actual controlled experiments have been made on this subject. Anyway at that time I had a salary of around $8000 a year. Twenty per cent of $8000 is $1600 — a possible $1600 worth of lost time every year. The capitalized value of $1600 should be around $25,000. On the other

Architectural Record, October 1947

Shortly after his departure from the firm of John W. Harris and Associates, Lathrop Douglass established his own office, Lathrop Douglass, Architect, in Greenwich, Connecticut in 1947. The architect quickly made a name for himself as an advocate of the standardization and professionalization of office building design. In 1947, Douglass published a pair of articles in *Architectural Record*, "New Departures in Office Building Design" and "Perhaps the Best Is Actually the Cheapest," in which he investigated the relationship between the modular design of office interiors and worker productivity.[1] In these texts, Douglass explored the use of standardized office suites, designed to fit within specific structural and glazing systems.

The firm got its start with several office buildings for oil companies in South America, including a headquarters for the Creole Petroleum Corporation, a subsidiary of the Standard Oil Company of New Jersey, in Caracas, Venezuela (1949–1956), and Edificio Esso in Bogota, Columbia (1956). In keeping with Douglass's investigations of efficiency in office building design, the Creole Petroleum Building was designed based on "(1) climatic considerations, (2) a planned scheme of private offices and desk placing in large open areas, (3) space flexibility according to departmental integration,"[2] and included horizontal shading devices to provide sun protection and make heating and cooling systems unnecessary. In this way, the building served as a continuation of Douglass's studies of the optimization of fenestration in relationship to the interior office module. In all, Lathrop Douglass designed more than fifty office buildings over the course of his career.

Lathrop Douglass, Architect also become known for its design of shopping malls, including one of the first malls in the eastern United States, the Cross County Center in Yonkers, New York, which opened in 1954. The firm went on to design numerous shopping centers and large department stores in the United States and Europe in the 1960s and 1970s. One of the most elaborate malls undertaken by the firm, the Parly 2 Shopping Center on the outskirts of Paris, near Versailles, opened in 1968. The project was large enough that Lathrop Douglass had a second office in Paris in this period. Marking a significant departure from the austerity of the firm's earlier work, Parly 2 included multiple fountains, sculpted plaster ceilings, and marble floors.

Lathrop Douglass, Architect continued to produce work until Douglass's death in 1981. His son continued to operate an architectural office in Seattle with a nearly identical name, Lathrop Douglass Architects, although there is no direct lineage between the two firms. — JJ

① Lathrop Douglass, "New Departures in Office Building Design" and "Perhaps the Best Is Actually the Cheapest," *Architectural Record* (October 1947): 119–123.

② "Edificio Creole, Caracas, Venezuela," *Architectural Record* (June 1955): 151.

1947–1998

Harry Weese & Associates

Headquarters
Chicago, IL

Founding and Key Partners
Harry Weese (founding principal), Ben Weese, Jack Hartray, James Torvik, David Munson

1947

1998

Harry Weese at his desk, c.1963. Harry Weese Papers, Ryerson & Burnham Archives, The Art Institute of Chicago. Digital File #200604.100524-01

Harry Mohr Weese graduated in 1938 from the architecture department at the Massachusetts Institute of Technology (MIT), where he studied with Alvar Aalto and met Eero Saarinen, J. Irwin Miller, and others who would influence his later career. Saarinen convinced Weese to spend a year studying at the Cranbrook Academy of Art, where he worked with and befriended Ralph Rapson, Florence Knoll, Charles Eames and Ray Kaiser, and Benjamin Baldwin. Following a fellowship from the Bemis Foundation at MIT to study prefabricated housing, a period of work for Skidmore, Owings & Merrill, and service during World War II as an engineer for Navy destroyer ships, Weese established his practice, Harry Weese & Associates, in Chicago in 1947. J. Irwin Miller became Weese's first major patron through his family's business, the Cummins Engine Company, providing Weese's firm with numerous commissions in Columbus, Indiana, where the company was based. Harry Weese & Associates designed over a dozen buildings in Columbus through the Irwin family, including the Lillian C. Schmitt Elementary School (1957), the Irwin Union Bank and Trust (1961), First Baptist Church (1965), and the Cummins Inc. Technical Center (1968). In the 1950s, Eero Saarinen also passed along commissions to Weese's office, including Goodwin-Kirk Residence Hall at Drake University, a campus for which Saarinen, Swanson, and Saarinen had produced the master plan.

Harry Weese & Associates gained prominence in the late 1950s, and it was in 1956 that the firm was approached to design a US Embassy in Accra, Ghana. Completed in 1959, the design is among the best examples of regionally-influenced modernism by US architects at the height of the embassy building program under the Foreign Buildings Operations (FBO) office of the US State Department. The project was one of only two buildings abroad by the firm, along with the US Embassy Staff Housing block in Tokyo, Japan (1979–1982), also commissioned by the FBO.

By the end of the 1970s, Harry Weese & Associates had become one of the largest architecture firms in the US, producing over 1000 projects during Weese's forty-year career. Chief among these was the firm's design for the 100-mile long Metro system of Washington, D.C. (1967 to 1976), which architectural critic Herbert Muschamp ranked in Weese's obituary as being "among the greatest public works projects of this century."[1] The firm's work included major restoration projects for landmark buildings by some of Chicago's most famous architects of the late nineteenth and early twentieth centuries, including Adler & Sullivan's Auditorium Building (1886–1890) and D. H. Burnham & Company's Field Museum of Natural History (1909–1912). Weese was also a juror for competition to design the Vietnam War Memorial in 1981, and has been credited with helping to select, and vigorously defend, the controversial winning entry by Maya Lin.

Harry Weese & Associates slowly dissolved over a period of two decades beginning in the late 1970s, as Weese struggled with health problems and his main partners, including his brother Ben Weese, left the office. Harry Weese died in 1998, and the firm was sold and incorporated into the Chicago offices of Gensler in 2000. — JJ

① Herbert Muschamp, "Harry Weese, 83, Designer Of Metro System in Washington," *The New York Times* (November 3, 1998): B11.

1948–2012

John M. Johansen

Headquarters
New Canaan, CT

Other Locations
New York, NY, Wellfleet, MA

Founding Partner
John M. Johansen

1948

2012

GA House, 1978. Photographer T. Kitajimu

After earning degrees from Harvard College in 1939 and the Harvard Graduate School of Design in 1942, John M. Johansen worked for Marcel Breuer, for the National Housing Agency in Washington, D.C. during World War II, and for Skidmore, Owings & Merrill (SOM) before establishing his own office in 1948 in New Canaan, Connecticut, soon after accepting an appointment in the School of Architecture at Yale University. There he became known as a member of the "Harvard Five" group of architects who practiced in New Canaan from the 1940s onward, along with fellow alumni Philip Johnson, Landis Gores, Eliot Noyes, and Breuer, who had taught at Harvard while Johansen was a student.

Johansen began his career with the design of a series of modern houses in southern Connecticut, including his own, that were prominently featured in architectural journals, popular magazines, and museum exhibitions. Following a trip to study Renaissance villas in Italy in the mid-1950s, Johansen's work took what he termed a "neo-Palladian" turn.[1] His subsequent house designs in this period featured cross-shaped and symmetrical plans, grottoes, and other classical elements, yet adapted to fit within the tenets of modernism in which he had been taught.

It was in these years that Johansen was asked to design his first nonresidential commission and his only building outside of the United States, the US Embassy in Dublin, Ireland, in 1956. Criticized by some for its highly sculptural concrete façade, the embassy design was forced to undergo several revisions before final approval in 1962, ultimately taking nearly ten years between Johansen's first design and the construction of the building in 1964. Despite these controversies, the embassy was generally well received in Ireland and contributed to Johansen's reputation at home as one of the leading young modernist architects in the United States. The project marked a turning point in Johansen's work in terms of both scale and language, and his firm went on to produce major buildings in the US in an even more robust aesthetic in concrete, including the Morris A. Mechanic Theater (1967) in Baltimore, Maryland, the Goddard Library at Clark University (1969) in Worcester, Massachusetts, and the Mummers Theater (1970) in Oklahoma City, Oklahoma.

As the scale and complexity of his firm's projects grew, Johansen relocated his office from New Canaan to New York City in the early 1970s. By this time his office had developed a language of buildings in concrete featuring fragmented, additive volumes connected dynamically by passageways, as manifested in the Mummers Theater and in the L. Francis Smith Elementary School (1969) in Columbus, Indiana. With a reduction in the firm's work in the 1980s, Johansen relocated his office to Wellfleet, Massachusetts. A series of four office buildings for SCI (1981–1988) in Quincy, Massachusetts were the last built projects completed by the firm. Johansen continued to write and lecture until shortly before his death in 2012. — JJ

①
John M. Johansen, *A Life in the Continuum of Architecture* (Milan: L'Arca Edizioni, 1996): 21.

Marshalling Resources: The Regulation of the Pax Americana

In a 1941 editorial, Henry Luce, chief editor of *LIFE* and vocal internationalist, labeled the century as "American."[1] Three years later, as World War II began to near its end, the need for diplomatic and economic instruments to bolster postwar reconstruction were presented to the US public in terms similar to Luce's advocacy for involvement in the war itself, as moral and historical imperatives of the nation. In 1944, nearly a full year before the official end of the war, representatives of 44 nations convened to design these instruments at the United Nations Monetary and Financial Conference in Bretton Woods, New Hampshire. Organized by the US government on behalf of the United Nations, representatives worked in three technical commissions. The first, led by senior US Treasury official Harry D. White, formulated the articles of agreement for an International Monetary Fund, while the second, led by Lord John Maynard Keynes of Great Britain, did the same for an International Bank for Reconstruction and Development (later the World Bank). The third, chaired by Dr. Eduardo Suarez of Mexico, considered other means of international cooperation. The gathering was symptomatic of both the hope for a speedy end to the war and the desire for financial mechanisms to stabilize the world economy, seen as key to preventing future conflicts.[2] In the wake of the conference the US dollar and other national currencies were tethered to an international monetary system of short-term fixed and long-term adjustable exchange rates backed by the gold standard, while the institutions launched at Bretton Woods—the IMF and the World Bank—have shaped global development since.

As the US emerged out of World War II as what Harry Truman called "the giant of the economic world," various diplomatic and monetary devices were put in the service of its aggressive quest for "peace and prosperity."[3] Indeed, the distinguishing feature of US architectural, engineering, and construction activities abroad in the period defined by the Bretton Woods exchange was precisely the involvement of the US government. At a time

① Henry Luce, "The American Century," *LIFE* (February 17, 1941). Luce also owned *Architectural Forum*, which Jane Loeffler has described as an explicit site of Cold War rhetoric. See Loeffler, *The Architecture of Diplomacy: Building America's Embassies* (Princeton: Princeton Architectural Press, 1998).

② Robert Skidelsky, "Globalisation and the Bretton Woods Institutions in the Light of Changing Ideas about Markets," *World Economics*, Vol. 6, No. 1 (January–March 2005): 15–30.

③ Thomas G. Paterson, *Soviet-American Confrontation: Postwar Reconstruction and the Origins of the Cold War* (Baltimore, London: The Johns Hopkins University Press, 1973).

1925

1929 The US Market crashes starting a world-wide depression

1934 Export-Import Bank of Washington

1944 Bretton Woods Conference

1945 • World Bank and IMF established • Arab League begins

1947 • Truman Announces The Truman Doctrine • General Agreement on Tariffs and Trade • International Basic Economy Corporation (IBEC), founded by Nelson A. Rockefeller

1948 • Organization for European Economic Co-Operation and Development • First loan by the World Bank - to Chile

1939–1945 World War II

when "most international construction was American," conducted through the "private hands" of large US companies, government involvement could be understood as providing protective "public gloves."[4] This occurred most directly through the operations of enablers like the US Army Corps of Engineers, which intensified during the war and continued in numerous locations afterward in the form of defense production.

Two such key mechanisms for facilitating architectural and engineering construction abroad were the Marshall Plan, publicly announced at Harvard University in 1947 and intended to provide aid to war-ravaged European countries, and the Point Four Program, from 1949, which set the terms of "technical assistance" for much of the developing world.[5] While the Marshall Plan was so effectively organized that during its existence it managed to briefly overshadow the World Bank in its impact, the Point Four plan proved to be more problematic in terms of its clarity of objectives and the domestic support it garnered.[6] Still, Point Four financed the construction of villages, sewage systems, transportation infrastructure, dams, and power plants from Burma to Ethiopia. Giants of trade and travel such as Sears and Hilton International benefited tremendously from these plans, as did large construction and engineering companies like Bechtel whose participation was often stipulated by the terms of economic agreements. US planners like Albert Mayer in India and architecture firms like Welton Becket & Associates, William B. Tabler, and Skidmore, Owings & Merrill (SOM) benefited from the postwar regulation of development and the expansive pursuit of free trade, raw materials, and political influence abroad.[7]

In 1955, *Architectural Forum* celebrated the participation of US architects in the construction of the Pax Americana: "we are building up the basic welfare of other nations, creating climates unfavorable to communism, readying countries for industrialization and democratic independence, making them prosperous enough to buy more of our products."[8] Though the regulatory and financial tools of development multiplied throughout the Cold War and in its aftermath, the particular perspective on progress and prosperity supported by these tools was consistently wedded to the American way of life, recruiting an expanding number of US companies for its global implementation. — AM

④ Jeffrey Cody, *Exporting American Architecture, 1870–2000* (New York, London: Routledge, 2003): 123.

⑤ The full text of the Bretton Woods agreement is available online at http://fraser.stlouisfed.org/docs/publications/books/1948_state_bwood_v1.pdf (last accessed October 26, 2014).

⑥ Reproductions of the Marshall Plan text are available via the National Archives and Records Administration website at http://www.archives.gov/exhibits/featured_documents/marshall_plan/ (last accessed October 26, 2014).

⑦ See Cody, *Exporting American Architecture.*

⑧ "US Building Abroad," *Architectural Forum* (January 1955): 99.

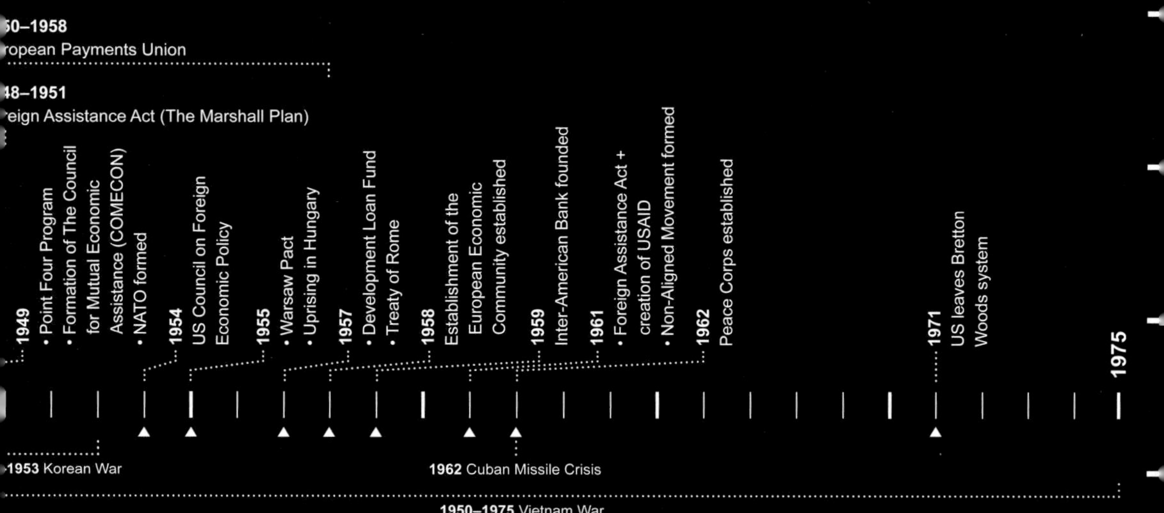

US Commitments Around the World

Redrawn from "Nation's Commitments All Around The Earth," *Life*, December 23, 1957

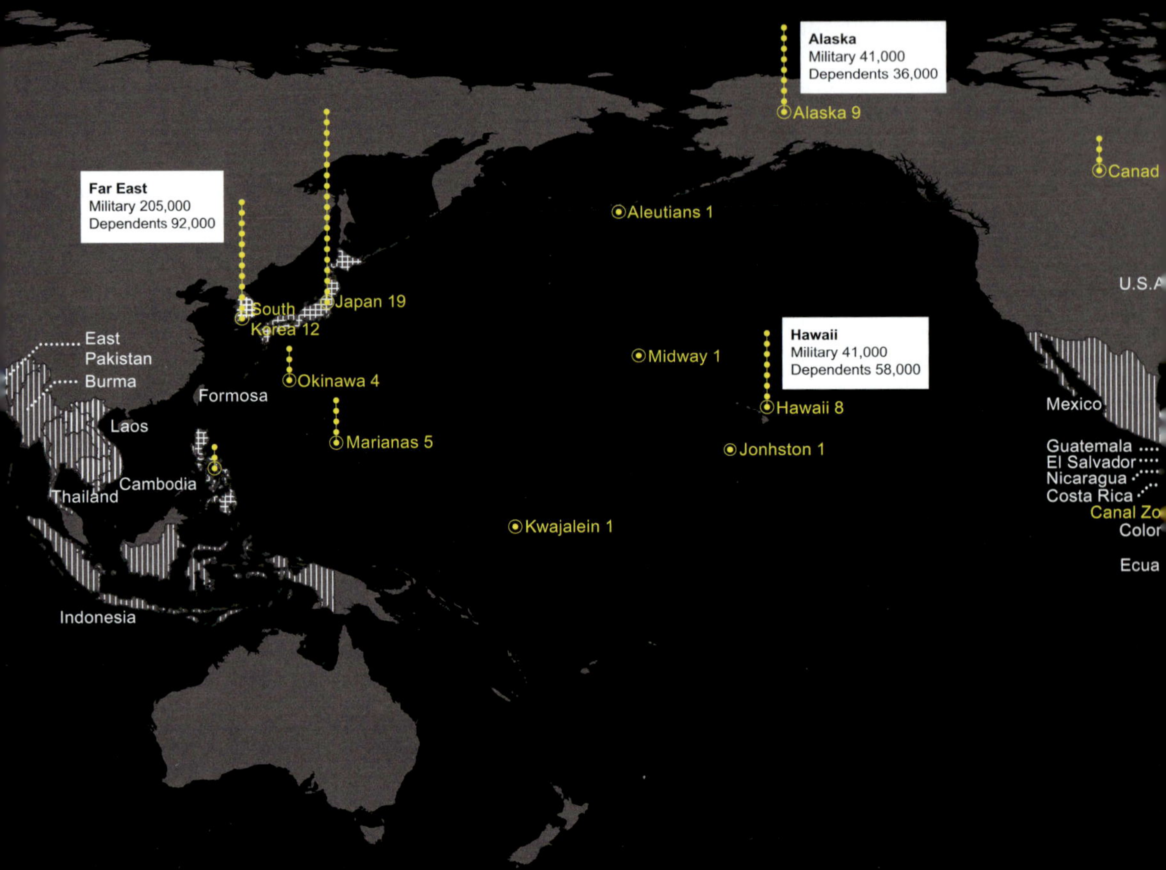

Legend

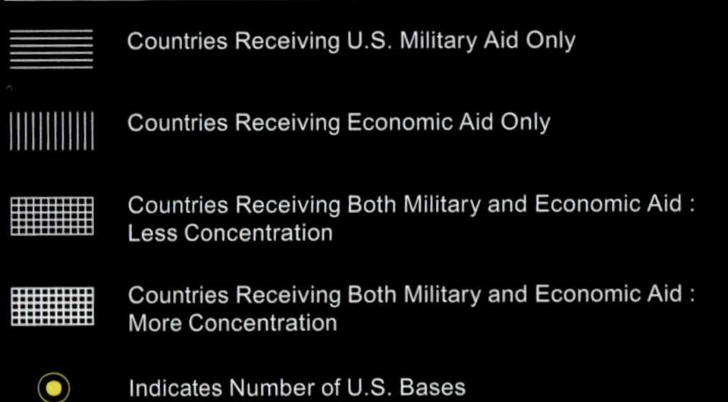

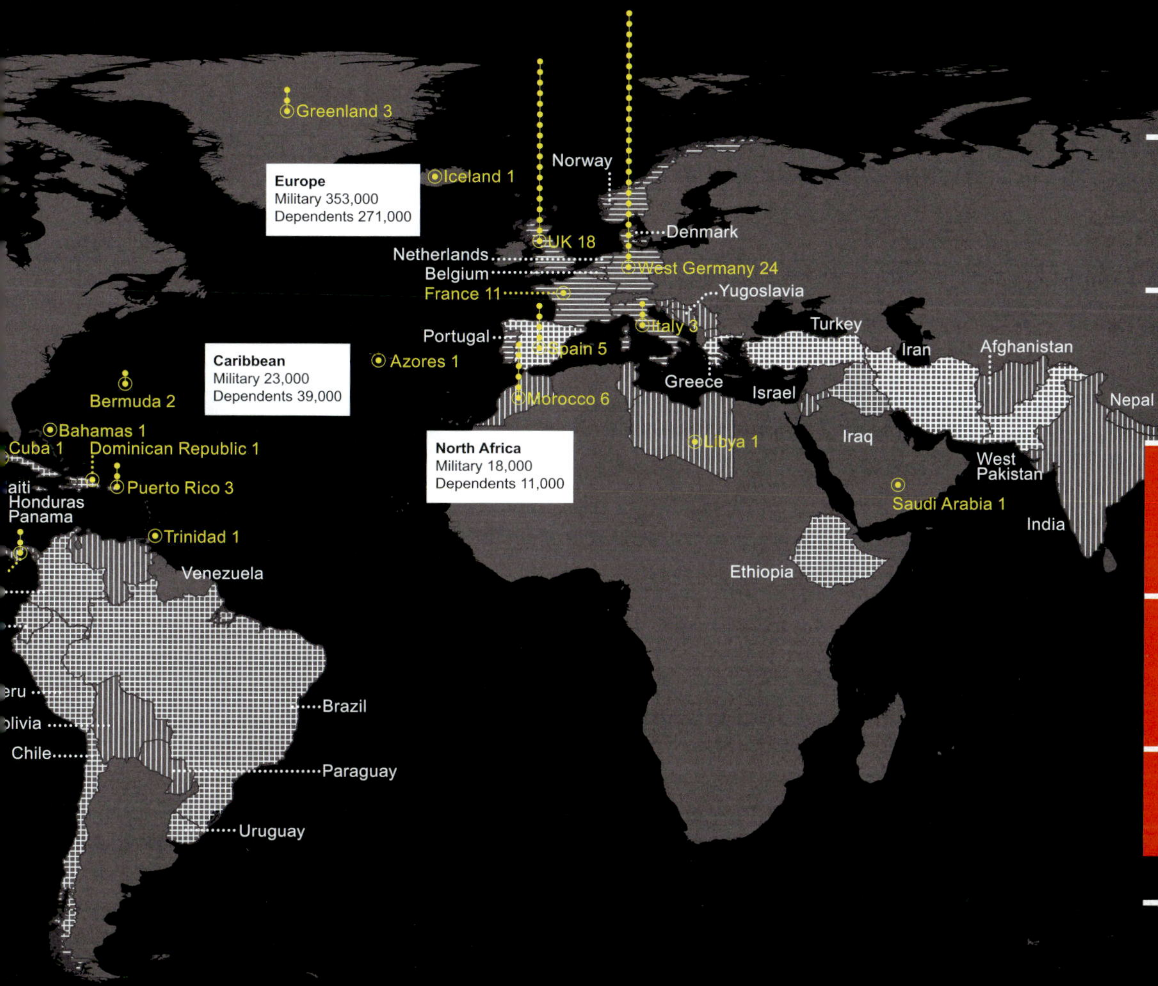

Greenland 3
Europe
Military 353,000
Dependents 271,000
Iceland 1
Norway
Denmark
UK 18
Netherlands
Belgium
West Germany 24
France 11
Yugoslavia
Italy 3
Turkey
Portugal
Spain 5
Iran
Afghanistan
Caribbean
Military 23,000
Dependents 39,000
Azores 1
Bermuda 2
Greece
Israel
Nepal
Morocco 6
Bahamas 1
Cuba 1
Dominican Republic 1
North Africa
Military 18,000
Dependents 11,000
Libya 1
Iraq
West
Pakistan
Puerto Rico 3
Honduras
Panama
Saudi Arabia 1
India
Trinidad 1
Ethiopia
Venezuela
Brazil
Chile
Paraguay
Uruguay

US BUILDING ABROAD

Studio R. R. Prabhu

In doing its share of a $100 billion postwar job,

the building industry has become a world-wide ambassador

The year 1955 finds the US building industry hard at work in almost every country of the free world. Our architects and planners are creating whole new towns from teeming India to tiny El Salvador. Our engineers and contractors are building new dams and power plants in Turkey and Afghanistan, new refineries in Sumatra and Ceylon, new highways in Colombia, new hospitals in Iran and Peru. We have opened gleaming new embassies and consulates in a dozen capitals, big luxury hotels in a dozen more.

What is the significance of this tremendous activity?

First, it means we are building up the basic welfare of other nations, creating climates unfavorable to communism, readying countries for industrialization and democratic independence, making them prosperous enough to buy more of our products.

Second, our industry and commerce are expanding in search of new sources of raw materials, new markets for finished products. To serve increased travel and trade, hotels and stores are springing up along the new commercial routes.

Third, we are helping build defenses for ourselves and our allies.

And fourth, we are keeping up strong governmental and public relations through our official missions: new embassies, consulates, libraries, information services.

In this vast development of the world community our planners and builders have ranged far and wide. In spreading wealth and knowledge they have also learned a few things about other climates, methods and materials —and other peoples. The best of them have learned how to be teachers, welfare workers, grass-roots ambassadors. Working closely with local government, professions, management and labor, they have been making friends—or, alas, sometimes enemies—for America in every country they have entered. Most have given a fairer picture of America than the picture painted by communist propaganda (and by some of our own Grade-B movies and Grade-B tourists). In many cases they have been able to show in concrete and steel that the kind of system practiced in America produces not only wealth, but technical and administrative abilities as well, and the willingness to share these assets with others.

On the following pages, FORUM presents, for the first time in a broad panorama, some of the best examples of jobs designed, financed or built by the US around the world. These structures, and the men who made them, are the face of America abroad.

But, first a summary of the over-all program, its financing and its accomplishments:

ECONOMIC AID. By late 1948, thanks to the Marshall Plan, Europe fairly crawled with members of the US construction industry. Architects went abroad to advise on the planning of industrial plants and housing, to give the benefit of their experience in expanding the US wartime industrial machine. In the early stages of the Marshall Plan—or until their local counterparts had time to bring their techniques up to date—US architects advised on better than half of the projects. In some of the less industrialized countries, US engineers are still being asked to draw complete plans or advise on locally produced schemes.

In the field of power facilities, the giant $116 million hydroelectric project in Greece—one of the biggest power jobs attempted under any aid program — was designed and supervised by Ebasco Services, Inc. Most of the cost came from local currencies, partly to pay for domestic workers and partly to pay for European materials and equipment used in the project (some of which came from factories built with Marshall Plan money). But Ebasco's receipts from the job, $13.8 million on a cost-plus arrangement, came out of US aid money allotted to Greece.

With the exception of the construction superintendents, the project engineers and some highly skilled equipment workers, Ebasco used mostly Greek personnel. Further, by the time the job is completed, Ebasco will have sent local citizens back to the US for training to operate and maintain the project.

An example of the kind of project stimulated by the combination of US aid and advice from US specialists is the housing program carried out in six western European nations. In just four years (1948-1952) the equivalent of almost $750 million was spent on housing projects in England, France, Italy, western Germany, western Austria and the Netherlands. All of the money came from counterpart funds.

In one area, the Ruhr Valley, this effort paid for eight housing projects for miners. Under the guidance of a special housing mission set up by the Marshall Plan (headed by James Butler and directed in its early stages by US Architects William Wittausch and Vernon DeMars, and later by Bernard Wagner), 15 teams of German architects, engineers and developers submitted plans and costs for the proposed units. Winning teams, awarded contracts to carry out their plans, used German workers, equipment and materials, and built the projects at a saving of up to 20% under usual construction patterns in the area. The program also introduced to this part of Europe a form of US installment home buying.

MUTUAL SECURITY. Most of the $15 billion in military aid extended so far to Europe has been paid out in the last three years. The US construction industry is part of this operation, too, since most new European installations are joint efforts of the North Atlantic Treaty Alliance.

Thus, military bases in Europe and North Africa have been designed and constructed on a cost-plus basis by US engineers and contractors with some of the contracts awarded by the Army Corps of Engineers, some by the Navy's Bureau of Yards and Docks, and a few by similar agencies of foreign governments.

Payment for the work can come from any one of three different sources (or a combination of all three): US foreign military aid funds; defense allotments of the US Defense Dept.; or foreign-subscribed NATO funds.

In the six-year period, 1950-1955, the engineers will have supervised construction of $1.8 billion worth of bases, barracks and similar military services in western Europe, North Africa and the Middle East. Much of this work has been done by US heavy construction firms such as Morrison-Knudsen Co., who had $185 million worth of foreign contracts outstanding in 1953.

These are good reasons why the work is done on a cost-plus basis. Every job is different; what the architects and builders learn in one country may not do them any good in another because of political, economic and climatological reasons. Then too, turnover of construction workers is high, sometimes running 40%, and the cost of shipping men and equipment is far greater than on domestic jobs. (M-K spent $15 million on transportation alone during 1953.)

LOAN PROGRAMS. Export-Import Bank loans have played a particularly important role in developing foreign power and transportation industries but they also have been widely used to build and equip many manufacturing plants in Latin America and Asia.

The equipment for Export-Import Bank loans generally comes from the US and the plant is usually designed and built by US engineers and builders. In many instances the actual construction is carried out in conjunction with a local firm but, in any case, most of the more highly skilled workers are recruited from US construction crews while most of the unskilled labor is performed by local employees. One of the distinctive features of these operations, however, is the training of native workers to do the more difficult work. Sometimes when a US crew departs from an area, it leaves behind what becomes the nucleus of a small construction company, manned almost completely with men who have received their training on the job—from engineers to bulldozer operators.

POINT FOUR. American advisers employed by Point Four have gone out in small teams to set up such projects as model farms in India and health programs in Iran, but money from this program has also paid for things like the two-year technical and economic survey supervised by the engineering firm of Knappen, Tippetts, Abbett, McCarthy for the government of Burma.

In some instances, the various US aid programs overlap. For example, in Afghanistan, a $75 million project calling for the construction of two dams was largely financed with Export-Import loans while Point Four technical assistance to the same country has been showing previously nomadic Afghans how to use the 400,000 newly irrigated acres that the dams will create.

This project, begun back in 1947 by Morrison-Knudsen, is just winding up and is typical of the kind of operations that US firms find themselves in when they work on aid projects. Examples: 1) M-K used 60 local workers for every US national employed and had some unusual problems to contend with as a result. For instance, the Afghan version of the coffee break consists of two prayer periods each day on company time in addition to three prayer sessions on the workers' own time. 2) The transportation difficulties were enormous and getting 17,000 tons of equipment into the middle of this backward Asian nation accounted for about 25% of the project's cost. 3) Despite the Point Four work in Afghanistan, M-K found it necessary to start its own model farm in one area just to show local farmers how to use the new land—certainly an unusual venture for a construction crew.

In addition to the aid programs carried out by the government and the technical assistance done by the big private firms in connection with their profit-making work, some US citizens, notably the Rockefellers, have established what could be called "private" Point Four programs. The Rockefeller's International Basic Economy Corp. (IBEC) has been trying to improve the economy of several Latin American states. Among other things, IBEC has introduced the supermarket technique of food distribution, opened farm machinery and food processing plants and engaged in town and regional planning.

PRIVATE INVESTMENT. Despite some obvious deterrents, private investment abroad is big. At the end of 1953 it totaled about $17 billion, up $10 billion from 1946. The graph and table (right) show that the manufacturing industry is the biggest of the private investors ($5.2 billion by 1953) and that the Latin American countries get the biggest share of the private investment dollar—about 37%.

Not all these private dollars go into industrial plants. For example, in building its Batangas Refinery in Indonesia, Caltex (California Texas Oil Co.) has had to put up mosques, schools and housing and provide virtually all the services a municipal government would supply at home. Similarly, Aramco (Arabian American Oil Co.) has pro-

A summary of the programs which have carried US building abroad

In the last 15 years the US has developed a series of programs, both public and private, that have put its architects, engineers and builders into almost every corner of the free world.

Following is a year-by-year and dollar-by-dollar summation of the most important of those steps:

LEND-LEASE. Started in 1940, this program was designed to give the allies the military hardware they needed to overcome the axis. Before the program ended in 1945, the US had spent $48.7 billion in the effort ($8 billion of which came back in reverse lend-lease after this country entered the war.

UNRRA. Destruction was the residue of the war and the US felt compelled to develop an aid program to alleviate human suffering. Under the United Nations Relief and Rehabilitation Administration (as the program was called), the US spent $3.5 billion in less than three years to feed, clothe and at least temporarily house the victims of war.

BRITISH LOAN. To pay its war bills, Great Britain liquidated great chunks of its foreign investments. To help the United Kingdom restore its shattered industrial empire and become a strong ally once again, the US loaned the British $4.4 billion in 1946.

MARSHALL PLAN. Just as Europe began to show signs of a start at recovery, a new enemy—communism—appeared and begain exploiting low living standards. The Marshall Plan was the answer. In its early stages, the program included large grants for foods, fibers and fuel. But, even at the start, the Marshall Plan had as its prime goal the raising of western Europe's productive capacity. This meant new factories, additions to and renovations of old plants, construction of power facilities and a host of related industrial projects.

The Marshall Plan—or its successors—required the expenditure of $15 billion by the US. It was the first aid program in which the US construction industry played a major role.

COUNTERPART PROGRAM. As a condition for receiving Marshall Plan funds, each recipient nation was required to put up a specified amount of its own currency in a fund to be used for roughly the same purposes as the dollar grants. To date, counterpart funds have amounted to more than $1 billion.

EXPORT-IMPORT BANK. Since 1945 this government bank has loaned over $3.5 billion to nations all over the world, mainly to finance projects that private investors shied vided schools and health facilities for native workers and houses which they can buy on the installment plan. It also has established an "Arab Industrial Development Dept." to ease the growing pains of Saudi Arabia, opened industrial training schools for 7,500 Arabs and let contracts with 700-odd native suppliers for everything from ice and laundry services to furniture and auto repair.

In the field of manufacturing and assembly plants, General Motors is probably the leader of all US investors abroad with its 27 plants in 17 nations and its $191 million expansion plan for Europe alone. Other fields are marked by other blue-chip investors: Pan American (through Intercontinental Hotels) with its 15 foreign hotels, *Reader's Digest* with its publishing plants in 14 countries, E. R. Squibb with 17 factories around the world and Coca Cola with its ubiquitous bottling plants.

HOW BIG THE FUTURE? Although the scope of our private operations abroad seems large, it is actually small when measured against the undeveloped state of most of the world and the prewar investments made by Britain when she occupied our present position as leader of the Western Alliance. If, as Britain did, we were to put 2.5% of our gross national product into foreign countries, it would mean stepping up our present rate from less than $2 billion to $5 billion per year.

What are the chances of our reaching this figure? No quick or easy answer is possible, but, based upon postwar experience to date, certain facts are obvious. While it will meet keener local competition, US industry should continue to flourish in such newly prosperous countries as Britain and west Germany. In other countries not so far along the road to recovery, government aid programs will continue to stimulate growth and thereby open new markets for private investment and private construction. This trend may be abetted by an International Finance Corp., a proposed adjunct of the World Bank, whose $100 million fund would help finance private industrial development in retarded areas.

Asia alone holds a big potential market for US construction, but the extent of our government aid to this continent is yet to be decided by the newly formed Council of Foreign Economic Policy.

On the other side of the ledger must be listed these hard facts which may tend to curtail our construction operations abroad: 1) European countries will capture a growing share of the foreign construction market; their

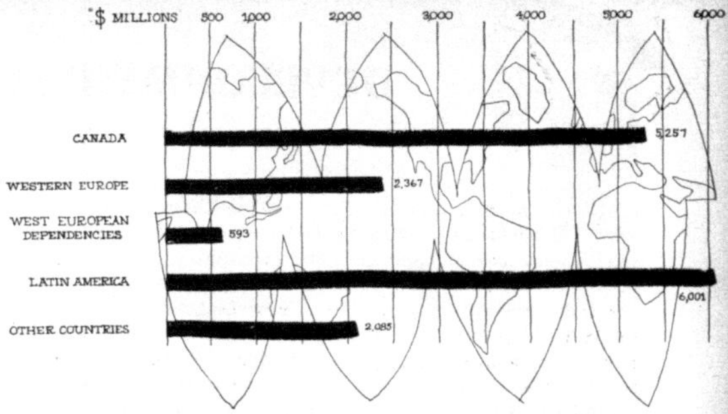

PRIVATE INVESTMENT ABROAD amounted to $16.3 billion by 1953. Graph (above) shows that bulk of it has gone into South America; table (below) shows that manufacturing industry has been biggest investor.

$ millions	1953	1950	$ millions	1953	1950
Agriculture	658	589	Public utilities	1,499	1,425
Mining and smelting	1,934	1,129	Trade	1,046	762
Manufacturing	5,242	3,831	Other	994	662
Petroleum	4,931	3,390	Total	16,304	11,788

Source: US Dept. of Commerce; Office of Business Economics

equipment manufacturers can offer longer term credit than the US competitors—thanks to their more generous government-backed loan programs, and they will take business away from US competitors because the contracts for the design and construction of plants usually go to the same nation that supplies the equipment. 2) Many European nations, unlike the US, are now willing to take payment in soft currencies. However, as these nations get closer to currency solvency, this problem will become less acute. 3) Whereas currency exchange problems have prompted US firms to plow back their foreign earnings in new plants and equipment, the growing opportunity to withdraw their profits may curtail plant expansion. 4) Russia is extending its efforts to beat the free nations to the foreign market.

On balance, these deterrents are more than offset by the simple truth that the world economy is growing fast and that the US will continue to sell a fair share of that growing market. Thus, US architects, engineers and contractors can look forward to more and more work abroad. And, as long as the US continues to play wisely its role as a major world power, the industry's role will continue to be that of ambassador as well as builder.

away from because of low profit possibilities. Usually, these same projects had to be established before profitable ventures could be attempted by private investors. The International Bank for Reconstruction and Development (World Bank)—to which the US as well as many other nations subscribe funds —serves much the same purpose. In the absence of any large-scale aid program designed specifically for Latin America, the Export-Import Bank and the World Bank have supplied most of the public money going south of the border.

POINT FOUR. In many cases, nations which we feel need our economic assistance are in such a backward state that they cannot qualify for Export-Import Bank loans. This is where the Point Four program enters the picture, designed as it is to lay the groundwork for future industrialization by increasing the food supply, improving sanitation and—in some cases—educational and housing facilities.

Since it began in 1949, the US government has spent less than $250 million on Point Four. Private citizens have engaged in similar overseas programs. Outstanding among these is the Rockefeller International Basic Economic Corp. (IBEC), which has tried to improve the economy of several Latin American nations by introducing more advanced techniques in the fields of agricultural, retailing and town planning.

Another aspect of private Point Four work is carried out by the big oil companies in and around their foreign fields and refineries. Since their work takes them into backward nations, they have found it necessary to build whole cities and provide educational, housing, health and municipal services for their workers and their families.

MUTUAL SECURITY. At about the same time that the Korean war started, it became apparent that economic assistance to friendly nations was not enough. Once mainly an internal threat, communism became an external one as well. To counter this, the US embarked on the Mutual Security military aid programs. To pay for the bases, arms and men needed for the defensive side of the alliance, the US has paid out $15 billion since 1951 and the program is still going on.

PRIVATE INVESTMENT. Despite the uncertainties of world politics—tangibly expressed in the very need for huge aid programs—the US private investor has, in the postwar years, been willing to invest more than $10 billion abroad.

DEVELOPMENT: NEW RESPONSIBILITIES

Helping underdeveloped nations realize their potentials has kept US architects, planners and builders busy on some of the biggest jobs of their careers: overhauling entire national economies, building new dams to create farmlands and power for industrialization; laying out new highways, tunnels and bridges to link scattered areas; building new harbors and airports to lure world trade, new housing, schools and hospitals to raise low standards of shelter, health and education.

Quite naturally a lion's share of this work has fallen to heavy engineering and construction organizations; but the impact has been at least as strong from the deeply humane enterprises of individual professionals. Among these, we find Mayer & Whittlesey, as architects and planners, doing the basic plans for Chandigarh, major capital of Punjab, India; Neutra and Alexander laying out a $25 million plan for rebuilding devastated Guam; Alexander with Indian Architect Sarma, planning under UN auspices a new "rural city" for 60,000—"Pallikkarana" in Madras State; Jacob Crane heading rural-tropical housing studies in southeast Asia; dozens of others working away quietly, as did Albert Mayer living in Indian villages to study how they could win improvement.

Contrasted with this work is the effort of vast engineering organizations such as Knappen-Tippetts-Abbett-McCarthy of New York, involved during the past five years in planning for $3.7 billion in overseas projects in 12 different countri

Three years ago KTAM, assisted by Robert Nathan As ciates (economic consultants), Pierce Management (mine experts) and $2 million in Point Four aid, launched an inclusive economic, social and engineering survey of Bur aimed at doubling gross national production by 1959. Th $1.5 billion plan calls for huge irrigation and power proje (two of which KTAM is now designing), rail, highway communications networks, new port facilities, new mining industries. Elsewhere in backward Asia KTAM is working a $555 million project to reclaim Iraq's Tigris-Euphrates ley and make it bloom with crops enough to feed the ent population of 5 million. In Korea they are consultants to United Nations on a $130 million rehabilitation program cluding three thermoelectric power plants being built by Be tel Corp. of San Francisco to double the nation's pov capacity. KTAM has been working on other power and irri tion projects in eight other countries.

Big Builder Morrison-Knudsen of Boise, with $560 mill in overseas contracts completed since the war, has carried $50 million in dam and irrigation contracts for the Afgh government, an earth-fill dam in Ceylon to double the islan water storage and provide new plots for 20,000 farmers; 1957 they will complete a power dam for the city of Teher

Photos: (below) UP; (opp. p.) LIFE—William Sanders

BOLIVIAN HIGHWAY (right and above) now links two halves of a nation split by the Andes mountains. Helped by Export-Import Bank loan, engineered by KTAM and built by Macco-Panpacific of Los Angeles, the $45 million, 312-mi. life line joins the food-producing plains with the populous tin mines of the Altiplano, also closes the last gap in a 2,000-mi. road and rail system across the continent. US engineers and contractors have built roads in Colombia, El Salvador, Belgian Congo; tunnels under Havana Bay and through New Zealand mountains; harbor facilities in Guatemala, Australia, Liberia, Thailand.

INDIAN POWER PLANT at Bokara is one of the first projects undertaken by the Damodar Valley Corp. in a five-year plan to irrigate 1 million acres and distribute electricity over a 250,000-sq.-mi. area in northeastern India. Designed and built by International General Electric Co. of India, with Harza Engineering Co. of Chicago, the hydro-electric plant is India's biggest power station. Elsewhere, power programs include four new plants in Greece built under supervision of Ebasco Services, Inc., who have also done power jobs all over South America and have designed and built India's first newsprint mill. Last year Stone & Webster completed Brazil's largest thermoelectric power plant near Sao Paolo with the help of a World Bank loan. Kuljian Corp. of Philadelphia are building the first two units of a $45 million power plant near Caracas, Venezuela.

SALVADOREAN DAM completed last year lights the streets of San Salvador, will help the coffee-dependent country broaden its industrial base and irrigate some of its 72% of uncultivated land. Project was partially financed with World Bank loan, designed by Harza Engineering and built by J. A. Jones Construction Co. of Charlotte, N.C. Harza has also planned power-irrigation projects in India, Jordan, Iraq, Surinam, Uruguay and the Philippines, is working on complete development of the Meric-Evros River basin on the Greek-Turkey border.

LOW-COST HOUSES with reinforced concrete frames are replacing entire communities wiped out in Salvador's 1951 earthquake. Regional rehabilitation of five towns is IBEC Housing Corp. project under Architects George Dudley, Edward Echeverria, and Planning Consultant Robert Burlingham.

BETTER HOUSING is a basic mission of the US abroad, both officially and unofficially. Under technical cooperation programs, there are currently some 40 US housing specialists working in the field on projects financed by the Foreign Operations Administration. Two recent programs are shown below, one in highly industrialized western Germany, the other in lesser-developed Formosa. Others include a survey of housing legislation and building techniques carried out by The Architects Collaborative for Costa Rica, assistance to Colombia by the Small Homes Council of Illinois University, advisory work in Burma, Italy and the Middle East. Among the unofficial programs are those in Puerto Rico (1,800 $6,000 houses and community facilities) and a 2,000-house, four-year plan for El Salvador (photo, left), both initiated by the Rockefellers' International Basic Economy Corp.

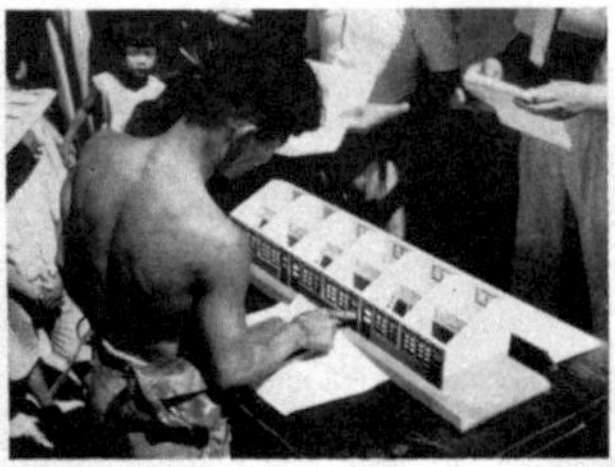

SOUND TRUCK, movie, exhibits and a soil-cement blockmaker demonstrate FOA self-help housing program to Formosan coal miners and dockworkers. Right: finished houses. Mobile unit first went on the road last August, has helped relieve critical housing conditions among refugee population.

IN NINE RUHR CITIES, counterpart funds and FOA technical assistance under US Housing Specialist Bernd Wagner have produced 5,337 row-house homes for coal miners, plus good will and increased coal production. All were designed and built by Germans, with Americans introducing competitive bidding and a FHA-type installment purchase plan. Above: row houses at Aachen.

MAP OF BERLIN (below) shows how US-guided housing has sprung up where needed all over Western zone, while in Eastern sector 90% of all new housing has been state-directed into grimly monumental "showpieces" along the Stalinallee (symbols represent 30 to 200 dwelling units each). Beside housing 190,000 refugees from the Soviet zone FOA is currently building an answer to Stalinallee: the 1956 Berlin International Building Exhibition, a complete redevelopment of a bombed-out area north of the Tiergarten with 8,000 permanent dwelling units shown in various stages of construction, architectural exhibits, festive pavilions and cafés in a landscaped park.

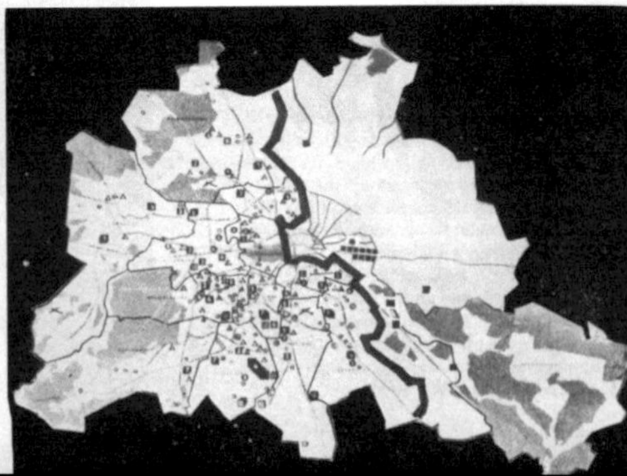

MODERN HOSPITALS for underdeveloped countries have been greatly aided by US architects and engineers and the US Public Health Service. At left is the Union Central Medical Center in Rangoon, biggest of nine hospitals designed by Litchfield, Whiting, Panero & Severud, architects and engineers, and paid for by the Burmese government. An Indian contractor has started foundations on the $11 million project, which includes a 600-bed hospital, 200-bed TB center, medical school (500 students), nursing school (400 students) and residences. Buildings are oriented, shaded, through-vented for climate control, designed for local materials and methods.

CENTRAL HOSPITAL in Lima has 500 medical and surgical beds and 350-bed maternity wing. Developed with help of USPHS and designed by Edward D. Stone and A. L. Aydelott, associated architects, the $12 million project will be operated by Peruvian government for 75,000 Lima white-collar workers under social security program.

NEMAZEE MEDICAL CENTER in Shiraz was built by Iranian philanthropist. Edmund J. Whiting, architect; Severud-Elstad-Krueger and Ernest Franck, engineers. Among other hospitals overseas, Whiting also designed Roosevelt Hospital, Guatemala, Methodist mission hospital in Southern Rhodesia.

AGRICULTURAL INSTITUTE at Allahabad, India (below) is the work of Architects Mayer & Whittlesey. The campus, almost completed, includes administration building (left) and library (right); concrete arches lead to school buildings, chapel, dormitories. The Institute will be more fully published in a future issue of FORUM.

Louis Checkman

INDUSTRY: NEW INVESTMENTS

Almost before the ubiquitous Coca-Cola first went abroad (in 1909), US planners, architects, engineers and builders have been hard on the heels of industrialist-explorers all over the world. The contract-engineering firm of Frederick Snare, for example, has in the past 50 years completed close to 850 jobs in Latin America and elsewhere. Bechtel Corp. has built pipe lines and refineries for a handful of oil companies in the Middle East (photo below). We have been designing and building for foreign interests too: Bechtel recently finished a $100 million refinery and town at Aden for British Petroleum Company, Ltd.; Stone & Webster engineered a new refinery near Milan for Italian investors; Ralph M. Parsons Co. is completing a refinery for the Turkish government and Morrison-Knudsen is working on a gas pipe line to Karachi.

As they invested billions of dollars in new sources of raw materials, big US extractive industries of oil and steel became even bigger clients overseas than they are at home, for planners and architects as well as engineers and builders. They also illustrated the great swing in capitalism, away from t old idea of simple "exploitation" toward the new idea th he who creates unprecedented prosperity among new grou of people creates thereby new *markets* for his product. get better workers meant building a great deal besides pr duction facilities, administration facilities, executive housin it meant housing or housing loans and floor plans for tho sands of native workers, schools and outside scholarships train employees and their children, and the community cente hospitals, churches, stores, recreation centers for new tow often in wilderness.

The bigger the industry and the more primitive the countr the more welfare and building become one, and the more mu be done that is not directly connected with the company, steer clear of the "imperialist" label, restrictive legislati or outright nationalization. As one US corporation preside put it: "We are trying to show them that we are real putting back into the country more than we are taking out

TRANS-ARABIAN PIPE LINE, built by Bechtel, carries oil to Mediterrane

RESEARCH AND DEVELOPMENT LABORATORIES on Bahrain Island, Persian Gulf, were designed for Bahrain Petroleum Co., Ltd. by Architect Chauncey Riley of New York. Long hood over windows of laboratory building at right keeps bright sunlight from penetrating interior and affecting products under test. On office building at left, lower halves of freestanding blinds slide up to allow more sunlight during winter. Buildings are part of refinery development started in 1936 by Bahrain Petroleum (wholly owned by California-Texas Oil Co.). Riley also designed housing, hospital addition, dining halls, theater, library, gymnasium, shopping center and small hotel in nearby company town of Awali. Last month Caltex opened the Philippine Islands' first refinery at Batangas Bay with housing, hospital recreation and school facilities by Riley. It also has communities in Rumbai and Perawang, Indonesia, an office building, cafeteria, housing and refinery in Holland.

ADMINISTRATION BUILDING is part of Standard Vacuum Oil Co.'s new Bombay refinery project, laid out by US Architects Mayer & Whittlesey and local associate Durga Bajpai, built by local contractors. Building has sunshade fins to reduce cooling load, private dining room and terrace on roof. In right foreground is patio for employee cafeteria and recreation building. (Housing for refinery workers is shown on p. 108.)

BOMBAY OFFICE BUILDING of Standard Vacuum Oil has fixed sun-louvers of precast concrete (important on northwest and southwest sides shown here) which cut air-conditioning loads, are less expensive than operating louvers and need not be adjusted by busy employees. Louvers and main entrance were designed by Chauncey Riley, building itself by local Architect John A. Ritchie. Arresting honeycomb exterior is floodlighted at night.

Courtesy Creole Petroleum Corp.

ELEMENTARY SCHOOL (left), town plan a houses were designed by Skidmore, Owi & Merrill for expanding refinery town b by Creole Petroleum Co., Jersey Standa big Venezuelan affiliate. Creole pays tuit for workers' children but, following i policy of integration, is turning over community facilities it builds to nation to run. Company shares costs with gove ment, offers house plans, loans to reside

SENIOR STAFF HOUSES in Tokyo (left) and Homoku, Japan, were built by Standard Vacuum Oil Co. for American employees. Architects: Antonin Raymond & L. L. Rado.

WORKERS' HOUSING (right) for Stanvac's big Bombay refinery was designed and built by local architects and builders on Mayer & Whittlesey's community plan, which includes staff and employee housing units, recreation center, cafeteria.

NEW PORT CITY for 40,000, *Puerto Ordaz,* and its companion, *Ciudad Piar,* new mining town in Venezuelan mountains, has cost the Orinoco Mining Co. (US Steel) $30 million so far. Architect-Planners Wiener & Sert, and Oficina de Planificacion y Vivienda, started wholly afresh, with civic center (separating the shopping center and public square, including church). Workers live in four zones: *obreros* in cement-block row houses reversing most US planning con tions—almost no cars, few roads, little pa ing but many pedestrian paths, close-by r reation; *junior staff; senior staff* (progr sively more space, cars); finally an inevita *service population*—not employed by Orin but responsibility assumed and precauti built in to prevent their creating typi fringe slums. (These are integrated tov and expansion is planned for.)

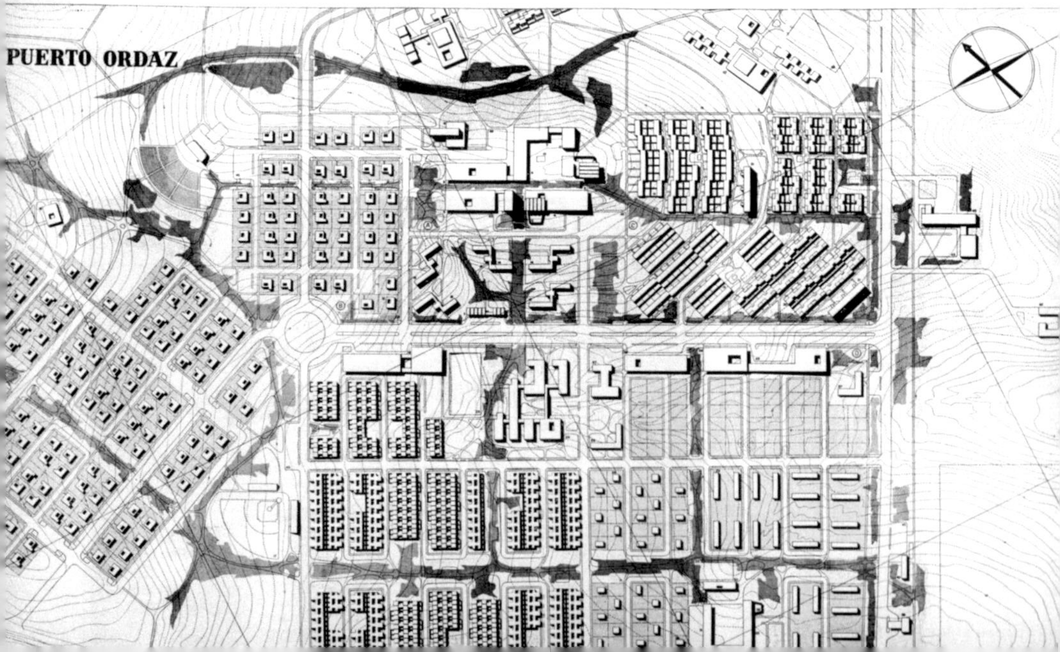

PHARMACEUTICAL COMPANIES are all over Latin America, expanding into Near and Far East as well. Last year Squibb completed a $1 million air-conditioned plant at Cali Colombia (left) by local architects, has also built in Argentina, Brazil, Cuba and Peru, Turkey and the Philippines. Abbott Laboratories, with operations in 38 countries, will open a new Caracas plant this spring. Sterling Drug has opened new factories in Brazil, Colombia and South Africa (architects: Barnum & Thompson). Pfizer, Lilly and Lederle are also active abroad.

RADIO CORP. OF AMERICA has built or added to plants in Argentina, Brazil, England, Greece, Italy. At left is the new Madrid factory of Inelsa, RCA associate in Spain. Left of tower is recording studio.

GENERAL MOTORS' new assembly plant at Antwerp was designed by Smith, Hinchman & Grylls in collaboration with Belgian Architects V. Cols, J. De Roeck & Associés. Behind glass showroom at left are offices, parts and new car warehouses. At right are assembly buildings, power plant. GM is spending $191 million to expand facilities in seven European countries, has built other new plants in Karachi and Montevideo.

FORD MOTOR CO. plant at Cologne, by German architects, engineers and builders, turns out 40,400 cars and trucks a year. Ford has other manufacturing facilities in England and France, new assembly plants in Alexandria, Egypt (1950) and Sao Paulo, Brazil (1953). Chrysler is building new offices in Mexico City. Local affiliates of Studebaker-Packard have opened plants and showrooms in Latin America, Africa and Europe. Kaiser-Willys has built an Israel plant, is looking into South America.

HABANA HILTON, designed by Welton Becket & Associates of Los Angeles, is scheduled for completion in 1956. Financed by Cuban pension union, the $13 million project will have 630 air-conditioned rooms and 42 de luxe suites, ground and rooftop swimming pools, 450-car garage, mosaic exterior.

COMMERCE: NEW MARKETS

With an eye on newly developing markets, US hotelm retailers, bankers and manufacturers are setting up sh overseas in bigger numbers than ever. Hilton, with 28 hot in the US and Puerto Rico, one in Spain, is under way five more abroad. Intercontinental Hotels and Sears, Roebu are adding to their South American chains. Foreign invest are calling on US architects for office buildings, shops a showrooms. And in trade promotion, a new Commerce De program is already helping US businessmen show off the tion's industrial achievements at international trade fairs, field in which most other governments have long helped th manufacturers compete (and in which communist countr have stolen more than one propaganda march on the US wi lavish, state-sponsored exhibits).

INTERCONTINENTAL HOTELS CORP., set up in 1946 as wholly owned subsidiary of Pan American World Airways, has taken over management of five South American hotels (of which it has remodeled three) and has built four new ones. Largest new hotels are the $7.5 million Tamanaco in Caracas (left) and the $8.7 million Tequendama in Bogota (below), both with 400 rooms and designed by Holabird & Root & Burgee. IHC is building a 120-room hotel in Curaçao and plans another of 100 rooms for San Salvador, both designed by IHC Architect Joseph Salerno and Engineer R. S. Smith.

ISTANBUL HILTON (above, below and left) was designed by Skidmore, Owings & Merrill, will open its 300 rooms to Middle East travelers this May. Turkish Pension Fund financed construction at $20,000 per room; Hilton provides working capital, pays two thirds of operating profits as rent. Hilton is also building new hotels in Mexico City and Acapulco, both designed by local Architect Fernando Parra, will soon start work on $7 million, 400-room luxury hotel in Rome, and in Cairo, will open Nile Hilton by Welton Becket.

SAVOY PLAZA HOTEL in Beirut, now in foundations, was designed for Lebanese investors by Edward Stone of New York and Elias & Dagher of Beirut. It will cost $4 million, have 221 rooms, pantry on every floor, roof grill and swimming pool.

Wyn Moroz

COMMERCE cont'd.

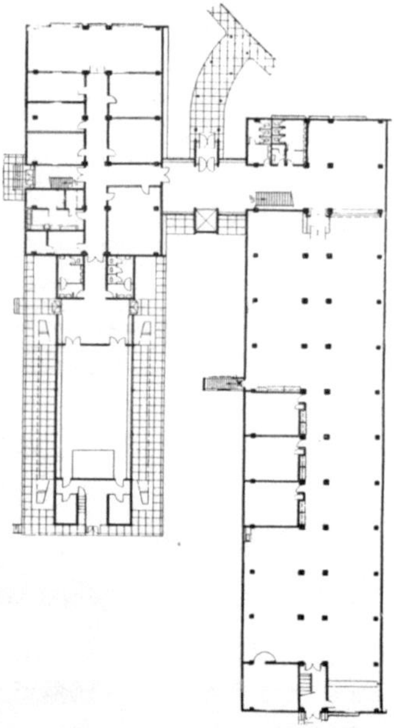

OFFICE BUILDING in Yawata, Japan, was designed for the Yasukawa Electric Manufacturing Co. by Antonin Raymond and L. L. Rado. Long center court with pool is flanked by offices (top), auditorium of shell cncrete arches (right). South- and west-facing windows are shielded by sun louvers. Tall element at right is elevator shaft.

Photos (above): K. Kanayama, courtesy "Kenchiku Bunka"

BANK BUILDING in Nagoya, Japan, was designed for National City Bank of New York by Raymond & Rado. National City, which started its expansion into Latin America in 1914, now has a dozen Asian branches among its 57 overseas offices.

FIRST SHOPPING CENTER in booming suburban Caracas opened last November with American-style supermarket, eight smaller shops, offices. It is second such project promoted by VBEC (Venezuelan Basic Economy Corp.), set up by Nelson Rockefeller and his brothers to join with local capital in developing agriculture and industries vital to economic advancement. The center was designed by Oficina Don Hatch, Caracas.

Rhys-Dorvyne

KNOLL ASSOCIATES of New York have opened seven overseas showrooms for furniture and fabrics, including one in Paris (above).

← **SEARS, ROEBUCK** has built or acquired 26 stores in Latin America, will open three more this fall (in Lima, Mexico City, Sao Paulo). Plans are prepared by Sears' Architects John Redden and John Raben with local architects. Left: new store in Barranquilla, Colombia.

AUTOMOBILE SHOWROOM for Studebaker-Packard and Morris cars was designed for Caracas dealer by New York's Roger Halle.

RENTAL OFFICE BUILDING designed by Lathrop Douglass for US and local tenants will be largest in Caracas, have ten office floors, penthouse restaurant, shopping plaza, basement parking for 200 cars. Construction on the $3 million project will start next month.

DEFENSE: NEW STRATEGY

Building a defense perimeter overseas has posed a wide range of problems for service engineers and their civilian partners. Contract architects, engineers and builders have had to adapt the necessary installations first to jungle heat and then to the icy winds of the Arctic barrens.

Bulk of the work abroad during the past three years has been for the Army Corps of Engineers, and the bulk of their work, in turn, has been for the Air Force: a band of bases across the top of the world (Alaska, Canada, Labrador, Greenland, Iceland) and another band across the middle (Bermuda, the Azores, French Morocco, Tripoli and the Middle East). The Navy's Bureau of Yards and Docks has had work of its own in the Carribbean and Pacific, work for the Air Force in Guam and recently in Spain. Here four airfields and two ports are being carried out by Architect-Engineers Frederic R. Harris, Metcalf & Eddy, Shaw, Metz & Dolio, Pereira & Luckman. Management contractors: Raymond Concrete Pile Co., Walsh Construction, Brown & Root.

ACCENT ON THE ARCTIC for advance bases ha meant working with totally new conditions temperatures ranging from 60° F. to —50° normal winds of 35 mph with gusts up t 125, permanently frozen earth and fossi ice down to 1,000′ or more. To avoid dis turbing the active surface layer, whicl would result in settling and cracking foun dations, B-36 hangars at the giant Thul base (right) have 4″ of foamed glass in sulation in their floor slabs, rest on hug gravel pads 9′ thick laced with forced-ai ducts to dispel heat transferred down dur ing winter. Thule architect-engineers fo Corps of Engineers were Metcalf & Edd and Alfred Hopkins & Associates.

Photos (below & top opp. p.): LIFE—George Silk

PRECAST WAREHOUSE at Iceland base is concrete frame and panels, shipped fro prefabricator in Holland. Same prefabr cator did Air Force buildings in Greenlan

←

"ICEBOX" BARRACKS at Thule are built insulated prefab panels (glass-fiber san wich of aluminum-clad plywood). To pr vent heat transfer, buildings are raise 2′-9″ on wood posts set on 3′ gravel pads.

SCHOOL for military and civilian childre at Port Lyautey, French Morocco, is of co crete frame and block. Architect was Jam C. Mackenzie.

SUBMERGING BARRACKS north of Thule were developed by Army engineers and Metcalf & Eddy. Towers are extended as metal pressure hull sinks slowly into deep snow.

CONCRETE NAVY BARRACKS at Guam were built of precast slabs with shutter walls by Pacific Island engineers (F. R. Harris, Inc., Blanchard & Maher, Keller & Gannon).

HOT-WEATHER DESIGN for Navy families at Guantanamo Bay, Cuba, has floor-to-ceiling jalousies, block walls. Architects: Fisk, Johnson & Perkins; Ossipoff & Preis.

HOSPITAL at Naval Air Station, Guam, was designed by Pacific Island engineers. Built of reinforced concrete, it is planned for expansion from 350 to 500 beds.

CHAPEL BUILDING is part of permanent Army town at Sukiran, Okinawa, designed by Architects Skidmore, Owings & Merrill for Army engineers.

DIPLOMACY: NEW PUBLIC RELATIONS

On the preceding 14 pages has been shown some of the great spread of planning and building by which we are furthering our ends and the ends of others all over the world —and by which other peoples are judging our motives and our abilities in all fields. The free nations have come to accept US partnership in world economics and world politics, and we are coming to accept the responsibilities that go with it. Yet some, especially in the older nations, still like to look upon Americans as a bunch of cultural cowboys. Here then, in conclusion, are some of the newest buildings that represent us officially in our economic and political roles, and in our cultural role as well. They bear the American flag, so they must represent us well. We believe they do.

COPENHAGEN EMBASSY (left and above) is set back among trees lining the Oster-brogade, one of the main arteries leading from the city to the northern suburbs. Auditorium and skylighted reading room (right) are readily accessible to public; the embassy offices are raised on columns, for security control as much as architectural effect. Both Copenhagen and Stockholm embassy (see overleaf) were designed by US Architects Ralph Rapson and John van der Meulen in the offices of Anders Tengbom, Swedish consulting architect, under the direction of Ides van der Gracht, US State Dept. regional director for foreign buildings operations.

ELEVEN OTHER EMBASSIES have been completed by FBO since 1945, with 97% of funds coming from debts owed US. Rio de Janeiro and Havana embassies were designed by Harrison & Abramovitz, Ankara by Eggers & Higgins, Saudi Arabia by the Byrne Organization. FBO with foreign architects designed the embassies in Iran, Liberia, Thailand, Brussels, Costa Rica, Australia, Ethiopia, and two more under construction in Spain and Nicaragua.

RIO EMBASSY

BRUSSELS EMBASSY

LIFE—N. R. Farbman

MADRID EMBASSY

Photo by Peter Blake

HOUSING at Bad Godesburg for German employees of US government. Designed by Apel, German associate of Skidmore, Owings & Merrill, built under Army Corps of Engineers.

AT BREMEN, staff apartments (above) and consulate (right) by Skidmore, Owings & Merrill.

DIPLOMACY cont'd.

STAFF HOUSING, a relatively small part of FBO program, has produced good architecture to repr sent the US, paid off in reduced quarters allowanc for foreign se rvice personnel. Aside from a ha dozen new homes for ambassadors or consul general projects have included staff apartments in Toky designed by Raymond & Rado (AF, March '53) ar apartments by Skidmore, Owings & Merrill to with their new consulate at Bremen (lower left).

FOURTEEN CONSULATES have been finished sin the war: Curaçao, Belgium, Newfoundland, Ita (Naples), Germany (Bremen and Frankfort France (Strasbourg and Cherbourg), Aden, Sau Arabia, Brazil (Natal and Belem), Canada (Queb and Toronto). Under construction: Port-au-Spai Trinidad; Le Havre, France (by Rapson and va der Meulen), Dusseldorf and Stuttgart, Germar (by Skidmore, Owings & Merrill).

PRIVATE DIPLOMACY: the Stoa of Attalos, shoppir cultural and social center of ancient Athens, is n being restored as an archaeological museum by t American School of Classical Studies, with $2 m lion donated by Rockefeller and other US friends Greece. Once the meeting place of poets, phil ophers and politicians, it will (by 1957) house rel excavated by US scholars under Homer Thomps and John Travlos. Architects: W. Stuart Thomps and Phelps Barnum.

Photos: Ateljé Sundahl

STOCKHOLM EMBASSY has drawn visits and praise from leading European architects (sample: "the best office building in Northern Europe"). Entrance lobby (above) and gallery (right) open on central garden court. Tall office block (below) faces narrow end to street to keep large building from overpowering other, more residential, embassies nearby. Below this, auditorium-cafeteria faces glass and balcony to southern sun. Architects Rapson and van der Meulen also designed Copenhagen embassy (shown on preceding pages).

Don Hatch (left) and Michael Hare, partners in both Oficina Don Hatch, Caracas, and Hare & Hatch, New York City, study a model.

Both the aerial photo and map acrosspage show how Caracas crowds its mountain-rimmed valley. Last remaining free area for development is a 1,200-acre tract to the east, where Oficina Don Hatch is doing the entirely new residential community of La Urbina. The map also shows the location of a number of the projects presented on subsequent pages.

Aerial photo: Hamilton Wright

the architect and his commun

Anyone who still thinks of Venezuela as a slow-paced, cocoa- and coffee-growing country has overlooked one of the most sudden and dramatic developments that has occurred anywhere. For in the early '20s, an oil gusher whooshed in the Maracaibo Basin area of this tropical, mountainous country—and today, Venezuela is second only to the United States among the largest producers and exporters of petroleum in the entire world. In 1947, the United States Steel Company found mountains of high-grade iron ore—sufficient resource, it is estimated, for the next 50 to 100 years. And even more recently, there has been either discovery or development of other of the enormous natural resources of the land—gold, diamonds, nuclear minerals, sulphur. In the Orinoco River Valley, there is a vast hydroelectric program going forward.

As Don Hatch, partner in charge of the Caracas firm of Oficina Don Hatch, comments: "Venezuela is a boom country, where the national pastime is literally 'grabbing a bull by the tail'—and I like it."

Oficina Don Hatch is but half of an exceptional, two-part-two-country office setup—the other half being the firm of Hare & Hatch in New York, which handles commissions in the United States as well as working closely with the Caracas office. The dual firm was formed in 1949 "to provide an organization capable of bringing the requisite professional technical skill to bear on building problems in Venezuela and to have the necessary staff available in New York or Caracas, as the need arose." Michael Hare, who is usually at the New York office, and Don Hatch, who lives in Caracas, are principals of both partnerships. The two served together in aviation, U. S. Marine Corps, during World War II and have been in close association ever since: "The Marine Corps, following the alphabetical rule, landed HAre and HAtch in adjacent bunks," Don Hatch points out, "and we've been there ever since!"

In the Caracas office, Dr. Claudio Creamer, an associate of the firm, is in charge of all structural engineering. Among the New York engineers who frequently serve as consultants are Henry Werner, on structural work, and Frederic E. Sutton, for special mechanical engineering.

Hatch went to Venezuela in 1948 for the Venezuela Basic Economy C tion, a Rockefeller project, as chi itect for their construction progr volving at that time 15 to 20 pr refrigerated warehouses, ice supermarkets, and retail stores. the program and management changed in 1949, Hatch took ov pletion of the program on his o opened the Caracas office.

"Whereas, stateside, an ar community may be his city, its e and his state," Hatch commer Venezuela, Caracas is my house, community is all Venezuela. . . I am a foreigner, I miss the stin of political activities. My con contribution, God willing, will b ing to find an architecture fo zuela." The following pages indic only how successful his search h but also to what a wide range o ing types he has applied his fin

With the enormous growth country, swift changes have als place in things architectural. " old hacienda houses are nearl Most of the old Caracas town have disappeared, and what is going." Inevitably, the fast gr

ficina Don Hatch: Caracas, Venezuela

Hare & Hatch, New York)

acas has brought typical problems in wake—smaller lots, higher rents, the alities that quick money invariably duces. Not the least of the city's blems is its physical limitations, con- d as it is in the valley setting among ntains that it can't climb.

ntil about 1948-49, the sort of pro- ional architectural service that is iliar in the States was almost un- wn in Venezuela, the nearest thing t being engineer-contractor offices were the main source of building gn. There were also a few Beaux- -trained architects, who worked nly for the government. At about time that Oficina Don Hatch was blished, several young U. S.-educated ezuelans and a number of Europeans opened architectural offices there. cated' who wander off on their own after short instruction . . . certain of the sub-contractors do not relish our strict supervision, and one job with us is enough for them." Hatch does feel that patience is establishing for the firm a reputation for integrity and professional ethics. Nonetheless, he still wonders if it may not eventually be necessary for the firm to do its own building. "What AIA would say is obvious," he comments.

Oficina Don Hatch started out with just Hatch as the architect and his wife as secretary. Today, they have a sizable staff, efficient personnel mostly acquired in Caracas, since Hatch found that imported U. S. draftsmen and/or their families lacked the frontier spirit and soon wanted to return home.

"We have a little United Nations in as well as sketches. With this detailed early study, working-drawing production is simplified, and work fast progresses to complete detailing, selection of materials, textures, colors, finishes, the lighting and landscaping, all developed as working drawings. Dr. Creamer, the associate engineer, keeps "working things over" and refining for better integration of structure and design. "All of our bones show," says Hatch, "and we are careful of their appearance": the structural drawings are "something to see." Each bar is shown, its position in the slab, beam or footing; its size, length, etc., all dimensioned on the drawing.

Oficina Don Hatch usually takes sealed bids from a selected list of contractors, based on exceptionally complete drawings and specifications, with the low bid-

y, "there are probably 20 to 30 itectural firms in the country."

nce the way a North American arch- s office operates was generally un- liar, achievement of well finished lings has required a continuous ess of explaining and educating new client, each new subcontractor, in not a few instances, the workmen selves—"quite a safari," Hatch calls One gradually builds up a fair list of 'in the fold,' " he goes on, "but there nsiderable mortality among the 'edu- the office," Hatch says. "The head draftsman is Canadian; the designer is a Russian without portfolio; draftsmen are a Panamanian, a Yugoslav, an Englishman. The engineer is an Ecuadorian; the office boy, a Venezuelan; one secretary, a German with a Guatemalian passport; the accountant a Trinidadian."

In developing a project, he explains, there is little differentiation between designing and production of working drawings. A very thorough preliminary study is made, usually involving models der awarded the contract, on a lump-sum amount. In some cases, though, "we have successfully used a contract with a guaranteed top and a distribution of any savings, between owners and contractor—this again by competitive bidding."

In the study that follows we show several of the recent jobs from Oficina Don Hatch drafting boards—a hotel, an automobile showroom; a group of shops; an office building; a house, a yacht club, and a shopping center.

THE ARCHITECTURAL FORUM

FIFTH AVENUE

34 ST. 34 ST.

X new address
march 1945

UERTO RICO

"colonial" Puerto Rico Richard J. Neutra designs a school and hospital system, first step in a nned program to meet the island's newly awakened sense of its independent destiny.

he West Indian island of Puerto Rico, last outpost J. S. sovereignty in the Atlantic, an impressive plan- g program is underway. Its goal: to set up a mini- n standard of living for every Puerto Rican family to improve their health, education and social out- . An integral and important part of this program is mplete new system of schools, hospitals, and health ers, both rural and urban, designed by Viennese- n, U. S. architect Richard Neutra, head of Califor- s State Planning Board and former professor of itecture at Bennington College.

eutra's assignment is of particular significance, for toward Puerto Rico that the eyes of South America turned. This small tropical island, strategically ted between the two hemispheres, is regarded as Latin American guinea pig in the hands of the th American experimenter. What happens in rto Rico may answer the question of all the Latin

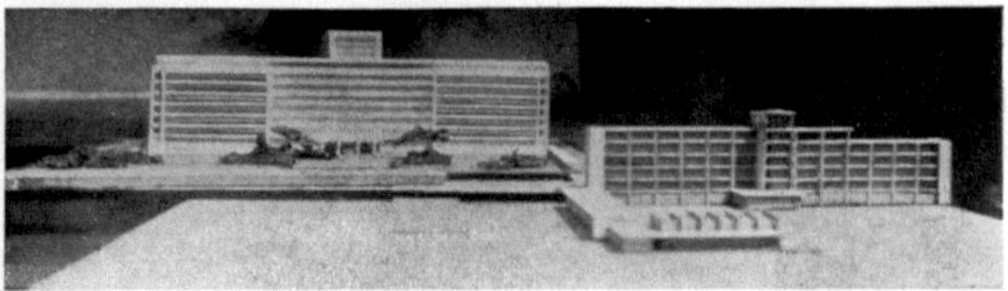

HOSPITALS rise as high as eight stories. Their breeze fronts have a porch-like openness, while the lee fronts permit exit of cleansing air currents.

SCHOOLS are oriented toward the prevailing breezes, classrooms open into shrubbery-enclosed courts by means of center-pivoted doors (above). Corridors (right) are cement walks under a roof projection.

countries surrounding the Carribean as well a British and Dutch colonies in this hemisphere. attitude is: What shall we look forward to if the gos or "yankis" have their way? Apart from pc are they in earnest about helping those who have been colonials to grow into peoples — indepe peoples capable of taking an independent place modern world?

So far Latin America has seen little in Puerto to encourage her about the gringos. A mount island only 100 miles long and 35 miles wide population of 2 million, Puerto Rico has been world-wide publicity for its *miseria y hambre*— and hunger. Certainly there is unrelieved overp tion, poverty in living and housing, undernourisl and disease, illiteracy, maldistribution of lands an to produce wealth and food. Nature, however, has of Puerto Rico a lovely island. Behind coastal f of cocoanut palms rises a skyline of interior mou towering into a sunny sky. A trade wind clima vails with neither extremes in temperature nor defined dry season. Showers usually last but minutes and are followed by brilliant sunshine temperature averages 76 degrees in winter, 80 i mer. These natural assets provide all the more inc for correcting the man-made deficiences which come about through centuries of colonial misrul

Under both Spanish government, which end 1898, and present American sovereignty Puerto has had limited powers of self-rule, but has no allowed representation in the national gove which makes decisions affecting its welfare. The has had no voice in determining tariffs, coastwis ping, labor laws and agricultural policy, although the Organic Act it has secured considerable in dence in the management of internal affairs. The has not taxed Puerto Rico for federal purpose has returned excise taxes collected from conti consumers of Puerto Rican goods in the U. S.

After taking Puerto Rico by force in 1898, the States until recently has shown a deplorable disi in its ward. Belatedly we are asking ourselves: the U. S. provide assistance on a basis compara that for a state? Provide only the type of assi associated with the "good neighbor" policy? P special help? Whether Puerto Rico's future is mined by itself, by the U. S. or by both countries ing together depends on the answer given to questions.

The Puerto Ricans themselves know that they

REXFORD G. TUGWELL, Governor of Puerto Rico
DR. RAFAEL PICO, Chairman, Planning, Zoning and Urbanizing Board
SERGIO CUEVAS, Commissioner of the Interior
SANTIAGO IGLESIAS, JR. Former Commissioner of Labor
PAUL EDWARDS, Chief, War Emergency Program
LOUIS STURCKE, JR., Chief, Bureau of Budget
DR. FERNOS ISERN, Commissioner of Health
DR. JOSÉ CANDARA, Department of Health

RICHARD J. NEUTRA, Architect
LUIS M. GUILLERMETY, JR., Exec. Director and Sec., Committee on Design of Public Works
JACINTO CALIB, Chief Assistant, Committee on Design of Public Works
STEPHAN V. ARNESON, Program Director
JOSEPH BLUMENKRANZ, Hospital Consultant

FRANK BECK, Head of Drafting Room
HENRY KLUMB, General Design
OSVALDO L. TORRO, Architect
PABLO REICHARD, Architect
MIGUEL FERRER, Architect
LUIS TORREGROSA, Chief Structural Engineer
ANTONIO CALDERON, Chief Civil Engineer
JAIME COBAS, Chief, Mechanical Electrical Section

xist without assistance from the U. S. However, like 'possessions" the world over, this island has outgrown ts status of complete domination by a larger power. The popular plan is to develop the island's resources nd expand its production to the greatest possible extent with protection and subsidies. This movement reached political success in the last November elections when he majority of legislative seats were won by the 'populares," the party founded by Luis Munoz Marin o awaken the peasant to his electoral responsibilities. This meant a reinforcement of planning aims and an ndorsement of Rexford G. Tugwell, for years hailed by the growing popular party as the best American governor ever sent to the Island.

Tugwell had been attacked and blamed by the oppo-ition coalition, a violently active minority of sugar planters and other special interest groups, for social-zing Puerto Rico. Like many an oppositional state-nent, this was mainly for continental consumption and was based on a measure of continental ignorance. Ac-ually democracy, in the form of the long-dormant peasant vote was making its demands heard. The power nd luxury enjoyed by the wealthy minority at the ex-pense of a miserably under-privileged peasant popula-ion was slipping away. For the first time the govern-nent was working hard and systematically on a most dvanced system of rural health centers, village schools, listrict hospitals, etc. These projects were given rgent priority before the institutions of higher pro-essional training which were also in the planning tage. To accomplish such an extensive program, Tug-well (under the auspices of the Planning Urbanizing nd Zoning Board) appointed a Committee on Design f Public Works with a goal of producing detailed plans or $50 million worth of building during a three-year planning period. It was this committee which chose Neutra as acting architect and consultant. In addition o his actual designing duties, it was the government's ntention that Neutra should train young Puerto Rican rchitects and engineers. This is an important factor n the integrated development plan of the island. When in operation, the public works' projects are xpected to turn out trainees to serve the island and its arious new industries fostered by the half-govern-nental "Industrial Development Corporation." The workers thus trained would also be encouraged to emi-grate to other countries in need of skilled artisans, preferably to parts of Latin America.

Starting in the fall of 1943, therefore, with the ever-growing help of Puerto Rican engineers and architects, Neutra embarked on a concentrated design program which put supposed tropical leisure to shame. Open air schools were designed for over 150 villages. One hundred twenty-eight rural health centers were planned, designed and redesigned to bring a preventive health program and a social service into the mountains of the interior. Four large district hospitals and an insular home for girls were also among the important projects, while a fifth hospital in the metropolitan area of the capital of San Juan was designed in conjunction with the medical college there.

The importance of these designs to the planning program as a whole results from Neutra's design approach. First, architectural treatment was completely compatible with the warm tropical climate. The outdoors was used as a space auxiliary with no additional building cube and no extra cost. Building types developed in the temperate zones were carefully restudied in their relationship to the function of heat economy. For example, it might be extravagant to propose in New York a pavillion for contagious diseases with an adjacent wing for services—janitor's and doctor's wash-rooms, serving pantries, sterilizing and utility rooms—all laid between two different corridors. One of them is the "contaminated" corridor used after contact with the patients and the other is the clean corridor for use after being disinfected. Such a double corridor is expensive to build, to heat and to ventilate. But in Puerto Rico these two "corridors" are simply two inexpensive roof projections. The scheme is therefore feasible.

The second feature of the Neutra approach is his unit design which allows a standardization of rooms to be used in different arrangements for different sites. According to the needs of the specific community, more or fewer rooms can be employed to form a complete building. The classroom units, for instance, can be used singly or in rows to form buildings of various lengths. Hurricane resistant reinforced concrete of standardized design is the favored building material. Besides hollow concrete tile, other shop or yard-made elements and a number of prefabrication schemes were studied to facilitate transportation over poor truck roads to scattered village sites, and to reduce work on the premises.

The Neutra designs were approved by the Public Works Committee last May and one of the schools has already been built. It is expected that Puerto Rico will be able to carry through its project if current expenses are kept low, normal federal participation continued and existing economic relations with the United States undisturbed.

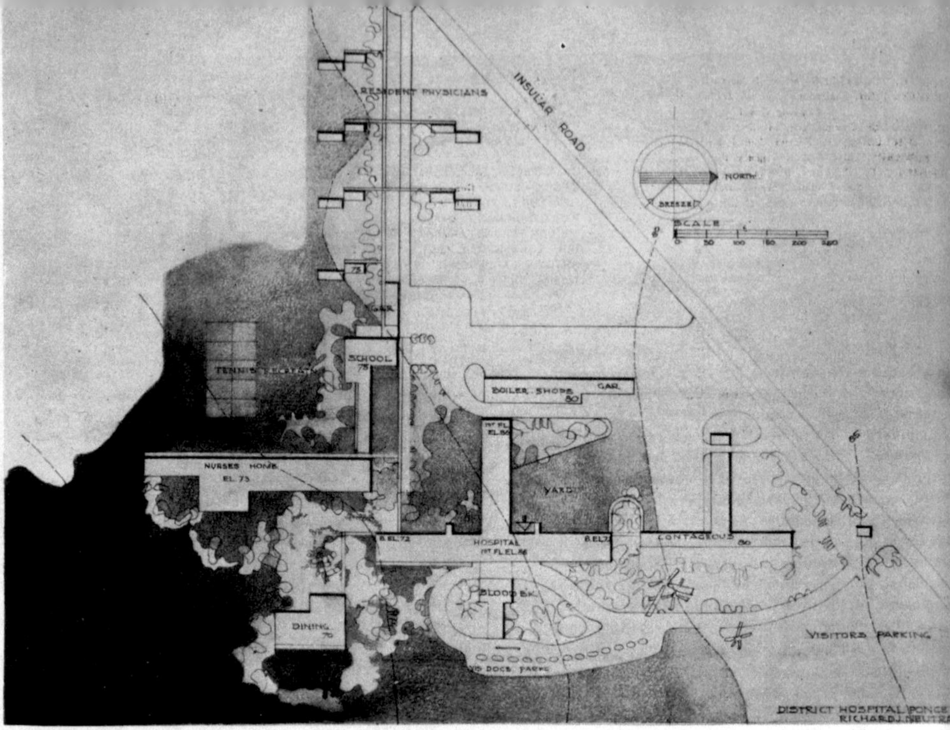

HOSPITALS are divided into separate units for varied grouping and future expansion

The Puerto Rican hospitals have been designed as a group of separately functioning but related units, thus allowing better isolation and more advantageous site arrangement. Scheduled for already purchased plots of thirty to forty acres in the midst of a magnificient tropical landscape, they are oriented to take advantage of trade winds, land and sea breezes during both night and day. Their thoughtfully executed design anticipates future expansion. Principal multi-story buildings for patients, nurses and nursing students are grouped together while the one-story dining building and resident physicians' dwellings branch from the central area. A contagious pavillion has also been designed although it will not be included in every group. In addition to the actual hospital buildings, a large consolidated laundry and other central facilities such as laboratories and a common drug center will service the institutions.

Among the most important projects of this sort are the large district hospitals for Ponce containing 600 beds, those for Mayaguez and Caguas with 500 beds each and for Guyama with a 300 bed capacity. Simplicity and economy of both initial cost and maintenance keynote of all these structures. They characterize a coming era when tropical countries will enter a level of advanced technology heretofore found only in temperate zones.

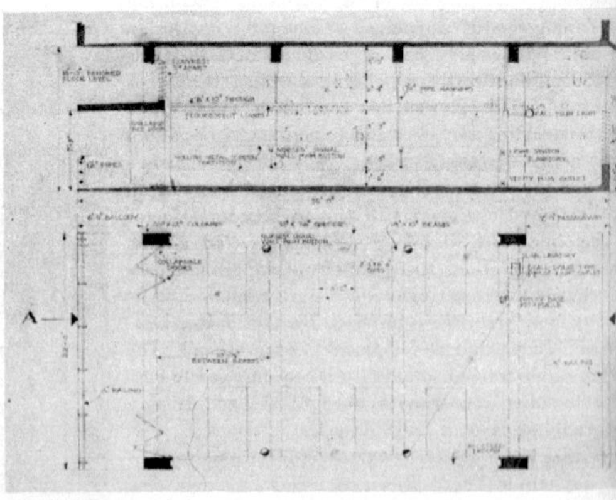

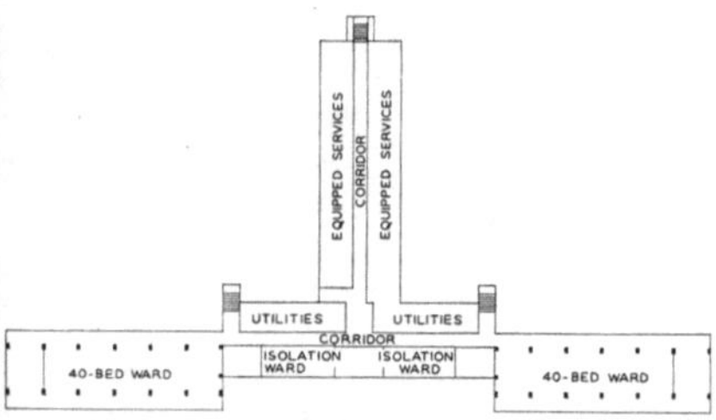

TYPICAL WARD

Wings of the extremely narrow main hospital buildings from back to front are open to breezes from both directions. Movable louvered blinds make these rooms no more than semi-interiors, but they are protected from tropical insects by non-corrosive screening which covers all open areas including balconies. A generous roof overhang excludes excessive sunshine. Glazed windows and mechanical air conditioning are used sparingly in the hospital buildings and are restricted almost entirely to the area of adjunct services such as surgical and delivery suites and certain isolation rooms.

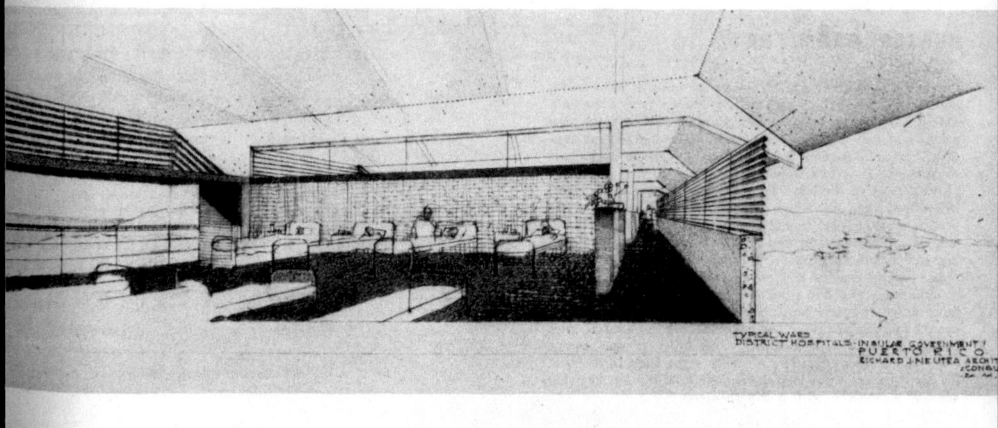

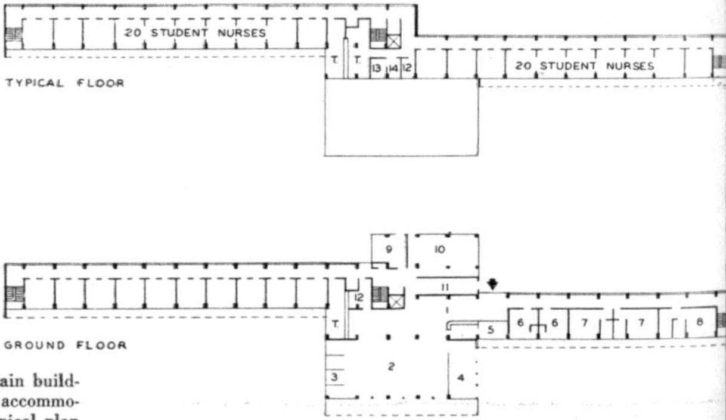

NURSES' DORMITORY

Living space for nurses necessarily occupies a main building in any hospital group, the one shown here accommodating 300 nurses, students and graduates. Its typical plan consists of two wings, six stories high, and a central area which extends beyond the building line at one-and-a-half story height to form a communal living room equipped with visitors' bays on the left side, a reading alcove on the right. Doors lead from this room to open courts. The rest of the central area on the ground floor is occupied by an information and mail center and two rooms at the rear for sorting and distributing linen. The right wing contains single rooms for instructors and an apartment for the matron in charge, while the left wing is divided into bedroom-living room units designed for two nurses. These rooms are repeated in both wings of the upper floors, the central area being equipped with a shower and toilet group, sewing room and kitchenette. The top floor right wing is reserved for night nurses who sleep during the day, the left remains open as a sundeck with a superb view.

1. Lobby
2. Living room
3. Reception bays
4. Reading room
5. Information and office
6. Individual room
7. Instructors room
8. Matron's apt.
9. Soiled linen.
10. Clean linen
11. Trunk storage
12. Kitchen
13. Sewing
14. Laundry

1. Nurse in charge
2. Examining Doctor
3. Bath
4. Nurse's station
5. Utility
6. Service pantry
7. Dish steril:zer
8. Nurses' toilet
9. Patients' bath
0. Doctors' toilet
1. Laboratory
2. Scrub-up
3. Sterilizer
4. Operating

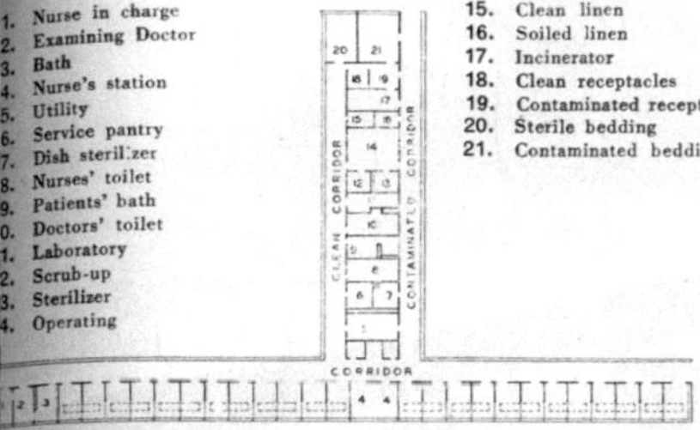

15. Clean linen
16. Soiled linen
17. Incinerator
18. Clean receptacles
19. Contaminated receptacles
20. Sterile bedding
21. Contaminated bedding

ONTAGIOUS PAVILION

solation for contagious diseases is provided by a separate ne-story building connected to the main hospital by a cov- red walk. Individual rooms for patients occupy the top ection of the T-shaped structure. An operating room, aboratory, sterilizing rooms, space for clean and soiled nen and bedding, toilets, baths and an incinerator are laced in a branch which extends from the center of the atients' section. This ingenious design makes possible the se of two separate corridors, clean and contaminated, laced on either side of the service rooms. As mentioned efore, these corridors eliminate the danger of spreading isease, since one is used after contact with patients, the ther only after nurse or doctor has been disinfected. Iade merely by extending the roof, they add little to the uilding cost.

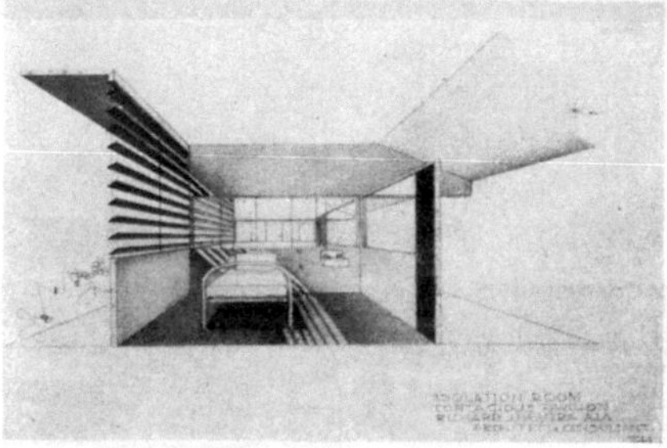

ILLAGE HEALTH CENTER

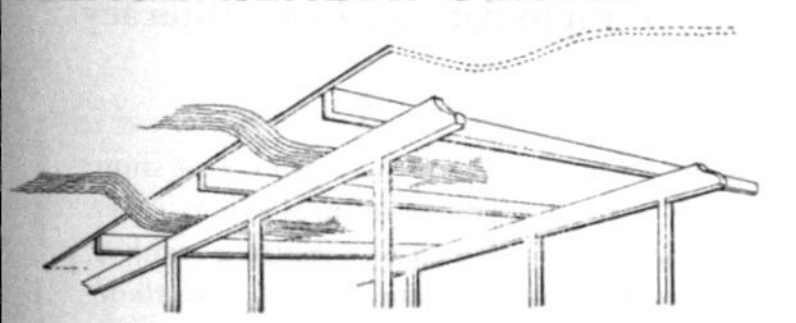

Ventilated roof construction

esigned to bring a social health service into the nall villages of the interior, the health centers are istinguished from hospital clinics in that they practice reventive medicine and "case holding"—attracting ersons with incipient tuberculosis, venereal disease or milar ailments to systematic repeat visits—rather than ealing with cases of acute illness. In addition to this nction, the health centers are intended as meeting laces where the "Jibaros," the poor mountain peasants, ay enjoy their own social life, play dominos in the vening, strum a guitar or dance on the spacious porch. eutra has provided a bench around the wide opening the milk dispensary, making it into a stage for teach- s or entertainers addressing the assembled community. uitable programs will teach the villagers about child re, diet, cloth making and housekeeping. Neutra's tent is to dissolve the "institutional" character of these nters and make the villagers—who for centuries had ttle reason to trust a distant government—feel that e buildings are their own community property.

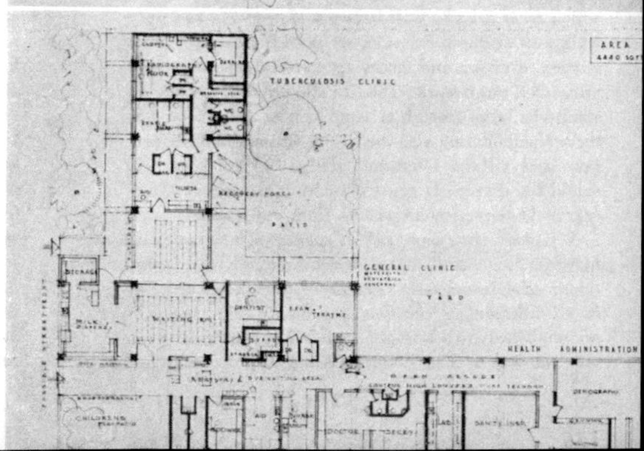

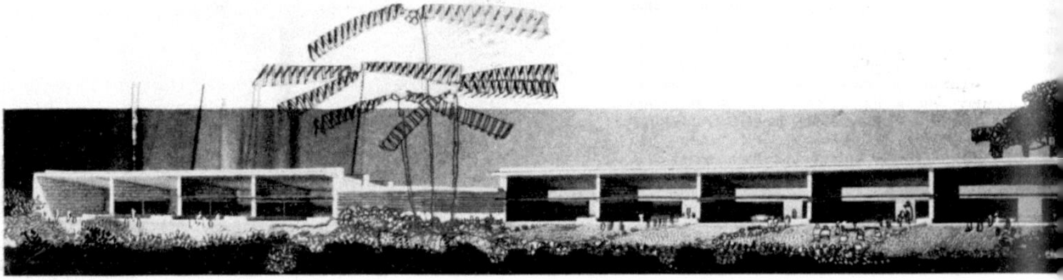

SCHOOLS are planned by the hundreds in Puerto Rico's campaign against illiteracy.

Of all necessary projects none will so profoundly influence the long-exploited peasant population as the building of rural schools. To insure educational facilities for the maximum number of communities, therefore, Neutra has designed his schools as classroom units complete in themselves, thus permitting the construction of one or many rooms according to specific needs and providing great flexibility of arrangement. Each classroom expands and opens into an outdoor court on one side, doubling the useful instructional area without increasing costly building cubage. Lockable compartments which form a baffle wall between classrooms and open walkways on the other side, are used for storing books, writing, drafting and modeling materials together with unfinished pupil work. The site allotted to these schools should be large enough to serve as a neighborhood center accommodating also the health station, milk dispensary and village fountain. Hedges of hibiscus will shield the extremely open plan from outside view and segregate the open air courts from each other.

A typical classroom **(1)** is airy and informal with movable stools and tables, reminiscent of the conventional schoolroom only because of its blackboard. As in all interiors, a continuous sub-soffit air change is accomplished with lowered spandrel spanning between the end walls. The sloping ceiling aids in reflecting light toward the work area. The industrial arts shop **(2)** is an open space under a roof projection, carefully planned for specialized use. Drafting tables, electric wiring tables, wood-working benches with their machine tools and a metal working bench are carefully segregated from each other. A gluing table, painting bench and blueprint tank are near the sink adjacent to the drafting area. Separated from the shop proper by a glass panel, a smaller room offers space for storage, a library, planning table, and instructor's desk. The home economics laboratory **(3)** is placed near the shop structure at some distance from the quiet academic areas. A well-articulated space idea provides a combined cooking and sewing area open to the living room where meal service and managing of living quarters is taught. This is one of the few classrooms having continuous fenestration and is further distinguished by a small porch and model garden at its entrance. Lunch facilities **(4)** are designed as cafeterias for quick serving. The children form a line which passes handwashing troughs on one side of the building, files into the interior past the serving counter, and scatters to tables. Scraping and stacking of their own dishes is done outdoors at the other side of the building and china, glasses and cutlery are then taken into the dishwashing department of the kitchen.

1. TYPICAL CLASSROOM

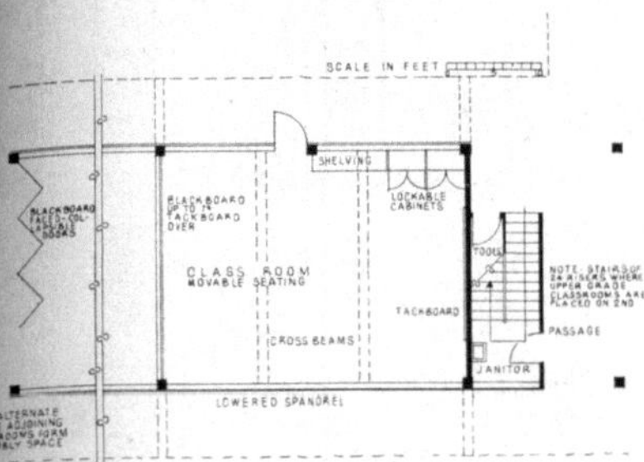

2. INDUSTRIAL ARTS

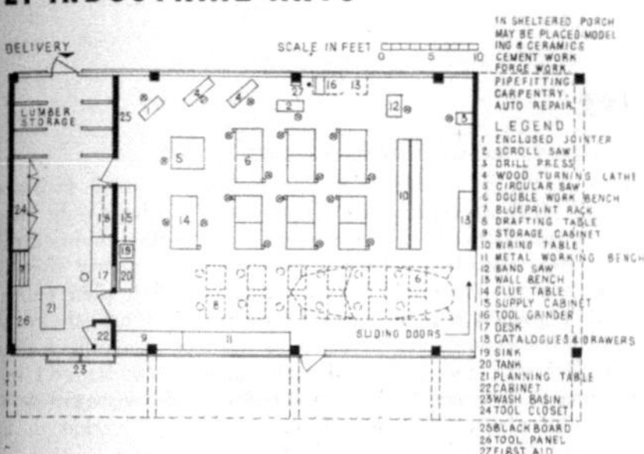

3. HOME ECONOMICS

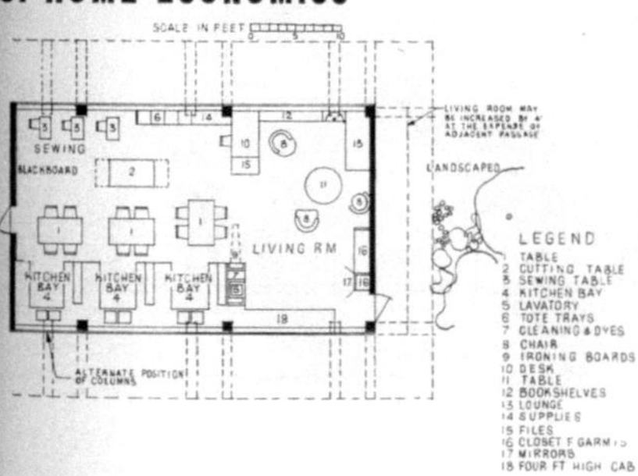

4. LUNCH FACILITIES

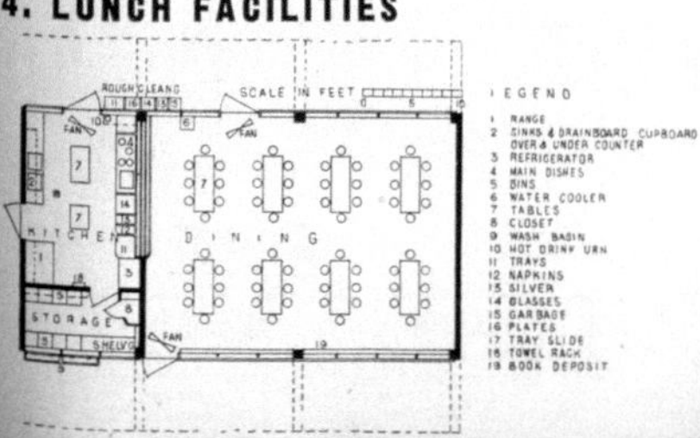

5. SCIENCE

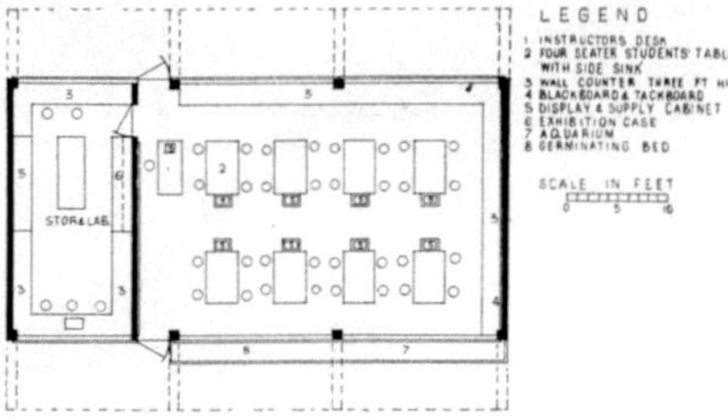

6. ADMINISTRATION

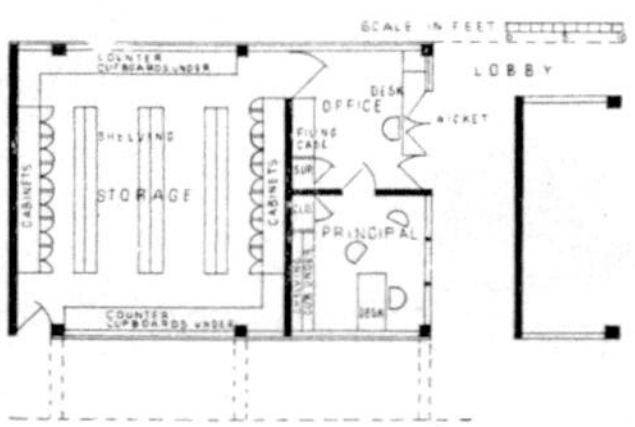

7. TOILETS

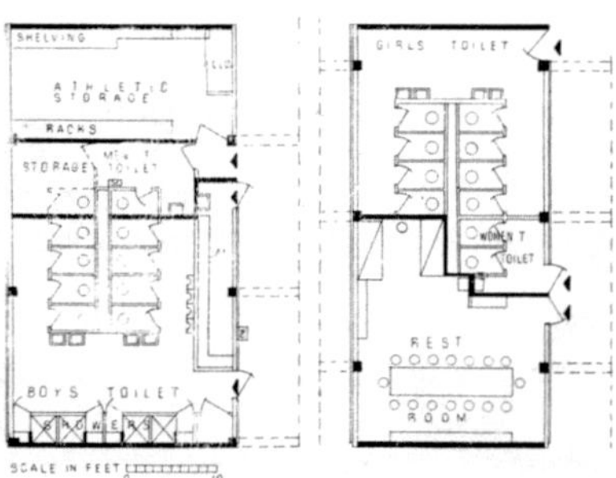

Science rooms **(5)** are not too specialized, but fit diversified programming without waste. Instead of distant storage for each science, extra equipment is kept in a small adjoining storage and laboratory room which may also serve for individualized experimentation. The main room is equipped with demonstration table, regular school seats and a bench along the window front. The outside science court is particularly important since it may be used to study soil cultivation and for observing living insects, reptiles, birds, etc. Administration offices **(6)** including a reception room for visitors, principal's office and teachers' restroom, are near the building entrance. Toilets **(7)** have separate sections for teachers and students. Showers and a space for athletic storage is included in the men's room.

GROUPING

School units can be arranged in innumerable combinations, but mus be oriented to catch the breeze. For this reason, enclosed patios an the conventional block arrangement of rooms with windows only on on side are never used. Instead, single rows or freestanding rooms are th rule. Of the many variations, three are shown to illustrate the flexi bility possible with the same schoolroom units. The first plan (above) an L-shaped arrangement plus a long separate row, is for a square plo Lower grades and restrooms are grouped in the free row, upper grade are in the parallel row, and industrial arts, home economics and lunc facilities are apart from quiet classroom areas. This segregation is keynote of all the plans. The second one (below) is varied to fit long, narrow site, the third (bottom) is a two-story plan.

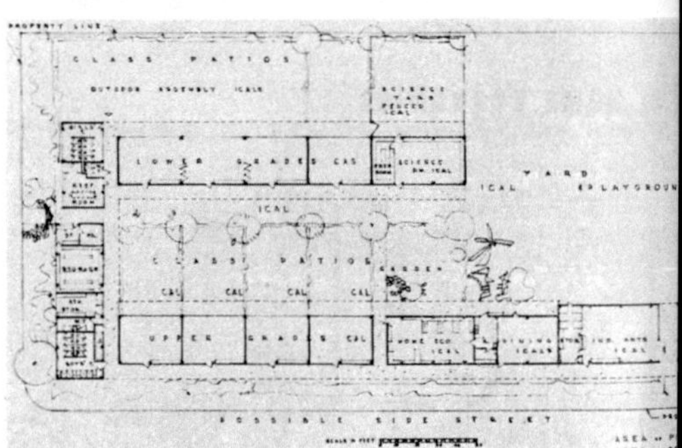

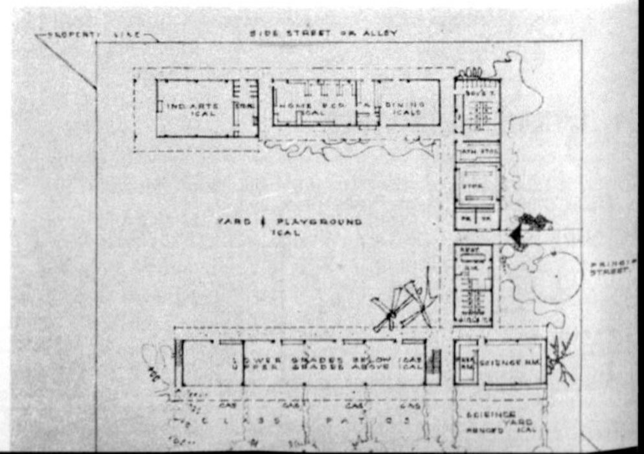

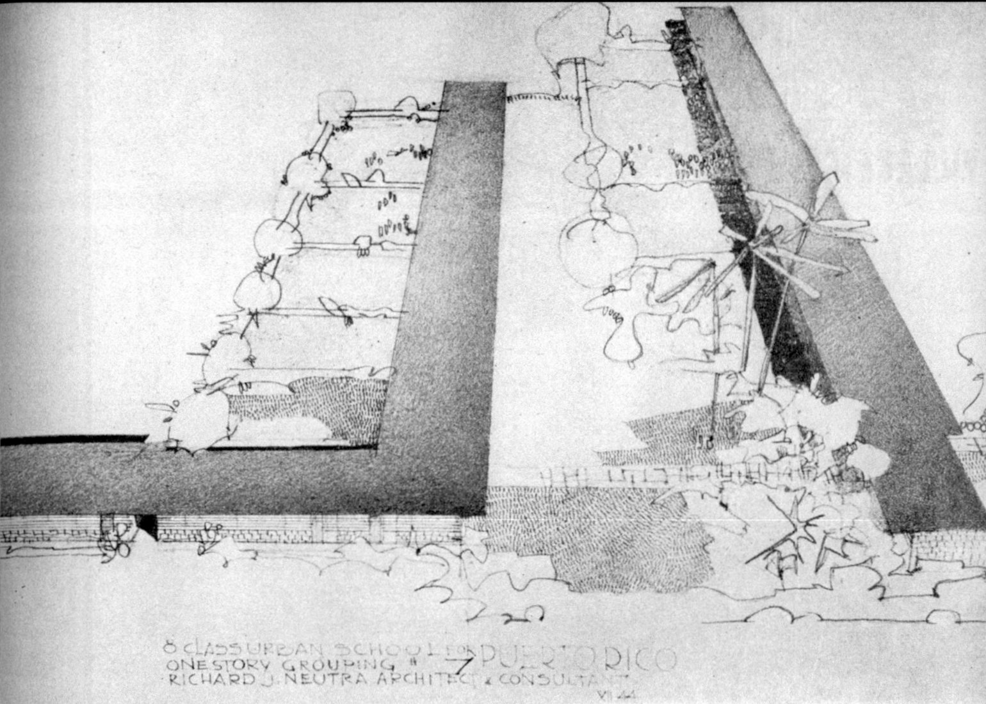
8 CLASS URBAN SCHOOL FOR PUERTO RICO
ONE STORY GROUPING # 7
RICHARD J. NEUTRA ARCHITECT & CONSULTANT
XII 44

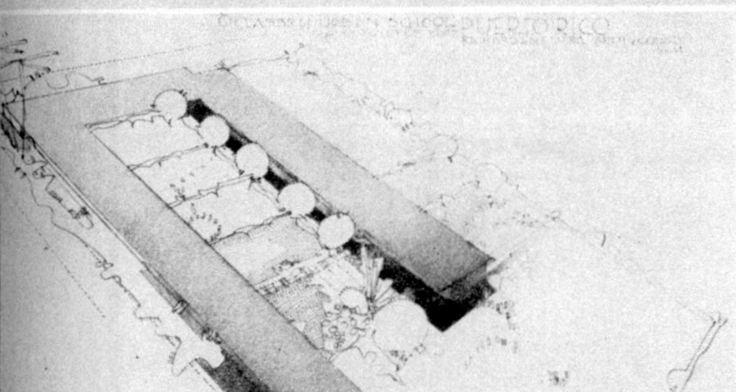
PUERTO RICO

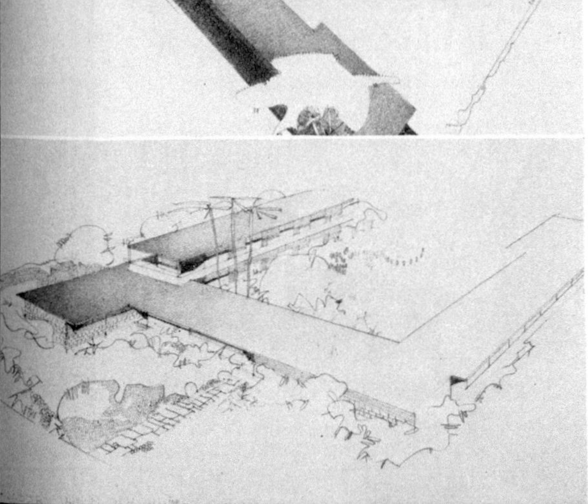

VILLAGE CENTER

One of the most important ideas in the Neutra plan is his grouping together of school, health center, and, in larger villages, a social hall to provide some real focus for community life. Here music and entertainment, partly provided by the villagers themselves, partly by teachers or professionals, will help to make the people feel that the center belongs to them. Adult education will also be carried on—sewing clubs, agricultural meetings, classes in animal husbandry, plus broadcast programs of news and civic issues. With this end in mind, Neutra has related the design of all the buildings to insure a harmonious group.

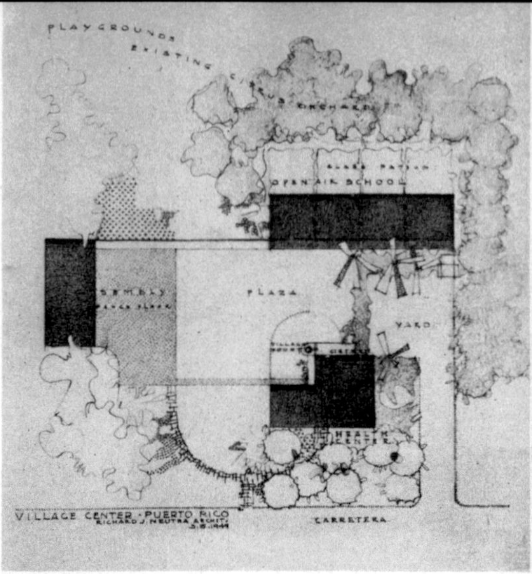

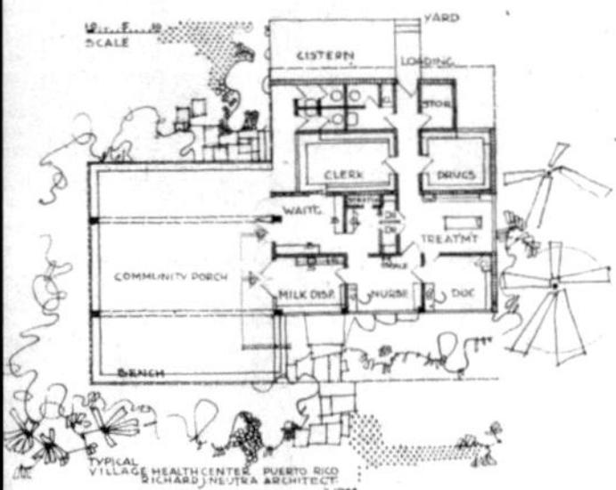

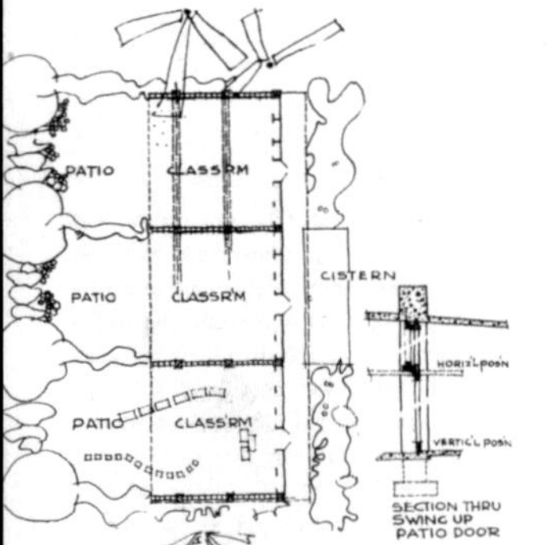

INTRODUCTION

Under date of September 8, 1945, The Standard Oil Development Company issued an "Invitation for Proposals for Architectural Work, Engineering and Construction, Employees' Housing Project at Turiamo, Venezuela, for the Creole Petroleum Corporation."

Subsequently, the Turiamo site was abandoned, and a new site selected for the refinery and housing project at Amuay Bay, on Paraguana Peninsula in northwestern Venezuela.

This housing project is to be a complete community for Venezuelan and expatriate employees and their families, and will be adjacent to the proposed refinery and terminal.

Not only must the completed project satisfy the letter and spirit of the Venezuelan labor laws pertaining to employees' living conditions but must also "conform to Creole's own employees' welfare policy and its desire to cooperate with the Venezuelan Government in its program of social advancement for the nation."

A study at first hand of the project site and the oil refinery and producing camps in Venezuela, Aruba and Curacao, was considered a prerequisite for the design of the new community.

To this end architects, site planners, and engineers, visited the site and also many oil camps. The management responsible for the operation of these camps, and the residents, were interviewed with regard to the sociological, economic, and maintenance problems encountered. Also discussed were ways and means of avoiding such problems in the future.

During the survey, extending over a period of five weeks, the following communities were visited:

1. Site of proposed Creole refinery and housing development, Paraguana Peninsula.
2. Shell Camp, El Cardon, Paraguana Peninsula.

3. Mene Grande Camp, Paraguana Peninsula.
4. Creole Camp, Quire Quire.
5. Creole Camp, Carapito.
6. Consolidada Camp, Santa Barbara.
7. Consolidada Camp, Guanta.
8. Mene Grande Camp, Puerto de la Cruz.
9. Creole Camp, Jusepin.
10. Mene Grande Camp, San Tome.
11. Socony-Vacuum Camp, Anaco.
12. Mene Grande-Creole-Shell Camp, Tia Juana.
13. Western Division Headquarters, Creole, Maracaibo.
14. Lago Oil & Transport Co. Camp, Aruba, N. W. I.
15. Creole Camp, La Salina.
16. Shell Camp, Palmarejo.
17. Richmond Development Co., Maracaibo.
18. Shell Central Headquarters, Maracaibo.
19. Mene Grande Camp, Maracaibo.
20. Shell Refinery, Curacao.
21. Pro Patria, Artigas, Paraiso.
    Belle Monte and Country Club, Caracas.
22. Urbaniacion "Caribe", Macuto.
23. Obrero Bank Housing Development, Maracaibo.

In addition to the above, construction methods and architectural trends were observed in many other Venezuelan communities.

The following study and report represents the recommendations of the engineering and architectural firms of Skidmore, Owings and Merrill-Philip Ives, Associated; Bechtel Brothers McCone Company; and the Raymond Concrete Pile Company; for the design and construction of the refinery community described in the "Invitation for Proposals," issued by the Standard Oil Development Company.

Skidmore, Owings & Merrill, Creole Petroleum Corporation, Amuay Bay, Venezuela, S.A.

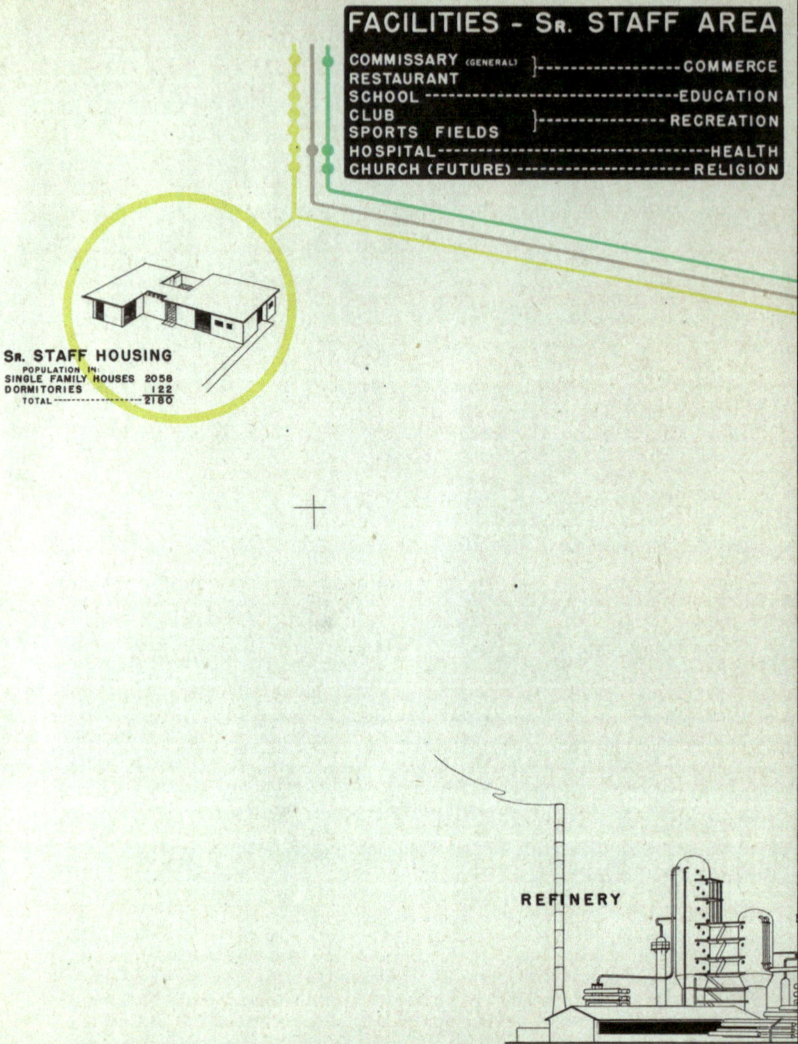

ORGANIZATION OF

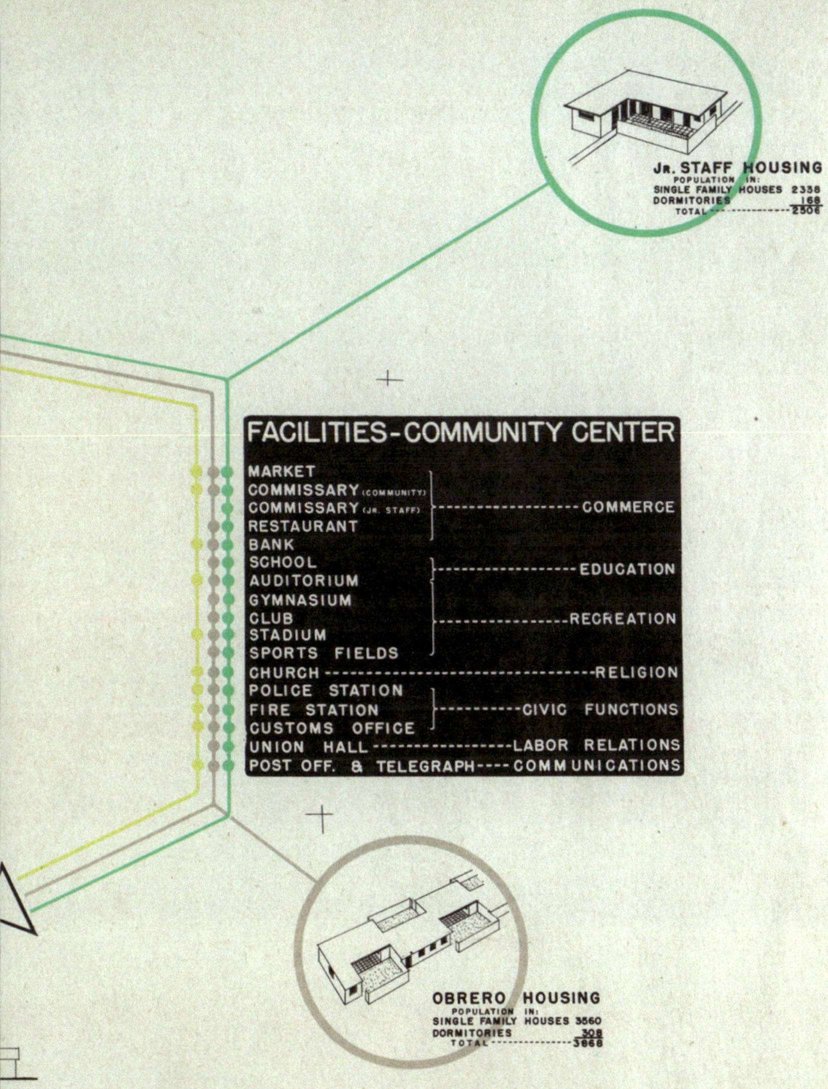

OMMUNITY FACILITIES

Skidmore, Owings & Merrill, Creole Petroleum Corporation, Amuay Bay, Venezuela, S.A.

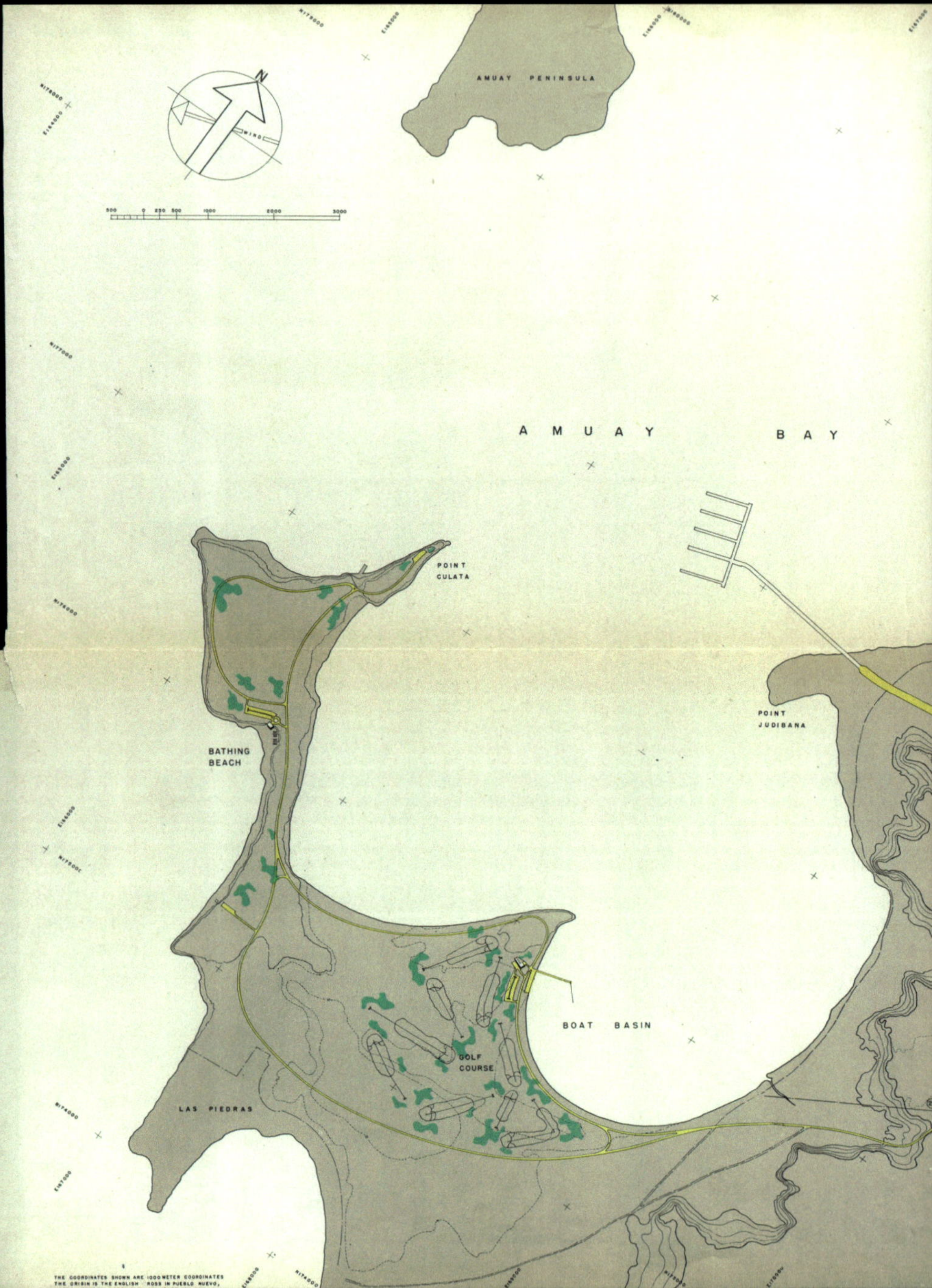

1946

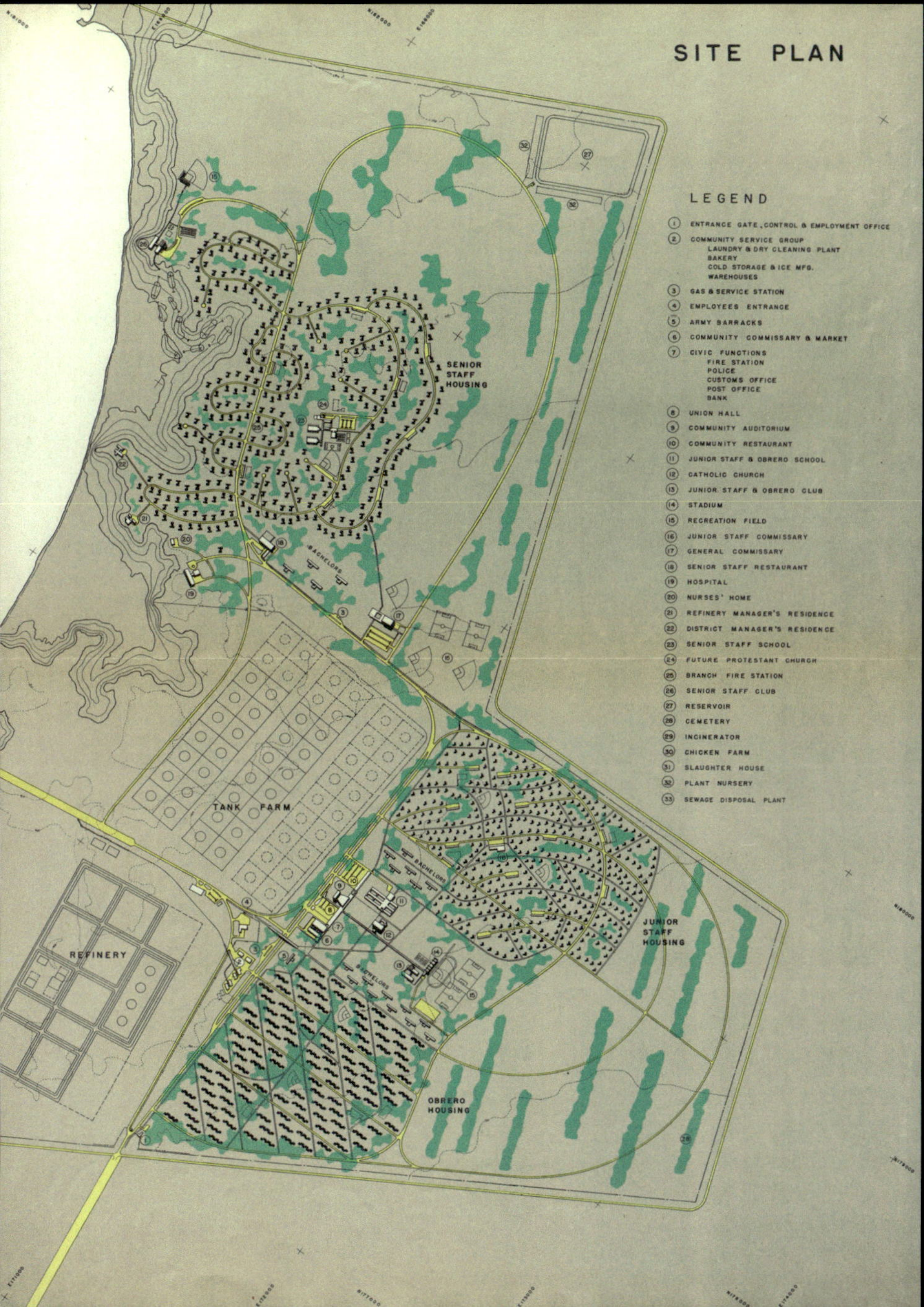
SITE PLAN
LEGEND
1 ENTRANCE GATE, CONTROL & EMPLOYMENT OFFICE
2 COMMUNITY SERVICE GROUP
LAUNDRY & DRY CLEANING PLANT
BAKERY
COLD STORAGE & ICE MFG.
WAREHOUSES
3 GAS & SERVICE STATION
4 EMPLOYEES ENTRANCE
5 ARMY BARRACKS
6 COMMUNITY COMMISSARY & MARKET
7 CIVIC FUNCTIONS
FIRE STATION
POLICE
CUSTOMS OFFICE
POST OFFICE
BANK
8 UNION HALL
9 COMMUNITY AUDITORIUM
10 COMMUNITY RESTAURANT
11 JUNIOR STAFF & OBRERO SCHOOL
12 CATHOLIC CHURCH
13 JUNIOR STAFF & OBRERO CLUB
14 STADIUM
15 RECREATION FIELD
16 JUNIOR STAFF COMMISSARY
17 GENERAL COMMISSARY
18 SENIOR STAFF RESTAURANT
19 HOSPITAL
20 NURSES' HOME
21 REFINERY MANAGER'S RESIDENCE
22 DISTRICT MANAGER'S RESIDENCE
23 SENIOR STAFF SCHOOL
24 FUTURE PROTESTANT CHURCH
25 BRANCH FIRE STATION
26 SENIOR STAFF CLUB
27 RESERVOIR
28 CEMETERY
29 INCINERATOR
30 CHICKEN FARM
31 SLAUGHTER HOUSE
32 PLANT NURSERY
33 SEWAGE DISPOSAL PLANT
SENIOR STAFF HOUSING
BACHELORS
TANK FARM
REFINERY
JUNIOR STAFF HOUSING
OBRERO HOUSING

Skidmore, Owings & Merrill, Creole Petroleum Corporation, Amuay Bay, Venezuela, S.A.

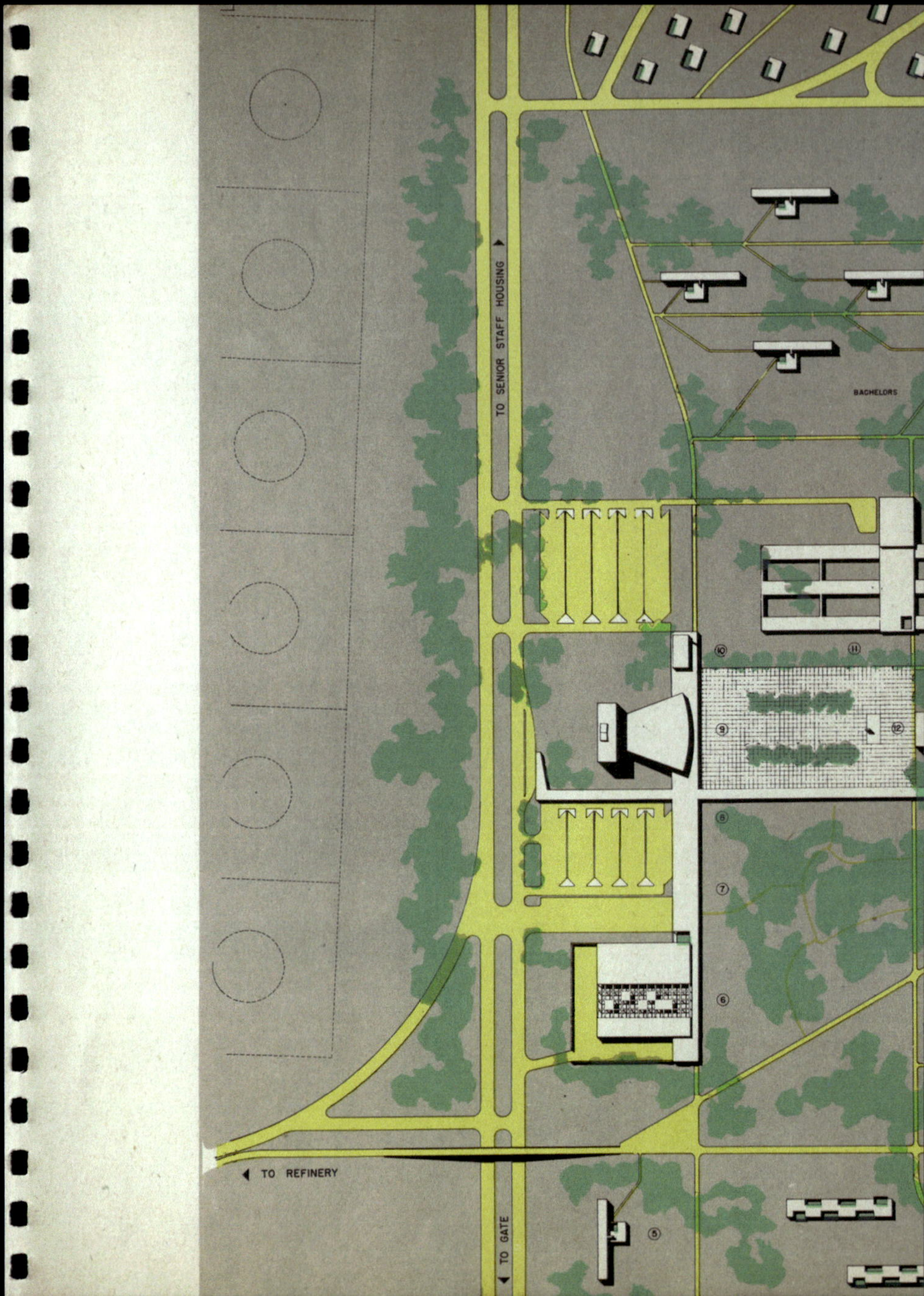

1946

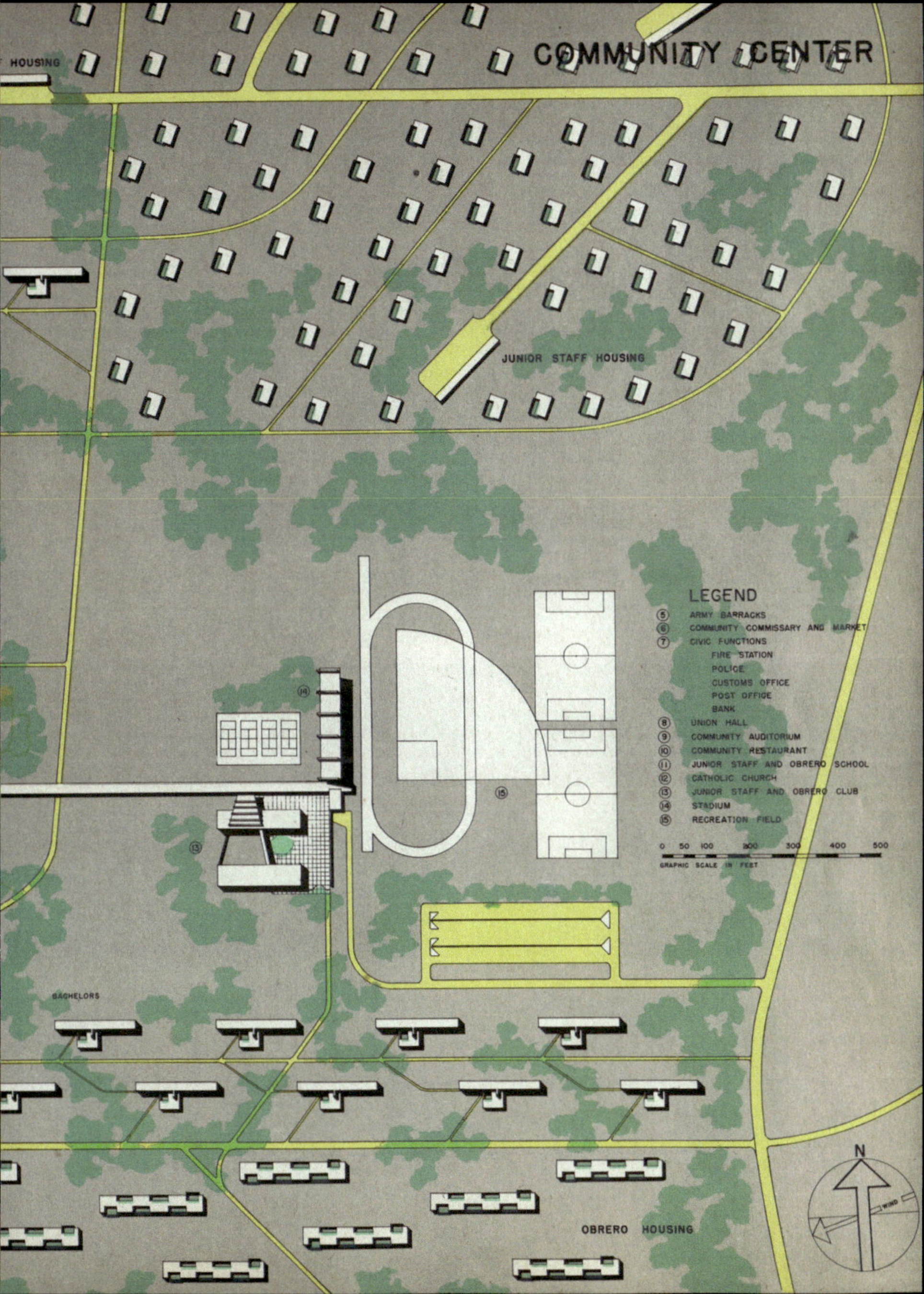
COMMUNITY CENTER
HOUSING
JUNIOR STAFF HOUSING
LEGEND
⑤ ARMY BARRACKS
⑥ COMMUNITY COMMISSARY AND MARKET
⑦ CIVIC FUNCTIONS
FIRE STATION
POLICE
CUSTOMS OFFICE
POST OFFICE
BANK
⑧ UNION HALL
⑨ COMMUNITY AUDITORIUM
⑩ COMMUNITY RESTAURANT
⑪ JUNIOR STAFF AND OBRERO SCHOOL
⑫ CATHOLIC CHURCH
⑬ JUNIOR STAFF AND OBRERO CLUB
⑭ STADIUM
⑮ RECREATION FIELD
0 50 100 200 300 400 500
GRAPHIC SCALE IN FEET
14
15
13
BACHELORS
OBRERO HOUSING
N
WIND

Skidmore, Owings & Merrill, Creole Petroleum Corporation, Amuay Bay, Venezuela, S.A.

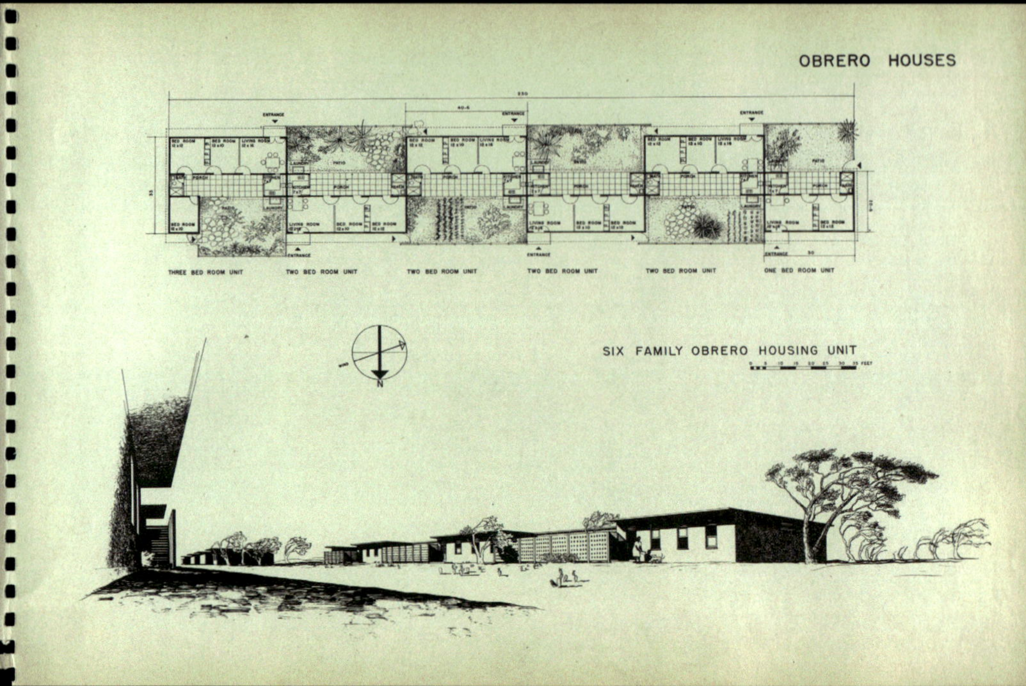

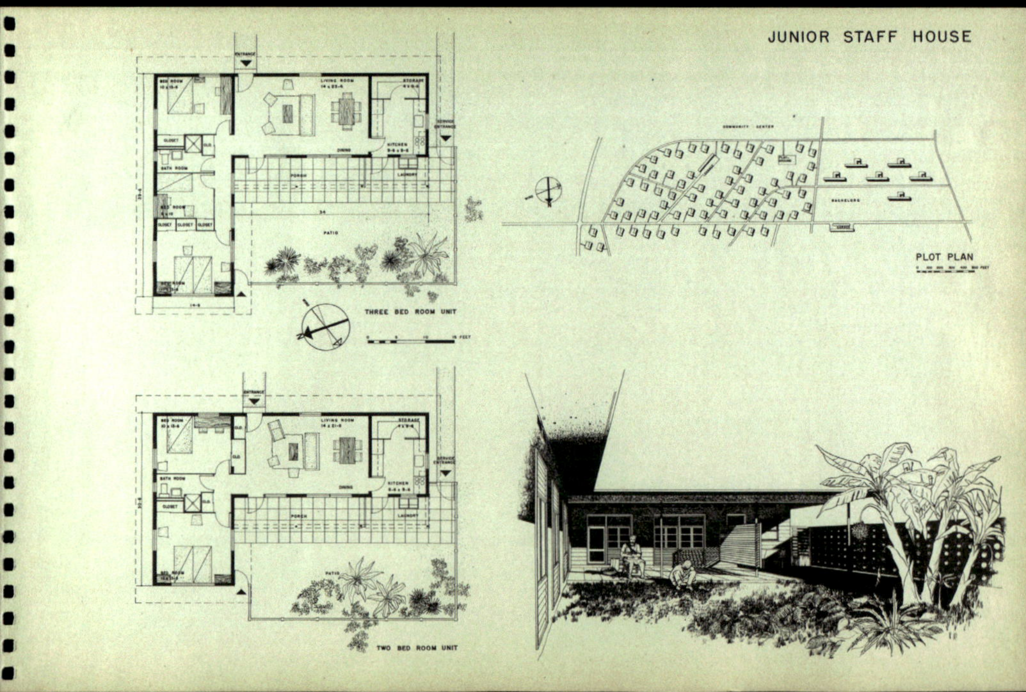

REFINERY MANAGER'S HOUSE

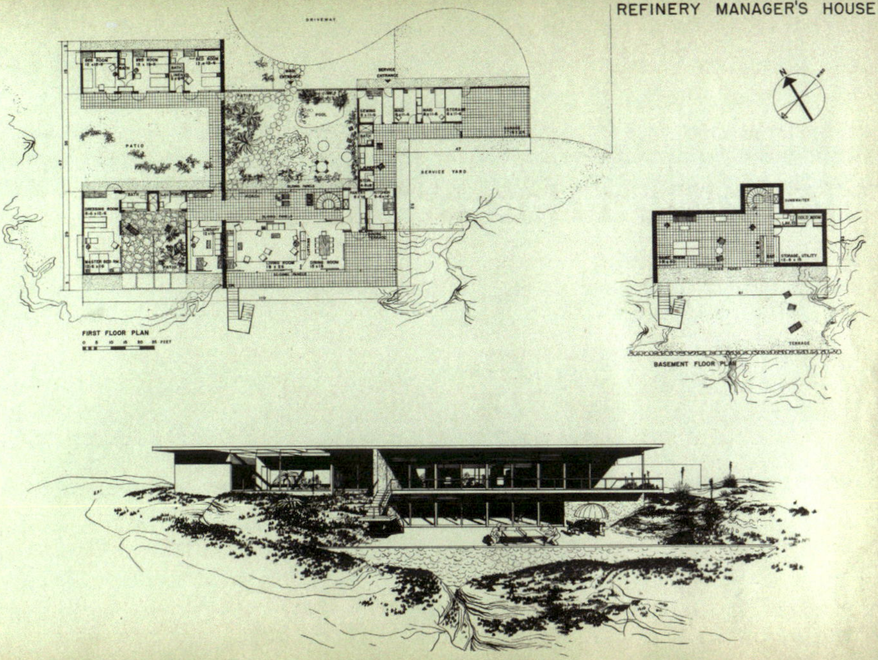

SENIOR STAFF CLUB

1948–1959

Oficina Don Hatch

Headquarters
Caracas, Venezuela; New York, NY

Founding Partners
Donald Hatch, Michael Hare

1948

1959

Progressive Architecture, March 1954

Oficina Don Hatch, founded in 1948, was one half of a two-part office structure that provided a permanent presence in Caracas for the architectural partnership of Donald Hatch and Michael Hare. The other half, Hare and Hatch in New York, handled national projects and provided support for the Caracas office. As Hatch put it, the dual office structure was created "to provide an organization capable of bringing the requisite professional technical skill to bear on building problems in Venezuela and to have the necessary staff available in New York or Caracas, as the need arose."[1]

The office was conceived after Hatch went to Venezuela in 1948 as the chief architect of the Venezuela Basic Economic Corporation (VBEC), a Rockefeller-funded project. After completion of multiple projects for the VBEC, Hatch and Hare, who had met while serving in the Marine Corps during World War II, simultaneously opened offices in Caracas and New York.

Although Oficina Don Hatch lasted only ten years and its staff never exceeded twenty, its production was prolific both for its quantity and diversity, including the Macoroma House (1951), Las Mercedes commercial center (1952–1955), Mobil Oil Corporation's Sucre Building (1959), Hotel Balneario, a Chrysler-Plymouth showroom, Galleria Don Hatch, NCR Building, and US embassies in Caracas (1957) and Port-au-Prince (1955–1959).

Oficina Don Hatch was one of the first professional architecture practices in Venezuela, and its most valuable import was the implementation of American construction and design standards. The work, driven by the oil boom in Venezuela of the 1940s and 1950s, was part of a larger narrative of foreign interventions in the city during the military dictatorship of Marcos Perez Jimenez. Soon after the end of the Jimenez dictatorship in 1958, Oficina Don Hatch closed its doors. — JJ

(1)
Don Hatch, quoted in "The Architect and His Community; Caracas, Venezuela," *Progressive Architecture* (March 1954): 100.

1949–
2010

Yamasaki and Associates

Headquarters
Troy, MI

Other Locations
Detroit, MI; St. Louis, MO

Founding and Key Partners
Minoru Yamasaki, George Hellmuth,
Joseph Leinweber (founding principals),
Gyo Obata, George Kassabaum

1949

2010

Ezra Stoller, Esto

The American-born son of immigrants, Minoru Yamasaki grew up in Seattle, Washington, a city in which he described suffering a strong racial bias against Japanese inhabitants. At the University of Washington he was denied a scholarship to attend the Society de Beaux Arts in Paris, despite having among the best grades in the history of the school, a slight he perceived as a blatant act of racial discrimination. After earning a graduate degree in architecture in New York in 1936 he took a position in the working drawings department of Shreve, Lamb & Harmon, architects of the Empire State Building. Following the attack on Pearl Harbor in 1941, his family joined him in the city to avoid relocation to Japanese internment camps on the West Coast. After working for Harrison, Fouilhoux & Abramovitz and a brief collaboration with George Nelson, in 1945 he became chief designer at Smith, Hinchman and Grylls in Detroit, the city where he spent the rest of his career.

In 1949 Yamasaki and two other principals of the firm, George Hellmuth and Joseph Leinweber, left to form the firm of Hellmuth, Yamasaki & Leinweber, with offices in Detroit and St. Louis. The firm's first major public building was the terminal for Lambert International Airport in St. Louis (1951–1956), an early example of the use of a repeating structural module of arched and vaulted elements that would characterize Yamasaki's later airports in Boston and Saudi Arabia. The commission to design the US Consulate in Kobe, Japan, in 1954 allowed Yamasaki to travel throughout Europe, India, and Southeast Asia, an experience he credited with beginning his introduction of historicist elements into his work.

In 1954 a near-fatal stomach illness forced Yamasaki to consolidate his practice in Detroit, the strain of running two offices having become too stressful. Hellmuth took the St. Louis office and joined with employees Gyo Obata and George Kassabaum to form the office of Hellmuth, Obata + Kassabaum (HOK), thereafter one of the largest firms in the country. Yamasaki consolidated his practice in Detroit as Yamasaki & Associates. Institutional and office projects in Michigan followed. In 1959 the office received the commission to design the US Pavilion for the Agricultural Industries Fair in New Delhi, India, featuring a module of gold onion domes supported on diagonal cross beams.

In the same year, the US Army Corps of Engineers and its contractor, the Parsons Company of Los Angeles, hired Yamasaki & Associates to design a civil airport terminal in Dhahran, Saudi Arabia. Donated by the US government in exchange for land to build a US air force base, the terminal was intended primarily to serve east-west international traffic, particularly leisure travel to Europe and the United States for Aramco employees based in Dhahran. The airport led to several other projects in the country, including the Eastern Province International Airport near Damman (1977) and the headquarters of the Saudi Monetary Agency in Riyadh (1978–1981).

With a staff of eighty employees by 1979, Yamasaki & Associates had become a large firm known equally for its international commissions and for corporate commissions in the United States. The office continued operation under the same name after Yamasaki's death from stomach cancer in 1986. In later years, Yamasaki's legacy became indelibly associated with the tragic fates, nearly thirty years apart, of two tower complexes designed by his firm: the demolition of the Pruitt-Igoe housing complex in St. Louis, Missouri, in 1972—an event famously labeled by critic Charles Jencks as the official death date of the modern movement in architecture—and the destruction of the World Trade Center towers in New York in 2001. In 2009, the office was forced to shut down amidst a number of lawsuits filed by clients for outstanding contracts and payments. —AWS & MK

1949–
1994

Edward Larrabee Barnes Associates

Headquarters
New York, NY

Founding and Key Partners
Edward Larrabee Barnes, Mary Barnes (founding principals), John M.Y. Lee, Percy Keck, Alistair MacFarlane Bevington

1949

1994

Architectural Record, June 1987

Edward Larrabee Barnes won the Sheldon travelling fellowship in 1942 upon his graduation from Harvard Graduate School of Design, where he had studied under Walter Gropius and Marcel Breuer. As his travel was limited by World War II he spent his fellowship year in Washington as an intern in the Division of Defense Housing. Following Pearl Harbor he enlisted in the US Navy and served as a naval architect until the end of World War II. Before he opened his own office in New York in 1949, Barnes spent a short period working for architect William Wurster in San Francisco, followed by a stint in the office of the industrial designer Henry Dreyfuss in Los Angeles. Two years after opening his own office, Barnes' wife, Mary Cooke, joined him as the interior designer in the practice after spending two years as a curator at the Museum of Modern Art (MoMA) in New York. The office designed a series of small, modern houses in the early 1950s before acquiring its first large commissions, the Haystack Mountain School of Arts (1962) on Deer Isle, Maine, and the El Monte Renewal Project (1958–1961) in San Juan, Puerto Rico. Other major commissions followed, including the Walker Art Center in Minneapolis (1971), the IBM headquarters in Manhattan (1983), and the Dallas Art Museum (1984). Barnes would come to be known for his lack of a signature style—the subject of both positive and negative critique in regards to his vast body of work.

Though they embody modernist principles, many of the office's projects also displayed a playful lack of adherence to them. Peter Blake praised Barnes for understanding "that a designed building in a participatory democracy, should respond to a great variety of factors and that its ultimate form should express those conditions and demands rather than provide a memorial to its architect or to those that pay the bill."[1]

His only two international commissions, the El Monte Renewal Project and the US Consulate (1958–1966) in Tabriz, Iran came early in his career. The El Monte Apartments was the office's first large-scale overseas project and the only instances in which Barnes engaged in a public housing project. The US consulate in Tabriz, a strange, if beautiful, one-story building of brick domes, is also singular in its style and program at the office. It is one of only two projects that Barnes produced for government institutions.

The office closed when Barnes retired in 1994. Over 500 architects and designers passed through the office during the four decades of its operation. Barnes continued to work as an architectural consultant until his death in 2004.

—JJ

(1) Peter Blake, "Introduction," in Edward Larrabee Barnes, *Edward Larrabee Barnes: Architect* (New York: Rizzoli International Publications, 1995).

1949–
2007

Hugh Stubbins and Associates

Headquarters
Cambridge, MA

Succeeded By
KlingStubbins (2007)

Founding Partner
Hugh Stubbins

1949

2007

The Hugh Stubbins Archive, Courtesy of the Frances Loeb Library, Harvard University Graduate School of Design

While an undergraduate student at Georgia Institute of Technology in Atlanta, Hugh Stubbins received a scholarship to the Harvard Graduate School of Design. Shortly after graduating in 1935, he began working for Boston architect Royal Barry Wills, who had carved out a niche as a designer of Cape Cod colonial houses and welcomed the young architect's input as the housing market started shifting toward modernism. The relationship, which lasted until 1938, was prosperous and beneficial for Stubbins, a junior partner who got equal credit with Wills for the work.

Following his partnership with Wills, Stubbins opened a firm in Cambridge with his classmate Marc Peter. Though the firm was publicly recognized for its work, it failed to receive any real building commissions and Stubbins had to take a job in his hometown, Birmingham, Alabama, with Miller, Martin and Lewis. He spent only six months there before Harvard beckoned him again. In 1940 he won the Wheelwright Traveling Scholarship, and Walter Gropius, who had never personally met Stubbins, invited him to take the role of his assistant in the master's class there. Stubbins chose Gropius over his Wheelwright trip to Europe and spent the rest of his architectural career in the Boston area. He moved through the ranks at the GSD, from teaching assistant to Gropius to assistant and associate professor and finally chair of the Department of Architecture from 1953 until Josep Lluís Sert took over the post.

During World War II, Stubbins left his teaching post in order to put his skills to use at the Harvard Radio Research Laboratory, where he worked on airplane camouflage devices, and later on a heat-sensing eye for the Navy with a team led by the founder of Polaroid. Together with his involvements in the war effort, Stubbins's relationship with Gropius proved decisive in receiving the prestigious commission to design the Congress Hall in Berlin in 1957.

Though he had opened his own practice, Hugh Stubbins and Associates (HSA), in 1949, Stubbins also briefly paired with The Architects Collaborative, working on the Back Bay Center in 1953. HAS's first commission was for the 100-unit Windsor Locks Defense Housing project in 1940, while his first commission over one million dollars, a county school in Weston, Massachusetts, opened in 1955. Around this time the Foreign Buildings Operations office of the US Department of State commissioned HAS to design the US Embassy in Tangiers, Morocco (1955–1961). The success of the firm at this point forced Stubbins to choose between academic work and practice, and he left the GSD for good in 1954. Three years later he incorporated his firm.

Though the Berlin Congress Hall (1955–1957) received a great deal of media attention, it failed to bring other international commissions to the firm, nor did it have any real stylistic effect on the firm's production. In fact, its formal expressiveness is anomalous among the 800 projects credited to HSA, corresponding neither to the atmospheric regional modernism of Stubbins's houses and early institutional work nor to the elegant austerity of the later office towers that marked the skylines of Boston and New York. Employing the largest span for which thin-shell concrete technology had been used up to that time, the Berlin project does belong to the string of "firsts and superlatives" credited to Stubbins. The Congress Hall was followed by Harvard University's Loeb Drama Center (1960). Over the years Stubbins built a series of buildings for Harvard and other universities in the United States. Starting with the construction of HSA's own office building at 1033 Massachusetts Avenue in Cambridge in 1969, the firm entered the realm of office buildings, culminating in two iconic towers: the Federal Reserve Bank in Boston (1977) and, a year later, the Citicorp Center in New York (1978).

From 1983 onward Stubbins began to withdraw from the firm, leaving the practice in 1992, a year before the completion of the Landmark Tower in Yokohama (1990–1993). At the time the building was Yokohama's tallest tower, using a flexible, earthquake-absorbent skeleton built according to HSA's plans. Renamed The Stubbins Associates in 2006, the firm eventually merged with that of another mid-century modernist, Vincent G. Kling, forming the successor firm KlingStubbins in 2007. The office was acquired by Jacobs Engineering in 2013. — AM

ROMA Design Group

Headquarters
San Francisco, CA

Founding and Key Partners
George T. Rockrise (founding principal),
Hervey Parke, John F. Beuttler,
Bob Odermatt, Bob Mountjoy, Jim Amis

1949

George T. Rockrise Collection, Environmental Design Archives, University of California at Berkeley

After graduating from the School of Architecture at Syracuse University, as had his father before him, George T. Rockrise earned his M.S. in Architecture from Columbia University in 1941. Immediately after graduation, he began working in Panama as an architect for the Corps of Engineers Office of the Caribbean Defense Command, the Panama Canal Service, and the US Navy. Rockrise returned to New York City in 1945, where he worked for Edward Durell Stone (collaborating for the first time with the landscape architect Thomas Church) and for Skidmore, Owings & Merrill (SOM). At SOM he worked on the United Nations project in New York City, through which he had direct interactions with Le Corbusier and Oscar Niemeyer, among others. Two years after returning to New York City, Thomas Church invited Rockrise to join him as an associate in his San Francisco practice. Two years later, in 1949, Rockrise established his own office there.

Rockrise worked independently at first, although he partnered with other architects for larger commissions. In its early years, the firm's projects included student housing at the University of California, San Francisco (UCSF) and the University of California, Davis (UC Davis), as well as the redevelopment plan for Market Street in San Francisco. In its early work, the office gained a reputation for landscape design and urban planning in addition to architecture projects.

In 1957, Rockrise joined with Hervey Parke Clark and John Frederick Beuttler, who had established an architectural practice together in San Francisco in 1946, to design the US Consulate in Fukuoka, Japan (1957–1960). The project was one of many awarded to young modernist architects by the Foreign Buildings Operations (FBO) office of the State Department during the 1950s. Although not a significant project in terms of size or complexity, the consulate was widely praised, and featured prominently in various FBO publications. The commission led to a lasting relationship between Rockrise and the FBO, which retained him as an advisor for other projects in Venezuela, Brazil, Germany, and Saudi Arabia. In 1981, the FBO hired Rockrise to design the US Embassy in Manama, Bahrain.

In 1968, Rockrise expanded his practice to include associates Robert Odermatt, Robert Mountjoy, and James Amis, and in 1980 the group founded a joint architecture and planning office, ROMA Design Group. The firm acquired several major commissions throughout the 1980s, continuing its rise as a leading urban design firm in the United States. ROMA has been heavily involved in the reshaping of the San Francisco waterfront since the early 1990s, and has exported its expertise to other countries, including Canada and New Zealand. In 2000, the firm won the competition to design the Martin King Luther, Jr. Memorial in Washington, D.C., and the project was finally completed in 2011. In the last decade, ROMA Design Group has worked on projects around the world, including several proposals for developments in Russia, the Philippines, Singapore, Turkey, and Azerbaijan.
— JJ

Creole Petroleum Town Plan
1946–1951

SOM

Architect
Skidmore, Owings & Merrill

Location
Amuay Bay, Venezuela

Client
Creole Petroleum, Standard Oil Company of New Jersey

El Panama Hotel
1946

Architect
Edward Durell Stone and Associates

Location
Panama City, Panama

Client
Hoteles Interamericanos S.A.

US Embassy
1947–1953

Architect
Eggers & Higgins

Location
Ankara, Turkey

Client
US Department of State, Foreign Buildings Operations

Club Ariston
1948

MBA

Architect
Marcel Breuer, Architect; Carlos Coire, Eduardo Catalano

Location
Mar del Plata, Argentina

US Embassy
1948–1952

Architect
Harrison & Abramovitz

Location
Rio de Janeiro, Brazil

Client
US Department of State, Foreign Buildings Operations

General Motors Assembly Plant
1948–1953

SMITHGROUP JJR

Architect
Smith, Hinchman and Grylls

Local Architect
V. Cols, J. De Roeck & Associes

Location
Antwerp, Belgium

Client
General Motors

Reader's Digest Offices
1949–1951

Architect
Raymond & Rado

Location
Tokyo, Japan

Client
Reader's Digest Association

Creole Petroleum Building
1949–1955

Architect
Lathrop Douglass

Location
Caracas, Venezuela

Client
Creole Petroleum Corporation,
Standard Oil of New Jersey
Foreign Buildings Operations

1946

1950

US Embassy
1950–1952

Architect
Harrison and Abramovitz

Location
Havana, Cuba

Client
US Department of State,
Foreign Buildings Operations

Hotel Tamanaco
1950–1953

Architect
Holabird & Root

Location
Caracas, Venezuela

Client
Intercontinental Hotel
Corporation

Hotel del Lago
1950–1953

Architect
Holabird & Root

Location
Maracaibo, Venezuela

Client
Intercontinental Hotel
Corporation

Hotel Tequendama
1950–1953

Architect
Holabird & Root

Location
Bogotá, Colombia

Client
Intercontinental Hotel
Corporation

Intercontinental Comfort: Little Americas Abroad

The dust of World War II had not yet settled in Europe before the impact of the new "American tourist" began to be felt internationally. In 1945 Juan Trippe, the owner of Pan American World Airways, began to offer new "tourist class" travel from New York to London, cutting the cost of transatlantic flights in half.[1] The following year Pan American established the InterContinental Hotels Group as a subsidiary division with its first hotel in Belém, Brazil.[2] With the official announcement of the Marshall Plan in 1947, understanding how its financial structure might benefit his business and upon encouragement from the US State Department, Conrad Hilton launched the international arm of his own hotel "group," Hilton International, with the Caribe Hilton in San Juan, Puerto Rico.[3] In the same year he bought the Waldorf Astoria hotel in New York, adding considerably to the recognition and esteem of the Hilton brand.

The growing demands of this new class of consumers—capable of jet travel from 1955 onward thanks to Trippe's then-risky purchase of Boeing 707s—were quickly met with new US chain hotels worldwide. Sheraton, InterContinental and Hilton, the three key players on the postwar hospitality map, all relied on US architects to provide the perfectly packaged elements of basic comfort that their customers had come to expect. As a 1963 article in *Life* suggested, the global expansion of these hotel companies, led by Hilton, was set off "by a matchless postwar combination: the burning sensation of money in the public's pocket, and the flames from jet transports, which have shrunk the earth to prune size."[4]

Contemporary US media made evident the ideological project of Conrad Hilton's international hotels.[5] Hilton was often recorded proclaiming that world peace would be reached "through international trade and travel;" each of his hotels would be "a little America," designed to show "the countries most exposed to Communism the other side of the coin—the fruits of the free

① Richard Branson, "Juan Trippe: Pilot of the Jet Age," *Time Magazine* (December 7, 1998).

② Owen Edwards, "Sky King: Pan Am founder Juan Trippe turned Americans into frequent fliers," *Smithsonian Magazine* (November 2007).

③ See Conrad Hilton, *Be My Guest* (New York: Prentice Hall, 1957).

④ Dora Jane Hamblin, "His Hotels Keep Conrad Hilton Hopping. In 19 Lands Instant America." *LIFE* (August 30, 1963): 68.

⑤ See Annabel Wharton, *Building the Cold War: Hilton International Hotels and Modern Architecture* (Chicago: University of Chicago Press, 2001).

1930

1936
• Pan American begins passenger flights across the Pacific Ocean
• the DC3 Designed with a galley to enable hot meals to be served to passengers

1939
Pan American operates its first passenger transatlantic flight

1945
"Tourist Class" offered on Pan American

1946
• Intercontinental Hotels Group founded
• Hilton Hotels Corporation founded

1947
• The Marshall Plan announced
• New York City's Roosevelt Hilton Hotel first to install TVs in guest rooms

1939–1945 World War II

world."[6] This ideological work was also financially lucrative. When investment for the construction of his hotels did not come from local sources (whether pension funds or local magnates), the US government provided Marshall Plan funding on the authority of the Economic Cooperation Administration. This financial structure meant that if anything went wrong—as when Fidel Castro took over the Havana Hilton as his revolutionary party headquarters in 1959—Conrad Hilton stood to lose very little personally. Local governments were often persuaded to provide the best public properties for the construction of what historian Annabel Wharton has termed the "monumental modernity" of the Hiltons and their architectural-symbolic function.

A definitive increase in US tourism was also ascribed to these hotels, adding economic to cultural value. The Istanbul Hilton (1952–1955), for example, was "given large credit for an electrifying 60% increase in tourism that took place in Turkey during the hotel's first year of operation."[7]

At the height of Hilton's expansion into the Middle East and Japan in the early 1960s, Hilton International had hotels in 19 different countries totaling some 60,000 rooms, including those in its US hotels. Though Sheraton had more rooms in total (64,000), it had hotels in only four countries outside of the US. Intercontinental, though equally present in 19 countries, had only 5,300 rooms and considerably less fanfare.[8] The media-savvy Hilton also claimed a few important standards, including bathrooms in every room and television sets in all guest rooms (1951), air-conditioning in every hotel (1955), and direct-dial telephone service in every room (1957). In each case, local color "was brought inside the hotel, tamed and adapted to live with such creature comforts as air conditioning, piped music, ice water taps and direct dial telephones."[9]

With their indoor comforts, tennis courts, and modern lines, these "little Americas" were built by a handful of US architectural firms including Skidmore, Owings & Merrill, Welton Becket & Associates, and William B. Tabler Architects, often in cooperation with local architects to ensure "local color" and smooth delivery.[10] All were well versed in the idiom and program required to supported the modern American traveler, one who, as an article in Time magazine suggested in 1963, "dares everything and risks nothing."[11]

—AM

⑥ Conrad Hilton, *Be My Guest*, quoted in Michael Wise, "The Ideological Coding Behind Hilton Hotels: A Cold War weapon disguised as a place to spend the night," *The New York Times* (July 21, 2001).

⑦ Hamblin, "His Hotels Keep Conrad Hilton Hopping."

⑧ Ibid. See also Ruth Sheldon Knowles, "Enterprise & Diplomacy: Pan Am Airways' Hotel Unit Helps Itself by Aiding Nations," *The Wall Street Journal* (April 14, 1964): 18.

⑨ Hamblin, "His Hotels Keep Conrad Hilton Hopping": 68.

⑩ See Margaret Arbanas and Ana Miljački, "Hilton Hotels: The Politics of Pleasure," in Eva Franch i Gilabert, Amanda Lawrence, Ana Miljački, Ashley Schafer, ed., *OfficeUS Agenda* (Zurich: Lars Müller, 2014): 254–265. The term "little Americas" is Hilton's. See Conrad Hilton, *Be My Guest*.

⑪ Andy Kopkind: "Hotels: By Golly!" *Time Magazine* (July 19, 1963): 66–72.

1949
- Hilton International founded
- Conrad Hilton appears on the cover of *Time*

1952 De Havilland Comet becomes the world's first commercial jet airliner

1955 Hilton launches program to bring AC to every guest room

1957
- Sputnik 1 flight
- Boeing introduces its 707 jet airline

1958 Pan American initiates its New York to London route with the Boeing 707

1963 Conrad Hilton appears on the cover of *Time* again

1967
- FAA is established as part of the U.S. Department of Transportation
- Trans World Airlines acquires Hilton International

1970

–**1953** Korean War

1962 Cuban Missile Crisis

1950–1975 Vietnam War

1946

1967

ISTANBUL, TURKEY... a city of fabulous beauty . . . presents a dramatic setting for the new Istanbul Hilton—the second Hilton Hotel in Europe. Overlooking the Bosphorus, this magnificent 300 room hotel with the most advanced conceptions of luxurious comfort and convenience opens an entire new area for world travelers. The landscaped gardens, terraces, tennis courts, reflecting pool and private balconies blend perfectly with the surging progress of Istanbul. In keeping with high Hilton standards, guests will enjoy fine accommodations, superb cuisine and friendly hospitality.

Consult your Travel Agent, write direct, contact Hilton Hotels International Reservation Office: 401 Seventh Avenue, New York 1, N. Y. Tel. LOngacre 3-6900; Teletype NY1-1234, or any Hilton Hotel. Credit accommodations are available for guests presenting Hilton and Statler Hotels Credit Cards.

EXECUTIVE OFFICES
THE CONRAD HILTON
CHICAGO 5, ILL.

Hilton Hotels
THE AROUND THE WORLD

Conrad N. Hilton, President

HAVANA, the glamorous, gay capital of Cuba, provides a sophisticated setting for the new 30-story high Habana Hilton. Overlooking Havana, historic Morro Castle and the harbor, this spectacular, completely air-conditioned hotel offers 630 lavishly appointed rooms and suites, each with a large private balcony, plus all the facilities of a magnificent resort. A swimming pool, colorful cabanas, an exciting Trader Vic's restaurant and a roof top cocktail lounge, the Sugar Bar, are just a few of the many outstanding features at Latin America's largest hotel, the fabulous new Habana Hilton.

Reservations: See Travel Agent or call New York, LOngacre 3-6900 • Chicago, FInancial 6-2772 • San Francisco, YUkon 6-0576 • Miami, FRanklin 9-3427 • Pittsburgh, COurt 1-5600 • Toronto, EMpire 8-2921 • Montreal, UNiversity 1-3301 • Havana, F-3296 or any Hilton Hotel.

EXECUTIVE OFFICES
THE CONRAD HILTON
CHICAGO 5, ILL.

Hilton Hotels
AROUND THE WORLD
Conrad N. Hilton, President

INTRODUCING GERMANY'S NEWEST HOTEL . . . DESIGNED FOR THE JET AGE

WEST BERLIN—Now, a Hilton Hotel for the *Jet Age,* as up-to-the-minute as Pan American's transatlantic 707 Jet Clippers. The new Berlin Hilton reflects the vitality of rebuilt, thriving, exciting West Berlin. The 14-story Berlin Hilton offers 350 attractive rooms, and famous Hilton service and hospitality. Its six glamorous restaurants and bars include the delightful Roof Garden with breathtaking panoramic views of Berlin. The Berlin Hilton is located at the center of this great crossroads of the world. The majestic Brandenburg Gate is about a mile away . . . adjoining the hotel is the lovely Zoological Garden. While the Berlin Hilton has its own Colonnade of fine shops, it is situated in the immediate vicinity of famed Kurfürstendamm, Berlin's business, shopping and theatre district . . . alive with all the gaiety and entertainment of a great European metropolis.

RESERVATIONS: *See Travel Agent or call* New York, *LOngacre 3-6900* • Chicago, *FInancial 6-2772* • San Francisco, *YUkon 6-0576* • Miami, *FRanklin 9-3427* • Pittsburgh, *COurt 1-5600* • Toronto, *EMpire 2-3771* • London, *Whitehall 2150, or contact any Hilton Hotel.*

EXECUTIVE OFFICES
THE CONRAD HILTON
CHICAGO 5, ILL.

Hilton Hotels AROUND THE WORLD

Conrad N. Hilton, President

NEEDHAM & GROHMANN, INC.
ROCKEFELLER CENTER • NEW YORK

THE NEWEST HOTEL IN CAIRO...MODERN AS A TWA JETSTREAM*

CAIRO—Another Hilton Hotel! New and beautiful as the mighty TWA JETSTREAM, longest-range airliner in the world today. The magnificent, 400-room Nile Hilton, on the banks of the majestic Nile, overlooks the Pyramids, the old Citadel and the city of Cairo with its mosques, museums and historic monuments. Completely air-conditioned, it is an ideal year-round meeting place for world travelers. Surrounded by symbols of ancient civilization and Pharaonic splendor, guests will enjoy every modern comfort, convenience and famous Hilton hospitality. And, TWA will fly you direct to Cairo.

RESERVATIONS: *See your Travel Agent or call New York, LOngacre 3-6900 • Chicago, FInancial 6-2772 • San Francisco, YUkon 3-0576 • Miami, FRanklin 9-3427 • Pittsburgh, COurt 1-5600 • Toronto, EMpire 2-3771 • London, Whitehall 3061 or any Hilton Hotel.* **CARTE BLANCHE**—*The Hilton All-Purpose Credit Card — Your Finest Credit Credential.*

EXECUTIVE OFFICES
THE CONRAD HILTON
CHICAGO 5, ILLINOIS

Hilton Hotels
AROUND THE WORLD
Conrad N. Hilton, President

...drich-Blessing Studio

HOTELS

HOLABIRD & ROOT & BURGEE & ASSOCIATES, Architects

WASHINGTON D.C. for Statler

SAUDI ARABIA . . .

LISBON . . .
TOKYO for Intercontinental

For anyone who wishes to learn how to build a successful hotel there is one clear path, and it leads to the door of a firm of architects in Chicago. In a field where failures have been frequent and notorious, the hotels of Holabird & Root & Burgee have the air of sweet success, and the latest ones are positively roaring with it. No wonder then that the hotel empire of "H & R & B" is rapidly encircling the world, and in a very few years the firm will be able to boast like the British Empire, that the sun never sets on it. At the moment the architects' international client is Intercontinental Hotels Corp. ("IHC"), subsidiary of Pan American Airways. The most advanced of its projects are three houses in Colombia and Venezuela, which can now be previewed in some detail. But IHC has 11 others in various stages of progress in the capital cities of Central and South America; it has them in Tokyo, Saudi Arabia, South Africa, Istanbul, Madrid, Lisbon, Stockholm and Copenhagen. No American architectural firm has so dominated a world-wide field of endeavor since the globe-circling industrial work of the late Albert Kahn.

Like many another successful outfit, H & R & B makes no secret of the major principles that guide its successful work—the principles that have so eluded others. If one examines this record, one fact stands forth instantly. The office has associated itself with those hotel men to whom building is a regular habit giving an opportunity for steady practice and the development of systematic research. The trouble with most hotels, to quote Byron Calhoun, the energetic vice-president of Intercontinental, is that the owner builds just one of them in a lifetime; he has no chance to apply what he learns from his mistakes, and there are very few architects who have designed more than one hotel. The consequence is that the ordinary operator and his architects work by rules of thumb which are worse than nothing if they are not true.

Why build at all?

The general situation was made apparent by FORUM's independent check of the hotel field. Failures have been notorious and the fact that 81 per cent of American hotels defaulted on their bonds during the depression has been ascribed "not to defects inherent in the business but to over building." It would be more accurate to ascribe it to the fact of bad building rather than over building. To protect themselves against those haphazard procedures hotel operators today have taken two different tacks of action. The Hilton chain in its 1949 Annual Report made it virtually a cardinal principle not to invest its own funds "in new construction under present high conditions," but "either to acquire going properties . . . or to induce others . . . to build properties" that can be profitably leased. By this means the investment base is broadened, Hilton's risk diminished.

Another approach has been Statler's policy of reinvesting its own funds in building comparatively few new hotels under a unified operating policy. In either event the key factor in assuring success is getting to be the research approach to building. In memory too recent for comfort there have been colossal boners perpetrated by one-shot amateurs. Statler formulated a concept of hotel service and built to it. This permits each subsequent hotel to be built on the experience of its predecessor, and develops a steady line of progress. It keeps the

circling the globe make Holabird & Root & Burgee, Chicago architects, the world's teachers of up-to-date hotel planning. Working closely with clients such as Intercontinental Hotels, they design from the inside out—starting with a workable daybed, ending with a favorable balance sheet

hotel man eagerly meeting new demand instead of fighting a grudging battle against obsolescence. The fact that new building, even at today's costs, can pay off is dramatically illustrated in Washington, where the new Statler built at war prices is reputed to be Washington's most successful hotel.

Though IHC is a new firm, its heads are experienced and successful men. President Wallace S. Whittaker and Vice President Byron Calhoun are proud to claim that, like Statler, they are devoted wholeheartedly to the research approach. And both of them, scanning the field for changes in demand, believe that changes in travel, advances in comfort standards, and ideals of service have been too rapid and radical for most existing buildings to keep up with through remodeling. In concentrating on the market potential rather than on stop-gap measures IHC is working hand-in-glove with its architects.

"The up-to-date American commercial hotel"

In the minds of these men the changes which tend to make existing buildings obsolete can be summarized as follows:

First, the public travels lighter. Guests come by plane and car as well as by train or ship and they weigh their luggage carefully by the pound. An H & R & B man tells of meeting a Sears-Roebuck representative in Saudi Arabia, on the other side of the globe, contentedly traveling with two nylon shirts as his complete change of linen. This lighter luggage means that large trunk rooms, inherited from the European hotel, are obsolete, and the old highboys in guest rooms can be replaced by a luggage stand and a few drawers. But in order to care for their fewer things, people now need a dependable valet service for quick laundry and dry cleaning.

Second, by far the majority of the hotel's guests arrive on rubber tires, and increasingly by highway. In 1948 the American Hotel Association published a pamphlet on *How to Sell the Motor Traveler* based on a poll which declared that 86 per cent of all travelers would prefer to come on rubber, and among vacationists the percentage was 91. The first effect of cars is to open up locations off the main drag or farther out. These sites are open, quiet, attractive, inexpensive, compared to the congested, noisy, costly situations of the main downtown corners (the land under the Plaza in New York is valued at $77.60 per sq. ft.). H & R & B's Tamanaco Hotel for IHC at Caracas (page 96) will lie five miles from the shopping center at a magnificent spot against a mountain background, but a new superhighway will make the distance not over ten minutes. Tamanaco therefore significantly becomes a "resort" hotel that can compete with the local "commercial" hotel for business travelers; and in future the combination of resort and commercial will be more frequent.

In U. S. towns of 100,000 or less, the car is credited with still another effect: it made the motor court so serious a rival that many hotels are contemplating their own outpost courts. But regardless of motels the effect of cars is to create tremendous leverage in favor of a new hotel with garage or parking attached. Even the guest arriving by plane may rent a drive-self car at the airport for the duration of his stay, choosing a hotel that gives him the chance to take care of it; and arrangements are now under way by which travelers may be able to drive such a car to the next town and leave it.

Still another effect of the rubber tire, and a tricky one, is the problem of correct access, involving not only the guest's own car but taxis. Even the motor entrance of the Washington Statler, nearly perfect in being situated off-street and under cover, has taught its architects something: taxis tend to ignore it and to land their charges at a less convenient second entrance because the motor entrance lands the driver in a back street where there is no chance to pick up another quick fare.

Third, travelers demand higher comfort. Air conditioning for guest rooms alone requires at least ¾ ton of refrigeration per room at an installation cost of $400 to $600 per room not to mention annual operation costs. Radio and television are far easier to install in new hotels than in old, and are rapidly becoming indispensable.

Higher wages and better working conditions. Payments to personnel may take up as much as 35 per cent (Statler) to 41 per cent (Knott hotels) of total income, and IHC reports that some wage scales abroad have increased 400 per cent in recent years. In some foreign countries where actual monetary wages are less than 20 per cent of the gross, lower efficiency offsets the lower wages; one maid may be expected to care for less than 10 rooms, while in the U.S. a maid is expected to make up from 14 to 18 rooms.

What outmodes the older hotel more rapidly than anything else is the labor cost of wasted steps. By careful planning which eliminates a single checking station in the kitchen of a large hotel, now abuilding, the labor budget has been cut $25,000 a year. Again, when H & R & B lay out their air conditioning, they try to concentrate fan rooms on single floors. In the Los Angeles Statler the usual pipe transfer space beneath the guest room wings has been enlarged to house all air handling equipment. The purpose is not only to save on pipe runs and ducts but to put the whole installation within easy supervision range of a single engineer instead of requiring several. Still further step-saving expedients are necessary in the kitchen. It goes without saying that a new step-saving building has first pick of the best hotel employees.

Higher materials costs might be considered a disadvantage in new building; they induce tight planning. But modern hotel men are convinced that the public, much as it loves space, loves new equipment more. To pay for new materials and services it is necessary to cut non-essential space to the bone. And this cannot be done without also improving the organization of the hotel plan. The result is to save not only on personnel time used in the daily operation of the building but also to save on maintenance items such as painting. So important is this compactness that H & R & B have set themselves a top figure of 6,000 cu. ft. per room as the total allowance for all facilities in the hotels of 400 rooms and more. (Some operators think the optimum hotel size is close to 500 rooms; others put it closer to 1,000.)

In looking over the many different plans for IHC as well as for the new Los Angeles Statler, plans done for so many countries, with different climates and different kinds of clientele, and done with different associates, one of the architects remarked thoughtfully, "I guess when you come right down to it they are all of them based on the American commercial hotel."

From their recent experience with the Washington Statler the architects learned about motor access.

Impressive lobbies leading to banquet rooms have helped make the war-built Statler wonderfully profitable; but on principle public areas are held down.

Photos: Hedrich-Blessing Studios

Whether or not it is physically combined with the lounge, the arrival-and-departure lobby should be a self-contained compact unit.

Rooms. To begin with, the American commercial hotel is designed to no preconceived architectural concept. In H & R & B's careful procedure, the design begins with a unit guest room. Indeed it begins farther back with the complete redesign of the bed and rearrangement of the furniture. John Root is still astonished at the way they tackled guest room planning in the Twenties. Room sizes were arbitrarily agreed on without study of the room's use. Column spacing, window arrangement and the like took charge. Afterwards there was hell to pay trying to fit in the furniture. The present technique of designing rooms with the aid of full-scale mockups is so important that it is more fully described farther on (pages 94, 95).

The guest room is so important because room rents are the backbone of the hotel's income. They normally account for about 70 per cent of the hotel's receipts, and Calhoun declares that the hotel should retain 70 to 75 per cent of its room receipts as an operating profit (profit before rent, taxes, interest, depreciation and insurance). (The corresponding rates of operating profit would be: food service, 20 per cent; beverages 30 per cent.) Hotel accountants, such as Horwath & Horwath or Harris, Kerr, Foster & Co., relate all hotel income factors to the room count of the hotel.

Once the basic room has been designed, column spacing can be determined. With maximum efficiency the up-to-date hotel assigns at least 60 of today's smaller rooms to the floor—though special reasons may cause a deviation. (The Bogota hotel, seen on page 100, has 28 rooms to the floor for the sake of a higher silhouette and better visibility from afar.)

Public areas. H & R & B try to keep the *total* cubage of the hotel within 6,000 cu. ft. per room, which takes some doing. Normally the cubage of public and service space must be held to 40 or 45 per cent of the total. This means smaller lobbies. Most of today's guests are embarrassed rather than pleased at entering a palace under the guidance of bellhops as heralds. In large hotels H & R & B like to separate off a convenient and limited entrance area to be devoted entirely to arrivals and departures. It contains the registration desk and the cashiers, the transportation desk, baggage checkroom, bell captain's post, and the desk or office of the assistant manager. The elevators, close by, serve as a dividing shed between the entrance lobby and the social lounge. The guest goes up from the entrance area to get settled in his room. He comes down and turns the other way into the lounge to find his friends or choose his dining room. With nice tact, H & R & B hold this public lounge area down. There are no dividends for the hotel in supplying a dating center for all of the community's cupids. In smaller hotels of 500 or fewer rooms there is less opportunity for such articulation.

Food service. Though it's all a hotel can do to break even and better in supplying food, without it the hotel would lose its chief revenue boosting devices, such as conventions. Just as old rules of thumb are useless in designing a modern guest room, where 3 in. one way or another make the difference between being able to accommodate the furniture or not, so the architects find no rule of thumb for sizing dining rooms and kitchens. Roughly, the dining area usually exceeds the kitchen area (including storage) slightly (Stevens, 123 per cent; Palmer House, 127 per cent; Boston Statler 118½ per cent; Washington Statler 96 per cent). But looking forward H & R & B can see the ratio varying all over the lot. And just as IHC in its guest room studies has abandoned rules of thumb and started with redesigning the bed, so in its kitchens it now abandons rules of thumb and starts always with the menu the hotel will offer. Obviously a menu that offers 30 entrees to choose among will require more square inches of cooking surface (and more cubic inches of storage) per seat than one which offers six. So, too, especially in working abroad, there are vast differences in availability of food—meat or vegetables, fresh or preserved—which completely change the processes of preparation and their space requirements.

Food prefabrication. In the U. S. itself, however, there impends a basic revolution: food prefabrication. Already Stouffer's restaurants, famous for their efficiency, get their potatoes delivered peeled. And Swift or Armour will be able to cut down kitchen operations tremendously for the hotels if numbers of hotels can get together and decide to have their chops and steaks cut to standard thicknesses and delivered wrapped. All of which means the elimination of butchering and saving of space in kitchens.

Today's and tomorrow's kitchens, as one may see them in H & R & B's plans, are turned broadside to the dining rooms, instead of being at one end, so that serving can occur quickly by short routes from numerous serving stations.

And today's dining areas, in direct contradiction to yesterday's, are broken by every open planning device—change of level, change of shape, change of placement—into smaller more intimate units, so that the diner and his friends may find a variety of seats to choose from and so that they may enjoy a degree of privacy while they are still part of the whole show.

Any dining space, especially a breakfast room is improved by being open to a sunny view out, as exemplified at the Statler . . .

Rules of thumb, or direct inquiry?

What H & R & B and their clients stress above all else is the need in hotel business for direct inquiry into the market to replace rules of thumb. Pairing up for their exhaustive preliminary surveys, H & R & B and IHC found that you can't even trust the census of available hotel rooms in the ordinary U. S. city, let alone abroad—it is better to have a field check. And such a thing as a fixed ratio between population and hotel beds does not exist; the market can only be established by on-the-spot inquiry into the travel habits of commercial and other travelers arriving by different conveyances. Such details as the labor situation and food and water sources are checked with industrial acumen.

. . . And the new Tamanaco shows the added effect of arranging the seating in varied patterns and on different levels, to give a grandstand effect.

Rules of thumb are unreliable. Supposedly every hotel should balance its guest rooms with "banquet" facilities—really places for local organizations to meet and eat in—but the successful new Terrace Plaza in Cincinnati virtually foregoes them and is little more than a dormitory (because its parent hotel the Netherland Plaza has them) and the Washington Statler on the other hand makes a terrific profit crowding only 850 rooms on a tight piece of land, because it has two floors of eating and meeting rooms, result of being aware that Washington was short of convention facilities. Even room rates don't follow the "rules." Twenty years ago a rule was established that the daily rate should be $1 for every $1,000 investment per room, and learned tabulations exist to prove it; but today's average construction cost alone, in the U. S., is estimated by H & R & B at between $10,000 and $12,000 per room on which average daily rates will nevertheless be closer to $8 than to $12. Percentage of occupancy is tremendously important to any hotel. Some authorities think 80 per cent occupancy is the break-even point. Yet this too depends on factors that are highly variable. For example the Stevens and the Palmer House in Chicago, that were bought in at a value greatly written down, would meet all costs today at 50 per cent occupancy, in the opinion of their operators; whereas the Waldorf, in the same hands, had to take in $17.6 million last year, despite 91 per cent occupancy, to keep $696,000 under its special circumstances. IHC figures that it will make a profit on the hotels H & R & B are designing for it, even at 60 per cent occupancy, because the buildings look forward into the future and are designed to a researched market, instead of trying by rule of thumb to adapt a structure designed many years ago for totally different conditions and purposes.

As Calhoun says, "Other industries build a plant to create some product. In the hotel business, once the plant is built the product has already been created. What the hotel man has to sell is the building he operates. It is of incredible importance that it be the right building. Under today's new conditions I will take a well-organized *new* building every time."

Step-saving in the kitchen is a cardinal requirement for efficient operation, and the up-to-date version is organized with well-defined serving stations.

KEY PLAN ELEMENT: improved unit bedroom has nice sitting room, and organized dressing space

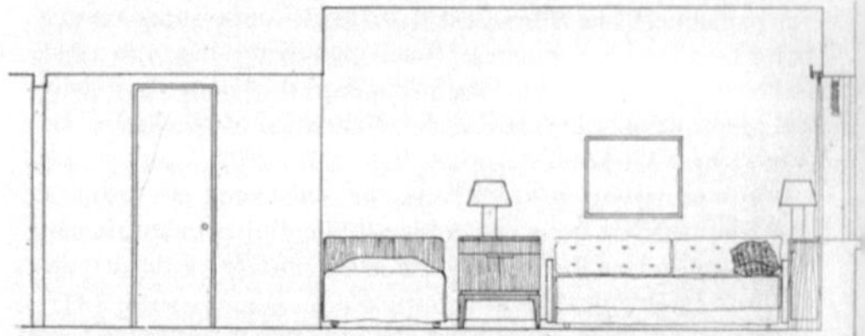

The revolution that has transformed today's hotel planning began in earnest at the Washington Statler through the conversion of the old-fashioned "bedroom" into a 24-hour guest room; this was achieved by the conversion of the "bed" into a "day couch." The next move was to rearrange the furniture, transforming the hotel room into a compact little one-room apartment. At Statler the conventional placement of twin beds with their heads to the partition wall (easy to occupy, easy to care for) was replaced by a conversational grouping within the same amount of space—actually in even less. Because beds were longside to the wall (photo below) the middle of the room was free and the room looked bigger. The

Hedrich-Blessing Studio

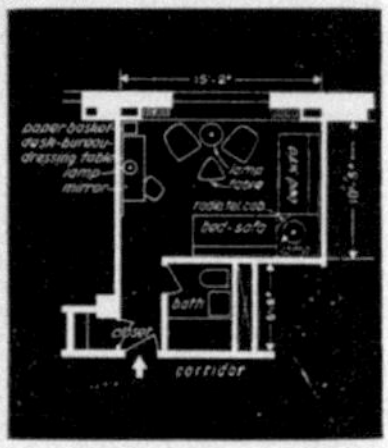

Statler bed was already an improvement on the familiar hotel "day-bed" which has so often been a makeshift affair, uncomfortable to sleep in, hard to make up, and unalterably attached to one spot where it has been "built in" for the sake of anchoring the heavy pull-out mechanism.

In working out still further improvements with IHC, the architects got the benefit of three years' collaborative development work by an important bed and mattress manufacturer. First, the bed was given a sturdy frame, entirely independent of the wall and easily movable. Next the bolster was attached to this frame. From either end the maid can trip a lever on top and release the powerful spring mechanism that sends the bed out, rolling on rubber casters. The rear casters move on a smooth track. The front ones move on the carpet and are 3 in. wide so as to leave no conspicuous marks. For use as a daytime couch the bed is pushed back in under the bolster, compressing the spring mechanism again until it locks. A ship-shape detail is that the head and foot boards move out with the bed instead of being fixed to the back. These boards can be removed altogether. Pillow storage is in a compartment at the window end of the bed.

Another very important reorganization of the room for IHC is the use of the vestibule, which the conventional hotel wastes altogether, as the dressing area logically situated alongside the bathroom. To do this, H & R & B have moved the dresser from its usual bump-against-the-wall situation (plan above) and incorporated it in an organized storage sequence, starting with the clothes closet next to the entrance door. This includes the luggage rack, the dresser drawers, and finally the combination writing desk and make-up table—all looking like parts of a single piece of furniture. The luggage rack has a stainless steel shelf that can be utilized as an improvised room-service bar.

Although the Tamanaco Hotel, for which this mock-up was made, lies in a perfect climate requiring neither heating nor air-conditioning, the window pattern fits to an air-conditioning standard—it reaches almost from wall to wall but is only 4 ft. 6 in. high to reduce possible cooling loads. Lamps are individual, portable. (Fixed lights produce fixed furniture arrangements; fixed arrangements produce worn spots in the carpet.)

DAY—The "day couch" seen above is part of a small sittin room, and will be made up as a bed only in case of doubl occupancy. The bed in the foreground is a standard singl bed. The furniture is scaled down in height to increase ap parent spaciousness of the room whose ceiling is less tha 9 ft. high. The dimensions of the room unit as a whole, in cluding bathroom and vestibule, are 11 ft. 5 in. by 21 ft. in.; of the room alone, 11 ft. 5 in. by 13 ft. 11 in.

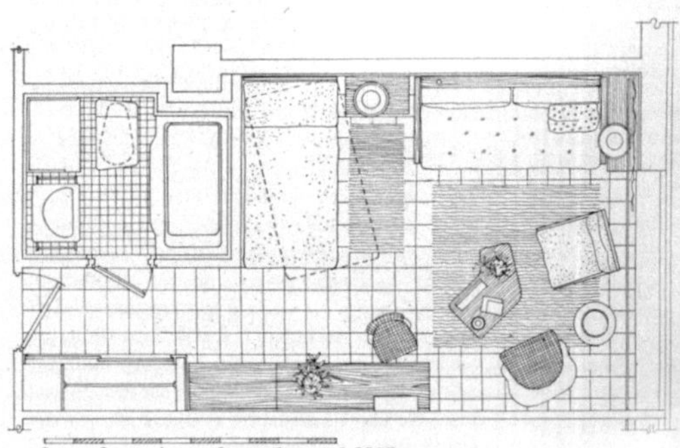

estibule, based on improved furniture

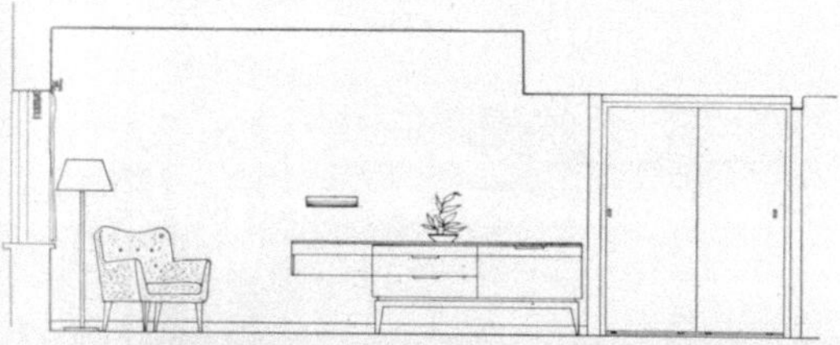

Photos: Schnall

NIGHT—bed is pulled out, makes a bedroom.

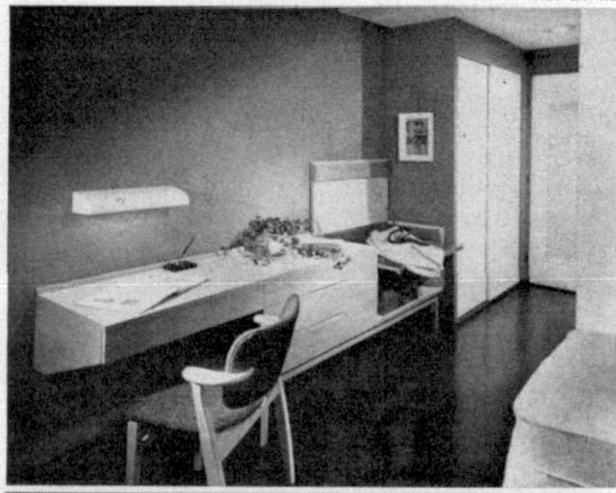

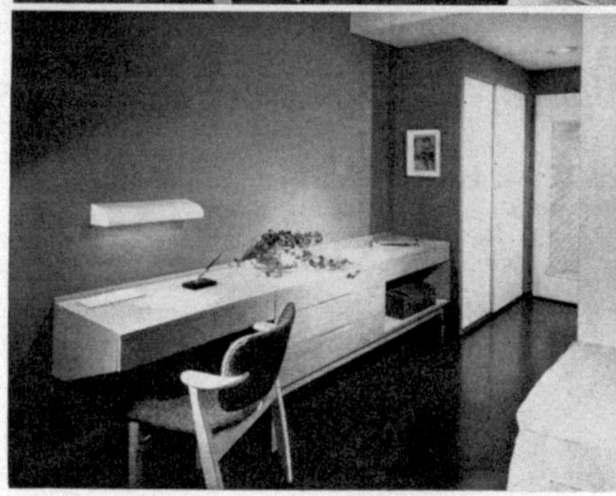

Entryway dressing room. Clothes closet, luggage rack, dresser drawers, combination writing desk and make-up table as a coordinated storage group.

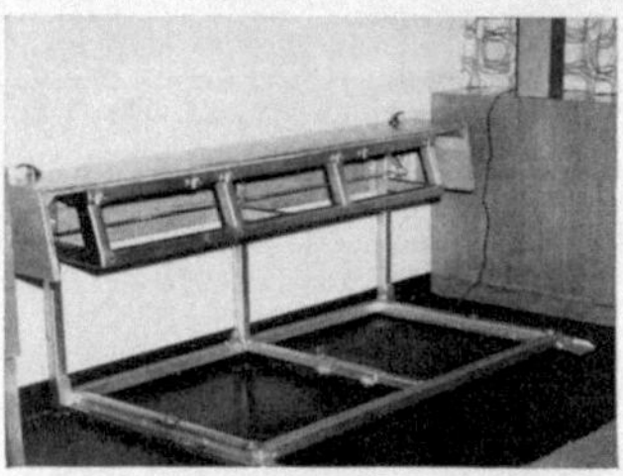

Sturdy frame, independent of wall has powerful springs and channel-shaped tracks.

Bed rolls out from under bolster, carries head and foot boards with it.

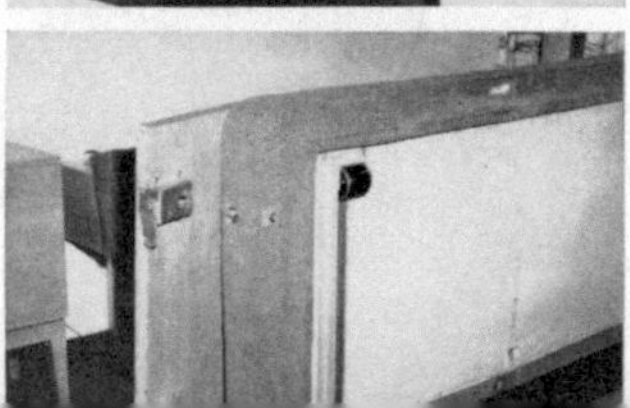

Bottom of bed shows wide hard-rubber casters, removable foot boards.

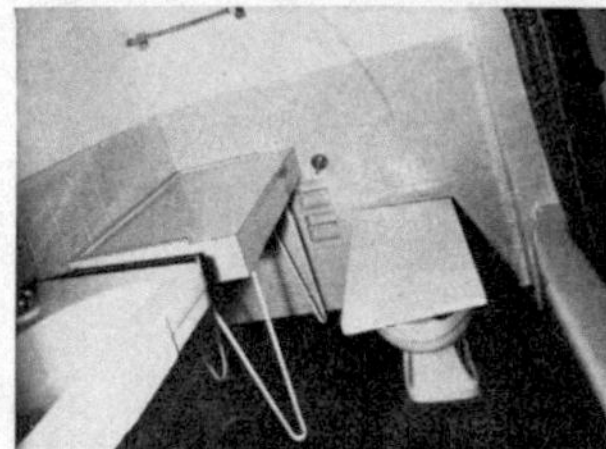

Dressing stand in bathroom was a bright idea, finally dropped to save cost of extra mirror, and align all plumbing fixtures back-to-stack.

Hedrich Blessing Studio

TAMANACO HOTEL has grandstand terrace suites and grandstand eating spaces but its basic rooms are

LOCATION: Caracas, Venezuela

GUSTAVO GUINAND, Architect and Engineer

HOLABIRD & ROOT & BURGEE & ASSOCIATES, Associate Architects

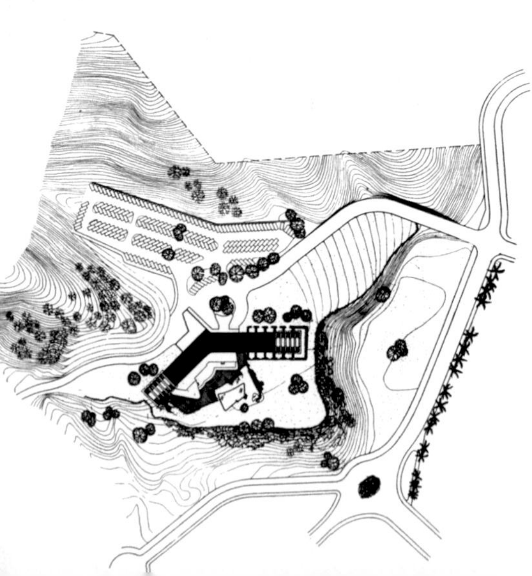

Better than any other example the terraced Tamanaco illustrates Intercontinental Hotel Corp.'s threefold appeal to tourists, business men, diplomatic emissaries. IHC, a wholly owned subsidiary of Pan American Airways, helps local investing groups get American loans through the U. S. Export-Import Bank, gives them help on planning, management, purchasing, to erect hotels wherever Americans travel, incidentally helping their respective countries build up dollar balances. IHC's architects are associated with local men.

Because of the pressing hotel need in oil-rich Venezuela, the Tamanaco supplements the Rockefellers' Harrison-designed Hotel Avila in Caracas (FORUM, June 1946).

The Inca-pyramid terrace profile exists to give premium exposure and outdoor living to top-priced suites, in a climate like Paradise—temperatures seldom vary outside a 60 to 85° range (and the hotel requires neither a heating system nor air conditioning). Rooms face approximately north and south, and the sun favors one side and then the other according to the season because the situation is so close to the equator. The plan is bent to fit topography and the bottom of one canyon is used for a parking lot. All rooms have magnificent views except south rooms in the east wing, which lies somewhat close to the hill-side; accordingly the low-rate rooms and singles are there. (The basic room is shown on the two preceding pages; variations on the next two.)

Using the ground slope, the architects have arranged a fascinating series of dining rooms, grills, and cocktail lounges in a falling series of levels, so all of them give an unobstructed grandstand view of the swimming pool and the big terrace. (See plan opposite.) Because virtually all food is imported, the kitchen has a large area devoted to storage.

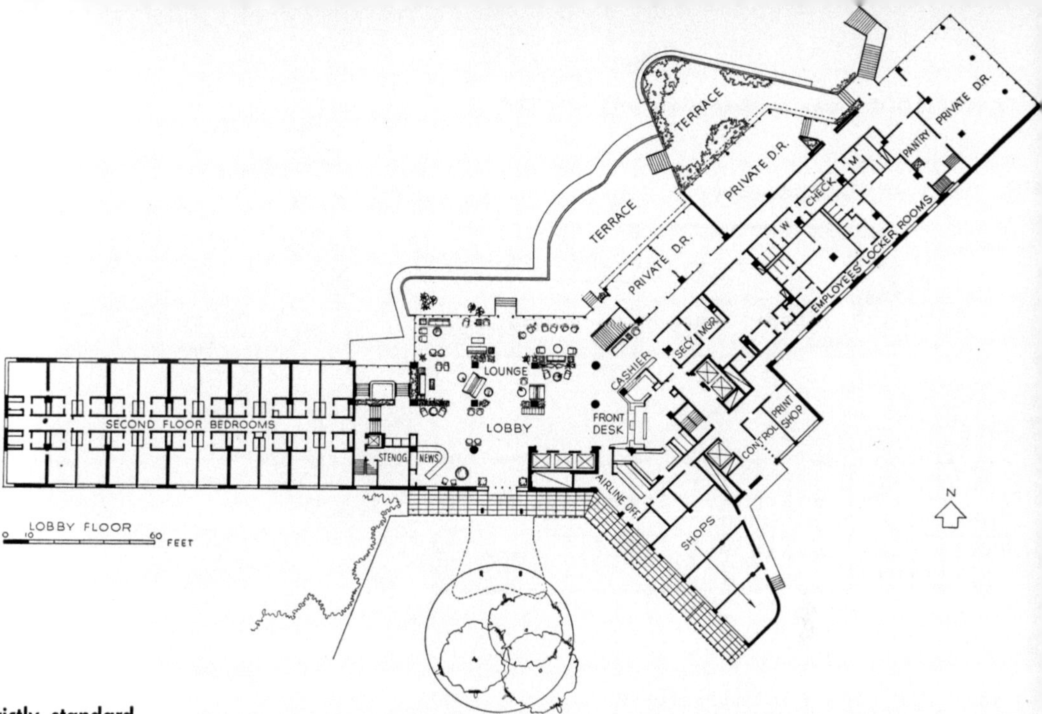

ictly standard

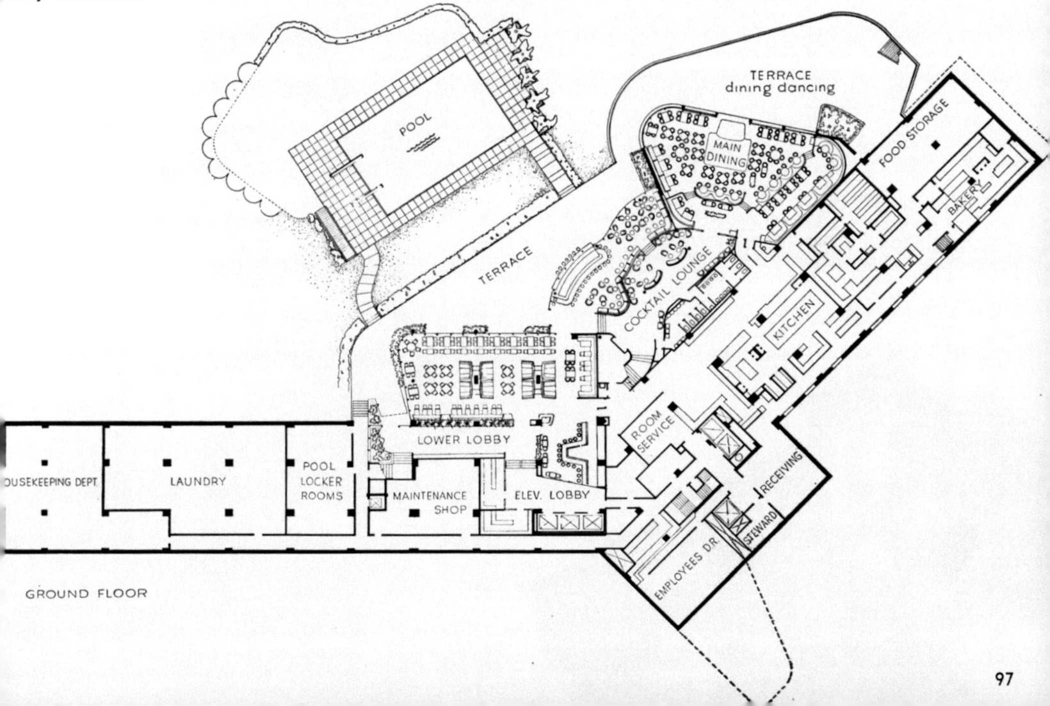

TYPICAL FLOOR shows standard rooms and variations

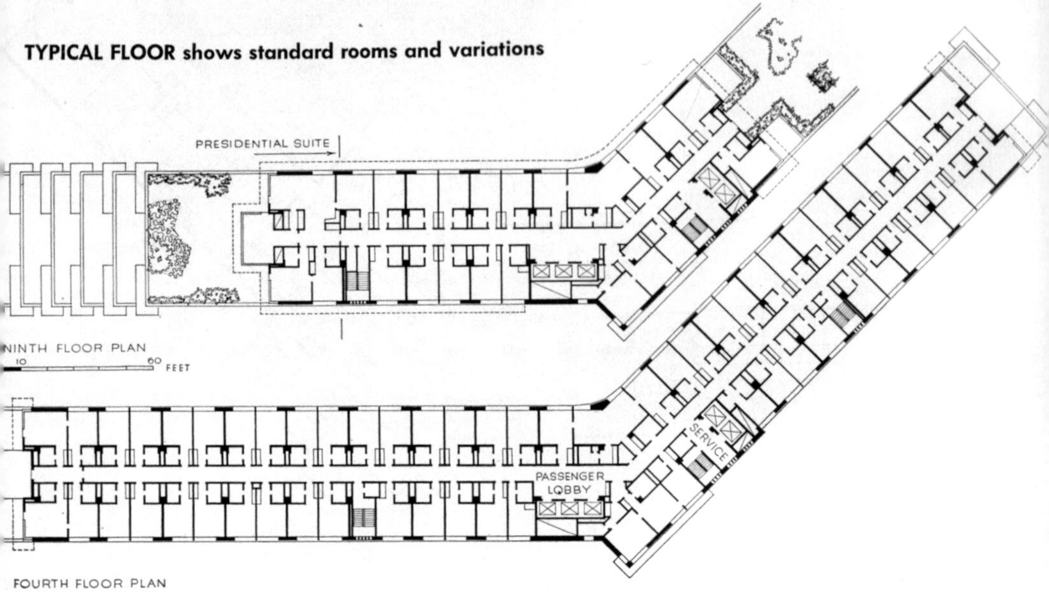

NINTH FLOOR PLAN

FOURTH FLOOR PLAN

The typical floor plan (above) shows at a glance the simplicity, regularity, and economy to be obtained from sticking almost exclusively to a single basic room plan. (This basic plan is shown at the extreme right in the plan at the bottom of the page. It corresponds with the mock-up shown on pages 94 and 95.) Variations occur in rooms at the ends, and along the south side of the east wing where they face the close-by hillside. These are shallower by 2 ft. than the others and contain single or double beds instead of two separate beds, and they carry a lower rate. (See middle row of room plans, right.) At the ends of wings, next to terraces, there are larger rooms that can be used as bedrooms but will more likely serve as the sitting room in combination suites (photo of model below). The guest room next door can then be opened into the suite to serve as its bedroom element—or it can be sold separately as a guest room to itself. The connecting door has been carefully placed by the architects so as to swing free of the day couch when it is extended for use as a bed.

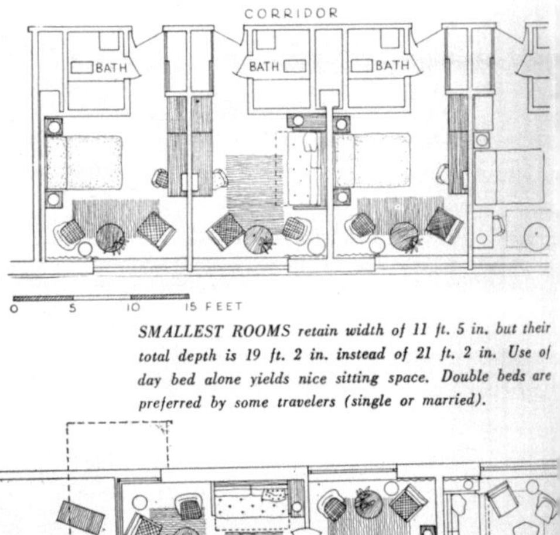

SMALLEST ROOMS retain width of 11 ft. 5 in. but their total depth is 19 ft. 2 in. instead of 21 ft. 2 in. Use of day bed alone yields nice sitting space. Double beds are preferred by some travelers (single or married).

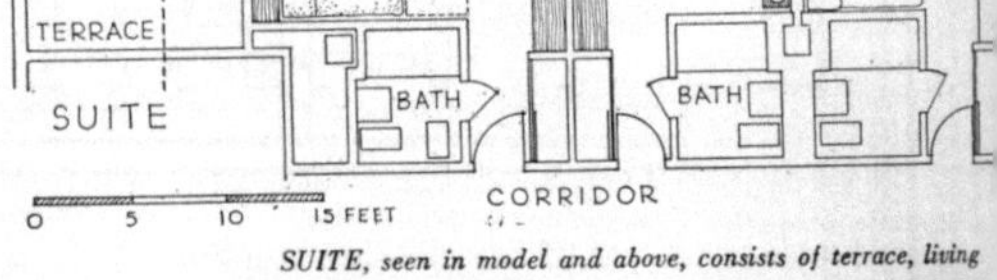

SUITE, seen in model and above, consists of terrace, living room, and conventional bedroom made up with twin beds. Each room has its own bath so they can be rented separately if desired. Room at right end is the basic type.

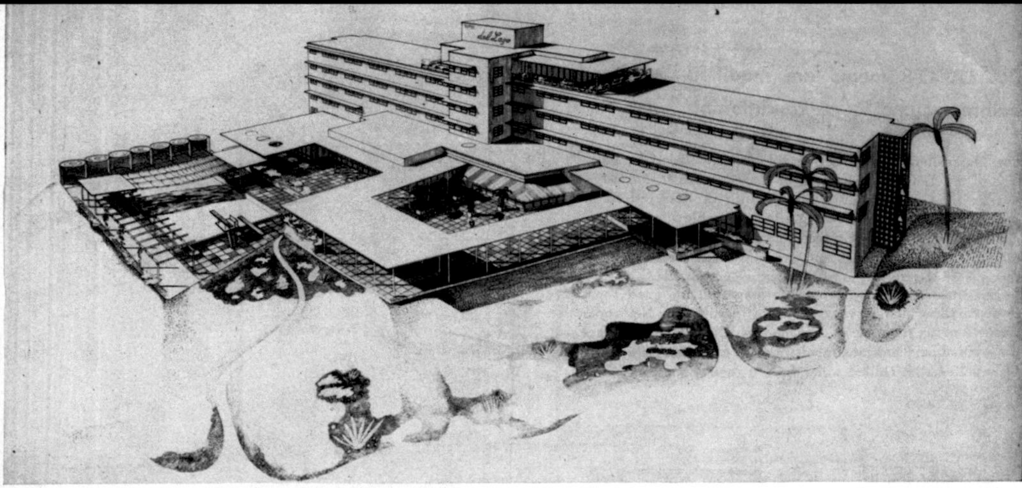

DEL LAGO HOTEL changes the typical rooms to suit the special needs of travelers in the tropics

LOCATION: Maracaibo, Venezuela

HOLABIRD & ROOT & BURGEE & ASSOCIATES
Architects and Engineers

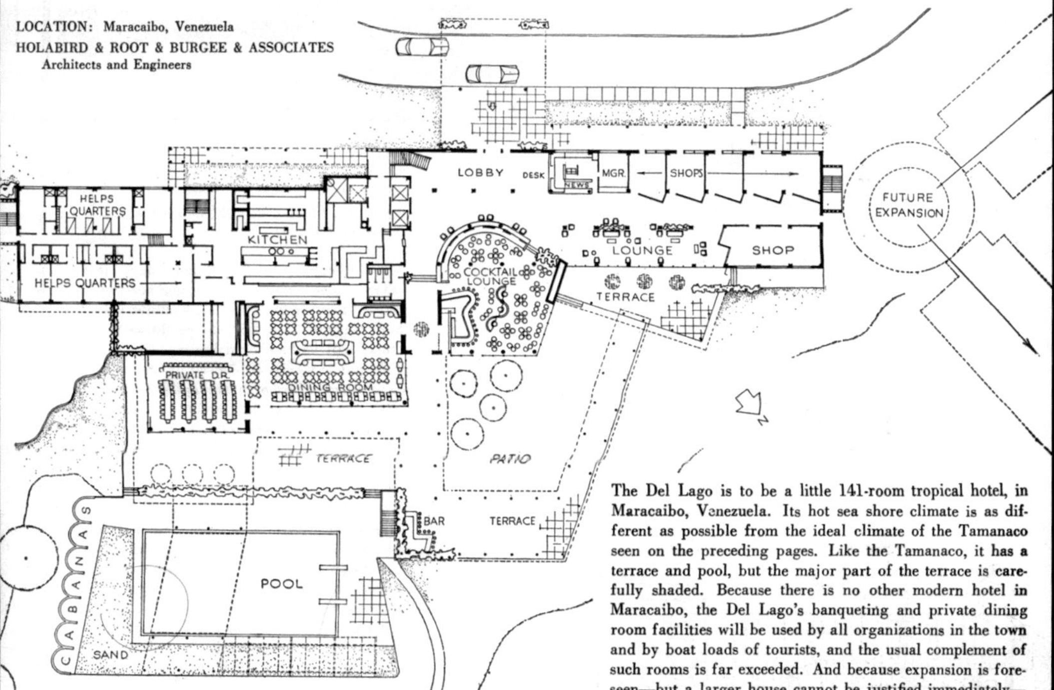

The Del Lago is to be a little 141-room tropical hotel, in Maracaibo, Venezuela. Its hot sea shore climate is as different as possible from the ideal climate of the Tamanaco seen on the preceding pages. Like the Tamanaco, it has a terrace and pool, but the major part of the terrace is carefully shaded. Because there is no other modern hotel in Maracaibo, the Del Lago's banqueting and private dining room facilities will be used by all organizations in the town and by boat loads of tourists, and the usual complement of such rooms is far exceeded. And because expansion is foreseen—but a larger house cannot be justified immediately—two future wings are indicated on the plan, radiating from a central patio; they can be built without disturbing the existing structure or the occupants.

This hotel serves a special situation and it has a special room plan, shown on the next page.

DEL LAGO'S rooms are modified by special bathrooms and by air conditioning

The Maracaibo rooms differ in some details from the basic type of the Tamanaco. Because of the hot weather and water scarcity most of them are equipped with showers instead of baths. The south rooms, facing a less desirable view, are specially designed for use by technicians enroute to or from the oil fields. The bathrooms and dressing areas are taken from the end of the guest rooms and put alongside. This gives a larger dressing room with ample storage but the guest room is deprived of the privacy given by vestibules. Net room dimensions are the same as Tamanaco's. The guests' desks face the window and are integrated with air conditioning units to be supplied with chilled water from a central source.

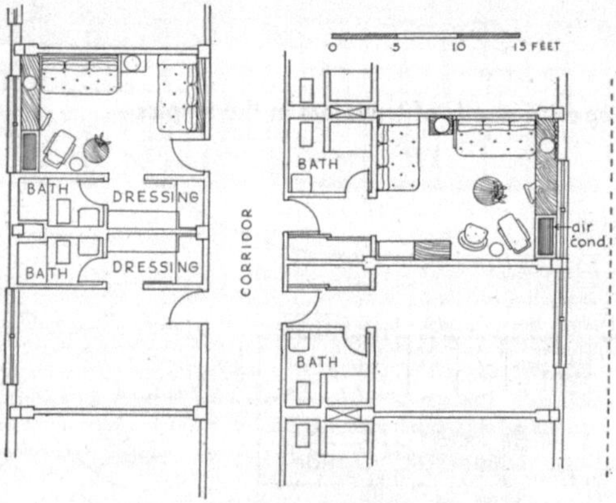

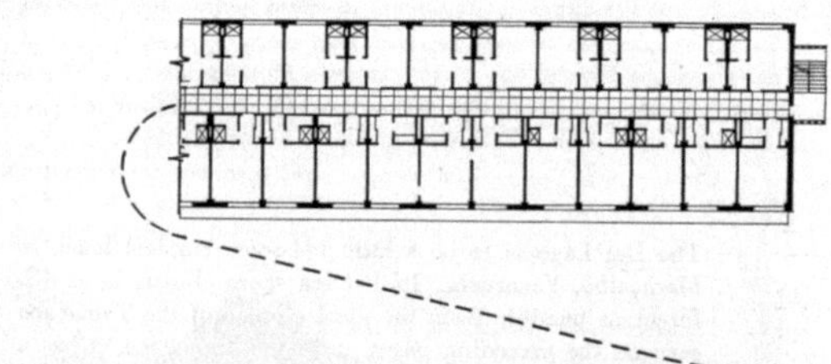

TYPICAL FLOOR PLAN
0 10 60 FEET

BOGOTA'S modern downtown hotel has s

LOCATION: Bogotá, Colombia

CUELLAR, SERRANO, GOMEZ y CIA., LTDA.
Architects, Engineers, and Builders

HOLABIRD & ROOT & BURGEE & ASSOCIATES
Associate Architects

In all its essentials this Bogota hotel might just as well a 400-room house downtown in some northwestern town the U. S. Because Bogota's temperatures vary only wit a short range of 33 to 65°, air conditioning is not nee but there will be baseboard heating, and the architect kept the public areas well glassed in. As a downtown ho this operation will count on recouping $40,000 of its ann $90,000 fixed charges by renting its street frontages stores. To the rear of the hotel is a parking lot. Not cou ing this rental space, the cubage of the hotel would f within H & R & B's standard of a total of 6,000 cu. ft. p room if it were not for the ballroom, demanded by t town, which puts the hotel over its cubage.

Four of the stores are given double frontage—to t street and to a long entrance ramp (see upper plan) a two of the hotel's four bars (an unusual number for t size of house) have attractive street entrances to entice to patronage. And in keeping with H & R & B's love for sun eating and drinking space, the main eating and drinki rooms, on two different levels, have three-way exposure the pleasant, park-like, entrance grounds.

In its guest rooms this hotel follows the same pattern the Tamanaco (page 96), except that the general shape more compact and consequently economical. In fact t compactness—where compactness counts—of the guest-roo stack contrasts interestingly with the open treatment—whe open treatment counts—of the public and commercial area

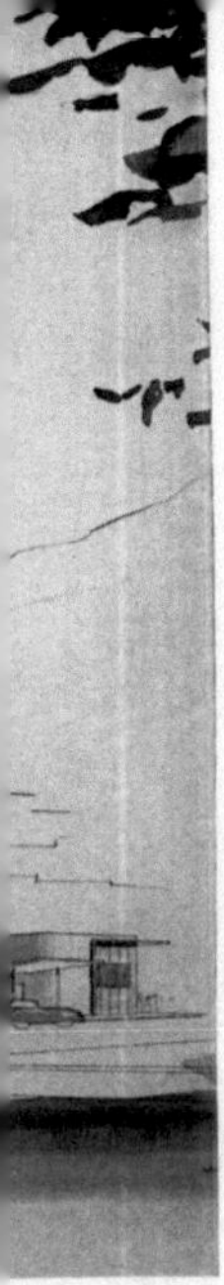

parking

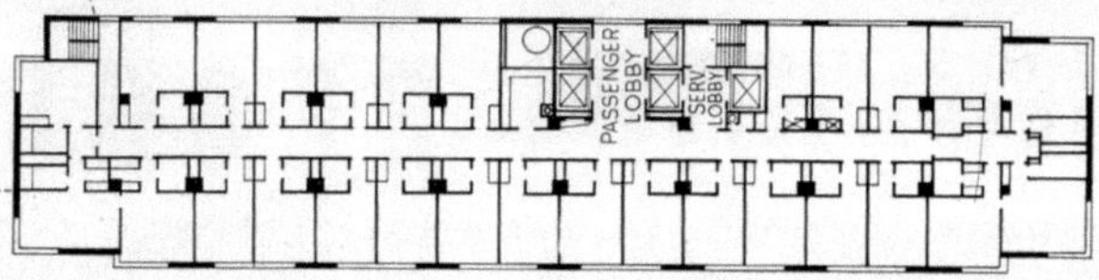

TYPICAL FLOOR PLAN

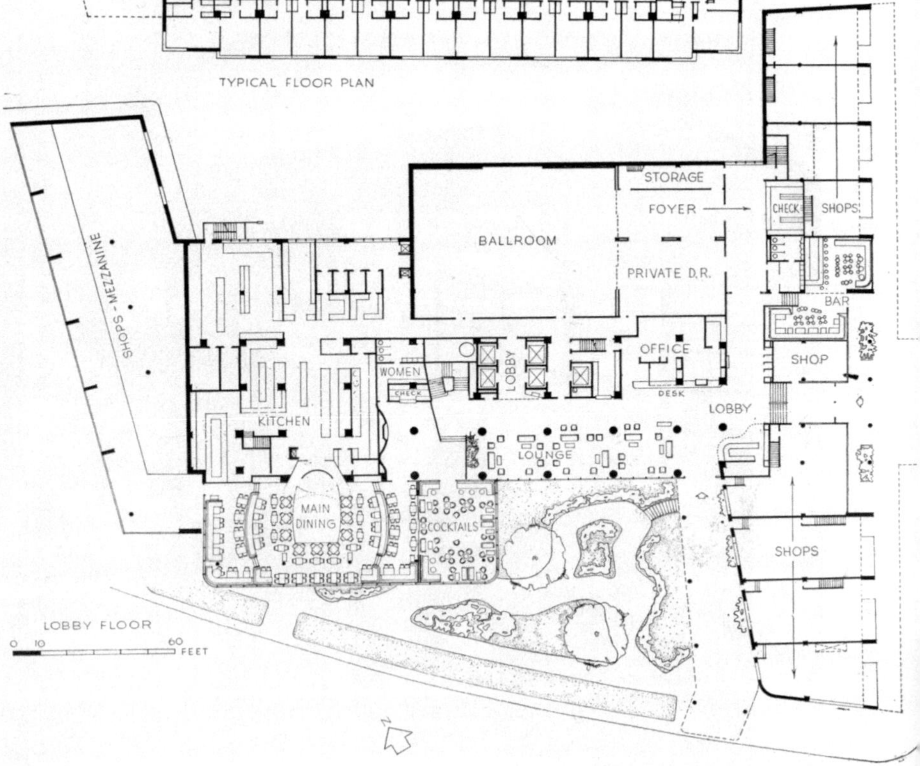

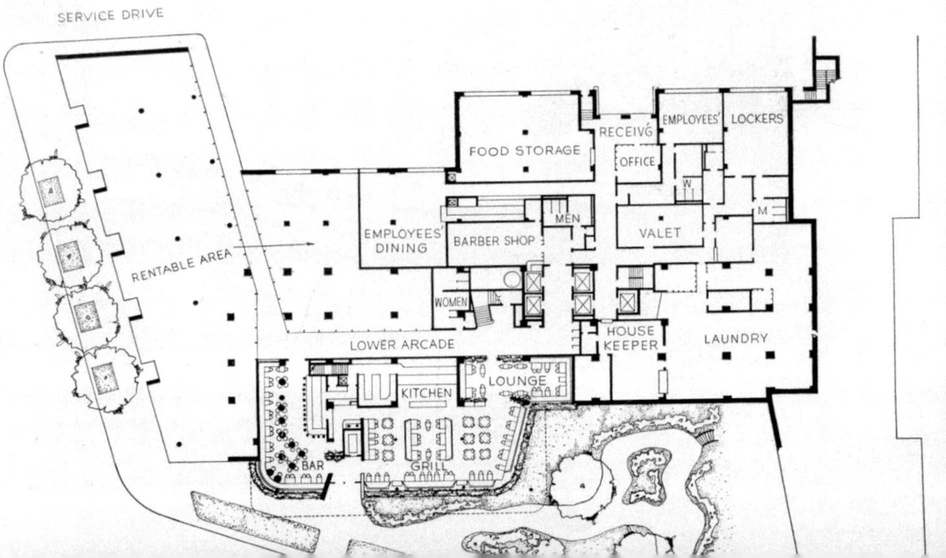

ARCHITECTURAL RECORD

BUILDING TYPES STUDY NUMBER 203

SHOPPING CENTERS

OCTOBER 1953

Hotel Copan, São Paulo, Brazil
Henrique E. Mindlin, Architect
Holabird & Root & Burgee, Associate Architects

INTERCONTINENTAL HOTELS: DESIGN FOR TOURISM

Above: Hotel Victoria Plaza, Montevideo, Uruguay, opened December 1952; 400 rooms; cost $5 million; collaborating architect, Frederico Perralta Ramos. Below: Hotel Tequendama, Bogota, Colombia, opened May 1953; 400 rooms; cost $8.75 million; collaborating architect, Cuellar, Serrano, Gomez and Company

ove: Hotel de Lago, Maracaibo, Venezuela, opened gust 1953; 150 rooms; cost $3 million; Holabird oot & Burgee had no associate. Below: Hotel Tamao, Caracas, Venezuela, opening this month; 400 ms; cost $7.12 million; collaborating architect, stavo Guinand

INTERCONTINENTAL HOTELS Corporation is one organization that probably rates the overworked adjective "unique." Founded in 1945 as a wholly-owned subsidiary of Pan American World Airways, I.H.C. has been responsible for financing, planning, design and construction of the four hotels shown on this page; it has a fifth, the Hotel Copan in Sao Paulo, Brazil (see pages 135–142) under way, and a sixth, as yet unnamed, under contract in Tokyo; and it manages five others.

The key to I.H.C. activities is a financing arrangement worked out through the efforts of the United States Government, which wished to encourage international tourism and recognized lack of hotel facilities in many parts of the world as a major barrier. The Export-Import Bank of Washington, D. C., agreed to make available, to groups in Latin American countries in particular and other countries in general, long-term loans to assist in financing hotel construction. I.H.C. finds local sponsorship for each new hotel project and then acts as agent for securing of necessary loans and credits in the United States. Although local products are used where possible, the larger part of materials and equipment required is not available locally; and it is estimated that well over half the funds expended for these items, including interior furnishings, is spent in this country.

New Tourists, New Hotels

The international tourist of today and tomorrow is the specific target of the I.H.C. program; and design of the hotels is carefully geared to I.H.C.'s concept of the "new tourist": a middle-income American whose regard for comfort and mechanical conveniences that work far outweighs his reverence for hand-carved furniture and crystal chandeliers.

Prelude to Planning

I.H.C. decides to build a new hotel only after a team of architects, engineers and men thoroughly versed in the operations side of hotel management has made a detailed, on-the-ground survey, including types of architecture, sales possibilities both as to food and rooms, climate and possible local trade.

Evolving the Design

I.H.C. architecture, for which Holabird & Root & Burgee and Associates of Chicago, as consulting architects on all I.H.C. projects, are mainly responsible, is the product of a painstaking application of that favorite maxim of the contemporary idiom — how often honored in the breach only its detractors like to say — designing "from the inside out." Design begins in fact with the selection of furniture for a single-unit guest room. After the requirements of furniture and equipment are determined, miniature scale furniture is built and moved around on a scale plan. Next miniature rooms are built and finally a full-scale mockup is constructed of plywood panels and temporary fasteners — a method which makes it possible to expand the walls while different layouts are tried. Suites and finally complete floor plans are developed with the unit rooms as a basis.

In the design of I.H.C. kitchens, the "inside" starts with the menu — types and quantities of food which will be required are estimated on the basis of a detailed survey of the hotel's potential customers, native, transient and tourist, and a typical week's menus are prepared. These are studied to determine the type and quantity of kitchen equipment needed and from this information space requirements are calculated.

Holabird & Root & Burgee work with I.H.C. staff architects and engineers and usually with a local collaborating architect. Contractors of any country can and do bid on the construction. Under a separate agreement I.H.C. will act as purchasing agent; and under a separate operating agreement I.H.C. manages the completed hotel.

Typical miniature model of a single-unit guest room complete with exact replicas to scale of all furniture to be used: early step in the design of every hotel as I.H.C. develops it

JANUARY 1953

ARCHITECTURAL RECORD

Istanbul Hilton Hotel

ARCHITECTS' OFFICES—BUILDING TYPES STUDY NUMBER

194

TOURIST HOTEL FOR ISTANBUL, TURKEY

MOSQUES AND MINARETS, earlier native architecture of Istanbul, will one day soon be scenic contrast to the latest American-aided project in the East, the Istanbul Hilton Hotel, done by Skidmore, Owings & Merrill and their Turkish associate, Sedad H. Eldem.

In architectural terms, the mosques and the minarets have little more significance than ancient and revered landmarks in this or any other country. For something like twenty-five years the Turks have wanted, in fact made a point of rather demanding, international styles of architecture. Virtually all of the large buildings of recent years have been modern in concept and styling, something that could be said of perhaps no other country.

The new hotel will nevertheless represent a new high, literally as well as figuratively. It will be the highest building to date, and the most important, for it will become the focus of business and diplomatic (and tourist) functions and activities. Designwise, it will no doubt stand out for a quality of assertiveness, partly because this is one of the

Ezra Stoller

natural products of the American portion of the design association, partly because that quality is inherent in any of the new hotels beginning to dot the travel maps and posters.

In this instance, however, the scheme of the hotel departs from the strictly tourist concept, for it is to fill a larger need in Istanbul. This is essentially a project of the Turkish government, as are most of the later buildings there, and one of its purposes was to provide facilities for official functions. It is really a combination of the great tourist hotel and the hotel version of a palace.

This thinking is readily visible in the model photographs. The main shaft of the building contains the sleeping rooms, and follows the logical form of many strictly tourist hotels. The lower portion, however, is greatly extended, including all of the lounges, bars, restaurants and shops, flowing outward to pools and gardens and sports facilities of a vacation resort, but also having the banquet and conference rooms of a hotel catering to business and government activities.

These purposes found their way into the architectural expression, though the interpretation is much more natural than the listing of the purposes might imply. The slick efficiency of the hotel-room shaft is manifest, and the extension of the two public floors offers no denial of this note. There is perhaps a gayer or more gracious note in the gradual movement outward of the lower floors, and there are motifs of definitely Turkish origin, these being suitable for tourist or diplomat alike. The picturesque quality of Turkish artistry will find its place in the interiors, even though the tourists have to take cabs to see the minarets.

From its beginning the hotel project seemed to accumulate a great deal of official attention, and was finally blessed with high-level approbation. Istanbul (Turkish government) had long sought to interest

Owner: Turkish Republic Pension Fund
Advisor-Operator: Hilton Hotels International
Associated Architects: Skidmore, Owings & Merrill
Sedad H. Eldem
Partners in Charge: William S. Brown, Coordination
Gordon Bunshaft, Design

Ezra Stoller

ISTANBUL HILTON HOTEL

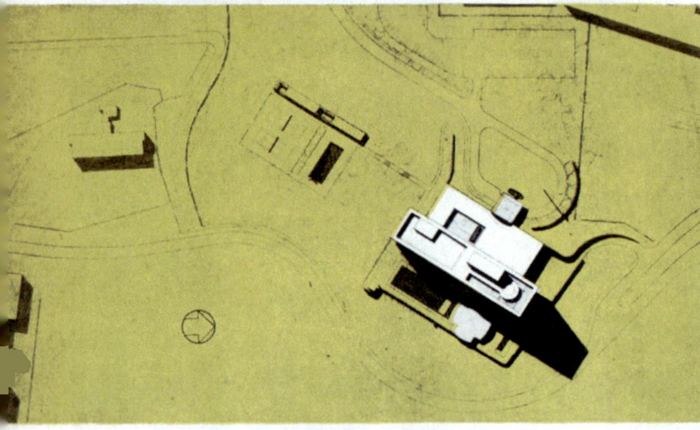

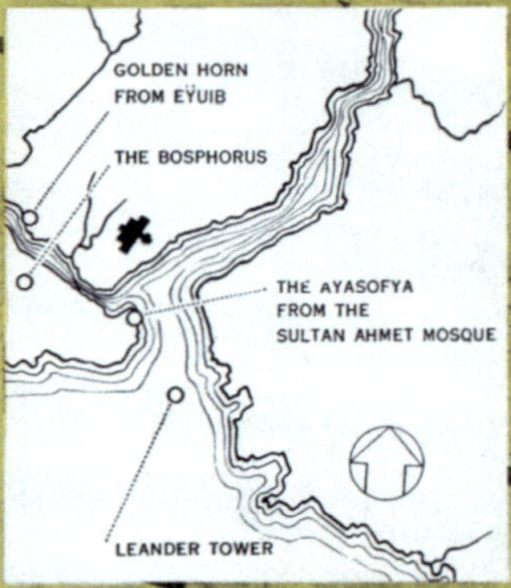

For all of the European influences that have been felt in Turkey in its recent history, the country is still visited for historic scenic attractions. The hotel will have for its site a high hill overlooking the famous Bosporus (left, below). Within range of this hill (telescopic range, perhaps) are such views as the Leander Tower (left, above), the Golden Horn (opposite page) and the mosque d'Ayasofya (page 103)

American capital in such a venture. ECA (now MSA) took an interest in this and other similar moves toward extension of commercial and tourist trade. An official tour was organized, with Conrad Hilton and John Houser of Hilton Hotels International, and Louis Skidmore and William Brown of the architectural firm, who visited London, Rome, Istanbul, Athens. Istanbul was the first city selected; there may be others. The enthusiastic cooperation of the Turkish government was a factor; funds and collaboration were made available. Also the choicest possible site; indeed the site is part of an ambitious park development for Istanbul, and but for official enthusiasm could not have been made available for any hotel, with or without international backing.

A contract with the Turkish government was signed by the Turkish minister of Foreign Affairs and Hilton Hotels International, and was subsequently assigned to the Turkish Republic Pension Fund for administration and for carrying out the provisions. The hotel will be operated under 20-year lease by Hilton Hotels International.

As a design assignment, the hotel had an unusual tie for Skidmore, Owings & Merrill, for the firm had previously been retained by the Turkish government to survey town planning, housing and building. Gordon Bunshaft, partner and design chief, had led a field group in a two-month trip through Turkey, culminating in a major set of recommendations to the Ministry of Public Works. The findings of the survey do not have too much bearing on this project, but the fact of the study did do much to smooth the planning procedures. Turkey does have much of modern technology, but like all Eastern cities is lacking in basic things like steel and cranes and tools and techniques.

Perhaps this hotel project will advance in some degree the firm's own recommendations about developing local industries. It is true that most of the materials will have to be brought in, but the project will have an unusual amount of participation by Turkish interests. Sedad Eldem, an award-winning contemporary architect, was an active participant in the early planning, spending many months in New York. Basic design was done in New York, also engineering. But working drawings were done in Istanbul by Eldem's office, with two S. O. & M. men working there for interpretations.

In design terms this is a normal project, affected by local shortages principally in steel-saving devices. The structural design, in reinforced concrete, was developed to use steel rods with exceptional economy. The structure will stand on continuous footing beams, with reinforcing rods carefully placed to match tension stresses, but designed without too much reliance on bonds. Beams throughout the building get over-sized, not only because of the steel saving, but also for an earthquake condition of second-degree magnitude.

The overall design takes full advantage of a site difficult to match in any of the tourist centers of the world. Bellevue Park, on the top portion of which the hotel will stand, is a high promontory overlooking the strategic Bosporus, with views and breezes to give the steamship and air lines much copy for their tourist folders.

Integration of indoors and outdoors, stressed so heavily in modern tourist hotels, is extensively but very naturally done. The upper (entrance) floor has an open patio in the center, surrounded by a group of shops on one side, main lobby on the other. Lobby opens on the other side to a very long cocktail terrace overlooking the garden, a modern version of the old front porch. Below, on the garden side the near visual focus is a reflecting pool, to be used also for skating. The hillside falls away rapidly toward a huge free-form swimming pool, with tennis courts and cabanas; farther still, to one side, is an amphitheater. And in the distance, those terrific views.

ISTANBUL HILTON HOTEL

Ezra Stoller

The multiple purposes of the hotel show more plainly from the front entrance side; the great extension of the lower floor contains shops, offices, lounges, encircling an enclosed patio, with vast terrace hanging outward toward reflecting pool and gardens

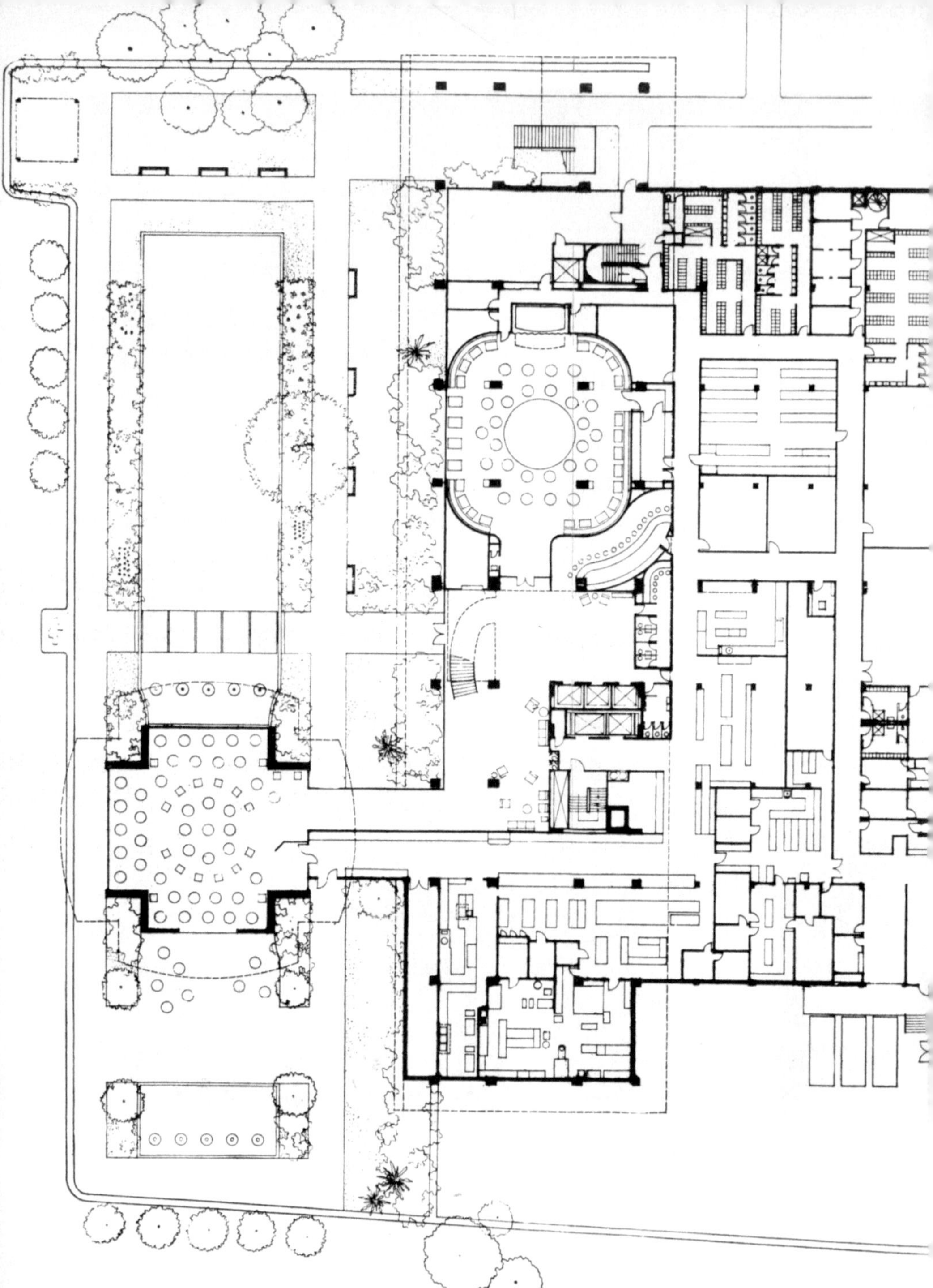

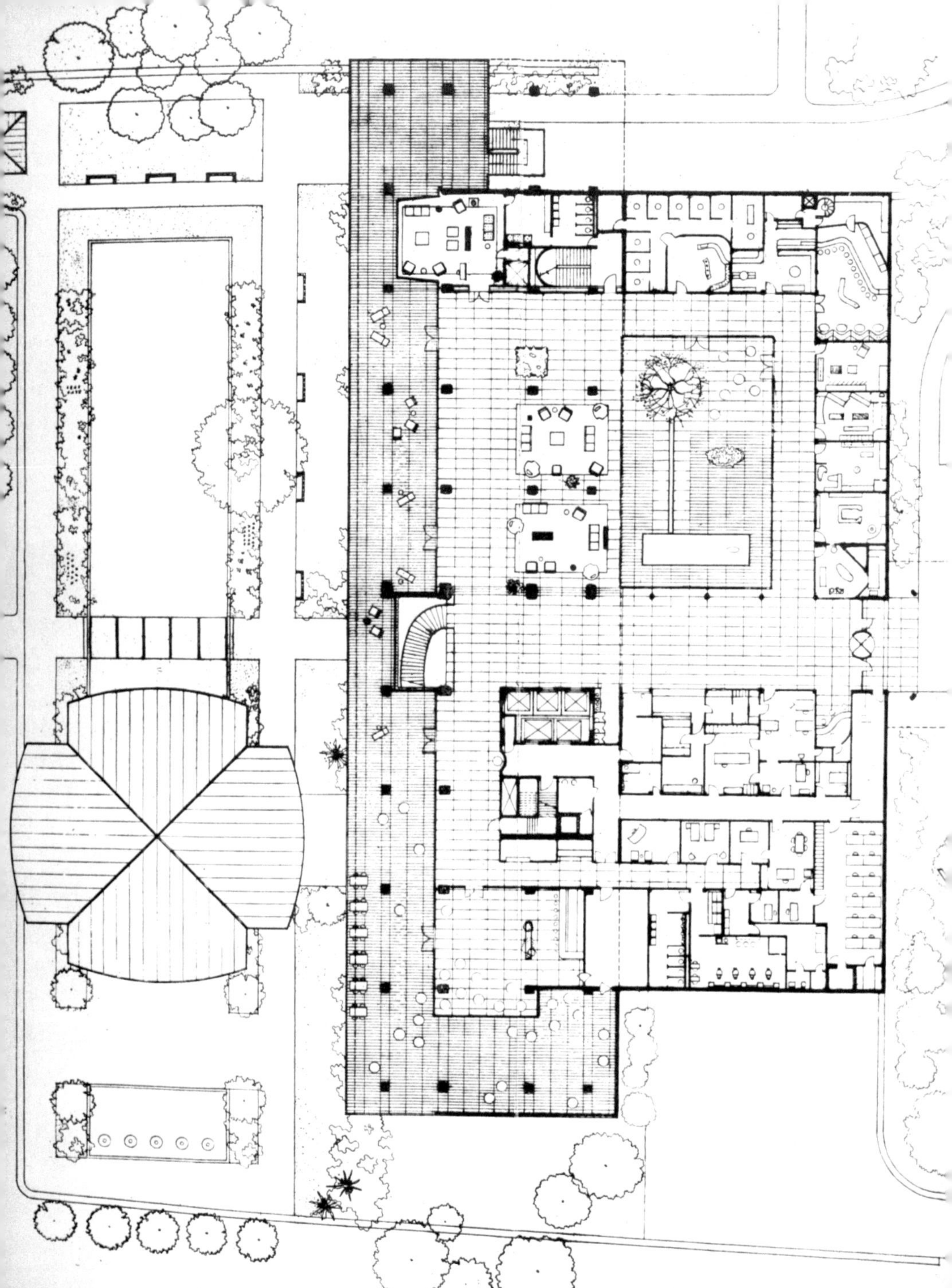

The architect of the pace-setting Hartford and Dallas Statlers has a half-dozen new projects on the way, from Pittsburgh's Golden Triangle to the slopes of a Salvadorean volcano. The difference with Tabler's hotels: even the towel hooks pay off

LENI ISELIN

Bill Tabler's hotel boom

)f all today's complex buildings, few resent more exacting design problems than a big commercial hotel. And there is probably no one who knows more of the tricks of this particular trade than William Benjamin Tabler, a genial 42-year-old New York architect with a pink-cheeked smile and a passion for check lists.

At the moment, Bill Tabler and his young associates are busy men —with some $50 million in construction on the boards. Preliminaries for an 800-room Pittsburgh Hilton (p. 120) have been approved, and the staff of 18 in offices atop the New York Statler is being more than doubled to push out working drawings. Also in the works are a 300-room annex to Denver's famed old Brown Palace, a 450-room hotel for the Meyer chain in Jacksonville, Fla., a 320-room hostelry at Idlewild airport for the Port of New York Authority and Knott Hotels, a 200-room business-tourist resort in San Salvador and another in Ponce, Puerto Rico for Intercontinental Hotels Corp. (pictures, pp. 116 & 117). In varying stages of study are IHC hotels for Guatemala City and Caracas, Venezuela, big motor hotels for Winston-Salem, N. C. and White Plains, N.Y.

If current trends hold, Tabler and other hotel architects will be even busier in the next few years. As railroads created the dozens of big downtown commercial hotels and automobiles the thousands of roadside motels, so the airplane has set off a world-wide hotel boom that hotelmen hope will get new impetus from the fleets of jet airliners scheduled to enter service next year. "Do you realize," Tabler asked a group of real estate men recently, "that just one of these jets will be able to carry as many people a year as the *Queen Mary?* For all but a few flying hours they'll need hotel accommodations."

What fascinates Tabler and others about hotels, aside from this prospect of big future jobs, is the challenge of organizing a whole cross-section of properties under one roof, and making the total both attractive and profitable. A big-city hotel today has the circulation problems of a major terminal, the housing problems of a dormitory with daily turnover, the feeding and entertainment problems of restaurants and meeting halls, the store rental problems of a fair-sized shopping center. "Back of the house" are the service, utility and maintenance problems of a miniature city: heating-cooling plants, laundries, employee dining rooms, furniture and TV repair shops. The new Dallas Statler Hilton, with 1,000 rooms, for instance, actually can hold something like 10,000 people, and its laundry room could serve a town of 25,000.

The big difference today, compared with the last great hotel boom of the tens and twenties, is, of course, labor—both to build and to operate. The rise in construction costs is well enough known. But in the last 20 years alone, hourly wages of hotel employees—always the largest single item of hotel expense—have increased 244%. In the same period, room rates, still the major source of income despite all the fancy bars and ballrooms downstairs, have increased only 172%.*

In today's hotel, economies of service and maintenance have to be built into every detail.

No crepes suzette

Here are the rules-of-thumb Tabler uses to check out a projected commercial hotel:

1. *Construction cost per room no more than $1,000 per dollar of average room rate.* If a hotel wants to make a fair profit on a **$10** average room rate, for instance, total contract cost, including all public and service areas, should not exceed $10,000 per bedroom. "Commercial hotels costing more than this," says Tabler, "must have other sources of revenue or be prepared to go through the wringer as they have in the past." Tabler's Hartford and Dallas Statlers (acquired by Hilton with the rest of the chain) were built just under the $10,000 mark and are reported to be making among the largest "house profit" percentages (before fixed charges) of any hotels in the country.

2. *Bedroom floor area equal to or greater than total public and service areas.* This is what for so many years kept the Statler chain out of secondary cities that could not support a hotel of 1,000 rooms or more; below 1,000 rooms Statler found it could not reduce public and service areas proportionately, and the result was less profitable (until Hartford, where eight years of research and tight planning made a 455-room hotel possible). "The necessary public and service areas," according to Tabler, "have

Design team: Bill Tabler (seated) helps one or two of his young associates develop and manage each hotel job from start to finish, calls in the others for frequent bull sessions. Associates and their jobs (l. to r.): David P. Dann, 32 (Dallas, Pittsburgh); John B. Robinson, 37 (Idlewild); Eugene R. Branning, 37 (Pittsburgh); Ray C. Giedraitis, 34 (junior associate in charge of Denver); John C. Mayer, 33 (Jacksonville and Salvador).

* 1956 year-end survey of 400 US hotels by Harris, Kerr & Forster, hotel accountants and consultants.

Bedrooms on a budge

been running up to 60 to 65% of total construction costs, and that is why we have had to reduce bedroom sizes in recent years to compensate. To some hotelmen it is glamorous to have the biggest night club or the longest menu, but we feel it will be more profitable in the future to have bigger bedrooms and fewer crepes suzette."

3. *Less than one employee per room.* Statler used to average about as many employees as there were bedrooms. In Hartford, though, rising labor costs finally forced design innovations that reduced this figure to 370 employees for 455 rooms, and in Dallas to 600 for 1,000 rooms. (In contrast, Houston's plush Shamrock opened in 1949 with 1,900 employees for 743 rentable rooms, gradually "shook down" to a mere 1,200. Originally laid out as a residential hotel, the Shamrock nearly cost Oilman Glenn McCarthy his shirt when converted to transient use. New owner Hilton has subdivided suites into smaller bedrooms, enlarged dining facilities and made other improvements, but the hotel is still not an outstanding moneymaker.)

4. *Land cost no more than 10% of building cost.* It is unwise to go above this unless you can get it back in unusually lucrative ground-floor rentals or other "outside" sources such as appreciation of surrounding property.

5. *Design to break even at 60 to 65% occupancy.* The national average of hotel occupancy sank to 61% in 1938, rose above 91% in 1945 to '46, in the last three years has leveled off at about 73%. When occupancy drops off over week ends, holidays or low years, Tabler's new hotels can reduce costs by shutting down floors, using segments of total kitchen equipment.

6. *Net bedroom area at least half of typical-floor gross area.* When bedrooms are widened above this point, resulting longer corridors and greater outside wall area make it uneconomical.

7. *At least a 20 sq. ft. difference in room size for two different price ranges.* Tabler has found through use of bedroom mockups and visual design tricks that the average guest cannot detect less than this differential. Recommended minimum bedroom sizes: 90 to 110 sq. ft. for singles, 130 to 150 sq. ft. for doubles, 160 to 180 sq. ft. for twins.

8. *The money is still in the bedrooms.* Departmental profit margins may be anticipated at 70% on rooms, 50% on beverages, 20% on rentals, and down to 0% on food. Today, meeting and feeding facilities exist primarily to bring people into the bedrooms, especially the convention trade. Most hotel operators and accountants try to show a small profit on food, but often they are not charging off the initial costs of dining rooms and kitchen equipment on their food statements. The big hotel dining room with its long menus and lavish entertainment is becoming a thing of the past; operators are turning more and more to "specialty" restaurants—"Rib Rooms," "Polynesian Villages," etc. —where a limited specialty menu can be served at high and profitable prices. Such rooms are, of course, excellent attention-getters, especially for local businessmen on whose patronage a hotel must depend.

Shakedown cruise

If Bill Tabler is being sought out as a leading specialist in hotel design, his background and methods may hold more than passing interest for other architects. After leading his Harvard class through civil engineering and a master's degree in architecture (a nine-year program telescoped into seven), Tabler joined Chicago Architects Holabird & Root in 1939 at $15 a week, worked up to field superintendent on their Washington, D.C. Statler (AF, June '43) before leaving for three years as a Navy construction officer in the Pacific. On his return, Statler Senior Vice President H. B. Callis, who had been impressed with Tabler's grasp of detail, took him on and sent him around Statler's chain of eight hotels to study them and suggest ideas for modernization. Tabler spent six months or

PHOTOS BELOW: ADOLF STUD

seven Tabler hotels

Hartford Statler, Tabler's first hotel job on his own, opened in 1954 opposite Connecticut's state capitol. The product of long research, this 455-room hotel pioneered a 1¼"-thick metal curtain wall, efficient bathrooms, flexible public spaces (see overleaf).

Hotel Robert Meyer in Jacksonville, Fla. will lure motorists downtown with 150 spaces in two parking basements, made possible by moving the mechanical service areas to the third floor (behind a band of air-intake louvers). The concrete frame and block walls are exposed.

International Hotel, designed for new York's Idlewild airport under N.Y. Port Authority control, is efficient but architecturally unexciting. Its 320 rooms, restaurants and meeting spaces for air travelers will be operated by the Knott chain.

Ponce, Puerto Rico job for Intercontinental Hotels Corp. and an investment group will have 204 semicircular balconies overlooking the swimming pool, the town and the Caribbean. The consulting architect was Henry J. Stojowski, a former Tabler associate.

Dallas Statler-Hilton, finished early in 1956 under the new owner's label, adapted many of Hartford's economies in its 1,001 rooms, brought construction cost below $10,000 per room with flat-plate concrete floors cantilevered from two inner rows of columns.

Brown Palace West in Denver will be a 288-room tower linked by a bridge to the parent hotel, echoing its rounded corners and brown masonry face. To be built for $10,000 a room, it will have a ballroom seating 650, and a garage for 80 cars underneath.

Hotel El Salvador, now rising on a volcanic hillside a thousand feet above city of San Salvador, has 204 balconied rooms, special frame and foundations against earthquake. Entrance is at near end between long rows of shops which will have corrugated roof.

© EZRA STOLLER

WILLIAM LANGLEY

LOUIS CHECKMAN

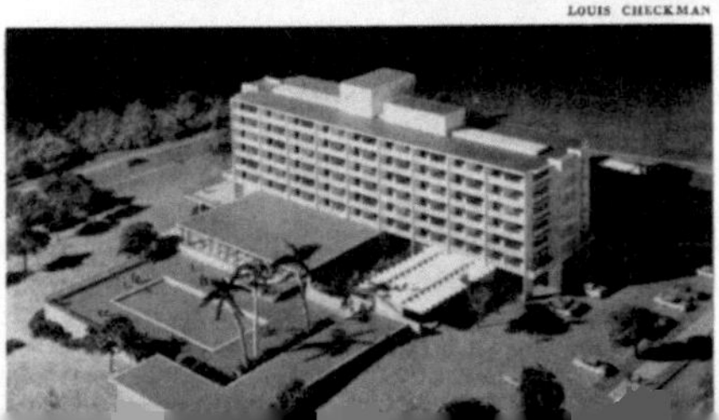

Tabler's design detail

more measuring all kinds of spaces, talking to department heads, questioning why a kitchen or service bar or laundry room in one hotel had to have twice the area to do the same job as elsewhere. When plans for a new Los Angeles Statler came under consideration, Tabler asked for the chance to use his sheafs of checklists and managed to cut a million cubic feet out of the design. A few years later he got the chance to do his own hotel, the Hartford Statler, and from his accumulated research turned out a building that became a model for medium-sized cities (AF, April '53). Between Hartford and the subsequent Dallas Statler (AF, June '54 and April '56), Tabler worked out an array of ingenious cost-saving features, some being adapted to hotels now on the boards:

A single central kitchen as near the hub as possible so that waiters have short walks in all directions to coffee shops, supper clubs, banquet rooms, room-service elevators. One-way circulation is carefully worked out so that waiters move fast and food is hot on arrival.

One huge ballroom, removed from under the bedroom tower and its forest of columns, and flexibly divisible by sliding or folding partitions into as many as five rooms for any sized meeting.

Simplified construction, as Tabler pioneered at Hartford in cantilevered flat-plate slab construction and thin (1½") porcelain enamel sandwich curtain walls. The concrete frame of his new Jacksonville hotel will be left exposed and will be infilled around the windows with a good grade of block that does not have to be plastered as so many local buildings are. Foundations are carefully studied to fit particular site conditions and save money: Pittsburgh will have an unusual "boat" basement, Salvador special earthquake pads that ride on a cushion of volcanic ash instead of going down to bedrock.

Repetitive economies, as represented in Tabler's now-famous bathroom (opposite). Plumbing is back to back and cut to a minimum; an elongated washbasin counter and angled toilet double as makeup table and chair; towel racks are next to the bathtub so guests will dry themselves in the tub instead of using bathmats; a towel hook is placed so they will reuse hand towels instead of reaching for a new one (which Tabler points out can save $7,000 a year alone in laundering costs, or enough to finance another $100,000 worth of construction). Single light bulbs and sinks with simple rubber stoppers are so easily accessible that maids can service them instead of having to call in maintenance. A 5" gap above bedroom closet door allows the closet light to double as hall illumination; windows swing in and up for quick washing from inside. In Denver, Tabler may even remove the "up" and "down" signal lamps from elevator doors on each floor and hang them from the entrance to the elevator cab itself, saving 100 fixtures at $50 each.

Chefs and clients

Tabler's acute cost-consciousness, animated by specific figures, often comes as a pleasant surprise to clients inclined to think of architects as expensive dreamers. He also performs a valuable function the client often cannot perform for himself: if a chef, for instance, squawks about too little space in the plans for his pastry department, Tabler can politely quote from his mental file that such-and-such a hotel has only 1,000 sq. ft. for pastry and does very nicely with it. In keeping the chef from swallowing the housekeeper and the maitre d' from swallowing the chef, Tabler's technique illustrates the balance-wheel value of the architect in any corporate building project.

Tabler is close enough to costs so that his approach to fees doesn't frighten away clients, either. In his projected addition to Denver's Brown Palace, for instance, he simply told the owner, C. K. Boettcher: "I think we can build this hotel, as we have done elsewhere, for about $10,000 a room, or $3 million for

Flexible function rooms in most Tabler's hotels allow one big space double as banquet and meeting rooms f groups of several sizes. Above, doub soundproof partitions are rolled into pla to subdivide the Dallas Statler-Hilton ba room. Below, diagram shows similar "fiv in-one" ballroom for the Meyer hotel Jacksonville.

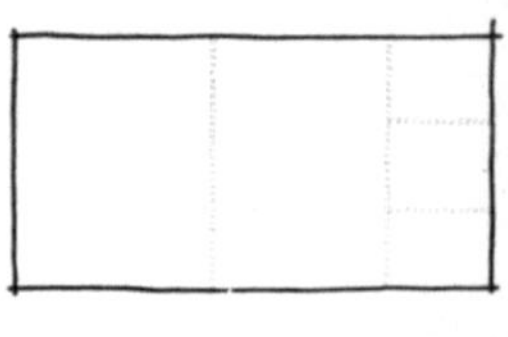

add up to big economies

MEISEL

Careful detailing means large savings when multiplied by 200, 500 or 1,000 hotel guest rooms. In Hartford and Dallas, for example, the closet lights (left) switch on at the room entrance, lighting the hall through the ceiling gap and eliminating an extra fixture and switch. Bathrooms (right) are reduced to 4'-10" x 6'-7", yet mirrors make them seem larger. The toilet is angled to let the door swing in and to serve as a seat for the makeup shelf extension of the special washbasin. The maid can change the single bulb over the louvered towel rack, and plumbing is easily accessible through the back of the cabinet.

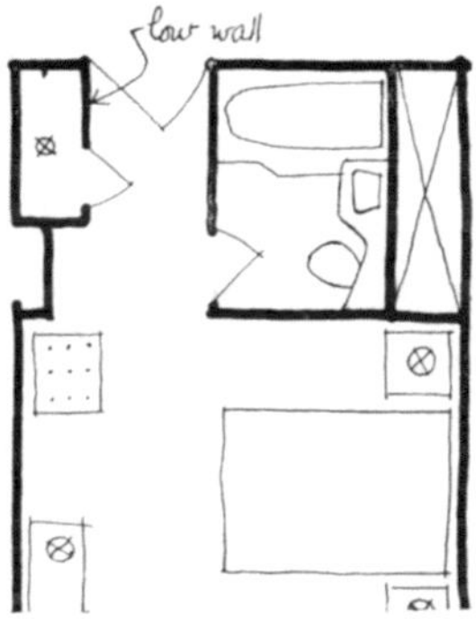

EDWARD SAXE STUDIO

Variety in bedrooms, vital to successful hotel operation, is worked out by Tabler within strict framework of standardized structure, equipment and furnishings. A segment of a typical floor for the Pittsburgh Hilton (above) shows how partitions and furniture are moved to yield many different room sizes and arrangements. The beds can even be placed along the outside wall where solid sections occur between floor-to-ceiling windows. The hollow triangular mullions house air-conditioning risers and TV conduit and give the façade a big "picture frame" pattern (overleaf).

Special foundations for the Pittsburgh Hilton were devised as an economical way of licking the water-pressure problem common to low river land. Whenever ground water rises, a basement not designed for pressure must be allowed to flood, risking damage to its contents (1, below). If dryness is required, the basement slabs and walls must be beefed up against pressure, but then the basement becomes a caisson or "boat" that will try to float up out of the ground with the rising water. To combat this, some Pittsburgh buildings are tied down by expensive tension piles driven to bedrock far below; this is particularly true for very low structures like underground garages which have insufficient weight above to hold them under (2). For the Hilton, however, Tabler and Engineers Seelye Stevenson Value & Knecht hope to have a cheaper system. Columns of the three-story ballroom section (3) will rest on spread footings which go down only as far as solid subsoil, and the ballroom weight will hold down a 12' pressure basement containing various storage and employee facilities. A deeper basement for the hotel's big machinery (4) is held down by the heavier bedroom tower, whose columns rest on a continuous spread footing.

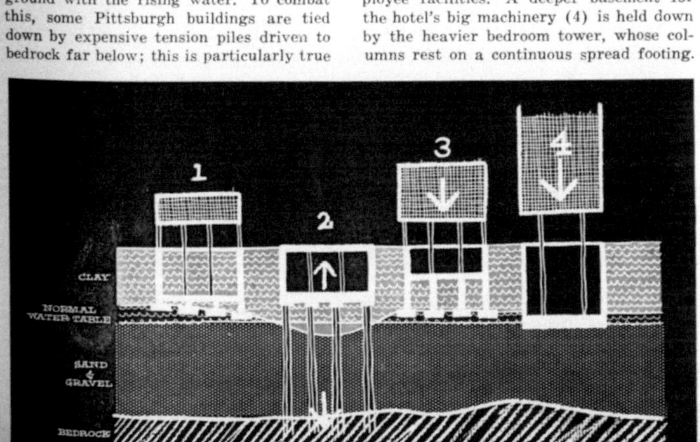

the 300 rooms. I'd prefer to do the job for a flat fee of $180,000 including engineering, which amounts to 6% of our estimate, instead of the usual 6% of actual construction cost. If we don't hold it to $3 million we shouldn't get 6% of the extra cost. But if we do, or bring it in under our estimate, we have certainly earned our fee."

Like other architects, Tabler often has to contend with a basic misunderstanding of his professional worth. One experienced hotel operator who had never actually built a new hotel before looked at a building Tabler had sweated down below $10,000 a room and asked what percentage fee he charged for it. "About 6%," replied Tabler. "About 6%," eh?" said the hotel man. "Why that's exactly what our other architects charge us—you don't save us anything at all!" It takes a bit of explaining that the real savings are in the building's lower cost now and for years to come, not in a smaller fee.

Back at the office . . .

In Tabler's office, unlike some others, one or two associates captain each job from start to finish, conferring with clients, developing the design, supervising production of working drawings, visiting construction in the field. There are no "design men," "office men" or "field men." The result is that each job captain, besides developing as a more rounded architect himself, can serve the client with a more intimate knowledge of the job. Tabler also makes a practice of taking on ten or a dozen college undergraduates every summer to help with working drawings, gives them their head to develop detailing and interior design ideas. He also has a program of 12 weekly talks (schemes for hotels, bedrooms, bathrooms, office practice, working drawings), last year took 30 staff members and wives on a week-end jaunt to Hartford for a critical room-by-room tour of the new Statler.

How about future hotels? Aside from the obvious trend to air conditioning, television and self-service elevators for old as well as new hotels, Tabler and others are looking to mechanization to cut down ever increasing payrolls. In addition to central reservations boards, such as those used by Hilton and Sheraton, chains are considering central accounting computers to reduce the large chit-counting departments and instantly relay bills when guests check out. (It has been suggested that one such computer might be shared by a group of nonchain hotels in the same city.) Direct-dial telephones are now being installed in Hilton's New York Waldorf Astoria on a pilot basis, may cut the number of operators required there and in the Pittsburgh Hilton by 30 or 40%. Other labor-saving ideas still aborning: message lights on guest-room telephones indicating a taped call awaiting; automatic tabulation of telephone charges; recorded good-morning - time - and - weather calls; room - number information lists flashed on television screens in front of operators; registration by two-way television from the curb or from railroad stations and airports; corridors and back entrances monitored by television "eyes" controlled by the desk clerk, house engineer or a single watchman; kitchen conveyor belts carrying complete prefrozen dishes under special quick-heating warmers out to waiters.

Some day the weary traveler may be able to drive directly to his tower-floor bedroom, take his own ice cubes out of a refrigerator without waiting half an hour for room service, recline on a mattress adjustable to hard, medium or soft, in front of a radio-televison screen that can also be turned on by the front desk to warn him of anything from an air raid to a noisy party. But if one trend toward efficiency continues, he won't be able to indulge in that most ancient of hotel pastimes: lobby-sitting. Lounges in new hotels are being tucked off to the side out of the way of elevators and front desk, and reduced in size to discourage free-loaders from the street. Soon there may be no free seats at all.

Tabler's big job:
Pittsburgh Hilt

In the golden triangle this fall excava
will start for the $15 million Pittsb
Hilton. It will rise in front of Equi
Life's Gateway Center office towers
land and mortgage lent by Equitable.
late 1959 guests in most of the hotel's
rooms will have a sweeping view of
State Park, the rivers and the new
pressways and bridges. The plans (o
site) are unusually open and clearly
ganized for a large, complex building.
and elevators are right up front and
ble; foot traffic from five entrances c
lates around an administrative core.
small kitchen serves a coffee shop to
the office buildings, an employee di
room liberated from the basement a
men's bar, which shares the main
with the lobby, the mezzanine and
supper club over the driveway. The bi
banquet kitchen above can be shut
over the week ends and slow period
save money. The ballroom, removed
under the tower and clear-spanned,
seat 2,600 and can be subdivided fo
many as four smaller groups. The
room floors, as in Dallas, are economi
cantilevered from two rows of colu
The curtain wall will be anodized al
num. For colorfastness (and to the jo
Hilton and Pittsburgh publicists) the
will probably be—gold.

Eight schemes of the 15 considered were made into models, dropped in place by Tabler to explain design's development.

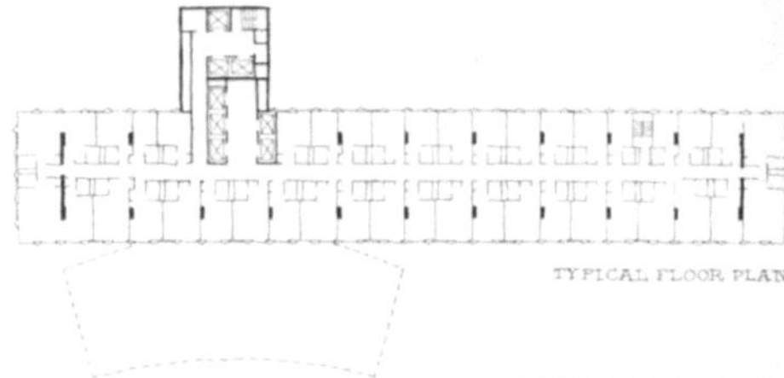

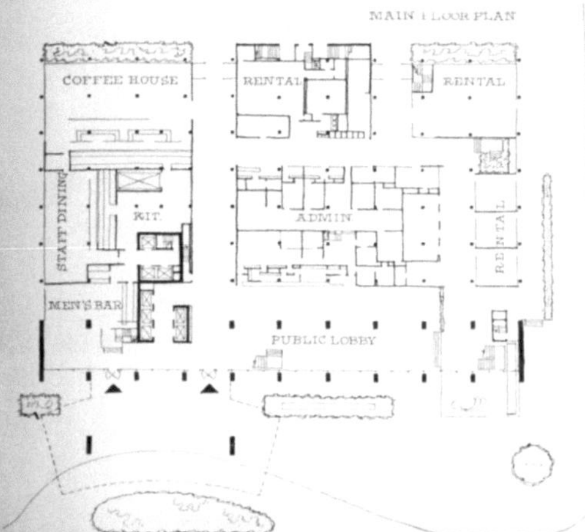

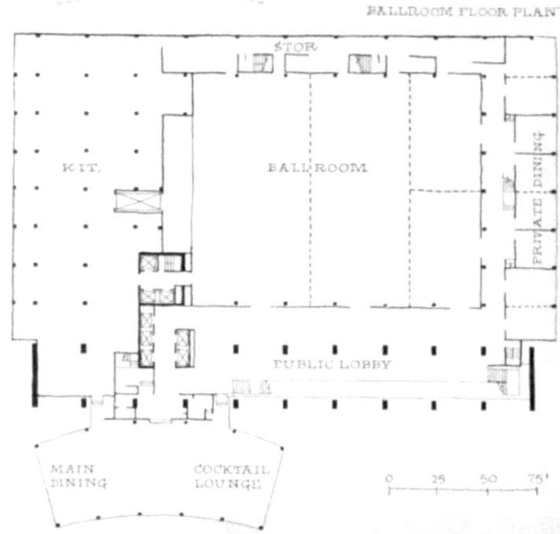

PHOTOS (BELOW & OPP. P.): LOUIS CHECKMAN; (ABOVE): ELI AARON

Welton Becket & Associates fill its cantilevered concrete shell with rich inter

Habana Hilton

Conrad Hilton is an enlightened as well as prodigious architectural cl New Hilton hotels are molded on lines dictated partly by economic ana partly by the untrammeled esthetic decisions of whichever top-ran architectural firm has the job. The $24,000,000 Havana Hilton, hou 630 rooms and suites in its 30 stories, is the 32nd hotel to fly the H flag. It was built by Hilton, and will be operated by him for a C restaurant worker's union which financed the program with its retire fund. Designed by Welton Becket & Associates in collaboration Cuban architects Nicolas Arroyo and Gabriella Menendez, it ranks the Istanboul Hilton of Skidmore, Owings & Merrill as one of Hilton's design triumphs - ornament to the city where it stands. Like all new Hilton hotels it is of reinforced concrete struction, and like all of them it exploits that construction to cantilever balconies all aroun guest tower, giving every room a balcony which — through its sheer glass wall — adds its space and a view of the Bay, Morro Castle, and the entire city to the assets of the decor. spreading lower floors are an intricate network of automobile ramp, landscaped grounds, ar inner skylighted Spanish court which lends outdoor effects to the public areas despite the that the hotel's location in the center of the city forces the lower floors to be walled off and tu inward. To this court, under round plastic skylights in a domed ceiling, guests drive their ca a huge-scaled setting of terrazzo walls, carved wood grilles, fountains, full-sized trees. Co lounges, shops, and other facilities are on this level. But the lobby's upper floor is the center which radiate the chief restaurants and ballrooms, and the cabana-rimmed pool. Furnitu modern and plushy, but art works by native artists, and charactertistic terrazzo and mosaic kling everywhere on walls and floor, set the exotic tropical mood. This combination of ultra-m planning, luxurious furnishings, and Cuban artifacts is typical of the entire enterprise. — (

all photographs by lionel

Habana Hilton *tropical materials and native arts ornament breathtaking modern s*

SECOND FLOOR PLAN

1 *lobby. Central portion is on lower l*

2 *bar terrace*

3 *casino*

4 *las antillas bar*

5 *el caribe supper club, with enclos rim for storage, control room, orch etc.*

6 *ballroom (salon de gala) with stag right and enclosable private dining area at inner corner (salon de los embajadores). Surrounding areas w permanent enclosures include stora space, ballroom lobby, foyer, banq manager's office, food and beverage manager's office, work room, check etc.*

7 *foyer of upper lobby level, leadin main check room, powder rooms,*

8 *elevator lobby, with service lobby a offices beyond*

9 *service areas*

10 *swimming pool, surrounded by ca and adjacent to the poolside antil*

Above: El Patio bar, sporting striped canopy, wood grille, and floral decorations, imaginative terrazzo floor, achieves openair effects on the lower lobby floor. Right: Sugar Bar terrace matches roof-top panoramas with pearl-shell-highlighted blue and beige terrazzo floor, blue and white walls, pearlescent black Swedish granite piers, a curved cast terrazzo mural panel by Portocarrero enriched with many embedments. White lacquered steel chairs have reversible Naugahyde cushions; low white lacquered steel tables have Marlite tops. Architectural lighting by Gotham and Marco. Fountain lighting by Kim Lighting, Pasadena. Luis Mion executed many of the terrazzo floors and ceramic murals in the Havana Hilton.

Las Antillas bar on the upper lobby floor is half indoors (as indicated on plan at left) half on the swimming pool terrace. Its scale enables it to carry the sparkle of rough cleft stone column cladding, Venetian mosaic bar front, a black and white terrazzo floor, and a brilliant Rene Portocarrero tile mural. More detailed descriptions and credits will be found in a special section overleaf.

Habana Hilton *guest suites are varied but always light and view-pervaded*

Salon of the Caribe Suite, one of the luxurious corner suites on the 22nd-24th floors, has a Tapetes Luxor rug from a painting Cuban artist Servando Cabrera Moreno.

Castellana Suite dining room

Castellana Suite terrace

Plan of the three floors which contain the luxury suites is basically the same as that of the rest of the floors in the guest tower, and the plan of the ordinary guest floors can be deduced from them, as well as from the plan of a typical guest unit — shown overleaf. In spite of generous room sizes, every visual device is used to make the rooms seem visually larger: casements are airy and simple, most of the furniture is low and light, flooring is continuous from indoors to terrace edge; window obstructions are absent; balcony rails are light.
Opposite page: Salon of the Caribe Suite has furniture of ebonized mahogany with cording of Chinese sea grass, covered in Boris Kroll fabrics. The floor is in pink-beige marble squares, the walls in beige plaster and beige and gold Kneedler-Fauchere paper, casements of yellow-gold David and Dash rayon gauze.
Above left: Dining room of the Castellana Suite has high-backed chairs made by Decoracion y Diseños of Havana to Welton Becket's design in tortoise-shell lacquered mahogany, gold leaf, and bronze, and upholstered in washable white Adams leather stamped with gold. Silver bowl and tray are part of the hotel's regular service, supplied by the International Silver Company. Lamps by Lamparas Futurama, Havana.
Above right: Terrace of the Castellana Suite has a marble floor which is a continuation of the interior flooring, a balcony railing with a silvery satin finish, an outside Cohn-Hall-Marx drapery of yellow and gold cotton brocade with David and Dash sailcloth lining with Tempo-Resisto treatment.

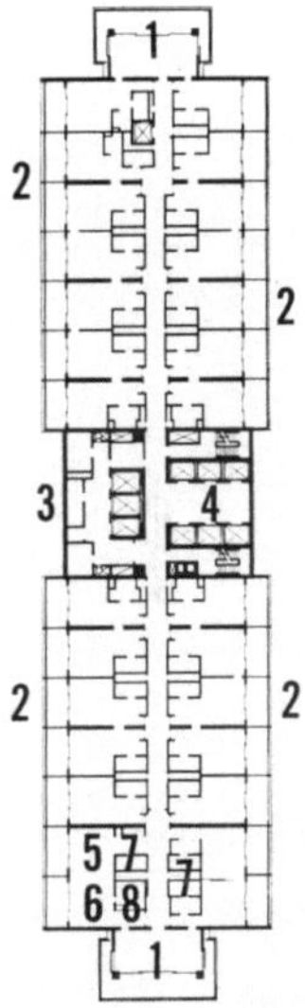

plan of 22nd-24th floors

1 *living room*
2 *bedroom*
3 *restroom*
4 *service lobby, storage, etc.*
5 *elevator lobby*
6 *library*
7 *dining room*
8 *dressing room*
9 *kitchen*

CONTRACTORS AND SUPPLIERS FOR THE HABANA HILTON

accessories
Ad-Pac Company
Baker Linen Company
Ceramica Cubana
Leon De Witt
Federal Seaboard Terra Cotta
Froelich Leathercraft Company
Ivan Gundrum
International Silver Company
Libbey Glass
National Serigraph Society

fabrics
Adams Leather Company
Henry Calvin Fabrics
Cohn-Hall-Marx
David & Dash
Decor Art Interiors
Dobeckmun Company
DuPont Fabrilite
Froelich Leathercraft Company
Golding Decorative Fabrics
B. F. Goodrich
Guilford Leather
Jofa, Inc.
Konwiser
Boris Kroll
La France Decorative Textiles
Jack Lenor Larsen, Inc.
Gene McDonald, Inc.
Moss Rose
W. B. Quaintance & Company
Stroheim & Romann
Morton Sundour
Thaibok Fabrics Ltd.
Tropicraft of San Francisco
United States Rubber Company
Vicrtex Sales Corporation
William Webb Textiles

furniture
Advance Design
Marta Arjona
Bielecky Brothers
Brown Jordan
Contempor
Decoracion y Diseños
Federal Seaboard Terra Cotta
Howe Folding Furniture
Knoll International
Mimbre Art Furniture
Simmons Company
Steinway & Sons Company (piano)
Straus-Duparquet
Troy Sunshade Company
La Esmeralda & Alberto Villablos

floor coverings
Bigelow Sanford
Cabin Crafts Needletuft
James Lees & Sons Company
Marmoles Santa Rita
Alexander Smith
Tapetes Luxor
V'Soske

Continued on Page 159

Habana Hilton *guest rooms boast mechanized comforts, lush decor, neat plans*

Studio bedroom. Detailed furnishings of this "standard fare" room are listed in special section beginning on preceding page mahogany and particle board sliding screen and hardly perceptible storage chest it hides in the dressing area were both Aristides Salgueiro.

1 Salon of the de luxe West Suite. Cuban Botticino marble floor covers the whole suite, balcony included. David & Dash pink rayon gauze curtains and beige and white washable rayon and cotton Cabin-Crafts-Needletuft rug set off furniture executed by Mimbre Art of Havana. Table tops are Parkwood and Kappa Shell.

2 Salon of the de luxe Castellana suite is floored in pink Rosado del Rio Cuban marble, walled in pale yellow Shiki silk from Kneedler Fauchere. Adjacent bedroom, not illustrated, has a huge baroque mirror headboard by El Espejo, Havana, behind the Hollywood twin beds, furniture in pale-finished mahogany, gold leaf and bronze designed by the Becket office, a Cohn-Hall-Marx-lined spread, Boris Kroll upholsteries.

3 Twin bedroom of the de luxe West Suite. Balcony and interior floor are white terrazzo from Luis Mion, walls are off-white painted plaster, casement curtains are pink color-set rayon gauze from David & Dash, outside draperies are white sailcloth from Quaintance treated with a Tempo-Resisto coating from David & Dash. Sliding screen of dark-stained mahogany and particle board by Aristides Salgueiro. The rug is a natural, white, and beige washable cotton and rayon from Cabin Crafts-Needletuft. Balcony chairs are gold aluminum and natural rattan from Troy Sunshade, the table from Marta Arjona, Havana. The Becket office designed the furniture inside. Contempor, Havana night stands have Parkwood tops. Wrinkle-resistant sky-blue rayon and cotton spreads from Stroheim & Romann; all other furniture coverings emerald green and bright pink heavy linen from Konwiser.

4 Salon of the de luxe Castellana suite is marble-floored to balcony-rim wall. Jack Lenor Larsen upholstery and casement fabrics run in the yellow-white and beige range. Hand-made saffron wool carpet from Tapetes Luxor, Texcoco, Mexico blends with pale yellow walls.

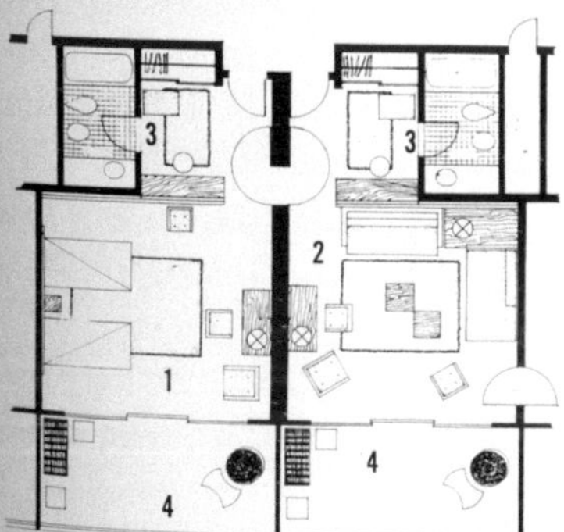

TYPICAL ROOMS ARRANGED AS A SUITE:

1 twin bedroom *3 dressing room opening to bathroom*
2 studio bedroom *4 balcony*

1

2

3

4

1951–2010

Eduardo Catalano

Headquarters
Cambridge, MA

Other Locations
Raleigh, NC, Buenos Aires, Argentina

Founding Partner
Eduardo Catalano

1951

2010

Courtesy MIT Museum

Eduardo Catalano, an Argentinian who studied at the University of Pennsylvania and the Harvard Graduate School of Design (GSD), returned to the United States in 1951 after his six-year tenure at the Architectural Association in London. He returned to take a teaching position at the University of North Carolina.

Prior to founding his office in Raleigh, North Carolina, Catalano collaborated on several projects and won various competitions with other Argentinian architects as well as colleagues from the GSD. The first project he built, his own home in Raleigh, was developed as a result of his research on the structural properties of hyperbolic paraboloids. The house—a thin-shell wood roof structure anchored at two points that enclosed a large glass volume—garnered significant press for the rising architect. In 1956, as Catalano relocated to Cambridge, Massachusetts, to take a teaching post at the Massachusetts Institute of Technology (MIT), the house in Raleigh was named the house of the decade by *House and Home Magazine*.[1]

Catalano continued his research on thin-shell structural systems at MIT but explored several different structural systems at his office. His work varied aesthetically during his five-decade career, but it was consistenly defined by his interest in structural and modular logics. In 1962, the office completed its first major commission, the Julius Stratton Student Center at MIT. Other major commissions soon followed, including the thirty-story tower for student housing at MIT, the Juilliard School of Music at Lincoln Center in New York, and several libraries around Boston. In 1969, Catalano's office completed one of its largest and most significant projects, the Government Center in Greensboro, North Carolina.

In 1970, Catalano received the commission for the US Embassy in Buenos Aires. The project provided the first opportunity for Catalano to build a prominent building in Argentina. The embassy—a large, cast-in-place concrete structure—follows the same structural systems that Catalano had developed in his previous work. In 1987, the office was commissioned again by the State Department to design the US Embassy in Pretoria, South Africa. The project was completed in 1993, as apartheid ended.

Catalano continued to work from his office in Cambridge until his death in 2010. He completed one of his last major works in 2002, when he partnered with Lockheed Martin to produce an enormous kinetic sculpture on the grounds of the National Museum of Fine Arts in Buenos Aires. — JJ

(1)
Jonathan Glancey, "Eduardo Catalano Obituary," *The Guardian* (February 15, 2010).

1951–1997

Paul Rudolph

Headquarters
New York, NY

Other Locations
Cambridge, MA; Sarasota, FL, New Haven, CT; Boston, MA

Founding Partner
Paul Rudolph

1951

1997

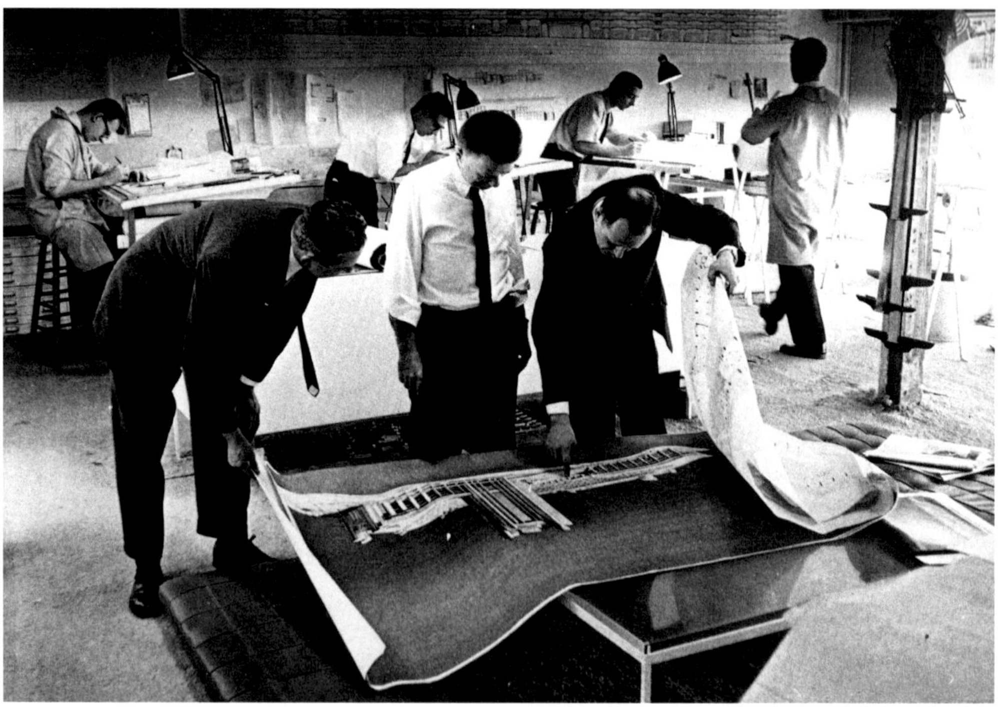

Architecture + Urbanism, January 1975. Photographer: Yuju Noga

In the title of his obituary in *The New York Times* in 1997, critic Herbert Muschamp summarized Paul Rudolph as a "Modernist Architect of the 60's."[1] Though he was born at the close of World War I and worked into the 1990s, Rudolph's legacy is most often associated with his Art and Architecture Building at Yale University, where he was Chair of the School of Architecture from 1958 until 1964. His long career spanned the rise and fall of modernism in the United States, and with it, the mannerist concrete style with which he is associated. Long after the building at Yale, though, much of Rudolph's most prominent work was built in Southeast Asia, where competitions and diverse tastes allowed him to further his ambitions.

After studying at Auburn and the Harvard Graduate School of Design, and serving in the Navy during World War II, Rudolph's career began in Sarasota, Florida, where he and partner Ralph Twitchell were among the members of the group that became known as the Sarasota School. After breaking with Twitchell to establish his own firm in 1951, Rudolph built homes and schools, most notably the airy, modern Umbrella House (1954). Prior to moving his practice to Yale, Rudolph had already been commissioned to design the US Embassy in Amman, Jordan, though it was never built. During his years at Yale, Rudolph saw large-scale academic buildings built in New Haven as well as in Florida, Massachusetts, and upstate New York.

Following the end of his tenure at Yale in 1965, Rudolph moved his practice to New York City, where he oversaw, among other projects, the completion of the State Services Center (1972) in Boston. Featuring the striated and bush-hammered concrete for which Rudolph had become famous at the Art and Architecture Building at Yale, Vincent Scully described the State Services Center as "one of the most inhospitable, indeed physically dangerous, ever devised by man... the building repels touch: it hurts you if you try."[2] Yet, like the architect's unbuilt Lower Manhattan Expressway plan, devised with Robert Moses in New York in the same period, these and other concrete projects represented a high-water mark for both Brutalism and Rudolph's career in the United States.

Rudolph began his overseas career wit the Daiei Building (1971–1973), a concrete corporate headquarters in Japan. Later, seeing in Singapore a nation "expanding their notions of how cities should be built," Rudolph was able to complete his Colonnade Condominiums there (1981–1987), a project reminiscent of his failed 1967 Graphic Arts proposal for a high-rise concrete tower on the Hudson River in Manhattan.[3] Rudolph's firm continued to expand its formal repertoire of towers in Southeast Asia, building in white concrete at the Dharmala Sakti Building in Jakarta, Indonesia (1982–1988) and in glass at the Bond Centre in Hong Kong (1984–1988). While *Progressive Architecture* had collapsed Rudolph's visage onto his signature "corduroy concrete" surface for a 1964 cover, Rudolph saw projects like the Bond Centre as developing an "intention that the building appear to inhabit the sky, and become dematerialized."[4]

While his image as an architect in the US remained fundamentally conflated with the concrete façades of his 1960s work even after his death, only in Asia did Paul Rudolph see some of his grandest plans realized. Summarizing the architect's long life in 1997, Herbert Muschamp acknowledged that, "while Rudolph's place in mid-century American modernism is assured, his role in the expanded culture of globalization remains to be assessed."[5]
— MW

① Herbert Muschamp, "Paul Rudolph is dead at 78; Modernist Architect of the 60's," *The New York Times* (August 9, 1997): 50.

② Vincent Scully, quoted in Tim Rohan: "Rendering the Surface: Paul Rudolph's Art and Architecture Building," *Grey Room* 1 (Autumn 2000): 86.

③ Paul Rudolph, "Enigmas of Architecture," *Architecture + Urbanism* 80 (July 1977): 318.

④ Paul Rudolph, "Bond Center, Hong Kong," *Architectural Record* (January 1989): 77.

⑤ Muschamp, "Paul Rudolph is dead at 78; Modernist Architect of the 60's."

Davis Brody Bond Architects & Planners

Headquarters
New York, NY

Other Locations
Washington, DC; Sao Paulo, Brazil

Founding and Key Partners
Lewis Davis, Samuel M. Brody, Chester Wisniewski (founding principals), Alan Schwartzman, J. Max Bond Jr.

Current Partners
Lewis Davis, Samuel M. Brody, Steven M. Davis, William H. Paxson, Carl K. Krebs, Christopher K. Grabé, David K. Williams

1952

Davis Brody Bond Architects & Planners

SERT, JACKSON AND ASSOCIATES

ARCHITECTS CAMBRIDGE MASSACHUSETTS

1953–1983

Sert, Jackson & Associates

Headquarters
Cambridge, MA

Founding and Key Partners
Josep Lluís Sert (founding principal), Huson Jackson, Ronald Gourley, Joseph Zalewski

1953

1983

Josep Lluis Sert Collection, Courtesy of the Frances Loeb Library, Harvard University Graduate School of Design

Josep Lluis Sert Collection, Courtesy of the Frances Loeb Library, Harvard University Graduate School of Design

The appointment of Josep Lluís Sert as dean of the Harvard University Graduate School of Design (GSD) in 1953 marked the end of the first phase of his career in the United States, which had followed his emigration from Paris to New York in 1939. The position meant both a change in geography from New York to Cambridge, Massachusetts and the revival of Sert's independent architectural practice, to which, by agreement with the University, he was able to devote half of his time. While he continued to work with Town Planning Associates (TPA), the consultancy group founded in 1942 by Sert, Paul Lester Wiener, and Paul Schulz, Sert's private architectural practice overlapped with these efforts until the end of TPA was formally announced in May of 1959.

1953 was also the year in which Huson Jackson was appointed professor at the Graduate School of Design. Jackson had received his architecture degree from the GSD in 1939 and worked with Carl Koch and Joseph Richardson on residential commissions in Boston afterward. He moved to New York In 1946 to establish an office with Harold Edelman, Judith Edelman, and Seymour Howard, a practice he continued to maintain following his return to Boston to teach at the GSD. In 1958, Sert invited Jackson and two associates who also taught at the GSD, Ronald Gourley and Joseph Zalewski, to join his firm, now renamed Sert, Jackson & Gourley. In 1963 the firm became Sert, Jackson & Associates (SJA), the name under which it practiced for the rest of its existence.

With Sert serving as a consultant to Harvard University on its campus planning, Sert, Jackson & Gourley and later SJA played a major role in the transformation of the Harvard campus in the 1960s. The firm's buildings for the University include the Holyoke Center (1958–1965), Peabody Terrace (1962–1964), and the Science Center (1969–1972). Sert also acted as the local architect for the Carpenter Center for Visual Arts at Harvard, Le Corbusier's only building in North America, after working to secure the commission for his former employer in 1961. SJA also completed a major complex of academic buildings for Boston University (1960–1965) including the Law Tower, Mugar Library, and George Sherman Student Union.

Sert, Jackson & Associates often collaborated with Hideo Sasaki, the head of the landscape department at the GSD and director of Sasaki & Associates, integrating architecture with landscape as an essential feature of the firm's designs. Sasaki's work included the landscape design for SJA's US Embassy in Baghdad (1955-1961), a key project in the program launched by the Foreign Buildings Operations (FBO) of the US State Department to build modernist embassies worldwide. Following the Baghdad project, SJA went on to produce numerous projects for clients in Saudi Arabia, including a master plan for the Saudi Arabian National Center for Science and Technology (1977) and a comprehensive study plan for Jeddah (1977–1982), in collaboration with SaudConsult and RMJM.

It was also through Sert, Jackson & Associates that Sert would return to building in Spain, halted by his exile in 1939, in the latter decades of the Franco regime. Following Sert's design of a studio for his friend, the artist Joan Miró, in Palma de Mallorca (1954–1957), SJA was commissioned over a decade later to design the Fundació Miró (1968–1975) in Barcelona. SJA also completed numerous projects in France in this period, including the Fondation Maeght (1958–1964) in Saint Paul-de-Vence, the Carmel de la Paix Convent (1967) in Mazille, and the Ecole des Beaux-Arts et des Arts Appliquées (1967) in Besançon.

By 1970, Sert, Jackson & Associates occupied the top floors of a self-designed building in Cambridge, part of the "Architects' Corner"—so named for the number of firms who also had offices there—which had been inaugurated by the construction of The Architects Collaborative's offices in 1966. SJA reached its largest size, around 60 employees, by the end of the decade, in part through its work for the New York Urban Development Corporation to design housing on Roosevelt Island (1976) in New York City. The firm closed following Sert's death in 1983, in Barcelona, Spain. — RW & MK integrus ARCHITECTURE

1953–

Integrus

Headquarters
Spokane, WA

Other Locations
Seattle, WA; Carmel, IN

Founding and Key Principals
Bruce Walker, John McGough (founding principals), Walt Foltz, Jack Lyerla

Current Principals
Gerald Winkler, Larry Hurlbert, Mark Dailey, Brian Carter, Thomas Corcoran, Preston Potratz, David van Galen, Rebecca Baibak

1953

AIA Spokane Archives

Bruce Walker and John McGough opened their office in 1953 in the abandoned elevator shaft of the Davenport Hotel in Spokane, Washington, shortly after Walker won a national home design competition. In Spokane, Walker joined a growing group of architects who had, like him, trained under Walter Gropius at the Harvard Graduate School of Design and had returned to the Northwest to design modern architecture. The firm, initially named Walker & McGough, designed a series of modernist houses around the city before acquiring its first major project in 1956. The Washington Water Power Building, designed in cooperation with another GSD alumni, Kenneth Brooks, cemented the firm's reputation in Spokane and spawned several additional projects.

Walker & McGough continued to grow throughout the 1960s, opening a second office in Seattle in 1963. Significant projects of the time include the New Spokane Hotel, the Spokane Public Safety Building, and several structures for the University of Washington. In 1966, the firm was renamed Walker, McGough, Foltz, and Nixon and became Walker, McGough, Foltz, Lyerla in 1970, before settling on Integrus in 1991. Along with architecture services, the firm has expanded to provide structural engineering, educational planning, and security consulting.

Beginning with the Washington Corrections Center in 1964, the firm developed expertise in the design of high security buildings. Integrus has completed more than a dozen correctional facilities, justice centers, and police departments and has defined the standards for integrated security design.

In 1987, the firm was approached by the Foreign Buildings Operations (FBO) office at the State Department to provide security upgrades at the US Embassy in Bogotá at the height of Columbia's drug war. Their relationship with FBO continued as it was reorganized and renamed into the Bureau of Overseas Buildings Operations (OBO). Since the OBO installed its Standard Embassy Plan in 1999, which was intended to respond better and more economically to the security threats to US embassies, the eight embassies and consular buildings that Integrus was commissioned for and completed by 2002, have been designed according to its protocols and guidelines. — JJ

John Portman & Associates

Headquarters
Atlanta, GA

Other Locations
Hong Kong, Hong Kong (1988);
Shanghai, China (1993)

Founding Partner
John Portman

Current Partners
John Portman, Grace A. Tan, Walter N.
Jackson, Walter E. Miller, Gordon R.
1953 Beckman, Lell E. Barnes III, John D.
Nipaver, Gregory A. Botsch (principals)

RIBA Journal, December 1977. Photographer: Monica Pidgeon

John C. Portman, Jr. started his architecture practice in Atlanta shortly after graduating from the Georgia Institute of Technology in 1950. In little more than a decade his early work in the center of the city, including the Merchandise Mart and the Peachtree Center, earned him the title of "Atlanta's One Man Urban Renewal Program" in a 1966 issue of *Architectural Record*.[1] The "one man" referred to Portman's multiple roles in the 1957 Merchandise Mart and many major projects: architect, landowner, financier, and developer. By 1966 Peachtree Street was dotted with a half-dozen buildings designed and developed by Portman's companies; the private bridges and promenades connecting his buildings together prompted *Architectural Record* to deem them "a new spatial pattern."

One part of the downtown Atlanta ensemble—the Hyatt Regency—displayed the signature glass capsule elevators and striking multistory atria that would become Portman's signature style. Twenty-two stories tall, the hotel atrium would be followed in 1973 by the HyattRegency San Francisco (part of Portman's Embarcadero Center complex and host to the Guinness-ranked largest atrium lobby) and later by Detroit's Renaissance Center (1977) and the Westin Bonaventure in Los Angeles (1976). While Portman's first atrium was constructed as part of a senior public housing project in Atlanta, it was in his 1970s hotels that the form found its apotheosis.

The voluminous interior spaces and intricate circulation systems allowed these projects to exist apart from the central city fabric. The "new spatial pattern" of Peachtree Street removed pedestrians from the street itself, as the sky bridges did in Los Angeles, San Francisco, and Detroit. The tendency was enough for philosopher Fredric Jameson to take aim at the Bonaventure as indicative of problems of the whole of postmodernism. In *Postmodernism, or, The Cultural Logic of Late Capitalism*, he famously proposes that the hotel "ought not to have entrances at all…for it does not wish to be a part of the city but rather its equivalent and replacement."[2] Portman, for his part, characterized the sky bridges in terms of Venice, spanning not canals, but the "vehicular rivers" that separate his properties from one another.

In 1979, President Jimmy Carter, a Georgia native, played host to Chinese Premiere Deng Xiaoping at Portman's Hyatt Regency in Atlanta. Impressed by the structure, Deng invited Portman to visit China later that year. The personal connection would eventually lead Portman to open the first American architecture office in Shanghai. While Portman's first buildings overseas were the Pavilion InterContinental Hotel and Marina Centre in Singapore, in 1989 the firm designed and developed its first mixed-use project in China—the Shanghai Center. A symmetrical, multi-tower complex, not unlike the Renaissance Center, the project became the tallest building in the city when it was completed. Into the twenty-first century, projects such as Tomorrow Square and the Bund Center in Shanghai and the Yintai Centre in Beijing would cement Portman's reputation as the first iconic American architect in China.

Even with offices in China, India, and Korea, Portman maintains a heavy presence in the center of Atlanta. Portman Holdings still owns the Merchandise Mart—eight million square feet of rentable space that he credits with helping him "get through the rough times."[3] — MW

① Jonathan Barnett, "John Portman: Atlanta's One Man Urban Renewal Program," *Architectural Record* (January 1966): 133–40.

② Fredric Jameson, *Postmodernism, or, The Cultural Logic of Late Capitalism* (Durham: Duke University Press, 1991): 40.

③ John Portman, Interview, "Not Everyone Can be a Successful Architect-Developer," *The Architects Newspaper* (January 21, 2010), http://archpaper.com/news/articles.asp?id=4164#.VFJj0eeQySZ (last accessed October 29, 2014).

Sasaki Associates

Headquarters
Boston, MA

Other Locations
Shanghai, China

Founding and Key Partners
Hideo Sasaki (founding principal), Paul Novak, Peter Walker, Richard Strong, Stuart O. Dawson, Kenneth DeMay

Current Partners
Steve Brittan, Fiske Crowell, Robert Culver, Mark Dawson, Ricardo Dumont, Linda Eastley, Gina Ford, Vinicius Gorgati, Michael Grove, David Hacin, Steve Hamwey, Greg Havens, Peter Hedlund, Jason Hellendrung, Joe Hibbard, Bryan Irwin, Gregory Janks, Dan Kenney, Katia Lucic, Bill Massey, Elizabeth Meek, Fred Merrill, James Miner, Tyler Patrick, Dennis Pieprz, Steve Roscoe, Pablo Savid-Buteler, Chris Sgarzi, Victor Vizgaitis, Alan Ward, Isabel Zempel

1953

SWA Group Office

In 1953, landscape architect Hideo Sasaki joined the faculty of the Harvard University Graduate School of Design (GSD) and established his design practice, Hideo Sasaki Associates, in Watertown, Massachusetts. Sasaki had received his degree in landscape architecture from the GSD in 1948, and taught at the school for eighteen years, serving as chair of the Department of Landscape Architecture from 1958 until 1968. Committed to expanding the conventional boundaries of landscape architecture, Sasaki emphasized teamwork and collaboration both in his practice and in his teaching at Harvard. He joined other in the postwar period in calling for a synthesis between landscape, architecture, and regional planning, arguing that "The landscape architect, because of his specialized knowledge, may contribute greatly to the field of urban design... He may, together with the planner, determine the relational aspects of the use of the land, and may further determine the design structure and form of the overall project."[1] Sasaki recalled that in the postwar years, "there was a spirit of inquiry and excitement, whether it was with architects or landscape architects.... We would work together to achieve a solution that we thought was the most appropriate or creative for a particular situation."[2] True to this collaborative ethos, the firm went through a series of changes in partnership over the next decade, adding Paul Novak to the firm's masthead in 1955 to become Sasaki & Novak, Peter Walker in 1958 to become Sasaki, Walker & Associates, Richard Strong in 1960 to become Sasaki-Strong & Associates, and finally Stuart O. Dawson and Kenneth DeMay in 1964 to become Sasaki, Dawson & DeMay Associates.

In these years, Sasaki collaborated frequently with Josep Lluís Sert, dean of the GSD, as the landscape architects for numerous projects by Sert, Jackson & Gourley (later Sert, Jackson & Associates) in the US and abroad including the Holyoke Center (1958–1965) and Peabody Terrace (1962–1964), both for Harvard, and the US Embassy (1955–1961) in Baghdad. From the 1960s onward, the firm's work included campus planning in addition to architectural and engineering projects. Among the firm's major international landscape and planning projects in this period was the master plan for Costa Smeralda (1968–1978) in Sardinia, Italy, a resort community developed for a consortium led by the Aga Khan. In 1975, the expanding multidisciplinary practice was renamed Sasaki Associates, and Hideo Sasaki remained president and chairman of the firm until 1980.

In recent decades, Sasaki Associates has expanded its practice overseas to Asia and the Middle East through a specialization in large master plans, often with a focus on "sustainable" landscapes. In 2002, Sasaki was selected to design the master plan for the 2008 Olympics in Beijing, China. The plan included the organization of athletic facilities and supporting buildings for the Games, as well as the design of connections to new transportation infrastructure built by the city, including a monorail. Aware of failures by previous hosts to continue the use of Olympic sites after the end of the Games, Sasaki Associates's plan included 1,700 acres of green areas on axis with the Forbidden City, designed to become public space for cultural and entertainment activities in Beijing following the conclusion of the Olympics.

Sasaki Associates has since expanded its expertise in such large-scale planning projects for numerous universities overseas. In 2008, the firm designed a master plan for the American University in Cairo, relocating the school from its historic campus, near Tahrir Square, to the new satellite city of New Cairo. In 2010, the firm was hired by the Singapore Government Ministry of Education to design the campus master plan for the Singapore University of Technology and Design, a new university established in 2009 and developed in partnership with the Massachusetts Institute of Technology (MIT). With over 230 employees, Sasaki Associates currently maintains an office in Shanghai in addition to its original offices in Watertown. — RW & AL

①
Sasaki Associates, *Integrated Environments* (Washington, D.C. and Cambridge, MA: Spacemakers Press, 1997): 9.

②
Sasaki Associates, *Integrated Environments*: 10.

US Embassy Staff Housing
1950–1953

Architect
Raymond & Rado

Location
Tokyo, Japan

Client
US Department of State, Foreign Buildings Operations

Standard Oil Vacuum Company Facilities and Housing
1951

SOM

Architect
Skidmore, Owings & Merrill

Location
Sumatra, Indonesia

Client
Standard Vacuum Oil Company, Standard Oil of New Jersey, Mobil

Ciudad Piar and Puerto Ordaz New Towns
1951–1953

Architect
Town Planning Associates

Location
Bolivar State, Venezuela

Client
Orinoco Mining Company (US Steel)

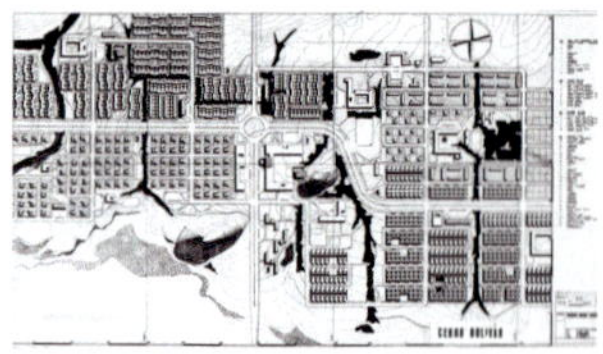

Neighborhood Unit in Pomona
1951–1953

Architect
Town Planning Associates

Location
Maracaibo, Venezuela

Client
Banco Obrero, Agencia Nacional de la Vivienda en Venezuela

US Embassy
1951–1954

Architect
Ralph Rapson & John van der Muelen

Location
Stockholm, Sweden

Client
US Department of State, Foreign Buildings Operations

Central Hospital of Social Security for Employees
1951–1956

Architect
Alfred L. Aydelott Associates, Edward Durrell Stone

Location
Lima, Peru

Client
Social Security for Employees (S.S.E.) General Manuel A. Odria, President of the Republic of Peru

Istanbul Hilton Hotel
1952–1955

Architect
Skidmore, Owings & Merrill

Location
Istanbul, Turkey

Client
Republic of Turkey

Centro Commercial Las Mercedes
1952–1955

Architect
Oficina Don Hatch

Location
Caracas, Venezuela

Client
International Basic Economy Corporation Foreign Buildings Operations

US Embassy Staff Housing
1952–1955

Architect
Ralph Rapson, John van der Muelen

Location
Paris, France

Client
US Department of State, Foreign Buildings Operations

US Embassy
1952–1955

Architect
Ralph Rapson, John van der Muelen

Location
Copenhagen, Denmark

Client
US Department of State, Foreign Buildings Operations

US Consulate and Staff Housing
1952–1955

Architect
Skidmore, Owings & Merrill

Local Architect
Otto Apel, Sep Ruf

Location
Bremen, Germany

Client
US Department of State, Foreign Buildings Operations

US Consulate
1952–1955

Architect
Skidmore, Owings & Merrill

Local Architect
Otto Apel, Sep Ruf

Location
Frankfurt, Germany

Client
US Department of State, Foreign Buildings Operations

US Consulate
1952–1955

SOM

Architect
Skidmore, Owings & Merrill

Local Architect
Otto Apel, Sep Ruf

Location
Dusseldorf, Germany

Client
US Department of State,
Foreign Buildings Operations

St. Anselm Church
1952–1956

Architect
Raymond & Rado

Location
Tokyo, Japan

Client
St. Anselm Church

Amerika Haus
1952–1957

SOM

Architect
Skidmore, Owings & Merrill

Location
Cologne, Germany

Client
US Department of State

UNESCO Headquarters
1952–1958

MBA

Architect
Marcel Breuer Associates,
Bernard Zehrfuss, Pier
Luigi Nervi

Location
Paris, France

Client
United Nations Educational,
Scientific and Cultural
Organization

US Embassy
1953–1958

Architect
Raymond & Rado

Location
Jakarta, India

Client
US Department of State,
Foreign Buildings Operations

The Image of Good Government: The Foreign Buildings Operations Program

The immediate postwar construction of US embassies for an expanding foreign service relied in large part on repayments of war retributions.[1] In the case of the US Embassy in Havana, Cuba by Harrison & Abramovitz (1950–1952), up to 30% of the total cost of the building was provided in materials shipped from various European countries: travertine from Italy, steel from Belgium, partitions from England.[2] Though this form of financing allowed for the rapid build-out of the program, together with high foreign currency assets that allowed the purchase of property abroad without dollar expenditure, it was the 1954 decision to introduce a panel of experts into the process of choosing architects and projects for US embassies that would have the most decisive impact over the following two decades.[3]

The era often referred to as the heyday of the Embassy program was inaugurated in response to mounting criticism and pressure from Congress, some of it directed at the modernism of the program's early postwar buildings. When Leland King, head architect of the Foreign Buildings Operations (FBO) program since 1941, became director of the program in 1953, he formed a rotating advisory panel of illustrious architects that initially included Pietro Belluschi, Henry Shepley of Shepley, Bulfinch, Richardson & Abbott, and Ralph Walker of Voorhees, Walker, Smith & Smith. The FBO's key objectives, as covered enthusiastically in architectural journals in the years after the formation of the Advisory Council, were for each of its buildings "1) to represent American architecture abroad; 2) to adapt itself to local conditions and cultures so deftly that is it welcomed, not criticized, by it hosts."[4] To these Belluschi added more specific design criteria, encouraging the avoidance of "obsolete or sterile formulae or clichés" or anything deemed "bizarre or fashionable."

① Two key histories of the US embassy program are Ron Robin, *Enclaves of America: The Rhetoric of American Political Architecture Abroad, 1900–1965* (Princeton: Princeton University Press, 1992) and Jane Loeffler, *The Architecture of Diplomacy: Building America's Embassies* (Princeton: Princeton Architectural Press, 1998).

② Information on the 1952 Havana Embassy building is available at http://www.docomomo-us.org/register/fiche/former_united_states_embassy_havana_cuba (last accessed September 10, 2014).

③ Jane Loeffler, "The Architecture of Diplomacy: Heyday of the United States Embassy-Building Program, 1954–1960," *Journal of the Society of*

1920

1924 Rogers Act creates the Foreign Service

1926 Porter Act creates Foreign Service Building Commission

1939–1945 World War II

1941–1953 Leland King chief architect of FBO

1946 Frederick Larkin founding director of Foreign Buildings Offices (FBO)

Instead, he advocated for "the sensitive and imaginative designer" able to provide a "directness and freshness of approach" with "a distinguishably American flavor." The task of the Council was to collect and vet a pool of just such "sensitive and imaginative" designers, and they favored younger, up-and-coming architects over established firms. In the period between 1954 and 1957 the committee also intervened directly in the design aspects of projects with specific questions about the necessity of louvers, the security intelligence of all-glass buildings, and the local capacity to pull off construction details.

In this period the priority for FBO buildings frequently went to "developing" nations, particularly in tropical climates, where questions of constructability and context often became the alibi for fashionable shading and screening devices. Though it was clear to those who submitted their credentials for US Embassy commissions that their designs were required to represent a young, forward-looking image, the actual architectural appearance of these buildings was never publicly stipulated by the Advisory Council. The results were diverse, sometimes even whimsical interpretations of the intersection between locality, modernism and Americanism, producing a collection of projects that G.E. Kidder Smith described as "the most brilliant series of official buildings" in 1961.[5] Reactions to individual embassies were more varied. Ada Louise Huxtable, for example, found Eero Saarinen's embassy in London "lifeless," whereas Edward Durell Stone's embassy in New Delhi was both "uniquely beautiful" and aesthetically "American."[6]

In 1957 the American Institute of Architects and the Architectural League of New York mounted an exhibition on the embassy program titled "Good Architecture is Good Government," while *Architectural Forum* echoed the positive evaluation of its products abroad: "Overseas the state department accepts the proposition that good architecture is good government."[7] Yet the financial situation of the program had already begun to deteriorate by this point. While some commissions that had been awarded before 1957 were only completed afterwards, maintaining the image of the program into the early 1960s, the activities of the Advisory Council began to shift as political events prompted a reorganization of the FBO and, as Jane Loeffler has shown, a "more cautious statement of design policy" abroad. — AM

Architectural Historians (September 1990): 255.

④ Key passages from Belluschi's memorandum were quoted in numerous articles that described the beginning of the program. See "Architecture to Represent America Abroad," *Architectural Record* (May 1955): 187; "American Architecture Designed for Export," *Architectural Record* (October 1957): 237.

⑤ G.E. Kidder Smith, *The New Architecture of Europe* (Cleveland: World Publishing 1961); cited in Jane Loeffler, "The Architecture of Diplomacy": 275.

⑥ Ada Louise Huxtable, "Sharp Debate: What Should an Embassy Be?" *The New York Times Magazine* (September 18, 1960): 42.

⑦ "USA Abroad," *Architectural Forum* (December 1957): 114. According to Jane Loeffler, both *LIFE* and *Architectural Forum* also supported the exhibit. See "The Architecture of Diplomacy," footnote 86.

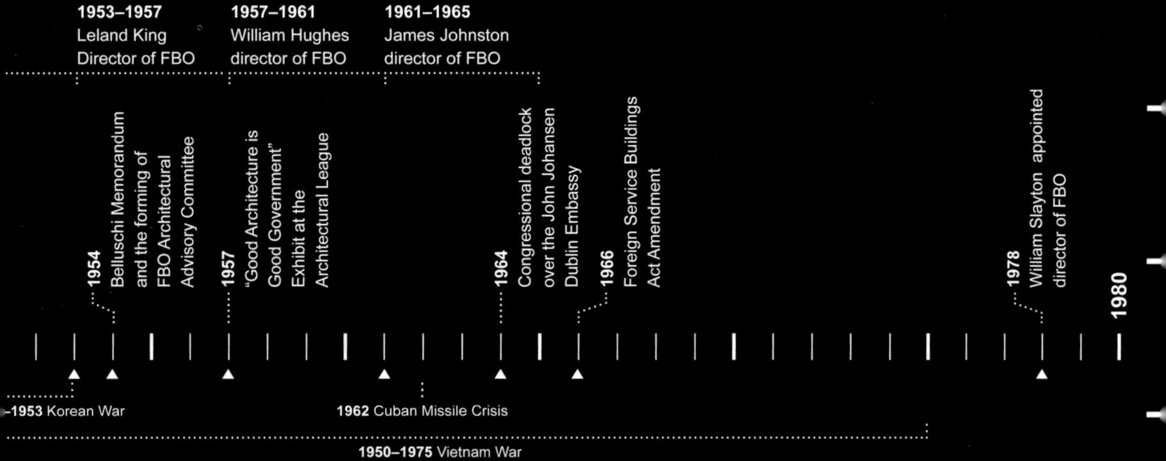

FBO Material Gains From Post-WWII Debt

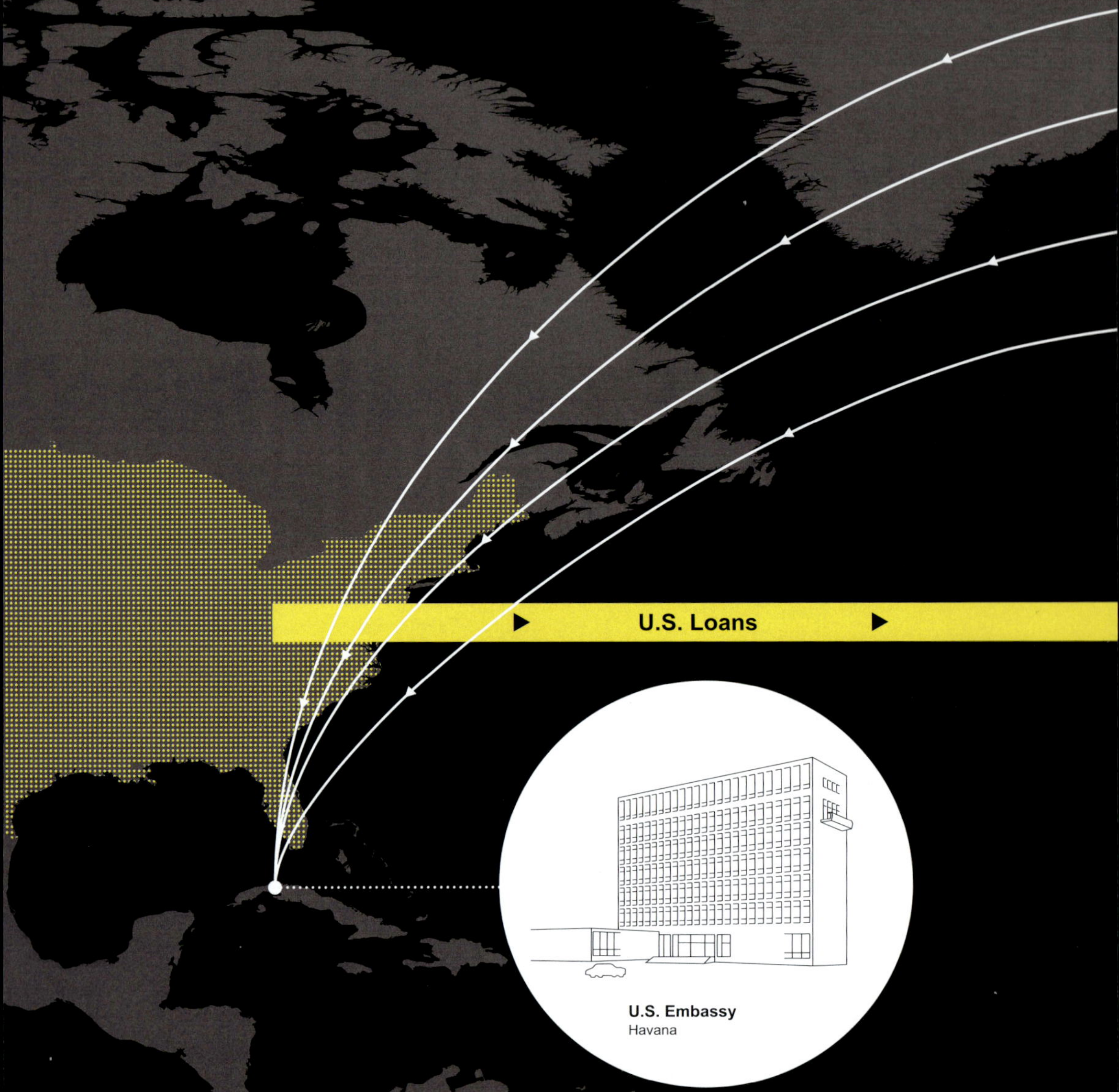

Payment in Materials
Elevator Equipment & Office Partitions
England
Steel
Belgium
Concrete & Furnishings
France
Travertine
Italy

MAGAZINE OF BUILDING

architectural **forum**

March 1953

New U.S. Embassy in Rio looks out toward famous Sugarloaf

U.S. ARCHITECTURE ABROAD

Modern design at its best now represents this country in foreign lands

We are known the world over for the quality of our exports. American automobiles still draw big crowds on European streets, and American airplanes, farm machinery or labor-saving devices are likely to make out well at any foreign industrial fair. Moreover, our technical slang has become part and parcel of many a foreign language: In Greece today, a really pretty woman is known as a "dynaflow girl. . . ."

Now, at last, we are beginning to export some of our best architecture as well. This, of course, is a good deal more important than exporting tractors: Americans have never felt self-conscious about the quality of American machinery—but we have felt very unsure of ourselves in the past where architecture was concerned. In 1893, we did not even trust our own Chicago School; instead, we imported Beaux-Arts architecture from Paris for the Columbian Exposition. In the early decades of this century, Europeans (rather than Americans) recognized the importance of Frank Lloyd Wright and of our engineers—while Americans continued to copy Paris, Rome, London and Athens with the utmost timidity whenever a representative US building had to be erected at home or abroad.

All this is about to change—has, in fact, begun to change already. No country can exercise political world leadership without exercising a degree of cultural leadership as well. Whether consciously or not, the US Government has now made US architecture a vehicle of our cultural leadership. That is the fundamental importance of the story on the next 14 pages.

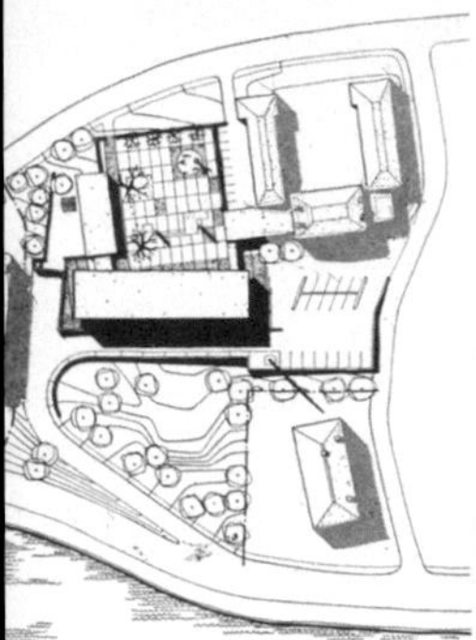

Finland: *Preliminary sketches for new U.S. Embassy in Helsinki, by famed Finnish-born modernist Eero Saarinen. Building will overlook Gulf of Finland. Below: The USSR's new Helsinki Embassy.*

This, incidentally, is the story of one agency of the U Government—the Foreign Buildings Operations (FBO of the Department of State—and its wise decision that onl the best US architecture and the best US architects shoul represent us abroad. In more than 50 embassies, con sulates, information centers and staff quarters now unde construction or completed in places as far apart as Madri and Tokyo, Helsinki and Rio, Berlin and Athens, FB is displaying to the rest of the world a colorful picture o a young, progressive and modern-minded America. Th lesson will not be lost upon those who may have receive a different impression from Soviet propaganda.

But this new crop of buildings is likely to be only th vanguard of a major "export drive" in American archi tecture. Before long, many a US corporation will be build ing headquarters overseas—like the *Reader's Digest* buil ing in Tokyo (AF, Mar. '52), Ford's offices and plant in th Low Countries, US oil companies' structures on the Persia Gulf and US steel companies' towns on the Orinoc And hand-in-hand with such private-enterprise export of American architecture will go technical assistance t many foreign countries in need of our building know-hov

Like all sound commerce, in goods as well as ideas, thi will be no one-way street. The more architects go abroa to design and construct these buildings, the more closel they will be brought in contact with good foreign arch tecture and building, and the more good ideas they wi bring home with them. Undoubtedly there are things th US architects, builders, and manufacturers of buildin materials can learn from abroad.

The questions raised by FBO's activities, therefor are not confined to the most obvious one—i.e. how FBO energetic young director, Lee King, managed to do suc an important and difficult job so very well—there a other questions relating to what US building can teac the rest of the world, what it can learn from the rest of th world, and what US architects and builders will be u against when they work abroad. The story on these page provides some of the answers.

Germany: *Skidmore, Owings & Merrill's Gordon Bunshaft designed new Bremen Consulate at left. Below: Soviet Monument in Berlin.*

Architecture makes a good ambassador:

Note the pretentious classicism

of official Soviet architecture abroad,

then compare it with the clean and friendly embassies, consulates, information c

Cuba: *Harrison & Abramovitz just completed the American Embassy in Havana. Right: The Soviet counterpart.*

De C. Arias

LIFE: *Rubino*

France: *Rapson & Vandermeulen designed these ne staff apartments for Neuilly.*

Doreyne

These are the men responsible for FBO's new buildings abroad:

LELAND W. KING, R.A., director and supervising architect for all projects

EDWARD J. KERRIGAN, deputy director for administration

REGIONAL FBO DIRECTORS:

Alan B. Jacobs, R.A.
Western Europe (except as indicated)

Ides van der Gracht, R.A.
Scandinavia and Russia

Beverley T. Nelson, R.A.
United Kingdom

Lorenz Berz
Austria and Satellites

Jack Gensemer, R.A.
Western Germany

Leo Riordan
Far East (except Japan)

Edward Callahan
Japan

Peter Collins-Cona
South America (Central America is handled from Washington)

Charles G. Osburn
Near East

SPECIFIC PROJECTS ILLUSTRATED:

Skidmore, Owings & Merrill (Gordon Bunshaft, partner in charge), *and the Architektengemeinschaft Apel Architects for all new consulates, America houses and housing in Germany*

Harrison & Abramovitz
Architects for embassies in Rio and Havana

Raymond & Rado
Architects for housing in Tokyo

Leon J. Stynen
Architect for consulate in Antwerp

Ralph Rapson and John Vandermeulen
Designers for embassies in Stockholm, Copenhagen, Athens; consulate in Le Havre; housing in France

Eero Saarinen
Architect on preliminary designs for embassy in Helsinki

Pericles Sakelarios
Consulting architect for embassy in Athens

Anders Tengbom
Consulting architect for embassies in Stockholm and Copenhagen

Garigues & Middlehurst
Consultant architects to Paris regional director, for embassy in Madrid

Knoll Associates
Consultants on interiors and furnishings for embassy in Havana

Thomas D. Church
Landscape consultant for embassy in Havana

Germany: *Skidmore, Owings & Merrill designed this "Amerikahaus" for Cologne*

d staff apartments now being built by the U.S. in many parts of the free world. For details, turn the page

Japan: *Raymond & Rado were the architects for staff apartments near Tokyo*

Brazil: *Harrison & Abramovitz designed our new Rio Embassy.*

EMBASSIES

DeC. Arias

Havana Embassy *is faced with travertine supplied by Italian government out of surplus property debts to US. Base of building is faced with a native coral called jaimanitas. Its color is pinkish-gray. Glass is green and heat-resistant. Structure is reinforced concrete, with 10" x 24" deep columns, 5' o. c., along east and west facades, and clear 40' floor spans across depth of building. These floors are ribbed concrete slabs whose over-all depth is only 12". Tile inserts are removed wherever recessed lighting fixtures are needed. Extra-deep (4"), aluminum Venetian blinds help reduce glare, add texture to facade.*

Embassy office buildings, as distinguished from the ambassadors' residences, are not unlike the headquarters of a small corporation. In addition to a great deal of flexible and secure office space, embassies must contain special departments open to the public and, occasionally, some staff and community facilities like auditoriums and cafeterias. Security regulations and the fact that these buldings are American "islands" on foreign soil have tended to make embassies self-contained and stern looking. FBO Director King, while retaining maximum security, has tried to give the new embassies a friendly and inviting look. Completed to date under the new, modern FBO program, are the embassies in Rio, Havana and Brussells; under construction are the new embassies in Stockholm, Copenhagen, Madrid and Ankara; in planning stage are new embassies for Helsinki, Reykjavik, the Hague, Athens and Jakarta (Indonesia). Seven of these buildings are shown on these pages.

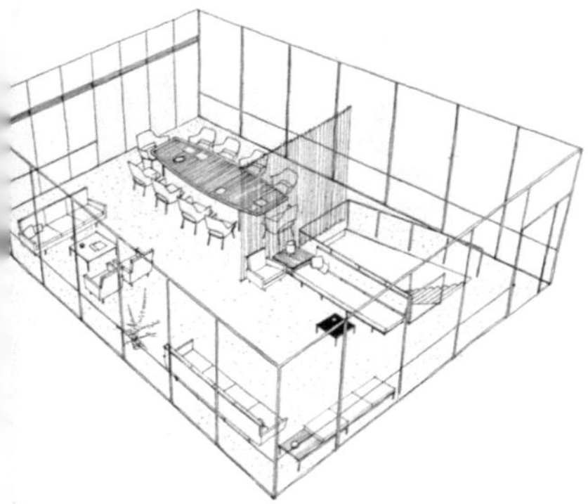

Havana interiors *are now being completed, were designed by Knoll Associates. Sketches show ambassador's modern office (top) and conference room (below). Interior design is important part of FBO program and considered integral part of architecture.*

Estudio Amen

Madrid Embassy *(above) was designed in FBO's Paris office by Regional Director Alan Jacobs, is now almost half finished. As in Havana Embassy, slab building rises out of one-story block which houses such functions as visa and passport divisions and information offices to which public must have ready access.*

I. Shenker

Brussels Embassy *(left), also designed in FBO's own offices, is still somewhat conservative but represented big step forward from earlier, traditional FBO work. There has been some criticism of this building's modern interiors, which the ambassador dislikes*

Stockholm Embassy *(above and right) is now under contruction, should be completed late this summer. One of the handsomest of the new FBO structures, this building occupies a distinguished (though somewhat difficult) site on the edge of downtown Stockholm, opposite British Embassy. Facilities include a small auditorium, lunchroom for staff, and staff garage.*

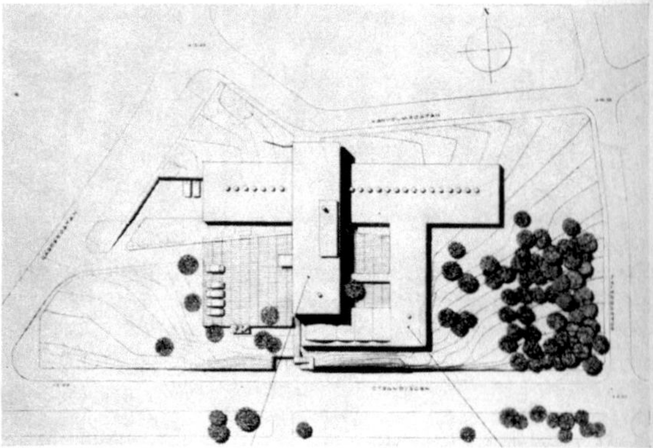

"secure" offices

public offices

offices

cafeteria and auditorium

Athens Embassy *(left and below) is still in the preliminary design stage, may have to be drastically revised for another site. Present plans call for patio-centered office block on stilts, lower building off to one side housing auditorium and staff lunchroom. Formal plaza between two structures is main approach. Designers Rapson and Vandermeulen were responsible for Stockholm, Athens and Copenhagen jobs (see opposite).*

Cost of FBO program is unusually low. State's Frederick Larkin, King's predecessor, and King himself worked out ingenious financing methods for each project, found that foreign governments are delighted to pay for buildings and sites to reduce their old debts to US (from Lend Lease, Surplus Property and Marshall Plan). This method enables our allies to discharge some of their obligations without touching their limited hard-currency reserves; it enables the State Department to acquire valuable property abroad; and it enables the Foreign Service to reduce its office rentals and the quarters-allowances to Foreign Service personnel, which are payable in hard dollars. To date the FBO program has cost $110 million—but 97% of this cost has been met by our allies in soft currencies and with other soft-currency funds. Only 3% of the cost of the program has to be met with new dollar appropriations. Congress is keeping an eye on these costs because of recent criticism of another US project in Germany, the housing of the High Commission staffs.

Copenhagen Embassy *(above) should be completed early next year. Notion of placing office blocks on stilts is not solely esthetic. Such separation of embassy offices from public areas emphasizes need for security control of the former.*

Rio Embassy *(right) by Harrison & Abramovitz was completed last year, is somewhat similar to later Havana building by same architects. Finish is Italian travertine also. Irregular-shaped building in front is small library.*

CONSULATES

Photos: ©—

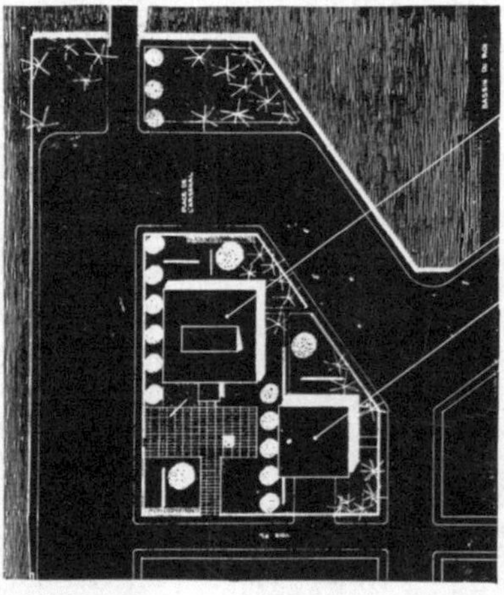

Le Havre Consulate *(left and below) is really two small buildings: one a single-story office structure; the other a two-story building to house the staff. Note that this Rapson & Vandermeulen design (like their embassies on the previous page) makes effective use of a formal approach-plaza.*

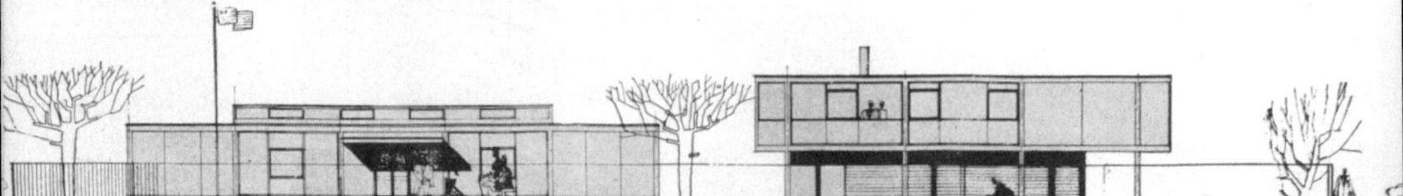

Consulates are really small embassies located in cities important enough to demand US representation. One of the earliest modern consulates was built at Antwerp (see next page), but there are now seven new consulates planned for Western Germany alone, and one small one will soon be built in the devastated French port of Le Havre (see opposite).

Consulates in Germany all follow roughly the same plan-formula: a low-slung, one-story structure (sometimes with a central patio) contains foyers and offices to which the public has access; out of this horizontal mass rises a vertical slab (generally supported on stilts), containing other offices with maximum security. Structure of these buildings by Architects Skidmore, Owings & Merrill and their collaborators will be of exposed steel, with glass or stone veneer panels set into the steel cage. FBO is working on such consulate buildings for the towns of Bremen (now under construction), Dusseldorf, Frankfurt, Munich, Stuttgart, Hamburg (an annex) and Bremerhaven. For typical plan, turn the page.

Bremen Consulate *(opposite and below) by Gordon Bunshaft is first of Skidmore, Owings & Merrill buildings to go ahead. It set the pattern for six more to come. Basic scheme in all is to put public-access areas into large, low-slung building, then straddle it with office tower on stilts. This gives offices in vertical slab better security, makes for excellent architectural composition. Consulate shown here has exposed steel frame, stone veneer and glass panels. Steel is first welded, then sand-blasted, then acid-etched, then zinc-coated and finally given three coats of paint. German process is guaranteed to resist rust for at least ten years.*

AMERICA HOUSES

"America houses" are US information centers in Germany. They are immensely popular, contain well-stocked libraries, reference files and auditoriums. Germans are particularly interested in US technical publications available in the large reading rooms.

Skidmore, Owings & Merrill's office near Bonn is currently working on plans for six such information centers in Cologne, Frankfurt, Hamburg, Berlin, Stuttgart and Munich. All consist of two rectangular units joined by a glazed entrance-link. One unit (all glass and steel) contains library, reading rooms and offices: the other (all brick) contains the auditorium. This plan is sufficiently flexible to fit almost any site. In Berlin's coming "Amerikahaus," the architects carefully screened reading rooms from the street to keep Soviet informers from noting down which Germans came to read "dangerous, war-mongering" books.

Working details reproduced at the right were actually drawn for Cologne's "Amerikahaus" by German draftsmen, show steel fascia and spandrel details in glass wing of building. German detailing of glass wall with hopper (left) and spandrel (right) demonstrates exquisite techniques used by the US architects' collaborators in Bad Godesberg. Material indications and dimensioning differ from US standards, of course, but rendered drawings such as this help overcome these barriers.

"Amerikahaus" Hamburg *(above) is typical of six of these structures now being planned. Solid brick wing at left contains auditorium, glass wing at right (with two-story area in rear) contains library and related offices. Last year more than 10 million Germans visited the few existing US information centers, proved how strong a force the "Amerikahaus" can be in the cold war.*

© Ezra Stoller

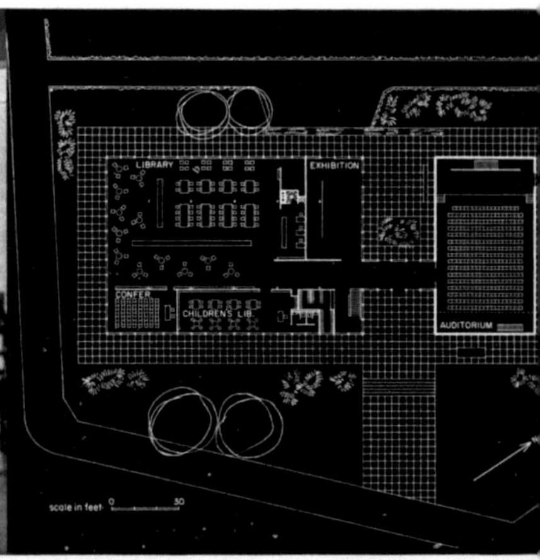

"Amerikahaus" Cologne *(above) will be first US information center to be constructed under new program. Detailing (shown also opposite) is similar to that of consulates, with specially treated, exposed steel very much in evidence. Designer Bunshaft is full of praise for German draftsmanship, for availability at low cost of special equipment and special sizes in windows, doors, etc.*

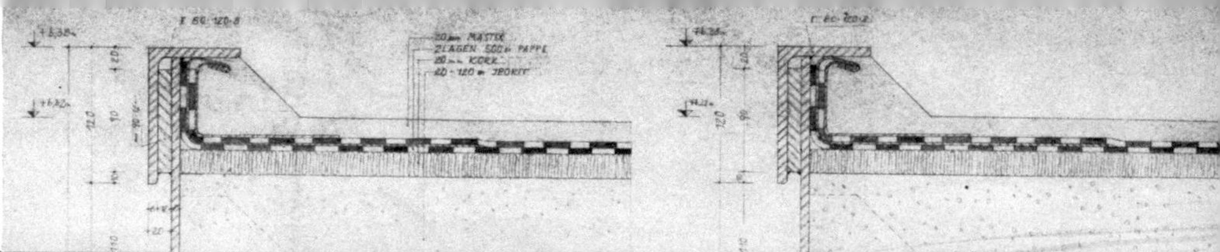

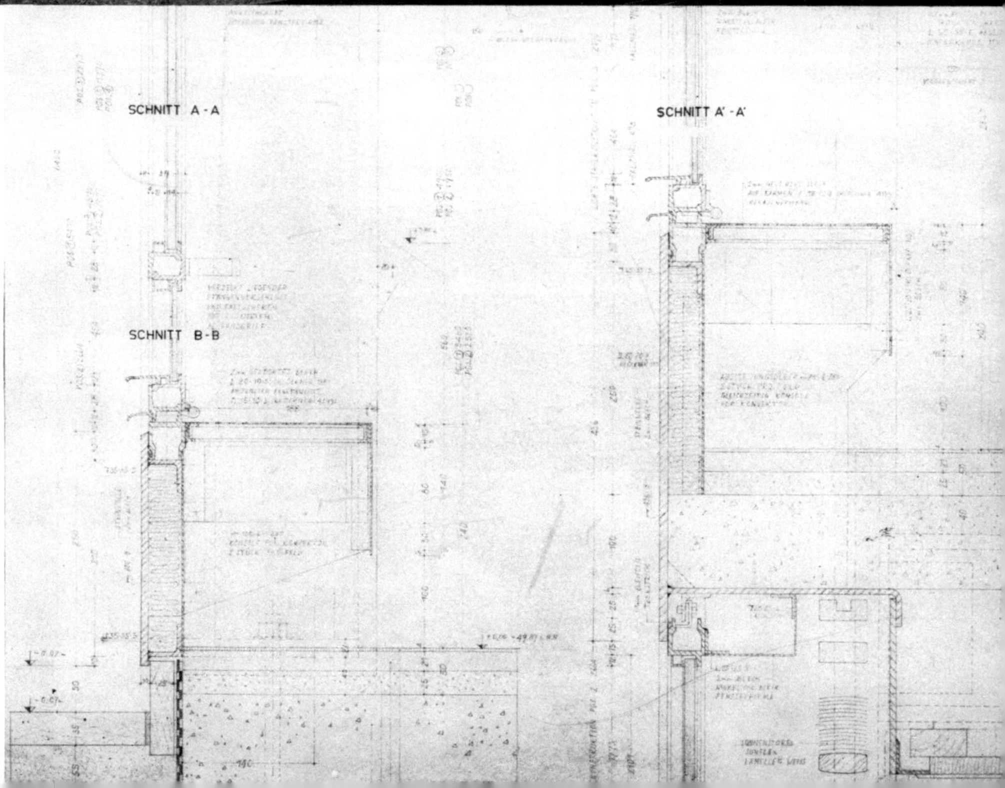
SCHNITT A - A
SCHNITT A' - A'
SCHNITT B - B

Frankfurt Consulate *(above and right) is very similar to Bremen scheme on previous page, but has patio-centered lower floor. Composition is not unlike Lever House in Manhattan, by same architects.*

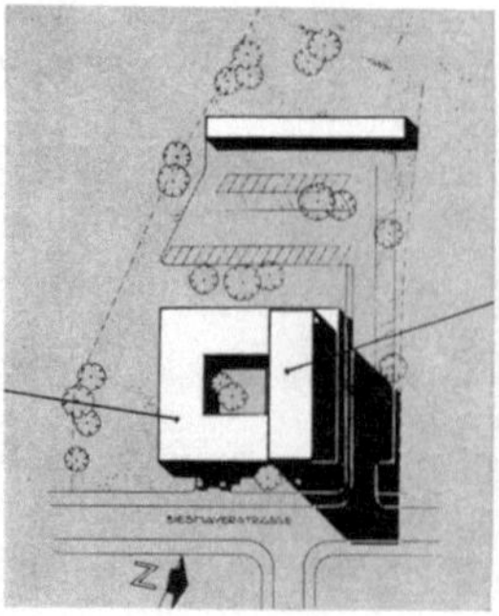

Antwerp Consulate *(below) by Belgian architect Stynen was one of earliest modern FBO jobs. Site is difficult (a middle-of-the-block lot between two streets, with two frontages) but facade treatment is clean and sensitive.*

STAFF HOUSING

'okyo Housing (above) by Raymond & Rado is a handsome apartment building detailed very much like the firm's famous Reader's *Digest Building, also in Tokyo. Japanese concrete formwork is so ine that architects could leave concrete unfinished. Below: Typical Rapson & Vandermeulen apartment for* **France.** *Bottom of page: Staff apartments for* **Western Germany.**

Staff housing is an important part of FBO's program since it will soon pay off in reduced quarters-allowances for Foreign Service personnel and help relieve acute housing shortages in countries like Germany, France and Japan. A handsome, modern apartment house has been completed in Tokyo under FBO's new program, and many additional staff housing units are currently on the drafting boards. In Germany alone, more than 200 apartment units are now in the planning stage. In addition, several new consulates will each require a so-called "principal residence" to house the consul general and his family. Such residences are now being planned for seven German cities whose acute housing shortages make it advisable that the Foreign Service provide its own housing to avoid causing resentment through requisitioning of German buildings.

Recent Congressional criticism of the extravagance of US housing near Bonn referred to the "Little America" projects built near the High Commission Headquarters (see News, p. 40), not to this FBO program. However, FBO is reducing its apartment sizes in the new projects to comply with Congressional demands.

U. S. ARCHITECTS ABROAD

FBO Director Leland King, pointing out Havana Embassy model to Deputy Director Kerrigan in Washington office.

Draftsman Hansgeorg Beckert (German) and Designer Paul Pippin (US) in FBO's Bad Godesberg office.

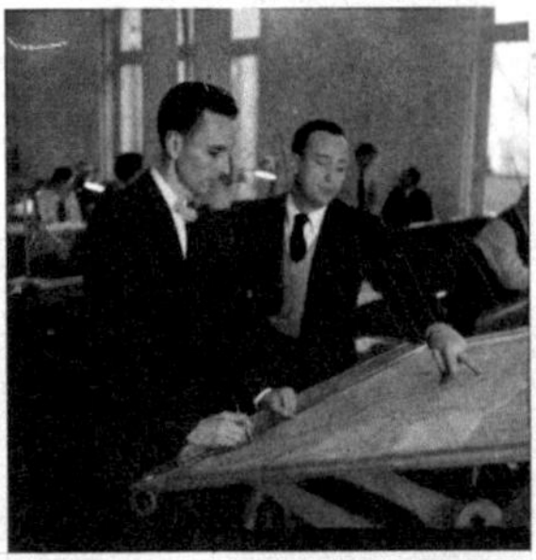

John Vandermeulen and Ralph Rapson (above) are chief US designers in Paris office of FBO. Picture at left shows them with French model maker and model of new staff housing units.

SCHNITT DURCH DIE BRÜSTUNG

One of chief designers in Bad Godesberg office is Natalie DeBlois (US) of Skidmore, Owings & Merrill. S. O. & M's Dave Hughes is the youthful chief of the Bad Godesberg operations.

Give and take between US and foreign architects is an important part of the FBO program. When asked what US building could *give* to the rest of the world, FBO architects listed a) better organization of the job, and b) better integration of the building process. When asked what "know-how" we could *take* from the rest of the world, FBO architects stressed a) better draftsmanship in detailing, and b) better workmanship in the execution of buildings. Said US Architects Hughes and Bunshaft: "Our drawings and specs for Bremen may have been the most complete set ever made in Germany. Hitherto, German architects would draw up plans, elevations, sections and a few assorted details, then start building. When the building was half up, they would then walk in and sketch out some additional details." Because the Bremen drawings and specs were so complete, bids came in very close. But while Bunshaft and Hughes think they taught their German friends a good deal about the organization of a job, they feel that they learned much about beautiful draftsmanship (see details for Bremen Consulate on these pages) and about hard work.

As to building craftmanship, most FBO architects are agreed that European and Japanese standards are often much higher than those in the US. Since there is so little real standardization of building parts abroad, architects can get exceedingly well-made windows, doors, ducts, radiators, etc. in any size and at low cost. This, together with much more liberal building codes, makes possible such slim and elegant details as the convector housing at left. Finally, all agreed that the ideal combination in working abroad is to have a US firm associate with a good local architect, and to utilize good local materials—custom-made, if necessary.

That, in any event, has been the FBO formula to date; and its success has been impressive.

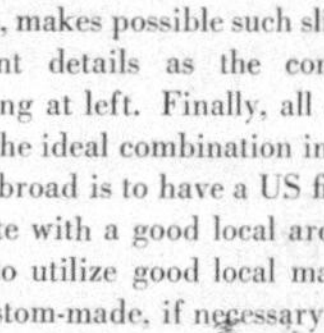

ARCHITECTURAL RECORD

HOUSES 222

MAY 1955

U. S. Legation Office Building
Tangier, Morocco

Hugh Stubbins Associates, Architects

While this rendering is rather dominated by the arches at the entrance, other features will perhaps contribute more to the overall expression: pierced concrete sun screens shading the large glass areas of the three-story building, marble facing at the ends, an arcaded patio landscaped with water pools and orange trees. The Consular Court at ground level will have a surround of glass at the ceiling line with a dado of colorful mosaic tile. The three-story building is roughly in the center of a one-and-a-half-acre site, is surrounded by one-story elements which with it form the entrance court on one side and an enclosed patio on the other. Open arcades provide circulation at ground level. One-story buildings are wall bearing, with stucco finish.

ARCHITECTURE TO REPRESENT AMERICA ABROAD

Regional Expressions of American Architectural Thinking are Sought for State Department Buildings

THE NEW PROGRAM for State Department buildings in foreign countries might be characterized as a significant experiment in regional architecture for diplomatic objectives. Really now just getting to the first-look stage, the refurbished operation has a panel of famous architects to guide it and a clear statement of purposes. A dozen or so American architects have had plans for various buildings approved, and an appropriation decision is now in the making.

Objectives are given as two: (1) to represent American architecture abroad; (2) to adapt itself to local conditions and cultures so deftly that it is welcomed, not criticized, by its hosts. Here is a clear mandate to develop a sympathetic, regional expression of our own architectural thinking, all to a purpose whose importance transcends the normal challenges in design.

This was the need that led to the formation of the rotating Architectural Advisory Panel for the Foreign Buildings Operation, consisting of: Pietro Belluschi, F.A.I.A., dean of the School of Architecture and Planning, Massachusetts Institute of Technology; Henry Shepley, F.A.I.A., of Shepley, Bulfinch, Richardson & Abbott, Boston; and Ralph Walker, F.A.I.A., of Voorhees, Walker, Smith & Smith, New York. The panel is chairmanned by Col. Harry A. McBride, former Foreign Service officer and Assistant Secretary of State, and, from 1939 until his retirement, administrator of the National Gallery of Art.

To state the objectives positively for the panel, Mr. Belluschi prepared this addendum to the State Department's instruction sheet:

"To the sensitive and imaginative designer it will be an invitation to give serious study to local conditions of climate and site, to understand and sympathize with local customs and people, and to grasp the historical meaning of the particular environment in which the new building must be set. He will do so with a free mind without being dictated by obsolete or sterile formulae or clichés, be they old or new; he will avoid being either bizarre or fashionable, yet he will not fear using new techniques or new materials should these constitute real advance in architectural thinking.

"It is hoped that the selected architects will think of style not in its narrower meaning but as a quality to be imparted to the building, a quality reflecting deep understanding of conditions and people. His directness and freshness of approach will thus have a distinguishable American flavor.

"The committee feels that if the above philosophy is adhered to, we need not fear criticism; on the other hand, if we act timidly, solely in the hope of avoiding any and all criticism from whatever quarters, we shall surely end up in dull compromises with the result that we shall have nothing but undistinguished buildings to represent us abroad. We would thereby have forfeited our opportunity to display the high American cultural achievements in the field of architecture generally recognized by architects of the more advanced nations of the world."

Architects invited by the Department of State — after consultation with the Advisory Panel — to participate in the program are sent to visit their assigned sites after intensive briefing by the department and the Panel. They normally then make two "presentations" before the officials and the panel: at the first, preliminary designs are presented and discussed; at the second, the final schemes incorporating any suggestions or amendments arrived at through the first discussion are submitted and — usually — approved. Architects are to visit sites a second time during construction. Although there has so far been no conflict of judgment, it should be noted that the function of the Advisory Panel is advisory only; and the State Department does not bind itself to accept Panel recommendations.

On following pages ten of the early projects in the new program are quickly shown in renderings or model photographs. The RECORD will report further as the program develops.

Office Building (above) and Embassy Residence, Asuncion, Paraguay

Keyes, Smith, Satterlee & Lethbridge, Architects

More than any other, this design was affected by difficulty of transporting materials. Both buildings will be of reinforced concrete columns and slabs with native brick interior partitions and stucco on brick exterior walls. Due to extreme heat, humidity and tropical rainfall, both buildings will have wide galleries and roof overhangs with an umbrella roof above the main roof. The entire office building and sleeping rooms of the residence will be air conditioned. Retaining walls and drainage ditches will be necessary to prevent excessive soil erosion.

U. S. Embassy Office Building and Residence
Tegucigalpa, Honduras

Michael M. Hare, Architect

Office building and residence in this instance are on two different sites, the office building in the city, the residence on a high site some miles away. Both buildings are similar in design, and employ such native features as small wall openings, high ceilings, patios and verandas, using materials and construction typical of the country. Structurally both two-story buildings will be wall bearing with reinforced concrete floor and roof slabs. No air conditioning will be used, as the climate is "ideal."

U. S. Embassy Staff Apartments
Manila, P. I.

Gardner A. Dailey, Architect

This apartment house, containing 30 units of from one to three bedrooms, is in effect four buildings around a planted court, joined together by interior corridor-balconies and a common roof. The open plan takes advantage of the prevailing breeze from Manila Bay. This will be the first of three proposed buildings on 23 acres.

© Ezra Stoller

U. S. Embassy Office Building and Staff Quarters, New Delhi, India

Edward D. Stone, Architect

To achieve a formal expression of both character and dignity, the general design of the office building resembles the traditional Greek or Indian temple. The two-story building encloses an open aquatic garden, which is to be covered by aluminum stripping suspended on cables. All offices are one bay in depth and all corridors become open balconies fronting on the central garden. The design employs the surrounding podium of the Indian temples in that locale. Exterior of the office building is of ornamental perforated tile, marble and concrete, with concrete frame. Space for a future residence for the ambassador has been provided adjacent to the office building. Buildings in the background are apartments for the staff, and quarters for servants. Central air conditioning will be provided for the office building; individual units for the staff quarters.

U. S. Consulate General
Office Building
Lagos, Nigeria

Weed-Russell-Johnson
Associates, Architects

Designed for an enervating climate, the building exhibits a variety of sun control devices and venting ideas. Here the patio is designed as an entrance element, especially to serve the information center, which attracts many visitors. The library will be featured on the street side in window displays. Local stone will be used for facing.

U. S. Consulate General
Office Building
and Staff Quarters
Dakar, French West Africa

Moore and Hutchins, Architects
Georges Pellisier, Assoc. Archt.

So far as local codes permitted, the three-story office building and the apartment building were oriented on the site to catch the prevailing breezes; all living units have through ventilation. Buildings have reinforced concrete frame: exterior facing is Italian travertine, marble and some tile. The design incorporates a great deal of glass, and glass jalousies behind the sunshades. Stainless steel was used for rails and trim, aluminum for windows and frames.

U. S. Consulate General
Hong Kong

Wurster, Bernardi and Emmons;
Feltham and Cumine; Architects

The office building is to be built on the side of a hill opposite the new Secretariat of the Hong Kong government in Victoria, and will overlook the harbor. It is of reinforced concrete construction with native granite facing. It has a fifth floor penthouse for the Consul General and his staff, can add complete fifth floor later.

U. S. Embassy Office Building
Djakarta, Indonesia

Raymond and Rado, Architects

The office building, of two stories, will have a reinforced concrete frame, faced with marble and stone and concrete overhangs. Underneath the sun shades there will be sun louvers of metal. Behind the office building there will be a service building housing generators, cooling towers and a garage. The service area will be separated from the office area by high open-type stone walls enclosing a garden court with reflecting pool and tropical planting.

U. S. Consulate
General Office Building
and Staff Quarters,
Kobe, Japan

Leinweber, Yamasaki & Hellmuth, Architects

This complex of office building apartment house and combined servants quarters and garage, will become an interesting addition to the search in Japan for contemporary methods combined with Japanese qualities in design. Office building will be reinforced concrete and glass, with fiber-glass sunshades to cut off direct rays of the sun but keep the light and views. In the apartments, living rooms will have sliding glass doors to balconies.

USA abroad

Overseas the State Dept. accepts the proposition that good architecture is good government—an idea too little followed here at home

The 15 embassy and consular build ings shown on the following page are a sampling of 50-odd curren projects in the program of the Stat Department's Office of Foreig Buildings (FBO). By and large, th overseas face they present for th US is a face of assurance, impor tance, tact and vitality.

Those last two qualities in partic ular have been so conspicuously ab sent from the federal government' architecture at home—and indee from the official architecture of mos modern governments elsewhere to —as to throw doubt on the ability o the contemporary architect to suc ceed with monumental governmen buildings. The FBO program, now large enough and solid enough t show it is no fluke, proves one thing even though the building with gov ernmental symbolic character is stil no easy assignment, good govern ment architecture *can* be done b US architects. In most of the exam ples shown here, the symbolism necessarily has a flavor of the exoti but to hit this right for Rabat o Accra or Bangkok has been no les

US ambassador's residence and embassy office building for Rabat, Morocco; Ketchum, Giná & Sharp, architects

nanding than it would be to ign for midtwentieth-century shington with vigor and diplo-cy.

To get these creative results from architects, and to raise the stand-ls of its program consistently ring four years, as it has, FBO been pretty creative itself in the ninistrative realm. It has evolved echnique for operating as an in-ligent client that could not only fit other government bodies, but t contains some useful tips for corporate client.

The key stroke at FBO was the ation in Jan. '54 of an architec-al advisory panel, composed of n of real stature* to serve not as igurehead but as a hard-working, sted "building committee." Origi-lly the chairman, appointed for a term, was a former foreign serv- officer. Now the chairmanship es to an active top career diplomat while he is on Washington assignment (usually about a year) between foreign posts. FBO has found this combination of fresh field experience with architectural authority the smoothest working arrangement.

The panel recommends an architect for each project, basing its recommendations on the evidence of brochures which architects who want FBO work must take the initiative of submitting. When congressmen with architect constituents find this apolitical selection hard to understand, FBO's policy and methods are patiently and firmly explained; this has always been accepted and indeed respected. "It is simple to stay unpolitical," says an FBO official, "if you just never, never, never make the first political decision."

The architect gets a full briefing on practical and diplomatic aspects of his project and a trip to the site. Nowadays it is a rare first scheme that does not need revision, perhaps several times, for the advisory panel functions far more as a critical body than in its early experimental days. In one round this fall, for example, revisions were recommended for three schemes on the grounds that one had subordinated too much to parking, another had fallen into the temptation of competition with adjacent commercial buildings, the third was considered too overtly exhibitionistic. But the advisory panel steers scrupulously clear of asking for any rubber-stamp solution. After a critical session, the architect is asked to send by letter his understanding of what was said. This is confirmed against the minutes. If he has misunderstood or forgotten a point, he is straightened out at once. This seemingly simple requirement was the fruit of much trial and error and has worked an enormous improvement in the planning process.

Official US building abroad, not many years ago, was a sorry affair. The change came because of foreign criticism sharp enough to worry the State Dept. into the successful solution. Sharp domestic criticism may be the only means that will force similar reforms at home.

---

resent members—appointed for two-year terms— Architects Richard M. Bennett, Edgar I. Wils, and Eero Saarinen. Their predecessors were tro Belluschi, Henry R. Shepley, and Ralph T. lker.

DELINEATOR: HELMUTH JACOBY

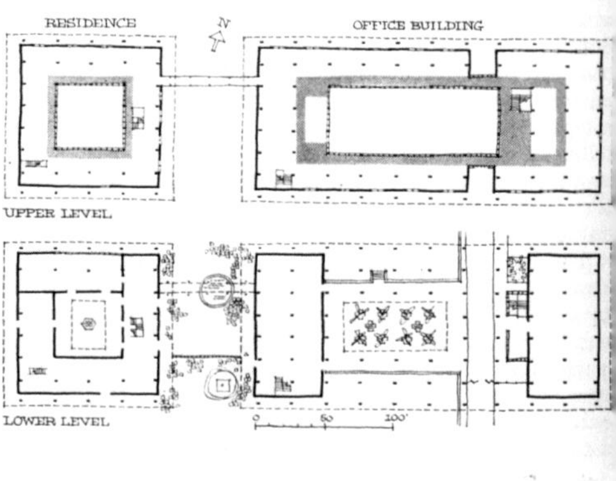

Rabat, Morocco is a city which delights in walled gardens, in intricate play with texture and color, and in surprises around the corner. For it Architects Ketchum, Giná & Sharp have designed an embassy group that overlooks the panorama of the city from an eminence and becomes, itself, a distinctive and harmonious accent in the panorama (p. 114). The embassy office entrance passes alongside a rubble wall, beneath the reinforced concrete roof, and opens into a palm-grove patio (above) with the view of the city glimpsed beyond, beneath the open first story. The second-floor office walls ringing the patio are screened with wood grilles set with colored glass inserts. Separated by another garden is the ambassador's residence (left in plan), the center for formal receptions. On the exterior, windows corresponding with the peaked sections of the roof are sun-screened with vertical aluminum louvers. Operating sash (including 40% of transom lights) catch the prevailing Atlantic breeze to make air conditioning unnecessary.

ARCHITECTS: KETCHUM, GINA & SHARP
PARTNER-IN-CHARGE: MORRIS KETCHUM JR.
STAFF ARCHITECT: OLIVIER DE MESSIERES
ENGINEERS: SEVERUD-ELSTAD-KRUGER, ASSOC.
LANDSCAPE ARCHITECT: THOMAS D. CHURCH & ASSOC.

oul, Korea: Embassy staff ısing by Architect Ernest Kump is designed in small ts (four apartments to a lding) so groupings may ommodate to oriental gar- ıs, some of which, like the in the rendering, already st on the site. Kump de- ned for common local meth- and materials: reinforced crete, masonry, terrazzo, ored tile. The overhangs icipate equinoctial rains summer heat.

akarta, Indonesia: This ıstruction view of the em- ıssy office building by Archi- ts Raymond & Rado is the w which will greet visitors, o approach beside the pool l turn behind the dark blue nted iron screen, beneath a n-shell porte-cochere de- ned by Engineer Paul eidlinger. The former US ısulate here, like all gov- ıment buildings, was of tch influence, now anath- a. The architects did not em as applicable the indig- ous architecture (which tures astonishing "buffalo rn" roof profiles). The new bassy is an example, in- ad, of what might be called ernational-tropical.

JOHN LAUNOIS—BLACK STAR

ıngkok, Thailand: Much ıt Architect John Carl arnecke admired both for auty and practicality in the ligenous architecture of ıngkok (FORUM, Sept. '57) echoed in his balconied em- ssy office building poised htly in a *klong* or lake. The sult is a distinctly nonimi- tive, yet sensitively evoca- ve, design. The structure is inforced concrete with pre- st concrete railings. The ass enclosed offices surround central light well. Cars ar- ve over the arched pilings of useways.

LOUIS CHECKMAN

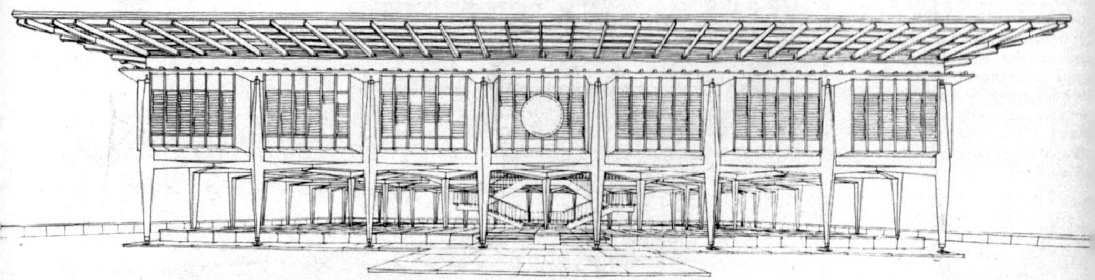

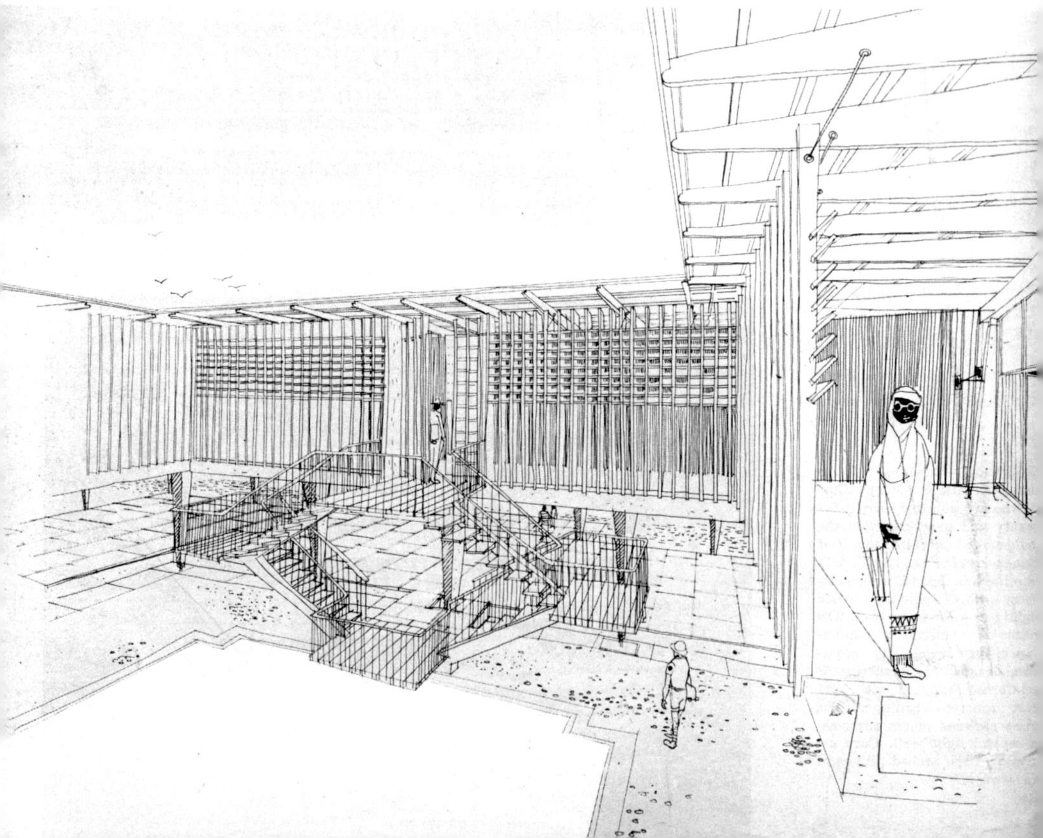

ra, Ghana (left): For embassy office building, er construction, Architect ry Weese had to depend imagination sparked by mon sense. Local inspira- was lacking in the monot- is landscape and the archi- ıre, consisting of imported onry clichés on the one d, and of tin roofs and on the other. Weese be- e convinced that, termites vithstanding, a chief Ghana ort, mahogany, could be d for building at home if it e raised off the ground aided by preservatives. mahogany parasol and rich- louvered walls are sup- ed on tapered concrete mns, cantilevered from an hquake - stable platform. es are one room deep for ilation; the corridor is a o gallery. The building de- ts African students who e seen it, as symbolic of ichness found most often ndigenous wood sculpture.

JOHN BRYSON—LIFE

Karachi, Pakistan (above): This embassy office building by Architects Richard Neutra & Robert Alexander is "straight-forward office, stripped for action," to fit the character of a determinedly modern, young port city. The thin-shell barrel vaults of the adjoining warehouse are echoed by the office penthouse. The warehouse arches into the adjoining pool.

ens, Greece (below): an embassy office building the city of the Acropolis, hitect Walter Gropius' , The Architects' Collab- ive, naturally enough chose lassic. But aiming at a lassic expressing freedom, architects extended the ', put the walls in retreat, permitted the interior t to flow all the way out he entrance.

ROBERT D. HARVEY STUDIO

R. SHIRK

Kobe, Japan: In bustling downtown Kobe, this walled compound with garden is a graceful acknowledgment of US appreciation for Japanese culture. Designed by Yamasaki, Leinweber & Associates, the group includes a consulate (center in model photo), servants' quarters (foreground) and staff housing (far right). The completed group will be shown soon in FORUM.

ANDREAS FEININGER—LIFE

London, England: This is the revised scheme by Architect Eero Saarinen for the embassy project which he won by competition (FORUM, April '56), the only competition, incidentally, which FBO has held or expects to hold. The main change, occasioned both by an 85,000 sq. ft. increase in space needs and Saarinen's discontent with his original proportions, is in the base, which is revised from one projecting story to two recessed stories. Diagonal beams, meeting in points, accent the separation of the base with its public spaces from the office floors above. The original fenestration, staggered precast floor-to-floor box frames, is retained.

R. SHIRK

:aghdad, Iraq: Sun control evices create rich, textured ast and west walls for an em- assy office designed by Archi- ect José Luis Sert. The ierced concrete piers support- ıg the overhanging third story ive vertical shade to the re- essed lower stories. White eramic tile screens and ce- amic glazed louvers screen ıost openings. The double roof onsists of troughs of rein- orced concrete topped with pen joint precast planks; when rains, which is not often, the roughs become drains. The aghdad compound is a large roject; the site sketch shows s center portion, the recrea- on court, with two senior of- cers' villas at left, servants' iesta house at rear, staff partments at right. The hous- ıg has vaulted double roofs. n upper right corner is a por- ion of the monitor-roofed util- y and warehouse building: ıe embassy office building is eyond this at the narrow ead of the compound. At the ther end, also not shown, is ıe ambassador's residence, its ardens running to the Tigris iver. The entire site has been onceived by Sert as a series of ourts, linked from end to end y the irrigation canal.

ROBERT C. LAUTMAN

ima, Peru: Direct and frank- oking, this reinforced con- rete embassy office building by eyes & Lethbridge illustrates ıe means by which many of ıese new overseas buildings eal with the troublesome prob- m of security. Instead of osing up, of becoming a for- ress with slits which literal ollowing of security require- ents would suggest, these ıildings clearly define their ublic areas and keep them ear the ground, then have arefully controlled access to pper security areas, with the hole arrangement unobvious. rom the exterior, even the ell-guarded areas make no -do over "Keep Out!"

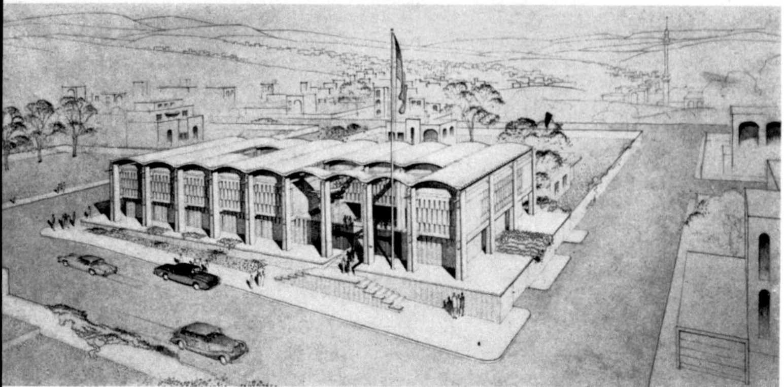

Amman, Jordan: This emba sy office project by Archite Paul Rudolph has unfortunat ly been suspended indefinitel because of Middle East unres Security demanded a wa around this site, and Rudolp ingeniously used the wall for podium, with gated vehicula and service access beneath th platform. The curved precas ribs form a parasol shadin the flat roof beneath; the co onnade is calculated also fo vertical sun shade.

Lagos, Nigeria: This consu lar office building by Weed Russell, Johnson Associates i deliberately relaxed to invit wide use of its library. Th climate is much like that o Florida; the favored buildin material is local stone. Struc turally the building is designe for a third story, anticipatin the day when Nigeria become independent and the consulat is raised to embassy status.

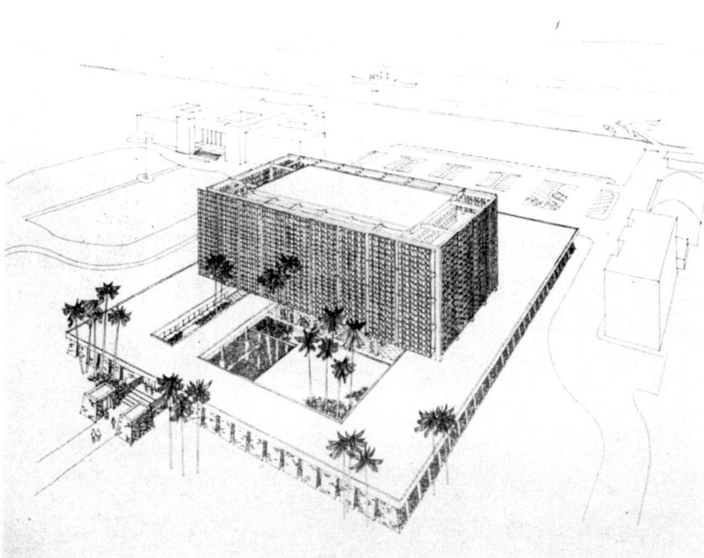

Manila, Philippines: For thi supplementary embassy offic building (the embassy prope is the existing building a upper left), Architect Alfred Aydelott harked back to the picturesque *Intramuros*, old Spanish-walled Manila. His base is of the same volcanic rock, used in the same rugged fashion. The offices, raised above pools and gardens, are glazed floor to ceiling and screened with precast concrete, inspired by laced bamboo screens which admirably protect huts from the sun.

New Delhi, India: Architect Edward D. Stone's already famed (and already ancestral) embassy office building is now under construction. The almost incredible serenity and grace of its façade is fulfilled within by the magical-shadowed water garden at the building's core. (Photos: © Ezra Stroller.)

John Hejduk

Headquarters
New York, NY

Founding Partner
John Hejduk

1954

2000

Gampe

John Hejduk began his architectural journey in 1947 at The Cooper Union, the same place where he ended it half a century later. Hejduk transferred from Cooper Union to the University of Cincinnati in 1950, and finally completed his architectural education at the Harvard Graduate School of Design in 1953. He later described his training as benefiting equally from his academic work and his work as a manual laborer, building tract houses with his uncle. Upon finishing his masters degree, Hejduk was promptly recruited by the new dean at the University of Texas at Austin, Harwell Hamilton Harris, and by Bernard Hoesli, Hejduk's colleague in the office of Fellheimer and Wagner in New York, where he had worked during his work-study program at Cincinnati. Hejduk joined a faculty of young dynamic teachers in Austin in 1954, completing the group later to be canonized as the Texas Rangers. Along with Hoesli, Robert Slutzky, Colin Rowe, and Lee Hirsche, Hejduk was involved in the reanimation of the school's curriculum.

It was in this experimental pedagogical environment—one that included discussions of two-dimensional and three-dimensional composition, color theory, and precedent analysis—that Hejduk developed the problem of the nine-square grid, first given to students at UT Austin in 1954. In Hejduk's architectural work the nine-square grid sponsored a series of studies from 1954–1963 collectively titled the Texas Houses. Hejduk spent only one year in Texas, moving back to New York in 1954 to work in I. M. Pei's office and teach at Cornell. After the Texas Rangers disbanded, each of its members continued developing aspects of this shared pedagogy in their respective corners of academia: Hoesli at the ETH in Zurich, Slutzky and Rowe at Cornell, Hirsche at Williams College, and Hejduk at The Cooper Union, where the nine square became famous as the first-year assignment under his tenure.

After joining the Cooper Union faculty in 1964, Hejduk began inflecting the school's pedagogy with these and other Texas experiments. The pedagogical results eventually appeared in the famous exhibition of Cooper Union student work, produced from 1964 to 1971, at the Museum of Modern Art and were published as *The Education of an Architect: A Point of View* (1971), followed by a second volume of student work from 1975 to 1982. Hejduk became dean in 1974 and remained in the position until his death in 2000. Over the course of three decades he was responsible for bringing important voices into both the school and the New York architectural scene in general, as evidenced by the many subsequently notable students who passed through the school under his tenure.

Hejduk began his own practice in New York a year after arriving at Cooper Union, in 1965. For decades to come the practice was involved largely in conceptual projects, some of which were published by the Museum of Modern Art in *Five Architects* (1972). Yet membership in the "New York Five" had little impact on Hejduk's building career. He was involved in the renovation of the Cooper Union at the time, but this "vagabond architect," as Anthony Vidler affectionately called him, was first and foremost a storyteller.[1] With twenty-one books of his architectural proposals containing entire architectural worlds, Hejduk's publishing production far exceeded the number of his constructed buildings.

Hejduk was eventually commissioned to design The Kreuzberg Tower and Wings (1988) near Checkpoint Charlie and Tegel Housing (1988), all as part of the 1987 International Building Exhibition in Berlin. Two of his buildings were executed posthumously in conjunction with twenty-six full-scale installations of Hejduk's designs built as temporary structures and put on display at various museums around the world, including the Institute of Contemporary Art in Boston, the Triennale di Milano, and the Prague Castle. Peter Eisenman incorporated a tower by Hejduk into his project for Galicia as a memorial to his friend, while Wall House II was realized by a private individual in Groningen in the Netherlands in 2001. — AM

① Anthony Vidler, *The Architectural Uncanny* (Cambridge: The MIT Press, 1992).

1954–

Robert P. Madison International

Headquarters
Cleveland, OH

Founding and Key Partners
Robert P. Madison (founding principal), Kevin Madison, Sandra Madison

Current Partner
Robert P. Madison

1954

Robert P. Madison

Robert Madison opened his office in 1954. It was the first architecture firm started by an African American architect in Ohio and only the tenth in the United States. The office got its start in Cleveland, Madison's hometown, after he left his teaching position at Howard University. Madison, a World War II veteran, was the first African American to study architecture at Case Western Reserve University, before continuing his studies at the Harvard University Graduate School of Design (GSD), where he studied under Walter Gropius, and as a Fulbright scholar at the École des Beaux-Arts in Paris. Some of Madison's first projects were small residential and commercial commissions, but by the late 1950s his practice was primarily in building churches across the country as the official architect of the African Methodist Episcopal Church. The office continued to grow throughout the 1960s and gained commissions for several schools, community centers, and cultural institutions.

Madison's most significant commission arrived in 1965, when he was selected by the Foreign Building Operations (FBO) office of the State Department to design the US Embassy office building in Dakar, Senegal. The complex project did not receive funding until 1972 and took an additional five years to complete, but it helped to shape the firm's global reputation. It also led to other significant international commissions, including government projects in Trinidad and Tobago, Jamaica, the Bahamas, and Nigeria. In 1982, Madison was also approached to compete for the design of the University of Abu Dhabi in the United Arab Emirates.

The office has continued to produce an extensive number of projects in Cleveland, including museums, stadiums, and airports, and has expanded its services to include interior design, urban design, and planning. Along the way, the office has trained and employed nearly two hundred African American architects and engineers, including Madison's son and daughter, Kevin Madison and Sandra Madison, respectively.
— JJ

1954–
1984

Victor A. Lundy

Headquarters
Sarasota, FL; Houston, TX

Founding Partner
Victor A. Lundy

1954

1984

U.S. General Services Administration

Victor Lundy's architectural beginning was interrupted by the onset of World War II. He had enrolled at New York University, joined the school's Beaux-Arts program and then four years into his studies he found himself on the battlefield in Europe. As the story goes, while in the army, he met a captured German architect with great knowledge of Mies and Gropius, which convinced Lundy to enroll at Harvard University's Graduate School of Design (GSD) upon returning to the United States. He earned his bachelor of architecture and his masters degree there under Walter Gropius's directorship. In the early 1950s Lundy worked at various architectural firms in New York. He received his professional license and completed his first commission in 1951.

His first house project was in Sarasota, Florida, where this New Yorker opened his own firm in 1954. Paul Rudolph, who had finished two years earlier at the GSD, was already in the area. Lundy, Rudolph, and a handful of other important modern architects would eventually constitute the Sarasota School of Architecture, though in a recent interview, the 85-year-old Lundy shrugged off this designation.

Upon moving to Sarasota, Lundy made contacts with the arts and religious communities, and through those connections and a few serendipitous alignments he won the commission for a small building for the new Chamber of Commerce, which was completed in 1956. A year later Lundy began a relationship with United States Information Agency (USIA), which would last through the 1970s and include a number of exhibits. In 1957 he was part of USIA's "America Builds" show at the Marshall House, and in 1965 he traveled to Moscow alongside Louis Kahn, Robert Venturi, Paul Rudolph, and Charles Eames in connection with the federally sponsored exhibit, "Architecture U.S.A."

Lundy completed a number of projects in Florida while still in his thirties. Two commissions in Connecticut for a Unitarian Church in Westport (1965) and a Unitarian Meeting House in Hartford (1964) both enlarged his operation and placed him on the national scene, effecting the gradual move of his practice from Sarasota to New York City. During the 1960s, other projects completed out of Lundy's office included unconventionally designed public schools in Westport and Queens, New York; pioneering examples of pneumatic structures; a commission for the US Embassy in Sri Lanka (1961–1984); and the 1965 IBM complex in Cranford, New Jersey.

Lundy developed a demountable pneumatic structure for the traveling building and exhibit of the US Atomic Energy Commission (1965–1967) in collaboration with Birdair Structures of Buffalo, New York. It housed a working nuclear reactor and a theater in its interior and it traveled throughout the world, starting with Rio de Janeiro in 1959. Reyner Banham, in *The Architecture of the Well-Tempered Environment*, discussed the project as a subversive reversal of the traditional roles of architecture and environmental management. A few years later, Lundy produced the inflatable "air balloons" for the New York World's Fair of 1964, which captivated Philip Johnson, also involved in the Fair at the time.

Lundy received the commission for the US Embassy in Colombo, Sri Lanka, in 1961, and its execution took twelve years, outlasting seven ambassadors. Once completed in 1984, the embassy won the Presidential Design Award. As in the case of his 1976 monumental US Tax Court Building in Washington, DC, funding cuts related to the Vietnam War stalled the embassy project. As the country and architectural discourse were transforming around him Lundy moved his office again to Houston, Texas, where he established Victor A Lundy & Associates in 1976. Eight years later in 1984, he became the design principal and vice president at HKS Inc. in Dallas. — AM

1955–

HOK

Headquarters
St. Louis, MO

Other Locations
Atlanta, GA; Beijing, China; Calgary, Canada; Chicago, IL; Dallas, TX; Denver, CO; Dubai, United Arab Emirates; Hong Kong, China; Houston, TX; London, UK; Los Angeles, CA; Miami, FL; Mumbai, India; New York, NY; Ottawa, Canada; San Francisco, CA; Seattle, WA; Shanghai, China; Singapore; Tampa, FL; Toronto, Canada; Vancouver, Canada; Washington, D.C.

Founding Partners
George Hellmuth, Gyo Obata, George Kassabaum

Current Partners
Bill Hellmuth

1955

HOK

In 1944, HOK founder George Hellmuth wrote a forward-looking memorandum, prior to starting out on his own. Author Walter Mcquade, architectural critic, summarized Hellmuth's points in the book *Architecture in the Real World*: "Never depend on just one building type," "diversify in location," "expand into architectural subspecialties," "set up a thoroughly systematic marketing group," and "organize the office for maximum efficiency."[1] These tenets—which focus on architectural practice, rather than design—formed and shaped the firm of Hellmuth, Obata + Kassabaum (HOK) through the decades. In 2013, the office was named the eighth largest US office by architectural revenue, and the firm continues to work across multiple typologies, maintain regional offices, and pursue international commissions.

HOK was founded in 1955 out of the Hellmuth, Yamasaki & Leinweber partnership, which dissolved after six years in business. The firm's Detroit branch became Yamasaki & Associates and Hellmuth took over the St. Louis branch. With employees Gyo Obata and George E. Kassabaum, graduates of Washington University in St. Louis like Hellmuth, HOK officially opened its doors with 24 staff members. The firm grew by dividing the founding partners' expertise: Hellmuth in marketing, Obata in design, and Kassabaum in management.

Despite Hellmuth's manifesto, in its early years HOK began like other corporate architecture firms: namely, by specializing in one typology (schools) and building prolifically in its hometown. HOK was "deep into the architectural grain of its home city," wrote Walter McQuade in 1984, occupying multiple levels of the Boatmen's Bank Tower (1976) that the firm had designed. Unlike Skidmore, Owings & Merrill, the firm to which HOK has been compared in scale and reach, the latter does not operate under a "studio" system, instead employing experts who collaborate on projects as needed, with only a project manager remaining on a single building design throughout its duration.

In the mid-1960s, HOK grew and expanded across the US, opening regional offices in San Francisco and later in Denver, Houston, Los Angeles, Boston, Washington D.C., and Portland. These regional offices operated under the central direction of HOK's St. Louis office, from which a central designer oversaw the firm's trajectory, paychecks were issued, and specifications—one of HOK's key means to streamline the construction process—were developed and disseminated. HOK also engaged in strategic acquisitions, including Kahn & Jacobs in 1973 and the large interior design firm BBG-BBGM in 2013.

HOK began its work internationally in 1975. Following the trajectory of American firms working in the Gulf Region during the boom in oil prices and the corresponding recession in the US, Hellmuth flew to Riyadh after receiving a letter regarding the design of King Saud University. According to McQuade, Hellmuth cold-called 15 offices before finally reaching the university directors to schedule a meeting; HOK was the only American firm among three finalists for the project. Ultimately, HOK was chosen, resulting in a 3.5 billion dollar contract over ten years. This lucrative project led to other projects in the region including King Khaled International Airport (1975–1984). By 2007, forty percent of HOK's billing consisted of international projects. The office continued its growth internationally by opening a branch in Hong Kong in 1984, followed by regional offices in Mumbai and Shanghai. Under the leadership of George Hellmuth's nephew Bill Hellmuth since 2004, the firm continues its marketing and diversification tactics while also entering into subspecialties in sustainable design and BIM technology. —AL

(1)
George Hellmuth, quoted in Walter McQuade, *Architecture in the Real World: The Work of HOK* (New York: Harry N. Abrams Inc. Publishers, 1984): 14–15.

Pei Cobb Freed & Partners Architects

Headquarters
New York, NY

Founding and Key Partners
I. M. Pei, Henry N. Cobb, Eason Leonard (founding principals), James Ingo Freed, Araldo Cossutta

Current Partners
Henry N. Cobb, Michael D. Flynn, George H. Miller, Ian Bader, Yvonne Szeto, Jay L. Berman, Michael W.Bischoff, José Bruguera

1955

Architecture, February 1990. Photographer: Serge Hambourg

The history of Pei Cobb Freed & Partners—and in particular its role in the export of U.S. architecture abroad—is perhaps best framed in relationship to the life and career of its founder. Ieoh Ming Pei was born into a wealthy Chinese family in 1917 and educated in elite Shanghai schools. In 1935 he was sent to the United States for college, first at the University of Pennsylvania and then MIT, where he studied architectural engineering. This was followed by graduate study at Harvard's GSD under Walter Gropius. In 1948 Pei took a position as Director of Architecture at Webb & Knapp, a real estate company owned by William Zeckendorf, which executed many important, large-scale projects throughout the country.

Pei's first independent commission, the Tunghai University Campus Master Plan in Taichung, Taiwan, arrived in 1954 while he was still at Webb & Knapp. This was the year Pei became a US citizen, though the selection of Pei for this project was doubtless a result of his personal ties to China. Tunghai University had been founded by the United Board for Christian Colleges and Pei had attended a United Board middle school in Shanghai, in addition to having consulted with Walter Gropius on an unbuilt United Board university planned for Shanghai.[1]

In 1956 Pei designed the structurally daring Luce Memorial Chapel for the Taichung campus. Taking nearly seven years to complete, the chapel quickly became the signature not only for Tunghai University, but for the nearby capital city Taipei as well. It also represented what were to become hallmarks of Pei's architecture: an innovative and sensitive use of technology, strong sculptural forms, and a connection to history.

While at Webb & Knapp Pei gained valuable experience not only in design but also in business and development. Nevertheless, technically working within a development company carried professional stigma, and prevented Pei from gaining licensure credits according to AIA regulations at the time. In 1955 the Pei-led design group at Webb & Knapp formed I.M. Pei & Associates. While independent from Zeckendorf, Pei & Associates continued to work primarily for Zeckendorf until the two officially separated in 1960. The practice rose to the top of the profession in the United States, gaining renown for its technical competence and ability to deliver high-quality design, especially to large corporate and institutional clients.

Boston's John Hancock Tower project (1976) presented the office with its most serious public relations test. Before completion, the tower's glazed curtain wall panels began falling off. While ultimately corrected, this was a public relations disaster for the office, and for a period of time the firm had difficulty securing projects in the United States. As a result, Pei and his partners began actively seeking international work, particularly in nations such as Singapore, Iran, Australia, and Kuwait. This, in addition to work Pei was invited to undertake in Hong Kong and on the Chinese mainland (in no small part thanks to his historic family connections to the Bank of China through his father), enabled the office to survive what ultimately proved to be a temporary setback. The selection of the firm by French President François Mitterand for the Grand Louvre project (Phase I 1983–1989, Phase II 1989–1993) was a watershed moment for the office. After completing the famous pyramid, Pei would retire in 1990 from what was then known as Pei Cobb Freed & Partners.

Pei's "retirement" marked the beginning of a new phase in his career. Working at various times independently or with his sons, since 1990 Pei has focused even more on projects abroad, particularly in Europe, Asia and the Middle East through commissions such as the Miho Museum in Shiga, Japan (1997), the Suzhou Museum in Suzhou, China (2006), and the Museum of Islamic Art in Doha, Qatar (2008). The Suzhou Museum in particular has been cited as an example of Pei returning to his roots (Suzhou being his ancestral home). These later projects exhibit the primary abstract forms of Pei's earlier work, again imbued with a connection to history and local context, and could be seen as a life and career which has spanned continents and centuries coming full-circle. — JR

①

Philip Jodidio and Janet Adams Strong, *I.M. Pei: Complete Works* (New York: Rizzoli, 2008): 59.

William B. Tabler Architects

Headquarters
New York, NY

Founding Partner
William B. Tabler

Current Partner
William B. Tabler, Jr.,
Sultan Sayani, Mark Dabbagh

1955

Architectural Forum, July 1957. Photographer: Leni Iselin

In 1955 William Tabler opened his New York-based architecture office, focusing almost exclusively on hotel design. Tabler had gained experience in the industry during his time at the offices of Holabird & Root, where he worked on the thousand room Statler Hotel in Washington D.C., and later, starting in 1946, as the in-house architect for Statler. By 1954, Tabler had designed three major hotels as the head architect of the hotel company and overseen the development of several others. Upon his departure from Statler in 1955, Tabler's newly formed firm immediately garnered several major commissions. By 1957, the office had over 50 million dollars in construction projects on the boards and commissions for several additional buildings. Two of those, the El Salvador InterContinental Hotel in El Salvador (1958) and the El Ponce InterContinental Hotel in Ponce, Puerto Rico (1975), would become the firm's first and second international projects.

Tabler gained prominence for his ability to produce a high return on investment for his clients. His hotels "traded charm for efficiency" and proliferated across the world as major hotel corporations sought to engage new economies.[1] The office developed a series of benchmarks for ensuring the viability of their hotel designs, which soon became industry standards. They included maximum square-footage costs per room, maximum land-costs, employee to room ratios, and break-even occupancy. Aside from technical innovations and efficiencies, Tabler Architects pioneered organizational strategies within the office to allow for a single architect and his team to lead an entire project from design through construction.

One of the largest changes in the design of hotels that Tabler Architects introduced was a reduction in the size of public spaces. According to their internal standards, total bedroom floor area needed to exceed total public and service areas in order to maintain profitability. Therefore, smaller scale lobbies and public spaces dominate many of the Tabler hotels.

The office produced hotels for several major hotel companies, including Hilton and Intercontinental, and had built over four hundred globally by the time of Tabler's death in 2004. His son, William B. Tabler, Jr., joined the office in the mid-1970s and has led the firm since his father's death. The firm continues to operate out of its New York offices but has diversified its portfolio to include residential and commercial buildings. — JJ

① David Dunlap, "William B. Tabler Sr., Architect of Hilton Hotels, Dies at 89," *The New York Times* (February 10, 2004).

Phoenicia Intercontinental Hotel
1954

Architect
Edward Durell Stone and Associates

Location
Beirut, Lebanon

Client
InterContinental Hotels Group

US Embassy
1954–1959

Architect
Edward Durell Stone and Associates

Location
New Delhi, India

Client
US Department of State, Foreign Buildings Operations

Esso Building
1954–1956

Architect
Lathrop Douglass

Location
Bogota, Colombia

Client
Colombiana S.A., Standard Oil of New Jersey

Tire and Footwear Plant
1954–1956

Architect
Oficina Don Hatch

Location
Guacara, Venezuela

Client
International Basic Economy Corporation

Joan Miró Studio
1954–1957

SERT, JACKSON AND ASSOCIATES
ARCHITECTS CAMBRIDGE MASSACHUSETTS

Architect
Josep Lluís Sert

Location
Palma de Mallorca, Spain

Client
Joan Miró

Quinta Palatino
1954–1957

Architect
Town Planning Associates, Arroyo and Menéndez

Local Architect
Rita Gutiérrez, Jorge Mantilla

Location
Havana, Cuba

Client
Pedro Abreu

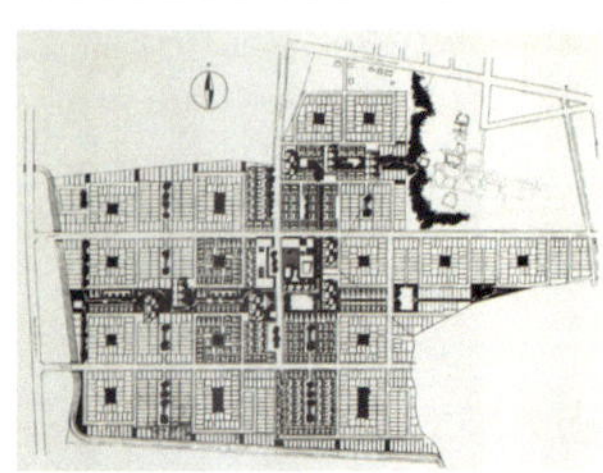

US Consulate
1954–1957

Architect
Yamasaki, Hellmuth and Leinweber

Location
Kobe, Japan

Client
US Department of State, Foreign Buildings Operations

US Embassy
1954–1960

Architect
Eero Saarinen and Associates

Other Architect
Yorke, Rosenberg and Mardall

Location
London, UK

Client
US Department of State, Foreign Buildings Operations

Luce Memorial Chapel
1954–1963

Architect
I. M. Pei & Associates

Location
Taichung, Taiwan

Client
United Board for Christian Higher Education in Asia

1954
1956

US Pavilion, Indian Industries Fair
1955

Project Lead
Jack Masey, USIA

Design
John Vassos (architecture), Jack Masey (exhibits)

Location
New Delhi, India

Aruba Caribbean Hotel
1955

Architect
Morris Lapidus Associates

Location
Aruba, Aruba

Client
Koninklijke Luchtvaart Maatschappij N.V. (Royal Dutch Airlines)

US Embassy
1955

Architect
Richard J. Neutra

Location
Karachi, Pakistan

Client
US Department of State, Foreign Buildings Operations

Congress Hall
1955–1957

Architect
Hugh Stubbins and Associates

Location
Berlin, Germany

Client
City of West Berlin

Interbau Housing Block
1955–1957

Architect
The Architects Collaborative

Location
Berlin, Germany

Client
Hansa A.G.

Hipódromo La Rinconada
1955–1959

Architect
Arthur B. Froehlich and Associates

Location
Caracas, Venezuela

Client
Instituto Nacional de Hipodromos,Presidente Marco Perez Jimenez

US Embassy
1955–1959

Architect
Eero Saarinen and Associates

Location
Oslo, Norway

Client
US Department of State, Foreign Buildings Operations

US Embassy
1955–1961

Architect
Hugh Stubbins and Associates

Location
Tangiers, Morocco

Client
US Department of State, Foreign Buildings Operations

Gunma Music Center
1955–1961

Architect
Raymond & Rado

Location
Gunma, Japan

Client
Gunma Music Center

US Embassy Baghdad *1955–1961*

SERT, JACKSON AND ASSOCIATES
ARCHITECTS CAMBRIDGE MASSACHUSETTS

Architect
Josep Lluís Sert

Location
Baghdad, Iraq

Client
US State Department, Foreign Buildings Operations

US Pavilion, Jeshyn International Fair *1956–1959*

United States Information Agency

Project Lead
Jack Masey, USIA

Design
R. Buckminster Fuller/Geodesics, Inc. (architecture); Jack Masey (exhibits)

Location
Kabul, Afghanistan

US Embassy *1956–1959*

Architect
Alfred L. Aydelott Associates

Location
Manila, Philippines

Client
US Department of State, Foreign Buildings Operations

Broadcasting USA: Soft Power and the United States Information Agency

In one of his earliest executive orders, President Dwight Eisenhower consolidated the foreign information activities of the US government into the United States Information Agency (USIA) in 1953.[1] An independent entity reporting directly to the president, the USIA's sphere of action was confined under the Smith-Mundt Act to activities outside of the US, while the Office of International Trade Fairs (another postwar entity dedicated to cultural and economic outreach) remained under the supervision of the State Department. Following intense internal discussions about the difference between the spreading of culture and of information, perceived as administratively and ideologically incompatible, the USIA would lean on the side of propaganda throughout its operation.[2] Yet its activities—from films and exhibits to full-fledged participation in Expos abroad—were never referred to explicitly as propaganda by its staff, according to Eisenhower's belief that for such dissemination to be successful "the hand of the government has to be carefully concealed."[3]

Domesticity and design, packaged to broadcast the allure of the "American way of life," were strategically deployed by the USIA and the OITF during the Cold War as soft, yet powerful, ideological weapons.[4] Already contained within the logic of the Truman Doctrine set forth in 1947, period discussions of the work of both agencies unapologetically described their tactics as "soft sell with hard facts."[5] The key venues for this "soft sell" were the international trade fairs featuring US participation from 1954 onwards. Formalized by the 1956 International Cultural Exchange and Trade Fair Act, the trade fair program became an opportunity to exhibit both products and ideas, with the government aiming to "establish its influence in politically uneasy countries, to promote capitalism as a system superior to communism."[6] The results were a series of pavilions and exhibitions from 1954 through the

(1) Reorganization Plan No. 8 and Executive Order 10477, National Archive Records of the USIA.

(2) See Richard T. Arndt, *The First Resort of Kings: American Cultural Diplomacy in the Twentieth Century* (Washington D.C.: Potomac Books Inc., 2005); Wilson P. Dizard, *Inventing Public Diplomacy: The Story of the U.S. Information Agency* (Boulder: Lynne Rienner Publishers, 2004); Jeffrey Cody, *Exporting American Architecture, 1870–2000* (New York, London: Routledge, 2003).

(3) Emily Pugh, *Architecture, Politics, and Identity in Divided Berlin* (Pittsburgh: University of Pittsburgh Press, 2014).

(4) See Greg Castillo, *Cold War on the Home Front: The Soft Power of Midcentury Design*

1935

1938 Division of Cultural Relations established

1945 President Truman transfers the activities of the Office of War Information to the State Department

1947 Truman announces the Truman Doctrine

1948 Smith Mundt Act - creates the US Advisory Committee on Information

1953 • President's Committee on International Information Activities established • United States Information Agency (USIA) established

1954 Special Emergency Fund (for Trade Fairs)

1956 International Cultural Exchange and Trade Fair Act

1958 • Brussels World Exposition • American National Exhibition in Moscow

1958–1960 Soviet-American Cultural Agreement (Lacy-Zaroubin Agreement)

1961 Fulbright - Hays Act (Mutual Educational and Cultural Exchange Act)

1967 Montreal World

1939–1945 World War II

1950–1953 Korean War

1962 Cuban Missile Crisis

1950–1975 Vietnam War

early 1960s on sites spanning from Latin America to Asia, Bogota to Bangkok.[7] Though their directives came from different sources, the OITF and the USIA presented a relatively unified front. US architects participated in this broadcasting as exhibition designers and curators (including Charles and Ray Eames, George Nelson, and Cambridge Seven Associates), pavilion designers (particularly Buckminster Fuller, introduced to the Expo program by Jack Masey), and occasionally as the content of the exhibits themselves (for example "America Builds," exhibited at the George Marshall House in Berlin in 1957).

For the first World's Expo of the Cold War, in 1958 in Brussels, the OITF had a budget of over $100 million, by far the highest of any US participation in such "Category One" World fair. Masey, who played an array of roles within the USIA's exhibits over his 28-year tenure—exhibition coordinator, commissioner, Chief of the East-West Exhibits branch—called this category the "Super Bowl of Expos."[8] To compete with the success of the Soviet space program just a year after the launch of Sputnik, the US spent its funds on a lavish pavilion designed by Edward Durell Stone & Associates, color television sets, Disney's Cyclorama, elements of US industry "called upon to indicate their respective contributions to American life," and a controversial exhibit (soon closed) on the country's "unfinished business" with racial inequality.[9] Subsequent Expos fell under the USIA's jurisdiction, where Masey was a key advocate for both architecture and the need to convincingly present American everydayness, from shoes and dishwashers to highways and Tupperware (as at the American National Exhibition in Moscow in 1959).

Governmental financing of Expos and trade fairs plummeted steadily over the course of the Cold War, with the budget for the Montreal Expo in 1967 reduced to half that of Brussels. Following the collapse of the Soviet Union, these funds evaporated completely by 2000. During its later years, the USIA's broadcasting tasks included the management of US participation in the Venice Biennale, and a slew of other proportionately less spectacular programs. Since the end of the USIA in 1999, subsequent Expos in Aichi, Seville, and Shanghai have all been financed by corporate entities with increasingly less direction in their message and design, with much of the USIA's former broadcasting strategies absorbed into the general modes of global cultural dissemination, without the need for top-down orchestration. — AM

(Minneapolis: University of Minnesota Press, 2010).

⑤ Irma Weinig, "American Exhibit Combines Soft Sell With Hard Facts," *Industrial Design* (September 1959): 66–73.

⑥ Jane Mitarachi, "Design as a Political Force," *Industrial Design* (February 1957): 39.

⑦ See Jack Masey and Conway Lloyd Morgan, *Cold War Confrontations: US Exhibitions and their Role in the Cultural Cold War* (Zurich: Lars Müller, 2008).

⑧ Jack Masey, presentation on the financing of Class One World Expositions, n.d., and email exchanges with Jack Masey and Beverly Payeff-Masey, May 2014.

⑨ "U.S. to Build Circular Pavilion For '58 World's Fair in Brussels," *The New York Times*, January 28, 1957: 25. On the Unfinished Business exhibition, see W.W. Rostow, "Some Unfinished Business Of The American Community," box 3, Jerome B. Wiesner papers (MC 420), Institute Archives and Special Collections, MIT Libraries, reproduced in this book.

1956

1989

1970 Osaka World Exposition

1978 Carter renamed USIA into United States Informational Communication Agency

1982 Reagan restored the old name USIA

1990–1991 First Persian Gulf War

1994 The International Broadcasting Act

1998 Foreign Affairs Reform and Restructuring Act

1999 USIA closes

2001 Afghanistan War

2003 Iraq War

2005

Funding for US Participation in Class I World Expositions

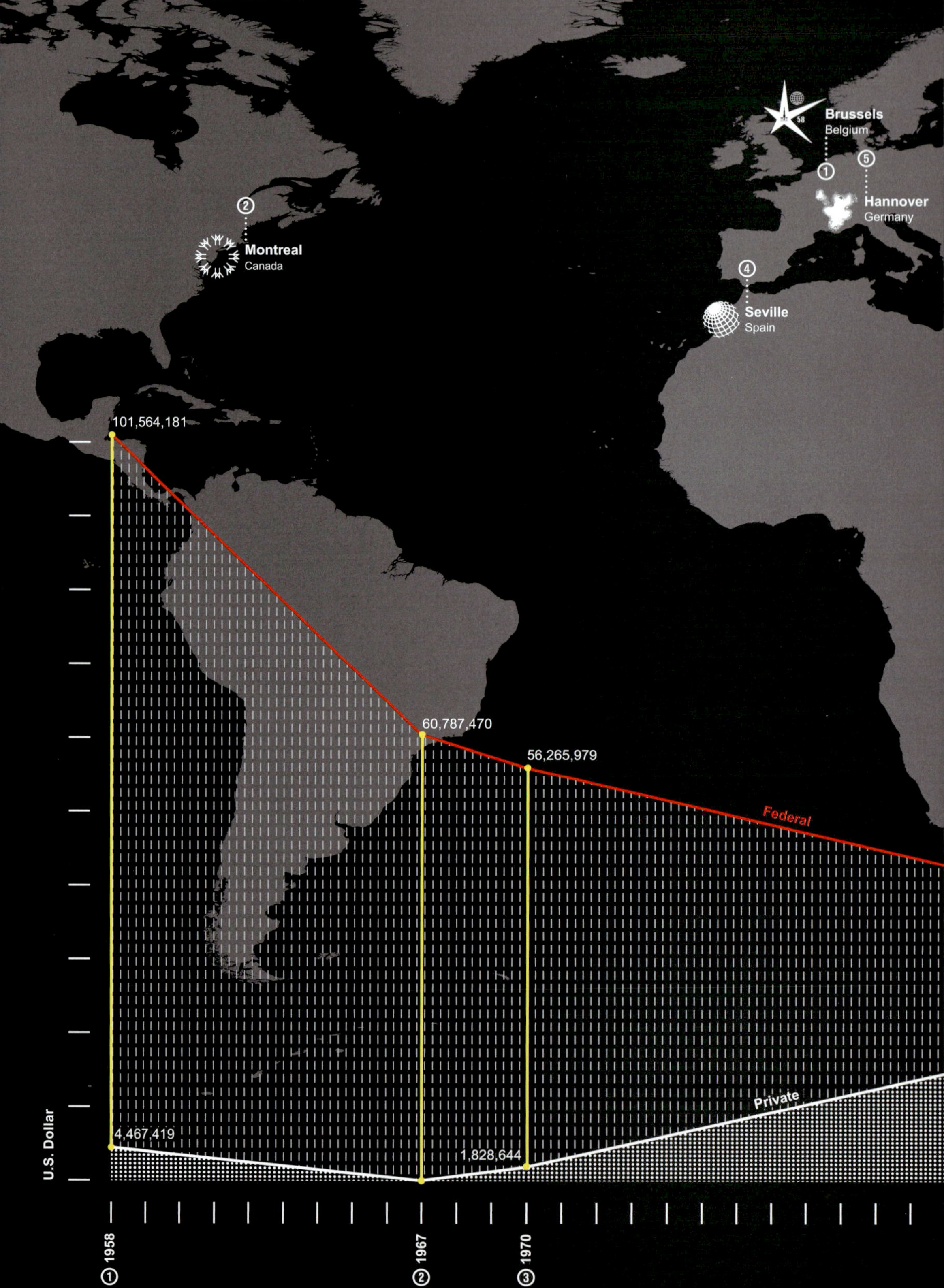

Osaka
Japan
③ ⑥
⑦
Aichi
Japan
Shanghai
China
61,000,000
37,670,837
32,094,821
25,343,212
④ 1992
⑤ 2000
⑥ 2005
⑦ 2010

INDUSTRIAL DESIGN

February 1957 $1.50 per copy 2

Design as a political force

Aids and sources for the designer: Modelmaking

Cars '57: review and questions

Martin Rosenzweig

The U. S. A. has plunged deeply into a new overseas Trade Fair program — constructing pavilions and designing exhibits to build trade and win friends throughout the world.

Design as a political force

These commercial fairs on foreign soil provide point-of-sale display for the American way. With the U. S. A. in direct competition with other governments, our products are a measure of our success as a nation; our presentation of those products is a crucial part of our success in getting across the American story. The designers chosen to create Trade Fair exhibits must work with the government on this challenging job of political communication — interpreting our country to people that are western and alien, civilized and backward, unfriendly and neutral. On the next 18 pages, we shall examine how they are pioneering a new policy for American commerce and a new role for American design.

pros and cons of America's program to win friends

by Jane Fiske Mitarachi

U. S. EXPANDS ROLE IN TRADE EXHIBITS

American Way to Be Shown at Fairs in Many Areas, Including One in Poland

The United States' program of official participation in international trade fairs became a "going business" last year.

Since its initiation by President Eisenhower just over two years ago, the project's dual aim has been promotion of two-way trade and better understanding of United States. Central exhibits and trade missions provided the method.

At the start, the United States was an uncertain newcomer to the foreign trade-fair circuit. For long it had been conspicuously absent from the great international exhibits in which other nations gained profit and prestige. The Soviet Union and other Communist countries for long have found them a ready-made propaganda medium.

Until recently, the new trade-fair program of the United States was on a temporary basis and a slim budget drawn from the President's emergency fund.

Under direction of the Commerce Department's Office of International Trade Fairs, and with substantial cooperation by American industry, the program's record is an impressive one. In relatively short time, the United States has become an "old pro" at trade-fair productions. To date it has participated in forty-five fairs.

Techniques Perfected

Last year, it perfected its tenchiques with participation in nineteen fairs. Ten more are on the schedule for the first half of 1957. This year, for the first time, the program will reach behind the slightly unhinged Iron Curtain with an official United States exhibit in the International Trade Fair at Poznan, Poland, June 9 to 23. It was during this fair last year that Polish rebellion against the Soviet Union first flared forcefully.

Last July, Congress made the trade-fair program permanent and provided it with a current fiscal year budget of $3,650,000, its highest to date.

Most of this is used for what the President has called "seed money," to create the basic central exhibits that provide the means for cooperative participation by private American business.

Some of the exhibits, which have drawn a total of some 30,000,000 visitors to date, have featured typical American homes, voting machines, "atoms for peace" applications, United States farm production, "do-it-yourself" workshops, American art and design, electronic devices and automated factories.

The central exhibit provides not only a means by which private business may display appropriate products but is also a main attraction to which individual private exhibits throughout a fair may be keyed. This "tying in" with the official exhibit also multiplies indentification of United States products elsewhere in the fair. So far, about 2,500 private concerns have contributed or loaned goods and display materials for the

New York Times, January 3, 1957

The clipping at the left was published only a mont ago, some 30 months after the start of a crash pr gram for American participation in overseas Trac Fairs. Since the original exhibit in Bangkok in D cember, 1954, the Department of Commerce's Offi of International Trade Fairs has engaged designe to create a total of 45 exhibits of American wares an American ways in countries from Yugoslavia to A ghanistan. That these exhibits have been totally su cessful has never been doubted by the American pres which has published numerous enthusiastic report like the one in *Time* in 1955: "Last week more tha 30,000 visitors a day poured through the gates to se the first TV show ever broadcast in Indonesia. Th U.S. Exhibit, from an aqua-green Thunderbird to a automatic voting machine . . . easily outdazzled com petition from Red China. . . ."

The whole matter of U.S. participation in thes shows is full of novelties. It has made the governmer an important client of the design profession; it ha given industrial designers — who have done much t create the American scene — an enormous challenge i presenting that scene to people abroad — a challeng verging at times on foreign policy planning. And has opened up a series of questions about the purpose of our participation and the effectiveness of the show we have sent abroad. Have they really "outdazzled the competition, and does design dazzle make success ful shows in the terms that the government now em ploys them?

What IS a Trade Fair?

Literally dozens of Trade Fairs take place all over th world every year. A Trade Fair, on a large scale, to European and Asian business roughly what th Housewares Show is to the small appliance industri — a week's chance to buy and sell and vie for com petitive advantage. One difference is the fact th Fairs are international: with countries of the Ea and West competing for commercial leadership, com petition has taken on a particularly strong flavo Another difference is the audience: most Fairs, ope to the public, are a good free show for the peopl They are attended both by businessmen and by worke and farmers and others who, having virtually no hop of owning the goods on display, come out of curiosit — an impressionable curiosity. What they see ma represent to them either fantasy or frustration.

The U.S. government makes no bones about th fact that the prime mover in its new program wa Russia. Alarmed that Russia had peddled its good at 133 Fairs in four years, while U.S. exhibitors staye home, the President obtained a grant in 1954 to buil

nce nations through Trade Fair exhibits abroad. Are we doing our best?

e and good will on the world Fair circuit. In its year, more than 12,000,000 visitors in 15 coun- saw the American exhibit, while 25,000 trade iries were received from foreign businessmen. In , 1956, after 18 months of experimentation, Trade s were given a permanent status by an act of gress. This year's appropriation was $3,650,000, the 8 fall exhibits alone drew 4,000,000 observers.

rica's motives at the Fairs

re is little doubt that measurable trade is only part hat the U.S.A. wants from its overseas exhibits. er exhibiting nations do need, and expect, to sell chandise; the U.S.A. wants and needs to establish nfluence in politically uneasy countries, to promote talism as a system superior to communism. The goal, then, is eminently political despite its com- cial garb. In the process of conveying this mes- , an exhibit also does a good deal to stimulate le for industry at home, both through its central onal display and through parallel side shows that ate business may sponsor. Business has, in fact, deeply involved in the entire program: over 3,000 cerns have contributed material for the exhibits late, and some firms have sent executives as part the trade teams that accompany each exhibit, to ruct foreign businessmen how to sell to U.S. mar- . The final purpose is to promote general good will ng our foreign neighbors — again, a goal seeming- uch closer to the aims of the State Department than hose of Commerce.

ecause it is eminently viewed as a propaganda olem, the preparation of a Trade Fair exhibit ht easily be a job for specialists — experts in for- trade, foreign relations, public relations, or eco- ics. The fact that interests us here is that, during past year, the problem has been thrown open in- d to designers, several of whom have been primarily ciated with product design. The story of why those gners were selected goes back to the beginning of Trade Fair program, and to recent changes in it.

hange of policy

first American exhibits, at the end of 1954 and 5, were designed and/or supervised by the Office Design and Production, maintained in Paris by the ce of International Trade Fairs; Roy Williams was Director of the OITF. These exhibits (ID: Au- , 1955) demonstrated a consistently tasteful, mod- style, and showed much of the same material. A ical display at the Paris Fair, for instance, included ouse (decorated by *House Beautiful*) in which ther'" prepared meals in a modern kitchen equipped with freezer, garbage disposal unit, dishwasher, mixer, and other gadgets. "Father" puttered with the car in the carport, worked with power tools in the home shop.

As the program gained momentum in its second year, the OITF was placed under the direction of former advertising executive Harrison T. McClung, and it soon showed a change of direction. Closing the Paris design office, OITF decided that design contracts should be put out for bid among designers and archi- tects of varied experience. Even more significant, it decided to seek outside advice on its approach. Mem- bers of OITF contacted various professional groups, among them the Advertising Council and the Ameri- can Society of Industrial Designers, asking them to form a committee to help them in reaching designers about bids. A.S.I.D. felt its Office could handle that job, and proposed a committee to advise OITF on profes- sional procedures. When the committee did not materi- alize, A.S.I.D. provided a list of members who might be capable of handling the jobs. In May of last year, the OITF issued, to over a dozen A.S.I.D. members and others, an open invitation to bid on Fairs that were to open in early September.

Behind this new tactic lay not only an unprecedented bulk of exhibition work, but a search for a new and better way to reach Fair-goers abroad. During its first round of shows, the Office had been able to record both attendance and attitudes among visitors, and felt it could do better in both. In throwing the problem open to designers, it not only gave members of the profession a good chunk of government work; it also gave them a new kind of responsibility for presenting America, and in some cases formulating America's approach to other nations. Designers were being asked to be propagandists; design became a tool of com- munication and the visual composition of an exhibition a secondary problem.

The paradox of leadership

The situation facing the OITF overseas is not basically different from the one that has been faced by every American diplomatic mission abroad since the war — probably the most difficult political role any nation has ever faced. The U.S.A., as a world leader, is in a posi- tion to be feared but not liked. It is an accepted para- dox that nobody really loves a leader, however much he may need or depend on him. When that leader also is the richest nation in the world, and everybody's benefactor to boot, it is all the more an object of resist- ance and resentment.

Because this role of world leader is one for which the U.S.A. was never formally schooled, the pains and perils of unaccustomed authority have been especially

(continued on page 52)

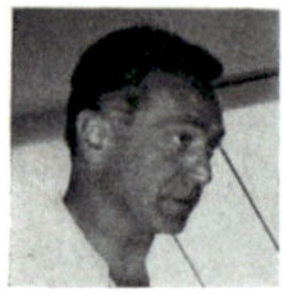

The Salonika Fair is the only trade fair of major size held regularly in Greece, and is by common consent a battleground for the Soviet bloc countries and those of the West. This year both Turkey and Great Britain withdrew from the Fair, leaving America the only major country representing the West.

Under these precarious conditions, designer Bernard Pfriem had the task not only of creating a strong statement of the American way of life but also a sympathetic one. Pfriem, who was Director of Design for the Trade Fair Program and now operates his own exhibit design office, presented the "Fruits of Freedom" theme with major emphasis on activated exhibits: every section of the American pavilion had one or more animated elements in which the U. S. objects were brought to life through actual demonstrations.

The U. S. Department of Agriculture joined with the Office of International Trade Fairs in illustrating how industrial and agricultural progress is refl Americans' work and leisure. Farm ment—including tractors, tillers, s fertilizers and methods of irrigati demonstrated in 15,000 square feet door display area, and the care stock and poultry was carried o appropriate setting.

Since most Greeks attending t would compare American consume with those of the Soviet bloc countr purpose was not merely to show o advanced products but to break aw the "department store" method of ing them. Major attention in ou square feet of indoor display was toward a closed-circuit television tion, a children's playground illust psychological approach to child tra completely equipped auto repai metal and woodworking shops, mod gery and dentistry installations, trains, and a home dressmaki fashion show.

SALONIKA, GREECE

A typical international fair: battleground of ideologies, ways of

U. S. pavilion at Salonika Fair (in yellow frame below) draws crowds of Greeks eager for a glimpse of American life. Panel at entrance brings together symbols of major sections in 29,000 square feet of indoor display area, while outdoor exhibits of agricultural machinery lead visitors on to extensive field demonstrations by Department of Agriculture.

1

2

Salonika posed a typical communications proble

3

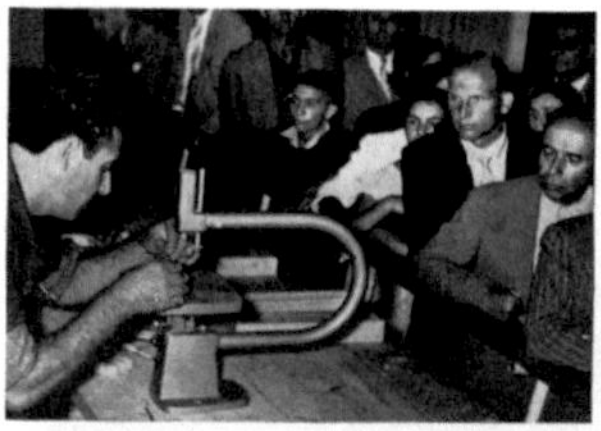

4

5

1. Main exhibit hall of U. S. Salonika pavilion, with ramp suspended above shallow pool, becomes scene of fashion show 2. with models parading dresses made by sewing machine on the spot. Miniature mannikins stud pool to symbolize home-dressmaking exhibit. 3. Power tools make up another feature of do-it-yourself displays. 4. Doughnut-maker proves popular, illustrates mass-production technique. 5. Children at play communicate benefits of America for the younger set, against background 6. of products of our ingenuity in keeping them amused. 7. Fully equipped surgical exhibit indicates high development of techniques for sustaining human life.

6

ıow to relate American achievements to Greek attitudes and needs

7

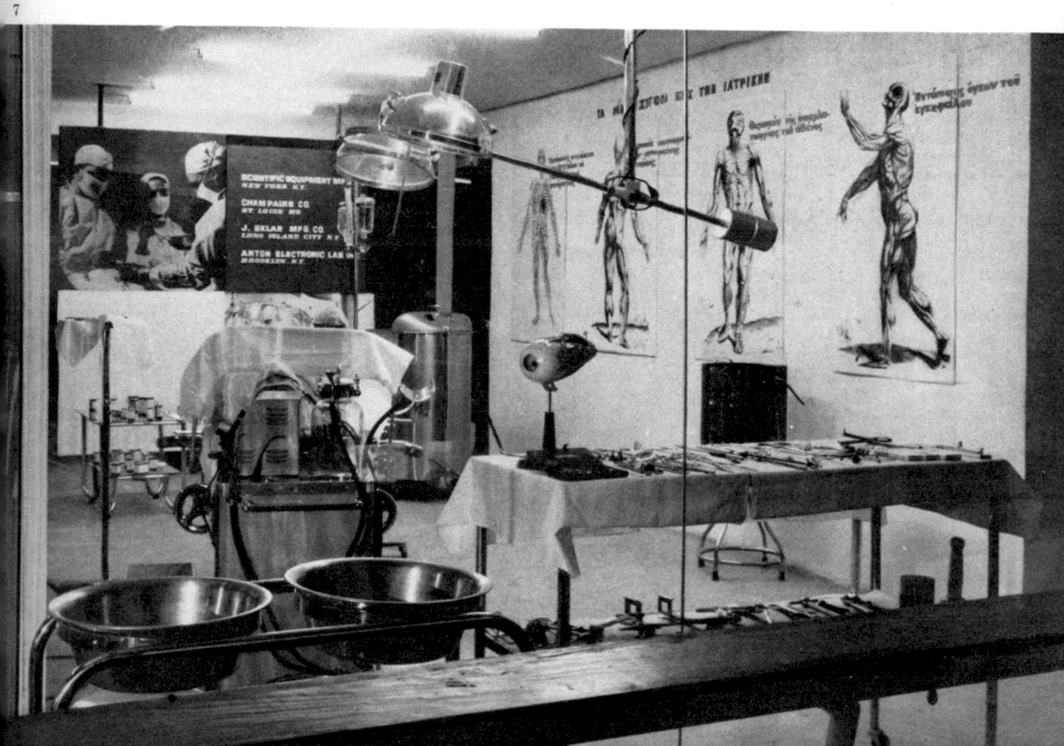

BARI, ITALY

At the annual Levant agricultural fair in Bari, the U. S. effort was to help Italian farmers by offering technical information on their pressing cultivation and marketing problems. The tone of our exhibit was one of sharing experiences: "Your agricultural problems are similar to ours—here's a sample of our work that may interest you." Designer Charles Shaw developed the show as a method of comparing notes, as well as a demonstration of new agricultural machinery. A photo-story gave the south Italian farmers an understanding of similar American regions with similar crops—the almond industry of Southern California being featured. The now-familiar tractor told a new story, answering questions from the audience by means of a lecturer with microphone, concealed behind a one-way transparent shield. And our display of Italian crafts sold on the American market seemed to say that we think they can help us too.

"Talking tractor" answers visitors' questions on agricultural probl… hi-fi mechanisms are exposed in transparent cases in garden; ch… wrapping machine (right) is demonstrated.

IZMIR, TURKEY

The exhibit at the Izmir trade fair was, like Bari, intended for information rather than trade purposes, but covered the entire economy of a nation disappointed in the slowness of its progress toward industrialization. Designers Henry Gardiner and Lothar Witteborg (right and left, below) spelled out the theme, "150 Years of American Industrial Progress," to show the Turks that industrialization is not an overnight process but the gradual result of planning, evolution and the cooperative effort of an entire people. Contrasting the earliest and latest models of familiar American inventions, they singled out specific resources of our economy for explanation—industrial design among them. Some 450 photographs and 250 tons of heavy machinery went into the show's panorama of industrial growth.

ason frames used in display are acked to form 100′ tower.

elephone exhibit explains slow rowth of modern technology.

Solar-battery-powered radios, tape recorders and other electronic devices display benefits of industrialization to Turks, many from agricultural areas.

DAMASCUS, SYRIA

The United States exhibit at Damascus was for a time one of the front-lines in the tense war of political influence in the Middle East, and the atmosphere in which it took place was made tenser by public demonstrations protesting our presence at the fair. In a nation of such poverty that the 30¢ admission fee to the fair grounds ruled out a majority of the population, our most direct channel of encouraging the Syrians to regard us as friends lay in setting a tone of mutual exchange. The exhibit and new pavilion by Raymond Loewy Associates, with William Snaith as project chief and Phil George, Joe Lovelace and Raoul Du Bruhl as design team, tried to build a bridge of understanding between Syrian and American life by emphasizing not only our spectacular technological resources but also Syrian products exported to the U. S. and valued here.

The display was divided into four categories: agricultural pursuits, woodworking and metal working, electronics, and consumer products. A wide range of products and techniques were demonstrated in an effort to show that Americans are engaged mainly in the production of peacetime goods, of the kind the Syrians might be able to use. Although many of these were new and bewildering, the designers refused to talk down to their audience and maintained interest by straightforwardly displaying them as advanced achievements.

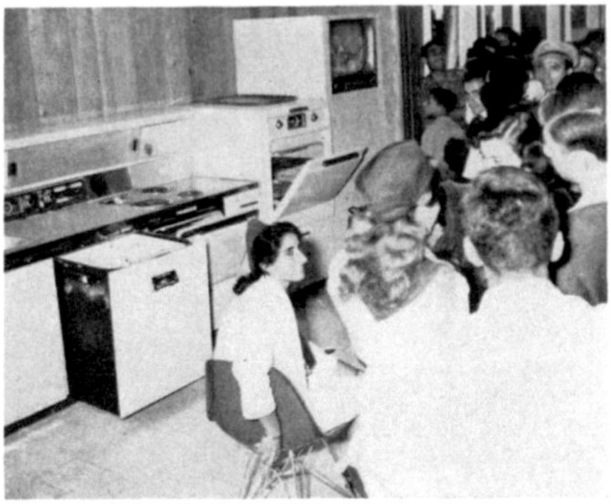

Syrian girl explains to her countrymen the complexities of a modern kitchen installation. Below, view of U. S. pavilion from Damascus street highlights TV exhibit under pentagonal form of intersecting parabolic arches; concrete structure was temporary.

ZAGREB, YUGOSLAVIA

e Zagreb International Trade Fair was e first opportunity the United States has d to stage an industrial exhibit in a mmunist country. While little was excted in immediate trade, the fair offered hance to counter Soviet propaganda and esent an approach to American life and sources.

Designers of Raymond Spilman's office, luding Don Waterman and David Wurr, developed the theme, "America at me," against the background of a photory of an average American industrial rker, Ed Barnes (which has been shown other fairs in the past). Displays of del prefabricated houses—one of them, John Johansen, of unusual design in ayed concrete construction—were comtely furnished and supplied with kitchen, rden and recreational equipment. The thod of approach was to invite the Yugovian worker to compare his daily life th that of his American counterpart.

The industrial equipment shown was ected for its applicability to Yugoslav oblems, and included a butcher shop in eration with modern refrigeration and kaging devices, a Department of Agriture display of dairy processing machin, and a sewing machine production line. -it-yourself tools, automobiles, cameras, hildren's playground, hi-fi and television uipment presented other aspects of erican life.

Marshal Tito, standing to right of his wife, watches demonstration of meat-processing machinery with obvious interest. Behind him is one of the exhibit designers, Don Waterman. Below, prefabricated sprayed concrete structure is shown in U. S. outdoor area, housing an exhibit of American architecture.

VIENNA, AUSTRIA

The cosmopolitan visitors at the Vienna International Fair needed no introduction to the refinements of Western culture, but in a country recently freed of the influence of Soviet occupation it was the U. S. exhibit's role to tell them "What's New"—what has been happening on the frontiers of American science, industry and daily living. Our exhibit, designed by Peter Harnden, former Chief of Design and Production at our Trade Fair office in Paris, concentrated on a relatively few large units of display. The most popular was a demonstration of the use of color television in surgery and medical education, in which a hospital operating room was built to perform a simulated operation on a mannequin patient. Advanced technical devices, including a high-fidelity phonograph built into the dashboard of a car, solar-battery-powered radios, and ultra-modern kitch equipment, introduced other recent livi habits to the Austrians. Modern transp tation developments—motels, jet passeng liners and radar landing-controls—w elaborated through models and illustra lectures on American travel trends. The d play technique itself was a subject of int est and a different way of providing visu attractions for a sophisticated audien

Linear elements of display materials are used to develop pattern of flags marking American exhibit.

Fashion show, in co-operation with Department of Agriculture, tells "What's New" in cotton fabrics as well as style.

Latest trends in daily living are reflected in choice of dining accoutrements.

STOCKHOLM, SWEDEN

Permanent U. S. pavilion modifies glassy international style with suggestion of Scandinavian use of wood at rear. TV monitors dot surrounding garden area. At right, scenes from a pantomime of do-it-yourself apartment decoration danced by Swedish couple. Interior view below shows mixture of "department store"-type displays, right, and theme of home craftsmanship developed in exhibit island at left.

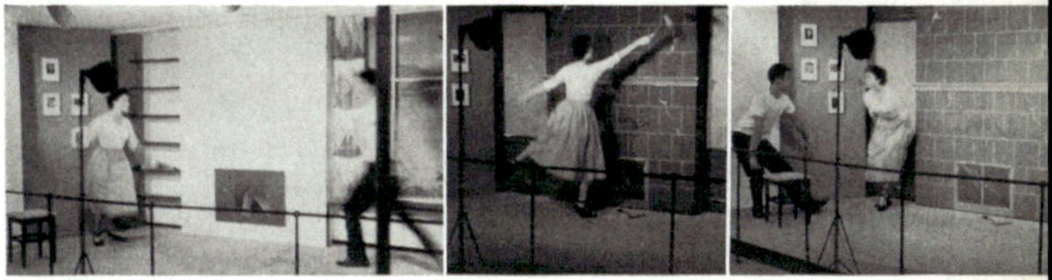

The U. S. exhibit at St. Erik's Fair, both architectural and display design by Scandinavian - American Reino Aarnio, managed to express both our debt to the Swedes' tradition of craftsmanship and our ability to make skillful use of their idiom and materials in our own culture. Our theme was the do-it-yourself trend in America, in which the craft-conscious Swedes have expressed an interest. Do-it-yourself on the sewing machine was made more engaging by a fashion-show of dresses produced on the spot; children were busy making model airplanes, creative paintings and prefabricated toys; a young Swedish couple danced a pantomime of apartment decoration. The tradition behind our skills was indicated by a display of colonial furniture, and two Navajo Indians — skilled workers in metal and fibres—showed another aspect of American resources that was unusually popular. The good-humored and sympathetic character of the show was summed up in a collection of cartoons spoofing the do-it fad, in which the graphic hand that symbolized the amateur artisan throughout the exhibit appeared for the last time—with the thumb bandaged. By such means, the exhibit suggested what Americans are really like.

KABUL, AFGHANISTAN

While some 200 Soviet technicians labored on a $2,000,000 pavilion for the Jeshn Fair at Kabul, the American pavilion was flown in on a single airplane and, with four Americans directing unskilled Afghan labor, completely erected in two days. It was the largest geodesic dome ever designed by Buckminster Fuller—100 feet in diameter—and its dramatically simple method of construction was an impressive demonstration of American ability to be ingenious rather than lavish.

This was the first American exhibit at an Afghan trade fair, and one of the first hints the Afghans have had about the Western world. Designer Jack Masey tried to create a panoramic view of American life, starting with such fundamentals as a photomural of the New York skyline. The exhibit featured the technological miracles that are synonymous with America throughout the world: TV, solar batteries, hi-fi, tape-recorders, model planes and trains. Perhaps our biggest drawing card was an outdoor Cinemascope theater adjoining the dome, which impressed the spectators with scenes taken in their own country. But the Afghans also showed interest in objects that help us perform tasks similar to their own—a miner's lamp, agricultural equipment, home heating stoves, water heaters, portable coolers and a textile handloom. Our selection showed that we can approach remote civilizations with objects on a human scale as well as with the merely colossal.

The fair pointed, too, to the long-range usefulness of a flexible and portable system of exhibit construction for the Trade Fair program. The Fuller dome, identifiably American, was used at our exhibit in Bangkok, Thailand, in December and will be used in the Tokyo fair this spring.

Stages in building exhibit dome show meeting of East West: Afghan workmen learn to assemble prefabric framework, U. S. technicians add finishing touches, and c pleted dome glows from interior lights near outdoor m

Display features at Kabul were selected for comprehensibility to unsophisticated audience. "Talking" cow and chicken below, giving interested farmers transcribed information on raising livestock, were animated to show internal processes. Mechanical equipment at right was explained by native guides, like the one third from top, who were used throughout.

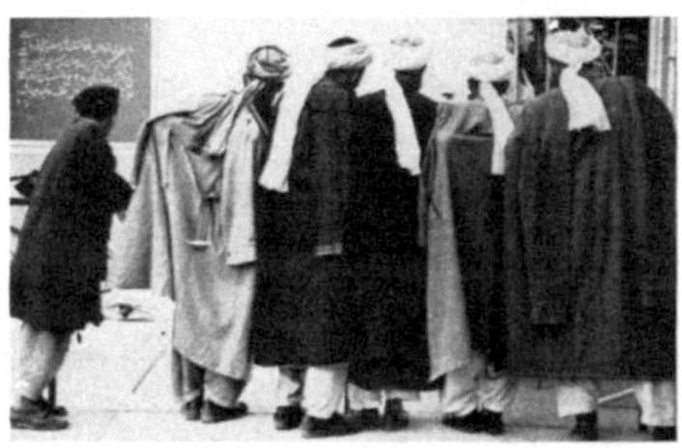

(*continued from page* 39)
disconcerting. Only at the war's end, when the country abruptly found itself in the center of the international stage, were our leaders forced to realize that the conduct of peace is even more of a psychological problem than the conduct of war. We learned, though experiences in postwar Japan, that physical conquest does not automatically change a way of life: to decree democracy by law did not produce a democratic people overnight. We faced the fact, too, that the presence of ambassadors does not always produce good will, just as the presence of information does not always constitute a desired communication. In the early days of its new and difficult role, the U.S.A. might easily have come to the conclusion that almost nothing it could do was totally right. And in some respects it would have been true.

Nevertheless, after 10 years of experience and error, the country has grown wiser in the techniques of leadership, and quicker in the perception of the fact that our own conduct — not only national policies but the conduct of servicemen and tourists and foreign service employees abroad — continually form the attitudes of other nations toward us. There is little doubt that today American politicans are more aware that people of the world, like any group of constituents, are deeply sensitive to America's attitude toward their own interests. What is best for a citizen of the U.S.A. may be entirely meaningless for life in Bangkok; an Afghan or Syrian may be deeply attached to his somewhat tedious and unsanitary life, too proud to want it disrupted by ideas that we may consider superior.

Soviet Pavilion, Kabul Fair

This point of view—based on a body of research in the increasingly important social science of anthropology —has almost had to find its way into America's foreign policy. But — whatever it is called — this viewpoint has made one fact inescapable at a moment when a bitter contest for world-wide "friendship" is being waged: friends are won and not bought; half the winning is in knowing how to overcome the obstacles to friendship, the other half is in the wanting to be friendly.

How others saw us

In terms of these subtle political problems, the OITF set about evaluating the pros and cons of its initial efforts. One of the hardest facts to face —and the most revealing — was the relative response drawn by Soviet and American exhibits. Despite the fact that U. S. shows and products did outdazzle the competition, they did not always provoke the most dazzling reactions. When Russia and the U.S.A. showed similar equipment — the Russian often technically inferior —the Soviets would be applauded while the Ameri suffered indifference or criticism. When both nat displayed helicopters in Damascus, for instance, th cident was reported by Henry Tanner in the New Y Herald Tribune: "Each afternoon, when the Rus (military) plane appears, the American (commerc follows, waves, wiggles, moves up and down, does the things the Russian can't do. The Syrians love it. do you think the United States really scores a po I watched the spectacle one afternoon with a gr of Syrians. They had nothing to say about the di ences in performance. They all agreed that the Rus plane was 'bigger,' hence by implication superior. . Part of this problem goes back to continual propaga and suppression of facts in Soviet-dominated ne papers. Another part can be traced to attitudes are more human than political. Many visitors in un developed countries can appreciate Russian achi ments because they *identify* themselves with pe who have recently overcome physical and econ handicaps. The same achievements by Americans like the work of a privileged nation with which have no personal identification.

Chinese Pavilion, Kabul Fair

On the positive side of the ledger, the OITF ha chance to analyze successful episodes: Sears, Roe catalogs on display in Berlin had been eagerly thum and frequently stolen. (Reason: a chance to actu visualize goods and compare prices without salesn ship.) A replica of an American supermarket had popular in Vienna. (Reason: a method close to w the Viennese knew, different enough to be interest in a relatively well-fed country.) And Cinerama been a hit in Bangkok and elsewhere. (Reason: with few economic overtones.) By and large, w other national exhibits gauged their extravaganza definite economic possibilities within the country, American spectaculars were being put on in the tradition of the Big Top. Thus, if they failed it not for lack of showmanship, or even of clear Am can identification. The underlying problem emer cleanly as one of *how we are being interpreted.* a young Italian said after the 1955 Milan Trade F "Americans show us beautiful refrigerators, and th only show us how poor and ugly our own are; Am cans overwhelm us with displays of products based abundance of electricity — when in Italy we never ow if the little costly current we have will operate all. The exhibits don't relate to the realities of our e, nor do they offer positive help — and they seem, thout meaning to, to cast a negative light on what have struggled to accomplish."

With this insight to help formulate the communica-ns problem, the OITF turned to outside designers help in solving it. Before final results can be ighed, it is necessary to examine in some detail how government, as the client, employed its designers.

w the program was organized

e fact that the eight fall Fairs shown on the preced- pages were able to open at all is perhaps the most markable thing about them. They were all created der virtually breakneck conditions as follows:

For each Fair, OITF prepared a budget. In some ses, such as Damascus ($124,000), this included a w exhibition building; in others it covered only the pense of installing an exhibition in a given interior outdoor space on the Fair grounds, including prod-ts that could be solicited from American business or rchased by local trade teams. In Salonika, for in-nce, the total appropriation for the 29,000 square t of indoors area was roughly $166,500. For Bari, was $110,000. For the recent Bangkok Fair, it was 40,000, including a new pavilion. Design fees and all nstruction had to be covered by these sums.

Late in May, 1956, the office issued an open invita-n to bid to a selected group of designers, on the basis their charge for "1) survey and preparation of a ncept of the exhibit and related preliminary plans; preparation of final, full and detailed plans, designs d specifications of the exhibit; and 3) assistance supervision of the construction, assembly, erection d installation of the exhibit, including selection of ilding firms and individual items for exhibit. Com-nsation is provided separately for each of these three ges and the Department may treat each stage as a parate contract."

In the letter of invitation, the Department outlined iefly its objectives and the material available for hibition. Because bids were submitted prior to the eliminary survey, this explanation was the basis on nich bid estimates had to be made. Within a few eeks, the eight bids were awarded on the basis of uality plus price." Of the designers awarded con-acts, only one was a native of the area involved 'innish-born Reino Aarnio worked in Sweden.) Peter arnden and Bernard Pfriem, exhibition designers the Salonika and Vienna Fairs respectively, had eviously headed design in the OITF's Paris office. The remainder were to be largely dependent on their survey trips, research, and embassy and governmental guid-ance for their acquaintance with local conditions.

Bid guesswork was just the first of their problems. The preliminary surveys, averaging several days to a week, permitted consultation with embassy officials, but the pressure of the schedule — with some contracts signed 60-70 days prior to the opening dates — did not make it easy to do basic research about national at-titudes and problems. (The Raymond Loewy organiza-tion was unique in sending two researchers for three weeks to explore the Syrian political scene and con-struction situation in detail.) Charles Shaw's Bari exhibit was entirely designed and installed within 60 days. Aarnio, in another instance, arrived on his Stock-holm visit to find that, by some oversight, there was no building to hold the American exhibit. He was able, by virtue of being an architect as well as an industrial designer, to design a permanent (as specified by Swed-ish law) American pavilion in four days. The time pressure was not the only obstacle: designing the ex-hibits was made even more complicated by the method in which the themes were developed and carried out. The contract, as previously noted, specified that the de-signers should work with the OITF in developing a particular theme for each country. These themes, without question, were actually the most critical aspect of the "design," for they established not only what ma-terial would be shown but at what *level* the U.S. chose to communicate with the foreign peoples.

And the themes had to be projected partially with ma-terial on hand from previous Fairs (if for no other rea-son than time) and partially from ideas that the de-signer might have — based on what he knew, was told, or could project about the country in question.

Facing the questions

There was no simple set of policies to guide designers about communication with foreign countries; no one individual had all the answers — in fact, there was no totally right answer. Each country posed a special situation, and the special answer — whether to be helpful, or impressive, or modest, or educational — had to grow out of the fact that the situations were varied indeed. Designers working in what we call "under-developed" countries faced the perplexity of 20th-century agrarianism: what is the view of those countries toward industrialization, and what is their best route to it? Some are equipped to develop it

from within; some in need of having it stimulated from outside; some will accept the atomic age directly, without romantic attachments to earlier technological eras. Western countries, while more familiar, pose another set of attitudes that are not perforce easier to cope with: by their very acquaintance with American ways, Europeans often have emphatic feelings about the difference between them and our traditions, manners, and general values. Audience literacy and construction conditions were considerations everywhere.

How they saw us

Successful design, under these conditions, is hard even for someone acquainted with local attitudes; for Americans accustomed to equating popular success with impressiveness and extravagance, it is full of hazards and surprises. The model kitchen, for example, with its washers and disposals and mixers, might seem like a legitimate statement of American accomplishment in Paris; but in Damascus, an electric kitchen actually has no relation to middle-eastern cookery. The electric mixer, on the other hand, could prove to have great meaning and influence to the Syrian audience if it were demonstrated as a tool for making the creamed and mashed chickpeas and eggplant that are a middle-eastern staple. The American supermarket, with its acres of disposable paper packages—a hit with westernized audiences — could easily annoy undernourished Greeks at the display both of waste and of plenty. Conversely, turbines and reactors and such technological miracles would probably have no effect on an Afghan herdsman, while in central Europe they would indeed symbolize American technical prowess — or, without the help of more humanly appealing material, they might represent another inviting display of American superiority to people who knew that, in their lifetimes, there would never be room for them on the U.S. immigration quota.

The subtlety of the situation extends in its most critical forms to decisions between foreseeable alternatives: our habit of giving out free doughnuts and ice cream, for instance, drew crowds in many countries and dramatically demonstrated our productivity and the effectiveness of our machinery. It also drew criticism in many quarters, particularly from other exhibiting nations who could not afford the lure of handouts. At a point like this, somebody has to decide which course best serves the total effort at international good will. It was frequently the designers.

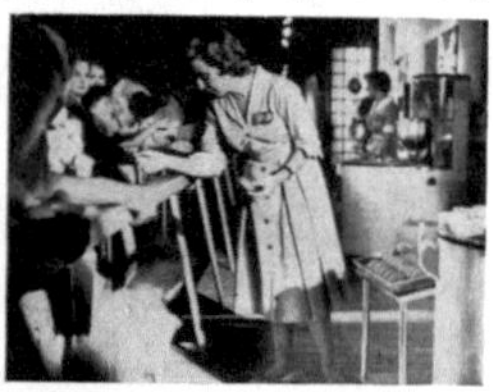

To evaluate the overall success of the fall Fairs at this time, virtually impossible except in relat terms: In 1956 Director Williams had claimed thusiastically, "In 1957 we'll double last year's atte ance or bust." At the eight recent fairs, most ne paper accounts here cited higher attendance at American exhibits than at any others; reporters a officials alike have stated that Americans have b much more popular than ever before.

Attendance figures, of course, are not a definit measure of the effectiveness of propaganda in minds of the viewing crowds. Perhaps nothing rea is. But in terms of the potential effectiveness of effort, there are a few conclusions to be drawn fr what we tried to do — and here the great range style and content of the fall shows reflects at leas sober acceptance of the specialness of each regio problem. In Afghanistan — one of the most diffic Fairs we have yet tackled — the U.S.A. was the o exhibitor to employ Afghan attendants throughout, explain the products in vernacular; the products the selves were modest and more workaday than elsewhe In Greece and Italy there were educational agricultural demonstrations on how Americans use farm machines and prepare foods for market. The Stockholm exhibit a pealed to the Scandinavian identification with han craft traditions by demonstrating what Americans with do-it-yourself. In Damascus, the U.S.A. purpose framed a sophisticated technical exhibit—despite t fact that the audience was not educationally equipp to grasp many of the electronic devices; the designe discovered in their local study that Syrians are high sensitive to being "talked down to" by Americans, a decided that addressing the Syrians as equals w more important than detailed communication.

Government as client

In selecting industrial and exhibition designers to p pare the Trade Fairs, the OITF expressed a belief their ability to solve an entirely new kind of proble — one on which others had already stubbed their to It is worth examining, in summing up, whether th role was a proper one for designers or whether it rather one for specialists and, in evaluating what h happened, to ask how it might be better done hereafte

An industrial designer is, by training and expe ence, a problem solver — whether the problems kles are in the area of products, manufacturing, rketing or communication. An exhibition designer, ugh working in a more specialized medium, is a blem solver in visual communication. Because each st solve a tremendous variety of different kinds of blems, what each has to offer is an *approach* to blem-solving; thus it seems entirely reasonable — remely perceptive, in fact — that the OITF assumed t a good designer could solve even a large and dif-lt communications problem — *provided that the blem was properly stated,* or that the information ded to formulate the problem was made available he designer.

t is part of the experience of every practicing de-ner, of course, to know that the first step with ny clients is to re-state the problem for him: a nt who thinks he wants a gas pump designed fre-ntly needs a re-evaluation of the way his gas sta-s function first. The situation was not much dif-ent in the case of the Trade Fairs, and the client generally aware of it: OITF needed not merely ger or bolder exhibit installations, but a fresh look its whole method of communications. It did look the designers for help in this area, and got some asurable results.

3ut, had the OITF been more experienced in the of a designer's client, it might have done more several areas to assure those results. In terms of ure programs, these might be outlined this way:

) **Guidance:** A designer, as a generalist rather than cialist, needs full information in order to com-nicate with an audience he does not know; if such ormation is not part of the statement of the prob- by the client, access to it should be provided. The TF could provide a variety of sources — political lysts and observers, government specialists, foreign isors — from whom the designers could compile icient information to make their *own* conclusions not only the safest but the most effective approach. ne such steps have already been taken.

) **Material:** Though the designers have not been ler obligation to utilize all the material pre-selected the OITF, there would be opportunity for better more consistent exhibitions if they were encour-d to exercise more control over all the material to presented. The freedom given to designers has been reciated, and could well be increased.

) **Evaluation:** As a client, government can evaluate e realistically what a designer's talent is worth oth time and money. The pressure of time, as previ-ly mentioned, need not be so bad again. But the t remains that design, as a creative as well as phys- activity, cannot be successfully conceived or ex-ecuted under pressure.

Though the fees for each exhibit are not, of course, public information, it is worth questioning whether the method of arriving at these fees is a workable one — and whether design should be selected on the basis of bids at all. The bid, of course, is a governmental convention for assuring an open and uncorrupted market and free competition. Bids certainly are workable when the problem is to select materials or even to contract for construction. But talent is not that easy to measure; the selection of designers on the basis of "quality plus price" is a vague criterion at best.

The problem of a governmental agency employing designers is not much different from that of any client: its job is to be a skilled enough judge of design, and of people, to select the talent that will best do its job. If, because of inexperience, it does not feel qualified to make such selections, it would be possible to form a committee of selected professional advisors to instruct or advise in its program. When the A.S.I.D. offered to form such a committee to advise on professional practices and on design policy for the Fair exhibits, it suggested one plausible answer. It is to be hoped that in the future, instead of approaching the design as a simple competition among individuals, OITF will also seek liason with groups that can provide the collective advice of experienced professionals.

4) **Criteria:** The OITF has made no statements on its choice of designers to date; neither has it defined its standards of "quality" or "price" or the relative weights of each. Hereafter, it would undoubtedly improve both design results and designer relations to have its standards more specifically aired.

The Trade Fair program has, in a sense, really just begun. On the basis of this crash program, and the success of the December Bangkok exhibit (Cushing & Nevell, designers) the OITF has high hopes for even better results in the 6 Spring shows for which designers have already been selected: Loewy Associates: Milan; Becker & Becker Associates: Paris; Charles Shaw: Casablanca, Barcelona; Cushing & Nevell: Tokyo; Reino Aarnio: our first exhibit in Poland in June. There will be a chance for designers and the government to perfect their working methods and their effectiveness in winning friends for the U.S.A. These improvements are more than desirable; they are essential. The Trade Fair program is undoubtedly one of the most serious responsibilities that the design profession has ever assumed.

U.S. ARCHITECTURE IN WEST BERLIN

AMERIKA BAUT

EXHIBITION WAS SHOWN IN PERMANENT U.S. PAVILION IN BERLIN. ENTRANCE WAS BY WAY OF SPIRAL STAIR LEADING TO CIRCULAR ROOM IN FOREGROUND.

"Amerika Baut" was the U.S. building industry's contribution to West Berlin's Interbau exposition, the biggest architectural show held anywhere in many years. During its two-week run, "Amerika Baut" was seen by more than ¼ million people from West and East Germany, from Western and Eastern Europe. The show was sponsored by the U.S. Information Agency; it was conceived and designed by Peter Blake; and it was held in the George C. Marshall House (left), an awkward, 25,000 sq. ft. exhibition pavilion which the U.S. maintains in West Berlin.

Although the form of the exhibition was dictated largely by the form of the available space, the content was determined by three general intentions:

first, to show how the vast dimensions of the U.S. have produced a building industry with special problems and special characteristics;

second, to concentrate upon those American building techniques that differ most radically from those of Europe;

and, third, to demonstrate that these industrial techniques have helped produce new forms of high architectural quality.

Since the exhibit was to be seen by a lay audience, the chief design problem was how to dramatize so technical a subject. Several devices, old as well as new, deliberately corny as well as elegant, were employed: for example, the circular tail-end of the Marshall House was transformed into a realistic replica of an observation platform on top of a Manhattan skyscraper—entered by spiral stair from below, and lined with a 360° panorama specially photographed for the exhibition (see opposite). Recorded sounds of Times Square traffic and flickering lights made the illusion complete.

SCRIPT & DESIGN: PETER BLAKE, ARCHITECT

ASSOCIATE: RICHARD S. STARK

SYMBOL & TYPOGRAPHY: BROWNJOHN & CHERMAYEFF

EXHIBITS OFFICER: JACK MASEY, U.S.I.A.

OF AMERICAN BUILDING OPERATIONS WAS DRAMATIZED BY 360° PANORAMA OF MANHATTAN SKYLINE PHOTOGRAPHED IN 5 SECTIONS BY J. ALEX LANGLEY.

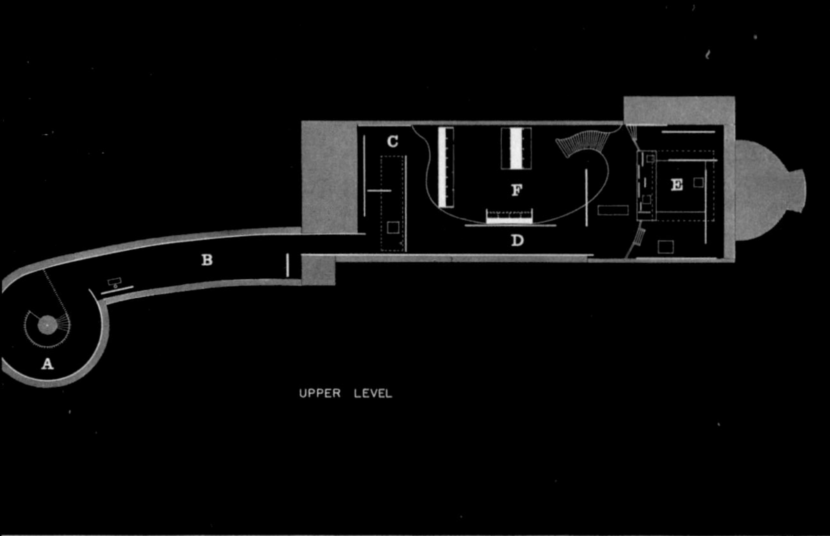

N OF UPPER LEVEL SHOWS ENTRANCE AREA WITH MANHATTAN SKYLINE AT LEFT, INTRODUCTION TO SHOW (B), EXHIBITS ON BALCONY (C, D & E)

The Marshall House consis
two areas: a long wing on
and a 2-story high room, 10
60′, overlooked by a free
balcony (see plan).

It was decided to enter th
hibit at the far end of the ele
wing; to use that wing for th
troduction to the show; the
lead visitors into the balcony
overlooking the tall, central
and, finally, to exploit the h
of that room for a dramati
max.

To show the exhaustive
planning that goes into the
struction of a typical U. S.
skyscraper, I. M. Pei's "Mile
Center" in Denver was select
a case in point. It was expl
how structural, mechanical
economic considerations all
bined there to form part o
final, esthetic expression. Her
elsewhere, the show made li
use of models, working draw

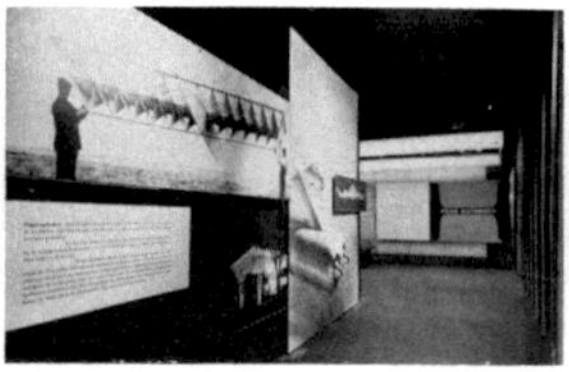

AREA B SHOWS INFLUENCE OF TRANSPORTATION TECHNOLOGY ON AMERICAN BUILDING

AREA C: "MILE-HIGH CENTER"

AREA D: NEW BUILDING PANEL

THE NEW WORLD OF FORM OPENED UP BY NON-SKELETAL STRUCTURES WAS EXPLAINED IN TERMS OF CURRENT U.S. EXPERIMENTS IN THIS FIELD

The following companies
a major contribution to the su
of this exhibition:

Aluminum Company of Americ
The Bettinger Corporation
The Browne Window Manufact
ing Company
Dearborn Glass Company
Filon Plastics Corporation
General Bronze Corporation
Hexcel Products, Incorporated
Integrated Ceilings Sales Co
International Molded Plastics,
Kawneer Company
The R. C. Mahon Company
McLouth Steel Corporation
Olin Mathieson Chemical Cor
Resolite Corporation
Reynolds Metals Company
Rigidized Metals Corporation
Southdale Center, Incorporate
Sweet's Catalog Service

ized photographs and actual ng materials (see opposite). example, hundreds of new ican sheet materials and pan- ere shown in a modular, one- grid-frame that formed the drop for areas C & D.

ea E of the exhibit dealt with forms created out of warped curved planes. There were ls and pictures of Saarinen's Yale ice hockey rink, Breuer's r College Library, Yamasa- St. Louis Airport, Catalano's house, and many others.

m several points in the bal- area, visitors were able to a glimpse of the tall, central below. This space had been formed into a full-sized, imag- American city, made up of les of existing U. S. skyscrap- Now, as they left the balcony visitors walked down a d stair to enter this imaginary

AREA C CONTAINS FULL-SIZE BLOW-UPS OF "MILE-HIGH CENTER." BALCONY RAIL IS VISIBLE AT LEFT. MODULAR GRID OF NEW MATERIALS IN REAR

CATALOGS

AREA E: NEW FORMS IN BUILDING BASED ON SHELL-PRINCIPLE. THIS AREA WAS BRILLIANTLY LIT BY NEW PLASTIC, LUMINOUS CEILING

AS VISITORS DESCENDED FROM BALCONY, THEY ENTERED A FULL-SIZE, MODERN AMERICAN CITY. FACADE-SECTION AT RIGHT IS SEAGRAM BUILDING

e, Incorporated
Incorporated
n Carbide International Co.
d States Korboard
d States Plywood Corp.
co Products, Incorporated
b & Knapp, Incorporated
Wilson Lighting & Display,
corporated

d the following publications institutions provided pictorial rial and models:

rchitectural Forum
Bettman Archive
d of Higher Education, City of
ew York
mbia University
ute of Aeronautical Sciences
Museum of Modern Art
National Geographic Magazine
Smithsonian Institution
University

PHOTOGRAPHS: GNILKA

SKYSCRAPER CITY IS SEEN ABOVE. PHOTOGRAPHS IN ONE-POINT PERSPECTIVE (BELOW) GAVE ILLUSION OF GREATER DEPTH TO AREAS UNDER BALCONY.

Six major U.S. skyscrapers w shown in the tall, central area of Marshall House: the bronze Seagr Building (Mies Van der Rohe & Ph Johnson), the stainless steel Un Carbide Building now under c struction (opposite page) and glassy Lever House (both by Sk more, Owings & Merrill.) In addit to these three New York structur there was the aluminum ALCOA Bu ing in Pittsburgh (Harrison & Abran vitz), the louvered Tishman Buildi in Los Angeles (Gruen), and the p celain-enamel Exchange Park in D las (Lane, Gamble & Associates).

These six facades were so plac as to create two interlocking "pi zas"—and to conceal the ugly fr form balcony and stair as much possible (see plan opposite).

To dramatize the height and wi of these buildings, the 2-story hi facades were set between mirrors floors, ceilings and on both sid

The resulting reflections *ad infinit* in all directions produced a startli climax to the show and effectively d stroyed the unhappy existing spa

"Amerika Baut" will be shown part at the Poznan Fair in the Spri of 1958. Elements of the show a being incorporated in the Bruss World's Fair and in a forthcomi exhibition in New Delhi.

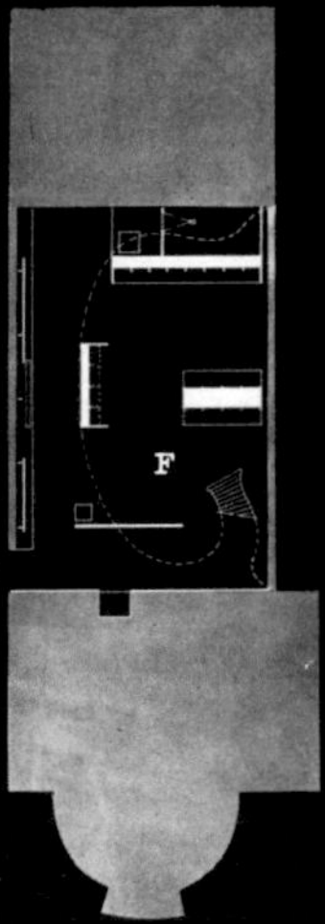
F
EXIT

"Man in America"

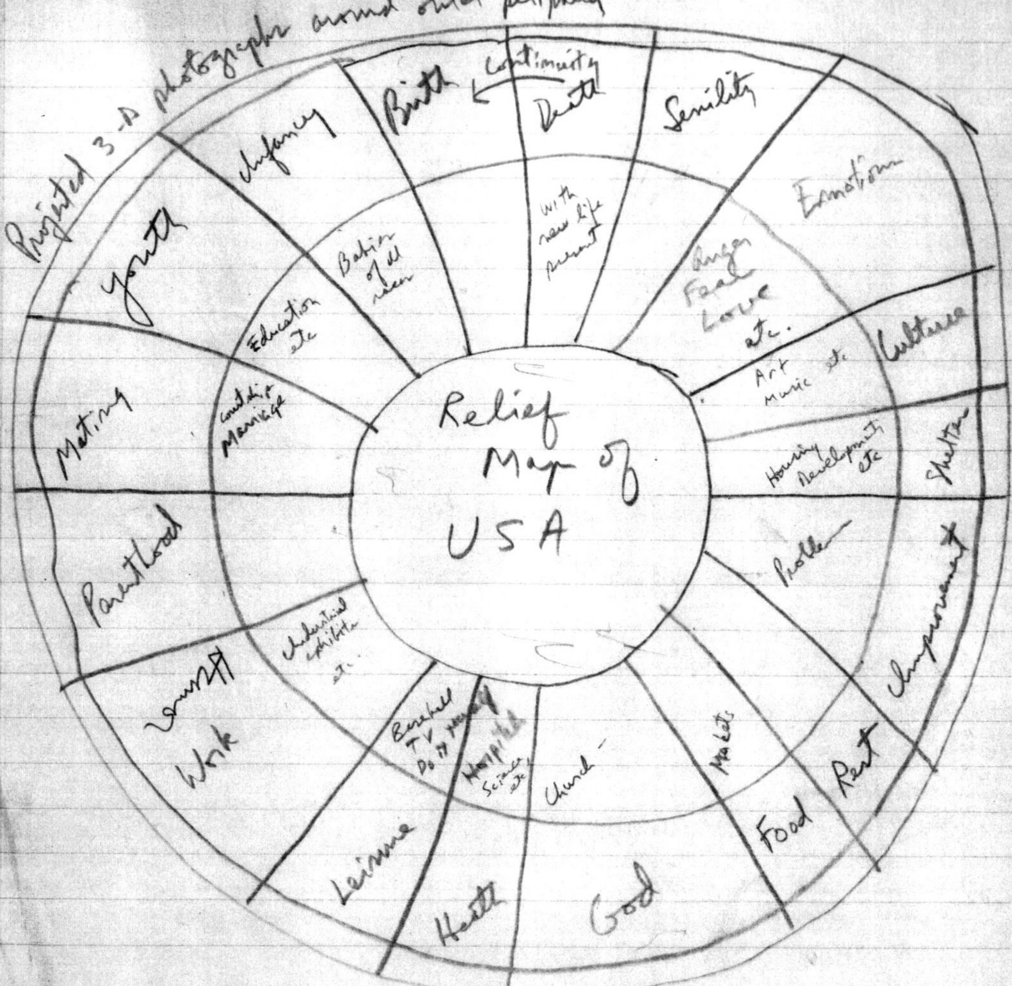

W.W Rostow

SOME UNFINISHED BUSINESS OF THE AMERICAN COMMUNITY

It became the deep conviction of those who evolved this exhibit that something like it must form an element in the Brussels' Fair. The projection of America in terms of various scientific, business, and leisure activities--without the element of active commitment to ideals--is not only inaccurate, but conforms to the worst European images. Moreover, the desegregation problem cannot be evaded. It will be underlined rather than evaded by omission. The correct setting for it is within the framework of the American commitment to struggle towards its peculiar version of common Western aspirations.

This memorandum sets out the proposed thematic message of the exhibit; and then suggests tentatively a few ideas about projection.

In extremely simple form the sequence of messages to be projected are these:

-- The United States has been and remains committed to aspire towards a set of ideals, special in their expression but deeply rooted in Europe and the Mediterranean world.

-- These ideals by no means govern all American behavior, but they suffuse American life in many ways.

-- They are brought into effect not merely by the formal action of American politics but by the way the American community is organized; for the American citizen is not merely an individualist, he takes active responsibility in the community through a maze of powerful voluntary associations.

-- These voluntary associations, acting responsibly, operate on both domestic and foreign policy.

-- For example, it is the wisdom and responsibility of citizens and their voluntary associations, rather than the Supreme Court decision itself, which is now bringing slowly into effect the desegregation decision, not by ukase, but by living social process at the local level. This can be observed in such difficult cases as Clinton, as well as such relatively successful cases as Louisville and St. Louis.

-- For example, the new American initiative in economic foreign policy, forecast in Mr. Dulles' recent statement, is rooted not merely in the decisions and deliberations of the Executive Branch and the Congress but in the responsible study, recommendation, and support of a maze of private groupings, representing business, labor, women, the churches, etc.

-- Like the rest of American life, these examples are unfinished, on-going business, a living process.

* * *

Following are some amateur ideas about how this sequence might be effectively projected.

This section of the exhibition should be quiet, sound-proofed, dignified without being over-solemn or pretentious. Although devices of vivid projection should not be rejected out-of-hand, there should be no straining for exciting effect, beyond clarity and substance. This is meant to be an exhibit only for those who are interested in serious matter.

In general, the effort is to elaborate the technique of, say, a LIFE story into exhibition terms, cutting down, if possible, the role of text, and exploiting potentialities for scale and movement denied a magazine.

First, the exhibit should contain a selection of the classic European texts which lie at the basis of liberty and democracy. It may or may not be necessary to go back to the Old and New Testaments, Greece, and Rome; but certainly there should be British, German, and French sources. Following these should be not merely selections from the Declaration and Constitution; but selected quotations from Jefferson, Hamilton, Lincoln. Despite apparent banality, there should be good pictures of the relevant men.

Second, there should be a chart of the American community showing not merely the President, Supreme Court, Congress, and the two parties; but also the maze of voluntary associations which surround them: business, labor, farmer, veteran, women, religious, etc., etc. These could be charted and a map could show their geographical spread, in moving sequence. There might be a few half-humorous quotations from European observers of the American scene commenting on the American passion for voluntary association, from De Tocqueville on: perhaps pictures of the President being photographed with a dozen or so representative groupings.

Third, there should be an exhibit on the desegregation problem. This might contain the following elements:

a. Some statistics and perhaps a racial chart, showing how the Melting Pot has evolved over recent decades.

b. A brief, compact exhibit on the progress made by Negroes in the past fifty years in terms of income and education levels, etc.

c. A desegregation exhibit focused on three cases, each told pictorially, LIFE-style: Clinton, where the fact of rioting

Advertising - The exhibit probably should show both the good and the bad. The control side of advertising is gaining, but we can show the variety, individuality, originality -- such as good cartoon type advertising.

Magazines and periodicals -- Europeans don't have any ideas of the variety and quality of our press. Most Europeans are not familiar with any of our magazines but TIME and LIFE. We should stress the good content of our magazines and present magazines as a new development.

Final overall thoughts.

The exhibit should have no slick answers. It must indicate that life here is a continuing search for the right answers - in that sense it is a continuation of the oldest search in the world. In this country we continue to explore new and uncharted worlds.

What the Russians will see

Anne Anderson runs exhibition kitchen (above) from a push-button panel (right).

A "miracle kitchen" with its own "brain" will be a high light of the U.S. exhibit in Moscow

FIVE MILLION RUSSIANS are expected to flock to Sokolniki Park in Moscow this summer to see a panorama of U. S. life displayed in the American National Exhibition. Vice-President Richard M. Nixon is scheduled to open the $5 million showcase on July 25. The exhibition is part of a unique cultural exchange. The Russian counterpart is a Soviet exhibition now being held at the Coliseum in New York City.

The Russians are showing "hard goods" (rockets and coal-mining machinery) as well as "soft lines" (fashions and furniture). The U. S. presentation will include an $11,000 ranch house, a Disney Circarama movie, U. S. automobiles, Leonard Bernstein and the New York Philharmonic and a fantastic $250,000 "miracle kitchen." One of three to be displayed in Moscow, the kitchen has an electronic brain designed and built by RCA Whirlpool. It promises to be a high light of the exhibit. At the 1958 Milan exposition, visitors rated it "outstanding." In charge of demonstrating the push-button kitchen will be Anne Anderson, Iowa editor and home economist. Here, in a preview for Americans, she shows how the domestic wonder takes the work out of cooking.

Produced by GEREON ZIMMERMANN Photographed by BOB LERNER

1

2

1 *A touch of the hand brings a refrigerated compartment to working level. Vegetable sink is located just below. The experimental kitchen has closed-circuit TV, air conditioning and a controlled system of colored lights.*

2 *Mrs. Anderson begins a salad on work surface of the free-standing range. The oven, which operates on the microwave principle, can bake a cake in three minutes.*

3 *She presses a button, and the dishwasher "walks" an electronic track to the dining table. Kitchen also has a robot floor cleaner and automatically adjustable sinks. By pressing buttons, Anne can prepare a complete meal without leaving the kitchen's control panel.*

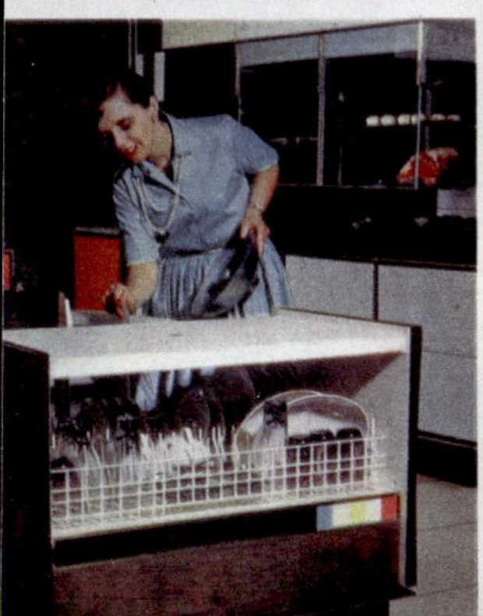

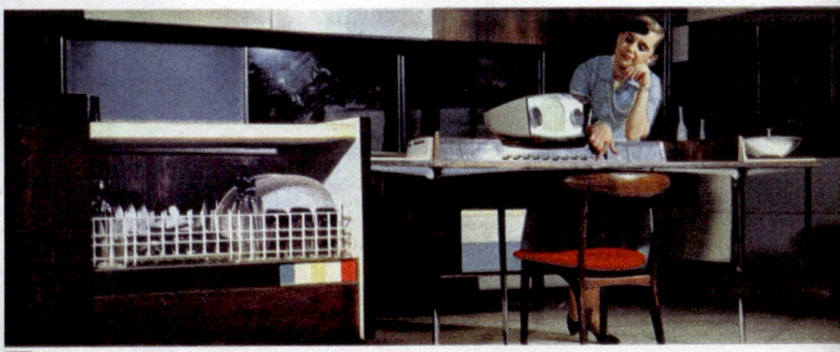

3

continued

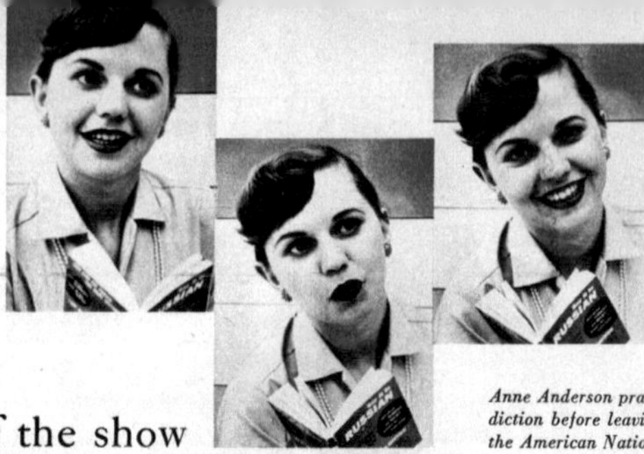

Anne Anderson practices her Russian diction before leaving for the American National Exhibition.

The wash will be part of the show

As steak sizzles, French fries sputter, and a dishwasher "walks" across the floor, Mrs. Anderson will tell Russians about the kitchen in their own language, which she has spoken fluently since her childhood in Argo, Ill. Anne Sonopol Anderson's parents were born in the Ukraine region of Russia, and two of her uncles still live there. She is a graduate of the University of Illinois, where she studied journalism and home economics. When Russian agricultural experts visited Iowa farms in 1955, she was one of the interpreters for the delegation. Once, meeting the visitors on Walnut Street in Des Moines, she hailed them in their own language. The result was a Russian-speaking foursome that wound up in a drugstore sharing ice-cream sodas and pop. She hopes she will see her Russian acquaintances again in Moscow this summer.

Crated for a ship's hold, the kitchen leaves its "home" in St. Joseph, Mich., for Moscow.

Anne's schedule is a crammed one. The kitchen will be in operation 13 hours a day. She will have five assistants; one of them is her sister, Tania Mandel, a Salinas, Calif., schoolteacher who also speaks Russian. The two are training four Soviet women to help them in operating the push-button kitchen, which will get the equivalent of five years' normal wear and tear in six weeks. (Altogether, 75 young Americans who are fluent in Russian have been chosen as guides at the exhibition.)

The food prepared in the kitchen of the future will include America's favorite dishes. A typical dinner will be steak, French-fried potatoes and onion rings, green salad with blue-cheese dressing and a strawberry angel-food loaf cake. Other U. S. preferences (fried chicken, corn on the cob and apple pie) will also be done to a piping turn in the other two kitchens in operation at the exhibition. In all, seven tons of American food will be prepared; they will include 110 varieties of edibles ranging from frozen beef pies to chocolate cake mixes.

Like all women, Anne Anderson worried about the wardrobe she will take on the trip. For the demonstrations, she and her sister decided to wear the popular shirtwaist-style dresses in pastel colors. The frocks are of wash-and-wear fabrics. The two are also taking along dresses for their Russian assistants. Of course, the clothes will be laundered in the exhibit's combination automatic washer and dryer during demonstrations. Russians thus will see the characteristic circus of activity that is an everyday occurrence in most U. S. kitchens.

Russian interest in the push-button kitchen was foreshadowed when Anastas I. Mikoyan, the Soviet Union's first deputy premier, visited the U. S. last year. "We have to free our housewives like you Americans! The Russian housewife needs help," he said. He knew the statistics about mechanical aids for housewives in the U. S. and the U.S.S.R. For example, 309,000 refrigerators and 377,000 washers were produced in Russia in 1957, compared to U. S. sales in 1957 of 3,350,000 and almost 4,000,000.

Another indication of Russian interest in the exhibition came recently when Premier Nikita Khrushchev visited the building site in Sokolniki Park, once a hunting preserve for the czars. He watched workmen hustling to complete the exhibition structures. Inspecting the gold-tinted aluminum geodesic dome for one of the two main buildings, he noted that the arresting structure had "many interesting technical innovations." Buoyantly, Khrushchev slipped one of the dome's brass bolts into his pocket and told an American official, "Look, I am stealing this." The Russians, incidentally, have agreed to purchase the two American exhibit buildings after the fair. Besides the dome-shaped one, there is a fan-shaped structure with an accordion-pleated aluminum roof.

The exhibition will bring to Moscow a transplanted slice of the American way of life. It will be a display that President Eisenhower has called "about the best investment the Government has made in a long time."

END

Bill Vitous, RCA Whirlpool exhibit specialist, has his apron tied by Marcia Corley. Vitous last year took the kitchen to Milan, where it was seen by 1,000,000 people. He anticipates similar favorable reaction in Moscow.

Montreal dome

Inside the bubble

Any exhibits designed to fill such a spectacular enclosure would appear doomed to obscurity. Yet the exhibit structure (left), designed by the Cambridge Seven may turn out to be almost as spectacular as the dome that will house it.

The structure will be a series of platforms on different levels, connected by escalators, bridges and elevators, and containing exhibits of American creativity in the arts, sciences and technology. The arrangement of the platforms will make possible some highly dramatic exhibition techniques: objects will be visible not only at eye level, but also from above and below, while the visitor is standing or in motion.

The Cambridge Seven—another rather far-out group not usually commissioned by bureaucrats to do important work for the U.S. Government — will draw upon other Creative Americans to help select material for their show. Much of that material, especially in the arts, is likely to be controversial, and some Members of Congress, undoubtedly, would prefer a Hallmark-type exhibit.

But those who selected the designers of the official U.S. Pavilion at Expo 67, and of the exhibits it will contain, understood one all-important fact: that next year, in Montreal, "Creative America" will be on view before an international audience that knows a great deal about where the action is in U.S. art, design, science and technology. To trot out mediocrity before such people would be an insult.

Left: Air view, with top of bubble removed, showing overlapping platforms of exhibit structure within the dome. Opposite page: Most recent model of the U.S. Pavilion with its gleaming space frame.

FACTS AND FIGURES

U.S. Pavilion for the Canadian Universal and International Exhibition, Montreal, 1967.
Organizing Agency: U.S. Information Agency. Pavilion Architecture: R. Buckminster Fuller, Shoji Sadao, Peter Flloyd, Geometrics Inc. Interior Platforms, Landscaping and Exhibit Architects: Cambridge Seven Associates Inc. (Ivan Chermayeff, Terry Rankine, and others). Engineers: Simpson, Gumpertz & Heger Inc. (structural); Paul Londe & Associates (mechanical and electrical). Canadian Associate Architects: John B. & John C. Parkin (Hugh F. McMillan). General Contractor: George A. Fuller Co., Inc. Appropriation for Pavilion and Exhibits: $9.3 million.

THE ARCHITECTURAL FORUM / JUNE 1967

FORUM

olitan's centennial in 1970. e proposed extension (above) been designed by Brown, wford and Forbes.

The Aswan High Dam will rtly flood the original temple . The fantastic eight-year-old cue operation, under the auspi- of UNESCO, has saved most the other temples. But $2.2 llion is still needed to secure u Simbel. Persons wishing to p save that temple should send ney to Roger L. Stevens at White House.

EXPO 67

OP-OUT

By the time this appears in nt, almost everything worth ring about Montreal's scrump- us Expo 67 will have been said. erything, we suspect, with one eption: no one is likely to have d the story of how it hap- ned that the stunning U.S. vilion, with its wonderfully so- isticated, witty, colorful exhibits er got built by any outfit as id-cult" as the U.S. Govern- nt.

We feel a trifle self-conscious out revealing the secret, for the ry involves someone who was ce—about 20 years ago—a drop- t from The Architectural rum's editorial staff.

Anyway: *some* people in this eat country of ours must have ndered, just a little bit, how came to pass that the rather n-swinging Administration of ndon B. Johnson built a 20- ry steel-and-plastic "skybreak bble" by that certifiable risk, cky Fuller; how our Govern- nt screwed up enough courage commission a crew of junior in- rrigibles known as The Cam- idge Seven to design the plat- rms and exhibits inside Bucky's bble; how a young Hollywood iter named James R. Silke was ked to compile the most amus- g exhibit on American movies date; how this same Adminis- ation hired an extremely controversial art critic called Alan Solomon to put up one of the most sensational Pop-Art exhibits ever shown anywhere; how the General Accounting Office was persuaded to pay a man called Art Kane, who had never made a movie in his life, to make an absolutely fabulous film for our pavilion; and how it happened that the Government of the U.S. commissioned somebody like James Rosenquist to paint a 33-ft.-high Pop job of two feet sliding down a firepole, or somebody like Claes Oldenburg to make a big, black, drooping ventilating fan.

Well, the answer is really quite simple. There was *one* man in the right spot at the right time who had the courage of his convictions, and stuck with the former and the latter, and made the whole thing come true.

His name is Jack Masey (below). After he was dropped from our staff some 20 years ago, Masey went to work for the U.S. Information Agency—in places like Delhi, Tashkent, Kabul, and—Ugh!—Washington. He happened to be available when Expo came up, and so the U.S. Information Agency made him chief of design for that particular enterprise.

For close to three years, Masey worked around the clock within that agency to make our Montreal pavilion just a little better than it would have been under normal circumstances.

To indicate what the pavilion might have been *without* Masey, just look at the USSR job. In the Moses-directed disaster, the 1965-66 New York World's Fair, there was a U.S. Government nothing-box, containing several million cu. ft. of nothing; the USSR Pavilion in Montreal is that same nothing-box, with the lid turned up just a little.

But our pavilion at Montreal is a triumph of architecture, engineering, interior design, display, dramatization, and all the rest; a demonstration of the ebullient spirit of the young people of our nation, and a triumph of sheer courage.

We do not wish to embarrass Jack Masey. But this is not only Bucky Fuller's pavilion, not only the pavilion of the Cambridge Seven, nor that of the other contributors. It is the pavilion of one Jack Masey, a drop-out from The Architectural Forum, and now a highly improbable bureaucrat.

BEAUTY

APPOINTMENTS

The First Lady's beautification drive was endorsed last month by Lassie, that well-known star of screen and television. Lassie is, of course, a collie, and will work in

the anti-litter section of Mrs. Johnson's campaign. He will be featured on a poster showing him deposit (by mouth) a piece of litter in a wire trash basket. Lassie, who has frequently demonstrated the prehensile capabilities of his teeth, presented the First Lady with a bouquet of flowers—also by mouth. Thereupon the official White House collie, Blanco, took violent umbrage and had to be removed from the premises.

OBSTRUCTING UGLINESS

Almost everyone is against ugliness—more or less. The White House certainly is, and after its Conference on Natural Beauty, in 1965, the President sent a strongly worded highway beautification proposal to Congress. Mrs. Johnson then made sure that a law was passed with some teeth in it.

Now, it seems, some members of Congress think that there were too many teeth in the law, and they are trying to pull them.

In month-long hearings by the House Public Roads Subcommittee it became clear that the beautification advocates, who had helped Mrs. Johnson get the bill passed in the first place, had gone home—while the full-time lobbyists for the billboard industry remained vigorously at work.

The bill, as originally passed in the House by 245 to 138, was written to ban billboards along the interstate system and certain primary roads by 1970, and provides, for the present, for the removal of 900,000 signs along the interstate highway system and the cleaning up of 17,500 junkyards.

A curious aspect of the apparent change of heart on this program in the House is the recent behavior of Rep. John C. Kluczynski (Dem., Ill.), who steered the original bill through Congress two years ago. Now Mr. Klu-

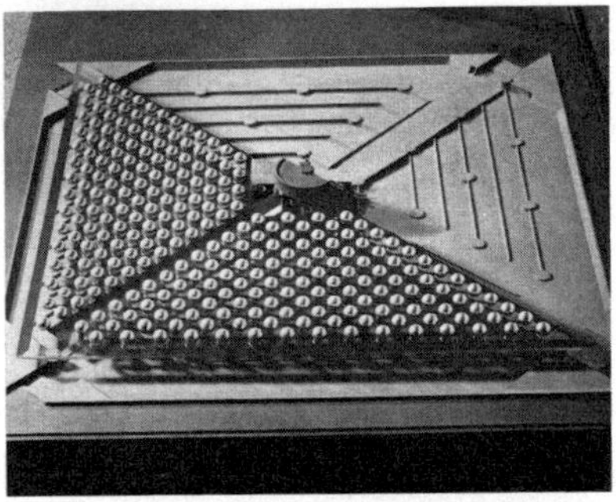
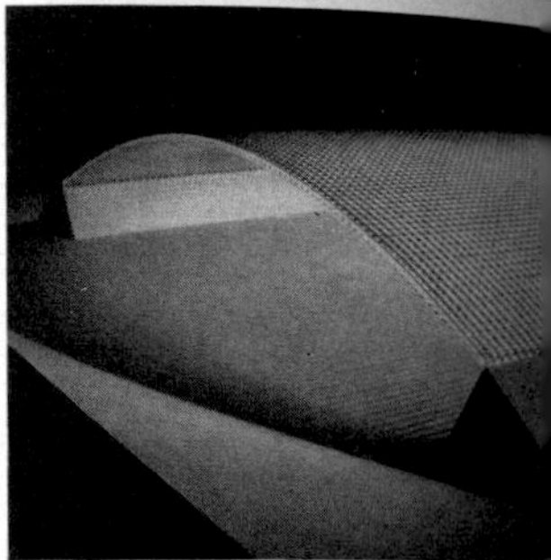

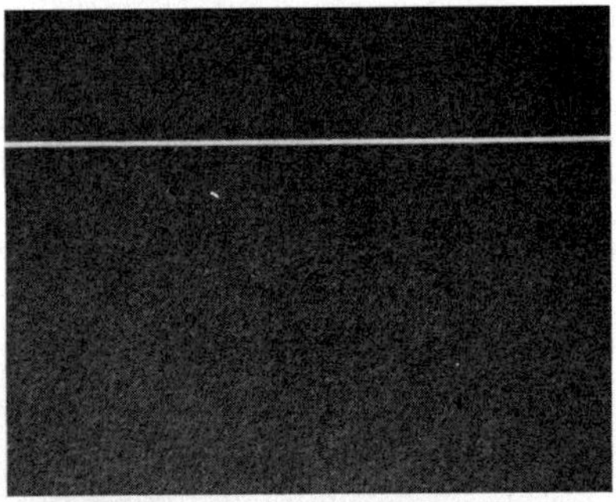
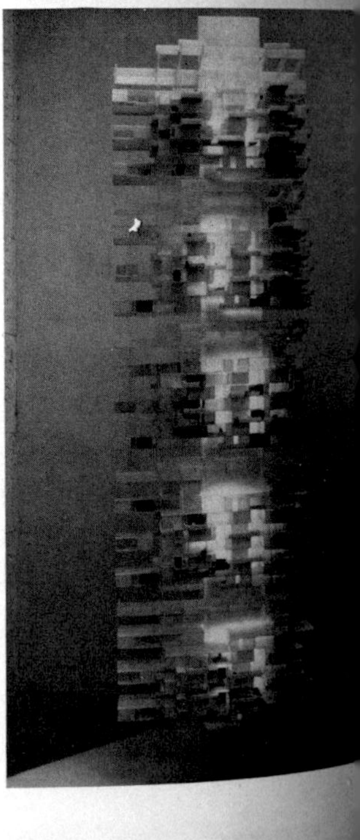

HE U.S. AT SAKA

1	2	3
	5	6
	8	
9	10	11

cepts submitted to USIA by participating design teams: 1. Minoru Yamki & Assocs. (a traditional pavil- with garden courts); 2. George on & Co.; 3. Hellmuth, Obata & with Ronald Beckman; 4. Noguchi with Pavilion Assocs.; nold Saks and James S. Ward ames Stewart Polshek; 6. Wil- Mouton Jr. with Philip John- Harper & George; 7. Myron , Skidmore, Owings & Mer- Morton Goldscholl Design Ulrich Franzen & Assocs. Forberg Assocs. (electron- vents—represented here by a beam—in an unspecified enclo- Gruzen & Partners; 10. Cher- Geismar and Rudolph De- Davis Brody & Assocs. d team); 11. Paul Rudolph aper of prefabricated units).

There will be many large, lavish structures at Expo 70 in Osaka, but the U.S. Pavilion will not be one of them. Our contribution to the world's fourth "first category" exposition (and the first in Asia, where the U.S. now seems deeply "committed") may be tasteful, informative, engaging, even delightful—but it is definitely going to be modest.

Planning for U.S. participation at Osaka started off well, as such things go in this country. The U.S. Information Agency was in charge of the whole undertaking, as it had been at the Montreal Expo (but not at previous world's fairs). Early in 1967, USIA began the process of selecting a design team, with the deliberate care of an enlightened client. A number of potential architects and designers were interviewed, and the most promising were asked to develop preliminary proposals. Those invited were encouraged to work in teams—either with other invited participants or with collaborators of their own choosing.

There were no limitations imposed by USIA on the type of pavilion or the nature of the exhibits. The best possible concept, it was hoped, would come from architects and designers given free reign. The "program" consisted only of a site (a very prominent one) and an estimated budget—for both structure and contents—of about $9.3 million.

Exhibition proposals

Eleven schemes were submitted to USIA last September. Each one was presented before an advisory panel representing government, the design professions, and the communications industry.*

The submissions they saw (opposite) ranged from Yamasaki's pointedly conventional scheme (1), which shunned all avant-garde concepts, to Franzen and Forberg's far-out proposal (8) which rejected the concept of a pavilion altogether. Eight of the more interesting schemes are shown in greater detail on the following pages—with notes on the panel's reactions to them.

The panel's job was to choose a design team, and it was unanimous in its selection: the team of Rudolph DeHarak and Chermayeff & Geismar, designers, with Davis, Brody & Associates, architects, which had proposed an inflated structure (10).

The pavilion's fate

Developments since the design team was chosen should make the other contenders feel relieved to be out of it all. The overall appropriation of $17.75 million originally requested by the USIA (to cover administration, as well as design and construction) was first trimmed to $16 million by the Bureau of the Budget, then slashed to $10 million by the economy-minded 90th Congress. (The overall budget for the U.S. exhibit at the New York fiasco of 1964-65 was $17 million.)

These budget cuts had the greatest impact on the portion allotted to structure and exhibits. For reasons best understood in Washington, the administrative budget (high to begin with because Osaka is so far away) could not be cut below $5.2 million. Only $4.8 million—less than half of the total—was left for the building and its contents. Of that, only $3.2 million has been earmarked for the structure itself—about the cost of the U.S. pavilion at this year's HemisFair (page 84)—and we already own Texas.

You can't just take a concept developed for a $9.3 million budget and shrink it to one-third of its original size; attendance at the pavilion—estimated at 30 million—simply will not decline proportionately. When you can't shrink the design to fit the budget, of course, you start all over from scratch, and that is exactly what the design team for the Osaka pavilion has had to do.

**William Bernbach, President of Doyle Dane Bernbach Inc.; Peter Blake, editor of* THE ARCHITECTURAL FORUM; *William N. Breger, chairman of the architectural design department at Pratt Institute; Howard L. Chernoff, acting commissioner general for Expo 70; Donlyn Lyndon, head of the department of architecture, MIT, and a* FORUM *correspondent; Jack Masey of USIA, director of planning and design for the exhibition at Expo 70; Robert Sivard, art director, USIA; Frank Stanton, president of CBS; William Walton, chairman of Washington's Fine Arts Commission; and Lloyd Wright (no kin), executive assistant to the director, USIA.*

A GRAND SPAN

Like some famous pavilions of the past, this one would have been memorable as a structural feat — a 3-ft.-thick space frame spanning an area 400 ft. square. Like Fuller's dome at Expo 67, the system would have had potential urban uses. Exhibits would have been focused on a single subject, space technology, featuring a vast simulated moonscape. Concrete abutment structures would have housed smaller-scaled exhibits. A major drawback of the proposal was its dependence on U.S. success in the "man on the moon" program. The sophisticated techniques required for climate control in an open-ended pavilion might also have posed problems.

William J. Mouton, Jr., engineer (invited); Philip Johnson, architect; Harper & George, designers.

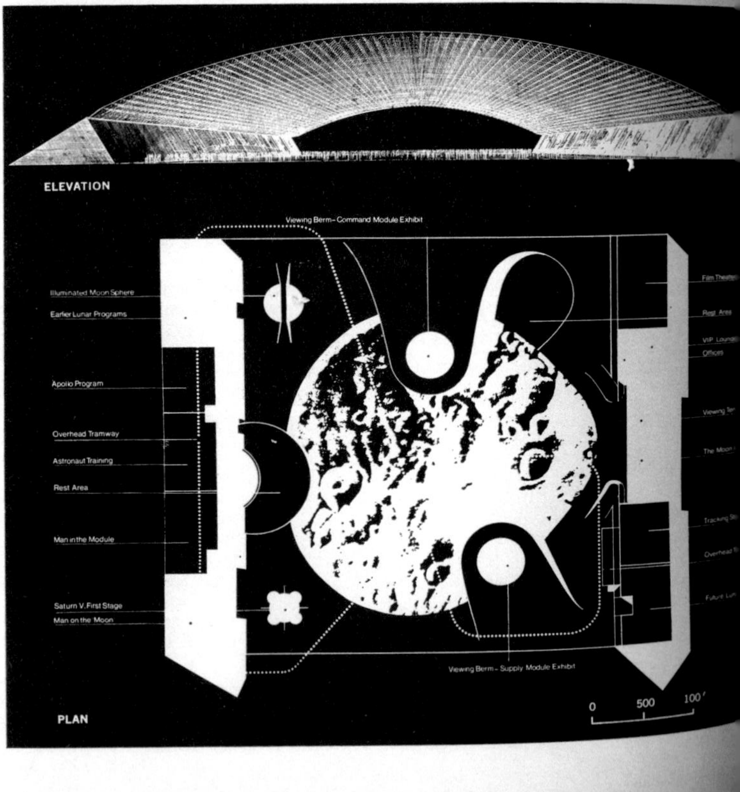

3 OF CABLES

sparent roof—260 ft. by and only 16 in. thick—have been held in place by supported on six masts. lines would have been t inside the pavilion, on a ine overlooking the exhibit Space below the mezzanine have housed 20 or more movie theaters, showing films varying widely in tech- and subject. Although un- edly elegant, the design d more appropriate for other purpose, and it would unnecessarily severe prob- of light and climate control.

Goldsmith, Skidmore, Owings ill, architects (invited); Morton oll Design Assocs., designers.

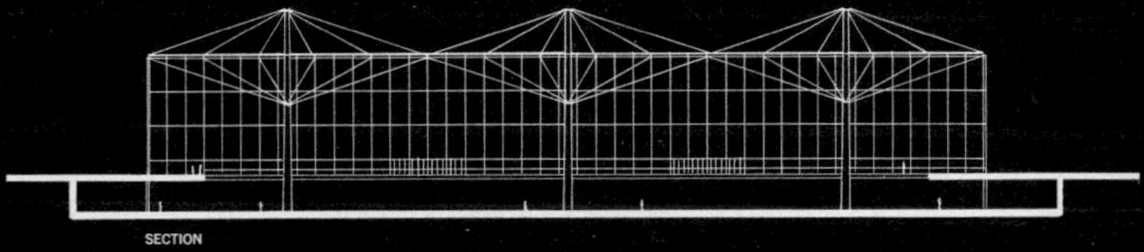

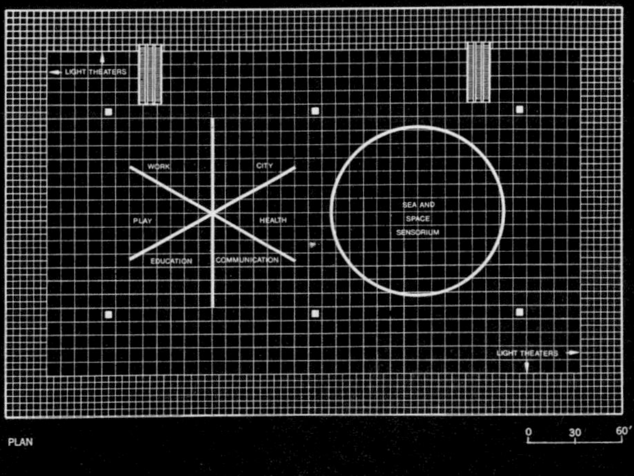

ABSTRACT MOONSCAPE

Instead of housing exhibits in an isolated building, this solution proposed placing them underground. Above ground, space would have been defined by undulations in the surface of the site—and forms projecting through it. The effect would be of an abstract garden, with all surface materials artificial and vividly colored—a garden in which children could play and adults rest in the shade of balloons. A single large space balloon, rising 240 ft. above a stone-clad mound, would identify the exhibit from a distance. Although the scheme was fascinating, the problem of visitor flow through the exhibits was thought to be poorly solved.

Isamu Noguchi, sculptor (invited); Pavilion Associates, architects and designers.

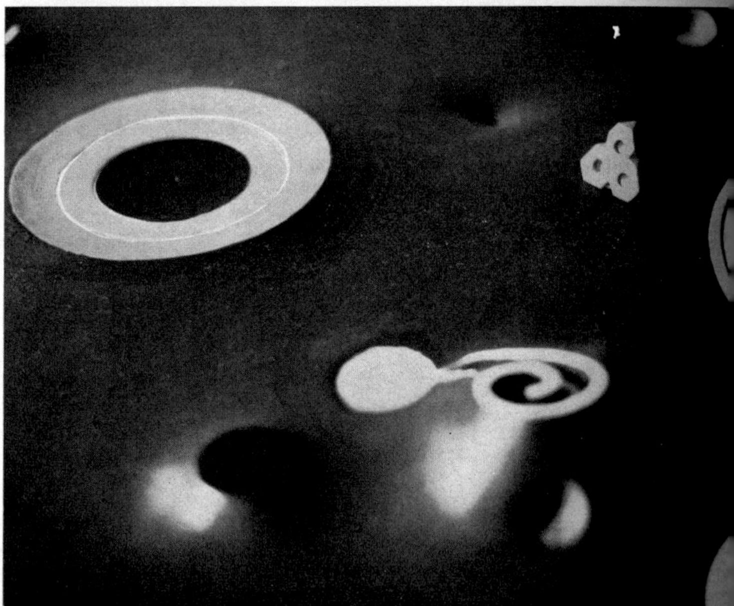

DED EARTHSCAPE

is scheme, cut-and-fill tech- es would have been used to e underground exhibit spaces a park on the surface. The ior massing has much in mon with that of Noguchi's me (opposite), but natural erials would have been used water introduced. The hours lly wasted by waiting crowds d have been used to inform entertain them through a s of color TV screens. The or's path through the pavil- (shown on plan) would have ved many changes of level spatial character (shown in section, which roughly follows route). Much of the pavilion d have been freely accessi- "unprogrammed" areas.

ge Nelson & Co., designers (in- .

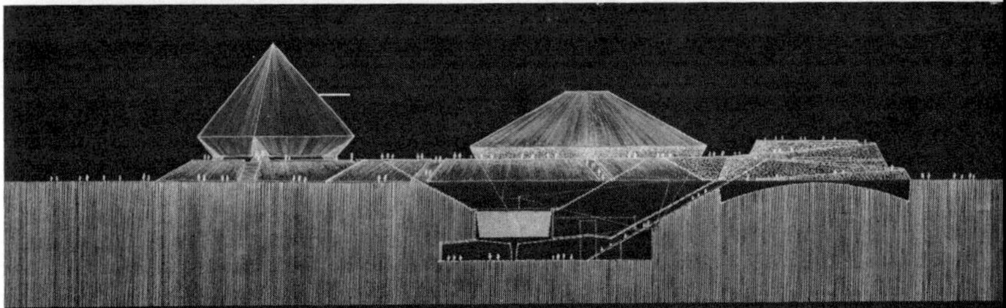

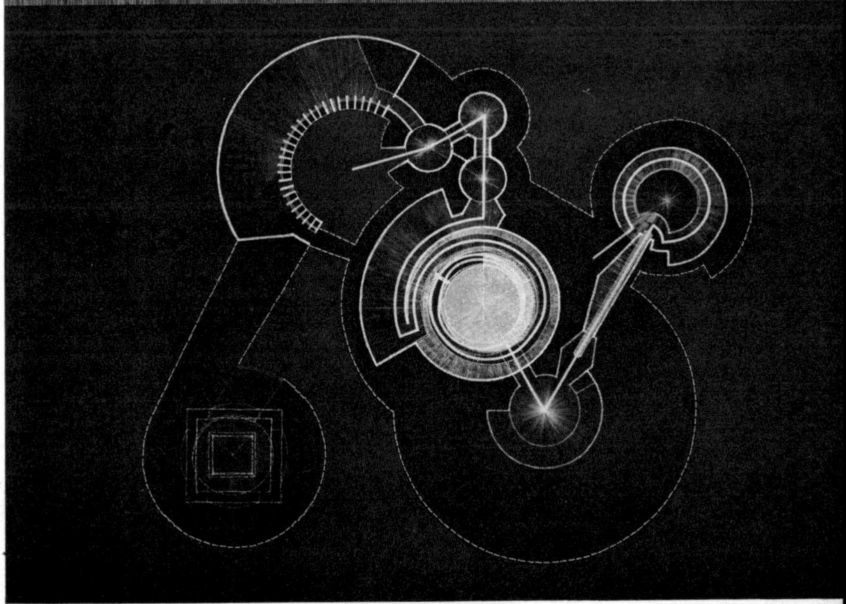

STRUCTURAL UMBRELLA

A deliberate diversity of objects and events would have been housed under a unifying structural frame 384 ft. long and 248 ft. wide. Visitors would have been offered a choice of degrees of freedom, ranging from random movement at ground level through various programmed sequences passing through, over, and under the steel trusses. Since the scheme relied heavily on sheer size for impact, it would have been quite vulnerable in case of budget cuts.

Hellmuth, Obata & Kassabaum, architects (invited); Ronald Beckman, Research and Design Inst. (designers).

ELEVATED CUBE

The cubic building, 162 ft. in all dimensions, would have straddled a walkway passing through an earth mound. The structure would have been assembled of 18-ft. cubic modules, prefabricated of steel. In plan, they would have formed a ring one module thick, leaving a court 126 ft. square in the center. The visitor's exposure could range from merely passing through below the cube to exploring the uppermost modules. The compartmentalization of exhibit space would have been too limiting, and the facades too reminiscent of conventional multistory buildings.

Gruzen & Partners, architects (Invited).

SEMBLAGE OF PODS

e "exhibits" in this case would
e been instant TV transmis-
ns of events and scenes in the
., relayed by satellite. The ef-
t would have been a unique
se of immediacy and an em-
asis on the open nature of U.S.
iety. The visitor would have
en asked to choose the situa-
ns he wished to observe for
alf-hour period; his selections,
into a computer, would have
ded an assigned time and lo-
ion among the 600 viewing
s, each of which would have
ted six viewers. While waiting
his time to ascend, the visitor
uld have viewed other televised
ibits in the parklike area under
aluminum space-frame struc-
e. The technical features of
scheme would probably have
en feasible, and it was admired
all members of the panel. But
behavioral problems created
the 600 enclosed pods would
e been formidable.

old Saks and James S. Ward, de-
ners (invited); James Stewart Pol-
, architect.

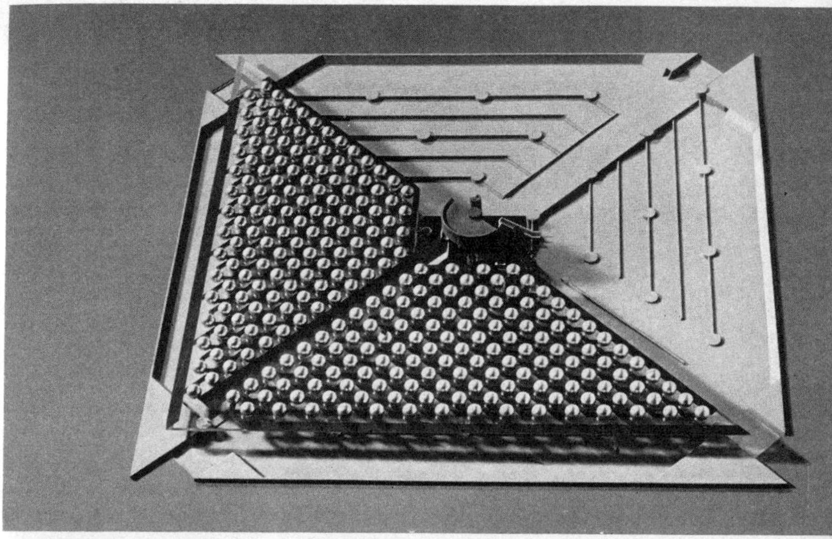

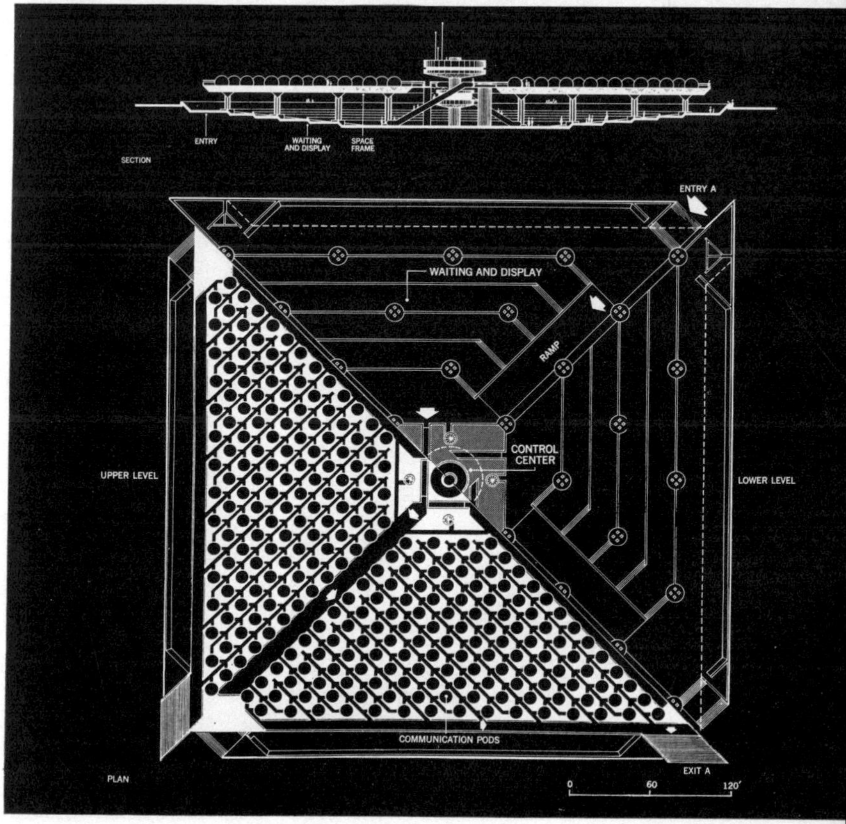

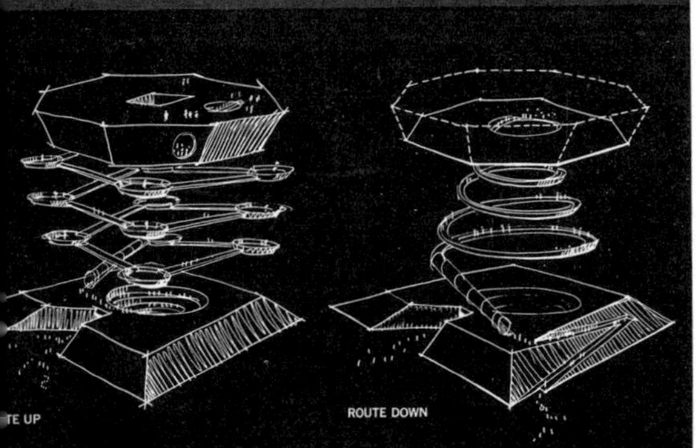

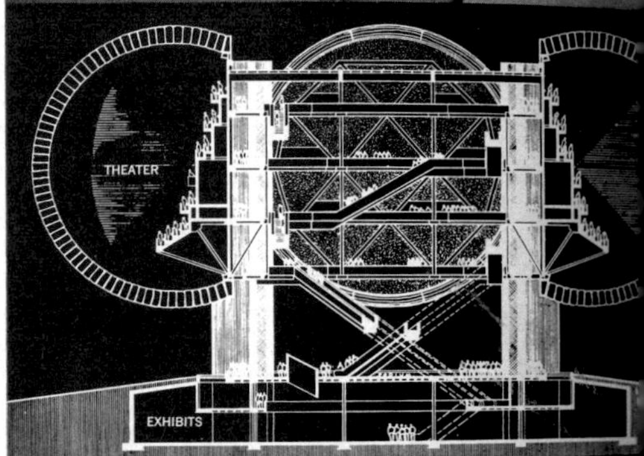

SECTION

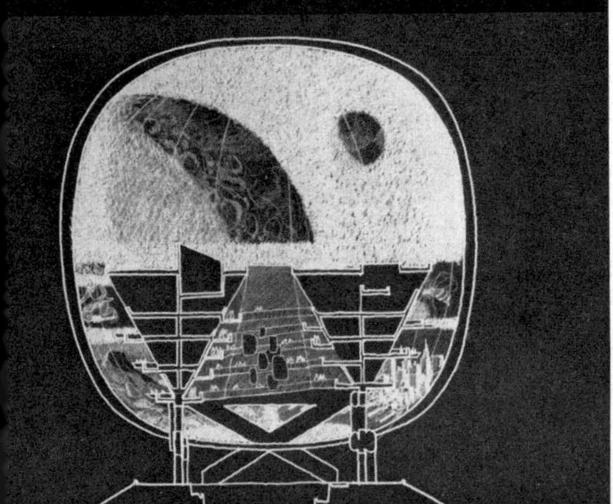

SCHEME 1 SECTION

SCHEME 2 PLAN

ᴇ GREAT BALLOON

vast air-supported pavilion left) by the chosen design n would have been outstand- for its economy of material, appropriately temporary look, its bold form—geometrical- etween a sphere and a cube. double-walled inflated en- pe, 275 ft. in diameter, ld have served both as efficient enclosure and as an rmous projection screen. Visi- would have entered by a al ramp, overlooking a plat- n for live performances, then ended through a sequence of forms, from which continuous s of U.S. scenes would be ved. At the top, they would e passed through an enclosed ce, with exhibits of real arti- ts, then emerged on a vast eau to view films of space ex- ation projected on the upper of the structure. From the cending spiral, they would e seen aerial films shown on bottom of the envelope.

. DIVIDED

ther investigation by the ected design team revealed t the 275-ft. inflated structure ld not be constructed within estimated budget for building d exhibits, which had declined m $9.3 million to $7.8 million. new scheme was developed ar left), with four air-sup- ted theaters (showing the ne film program in rotation). visual impression of un- unded projection surfaces uld have been preserved, along h such features as the en- nce spiral.

. AND DEFLATED

e pavilion that will actually be ilt at Osaka will hardly be ible to passers-by. Its vast of—a cable-restrained, air-sup- rted dome spanning an area 0 ft. by 470 ft.—will not be vealed until the visitor has en- ed the exhibition area.

This vast, unexpected canopy, eltering two acres of heavily nted terraces, will have con- derable impact. So, hopefully, ll the movies and other ex- bits in the pavilion. Not even hint will remain, however, of at we might have built.

ermayeff & Geismar Assocs., de- ners (invited); Rudolph DeHarak, signer (invited); Davis, Brody & socs., architects.

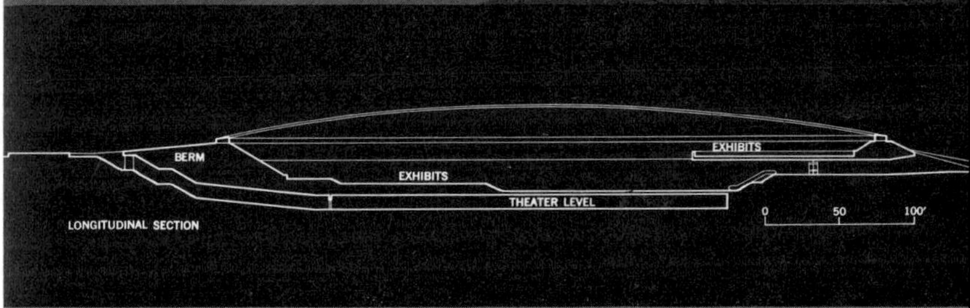

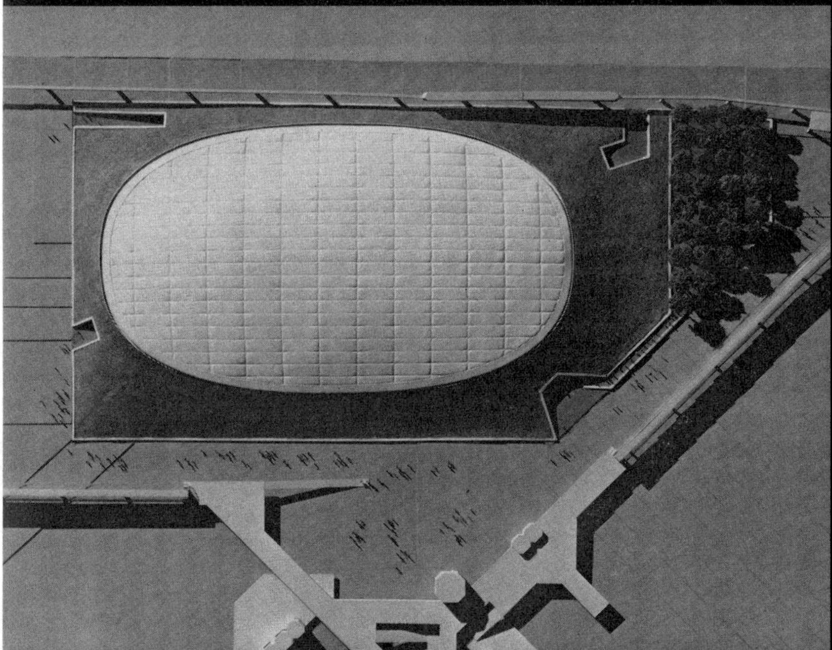

1957–2009

Brown Daltas and Associates

Headquarters
Boston, MA

Other Locations
Tehran, Iran; Rome, Italy;
Harrisburg, PA

Founding Partners
Benjamin Brown, Spero Daltas

1957

2009

Architectural Forum, October 1962. Photographer: Robert Moore

Benjamin I. Brown and Spero Daltas first met in Iran as consultants for Ammann & Whitney-Husted, a joint-venture engineering and architecture firm responsible for the design of military bases abroad for the US Army Corps of Engineers. Daltas, a son of Greek immigrants to the United States from St. Paul, Minnesota, served in the US Navy during World War II before graduating from the University of Minnesota in 1943 and the Massachusetts Institute of Technology (MIT) in 1948, where he received both the Prix de Rome and a Fulbright fellowship to study in Rome. He later spent five years working for Eero Saarinen and Associates, serving as job captain for the US Embassy in London (1954–1961), before moving to Tehran in 1956 to work for Ammann & Whitney-Husted. Brown, a native of Albany, Georgia, had been a partner for Alfred L. Aydelott Associates in Memphis before moving abroad to work for Ammann & Whitney-Husted in 1953, first on projects in France and Greece and later in Iran. In 1957, the pair joined to establish their own practice, Brown & Daltas, in Tehran, with Daltas described as the creative partner among the two.

By 1962, Brown & Daltas had undergone what was described in the US architectural press as "a five-year adventure in expatriate architecture" in Iran, beginning with the design of a Coca-Cola bottling plant in Meshed.[1] The square brick vaults used in the factory, built by skilled local bricklayers to reduce the use of imported steel, were developed into an octagonal system of vaults in the firm's second project, a palace for Princess Fatemah in the royal gardens in Saadabad, north of Tehran. An office tower and shopping center in Tehran featured a five-story arcade with a bazaar at ground level and offices above.

By this time, Brown & Daltas had established a US office in Harrisburg, Pennsylvania to produce its growing number of overseas commissions. By 1974, the firm had relocated its primary office from Tehran to Italy, and thereafter the firm, eventually renamed Brown Daltas and Associates, maintained offices in Rome and Cambridge, Massachusetts. When the University of Minnesota began a foreign-study program in Rome for architecture students, the office became a waystation for students from the university, many of whom were subsequently hired to work on the firm's commissions in the Middle East.

The firm had already begun to supplement its work with the design of military bases for the US Army Corps of Engineers (USACE) during its first two years of practice in Iran, and the USACE continued to be a major source of commissions for three decades afterwards. Chief among these commissions in scope and scale was King Khalid Military City (1974–1986) in Saudi Arabia, a massive desert complex that was at the time the largest military construction project ever undertaken by the USACE. Referred to by US soldiers as the "Emerald City," the octagonal city was designed to house 65,000 people at a cost of over $9 billion dollars, including schools, hospitals, airfields, housing, and underground utilities. The project was built for the Saudi Arabian Ministry of Defense and Aviation as part of an extended oil-for-security exchange in which the US Army Corps of Engineers held a long-term contract to build facilities for the Saudi Arabian army, navy, and air defense forces as well as for the US military.

By the conclusion of the King Khalid Military City project in 1986, Brown Daltas and Associates had grown to over 110 employees. The firm continued to build heavily in Saudi Arabia in the 1970s and 1980s. Other projects in the country included the Saudi Arabian National Centre for Science and Technology in Riyadh, a complex of four major universities including housing, schools, and community facilities; the headquarters of the Saudi Arabian Monetary Authority (SAMA) in Riyadh, and Markaz Al Mahmal Commercial Centre in Jeddah. Other countries in which the firm completed projects prior to Spero Daltas's death in 2009 included Burma, Uganda, Turkey, Somalia, and Mexico. — MK

(1) "Americans Abroad: Brown and Daltas in Iran," *Architectural Record* (October 1962): 127.

Mitchell/Giurgola Architects

Headquarters
New York, NY

Other Locations
Philadelphia, PA; Canberra, Australia (1981–1988)

Founding and Key Partners
Romaldo Giurgola, Ehrman B. Mitchell Jr., Warren W. Cunningham (founding principals), Richard Thorp

Current Partners
Steven Goldberg, Jan Keane, Paul Broches, John Kurtz, Carol Loewenson, James R. Braddock, Stephen Dietz,
1958 Susan Stando, John Doherty

AIA Journal, April 1976

Romaldo Giurgola, Ehrman B. Mitchell Jr., and Warren W. Cunningham established the Philadelphia office of Giurgola, Mitchell & Cunningham in 1958 in order to work on their first major commission, a visitor center for the Wright Brothers Memorial for the US National Park Service in Kill Devil Hills, North Carolina. Mitchell had received his degree in architecture from the University of Pennsylvania (Penn) in 1948, while Giurgola, born in Rome, received his bachelor of architecture from the Sapienza University of Rome a year later. After completing his graduate degree at Columbia University in 1951, Giurgola began teaching, first at Cornell University and then at Penn after 1954, where he remained for 12 years. The pair split from Cunningham in 1960 to establish Mitchell/Giurgola Associates, with Mitchell responsible for landing commissions and Giurgola in charge of design.

The success of the Wright Brothers Visitor Center and a series of prominent competition entries led to other commissions and to the firm's frequent presence in architectural journals after the 1950s. Much of the work of Mitchell/Giurgola Associates over the next two decades was centered around Philadelphia, where by the 1960s, academic and religious institutions sought out the firm for its growing expertise in campus planning and buildings ranging from elementary schools to universities. In 1961, critic Jan Rowen named Mitchell and Giurgola among the protagonists of what he termed the "Philadelphia School" of architects, along with Louis I. Kahn, Robert Venturi, Patrick Geddes, and others who sought an architecture that was more historically grounded than the prevailing examples of orthodox modernism.[1]

In 1966, Giurgola became the chair of the architecture department at the Graduate School of Architecture and Planning at Columbia University. The appointment necessitated a move from Philadelphia to New York, where Giurgola established a branch office of Mitchell/Giurgola Associates in 1968. The firm's work in the 1970s included numerous commissions for academic buildings and master plans in the United States, including student residences at Williams College (1972), a campus plan, gymnasium, and music building for Swarthmore College (1973) in Pennsylvania, and a biology building for Columbia University (1977). The firm's first international projects included the Volvo Headquarters in Gothenburg, Sweden (1977–1984) and a series of school facilities in Italy for the US Agency for International Development (USAID), including a secondary school complex in Aviano (1978–1981), student housing in San Pietro al Natisone (1981), and a technical high school in Maniago (1981).

In 1980, Mitchell/Giurgola and Richard Thorp, an Australian architect, won an international competition for what became the firm's most monumental commission, the Parliament House of Australia in Canberra. Occupying the circular government center envisioned by Walter Griffin and Marion Mahony at the center of their master plan for the new federal capital of Australia in 1912, the scale and significance of the project prompted Giurgola to move to Canberra, where he and Thorp established Mitchell/Giurgola-Thorpe in 1981 to undertake the commission. Mitchell retired in 1984, four years before the complex was completed in 1988. Giurgola has remained in Australia since, receiving his Australian citizenship in 2000.

The current firm of Mitchell/Giurgola Architects, based in New York, is a descendant of the office established by Giurgola there in 1968. Working in Europe, the United States, and Australia, the firm's work continues to include an array of academic and institutional buildings, such as the Smilow Center for Research at the New York University School of Medicine (2006) and the Laufer Center and Library at Stony Brook University (2012). With approximately 50 employees, the firm is headed by a number of partners, many of them former students of Giurgola's from Penn and Columbia. — RW & AM

① Jan C. Rowen, "Wanting To Be: The Philadelphia School," *Progressive Architecture* (April 1961): 130–163.

1958–
1999

Parker Design Group

Headquarters
Minneapolis, MN

Founding Principal
Leonard Parker

Current Partners
Stephan Huh, Gary Mahaffey, Francis Bulbulian, Raymond Greco, David Dimond, Carol Schu

1958

1999

David Brewster, *Star Tribune*

Shortly after his departure from Eero Saarinen and Associates, Leonard Parker opened his Minneapolis office in 1958. Parker joined a growing group of modernist architects in Minneapolis, led by Ralph Rapson, that eventually transformed the skyline of the city and influenced hundreds of Midwest architects through both their offices and teaching posts at the University of Minnesota. The office got its start with a series of small projects, including several residences and the Jewish Community Center of St. Paul in 1964, but garnered commissions for several large buildings in Minneapolis in the 1970s, including the University of Minnesota Law School and the Minneapolis Public Radio building.

Parker, like many of his contemporaries, studied under some of the leading figures of European modernism on the East Coast, including Alvar Aalto at the Massachusetts Institute of Technology (MIT). After graduation, he joined the offices of Eero Saarinen, were he worked with Gunnar Birkerts and others on the design of several of the office's key projects, including the St. Louis Arch. Although Parker's schooling and time at Saarinen's office stylistically impacted his firm's early projects, Leonard Parker Associates became famous for its regional aesthetic, and later for its post-modern work.

The Foreign Buildings Operations (FBO) office at the State Department commissioned Leonard Parker Associates in 1987 to design the US Embassy in Santiago, Chile. The project was part of a wave of buildings commissioned by the FBO after the bombing of the Beirut Embassy in 1983 circumscribed by stringent new safety regulations. The building, one of only two instances in which the firm built abroad, was completed in 1994 and sits inside a compound on the outskirts of Santiago.

The office continued to produce major projects regionally during the 1990s. The firm completed work on the Minneapolis Convention Center in 1992, and finished the Minnesota Judicial Center in 1998. In 1999, Leonard Parker Associates merged with Durrant to create a large national firm. Parker Durrant operated until 2006, at which point Parker Design Group was spun off. The firm currently operates out of Minneapolis. — JJ

1958–

Venturi, Scott Brown and Associates

Headquarters
Philadelphia, PA

Founding and Key Partners
Robert Venturi, Paul Cope, H. Mather Lippincott (founding principals), William Short, Paul Rauch, Denise Scott Brown

Current Partners
Robert Venturi, Denise Scott Brown

1958

Venturi, Scott Brown and Associates

The firm known today as Venturi, Scott Brown and Associates (VSBA) was first established in 1960 by Robert Venturi and John Short. John Rauch, an architect who joined the firm shortly after its launch, replaced Short as partner in 1964. Denise Scott Brown joined the office five years later, and the firm became Venturi, Rauch & Scott Brown, operating under that name for two decades until Rauch's resignation. After a succession plan ten years in the making, VSBA is currently led by partner and principal, Dan McCoubrey. While Venturi has retired from practice, Scott Brown continues to publish and speak on her work.

Venturi was born in Philadelphia and studied architecture at Princeton, where he also received his MFA, working for Eero Saarinen and Associates and Louis I. Kahn prior to establishing his practice with Short. Scott Brown was born in Zambia, South Africa, and received a diploma from the Architectural Association in London before pursuing postgraduate studies in city planning at the University of Pennsylvania (Penn), where she and Venturi met in 1960. They taught their first course together at Penn in 1962, beginning their lifelong collaboration. While within the firm, Venturi has been listed as the principal in charge of design and Scott Brown as the principal in charge urban design and planning, their collaboration has often spanned disciplinary lines.

Throughout their practice, the work of both partners has remained inseparable from their academic and theoretical contributions to the discipline. In 1969, Venturi and Scott Brown led a design studio at Yale to study Las Vegas, culminating in the seminal book *Learning From Las Vegas* (1972). A collaboration between Scott Brown, Venturi, and Steven Izenour, the study embraced what they called "the everyday and ordinary," positioning symbolism, iconography, and inclusive heterogeneity against what they critiqued as the anti-populist language of high modernism.

VSBA's architectural and urban planning practice has included numerous projects for university clients, including laboratory buildings, such as the Lewis Thomas Laboratory at Princeton (1986), and libraries, such as the Baker Berry Library at Dartmouth (2002). The firm's major institutional commissions include their well-known Franklin Court (1976) in Philadelphia, additions to the Museum of Contemporary Art (1996) in San Diego, and the Sainsbury Wing of the National Gallery in London (1986–1991). The office's urban planning projects, fuelled by Scott Brown, have included plans for South Street and the Old City neighborhood of Philadelphia, as well as for numerous other towns across the United States. VSBA has also practiced in the Middle East, designing the Khulafa Street Building (1982), a mixed-use city block in Baghdad. Sited in a space carved out by a master plan for Khulafa Street by The Architects Collaborative (1979–1983), the building was commissioned under Iraqi architect and planner Rifat Chadirji, prior to the end of the Iraqi building boom in the latter stages of the Iran-Iraq War. Though VSBA ceased work on the project as the war escalated, the building was eventually completed by a local office in partnership with a Yugoslavian firm.[1]

Throughout her career, Denise Scott Brown has advocated for the recognition of women in the profession, both through the strength of her presence wthin the field and in her writing. Her essay, "Room At The Top? Sexism and the Star System in Architecture," for example, was circulated widely between sympathetic hands before it was published.[2] Scott Brown recently became a symbol for the fight against what she terms the "petty apartheid" of sexism in architecture, when a group of Harvard students collected over 18,000 signatures in a petition to have her name added to Venturi's 1991 Pritzker Prize. The petition was ultimately denied. — DR

① Benedict Clouette and Marlisa Wise, "The Undecorated Shed: Venturi and Scott Brown's Project for a Commercial and Residential Block on Khulafa Street, 1981–82," *San Rocco 6* (Spring 2013).

② Denise Scott Brown, "Room at the Top? Sexism and the Star System in Architecture," in Ellen Perry Berkeley, ed., *Architecture: a Place for Women* (London: Smithsonian Institution Press, 1989): 232–246.

1959–

Gunnar Birkerts and Associates

Headquarters
Birmingham, MI

Other Locations
Ann Arbor, MI; Wellesley, MA

Founding and Key Partners
Gunnar Birkerts (founding principal), Frank Straub, Barbara Bos, Charles Fleckenstein, John Hillberry, Almon Durkee, Vytautas Usas, Harold Van Dine, Gunars Ejups, Anthony Gholz, Kenneth Rohlfing

Current Partners
Gunnar Birkerts

1959

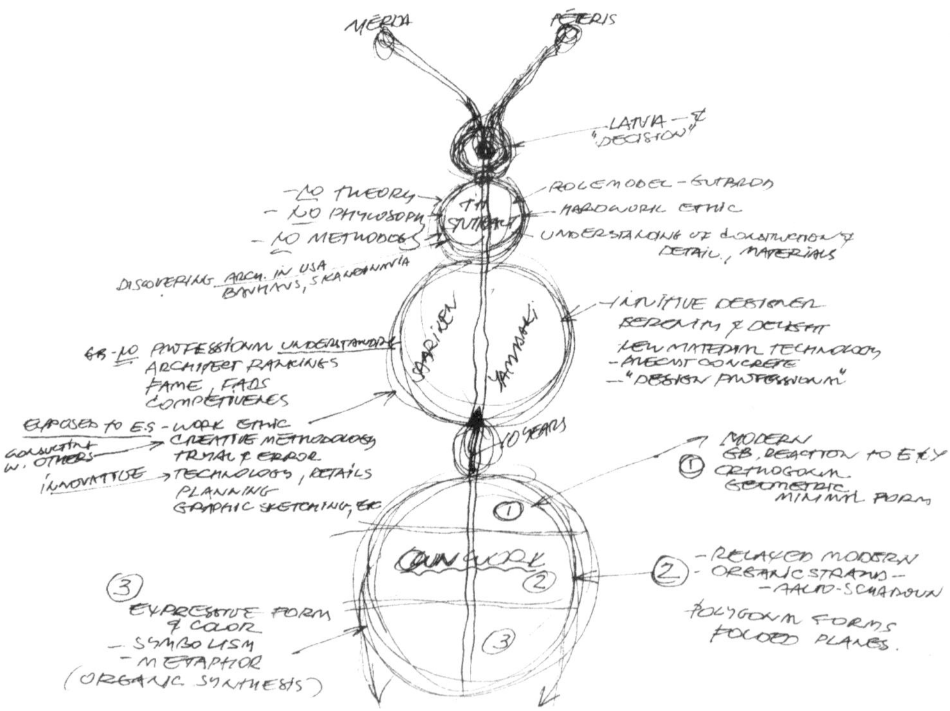

Gunnar Birkerts

Latvian born émigré Gunnar Birkerts opened his office in Birmingham, Michigan in 1963 after he split with his partner, Frank Straub. Birkerts and Straub had met in the office of Yamasaki and Associates, where they both worked as senior designers in the late 1950s before launching a firm together. Birkerts would get his start with a series of projects in and around Detroit. The majority of his initial commissions were garnered from relationships established during his time at Yamasaki's office and at Eero Saarinen and Associates. However, the commission for Birkerts' first major project, the University Reformed Church in 1964, resulted from his teaching post at the University of Michigan School of Architecture. Other significant commissions followed, including the Minneapolis Federal Reserve Building (1967), the Lincoln Elementary School in Columbus, Indiana (1967), and the Duluth Public Library (1969). By the late 1960s, Birkerts had established himself as one of the leading modernist architects in the United States.

Birkerts fled Latvia to study architecture in Stuttgart shortly after the end of World War II, as Russian forces took control of his country. It would be several decades before he returned. From Stuttgart, Birkerts immigrated to the United States in 1949, where he landed at the Chicago offices of Perkins and Will. Birkerts visited Latvia several times after the 1960s, but it would not be until 1989 that he was awarded a commission in his home country. His winning entry for the Latvian National Library in 1989 remains one of the defining achievements of his career. Although the project was put on hold shortly after its approval, it was completed and will be inaugurated more than twenty years after its commission, in 2014.

The US Embassy in Venezuela is one of the few other international projects built by Birkerts' office. The office received the commission in 1989 and the project was completed in 1996. The embassy is part of the generation of buildings for the Foreign Buildings Operations (FBO) office that was commissioned following the bombing of the Beirut Embassy in 1983. As such, it follows strict security protocols; however, the building maintains a distinct character from many of its more standard contemporaries.

Gunnar Birkerts and Associates continued to produce significant work throughout the 1970s and 1980s before a slight slowdown in commissions during the 1990s. Significant projects in these decades included the headquarters for Domino's Pizza in Ann Arbor, Michigan, the expansion of the Law School at The Ohio State University, and the Dr. Martin Luther King Jr. Library in San Jose, California. In 2006, Birkerts closed the office in Birmingham and relocated to Wellesley, Massachusetts. He continues to operate out of his office there, largely as a consultant for various Latvian organizations. — JJ

ZIMMER GUNSUL FRASCA ARCHITECTS LLP

1959–

Zimmer Gunsul Frasca Architects

Headquarters
Portland, OR

Other Locations
Seattle, WA; Los Angeles, CA; Washington, D.C.; New York, NY; Vancouver, Canada (as ZGF Cotter)

Founding Partners
Norman Zimmer, Brooks Gunsul, Robert Frasca

Current Partners
Braulio Baptista, Kathy Shaloo Berg, Larry Bruton, Joseph Collins, Kelly Davis, Margaret DeBolt, Mark Foster, Robert Frasca, Dan Huberty, Ted Hyman, Robert Packard, Doss Mabe, Eugene Sandoval, Allyn Stellmacher, Karl Sonnenberg, Todd Stine, Jan Willemse

1959

Zimmer Gunsul Frasca Architects

1962–

Tigerman McCurry Architects

Headquarters
Chicago, IL

Other Locations
Orlando, FL

Founding and Key Partners
Stanley Tigerman, Norman Alfred Koglin (founding principals), Laurence Ogden Booth, Robert Fugman, Margaret McCurry

Current Partners
Stanley Tigerman, Margaret McCurry

1962

Interiors, May 1981. Photographer: Balthazar Korab

Cambridge Seven Associates

Headquarters
Cambridge, MA

Founding Partners
Lou Bakanowsky, Ivan Chermayeff, Peter Chermayeff, Alden Christie, Paul Dietrich, Tom Geismar, Terry Rankine

Current Partners
Ronald D. Baker, Stefanie Greenfield, Steven Imrich, Patricia E. Intrieri, Gary C. Johnson, Peter G. Kuttner, Timothy D. Mansfield, Charles Redmon, Marc Rogers (principals), José Silveira (CFO)

1962

Cambridge Seven Associates

The group of architects, graphic designers, filmmakers, and exhibition designers who joined together to form Cambridge Seven Associates in 1962 came from two professional and personal lineages. The first was The Architects Collaborative (TAC), the team-based practice established in 1945 in Cambridge, Massachusetts by seven young architects along with the German émigré Walter Gropius. Architects Terry Rankine, Paul Dietrich, Lou Bakanowsky, and Alden Christie were all colleagues at TAC, working under founding partner Benjamin Thompson, and had discussed leaving to form a practice that would combine TAC's collaborative approach with an even more multidisciplinary focus. The second lineage was represented by Peter and Ivan Chermayeff, the sons of Serge Chermayeff, the British émigré who had led the New Bauhaus School of Design in Chicago from 1946 to 1951 before moving to Cambridge to teach at the GSD in 1953. Ivan had studied graphic design at Yale and established a thriving graphic design firm with Tom Geismar, Chermayeff & Geismar, in New York City in 1957, while Peter received his architecture degree from the GSD in 1962.

In the summer of that year, Dietrich approached Peter Chermayeff, then working on an anti-war film about the effects of nuclear weapons, about joining his colleagues to form a collective, multidisciplinary design practice. Assured that exhibitions, graphics, and film would be equal parts of the work to be undertaken by the new firm, Peter agreed to join, and Ivan Chermayeff and Tom Geismar soon came on board as partners, in parallel to their ongoing work with Chermayeff & Geismar. Faced with the task of naming a group of seven equal partners, the colleagues christened themselves Cambridge Seven Associates, or C7A.

The formation of the office took place in parallel with obtaining the commission that established Cambridge Seven's reputation, the New England Aquarium (1962–1969) in Boston. Acquired through the firm's interest in zoos and aquariums, as environments in which architecture, exhibits, and graphics could be integrated as part of a holistic visitor experience, the building was the first multilevel aquarium, organized around a massive, vertical tank around which visitors ascended along a continuous, spiraling ramp. The young firm also played a major role in modernizing the navigation of Boston's cityscape through their commission in 1965 to direct the first comprehensive transit design program in the United States, included the naming and logo for the expanded regional network—thereafter known as the T—the color-coding of its subway lines, and comprehensive signage, wayfinding, and maps throughout the system.

The firm's first project abroad, the spectacular, multimedia exhibition design for the US Pavilion at the Canadian World Exhibition in Montreal in 1967, came through Jack Masey, Chief of Design and Operations for the United States Information Agency (USIA). Cambridge Seven worked closely with Buckminster Fuller, the designer of the US Pavilion, to design the enclosing structure as a continuous three-quarter sphere, an unprecedented type that expanded on Fuller's previous vaulted domes for the USIA at the Jeshyn International Fair in Kabul, Afghanistan (1956) and the American National Exposition in Moscow (1959). Among Cambridge Seven's most notable commissions in the US and abroad after the 1970s were several extending from its expertise in aquariums, including the National Aquarium (1976–1981) in Baltimore, the Ring of Fire Aquarium and Tempozan Marketplace (1987–1990), in Osaka, Japan, and the Oceanaria de Lisboa (1993–1998) in Lisbon, Portugal.

Since the 1990s, Cambridge Seven has expanded its international practice to include a series of projects in Kuwait and Saudi Arabia, partly through contacts acquired following the demise of The Architects Collaborative, which had built extensively in both countries, in 1995. True to the firm's multidisciplinary expertise, its first project in the Gulf, the Scientific Center of Kuwait (1993–2000), included an aquarium, an IMAX theater, and a children's science museum. Subsequent commissions in Kuwait have included the College for Life Sciences and the College of Engineering for Kuwait University, the Ministry of Education Headquarters in Kuwait City, and the Fahaheel Waterfront. In Saudi Arabia, C7A is currently designing both buildings and exhibits for an Aquarium and Geo-Science Centre for King Abdullah Financial District, near Riyadh. — MK

Gehry Partners

Headquarters
Los Angeles, CA

Founding Partner
Frank Gehry

Current Partners
Frank Gehry, Brian Aamoth, John Bowers, Anand Devarajan, Jennifer Ehrman, Berta Gehry, Meaghan Lloyd, David Nam, Tensho Takemori, Laurence Tighe, Craig Webb (Gehry Partners), Dennis R. Shelden (Gehry Technologies)

1962

After cutting short his studies in urban design at the Harvard Graduate School of Design in 1957, Frank Gehry returned to Los Angeles, the city to which he and his family had moved from Toronto ten years earlier. He had already received a Bachelor of Architecture from the University of Southern California, and though he soon took a job in Victor Gruen's Los Angeles office, he did not stay there for long either. In 1961, Gehry spent a year in Paris working in the office of André Remondet, then returned to the US to open his own practice, initially in partnership with Greg Walsh.

With the exception of these early forays, Gehry has spent his entire career in Los Angeles, a setting formative enough that Rafael Moneo has suggested that one cannot talk "about Frank Gehry without immediately mentioning his city."[1] The office first sustained itself with small residential and commercial projects in California, where Gehry's reliance on a form of LA vernacular echoed the local art scene in its use of materials such as plywood, chain link, and corrugated metal. The culmination of this period was Gehry's remodeling of his own house in 1978, in which the composition of crude industrial materials offered a challenge to the syntactic and historicist postmodernism that increasingly ruled academic architectural circles.

In the early 1980s, Gehry started building his first fish sculptures, including the Fish Dance restaurant in Kobe, Japan (1986–1987). The competition-winning entry for the Walt Disney Concert Hall in Los Angeles in 1988 was followed by the design of a shopping mall at the Euro Disney Resort (1988–1992) near Paris. After receiving several commissions in Europe, including the Vitra Design Museum (1989) in Germany and the American Center in Paris (1994), the firm's work abroad began to increase exponentially, transforming the office into a global player.

At the end of the 1980s, there were purportedly only two computers in Gehry's office, neither dedicated to design uses. To deal with the extreme financial and construction problems surrounding the geometrically complex Disney Concert Hall, Gehry turned to Jim Glymph, who joined the firm on the condition that the office would internalize all aspects of project development. A fish sculpture for the Villa Olympica in Barcelona, developed for the 1992 Summer Olympic Games, proved equally important for the subsequent development of technology in Gehry's office. In order to solve the design and construction of the fish, Glymph found a French aerospace software, CATIA, which, when modified, helped coordinate the work of all parties involved in the project. Though Gehry Technologies was officially established in 2002, its real beginnings lay with these attempts to integrate the representational mechanisms by which design, calculation, and final execution occur. With Glymph serving as president, Gehry Technologies currently provides global services from offices in Los Angeles, New York City, Hong Kong, Abu Dhabi, Mexico City, and Paris, and was recently sold to Trimble Navigation, Ltd. in September 2014.

When Gehry received the Pritzker Architecture Prize in 1989, it was already imaginable that his firm's then-nascent embrace of digital technologies would transform the practice of architecture. Yet the first commission to become truly emblematic of the firm's use of these technologies, the Guggenheim Bilbao (1991–1997) was still yet to come. Beyond its much-debated effects on the economy and on the imaginations of mayors and other public officials worldwide, the Guggenheim Bilbao was seen by numerous critics as impacting architectural consciousness on a more fundamental level. For example, Herbert Muschamp, then critic for *The New York Times*, saw in it a specifically American form of empathy and generosity towards the users of architecture.[2]

Gehry Partners currently includes over 160 people in its Venice, California headquarters, including many senior architects with extensive experience in developing and managing complex projects. According to the firm, every building in the office is designed personally by Frank Gehry. — AM

① Rafael Moneo, *Theoretical Anxiety and Design Strategies in the Work of Eight Contemporary Architects* (Cambridge, MA: The MIT Press, 2004): 254.

② Herbert Muschamp, "The Miracle in Bilbao," *The New York Times* (September 7, 1997).

KMW Architecture

Headquarters
Boston, MA

Founding and Key Partners
Gerhard Kallmann, Michael McKinnell, Edward Knowles (founding principals), Henry A. Wood

Current Partners
Michael McKinnell, Bruno Pfister, Bruce A. Wood, Alicia Crothers

1962

KMW Architecture

Gerhard Kallmann, Michael McKinnell, and Edward Knowles opened their office in Boston in 1962 after a successful bid to design the Boston City Hall. Their enormous and technically complex first project catapulted them to immediate stardom. At the time of the competition, Kallmann was a professor of architecture at Columbia University and McKinnell was his teaching assistant. Henry Wood joined the firm in 1965 as they transitioned from New York to their permanent Boston office. Several other brutalist projects immediately followed City Hall, including the Boston Five Cents Savings Bank and the Phillips Exeter Academy athletics facility, before work in the office began to dry up in the mid-1970s.

The downturn is generally attributed to the office's association with brutalism and the fall from prominence of that style at the dawn of post-modernism. During this period, Kallmann & McKinnell both taught at the Harvard Graduate School of Design. In 1977, the office received a commission for the American Academy of Arts & Sciences, which marked a significant aesthetic departure from their previous work, garnering national attention for the firm once again. Various significant projects followed, including their first international project, the US Embassy in Dhaka, in 1983.

Kallmann, McKinnell & Wood maintained a close relationship with the Federal Buildings Operations (FBO) office of the US State Department, and in the late 1980s the firm was invited to submit proposals for the US Embassy in Berlin as well as the US Embassy in Bangkok Although it was not ultimately selected for the Berlin project, the office completed the US Embassy in Bangkok in 1996. The chancery in Bangkok was widely publicized by the FBO as part of a new wave of designs that complied with stringent security requirements. In 1998, the office completed its latest international project, the headquarters for the Organization for the Prohibition of Chemical Weapons in The Hague.

Until 2006, Kallmann, McKinnell & Wood maintained a clearly delineated hierarchy, with Kallmann and McKinnell as the lead designers for all major projects at the firm. However, due to the scale of the Howard Hughes Medical Institute commission in 2006, the office was forced to create a more collaborative team-based workflow. Since then, the firm has incorporated the team based structure in order to foster expertise across multiple project types, including civic, higher education, research labs, and corporate buildings. Kallmann, McKinnell & Wood continues to operate out of its offices in the historic Tennis and Raquet Club building in downtown Boston. — JJ

US Embassy
1956–1959

Architect
Harry Weese

Location
Accra, Ghana

Client
US Department of State, Foreign Buildings Operations

Soreq Nuclear Research Center
1956–1959

Architect
Philip Johnson

Location
Rehovot, Israel

Client
Israel Atomic Energy Commission

US Embassy
1956–1959

Architect
The Architects Collaborative

Location
Athens, Greece

Client
US State Department, Foreign Buildings Operations

US Embassy
1956–1960

Architect
Vincent Kling Associates

Location
Quito, Peru

Client
US Department of State, Foreign Buildings Operations

Place Ville-Marie
1955–1962

Architect
I. M. Pei & Associates

Associate Architect
ARCOP Affleck Desbarats Dimakopoulos Lebensold Michaud & Sise)

Location
Montreal, Canada

Client
Webb & Knapp (Canada), Ltd.

US Pavilion, International Trade Fairs
1956–1963

Location
Zagreb, Yugoslavia; Damascus, Syria; Casablanca, Morocco; Bari, Italy; Salonika, Greece; Poznan, Poland; Izmir, Turkey; Lima, Peru; Madrid, Spain; Barcelona, Spain; Valencia, Spain

Sponsor
Office of International Trade Fairs (OITF)

US Embassy
1956–1964

Architect
John M. Johansen

Location
Dublin, Ireland

Client
US Department of State, Foreign Buildings Operations

Banque Lambert
1956–1965

SOM

Architect
Skidmore, Owings & Merrill

Location
Brussels, Belgium

Client
Banque Bruxelles Lambert

George C. Marshall House, "America Builds" Exhibition
1957

United States Information Agency

Project Lead
Jack Masey, USIA

Design
Peter Blake, Julian Neski (architecture); Peter Blake, Julian Neski, Jack Masey (exhibits)

Location
West Berlin, Federal Republic of Germany

1956

1962

Arawak Hotel
1957

Architect
Morris Lapidus Associates

Location
Negril, Jamaica

US Embassy
1957–1959

MBA

Architect
Marcel Breuer and Associates, Architects

Location
The Hague, Netherlands

Client
US Department of State, Foreign Buildings Operations

US Consulate
1958–1960

ROMA

Architect
G.T. Rockrise

Location
Fukuoka, Japan

Client
US Department of State, Foreign Buildings Operations

Hotel Ponce Intercontinental
1957–1960

Architect
William B. Tabler Architects

Location
Ponce, Puerto Rico

Client
Ponce Hotel Corporation, Intercontinental Hotel Corporation

Ron Bacardi y Compania Building
1957–1962

Architect
The Office of Mies van der Rohe

Location
Mexico City, Mexico

Client
Ron Bacardi Company

University of Baghdad
1957–1983

TAC

Architect
The Architects Collaborative

Local Architect
Hisham A. Munir & Associates

Location
Baghdad, Iraq

Client
Iraq Development Board

US Pavilion, Universal and International Exposition
1958

Design
Edward Durell Stone, Leo Lionni (architecture); Peter Harnden, Bernard Rudofsky, Chermayeff & Geismar, Saul Steinberg, Cambridge Study Group (exhibits)

Location
Brussels, Belgium

Sponsor
US Department of State

Habana Hilton Hotel
1958

ELLERBE BECKET

Architect
Welton Becket

Local Architect
Arroyo y Menendez

Location
Havana, Cuba

Client
Hilton Hotels Corporation

Berlin Hilton Hotel
1958

Architect
Pereira and Luckman

Location
Berlin, Germany

Client
Hilton Hotels Corporation

El Monte Apartments
1958–1961

Architect
Edward Larrabee Barnes

Location
San Juan, Puerto Rico

Client
James H. Scheuer

Civil Air Terminal
1958–1961

Architect
Yamasaki and Associates

Location
Dhahran, Saudi Arabia

Client
US Army Corps of Engineers

Fondation Maeght
1958–1964

SERT, JACKSON AND ASSOCIATES
ARCHITECTS CAMBRIDGE MASSACHUSETTS

Architect
Sert, Jackson and Gourley

Location
Saint Paul-de-Vence, France

Client
Fondation Maeght

US Consulate
1958–1966

Architect
Edward Larrabee Barnes

Location
Tabriz, Iran

Client
US Department of State,
Foreign Buildings Operations

American National Exhibition
1959

United States Information Agency

Project Lead
Jack Masey, USIA

Design
Donald Richter (Kaiser/Fuller Dome), Welton Becket & Associates (Glass Pavilion), George Nelson & Co. (Fiberglass Umbrellas); George Nelson & Co., Charles and Ray Eames (exhibits)

Location
Moscow, USSR

Nile Hilton Hotel
1959

ELLERBE BECKET

Architect
Welton Becket & Associates

Location
Cairo, Egypt

Client
Hilton Hotels Corporation

Britz-Buckow-Rudow Master Plan
1959–1967

Architect
The Architects Collaborative

Location
Berlin, Germany

San Juan Intercontinental Hotel
1960–1961

Architect
Morris Lapidus Associates

Location
San Juan, Puerto Rico

Client
InterContinental Hotel Group

India International Centre
1960–1962

Architect
Joseph Allen Stein and Associates

Location
New Delhi, India

Client
India International Centre

IBM Research Center
1960–1962

Architect
Marcel Breuer and Associates

Location
La Gaude

Client
International Business Machines

BEWO-Bau Development I + II
1960–1965

Architect
Richard J. Neutra

Location
Morfelden-Walldorf, Quickborn, Germany

Client
Bewobau GmbH

US Embassy
1960–1967

Architect
Adrian Wilson Associates

Location
Saigon, Vietnam

Client
US Department of State, Foreign Buildings Operations

Ellinikon International Airport
1960–1969

Architect
Eero Saarinen and Associates

Location
Athens, Greece

US Embassy
1960–1969

PEI COBB FREED & PARTNERS Architects LLP

Architect
I. M. Pei & Associates

Associate Architect
John LoPinto and Assoc.

Location
Montevideo, Uruguay

Client
US Department of State, Foreign Buildings Operations

American International School
1960–1970

Architect
Joseph Allen Stein and Associates

Location
New Delhi, India

Client
American International School

University of Tunis School of Law
1961

TAC

Architect
The Architects Collaborative

Location
Tunis, Tunisia

Client
University of Tunis

Nanzan University Campus
1961–1964

Architect
Raymond & Rado

Location
Nagoya, Japan

Client
Nanzan University

American Traveling Exhibitions
1961–1965

United States Information Agency

Project Lead
Jack Masey, USIA

Design
Jack Masey (Plastics USA, Medicine USA, Technical Books USA; George Nelson & Co., Jack Masey (Transportation USA); Chermayeff & Geismar (Graphic Arts USA)

Location
USSR (6 cities); Belgrade, Yugoslavia

Hotel La Flaine
1961–1976

MBA

Architect
Marcel Breuer and Associates

Location
Flaine, France

Client
Societe d'Etudes de Participation et de Development

US Embassy
1961–1984

Architect
Victor A. Lundy

Location
Colombo, Sri Lanka

Client
US Department of State, Foreign Buildings Operations

Palace of Princess Fatemah
1962

Architect
Brown Daltas and Associates

Location
Tehran, Iran

Client
Her Imperial Highness Fatemah

Coca-Cola Plant
1962

Architect
Brown Daltas and Associates

Location
Meshed, Iran

Client
The Coca-Cola Company

Office Tower and Shopping Center
1962

Architect
Brown Daltas and Associates

Location
Tehran, Iran

Teijin Institute for Biomedical Research
1962–1963

Architect
James Stewart Polshek Architect

Cooperation
Design Section, Kajima Construction Co., Ltd.

Location
Tokyo, Japan

Client
Teijin Limited

Dublin Intercontinental Hotel
1962–1964

Architect
William B. Tabler Architects

Location
Dublin, Ireland

Client
Intercontinental Hotel Corporation

Society Verbi Divini Seminary
1962–1965

Architect
Raymond & Rado

Location
Nagoya, Japan

Client
Divine World Seminary Chapel

Parly II Shopping Center
1962–1968

Architect
Lathrop Douglass

Location
Le Chesnay, Seine et Oise, France

Client
La Societe des Centres Commerciaux

Neue Nationalgalerie
1962–1968

Architect
The Office of Mies van der Rohe

Location
Berlin, Germany

Client
Neue Nationalgalerie

Indian Institute of Management
1962–1974

Architect
Louis I. Kahn

Location
Ahmedabad, India

Client
Indian Institute of Management

National Capitol of Bangladesh
1962–1983

Architect
Louis I. Kahn

Location
Dhaka, Bangladesh

Client
Government of Pakistan

Nation Buildings: Post-Colonial Symbols and Infrastructures

In their new role as "development experts," US architects and planners arrived in India, East and West Pakistan even before these countries gained independence following the partition of the British Indian Empire in 1947. Albert Mayer appeared several months before the creation of the independent Dominion of India on August 15, 1947, when he was appointed Planning Advisor to the Government of Uttar Pradesh.[1] Inheriting Mahatma Gandhi's vision of a revitalized and modernized Indian village, the first Prime Minister of independent India, Jawaharlal Nehru, sought a transformation of the land and of daily life through numerous initiatives launched in the wake of the partition. Such transformations would prove to be, as architects Charles and Ray Eames wrote in their *India Report* in 1958, both "of degree" and "in kind."[2]

The Ford Foundation launched its operations in the Indian context through a series of projects following the partition, many of which were entangled with the US Point Four program and UN development funds under the Bretton Woods system of exchange.[3] Such development projects served to draw these territories deeply into international monetary structures, preparing local economies for an ultimately problematic inclusion in the liberalized global market.[4] The first Ford-sponsored project to employ Mayer's planning expertise was for the unprecedentedly large rural development scheme later known as the Etawah Project, including 15 pilot projects for 300 villages.[5] Intended as a model for other development projects in India, its deployment was messy, problematic, and transformative, for both India and the Ford Foundation itself. Greek planner Constantinos Doxiadis engaged in a similarly systematic "computing" of the territory as advisor for the selection of a new capital for West Pakistan, which moved following a military coup in 1958 from Karachi to Rawalpindi prior to the establishment of Islamabad.[6] Doxiadis explained his involvement simplistically, asserting that "Many countries which

(1) Robert C Emmett, *Guide to the Albert Mayer Papers on India in the University of Chicago Library* (Chicago: The University of Chicago, 1977).

(2) Charles and Ray Eames, *The India Report* (April 1958), reprinted in 1997 (Ahmedabad: National Institute Of Design Ahmedabad): 7.

(3) See Francis X. Sutton, "The Ford Foundation: The Early Years," *Daedalus*, Vol. 116, No. 1 (Winter 1987): 41–91.

(4) Ijlal Muzaffar, *The Periphery Within: Modern Architecture and the Making of the Third World* (Ph.D. Dissertation, Massachusetts Institute of Technology, 2007).

(5) See Albert Mayer and Associates et al., *Pilot Project, India: The Story of Rural Development at*

1945

1947
- British Dominion ends; Partition of India establishes India and West and East Pakistan as independent states
- Albert Mayer appointed Planning Advisor to the Government of Uttar Pradesh

1947–1951 Albert Mayer produces urban plan for Chandigarh

1948 Burma, Sri Lanka gain independence

1950–1953 Korean War

1951 First nationwide rural/community development programs in Indian begin with Ford Foundation assistance

1952 Joint Indo-American Technical Cooperation Agreement (Point Four Program) begins in India

1955
- East Bengal becomes East Pakistan
- Pakistan, Turkey, Iraq, and Iran form Baghdad Pact (Middle East Treaty Organization)

1958
- Military coup by Commander-in-Chief of the Pakistan Army, Ayub Khan
- Charles and Ray Eames, India Report

have recently become independent have no capital cities, either because the capital city of their area remained in another country...or because there was no capital in its territory with the necessary facilities or in a proper location."[7]

Foreign architects soon participated in the construction of modern national images for India, Pakistan, and after a civil war in 1971, Bangladesh. Development organizations employed architects and planners at different levels of visibility, aligning with local governments in appealing to narratives of self-help, coordination, and modernization.[8] Mayer was involved in the planning of Greater Bombay as well as for a new city at Chandigarh to be the capital of East Punjab after its previous capital, Lahore, ended up on the side of Pakistan after the partition. US institutions were represented directly through the construction of trade fair pavilions, embassies, and buildings for aid organizations including the Ford Foundation and USAID.

Other US architects arrived via different avenues. Muzharul Islam, a leading architect and director of the Public Works Department in East Pakistan (later Bangladesh), introduced an "American trio" of architects into the country—Paul Rudolph, Stanley Tigerman, and Louis Kahn—who had all been his teachers and classmates while a student at Yale.[9] Rudolph produced the master plan for an agricultural university at Mymensingh (1966), while Islam and Tigerman joined to design polytechnic institutes for five cities (1965–1975). Kahn, already at work on the Indian Institute of Management in Ahmedabad, was enlisted to design capital complexes for both East Pakistan at Dhaka (1963–1983) and West Pakistan at Islamabad. After abandoning the Islamabad portion of the project, the commission went instead to Edward Durell Stone, whose US Embassy in New Delhi (1954–1959) had already led to commissions for other technical and institutional buildings in Pakistan.

Contemporary architectural discussion about such representative national projects revolved around questions of modern monumentality and the construction of regional modernisms.[10] Both concerns were deeply implicated in the interests of both local and foreign actors in the post-partition context. Kahn's optimism about the ability of his governmental buildings to embody and project "the majesty" of the democratic process, in this sense, was echoed by the faith of local administrators in the reverse: a modernization project able to deliver both nation-buildings and the nation, via the magical powers of US agents of progress. — AM

Etawah, Uttar Pradesh (Berkeley: University of California Press, 1958).

⑥ See Arindam Dutta, "Computing Alibis: Third World Teratologies," *Perspecta 40: Monster* (2008): 54–69.

⑦ Constantinos Doxiadis, "Islamabad: The Creation of A New Capital," *The Town Planning Review*, Vol. 36, No. 1 (1965): 1.

⑧ See Ijlal Muzzafar, "The World on Sale': Architectural Exports and Construction of Access," in Eva Franch i Gilabert, Amanda Lawrence, Ana Miljački, Ashley Schafer, ed., *OfficeUS Agenda* (Zurich: Lars Müller, 2014): 227–239.

⑨ Kazi Khaleed Ashraf, "Muzharul Islam, Kahn and Architecture in Bangladesh," *Mimar* 31 (March 1989): 55–63.

⑩ See Josep Lluís Sert, Fernand Léger and Sigfried Giedion, "Nine Points on Monumentality" and Giedion, "The New Regionalism," in Giedion, *Architecture, You and Me* (Cambridge, MA: Harvard University Press, 1958): 48–52, 138–151.

1947

1983

1959 • Dhaka declared as Eastern capital of Pakistan • C. A. Doxiadis named advisor to the Special Commission for the Location of the Capital in Pakistan

1960 Islamabad, new capital of Pakistan, established at Rawalpindi

1961 Ford Foundation team directed by Mayer publishes a plan for New Delhi

1962 • Louis Kahn was commissioned to design the Indian Institute of Management in Ahmedabad • Muzharul Islam (Senior Architect of the Government of East Pakistan) invites Le Corbusier, Alvar Aalto, Louis Kahn as candidates for new capitals of Pakistan at Islamabad and Dhaka

1963 Louis Kahn awarded commission for western capitals of Pakistan at Islamabad

1966 Commission Islamabad transferred from Louis Kahn to Edward Durell Stone

1971 Civil war between West and East Oakistan; independent state of Bangladesh established

1975

1962 Cuban Missile Crisis

1950–1975 Vietnam War

US Architects in India, Pakistan, and Bangladesh 1947–1975

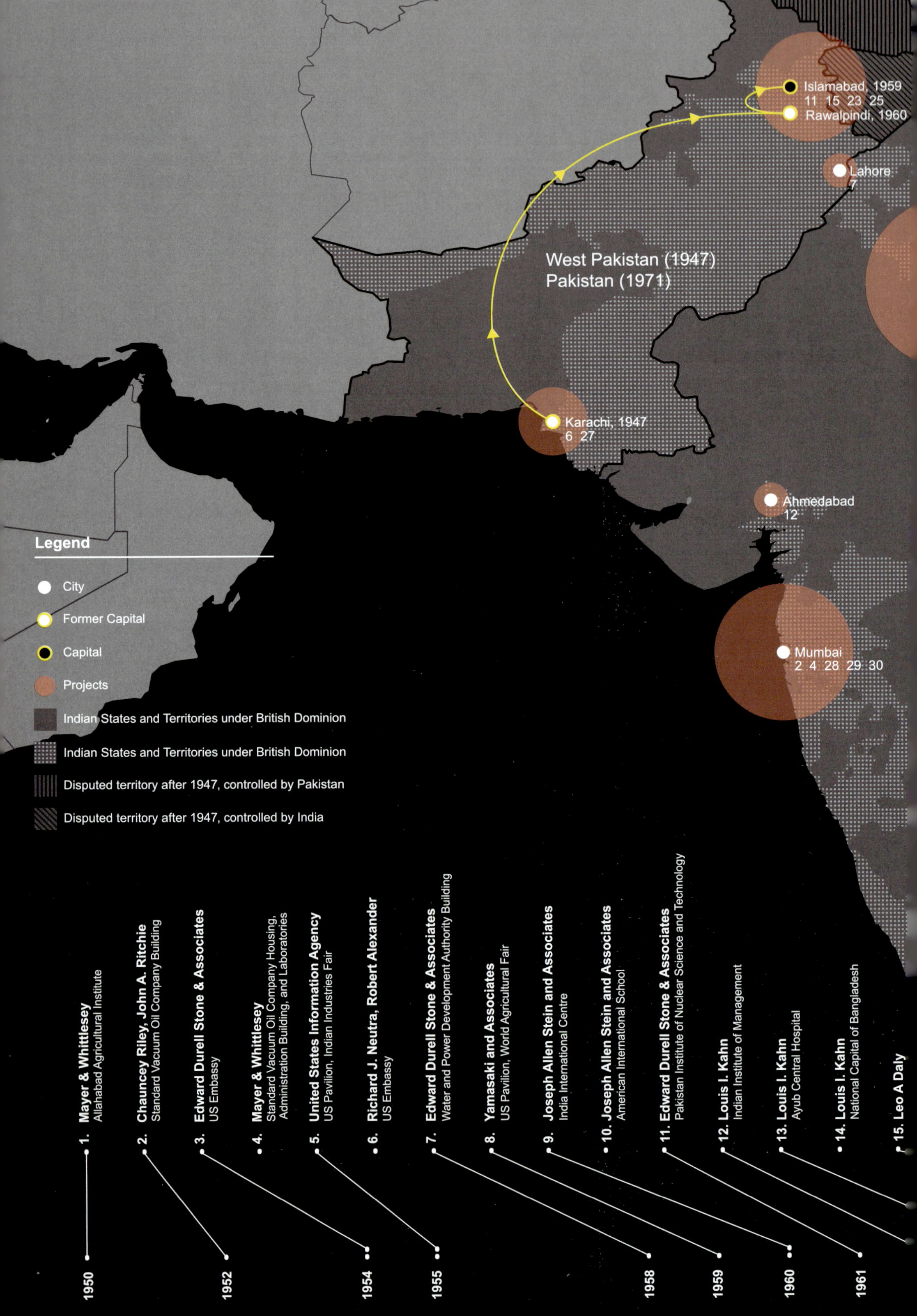

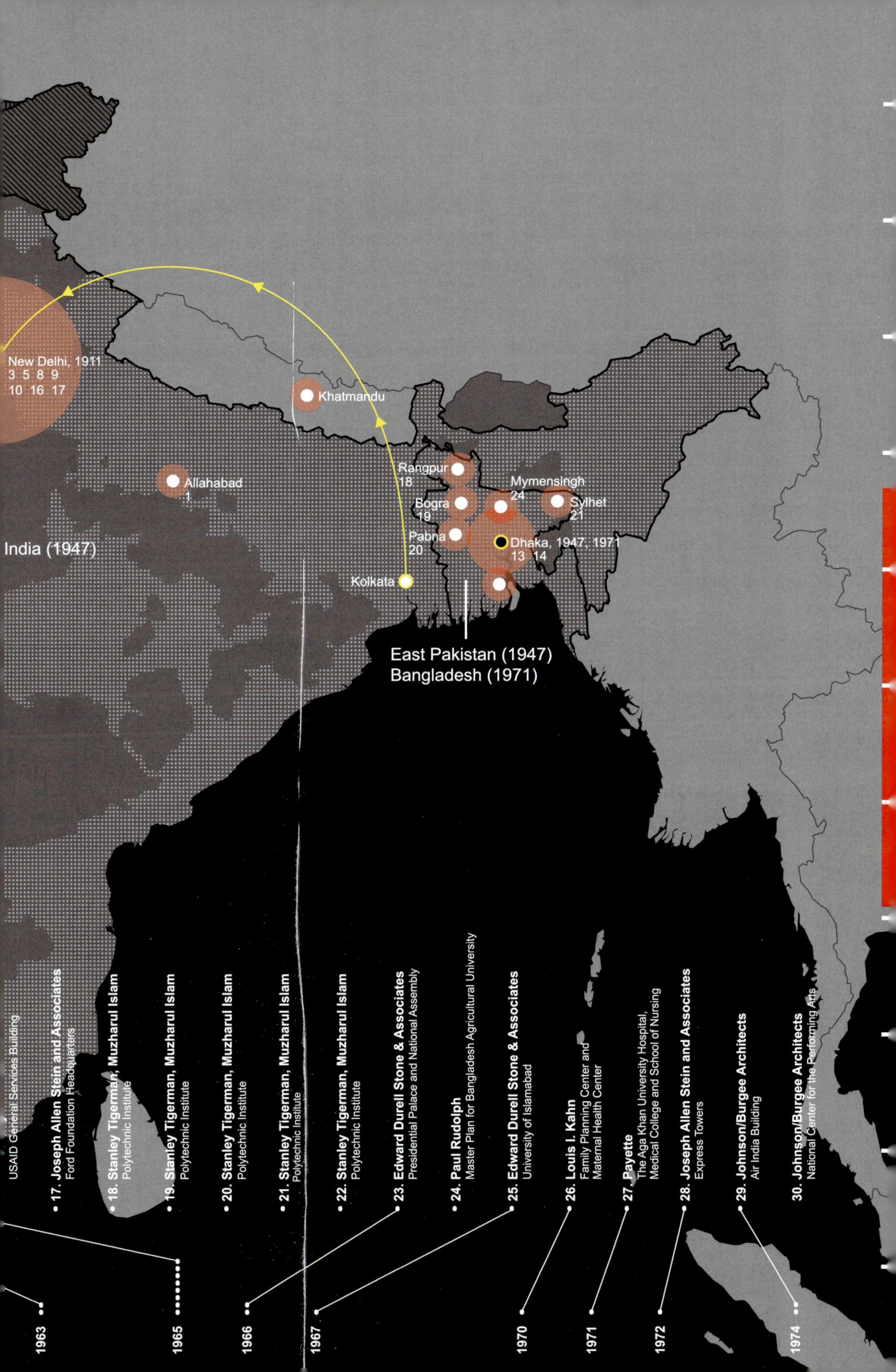

New Delhi, 1911
3 5 8 9
10 16 17
Khatmandu
Allahabad
1
India (1947)
Rangpur
18
Bogra
19
Pabna
20
Kolkata
Mymensingh
24
Sylhet
21
Dhaka, 1947, 1971
13 14
East Pakistan (1947)
Bangladesh (1971)
USAID General Services Building
17. Joseph Allen Stein and Associates
Ford Foundation Headquarters
18. Stanley Tigerman, Muzharul Islam
Polytechnic Institute
19. Stanley Tigerman, Muzharul Islam
Polytechnic Institute
20. Stanley Tigerman, Muzharul Islam
Polytechnic Institute
21. Stanley Tigerman, Muzharul Islam
Polytechnic Institute
22. Stanley Tigerman, Muzharul Islam
Polytechnic Institute
23. Edward Durell Stone & Associates
Presidential Palace and National Assembly
24. Paul Rudolph
Master Plan for Bangladesh Agricultural University
25. Edward Durell Stone & Associates
University of Islamabad
26. Louis I. Kahn
Family Planning Center and
Maternal Health Center
27. Payette
The Aga Khan University Hospital,
Medical College and School of Nursing
28. Joseph Allen Stein and Associates
Express Towers
29. Johnson/Burgee Architects
Air India Building
30. Johnson/Burgee Architects
National Center for the Performing Arts
1963
1965
1966
1967
1970
1971
1972
1974

New work in the office of Ed Stone

Whether they are monks or millionaires, Architect Edward Durell Stone's clients come to him for a quality that is peculiarly his own. That quality is best described as "romantic elegance." It can be found in a Stone factory as well as in a Stone cathedral; in a Stone hotel as readily as in a Stone laboratory. It is a quality that has earned him the admiration (and the envy) of his profession, for the ingredients of that quality seem to be totally resistant to plagiarism.

Monks (see page 127) and millionaires are not the only new clients who have recently wandered into Stone's opulent townhouse office (photo, right) on Manhattan's upper east side. Commissions have come also from as disparate a group of organizations as a U.S.-sponsored college in Lebanon (the design of an entirely new campus, page 128) to the nation of Pakistan (a nuclear research complex, opposite and page 120). Others: a legislative building in North Carolina (page 123, a hotel for Laguna Beach, Calif. (page 124), a civic center for Tulsa (page 125), and a combined office and hanging garden in Los Angeles (page 126).

Linking them all is the familiar Stone feeling, but some new deletions and additions to Stone's technique. In the last couple of years, for instance, he has moved away from the grilles of masonry or metal which were almost his trade-mark. He still favors circular plans, however, with interior courts, and the play of water. If anything he is even more fond of planting flowers and foliage. His hatred of the automobile is more evident than ever; he has taken to using the familiar podium on which he stands various buildings, as an out-of-sight garage. To roof over his buildings—or to shade his roofs—Stone is using soaring concrete shells held high up on thin-stem columns, delicate parasols against the sky.

The truest consistency actually is in the elegant, fanciful flavor of his work. Once a staunch enlistee in the New York division of the International Style—and considered one of its brightest lieutenants, at that—he mustered himself out about ten years ago. Today, with the help of his wife and chief assistant, Maria Torch Stone, he continues happily to stalk his own kind of sparkle and expansive style in architecture.

PHOTOS: WALLACE LITWIN; RENDERING (OPPOSITE): GRAHAM BUST

Nuclear institute

1. REACTOR
2. NUCLEAR PHYSICS
3. ELECTRONICS
4. NUCLEAR ENGINEERING
5. THEORETICAL PHYSICS
6. RADIO BIOLOGY
7. CANTEEN
8. AUDITORIUM
9. LIBRARY
10. RADIO CHEMISTRY
11. FUEL FABRICATION

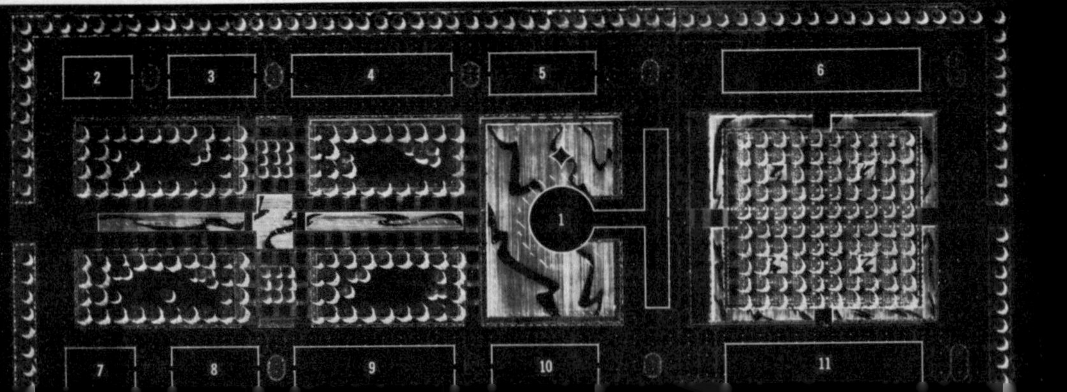

RENDERINGS BY GRAHAM RUST

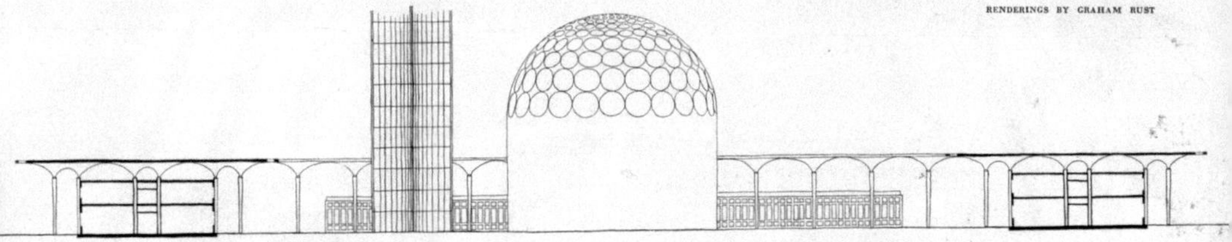

As the first building of its new capital, Islamabad, in the northern part of West Pakistan, the Pakistani government significantly has decided to build an Institute of Nuclear Science. To assist, they—also significantly—have called in American engineers and suppliers, plus a firm of German engineers in the atomic field, plus both Ed Stone Sr. and Jr. The younger Stone, 29, whose headquarters are in Fort Lauderdale, Fla., will do the landscaping, and is already establishing nurseries on the site in Pakistan to provide materials.

Stone Sr., for this design, looked upward to the sun for inspiration. To fend off its blazing heat in summer he will first build an immense concrete parasol, then tuck all his buildings in the shade underneath. The parasol will also extend out to provide a colonnade walk on both sides of the building group, and, of course, will neatly tie together the various architectural units as well.

Stone will use a podium for buried parking and services, and will house the reactor in a circular building. There will be some translucent domes to enliven the parasol's shade. For the landscaping and pools, Stone has in mind the effect fancied by the Mogul emperors in the delectable water gardens they built in centuries past.

Engineers: Burns & Roe, Inc.

Reactor supplier: American Machine & Foundry Atomics.

Nuclear engineers: Leybold, G.M.B.H.

Islamabad: a progress report on Pakistan's new capital city

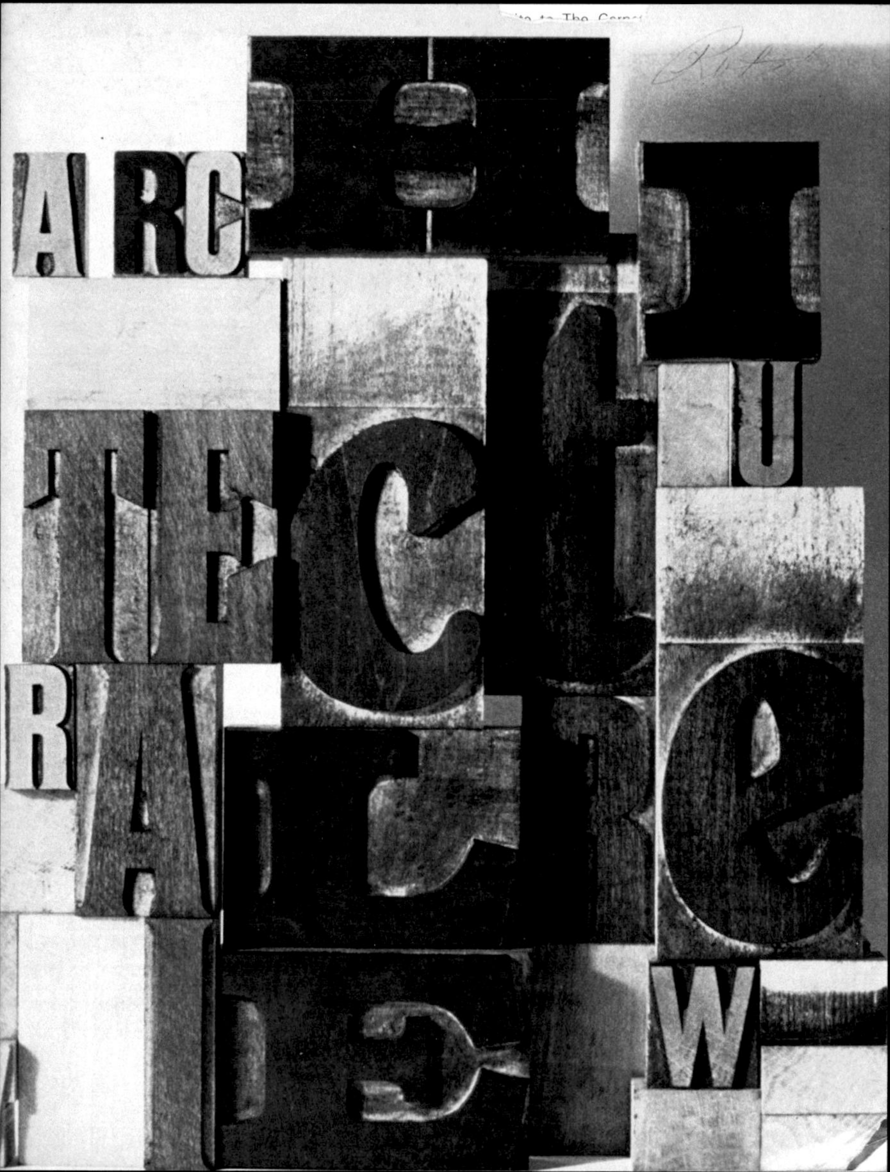

:HANGEABLE

'hough they were studios) over repeti-ve stacks of classrooms; these are nked across a central pedestrian way y a first floor bridge with an ppropriately light parasol roof. In ne same town, next to a Medical Hall e designed for Tange in 1960, Isozaki as recently completed a library, 17, vith a ruthless box-beam combination f structure and services, poking out of he volumes to give a suggestive im-ression of incompleteness. Whether

18

such a combination succeeds internally in being either functionally flexible or visually in scale is another matter, 18.

19

EAST IS EAST

The non-Communist East is in no less of a cultural turmoil than China itself. In Japan, for example, the Free World can easily appreciate the out-stepping image of the Tsuyama Culture Centre, 19, designed by Koshi Kawashima (out of Boston City Hall). But what can be made of the historicist styling by Kenji Imai of the Music Hall in Tokyo, 20, built in honour of Her Majesty the Empress's sixty-first birthday? At Islamabad, the new capital city of Pakistan (see pages 211–216 of

25

this issue), Arne Jacobsen had no cultural doubts: his Parliament Building, 21, was to have displayed pure geometry, a masonry cube surrounded by a light steel-framed palazzo. It was nonsense on grounds of cost and technique, so why did he try it? The Islamic authorities can at times be just as obscurantist, though it was Derek Lovejoy Associates, the English landscape consultants, who suggested that the pretty shrine at the existing village of Noorpur Shahan, 22, should be retained as a foil to the new city on the plain below. Meanwhile, new mosques are 'stripped traditional'; this one by Khwaja Zaheer-ud-Deen, 23, is in the

20

Class V centre of G6 close to the Municipal Offices (see page 215), with paving by Lovejoy.

Confusion of cultures has reached its climax at Islamabad in Edward D. Stone's deplorable design for the President's Palace, 24. In the Matthew plan for the administrative sector, 25, it faces symmetrically down the 'spine' of Capital Avenue between the Cultural Group to be designed by Robert Matthew, Johnson-Marshall and Partners (top of 25) and Rosselli's Secretariat (right of 25 and page 213). It will be flanked by colonnades leading to symmetrical pavilions, also by Stone, each with fifteen little domes, for the Foreign Affairs Ministry and for the Parliament Building. Stone arrived at the Islamabad as architect of the American-financed Institute of Science and Technology which lies in the National Park to the east of the city. A mosque-like minaret, 26, covers the exhaust system of the domed nuclear reactor next to it.

It is in Lovejoy's landscaping that

26

27

ISLAMABAD

East and West have most happily joined at Islamabad; 27 is the courtyard of the National Health Laboratories (next to Llewelyn-Davies's teaching hospital—see AR Preview, 1967), which were designed by John Musgrove but recast by local officials. In a G6 public park is a delightful Japanese garden by S. Tabata, 28. Yet one firm of local architects, Naqvi and Siddiqui, has shown in the Telephone Exchange, 29, that modern cubic shapes can be contrasted happily against natural contours. Response to the East must above all be environmental, as the work of the Colombo Plan team has proved: the climate can be controlled by *jali* screens, 30, as at Gerard Brigden's Government Hostel, 31 (see also page 214), and strong and simple enclosures, indirectly lit, can be made to stand out under the vast sky—

28

29

a primary school by Brigden, 32, shows this truly local and Oriental architecture without pretension.

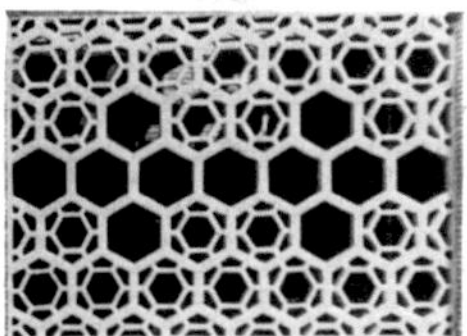

30

31

32

DACCA

In spite of Louis Kahn's unhappy interlude at Islamabad between Jacobsen and Stone, he is busy with actual construction of the major buildings for East Pakistan's capital at Dacca. The model of the Assembly Hall, 33, displays his extraordinary mixture of naivety in perforation and massing of the elevations with great sophistication in the complicated rooflighting, 34.

The consistent brick masonry cor struction will no doubt give the scal which the model lacks.

PONTI

Contacts with the East seem to have fixed Gio Ponti in a mannerism of random slits and thin verticals. 35 is the Denver Art Museum in the United States, designed by Ponti with James Sudler Associates. 36 is the interior of Ponti's chapel at the San Carlo Hospital in Milan, slits to the south, 38, and hexagons to the north, 37.

37

38

ISLAMABAD

rogress report on Pakistan's new capital city

en partition in 1947 gave India the vens-designed city of New Delhi, istan needed a new metropolitan s to express the distinctive aspira- s of a separate Islamic nation. en Field-Marshal Mohammed Ayub n established strong leadership in 3, one of his first acts was to appoint ommission for the Location of the ital, with Dr. Constantine Doxiadis, Greek architect-planner, as adviser.

Commission recommended two ible sites. One was just outside the porary capital of Karachi; but, e apart from its chronic congestion refugees and with the commerce Vest Pakistan's only modern port, achi was badly situated for a capital, ng a very hot and humid climate a hinterland of desert.

he other possible site was chosen: Potwar plateau, lying to the north ne country in a less steamy atmos- e 1,600-1,900 feet above sea-level the foothills of the Himalayas g another 3,000 feet as a backdrop. existing town of Rawalpindi nine s to the south, besides having good and rail links to the rest of the ntry, lies on the Grand Trunk Road ch connected Teheran and Kabul Peshawar, Lahore, Delhi and Cal- a—a linear growth of historic itals which Doxiadis was quick to tify as the basis of a future Asian menopolis.' Another ancient road, sadly a cul-de-sac, runs north to hmir and Central Asia. In February.), Ayub Khan named the Potwar site nabad (city of Islam). Rawalpindi me the second temporary capital 1965 when Islamabad took over ially from it.

DOXIADIS PLAN

iadis Associates were appointed in to prepare the new capital's er Plan, approved in May, 1960, and wed in most of its essentials ever e. The basic idea, which Doxiadis 'dynapolis,' is of a city expanding in ear fan-shape from an initial focal t. In the case of Islamabad, there to be two foci: the old centre of alpindi and the new administrative e of Islamabad, situated directly w the escarpment of the Margala . A linear layout made sense of the which, besides the Margalas, was ded to the east by more hills and to outh by the Sohan River. Doxiadis pted the uncertainty of dynamic th, his population graph, showing ncrease of 400,000 people in twenty s and a total of 2,250,000 by the of the century, being open to constant revision. In having a tightly built up nucleus constantly expanding, Islamabad is a Mark II capital compared to the Mark I of Brasilia and Chandigarh (and New Delhi), where an essentially static layout of monumental buildings and zoned uses will only gradually have its gaps infilled over the years. In one major respect, however, Doxiadis has compromised his own principles: whereas the buildings for local government will expand gradually with offices and shops as the spine of the linear layout, the buildings for national government and national culture have been treated as a fixed 'focus' at the point of the fan, with only the National Park and the enormous artificial Rawal Lake to the east of it. Islamabad will for some years be a one-industry city of Government, and there may be increasing difficulties of 'tidal flow' and congestion of transport as the growth of the whole city moves increasingly away from this focus. The administrative centre includes the main Government Secretariat buildings, the President's Palace, the Parliament Building, the National Library and Museum, and the Armed Services Museum. To the south is the diplomatic enclave of embassies and high commissions. To the west are sites for various 'buildings of national importance' and an exclusive residential area for high officials. Only to the west of these do the residential sectors around the main spine start.

These residential sectors are built on a disciplined hierarchy of communities. Each sector, housing 30-40,000 people, is known as a Class V community, the centre of which contains municipal offices, large shops, health centre, cinema, fire station, police station, post office, Jamia Masjid (Friday mosque), dhobi ghat (central laundry area), sports centre and recreation areas. Each Class V community is subdivided into three or four Class IV communities of about 10,000 people, with centres containing shops, covered food market, mosque, secondary school, health clinic, restaurant, local police point, municipal maintenance office, and sub-post office. Each Class IV is again subdivided into three or four Class IIIs of about 2,500 people each; these contain local shops, primary school, tea house and praying place. A Class II community is a group of about a hundred people served by a corner shop; Class I is the family itself or 'any gathering of two or three people.' This hierarchy is not perhaps very different from Gibberd's at Harlow, and the range of facilities contained in a Class V centre (essentially radial in its focusing of traffic, not linear) seems to leave remarkably few activities over for the 'main spine.'

The test of Doxiadis, however, is not his diagrams but the environment he has created; and there can be no doubt as to what he intended, as his firm did detailed designs for the first four Class V communities, and in one of these, G6, a large quantity of housing to these designs was actually built in 1961 and 1962. The whole layout is based on the most rigid grid of squares, each Class V sector having a side of about 1¼ miles. 'There is no reason for the main roads to be curved,' Doxiadis has said, 'unless the form of the landscape compels us to do so'—and in fact he has allowed virtually no curves, even though the Potwar Plain is undulating, being eaten into by deeply eroded water courses. Sometimes the grid results in roller-coaster gradients for straight roads, and in a city where the housing is almost entirely single-storey, the failure to follow the natural contours sufficiently means a monotony of aspect and an excessive dictation of pedestrian movements, even though vehicles and pedestrians are meticulously kept apart. Standard house plans were evolved by Doxiadis for the eight established levels of Government housing (A to H), corresponding closely to income and status. Each man moves to an appropriate house on being promoted in the civil service. The climate runs to extremes, from 30 deg. F. in winter to 115 deg. F. in summer, with 40 inches of rain per year, mostly in the July-August monsoon but also in the spring rainy season. Doxiadis has aimed, so he told the REVIEW in a recent statement, at 'creating types of spaces which have two characteristics: (a) they should have a small exposure to the winds which can make living outside during the sunny winter days very unfavourable when man needs the sun but avoids the wind; (b) people tend to forget the necessity to create as many shaded places as possible, which will be indispensable during the summer when greater exposure to the sun means much more unfavourable conditions.'

MUSLIM OR MODERN?

Unlike India, Pakistan has very few qualified architects and fewer still of talent. There are five local firms at Islamabad and an American from Karachi, William Perry; but up to last autumn the Capital Development Authority—the equivalent of Nova-Cap at Brasilia—had recruited only one qualified architect-planner, one architect and one town planner of Pakistan nationality. No one can say the CDA did not go to big outside names: Sir Robert Matthew, Gio Ponti, Arne Jacobsen, Louis Kahn, Lord Llewelyn-Davies. Matthew and Percy Johnson-Marshall have done the overall plan for the administrative sector with Derek Lovejoy Associates as landscape architects. Matthew's superlative diplomacy has faced unequal odds. In the first place, Dioxiadis's layout for the area showed

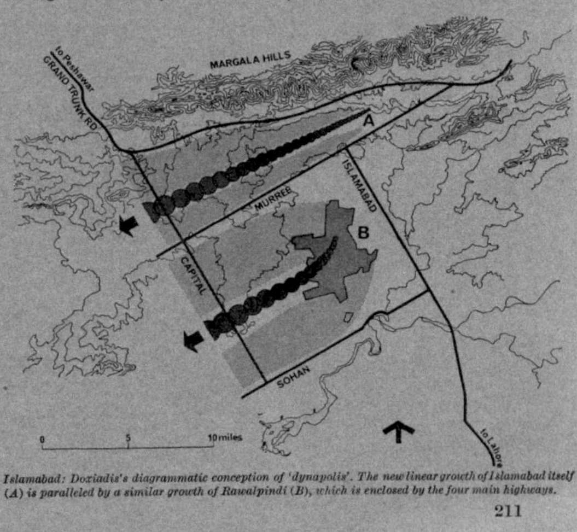

Islamabad: Doxiadis's diagrammatic conception of 'dynapolis'. The new linear growth of Islamabad itself (A) is paralleled by a similar growth of Rawalpindi (B), which is enclosed by the four main highways.

just how irrational 'rationalist' planning can be: along National Avenue were to be serried ranks of ten-storey slab blocks for the Ministries, inflexibly subdivided for a rapidly evolving country and wildly optimistic for a technology of cheap manual labour still geared very largely to single-storey structures of brick and stone. Doxiadis nevertheless stated that these block shapes were based on 'detailed calculations . . . covering both present and future requirements.'

Matthew and Johnson-Marshall kept Doxiadis's zoning but laid it out again with more regard to the contours of the landscape. Gio Ponti had already designed the first public building built in the miscellaneous area to the west—Pakistan House, an hotel now renamed the Shehrzad and considerably re-decorated. His partner Alberto Rosselli then began work on the Secretariat buildings to go on Doxiadis's Ministries' site. The first phase of these, now nearing completion and partially occupied, consists of two groups of four L-shaped blocks, containing about 1,000,000 sq. ft. in all. Space is so arranged that Ministries can rapidly expand and change places. Visually the expression of the lift and stair towers at the corner of each 'L,' together with the placing of the blocks at different levels on the slope, enables the buildings to blend with their mountainous background. Rosselli rejected local brick as too small in scale and local stone as too costly—and both gave inadequate earthquake-proofing; but, having chosen instead to use an infill of precast concrete within an in situ concrete frame, he discovered that precasting had to be taught from the beginning and lifting tackle was non-existent. The primitive lifting method ultimately adopted consisted of a pulley wheel fixed high up and worked by driving a tractor away from it with the cable attached. Rosselli points out that the buildings were intended all along to have an educational effect on the local building industry. Nevertheless, he admits, 'the technology adopted betrayed its origins and was difficult to graft into the country with its particular climate; technology was revealed as a product designed for a given society rather than a mass of universally valid techniques.' The close-up photographs of the buildings, handsome as they are, reveal many jagged edges to the precasting, eventually rendered over. A major problem was the filing and accurate reading of the architect's drawings sent out from Italy.

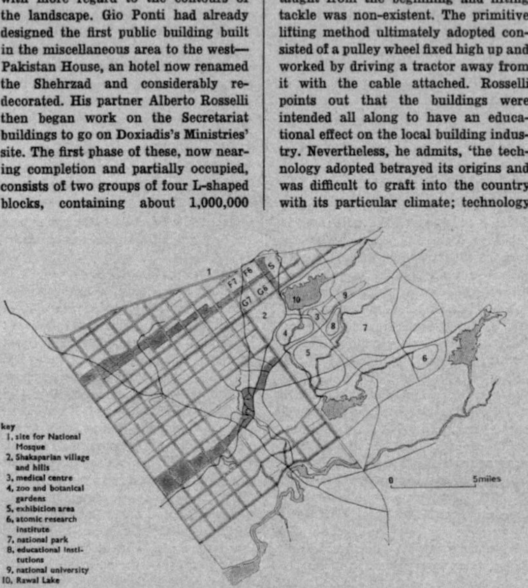

The Doziadis master plan for Islamabad. Civic and commercial areas are hatched. F6, F7, G6, G7 are the first four housing areas, and S is the secretariat—see the detailed plan below.

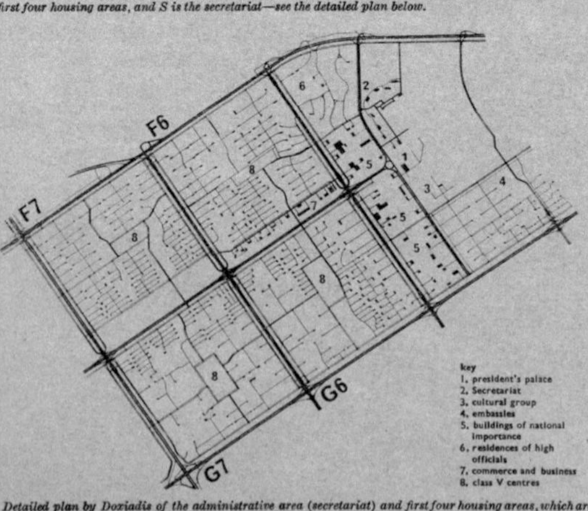

Detailed plan by Doxiadis of the administrative area (secretariat) and first four housing areas, which are illustrated on the following pages. The hierarchical division of communities (classes I-V) can clearly be seen, as can the almost total separation of pedestrians from motor traffic. There are few cars at present, but main roads are planned for massive flows of traffic later in the century.

Much more challenging than mechanical functioning or technological sophistication is that deeper level of aspirations, which a nation looks to find expressed in its capital's monuments. 'Being Western architects designing for the East,' says Rosselli, 'we tried to establish a method of approach to Muslim tradition: we interpreted it as not bounded to the "forms" of the past but to its general ambience, to present culture, to the actual way of life and to the local climate. We went beyond rationalism [i.e. Doxiadis] as regards our interpretation of the environment. But on the other hand we had too to keep a rationalist position before the problems of technology, economy and structure. . . . They are not imported European buildings and are completely different from what we have designed for Italy or abroad.'

Yet in spite of Rosselli's slightly Oriental precast panels, the Secretariat has been fiercely criticized for being too Western in style. Delay and lack of funds gave the opportunity for a wholesale change of consultants. Jacobsen was the first to go: his sleek and serene Parliament Building was as remote from Muslim culture as a sauna bath. He was replaced by Kahn, who produced three different schemes for the President's Palace and the Parliament Building in that extraordinary style with holes punched in it which is actually achieving splendid results at Ahmedabad in India and at East Pakistan's capital of Dacca (see AR World, November, 1966). But at Islamabad he was not acceptable. Last November a third architect was appointed: Edward D. Stone. His design for the President's Palace, which has been accepted, flatters Islamic grandeur in the crudest way (see World, pages 169-170, for illustrations of this and other buildings attempting local character).

TROPICAL COMMUNITIES

That it is not impossible successfully to create new communities in Pakistan which are both Muslim and modern can be seen in the work carried out at Islamabad in 1962-66 by the team of experts provided by Britain under the Colombo Plan, with Gerard Brigden as chief architect. Their work reached maturity in designs for the Government Hostel, the State Guest House and the Supreme Court, of which the first has been completed, but principally they have built up the residential sectors. Of these, G6 is virtually finished and parts of G7 and F6 are ready, accommodating about 60,000 people in all, together with shopping centres, food markets, primary and secondary schools, health centres and municipal offices. Doxiadis had laid down for G6 a two-dimensional plan wh overestimated actual requirements much as his plan for the administra centre. Development thus became low or too broken up. In his comp area of G7 by contrast Brigden was to move away from the rigid pa lines of housing in the Doxiadis The Colombo Plan team have atte to develop an appropriately reg domestic architecture, extracting functional principles that originally behind the motifs of Islamic ornamen in particular, those of climatic cont They have used open-work scre (known as 'jali') which give shade admit cross-ventilation, water garde which give coolness and relaxation the heat of summer, and geomet forms which stand out in the sun wi out glaring reflections. Domestic bui ings were traditionally built wh possible with 15-20 ft. ceilings so t cold air could be let in at night s stored during the day. The Colon Plan architects have instead develo a form of double roof construction which the upper roof of shell concr shields the main roof from the sun a parasol; with this method rooms be given lower ceilings and can heated more easily in winter.

Doxiadis's provision of generous pu spaces in graduated amounts for e class of community was paralleled a careful ecological analysis of the main categories of natural landsca the mountains, the hillocks, the p and the ravines. The Colombo P landscape consultants, Derek Love Associates, who are employed throu out the city, have been allowed la funds for their work, which extended from afforestation to c solidate the seriously eroded hills and ravines to the hard brick pa of urban squares. In some of public buildings such as the Gove ment Hostel and the National He Laboratories they have created wa gardens which successfully trans traditional ideas into modern forms.

Much more difficult has been the tr ment of the major highways; w Doxiadis drew them straight ac the ravines, he forgot that the probl of cut and fill would have to be sol without the use of earth-moving chinery, thus leaving the ugly scar labourers' 'borrow pits.' Even in la scaping the problem of Muslim ve modern has arisen: the Director Horticulture wished to plant the with flowering cherries rather t forest trees and to lay out urban squ with rosebeds. However, the enthusi with which the Director and the habitants have smothered the cere grid of Doxiadis's first terrace ho in an emotional frenzy of foliage flowers is one of the most encoura signs at Islamabad that living c munities have been delivered from birth pains.

ACKNOWLEDGMENTS
This article has been made possible by help the architects concerned, in particular from G Brigden of the Colombo Plan team, Michael caster of Derek Lovejoy Associates, Alberto R of PFR International Consultants and Dr. stantine Doxiadis.

The landscape of Islamabad has natural ravine-pitted plains framed by the majestic Margala Hills. 1, the Government Secretariat, designed by the Italian architect Alberto Rosselli—the *raison d'etre* of what is at present a one-industry town. 2, aerial view of western half of G6 housing sector (with the Margala Hills behind). The Class V centre is on the extreme right. The two slab blocks are municipal offices: architect, E. Harvey Foster. Courtyard housing designed by Gerard Brigden contrasts strongly with the terrace housing beyond it, mostly by Doxiadis Associates. To the left of the Brigden housing is the Class IV centre designed by E. Harvey Foster (see page 215). Further left is the prominent rooflight of a primary school by Gerard Brigden (assistant, Colin Franklin), illustrated in World, page 170. In the background can be seen the first housing in G7, by Brigden (see page 216). The 'linear spine' of Islamabad will run along the Murree Highway (bottom left).

1

2

3

ISLAMABAD

4

5

3–5, the Government Secretariat: architects, PFR International Consultants—Gio Ponti, Antonio Fornaroli; Alberto Rosselli: Structural engineers, Pietro Locatelli and Mario de Bernardinis. 3, detail of façade, showing sophisticated precast detailing and unsophisticated constructional equipment. 4, two kinds of façade, both oriented similarly, and service towers with a touch of applied arcading. 5, entrance forecourt, landscaped by Derek Lovejoy Associates, giving access to ground floor cloister.
6–8, Government Hostel: architect, Gerard Brigden. Environmentally the most successful building yet erected in Islamabad, it provides single rooms and suites for members of the National

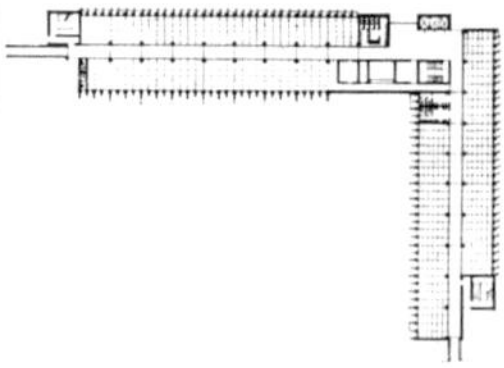

plan of typical secretariat block

Assembly and senior civil servants, planned round two courtyards. 6, three-storey residential wing, showing vocabulary of materials: brick cross walls, in situ concrete floors, teak windows, precast jali screens to verandahs, tie-beams for earthquake resistance in front of service room recesses. 7, view from courtyard, landscaped by Derek Lovejoy Associates, back to entrance wing containing reception on ground floor, lounge and dining room on first floor. The shell concrete canopy roof, for extra protection in winter and extra insulation in summer, springs 1½ in. above the main roof. 8, detail of landscaping, with brick paving and seat of local white marble. Note circular depressions for watering newly planted shrubs and coverings of straw protecting them from the sun.

6

7

8

9

9, typical housing by Doxiadis Associates, showing the straightness of the grid. Pedestrians and vehicles are carefully segregated; the heavy bars make the windows of the houses burglarproof. The flat concrete roofs have been criticized for inadequate insulation. 10, Doxiadis-designed street, showing overwhelming effect of barely five years' growth of vegetation. Each house is given one tree and one creeper. 11, covered bazaar: architect, Gerard Brigden; assistants, David Williams and Roger Guise. Four of the six rooflit hexagons have peripheral shops; the others contain restaurant and food market. The structure of concrete columns incorporating water shutes has infill walls of yellow-brown brick and double doors for dust and fly screening. 12, Class IV centre: architect, E. Harvey Foster; assistant, Robert Goodyear. Shops below, office and flats above, with precast jali screens and panels of rendered concrete. Brick paving to pedestrian square, with dark

elevation of type A house, designed by Doxiadis Associates

plan of type A house (300 sq. ft.)

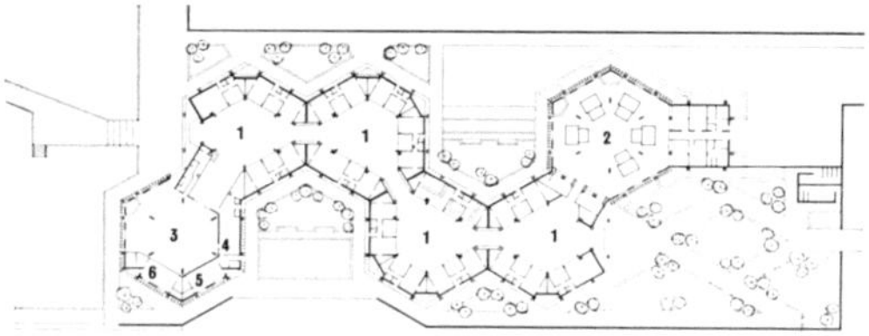

plan of covered bazaar: key, 1, general market. 2, food market. 3, restaurant. 4, kitchen. 5, 6, market superintendant. bank.

12

14

15

ISLAMABAD

blue tiled surrounds. 13, primary health centre: architect, Gerard Brigden; assistant, Derek Bradford. This has the same system of shell concrete outer vaults as the Government Hostel. Paved square landscaped by S. Tabata (Japan). 14, Class V square, with terraces and pool: landscape architects, Derek Lovejoy Associates. In background, principal municipal office block: architect, E. Harvey Foster—concrete-framed, faced in brick.
15, E type housing in G6 for middle classes: architects, William Perry Associates. In background, Secretariat (see page 213) and Margala Hills.
16–19, First quarter of G7 housing area: architect, Gerard Brigden. 16, B type houses—the second smallest, 450 sq. ft. each—see plan. The entrance rooms for receiving guests project, so as not to infringe purdah in the inner rooms. Reddish-brown brick walls, of 9 in. semi-cavity construction, support

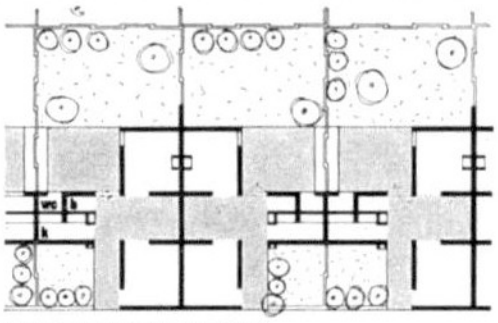

plan of type B housing, G7 area

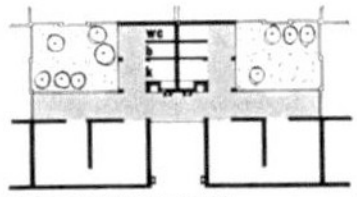

plan of type A housing, G7

brick vaults on concrete beams which (unlike the purely decorative canopies on the Perry housing, above) allow air to circulate freely for insulation as well as shading windows on the garden side. Pedestrian way has precast paving and brick water channels (shown unfinished); the serrated walls are a deviation from the architect's plan. Assistants: Robert Goodyear and Derek Bradford. 17, A type houses, looking along pedestrian way towards mosque adapted from similar form by a local architect, Rizvi—a tribute to Brigden's assimilation of the genius loci. The bricks here are rendered. 18, A type housing of two different designs—that on left with projecting blocks to shade windows (partially). 19, Class III centre by Brigden: assistant, Colin Franklin. The colonnade of rendered brick vaults on concrete columns surrounds a landscaped courtyard—see plan.

16

18

19

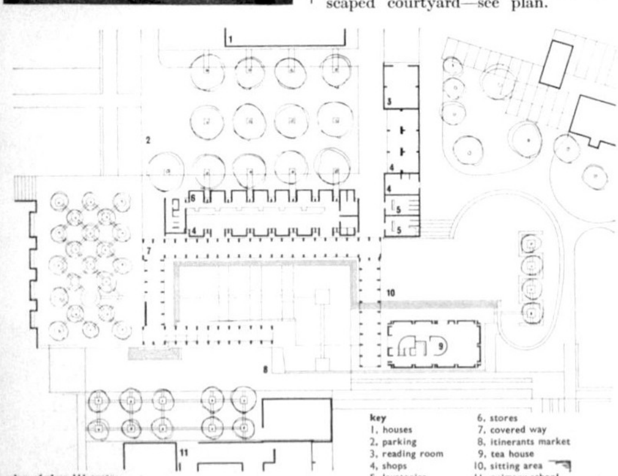

plan of class III centre

The Colombo Plan team consisted of Gerard Brigden, Eric Harvey Foster and Kenneth Mitchell, architects; W. Hamilton, architect-planner; John Sutherland, structural engineer; L. Fowler, quantity surveyor; J. Biggar, clerk of works. The landscape consultants, also employed directly by the Capital Development Authority on other areas, were Derek Lovejoy Associates: associates-in-charge, Michael Langlay-Smith, Anthony Walmsley, Michael Lancaster and M. J. Heath. The team was augmented at times by young British architects who travelled overland to Pakistan, including Robert Goodyear, Derek Bradford, Colin Franklin, David Williams and Roger Guise.

OFFICE BUILDING DESIGNED BY YAMASAKI FOR HIS OWN FIRM
SHOWROOM INTERIORS CONCEIVED AS ARCHITECTURE
APARTMENT COMPLEX THAT COMBINES TOWER AND GARDEN UNITS
SPECIAL REPORT: SOME PARTICULAR PROBLEMS OF NOISE CONTROL
BUILDING TYPES STUDY: COLLEGE BUILDINGS

FULL CONTENTS ON PAGES 4 AND 5

ARCHITECTURAL RECORD

[SE]PTEMBER 1968 **9** A McGRAW-HILL PUBLICATION TWO DOLLARS PER COPY

By Raymond L

MASTER PLAN STUDY GIVES ST PAKISTAN NEW APPROACHES FOR TROPICAL ARCHITECTURE

A unique master plan has recently been completed for the expansion of five technical institutes in East Pakistan. When built, the new facilities for existing institutions in the cities of Pabna, Rangpur, Sylhet, Barisal and Bogra will represent more than additional accommodations. They will demonstrate architecture as rational building, for they were conceived of as congruous forms, based upon a sympathetic understanding of the country's environment and the way of life enjoyed by its people.

Formulation of the master plan has taken two and one-half years
mplete. Design and working drawings, related to work on the various sites, are now in process, and construction
egin this year. The study which backs up the master plan represents an achievement of architectural significance
nly to Muzharul Islam and Stanley Tigerman, the project's architects. They believe that when available in book
the study will be of considerable use to architects and builders of East Pakistan, whether or not they are spe-
lly interested in designing polytechnic schools. Their research, meticulously organized, is the first of its kind com-
for that country. It should become an especially valuable tool for native builders in a country that suffers, like
others, a kind of architectural schizophrenia: the result of rational native practices in conflict with European
imported during generations of foreign domination. In having produced such a study, the architects now be-
they will leave something behind them other than buildings: a work that could be part of a continuing process.

he study from which the specific building programs were written is comprised of several parts. These deal with
rmulation of design criteria based upon the exploration of the unique problems of this geographical locale and
ople. When they first undertook the project, the architects quickly discovered that there was neither doc-
tation of existing standards nor of performance or quality of work, and they set out to collect such information.
laving completed their basic research, the architects then proceeded toward a synthesis of their findings as built
. The result was a compendium of construction details, spatial arrangements and siting configurations that could
ted against the country's unique problems and environment. It was only after these initial steps were accom-
d—qualifying architectural forms in terms of all determinants—that the specific requirements for polytechnical
ng were introduced. Throughout the study, existing practices were often challenged by the architects in an effort
t out current educational intentions from a morass of old practices and prejudices. Ultimately, a set of building
was arrived at that is well-related to accommodating teaching, administrative, recreational, social and housing
: a *kit of parts* which will contribute to the future development of all of East Pakistan's polytechnic institutes,
erhaps to the betterment of architecture in all places with similar problems.

ocial habits and customs, physiol- ducation, family structure and rec- ed idiosyncrasies of the East Paki- were recorded wherever they ap- d relevant to making suitable ac- nodations. The Pakistani's concept public" and "private" had to be erstood both in terms of accepted cul- patterns, determined largely by eco- ic exigencies, and the future of these erns in light of sociological change as esult of education, urbanization, and sperity.

Statistics on labor, materials and con- ction costs were compiled. These fig- were given a specific architectural text in relation to economical build- forms and mechanical systems in gen- use in the country. Good practices n of native ingenuity were brought focus, especially when exploring the blems of construction and materials the monsoon season. Figures A-L are ne of the 22 diagrams explaining *form ough structure and form through ma- als.* These illustrate various combina- ns of columnar and wall and/or com- ite systems, employed to achieve her flexible or fixed spatial systems. ults, domes and arches, and folded tes are illustrated because of their rele- ce to building techniques in East istan.

Form through environment is illus- ed by diagrams (M-S) that show hypo- ical building sections under different ther conditions: sun, wind, rain, air ement, flooding, etcetera. In the ics, a building's relation to climate is emely important. Mechanical air-con- oning systems are seldom used be- e of their high initial expense and op- ing cost. During the winter, the tly-clothed East Pakistani may experi- some discomfort at night when the perature is 45-50° F. minimum. He pensates for the problem by closing openings of his home to keep out the t air. During the hot, humid monsoon on, natural ventilation is the basic ns of maintaining comfort, facilitated rge building openings. But when this electric fans are sometimes used.

In the study Tigerman offers a section d *form through form* (figure Y). Un- other sections in the book, this one, nsists, is not to be translated "liter- He explains, however, that formal gurations, extended from the ab- t, may form a basis of architectural tics and esthetics are important in Pakistan, where, as in most places, espect is heightened by beautiful tecture.

For those who may be doubtful, the lness of this kind of "formal analy- (as illustrated in the diagrams at will be found in the buildings.

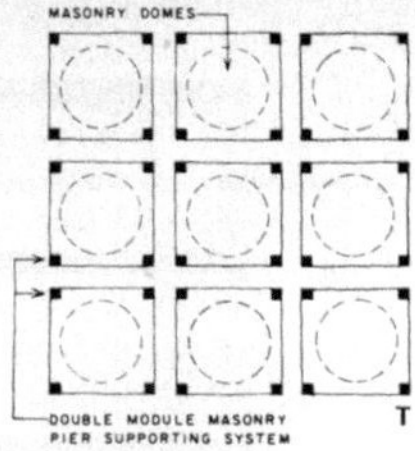

T

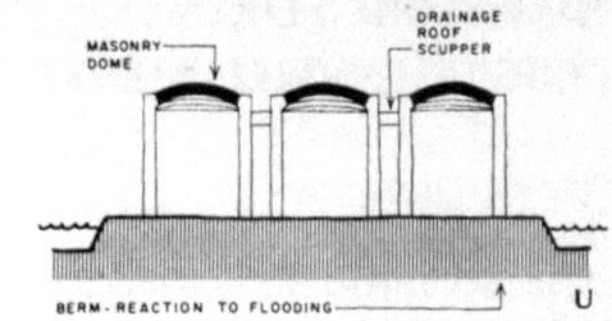

U

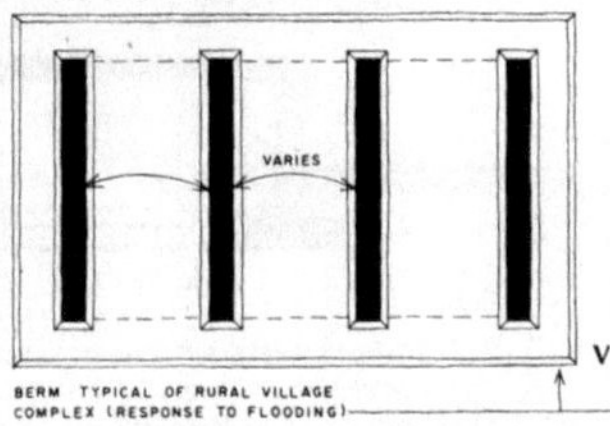

V

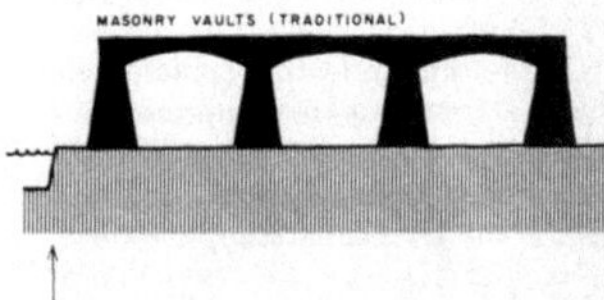

W

THE DIAGRAMS below are abstract only to a certain extent; they are based upon the pinwheel, which increases the perimeter for the amount of area enclosed. The pinwheel lends itself to the form of a convoluted single-loaded corridor, which is ideal for purposes of maximum cross ventilation. In the pinwheel plan a number of slots are developed through which wind is squeezed, utilizing Bernoulli's principle of forcing ventilation through the building by reducing and then enlarging the size of passageway.

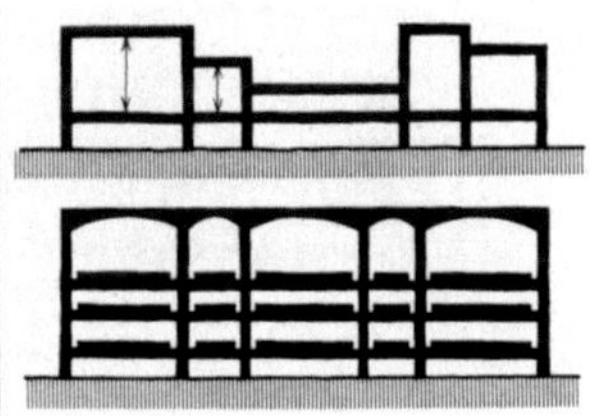
X

FORM *through cultural and sociological patterns* is examined in examples of indigenous institutional and genre constructions of mosque and domestic architecture (figures T-X). *Form through function* is illustrated by structural systems manipulated to provide for the desired degree of flexible space. Figure Z belongs to the section that develops *form through economics and construction methods.* This section provides an illustrated, thumbnail review of basic construction forms, their best (local) application, and some determining factors for their employment.

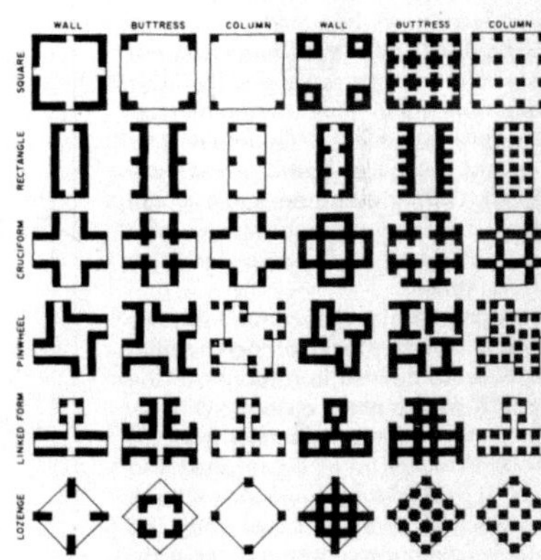

Y

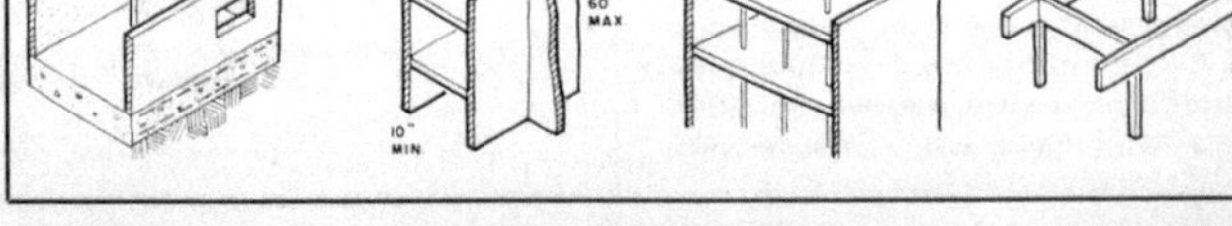

Z

BUILDING CONCEPTS SYNTHESIZED FOR A TROPICAL ENVIRONMENT

The primary synthesis of built form and environmental determinates is illustrated by a schematized typical building section shaped in response to the varying seasons of the country: monsoon, winter, and summer. The same diagram is then used to illustrate a secondary synthesis: that of a building's response to materials, vegetation, and pests.

Natural forces affecting climatological human comfort—temperature, humidity, air velocity, and light—are commonly acknowledged as design determinates. The master plan study points out, however, that factors of age, sex, skin pigmentation, clothing, general health, and acclimatization are also critical factors.

The climate of East Pakistan is of the tropical monsoon type. Winter (November through mid-March) has temperatures ranging from 45° to 90° F., clear skies, little rain, wind velocities from one-half to two and one-half mph, and low humidity. Summer (mid-March through mid-May) has the highest temperatures (100° F.), 15 per cent of the total annual rainfall (100-220 inches), and frequent violent thunderstorms with wind velocities up to 120 mph. During the monsoon (mid-May through October) over 80 per cent of the annual rainfall occurs. Frequent storms are characterized by steady, moderate rain lasting from several hours to several weeks. Wind velocities are slightly lower than during the summer; maximum temperature is above 90° F., humidity is at its annual peak, and skies are generally overcast. During monsoon, most of the tropical cyclones occur bringing storm winds in excess of 75 mph and very heavy rainfall.

Appropriate architectural form, its critical dimensions and proper orientation, is to be derived in response to the specific demands of the country's climate. Also, certain building practices must be observed: topsoil must be stripped and replaced by sterile silt to control growth of vegetation; ground cover must be planted to reduce reflected solar gain; house traps must be water-sealed to exclude rats and cockroaches; windows, doors and vents should be screened to exclude vermin. The living platform of all structures must be elevated above monsoon flood level. Large overhangs and louvered openings are to be oriented to allow for control of wind, light, and rain in the different seasons. Massive roofs are useful in winter as a solar heat reservoir for night time reradiation.

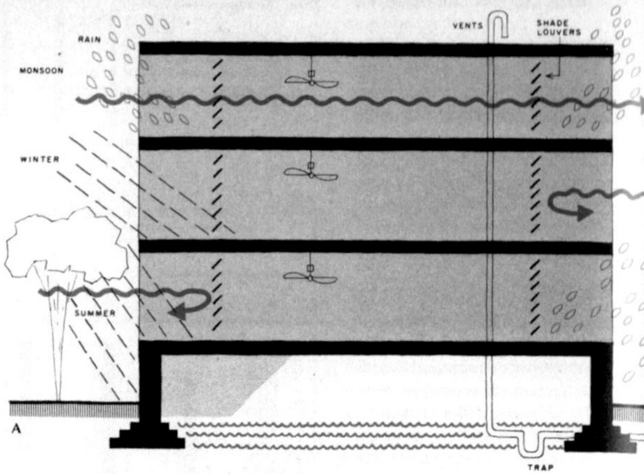

A

SCHEMATIZED TYPICAL BUILDING PLANS are shaped in response to climatological forces of East Pakistan. Certain rules-of-thumb are established for good building practice. All wall openings should be maximum size for maximum ventilation; closures should be of materials affording minimum interference with ventilation, such as screens and nets. A north-south orientation of walls takes advantage of prevailing winds. Exterior galleries facilitate dry, ventilated interiors and also promote air circulation. Many variations of the ideal linear form are possible. The continuous gallery can be interpreted both for public service and as a private veranda (fig. D), depending upon the disposition of interior spaces. Masonry walls should, at least at one point, make one right angle turn for seismic stability. Windows and doors should be louvred. Eaves are extra-heavily anchored and weather joints are designed for high wind-driven rain. All sanitary and cooking facilities should be placed to the leeward side of the building.

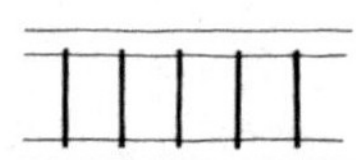

B

SCHEMATIC PLAN - TYPICAL BUILDING (MONSOON SEASONAL RESPONSE GOVERNING FORM)

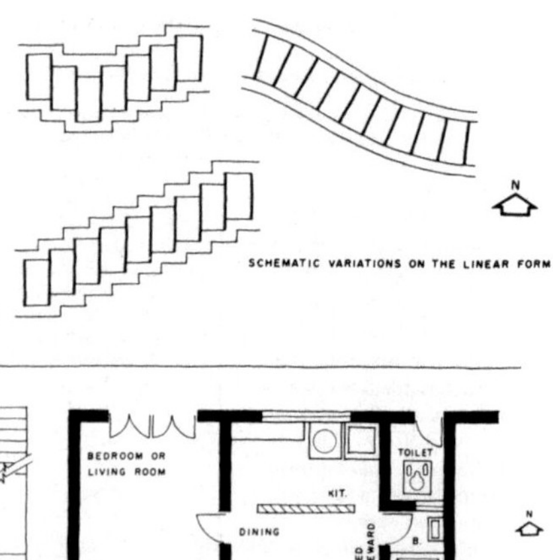

SCHEMATIC VARIATIONS ON THE LINEAR FORM

C

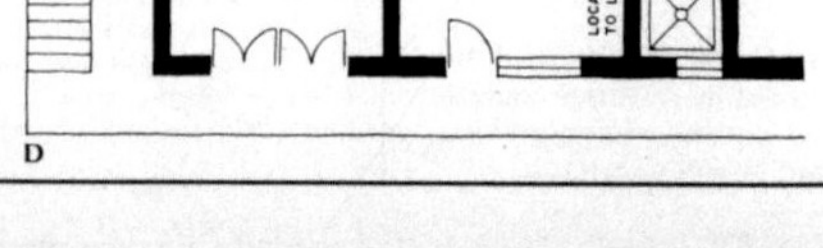

D

[K]IT OF PARTS FORMS [TH]E PROTOTYPICAL [PO]LYTECHNIC INSTITUTE

[Und]ertaking the existing and future pro-[gram]s of the Director of Technical Edu-[catio]n, the architects developed compo-[nent] parts for a prototypical polytechnic [com]plex. Spaces were developed for ad-[mini]stration, classes, twelve kinds of lab-[orat]ories, seven kinds of shops, ten kinds [of st]aff housing, student housing, recrea-[tion], medical and religious facilities.

What evolved was a "kit of parts". [The] elements are rationally formulated [con]figurations in themselves, but they re-[mai]n to be interpreted as architecture in [resp]onse to the specifics of a given site [and] program. For example, traditionally [ten] different housing units were con-[sid]ered necessary to accommodate the [vari]ous ranks of teaching staff (figure A). [Up]on evaluation, the architects decided [this] distribution to be excessive and un-[just]. They were able to modify their de-[sign]s to only four types, providing ap-[pro]ximately the same accommodations [for] all, varying them only in space.

The individual modules of space for [eac]h program type were developed in [suc]h a way as to allow for interpretation [in] response to environment or esthetic [pre]ferences (figure B). Tigerman consid-[ers] this the "exciting part of systematic [thi]nking, of working in systems analysis [an]d permuting multiples. To achieve di-[ve]rsity is a desired goal. Normally diver-[sit]y is achieved only by the intuitive [mi]nd. But if the problem, let us say, is [ho]using for the poor of East Pakistan—I [m]ean dealing in something where cost is [an] issue—then you have to somehow find [a s]ystem, a really taut plan, a taut module, [so] that that module may be repeated to [for]m many varieties which would not [loo]k 'project-like'; forms which will not [ne]cessarily reveal the individual modules [tha]t made them up. Thereby the analytic [mi]nd can be at work on something to [ach]ieve the end of diversity, which is one [of] those things sought by human beings: [so]mething different that is theirs, their [pla]ce of *terra firma,* their house, their [thi]ng. And there is no way to do this out [of] the intuitive mind alone through form [or] esthetics while still trying to be opera-[tiv]e in the taut planning context of solu-[tio]ns dealing with the poor."

A large reservoir or tank is incorpo-[rat]ed into the plan of each prototypical [site]. The tank serves to collect some of the [ann]ual rainfall of 100 to 220 inches. Such [tanks] are to be found in every village. At [the s]chool, as in the towns, they will be [use]d for recreation and bathing.

CHARACTERISTIC SPACE ALLOCATION RELATED TO ACADEMIC STATUS

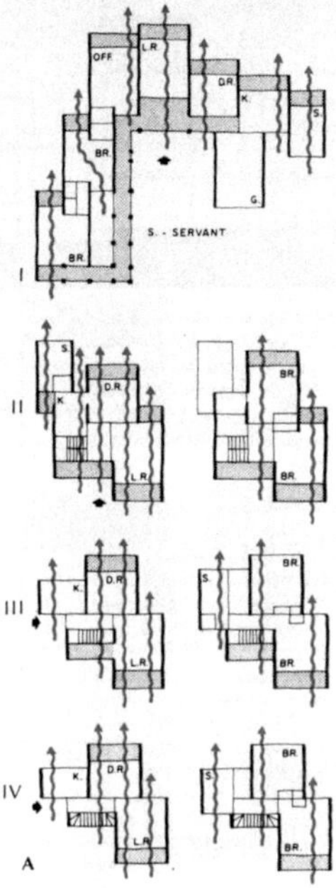

I One story dwelling
Net Area—1500 sq ft
Gross Area—2400 sq ft

II Two story row house
Net area—1125 sq ft
Gross Area—1600 sq ft

III Four story stacked maisonette
Net Area—1025 sq ft
Gross Area—1300 sq ft

IV Four story stacked maisonette
Net Area—1025 sq ft
Gross Area—1300 sq ft

V Three story flat
Net Area—840 sq ft
Gross Area—1000 sq ft

VI Three story flat
Net Area—510 sq ft
Gross Area—700 sq ft

VII Two story flat
Net Area—190 sq ft
Gross Area—286 sq ft

VIII Two story flat
Net Area—150 sq ft
Gross Area—225 sq ft

IX Two story flat
Net Area—90 sq ft
Gross Area—150 sq ft

X Two story flat
Net Area—90 sq ft
Gross Area—150 sq ft

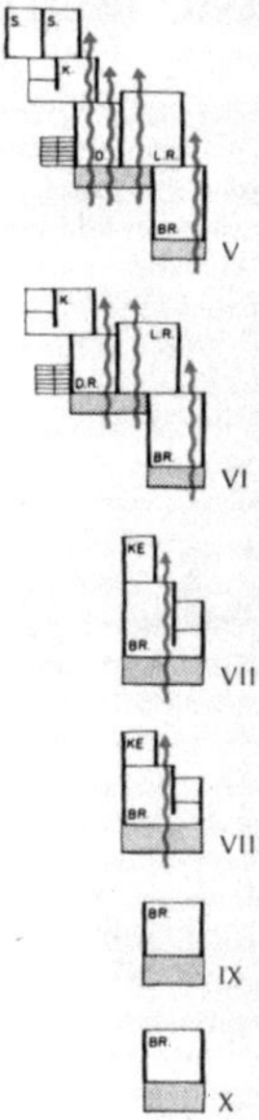

POSSIBLE GROWTH PATTERN OF BASIC UNITS

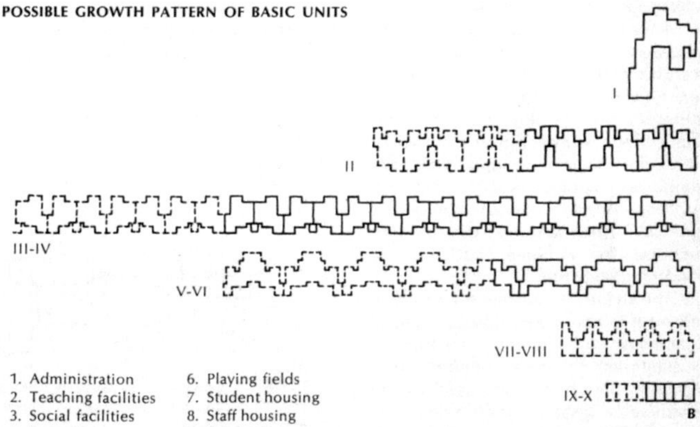

1. Administration
2. Teaching facilities
3. Social facilities
4. Recreation
5. Water tank
6. Playing fields
7. Student housing
8. Staff housing
9. Reservoir

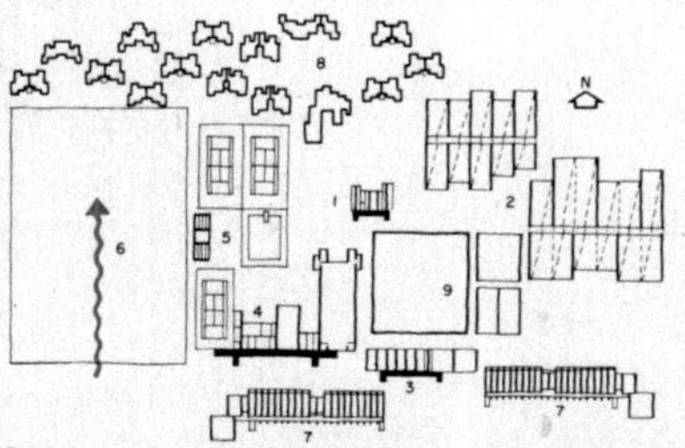

THREE PROTOTYPICAL POLYTECHNIC SITES were developed. These are considered site diagrams based upon function, environmental determinates and expansion possibilities. Each one is developed in terms of land-use flexibility: phasing building programs, indeterminate growth patterns, obsolescence. They are not based upon any relationship with outside facilities, such as a town or other educational institutions. Actual site relationships—physical, social and cultural—will shape each institution into a unique environment. Typical plan shown, left.

PROTOTYPICAL DESIGNS CONSOLIDATED INTO BASIC BUILDING TYPES

Out of the numerous programs to be spatially accommodated, four building types were established: housing for students, faculty and administration; laboratories, offices and classrooms; shops; and recreation facilities of all types.

To refine the requirements for living accommodations, questionnaires were sent to all students and faculty at existing institutions. The architects were especially interested to know current attitudes toward Western conveniences. To many Pakistani Western models are equated with modernization. In Pakistan cooking facilities and sanitary conveniences are radically different than those in the West, and it was decided, on a purely pragmatic level—because many of the residents will spend much of their professional life abroad—that they be introduced to the differences. This meant that both traditional hearth stoves and Western appliances, flush valve and squat toilets would be provided.

The boys' hostel includes common facilties for dining, a dispensary, prayer hall, and various public rooms. The basic living unit is a split-level room which sleeps four. In two of these rooms eight boys have their own veranda. Four rooms receive a toilet and stair. Each floor, with its cluster of rooms, is meant to represent a tiny neighborhood. Separated from their homes and having little social intercourse with either townspeople or families of the faculty, the boys rely upon congenial groupings for companionship. Socializing with one's peers in a meaningful way is particularly important in Pakistan, where the boys, when at home, had led a very cloistered family life.

The architects consider it an accomplishment to have been allowed to group apartments for different categories of teaching staff into one building form. Normally, since the various ranks carry certain social distinction, the groups are separated. The architects hope that proto-

THE HOUSING UNITS are an adaption of the single-loaded corridor plan, and are oriented to take advantage of the prevailing south wind. All rooms can be opened to allow for cross-ventilation through the building.

The student's rooms are split-level. The levels are stepped in ascending form from north to south. Each level provides a place for two boys to sleep. The beds for each pair of boys are slightly elevated, exposed to the wind, and thus afforded maximum ventilation. Stairwells serve as a kind of ventilation chimney. These open on to roof decks, which are popular in summer for communal sleeping.

Economically, no glass sections could be used in openings. The most appropriate section for a closure is a louvred panel with operable slats. Tests show that entire walls made of such panels are best for optimum ventilation.

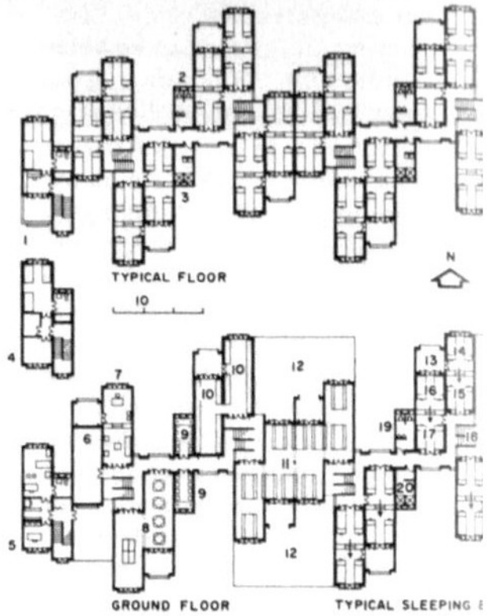

1. Dispensary
2. Toilet
3. Shower
4. Dispensary (upper level)
5. Dispensary
6. Prayer hall
7. Lounge
8. Recreation
9. Lavatory
10. Kitchen
11. Dining
12. Dining terrace
13. Veranda
14. Bedroon
15. Bedroon
16. Bedroon
17. Bedroon
18. Access
19. Toilet
20. Shower

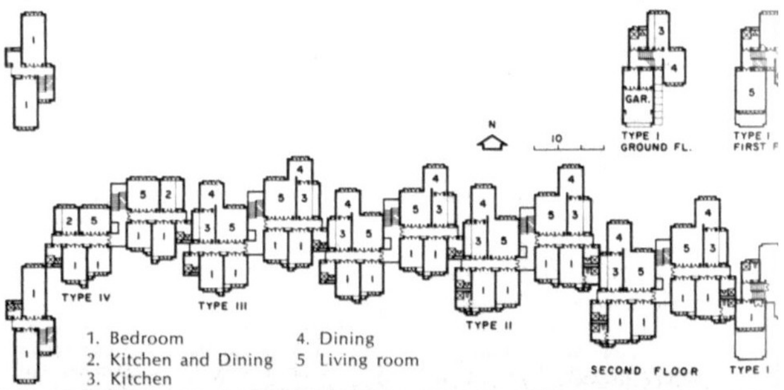

1. Bedroom
2. Kitchen and Dining
3. Kitchen
4. Dining
5 Living room

may eventually give way as residents
nce upon one another.

No common facilities are provided faculty and staff (opposite). Entertainit for the residents takes place at ne, to which relatives and friends are uently invited. Typically, women and dren occupy certain rooms and the others when there are guests.

igerman points out that purdah as a em is not so pronounced as it once , but many of the traditions remain. we had to accommodate in the hous- as you see in the various plans, a way women can move around in the hen and dining area, where they nd most of their day, and a place for n to retire after meals, especially when re are invited guests. No matter what ial position a family may hold in Paki- , individuals would expect this kind accommodation. Custom necessitates riety of separate spaces within a home ich serve the entire family on many els of sociability. Friends and relatives p in at all hours, and as there are gen- lly no telephones, a family must be dy to receive them. Traditionally, im- mptu visiting is in bad taste during al time, so it is important, to prevent barrassment, that all dining may be ne privately, separate from the other blic areas of the house. However, since Pakistani family is always blessed with presence of some relative, every cor- of the house, no matter how assigned, ikely to be someone's bedroom."

When the 10 prototype living units re reduced to four, the architects were e to appreciably improve upon the erall design concept for staff housing.

Each unit now has the same number rooms, with the exception of the prin- al's, which has an office and servant's m. Now, they believe, there is a cer- n equality for the four staff grades in housing. By Pakistan standards, the arters are considered quite adequate. wever, distinctions of rank are quite d, and it would not be possible—in foreseeable future—that a person of ver rank, but with a large family, might oy the increased spaciousness of a her-ranking apartment.

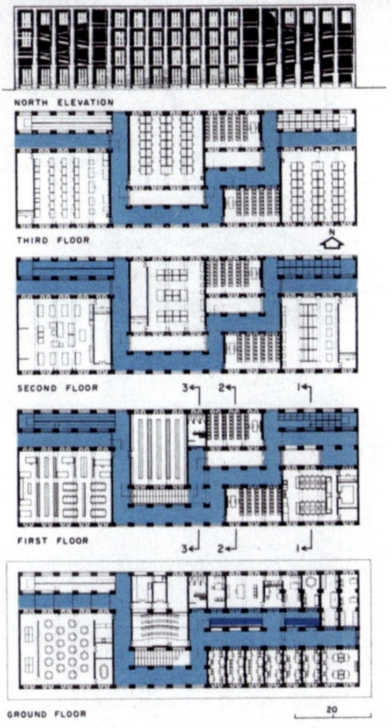

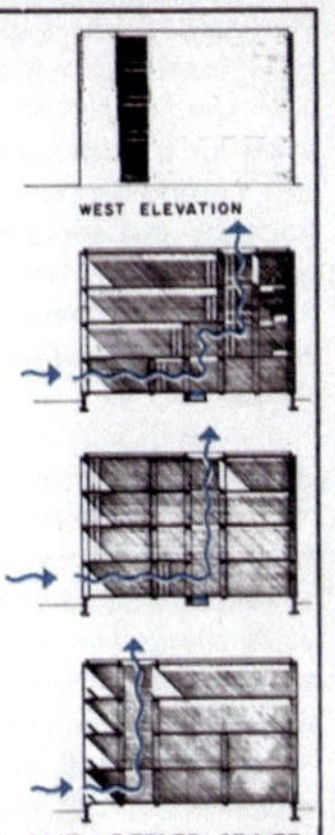

CLASSROOM AND OFFICE SPACE is housed in a building (left) patterned on a pinwheel *parti*. Corridors are extended as open slots to the outside walls of the building. Prevailing wind from the south enters the building through either the exposed corridor or through the louvred walls. From here the wind is moved vertically through a system of staggered openings (above). All areas in which odors are likely to occur—laboratories, toilets —are placed to the leeward side of the building. The shops (below) are grouped around open courts.

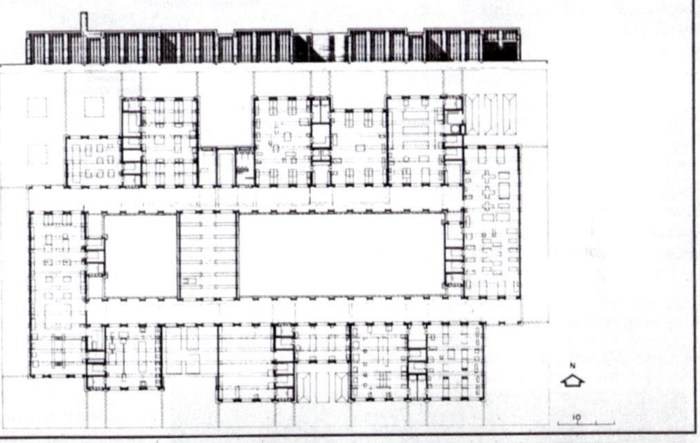

The sites for the expansion of the technical institutes are in existing towns. Resident families and students rely upon the town for a certain amount of socializing and entertainment. Family marketing is done by the servants and male householders at the bazaar. Restaurants are the principal meeting places for male companions. Everyone attends the movies.

Even though at this time the five sites are little more than small towns, the architects have now turned their thoughts to multi-storied forms to meet the needs of future urbanization. The Master Plan study allows for such an open-ended interpretation in making the final decisions about design. When Tigerman was in Dacca at the end of June, he and Islam designed the first multi-purpose form to come out of the Master Plan: they amalgamated the classrooms, shops, and administrative offices into one three-story building. This form will provide for a huge open space on the middle several floors. At the outset, the building may seem unfinished; only a certain amount of floor space will actually be filled in.

The unbuilt space will allow for expansion, but meanwhile, it will serve as a large veranda. Perhaps the next step is to place the housing above teaching space, shops, etcetera, which would certainly make sense in smaller sites than the ones selected. The multi-storied building will cost less, maintenance will be less, and the students will, in terms of climate, have a better environment.

This kind of planning and changing has occurred time and again, and has been allowed for in the way information in the Master Plan has been assembled. Tigerman has confidence in the quality of these changes. "We all keep growing and I keep learning more and more about the particular problems of East Pakistan. The designs, as they change, begin to solve the problems, in our judgment, in a better way."

FIVE POLYTECHNIC INSTITUTES AT BARISAL, BOGRA, PABNA, RANGPUR AND SYLHET, EAST PAKISTAN. Client: *Directorate of Technical Education, Government of East Pakistan.* Architects: *Stanley Tigerman and Muzharul Islam.*

1 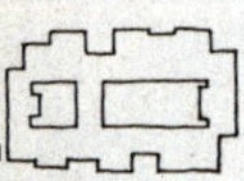

2 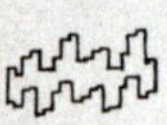

3 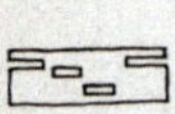

4 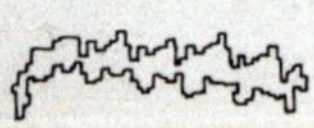

KEY LEGEND
1 Shops
2 Staff housing
3 Classrooms/Administration
4 Student housing

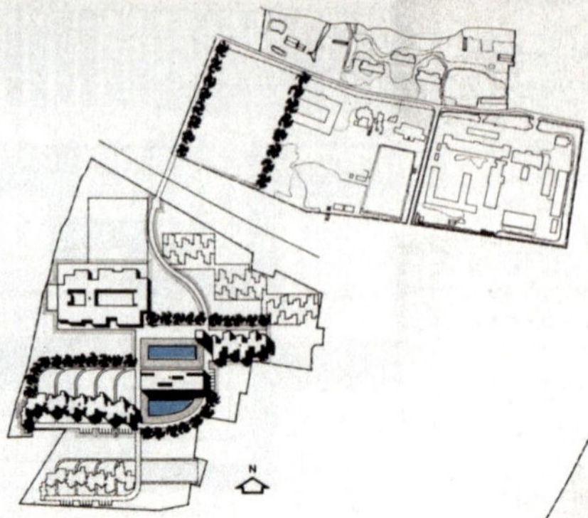

SYLHET MASTER PLAN

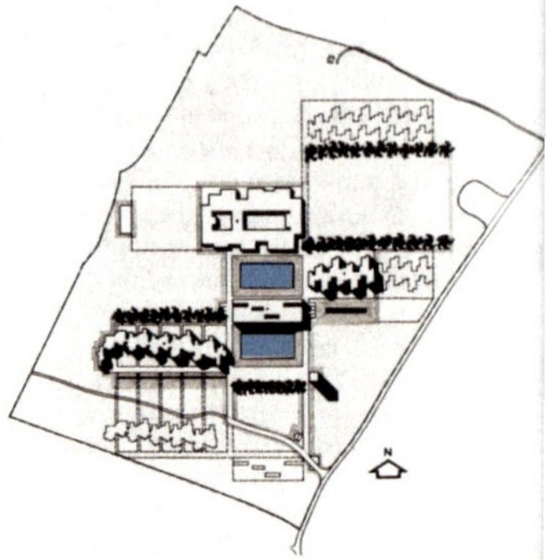

PABNA MASTER PLAN

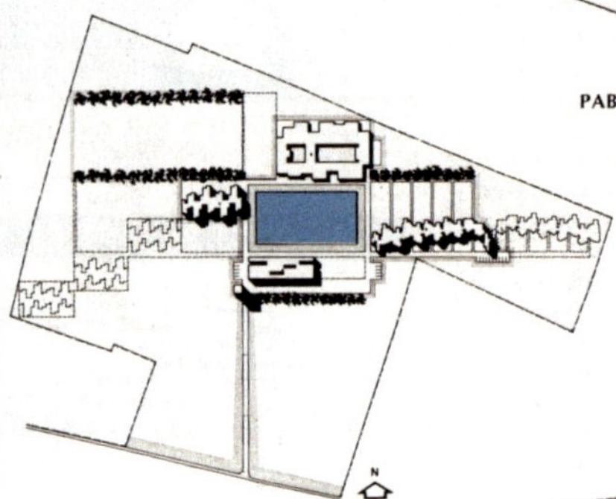

RANGPUR PLAN

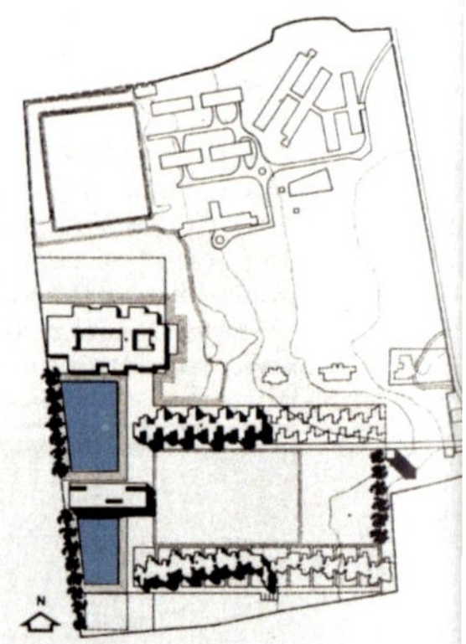

BOGRA MASTER PLAN

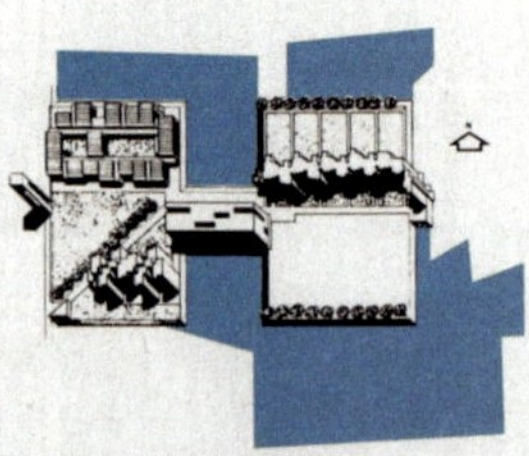

BARISAL MASTER PLAN

MIMAR
ARCHITECTURE IN DEVELOPMENT

MIMAR 6 · 1982

Visions of Grandeur

Brian Brace Taylor

Following on the heels of the theme of MIMAR 5, "Open-to-Sky Space", we are taking up again but in an entirely different way, a subject broached in MIMAR 1: namely, the relevance of imported expertise and technology for the client culture in countries of the developing world. In so doing, our attention is turned towards two capitals in the Muslim world, Baghdad, Iraq and Dacca, Bangladesh, where efforts are underway to give expression through building to a national identity. Although the two operations, renewal and expansion of ancient Baghdad begun some three years ago and the construction of the capital complex, Sher-E-Bangla Nagar designed by Louis I. Kahn some 20 years ago, are very different in nature, in available resources, and in approach, a number of parallels suggest themselves and warrent discussion.

Exterior detail of the east facade of the National Assembly Building, showing government offices. White strips of marble cast shadows at regular intervals, thereby modulating and giving rythmn to the concrete surfaces.
Photograph: B. Taylor.

Above, left: Building in the Bangla Bazaar of Dacca whose facade was inspired by the architecture of Kahn's capital complex.
Above: Paving with concrete one of the narrow lanes in Bangla Bazaar, Dacca's eldest. The contrast between this most basic kind of improvement with the stupendous scale of the capital undertaking bespeaks the inherent contradictions often present in the development policies of countries like Bangladesh.
Photographs: B. Taylor.

Before setting out to enumerate those fundamental issues that allow one to meaningfully compare contemporary architectural transformations in an Iraqi and a Bengali city, our position as critic can be formulated as follows: The type of architecture, like the type of technology, a government client chooses to finance is an indication of its overall policy for national development. The selection of an architect, for example, either foreign or indigenous, reflects a decision on the part of the powers that be to promote one or another strategies for modernisation. Modernisation has, as a rule, generally come to be synonymous with Westernisation as opposed to reliance upon locally-available intellectual and material resources. Political regimes, as is the case with both Iraq and Bangladesh, have tended in the past to adopt Western architectural models, including the necessary technology, expertise and materials, even when these are at variance with the economic and political realities of the nation.

The case of Louis Kahn's National Assembly building in Dacca is a case in point. Nearing completion earlier this year, the exterior facades were cleaned and scraped, window glass installed, and a portion of the edifice — the actual assembly chamber — was inaugurated in February, 1982. Although much of this interior finishing work still remains to be done in the rest of the building, the major construction is done and reflects what might justifiably be termed a super-human effort on the part of the Bangladeshi certainly in terms of their national budget, to see the Assembly through to completion. But have the ends, after all, really justified the extravagant means required?

As recent photos presented in this issue partially suggest, the assembly is an awe-inspiring and humbling mass of concrete. Above all the scale, vast and difficult to relate to as a human being, the proportions of certain spaces, and certainly the spectacular mingling of light and darkness in the cavern-like interior produce marked emotional reactions to this monument of contemporary architecture. However, the kinds of reactions the assembly provokes, it would seem, ought in some way to be related to the original intentions of the architect and/or of his client. What were these?

If the government client in 1962 initially wanted a tangible symbol of unity between east and west Pakistan, where parliamentary democracy was to prevail as a form of government, the authorities in Dacca at various moments since independence, have pursued work on the capital complex as a sign of Bangladesh national identity and cultural itegrity. Kahn himself, on the other hand, expressed his intentions differently: "... the idea which is still the prevailing idea of the plan. This came simply from the realisation that assembly is of a transcendental nature. Men came to assemble to touch the spirit of commonness, and I thought that this must be expressible". Further in the same text Kahn wrote: "What I am trying to do is to establish a belief out of a philosophy I can turn over to Pakistan so that whatever they do is always answerable to it." Whatever concordance there may have been between the high objectives of Louis Kahn and his governmental client, little of either of the above mentioned frames of reference seems to have survived in the end result.

As a symbol of national unity for a modern nation-state, whose constitution includes many of the basic principles of parliamentary democracy but whose actual governing powers since independence from the British have most frequently been martial law authorities, Kahn's "Citadel of Assembly" (the architect's own terminology) has a questionable relevance. The extent to which the people of Bangladesh, one of the very poorest (average per capital income US$90.00 a year) populations in the world economically-speaking, find anything in the architecture of assembly building to identify with *culturally* has yet to be shown.

This is not necessarily the case for the red-brick residences, for ministers and administrations, situated on either side of the assembly, where in fact the smaller scale, the exposed brickwork and presence of interior courts have a definite relationship with earlier Bengali architecture. The assembly, of reinforced concrete and white marble strips, has none of these aesthetic characteristics, nor does it symbolise indigenous social institutions. One is left with the conviction that the assembly building, so clear when reading the plan and so baffling as one tries to move through it, reflects the somewhat authoritarian policy decision to provide Bangladesh with a grandiose landmark of political, social, and perhaps technological, progress at whatever cost.

The decision to adopt a modernised form of Western construction technology for the Assembly illustrates a choice typical of many third world countries to adhere to foreign concepts and values related to that ubiqituous phenomenon called "Progress". Portions of the report by Mr. Fred Largford published in this issue, who was the engineer sent by the architect to Dacca to experiment with adapting Western construction standards to the local situation and to train workers, reveal the kinds of logistical and organisational problems involved in what was an attempt at transfer of technical know-how. The Dacca complex was not a classic "turn-key" operation like so many others in the 1960's and '70's; Bengali workers in large numbers were actually trained on the job by the department of public works. This fact not only explains, in part, why the building has taken so long to complete, but also how it is that Bangladesh construction companies are operating successfully in the Middle East market — as Mr. Cantacuzino points out in his article on Baghdad.

Our argument clearly is *not* that Kahn's assembly building was a unique (or single) case of training manpower for a modern construction industry which was then exportable. Rather it is precisely the fact that the technology selected for such an enormous and prestigous undertaking did not contribute significantly to developing the overall economic infrastructure of the country. Unskilled and semi-skilled labourers prefer to leave the country for abroad, where they can earn more, while their remittances (as in Yemen and many other countries) tend to encourage a consumer as opposed to a producer economy. These are but several observations of a *structural* nature.

On a cultural level, Louis Kahn's assembly complex and more exactly the Ministerial Hostels have had noticeable repercussions locally over the last decade. Numerous villas in Dacca's most exclusive, upper-class suburbs sport Neo-Kahnian facades of red brick with apertures of pure geometric form: circles, semi-circles, triangles. Even more astonishing was the multi-storey building with such a facade to be seen in the heart of Dacca's Bangla Bazaar. The proprietor clearly hoped to benefit from such a decorative allusion to the capital in terms of his social and commercial status. The Kahnian architectural idiom, when confronted within the social and economic context of the old bazaar or that of predominently *rural* Bangladesh, seems to suffer from the effects of a radical dislocation, or displacement. There is a surrealistic dimension, almost like the 'readymades' of Marcel Duchamp, to the whole exercise.

In the final analysis, what has transpired in Bangladesh with a *good* architect who produced a stunning gesture in space and form has also occurred elsewhere in the developing world with less good results, (and might happen in Baghdad if one is not attentive) namely, architecture and the technology employed to achieve it, become vehicles for expressing something (eg. national 'identity', 'progress', political or religious doctrine, etc) which bears little relation to popular aspirations and capabilities. The processes by which acceptable, even good, architecture comes into being materially are every bit as crucial for our judgement of the final product as the intrinsic qualities it may have. To have selected designers of talent for public commissions such as Dacca or Baghdad is already a 'plus' to insist as well that the building-to-be demonstrates coherent links with the *structural* elements of a given society is even better.

Curzon Hall, built by the British colonial administration in Ramna, a new suburb of Dacca, in the early 20th century. Constructed of red brick, a relatively durable material employed in Bengal in the past, the hall possesses deep, protected galleries whose scale and openings evoke those of Kahn's ministerial residences in the capital complex.
Photograph: B. Taylor.

National Assembly Hall, Dacca

Project Data

National Assembly Hall, Sher E Bangla Nagar, Dacca, Bangladesh.
Client: Public Works Department, Government of Bangladesh.
Architect: Louis I. Kahn.
Started: 1962, inaugurated February 1982 (but still incomplete).

The Sher-E-Bangla Nagar, or National Assembly Complex in Dacca, Bangladesh edges slowly towards completion. Louis I. Kahn (1901-1974) the American architect, designed the principal buildings, including the official residences, as well as the Ayub hospital (1963), and supervised construction through regular visits until his death eight years ago. The Public Works of Bangladesh Department has carried on the site work, with unfailing counsel of David Wisdom and Henry Wilcots, architects in Philadelphia and long-time associates of "Professor Kahn" — as he is still affectionately referred to in Dacca.

The assembly chambers were inaugurated and used earlier this year. It was a highly symbolic event after the vicissitudes of war, of political instability and assasinations, not to mention the actual hardships of acquiring adequate supplies of materials in order to achieve the building. Highly controversial in more than one respect, the edifice now must find its place as a stunning statement of architectural excellence within the totality of Kahn's work itself as well.

While the colour of the carpeting that was put down does not correspond to Kahn's original specifications, nor that of the chairs for the Members of Parliament, the teak of the desks and rostrum lend a warm touch to the atmosphere of the central meeting space. (The carpet will be changed eventually we are told). The prayer hall, the various smaller meeting rooms, interior promenades lit artifically as well as by daylight, and the two major entries on the north and south are practically complete. The lakes have been drained in order to execute the necessary brick works on the banks. Now, for the first time the building can be viewed from the outside without the cranes rising above the 40 metre high structure, perennially testifying to its unfinished character. MIMAR wishes to celebrate the occasion of its inauguration by bringing the following images to its readers.

Below: The architect, Louis I. Kahn, lecturing in Dacca in January, 1973.
Photograph: A. Hossain.
Bottom: The National Assembly Complex, viewed from the west, is set in a rural landscape, away from the centre of Dacca.
Right: An internal walkway in the Assembly Building.
Photographs: B. Taylor.

Text and photographs by Brian Brace Taylor. Additional photographs by Anwar Hossain.

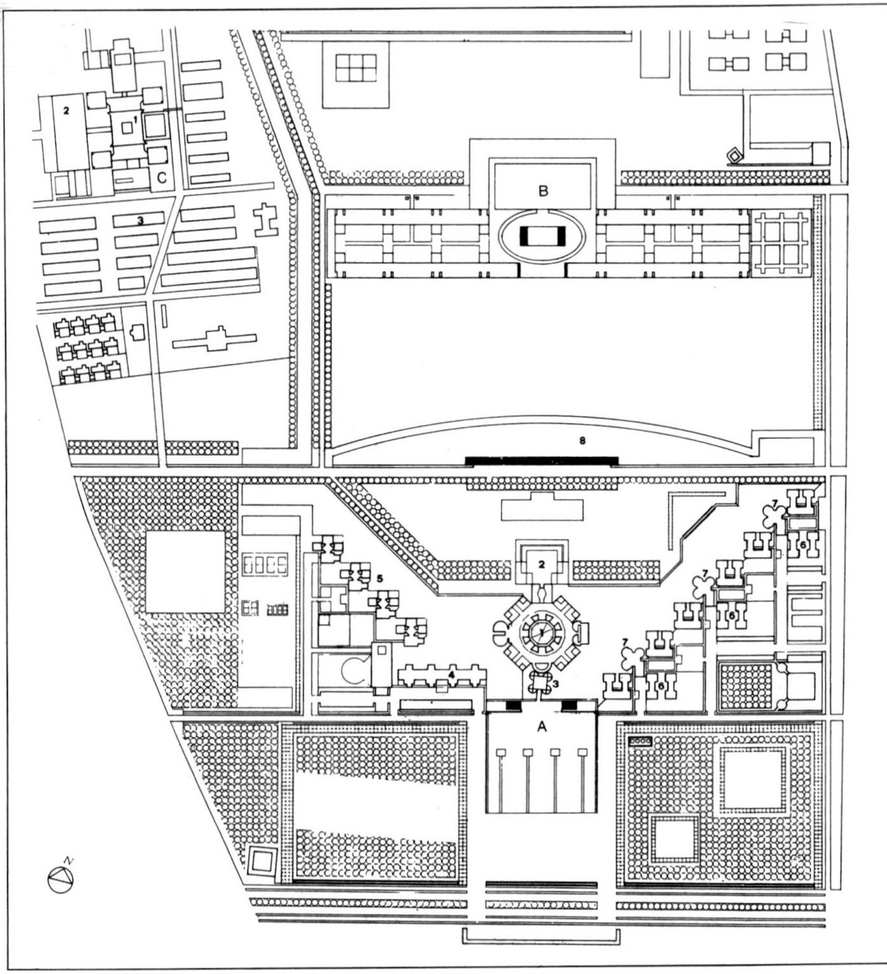

Master Plan, Sher-E-Bangla-Nagar

Of the Sher-E-Bangla Nagar (Capital Complex) Master Plan, Louis Kahn said: "I was given an extensive programme of buildings: the Assembly, the Supreme Court, hostels, schools, a stadium, the diplomatic enclave, the living sector, a market, all to be placed on a thousand acres of flat land subject to flood. ... the prevailing idea of the plan came from the realisation that assembly is of a transient nature. Men came to assemble to touch the spirit of community, ... thought that a mosque woven into the space fabric of the assembly would reflect this feeling.

The Supreme Court was the test of the acts of legislation against the philosophic view of the nature of man. The Assembly, Mosque and Supreme Court became inseparable in thinking of the transient nature of assembly.

My design at Dacca is inspired, actually, by the Baths of Caracalla (the great Roman public baths), but much extended. The residential spaces ... are an amphitheatre. This is residual space ... a court. Around it are gardens, and in the body of the building are interiors, and in the interiors are levels of gardens and places ... that honour of the knowledge of how you were made. All these are places of well-being and places for rest and places where one gets advice about how to live forever ... and so that is what inspired the design."

Plan

A. *Citadel of the assembly*
1. *Assembly building*
2. *Presidential square*
3. *Prayer hall*
4. *Hostels for ministers*
5. *Hostels for secretaries*
6. *Hostels for members of the assembly*
7. *Dining halls*
8. *Lake*

B. *Secretariat*

C. *Hospital complex*
1. *Hospital*
2. *Out-Patient department*
3. *Staff housing*

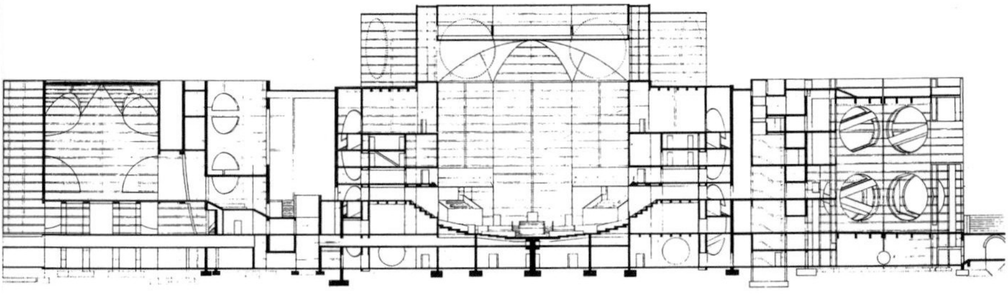

Section

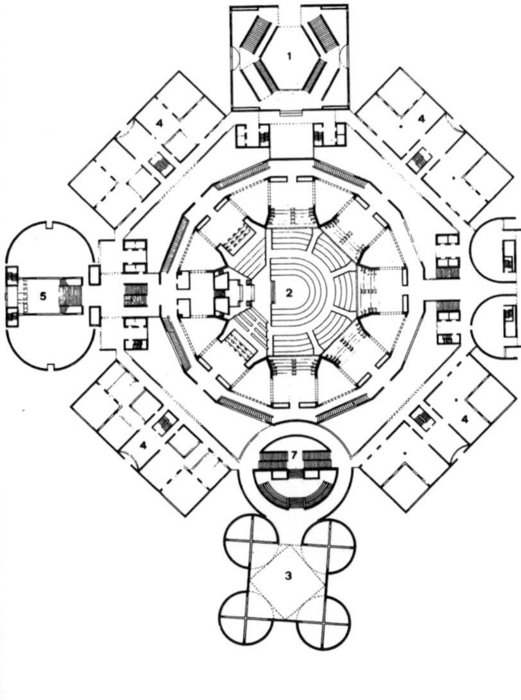

Plan

1. *Entrance hall*
2. *Assembly chamber*
3. *Prayer hall*
4. *Offices*
5. *Ministers' lounge*
6. *Dining and recreation*
7. *Ablution court*

Above: A great hall is the centre of the National Assembly Building. The roof structure has large openings which bring in natural light into the complex.
Overleaf: The strong sculptural structure creates a sequence of planes, the surfaces of which are concrete banded with marble.
Photograph: B. Taylor.

Above: Aerial view from the north, of the presidential plaza and National Assembly, flanked by ministers' housing (right) and legislators' housing (left) and the man-made reflecting lakes.
Right: Legislators' residences, with the circular dining/ lobby sections viewed from the north.
Photographs: A. Hossain

Above: Roof of the Assembly Hall viewed from below.
Above, right: Interior of the National Assembly Hall.
Right: Podium and focal wall of the Assembly. The hyperbolic roof meets the walls to create a recess which allows for indirect natural lighting.
Photographs: B. Taylor.

1963–2010

Polshek Partnership

Headquarters
New York, NY

Founding Partner
James S. Polshek

1963

2010

Polshek Partnership

James Stewart Polshek founded his practice in New York City in 1963. The firm modified its name numerous times as it grew and underwent changes in organization, and in 2010 Polshek Partnership's nine partners (Polshek himself having retired from the Partnership in 2005) created Ennead Architects LLP, reflecting "a gradual and continuous transition in leadership from the studio's identification with a single design leader to an alliance of partners."[1] Over the years, the office has developed a reputation as a quintessentially American firm, particularly respected for its expertise designing and executing cultural and institutional work in the United States. Nevertheless (and little-known to many familiar with the firm's work) Polshek's earliest significant opportunities to build came abroad.

In 1961 Dr. Gerald Oster—Polshek's first client, for whom he had recently designed two residences—introduced the young architect to the chairman of Teijin Ltd., a Japanese textile manufacturer. At this first meeting, Chairman Shinzo Ohya explained to Polshek his ambition to build the most advanced laboratory in Japan at the time, and then proceeded to ask Polshek if he would like to design the facility in question. As improbable as it may seem that a young architect with only six months' experience as a junior intern with I.M. Pei and a limited amount of residential and office interior design with Ulrich Franzen could undertake such a commission on his own, four months later Polshek was on his way to Japan.[2]

In 1962, after visiting the proposed site in Tokyo and beginning concept design, Polshek moved with his young family to Japan to undertake the design and construction of the Teijin Institute for Biomedical Research. Polshek had the full in-house architectural and engineering support of Kajima Corporation—the construction company hired for the project—which provided him with the resources of an established office. The research facility was completed in 1963, and a satisfied client offered Polshek a second commission for the Teijin Applied Textile Science Center, which was completed a year later halfway between Kyoto and Osaka.

Following this work, Polshek returned to New York City. While in his telling "the collaborative spirit behind Japanese design affected me for a lifetime,"[3] the impact of these two projects on his professional career in the United States was virtually nonexistent. As he stated, it was "back to designing kitchen renovations and apartments in New York."[4] The office would eventually execute a handful of additional projects abroad such as the United States Embassy in Muscat, Oman (1984–1991); the Government Office Building, Chambery-le-Haut, France (with Alain Salomon) (1991–1995); and the Cheil Building, Seoul, Korea (1995–1997). However, the overwhelming focus of Polshek/Ennead's sizeable output has—until recently—remained in the United States. That said, with the establishment in 2012 of "Ennead Architects International" which "expands the studio's geographical reach and formalizes our pursuit of opportunities to make significant architecture throughout the world,"[5] the 170-person office has, in a way, returned to its beginnings. — JR

① "Ennead History," http://ennead.com/#/history (last accessed October 25, 2015).

② James Stewart Polshek, *Build, Memory* (New York: Monacelli Press, 2014): 23.

③ Polshek: 35.

④ James Polshek in conversation with author (April 18, 2014).

⑤ "Ennead International," http://ennead.com/#/international (last accessed October 25, 2014).

Richard Meier & Partners
Architects LLP

1963–

Richard Meier & Partners Architects

Headquarters
New York, NY

Other Locations
Los Angeles, CA

Founding and Key Partners
Richard Meier (founding principal), Michael Palladino

Current Partners
Richard Meier, James R. Crawford, Bernhard Karpf, Vivian Lee, Reynolds Logan, Michael Palladino, Dukho Yeon

1963

Ezra Stoller, Esto

After receiving his undergraduate degree in architecture from Cornell University in 1957, Richard Meier, a native of Newark, New Jersey, moved to New York City, where his practice has continued to be based. There he interned briefly for Davis, Brody and Wisniewski and then at Skidmore, Owings & Merrill (SOM) before working for Marcel Breuer and Associates (MBA) from 1961 to 1963. He established his own firm in New York in 1963, and proceeded to build the reputation of the office through a series of high-end residential commissions in New York and the surrounding area.

As a professor at the Cooper Union after 1962, Meier was among the founding members of the Committee of Architects for the Study of the Environment (CASE), an academic working group that included various members of the East Coast architectural scene. Meier's Smith House, completed in 1967, and Saltzman House, completed in 1969, were among the projects included in a CASE conference and exhibition at the Museum of Modern Art (MoMA) in 1969 which were eventually collected in *Five Architects* (1972), the publication which labeled Meier and a diverse group of colleagues—Peter Eisenman, Michael Graves, Charles Gwathmey, and John Hejduk—as the "New York Five." Among the group, Meier's house projects perhaps most fully embodied the formalist neo-Corbusian mode which critics Colin Rowe and Kenneth Frampton, authors of the book's introductory essays, sought to identify in the work of the group as a whole.

Richard Meier's office continued to design a number of houses as well as commissions for a range of mid-sized institutional projects throughout the 1970s, including schools, a seminary, and offices for Olivetti. The firm's first international project, the Museum für Angewandte Kunst (Museum for the Decorative Arts) in Frankfurt am Main, Germany, was commissioned in 1979 and completed in 1985, the first of many international museum commissions the firm would produce in the following decades. This and other cultural commissions for the Athenaeum in Indiana and the High Museum in Atlanta (1983) shifted the overall scale and audience for Meier's works. So too did a series of high-profile research, technology, and office facilities for European corporations, including Siemens and Daimler-Benz in Germany. Yet even at these larger scales, Meier's techniques remained consistent: a play of platonic geometries and grids.

Meier won the Pritzker Prize in 1984, as the Frankfurt museum was being completed. These two events solidified his career as a prolific designer of cultural institutions, and commissions including the campus of the Getty Center (1984–1997) in Los Angeles, the contested City Hall and Library (1986–1995) in the Hague, Netherlands, and the Museum of Contemporary Art of Barcelona (1987–1995) soon followed, though all were only realized in the second half of the following decade. More recently, the office has completed a range of cultural commissions in Europe, including the Arp Museum (1989–2007) in Rolansdeck, Germany and the controversial Ara Pacis Museum (1995–2006) and the Jubilee Church (1996–2003), both in Rome. In the last ten years, Richard Meier & Partners Architects has become a truly global practice, with seven partners, a staff of 90 employees in offices in New York and Los Angeles, and projects in Europe, South America, and Asia. — WX & AS

1964–

Michael Graves & Associates

Headquarters
New York, NY

Founding Partner
Michael Graves

Current Partners
Michael Graves, Patrick Burker, Gary Lapera, Karen Nichols, Tom Rowe

1964

Michael Graves & Associates

Currently as much product designer as architect, Michael Graves first studied to be a painter before receiving his undergraduate architecture degree at the University of Cincinnati in 1958. After graduating from the Harvard University Graduate School of Design (GSD) in 1959, he received the Prix de Rome fellowship the following year to study in Rome. When he returned to the US in 1962, he began teaching at Princeton University, where he has remained for over 40 years. It was in Princeton that Graves established his architectural practice in 1964, and while Michael Graves & Associates also maintains an office in New York City, the New Jersey office continues to function as the firm's primary studio.

Like many architects of his generation, Graves began his practice with experimental unexecuted projects and competition entries. Graves was a member of the academic working group Conference of Architects for the Study of the Environment (CASE), and was among the participants in a CASE conference and exhibition at the Museum of Modern Art (MoMA) in 1969, including work by Graves, Peter Eisenman, Charles Gwathmey, John Hejduk, and Richard Meier, that eventually led to the publication of *Five Architects* (1972). Graves's first built projects, the Hanselmann House (1969), designed for two high school friends in Fort Wayne, Indiana, and the Benacerraf House (1969), in Princeton, New Jersey, were included in both the conference and the subsequent publication, marking a moment of continuity with his CASE colleagues prior to the postmodern turn that would mark his later work.

By the mid-1970s, Graves had moved away from the neo-modernist formal investigations that had characterized the grouping of the "New York Five," and his work featured increasingly mannered and playful historical references and juxtapositions. The Portlandia Building (1982), his first major public work, is often cited as the epitome of this genre of postmodernism, appearing on the cover of the fourth edition of Charles Jencks's *The Language of Post-Modern Architecture* (1984). The populist appeal of the firm's language garnered it commissions from a range of commercial clients, most notably the Walt Disney Company, with which Graves began a long relationship with the design of the Swan and Dolphin Hotels (1990) in Orlando, Florida. The relationship would continue at Euro Disney Resort, on the outskirts of Paris, where the firm's Hotel New York (1988–1992) was one among the fantasy environments modeled after historical US cities and towns. Graves had already begun his involvement with industrial design as well. His first project to appear abroad, in fact, was not a building but an object, the iconic Teakettle for Alessi, known as model 9093, designed in 1985. Over 1.4 million kettles have since been sold.

The first building Michael Graves & Associates completed abroad was the Nexus/Momochi housing block (1989) in Fukuoka, Japan. The project formed part of the larger urban development for the Asia-Pacific Exhibition in Fukuoka in 1989, led by Arata Isozaki, in which pairs of international architects were invited to develop residential blocks on adjacent sites; Graves was paired with Tigerman McCurry Architects. On the heels of this project, the firm's subsequent commissions in Japan included the Hyatt Hotel and Office Building (1990) and Momochi District Apartment Building (1993), both in Fukuoka, and the Tajima Office Building (1988–1993) in Tokyo. In the Momochi tower, the firm's expertise involved the development of a prefabricated clip-on façade system to remediate a partially finished apartment tower that had failed to sell sufficient numbers of units to support the project.

By the late 1980s, Michael Graves & Associates had expanded its practice to include furniture and a wide range of product designs, including shopping bags for Bloomingdale's. In the 1990s, Graves established Michael Graves Design (MGDG) as a product design, graphic design, and branding division of the office. In 1999, a collaboration with Target included the design of scores of household items, from brooms to bottle openers. Michael Graves & Associates currently has six principals and over 100 employees, and is designing projects in Europe, Asia, and the Middle East.
— WX & AS

Eisenman Architects

Headquarters
New York, NY

Founding Partner
Peter Eisenman

Current Partners
Peter Eisenman, Richard Rosson

1964

Eisenman Architects

Peter Eisenman's long career in academia and practice began at Cornell University, where he received his undergraduate degree in architecture in 1955. After working briefly for The Architects Collaborative (TAC) in Cambridge in the summer of 1959, an experience he later credited with his disillusionment from mainstream practice in these years, he completed his master's degree at Columbia University in 1960 and left the US to study at Cambridge University in England under Colin Rowe, whom he credited as a key critic and mentor for his work thereafter. His Ph.D. thesis at Cambridge, titled "The Formal Basis of Modern Architecture" (1963), announced the interest in the semiotic and philosophical investigation of architectural form that would mark his later career.[1]

When he returned to the United States in 1964, Eisenman continued his analysis of the formal basis of architectural language through drawings, writing, and building, manifested in the abstract series of houses that would establish his reputation. The first of these projects to be built, the Barenholtz House (1967) known as House I, and the Falk House (1969), known as House II, were famously included in *Five Architects* (1972), the publication through which the Museum of Modern Art (MoMA) promoted a diverse group of architects — Eisenman, Michael Graves, Charles Gwathmey, John Hejduk, and Richard Meier — as a formalist neo-avant garde, branded as the "New York Five."

The publication grew out of a 1969 meeting at MoMA of the Committee of Architects for the Study of the Environment, or CASE, an academic working group of which Eisenman was a founding member and primary instigator. Through a series of meetings and conferences at academic institutions along the East Coast after 1964, CASE included at various points among its key interlocutors Stanford Anderson (MIT), Henry Millon (MIT), Michael McKinnell (Columbia), Graves (Princeton), Hejduk (Cooper Union), Kenneth Frampton (Princeton), and Rowe.[2] The CASE conferences soon led Eisenman and fellow members of the group to establish the Institute for Architecture and Urban Studies (IAUS) in New York City in 1967. A non-profit, independent agency that operated between architectural practice and education, the IAUS launched two important journals, *Oppositions* and *October*, along with a series of exhibitions, lectures, and conferences that established New York City as a center of architectural theory and criticism after the 1970s.

By the time the Institute closed its doors in 1982, Peter Eisenman had already started his own full-time architectural practice, joining in 1980 with architect and planner Jacquelin Robertson to establish Eisenman Robertson in New York. The following year, the firm entered the international competition for the Internationale Bau-Ausstellung (IBA) social housing program in Berlin, directed by Josef Paul Kleihues. The office received Special First Prize and the project, known as the Checkpoint Charlie housing (1981–1985), constituted both the firm's first major built work and its first international project. In 1983, Eisenman Robertson won the competition to design the Wexner Center for the Visual Arts at The Ohio State University (1983–1989). By 1988, however, the firm had dissolved, and the project was completed under Eisenman's subsequent solo practice, Eisenman Architects.

Eisenman Architects has continued to compete for prominent commissions around the world over the last 25 years, working on over 40 international projects, though only a small fraction of these have been realized. The firm's projects abroad have included headquarters for the Koizumi Sangyo Corporation (1988–1990) and the Nunotani Corporation (1990–1992), both in Tokyo, and the Memorial to the Murdered Jews of Europe (1997–2005) in Berlin, originally in collaboration with the artist Richard Serra. Eisenman Architects' largest commission, for the City of Culture of Galicia in Santiago de Compostela, Spain, came as the result of an international competition in 1999. After numerous delays, the project was halted in 2013 after more than a decade of construction, with costs having nearly doubled relative to the original budget. Despite such large-scale international work, Eisenman Architects has remained a small to mid-size office, currently employing a staff of 25.
— WX & AS

① See Peter Eisenman, *The Formal Basis of Modern Architecture* (Ph.D. Dissertation, Cambridge, 1963), republished in 2008 (Zurich: Lars Müller).

② See Stanford Anderson, "CASE and MIT: Engagement," in Arindam Dutta, ed., *A Second Modernism: MIT, Architecture and the 'Techno-Social' Moment* (Cambridge, MA: MIT SA+P Press and MIT Press, 2013): 578–651.

1964–

Gwathmey Siegel Kaufman Architects

Headquarters
New York, NY

Founding and Key Partners
Charles Gwathmey, Robert Siegel
(founding principals), Gene Kaufman

Current Partners
Robert Siegel, Gene Kaufman

1964

AIA Journal, February 1982

After graduating from the School of Architecture at Yale University in 1962, Charles Gwathmey's first commission was a house for his parents on Long Island. Though the project was designed with Richard Henderson, Gwathmey's partner in practice at the time, the partnership dissolved shortly after the project was completed in 1966. Following a commission in 1968 to design a dormitory for the State University of New York at Purchase, Gwathmey invited Robert Siegel, an architect with experience in university projects, to form the partnership that became Gwathmey Siegel & Associates in the same year.

A series of residential commissions in the New York area established the firm's early reputation. Both the Gwathmey Studio and Residence (1966–1967) for Gwathmey's parents, in Amagansett, and Gwathmey Siegel & Associates's Bridgehampton Residences (1970), in Bridgehampton, were included in the meeting and exhibition at the Museum of Modern Art (MoMA) in 1969 by the Conference of Architects for the Study of the Environment (CASE), an academic working group, that was eventually published as *Five Architects* (1972). Presenting the firm's early work along with that of young practitioners Peter Eisenman, Michael Graves, John Hejduk, and Richard Meier, the publication marked a brief moment of overlap between the abstract, neo-vernacular language of Gwathmey's houses, clad in vertical cedar siding, and the diverse formal motivations of the other members of the so-called "New York Five."

Moving from residential to institutional work, Gwathmey Siegel & Associates had already received the commissioned in 1970 to renovate Princeton University's Whig Hall after it had been damaged by fire. The firm went on to to develop a series of high-profile institutional and cultural projects in the United States, including the extension and renovation of Frank Lloyd Wright's Solomon R. Guggenheim Museum in New York, a project that kept the office occupied for nearly a decade, from 1982 to 1992. The work of Gwathmey Siegel & Associates was marked thereafter by a balance between such commissions and a continued commitment to residential work, with Gwathmey as the lead architect for the majority of residential projects and Siegel as the partner responsible for larger institutional and commercial projects.

While the size and complexity of the firm's projects increased over time, the work of Gwathmey Siegel & Associates continued to remain largely based in the Northeastern United States in the 1970s and 1980s, in contrast to the other practices with which the firm had been grouped in Five Architects. The firm's first project abroad was a golf clubhouse for the Euro Disney Resort (1988–1992), on the outskirts of Paris. Gwathmey Siegel & Associates went on to design large-scale projects abroad including a 2.5 million square foot, $300 million dollar campus for Nanyang Polytechnic University (1993–1999) in Singapore.

Following Charles Gwathmey's death in August 2009, architect Gene Kaufman joined Siegel as a partner, and the office continued under the name Gwathmey Siegel Kaufman Architects. The firm's recent projects have included a Miesian condominium near Union Square in New York in 2006 and an addition and renovation to Paul Rudolph's iconic Yale Art and Architecture Building, completed in 2011. — WX & AS

Bohlin Cywinski Jackson

Locations
Wilkes-Barre, PA; Pittsburg, PA; Philadelphia, PA; Seattle, WA; San Francisco, CA

Founding and Key Partners
Peter Q. Bohlin, Richard Powell (founding principals), Bernard Cywinski, John Larkin, Jon C. Jackson

Current Partners
Peter Q. Bohlin, Jon C. Jackson, Frank Grauman, Cornelius J. Reid III, Karl A. Backus, Greggory L. Mottola, Roxanne Sherbeck, Robert E. Miller, Raymond S. Calabro, Steven D. Chaitow, David Murray

1965

Nic Lehoux

Peter Bohlin and Dick Powell first opened an office in Wilkes-Barre, Pennsylvania in 1965 when they received a commission to build a home for Bohlin's parents. The office garnered local recognition for a series of residences throughout Pennsylvania before receiving its first large commission, the Ten East South Street Apartments, in 1973. In 1975, architecture critic Paul Goldberger featured a second home that the office designed for Bohlin's parents in the *New York Times*.[1] The house remains one of the most significant projects that the office developed, and it helped define the firm as one of the leading residential practices in the country. In 1980, the office joined with Larkin Cywinski to form the partnership of Bohlin, Powell, Larkin & Cywinski. Although the office continued to work on single-family homes during the 1980s, it increasingly won commissions for commercial and institutional projects.

In 1991, the office was once again restructured, as both Dick Powell and John Larkin left and Jon Jackson was made a principal. The new firm was named Bohlin Cywinski Jackson. The office continued to expand during the 1990s, opening offices in Pittsburgh and Philadelphia first and later in Seattle and San Francisco. Major projects during this time include the Center for Biotechnology and Bioengineering at the University of Pittsburgh, the Science and Mathematics Building at St. Mary's College in Maryland, and the Pennsylvania Higher Education Assistance Agency.

In 1999, Bohlin Cywinski Jackson was awarded the commission for the Pixar Headquarters in Emeryville, California by Steve Jobs, then the company's CEO. The successful completion of the campus led to a close relationship with Jobs, who once again retained the firm as Apple looked to design its flagship stores. In 2004, Apple opened its first retail store in SoHo New York, which was soon followed in 2008 with the now-famous glass cube design at the corner of 59th Street and 5th Avenue in New York. The projects would cement the partnership between Apple and Bohlin Cywinski Jackson. Since those first projects, the office has completed eighteen stores for Apple, nine of which are overseas. They represent, along with the recent Uniqlo flagship store in Shanghai (2010), the only projects that the firm has completed abroad.

The office has continued to design houses and small residential buildings, but now receives most of its business from commercial, retail, and institutional projects. Most recently, the office has finished work on the Apple Store in Palo Alto (2013), the Marquez Hall at the Colorado School of Mines (2012), and Apple stores in Pudong, Shanghai (2010), Aix-en-Provence, France, Omotesando, Tokyo, and Puerta Del Sol, Madrid (2014). — JJ

① Paul Goldberger, "At once a rugged cabin and a glass box," *The New York Times Magazine* (September 26, 1976): 23, 68–69.

Gensler

Headquarters
San Francisco, CA

Other Locations
Atlanta, GA; Austin, TX; Baltimore, MD; Boston, MA; Charlotte, NC; Chicago, IL; Dallas, TX; Denver, CO; Detroit, MI; Houston, TX; Lacrosse, WI; Las Vegas, NV; Los Angeles, CA; Miami, FL; Minneapolis, MN; Morristown, NJ; New York, NY; Newport Beach, CA; Phoenix, AZ; Philadelphia, PA; Raleigh, NC; San Diego, CA; San Jose, CA; San Ramon, CA; Tampa, FL; Washington, DC; San Jose, Costa Rica; Sao Paulo, Brazil; Toronto, Canada; Mexico City, Mexico; Bangalore, India; Bangkok, Thailand; Beijing, China; Honk Kong; Seoul, South Korea; Shanghai, China; Singapore; Syndey, Australia; Tokyo, Japan; London, UK; Abu Dhabi, UAE; Dubai, UAE; Doha, Qatar

Founding Partners
Art Gensler, Drue Gensler, Jim Follett

Gensler

M. Arthur Gensler founded his three-person San Francisco practice in 1965. Nearly fifty years later, Gensler—with 3,500 current employees distributed across forty-three offices in fourteen countries—consistently ranks at or near the top of "World's Largest" lists of architecture firms. The remarkably successful organization that "Art" and his partners have built, and which continues to grow, benefitted from a combination of luck, entrepreneurial spirit, and good business sense, representing a case-study in the defining characteristics of large-scale, international American architectural practice.

The firm's first project consisted of interiors work at the SOM-designed Alcoa Building in San Francisco, and interior architecture would remain a primary focus at Gensler for many years. The office's first building commissions, including a 60,000 square-foot project for MasterCard, followed soon after. Luckily for Gensler, two of the firm's earliest interiors projects involved local businesses that became enterprises with national and international reach—first for the tenants of the Bank of America Headquarters and next for a new denim store which became The Gap. In Art Gensler's telling, Cushman & Wakefield—the real estate broker for the Bank of America Headquarters—commissioned Gensler to do the First National Bank of Denver and the Houston headquarters for Pennzoil. Eventually, the Mobil Oil Company leaders familiar with Gensler's work for Pennzoil in Houston invited the firm to New York. New York-based Goldman Sachs then commissioned Gensler for a new Headquarters. In 1988, Goldman Sachs commissioned Gensler to take on work in London.[1] Gensler had gone international.

The firm has always prided itself on its responsiveness to client requirements. If a "Gensler style" is difficult to define, it is not unintentional. A principle that has guided the firm's client relations since the beginning is the so-called "rubber band theory," in which the goal is to remain flexible and cautious with regard to how far one pushes a client outside their comfort zone. Not surprisingly, Gensler has maintained over the years a consistently high level of client satisfaction, demonstrated by repeat commissions.

In 1991 Jun Xia, a young and talented Chinese-born architect, joined Gensler's Denver office. After a trip to Shanghai in 1998, he convinced Gensler's leadership that it was time to establish a presence in China. Xia went on to become the design director of Gensler's Shanghai office, which is now completing China's tallest building, the Shanghai Tower. Having learned from this example, Gensler is actively recruiting intern architects from countries such as Brazil, Argentina, India, China, and the Middle East in the expectation that future opportunities abroad will likewise emerge from a broadly-connected workforce (and if judging by precedent, a degree of luck).[2] Despite its extraordinary growth, in many ways, what Art Gensler said when reflecting on the early days of the firm remains true to this day:

[O]ur new offices were really just an extension of the family—never a separate, competing organization...I was very lucky to find some terrific young people who were willing to move and travel much more than today. In those days if I said, "Let's go," you would jump on the plane and do it. There were no contracts. Maybe we were young and naïve, but we were all trying to build something and have fun. All we did was respond to client demand rather than push into a community. By and large that has been the basis for every office that we have.[3]

—JR

① "Interview with Gensler," *Perspecta* 40: (August 2008): 186–193.

② "The Secrets of the Talent Scounts," *The New York Times* (March 14, 2009).

③ "Interview with Gensler."

Hartman-Cox Architects

Headquarters
Washington D.C.

Founding Partners
George Hartman, Warren Cox

Current Partners
T. Lee Becker, D. Graham Davidson,
Mary Catherine Lanzillotta

1965

Hartman-Cox Architects

KRJDA
KEVIN ROCHE JOHN DINKELOO AND ASSOCIATES LLC

1966–

Kevin Roche John Dinkeloo and Associates

Headquarters
Hamden, CT

Successor Firm To
Eero Saarinen and Associates (1941–1961)

Founding and Key Partners
Kevin Roche, John Dinkeloo (founding principals), Joe Lacy

Current Partners
Kevin Roche, John Dinkeloo, Philip Kinsella, James Owens, Christiaan Dinkeloo, Steuart Gray, Jon Carr, Garry Leonard, Wesley Kavanagh

1966

Kevin Roche John Dinkeloo and Associates

1966–

Studio Hillier

Headquarters
Princeton, NJ

Founding Partner
J. Robert Hillier

Current Partners
Barbara A. Hillier, J. Robert Hillier

1966

Taylor Photographics

BTA Architects

Headquarters
Boston, MA

Founding and Key Partners
Benjamin Thompson (founding principal), Jane McCullough Thompson, Thomas Green, MacGregor Freeman, Henry Haff

Current Partners
Philip Norton Loheed, MacGregor Freeman, Dennis C. Rieske

PROCESS:Architecture, June 1990

Antoine Predock Architect PC

Headquarters
Albuquerque, NM

Other Locations
Beijing, China; Taipei, Taiwan;
Los Angeles, CA

Founding Partner
Antoine Predock

1967

Architecture & Urbanism, November 1988. Photographer: Roberi Reck

1967–

Center for Environmental Structure

Headquarters
Berkeley, CA

Other Locations
West Sussex, England

Founding Partner
Christopher Alexander

Current Partners
Christopher Alexander, Artemis Anninou, Hajo Neis

1967

Center for Environmental Structure

JAHN

1967–

JAHN

Headquarters
Chicago, IL

Other Locations
Berlin, Germany; Doha, Qatar;
Shanghai, China

Founding Partner
Helmut Jahn

Current Partners
Helmut Jahn, Francisco Gonzalez-Pulido,
Phillip Castillo, Steve Cook,
Arthur Herbstman

1967

JAHN

German émigré Helmut Jahn went to work as an assistant for architect Gene Summers in Chicago in 1967, shortly after graduating from the Illinois Institute of Technology. Summers, known as Ludwig Mies's van der Rohe's right-hand man in The Office of Mies van der Rohe, had recently left to open his own office. Shortly after Jahn's hiring, Charles F. Murphy invited Summers to join his firm to design a major commission for McCormick Place II (1968) in downtown Chicago. Jahn followed Summers and began a rapid trajectory upward through the firm. Murphy had himself begun his career at D. H. Burnham & Company in 1911 as a private secretary while moonlighting in architecture school, remaining briefly with Burnham's successor firm, Graham, Anderson, Probst & White, before striking out with two other young architects in 1937 as Shaw, Naess & Murphy. Named C. F. Murphy Associates by the time of Jahn's arrival, in the 1960s the firm was one of Chicago's largest, known unofficially as the in-house architect for the City of Chicago and employing up to 450 people at its peak, with subsidiaries in engineering and interiors.

Following the departure of Gene Summers, Jahn became vice president and director of planning and design at C. F. Murphy Associates, marking a shift in the office's work from its Miesian roots to a broader, more technological, and occasionally more colorful palette of architectural elements. By 1981, Jahn was president of the firm, now known as Murphy/Jahn. The following year he became CEO after purchasing 51% of the office's stock, leaving him the unquestioned owner of the company. In 2005, the firm became known simply as JAHN.

Today, JAHN has broadened its work from Chicago to overseas, with a particular focus on office towers and airports. The firm has become known for its expertise in designing technologically sophisticated curtain wall systems. Though the office no longer employs engineers in-house, it is still known for "archi-engineering," a term the firm uses to describe its brand of technically driven design. JAHN maintains an office win Germany with up to 15 staff members to oversee local projects. Helmut Jahn continues to lead the concept design stage of all projects and speaks strongly about maintaining an office culture in which hand drawings precede computer-aided documentation. The office culture is known to be fast-paced and require long hours of its employees, reflecting the work ethic of its guru-type leader.
—AL

GP GOETTSCH PARTNERS

1969–

Goettsch Partners

Headquarters
Chicago, IL

Successor Firm To
The Office of Mies van der Rohe (1938–1969)

Founding and Key Partners
Joseph Y. Fujikawa, Bruno Conterato, Dirk Lohan (founding principals), Joseph Caprile, James Goettsch

Current Partners
James Goettsch, James Zheng, Steven N. Nilles, Michael F. Kaufman, Joseph Dolinar, Lawrence C. Weldon

1969

Goettsch Partners

In 1969, The Office of Mies van der Rohe in Chicago closed upon the death of its founder. A successor firm was established by three senior members of the office, Joseph Fujikawa, Bruce Conterato, and Dirk Lohan—Mies's grandson, who had himself emigrated from Germany in 1957 before going to work for his grandfather in 1962. Conceiving of themselves within the legacy of Mies's practice, Fujikawa, Conterato, Lohan & Associates continued until 1982, when Fujikawa left the office and Conterato retired. Lohan continued practicing as Lohan Associates through 2002. Following a brief two-year partnership as Lohan Caprile Goettsch, in 2005 the office became Goettsch Partners, led by James Goettsch, who had previously been an executive vice-president at a competing Chicago firm, Murphy/Jahn (today JAHN).

The lineage of partnerships that led to Goettsch Partners reflects the changing styles and structures of professional practice in Chicago after Word War II, from the so-called "Second Chicago school" under Mies's guiding example to the work of his legatees. In the 1970s and 1980s, the firm focused on large corporate campuses in the United States for clients including McDonald's, Frito Lay, and TRW. The office's more recent projects reflect the continued demand in Chicago for firms with expertise in tall towers, including the headquarters of Blue Cross Blue Shield and a landmark tower at 111 South Wacker (2005).

In 1999, Goettsch Partners began working in Asia with their design of the Suzhou International Tower. According to the firm, sixty-five percent of their current work is in Asia, versus twenty percent in the US and ten percent in the Middle East. The turn to East Asia in particular over the past decade is one that has been shared by other large Chicago offices. The focus on Chinese projects has been reflected in the promotion of James Zheng, previously Director of International Projects, to President of the firm in 2013. Goettsch Partners also operates offices in Shanghai and Abu Dhabi, totaling around 90 employees, including groups for both interiors and architectural design. The office's architectural services exceed $22 million annually, positioning Goettsch Partners as the 127th largest in the world by revenue. Occupying the top two floors of the historic Santa Fe building in Chicago, the office of Goettsch Partners today overlooks a city built in part by a complex genealogy of architectural offices, of which it is one of the key inheritors. —AL

RAMSA
ROBERT A.M. STERN ARCHITECTS

1969–

Robert A.M. Stern Architects

Headquarters
New York, NY

Founding Partner
Robert A.M. Stern

Current Partners
Robert A.M. Stern, Augusta Barone, Gary L. Brewer, Randy M. Correll, Melissa DelVecchio, Sargent C. Gardiner, Preston J. Gumberich, Michael D. Jones, Alexander P. Lamis, Daniel Lobitz, Grant F. Marani, Meghan L. McDermott, Roger H. Seifter, Kevin M. Smith, Paul L. Whalen, Graham S. Wyatt

1969

Maris/Semel

Robert A. M. Stern graduated from the School of Architecture at Yale University in 1965, where he made an early name for himself as much for his scholarly and editorial interests as for his design acumen. While at Yale, Stern edited the influential volume 9/10 of *Perspecta*, the Yale architectural journal, notable for reflecting the interests of a new generation of architects and critics, centered at Yale, in architectural history and popular culture beyond the confines of the modernism of the time. Among the contributors to the volume were Charles Moore, Louis I. Kahn, Philip Johnson, Henry-Russell Hitchcock, Vincent Scully, and Robert Venturi, including the first publication of excerpts from Venturi's forthcoming book, *Complexity and Contradiction in Architecture* (1966).

In 1966, Stern briefly joined the office established by Richard Meier in New York five years earlier. By the following year, Stern had already completed his first solo project, the Wiseman House in Montauk, New York. In 1969, Stern and a former classmate, John Hagmann, established the office of Stern and Hagmann in New York. The two worked primarily on residential projects in the New York area, including renovations to prewar apartments in the city and houses in the surrounding region. The firm was no doubt aided by the connections of Lynn Stern, Robert's wife: her father was the president of the Whitney Museum of American Art and her mother was a member of the Gimbel's department store family.

Stern left Hagmann and established Robert A.M. Stern Architects (RAMSA) in 1977. By the 1980s, the firm had added considerably to its steady resume of residential projects with larger institutional commissions, such as the Ohrstrom Library for St. Paul's School in New Hampshire. Even as the firm expanded, its work remained firmly rooted in the New York and New England regions.

In 1987, RAMSA was invited to design an expansion to the Mexx International Headquarters in Voorschoten, the Netherlands. The firm's reputation for preservation and the reinterpretation of historical vernacular styles gained them the commission, which called for the addition an annex to an original structure from 1858. The office expanded rapidly in the following years from predominantly regional work to international projects. Within five years of completing the Mexx headquarters, RAMSA had designed the US Embassy in Budapest and two large projects for the Euro Disney Resort (1988–1992) near Paris, the Cheyenne Hotel and the Newport Bay Club.

The firm's work for the Walt Disney Company has since been followed by other international commissions based on the recreation of US leisure and retail environments abroad, including the Diagonal Mar Entertainment and Retail Center (2001) in Barcelona, Spain, and numerous completed and ongoing commissions in China. Some of these projects explicitly invoke canonical New York buildings and urban spaces, such as the Dalian AVIC International Square in China, a development of four city blocks whose architecture and site strategy directly reference New York's Rockefeller Center. The RAMSA office on 34th Street is currently run by sixteen partners, with a staff of over 300 employees, and has projects in Europe, Asia, and South America. — WX & AS

S | I | T | E

1969–

SITE

Headquarters
Philadelphia, PA

Founding Partner
James Wines

Current Partners
James Wines, Denise McLee, Sara Stracey

1969

SITE

SITE was founded in 1969 by James Wines, a sculptor by training, with Alison Sky, Emilio Sousa, and Michelle Stone as original partners. Influenced by the political, cultural, and social upheaval of the late 1960s, SITE advocated for the erasure of conventional distinctions between landscape, environmental art, and built spaces.

Much of SITE's work constituted a critique of late modernist architecture and particularly its treatment of public space, rejecting it as prescriptive and formulaic. Instead, SITE proposed a more inclusive set of references and a seamless integration of landscape, art, and architecture. Their work in this period included a series of iconic designs for the BEST Products Company around the United States between 1971 and 1984. One of the largest mail order companies at the time, BEST commissioned SITE to design twelve showrooms for the company's merchandise. SITE's response was to design each showroom as one in a series of semiotic exercises that played on the generic box-like quality of the type, alternately peeling, tilting, eroding, and cracking the facades of the different buildings to reveal the envelope as a thin applique. The recognition from these projects provided a stable set of commissions that allowed the firm to pursue more speculative work like the 1977 Ghost Parking Lot in Hamden, Connecticut, in which twenty automobiles were buried underneath a layer of asphalt in an existing parking lot to create an artwork inseparable from its environment.

From the 1970s to early 1980s, SITE was recognized for such acts of building as a form of architectural critique. The group participated in the Venice Biennale in 1975 and held their first retrospective in the same year. At the same time, SITE continued to propose projects that inverted an accepted understanding of residential or commercial spaces. The High-Rise of Homes, published in 1982, proposed single-family homes within a Corbusian concrete and steel high-rise structure; the Floating McDonald's, built in Berwyn, Illinois in 1983, suspended a typical McDonald's drive-through above the ground.

In the early 1980s, SITE changed its name to SITE, Environmental Design. This shift in focus to environmental concerns was followed by an increasing number of public projects. Highway 86 Processional, a competition-winning entry for the Vancouver World Expo in 1986, reimagined the traditional Expo pavilion as an undulating exterior plaza, 700 feet long and 30 feet wide, extending from the ocean under a highway and over a viaduct. The project's success led to a series of commissions for large public spaces for world expositions, including the Four Continents Bridge, designed for the Hiroshima Sea and Island Expo in 1989, and Avenue Number Five for the Seville World Expo in 1992.

More recently, SITE's environmental interests have evolved into an increasing focus on green design. Their most recent international project, the Fondazione Pietro Rossini Pavilion, a visitor's center for a sculpture park, is literally encrusted in a heavy green roof. In the firm's own words, "SITE believes that buildings and public spaces should move beyond Industrial Age Traditions — inclusive of their conceptual, functional and aesthetic origins — in order to respond more effectively to the Twenty-first Century Age of Information and Ecology."[1] — WX & AS

① "SITE History, Profile," http://sitenewyork.com/frame/index.htm (last accessed, October 25, 2014).

1972–

Morphosis Architects

Headquarters
Los Angeles, CA

Other Locations
New York, NY, Shanghai, China

Founding and Key Partners
Thom Mayne, Livio Santini, Jim Stafford, Michael Brickler (founding principals), Michael Rotondi

Current Partners
Thom Mayne (design director), Brandon Welling, Arne Emerson, Ung-Joo Scott Lee, Eui-sung Yi (principals)

1972

Iwan Baan

Founded in 1972, Morphosis Architects has evolved into an international practice led by Pritzker Prize laureate Thom Mayne, with offices in Culver City and New York and large-scale commissions in the US and abroad. However, much of the popular and architectural press on Morphosis highlights both "then" and "now" at the firm, returning to the firm's roots in the radical Los Angeles architectural scene of the 1970s.

Emerging from the collaborative practice of Mayne, Livio Santini, James Stafford, and Michael Brickler in 1972, the early days of Morphosis have been compared to the jam sessions of a garage band. "We mowed lawns to stay alive," says Michael Rotondi, who joined the partners in 1975.[1] The group also co-founded the Southern California Institute of Architecture (SCI-Arc) in 1972, the architects themselves fresh out of their undergraduate studies. The early days were raucous and idealistic, poignantly described by Mayne as an "extended childhood."[2] Marked by growing up as a member of the "Vietnam generation" against the backdrop of the civil rights movement, in his early practice Mayne was uncompromising about construction quality and adherence to the firm's ideas, literally taking a jackhammer to a poorly installed concrete wall.[3]

Despite the firm's early, unorthodox manner, Morphosis quickly gained recognition for their built projects in the Los Angeles area, including the 2-4-6-8 House (1976) and Venice III (1986). By the late 1980s, the firm seemed poised to cross into larger projects, and Morphosis was described as "in the process of designing mega-projects in America and abroad."[4] Instead, the firm suffered both a split between Thom Mayne and Michael Rotondi, with Mayne retaining leadership of the office, and the economic crash of the 1990s, which left Mayne an estimated half a million dollars in debt. The loss of Rotondi, who had served as the firm's public face and interacted closely with clients, required Mayne learn to do the work of his former partner. "I realized within six months," Mayne said, "that I had no one to lean on."[5]

Despite these setbacks, Morphosis rebuilt and grew again after the late 1990s. Beginning with the design in 1999 of the Wayne Lyman Morse United States Courthouse in Eugene, Oregon, Morphosis received a series of large governmental commissions, including the San Francisco Federal Building (2000) and the NOAA Satellite Operation Facility (2001) in New Orleans. Thom Mayne earned the Pritzker in 2005, officially leaving behind his reputation as a "bad boy" of architecture. Morphosis began to turn its gaze beyond California, opening a New York office in 2007 and undertaking a series of large-scale international projects, including the Giant Interactive Group Headquarters (2005–2011) in Shanghai and the Phare Tower (2006–) at La Defense, France.

In recent projects, Morphosis Architects has engaged the discussion of sustainability in architecture, beginning with the "living skin" façade of the San Francisco Federal Building, while research by Mayne and the office has explored the idea of "combinatory urbanism" as a response to increasingly large and complex projects.[6] Critic Jeffrey Kipnis has suggested that the firm's current production has managed to retain "the vigor of the early work," while growing "bolder, less fussy, conceptually more adroit."[7] — AL

①
Arthur Lubow, "How Did He Become the Government's Favorite Architect?," *The New York Times* (January 16, 2005): 3.

②
"Thom Mayne Interviewed by Jeffrey Inaba," *Volume* 13 (2007): 112.

③
Ann Gray, "The Mayne Idea," *Form Inspiration* (2011): 31.

④
Nayana Currimbhoy, "The Making of Mega-Morphosis." *Interiors* (October 1989): 99.

⑤
"Thom Mayne Interviewed by Jeffrey Inaba": 113.

⑥
Thom Mayne, *Combinatory Urbanism: A Realignment of Complex Behavior and Collective Form* (Culver City, CA: Stray Dog Cafe, 2011).

⑦
Jeffrey Kipnis, "A Question of Qualities," in *A Question of Qualities: Essays in Architecture* (Cambridge, MA: MIT Press, 2013): 1.

US Embassy
1963

Architect
Welton Becket and Associates

Location
Warsaw, Poland

Client
US Department of State,
Foreign Buildings Operations

ELLERBE BECKET

Teijin Applied Textile Science Center
1963–1964

Architect
James Stewart Polshek Architect

Associate Architect
Ohbayashi-Gumi Construction
Company Design Department

Location
Osaka, Japan

Client
Teijin Limited

National School of Agriculture
1963–1967

Architect
Perkins + Will

Location
Chapingo, Mexico

Client
National College of Agriculture

PERKINS+WILL

Toronto-Dominion Centre
1963–1970

Architect
The Office of Mies van der Rohe

Location
Toronto, Canada

Client
Cadillac Fairview Corporation
and Toronto-Dominion Bank

University of Guelph Long Range Development Plan and Buildings
1964

Architect
Sert, Jackson and Associates

Location
Ontario, Canada

Client
University of Guelph

SERT, JACKSON AND ASSOCIATES
ARCHITECTS CAMBRIDGE MASSACHUSETTS

Westmount Square
1964–1968

Architect
The Office of Mies van der Rohe

Location
Montreal, Canada

Client
Ron Bacardi Company

Carlton Centre
1964–1973

Architect
Skidmore, Owings & Merrill

Location
Johannesburg, South Africa

Client
Carlton Centre

King Fahd University of Petroleum and Minerals
1964–1982

Architect
CRS Inc.

Location
Dhahran, Saudi Arabia

Client
King Fahd University of Petroleum and Minerals

USAID and United Nations Building
1965

Architect
Leo A Daly

Location
Islamabad, Pakistan

Client
United States Agency for International Development, United Nations

USAID General Services Building
1965

Architect
Leo A Daly

Location
New Dehli, India

Client
United States Agency for International Development

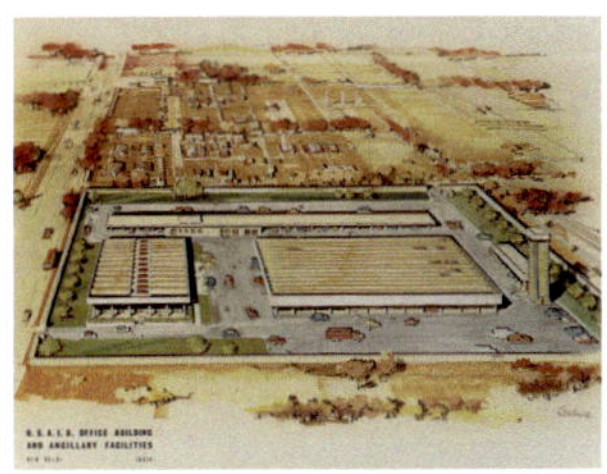

Heinz Headquarters
1965

Architect
Skidmore, Owings & Merrill

Location
Hillingdon, England

Client
Heinz Corporation

Jeddah International Airport
1965

Architect
Edward Durell Stone and Associates

Location
Jeddah, Saudi Arabia

Pakistan Institute of Nuclear Science and Technology
1965

Architect
Edward Durell Stone and Associates

Location
Islamabad, Pakistan

Client
Pakistan Atomic Energy Commission

Ford Foundation Headquarters
1965–1968

Architect
Joseph Allen Stein and Associates

Location
New Delhi, India

Client
Ford Foundation

Master Plan of Tehran
1965–1969

Architect
Victor Gruen International

Location
Tehran, Iran

Client
The Plan and Budget Organization of Iran

Kuwait Fund for Arab Economic Development
1965–1971

Architect
The Architects Collaborative

Consultant
Pace

Location
Kuwait City, Kuwait

Client
Kuwait Fund for Arab Economic Development

US Embassy
1965–1977

Architect
Robert P. Madison International

Location
Dakar, Senegal

Client
US Department of State, Foreign Buildings Operations

Pakistan Presidential Palace
1966

Architect
Edward Durell Stone and Associates

Location
Islamabad, Pakistan

Client
Goverment of Pakistan

Cummins Engine Company Component Plant
1966

Architect
Kevin Roche John Dinkeloo and Associates

Location
Darlington, England

Client
Cummins Engine Company

Master Plan for East Pakistan Agricultural University
1966

Architect
Paul Rudolph

Location
Mymensingh, East Pakistan

Client
East Pakistan Agricultural University

US Pavilion, Canadian World Exhibition
1967

Project Lead
Jack Masey, USIA

Design
Fuller & Sadao Inc./Geometrics Inc. (architecture); Cambridge Seven Associates (exhibits)

Location
Montreal, Canada

Carmel de la Paix Convent
1967

Architect
Sert, Jackson and Associates

Location
Mazille, France

Client
Centre de Culture Catholique

Ecole des Beaux-Arts et des Arts Appliquées
1967

Architect
Sert, Jackson and Associates

Location
Besançon, France

Client
Ecole des Beaux-Arts et des Arts Appliquées

University of Islamabad
1967

Architect
Edward Durell Stone and Associates

Location
Islamabad, Pakistan

Client
University of Islamabad

Canadian Imperial Bank of Commerce
1967–1973

Architect
I. M. Pei & Partners

Associate Architect
Page and Steele, Architects

Location
Toronto, Canada

Client
Canadian Imperial Bank of Commerce

PEI COBB FREED & PARTNERS Architects LLP

Bielefeld Kunsthalle
1968

Architect
Johnson/Burgee Architects

Location
Bielefeld, Germany

Client
Kunsthalle Bielefeld

PJAR

Manila Hilton Hotel
1968

Architect
Welton Becket

Local Architect
C. D. Arguelles

Location
Manila, Philippines

Client
Hilton Hotels Corporation

ELLERBE BECKET

Boots Pure Drug Company Headquarters
1968

Architect
Skidmore, Owings & Merrill

Location
Nottingham, England

Client
Boots Pure Drug Company

SOM

Cap 3000 Shopping Center
1968–1970

Architect
Victor Gruen International

Local Architect
Antoine Dory

Location
Saint Laurent du Var, France

Client
Societe Francaise des Nouvelles Galeries

VICTOR GRUEN INTERNATIONAL

Louvain la Neuve Master Plan
1968–1971

Architect
Victor Gruen International

Location
Ottigines, Belgium

Client
University of Leuven

VICTOR GRUEN INTERNATIONAL

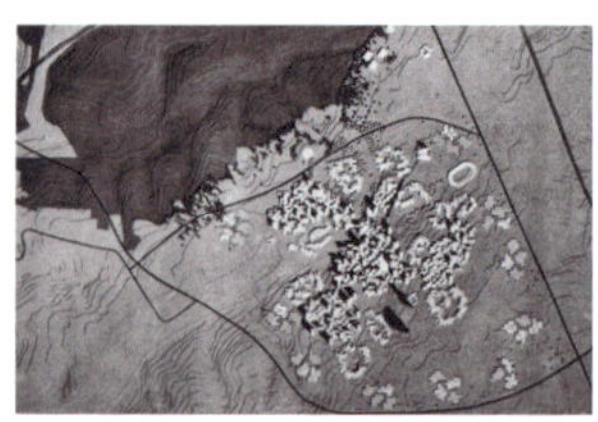

Baldegg Convent
1968–1972

Architect
Marcel Breuer Associates, Carlos Coire, Eduardo Catalano

Location
Baldegg, Switzerland

Client
Baldegg Convent

MBA

Wolfson Center for Mechanical and Transportation Engineering
1968–1974

Architect
Louis I. Kahn

Location
Tel Aviv, Israel

Client
Tel Aviv University

Fundació Joan Miró
1968–1975

Architect
Sert, Jackson and Associates

Location
Barcelona, Spain

Client
Fundació Joan Miró

SERT, JACKSON AND ASSOCIATES
ARCHITECTS CAMBRIDGE MASSACHUSETTS

Costa Smeralda Resort Master Plan
1968–1978

Architect
Sasaki, Dawson, DeMay Associates

Location
Sardinia, Italy

Client
His Highness the Aga Khan

SASAKI

US Embassy
1968–1985

Architect
Skidmore, Owings & Merrill

Location
Moscow, Russia

Client
US Department of State, Foreign Buildings Operations

SOM

Chase Manhattan Bank
1969

Architect
Skidmore, Owings & Merrill

Location
San Juan, Puerto Rico

Client
Chase Manhattan Bank, N.A.

SOM

Pacific Centre
1969–1973

VICTOR GRUEN INTERNATIONAL

Architect
Gruen Associates, Inc.

Local Architect
McCarter, Nairne & Partners

Location
Vancouver, Canada

PREVI Lima Proyecto Experimental de Vivienda
1969–1980

Architect
Center for Environmental Structure

Location
Lima, Peru

Client
The Peruvian Government and the United Nations Development Programme (UNDP). Invited by Peter Land

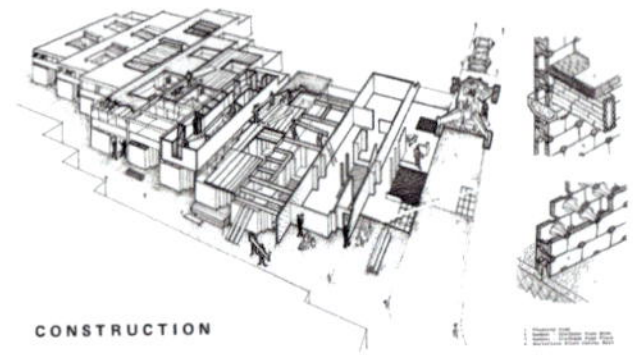

US Pavilion, Japan World Exposition
1970

United States Information Agency

Project Lead
Jack Masey, USIA

Design
Davis Brody Inc., Alan Schwartzman, David Geiger (architecture); Chermayeff & Geismar, Rudolph deHarak (exhibits)

Location
Osaka, Japan

US Embassy
1970

Architect
Eduardo Catalano

Location
Buenos Aires, Argentina

Client
US Department of State, Foreign Buildings Operations

Rosenthal Glass Factory
1970

TAC

Architect
The Architects Collaborative

Location
Amberg, Germany

Client
Rosenthal GmbH

Family Planning Center and Maternal Health Center
1970–1975

Architect
Louis I. Kahn

Location
Khatmandu, Nepal

Client
Goverment of Nepal, The Agency for International Development

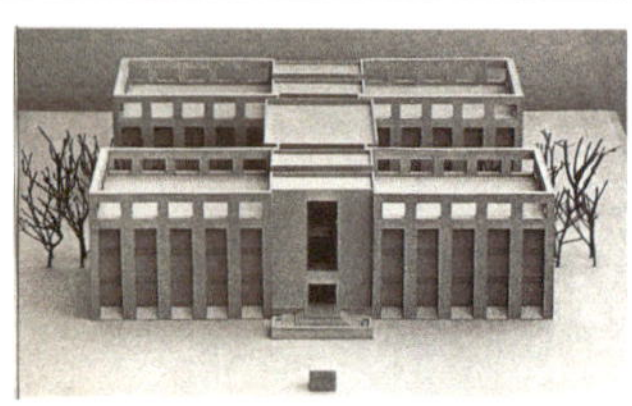

W.D. & H. O. Wills Tobacco Processing Plant and Headquarters
1970–1975

Architect
Skidmore, Owings & Merrill

Location
Bristol, England

Client
Imperial Tobacco Group, Ltd.

Oversea-Chinese Banking Corporation Centre
1970–1976

Architect
I. M. Pei & Partners

Location
Singapore, Singapore

Client
Oversea-Chinese Banking Corporation, Ltd.

Union Oil New Town
1971

Architect
Leo A Daly

Location
Balikpapan, East Kalimantan, Indonesia

Client
Union Oil Company of California

Daiei Building
1971–1973

Architect
Paul Rudolph

Location
Nagoya, Japan

Client
Daiei Corporation

Tour FIAT
1971 –1975

Architect
Skidmore, Owings & Merrill

Location
Paris, France

Client
Societe Civile Immobiliere de la Tour Fiat

The Aga Khan University Hospital, Medical College and School of Nursing
1971–1985

Architect
Payette Associates

Location
Karachi, Pakistan

Client
Aga Khan Hospoital and Medical College Foundation

Money Matters: Architectural Competition on the Open Market

In 1968, an editorial in the *Architectural & Engineering News* lamented the "Decay of the Old Ethics," predicting that "the huge public-private client of the future will know little, and care less, about many of the ins and outs of architects' professional ethics."[1] Sure enough, over the next decade the profession underwent a series of fundamental shifts in the legal and economic conditions of architectural practice in the US, one which saw the dismantling of over a century of anti-competitive regulations based on the definition of architecture as a disinterested, liberal profession.

The crucial event in this shift was the consent decree signed by the American Institute of Architects (AIA) with the US Department of Justice in 1972 to remove mandatory fee schedules from its standards of professional practice, a major stake in its charter to protect the interests of US architects as a community of expert practitioners. The consequences of allowing architects to compete for services on the basis of price were immediately clear to critics, who warned that "agreeing to the consent decree reduces the concept of professionalism to the level of a commodity."[2] Caught between consumer advocates who sought to democratize access to professional services and laissez-faire economists in favor of deregulating markets, by the end of the decade most of the AIA's ethical protections against competitive practice had been dismantled, including its long-standing ban on advertising and rules to prevent any architect from attempting to supplant another with potential clients.[3] Studying the impact of these changes, sociologist Robert Gutman held that architects' self-conception as a liberal (rather than entrepreneurial) profession was anachronistic, a sign that "the theoretical underpinnings which have held the field together no longer appear valid."[4]

Other factors further exacerbated the need for firms to grow bigger in order to meet the demands of open market competition. The effects of prolonged recession, the reduction of architects' authority over building construction, the

① Stephen A. Kliment, "Decay of the Old Ethics," *Architectural & Engineering News* (December 1968): 3.

② Walter F. Wagner Jr., "The AIA and the Justice Dept.: Do you know you're almost slightly pregnant?" *Architectural Record* (May 1972): 9.

③ Jay Wickersham, "An Accidental Revolution: The Transformation of Architectural Ethics in the 1970s," paper delivered at the Society of Architectural Historians annual conference, April 2011.

④ Robert Gutman, "Architecture: The entrepreneurial profession," *Progressive Architecture* (May 1977): 55.

1920

1927 American Institute of Architects (AIA) Code of Ethics formalizes ban on advertising

1941–1942 AIA relaxes bans on advertising

1941 Richmond H. Shreve replaces Edwin Bergstrom as President of the AIA

1949 AIA bans architects from engaging directly or indirectly in building contracting

1950–1953 Korean Wa

increased specialization of building types, and expanded litigation and the resulting liability protection that firms were obliged to carry, all led to a steady decline in the net profitability of US architecture firms after the 1950s.[5] The net effect was the consolidation of a smaller number of large firms with an increasing proportion of the architectural market, split from a sea of smaller practices with an evermore marginal share of the field.

Firms responded in different ways to these shifts in the economics of architectural practice. The largest offices were pushed both to diversify and specialize their services, often in highly technical building categories, or to look for commissions abroad, particularly the expanding markets of Southeast Asia and the Middle Eastern Gulf States. Caudill, Rowlett Scott (CRS) became the first publicly traded architecture firm in 1971, initiating a series of acquisitions that transformed the company into a vast global engineering and construction conglomerate over the next two decades.[6] The new market landscape in the US was also reflected in a growing category of national architectural competitions for private, often corporate clients. Emblematic was the AIA-sanctioned competition in 1973 for the headquarters of the Johns-Manville Corporation (a major manufacturer of asbestos products) outside of Denver, Colorado, won by The Architects Collaborative over CRS, Welton Becket & Associates, Vincent G. Kling & Partners, William L. Pereira Associates, I. M. Pei & Partners, RTKL, and Sert, Jackson & Associates.

Confronted with such structural shifts in the economics of architectural practice, contemporary critics like Manfredo Tafuri and Francesco Dal Co lamented a condition in which the field had become "dominated not by individual architects intent on communicating their opinions of the world but by large studios in which the tasks were parceled out with virtual assembly-line standards."[7] For Tafuri and Dal Co, such modes of practice could only produce buildings "as anonymous as the architectural concerns that build them." By the time of "Transformations in Modern Architecture," a comprehensive survey of the previous two decades of production held at the Museum of Modern Art in 1979, curator Arthur Drexler could only point (following the historian Peter Collins) to the "archaeologically unclassifiable" variations of late and post-modern buildings on display — much of it produced by corporate firms, for corporate clients — declaring the result to be "bewildering, profuse, overloaded, contradictory, inconsistent, largely mediocre."[8] — MK

(5) See Anne Filson's research on the separation of architects from building construction after 1949, presented in the historical graph of net profits of US architecture firms included in this volume.

(6) See Paolo Tombesi, "Capital gains and architectural losses: the transformative journey of Caudill Rowlett Scott (1948-1994)," *Journal of Architectural Education*, Vol. 11, No. 2 (2006): 145–168; Peggy Deamer, "Office Management," in Eva Franch i Gilabert, Amanda Lawrence, Ana Miljački, Ashley Schafer, ed., *OfficeUS Agenda* (Zurich: Lars Müller, 2014): 52–63.

(7) Manfredo Tafuri and Francesco Dal Co, *Modern Architecture/2* (Milan: Electa, 1976): 339.

(8) "Response: Arthur Drexler on Transformations," interview with Drexler conducted by Andrew McNair, *Skyline* (Summer 1979): 6.

1957 AIA establishes Professional Liability Insurance Program

1961 AIA Contract Documents revision reduces architects' authority over construction

1971 CRS Inc. becomes first publicly traded US architecture firm

1972 AIA signs consent decree with US Department of Justice to cease publishing standard fee schedules

1973 First US Class-A architectural competition for private client (Johns-Manville)

1975 AIA bars employment discrimination on basis of sex, race, creed, or national origin for first time

1976–1977 US Supreme Court bars no-advertising rules for professional organizations

1979 US Supreme Court strikes down AIA anti-supplanting rules

1981 Economic Recovery Tax Act accelerates depreciation schedules for US construction

1987 Revised AIA Code of Ethics and Professional Conduct renounces earlier bans on economic competition and involvement in construction

1990

1962 Cuban Missile Crisis

1950–1975 Vietnam War

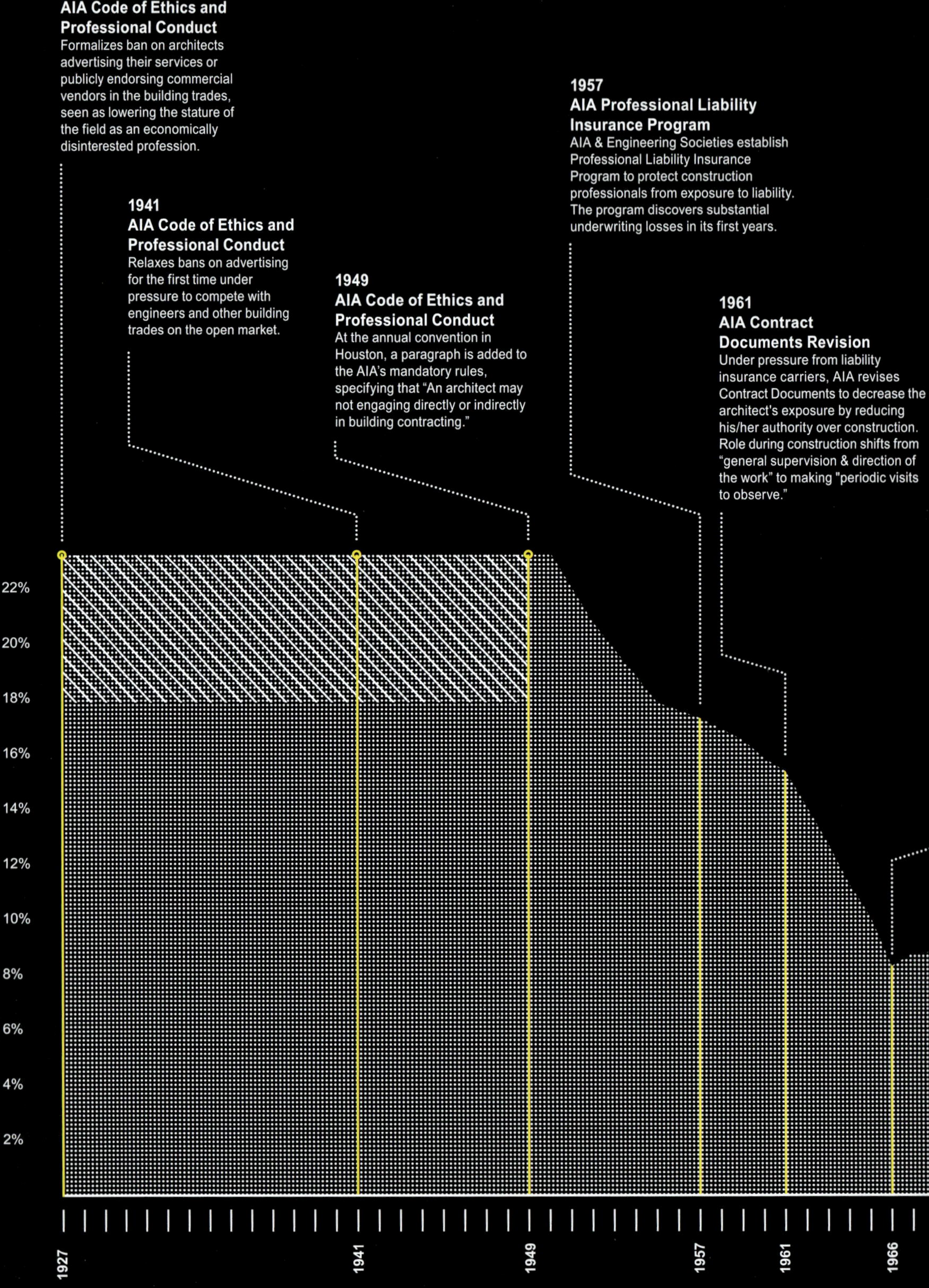

Research: Anne Filson
Sources: Birnbridge Associates Reports, AIA Publication: The Economics of Architectural Practice (1968), AIA Economics & Compensation Task Force Report (1986), Engineering News Record, PSMJ, AIA Business of Architecture Publications, US Census, US Bureau of Labor of Statistics

In the 1950s architectural practitioners in the U.S. were caught off guard by a precipitous drop in net profitability. Initial profit declines were due to an increase in the costs of architectural production. In the decades that followed, fee-based revenues remained relatively static, suggesting the architect's declining value proposition.

This chart plots external events that further contributed to the architect's diminished value: the rise of litigation that led to the AIA's legal dismantling of the architect's role as master builder, anti-trust settlements, recessions, and 1980s tax policy that reduced the demand for program-rich, site-specific architecture. Remarkably, the profession's collective reaction to these legal, political, and economic events had the effect of keeping architectural practice and its business model unchanged over decades. Contemporary practitioners are the beneficiaries of this continuity, and for better or worse, the diminished value and stature of the profession that it provoked. — Anne Filson

Legend

Estimated range of net profits before 1949

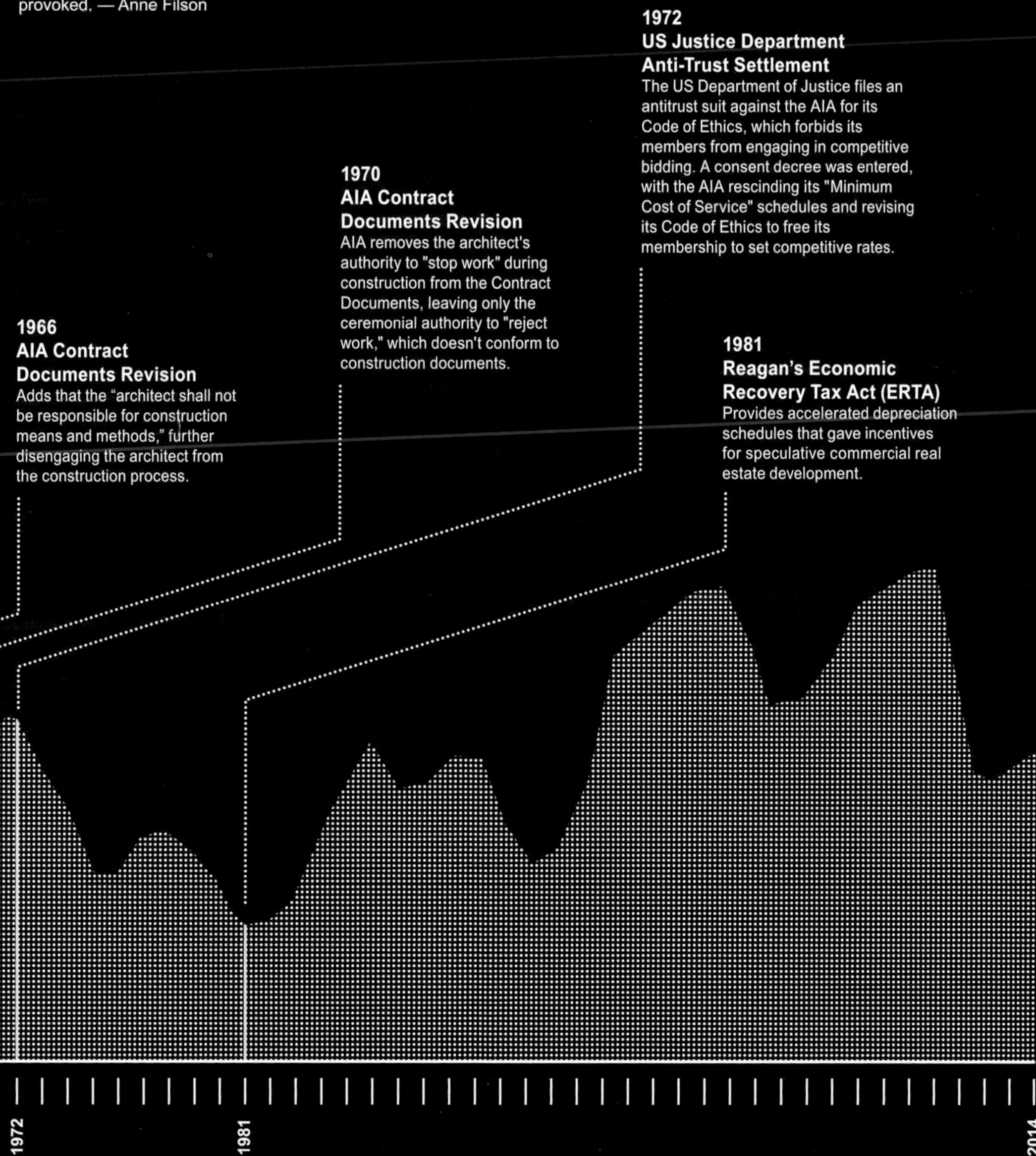

RCHITECTURAL & ENGINEERING NEWS DECEMBER 1968
CHILTON PUBLICATION
RACTICE
NEWS
12 TABLETS
BAYER
ASPIRIN
FAST PAIN RELIEF
Genuine
12 TABLETS
ANACIN
ANALGESIC TABLETS
FAST PAIN RELIEF
29
HEADACHE · NEURALGIA
BODY ACHE · COLDS
SAFE AS COFFEE
NoDoz
BROMO
SELTZ
BUSINESS
UNIT IV
Law of Corporations

12

ITENTS

VER

A&E NEWS' *annual office practice is- cover, Ivan Chermayeff reassembled contents of a desk drawer belonging to pical architect. Off camera are the 's books which reveal how much, if money has been made this year (p. and a letter explaining what he really it by those verbal instructions issued he job site yesterday (p. 42).*
her articles take a look at bridging rences between architects and con- tors, office equipment that saves time, the new URBS designs. The fourth t on US Steel's big office building rch project shows how Skidmore, ngs and Merrill, together with several neering consultants, organized the re- ch team (p. 74) (cover photo by Car- Macedonia).

EDITORIAL

DECAY OF THE OLD ETHICS

Developments over the past year or two threaten to pound the final nail into the coffin of traditional ethics, that ritualistic amalgam of statutes made up in equal parts of custom, self-interest and plain common sense.

It doesn't take an especially acute mind to look back and spot the signs. Several firms, both architectural and engineering, have in the past two years become part of larger outfits whose management does not have a majority of professionals as owners. This goes against most professional codes. Because the merging offices were larger ones, they got away with it. Individual architects in smaller firms have been censored, or worse, for far less.

There is another 'rule' followed more in the breach than the observance. That's the one which warns against knowingly injuring the professional reputation, prospects or practice of another architect. Insensitive design review boards with architects as members ignore this provision day in and day out. It is unfair to overlook infractions of this clause by official bodies and to permit transgressions by individual architects.

The rule that bars the architect from contracting is becoming increasingly meaningless. For one thing, the architect is in many cases taking over some of the general contractor's duties, especially when coordinating a separate-bid contract. For another, the clause implies that all contractors are dishonest, and that the architect cannot do contracting without compromising the client's interests. In actual practice, a growing proportion of the nation's building is being done by design-build firms; and while the quality of original design thinking is often mediocre, there is little evidence, AIA declarations notwithstanding, that the client suffers any more leaky roofs or ill-fitting partitions that way than he would if he obtained his building through more traditional (and ethical?) channels.

As we said before in this column, the day is at hand when more and more of America's annual $89 billion worth of building is going to be done by huge industrial builder firms, especially so if reduced military and space spending frees personnel and equipment of big firms for these purposes. These firms are organized to work all the way through from feasibility study to finished object, using systematic procedures and ending up with system-based products. The huge public-private client of the future will know little, and care less, about many of the ins and outs of architects' professional ethics. Moreover, system construction, in which Ezra Ehrenkrantz and his associates led the way with the California schools, has now spread to Florida, Montreal, Toronto, Pittsburgh, Georgia, Illinois, possibly soon Philadelphia. In it, the distinctions between designing, contracting and manufacturing are changing, which makes the appropriate ethical code clauses all the more outdated.

As Baltimore architect Rogers wrote to us the other day: "The underlying assumption behind most articles in a code of ethics is that there is less work to be done than there are practitioners to do it, and that there is thus pressure to 'get the job' improperly. This probably stems from the bitter experience of the design professions during the depression. In general, however, this is simply untenable today, even though in individual cases such pressures do exist. There is in fact far more work to be done than the design professions can possibly execute in the time required."

We have always had a qualm or two about the architect's Standards of Practice, mainly because a) they tend to imply members are dishonest, b) they are based on the doubtful assumption that a man will be honest with a Code but dishonest without one, and c) such ethics tend to be inflexible and to codify customs that belong to a past way of doing things. In a fast changing world, this is unrealistic; it also is unfair to those practitioners who closely adhere to the standards while others ignore them.

We live in an age marked by a lack of morals and an excess of moralizing. In the end, each architect must police his own professional behavior.

The architect can contribute to the building process originality, human concern, aesthetic vision, social judgment. If our environment is to be worth living in at all, it must have these qualities. The architect must feel free to play his part without being hamstrung by a set of outdated rules from the past. *Stephen A. Kliment*

NAMES

A unique design process developed by **Rogers, Taliaferro, Kostritsky, Lamb,** architects and planners, of Baltimore, relies on the client for final decision-making. Developed on a trial and error basis over several years, it was not until RTKL was selected to plan the central business district of Cincinnati in 1964 that the firm could prove its value. The process worked so well, in fact, that within a year a complete downtown renewal plan was achieved—not only in a planning sense, but politically as well.

Basically the process is a programmed series of choices which presents to the client valid alternatives from which he must choose and thus direct the next area of investigation. In this point by point manner discussion, suggestions, and, most of all, criticism can be constructively woven into the final plans. In the case of Cincinnati each decision was ratified by the City Council and the Planning Commission as the studies progressed; when the plan was completed it had already been adopted.

Looking back

Archibald C. Rogers, who founded the firm in Annapolis in 1946, sees RTKL's evolution in several phases, consisting of formation of and then additions to the partnership. Before 1949, when the first partnership was formed with Francis T. Taliaferro, who had been with Rogers from the beginning, the practice consisted of only minor residential and remodeling work in the Annapolis area. Charles E. Lamb joined the firm in 1950 and became a partner in 1954.

From 1954 to 1962 the firm expanded to about 20 people and received its first national honor award. Toward the end of this period a Baltimore office was established and the firm obtained its first urban design and planning commissions—a downtown plan for Hartford and the Charles Center Project in Baltimore.

George E. Kostritsky worked with the three partners as director for the planning council of the Greater Baltimore Committee on the Charles Center Project and as a consultant on the downtown plan for Hartford. Joining the firm in 1961, he became a partner the following year. Since then the firm has expanded to its present size of about 60 people.

Organization

RTKL feels the only way it has been able to fulfill its goals has been through the development of an organizational process and sound management techniques. All business is first funneled through a managing architect (an associate), with projects then divided into four studios, each headed by a partner. The partners are assisted by key associates (assistant directors) who together direct the several architects (project directors) on each team.

While the partners are available for key decisions and to work with the client, the project directors are responsible for day-to-day progress. The partners also form an advisory committee for the non-production wing of the business, and are joined by the associates to advise on production control.

In addition to their office duties, all partners are deeply involved in local problems of the Baltimore area. Rogers has served both as county zoning commissioner and executive director of the Greater Baltimore Committee; Taliaferro serves on the County Architectural Advisory Committee; Kostritsky is past director of the Baltimore AIA, and is now on the Maryland Architectural Review Board; and Lamb is chairman of the Baltimore AIA chapter's Urban Design Committee.

Research seminars

As a continuing part of research and its concern with environmental design, RTKL has for the last two years conducted private seminars for the benefit of its staff. Seen as a research program, these seminars allow the firm to test new concepts and technologies.

RTKL is one of a small handful of firms in the country involved with actual urban design projects of substantial scale. One of the most ambitious projects, begun last year, is Brooklyn's 'Linear City' which ultimately will cost an estimated total of $1.3 billion. Thus, RTKL's decision-making process is proving more successful than most in translating urban plans into actual architecture. *David Vachon*

Archibald C. Rogers

Francis T. Taliaferro

George E. Kostritsky

Charles E. Lamb

IDUCING INNOVATION BY MECHANICAL ENGINEERS

he author brings out reasons for the slow pace of innovation in mechani-l engineering and suggests ways to encourage the process. He is a partner the consulting engineering firm of Fred S. Dubin Associates.

Norman D. Kurtz PE

ıe present climate in which mechanical engineers must perform tends to inhibit ther than stimulate innovation. Consequently, the rate of progress in the develop-ent of new mechanical engineering techniques and systems, in the *construction dustry,* is quite slow compared to mechanical engineering developments in other elds, such as space.

The research and development capacity of most engineering firms is quite lim-ed. This is tied to economics, since most engineering commissions and fees are rely adequate for pure design costs. There is also a limit on the amount of in-me producing research work in the field. As a result, the profession as a whole is t well organized for this type of work. Systems for collecting and disseminating chnical information are not efficient, and it is difficult to establish standards performance. Adequate independent research and testing facilities are rare. The m of these factors makes it difficult for the engineer to develop with any assur-ce new concepts in a field which is largely based upon empirical data, practical perience and 'engineering judgment.'

Resulting innovation is often merely a gradual departure from the engineer's evious experience, or else a new idea of a product-oriented nature. Since most of e research effort in the field is by product manufacturers, engineers are overly pendent upon them for new ideas. They are thus forced to judge between claims d counterclaims of manufacturers and competitors. When the new products are corporated into a new system, the system is of necessity 'debugged' in the field ther than in a laboratory.

ability won't go away

spite these limitations upon the engineer's ability to test his ideas and find if ey are reliable, his liability before the law is not limited at all. He is extremely lnerable to criticism and legal action if performance is not up to the mark. This kes for uncertainty, since performance standards are nebulous. If comfort is standard, the decision could vary depending upon the judge. In recent years s has become serious with the trend to suing professionals and other third rties. In such a volatile atmosphere the engineer should be fairly sure of the ındness of his idea before venturing forth. Very often new concepts are devel-ed around new products which have been so 'well sold' that the engineer will take hance, encouraged by reassurances from the manufacturer. If the system does t fully perform, the fault is very difficult to assign, and it is usually the engi-r who must bear the responsibility.

Another incentive for many new ideas is construction cost reduction. Imagina-e thinking often fashions ideas whose inherent simplicity promises obviously ver material and/or labor cost. This could involve new equipment, materials or new system approach combining known equipment components in a different nner. Nevertheless, the newness factor in the design could cause contractors to omit bids with big contingencies—enough to offset the savings attributable to design. By the same token, new concepts designed to improve performance integrate the system with the architectural design could also cause contractors add to the bid to cover the unforseen. While many of these schemes should t no more than conventional schemes, the bids can result in the paying of an necessary premium for innovation.

couraging innovation

hough this would seem to give a good excuse not to innovate, it in no way re-ves the design professions (architects and engineers alike) of the duty to im-ve the situation. A good beginning is to create the atmosphere of oneness and iprocity among all members of the design team, fully recognizing the contribu-

Continued on p. 80

Cast of characters

A company of pros

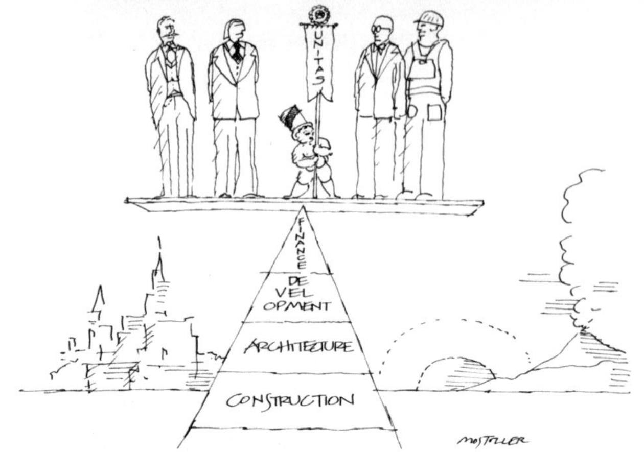

The players in the building production have overlapping and shifting roles, but however organized, the effort will always demand the same of talents.

Of all the performers in the construction process, architects have had remarkable success at being both directors and stars (a combination that rarely works in the theater itself). While these old "leader of the building team" claims may have become tiresome, the architect *is* the only one responsible for coordinating the process from programming to occupancy. As for stardom, even outside the architectural press, buildings may be referred to as "Kahn's" or "Johnson's"—rarely as "Fuller's" or MBM's."

Behind the entire team, of course, stand the backers—the clients. It is they who choose the date and place of performance, and choose, or at least accept, the key performers. But there is an even higher power that controls the whole theater—big government. As mentioned on the previous page, government has long controlled the economic cycles to which the building industry is so vulnerable—and done it off-handedly, making construction the inadvertent victim of money market strategies and on-again-off-again public programs that presumably serve higher economic (and political) goals. One result is that no portion of the industry—contractors, labor, or professional firms—enjoys the stability required for adequate capitalization and sound long-term management. Labor traditionally compensates for the unpredictability of work by seeking extreme increases in prosperous times, which contractors merely pass on to clients; but then the industry as a whole threatens to become overpriced.

Another area of government involvement that has been ballooning recently is agency *control* over development and building—as federal and state officials monitor everything from safety of stair rails to the runoff of rain water. The latest arena of monitoring is, of course, energy consumption. As presently administered, all of these protective processes demand vast hours of professional time—seen as boons or burdens depending on who is paying. Daniel Bell, in *The Coming of Post-Industrial Society,* foresees the dominance of a "professional class"—a class "based on knowledge rather than property." He distinguishes the professions (from business) as certified by and accountable to their peers (rather than their customers) and embodying "a norm of social responsiveness." Ironically, all of the peer-group controls among architects are being questioned—at the AIA convention next month, in the law courts, and on the following pages here. The courts and the federal Justice Department have been overturning the fee-setting and other mutually supporting restrictions among lawyers, physicians, engineers, and architects as unlawful "restraint of trade." Whether these organization rules are really "ethics" or mere vestiges of a guild mentality, the professions will have to do without them in the future. Ironically again, this may actually free them to play the roles Bell has in mind.

Among the numerous professional specialists that have been proliferating in the building design field—cost consultants, graphics consultants, zoning analysts, etc.—none has been more controversial than the construction manager. Construction has always had to be managed—traditionally by the general contractor, under the architect's overview. But the urgencies, material scarcities, and cost escalations of the 1960s caused the emergence of construction management as a separate activity—not a certified profession (Feb. 1976 P/A).

Whether CM is answerable to the architect, or reverses the position by acting as the client's agent, his position is ambiguous: he can and does make authoritative recommendations, but legal liability for all decisions remains with the architects, engineers, and contractors. For all its recent growth, construction management may already have passed its peak: in an economy of more predictable costs, interest rates, and material supplies, the virtues of the old competitive bidding system—no CM fee, for one—may reemerge. Architect John Portman sees valuable fallout from the emergence of the CM; his own office has a construction management department that monitors everything the general contractor does, and he recommends one for all firms large enough to sustain it. But he does not believe in administering construction by CM; only the competitively bid contract, he reminds us, gives the client an assured total cost.

One procedure that gives the client assured cost is design/build. The hitch, of course, is that nobody is necessarily defending quality, as against expediency. By working in or with design/build firms—or forming such firms themselves, as they increasingly will—architects may be able in some situations to give a performance that is both professional and businesslike—admittedly a very tough act to carry off.

The architecture troupe

As Robert Gutman points out on the following pages, architecture firms seem to be undergoing bifurcation—into large, comprehensive firms on one side and small, specialized firms on the other. And within the large firms, there will be more and more division of labor. This raises questions about the education and certification of architects: What knowledge is required for a professional degree? How will licensing standards cope with specialization? These issues must be resolved if the profession is to remain effective.

As Gutman also points out, we are going to have more trained professionals than traditional practice can absorb. One happy result may be that we will find many more architecturally educated people in business and government. And other opportunities may emerge in the area of *information.* As Alvin Toffler has reminded us (*Future Shock,* Random House, 1970) we are already encountering an advance wave of 'information overload,' 'overchoice,' and 'decision stress.' The research and interpretation needed to make this information glut manageable may add some new roles and many valuable members to the cast. [John Morris Dixon]

Architecture: The entrepreneurial profession

Robert Gutman

Research on the role of the architectural profession in society yields revealing comparisons with other professions and shows why architects must take initiative for their services to remain essential.

Even a brief conversation with architects these days soon reveals their concern about the future of the profession. Two conditions seem to have generated the air of crisis. The first is the rise in the number of professionals who now are unemployed, compared with three or four years ago. The situation is exacerbated because many of the larger, well established, and prestigious firms have had to cut their staffs by 30 to 50 percent. Architects are going about wondering whether the market for their services will ever approach the levels of the late 1960s. Some have even begun to ask how well the profession can withstand the changes that are going on in the construction industry.

The other disturbing condition is that the theoretical underpinnings which have held the field together no longer appear valid. Architecture made its claim for a place in industrial society by arguing that the way in which buildings were designed could improve the quality of life. Clients and users responded to this argument and sought out architects to help them provide housing, communities, schools, hospitals, parks, and other public amenities. Many of the designs which the architect proposed did not fulfill either the architect's promises or the user's expectations. This was a typical outcome in the field of housing and has led many public authorities in both the U.S. and Europe to become disenchanted with concepts put forth by the profession.

At the same time the profession itself has lost its conviction that principles of form and style could be derived by synthesizing the aesthetic element in professional work with the functional requirements of buildings. Architects themselves now don't know what general ideas should regulate their approach to their task.

The despair among the architects is understandable, but it is hard to believe that the profession will not recover. It should be realized, for example, that architecture often has been an underutilized profession. Recent unemployment rates are below those that prevailed earlier in the century (**table A**). In periods such as the present, when the industrial state is in a fragile condition, the concern of architects for building form and social benefit tends to be passed over in favor of an emphasis on the contribution of building to the increase in economic productivity. When the government fiscal situation is more relaxed and when corporations regain confidence in their survival, the skills which are unique to architecture among the design professions generally receive more attention. However, in order to make some guesses about what the profession may look like when the situation improves, it is important to identify the underlying forces that are shaping architecture today. It is important also to clear the terrain of a number of misconceptions about the field.

Architecture and the other professions
Architects like to think of themselves as similar to doctors or lawyers. Law and medicine are the two most powerful and prestigious professions in America, so it is natural that any other profession would choose to compare itself to them. Given

Author: Robert Gutman is professor of sociology at Rutgers and visiting professor of architecture and planning at Princeton. He has written widely over the last decade on social aspects of building design and architectural practice. The present article rose out of a study which he and his research group concluded last year on major trends in architectural practice for the Consortium of Eastern Schools of Architecture, results of which will be published at greater length in forthcoming papers and books. The views expressed in this article are those of the author alone and do not necessarily represent the opinions of other members of the Consortium.

	Architects	Draftsmen	Designers	Civil engineers	Lawyers & judges	Physicians & surgeons
1890	[4.5		]	—	1.8	1.4
1900	[6.8		]	—	2.6	1.9
1940	4.63	[5.25	]	5.03	1.03	0.39
1950	3.29	2.61	2.66	2.23	2.81	3.06
1960	0.84	7.67	0.92	0.51	0.42	0.45
1970	1.37	3.46	2.37	1.10	0.33	0.22

Table A: Unemployment of the male experienced labor force 1890-1970 (percentages)
Source: Forthcoming study "Architecture among the Professions," by Robert Gutman and Barbara Westergaard.

Cast of characters

this standard, architects are puzzled when they discover that their incomes are lower than physicians and lawyers, that they are less admired, and most of all, that they have difficulty keeping employed when doctors and attorneys still are doing so well. The discrepancy surely is one of the major factors which leads architects to be anxious about their prospects.

It would be helpful in thinking about their profession if architects were more realistic about the special features of their work which distinguishes it from the work of physicians and lawyers. Several factors are important to consider in this context.

First, what gives lawyers and physicians their eminence in this country is that they fill needs which are recurrent and to which American culture assigns top priority. This is true especially of the medical profession: ever since medical science became successful in preventing and curing illness, and the populace was alerted to the need for health care, the physician has become indispensable. Although in many countries the services of a lawyer may not be regarded as so necessary for enabling an individual to function in society, the normative system under which we conduct public and private transactions makes the services of an attorney a condition for the resolution of disputes. There generally is nothing in the field of architecture or building which can match the critical needs for legal and medical services. Only a small proportion of the public has direct contact with architects. And once their demand has been satisfied it usually is not repeated for many years.

Second, the right to dispense legal and medical services is restricted to members of the legal and medical professions. However, the architect's right to practice design and the supervision of building construction must be shared. In most states, civil engineers are permitted by statute to perform most of the same services as architects. For some kinds of building types, such as single-family houses, the owner can do the design work himself. In a study we completed recently, we found that architects do more of the design work for multi-family housing and for nonresidential buildings, a category including commercial structures, schools, hospitals and other community facilities (**table B**). Engineers dominate the market for factory building—an area which tends to recover from recessions more rapidly—and also do more of the preparatory work involved in single-family house developments. We also examined the results compiled annually over a period of 11 years by the *Engineering News Record* of the billings of the top 450 or so design firms. These data indicate that among large firms the share of the market held by purely architectural firms has been diminishing, while firms that combine both architectural and engineering are increasingly prominent (**figure 1**).

Third, much of the work of the architect, like that of most other professionals, consists in giving advice and making proposals for the benefit of his client. But architects generally are more circumscribed than physicians or lawyers in their capacity to make certain that what they propose is what actually will take place. In part, the reason is that the patient for a building is a client whose needs are acknowledged to be subjective. They can be met equally

	Receipts in dollars (percent)		
	Architecture firms	Engineering firms	Total
Single-family dwellings	21,529 (36.1)	38,035 (63.9)	59,564
Multifamily dwellings	53,840 (61.3)	34,003 (38.7)	87,843
Nonresidential building	586,394 (69.8)	253,615 (30.2)	840,009
Water supply	9,245 (5.2)	167,427 (94.8)	176,672
Industrial plants	46,926 (15.0)	266,205 (85.0)	313,131
Road, bridges, railroads	9,743 (4.6)	204,099 (95.4)	213,842
Civil airports	9,471 (25.6)	27,543 (74.4)	37,014
Power generation	7,976 (7.2)	102,298 (92.8)	110,274
Flood control, navigation	6,843 (13.6)	43,540 (86.4)	50,383
Mining and metallurgy	6,833 (16.5)	34,543 (83.5)	41,376
Other	30,127 (9.6)	284,389 (90.4)	314,516

Table B: Receipts for professional services by type of construction, 1967.
Source: Robert Gutman, Barbara Westergaard and David Hicks, "The Structure of Design Firms in the Construction Industry," *Environment and Planning B: International Journal of Architectural and Building Research*, April 1977.

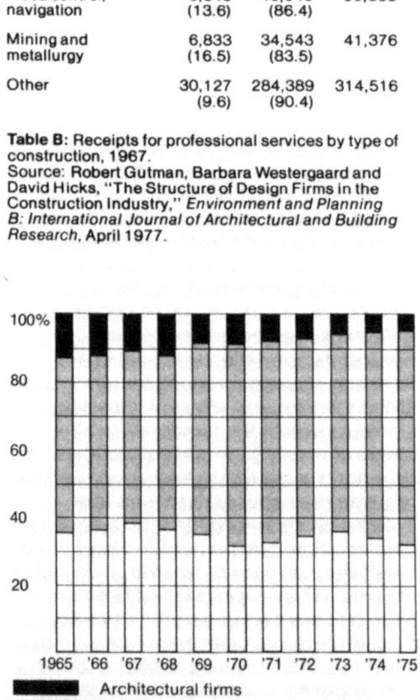

Figure 1: Percentage of receipts by type, top 450 design firms in terms of billings
Source: *Engineering News-Record*, Annual Design Buildings Survey, 1965-1975.

Note: Increase in billings of A/E and E/A firms relative to single-profession firms—from 51% to 62% over a ten-year period—reflects some real tendency toward combining these two services in single organizations. It also reflects, however, the inherently greater probability that a two-profession office will have receipts ranking among the top 450, hence has no definite implications for smaller firms.

well by several different prescriptions and the client or user is allowed to have a voice in choosing which one might be best for him. The situation is very different in law or medicine in which the practitioner usually assumes the right to say what is best for the patient or client on the grounds of scientific or objective knowledge. Another reason why the authority of architects is restrained is that they have less control over the institutions that execute buildings than physicians, say, have over the system which dispenses medical care. By tradition and by statute pharmacists, nurses, and hospital employees take their orders from the doctor; contractors, plumbers, and carpenters are independent tradesmen whose collaboration in the building process results from a lengthy process of negotiation and bargaining. Although architects are protected by a written contract in their relations to the building trades, they must often compromise with the builder's interpretation of what is an appropriate detail for a specific circumstance.

Fourth, the demand for architectural services is a function of the market demand for buildings, and at least up to now the architect has not been resourceful enough in freeing himself from dependence upon the construction industry. The link between architectural practice and this industry is especially unfortunate because, as is well known, this sector of the economy takes much longer to recover from recessions than do other sectors, such as automobile production. The sluggish demand for architectural services now, more than a year after the economy has turned upward, is an illustration of this problem. The situation is even somewhat more adverse than this statement indicates because architectural practice is tied not simply to the level of construction in general but to the demand for nonresidential buildings and multi-family housing, which recover even more slowly than total construction demand.

Creating demand

This comparison of architecture with law and medicine indicates that architecture is really more of an entrepreneurial profession than a liberal profession. The architect must go out into the community and seek work; he cannot expect to rely on people coming to him, as lawyers and physicians generally can. The challenge to the architect is to find a way of creating a desire on the part of the public to use his services in preference to the services of another type of building designer. The strategy of the American Institute of Architects in urging architects to become developers (still to be confirmed by a change in their code of ethics) will help in part to reduce their vulnerability to the vagaries of the market and the whim of clients. Since under the new arrangements which the relaxed code of professional ethics would permit, the architect could be his own client, obviously the chances improve immeasurably that the architect, will have tighter control over certain work. Howeve

708

becoming a developer does not eliminate his continued dependence on construction demand. Somehow, the architect must also make an effort to detach himself from the construction industry and begin to provide services which are useful to other, less cyclical sectors of the economy. Some firms now sense this requirement and present themselves as audiovisual specialists, media experts, exhibition designers, and experts in graphics and visual communication. This seems an astute move on the part of an entrepreneurial profession.

The romantic loner

There still is a powerful image in the profession which encourages the architect to think of himself as a free, independent practitioner, operating more or less on his own, and cultivating personal relationships with an understanding and appreciative client. The source of the image is a romanticized view of the architect-patron relationship that is supposed to have prevailed before the 19th Century.

A good deal of architecture continues to be practiced in this way. Some 60 percent of the firms which file business tax returns in this country are of this type. However, the average annual billings of these firms is only $10,000, which would suggest that most of them are run by architects whose major income comes from some other work, probably as a staff architect in a public office or larger private firm.

In a study we did of the settings in which architects work, a more important fact about the profession turned up. More than half of the architects in the U.S. are wage-earning and salaried workers employed in private architectural and engineering firms. Another 10 percent are employed in government agencies. Both groups have been increasing over the last few decades at a faster rate than self-employed architects (**figure 2**). These trends probably will continue so that some time soon as many as three-quarters of the profession will be holding staff or technical positions in design organizations.

The same tendency is visible among doctors and lawyers but it probably is more pronounced among members of the entrepreneurial professions, which in addi-

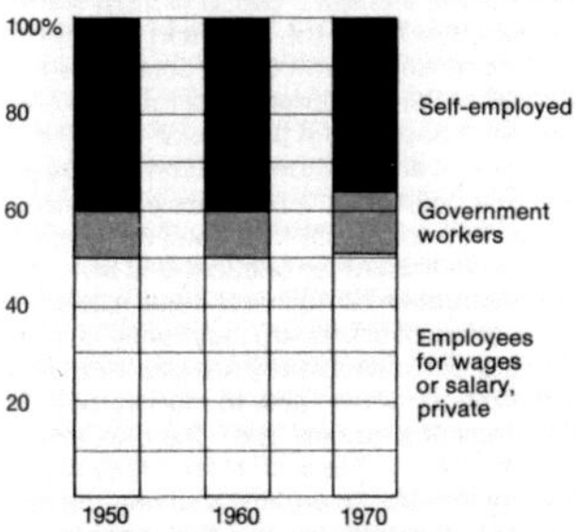

Figure 2: Employment status of architects (male), 1950-1970
Source: U.S. Bureau of Census

	Number (percentage of full-time employees)			
	Architects and engineers	Technicians	Other	Total
$1,000,000 or more	3,280 (29.8)	5,428 (49.4)	2,288 (20.7)	10,996
$500,000-$999,999	2,450 (33.2)	3,445 (46.7)	1,489 (19.9)	7,384
$250,000-$499,999	2,776 (35.5)	3,439 (44.0)	1,602 (20.3)	7,817
$100,000-$249,999	4,113 (41.2)	3,901 (39.0)	1,976 (19.4)	9,990
less than $100,000	1,621 (43.7)	1,314 (35.4)	774 (20.7)	3,709
Total	14,240 (35.7)	17,527 (43.9)	8,129 (20.2)	39,896

Table C: Type of employee by size of firm
Source: Robert Gutman, Barbara Westergaard, and David Hicks, "Structure of Design Firms in the Construction Industry." Based on U.S. Bureau of Census data, 1967.

Note: part-time employees listed in the same census data included 279 professionals, 1064 technicians, and 1529 others, totals for all firms.

tion to architecture, include engineering and accountancy. The trend reflects an underlying social process which accompanies the advance of industrialization and which is called the "dequalification of labor." The process can be defined as the historical tendency of work to be broken down into smaller and more limited tasks requiring less sophisticated training and expertise, at the same time elevating the responsibility of a tiny segment of the professional labor force that has the task of coordinating and managing.

The effect on the architectural labor force of the dequalification process is revealed not only by the reduced proportion of professionals to technicians in the design industry but also by the incorporation into the larger firms of many nontechnical personnel who have proven enormously useful in turning out program documents, working drawings, and specifications and filling other technical and supervisory roles. Among the firms in this country with four or more employees, only 40 percent of the payroll goes to the higher salaried professional staff, with the remainder paid to less expensive technical and support personnel (**table C**). To the extent that architectural work becomes more mechanized and standardized, the use of the latter type of labor will prove relatively more advantageous.

These shifts in the composition of the staffs of the leading architectural firms obviously present a great threat to the speedy revival of employment opportunities for architects. There is a good chance that for the first time since the decade of the Great Depression we will witness a major exodus from the profession. Between 1960 and 1970, the profession increased at the unprecedented rate of about 8 percent annually, resulting almost in a doubling of the number of architects in that ten-year period. For the years 1970 to 1975, the annual rate of increase was about 6 percent, but this rate of increase will become a negative value by 1980 (**table D and figure 3**).

These prospects offer a real challenge to the schools of architecture, to put it mildly. There are now about 25,000 students in the schools, about 3000 of whom are scheduled to receive first professional degrees this June. Twenty-five thousand students equal 40 percent of the registered architects in the country. If these enrollments were to keep up, and if the usual ratio of graduates to total enrollment remained what it has been in the years since World War II (by no means all those enrolled graduating), this would result in the addition of approximately 15,000 new architects to the ranks of the profession over the next five years. Obviously this number exceeds the absorptive capacity of the design industry, unless there is a radical and quick redefinition of the role and function of architects.

The organization person

Given the fact that architecture is an entrepreneurial profession, also recognizing the impact on the architect of the process through which work is becoming routinized and dequalified, it is not at all surprising that practice should exhibit still another feature of modern industrial organization. The distribution of architectural

Year	Number of architects	Architect per 10,000 urban population
1900	10,581	3.50
1910	16,613	3.94
1920	17,185	3.17
1930	22,850	3.30
1940	21,867	2.93
1950	25,359	2.62
1960	30,028	2.40
1970	56,284	3.77
1975	74,000	4.48

Table D: Number of architects and ratio of architects to urban population, 1900-1975.
Source: All years except 1975, forthcoming study, "Architecture among the Professions," by Robert Gutman and Barbara Westergaard. For 1975, National Endowment for the Arts Research Division, Report No. 1.

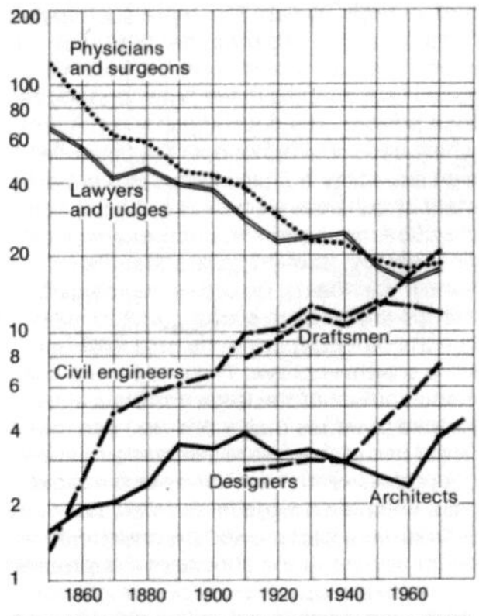

Figure 3: Numbers of specific professions per 10,000 urban population, 1850-1970
Source: Forthcoming report, "Architecture among the Professions," by Robert Gutman and Barbara Westergaard.

Cast of characters

work is now heavily weighted toward the top of a pyramidal structure. A large number of small firms do a small share of the work, and a small number of large firms do a large share of the work.

This is evident from an analysis of the relation of the size of architectural firms to their share of the annual receipts of the industry in 1967 and in 1972 (**table E**). In 1967, firms with three or fewer employees comprised 70.6 percent of all firms with a payroll, but they received only 21.5 percent of the total receipts of all firms. The firms with 50 or more employees commanded 20.4 percent of the total billings for design services even though they comprised only 1 percent of the firms in the field. By 1972, the firms with three or fewer employees made up a smaller proportion of the industry, and the larger firms had increased slightly, to 1.5 percent of the industry. The few large firms had increased their market share of the total billings.

The increasing dominance of the large firms accelerates the transformation of professional practice into an industrial type of organization. The more successful firms expand in order to offer potential clients a broad mix of services, and this mix in turn enables these firms to stabilize their position in a declining market. A firm which can provide not only the usual design capability but also includes a department or subsidiary which is expert at construction management, another which can do graphics, and still others that can handle interiors or do urban planning can use the profits from a strong unit to maintain the other departments until their balance sheets improve. The endurance and market power of the large firms is also enhanced because their work load can make better use of the less skilled and cheaper nonprofessional labor force. At the same time, because a large firm usually possesses more capital, and therefore can better withstand the shocks of a depressed market, it also is more adept in implementing the entrepreneurial definition of the role of the architect. For example, it is no secret that the larger firms are the ones pushing the AIA to relax its ban on advertising. The smaller firms generally oppose it because they realize that the use of advertising and agents as marketing techniques will further undermine their competitive position in the industry.

The issue that inevitably arises in any revelation of the dominance of architectural practice by the large firms is how far it will go, and will it swallow the offices made up of two or three partners and a professional staff of a couple of other architects working full or part-time. There is considerable sentimental attachment to these smaller firms. They are seen as the backbone of the profession, many architects much prefer to work in this kind of setting, and it is widely believed that they are the source of innovation in design (whether the belief is valid or not depends to a large extent on what one regards as architectural innovation). Certainly it is true that a stage will be reached eventually at which the economies of scale exhaust themselves. However, it is not evident that architectural practice has yet reached the point at which diseconomic effects set in; and there is continuing pressure from the dominant clientele of architects, which itself is industrial in character, to achieve greater economies and efficiencies in design through the expansion of the staff available to service it. On the other hand, it is also true that there are clients who are intimidated by the bureaucracy of the large office and who expect to have regular contact with principals and partners. If they cannot get the response they seek from the large office, they will turn to a smaller one. Clients often have surprisingly strong feelings on aesthetic issues; there may be no good way of communicating these feelings, or conducting negotiations about them, except through a personal relationship with the architect.

Number of employees	Percentage of all firms with payroll		Percentage of annual receipts	
	1967	1972	1967	1972
0-3	70.6	54.1	21.5	17.6
4-7	14.8	23.5	15.4	16.6
8-19	10.4	15.7	24.1	24.3
20-49	3.2	5.2	18.6	19.4
50+	1.0	1.5	20.4	22.1
Total	100.0	100.0	100.0	100.0

Table E: Distribution of U.S. architectural firms and annual receipts by number of employees, 1967 and 1972.
Source: Robert Gutman, Barbara Westergaard and David Hicks, "The Structure of Design Firms in the Construction Industry," *Environment and Planning B: International Journal of Architectural and Building Research*, April 1977.

The introspective professional

At the outset I mentioned the profession's anxiety about its future and identified two conditions which were symptomatic of this concern: the worry about the cutback in work and the architect's publicly acknowledged doubts about the ideas that guided design during the first century of industrial society. Our analysis of the development of architecture into an entrepreneurial profession has treated this process in the context of the first of these concerns, but we have said little about how the distressing loss of intellectual conviction has been reflected in strategies formulated by the profession to deal with its future. There is no space here to discuss the latter aspect of the current crisis in the depth it deserves. However, it should be noted that the theoretical problems of the field perhaps pose an even greater threat to the profession than does its industrialization. We see this instantly if we ask the question: what makes the architectural profession architectural? Certainly it is not the fact that it gets buildings up on schedule, or that it designs buildings which are economical to construct and maintain, or that its products may be durable and pre sent a salubrious and convenient environment. Such tasks could be handled as well by good contractors and engineers. The architectural profession merits this title because it alone is expected to coordinate the achievement of these ends with an aesthetic element, producing a design which responds to the canons of order, form, function, and convenience all in a single solution.

The difficulty at the moment is that neither the profession nor its clients are certain about how well it can fulfill this objective. A major battle has erupted again over style. It is much more dangerous this time than the last battle (c. 1940) because the mass media spread news of it to the potential clients of architects, and also because other design professions are poised ready to wrench away the architects' market. The profession advertises its confusion, too, when some of its members treat seriously the view that architecture is primarily an art form which has little to do with satisfying user requirements. This doctrine, autonomous architecture, borrows its rationale from 20th-Century trends in avant-garde painting and sculpture, and it also gets a lot of attention because of mass society's fascination with new ideologies of self-expression.

Confronted with this chaotic situation in the architectural culture, it is not surprising that the entrepreneurial side of the profession should compensate for the absence of a coherent philosophy of design by emphasizing with a vengeance the practical skills of the architect. Still, one must wonder whether either the definition of architecture as an art form or the determined pursuit of the entrepreneurial role can offer much hope to the profession over the long run. If architecture accommodates itself to a position as a business enterprise, doesn't it run the risk that it will be indistinguishable from other occupations involved in construction? And if architects adopt the identity of artists, do they really believe that the galleries already are overstocked with objects, will be able to market their drawings and models, too? The only effective course open to architects if they want their profession to endure is to resume authority in the area which is their unique province, as makers of buildings who are also makers of form. □

Multiple protagonists

In this long-term large-scale production many leading actors will be occupying center stage at one time or another. But who will finally gain the spotlight?

For this trial run, certain actors (in the metaphorical sense of course) have been designated to represent some of the *types* of protagonists occupying the stage on which "The Future of Architecture" is to be played. This group, unknowingly slotted for the roles in this extravaganza, has been selected because of the closeness with which their real lives coincide with parts in the production. Because these parts or roles could conceivably serve as examples to the rest of the profession, we have identified them as role-models.

Not all role-models are investigated; among those not covered here are the architect-developer, architect-researcher or architect-who-has-chosen-to-leave-the-field. Those involved in this trial run are limited to the more traditional or commonly shared definitions of the architect roles that continue to have a vital appeal to both performers and audience. (For a richly detailed account of the history of these roles, see *The Architect,* edited by Spiro Kostof, Oxford University Press, 1977).

One traditional role-model that was eclipsed during modern architecture's advent is the "gentleman architect." The species still survived of course, but in various guises and updated versions tailored for the new zeitgeist. The authentic gentleman architect, of true Beaux-Arts pursuasion disappeared into obscurity.

Now that the premises of modern architecture are being severely scrutinized, now that history has been retrieved through the efforts of theoreticians and preservationists, the type perfected in the late 19th Century has begun to have renewed interest. The closest correlative to be found is John Barrington Bayley, an architect who, with Harry van Dyke, recently completed an addition to the Frick Collection in New York City. In designing this addition the architects chose to loosely *replicate* the original Carrère and Hastings style, rather than *refer* to it.

Bayley becomes all the more intriguing when one learns he received his B. Arch from Harvard Graduate School of Design in the early 1940s under Gropius. He was a classmate of such modern luminaries as John Johansen and Philip Johnson. Shortly after, however, Bayley, who spent several years at the American Academy in Rome in the late 1940s became a dyed-in-the-wool classicist. His thinking, as expressed in *Unbuilt America* (McGraw-Hill Books, 1976): "Roman architectural surfaces improve with age. . . . They gain patina, high places are polished and low ones are darkened. The modern building does not improve with age. Unbroken surfaces of glass and steel are at their best when brand new."

In this period of intense questioning, perhaps this figure, heretofore anachronistic, will once again be summoned up on the stage.
[Suzanne Stephens]

Role models

The individual: Richard Meier

With the gradual takeover of architecture by the Modern Movement in the 20th Century, a new role for the architect emerged. The battle of the styles required a crusading spirit—a defender of Modernism's purity and idealism in the face of public resistance and lack of comprehension. "If there is any ideal preserved in the image of the modern architect," writes Bernard Boyle in *The Architect* (Oxford University Press, 1977) "it is the somewhat anachronistic one of the romantic hero struggling against the unheeding force of philistine society to fulfill his unique and prophetic destiny." Frank Lloyd Wright of course achieved that recognition most spectacularly in this country, le Corbusier in Europe. Ayn Rand helped immortalize (in melodramatic fashion) the role in *The Fountainhead;* Gary Cooper turned it into a legend in the 1949 film.

As a type of role-model, however, the "individual" has had a rough time of it ever since. Once modern architecture's battles were won, the Post-War building boom, the proliferation of materials and technologies plus the growth of "big business" gave the form-giver enough rope to hang himself. There was always the danger that pressures of work and proliferating technologies meant that too little attention was paid to the continuous working out of the design. Too large a project and too many compromises entrapped even the most careful architects trying to wed formal ideals with the realities of building. It was desperately hoped that the architect-as-individual could be played out successfully within the framework of the large office. The newly emerging role-model, the corporate architect, however, tended to keep the individual in the closet. Offering a full range of architectural services to the client, he anonymously captured commissions and left the high-design architects sitting targets for a disappointed public's accusations of being elitist, anti-social, monumental, and formalistic.

With his loss of face the individual architect as a romantic hero wasn't so romantic. Types have a way of enduring, however, especially if the need or desire

persists. And the individual architect, with his invincible faith in pure lofty ideals, his adherence to standards of quality as he rises above the morass of mediocrity in the built environment, still arouses professional and public longing. If the *morality* of Modernism's functionalist credos is no longer the crucial issue, a new kind of morality has sprouted up around architecture's formal and aesthetic obligations.

Re-enter the individual architect
Now, when it is especially clear that large offices have seized control of the greatest proportion of architectural work, the individual architect seems even more anachronistic. Nevertheless, the hardy stubborn breed, found principally on the East and West coasts, more rarely in between, thrives (or survives) in reasonably numerous quantities, teaching, talking, theorizing—and designing.

Of this breed Richard Meier might be the purest and most prolific representative in terms of translating ideas into built form. The haunting evocative quality of his kind of formalism—not too cerebral, not too polemical—appeals to a public that has often seen the modernist aesthetic, but not in a refined, rarified state. Faced with the limitless erosion of quality in daily life, the desire for a setting that transcends all by the sheer force of its incorruptible belief system can secretly possess the most realistic of souls. The astringency and purity of form, the rigor of a superb composition of unswerving discipline can be painfully seductive to the most pragmatic psyche. Not to be ignored of course is the status-conferring powers of pure form. Sign of enlightened, noncommercial values, architecture-as-art-object attests to the client's own powers of sensitivity, understanding, and cultivation.

After getting his architecture degree from Cornell University in 1958, Meier worked for Davis, Brody & Wisniewski (1959), Skidmore Owings & Merrill (1960), and Marcel Breuer & Associates before opening his own office in 1963. He was warned: One of the most successful design partners of a large corporate architecture office told Meier he was a fool, for the individual practice was no longer a viable way of making architecture in America.

Yet in the last ten years, since the completion of the Smith House in Connecticut in 1966, his success has been enviable: published, awarded, and copied, Meier's work has placed him in the forefront of architectural effort. Not that he isn't accused of being elitist, exclusivist, purist to the point of creating uncomfortable living environments. Or that any of the above isn't true to some degree. But he has proved that it is still possible to create Architecture—the kind of environment that is more than "nicely designed," the kind of environment that lets you know that Architecture as a special category lives.

Meier has also demonstrated to a certain substantial degree that it is possible for the individual architect to move out of the small-house category and capture

Photo: Ezra Stoller © Esto.

Meier's installation of the exhibit of his work at Cooper Union, New York City, October, 1976.

Photo: Ezra Stoller © Esto.

Shamberg House, Mt. Kisco, N.Y., 1976 (above), Bronx Developmental Center, 1977 (below).

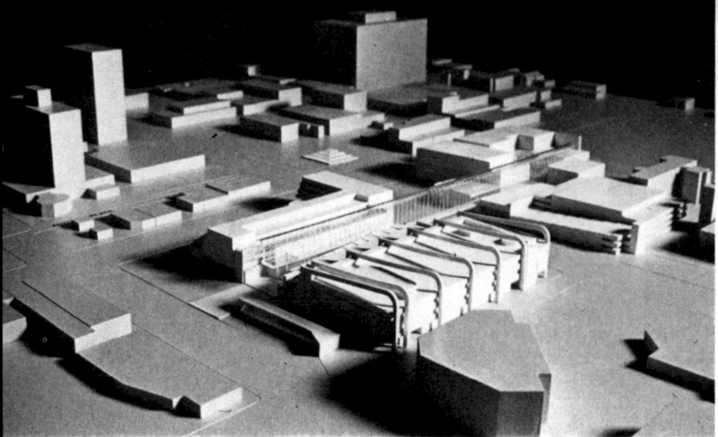

Multi-use civic center project in Colorado Springs, for Mondev International.

Photos: Ezra Stoller © Esto.

Multi-use project in Springfield, Mass., for Mondev.

large-scale major commissions. With his moderate- and middle-income housing for the New York State Urban Development Corporation in the Bronx, his Bronx Developmental Center for retarded children for the State Department of Mental Hygiene, his training center projects (unbuilt) for Olivetti, and his multi-use urban centers for Mondev (in project form) Meier has been able to gradually attract large-scale work with a small office—never over 35. Of course many projects don't get built; he loses commissions to larger architectural firms, and suffers more acutely than other firms in periods of economic slump and sluggish building. This isn't the movies.

Meier knows his high ideals won't bring in a lot of work, but is reconciled to the disadvantages of an office not organized as a business, even to bringing in partners.

"Architecture is a lousy business," Meier answers succinctly. "Anyone who has made it a good business is not usually making good architecture." Meier also believes in working on one project at a time, fearing that too much work or too large an office would diminish the design quality. (For the lags between projects, he turns to teaching).

Obviously this kind of principled attitude would seem almost self-destructive from a hard-core pragmatic view. Then how, one wonders, does this kind of architect attract a big-time developer like Mondev International of Montreal? Mondev's in-house architect Marco Ottieri, who was instrumental in Mondev's commissioning Richard Meier for multi-use projects in Colorado Springs and Springfield, Mass. (plus Mitchell/Giurgola in Seattle), explains that Mondev likes the one-to-one working relationship they have in working with these architects. "You know you're getting the person who did the work that made the firm worth going to in the first place—and you don't have all that bureaucracy to contend with," he explains. Also he adds, "Mondev knows Richard Meier will produce a beautifully detailed building with every part perfectly worked out. You don't have to worry about things falling apart 15 years down the line. He designs the hell out of every detail."

Since Mondev generally obtains private financing for 80 percent of its projects, hiring Meier initially created a problem with the banks. Bankers' predilection for big corporate firms who are well known has increasingly been a major obstacle for small individual practices. Ultimately Mondev convinced the banks that the gamble wasn't that great, since Mondev's very strong construction department plus its architectural department would guarantee money is being well spent.

Of course that old question of "compromise" looms up in these situations. Mondev and Meier vouch for the necessity of both sides respecting each other's position, whether pragmatic or formal. Ottieri comments that Meier is not rigid, surprisingly, about changes, even though one might think it to look at his architecture. However, Ottieri notes that Meier does not compromise his design principles: For example, if Mondev finds fault with one part of the solution, Meier will take the design home and rethink the entire concept. He will even go to the point of reworking the parti to keep the design integrity while solving the client's own problems.

In both projects Meier has executed for Mondev, a multi-use hotel/office/retail and mall complex in Springfield, Mass. and a hotel/retail/office/civic center in Colorado Springs, the company found this resilience. As Meier reasons, there is no one way of doing things. It is possible for the pragmatic considerations and the formal concerns to both be successfully meshed, as long as both parties are willing to acknowledge that a small change from one side may require more changes on the other side.

For all of its intentions, Mondev seems to be a different kind of developer. (Whether Meier succeeds in convincing them to allow him control over the interiors—usually the case with his houses—remains to be seen.) Since both Mondev projects are bogged down in the slow, arduous approval process, it may be a while before the outcome is apparent.

With a light workload in the office, Meier spends more time lecturing and teaching (at Harvard's Graduate School of Design) these days. Nevertheless, he remains optimistic about the future for the individual architect. Clients are more sophisticated, he argues, bureaucracy better educated, and the public demanding more. Discerning clients may still be few and far between but he remains convinced that too will change. [Suzanne Stephens]

Role models

The corporate architect: Paul Kennon, CRS

CRS President Paul Kennon (above), and a view of the firm's constantly changing open office in Houston.

Possibly no firm in the U.S. has been a more influential role model for medium-to-large practices than Houston-based CRS and its affiliate companies. The firm's 30-year history has embraced change in management process, in project delivery practices, and in technological advances. CRS procedures are copied, with varying degrees of success, by firms all over the country. And well they might be, because architectural practice—and all that that entails—is becoming more complex, clients more sophisticated and demanding, and the time element more crucial. CRS has demonstrated repeatedly that to live and grow a company has to stay loose, to adapt, to be willing to take risks.

As of about 18 months ago, CRS was reorganized, and Paul Kennon became the first elected president of the firm. What this portends for the present and future of CRS will be taken up as this article goes on. First, however, it is essential to briefly recall some previous accomplishments.

Architecture is truly practiced by team at CRS, more clearly than anywhere else. This has been true throughout the firm's history, whatever the other organizational aspects adopted. While there were always prominent names within the firm, there has been a continual commitment to sharing the responsibilities and the glory. Says CRS Board Chairman, Bill Caudill, "To run a firm like ours, you have to be a little bit permissive. When you delegate responsibility, you increase the life of the firm. And when you delegate responsibility, you have to be a little permissive, because you know damn good and well that you can do a better job than the guy you're delegating to; but he'll never grow if you don't, and in two or three years, he's going to be a lot better than you in that responsibility." Kennon adds, "I guess what we're saying is that there is a hell of a lot of ego to go around, and we're trying to spread it around. If we can continue to do that, we're going to survive."

Another CRS trademark is the intensively focused process they call 'Squatters'. Originating with groups of architects meeting clients, usually on site, to settle design objectives, quickly and objectively, the squatter concept has evolved. Over the years, the same process has been expanded, and continues to change in timing and intent. The evolution has taken the idea back in the project timetable to programming, and may occur several times during design, construction documents, or owner move-in phases. Post-occupancy squatters sessions to gather user feedback have been held, and CRS hopes to refine information from these continued efforts.

As the first architectural firm to go public, CRS spun off a holding company, CRS Design Associates (CRSDA), currently headed by Tom Bullock, Chairman, and Herb Paseur, President. The company, with separate offices, also holds CM Associates, the CRS-spawned construction management firm, and two companies with heavy engineering and environmental capabilities, A.A. Matthews, Inc., and Stevens, Thompson & Runyan, Inc. All CRSDA companies may undertake con-

Role models

tracts with outside firms, or with each other, as best fits project needs. Management sophistication has obviously not been an accident in the CRSDA group, which employs over 700 people in all. Of that number, CRS accounts for some 240 in Houston, the only CRS office now.

Current directions
Spirit at CRS runs high this spring. It is so infectious that it would almost be suspect, if it weren't for the fact that it is shared by everyone P/A interviewed. It's change time again. As Chairman Caudill puts it, "We're quite aware that a 30-year-old firm can get hardening of the arteries. We want to build a new CRS in the *Design* image; it has to be a little bit of a shocker this time. This is a new beginning. We want a new symbol; but at the same time, we'd be damned fools if we threw away everything we've got going for us." And, in a characteristic act, the CRS board elected Paul Kennon to make it happen. The more-than-conscious emphasis is on design quality, on making CRS the leader in design innovation that it has been in management.

Kennon, who came to CRS in 1967, was educated at Cranbrook Academy and served as a senior designer on major projects for Eero Saarinen & Associates. As he sees his challenge," what it takes is a commitment of an entire firm to the design focus. It's tough enough to do if everybody's pulling together; if that commitment is divided, then it's completely watered down. So our focus is on the design issues that will be facing society in the next 5-10 years. I think that never before in the history of Modern Architecture has that been so critical; never before have the times demanded as much creativity and as much innovation as is demanded today."

As currently organized, CRS comprises three architectural groups: international, commercial, and health and education. These are, of course, supported by other functions such as an engineering service group—centrally led, but working directly with project teams. The International Group, which will have over 100 people, is headed by Charles Lawrence (Director), Truitt Garrison (Manager), and Joe Griffin (Technologist). The Commercial Group heads are Norman Hoover (Director), Jay Nayland (Manager), and Jim Gatton (Sr. Vice President). Leading the Health and Education Group are Frank Lawyer (Design Leader), Jim Hughes (Director and Manager), and Nat Firestone (Technologist).

Emphasis is thus placed on design by virtue of the strongly design-oriented leadership, an active participation by these group leaders under an active design president. Kennon feels that CRS's design strength lies in its diversity—of talents, of projects, of working as a national firm within the U.S., and of working internationally to serve the third world. Quality control on design will be stepped up through a series of design reviews. Dates for these reviews are established in advance, and occur at project initiation phase (to establish design and corporate goals), possibly at the programming phase or before or after a design squatters. Other reviews accompany the schematic design, design development, and construction documents phases.

The process is one Kennon describes as a synergistic jury. "I'm convinced that we can design better buildings," he says, "if we communicate the problem and if we bring in fresh points of view. We're responsive. We try to find people to come into the firm who have flexibility. There's a difference between being responsive and being wishy-washy. I can be a flexible S.O.B.! It takes great courage to be responsive; as a designer you've got to get out of the mindset that you've got it all under control going in. Most architects try to play the game without all the cards on the table; they start playing too soon, without all the issues involved. If you just let those issues bubble up, you get all the cards, and the game becomes almost possible. But it's impossible the other way."

Other concerns
Along lines other than design, CRS's business development efforts center, as they always have, on both the international and the domestic markets. During the slowdown on domestic work, the overseas work has been going along nicely for CRS. According to Business Development head E.C. Kobs, "These projects are generally of a larger scope than we're used to in the U.S.—virtually to build infrastructure, to build cities. It's an exciting world, and we perceive the world to be our marketplace. It's not too hard to identify international markets these days, because generally speaking, they're where the oil is, the OPEC countries." Kobs' first criterion of successful Business Development is *to produce the quality of architecture that you sold the client in the first place.* Continuity of personnel and the commitment of the top team to the client's project is extremely important, he stresses. "You can't afford many mistakes, especially internationally. You're looked on in developing countries as the expert, and they lean heavily on your expertise."

For CRS, heavier involvement in the Middle East began with a 1963 project for Saudi Arabia's University of Petroleum and Minerals. International Group leader Charles Lawrence feels that having to organize and lead the decision-making process on a project the scale of the UPM has built in a better understanding of that process as applied to smaller projects, UPM is still growing, but the firm's commitment in the built work is paying off. Because CRS quality control was so stringent, top people and a careful building crew were brought to Saudi Arabia, and the result has become a showplace for the country.

Kobs also stresses a sincere commitment to the country in which the job is being done. "Our commitment is for more presence, for longevity," he says. This normally leads CRS to form professional companies within the country, in association with local firms. Before teaming up with another architect, CRS does its homework to find out who could best fit the requirements of each commission. Kobs feels that the emerging nations have work for which outside expertise will be needed for at least 20 years. "I wish the United States would regain its interest in world leadership," he says. "I feel we've lost that a little bit, partly because of energy, Watergate, and the rest of it, which have turned us somewhat inward. I wish we'd look outward again, because the world really does crave our expertise, our leadership."

On client services
To assure proper communication with clients, CRS has launched increased efforts to control client service quality. As Kobs puts it, "We see the marketplace as asking something different from architects than it has asked in the past. It's asking for *responsibility,* and responsiveness, and a commitment of key people. It's no longer possible to market architectural services through a professional "salesman," if you will; it's got to be through the people who

are going to do the work. The client today is much more sophisticated than he's ever been in the past." CRS co-founder Wally Scott agrees: "It's going to become a more and more specialized profession, where you're really going to have to deliver. The architect is going to become more and more accountable; there will be a need for higher and higher quality personnel. Your organization will have to be structured to allow the architect to be involved with the client, to communicate.

Frank Lawyer comments that clients will want buildings faster and for less money. Paul Kennon asks, "Can a client wait five years to design and build a project?" We think not; those days are *gone.* We're looking at all available technologies (such as computer-aided drafting) so we can gain more time to design with higher quality in a compressing time-frame of design/build."

Client services are now being reviewed with a quality control process not unlike the design reviews, relying heavily on the project manager's experience to identify problem areas. As Kennon puts it, "Are we serving the client better than any other architectural firm in the country? That's the mission." Careful attention is paid to areas the client isn't clear on, or has anxieties about. The individual project has been set up as the profit center at CRS. Because of the firm's size and the competitive market, CRS finds the client contact much needed.

Coming attractions

As Paul Kennon and CRS see it, design innovations, backed by sound technical and managerial policies, *are* the future. "As long as we focus on design innovations as the thrust of our firm, CRS will not only survive, but prosper," he projects. Kennon believes that his firm has the diversity to do both small and large projects. But size of firm need not diminish the opportunity to delivery quality, he feels. "I would hate to see the small firm go out of business," he says. "Our bigness can allow us to gather the expertise to specialize in various building types, to deliver quality design. But the small firm plays a very strong role in architecture. The Graves, The Meierses, The Gwathmey/Siegels, and The Venturis are leaders of design theory. The attitude of the firm is more important than size."

One thing that emerged in conversations with several CRS leaders is that specialization and flexibility will be key ingredients in future success. Norman Hoover feels that "architectural education is going to have to pay more attention to two aspects, the management and technical delivery functions." But what also comes out is the need for the balanced talent, what Kennon describes as "A designer who can also do production documentation, who's also a good technologist, and perhaps has management skills as well."

Another Kennon projection: CRS will continue its current practice of associating with other architectural firms. Having done so with over 200 firms around the U.S., CRS finds it an ideal form of practice, teaming with local professionals to add the clout it takes to get local work.

Another essential, E.C. Kobs adds, is the firm's contribution to the profession. "We do this all the time," Kobs says. "We train foreign nationals in Houston. We give to students, we give to the profession, we share everything we know. That's part of it; you have to give in order to grow. That's paid off handsomely for CRS. We *contribute,* damn it, and I think it's been a key factor in our success."

Kennon sees the important areas of concern as retrofitting, energy, consumerism, lifestyle values, life-cycle planning, project delivery, government involvement, and building management. Yes, management and operation by architects. Included in that is a software package on how to operate a facility, once you've moved in, from an energy standpoint and from a management point of view.

Up front, Kennon estimates that nine out of ten projects CRS undertakes get built. As part of the design process, the firm builds in implementation. "The one constant about us," Kennon notes, "is our willingness to change. If you want to look toward the future, we'll still be changing, taking risks. We make a lot of mistakes that way, but the greater the risk, the better the opportunity to improve."

Norman Hoover sees the trend toward moving out of the cities as producing fewer major projects, more renovating and remodeling. He feels that more efficient and sophisticated analysis of the building operation costs will probably change the form of what we build—that instead of an aesthetic expression of what *looks* like it uses less energy.

But Paul Kennon sets it out most dramatically: "The future of our profession lies in design excellence." [JM]

CRS has not slighted design in the past, but new projects undergo even more thorough quality review. One current design, a demonstration center for continuing education, U. of Washington in Seattle turns a sweeping arc façade to views, with stepped roof plazas for pedestrian use.

Firm profile

SOM at midlife

As SOM changes its leadership, it continues to attract major commissions to expand. Where growth takes the firm, will form follow?

Underwood & Underwood

Hedrich-Blessing

William Rudge's Sons

Above: Wonder Bread pavilion, New York World's Fair, 1939; Oak Ridge New Town, Tn, 1942; SOM meeting, Santa Fe, c. 1950: (last row, l. to r.) Gordon Bunshaft, John Rodgers, Marshall Sampsell, Walter Netsch, Arthur Christy, Jack King, William Brown, Frederick Kraft, Walter Severinghaus, Edward Mathews, and William Hartmann; (front row, l. to r.) Louis Skidmore, Elliott Brown, Robert Cutler, Nat Owings, James W. Hammond, and John Merrill, Sr.
Opposite: Toffenetti's Restaurant, New York, 1949; Lever House, New York, 1952; Manufacturer's Hanover, New York, 1954; Air Force Academy (chapel), Colorado Springs, 1962. Union Carbide, New York, 1961.

"I think we've just about reached our limit in physical size. From our four offices we can blanket the country, and we don't want or need any more. As for the partners, I doubt very much if the group will ever exceed 16 or 20, and most of the new men coming up will be replacements for us older guys." So spoke Nat Owings of Skidmore, Owings & Merrill in 1958. Only the last part of the statement has proved true. In 1958 the firm had 14 partners and 1000 people working in its four offices. In 1981, 34 partners run nine offices and 2000 employees, which include 93 associate partners and 212 associates. In 1980, *Engineering News Record* estimated that SOM's billings for the previous year totaled $35 to $50 million in construction dollar volume. While SOM won't divulge the actual current figures, Gordon Wildermuth, managing partner of the New York office, observes the estimate is a "little low." After all, the Jeddah airport (P/A, Jan. 1981, p. 120) costs several billion dollars, only one of a few such projects on which SOM is working. Whatever the figures, according to ENR last year SOM was second only to CRS, Inc., among architectural firms, and still is the largest *privately* owned architectural office with this kind of volume.

The founding members of the firm, Louis Skidmore, Nathaniel Owings, and John Merrill, developed a group of offices that evolved into the paradigm of corporate practice for 20th-Century architecture. Their organization, which included the establishment of self-contained offices in Chicago (1936), New York (1939), San Francisco (1946), and Portland (1951), was skillfully fashioned to allow the firm to thrive when the founding fathers were no longer around. And now the succeeding generation of SOM partners—Gordon Bunshaft, Walter Netsch, Walter Severinghaus, Roy Allen, Whitson Overcash—has retired, and others like Myron Goldsmith, William Hartmann, and Charles Bassett are soon to follow because of the partners' mandatory retirement age of 65.

Yet SOM pushes onward. With the exception of Bruce Graham, most of the design partners in SOM belong to yet another younger generation. A good half of these partners, in charge of design, management,

and engineering, range in age from their l thirties to their mid-forties. The average of all the design partners is 45. A few sma offices are headed by design partners quit bit under the average age: the 150-mem Houston office, for example, which ope in 1976, is run by 37-year-old Richard K ing; the 150-person Washington office, wh opened in 1967, is now directed by archi David Childs (age 40) and planner Wa Arensberg (42). Other offices that have b spawned in the last decade include the member Boston office headed by Peter H kinson, started up in 1971; the 60-per Los Angeles office, established in 1974; the 150-person Denver office, which offici opened in 1977. There is even a 15-mem office in Saudi Arabia to administer the J dah project and other work.

The question that now faces SOM, m then ever, is should a large firm continu grow? Can it go on producing large-s work of "quality" design? As Robert Gutr has observed (P/A, "The Future of Archi ture" issue, June 1977, p. 55), the profes is becoming increasingly divided into camps: a small number of large corporate fices who are assuming control over largest percentage of architecturally desig work, and the large number of firms sma size, doing small-scale buildings, and a p portionately smaller percentage of ar tecturally designed projects.

The split has affected design. Large-s work has come increasingly to signify the dinary, commonplace, and mediocre in ar tecture; small-scale design work more t ever may be the only occasion for seeing novative architectural form. Of course level of risk-taking allowed in small-scale sign in contrast with large-scale work mus taken into consideration. And joint ventures do allow new architectural thinking to permeate the built world—as Michael Graves's Portland office building (P/A, May 1980, p. 25) that he is doing with Emery Roth & Sons illustrates. Nevertheless, the trend definitely s there: large firms that produce quantities of buildings, with the efficiency with which Doubleday publishes and sells books, have seized the day. As a wider distinction has developed between literature and fiction, the same holds true for architecture and building.

Smooth management

While SOM designers constantly talk of their avowed interest in design ("Design is the hing we care most about" says Maris Peika, young associate partner in design for the Los Angeles office.), other qualities of SOM dazle. SOM's management skills and its ability to leliver a product with a high level of compeence and according to a predictable standard ave long stood out. As the firm has exbanded, it has made shifts in the organization o strengthen the standards while it accomnodates that growth.

Tom Eyerman, management partner in the Chicago office, recounts three periods of the irm's organization leading to the current ne. In the first phase, 1936 to 1948, the firm ould be characterized as an entrepreeurship, led by Nat and Skid and John Merill. These were the days of gutsy selling—onvincing companies they needed an SOM nterior or building. But it was their landing he job of designing and planning the defense ommunity of Oak Ridge, Tn, that gained the rm entry into major leagues in the 1940s.

From 1948 to 1960, the firm really began to stablish itself as a group practice. The approach sharpened up somewhat as the firm rganized itself into departments according the various phases projects underwent rom design to construction. Most of the work eflected the tastes and attitudes of the lients, culled from the Fortune 500.

These were the years that the New York ffice came to the fore. Started by Louis kidmore in 1939 with an interiors assignment, it emerged as the major SOM office hen Gordon Bunshaft and Walter everinghaus began obtaining a number of ssignments following the completion of the ndmark Lever House in 1952.

The next stage, from 1960 to 1972, saw the nergence of the Chicago office, with the npact made by Walter Netsch (Air Force cademy, University of Illinois at Chicago ircle) and Bruce Graham (Hancock Tower, ears Tower), in tandem with structural enineer Fazlur Khan. The departmental setup this point had evolved into project team ganization so that one group would carry e project all the way through from start to nish. In 1972, Bruce Graham initiated the udio concept for the Chicago office. Here veral projects would be executed by one oup, rather like a small office, a method of ganization adopted not only in Chicago, but also in the Washington office. The other offices still adhere to the departmental division where project teams are led by the usual two partners, one for design, the other for management.

Eyerman suggests that in recent years (1972 to 1980) the company has been moving from the entrepreneurial format—of making buildings—to a service organization that can tackle a range of problems, such as planning and research, related to building. Instead of a vertical management structure where the hierarchy assumes the shape of a pyramid, the service nature of a business implies a horizontal structure where the hierarchy of personnel takes on the shape of a trapezoid.

The choice of a trapezoidal distribution of power should do more than allow unimpeded growth, presumably until the firm successfully penetrates just about every crevice of the built world. It also will enable architects in the firm to become more involved with its management.

Traditionally, twice a year all the general partners meet; two more times they meet with associate partners. Up until last year, a nine-man committee, carefully representing each discipline and each region, would meet in between to discuss policy questions. Last May, however, the partners decided that more committees needed to be formed to include more partners in the firm's affairs. Besides the steering committee, there are now committees to address such issues as project management, technics, engineering, long-range planning, civic and professional services, financial services, and so on. Design meetings are now structured to include selected young architects in the discussions.

In March, the Design Committee staged a two-day meeting in San Antonio to discuss housing. The choice of the topic was unusual, since the firm doesn't have a lot of housing work right now, with the exceptions in Chicago and Calgary. The design partners from the various offices converged, however, to hear presentations by the young architects and to lead discussion groups. The remarkable range of presentations tended to divide up along regional lines: for example, presentations by East Coast offices analyzed historical examples for types of housing forms applicable today; the Midwest offices concentrated on more pragmatic issues like housing needs, possibilities of supply, and so on; while the West Coast offices gave more free-wheeling, intuitive presentations about the sort of images people had about housing, or the regional forms found in California.

The comments from the partners themselves were also enlightening: Marc Goldstein (San Francisco) quoted Viollet-le-Duc about "rational" architecture requiring both functional and emotive content. Bruce Graham called the architects to action, stating that they have the power and the ability to build cities; they know how to do it, and therefore

Ezra Stoller

Ezra Stoller

Ezra Stoller

J. Alex Langley

S.C. Valastro

Ezra Stoller

Ezra Stoller

© ESTO

Ezra Stoller

© ESTO

they should not just talk about it, but go out and do it. David Childs (Washington) suggested that architects could form ateliers to execute small housing projects, adding that part of the failure of housing in the past two decades has come from a misunderstanding about the kind of building scale appealing to the occupants.

Organization by conflict

Obviously diversity of thought occurs within the confines of SOM. While the new committee structure should foster dialogue and discussion, Tom Eyerman worries that the committee membership will become solidified. Since no mechanism exists for changing members, power lines could harden. Eventually, little pyramids will sprout up along the top of the trapezoid. Gordon Wildermuth, (management partner in the New York office) does not agree, contending that the committee structure is still too new to think about sclerosis.

Communication and cooperation between offices seems more highly valued now than it was in the past. Still, the branches will go after the same job or find work in the same city. The Chicago office is designing a highrise on New York's Third Avenue, while the New York office is doing another tower down the street. Both Chicago and New York, however, are pooling their talents for a housing project being planned in West Midtown Manhattan. And the New York office is working with the Portland office—one doing offices, the other housing—in Calgary.

Then too, are the many interoffice consultations that occur: LA may consult Washington on matters of transportation, and any of the offices may use Chicago's engineering capabilities. All of SOM makes use of the computer system, centered in Chicago, although San Francisco has its own network for the West Coast. Four different systems enable SOM to use computers for working drawings, engineering calculations, and graphics. The firm is even able to compute shadow studies for its highrises—a service capability many city planning agencies could well use.

More is discussed at partners' meetings than how all the offices can cooperate with each other. For one thing, they provide an opportunity to review each other's work—a staggering amount usually, recalls Chuck Bassett. But much of the discussion centers on the architects who will be made partners next. General partners must be voted in unanimously. Most of the general partners have gone through the ranks of becoming an associate—a decision made on the local level—then an associate partner, before being put up for general partner. When asked how an aspiring architect makes it known that he or she would like to be considered, Graham replies that if an architect has to lobby, he isn't partner material. Most partners agree with Raul de Armas's assertion that you will be spotted "if you are worth your salt." (After all, *they* were.)

Still, 400 to 500 architects are hired ea year. The pattern that prevails among t new generation of partners is tenure co bined with youth: most of the gene partners have been with SOM 15 to 20 yea almost from the time they got out of archite ture school. Not everyone who hangs in the makes it. But all who *have* made it have hu in there. And it is *very* rare to see a newcom brought in at a top level. While SOM stress putting young architects in important p sitions, most of the current partners now ha a good 20 or more years of career life left SOM—another reason many of the growt oriented partners want to see the firm e pand. The absence of women at the gener partner level is also seen as being rectified making more room at the top.

Attracting the young

Growth still remains a troublesome issue f many at SOM. Some partners think that t firm has expanded enough; if it gets a larger, the principals will lose contact with t employees. Yet attracting younger talent r mains a common concern. The firm is s trying to get over its past reputation of sw lowing up young architects and placing the on working drawings on one project for i numerable years. (An unfounded reputatio according to partners interviewed.)

Besides the in-house activities, the firm h been reaching out to the architectural co munity through the SOM Foundation esta lished in 1980. Already the Foundation h given grants to a number of architectural ganizations, such as San Francisco's Weste Addition, The Chicago Architectural Fou dation, and the National Building Museu being planned in Washington. As if to sp more efficiently up-and-coming talent, t SOM Foundation has established a traveli fellowship for students nearing the end their architectural graduate school traini The grants, reasonably hefty, go to applica from a limited number of schools that SO considers good. They say the list will chan from year to year.

Design image

As far as the organizational image goes, o often wishes cities or countries could run smoothly as information is retrieved a presentations made at the various SOM fices. It is not the false patinated-in-plastic ficiency of an airline service. At SOM o senses one is dealing with very focused, ganized people. That in itself can be scary

Design is another matter. The designs t firm turns out are uneven. In spite of t partners' enthusiasm about the work, such Donald Smith's avowal that "SOM has t best talents and highest quality buildings, good number of the buildings are frozen i geometrical mold.

The firm's attachment to clustered geo tries that are best comprehended from ae perspective and to towers that are chisel chamfered, cut, and carved is much in e dence. The idea that people experience bui ings on foot, looking straight ahead or sligh up, doesn't seem to bear much weight w ese designs. Still, a number of buildings stay ithin the Modernist approach that SOM elped pioneer and produce creditable re- lts. For example, the Commercial bank of uwait in Saudi Arabia, designed by Michael cCarthy (New York office) proposes a reamlined glass-and-aluminum tower han- ed with elegance. Then too, the linear and ticulated curtain wall of the Modernist ilding Raúl de Armas is adapting as part of 1 energy-conserving experiment with Alan himacoff and Princeton University's School Architecture, merits attention. Both of ese projects are polished refinements of a 1own type. They may be "predictable," but ey seem convincing testaments to de Ar- as's contention that "predictable buildings n be great."

Still, it is no secret that in large-scale design ork SOM has lost ground in the last decade so to other firms such as I.M. Pei & rtners, Philip Johnson/John Burgee, and sar Pelli. And these firms often get outdis- nced in the popular press by the smaller fices of Hardy Holzman Pfeiffer, Michael raves, Gwathmey/Siegel, and Richard eier. This situation exists in spite of SOM's nding four awards in the P/A Awards pro- am this year.

dividuality versus anonymity

ne weakened design reputation can be ex- ained in part by the issue of individuality rsus anonymity. Architects who are going risk incurring professional and public ath by braving new formal terrains 1) want do it on their own and 2) are forced to do it their own. Yet in these smaller offices one tices a spark, the sense of being at the edge chaos or delight, and the temperamental va quality of the leadership, all of which emed to have existed in the earlier days th Owings and Bunshaft. In the 1950s you re dealing with individuals—in their man- r and architecture—SOM's corporate style the contrary. In the 1980s, individuals such Graham remain, but the others, such as De efano, Adrian Smith, or Larry Doane, have t emerged as known architectural iden- es—yet.

Not only should these identities emerge, in der to give the personal imprimatur to a ge firm, but it will probably happen any- y, if the current work, much of which is der construction, turns out to be at the ality level of a Weyerhaeuser headquarters ilding.

But obstacles to that formulation of "high ality design," obstacles common to most ns, especially large ones, do crop up. The st obstacle is that formally this period is so ferent in its thinking from the decades in ich SOM created its memorable work. M took the basic tenets of Modern hitecture—its structural and functional erminants of form—and made those into a rvading architectural statement without losing the subtleties, and in some cases improving on them. But the ideas about meaningful architectural form have shifted away from those tenets, and here SOM is in trouble. The Modernist prototype no longer exists as a viable model to adapt or refine. New kinds of architecture are called for, and the formulation must go beyond chiseling and chamfering, or designing buildings in the shapes of triangles

On top of that, the enormous amount of work the firm has been attracting doesn't always permit a great deal of time to be spent on working out different kinds of design ideas. As one partner recalls, Bunshaft would personally involve himself in every single detail. But he usually worked on three or four projects at one time. Now design partners may be working on three times that number. SOM can still guarantee the client that what he sees in the project presentation is what he gets in real life. But the creative thinking that addresses issues of, say, contextual form, embodying emotional content, doesn't always appear to be on the schedule.

Another problem that affects SOM—and other architects in their working procedure —is the lack of a truly critical dialogue among partners on their own designs. The New York office must be applauded for arranging a symposium last winter with some highly talked about architects—Michael Graves, Robert Stern, Jorge Silvetti, and Steve Peterson. But a symposium is too soft. Critical jurying needs to be made a part of the in-house design process. Partners at SOM vary in their estimates about how much they now discuss each other's work. But most concede such reviews happen very informally, or not at all.

Designing buildings, of course, is not SOM's only concern. As it expands into its service role, it has set its sights on cities, infrastructure, large-scale planning. Jim De Stefano of the Chicago office points out that this overall conceptual approach, where major buildings as such are not the goal, is indicative of the direction.

The planning work of the San Francisco, Washington, and Boston offices represents the firm's comprehensive approach in this area, as does the Baltimore Transportation Planning Review project initiated by retired partner Nathaniel Owings and led by Peter Hopkinson (Boston). With regard to these efforts, Owings recently commented that though results are not always visible, he feels happy when SOM can stop something like an expressway going through the Baltimore Inner Harbor.

The architecture of SOM, particularly its skyscrapers, is another matter. Owings contends: "SOM is taking orders, not creating new ideas. We are putting up office building after office building. Until recently, the firm was praised for its quality. I don't know if we still have that quality. We are doing piecemeal work on a rational basis and getting paid for it." By these comments, Owings hastens to add, he does not mean to be "critical" of the firm. "It is just where I part from SOM." Meanwhile, the next generation moves on. [Suzanne Stephens]

Cervin Robinson

Ezra Stoller

Ezra Stoller

Ezra Stoller

Owens-Corning Fiberglas Corp.

Drafting room, 1940s; drafting room, 1960s; Inland Steel, Chicago, 1958; Beinecke Library, Yale Univ., 1963; IIT Gym, Chicago, 1967; Mauna Kea Hotel, Kaunaoa Bay, Hawaii, 1965; Hancock Tower, Chicago, 1970; Marine Midland Grace Trust, New York, 1967; Bank of America, San Francisco, 1969; American Can, Greenwich, Ct., 1970; Kitt Peak Observatory, Pima Co., Az, 1972; New Jeddah International Airport, Saudi Arabia, 1977–82.

HOK: an American recipe for success

RIBA JOURNAL

MAR 1982

The search for the London street

The properties of timber

How American architects do it

HOK: an American recipe for success

Hellmuth, Obata & Kassabaum are among the most successful of America's giant architectural practices. They have a reputation for building on cost, on time and to demanding schedules. An exhibition of their work will be held at the RIBA from April 14-May 12. *Stephen Trombley* visited them in their New York offices.

HELLMUTH, Obata & Kassabaum are one of the great success stories of American enterprise. Founded by three graduates of Washington University in 1955, with a staff of 28, the firm now employs in excess of 800 people. The original office was started up in St. Louis, Missouri, and this remains HOK's headquarters. HOK now have regional offices in New York, Washington DC, San Francisco, Houston, San Diego, Dallas, Belleville (Illinois), Denver and Riyadh.

HOK's growth has been spearheaded by the three founding partners, each of whom brings to the practice of architecture separate but complementary skills. George F. Hellmuth's expertise lies in the area of management and new business development. Gyo Obata is a designer of forceful imagination. George E. Kassabaum is the nuts and bolts man *par excellence* in charge of construction administration: he makes sure the building is built, on time, on cost. The tripartite division of labour works.

Hallmark of success

HOK have never been short of work, even during the slack periods of the last few years. Building within the constraints of time and cost is an HOK hallmark, one of which they are justifiably proud.

The list of HOK projects is impressive and varied. It includes corporate facilities for companies like Citibank, Dow Chemical, IBM, Mobil, Sony, Xerox and a host of others, as well as schools, universities, convention centres, prisons, hospitals and airports. Obata's designs are remarkably diverse, and express the truthfulness of his proclaimed commitment to each project as a separate process in which client, architect, environment and other factors work together to achieve success in terms of function and design.

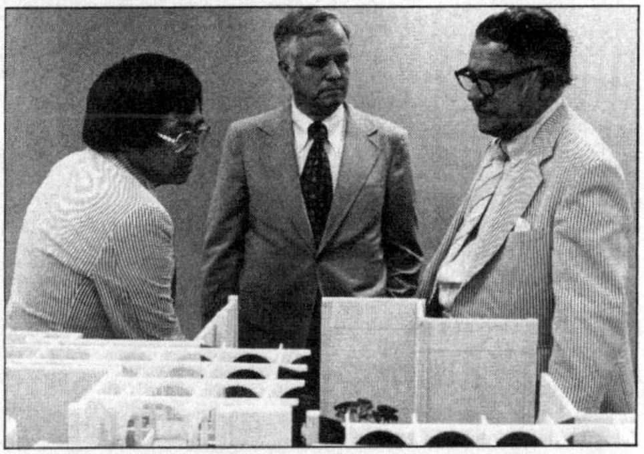

Gyo Obata *(left)*, George E. Kassabaum *(centre)* and George F. Hellmuth *(right)* inspect a model of part of their design for the massive 2,400-acre King Saud University development.

HOK's first successes were schools designed and built in the St. Louis area. They soon earned a reputation for excellence in this field, and graduated to the design of university buildings. HOK have designed 6 university campuses across the continent, and are currently heading a consortium which is building the King Saud University — one of the largest current construction projects in the world. They have built convention centres in St. Louis, Decatur (Illinois), San Francisco, San Diego and San Jose. Their prisons are sprinkled throughout the country, as are their hospitals. They are responsible for airports at Dallas/Fort Worth, St Louis, Lubbock, works at Dulles International Airport and Riyadh International Airport.

During the 1970s, HOK came of age. In 1973, they completed work on the worldwide headquarters (in Princeton, N.J.) of E.R. Squibb & Sons, the pharmaceutical manufacturers. This complex houses the company's administrative, marketing, personnel and research departments. The elegant three-storey structure is composed of rectangular shapes in limestone, brick and bronzed glass, and merges sympathetically with the gently rolling terrain on the 273-acre site.

Simultaneously, HOK had completed the Penrose Library of the University of Denver in Colorado. Again exploiting rectangular masses, the Penrose Library is on three levels.

Early completion

In 1970, the University decided that it wanted a 150,000-sq ft library at a fixed cost of $4.5m. HOK presented its final design in April 1971. Work began on site at the end of July 1971. The building was completed on August 18, 1972 — less than 13 months later. Obata commented that normally a building of this size would take HOK 18 months to complete. Not only did HOK complete in a year, and within the $4.5m budget, but they gave the University a bonus. The contract specified that of the 150,000 sq ft total, 100,000 sq ft were to be "for library use". HOK provided 27,000 sq ft of additional space *and* carpeted and furnished the space within the budget.

1974 saw the opening of the Dallas/Fort Worth International Airport. HOK, in collaboration with Brodsky, Hopf & Adler, had overall design responsibility for the four passenger terminals. The airport has been described as "an air transportation probe into the 21st Century". Passenger volume is expected to top 30 million by 1985. Like most things in Texas, the airport is big: sprawling over 17,000 acres, it is larger than the island of Manhattan. In all, 24 major consulting firms were involved in the planning, design and construction.

Obata revamped the original scheme for the terminals, and provided a group of semicircular structures ranged on either side of the main road.

] pace museum

Each terminal has 18 gates, yet all four terminals are linked by automated transit and baggage systems. However, Dallas/Fort Worth is only in its infancy: a further nine terminals will be completed by 2001.

One of HOK's great successes of the 70s is the National Air and Space Museum in Washington DC. Here the brief was to produce a design which, while possessing its own individual character, blended in with the overall design of the Mall in which it is situated. In addition, the practical requirements of the building were rigorous. The museum boasts the highest attendance rate of any museum in the United States, and the brief estimated that the building would serve 50,000 visitors per day. The forecast was not extravagant: over 40 million people have viewed the exhibitions on show since the museum opened in July 1976. Apart from having to contend with the enormous volume of users, the building had to meet the stringent structural requirements imposed by the nature of the exhibits. Aircraft are both large and heavy, and the brief demanded a structure which could support them in terms of both space and stress.

The client required a building which would play frame to the museum's picture. The museum's site is situated directly opposite the imposing National Gallery of Art. Obata solved the problem by creating a series of cubical structures linked by steel and glass areas which supply natural light in abundance. While the main lines of the structure harmonise with the National Gallery, the materials chosen by Obata complete the relation between the two. The core of the building is a sturdy steel frame, on which a curtain wall of Tennessee marble (matching the National Gallery facade) is hung. Obata's choice of materials played a significant role both in the speed with which the project was completed, and in keeping building costs down. Working in partnership with the contractor and the Government agency managers, HOK saved, by Government estimates, 26 months of construction time. Building commenced in November 1972, and the museum opened in July 1976.

Consortium

HOK have made an enormous impact in the Middle East with their work on the new King Saud University at Riyad, north-west of the Saudi capital. Building a university from scratch on a 2,400-acre site is a brief bound to test any architectural practice, no matter what their size or previous experience. In fact, it is probably too large a job for a single practice to tackle. The contract is worth well in excess of $3 billion. Consequently, the project is being executed by a consortium of five architectural practices led by HOK which goes under the name HOK + 4. (The other members include Dames & Moore, Los Angeles; Caudill Rowlett Scott, Houston; Gollins Melvin Ward Partnership, London; and Syska & Hennessey, Inc., New York). Under the terms of their contract, HOK + 4 are responsible for the design and construction administration of 12m sq ft of building space. While the Dallas/Fort Worth Airport is larger than the island of Manhattan, the King Saud University is 12 times larger than the Dallas/Fort Worth Airport.

The story begins in September 1974, when George F. Hellmuth received an unsolicited questionnaire from the university. Eleven trips to Riyadh and four months later, HOK were not only prequalified to work on the project, but were invited to form the consortium which competed successfully for the design contract. What happened in between would fill this article and more. Hellmuth and HOK outshone top competition from around the world.

Having got the job, HOK + 4 met for two weeks in the spring of 1975 and prepared a two volume proposal designed by HOK's graphics department. The proposal was bound in Morocco leather and stamped in gold: the leather alone cost more than $4,000. As Hellmuth explained to one American journalist, "You have to be a little forward in a situation like this."

HOK and Gollins Melvin Ward are responsible for the design and construction of 11 colleges, and more than 14 other buildings, including a library, mosque, auditoria, computer centre, museum and sports stadium. *Engineering News-Record* described Obata's plans as "a compact, densely arranged group of low-rise buildings modelled after Njad architecture that will be constructed almost entirely from a repetitive modular system of precast concrete elements, both structural and architectural, produced at a huge two-plant complex on site. "It's a simple system . . . put together like Tinker-toys", says Obata.

Co-existence

The traditional Njad architecture of central Arabia is beige in colour, and the individual buildings are placed close together, with small windows and flat roofs. Obata's design should, once again, provide a series of buildings which co-exist peacefully with their surroundings, yet which combine a high degree of individual style and advanced technology. The project is expected to be completed in 40 months.

J.C. Ryder-Richardson of GMW Partners relates how the architectural responsibility on the job is split 50-50. From early 1975 until the spring of 1976, GMW had between 12 and 15 people at work full-time at HOK's St. Louis headquarters. Part of GMW's job turned out to be educating HOK in what Ryder-Richardson calls "the intricacies of metrication". GMW felt that they were unable to take on a full range of additional staff for the job, and so developed a computer program

)pposite: Levi's Plaza, San ·rancisco, headquarters of the eans manufacturers, consists f three office buildings of 'our, five and seven storeys. The 750,000 sq ft development choes the natural and man-nade shapes of Telegraph Hill, which slopes towards the vaterfront. The low massing of the brick-clad building fits n well with the nineteenth-century buildings which urround the site.

Above: Model of HOK's lesign for the Dallas Galleria, 4m sq ft multi-use complex n a 42 acre site. The central ourt features a 150 ft liameter domed skylight and n ice skating rink. Right: The Galleria will consist of a hopping mall, two major lepartment stores, a 450 room otel, an office block and arking for 12,000 cars.

which could assist in the enormous bulk of drawing work required. They developed a program known as RUCAPS (Really Universal Computer Aided Production System) which they are now marketing. Ryder-Richardson describes GMW's working relationship with HOK as "very satisfactory". He says, "Gyo Obata and Brian Mayes, his opposite number with us, get on very well. They developed an extremely good rapport which made the whole thing possible, and which set the tone for other working relationships in the consortium."

HOK's successful conclusion to the 70s was the Olympic Center for the XIII Winter Olympic Games at Lake Placid, N.Y. Lake Placid is a tiny mountain community located deep in the Adirondack Mountains of New York State. The 1932 Winter Olympics had been held there, but the old facilities were hopelessly inadequate as the site of a modern Olympiad. The task facing HOK on this job was to design a facility to the highest standards, but one which would not be so specialised as to be redundant when the Olympic Games were over.

External trusses

The HOK solution occupies a hillside site adjacent to Lake Placid High School, and is connected to the old arena by a shared entry. The main arena includes a 30 m by 60 m Olympic-sized skating rink, as well as a smaller rink designed to United States competition specification. The arena has 5,000 permanent seats and temporary seating can be found for a further 3,000 spectators. The building was a success from the point of view of spectators and competitors alike. Excellent sight lines and bold use of the American colours of red, white and blue create a bright incentive to the enjoyment of sport.

The arena's most striking and controversial feature is the series of 11 external trusses which run vertically down the south face of the building. Inside, the trusses span the main arena over 240 ft, while the grandstand structure is independent of these. The system of external trusses was controversial not only because of its appearance. Two objections to the design on the grounds that support systems of somewhat similar appearance had proved inadequate were raised. In both cases, independent structural surveys led to minor design corrections and a successful completion of the Olympic arena.

In discussing HOK's success during the past decade with William B. Remington, Senior vice-President and Director of Public Relations, two explanations presented themselves. One has to do with the general nature of the American building industry; the other with HOK's own unique brand of marketing. Many of the issues which are problematical in the British industry present no difficulties in the United States. The architect usually enjoys a happy and productive relationship with the construction industry; there is a choice of union or non-union labour, and the industry sees itself as developing its own interests by building quickly and on cost. The harsh winter which has brought much of Britain to a halt is a pale shadow of the four month siege which has always been a perennial certainty for much of North America.

It doesn't halt the building process. One eminent New York architectural critic put it like this: "Our attitude enables buildings to be built on time, regardless of the conditions. Americans work harder than anyone, with the possible exception of the Japanese".

As for HOK's individual brand of marketing, Remington acknowledges that their reputation for building on time and on cost does much of the work for them. But, he admits, "it's tough at the moment. You need a strong marketing department to back you up."

HOK's tripartite division of labour ensures that design does not get lost in the hustle for work. Gyo Obata's basic design principle is "to solve problems concerning the space needs of people. Solutions must not only meet the functional requirement of owners and users, but must go beyond pure function to provide spaces that will enrich the lives of their occupants."

HOK marketing effort pays off

HOK are renowned in the US for their marketing skills. *Peter Sandy* talked to William Remington, Director of Public Relations, in his New York office.

BRITISH architects are still debating whether or not to take the marketing plunge; that debate is over in the USA. The discussion there centres on who does it best, and who, if anyone, does it better than HOK.

The firm's statistics tell only part of the story, although they are impressive. Some 40 people on the payroll of 800 are concerned with marketing and intelligence gathering. In addition each of the seven HOK American offices pay local PR firms up to $3500 a month each for publicity work. Recently the firm spent $40,000 just on the screening process to secure the contract for a new $160m headquarters for the Exxon Corporation.

That sort of money is only spent when a strong attitude towards marketing is held. Graham Whitelaw, Director of HOK's New York office, put it succinctly: "Essentially you have to understand what it is that you do, what it is that the client perceives that you do, and what he thinks he wants you to do. The trick is to put those together." This "trick" has nothing to do with advertising. Bill Remington considers advertising "demeaning and unprofessional", as it seems to the vast majority of American architects since they rarely bother with it. The trick has much more to do with combining design ability with flexibility where a client's needs are concerned — often before he even decides that he is a client.

Whitelaw describes a situation familiar to many British architects — the cost-conscious client who is not interested in design. "This guy was not interested in anything to do with the design; he had not one shred of a response to it. All he worried about was how many square feet could be got onto the site and how cheaply and how quickly it could be built. So we have to respond with what he wanted, which was an efficient, well thought-out, inexpensive process delivered by a pragmatic group of people. I

Opposite: The National Air and Space Museum, Washington, DC. Top- and side-lit galleries are designed for maximum space and structural robustness. Curtain wall of Tennessee marble helps the new building to harmonise with the National Gallery. Top: View of the vertical trusses on the south face of the Lake Placid Olympic Stadium. The design proved controversial, but HOK won out in the end after two independent inquiries. Above: The George R. Moscone Convention Centre in San Francisco. The building features 8 pairs of post-tensioned arches spanning 275ft. These support a roof which covers 6.3 acres of exhibition space.

said to him: " 'We'll give you all of that' and under my breath I added 'and we'll give you a damned good building too, only you'll never know it until two years later when you get a design award' ". Here Whitelaw leaned across the table for extra emphasis and said: "But don't ever talk design to that guy because he'll say, 'Design, what's this? That costs money. I don't want to talk to these people' ". Encounters of this kind are of course common on both sides of the Atlantic, but I sense that nine times out of ten, HOK would be able to beat their British equivalent in a race to get onto the same wavelength as a client, whether he was excessively cost-conscious or not.

Clients' needs

Marketing means more than just selling. It also involves a considerable amount of intelligence gathering. HOK do a lot of this, not only to find more clients to feed a very large mouth, but also in an effort constantly to learn how the firm can focus itself around clients' needs and expand and adjust its range of services. With regard to information gathering, it is interesting to note that shortly after the American construction industry's recession in the mid-1970's, a number of marketing firms emerged which specialised in providing marketing facilities for architects. This is beginning to happen now in the UK. HOK do this work themselves.

There is little mystery surrounding the operation: it's more or less a question of being thorough. They pay great attention to all relevant government publications, they scan the press and routinely follow up leads with written presentations.

An example of HOK's dedication to marketing is their quarterly newsletter, which carries information about current work. It has a print run of around 6,000, and a mailing list of some 3-4,000 names has been compiled. It is sent to decision makers at *Fortune* magazine's top 500 companies, along with developers, bankers and other investors.

HOK seem to be particularly inventive when it comes to developing new services, for instance their "Industrial Planning Service". This developed from an invitation in 1972 from Dow Chemicals in Michigan to assist them in making general environmental improvements to their 1500 acre plant site.

HOK came up with what appears to have been the first study of its kind which they called "An Industry/Community Interface Study". In essence it was a programme of landscaping, traffic concealment, painting, and small improvements. Most importantly it was planned to run over a period of several years and to fit in with the company's own plans. HOK's people had to be fully informed about Dow's future plans, and to carry it out they had to remain in close contact over lengthy periods of time. All very useful to both architect, client and the community. As the brochure puts it: "Increasing concern on the part of industries for the visual environment leads to marked benefits not only for the industrial plant, but for the entire community. Extending the life of older industrial facilities — rather than relocating to new sites — has proved viable in terms of economics, personnel contentment and overall property values."

This experience led to a similar request from Dow's sister company, and it was clear that a larger market might exist for a service of this kind. HOK people attended a great number of plant management conventions, they wrote a lot of letters and they managed to place two articles in chemical industry magazines. And so it spread; improvement plans for 18 major industrial corporations in 33 locations have been completed.

Success story

It was a considerable success story which Bill Remington enjoys telling: "A new discipline was spawned and we got a new kind of work as well as new architectural assignments."

I suspect that if and when HOK's kind of powerful financial expertise combined with architectural skills is adopted by British practices, then not only will those practices prosper, they will also make a significant contribution to increasing the influence of the profession.

The shrinking workload of the profession in the UK adds a certain edge to our discussions about marketing. "How many architects are unemployed in the UK?" asked Graham Whitelaw. "3 per cent and rising," I replied. "Yes, and the point is," said Whitelaw, "that marketing won't change that figure; it will just change who is included in the figure."

COVER STORY

PORTMANIA

The Atlanta-based architect-developer surveys an empire with $5 billion plus price tag.

BY MAEVE SLAVIN

John C. Portman, Jr. FAIA, is a softspoken, unassuming Atlanta man with a global reputation. As he turns 60 this year, he also approaches the 25th anniversary of his controversial debut in 1960 as an architect-developer. His gift for realizing visionary architecture is combined with the imagination and energy of a singularly audacious business tycoon, meeting on a peer level with Henry Ford II and David Rockefeller on vast scale urban development projects. His megastructures have brought coherence and exuberance to downtown America in Atlanta, San Francisco, Los Angeles, Detroit and soon New York's Times Square. In the course of this unrivaled achievement, he has revolutionized the design community attitude toward entrepreneurship, leading the way to professional acceptance of architect/developer practice. His astronomical success is convincing proof that architects can be one of their own best clients. Approximately half of all Portman projects are designed for outside clients.

Between 1960 when his Atlanta Decorative Arts Center (ADAC) opened, and 1984, the construction value of in-place Portman projects, including the Pavilion Inter-Continental Hotel, Singapore, shown here, exceeded $4 billion. In 1985, completion of six more will increase that figure by a further $1 billion. Peachtree Center, the 12-acre mixed-use complex credited with revitalizing downtown Atlanta, accounted for $200 million in 1973. San Francisco's Embarcadero Center (1974-81) reportedly cost $250 million, Detroit's Renaissance Center (1976) $500 mil and the Los Angeles Bona ture Hotel (1977), $90 mill

To be unveiled next are: Marina Square in Si pore, with three hotels 800,000 square feet of r facilities including four partment stores; the 50-s

Above: The 12-story, 450-room Pavilion Inter-Continental Hotel in Singapore by JP&A.

Right: Portman signature flourishes: glass elevator, greenery, skylight.

PHOTOGRAPHY BY JAIME ARDI

First level

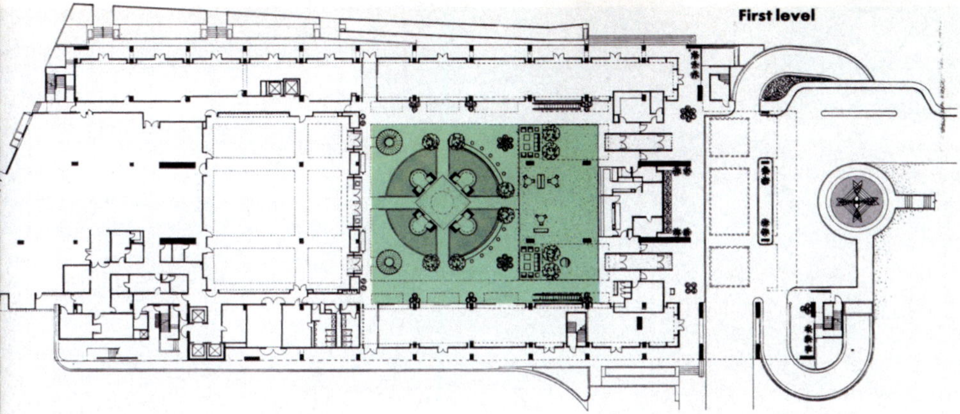

Second level

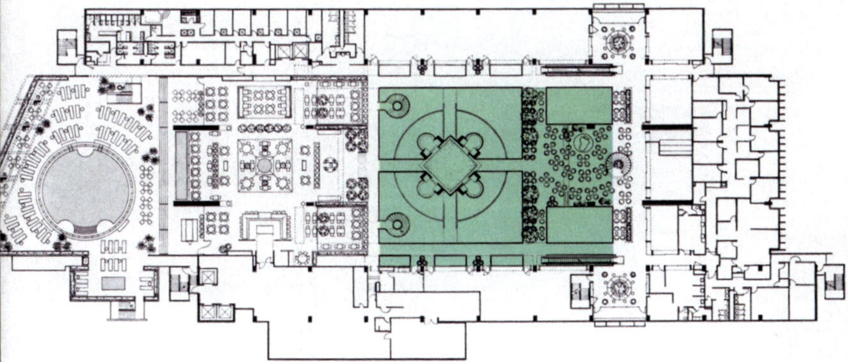

Typical guest floor

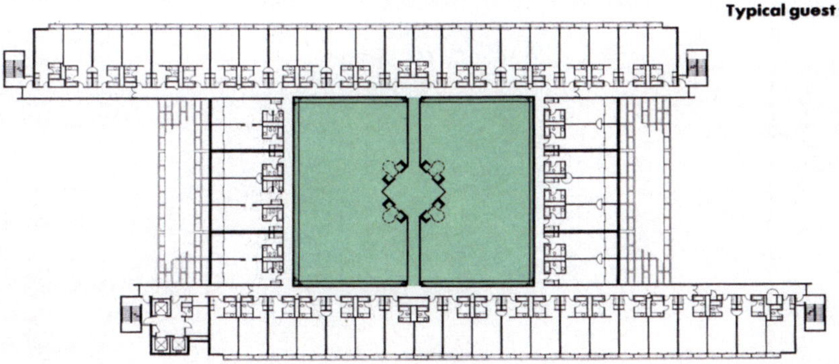

)n the atrium second the Lower Bar is in the round. Suspended ure is by Michio Ihara.

Above: Green shaded areas indicate location of atrium.

New York Marriott Marquis, with 1878 rooms and suites, a 46-story atrium, nine restaurants and lounges, and a 1500-seat theatre; the 52-story Atlanta Marriott Marquis, with a 47-story atrium (Portman's tallest atrium yet); the adjoining Marquis I office tower; and the first tower in Northpark Town Center, a 44-acre mixed-use urban center in suburban Atlanta. Late 1985 will see the opening of the 22-story, \$50 million, 600,000 square foot addition to the two million square foot Atlanta Merchandise Mart, with

Above: On the first floor level The Royal Pavilion (main dining room) is seen from the atrium. Swirling staircase rises to three atrium levels.

Left: Gilded gazebos on the terrace of The Chinese Restaurant on the atrium's third level. Glass elevators afford spectacular views of the atrium panorama.

special emphasis on the contract industry. This expansion, the third in the Mart's history, will give a permanent home to Conexion, the annual Southeast contract market, launched to great acclaim in 1983. When the 750,000 square foot computer mart, Inforum, joins these facilities in 1986, the Mart will comprise over 5 million square feet of permanent showrooms and temporary exhibition space. Finally, three hotel projects in San Francisco, Jakarta and Kuala Lumpur are now on the boards and scheduled for completion in 1986 and 1987.

Backing up this formidable real estate empire are nine component companies which serve Portman's wide ranging activities in design, development, investment, administration, construction management, purchasing and trading. These are: John Portman & Associates (JP&A), the architecture and engineering entity which literally shapes the total corporate configuration; the Atlanta Market Center (AMC) which includes the Atlanta Merchandise Mart, the Atlanta Apparel Mart and ADAC; Peachtree Center Management Company; Portman Properties and, Portman-Barry Investments, two real estate development companies; Peachtree Purchasing; Project Time & Cost; and the Atlasia Trading Company.

Portman presides over his multi-national enterprise with imperturbable aplomb. Whether he wears the hat of the architect, interior and furniture designer, art connoisseur, investor, developer or financial wizard, he applies

1960

Above: Pedestrian bridges connect the buildings of Atlanta's Peachtree Center, the 12-acre mixed-use ongoing Portman development started in 1960, which launched the urban Megaplex concept.

Top: Peachtree Center Garden Cafe is an example of Portman's belief that people respond intuitively to nature.

1967

Above: Portman's landmark hotel, The Hyatt Regency, Atlanta, introduced his spectacular atrium concept.

1971

Above: Justin Herman Pl in Embarcadero Center, S Francisco, puts Portman' "people watching" theo into practice.

Top: The Hyatt Regency O'Hare, Chicago, display kite sculpture by John Po man, adding color to the atrium scene.

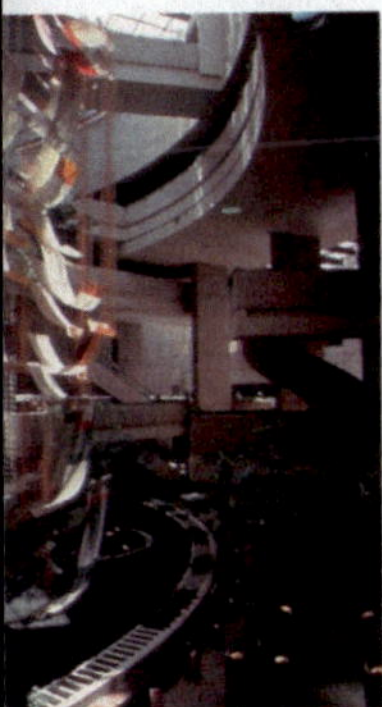

ALEXANDRE GEORGES

:: In the Westin Detroit
Hotel, Portman places
ure to take best advan-
f light from atrium sky-

e Westin Detroit Plaza
s one unit in Portman's
own complex which
es four office towers.

1977

ALEXANDRE GEORGES

Above: Portmanesque use of trees and water in the Los Angeles Bonaventure Hotel emphasizes nature in the interior environment.

1984

BERNARD KOH

Above: John Portman's Atlanta Marriott Marquis Hotel introduces a curvilinear shaped atrium 47 stories tall, the largest so far.

Top: The Pavilion Inter-Continental Hotel, Singapore, brings Portman luxury on a smaller scale: nine guestroom floors, three floors of public space and a 12-story atrium.

1985

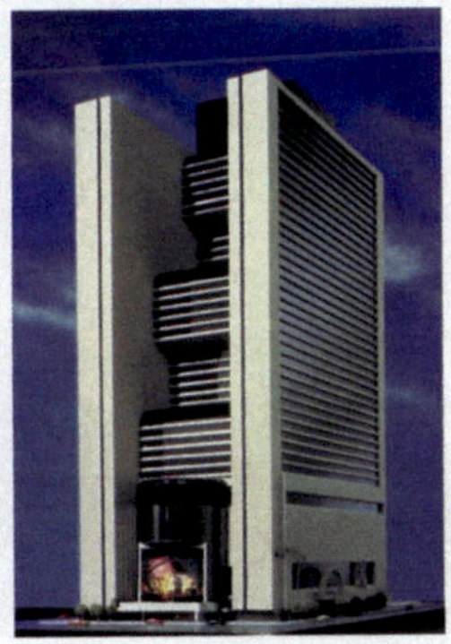

Above: Under construction, Portman's New York blockbuster Marriott Marquis will contain a 1500-seat theatre in addition to a 46-story atrium and 1878 rooms including suites.

raordinary concentration
l perception. No detail es-
pes his vigilant scrutiny.
n Portman is first and fore-
st an architect. He pro-
ses, however, that he is fun-
nentally a philosopher.
From a philosophical view-
nt, then, Portman studies
l analyzes human response
the environment. In a pro-
s he compares to zero base
lgeting techniques, starting
m often basic common-
ce issues, he reconciles con-
nt and variable elements of
esign problem. His conclu-
ns lead to his now well-
own and repeated-with-
riations hotel formula
ich creates the effect of the-
e in the experience of space.
ass elevators "explode,"
nging the thrill of the roller-
ster. Rooftop restaurants
ate, as the 360-degree pan-
ma of the city below gently
olds between soup and
s. Soaring atria are be-
ked with banners and cas-
ing plants, reflecting pools
l tumbling waterfalls.
lpture and clusters of ficus
es are introduced to define
man scale proportions.
dges, ramps, escalators and
ral stairways wind paths
ough interlocked levels of
aurants, bars and glamor-
shops. The drama of volu-
nous space is accentuated
tunnel-like "people scoop"
roaches from entry lobbies.
The word "Portmanesque"
been coined to describe
myriad effects of his inter-
ciplinary bravura. It is used
ratively (flamboyant, vul-
) as often as appreciatively
namic, people-oriented), a
which Portman accepts
h stoicism. His position,
te simply, is that architec-
e is public and non-elitist,
l should appeal to the com-
n denominator of society.
ile his projects are de-
ned on a generous urban
le, like walled medieval
ns, they offer small worlds
hin their gates. Open plazas
l terraces provide places to
and watch the passing
ade. These flower-filled ex-
aganzas are arranged with
les under gaily-colored um-
llas in interior courtyards
noved from traffic sounds
l pollution. The comings
l goings of pedestrians cre-
a spontaneous theatre of
Portman himself is an
avid "people watcher." The continuous interaction of people observing other people in Peachtree Center or Embarcadero Center is Portman's own restaging of the cafe life of the Champs Elysées, Tivoli Gardens or the Via Veneto.

Back in the mid-1960s, when Atlanta's Hyatt Regency, the epitome of "Portmanesque," was still in construction, the great hotelier Conrad Hilton predicted "that concrete monster will never fly." Portman has shown that when the architect is at the controls, projects take off and remain airborne. Expanding the scope of the architect into the development business also enlarged Portman's vision from single buildings to complete cities. His visit to Brasilia in 1960 convinced him that a sterile environment is hostile to the human spirit. He anticipated the decline of glass box architecture decades before what he calls "that Post Modern stuff" became a prevalent obsession. How history will evaluate Portman's contribution to the urban scene remains to be recorded. When a visitor mentions that the BBC has identified Michael Graves and Philip Johnson as America's greatest living architects, Portman's response is quiet laughter: a sound which reverberates all the way to the bank. ■

Rate this article, page 170.

Left: The Royal Pavilion is richly paneled in rosewood. Banks of chandeliers are custom-designed by JP&A.

Below: The Tea Garden is an opulent sidewalk cafe. The terrace of the elegant Chinese Restaurant is immediately above.

PROJECT: PAVILION INTER-CONTINENTAL
ARCHITECTS: JOHN PORTMAN & ASSOCIATES (DESIGN), BEP AKITEK (ASSOCIATE ARCHITECTS)
INTERIOR DESIGN: JOHN PORTMAN & ASSOCIATES (PUBLIC SPACE), HIRSCH BEDNER & ASSOCIATES (GUEST ROOMS)

Contractors: Takashimaya Co. Ltd. (interiors), Kajima Construction (general)
Consultants: Belt, Collins & Assoc. (landscape), William Hobbs Ltd. (pools & fountains), William C. Lam & Assoc. (lighting), Morris Harrison & Assoc. (electrical), Britt Alderman & Assoc. (mechanical)
Floors, floorcovering: Singapore Carpet, Marvin L. Walker & Assoc., Brintons
Ceilings: Simplex panels (ballroom), brass frames with Award fabric elements (coffee shop)
Partitions: Modernfold
Lighting: Lumen Designs, Seng Hup Electric Company (chandeliers), Sentinel Lighting
Furniture: Artifort, Architectural Supplements, Inc., Shelby Williams, Howe Furniture, Tropitone
Upholstery materials: Lackawanna Leather, Knoll Textiles, Ben Rose, Maharam
Custom fabrication: Cheng Meng Furniture
Accessories: Architectural Supplements Inc., California Umbrella, International Terra Cotta
Artwork Sources: Allrich Gallery, American Art Inc., Maxine Asch, Estelle Dodge Assocs. Inc., Eve Mannes Gallery, Hunsaker/Schlesigner

BTA IN THE 1990's: The Place, The People, The Culture

場所, スタッフ, 文化

Top Photos: Jon Goell

It's difficult to imagine Benjamin Thompson & Associates in any other place. Just across the Charles River from Boston, one of the most European of American cities, is Cambridge (pop. 100,000) whose heart is Harvard Square. On one side of the Square is the hushed, tree shaded precinct of Harvard Yard. On the other side is one of the more urban enclaves in America — and, despite rising rents, the center of a remarkable concentration of architectural firms.

A three minute walk from The Square itself, past coffee houses and art cinemas, brings one face to face with some of Harvard Square's architects. Here, in the 'sixties, when the Brutalist attack on the traditional urban fabric was at its height, four Cambridge architectural firms achieved a remarkable consensus as to the urban nature of this place. Facing Brattle St., one of the Square's principal arteries, and continuing around the corner down the narrower Story St., four adjacent buildings maintain the same floor heights, parapet lines, and slab thicknesses, share the same restrained pallet of colors, textures, and materials, and contribute to the shaping of a pleasant, very urban, interior walkway/lightcourt. This walkway gives access to shops and to a restaurant called Harvest.

Photos Below: Rex McManamy

The corner building — all faceted glass and centerpiece of the group — is principally occupied by a store filled with well designed home furnishings and fabrics. The store probably looks much as it did when the building was first published twenty years ago, although the name has changed. This is the D|R building (now Crate & Barrel), once the flagship of Benjamin Thompson's Design Research group of stores. In the 'fifties and 'sixties D|R was an oasis of good design, at a time in America when the otherwise available options ranged from the frumpy to the tacky.

Although D|R is long gone, Benjamin Thompson & Associates remains here, but not in the BTA designed D|R building. Across the street a bright yellow awning on a nondescript brick building proclaims "ONE STORY STREET/BENJAMIN THOMPSON & ASSOCIATES" in big bold, traditional serifed letters. Beneath it is a bright yellow door, with "BTA" on the transom in similar letters of an equally intense blue.

Up a flight of stairs is a reception room dominated by two un-expected images. One is a large colored lithograph of the interior of the Crystal Palace Exhibition of 1851. Clearly, from its frame and condition, it is no reproduction. Immediately one realizes that that icon of *Space, Time, and Architecture* is also, spiritually and architecturally, a primary ancestor of BTA's marketplaces. On the wall opposite is a familiar photograph — and, again, not of a BTA building. It is an interior view of an almost organic appearing dome in Isfahan, from Bernard Rudofsky's epochal exhibition and book, "Architecture Without Architects." (Is there another architect who would have an image, from such a polemic against modern professional architecture, as the frontispiece to his office?) In fact Rudofsky gave the entire original exhibition to Thompson, and its panels are now scattered throughout BTA's offices and the Thompsons' home.

BTA's staff of about 90 occupies two floors of offices at One Story Street, as well as space in a nearby building. The first impression is of a lack of artifice. There is a remarkably straightforward, comfortable quality about the place. Someone, meaning to be complementary, once used the term "old shoe" to describe it. Most surfaces are white, but where color occurs it is pure and saturated. No muddied PoMo drabs here. And, while this is not "architecture without architects," it has seen some construction without contractors. There is a sense that this is a self-made, and often remade, environment. One wall is a "library" of shelves of building materials. On another, above a FAX machine, is a wall clock, set five hours ahead. Below it a large hand lettered sign says "Dublin." Elsewhere in the office are other clocks labeled "Tokyo," "Los Angeles," "Auckland" — and, with a touch of irony, "Buffalo!" Other walls are covered with an eclectic variety of posters, maps, favored images, and old shop signs: mostly artifacts of past and present projects.

Much of the lower floor is given over to a big, somewhat cluttered studio in which there is more than a hint of the academic atelier. Around its perimeter are desks, often separated by ad hoc tackboard partitions. In the center are dozens of models of current projects in various states of creation and re-creation, including representations of waterfronts in half a dozen cities around the world. Some of the models are at a small scale. But many — of streetscapes, interiors, and entire buildings which can be disassembled floor by floor — are at larger scales.

At BTA there is not much interest in the small scale, abstractly monochromatic plug-in massing model, nor in the beautifully crafted, but immutable, presentation model in a

Photo: Jon Goell

Jamshid Kooros; source: **Architecture Without Architects** by Bernard Rudofsky

Sketches: Ben Thompson

THE STUDIO DESIGN PROCESS — RECONSIDERED

BTAのスタジオプロセスについて

BTA partners talk candidly about design collaboration and social values that lead to the making of "places that people like to inhabit"

BTAのパートナーは人々が喜んで住む場を生み出すためのデザインや社会的価値について率直に話し合う.

On a sunny day in May, a group of BTA's partners and associates took a day off to talk about what they have come to call the Studio Process. The participants included Ben Thompson, founder of BTA, Jane Thompson, his wife and partner in all ventures, who guided the discussion from time to time, BTA Partners Mac Freeman, Herb Gallagher, Tom Green, Hank Haff, Phil Loheed, and Ben Wood as well as Senior Associates Diana Tracey, John Shank, Jim Van Sickle, and Rick Fawell, and Dennis De Witt, an architectural critic and consultant.

The following has been extracted from some five hours of discussion about the process of design at Benjamin Thompson & Associates. If what you read is not exactly what you expect, it is because this is more about the facts of practice than the myths that come out of schools. and books. Call it, "The way we work."

Photos: Rex McMamamy

The BTA partners gathered for a meeting at the Thompson's house on Cape Cod. Standing, left to right: Hank Haff, Tom Green, Herb Gallagher, Phil Loheed, Mac Freeman, and Ben Wood. Seated: Ben and Jane Thompson.

トンプソンの家に集まったパートナーたち. 左からハンク・ハフ, ハーブ・ギャラハー, フィル・ロヒード, マック・フリーマン, ベン・ウッド. 座っているのがベンとジェーン.

出席者

ベン：ベンジャミン・トンプソン

ジェーン：ジェーン・トンプソン

マック：マクレガー・フリーマン

トム：トーマス・グリーン

フィル：フィリップ・ロヒード

ベン・W：ベンジャミン・ウッド

ダイアナ：ダイアナ・トレーシー

ジム：ジム・バン・シックル

デニス：デニス・デ・ウィット（オブザーバー）

以下は, 89年5月のある1日, BTAのスタジオプロセスについて話し合うために, 1日休日として5時間余をかけて繰り広げられた大熱戦の記録である. 出席者はもっと多かったのだが, 抜粋する中で発言が残された氏名のみを挙げた. 読者諸氏がこれを読んで,「オヤッ, ちょっと違うぞ」と感じるとすれば, それは学校や本からの神話ではなくて, 生きた実際の活動からの言葉であるからだろう. すなわち「私たちの仕事のやり方」そのものである.

Ben: If there is a "Studio," it isn't a room to which people bring their work and get chastised. That's the normal architectural jury system. Phil has defined it best by saying it isn't anywhere, it's everywhere.

Tom: The process was articulated in a specific way during BTA's first year. We were twenty people working on five or six different projects. Once a week each project was formally reviewed in the conference room. Three associates and the whole team were there. No one felt that they "owned" a project. No matter how uptight people got at points, there was an appreciation of the criticism and input of the other people in the office. People very quickly learned that the product was owned by everybody, and that a person's input was incorporated if it was good. It was an open forum. And the drafting room was set up with six alcoves for twelve people and a space in the middle for models — which was our "model shop."

Ben: Everybody had to have a model.

Tom: People were building models instead of making little drawings. Everyone knew what you were working on when you where building models, particularly when the whole middle of the room was filled with them.

Ben: Hank is working now on Cardiff, and there are models and things from Cardiff all over his area — a beautiful, incredible harbor and some wonderful buildings. It's important, that he's sitting amidst all that. You've got to be living in the middle of the environment, whether you're working on Cardiff or Buffalo or Rotterdam. The first principle, from the start, is that you work in an aesthetic environment. That creates an aesthetic standard.

Ben W: Our office is still a more sensual experience than most other offices. There's more color, more display, more different types of furniture — some would probably think too many!

Ben: The Studio is an attitude. When we moved in 1966, we had no projects to hang and Bernard Rudofsky gave us "Architecture Without Architects," the whole traveling show. That is what hung in the office and influenced the creative environment. Symbolically it kept us down to earth, thinking about real life and not about building monuments.

How We Begin

Tom: The first step may be to go around and interview people in their existing setting to find out what is working and what isn't working, what they want, what is their ideal space to work in.

Diana: It's broader than that, isn't it? Just where is this place? What is it? Why is it there? What is the character of the place? That affects the building, it affects the people, and a lot of other things too.

Photo: Bernard Rudofsky

A very systematic background search is typical of how we actually begin to develop alternatives.

Ben: Another essential issue is time. Your brain needs time to make judgements. If you don't have that time to deal with a problem you can develop twenty-seven different schemes, but they're all lousy. "Alternatives" don't mean anything. The time needed is incubation time.

Jim: In the process of designing you produce *things* — models and drawings. You have to go "around the world," try many things, and let them sit. After a time you realize that, out of all this stuff you've produced, there is maybe one model and two drawings which you've been looking at all the time that are *right*. When you first drew those you didn't know they were going to be the ones. Again, it takes time.

And that's why we need our kind of quick models. They do things a drawing can't do, in terms of showing you the reality of a situation. You can make seven variations, make a quick decision, then change it instantly.

Phil: One function of the model is to recruit support for ideas. The more support you can get, the more consensus you can build. One day Ben looked at something I was doing and said, "I don't understand that." Then he said, "Look, if you can't figure out how to explain this idea to your mother, forget it, it's not a good idea." I've always taken that as a very important principle. You can't make something so arcane that nobody but you can understand it, because then nobody can help *you* solve the problem.

Mac: The first thing that I like to see used is the scale comparisons. The richness of the scale comparison — places you've been and know — is really extraordinary for *immediate* understanding. Just superimpose something you know on the plan and you already know so much about the site.

Diana: A great feature of BTA is sensitivity towards maximum communication regardless of who is being shown a project. Most people have difficulty reading two-dimensional drawings of three-dimensional things. But I have yet to have failure with a model. People from any background can come to them, move around some furniture and sort of understand the space and the nature of the problem in ways they just can't grasp from flat drawings.

Ben: The difficult half of the problem in this Studio Process is trying to get the information down visually. If the basic facts and conditions are shown, one can under-stand the problem just like *that*. I tell people, "Get the basic material before we discuss it" — over and over again, like a music teacher who's driving a student to practice. That's the discipline that should be behind what we're calling the Process. The model is just another element of understanding. It doesn't mean the design is any good. It just means *you* understand it a little more. Whatever early ideas you have — in making a movie or doing anything else — are explorations. But a model can be fundamentally very irresponsible unless it clarifies the basic conditions and possibilities.

If you're honest with yourself, this is not for presentation but *is* for your own understanding. If you're trying to please somebody else all the time, that gets off the track.

Imagistic Techniques

Ben: Slide techniques help me see. I'm doing *that f*or myself because I enjoy looking at things and also like telling other people about them. It's a great pleasure to discover a place and make a story about it — to say, "Look at this — It's a great place."

Tom: Looking back at the "City of Man," which is the earliest of the slide shows, Ben was trying to create an exciting image of a way of life in cities. When people in the office first saw that, it was before we had done any large master planning projects, any retail projects, any of this city-scale work. It was a statement of aspirations, specific, but abstract enough that it wasn't limited to a particular building project. It made us think.

Jane: In making a slide show, reaching for images, and making everyone look at them, Ben is communicating with everybody and also keeping the team focused on goals. It's a fundamentally non-verbal cycle of the mind, working very differently from what you're doing with the program and measurements and scale and all those objective quantitative things. Again, it's explaining what can't be explained in drawings.

Phil: The constant theme of the Studio Process is one of communication with people outside of BTA. Part of the attitude of the Studio is that architects can't *do* anything much, except with the involvement of a heck of a lot of other people. It's a social art.

It wouldn't occur to us to make a door that didn't look like a door. We're not into playing those kinds of jokes on people. Or make a chair that looked like a pin cushion. How are you going to explain that to your mother? It's just dumb. If you want people to use the door as a door, they have to be able to recognize the darn thing. It does go far beyond satisfying your own testing process. The belief that it does work is the basis of this partnership. We're all different, but there's a common point of view and a conviction that forms the basis of something which will carry on through us to the next era.

Ben W: The way we work is not solely a way Ben has taught us. We have all contributed. Some of us work in quite different ways.

Phil: What's important to the survival of the Studio Process is the attitude toward the *next* problem. The "we don't know" factor — resisting becoming "organized" and codified — is a principle unto itself. Also, we're not set up in a hierarchy. Anyone in the office can talk to anyone else. Free access has always been a fundamental principle in the office, and there is no "pecking order."

Ben W: The thing that attracts our best people is the work we produce. Most people who come here without an interest in that work don't do very well in our terms. It's our way of working which produces those environments with the more sensual public experience that distinguishes our design.

The only way I have ever worked is with models. Jim probably builds fewer models than other people here. What Jim and I share is that we liked the work BTA did even before we got here. If we were producing work I didn't like now, I wouldn't want to be in the firm. If I thought we were going to produce work in the future that didn't have these shared values, I wouldn't want to be in the firm.

Photos: Rex McManamy

The one thing other people always say about our work is that we make places for people to enjoy. You ask your mother why she likes our work, and she'll probably say, "Because a lot of people like to go there." People don't pick it apart analytically.

Jane: What you're saying is that our values as such *are* the process?

Ben W: Yes. As a relative newcomer to this firm, when I go out into the world to represent BTA I have to understand as much as I can about what it represents. That's my charge, the integrity of the work, keeping that kind of work flowing, and making sure the process continues to produce that kind of work. I get nervous, if I think I see processes that are incompatible with that kind of work. I don't mean to say we should just be replicating our old stuff. We're constantly innovating. Some of the more recent projects — Tokyo and Rotterdam — are evidence that the process is bigger than any of us — even Ben.

Jane: We don't make "people places" by accident. The primary value system has to do with feeling, sensory experience, a sense of totality in architecture, and a lot of perceptions that are basically subliminal and intuitive.

Ben: You've always got to think about creating an open environment so things can happen, not a closed environment in which every ten minutes you tell people, "There is a deadline here. You've got to get this thing in — and it's probably going to be too expensive anyway." You've got to create a situation where people can work with some kind of equanimity.

Jane: The BTA process has a lot to do with teams of people complementing each other through *collaboration.* It's about creativity *within teams* and *within groups.* It encourages openness and flexibility. And it has to do with bringing the best out in everybody and getting the best design result.

I think we all believe that collaboration in architecture has a particular creative importance in achieving fresher and more innovative results. Architecture *is* both verbal and visual; most people are not. Architecture demands both information and intuition, both logic and poetry, both mind and heart, and requires an ability to cross between right and left brains. When different people work on complex problems and face difficult dilemmas, they come up with different views and alternatives. These challenge the mind to resolve the conflicts and become the raw material for new connections. I think this serves a team in the same way that free association serves the individual mind. It prepares the way for the "creative leap."

Ben W: You could say the same thing about the way Frank Gehry and Richard Meyer or any truly creative person works — if you were just going to list black and white techniques. But they may not share the same values we do. And that's the crux of the matter. It's not this process. All creative people go through the same things.

I could say the same things about fishing. What really distinguishes a good fisherman from a bad fisherman is true dedication to getting the darn fish in the boat: going out day after day after day and not catching anything, but continuing to try. What distinguishes our work is the way we try, test, and tirelessly network, and our dedication to a *value system* which is concerned with the tactile sensual qualities of the environment, versus more formal, academic, or intellectual characteristics. I think that's all there is.

Jim: I've worked for three major architects, and all three use everything they can lay their hands on to solve the problem: drawings, models, full scale mock-ups. So I'm agreeing with Ben Wood. This is not necessarily a unique process, but it is unique to a few unusual people.

Beyond Formalism

Ben W: I believe Ben is the only American architect of international stature whose work can't be described in purely formal terms. From Faneuil Hall on it's

Photos: Rex McManamy

very difficult. Remember that in the late 'sixties there was a lot of emphasis on values in architecture. Whole schools abandoned formal architectural design altogether in favor of live-in activism. A lot of architects who adopted that philosophy didn't produce any work and didn't survive. Ben survived with his values intact. And that is the source of the problem I have to deal with every day. The young people we hire, although somewhat selectively, still come to us with very formalist training, without those values.

Diana: And students in American architectural schools are not educated to understand that flexibility is OK.

In our design process we're always changing things, looking at things, exploring things. Most people either feel they're doing it "right" or they're doing it "wrong." Because there is changeability and flexibility in the way we work, new people can feel they're being asked to do something "wrong." And that's terrible.

Phil: The point you are making, Diana, illustrates the frustration of having someone come along and say, "That's a great solution, now do another." They feel they were asked to do something and they did it in what they consider to be the right way — the best way. Then somebody arbitrarily says, not whether it's right or wrong but, "Try something else." Meanwhile this person is thinking, "I did the 'right' thing already." By definition, any new scheme has to be "wrong" because he did the "right" thing already.

Mac: It's a question of being flexible enough to deal with uncertainty, to deal with chaos, to deal with complexity, to mistrust the first easy answer.

Ben W: I think it's a much more personal thing. It's just basically in Ben's character that he has been able to transcend the strictly formal pursuit of architecture. He's managed to attract people who agree with that philosophy. I don't think it's relevant whether he had to educate them or whether they came that way.

Phil: In another sense Ben has transcended ego — his own and others' — to achieve a true collaborative effort. That's an extremely difficult balancing act.

When I came to BTA what I found was rather shocking: work of integrity being produced by a *collaborative* process. We were taught that couldn't happen. But Ben's prodding and pushing has a way of channeling, deflecting, or somehow avoiding arrogance, so that people can work with others and gain some strength. This is what has been the key to the social aspect of the work.

Tom: Ben is a teacher. He's not a designer in the sense that some other architects are — someone who makes a little sketch and brings it in the next morning for a draftsman to draw up. Ben creates a work environment in which individuals become aware of themselves and their world. And it's not just the world of the T square, it's a world of food, of birds, of flowers, of all these things. You can't teach a value system — but, through example, you can open people to a value system. Albers was a teacher in that sense. You didn't learn how to draw in his drawing classes. You learned how to look.

Phil: That's not quite right. Ben *is* a designer too. But he's been willing to be stronger in a broader area — and sublimate his ego as well.

Ben W: The importance to me of working with the firm is that it affirms and uses certain of my instincts, in spite of my education. I grew up on a farm. I lived a very informal life. But I came to believe that to be an architect you had to be a kind of artist, making very formalistic sculptural resolutions of problems. That was contrary to my nature, even though I did quite well in school. It was a great relief to come to this firm and realize that yes, a guy as informal as Ben can have an impact and be a success in the profession.

A Personal View

Ben W: The first time I ever came here, to Ben and Jane's house on the Cape, I had only been at BTA about three weeks. I had been given a house to do on Martha's Vineyard. And, of course, I was not on the right track. It was not because I hadn't done houses. I had done houses like this: wood, big living room, spacious simple spaces. But I didn't yet know Ben and I thought he expected something much more formally complex. He was trying to tell me he didn't, but I wasn't listening. So I was into rotated geometry, "transformations of form of the third order," and the relationship of the house with God, country, and whoever else mattered.

Then I came down here. The first thing I encountered was a meandering dirt driveway. You had to park your car some distance from the house. Then you got a Gardenway cart to move things: it didn't matter if it was raining or not, or if the cart had recently been used for manure. The barn door was open. It smelled just like the place I knew as a kid, and it had old machinery and buckets full of bolts that you'd never ever use — just like the farm I grew up on.

Very early the next morning I walked over to the main house. In the kitchen Ben has stacked up a bunch of fruit from the garden to make a sort of marker — like a trail marker. On top of the fruit was a note that told me where the coffee was. He could have just left a note. Instead, he made this colorful expression out of it.

Later, before we had breakfast, we had to take a tour through all these paths he had made. We went on every path. They weren't manicured, and they didn't have formal archways and trellises and pediments and all that. They just sort of went around. But there was always a nice vista or a little intimate space or something happening.

When we got back Ben made breakfast. He just threw all the stuff together. He didn't cut the potatoes up but once — maybe not even once. He didn't chop the onions into a million pieces. He took a can of tomatoes but he didn't chop them up. And he put all of this into a pan. This is the way I always thought you ought to cook. But no one would ever let me. You always had to chop everything up, dice everything, make it into something fancy.

From that day on, I decided to cure myself of what I had learned. I know that how I work and contribute at BTA is a much more personal matter than any of these design process theories. And I think that's the way it is with each of us.

VISUALIZING ENVIRONMENTS

環境の視覚化

Thompson's way of simulating design ideas by projecting slide collages has built a powerful communication tool — and a poetic art form

スライドを映してデザインアイディアをまとめるトンプソンのやり方は強力なコミュニケーションの武器であり，詩的な芸術である．

A unique aspect of BTA's "Studio Process" of design is the use of photo-imagery for visually exploring and presenting not just the design project itself, but the ideas and ideals associated with it. Sometimes called "image modeling," these productions are more often simply referred to by BTA staff as "slide shows."

Following the 1968 assassinations of Martin Luther King and Robert Kennedy, Ben Thompson felt challenged to present a positive new view of urban life in response to a chronic sense of hopelessness about America's cities. Using triple slide images accompanied by music, he created a visual metaphor of an ideal city, calling it "A New Vision of the City of Man."

It combined images of the people and architecture from many cities, from Venice to Helsinki, London to San Francisco. The images captured texture, color, scale, and human drama in buildings and public places — projecting them on three large screens like a living collage. "The City of Man" became the reference point for design within BTA: a tool for teaching and for communications with staff, clients, agencies, and students. Since there is no single ideal city for studying the issues of urban life, it was a composite of the best experiences — an urban montage in which the relationship of human scale to building scale was always apparent.

This form of visual simulation — usually accompanied by music and some informal commentary — has become a standard BTA technique for analyzing site character and building context at every stage of the design process from conceptual exploration to completion, from model to reality. The final show is usually a "you are there" visual recreation of a gala opening event.

Photos: Rex McManamy

BTA's slide library contains 250,000 images.

BTAのライブラリーにある25万枚のスライド．

BTAのスタジオプロセスの特徴の1つにスライド写真の活用がある．これは，スライド写真を使ってデザイン行為そのものをするというより，ビジュアルに問題を展開したり提示するために，考えを引き出し，まとめ上げていくのを助けるものだ．ときには，これはイメージづくりとも呼ばれるが，BTAのスタッフの間では単にスライドショーと呼ばれている．

1968年，キング牧師とロバート・ケネディが暗殺されたことに触発されて，トンプソンはアメリカの都市につきまとう慢性の絶望的な状態に対して積極的に新たな都市生活像を描こうと決心した．3枚同時に映写する音楽入りのトリプルスライドで，彼は理想とする都市像を描いて見せた．それが新版「人間の都市」である．

世界のあらゆる都市，ベニス，ヘルシンキ，ロンドン，サンフランシスコなどから人と建築の結びつきをイメージして見せる．素材，色彩，スケール，人間のドラマがそれぞれの場所で演じられる．3重のスライドはまるで生きたコラージュである．「人間の都市」は，スタッフだけでなく，施主や関係者や学生たちすべてに教え，コミュニケイトするBTAのデザインの教科書である．都市生活の問題をスタディするのに参考となる格好の都市が存在しないため，このスライドは人間のスケールと建物のスケールの関係を明らかにする都市モンタージュとして，最良の手段といえる．

ときには音楽や解説も入ったこうしたビジュアルなシミュレーションは，BTAの敷地の分析や，プロジェクトの基本計画から完成にいたるまでの，模型から実物になるまでの，さまざまな分析の方法として定着している．プロジェクトの仕上げは，「さぁ，ここだよ」というオープニングのイベントでいつもやって見せるビジュアルショーである．

"A New Vision of the City of Man" 新版「人間の都市」

“The Ambiance of Paris” パリの雰囲気

16

Hotel Babin Kuk
1972

Architect
Edward Durell Stone and Associates

Location
Dubrovnik, Yugoslavia

Client
Hotelsko Touristicki Centar

Express Towers
1972

Architect
Joseph Allen Stein and Associates

Location
Mumbai, India

Client
Indian Express Limited
University of Petroleum and Minerals

Tour Gan
1972–1974

Architect
Harrison and Abramovitz

Location
La Défense, France

Client
Groupe des Assurances Nationales (GAN)

US Embassy
1972–1976

VICTOR GRUEN INTERNATIONAL

Architect
Gruen Associates

Location
Tokyo, Japan

Client
US Department of State, Foreign Buildings Operations

Torin Corporation
1973–1974

MBA

Architect
Marcel Breuer Associates

Location
Penrith, Australia

Client
Torin Corporation

Polimex-Cekop Meat Processing Plant
1973–1975

EPSTEIN

Architect
A. Epstein and Sons Inc.

Location
Ostrada, Poland

Client
Polimex-Cekop Ltd.

Souk Al Safat
1973–1979

TAC

Architect
The Architects Collaborative

Location
Kuwait City, Kuwait

Consultant
Pace

Client
Kuwait Investment Company

Souk Al Manakh
1973–1979

TAC

Architect
The Architects Collaborative

Location
Kuwait City, Kuwait

Client
Kuwait Investment Company

Souk Al Wataniyah
1973–1979

TAC

Architect
The Architects Collaborative

Location
Kuwait City, Kuwait

Consultant
Pace

Client
Kuwait Investment Company

Saudi Arabian National Guard Headquarters
1973–1980

LEO A DALY

Architect
Leo A Daly

Location
Riyadh, Saudi Arabia

Client
US Army Corps of Engineers, Saudi Arabian National Guard

Royal Saudi Air Force Headquarters Building
1973–1981

SMITHGROUPJJR

Architect
Smith Hinchman and Grylls

Location
Riyadh, Saudi Arabia

Client
Royal Saudi Air Force

National Library
1973–1981

TAC

Architect
The Architects Collaborative

Location
Abu Dhabi, United Arab Emirates

Client
Abu Dhabi Tourism & Culture Authority

Crude Ideals: Architecture and Oil in the Gulf States

The work of the largest US offices after the 1930s frequently followed the path of petroleum, first in Venezuela, Colombia, India and Indonesia (the first major sources of foreign oil) and then in the Middle Eastern Gulf States after World War II. As newly wealthy states sought to place themselves on the world stage, US architects chased the specter of petroleum-fueled development and the speculative finance economy to which it gave rise. Governmental complexes, vast military cities, new towns for oil workers, airports, banking towers, commercial centers, and luxury hotels were financed by oil companies and institutional clients made rich by national oil revenue, often enabled by Western conglomerates like Bechtel or federal entities like the US Army Corps of Engineers. The US Embassy in Baghdad by Josep Lluís Sert (1955–1961) and the University of Baghdad by The Architects Collaborative (1957–1983) were among the earliest examples of what quickly became a heavy involvement in the region by US firms including Brown Daltas & Associates, Caudill Rowlett Scott (CRS), Minoru Yamasaki Associates, Skidmore, Owings & Merrill (SOM), Leo A Daly, HOK, William Pereira & Associates, and others.[1]

The presence of US firms reached its peak during the boom in crude oil prices that followed the OPEC oil embargo in 1973, a shift in clientele that formed a corollary to the corresponding decline in building practice in the United States. By mid-decade, a raft articles in the US press speculated about the new, "oil-rich Middle East… the new frontier for professional services." *Architectural Record* asked, with both anticipation and unease: "is this the new client?"[2] Written in the manner of wary but hopeful field guides, such articles sought to outline the intricate foreign protocols which architects would have to negotiate if they hoped to work with Gulf clients. Concrete was the material of choice for many of these firms, a synthetic composite of foreign technics

① For a timeline of US firms and projects in the Gulf in this period, see Michael Kubo, "Petroleum Power: Architecture and Oil," in Eva Franch i Gilabert, Amanda Lawrence, Ana Miljački, Ashley Schafer, ed., *OfficeUS Agenda* (Zurich: Lars Müller, 2014): 160–167.

② Charles Hoyt, "The Oil-Rich Mideast: The new frontier for professional services?" *Architectural Record* (June 1975): 101–108.

1945

1948
- Bechtel completes Trans-Arabian Pipeline (Tapline)
- Standard Oil of New Jersey, Socony-Vacuum Oil join Socal and Texaco as owners of Arabian-American Oil Company (ARAMCO)

1950
Iraq Development Board created to spend 70% of national oil revenue on development

1951
Iran's oil industry nationalized from Anglo-Iranian Oil Company

1953
August 19
Coup in Iran orchestrated by UK and US governments; US-supported Pahlavi dynasty assumes power

1955
Turkey, Iraq, Pakistan and Iran form Baghdad Pact

1958
July 14
Coup in Iraq; pro-Western Hashemite monarchy overthrown

1959
Iraq leaves Baghdad Pact

1960
Organization of Petroleum Exporting Countries (OPEC) begins

1961
- Iraqi oil industry nationalized
- Kuwait becomes independent state

1950–1953 Korean War

1962 Cuban Missile Crisis

1950–1975 Vietnam War

and on-the ground matter and labor. CRS, for example, described the sand-blasted concrete of its University of Petroleum and Minerals in Dhahran (1964–1982) as "a Saudi product" despite its reliance on imported protocols of sourcing and assembly.[3]

For Western architectural critics, the built products of this exchange proved difficult to evaluate. For Manfredo Tafuri and Francesco Dal Co, projects like the University of Baghdad, begun by The Architects Collaborative in 1957, were no more than "typical American export products with their puerile environmental touches, which in reality are strictly from Disney."[4] By 1983, Charles Jencks lamented in the revised edition of his *Modern Movements in Architecture* that "when our biggest offices… perpetrate a form of historicist kitsch in the Middle East… it is time to reassess our recent past and Western culture together: criticize the unthinking modernism and historicism which are so commercially successful."[5]

The volatile nature of this exchange manifested itself in the rise and fall of corporate US firms that grew in size largely due to work in the Gulf, but which also suffered the consequences of this involvement following the end of the oil boom. Emblematic of this rise-and-fall trajectory was TAC's design of the Souk Al Manakh (1973–1979), one of a series of parking garages with ground-level markets in the city center of Kuwait. Within a year of its completion the souk became the center of a vast unregulated stock exchange for trading non-Kuwaiti (mostly fictional) companies, which ballooned to absorb over $90 billion in excess speculation by Kuwait's oil-rich citizenry.[6] The sudden collapse of the Souk Al Manakh stock bubble in the fall of 1982 caused a fifty percent decline in construction in Kuwait within the year, a first blow to firms that had overcommitted to work in the country.

The Iranian Revolution, the economic fallout of the Iran-Iraq War, the beginning of OPEC quotas on oil production, the Iraqi invasion of Kuwait, and the first Persian Gulf War spelled the end of the first boom of US architects working in the Gulf. The next wave of oil-fueled development would take place after the economic boom of the 1990s, now in the United Arab Emirates, Qatar, Bahrain, Azerbaijan, and other new inheritors of the petroleum ideal. — MK

③ Jonathan King and Peter Langdon, ed., *The CRS Team and the Business of Architecture* (College Station: Texas A&M University Press, 2002): 143; Charles E. Lawrence, *Saudi Search* (Houston: CRSS Research, 1986).

④ Manfredo Tafuri and Francesco Dal Co, *Modern Architecture/2* (Milan: Electa, 1976): 307.

⑤ Charles Jencks, *Modern Movements in Architecture*, 2nd ed. (London: Penguin Books, 1985): 8.

⑥ Ihsan A. Hijazi, "Kuwait in Bailout Effort After Market Collapses," *The New York Times* (December 20, 1982): 29, 32.

1973

1991

1980–1988 Iran-Iraq War

1979–1981 Iran Hostage Crisis

1965 US Army Corps of Engineers contracted to build military facilities in Saudi Arabia

1973 OPEC oil embargo begins

1975 Kuwait Oil Company nationalized

1979
- Iranian Revolution; Pahlavi monarchy overthrown
- Saddam Hussein comes to power in Iraq, launches major building program in Baghdad

1980 Saudi Arabian government acquires 100% percent ownership stake of ARAMCO

1981
- East–West Pipeline linking Jubail and Yanbu industrial port cities completed
- Oil glut; first OPEC quotas on oil production

1982 Souk al Manakh black-market stock exchange collapses in Kuwait

1990 Iraq invades Kuwait

1995

1990–1991 First Persian Gulf War

US Architects in the Gulf States 1945–1991

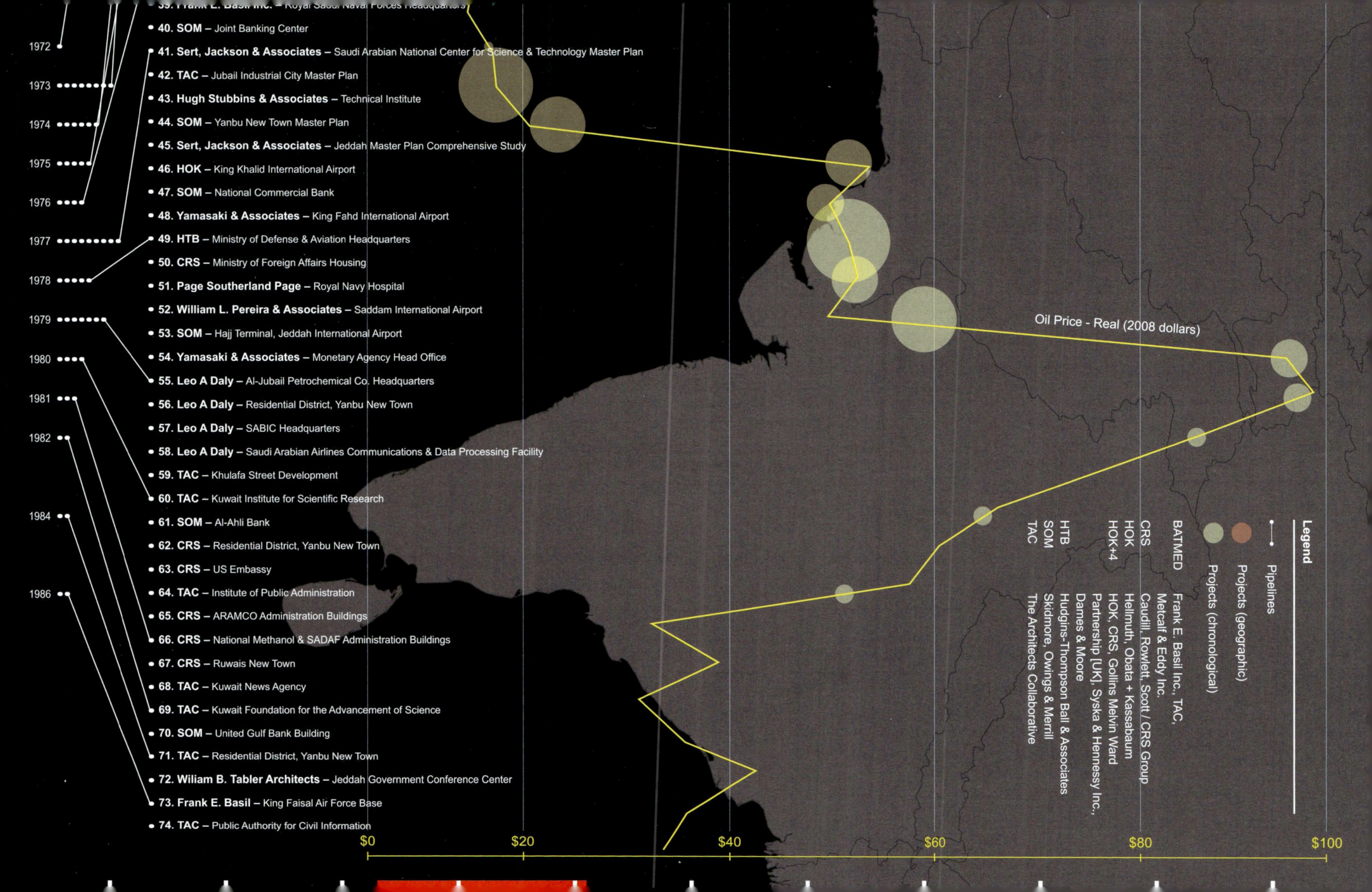

1972
1973
1974
1975
1976
1977
1978
1979
1980
1981
1982
1984
1986
40. SOM – Joint Banking Center
41. Sert, Jackson & Associates – Saudi Arabian National Center for Science & Technology Master Plan
42. TAC – Jubail Industrial City Master Plan
43. Hugh Stubbins & Associates – Technical Institute
44. SOM – Yanbu New Town Master Plan
45. Sert, Jackson & Associates – Jeddah Master Plan Comprehensive Study
46. HOK – King Khalid International Airport
47. SOM – National Commercial Bank
48. Yamasaki & Associates – King Fahd International Airport
49. HTB – Ministry of Defense & Aviation Headquarters
50. CRS – Ministry of Foreign Affairs Housing
51. Page Southerland Page – Royal Navy Hospital
52. William L. Pereira & Associates – Saddam International Airport
53. SOM – Hajj Terminal, Jeddah International Airport
54. Yamasaki & Associates – Monetary Agency Head Office
55. Leo A Daly – Al-Jubail Petrochemical Co. Headquarters
56. Leo A Daly – Residential District, Yanbu New Town
57. Leo A Daly – SABIC Headquarters
58. Leo A Daly – Saudi Arabian Airlines Communications & Data Processing Facility
59. TAC – Khulafa Street Development
60. TAC – Kuwait Institute for Scientific Research
61. SOM – Al-Ahli Bank
62. CRS – Residential District, Yanbu New Town
63. CRS – US Embassy
64. TAC – Institute of Public Administration
65. CRS – ARAMCO Administration Buildings
66. CRS – National Methanol & SADAF Administration Buildings
67. CRS – Ruwais New Town
68. TAC – Kuwait News Agency
69. TAC – Kuwait Foundation for the Advancement of Science
70. SOM – United Gulf Bank Building
71. TAC – Residential District, Yanbu New Town
72. Wiliam B. Tabler Architects – Jeddah Government Conference Center
73. Frank E. Basil – King Faisal Air Force Base
74. TAC – Public Authority for Civil Information
Oil Price - Real (2008 dollars)
$0
$20
$40
$60
$80
$100
Legend
Pipelines
Projects (geographic)
Projects (chronological)
BATMED Frank E. Basil Inc., TAC, Metcalf & Eddy Inc.
CRS Caudill, Rowlett, Scott / CRS Group
HOK Hellmuth, Obata + Kassabaum
HOK+4 HOK, CRS, Gollins Melvin Ward Partnership [UK], Syska & Hennessy Inc., Dames & Moore
HTB Hudgins-Thompson Ball & Associates
SOM Skidmore, Owings & Merrill
TAC The Architects Collaborative

The Persian adventures of two U.S. architects range from a Coca-Cola plant to a princess's palace

AMERICANS ABROAD: BROWN AND DALTAS IN IRAN

Few architects have among their first commissions a palace for a real-life princess. For Benjamin I. Brown of Albany, Ga., and Spero Daltas of St. Paul, Minn., it has been the high light of a five-year adventure in expatriate architecture. Their firm of Brown & Daltas, Teheran, Iran, has specialized in a modern adaptation of native materials and techniques. Their architecture, in the words of an admirer in the Iranian royal family, is "more Persian than the Persians'."

If this is the case, it is partly because Iranian architects want to be anything but Persian in these days of rapid Westernization. But it also reflects the two young Americans' sensitivity to the ancient arts of the Middle East. Brown & Daltas have used the marvelous geometric patterns of the Persians in tilework, masonry walls, coffered ceilings, light grilles, and even a heavy steel structural frame. They have exploited the Iranians' traditional skill at building brick vaults, and revived the dormant art of glazing. Finally, they have gratified the Persians' reverence of water by making it an integral element of both buildings and gardens.

Brown, 37, and Daltas, 42, met in Iran when both were architectural consultants to the engineering firm of Amman & Whitney-Husted on $60 million worth of military bases for the U.S. Army Corps of Engineers. Brown had been a partner in the Memphis firm of A. L. Aydelott & Associates, and had come overseas in 1953 as chief architect for several Amman & Whitney projects in France and Greece. Daltas came directly to Iran in 1956 after five years with Eero Saarinen (he had been job captain for the successful Saarinen entry in the London embassy competition). Brown & Daltas soon found that they shared the feeling of having worked for other people long enough, and their office opened in January 1957. Their first major project was a Coca-Cola bottling plant, their second the palace of Her Imperial Highness Fatemeh, sister to the Shah, in the royal gardens of Saadabad above Teheran. The firm was off to an auspicious start.

At the outset, however, Brown & Daltas found the difficulties of practicing in Iran formidable. Drafting-room talent was hard to find (eventually they developed a hard core of a dozen men, mostly Armenians, and farmed out most production work on large projects). Brick and gypsum were literally as cheap as dirt, but anything that had to be shipped in was exorbitant. The Iranian bricklayers (many in their early teens) were masterful, and refinery projects had developed a pool of skilled steelworkers. Even they had to be closely supervised, however, and the Iranians had to be taught other building crafts almost from scratch.

But the most persistent problem was financial. Building costs are amazingly low—hence, so are fees. Moreover, the French-trained Persian architects charge from 3 to 5 per cent, making it hard to convince hard-bargaining Iranian clients that they should pay at a state-side level. Even 8 per cent is unrealistic considering the amount of supervision required to do a conscientious job. After two struggling years, however, Brown & Daltas began to get some of the Army bases on which, mercifully, the Corps of Engineers does its own supervision. "It was the military work that kept our heads above water," Brown frankly admits.

The firm is now beginning to branch out. The partners are completing negotiations for a series of U. S.-aided college projects in tropical Africa, and starting a new 6,000-student campus for Rangoon University financed by the Agency for International Development; it will be designed in conjunction with the Burmese national building bureau, and used as a training ground for the university's architectural students. Full use will be made of local skills and materials: Daltas is experimenting with glazed, prestressed sections of Burmese terra cotta as both structure and finish.

Brown & Daltas recently established an office in Harrisburg, Pa., and plan to open another in Europe. There is still work to be completed in Teheran, but continuance of their Iranian practice will depend on the future course of the nation's presently sluggish economy. The Harrisburg office is more for production of the overseas work than for U. S. projects: Brown & Daltas are enjoying their role as ambassadors of American architecture abroad.

Mr. Daltas (left), Mr. Brown, the princess, and her new palace (opposite)

ROBERT MOORE

The palace of Princess Fatemeh is roofed by a composite canopy of concrete, steel, and glazed-brick vaulting

PHOTOS: RON PARTRIDGE

The roof of Princess Fatemeh's palace is composed of 24 octagonal umbrellas whose undersides are graceful brick vaulting. The umbrella frames are 2-inch pipes which cluster as central supports, then flare outward. The vaults were built from their outer edges in, without formwork—Iran's dry climate allows use of a gypsum mortar that bonds almost instantly. The bricks doubled as finished ceiling and forms for a layer of concrete. The concrete, in turn, was tied to the ribs with shear bars to create a composite structure.

Exposed sides of the handmade bricks, shaped to provide acoustical recesses, were glazed by an Iranian craftsman trained under an Italian technical-assistance program. They were given eight muted and closely related colors. During the day the greens predominate, and at night the brick vaults take on a golden glow.

The central portion of the palace is one great space, divided into an alabaster entrance terrace, a central reception room, and the large living room. On either side of the reception room, ramps bridge across a series of staggered pools to two-story wings on either side of the main volume. The water, brought from a mountain stream, cascades through glazed tile courses which ring around the driveway and meet at the entry. It continues through the palace's interior, feeds the air-conditioning system, and is thus warmed for the large swimming pool. Finally, it winds up in a complex network of fountains and reflecting pools in the rear gardens.

Construction cost was $14 per square foot. Engineers: Frank Newby and G. Megeroumian (structural), F. & R. Farman-Farmaian (mechanical). General contractor: Hoch-Tief Irranieane.

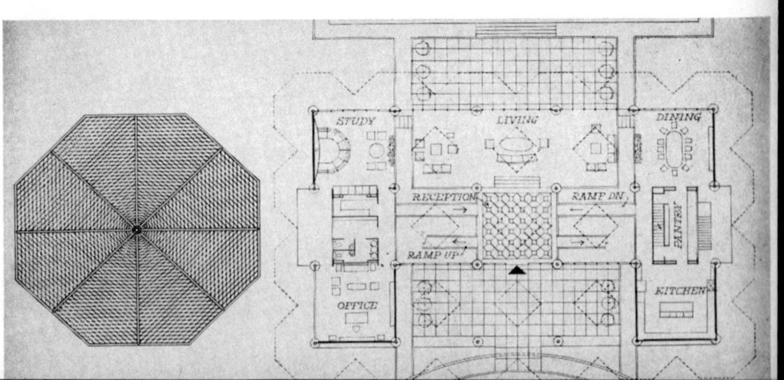

Swimming pool reflects the play of light on the glazed-brick vaults of the glass-walled palace. The garden site is in the foothills of Teheran

Ramps to the palace's two-story sections bridge over multilevel pools

The voluminous living room: skylights join clusters of four umbrellas

The ceiling of the Coca-Cola plant at Meshed, a glass-walled pavilion on the arid plains, is almost equally palatial

East meets West on the road to Meshed. Below, the composition of building's vaulted, steel-ribbed roof.

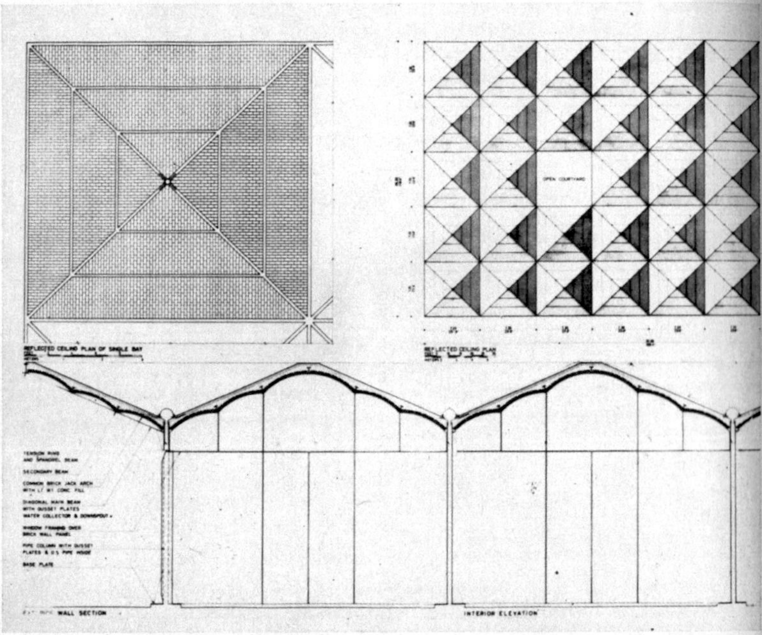

The plant sits pavilion-like in a subdivided octagon of land. Project also included employee housing.

The owner of this Persian Coca-Cola bottling plant wanted something different—and certainly got it. The usual way to put up a small industrial building in Iran is to have a prefabricated steel structure shipped in. Brown & Daltas' client, however, wanted to make his plant a pavilion, the focal point of a new development on the outskirts of Meshed (400 miles from Teheran toward the Russian border) including subdivisions and housing for his 385 employees. But he preferred to do so without paying a premium price.

The voluptuous ceiling which raises the building considerably above the architectural level of most bottling plants is similar in concept to that of the palace—a tightly knit composite structure of steel, concrete, and brick vaulting. Here the bricks are common bricks, left unglazed, but they were built with the same native skill in shallow arches with a lightweight concrete topping. They are supported by a wiry frame of steel bars which doubles as a tension ring, resulting in a continuously framed building of surprising strength and economy. The roof tested to six times its design load. The cost figures are other-worldly: 15 cents per square foot for the bricks in place, 2½ cents per pound for fabrication of the steel members, and $3.90 per square foot for the completed building.

Except in the warehouse, the walls are glass, and a steady stream of travelers and pilgrims stops to watch the bottling process in operation. At the main entry is a wide reflecting pool. The surrounding land is laid out in an octagonal pattern, and sale of the subdivided parcels more than paid for the building.

Engineers: G. Megerdoumian (structural), M. P. M. Engineers (mechanical and electrical).

e ceiling rises in an undulating series of brick arches. Thinness of the frame was a key cost-saving element—steel is expensive to ship in.

wide reflecting pool flanks the walkway to the plant's front entry

The bottling equipment was put on public display behind glass walls

A lofty and exotic bazaar opens from a Teheran office tower that is wrapped in a rigid structural steel grille

The spectacular arcade (opposite) leads directly from the tall, glazed lobby of the square office tower

A 16-story office tower and shopping center are, of course, far more difficult to relate to Persia's exotic heritage than is a palace, but Brown & Daltas have tried. The tower is on a narrow frontage along Teheran's teeming main commercial street, and the shops are in a five-story arcade on a thin finger of land behind.

Around the tower's exterior is a stiff frame of steel columns and X-braces—last month's tragedy in Iran was fresh evidence of the need to respect earthquake forces. And around the Xs Brown and Daltas have developed a geometric Persian pattern in steel which provides additional seismic bracing and a degree of sun control. Main trusses run through the square tower at third points, supporting secondary trusses on 4-foot 5-inch centers. A coffered concrete slab is cast around the top chord of the secondary truss to create a composite floor structure; the angles of the bottom chord are used to support a cast-in-place gypsum ceiling, with utilities in the space between. At right angles to the secondary truss, on the same 4-foot 5-inch module, is a suspension cable anchored to ends of the floor slab.

In the arcade, a similar structure produces a spectacular space. Its roof is a continuous, steel-framed, opaque glass skylight; its floor is a series of alabaster-rimmed pools. The first two stories are a flavorful bazaar, the upper three are offices. Railings of the balconies and bridges repeat the pattern of the tower's grille.

Construction costs were $7.50 per square foot for the tower and $5.50 for the arcade. Engineers: Newby, Megerdoumian, and Walter Mahkan (structural), R. Costain (mechanical and electrical). General contractor: Rah-Bana Co.

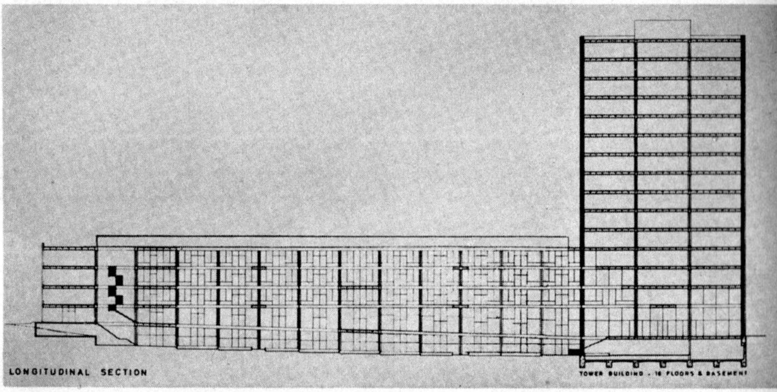

Geometric pattern in steel makes a Persian grille of the tower's frame. Spandrels are sky-blue mosaic tile.

EARL W. BRYDGES PUBLIC LIBRARY, NIAGARA FALLS, NEW YORK, BY PAUL RUDOLPH

ARCHITECTURAL RECORD

JUNE 1975 6 A McGRAW-HILL PUBLICATION FOUR DOLLARS PER COPY

THE OIL-RICH MIDEAST:

The new frontier for professional services?

Most of the photos in the following article are by architect Der Scutt, who is well traveled in the Mideast and who has just returned from his latest trip.

Suburban Riyadh: "waiting for housing?"

is this the new client?

Symbolizing the often-present wall between architects and the pyramids of bureaucracy in Mideast governments, Saudi Arabians open the University of Petroleum and Minerals designed by architects Caudill, Rowlett and Scott.

With so many architects and engineers from the United States involved in work in the Mideast, less adventurous professionals may reasonably wonder if they are missing untapped opportunities. But, before he or she purchases a plane ticket to seek out "the new client", here are a few points to consider:

Professional services from the United States are in continuing demand, but . . .

Firms that are new to the area will not be as easily accepted today as they were only a few years ago. The competition from all nations has become too sharp. "The days when American architects were treated as kings are gone." Still, according to Hans Neumann, president of Perkins and Will International: "The prestige of the American professional is unexcelled." This thought is seconded by many with good cause: the fast pace, with which Arab and Iranian leaders want to develop their countries, can only be facilitated by those offering the greatest efficiency.

These leaders are also conscious of their image, and the superficial image that many want—for better or for worse—is that of America. According to Dr. Charles Adams, Director of Islamic Studies at McGill University: "They have a love-hate relationship with us." Especially, the Arabs do not like many Americans' demeaning attitude, but their money now evens the score. One cynic comments that they would like U.S. technology by remote control, without the U.S. presence, which is disrupting to their entrenched patterns—"Our unshrouded women are considered practically naked."

Even so, all evidence is that the Arabs prefer doing business with Americans, because most are honest and open. For many years, the buying patterns of the American-Arabian Oil Company has strongly influenced those of the Saudi Arabian government, which is currently spending money at the rate of $200 million a month, and the amount is going up fast and steadily. The government employs American advisers at every level. The flow of materials and equipment to all of these oil-rich countries has reached a record-breaking, accelerating rate; who will determine the results?

While the immediate potential is enormous, it will require ambition

To obtain their goal of national self sufficiency and desirable living conditions for all of their people, each of these developing countries has a long way to go. Despite national incomes that have recently become staggering, almost all of the populations live in deplorable conditions, and almost every commodity is imported.

In Saudi Arabia, the last five-year plan produced 175,000 units of housing in a country variously estimated to contain between 3 and 8 million people. In an announcement in *The New York Times* on April 19, 1975, Crown Prince Fahd Bin Abdul–Aziz stated that the next five-year plan would find every citizen in comfortable housing with running water and electricity. While the actual goals of the next five-year plan may not be so optimistic, all kinds of projects to be built in the Mideast are conceived on an enormous scale (some can be measured by a cost in excess of a billion dollars). And there is an obvious reason; according to Saudi Planning Minister Isham Nazer: "There isn't a moment to be lost." The national economies must become self-sufficient and diversified before the oil income disappears.

Accordingly, much government work (which is most of the Mideast work) is going to firms which have a proven capacity—on their own or in consortium. There will be many commissions for smaller-scale work, but the already sharp competition will rise inversely to size.

It will not always be easy to identify a possible client

Ostensibly, a client may be a representative of the government in his country, although this is not necessarily the full situation. The ments' present dependency on Wester agement techniques causes alliances w lic and private organizations in almo major city of Europe and America.

It is possible to meet "half" of a M ern client in New York City (where t U.S. banks managing Arab developme porations in joint venture on Iran's i projects, and the boards of various American universities) or in Livorn where the U.S. Army Corps of Enginee ages a volume of Saudi Arabian con that will exceed $4 billion by 1980. Hyatt, Sheraton and Holiday Inn b operate hotels for local governments vate developers; Inter-Continental ha 15 hotels in design or construction in Private developers and contractors f U.S.—including Bechtel, Turner, a rett—are building many Mideastern on a "turn-key" basis. All of these zations, and many more, commissio ommend architects and engineers.

Still the decision maker in award professional service contracts will be owner, in both private and public wo Mideastern capital has a telepho (Tehran has a partial listing in Farsi), uals are difficult to identify and locate officers in financial institutions and n is contained in the Middle East Fina rectory and can be obtained by send quest and 8 pounds sterling to the Di 84 Chancery Lane, London WC2A 1D ever, the person whose title indicate sibility may not be in actual charg reorganizing the national civil service a clear chain of command, but—as Arabia— the Minister for Commu may be responsible for highways.

But, recognition of the client will do little good if that client is not reache

It will be almost impossible to obtai mission from a Mideast client withou

ized Beirut (top) is "home base" for many ns' foreign operations. In the harbor of tiny bottom), almost every building has been built he last five years, and more are coming.

The governments will work at top speed to provide every citizen with new, low-cost housing like Kuwait's (top), as long as the majority of the population lives in facilities like those outside of Riyadh (bottom)—or worse.

But, will the high qualities of indigenous architecture be lost in the rush? Top: Isfahan, back of the Friday Mosque. Bottom: Dubai, wind traps for natural air conditioning.

d being interviewed; the trip will be onsuming and expensive. Hotel reserva- xcept in Beirut) are often not honored. "American style" rooms cost at least 50 a day, the professional may be ex- to wait for days—even weeks—before interview. In the Arab countries, there few diversions. Alcohol, movies and are forbidden in Saudi Arabia and . And—if a commission is obtained— nt will expect to see the professional business is always "face to face"). Do on weekends (Thursday and Friday) or the summer (the clients are away). And, in the interview. . . .

cording to the U.S. Department of rce, firms wishing to do business with di Arabian government must have a na- s a representative, and the key to suc- failure hinges on the choice. This can to be true to a greater or lesser degree out the area. Good agents can arrange ing from visas to ministerial appoint- they will know of upcoming contracts nd up for their absent employer. The rce Department does not report that will also negotiate any gift required to he work, which is an accepted practice out the Mideast—to the point that it is nes included as an item separated from fessional's fee in applicable contracts. epartment has a "Near East Action in Washington.) According to others, nt is effective only through his personal s, and the wrong choice can lead to an ve dead end.

finally entering the interview, the pro- al *must* understand the traditional pro- At least one architect, Ellerbe's pres- en Mahal, is known to have taken a offered by Harvard in Switzerland. s is never discussed until the social es are observed; the process may take he potential client will be painfully po- tradition), probably embarrassingly in- and shrewd (he will respect the professional who tries to drive a hard bargain). He will almost always speak English well—and often with an American accent. On politeness in Arab countries, "My eyes are your sacrifice" means "thank you." Patience will be the test. And finally, the professional should be confident and enthusiastic.

And what will the client expect to find in the professional's background? The governments are sophisticated enough to have criteria for pre-qualifying architects and engineers on the basis of technical competence. Beyond technical competence, the public and private client will look for familiarity. Those educated in America will prefer Americans, and those educated in Europe, Europeans. Firms which have proven their abilities are favored; the first project is the critical one for any architect or engineer. Specialists (in, for instance, hospitals) will find a more "ready-made" market for services.

And the client will be looking for performance. He will want firms with an established presence—capable of on-going responsibility for their work. On the religious issue, Israeli firms are doing work in Iran, and firms with Jewish principals are doing work throughout the Mideast—despite the official stance to the contrary.

Although the first one may be negotiated at a disadvantage, the contract is all-important

After the polite interview has ended, many professionals from all over the world are using tactics to obtain contracts which more than one observer describes as "cut-throat." Some Iranians (in particular) have not been slow to exploit this situation—issuing multiple letters of intent for single projects, and using preliminary designs by one firm for completion by another. Still, a signed contract is collateral for a loan for up to one-third of its value in most Arabian banks, and—after signing—it is not uncommon for the professional to receive up to another third as payment for starting the project.

When a commission is received, the most important issue for the professional and the client will be the contract. Despite the existence of final agreements which consist of single-page letters, a contract should describe responsibilities and payment procedures in detail; it should be written by a local lawyer. Because professionals from many countries work in the area, there are many different services offered, and the lack of a good contract will lead to confusion. The European professionals, who were in the area before most American firms, generally prepared preliminary plans that were turned over to a builder. Accordingly, standard contracts now try to place all of the responsibility for the builder's performance on to the designer. The Syrians and Iraqis (in particular) would like a completed building delivered under a "turnkey" system, and architects are taking this responsibility—on their own or in consortium with developers. But, there is an obvious danger in turnkey: there is no way to know what a building will finally cost. Material and equipment can double in cost in one day, if they are in demand (and can be found).

Most contracts in Arab countries are written according to Lebanese law, which prevails except in the Emirates, which use British law. But it is possible to call for arbitration by the International Chamber of Commerce in Paris or the Institute of Engineers in London. Professionals have successfully called for protection clauses on losses due to acts of war, God and devaluation. In those countries that do not have freely convertible currencies, the design fee should be paid in dollars, although—without a devaluation clause—money may be lost (most Mideast countries severed their currencies' links with the dollar early this year). A good contract will describe the machinery for payment which—in the case of government work—can be circuitous and—in any case—possibly delayed. And finally, a government contract must clear all of the necessary regulations and agencies *after* signing to become legal.

There is no one market

Each country and state is culturally unique, and relative areas of land are not directly related to needs or to the ability to cope with needs.

And—when it is all over—the first work will probably cost the designer money

Since the first project is the critical one in securing future work, architects and engineers will want to make a special effort to assure its success. At the same time they will be working in unfamiliar circumstances with contracts (negotiated at a disadvantage) that usually do not provide reimbursement for research, consultants or travel. Still, on-site supervision is much more critical than in the U.S., and consultants on everything from the survival of plant life to concrete mixes will be required. There are few construction standards and minimal records on temperatures and wind (see page 108). As for extra costs being absorbed, almost every architect, contributing to this article, stated that their total fees were approximately the same or below comparable base fees at home.

Does the future potential warrant all of this effort?

At their present rate of expenditure and income, Saudi Arabia, Kuwait, Qatar and the Emirates would hold a recently estimated 333 billion dollars in reserves by 1980, which is more, by a half, than those held by the entire world today. But this amount will probably not materialize because of the accelerating rate with which these countries are rushing toward development for self-sufficiency, before the oil disapppears—possibly by the year 2000. If the area remains politically stable, the potential for construction should go on for some time. After every citizen and organization is decently housed, there will be redevelopment to meet the "revolution of rising expectations." But it is not likely that the West will participate as strongly as at present. The number of technically trained Saudis (estimated at 2,500) is exceeded by the number *currently* in Western schools. Iran requires local participation in any business venture and the other countries encourage it. In all of the countries, capabilities are bound to catch up with demand. If the situation still seems worthwhile. . . .

"The most important thing is to know where you are going"

There is no homogeneous demand for architectural or engineering services in the Mideast. The character of the potential client and his needs is extremely different in every country. According to George Rice, former head of McKee-Berger-Mansueto's Beirut office: "The assumption that the countries are alike is the most common mistake of Western businessmen—as incorrect as lumping the United States, Mexico and Canada." An expectant professional will want to know the pertinent characteristics .

The most pronounced difference is between Iran and the Arab countries. To relatively judge each block's long-range economic importance, an oil company executive states that—at present—the West could survive without the production of oil in all of the Mideast and African countries except Iran and Saudi Arabia (the leader). While Kuwait has produced oil at almost half of the rate of Saudi Arabia, the latter's known reserves are infinitely larger. Until recently, the gross national product of Iran approximately equaled that of all of the Arab countries together. But it has a much broader economic base, and the quadrupling of oil prices has thrown the balance to the Arabs. On the short range, one of the most important determinates of the ability to build buildings, is the national income per capita. Here, the smaller Arab states clearly take the lead. The Emirate state of Abu Dhabi had the world's highest per capita income in 1974: $28,000 for each man, woman and child (vs.$4,500 in the U.S.). Kuwait had a lesser per capita income, but one that is still approximately ten times larger than Saudi Arabia's. The other United Arab Emirates, and Qatar and Bahrain had substantially larger proportional incomes (in descending order) than the two larger countries.

Islam, the common religion, has different influences on each country. In Saudi Arabia, where the King is also the Defender of the Faith for all of Islam, the influence colors every sentence and act. There are few l versions of any kind, and public exe (including stoning) are common. We are not exempt from unusual punishme are considered at fault in (for instance automobile accident. Accordingly drunkenness and adultery are almo known. Women, who are segregated in cannot work in offices. Secondary routes for women are still commonly p from every room. But there is eviden strict segregation may disappear, as it h new hotel in Riyadh. Kuwait is similar servative while the citizens of the Emira considerably more tolerant. They have tation for independence and influence English. There is an endless demand f hotels in all Arab countries, as these s the only social centers.

The country least influenced by I Iran, which allows many religions, and the high rate of theft causes at least one tectural office to keep live-in servants. thing disappears: light bulbs in new bu and reinforcing rods from construction Urban women are active in the professio fully Western. Comparing the two countries:

Saudi Arabia

The gross national product in 1974 wa $46 billion, of which more than half income: and its growth is 25 per cent (the fastest in the world). Only estimate population exist: 8 million (by the g ment), 3 million (by resident foreigne though the government is making ever to broaden the base of income with i and exploration for gold and iron, it is little effort to conserve fuel or water. new buildings have little insulation or s tection despite normal 110-degree te tures; the only source of water for the Riyadh, is a fossil aquifer which will b tied if ways are not found to fill it. A n

evard in "culturally liberal" Abu Dhabi (top) or expected development similar to that in vntown of "strict" Kuwait (bottom).

High-rise housing (top) and a typical private "villa" (bottom) in Kuwait; the variety of character is as diverse as the architects and clients.

Women flee the camera in "modern-appearing" Dubai, while a stylistically traditional royal palace in Riyadh contains every current standard for Westernized comforts. The contrasts in life-styles are unnerving for Westerners.

of Western technicians and foreign la- , (about 50 per cent of the total) has d shortages of everything and is bound to a long-term effect on strict local customs. uction firms representing 47 different ries work in the capital which—along Mecca (forbidden to non-Muslims) is the of the conservative regime. Jiddah is Westernized, but is too isolated for the ct of government business.

While interested in value for their money, rabians are far more concerned with s-image" in their buildings than the Iran- Construction costs on two hotels in n and Mecca have been $150,000 a and another building in Rijadh is de- d by its architect as the most expensive uare-foot project in the world. While are building permits, they are not re- for construction by the government or the 5,000 princes; it is impossible to the real volume of construction.

s developed by the Central Planning Or- tion (which includes 10 Stanford Re- Institute consultants), the new five-year alls for government spending on con- on of $27 billion a year by 1980—com- to three at present. While much of the onstruction will be on heavy-industrial ations and the support systems of roads wers, all types of buildings (particularly g) are included. A draft transportation by government consultants recom- four new airports and the improvement more. As reported by *Engineering News d*, military installations will include two bases to cost $1 billion, an army base to e same, and five others whose cost will early another $1 billion. A new indus- y on the Persian Gulf is planned to cost lion. An Arab Investment Company has reated to stimulate private housing con- on by forgiving the last 25 per cent of ges. Two massive medical facilities CORD, page 41, May 1975) are the first ries expected to be built by 1980.

Iran

In 1974, the gross national product was $41 billion; the population was 31 million people, who are multiplying at an accelerating rate of almost 4 per cent (compared to Saudi Arabia's steady 1.3 per cent). The country is clearly feeling the pressures (and possible assets) of the mid-twentieth century West.

Until recently, the government has been in debt to support a program of development, which (with increased oil revenues) has been rebudgeted to equal that of Saudi Arabia in 1980. The capital city alone, Tehran with 4 million inhabitants, may be more populous than all of Saudi Arabia. The basically rural population is moving to the cities, and morato- riums on construction have been necessary be- cause of developed-land and material short- ages (which have dictated a masonry-braced steel construction for low-rise buildings). In order to diversify the pressure on Tehran, the government has established eight new indus- trial centers around the country. Isfahan (page 103), long regarded as important for its older architecture, has implemented a development plan (which includes a subway) limiting the population to one million people. To the south, Shiraz is in a similar situation.

While this is the 2001st year of Persian monarchy, private development is much more usual than in most Arab countries. Because of speculation, small sites for residences in Tehran can cost up to $150,000. "Everyone is crazy for profits." Accordingly, there is much more "shopping around" for professional serv- ices than there is anywhere else in the Mideast, and there are many more competent nationals to handle the demand.

Iran's pressures for speed in development are the greatest in the Mideast. Architects have been called in as foundations were in excava- tion. But the country is sophisticated enough to have its own critics who question their emerg- ing environment: In the words of architect E. Nader Khalili, "a national architecture can and will emerge."

Are currently involved professionals happy with their experience?

In order to do work in the Mideast, it will be necessary to have an office there or to make frequent trips. What have been the experiences of some of the architects, engineers and con- sultants who are there regularly? The con- sensus is that everything is expensive, scarce and difficult. A minimal house, by Western standards, is $1,000 a month in Saudi Arabia, and it can take up to three days to place a tele- phone call out of the country.

While Beirut and Tehran are the most Westernized cities, Beirut is favored for foreign offices because it is not the victim of the high- est inflation and does not bias Arabs who re- gard Iran as a more foreign country. Beirut is the only city in the Mideast where living costs and conditions don't require salaries for West- erners that are up to two and a half times nor- mal for the U.S. (some local draftsmen are available everywhere, but local labor laws make it difficult to terminate employment). But, the competition in Beirut is stiff, as it is estimated to contain up to 4000 architectural offices—some employing 500 people. High costs and local personnel shortages have caused Western joint ventures within joint ventures. Because of bad communications of every form, it will be necessary to have field offices, or affiliates on projects of any size.

Part of the problem in finding out about the Mideast is getting people to discuss their activities there. Aside from the obvious cause of warding off competition, there is—accord- ing to one architect—"a ridiculous net of polit- ical veils" whereby work cannot be published. There is a "mania" about security, on com- pleted buildings, and a love of waiting for the official announcement on others. One New York City architect, who denied having any work in the Mideast, is at work on a project of 10 million square feet in Tehran.

▪ Architect John Welsh heads the Beirut office of construction managers McKee-Berger-Man- sueto, who also have offices in Kuwait, Abu

learning from experience

Architects Caudill, Rowlett and Scott have been successful in producting an evolvement of indigenou architecture in their University of Petroleum and Minerals; visual similarities to the photo at right are obvious. But much of the new architecture (as seen on the last page) has not been so succ

Dhabi and Saudi Arabia. He said that much of their work is for governments, although there are seven or eight outstanding proposals to private developers. In Algeria, MBM is organizing a construction company for growth to some 56,000 employees. On their construction projects, MBM strongly believes in the turnkey process as the most effective method of producing what the clients want: completed projects. George Rice of MBM says that construction management is completely new to the Mideast, but the need is enormous.

▪ Engineer E. C. Kobbs handles business development of Middle East work for Caudill, Rowlett and Scott (CRS in 1964 was one of the first firms in Saudi Arabia, and the firm is working on projects of costs totaling close to $1 billion with an equal amount pending). Clients include the governments of Qatar, Bahrain and Saudi Arabia; plus ARAMCO and the Corps of Engineers. He credits the firm's success to their interdisciplanary skills, including construction management which is in growing demand. Detailed drawings are found to be more important than in the U.S.—contrary to Mideast practice. CRS/DA maintains an office of about 20 persons in Beirut and has an associate office in Riyadh with Rashid Engineering.

▪ Kathleen Kelly has just returned from Saudi Arabia (RECORD, October 1974; she was formerly with UDC) with a team of landscape architects consisting of Terry Schnadelbach, William Johnson and Grace Kirkwood. She says that, for the landscape architect, the area is unexplored territory. "There isn't even a list of plants that grow there or can survive." The sun and constant wind are predominant factors. Most of the top layer of soil is not sand, but many materials including cement; every soil is saline." The team's findings will be available shortly as a report.

▪ Hans Neumann is president of Perkins & Will International and maintains a Tehran office, with Iranian partners, of up to 80 people. Production work on larger projects is done in the Chicago office. Among the current projects are the Jondi Shapour University for 12,000 students on the Persian Gulf, a resort, and two hospitals. A new town on 3,000 acres near Tehran (photo, right) was carefully planned by P&W to consider traditional patterns of local life. But—according to Neumann—this plan was rejected by the clients because it was not Western. "They didn't want to hear the word bazaar. It was a shopping center. Many decision-makers are making the same mistakes that the West has, but the results will be worse."

▪ Architect Hugh Jacobsen, whose library in Cairo (RECORD, May 1974, page 120) is under construction, does not maintain a local office. He estimates that the library will take four years to build: excavations were made completely by hand. "Workers live on buildings as they go up." The library was dedicated with sacrifice of a water buffalo.

▪ Architect Walter Rutes is a vice president of Inter-Continental Hotels, which is building many facilities in the area. Its hotel in Abu Dhabi (photo right) was designed by Ben Thompson: "When the Sheikh saw Thompson's original model, he doubled the size of the project and moved it to a prominent position on the harbor. Our clients want good architecture that reflects local traditions (which are not always what Americans think they are)."

▪ Architect Michael Moss, partner in Haines Lundberg & Waehler, says that—despite a 20-year involvement in the Mideast—the firm is opening its first permanent office in Beirut which will have about 10 people. He states that the clients want American expertise which usually includes producing design here. Short schedules can be met with multi-disciplinary teams working on the site.

▪ Architect Gyo Obata has just returned from Iran where he was asked to produce a schematic presentation in Tehran in three days. Hellmuth, Obata and Kassabaum are opening an office in Beirut with Benham Blair and Abbot Merkt.

▪ Architect Hugh Stubbins is designing a nical school in Iran. He does not have an there but is associated with an Iranian tect. Contrasted to others' experience, h able to do a thorough program. On desi says: "They wouldn't have hired me, wanted an indiscriminate application c standards."

▪ Jim Shilstone of the Architectural Co Consultants says that the only key to struction's success is on-site study. "Yo to go back to fundamentals, when there standards for anything. How do you mak crete when the water is 100 degrees and salt?"

▪ Architect George Batori is an assoc Rader Mileto in Rome, which designs p in both Iran and the Arab countries. The recently completed a palace for the S Iran, and have a Horsemanship Club construction in Riyadh (photos, opposit much of their current design work is for U.S. hotel corporations. "The lack of e mental data everywhere, except Ira make the job more difficult." They an construction to take about two years.

▪ Architect John Harkness of TAC was sible for the University of Bagdad at when the firm had offices in Rome and tained day-to-day contact with Iraq by (communications could have been hel TAC personnel who speak the languag office gives courses). The success o Kuwait Fund Building (photo, opposite tially attributed to good on-site manag TAC has a small office in Kuwait.

▪ Architects who have gone to work f firms find living conditions difficult and sive. Alluringly high salaries are son "eaten up" by the costs of self-prese On professional satisfaction, one unhap ployee writes, "My feelings oscillate b excitement from planning a really big and despondency from having circum keeping me from doing a profession Everyone on a team does his thing."

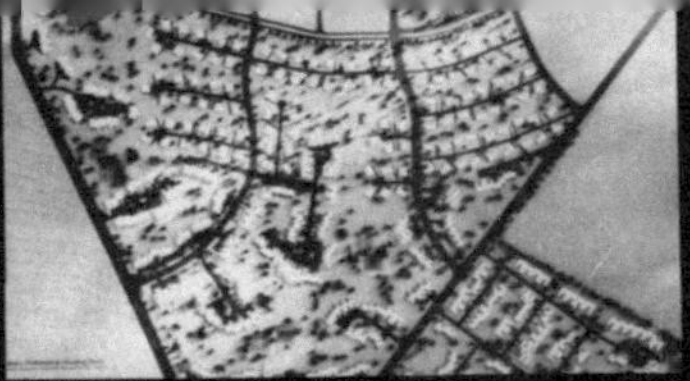

or corridor in the Friday Mosque in
characterizes some of the best qualities
enous architecture.

CRS's plan (top) for ARAMCO housing in Dhahran combines low-rise housing, which is characteristic of the area, and high-rise (bottom). It also combines tight-knit planning with more open Western concepts.

A vacation palace by Rader Mileto for the Shah of Iran (top) is on Kish Island. Jondishapur University (bottom) is by Perkins & Will.

ts in client acceptance: Perkins & Will's plan for a new
ear Tehran (above) was rejected by the clients because of its reliance on
nal living patterns, while Ben Thompson's Abu Dhabi hotel (bottom)
rcontinental (which prides itself on indigenous design) was
d in size when the pleased local owner saw the first model.

Emphasizing the necessity for on-site control of construction, the architects TAC for the Kuwait Fund Building (above) and Rader Mileto for the Horsemanship Club in Riyadh (below) are producing successful, finished products—despite construction limitations (see next page).

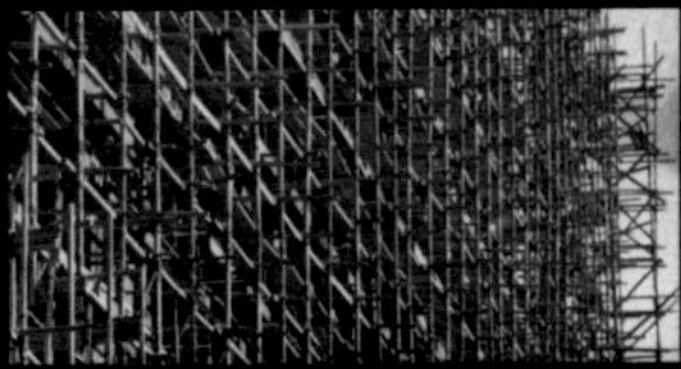

Scaffolding for high-rise buildings, is commonly tied together with rope (top). A Tunisian hotel (bottom) by Ahrens di Grazia Frizzell successfully utilizes local construction techniques.

Top: A new market in the Abu Dhabi accommodates traditional life-styles. Bottom: local material shortages are created by low-volume production, as in the making of concrete block in Jiddah.

Are Western services relevant to the Mideast?

The pragmatist will say that any services that are desired are important. But—while there is no doubt that there is much to be done in raising the average Middle East standard of living—it is possible that the Western professional will over-achieve—by imposing alien standards on countries with their own unique cultures. With the exception of Iran, which has seen some evolvement, Westerners are helping countries that have their own high and varied standards leap into the twentieth-century Western concept of alikeness. While thinking Americans ponder the desirability of our own rapid development, the changes in the Mideast are infinitely swifter and more radical. Hans Neumann says: "They need an immediate warning before they destroy their heritage."

While the photographs on this and the last two pages typify the best examples, much of the recent construction by Westerners is poorly planned and built, and its designers have copied the appearance of (for example) Miami in the 1950's—despite a relatively unencumbered ability to produce good architecture. And these buildings have sometimes been built to house programs that never materialized (such as hospitals without staffs—or high-rise buildings without operable elevators).

According to another architect with local experience: "One of the big problems will be moving too quickly without proper analysis." Projects are commonly doubled and tripled in size during design, and often there can be no redesign of basic support facilities or a new relationship of the parts.

Unfamiliarity with planning requirements and construction limitations is a common problem for many foreign professionals. U. S. architects are just not accustomed to the special requirements generated by social mores. For example: the circulation patterns and duplications of facilities required for segregation of the sexes can add 30 per cent to the area of a building. Where hotels are social and business centers, they require unusual support facilities such as vast storage areas. Royal boxes and machine-gun emplacements are required in public spaces.

On construction, a U.S. consultant says that architects can be "badly burned." Orders for expensive materials from the West take up to six months for delivery, and bad roads with weak bridges sometimes make transportation next to impossible. "Standard specifications used in the U.S. are useless. What you are used to here, you have to assume is not there." Other observers report that local contractors change plans on whim, and that labor—although still cheap—is practically non-existent.

The most dissatisfying experience for many designers will be the lack of accustomed perimeters, which leaves a sense of operating in a vacuum. Where do you site a building in flat sand as far as the eye can see? An architect reports that he is working on school buildings without a program and has no time to establish one. Colin Buchanan and Partners did a master plan for Kuwait four years ago, and that plan has remained in a locked room ever since. Director of Kuwait Planning, Ghazi Sultan, states that the bureaucracy is unable to translate the plan into activating legislation because the plan is not understood. While a height limitation has been imposed in the capital (see photo, page 103), most construction continues totally uncontrolled.

Still, many architects believe that the opportunities to do relevant and satisfying projects exist. One states that—because the client is often a powerful individual—it is easier to discuss alternatives and processes. Others state that the chances of realizing a project as it was conceived are far better than elsewhere. Some clients appreciate what concerned professionals are doing, and—in every case—they have the money to pay for good architecture. And—as a last quote: "Just because rain is unpleasant while asleep in the open, it is important that basic needs are not met indiscriminately."

—*Charles Hoyt*

Partners in Growth: The Gul

The Arab East is the fas growing market in the w for Western goods, services technology. Its ports are awash v imports, its cities are jungles of c struction, and its governments handing out contracts like newsb selling extras. As one diplomat pu never have so few people tried to vest so much money so profitabl so short a time.

To the United States this has b beneficial. During 1975, for exam when total world trade tumbled percent, business in the Middle I climbed by 15 percent and in 1976 United States alone sold $7 bil in goods and services to A countries.

The future, moreover, se equally bright. With billions of lars earmarked for capital expe tures, economists predict exceptio opportunities for foreign businessn willing and also able, to do busir with the Arab countries.

There is, of course, no guarar that American business and indus will continue to share in the bo According to both Arab and Ameri spokesmen, restrictions—which co seriously affect U.S.-Arab trade—h sent a wave of concern sweep through the American business c munity in the Arab world. As one U contractor put it, "The Arabs like goods, but not our restrictions".

Some American businessmen, fact, have hesitated to bid on portant projects—because of un tainties about possible restraints. a result, foreign competitors in m areas are flourishing.

At the moment, however, Ameri businessmen and industrialists still trying—and still hoping—p ticularly those who have entered lists in countries such as Abu Dh Dubai, Kuwait, Qatar and Shar where, a recent survey shows, stakes are high and the combata numerous.

"...never have so few people tried to invest so much money so profitably in so short a time."

Altogether, construction work worth about $2 billion is underway with another $600 million worth under consideration.

Abu Dhabi. "Compared to here," said Norman L. Richardson, gesturing towards Abu Dhabi's scaffolding-draped skyline, "construction in the United States is penny ante stuff. Abu Dhabi has money and the Abu Dhabians are willing to spend it."

Richardson should know. His firm, C. & O. Developing Co. of South Kenly, North Carolina, has just completed Abu Dhabi's first government owned hotel, the Ramada Airport Inn.

"They asked for an all-American hotel and we gave it to them," Richardson said. "Everything, including the bricks, came from the United States."

By "everything," Richardson did mean everything. Knapp of Phoenix, Arizona made the bar, Thomasville Furniture of North Carolina made the beds, Triangle Brick of Durham, North Carolina made the bricks, Nello L. Teer of Durham did the building, J. G. Hopkins of Roanoke, Virginia the plumbing, and Ramada, which will manage the hotel, the engineering and design. "Altogether, 600 American subcontractors and suppliers were involved and revenue for the States totaled $10 million."

And that sum, Richardson went on, does not include the $1,000-a-week wages for 75 Americans brought to Abu Dhabi to do the skilled work—wages which were apparently both needed and appreciated. "I've had calls from those who went home. They're begging to come back. They can't find jobs in the States."

Two Alabama competitors, who joined forces to tackle a venture in Abu Dhabi, have a similar story to tell. Faced with declining revenues during the U.S. recession, Harbert Construction Corp. of Birmingham, Alabama, and the Paul N. Howard Co. of Greensboro, North Carolina, decided to stop competing and start cooperating. As a result they won a $50-million contract to build a three-lane pipeline that today carries drinking water from a desalination plant to Abu Dhabi City.

As another result they kept the employees of the American Cast Iron Pipe Company of Birmingham, Alabama, busy for months manufacturing 68 miles of pipe, the largest single consignment—five shiploads—ever handled by the Port of Mobile.

And there may be more to come. Having completed the job almost one year ahead of schedule, Harbert-Howard expect to win another $45-million contract to lay pipe to the inland town of al-Ain.

"It's one of those American success stories," says Daniel Dolan of the U.S. Embassy in Abu Dhabi. "It proves that not only the big multinationals, but small firms too can succeed in business in the Middle East."

As in other countries of the Arabian Gulf, Abu Dhabi, the major partner in the United Arab Emirates, is spending substantial portions of its oil earnings

—more than $5 billion a year—in the United States and, as a result, providing jobs from Massachusetts to Minnesota. In early 1977, for example, S. J. Groves and Sons of Minneapolis, Minnesota was building roads, Bechtel of San Francisco, California was building an airport and The Architects Collaborative (TAC) of Cambridge, Massachusetts was designing a public library in Abu Dhabi and a hospital in al-Ain.

As American contractors almost invariably choose American machinery and vehicles, such contracts generate sales and jobs in the United States. "You use what you are familiar with," says George M. Meyer, area manager of Harbert-Howard, who bought $2.5 million worth of Caterpillar, Koering and General Motors vehicles and equipment to complete their pipelaying contract. And this, in turn, boosts U.S. exports, currently topping $500 million a year to the United Arab Emirates.

Future possibilities, furthermore, are "staggering," according to Francis X. Crowley, president of the Natgun Corp., water-tank builders in Wakefield, Massachusetts. As an example, Crowley listed the results of a visit to the Emirates in January by a 12-man U.S. trade mission. In three days it made $5.2 million in direct sales and reported $48.4 million worth of projected business during the next 12 months.

"It was the most successful U.S.

trade mission ever to visit the Emirates," says Dolan. "It was way off the chart." The Emirate traders were so keen to do business with the United States, he went on, that one of the delegation who was too ill to fulfill appointments "just lay on his bed all day taking orders."

During the same visit Oman sent three senior government representatives to Abu Dhabi for the first-ever contact with a U.S.-Government-sponsored trade mission. Even Iraq, which stopped buying American goods following the 1967 Arab-Israeli War, gave the delegation a red-carpet reception.

Not all of Abu Dhabi's plans are firm, of course, but those that are,

according to the U.S. State Department, "offer significant opportunities to U.S. businessmen, particularly planners, architects and builders."

That would seem to be the case already. In 1976, says chief city planner Dr. Azmi Abu Taleb, more than 400 construction licenses were granted for multistory blocks. And even now buildings are sprouting skyward—the houses, apartments, offices, schools, hospitals, mosques and hotels that are turning the scorched little island into a mini-Manhattan.

Dubai. As in Abu Dhabi, the skyline of Dubai is showing the effects of growth. Along the fast straight road to the famous Dubai Creek last month, a forest of cranes at Jabal Ali outlined a new port, a vast industrial complex and—limned by saucer-shaped antennae—a satellite communications center. Nearby there was also a towering concrete shell showing the location of Dubai's 33-story trade center. When completed, it will be the tallest building on the Gulf.

There were other signs of growth too. On the creek where, in earlier times, seamen sailed off to the Indian Ocean, trading dhows and service vessels for American offshore oil rigs inched past a Greek cruise ship that had just opened as a floating hotel—and was already full. Not far away, taxis fought their way toward the 700-bed Inter-Continental where harried businessmen hustled off to one of Dubai's 30-odd banks, including Citibank and Chemical from New York and the First National Bank of Chicago.

Growth, in fact, is the name of the game in Dubai and American companies seemed to be doing most of the growing. On the lower part of the creek, for example, a Sheraton hotel was rising against the skyline and an American-made drilling platform was moving out to sea; enroute the platform passed what will be the world's largest dry dock, also a brainchild of U.S. technology.

The dry dock, which will be able to provide repair and maintenance work on several large ships simultaneously, typifies the opportunities open to American companies throughout the Middle East. Another American company hopes to land the contract to manage it.

But there are numerous other examples as well. One is the $765-million, 74-berth port being built nine miles north of Dubai City. A second is the projected industrial complex at Jabal Ali. It will include a $500-million aluminum smelter—with 7.5 percent of it owned by the Southwire Corp. of Atlanta, Georgia, a company that will also provide technology in construction. Also planned for the complex is a $394-million gas-liquefaction plant for which Hudson Engineering of Houston, Texas, will provide engineering, equipment and design. Altogether, construction work worth about $2 billion is underway with another $600-million worth under consideration.

Contracts of those magnitudes are not easy to come by and for the United States they mean jobs. Most of the jobs are in U.S. production and design centers, but some of them are right in Dubai itself. J. Ray McDermott & Company, Inc. of New Orleans, Louisiana, maintains a 650-man work force of Americans in the Middle East, half of them in Dubai—and needs them. In 1976, according to Charles L. Davies, group vice-president, the McDermott Company won $200 million in offshore construction work in the Arab world, much of it done in McDermott's 80-acre construction yards on the bank of the Creek.

In Dubai, however, construction is not the whole scene. For Dubai also has plans to develop as a financial center of United Arab Emirates, and as the U.A.E. Eurodollar and dollar investments already total nearly $7 billion, there are almost unlimited opportunities for U.S. bankers, according to J. C. Green, an American working with the Commercial Bank of Dubai. "There is a tremendous demand for corporate finance, term credits and the more sophisticated banking services," he said.

"There is virtually no limit to what American businessmen could do in Kuwait."

Kuwait. At first glance attractive opportunities seemed equally available in Kuwait last month. In the kilometer-square grounds of Kuwait City's Salim al-Ali center, for example, the hot Arabian sun glinted off the gleaming coachwork of the 6,000 brand new American automobiles parked wall-to-wall in the center's parking lot.

"We sold 16,000 of them last year," said Suhail al-Haraish of Yousuf A. Alghanim and Sons, the largest General Motors dealer in the world. "And this year," he said, waving toward a convoy of new Chevrolets pulling into the lot, "we should sell more."

With an $8-billion-a-year income from oil—plus interest on its petro-dollar investments—Kuwait is one of the more attractive markets in the Gulf for American-made goods. Indeed, since the Middle East development programs began, U.S. exports to Kuwait—of everything from Sara Lee cakes to Boeing jet liners—have shot up 400 percent and in 1976 topped $414 million.

In addition, scores of U.S. construction firms, employing hundreds of American architects and engineers, are contributing to the vast development program that is transforming Kuwait from an ancient fishing and trading community into a modern, industrialized state.

Altogether more than 60 U.S. companies—including Bechtel, Honeywell, Otis and Merrill Lynch—have permanent offices in Kuwait to handle a wide variety of important—and profitable—projects. They include hospitals (Perini Corp.), housing (Perkins & Will), airport facilities (Stanray and FMC), a municipal fish market (Marcel Breuer), highways (DeLeuw, Cather) and a Disneyland-style amusement park (VTN). Recent orders placed by Kuwait with U.S. firms total $370 million. They are: Kellogg International—$250 million for a natural-gas processing plant; Foster-Wheeler—$70 million for oil refinery expansion; General Electric—$40 million for gas turbine engines; Parker Drilling Company—$10 million dollars to drill a 20,000-foot deep test well in the Burgan oil field.

And even that is just part of the picture.

Kuwait Airways operates a jet fleet of seven Boeings—all built by U.S. craftsmen—and is considering buying more. In addition, 80 percent of all the construction equipment used by the Ministry of Public Works is manufactured in U.S. plants—along with the parts Kuwait will need in years to come.

"...Since the Middle East development programs began, U.S. exports to Kuwait–of everything from Sara Lee cakes to Boeing Jet Liners –have shot up 400 percent."

For Americans, still shaken by the soaring and still uncertain unemployment figures of the recent recession, such statistics are unquestionably encouraging. But there are, according to U.S. officials in Kuwait, clouds on the horizon.

One is the alarm about new U.S. restrictions on trade. Like Arabs in the U.A.E. and Saudi Arabia, the Kuwaitis fear that artificial restraints will disrupt U.S.-Kuwait trade relations. Already, in fact, the previous tide of American businessmen pouring into Kuwait has slowed—apparently because of uncertainties in the U.S. about futu American trade relations with the Ara world.

Another cloud is competition—es pecially from Europe and Japan. Acros town from Alghanim's wall-to-wa Chevrolets, astute Kuwaiti salesmen, un troubled by any uncertain trade policie display hundreds of Toyotas that, thei signs suggest, they would be very please to sell to would-be GM customers. An atop Kuwait City's high-rise apartment commanding neon signs tell Kuwait th companies like Sony of Japan and Philip of Holland are quite eager to sell Kuwa whatever they might need.

In 1975 American businesses an industries had begun to improve the position in Kuwait. Admittedly, the were still a long way from matchin Europe's nine Common Market coun tries—who provided a whacking 38 pe cent of all Kuwait imports. But for th first time in a decade American expor to Kuwait had outstripped those o Japan—18 percent to 16.2 percent.

And the future, say U.S. official was looking even better. Past an present U.S. earnings from Kuwait ar peanuts, they claim, compared wit future prospects. The billion-dollar con struction boom in Kuwait, for exampl will probably last for decades. In shor a U.S. State Department spokesma put it, "There is virtually no limit t what American businessmen could do i Kuwait."

The key word there, of course, i "could." Because, as one observer addec "If U.S.-Kuwait trade relations go sou for any reason, there's damned fe imports that Kuwait can't get some where else and other countries—such a Japan or Britain—would be only to willing to provide them."

And Doha, the capital boasts such American institutions as a branch of New York's Citibank...and even a Colonel Sanders' 'finger-lickin' good' fried chicken emporium.

Qatar. In Qatar that has already happened. For nowhere is the cut and thrust of competition for rab petrodollars more plainly illustrated han in the foreign trade figures of Qatar, vhere the United States, Great Britain nd Japan jockey for supremacy in import eague standings.

In 1974, Japan ousted Britain as)atar's major foreign supplier and relegated the United States, previously the unner-up, to third place. Britain ounced back in 1975—capturing 21 ercent of Qatar's total imports to apan's 15 percent—but the United States, with 12 percent, stayed where it vas.

In absolute terms the figures on U.S. xports to Qatar might not seem disouraging. In 1975 they increased 80 perent: to $50 million, mainly in sales of igarettes, automobiles and heavy equipnent. And Doha, the capital, boasts such

merican institutions as a branch of New 'ork's Citibank, a fully automated AMF owling alley and even a Colonel Sanders' finger-lickin' good" fried chicken emorium. It will also soon have a pyramidhaped Sheraton on its white-sanded hores.

American firms, moreover, are actively articipating in, or bidding for, multimillion dollar contracts arising from the small shaikhdom's billion-dollar-a-year development program. Price International of Bartlesville, Oklahoma, for example, is coating sections of a 222-mile natural-gas pipeline, William F. Pereira of Los Angeles, California is planning a prestigious new suburb at the end of Doha Bay. And The Architects Collabora-

tive of Cambridge, Massachusetts (TAC) is competing for a $105 million building contract.

American companies are also involved in, or bidding on, even bigger projects. One is a $260-million university. Another is a $2.6-billion industrial complex rising like a mirage from Qatar's eastern seaboard salt flats at Umm Said which will include petrochemical facilities, a steel mill and an aluminum smelting plant.

Nevertheless, U.S. officials in Qatar are worried. Sent to Doha two years ago, when the United States first opened an embassy in Qatar, they had hoped to improve U.S. trade. But so far, Qatar's import figures show, other countries are doing better.

They asked for an all-American hotel and we gave it to them. Everything, including the bricks, came from the United States.

One reason, according to Kamal Ali Saleh, the director general of the Qatar

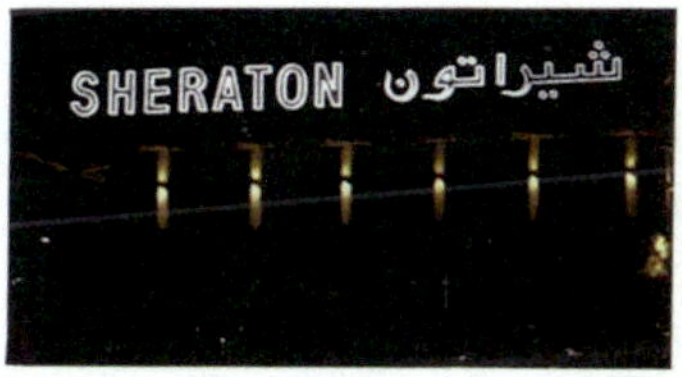

Chamber of Commerce, is that British and Japanese businessmen are often more aggressive and flexible than their American counterparts. "We had lots of visits by U.S. trade delegations, but no follow-up," Saleh says. "Some U.S. companies just have a take-it-or-leave-it attitude."

U.S. Ambassador Robert Paganelli agrees. "Some American businessmen think they can sell anything here at any price on any terms. In actual fact, the Qataris are extremely price and quality conscious and competition is fierce."

Another reason is that although Qatar

Continued trade with the Arab states is more in America's interest than ours...

businessmen and officials are favorably disposed to American products and technology, they know—and make it plain—that Qatar can survive without U.S. trade.

"Continued trade with the Arab states is more in America's interest than ours," says Mohammad Shabana Ali, economic adviser to the Ruler of Qatar.

That situation, they conclude, plus changes in U.S. attitudes toward U.S. firms doing business with the Arabs, could leave the U.S. in third place—or lower—for years to come, at least in Qatar and possibly, they imply, the entire Arab world.

DESIGNERS INFLUENCE LIFE-STYLE OF MILLIONS ABROAD

Los Angeles Companies Create Worldwide Impact

BY RUTH RYON

It is no secret that foreign investors have invaded the Southern California real estate market. On a more subdued level, Los Angeles area architects, planners and engineers are being retained overseas on varied projects.

Their impact, represented in billions of dollars in construction, will be felt worldwide and their designs and work will influence the life-style of millions abroad.

Consider, for instance, city planners.

Abraam Krushkhov, director of planning for Van Nuys-based ArchiSystems, was instrumental in putting together a team of U.S. experts to plan the future capital of Nigeria.

Hailed by Krushkhov as "the first national capital in world history to be planned entirely on ecological/environmental as well as social and economic principles," the multi-billion-dollar, yet-unnamed metropolis is expected to be under construction this year with inauguration, including completion of housing and offices, scheduled for 1986.

"They want to sign the constitution in 1979 on the site of the new federal capital," Krushkhov said.

Krushkhov is overall project director for the consortium called International Planning Associates, which includes Philadelphia-based Wallace, McHarg, Roberts and Todd Inc. and McLean, Va.-headquartered Planning Research Corp. (PRC) besides ArchiSystems.

According to Krushkhov, Walter G. Hansen, president of Alan M. Voorhees Associates (a subsidiary of PRC), is in charge of economic, demographic, infrastructure, engineering and transportation studies, while Thomas A. Todd, a partner in Wallace, McHarg, Roberts and Todd Inc., is in charge of environmental, ecological and site selection studies as well as urban design concepts.

"The present capital of Lagos was so congested it was no longer operable as a federal capital," said Krushkhov. Nigeria is black Africa's most populous country.

The team selected a site 200 to 300 miles inland but centrally located for the state capitals of the 19 new state governments. Based on tribal considerations, a 3,600-square-mile area for site selection was chosen by the government as neutral territory. Krushkhov indicated the new capital is being designed to help unify the country.

With its new-found wealth stemming from production of nearly 2 million barrels of oil a day, Nigeria has been developing rapidly and seeking national unity, particularly in the wake of the 1967 civil war when 10 million Ibos tried to create the separate state of Biafra.

'Beautiful Views'

In choosing the new capital site, Krushkhov said the team considered climate, geology and contour. "It's on high ground," he added, "with beautiful views."

By inauguration day in 1986, he estimates 150,000 to 300,000 people will live there. By the year 2,000, he figures the population will reach 1.6 million. The land should be able to support a population of 3 million, he added.

Since it was under British rule until 1960, the national language, English, gave the U.S. team an advantage when it competed with about 100 companies from around the world for the initial consulting contract.

Krushkhov gave another reason for the team's selection, saying, "The Nigerians love American technology and the way we organize."

Although Americans are involved, Kruschkov says the team will not impose Western standards on planning. "The Nigerians want to plan and build," he said. "We're their consultants, but this is their city. Nigerians stress participation in all aspects of the program. They have top Nigerian professionals in many fields."

A major consideration is housing.

Family Units Extended

Krushkhov says kinship patterns in Nigeria are so strong that family units often include more than a husband, wife and children. Social needs will dictate type of residences planned, he asserts, and the U.S. team is working with Nigerians to determine the form.

In Qatar, a 4,000-square-mile country, slightly smaller than the Los Angeles metropolitan area, off the south coast of Saudi Arabia on the Arabian Gulf, family units are extended like those in Nigeria. And they like privacy.

Considering those needs and desert winds, William L. Pereira Associates, based in Los Angeles, has planned housing with walls surrounding each unit.

"Each house is a little kingdom," said Pereira, chairman of the board. "Most of the construction in Qatar will be in housing, and it will be reflective of the culture.

"One of the most important aspects of planning is understanding the people. We don't want to change their life-styles. You can't put tract houses in there.

"The architecture will be a happy marriage between old and new, reflective of a culture dating back many centuries."

Pereira Associates is drafting a national plan for the entire country in addition to master plans for the new district of Doha and the new town of Umm Said, both in Qatar.

Construction has started on Umm Said and is expected to cost $25 billion. The new district is expected to cost $50 billion.

Please Turn to Page 9, Col. 1

DOHA TOWER—William L. Pereira Associates, Los Angeles-based firm, designed $50-million, 340-foot-high tower which will mark Doha like Statue of Liberty or Eifel Tower.

JAKARTA PROJECT—L.A.-based architectural firm of Daniel, Mann, Johnson & Mendenhall designed Gajah Mada Plaza, $35-million shopping center which will occupy a city block in the Indonesian city. Its 200,000 square fee of commercial space will be leased in space as small as 150 square feet. There will be n anchor or chain stores in the project

TOWER ADDITION—Welton Becket Associates, headquartered in Los Angeles, designed 23-story, 587-room addition to 4-year-old, 18-story, 204-room Arya-Sheraton hotel Teheran, Iran. The $87-million project scheduled for completion within 18 month

NFLUENCE OF LOS ANGELES FIRMS

ntinued from First Page

Pereira's firm also has designed a 50-million, 430-room, 850,000-uare-foot hotel and conference nter in the town of Doha on the Bay Doha, called a terminal point for ssing the vast deserts, the end of a k for the trade route through Ara- to the Arabian Gulf.

Construction on the hotel and con- ence center has begun and is eduled to be completed about 1981. "It will have the ability to be the siness, social and diplomatic center the country," said Pereira. "It will as much a symbol of the state as a ctical series of accomplishments."

The hotel and conference center being built on a promontory on Arabian Gulf and will be seen for es.

"From an esthetic standpoint, it l be a piece of sculpture," Pereira tinued, "pyramidal in form, trian- ar in shape."

The conference center will contain large ballrooms, exhibition and meeting rooms and facilities for translators and the press. Especially designed for the heads of state who stay there, two-story apartments Pereira describes as "like fair-sized houses" will feature sizable accommodations for private meetings. A penthouse restaurant also is planned.

Like the hotel, Doha Tower is envisioned as a symbol. It is still in design but is expected to cost $50 million to construct.

Ralph Jackson, in charge of public relations for Pereira, says it will be "one of the world's spectacular structures, being formed by two large, toroid shells joined at their apexes.

"The shells are lattices of intersecting concrete beams, producing a honeycomb effect and creating a complex play of light and shadow that changes continuously and keeps the huge forms light and airy in appearance."

When completed, the tower will stand 340 feet high.

"It will mark Doha on the Gulf like the Statue of Liberty," said Pereira. "Its design combines Arabic form with modern technology.

"Everyone who goes to Doha will want to see it, as people who go to Paris see the Eifel Tower."

Other overseas projects of Pereira Associates include planning employe housing in Saudi Arabia for a total construction cost of $60 million for three locations, space planning and interior design for the corporate headquarters of the petroleum industry in Caracas, Venezuela, at a construction cost of $2 million and transformation of an old Jesuit seminary in Caracas into a $60-million administration unit for the Venezuelan Institute of Petroleum Technology (INTEVEP). (INTEVEP is the research and development center of the national petroleum holding company Petroleos de Venezuela, S.A., founded in 1976 by the government to promote domestic production of technological information and support to reduce Venezuela's technological dependence on foreign resources.)

Referring to the employe housing project, Pereira said, "The houses vary from single family detached to apartments, not helter skelter but well designed. It is possible to achieve privacy and not look like apartments on Wilshire Blvd. These apartments will look more like a complex of houses stacked up with individual porches and patios."

With Medical Planning Associates of Los Angeles as facilities consultant, Pereira Associates designed the $160-million Imperial Medical Center of Iran, which is under construction and is scheduled to be completed about 1985.

The 2-million-square-foot complex will include a 600-bed teaching hospital expandable to 1,800 beds, according to Pereira, who called the project "the tip of the medical pyramid in Iran."

"This will be a center of excellence and will provide post-graduate experience for doctors in Iran," he explained.

Thornton Stewart of Medical Planning Associates said the hospital will contain a complete medical school, research facilities and a medical library that will be the central medical library for the country.

"It will be Type 1 construction," he added, "similar to what we use here for hospitals."

The U.S. system of health care delivery is different from that employed in Europe, he continued, citing variations in method of practice and layout of facilities.

"In Europe, they have larger, open wards," he said. "Our hospitals have double or single rooms. In Europe the hospitals tend to be more spread out. American hospitals are more concentrated and are fully air conditioned.

"British hospitals are especially spread out with courtyards between. It's a pleasant environment but big and sprawling."

Stewart pointed out that the Middle East is striving earnestly to upgrade health care. Besides working with Iranian architectural firms on nine other hospitals and an Atlanta, Ga. firm on a hospital in Jordan, Medical Planning Associates is consulting with Gruen Associates, headquartered in Los Angeles, on hospital planning and schematic drawings for a 1,050-bed teaching hospital in Tabriz, Iran.

That hospital will be part of the 2.5 million-square-foot Farah Pahlavi Medical Center and school expected to be under construction next year. Excavation operations started in March.

Stuart Lottman, in charge of public relations for Gruen Associates, indicated that when finished, it may be one of the largest medical centers in the world. A partner in the firm said $250 million is currently budgeted for the project, which is expected to take 4½ years to complete.

Gruen Asociates also has designed an office building for a life insurance

Please Turn to Page 10, Col. 1

INFLUENCE OF LOS ANGELES FIRMS

Continued from 10th Page

At least two of the company's current projects will make a major impact on the hotel industry because of their architectural contributions, according to Edward A. Killingsworth, president of the firm. Both will be located in Saudi Arabia.

Soil preparation studies are under way in Al Khobar on a hotel Killingsworth describes as the "queen of the bunch."

When completed, it will have 570 rooms, 50 villas (some with private swimming pools), a lagoon, theater, ballroom, bowling alley, health club, sauna, tennis courts, dining halls and, Killingsworth claims, "more luxury than you can possibly imagine." It will front the Arabian Gulf.

Less than a mile inland at Al Jubail, a 400-room hotel has been designed with a bowling alley, theater and restaurants.

"It started out more modest, but it's not working out that way," said Killingsworth, who noted that drawings have been completed but construction has not begun yet. Turner International Industries Inc., based in New York, will build both hotels, and Hilton International will operate them.

Separate cost estimates were not available, but those hotels and another designed by a New York architectural firm for Riyadh are expected to cost more than $200 million to construct. According to Robert D. Kupfer, president of Turner International Industries, the three hotels are expected to be completed by December, 1980.

OFFICE BUILDING IN SEOUL—Construction is under way on a headquarters complex for Daehan Kyoyuk Life Insurance Co. Ltd. in Korea. Gruen Associates designed the 22-story project that will contain offices, banking facilities, restaurants, underground shops, parking accommodations and four-story Garden Galleria.

Killingsworth's firm is also a consultant on the design of a 620-room, $50-million Hilton in Korea that is scheduled to be under construction in June with completion due in December, 1979.

"What we try to do, even in consulting, is to bring the indigenous architecture of the country into play," said Killingsworth. "We are the architects as a collector of cultures."

For instance, he explained, at the Jakarta Hilton, finished last year, about 300 Balinese sculptors worked on the shopping bazaar for more than a year.

Killingsworth's firm also is designing a 350-room Hilton hotel in Bali. "That hotel will have guest rooms that will give an overall appearance of a native village," he said.

In Medan, a town on the island of Sumatra in Indonesia, the company is designing a 300-room, 12-story hotel that will be "Moslem in character," according to Killingsworth. Owned by Moslems, it will have pointed arches, painted ceilings, beautiful tiles and, Killingsworth says, "all those wonderful things you see in the classic book 'Arabian Nights.'"

Speaking of other projects, Killingsworth remarked, "One problem we have with architects of other countries is that they have contempt for their own architecture. They want something slick and shiny. In Indonesia, they wanted to do the hotel in post and beam like California architecture. But I said, 'Why don't you take the cultures of Indonesia and develop them by using, for example, a temple gate or a Balinese theater?'

"In Korea, they have polychrome roofs like poster paint in brilliant reds, greens and blues. The architects did not want a Korean roof, but I talked them into it."

Tracy Price of Trace Price and Associates, based in Los Angeles, also is designing hotels overseas: a 300-acre, $15-million beachfront hotel in Panama, a 400-acre, $8-million second-home and hotel project with marina in Nicaragua and a 450-room, $32-million hotel in Taipei. Construction on each is expected to start at the end of this year or the beginning of 1979, according to Price, president of the firm.

Price says his company also was designated prime consulting architect on the reconstruction of the downtown core of Managua, Nicaragua following the 1972 earthquake there.

One year of a two-year contract has been completed and, according to Price, the Nicaraguan government has approved his company's plans.

Demolition is under way, he said, and the "phasing project" is expected to take 20 years to complete for a total construction cost of $200 million.

Please Turn to Page 20, Col. 1

OVERSEAS PROJECTS

ntinued from 11th Page

rice and Pereira are not the only ar-tectural firms involved in designing ldings as well as planning part or all of a n. Besides participating in the design of new federal capital of Nigeria, Archi-tems is designing a $50-million, 350-m hotel in Kuwait, a $15-million Hyatt el in Trinidad and the $200-million Min-r of Interior Building (a joint venture h the Saudi architectural firm Al Sharif ar Al-Mandily) in Saudi Arabia.

ohn Nalbandian, ArchiSystems general nager, said the Saudi building will "con-r the Arabian heritage and culture in design."

onstruction on the 1-million-square-t structure is expected to begin in about months, the same time building is eduled to get under way on the Kuwait el.

alled The Taj Mahal, the hotel will con-n 10 stories and three wings but will not k like the famous monument in India.

It will be a five-star hotel, meaning it is y plush," said Nalbandian. "Maybe the ne Taj Mahal connotes this."

rchiSystems also is negotiating a con-t to design, program and plan a $40-lion, 200-room hospital in Tehran, and firm has been awarded a contract to n a complex of two hotels linked by a ino on a 350-acre parcel in Antiqua, st Indies.

Championship Golf Course

roject director Al Martin said the com-x will include a 300-room hotel operated Loews, a 300-room hotel operated by rriott, an 18-hole championship golf rse, a tennis club with 12 courts, three ches, a marina and tourist condomini-s. Estimated cost of construction is from million to $70 million.

The Antiguan government has granted development group the exclusive nse for new casino facilities in Antigua a 10-year period," said Martin. He fig-s the start of construction is about a r away with completion expected in 0.

hen completed, it will be the only casi-complex in the country. MAT Associ-s, based in Chicago, is the developer.

he Beverly Hills office of John Carl rnecke & Associates also has been in-ved in overseas projects, specifically in nce and Guam.

he Guam project, a 165,000-square-foot, million Bank of America office building, completed last year.

recast concrete sunscreens were used re to shield the glass from the sun and hold plywood panels for protection from hoon winds and flying debris. Because of floods that accompany typhoons, the lobby was set 3 feet above grade.

The American Hospital in Paris is the other project. When completed, the new hospital unit will provide 160 beds and 180,000 to 190,000 square feet. The old hospital eventually will be converted into offices.

Phase 1, providing 75 beds, is under construction. Total building cost is estimated at $9 million.

Saudi Sports Complex

Daniel, Mann, Johnson & Mendenhall (DMJM), headquartered in Los Angeles, also is designing projects overseas.

The largest is the Saudi Youth Welfare Special Hospital Complex, a joint venture with Riyadh architect Victor Tarazi.

Expected to cost more than $100-million to construct, the complex will be part of the 1,300-acre Sports City to be built outside the Saudi capital. Sports City will be a self-contained complex providing facilities for a variety of athletic activities.

The complex will not be a conventional hospital by American standards. The 102-bed hospital will include rooms and equipment for health training, athletic development and evaluation. Construction is scheduled to begin this year.

DMJM also has designed the Gajah Mada Plaza, a $35-million shopping center for downtown Jakarta.

Mall Goes Upward

The center might be called an enclosed mall but it goes up rather than out like American versions.

Patrick Flynn, manager of communications, explained why: "Contrasting with the Fox Hills Mall in Culver City, which has 150 acres for spreading, the Gajah Mada Plaza has one city block, so it has to go up."

There will be no anchor or chain stores, either.

"Evidentally, they figure things differently over there," said Flynn. "Even a large department store figures revenue on a per-square-foot basis. In the Gajah Mada Plaza, they will have a lot of little shops."

In the arcades there will be a total of 200,000 square feet of commercial space that will be leased in spaces as small as 150 square feet.

The Los Angeles office of Wallace McHarg Roberts and Todd, Inc. has been involved on a project in Tehran with an office there now handling most of the work.

Environmental Complex

Called Paradisan, the project has been described as a "campus that incorporates recreational and educational facilities, institutes, zoological gardens, planetariums, a regional park, sports facilities, a wildlife preserve and observatories."

One source at the company called it "a sophisticated kind of Marineland."

Something like Balboa Park in San Diego but on a gigantic scale, he said, it will recreate the seven biogeographic zones of the world.

A major emphasis will be to "transform the Iranian attitude toward environment," he continued. "Modern cultures in that part of the world have not always been sympathetic to environment, and a lot has been lost because of poor agricultural practices and over-grazing."

Please Turn to Page 21, Col. 1

ealty Offices Open

obert and Joan Miller have formally ned their 100% commission Certified idential and Income Properties Corp. ces at 875 Via De La Paz, Pacific Pali-es, after operating four years in Santa ica and North Hollywood.

sing the principal broker's license, 15 ependent sales representatives work out he new corporate headquarters, paying onthly fee and receiving full commis-at close of escrow.

INFLUENCE OF LOS ANGELES FIRMS

Los Angeles Times Sun., June 4, 1978 —Part VIII 2

Continued from 20th Page

Occupying about 1,000 acres, Paradisan is expected to be under construction within a year.

Another area firm, Ralph M. Parsons Co. in Pasadena, was involved in planning a project abroad but is now going to manage construction of it.

The company has been designated "management services contractor" for the Yanbu industrial complex to be built on Saudi Arabia's west coast. The complex will include oil and petrochemical plants, a harbor, an airport and a new city. Construction is expected to take about 28 years to complete, and industry sources have estimated its cost at about $10 billion.

Parsons completed a master plan for the complex last August.

Specialized Firms Active

According to one industry source, Parsons is better known as an engineering firm, but it has an architectural department. Bechtel Corp. is similar.

In Norwalk, the Bechtel office, known as the Bechtel Power Corp., is involved in designing overseas power plants. The firm's San Francisco office is preparing the master plan for the Jubail (Saudi Arabia) industrial complex, a city for 300,000 persons. Construction on the 20-year, $20-billion to $30-billion project already has begun.

Like Bechtel's office in Norwalk, several other Los Angeles area firms are active in designing overseas projects but in specialized fields.

Howard Hirsch and Associates concentrates on interior design; Dames & Moore, geotechnical and environmental studies, and Adrian Wilson Associates, a division of HNTB, is conducting a $9-million safety survey of a building complex, the world headquarters for Asian Development Bank, in Manila. Through the study, recommendations will be made on how to protect the complex from earthquakes.

"We did some 70 buildings for identification of seismic needs after the 1972 earthquake here," said Carol Cushing, personnel manager for Adrian Wilson. "So that will help with this study.

"Our electrical engineers can spot faulty wiring, overloaded or outdated areas that could cause safety problems. The same is true with mechanical problems, and structurally, we will be able to tell how the building is built to withstand movement and load. The architectural end will come up with master planning of space and needs: how the space can be carved into a usable design and still be safe."

A contract will be awarded to complete the modifications Adrian Wilson Associates suggests.

The firm also is master planning a section of Managua, Nicaragua, in a government-sponsored $6.5-million project.

Howard Hirsch and Associates of Beverly Hills has been awarded a contract for the total interior design concept for a $27-million, 481-room hotel to be built in Tsimshatsui, Kowloon. Scheduled for completion in January, 1980, the hotel will be operated by Sun Hung Kai.

Engineers Involved

Hirsch and Associates also is providing the interior design plans and installation for a $24-million, 300-room hotel being developed by Tokyu Hotels International of Tokyo, Japan, in Dacca, Bangladesh. A blend of mughul and international architectural styles, the hotel will feature several restaurants, meeting rooms and a 1,000-seat ballroom with facilities for translators. It is expected to be completed by December, 1980.

Dames & Moore Civil Engineers, based in Los Angeles, is involved in many overseas projects, providing seismic studies, soil and rock mechanics and even oceanographic research.

Among the developments are the University of Riyadh, a $3-billion campus with a mosque expected to be under construction by summer; a $14-million shopping center in the Queensland area of Australia; a $100-million residential project under construction in Kuwait; a 1,200-room 28-story tower-like hotel expected to be completed in July in Jakarta; the Hyatt Regency and a banking center of three 18-story towers and a double-basement car park in Kuwait; port expansion valued at $50 million in Indonesia; a shipyard and grain silos in Iran, and the hotel designed by Pereira in Qatar.

"The hotel will be on a 100-acre site created by dredging material from Doha Bay," said Jill Tenney, publicity manager for Dames & Moore. "We did the geotechnical work to be sure the fill would support the hotel.

"The hotel also will be supported by piles. We will inspect installation to see that it is done properly."

The residential project in Kuwait is of interest because it is cluster housing, which Ms. Tenney called "a relatively new phenomenon there, going up rapidly to support the petroleum industry."

The shopping center in Australia also will have an impact. "It will change shopping habits there," said Ms. Tenney, "because shopping centers like ours are new to Australia."

She described the center as large, covered and air conditioned with a parking area.

New Town in Ontario

As part of a consortium, Dames & Moore is preparing an environmental study for the site selection of a new town in Ontario near Lake St. Joseph. Planned to support an iron mine that will be developed, the town site must be capable of supporting a population of 10,000, according to Ms. Tenney.

About a month ago International Consolidated Investment Group, an investment firm and its subsidiary brokerage company, opened an office in Beverly Hills. Its promoters said the group "was established to handle substantial investment funds that are flowing into the U.S. and California, in particular, from the Middle East and Europe."

Substantial investment funds are being spent by foreign investors on overseas construction as well, and a number of California firms are sharing the rewards.

Mrs. Ryon, a Times copy editor, is a regular contributor to the real estate section.

American designers in Arabia

August 1985

في الشرق الأوسط

MEC

MIDDLE EAST CONSTRUCTION

American designers in Arabia

ALTHOUGH American construction industry design firms are involved in practically all parts of the world, it is the Middle East which is by some way their most important market, both in terms of professional fee earnings and proportion of prestige projects. During 1983, informs *Engineering News Record ENR* (New York) in its annual review of professional fee billings for the top 500 design firms in the USA, "Mideast billings rose two per cent to $553.6 million — or about 44 per cent of all foreign billings." This followed a slight decline in 1982 (after the Middle East, the totals for other markets were led by Asia ($199.5 million), Latin America ($141.3 million), and Africa ($130.6 million) which includes the North African countries forming part of *MEC's* Middle East market region).

Relating the work of US design firms at home and abroad, *ENR* explained that "billings from foreign sources totalled only $1.26 billion for the top 500 firms during 1983: an 8.7 per cent decrease from 1982's level. Faced with weak market overseas, the top US designers found domestic clients generating a greater proportion of their work...". This downturn in foreign earnings was the first since 1969, when *ENR* commenced its annual survey of the work of US designers abroad.

During 1983, US architectural firms billed foreign clients for $49.6 million — approximately 7.8 per cent of their total; while engineer-architect firms took $619.1 million, almost half of the total US foreign design market. (This second category of designer firm is where architecture follows on from an engineering contract, often of extremely large size and value. The parentheses are not intended to be derogatory in respect of architectural quality emanating from engineer dominated firms; few, however, are renowned for their architecture as such.) Respectively, as third and fourth categories, architect-engineers earned $206.9 million (12.7 per cent), and consulting engineers $383.2 million (15.6 per cent).

The first four firms in the *ENR* top 500 all have industrial specialisations in which Sargent and Lundy (Chicago) and Gilbert and Commonwealth Cos (Reading, Pa), respectively second and third, are exclusively involved. Neither, it is believed, are particularly active in the Middle East and North Africa. The top firm is CRS-Sirrine (Houston) — the August 1983 amalgamation of the CRS Group (Caudill Rowlett Scott) and J E Sirrine Company (see *MEC/SAC* April 1985). In 1982 these firms were separately ranked 11th and 16th. With a longterm major Middle East commitment, CRS-Sirrine was 50 per cent industrial and 33 per cent other construction by fee fillings. From the 1960s, predominantly in Saudi Arabia, CRS has been producing top-quality architecture in the Middle East, examples of which are illustrated in this review.

The El Gezirah Sheraton Hotel, Cairo. (CRS Sirrine)

The two other design firms included in the total of 14 with billings worth more than $100 million, whose Middle East work is also mentioned below, are SOM (Skidmore Owings and Merrill) and Daniel, Mann, Johnson and Mendenall (DMJM), respectively ranked 12th and 10th. SOM's Middle East work will justifiably be familiar to regular *MEC* readers, notably through the Aga Khan award-winning Haj Terminal in Jeddah, and the newly completed prestigious National Commercial Bank tower, also in Jeddah. DMJM, on the other hand, is a newcomer to these columns.

On this occasion, however, pride of place is given to the two Saudi Arabian projects designed by Hellmuth, Obata & Kassabaum (HOK, of St. Louis) which have not previously appeared in *MEC:* first, the King Khaled International Airport; and second, the King Saud University (with four other design firms, as below), both at Riyadh. HOK was ranked 29th in 1983, and another newcomer, Leo A Daly (Omaha) with strong Saudi Arabia National Guard client connections, was 40th.

TAC (The Architects Collaborative, Cambridge, Mass) is another *MEC* familiar; its Middle East connections dating back to the founding partner Walter Gropius's work at Baghdad University. Whereas in a listing of firms by consistent architectural quality, particularly so in the Middle East, TAC would be in everybody's top ten, its position at 89 in the *ENR* table reflects merely the fact that others do more work. Similarly the Brown Daltas Group (Cambridge, Mass) at 294; and Sasaki Associates Inc — with its Kuwait waterfront landscaping speciality, at 156.

The following review of work, both completed and at various design and construction stages, is on the basis of a variety of building types, by the six firms concerned. The range of countries on this occasion is limited to Saudi Arabia — where American designers have creamed off most of the major prestigious projects; Kuwait, where they have a strong presence; and Egypt. US Aid programmes, the World Bank, other funding connections, oil industry links, the involvement of construction giants such as Bechtel, and last but by no means least, the US Army Corps of Engineers, have all combined to favour selection of American designers in Saudi Arabia and other Arabian markets. In the Lower Gulf and North Africa their penetration has been limited, in face of ▶

The Arab world, in spite of recent downturn in major construction activity, remains the most important market in terms of professional fee earnings for American consultants. In this context Tony Morris reviews work, completed and at various design and construction stages, of six practices whose examples include projects in Saudi Arabia and Kuwait.

Above: The superbly spacious central forum of King Saud University, Riyadh, Saudi Arabia. (HOK + 4)
Below: One of the four terminal buildings at King Khaled International Airport, Riyadh, Saudi Arabia. (HOK)

British, French and other European presences.

Hellmuth, Obata and Kassabaum Inc
HOK, based in St Louis, originated in 1955 when the firm of Hellmuth, Yamasaki and Leinweber split up, with Minoru Yamasaki taking the Detroit office, and Gyo Obata, the firm's erstwhile chief designer joining George Hellmuth and George Kassabaum in the new firm. HOK and Yamasaki were to cross paths in Saudi Arabia in the field of airport design: Yamasaki was responsible in 1961 for the Kingdom's first international terminal at Dhahran, and he is also the architect for the last of Saudi Arabia's major airports in Eastern province; in between, HOK designed the prestigious King Khaled Airport at Riyadh which was inaugurated at the end of 1983. In addition to the Riyadh Airport — which alone would ensure a Middle East reputation — HOK is also the mastermind behind the architectural consortium HOK +4 which is responsible for the King Saudi University at Riyadh.

The university project came first, when in early 1975 the Saudi Ministry of Higher Education invited HOK to form an international design consortium which, in competition with others, was awarded the design contract in the June. The other firms are Gollins Melvin Ward Partnership, London; Dames and Moore, Los Angeles; CRS, Houston; and Syska & Hennessy, New York City. The airport followed when, already established in Riyadh, HOK was commissioned by Bechtel, the Saudi Ministry of Defence and Aviation's chief Western consultant.

Space precludes other than summary descriptions of these two exceptional projects. The university was originally designed for a total of 20,000 students, in accordance with the academic master plan proposals, but in 1977, when documentation for the academic area construction was complete, the client was obliged to reduce the scale of the project in face of escalating costs. A contract was eventually signed with the Bouygues-Blount joint venture in April 1981 which produced in 40 months a total floor area of approximately 0.62 million m² of academic buildings on time for the commencement of the 1984 school year. At the peak, 12,000 workers were placing $4 million worth of construction a day; or, as HOK's Liebold commented, "the equivalent of three 10-storey office buildings a month in St Louis".

Used on a scarcely precedented scale, if ever, it was precast concrete technology that made such speed possible, with more than 78,000 components of 5,500 different types produced by a consortium known as the Precast Construction Group, in four plants in one of the world's largest precasting yards. The attractive tan colouring of the concrete is an immediate reference to the traditional material of Nejdi buildings.

King Khaled International Airport is situated 22 miles north of Riyadh where it replaces the original city airport. By the year 2000 it will be handling an estimated 15 million passengers per year, when Riyadh's rapidly increasing population is expected to be around 2.5 million. The airport has four triangular shaped terminals; two for domestic flights and two for international traffic. They are equipped with jetways capable of accommodating any commercial aircraft, which are linked by short air-conditioned halls for transfer passengers. There are two 4,328 m runways; a royal pavilion in the form of a small palace; a mosque for 5,000 worshippers inside, and a further 5,000 outside. The full site covers 243 km², making it the world's largest airport.

The distinctive roofing system used on all terminals consists of tiered curving triangular sections supported on columns. Arched clerestory windows between the roof sections filter the intense desert sunlight and create airy spaces without glare or overheating. The mosque, located in the centre of the terminal complex, acts as an anchor for the Islamic design motif, based on a 60 degree triangle, further echoed in the details of the paving, ceiling finishes and mosaics.

DMJM Phillips Reister Haley Inc

This architectural office in Denver, Colorado, is a subsidiary of Daniel, Mann, Johnson and Mendenhall (DMJM) of Los Angeles, the architect-engineer firm ranked 10th in the *ENR* billings league; and after CRS-Sirrine, the second largest in this category. Their work-base is diversified with a 30 per cent transportation emphasis, which includes their joint venture contract for the Saudi Arabian Public Transport Company (Saptco) to manage and operate the kingdom-wide bus system for Saudi Arabia.

In Egypt, as part of the Urban Health Delivery System Project for the Ministry of Health, funded by USAID, the firm's Denver subsidiary is on site in Cairo with a total of eight general urban health centres (GUHC) which are located throughout the metropolis each having a catchment population of about 150,000. Each GUHC is a neighbourhood health centre concerned with the complete health of the community, with a special emphasis on child health. After a first contract to construct four GUHCs was awarded to Armco, subsequent negotiation has awarded four more to that firm.

In addition, DMJM is also architect for the Centre for Social and Preventive Medicine (CSPM), forming part of the University of Cairo Medical Centre, and included in the Urban Health Delivery ▶

Above: A view along one of the pedestrian spines at King Saud University.
Below: The interior of one of the terminal buildings, King Khaled International Airport.

System Project. The CSPM will fulfill four major functions: the provision of health care services; the training of future health care staff; the continuing education of health care professionals; and research specialising in the health problems of Egyptian mothers, infants and children.

Leo A Daly

The professional association between Saudi Consulting House, and Leo A Daly (Omaha, Nebraska) — SCH/LAD — was formed in 1979 and has successfully completed numerous projects in the Saudi Arabia, including the well-known the Al-Jubail Petrochemical Company headquarters building. The American firm was founded in 1915 and has now worked in more than 50 countries, including Saudi Arabia, Jordan and Kuwait, on a wide range of projects. Arguably their most important design is the headquarters complex for the Saudi Arabian National Guard (SANG) on a 20.23 ha site alongside the Riyadh-Dhahran highway, on which they worked with the Middle East Division of the US Army Corps of Engineers.

The SANG project comprises twelve buildings dominated by the massive five-storey curved headquarters building, 227 m in length and providing 35,117 m^2 office space and including the executive office building which contains the office of HRH The Commander of the National Guard; and the auditorium (linked by glass-enclosed walkways); the mosque, which accommodates 1,000 worshippers inside and a further 1,000 on shaded landscaped plazas; and a military police barracks and dining facility. These buildings are constructed with insitu and precast concrete technology of a consistently high standard.

University of Petroleum and Minerals, Dhahran, Saudi Arabia; the mosque seen beyond the reflecting pool. (CRS Sirrine)

Interior view of the Al Jubail Petrochemical Company Headquarters Building. (Leo Daly)

The Al-Jubail Petrochemical Company headquarters building, at Al-Jubail, Saudi Arabia, belongs to the company formed by Sabic (Saudi Arabian Basic Industries Corporation) and Exxon (USA) for the production of low-linear density polyethylene pellets. SCH/LAD was retained by the Fluor Company (designers and constructors of the processing plant) to design the two-storey, 7,470 m^2 administrative headquarters accommodating about 180 staff. "From the beginning of the conceptual planning for the office building," explains John Free, "we made every effort to provide the user with the kind of environment one would experience if he were to explore the indigenous traditional architecture of Al-Jubail." Construction has a structural steel frame faced with Riyadh limestone and architectural precast concrete.

Other SCH/LAD projects include the Saudi Arabian Airlines Communications and Data Processing Facility, at Jeddah; Residential Community-Madinat Yanbu Al-Sinaiyah Industrial City for 2,000 inhabitants (see Housing Review article page 37 in this issue); Headquarters for Sabic, Riyadh; and the Pediatric Hospital, King Hussein Medical Centre, Amman.

The SCH/LAD co-operation agreement confirms two main objectives: first, to provide a high quality professional service to clients; and second, to train Saudi technical staff for the future development plans of the kingdom. Since 1979 more than 65 Saudi university graduates and draftsmen/technicians have completed an intensive one year on-the-job training programme. Two design/production teams have been established in Riyadh staffed entirely by employees of SCH.

The Architects Collaborative

The Middle East work of TAC — one of the most readily recognised acronyms in the business — is rated most highly by your correspondent, hence their regular appearances in *MEC*. The last occasion was in March 1984, when the *Innovation Design* column described the Institute of Public Administration Building in Riyadh as the result of "an extraspecial architectural commitment to impeccable detailing and meticulous control of material finishes". This predominantly insitu concrete building is designed around a currently fashionable atrium — which was the topic covered by the column; and it is illustrated here by the attractive night view.

In Kuwait, where TAC continue to be strongly active, a recent competition success, in face of strong local and international rivals, was for the new headquarters buildings of the Ministry of Public Works, and the Ministry of Electricity and Water. TAC's design was

Above: The National Methanol Company Headquarters Building, Jubail. (CRS Sirrine) Below: The Headquarters Building at the SANG complex, Riyadh, Saudi Arabia. (Leo Daly)

prepared in association with The Kuwait Engineering Bureau, for the complex of Ministry buildings housing approximately 69,677.25 m² of automated office space for 4,500 employees, with structured car parking for 3,500 vehicles. Future phases will include a mosque, computer centre and headquarters for the Ministries of Education and Interior. (The other four Kuwaiti firms invited to submit designs were Pan Arab Consulting Engineers, with SOM; Almarzouk & Abi Hanna, with Arthur Erikson; Kuwait Engineering Office; and Technical Engineering Studies.)

Model photograph of the Markaz Al Mahmal Commercial Centre, Riyadh. (BDA)

Brown Daltas and Associates Inc

BDA is based in Cambridge, Mass, and Rome, Italy. Its early work in Saudi Arabia was for SAMA (Saudi Arabian Monetary Authority) for whom the practice designed a number of provincial branch banks, which were illustrated in *MEC*. Its largest project in the kingdom is the King Khalid Military City, designed with the US Corps of Engineers for the Saudi Arabian Ministry of Defence and Aviation. Construction is 60 per cent complete.

A second extremely large project, for which the master plan of the science complex is complete, is the Saudi Arabian National Centre for Science and Technology, at Riyadh. This centre is planned to co-ordinate all of the scientific activities of the four major universities in the kingdom, in addition to carrying out its own on-site research work and engaging in joint research with some twenty other countries. The master plan includes a community with more than 500 units of housing, schools, community facilities, recreation and leisure areas, and a mosque. The several major public buildings include the administrative headquarters which has been planned as a sequence of public and private spaces, including 74,322.4 m² of office space, with 37,161.20 m² of parking below. The flexible layout administrative offices for a staff of approximately 4,100 persons are planned around garden courts. The insitu concrete structure is clad with travertine externally; with interior granite paving and carpeting.

BDA is also architect for the Markaz Al Mahmal Commercial Centre, which is to form the northern side of the principal square in Jeddah. This project is at the early construction stage. The complex of buildings includes a 20-storey 12,000 m² office tower; a seven-storey, 20,000 m² shopping centre and world trade centre, and other buildings, all linked by pedestrian bridges. The bridge between the tower and the shopping centre, across King Abdul Aziz Street, forms an entrance portal into the main city square. The architectural design is one of the earliest examples of what, to coin a phrase, can be regarded as post-modern Islamic traditional.

CRS-Sirrine Inc

The origins of this, the largest of the US design firms in fee billing terms, have been described, and the CRS (Caudill Rowlett Scott) designed University of Petroleum and Minerals, at Dhahran — its best known work — has been illustrated before in *MEC*. This project dates back to 1965 when the master plan was commenced, with the first class graduating in 1971. By 1982, when the second phase was completed, the university had complete facilities for the instruction and housing of 3,000 students. The mosque alongside the reflection pool is illustrated here.

Two other projects of interest are first, the El Gezirah Sheraton Hotel, Cairo — the 30-storey circular hotel tower already one of the city's Nile-side landmarks; and second, The National Methanol Company's corporate headquarters and production facility, Jubail — comprising a 13,145 m² area of office accommodation, cafeteria, guardhouse, laboratory and training buildings, utility building and two warehouses, completed in August 1983. ●

Machado and Silvetti Associates

1974–

Machado and Silvetti Associates

Headquarters
Boston, MA

Founding Partners
Rodolfo Machado, Jorge Silvetti

1974

Machado and Silvetti Associates

Rodolfo Machado and Jorge Silvetti, both Argentinians born in 1942 in Buenos Aires, overlapped at key institutions in Argentina and the US before forming their practice together in 1974. Both received their diplomas in architecture at the Universidad de Buenos Aires and their Master of Architecture degrees at the University of California, Berkeley, and both pursued postgraduate work in architectural theory after completing their architectural training. The pair's prolific theoretical production, both individually and collectively, placed them at the center of discussions of postmodernism in architecture throughout the 1980s. Their prominence within these disciplinary debates ensured a series of important pedagogical and administrative positions in turn for both Machado and Silvetti. The highest among these were Machado's appointments as Chair of the Architecture Department at the Rhode Island School of Design (1978–1986) and Chair of the Department of Urban Planning and Design at the Harvard Graduate School of Design (2004–2009), and Silvetti's appointment as Chair of the Architecture Department at the Harvard Graduate School of Design (1995–2002).

In lectures on their work and their pedagogical activity in the 1980s, Machado and Silvetti began to articulate a complex position on architectural production, involving the imperative to develop a sustained "criticism from within," to create a "personal iconography" of architectural form, and to achieve a "convincing technical materiality." The architects coined an appellation for this particular constellation of concerns, terming it an "aesthetic-pragmatic strategy of unprecedented realism." Accepted and consequently championed by many critics of their work, this "unprecedented realism" has been explained in a variety of ways.[1] Its effects, however, have been consistently understood to involve a disciplinary demonstration of the possibility of unprecedented conditions. In 1989, on the occasion of an exhibition of their work at the Harvard Graduate School of Design, architect Jaquelin T. Robertson described the firm's unique contribution to the field as one that involves regarding the "architecture and the design of the city as a singular investigation in which inquiry and realization, poetry and practicality, history and invention are inextricably entwined."[2]

Incorporated in 1985, Machado and Silvetti Associates has been involved in numerous architectural and urban projects over the last three decades. A 1997 article in *Architecture* described "the intellectual pair" as running "a busy Boston office, designing major buildings and master plans for universities and institutions."[3] Though currently numbering 20 employees, at their largest, Machado and Silvetti Associates had 60 employees. The office's self-description currently includes expertise in art museums, educational institutions, and urban design and planning, and the firm's projects have taken them worldwide to Berlin, Beirut, Buenos Aires, Sicily, Frankfurt, San Juan, Pamplona, Rome, Seoul, Singapore, Tenerife, Venice, and Vienna. In the United States the firm has completed numerous major commissions in Boston and New England as well as in New York, Texas, California, Utah, Wisconsin, North Carolina, and Arkansas. Although the same 1997 article in *Architecture* described the booming practice of Machado and Silvetti Associates as searching for a "new pragmatism" commensurate with their expanding volume of work, both Machado and Silvetti have maintained "unprecedented realism" as their aesthetic agenda, even as the particular vocabulary of their built projects has become more responsive to the local context and circumstances of each project. — AM

① See K. Michael Hays, ed., *Unprecedented Realism: The Architecture of Machado and Silvetti* (New York: Princeton Architectural Press, 1995).

② Jaquelin T. Robertson, "On Teaching and Practice," in Peter G. Rowe, ed. *Rodolfo Machado and Jorge Silvetti: Buildings for Cities* (Cambridge, MA and New York: The Harvard Graduate School of Design and Rizzoli International Publications, 1989).

③ "Machado and Silvetti Get Real," *Architecture* (April 1997): 80–83.

KPF

1976–

Kohn Pedersen Fox Associates

Headquarters
New York, NY

Other Locations
London, UK; Hong Kong, Hong Kong; Shanghai, China; Seoul, South Korea; Abu Dhabi, United Arab Emirates

Founding Partners
A. Eugene Kohn, Sheldon Fox, William Pedersen

Current Partners
A. Eugene Kohn, William Pedersen, William Louie, Paul Katz, James von Klemperer, Jill N. Lerner, Michael Greene, Anthony Mosellie, Douglas Hocking, Robert C. Whitlock, Lloyd Sigal, John Bushell, Mustafa Chehabeddine, Dominic Dunn, Josh Chaiken, Brian Girard, Inkai Mu, Richard Nemeth, Trent Tesch, Shawn Duffy, Crisitina Garcia, Charles Ippolito, Hugh Trumbull, David Malott

1976

Kohn Pedersen Fox Associates

A. Eugene Kohn, Sheldon Fox, and William Pedersen, three classmates from the University of Pennsylvania, founded Kohn Pedersen Fox Associates (KPF) on July 4, 1976, during a period of economic recession in the United States. All had been working in the office of John Carl Warnecke and Associates, where Kohn was president and partner and Pedersen and Fox were both vice-presidents. KPF established itself by focusing on procuring projects domestically, while other large architectural offices looked toward the Middle East for work during the boom in crude oil prices after 1973. Kohn, Fox, and Pedersen—a business developer, a management director, and a lead designer, respectively—campaigned in person for projects that might have seemed beyond the reach of a newly-fledged firm. This strategy proved successful when, after a few small interior design projects, the trio landed the design of the American Broadcasting Company headquarters in New York City (1976–1979), a large-scale project which set the stage for the firm's later growth.

In 1987, Gene Kohn reportedly attended a business seminar, held by the American Institute of Architects (AIA), in which an economist told audience members that if they did not begin to work overseas, fifty percent of them would be out of business in five years. Kohn seemed sympathetic to the message. KPF opened an office in London in the the following year to work on its first overseas building, an office for Goldman Sachs (1987–1991), a project that served as a catalyst for the office's future international work. KPF's London office served as a place for young designers to rise and grow as designers, beyond the auspices of the New York headquarters—a strategy that served all too well when, in 2009, five of KPF's London office partners attempted to buy out the office's UK operations and, after failing to do so, subsequently split from the office to start PLP Architecture. By 1996, up to 65% of KPF's total fees were estimated to come from work overseas. The completion of Tokyo's Roppongi Hills (1996–2003), a collaboration with developer Monoru Mori, CEO of Mori Building, was followed by an even larger commission for Mori, to design the Shanghai World Financial Tower (1994–2008), the tallest building in the world at the time of its construction.

Today, KPF operates six global offices with over 600 staff members. The firm has added more partners to its masthead, totaling 24 today, a strategy intended to move the office away from a pyramidal corporate structure toward a more horizontal organization. Unlike other large architecture firms, which operate either in small studios or with a single person at the helm, KPF's organization is based on a structure of teams in which partners might work in different capacities on multiple projects, with new collaborators over time. The office has expanded to include KPFIA, an interiors group within the firm. Despite its relative youth compared to its competitors, KPF continues to compete internationally for large-scale projects. —AL

Steven Holl Architects

Headquarters
New York, NY

Founding Partner
Steven Holl

Current Partners
Steven Holl, Chris McVoy, Noah Yaffe

Andy Ryan

Gluckman Mayner Architects

Headquarters
New York, NY

Founding and Key Partners
Richard Gluckman (founding principal),
David Mayner

Gluckman Mayner Architects

Arquitectonica

Headquarters
Miami, FL

Other Locations
New York City, NY; Los Angeles, CA; Madrid, Spain; Paris, France; Hong Kong, Hong Kong; Shanghai, China; Manila, Phillipines; Dubai, United Arab Emirates; São Paulo, Brazil; Lima, Peru

Founding and Key Partners
Bernardo Fort-Brescia, Laurinda Hope Spear (founding principals), Andres Duany, Elizabeth Plater-Zyberk, Hervin Romney

1977

Arquitectonica

Arquitectonica, founded in 1977 by five partners, is a prominent architecture and interior design firm, headquartered in Miami with over 300 employees working in offices in New York, Los Angeles, Paris, Hong Kong, Shanghai, Manila, Lima, Sao Paolo, and Dubai. While the firm in its earliest years included Andres Duany and Elizabeth Plater-Zyberk later of the planning firm DPZ, and architect Hervin Romney, the remaining founding partners—Laurinda Spear and her spouse Bernardo Fort-Brescia—now lead the worldwide organization.

Once referred to by Philip Johnson as the "gutsiest team in the business," Fort-Brescia and Spear's firm began in Miami, and came of age as that city did. Its first major work was a home for Spear's parents, designed in partnership with Rem Koolhaas, and featuring the bold colors, geometric forms and up-to-the-minute material touches that would become the firm's trademark. Arquitectonica's early multi-family work, including the Babylon building in 1977 and especially the Atlantis Condominium tower in 1982, defined a slick, neon Miami in the cultural consciousness. Prior to the construction of these forward-looking buildings, the city was something of a backwater, its Art Deco district only to beginning the process of restoration and landmark recognition in the late 1970s. With its bold primary colors, an iconic balcony cut from the glassy facade, and a prominent spot in the opening credits of TV's Miami Vice, the Atlantis defined luxury in Miami.

As Miami grew to play an increasingly crucial role as intermediary between Latin America and the United States, Arquitectonica's reputation grew as well, and found its first opportunity to build abroad: the headquarters of the Banco de Crédito in Fort-Brescia's native Peru. The resulting project, completed in 1988, was published widely, and demonstrated the firm's ability to build large commercial projects internationally. Like the Atlantis, the project is playfully avant-garde, with dazzling shapes and textures, while remaining decidedly client-conscious. Like the US Embassy in Lima that the firm completed several years later, the building's ability to work within security circumscriptions was admired as much as its stylistic touches.

Through the 1990s and into the early 2000s, Arquitectonica built many more large commercial and residential projects in Florida, Hong Kong, Europe, and throughout the United States. In the last ten years, the firm's work in Asia, especially malls in the Philippines and office towers in China and Korea, have propelled the firm's practice forward, and allowed it to weather the economic decline of 2008 and emerge in the 2010s with high profile projects from Miami Beach to Macau. — MW

moore ruble yudell
architects & planners

1977–

Moore Ruble Yudell Architects & Planners

Headquarters
Santa Monica, CA

Other Locations
Shanghai, China

Founding Partners
Charles Moore, John Ruble, Buzz Yudell

Current Partners
John Ruble, Buzz Yudell (partners), James Mary O'Connor, Mario Violich, Krista Becker, Jeanne Chen, Michael S. Martin, Neal Matsuno (principals)

1977

Moore Ruble Yudell Architects & Planners

One of several offices started by Charles Moore, Moore Ruble Yudell opened its doors in Santa Monica, California in 1977. Moore had recently moved to Los Angeles to teach at the University of California, Los Angeles (UCLA) after more than ten years at the Yale University School of Architecture. Buzz Yudell and John Ruble had both studied under Moore — Yudell at Yale, Ruble at UCLA — before the three established the firm. Moore, a prominent postmodernist, gained early notoriety for his use of playful historical references, and, through his multiple practices with various collaborators during the 1960s and 1970s, for the contextualism and vernacular language of his work. Moore Ruble Yudell continued some of these investigations, particularly in the firm's early housing complexes at Berlin and Malmö.

The office got its start with several private residences but soon began to work internationally on various large housing developments. Its first major project abroad was the Tegel Harbor Housing in Berlin. Initial work began in 1981, but the project would not be completed until 1987. By the mid-1990s, a majority of Moore Rubll Yudell's work came from international housing developments, including the Nishiokamoto Housing (1988–1996) in Kobe, Japan, the Potatisakern Housing and Villas (1988–2002) in Malmö, Sweden, and the Berliner Strasse Housing in Potsdam, Germany.

In 1995, as a result of their extensive work in Germany, Moore Ruble Yudell was invited to participate in the competition to design the US Embassy in Berlin. The firm's design was selected as the winner in 1996, but it would be eight years before construction began, and twelve before the project was finally complete. At the time of its opening in 2008, the embassy was heavily criticized for its heavily securitized appearance in the German press.[1]

Moore Ruble Yudell continues to produce a large number of international housing developments, with several projects currently underway in China. Since the completion of the Berlin Embassy, the firm has also developed a fruitful relationship with the Bureau of Overseas Building Operations (OBO) of the US State Department that has led to several additional embassy projects. These include commissions for US embassies in The Hague, Netherlands; Santo Domingo, Puerto Rico; Helsinki, Finland; and N'Djamena, Chad.
— JJ

(1)
Hans Stimmann, "Hässlich aber sicher – die neue US-Botschaft," *Die Welt* (May 23, 2008), http://www.welt.de/kultur/article2027722/Haesslich-aber-sicher-die-neue-US-Botschaft.html (last accessed November 23, 2014).

1977–

1977

Pelli Clarke Pelli Architects

Headquarters
New Haven, CT

Other Locations
New York, NY; San Francisco, CA; Los Angeles, CA; Shanghai, China; Tokyo, Japan; Abu Dhabi, United Arab Emirates

Founding and Key Partners
Cesar Pelli (founding principal), Fred W. Clarke, Rafael Pelli

Current Partners
Cesar Pelli, Fred W. Clarke, Rafael Pelli (senior principals), William E. Butler, David P. Chen, Mitchell A. Hirsch, Gregg E. Jones, Mariko Masuoka, Lawrence S. Ng, Mark R. Shoemaker (principals)

Pelli Clarke Pelli Architects

Born and educated in Argentina, Cesar Pelli began his career in the office of Eero Saarinen and Associates before becoming the first director of design at Daniel, Johnson, Hall & Mendenhall (DMJM) in Los Angeles in 1964. He was appointed design partner at Victor Gruen Associates in Los Angeles in 1968 upon Gruen's return to Austria. In these years Pelli gained recognition as a member of the group known as the "LA Silvers," so-called for their use of steel and mirror-glass curtain wall systems. The epitome of this slick-skin aesthetic was Pelli's monolithic Pacific Design Center in Los Angeles (1975), designed for Victor Gruen Associates and known as the "Blue Whale" for its scale and shimmering blue mirror cladding. Pelli left Los Angeles and established Cesar Pelli & Associates in New Haven, Connecticut in 1977, the year he became dean of the School of Architecture at Yale University.

While the firms's portfolio of built work is notable for its wide range of building types, Cesar Pelli & Associates became most recognized for its designs of iconic skyscrapers, many of which define city skylines around the world. The firm's first major tower complex was the World Financial Center in New York City, adjacent to the World Trade Center, completed in 1988 and consisting of four towers, each of a different height and crowned by a different geometrical form — dome, pyramid, stepped pyramid, and chamfered pyramid. Anchoring the southern tip of Manhattan on the Hudson River, these were the first buildings built on the reclaimed land that would become Battery Park City in New York. Pelli's tower for One Canada Square in London (1987–1991) featured a similar pyramid at its top as the pinnacle of the Canary Wharf development at London Docklands, planned by Skidmore, Owings & Merrill (SOM) and including office buildings by Kohn Pedersen Fox Associates (KPF), HOK, Perkins+Will, Pei Cobb Freed & Partners, and other US firms.

Perhaps the tallest and most prominent buildings completed by the firm in the last two decades are the linked Petronas Towers in Kuala Lumpur, Malaysia (1992–1998). The tallest buildings in the world until 2004, the towers quickly became both icons in the city skyline and emblems for the nation of Malaysia, as recognizable as its flag. Inspired by Malaysian ornamental geometries, the towers feature stepped profiles, ornamental crowns, and floor plans composed of a pattern of interlocking squares and circles. Other supertall buildings by the office include Two International Finance Centre (1997–2003) in Hong Kong, among the ten tallest towers in the world. More recently, the Torre de Cristal (2004–2011) in Madrid, Spain, the Iberdrola Tower in Bilbao, Spain (2007–2011), and the Shanghai International Financial Centre (2007–2011) in Pudong, China have continued the firm's signature for sharply faceted tower profiles and technically sophisticated glass facades.

In 2005 the firm was renamed Pelli Clarke Pelli Architects to recognize the role of principals Fred Clarke and Rafael Pelli, Cesar's son. The firm also has a smaller satellite studio in New York, led by Rafael Pelli. Despite the global reach and scale of the firm's work, Pelli Clarke Pelli Architects continues to practice in the same office space in which it was founded, an unassuming second floor office space above Chapel Street, on a modest commercial strip in downtown New Haven. — FT

JERDE

1977–

Jerde Partnership

Headquarters
New York, New York

Other locations
Los Angeles, CA; Hong Kong, China; Shanghai, China

Founding Partner
Jon Jerde

1977

Jerde Partnership

In his preface to the Jerde Partnership's monograph, the famed Los Angeles science fiction writer Ray Bradbury wrote of the firm's iconic Horton Plaza shopping center in San Diego: "Yeah, Gangway! I want to be lost."[1] Jon Jerde's LA-based firm, which prides itself on its "creative placemaking" practice, has, since gaining early prominence for its dizzying Southern California malls, become an international force for retail architecture.

Upon graduation from the University of Southern California with a Bachelor's of Architecture in 1966, principal Jon Jerde worked for larger firms designing American shopping malls. After "a frustrating ten years," he struck out on his own, founding the Jerde Partnership on the strength of a commission from a San Diego-based mall developer, Ernest Hahn. That project—to design a mall in a corner of the city's downtown targeted for urban renewal—would be completed in 1985 and dubbed the Horton Plaza. A collage of styles, materials, and reportedly of 39 different colors, the mall veered dramatically away from the standards of retail design as exemplified by the work of James Rouse and Victor Gruen on the East Coast. The architecture of the mall was no longer constrained to quietly hosting the store displays, but from then on a spectacle in and of itself. The 1.5 million square foot mall is often credited with triggering a renaissance in the downtown San Diego real estate market, and launched the firm toward a long career in stylish, unrestrained mall design.

Daniel Herman, in the *Harvard Design School Guide to Shopping*, credits Jerde's innovations in the "urban shopping/entertainment hybrid" with bringing "shopping to an environmental climax."[2] Jerde himself has described the project, and those that would follow, as "experiential architecture." Whatever the nomenclature, the Horton Plaza was a quick financial success, and the firm went on to design large-scale inner-city retail projects throughout southern California, in Las Vegas, and the landmark, five million square foot Mall of America in Minnesota.

By the mid 1990s, the Jerde Partnership was tapped to design large, exuberant shopping centers overseas—notably the Canal City Hakata, a targeted catalyst project for a declining industrial neighborhood in Fukuoka, Japan and the Beursplein in central Rotterdam. Jerde's stated belief that one "can't pull retail out separately from the rest of life...[that] everything is in collusion," led to projects that took on an increasingly greater urbanistic scope.[3] Namba Parks, in Osaka—another million square foot project—took on, in 2004, an almost Landscape Urbanist style, mixing ground planes, roofs, and landscaping together. Plans for the 15-story Langham Place Mall in Hong Kong displayed, in 2005, an eye for vertical, single-structure public space. Stylistically and geographically disparate, the body of work can still be summed up in the architect's words as "experiential architecture." In an interview in 2001, Jerde recalled that upon graduation from architecture school, he realized that he wanted to "build stuff for ordinary people."[4] By a more recent account, though, his firm goes further: the Jerde Partnership "puts people in a popular and collective environment in which they can be most truly and happily alive." — MW

①
Ray Bradbury, "Preface," in Frances Anderton, ed., *You Are Here: The Jerde Partnership International* (Phaidon Press, 1999):

②
Daniel Herman, "Jerde Transfer," in Chuihua Judy Chung, Jeffrey Inaba, Rem Koolhaas, Sze Tsung Leong, ed., *The Harvard Design School Guide to Shopping* (Cologne: Taschen, 2001).

③
Jon Jerde quoted in David Koch, "The Doyen of Design," *National Real Estate Investor* (September 1, 2004), http://nreionline.com/mag/doyen-design (last accessed November 8, 2014).

④
Jon Jerde, interview with Shashank Bengali, "Urban Legend Jon Jerde," *USC Trojan Family Magazine* (Summer 2001).

FXFOWLE Architects

Headquarters
New York, NY

Other Locations
Washington, DC

Founding Partners
Bruce Fowle, Robert Fox

Current Partners
Guy Geier, Sudhir Jambhekar, Dan Kaplan, Sylvia Smith, Mark Strauss, Heidi Blau, Tim Milam, John Schuyler (partners), Bruce Fowle, Elizabeth Finkelshteyn, Nicholas Garrison, Ann Rolland (principals)

FXFOWLE

KOETTER | KIM & ASSOCIATES | INC.
ARCHITECTURE URBAN DESIGN

1978–

Koetter Kim & Associates

Headquarters
Boston, MA

Other Locations
London, UK (1988)

Founding Partners
Fred Koetter, Susie Kim

Current Partners
Fred Koetter, Susie Kim, Mark deShong

Koetter Kim and Associates

1978

MACK Architect(s)

Headquarters
San Francisco, CA

Other Locations
Los Angeles, CA
Judenburg, Austria

Founding Partner
Mark Mack

1978

MACK Architect(s)

SafdieArchitects

1978–

Safdie Architects

Headquarters
Boston, MA

Other Locations
Toronto, Canada; Jerusalem, Israel; Singapore, Singapore

Founding Partner
Moshe Safdie

Current Partners
Moshe Safdie, Gene Dyer, David Brooks, Isaac Franco, Rainer Goeller, Paul Gross, Michael Guran, Jaron Lubin, Warren Mathison, Charu Kokate, Christopher Mulvey, Hugh Phillips, Greg Reaves, Sean Scensor, Carrie Yoon

Safdie Architects

1978

DS+R

1979–

Diller Scofidio + Renfro

Headquarters
New York, NY

Founding and Key Partners
Elizabeth Diller, Ricardo Scofidio (founding principals), Charles Renfro

Current Partners
Elizabeth Diller, Ricardo Scofidio, Charles Renfro, Benjamin Gilmartin, Scott Johnson

1979

Diller Scofidio + Renfro

In 1979, when Liz Diller and Ricardo Scofidio established Diller + Scofidio in New York, the city was still recovering from a brush with bankruptcy, Times Square was still a notoriously gritty place, and, with the exception of a few well-established large firms, US architects were simply not building. Intent on realizing their designs rather than committing them to paper, Diller + Scofidio directed their energies toward installations, exhibitions, video projections, and live performances "in real space," as Diller has remarked.

In this niche between conceptual art and architecture, the pair worked out of their loft on Cooper Square, directly over the offices of the Village Voice. Their firm designed over 50 works in its first 20 years, hiring architectural students and recent graduates on an as-needed basis. By 1998, Diller+Scofidio still only had one full-time employee, but the roster of designers who spent time in the studio included some of the most innovative members of the next generation of East Coast practitioners, such as Paul Lewis, Lyn Rice, Mark Wasiuta, Nicholas deMonchaux, Eric Bunge, and Eric Höweler.

Diller + Scofidio's first project abroad, Slither Housing (1994–2000) at Gifu, Japan, was also their first substantial built project, with the exception of a small house completed in 1981. Part of a government-subsidized housing development master planned by Arata Isozaki, the project was not widely published at the time and had little impact on the office's operations.

In 1999, Diller and Scofidio were jointly awarded a MacArthur Foundation fellowship, which provided them with previously unknown financial stability. By 2000, the firm was beginning to produce as many design competition entries and project proposals as grant applications for art works. A successful proposal to Restaurant Associates resulted in the commission to design the renovation of the Brasserie restaurant in the basement of the Ludwig Mies van der Rohe's Seagram building in New York, including a video installation, the "bar beam," as part of the project. Other winning competition entries in this period included designs for the Institute of Contemporary Art (ICA) in Boston and the Eyebeam Museum of Art and Technology in New York.

It was the Blur Building, the firm's second project abroad—an open platform with 33,000 fog nozzles, designed for the 2002 Swiss Expo on Lake Neuchatel, which the architects referred to as "the making of nothing"—that projected Diller + Scofidio into the international media. The firm grew rapidly, building the ICA in Boston and receiving the commission to renovate Lincoln Center in New York. Charles Renfro, who had worked with Diller and Scofidio since the mid-1990s, was made partner in 2004, and the firm was renamed Diller Scofidio + Renfro (DS+R). In 2006, with 40 employees, they moved to West 26th Street in Chelsea.

Today, Diller Scofidio + Renfro have over 100 employees and have expanded onto a second floor of their Chelsea headquarters. Yet the phone is still answered modestly, as it always has been: "studio." While DS+R continue to produce more experimental works, the balance of the practice has tipped largely toward architectural design. —AS

Santos Prescott and Associates

Headquarters
San Francisco, CA; Somerville, MA

Other Locations
Philadelphia, PA (1990–2002)

Founding and Key Partners
Adèle Naudé Santos (founding principal),
Bruce C. Prescott

1979

Santos Prescott and Associates

The architectural and urban design practice of Santos Prescott and Associates was formed in 2002 by Adèle Naudé Santos and Bruce Prescott in San Francisco. The practice has headquarters on each coast of the United States, in San Francisco, California and Massachusetts. The firm has inherited the legacy of Adèle Santos's previous three decades of architectural work, produced through the offices of Adèle Naudé Santos and Associates in San Francisco and Santos Levy and Associates in Philadelphia (1990–2002), Adèle Naudé Santos Architect (1979–1999), Interstudio in Houston, Texas (1974–1979) with Antonio de Souza Santos, and Adèle and Antonio de Souza Santos (1968–1972) in Cape Town, South Africa.

Santos Prescott and Associates has recently offered that the firm's architectural solutions derive from "knowledge gained from both professional practice and academic research."[1] Whereas both partners have been engaged in teaching, Adèle Santos's pedagogical and administrative careers have been in the spotlight for over three decades and have in part contributed to the changing nature and geographic location of her architectural offices. She has taught in institutions across the United States, occupying key leadership positions as Chair of the Department of Architecture at the University of Pennsylvania from 1981 to 1987, the founding Dean of the School of Architecture at the University of California, San Diego from 1990 to 1995, and Dean of the School of Architecture and Planning at the Massachusetts Institute of Technology from 2004 to 2014.

In an interview in *Perspecta* published in 1997, Santos described her mode of working as one deeply reliant on locale, including social, climactic and morphological conditions.[2] She proposed that concentrating on both the contextual and internal needs of a project meant that the firm's architectural language evolved from project to project. Endorsing this view, critics of Santos's work have identified issues of landscape and light as the key registers for her projects. Her treatment of these conditions across a series of international projects, from early houses in South Africa through housing projects in Japan and more recent institutional buildings in the United States and Guatemala, have been described as marked by Santos's South African sensibility. The blurring of indoor and outdoor boundaries continues to fuel the architecture of Santos Prescott and Associates' designs for private homes, housing, and civic and cultural buildings across Africa, Asia, and South and North America. — AM

①
Santos Prescott and Associates website, http://www.houzz.com/pro/bcprescott/santos-prescott-and-associates (last accessed November 23, 2014).

②
Adèle Naudé Santos, "Excerpts from a Conversation with Michael Meister," *Perspecta* 28 (1997): 87–93.

DPZ

DUANY PLATER-ZYBERK & COMPANY

ARCHITECTS AND TOWN PLANNERS

1980–

Duany Plater-Zyberk & Company

Headquarters
Miami, FL

Other Locations
Gaithersburg, MD; Charlotte, NC

Founding and Key Partners
Andrés M. Duany, Elizabeth Plater-Zyberk

Current Partners
Andrés M. Duany, Elizabeth Plater-Zyberk, Francisco Xavier Iglesias, Galina Tachieva, Marina Khoury, Matthew John Lambert, Senen M.A. Antonio (partners), Duane Phillips (principal, DPZ Europe)

1980

Residential Architect, July 2009. Duany Plater-Zyberk & Company. Photographer: Danny Turner

Three years after co-founding the firm Arquitectonica, Elizabeth Plater-Zyberk and Andres Duany founded their own architecture and planning firm, Duany Plater-Zyberk & Company. The pair's 1980 master plan for Seaside, Florida, begun while still part of Arquitectonica and finished by the nascent DPZ, catapulted the new firm to fame and ushered in the heyday of New Urbanism. Duany and Plater-Zyberk, as educators and designers, became important proponents of the school and its tenets of walkability, mixed-use, and contextual, tradition-minded architecture.

Seaside, built on virgin beachfront in concert with the designers' research into successful Southern towns, formalizes a number of the firm's concerns. Narrow roads lined with postmodern homes designed by the likes of Léon Krier and Robert A.M. Stern radiate out from a central square. The design of the various residences is unified by a strict form-based code developed by the firm. Siting referential architecture within a pedestrianized zone, the town—while fundamentally a summer resort—inspired many civic leaders across the country, and led the partners to dozens of other urban-scaled commissions in the U.S. and abroad.

From their offices in Miami, DPZ has unified what they call "Traditional Neighborhood Design" with shopping malls, as in the Kentlands (population 4,500) in Maryland and with existing urban cores, as in Providence, Rhode Island.[1] The firm prides itself on its design charrette process, wherein residents and business owners are invited to participate in structured planning and design discussions throughout the development process. The firm has also worked at the citywide planning scale, leading in 2005 the development of a general land use code for Miami. An attempt to bring the unity and pedestrian sensitivity of Seaside to the metropolitan scale, the Miami plan ("Miami 21") instituted formal restrictions meant to ensure architectural predictability and urban walkability across the city's 35,000 acres.

Duany and Plater-Zyberk's work abroad is often more explicitly linked to their early resort urbanism. The firm designed pedestrian-centric neighborhoods in more or less local styles in Loreto Bay, in Baja California (2003–2008), and at Schooner Bay in the Bahamas (2006–2009). Indeed, across their commissions in Europe, Asia, the Middle East, and South America, a shared theme of resort programs or resort-inspired living emerges. — MW

(1)
The notion has traveled from theoretical texts into numerous city codes across the US. See Andres Duany, Elizabeth Plater-Zyberk, and Jeff Speck, *Suburban Nation: The Rise of Sprawl and the Decline of the American Dream* (New York: North Point Press, 2000).

Raffles City
1973–1986

Architect
I. M. Pei & Partners

Location
Singapore, Singapore

Associate Architect
Architects 61

Client
Raffles City (PTE) Ltd., Singapore

PEI COBB FREED & PARTNERS Architects LLP

Dow Chemical Executive Housing
1974

Architect
Leo A Daly

Location
Hong Kong, Hong Kong

Client
Dow Chemical Co.

LEO A DALY

SABIC Headquarters
1974

Architect
Leo A Daly

Location
Riyadh, Saudi Arabia

Client
Saudi Basic Industries Corporation (SABIC)

LEO A DALY

Montego Bay Hospital
1974

Architect
The Architects Collaborative

Location
Montego Bay, Jamaica

Associate Architect
Chambers, Gibbs & Associates

Client
Montego Bay Hospital

TAC

Imperial Medical Center of Iran
1974–1976

Architect
William L Pereira & Associates

Location
Tehran, Iran

Client
Imperial Medical Center of Iran

Centro Banaven
1974–1978

Architect
Johnson Burgee Archtitects

Location
Caracas, Venezuela

Client
Banaven

PJAR

National Center for the Performing Arts
1974–1980

Architect
Johnson / Burgee Architects

Location
Mumbai. India

Client
National Center for the Performing Arts

PJAR

Hajj Terminal, Jeddah International Airport
1974–1981

Architect
Skidmore, Owings & Merrill

Location
Jeddah, Saudi Arabia

Client
Saudi Arabia, Ministry of Defense and Aviation

SOM

King Khalid Military City
1974–1986

Architect
Brown Daltas and Associates

Location
Saudi Arabia

Client
US Army Corps of Engineers

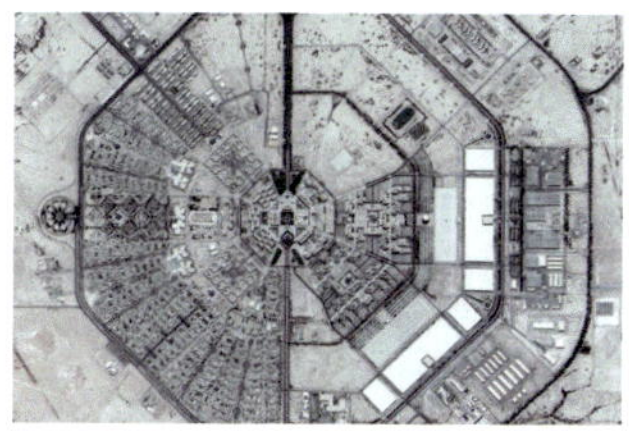

Torre Picasso
1974–1988

Architect
Yamasaki and Associates

Location
Madrid, Spain

Local Architect
Jorge Mir Valls; Rafael Coll Pujoi

Client
Unión de Explosivos Río Tinto, S.A.

Al-Jubail Petrochemical Co. Headquarters
1975

Architect
Leo A Daly

Location
Jubail, Saudi Arabia

Client
The Fluor Company, Al-Jubail Petrochemical Co., Saudi Basic Industries Corporation (SABIC), EXXON

LEO A DALY

Union Carbide Cellulose Casings Plant
1975–1977

Architect
A. Epstein and Sons, Inc.

Location
Thaon-les-Vosges, France

Client
Union Carbide Corporation / Viscora, S.A.

EPSTEIN

Sharjah Intercontinental Hotel
1975–1979

TAC

Architect
The Architects Collaborative

Location
Sharjah, United Arab Emirates

Client
InterContinental Hotels Group

ARAMCO Workers' Housing
1975–1980

CRSS

Architect
CRS Group

Location
Dhahran, Saudi Arabia

Client
Arabian-American Oil Company (ARAMCO)

King Khaled International Airport
1975–1984

Architect
Hellmuth, Obata + Kassabaum

Location
Riyadh, Saudi Arabia

Client
International Airports Projects (1AP), Ministry of Defense and Aviation, Jeddah

King Saud University
1975–1985

Architect
HOK+4 Consortium(HOK CRS Group; Gollins Melvin Ward Partnership [UK]; Syska and Hennesy, Inc.; Dames & Moore)

Location
Riyadh, Saudi Arabia

Client
King Saud University

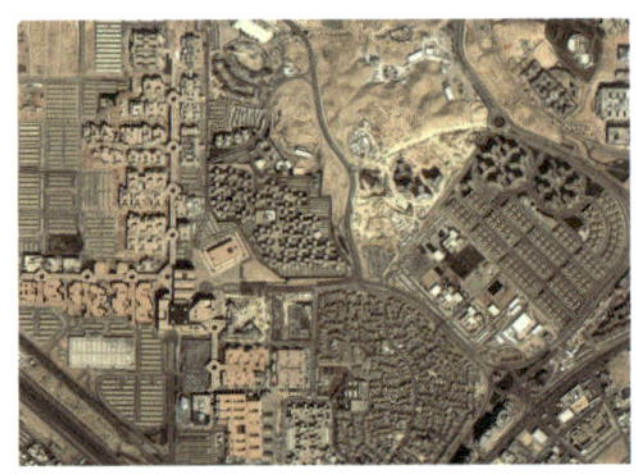

University of Blida Teaching Hospital and Housing Communities
1975–1986

SOM

Architect
Skidmore, Owings & Merrill

Location
Blida, Algeria

Client
Government of Algeria/ Ministry of Education and Scientific Research

King Abdulaziz Military Academy
1976

CRSS

Architect
CRS Group

Location
Riyadh, Saudi Arabia

Client
US Army Corps of Engineers

Hotel Bernardin Resort
1976

TAC

Architect
The Architects Collaborative

Location
Piran, Yugoslavia

Client
Hotel Bernardin Enterprise

Moscow World Trade Center
1976–1980

ELLERBE BECKET

Architect
Welton Becket Associates

Location
Moscow, Russia

Local Architect
Mosproskt-2

Client
Occidental Petroleum Corporation

Abu Dhabi Intercontinental Hotel
1976–1981

Architect
Benjamin Thompson Associates

Location
Abu Dhabi, United Arab Emirates

Client
InterContinental Hotels Corporation

Joint Banking Centre
1976–1982

SOM

Architect
Skidmore, Owings & Merrill

Location
Kuwait City, Kuwait

Client
Bank of Kuwait and the Middle East, Industrial Bank of Kuwait, Kuwait Real Estate Bank

Yanbu New Community Master Plan
1977

SOM

Architect
Skidmore, Owings & Merrill

Location
Industrial City, Saudi Arabia

Client
Royal Commission for Jubail and Yanbu

Yanbu Industrial City Residential District
1977

LEO A DALY

Architect
Leo A Daly

Location
Yanbu, Saudi Arabia

Client
Royal Commission for Jubail and Yanbu

Yanbu Industrial City Residential District
1977

Architect
Change to CRS Group

Location
Yanbu, Saudi Arabia

Client
Royal Commission for
Jubail and Yanbu

Yanbu Industrial City Residential District
1977

Architect
The Architects Collaborative

Location
Yanbu, Saudi Arabia

Client
Royal Commission for
Jubail and Yanbu

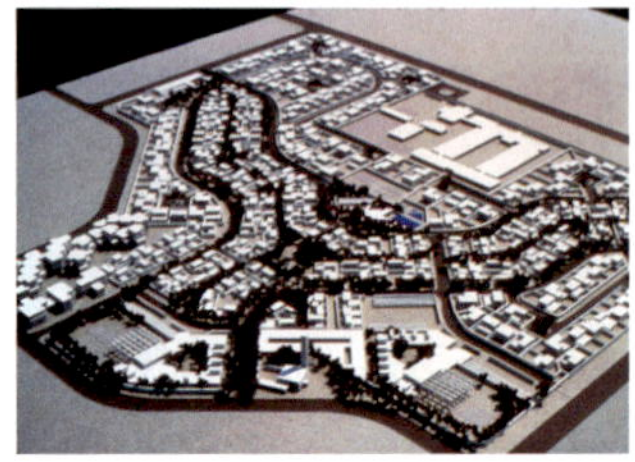

Shiraz Technical Institute
1977

Architect
Hugh Stubbins and Associates

Location
Shiraz, Iran

Client
Shiraz Technical Institute

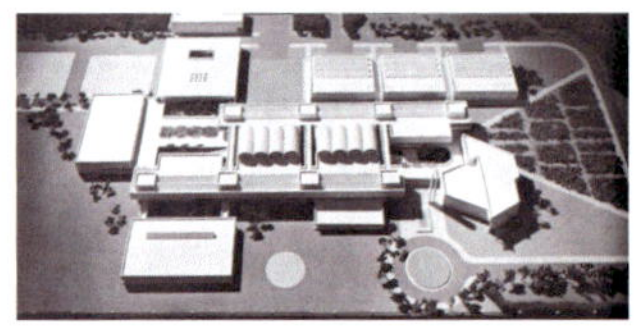

Jubail Industrial City Master Plan
1977

Architect
The Architects Collaborative

Location
location should be Jubail,
Saudi Arabia

Consultant
Pace

Client
Royal Commission for
Jubail and Yanbu

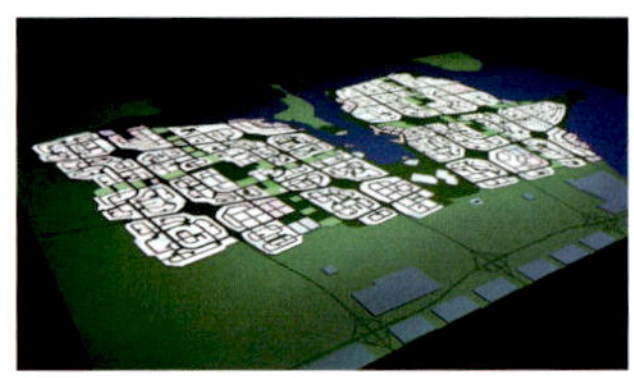

US Embassy
1977–1983

Architect
Fred Bassetti and Company

Location
Lisbon, Portugal

Client
US Department of State,
Foreign Buildings Operations

National Commercial Bank
1977–1983

Architect
Skidmore, Owings & Merrill

Location
Jeddah, Saudi Arabia

Client
National Real Estate Company
of Jeddah, National Commercial
Bank (owner)

Tnuva Dairy Processing Plant
1978–1981

EPSTEIN

Architect
A. Epstein and Sons, Inc.

Location
Rehovot, Israel

Client
Tnuva

Monetary Agency Head Office
1978–1981

Architect
Yamasaki and Associates

Location
Riyadh, Saudi Arabia

Client
Saudi Arabian Monetary Agency

Ministry of Foreign Affairs Housing
1978–1983

CRSS

Architect
CRS Group

Location
Riyadh, Saudi Arabia

Client
High Executive Committee,
Bureau for the Project of
Ministry of Foreign Affairs
and Diplomatic Quarter

US Embassy
1978–1983

HARTMAN-COX ARCHITECTS

UNITED STATES OF AMERICA EMBASSY

Architect
Hartman-Cox Architects

Location
Kuala Lumpur, Malaysia

Client
US Department of State,
Foreign Buildings Operations

Australian Parliament House
1978–1988

Architect
Mitchell/Giurgola Associates

Location
Canberra, Australia

Client
Parliament of Australia

Sheraton Miyako Hotel
1979

Architect
Yamasaki and Associates

Location
Tokyo, Japan

Porto Carras Resort
1979

Architect
The Architects Collaborative

Location
Sithonia, Greece

Israeli Air Force Bases
1979–1982

Architect
A. Epstein and Sons, Inc.

Location
Ramon & Ovda, Israel

Client
US Army Corps of Engineers, North Atlantic Division

EPSTEIN

US Embassy Staff Housing
1979–1982

Architect
Harry Weese

Location
Tokyo, Japan

Client
US Department of State, Foreign Buildings Operations

Khulafa Street Development
1979–1983

Architect
The Architects Collaborative

Location
Baghdad, Iraq

Local Architect
Hisham A. Munir & Associates

Client
Municipality of Baghdad

Kuwait Institute for Scientific Research
1979–1983

Architect
The Architects Collaborative

Location
Kuwait City, Kuwait

Client
Kuwait Institute for Scientific Research

Founders Hall (Meishusama Hall)
1979–1983

Architect
Yamasaki and Associates

Location
Misono, Japan

Local Architect
Itoh Architects and Associates

Client
Mihoko Koyama of Shinji Shūmeikai

Frankfurt Museum for the Decorative Arts
1979–1985

Richard Meier & Partners Architects LLP

Architect
Richard Meier and Partners Architects

Location
Frankfurt, Germany

Client
Museum Angewandte Kunst

Al Ahli Bank of Kuwait Headquarters
1979–1987

SOM

Architect
Skidmore, Owings & Merrill

Location
Kuwait City, Kuwait

Client
Al Ahli Bank

Institute for Public Administration
1980

TAC

Architect
The Architects Collaborative

Location
Riyadh, Saudi Arabia

Client
Institute for Public Administration

US Embassy
1980

CRSS

Architect
CRS Group

Location
Riyadh, Saudi Arabia

Client
US Department of State, Foreign Buildings Operations

Tanjong Jara Beach Hotel
1980

WATG

Architect
Wimberly Allison Tong & Goo

Location
Terengganu, Malaysia

Associate Architect
Arkitek Bersikutu

Client
Tourist Development Corporation of Malaysia

Basrah Sheraton Hotel
1981

TAC

Architect
The Architects Collaborative

Location
Basra, Iraq

Client
Ministry of Tourism and Resort Administration

Command Line: The Computer-Aided Office

In the 1960s, two academic conferences speculated on the new computational changes taking place within architecture offices and their implications for the future. *Architecture and the Computer*, convened at The Boston Architectural Center in 1964, brought together figures including architect Walter Gropius, historian Henry A. Millon, and cognitive scientist Marvin Minsky to assess the implications of the challenge, posed by Minsky, that soon "Architects will have to face the automation of design."[1] Four years later Murray Milne, an architecture professor at Yale, gathered attendees at the Yale Conference on Computer Graphics in Architecture (1968) to consider a potentially "fantastic" future in which the computer might become a "willing and capable partner" in design practice.[2] Participants included Bruce Graham of Skidmore, Owings & Merrill (SOM) and Nicholas Negroponte, a founder of the Architecture Machine Group at the Massachusetts Institute of Technology, whose interests already lay more broadly in the potential of computation to respond "intelligently to the tiny, individual, constantly changing bits of information that reflect... the coherence of the city."[3]

The Yale conference represented changes which had already begun to take place within the architectural profession across the previous decade. In 1958, Ellerbe Associates had acquired a Bendix G-15, an early computer the size of a refrigerator, to perform tasks ranging from personnel management to structural calculations and the drawing of floor plans and details.[4] Other large US architecture firms soon entered their own periods of digital experimentation. In 1969, Caudill, Rowlett, Scott (CRS) formed a separate company, Computing Research Systems 2 (CRS2), to develop a suite of applications for in-house use and sale, including streamlining cost analysis, project scheduling, and equipment specifications. Skidmore, Owings & Merrill (SOM), whose offices operated in a studio model, formed a 15th "studio," dubbed the Computer Group, to develop applications specific to the firm's needs and direct the office towards

① Marvin Minsky, in *Architecture and the Computer: Proceedings, First Boston Architectural Center Conference, December 5, 1964* (Cambridge, MA: 1965). See Jonathan Barnett, "Will the Computer Change the Practice of Architecture?" *Architectural Record* (January 1965): 143–150.

② Murray Milne, ed., *Computer Graphics in Architecture and Design; Proceedings* (New Haven: Yale School of Art and Architecture, 1969).

③ Nicholas Negroponte, *The Architecture Machine: Toward a More Human Environment* (Cambridge, MA: The MIT Press, 1970).

④ Kristine.K. Fallon, "Early Computer Graphics Developments in the Architecture, Engineering and Construction Industry," *IEEE Annals of the History of Computing* (June 1998): 23.

1955

- **1957** Univac 1 becomes first commercially available computer
- **1958** Ellerbe Associates buys Bendix G-15 computer
- **1963** "Symposium on the Use of Computers," at Arup headquarters in London
- **1964** • SOM founds the Computer Group • "Architecture and the Computer" conference at Boston Architectural Center
- **1965** IBM 360 and 1130 released
- **1966** Design Systems founded in Boston by Harvard GSD student Eric Teicholz
- **1967** • Nicholas Negroponte founds the Architecture-Machine group at MIT • SOM develops Building Optimization Program (BOP) for commercial office buildings
- **1968** Yale Conference on Computer Graphics in Architecture
- **1969** • Caudill Rowlett Scott (CRS) founds Computing Research Systems 2 (CRS2) • "Appalachian Conference" on computer integration held by SOM at IBM Sterling Forest, NY

1962 Cuban Missile Crisis

1950–1975 Vietnam War

a "methodology of the future."[5] Hellmuth, Obata + Kassabaum (HOK), Jung/Brannen, and Albert C. Martin & Associates soon developed their own architectural applications. At the same time, computer companies including Digital Equipment Corporation, Tektronix, and IBM were independently developing the potentials of "computer-aided design," or CAD, as commercial applications of military technologies for office use.

The development of commercially available drafting software soon put an end to the era of architects-as-programmers operating under the aegis of large offices. In 1986, SOM sold its AES system, the crown jewel developed by the Computer Group, to IBM, which repackaged it as SKYLINE. Yet the software never took off, as it was over ten times as expensive as the drafting software developed in the meantime by a new market competitor: Autodesk.[6] Founded in 1982, Autodesk rose quickly with their flagship program, AutoCAD—a "word processor for drawings"—by targeting small architectural firms with more limited budgets and drafting needs.[7] Other independent software companies emerged to compete, including McNeel, which released an AutoCAD-based modeling tool for curve-based surfaces in 1998 as the program Rhinoceros. Other companies drew on non-architectural industries, such as Wavefront Technology (later Alias|Wavefront), whose program Maya was used by both architects and Hollywood computer graphics and industrial design houses in science-fiction films such as *Stargate* (1994).[8] Gehry Partners LLP adapted CATIA, a program from the aerospace industry, into new software for the firm's formally complex buildings, criticizing existing commercial programs for remaining "entrenched in a paper-based, two-dimensional world."[9] The results of this adaptation eventually led to the establishment of Gehry Technologies in 2003 as a technology company independent from Gehry's architectural practice.

By the early 1990s, architecture practices across the US had substantially confirmed the predictions of Minsky and Milne some thirty years earlier about the computer as a willing design partner. The form-making potentials of digital design were soon evangelized by a generation of young architects as heralding an era of "voluptuous forms, stochastic and emergent properties, and intricate assemblages."[10] The moment when computation would be reclaimed by the academic design studio, most conspicuously under the deanship of Bernard Tschumi at Columbia through a series of "paperless studios" taught by Stan Allen, Scott Marble, Greg Lynn, and Hani Rashid after 1994, was just around the corner. —AL

⑤ See Bruce Graham, "Computer Graphics in Architectural Practice," in Milne, ed., *Computer Graphics in Architecture and Design*: 23–30; "SOM's Computer Approach," *Architectural Record* (August 1980): 84.

⑥ See Nicholas Adams, "Creating the Future (1964–1986)," in Peter MacKeith, ed., *SOM Journal 8* (Ostfildern: Hatje Cantz, 2013): 132.

⑦ John Walker, ed., *The Autodesk File: Bits of History, Words of Experience* (Thousand Oaks: Que Pub, 1989).

⑧ "Bill Kovacs, 56; Shared an Oscar for Work in Computer Animation," *The Los Angeles Times* (June 4, 2006).

⑨ Deborah Snoonian, "New Gehry Technologies will enable many to boldly go where only Frank has gone before," *Architectural Record* (October 2003): 12.

⑩ Greg Lynn, ed., *Folding in Architecture*, revised edition (Chichester, West Sussex; Hoboken, NJ: Academy Press, 2004): 9.

WestWorld, western-themed sci-fi movie is the first to use computer graphics

1975 Altair 8800 introduced as first "personal computer"

1980 IBM PC and Microsoft MS-DOS released

1982 Autodesk is founded

1983 HOK develops HOK Draw

1986 • SOM sells AES (Architectural Engineering System) to IBM • Bentley Systems, Inc. releases MicroStation

1992 AutoCAD is released for PC platforms

1994 "Paperless" studios at Columbia's GSAPP begin

1998 McNeel releases Rhinoceros

2002 Gehry Technologies is founded

1990–1991 First Persian Gulf War

2001 Afghanistan War

2003 Iraq War

1964 — **2005** — **2014**

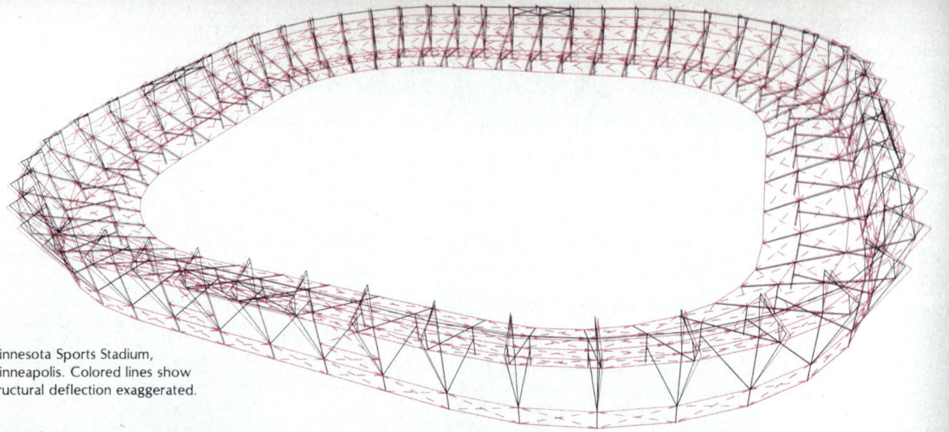

Minnesota Sports Stadium, Minneapolis. Colored lines show structural deflection exaggerated.

SOM's computer approach

The Chicago office sees the computer helping with three key issues of the 1980s: 1) enhancing employee ski deal with increasingly complex buildings, 2) keeping a competitive position by increasing productivity, ar developing staffing flexibility to react to changing business conditions.

Computer applications are becoming an integral part of the practice of Skidmore, Owings & Merrill in Chicago. That they have been successful in this, says computer group head Douglas F. Stoker, stems from "being able to identify pertinent problems and constructing appropriate solutions, instead of coercing problems to conform with available solutions." The systems do not require computer people to run them, but can be used by architects working as architects.

As long ago as 1963, the firm installed an IBM 1620 in the Chicago office to assist in engineering design. Since then, the office has tripled in size to 875 employees, and now has extensive computer hardware comprising three computers, two plotters, and over 70 terminals. The computers are a pair of Digital Equipment Corporation PDP 11/70 computers and a brand new VAX 11/780 also made by Digital. This one is a "virtual" computer that "thinks" it has a million times more memory capacity—which means it can accept an input overload and defer decision-making until the capacity is available.

The firm's approach in utilizing the computers is oriented toward the design professional, with applications responding to the needs of the 14 design studios and the four different disciplines of engineers comprising the firm. SOM started the design studio concept in 1972, when the firm had 300-400 people, as a means of solving an organizational, and "identity" problem. Each studio operates as an independent design office, undertaking its own projects, servicing them from start to finish. The computer group, also organized like a studio, treats design studios as if they were 14 customers.

Because the studios have at least 10 and as many as 100 professionals, and because the studios are diverse in building-type capability and interests, developing computer solutions could "get a little free form," Stoker muses. But, he says, the computer group tries to be efficient by applying the computer tools to specific problems, and solving them generically.

The SOM Chicago computer group combines training in architecture and engineering with computer programming skills, and is staffed by eight architects and engineers, three financial-oriented programmers, four operations people and one secretary. Its skills in the vocabulary of design permit close coordination between programming and design.

The key to using a computer on a project, SOM's computer group believes, is having a contiuum of information to utilize for a variety of end applications. "You want to avoid," says Stoker, "the discrete event approach where you do a drawing, take it out and throw the data away. Then you do a different drawing, take it out, and throw that data away, and so on." What you want to do, he says, is to build up a complete description, the ultimate goal being "every nut and bolt in the world." The data then can be used as the basis for a perspective, a set of working drawings, or modified to assist in structural analysis, or for calculating energy loads, or simply making a quantity estimate.

"An extreme test, a tough nut to crack," is how members of the firm describe the use of computers to produce 400 plan sheets for King Abdul University in Saudi Arabia. The first phase of the project, totaling one million square feet of space, required 80 different basic plan sheets which, multiplied by different architectural and engineering plines, yielded 400 sheets the compute involved with. About 80 per cent of the on the plan sheets was done by com and the remaining 20 per cent was drafted on overlays. The computer dr approach allowed the architects to easily sue base sheets to other discipline changes were made.

Experience with this project de strated that for the computer to be effe it has to be integrated into the studio sc people connected with design develop and evolution of the project are inv with the actual input of information. No does this put them in a better positic make decisions, but they feel they are p the process.

Beyond current applications, the u computers at SOM is being encourage the firm's belief that the number of p available to do drawings is going to thus the need to give really good tc especially the computer—to those peo the drawing activity. Further, if an arc can produce twice as many drawings wi computer, he can switch more of his tir design.

"It's important at SOM to keep th tems 'friendly'," says Stoker. We war systems to be easy to use, not hostil reasonable to deal with . . . English lan back and forth . . . a friendly and warm ronment. If the architect is not threat he's happy. The fact that the informat from the computer should be comp incidental. But we're not completely the because computers are still computers.'

the first phase of the King Abdul
University project (1 million sq ft)
Mecca, the SOM studio assigned
project developed over 400 com-
er-coordinated and -drawn plan
ets. Separate disciplines were able
hare data and overlay information
ny desired combination. The arch-
ural, mechanical, and structural
sheets were completely com-
er-generated. Common data of
mns, centerlines and walls were
ed in separate data "files" in the
puter, and overlayed on each of
sheets when plotted. Finish
edules also were generated.

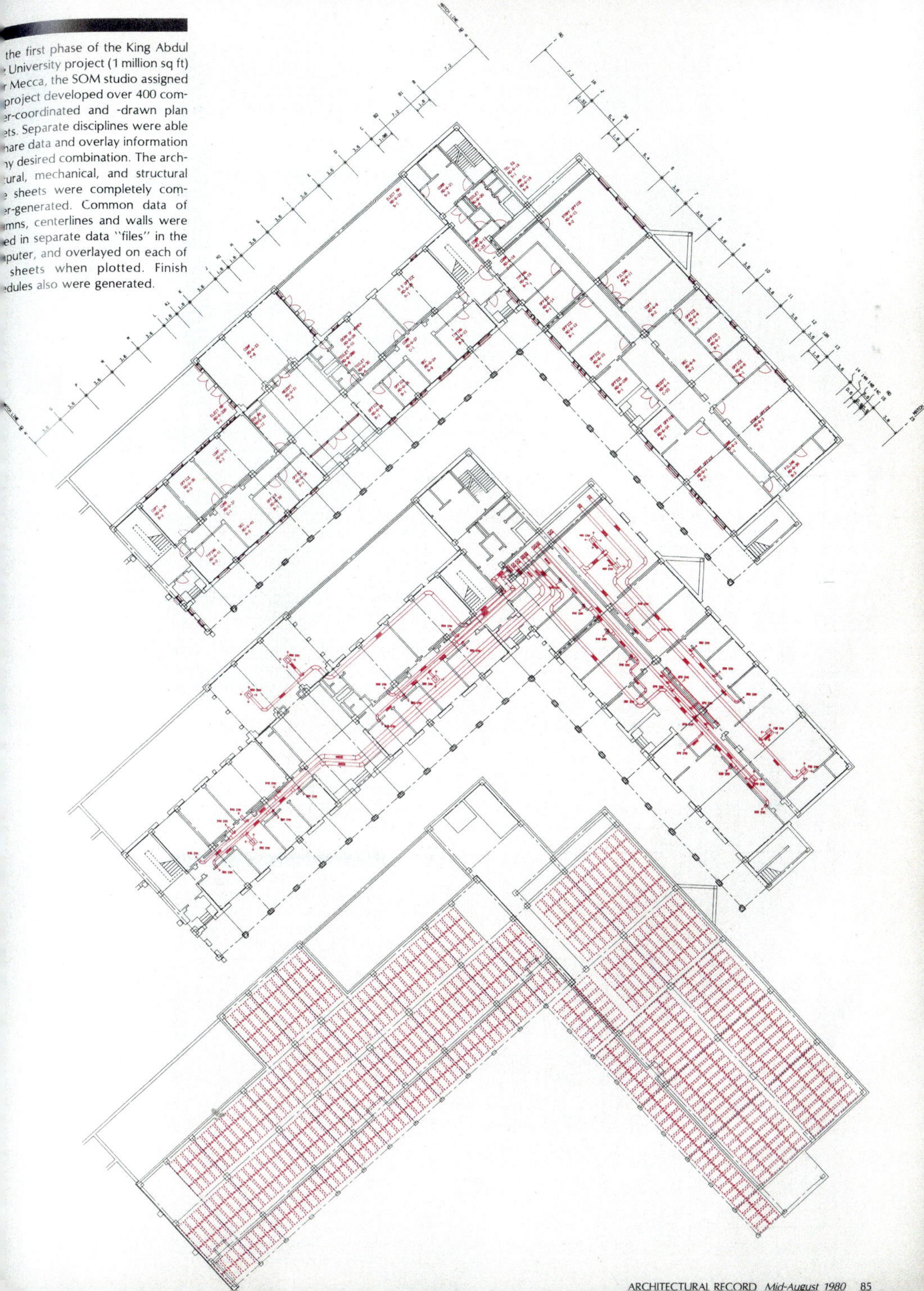

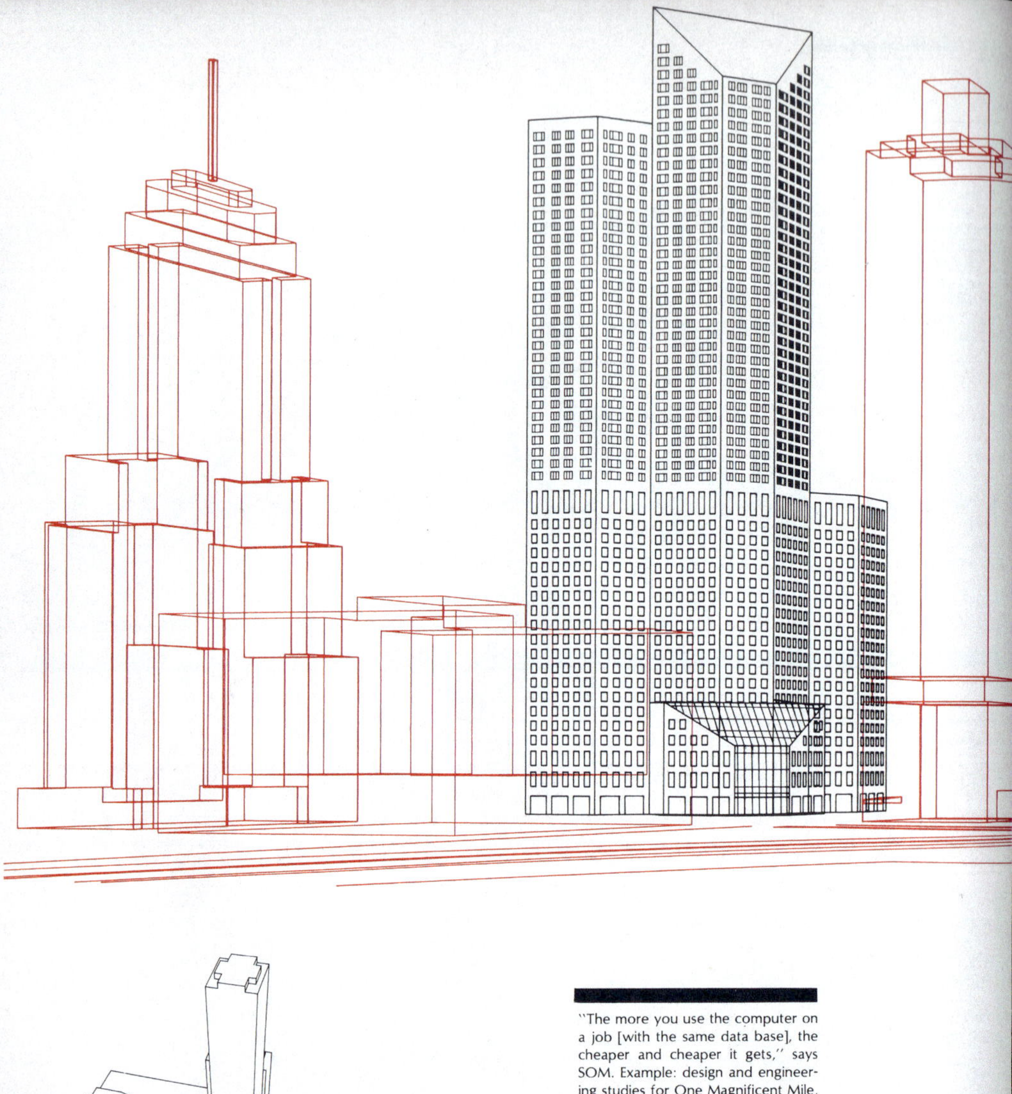

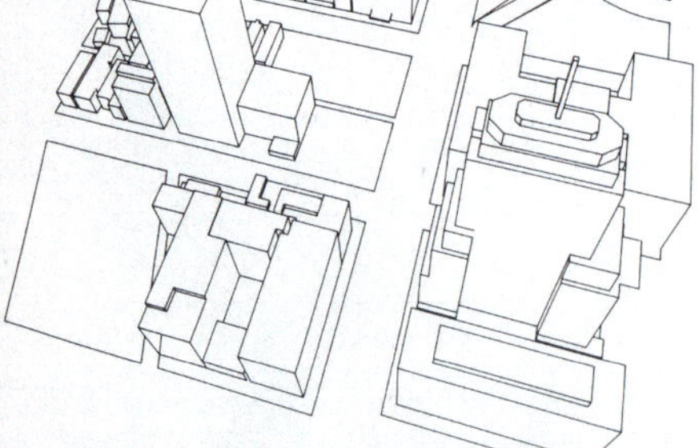

"The more you use the computer on a job [with the same data base], the cheaper and cheaper it gets," says SOM. Example: design and engineering studies for One Magnificent Mile, a 57-story multi-use tower at the head of Michigan Avenue on Chicago's near North Side. A proposed site was viewed from many angles to study the effects of building massing (left). Then the proposed form of the building was described to the computer and merged with the site description to construct pedestrian views (above). To convince the city that the building would not cast undesirable shadows on Oak Street Beach, the same data base was used but extended to include positions of the sun at various times of the day and year. A program was used that "went into the data base, looked at where the sun was, took positions of the sun, and generated shadows," (drawing across page).

One Magnificent Mile comprises three hexagonal concrete tubes bundled together for structural stability. Using the same computer graphics system as for the other studies shown here, the structural engineers were able to display the deflected shape (exaggerated) of the building under wind loading.

The drawing was created utilizing SOM's Structural Data Management System (SDMS) that was initiated 10 years ago. With the system, a data base is developed that describes the structure, its elements, and the loadings placed upon them. A standard language was developed to describe structures of all kinds regardless of the analysis techniques or programs to be employed. This language can deal with all sorts of "goofy" geometries. It has a library of standard elements: configurations, properties of sections, load distributions, etc. The SDMS can take a list of all the members that have loads on them and turn it into input for STRUDL, STRESS or other analysis programs. The engineer never has to deal with understanding the specific formats for all the different analysis programs. SDMS produces input that is sent to whatever computer happens to run that program.

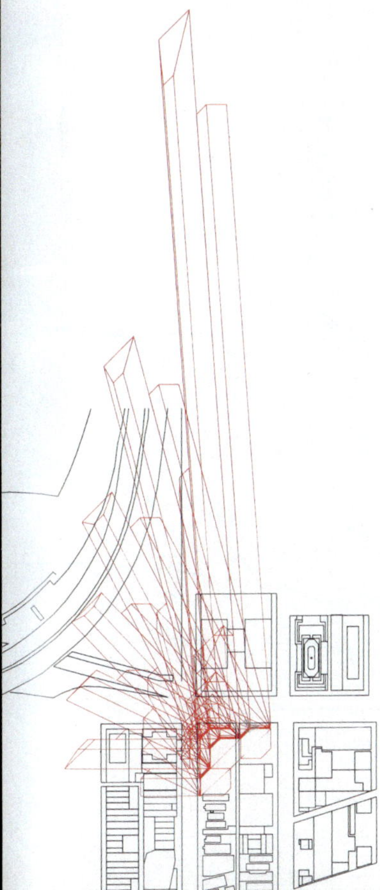

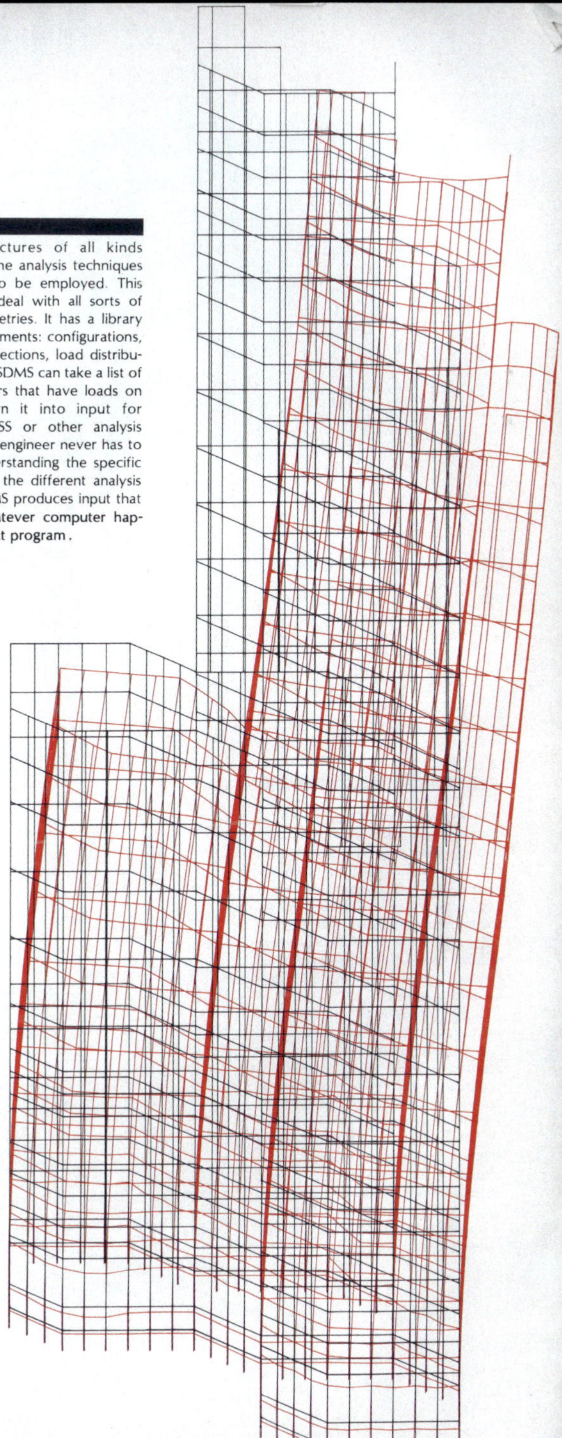

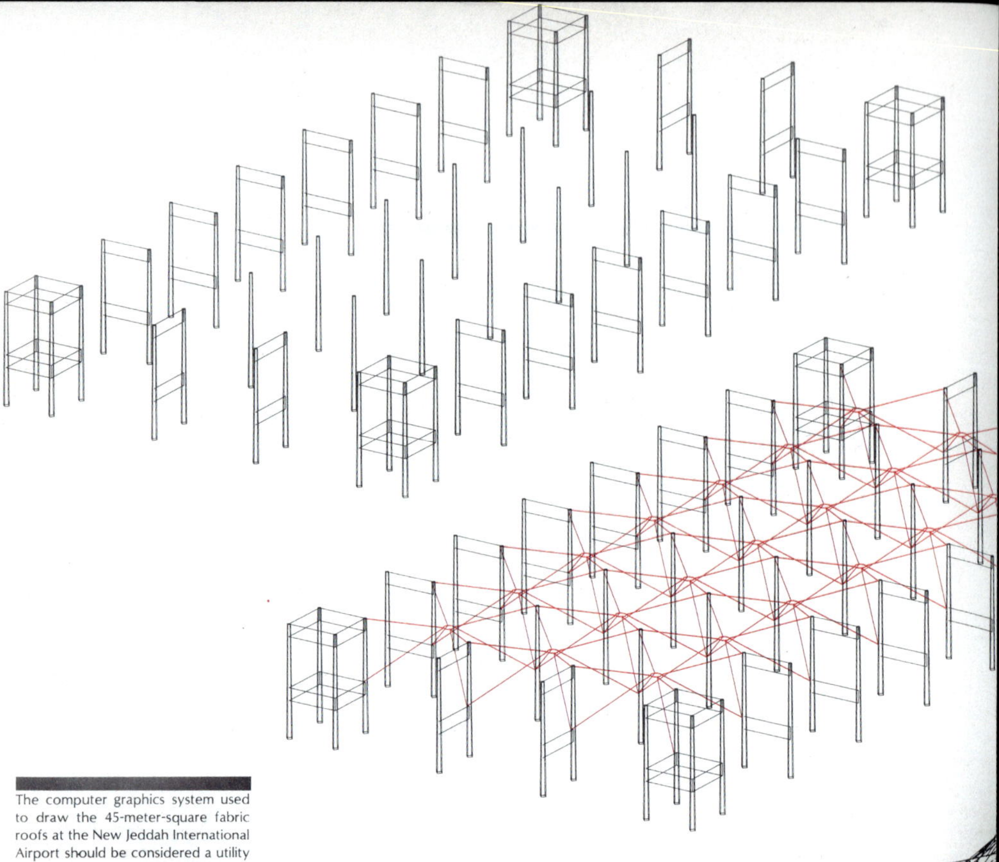

The computer graphics system used to draw the 45-meter-square fabric roofs at the New Jeddah International Airport should be considered a utility rather than a specific technique, according to SOM's computer group. They draw a parallel with an electric utility: the electric utility sells power, but does not care how the customer uses it. The computer stores data, but does not care what kind of pictures are drawn using it.

The same graphic system used for the plans shown earlier was used for these drawings. The pylons, cables and fabric elements were built up using graphic check points along the way. The composite was used for dynamic structural analysis.

The approach at SOM is to put the data into the computer so it is accessible for a variety of uses—drafting, structural design, sun studies, mechanical design, etc. The data is assembled and organized so that one can get at rationally.

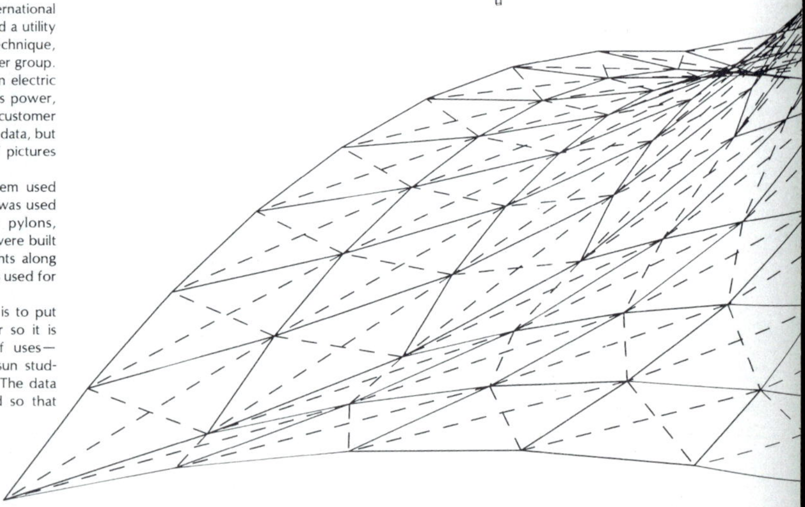

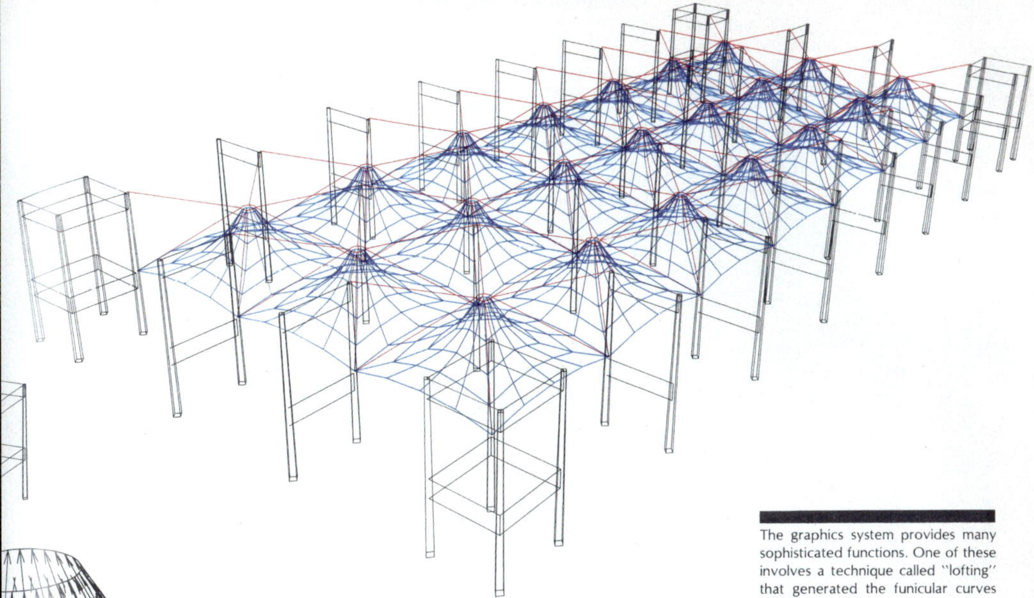

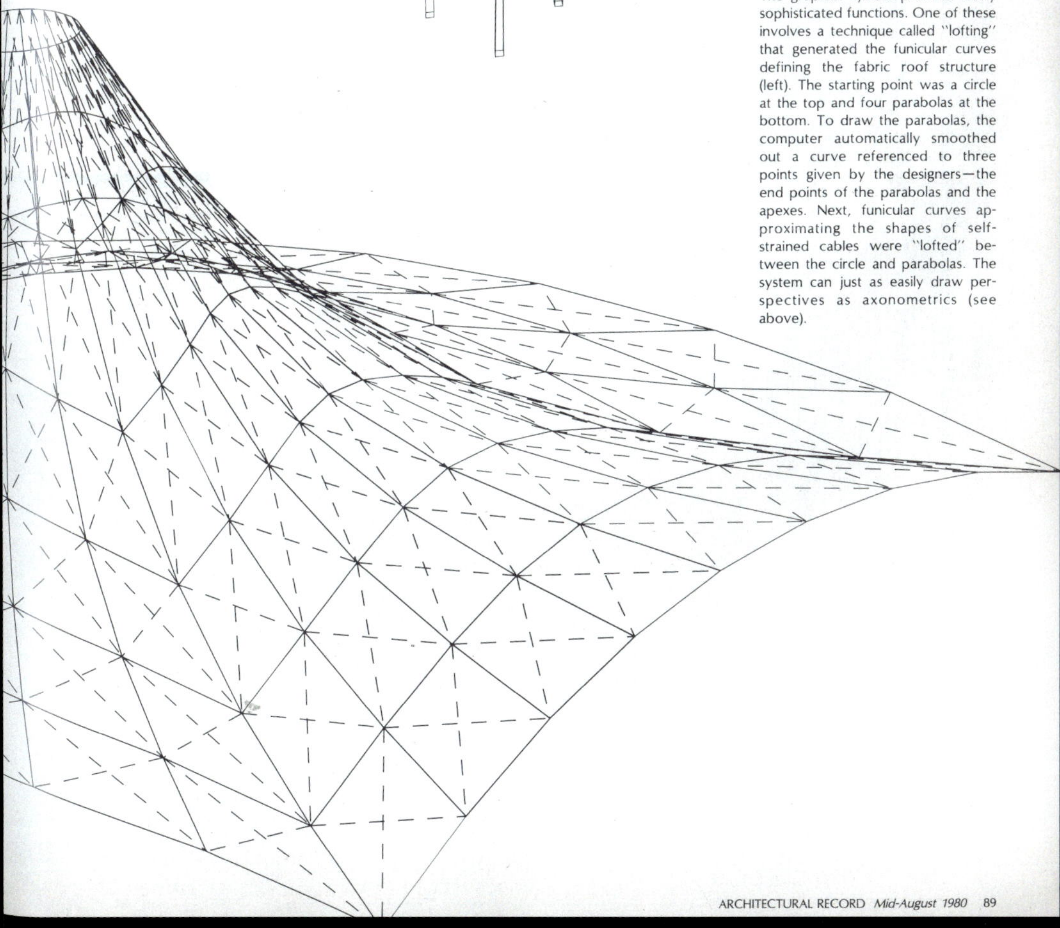

The graphics system provides many sophisticated functions. One of these involves a technique called "lofting" that generated the funicular curves defining the fabric roof structure (left). The starting point was a circle at the top and four parabolas at the bottom. To draw the parabolas, the computer automatically smoothed out a curve referenced to three points given by the designers—the end points of the parabolas and the apexes. Next, funicular curves approximating the shapes of self-strained cables were "lofted" between the circle and parabolas. The system can just as easily draw perspectives as axonometrics (see above).

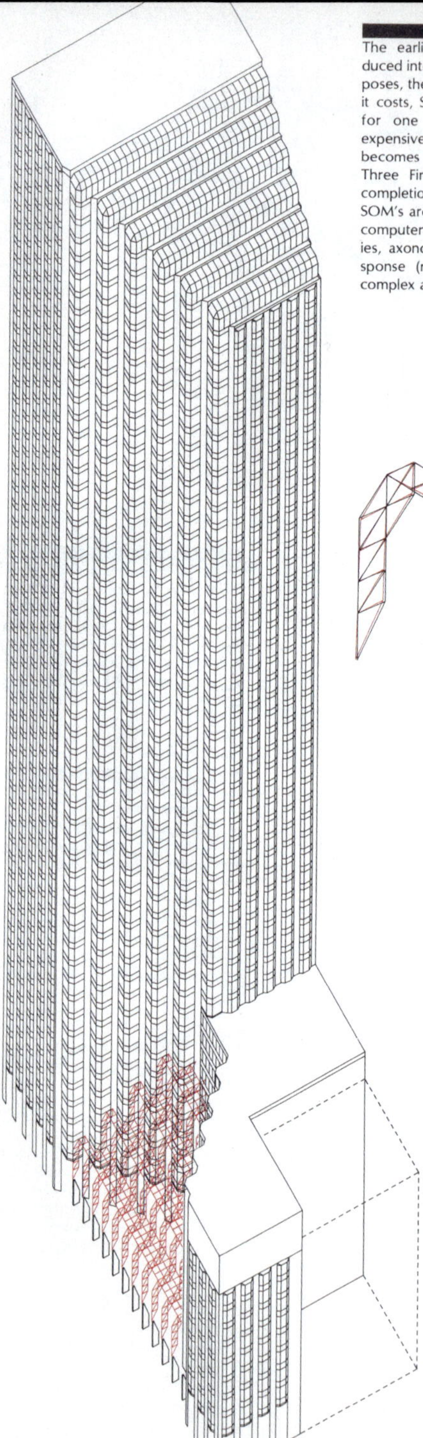

The earlier the computer is introduced into a project for graphics purposes, the larger the benefit for what it costs, SOM has found. Used only for one chore, the computer is expensive. Used for three or four, it becomes cheaper and cheaper. For Three First National Plaza, nearing completion in downtown Chicago, SOM's architects and engineers used computer graphics for elevation studies, axonometrics (left), structural response (right), and studies of the complex atrium truss.

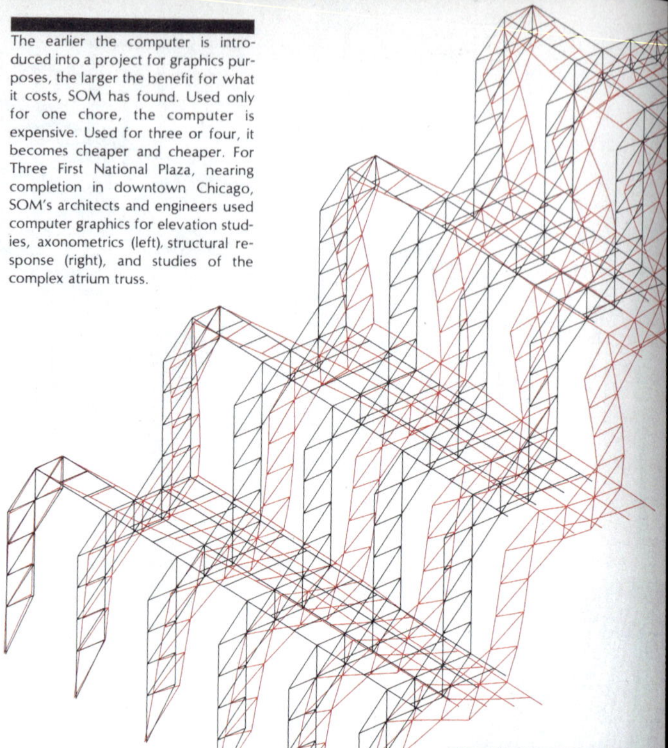

The interaction of building form atrium truss (red in drawing, left) studied in the axonometric. describing the truss was used to culate and display the struct response (exaggerated) above. typical connections used in the tu lar members of the truss were m eled to study the intersection members from a variety of ang Though round, the truss memb were shown square (across page simplify computer work.

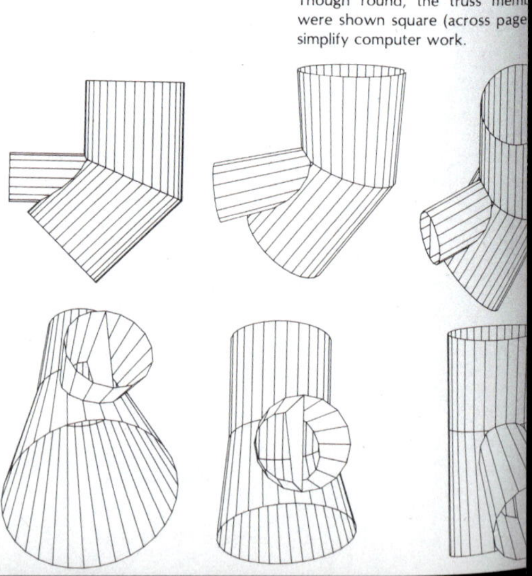

addition to the graphic computer dies shown here, a solar study was nducted to justify the use of clear ss in the atrium. The study showed at sun will shine on the atrium roof marily during midmorning hours. In gust, for example, the atrium will in the sun for 1½ hours in mid-orning, and for 30 minutes in the e afternoon. This study drew on ormation already in the computer. age of the computer seems to ild on itself a lot, says one of the rtners.

The wide diversity of computer plication in graphics can be further preciated by how SOM used com-ter drawings in the design of a eiman Marcus store. At least 16 ferent elevation alternatives were udied for the building. The design evations became the working draw-g elevations that became the silk reen pattern for the model.

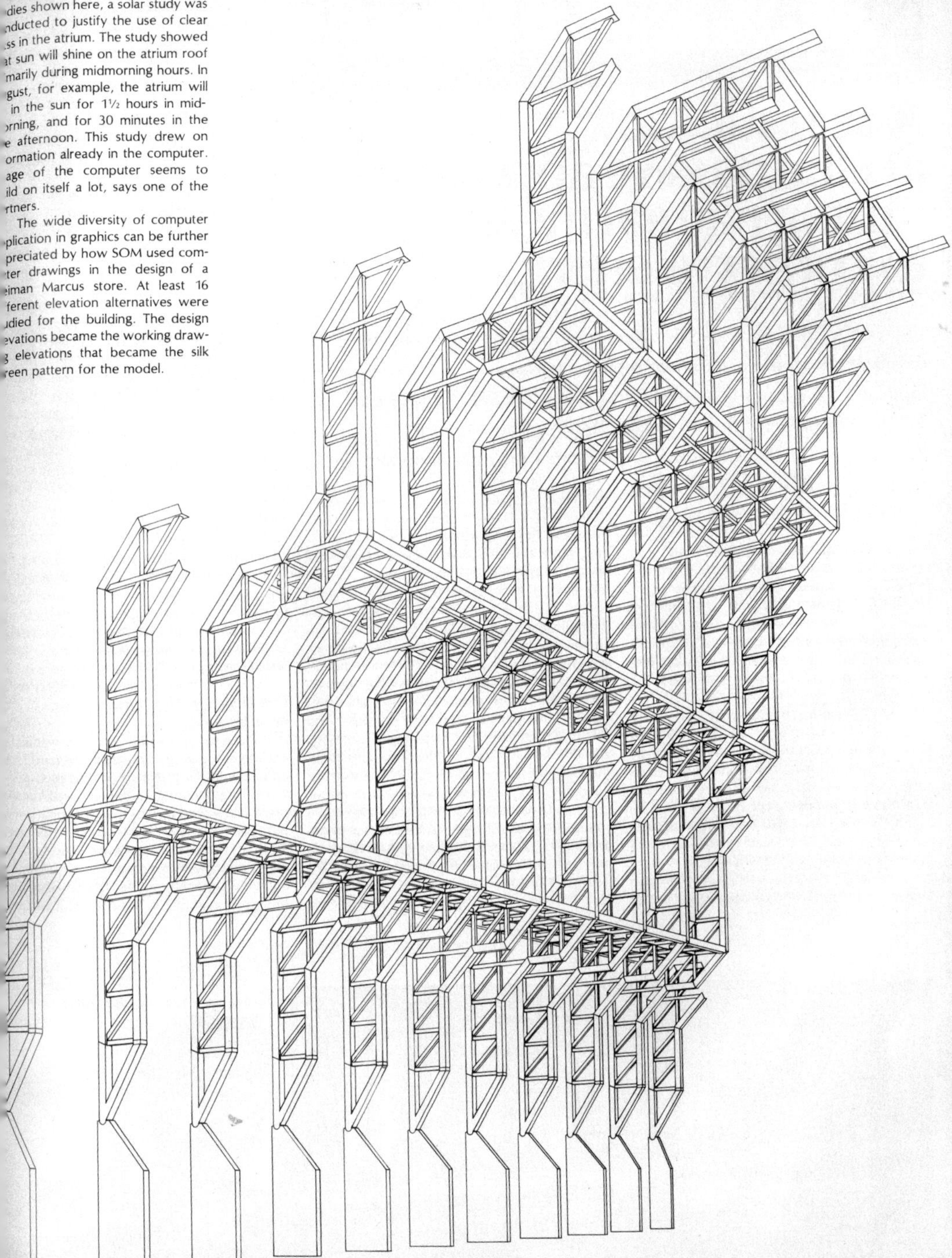

Architects have become involved with computers in a variety of ways—with important implications.

It has been said that with the computer, the numbers of architects needed will diminish drastically.

It has been said that with the computer, the small office will entirely disappear.

It has been said that building design will be taken more and more out of the hands of even medium-sized architectural design firms, to be executed only by large A/E companies that alone can afford very large computer systems.

Are we facing a crisis in the profession?

There is little doubt that a modern world without architects—or with lame-duck architects—would be a grim place. Architecture is the profession whose training encourages the student's social conscience and cultural and historical understanding to bloom, to take physical form, and to make an imprint on this earth, affecting everyone.

The computer itself will guarantee neither the salvation nor the destruction of the special role that architects have played in forming our civilization. Curiously, however, the machine can be used to hasten the passage towards either destination. On the one hand, there is a harmonious fit between architects and computers: both excel in finding simultaneous solutions to problems at several scales. On the other hand, if architects abdicate all but a cosmetic role; if they hide their heads in the sand regarding expert systems of all kinds; if they play the befuddled artist, eschewing business wisdom; and if they neglect to harness technology to assist them in their work and to free them to develop more humane and beautiful products; then indeed they will become inconsequential. There will always be room for the handcrafted object, but if the norm is technically sophisticated buildings, let architects be prepared to direct the process.

In P/A's first computer issue (May 1984), we were determined to shatter the stereotyped image of computer output as "boring" and predictable, and concentrated on the computer as a design tool. This year we compare the current situation with the predictions of doom reported in the first paragraph above, and have examined the range of ways in which architects use the computer—architects who not only learned to live with it, but benefit from it.

We found small firms that have flourished and have become more able to compete with the larger firms as a result of their new tool. We found medium-sized firms which, rather than reduce their numbers, increased the services they offer. We found firms that have expanded the limits of their design efforts because of the computer. We found architects forgetting their rivalry and sharing their knowledge. We found architects networking with other professionals to extend their field of practice. We found architects who have left the traditional profession and joined the computer industry, as their way to make a significant contribution to the field of architecture.

We looked into various ways universities are training architects for a world with computers. We asked the CAD vendors how they are meeting the needs of the changing profession. And we include, for your reference, a directory of useful books, periodicals, and conferences.

In every case, "imagination" meant more than designing a pretty façade. It meant pushing languages further, to create more subtleties as well as more standards to improve communication. It meant keeping one's financial house in shape, the better to accomplish one's goals. It meant examining the realities and resources of the contemporary world, and dealing with them in an enlightened way. ***Susan Doubilet, Thomas Fisher*** ■

The Traditional Office is Transformed

Architects with computers either broaden the range of services they offer, or deepen their investigation of solutions in one area.

Architects whose traditional practices have been transformed by the computer have been interviewed to see how their problem-solving skills have been applied to a variety of disciplines, some not usually associated with architects. Facilities management has turned a large profit for a small firm and helped balance the traditional side of the practice. Computerized methods have rendered a moderate-sized firm influential nationwide in hospital design. One large firm has become very efficient in production drawings, another has developed custom software for the design of complex structures, while a third is marketing its own software. Nevertheless, there is no fast buck solution for everyone. Facilities management is profitable, but requires specialized experience, not just an off-the-counter package. And software marketing has its own concomitant requirements—of transferability, broad market suitability, service, maintenance, and updating. *Susan Doubilet* ■

HOK

Over the past four years, Hellmuth, Obata & Kassabaum (HOK) of St. Louis has created its own CAD software using Digital Equipment Corporation (DEC) VAX/VMS computers and a relational database management system (INGRES) from Relational Technology, Inc. Since its first application—working drawings for the nearly completed Edison Brothers headquarters in St. Louis—the HOK system has been used on 150 projects within the firm's five offices. Last January, the firm decided to sell and service its system to other architectural firms through the HOK Computer Service Corporation (HOK/CSC).

Key to the potential success of HOK/CSC is its President, Charles Atwood, and its Vice President and Director of Product Development, Nathan Huebner. Since 1981, they have developed HOK's system from prior experience in architectural CAD, including work for SOM. In the following interview conducted by Deborah Dietsch, Atwood, Huebner and HOK Vice Chairman Jerome Sincoff discuss CAD within HOK, the firm's decision to market its system, and its ability to service it.

DD: What made you decide to market your CAD system to other firms?

Sincoff: It wasn't until last year that we started to think about it. By that time, we had used it successfully in our St. Louis, New York, Dallas, Washington, D.C., and San Francisco offices. As an architectural firm with a wide range of experience, we thought we could make a strong case for other firms to use it.

DD: How is the new CSC structured?

Atwood: From a financial and legal perspective, we are completely separate from HOK. We license software to them; they own their machines and are treated like any other client.

Huebner: We have grown from 4 to nearly 30 people in software and hardware development, educational services, and regional marketing. Over $2.5 million has been invested in our system.

DD: Why did you think other architectural firms would be interested in your software?

Sincoff: Our system is designed by architects for architects. It is an integrated system that can be used for a wide range of applications from schematics to the bidding process.

Huebner: I don't think that there's any one thing that our system does that the rest of them don't do. I think it's a well thought-out collection of the better features of a lot of other CAD systems. It probably has the strongest command language interface available with alternative definitions for components. If you draw a chair, for instance, you get a plan and a 3-D object. We have generators for walls, contours for land planning, and other features architects need.

Atwood: Its major strength is its 3-dimensional capabilities.

Sincoff: The most compelling argument to use our software is that we've tested it here and it works.

DD: Have you tested it outside the firm?

Atwood: No, but we tested in our five branch offices, which gave us the experience of trying to support our system from a distance.

DD: Who is a potential user of your system?

Atwood: I see it being used by medium (50-100 people) and large firms. I think the only firms that wouldn't buy our software are those that have developed their own.

DD: By marketing your software, don't you feel that you're giving the competition an edge? How do you dispel the idea that by using your software, the resulting designs will look like HOK's?

Huebner: It's pretty generic software; it doesn't design like Gyo Obata. Because we've used and developed it for three years, we are ahead of firms trying it out for the first time.

DD: As a CAD vendor, how is CSC going to

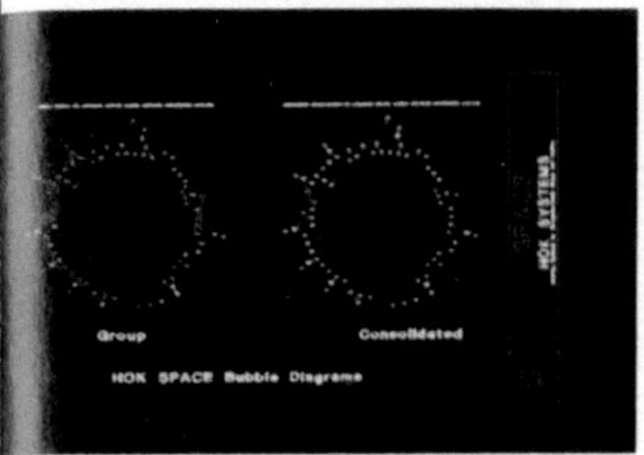

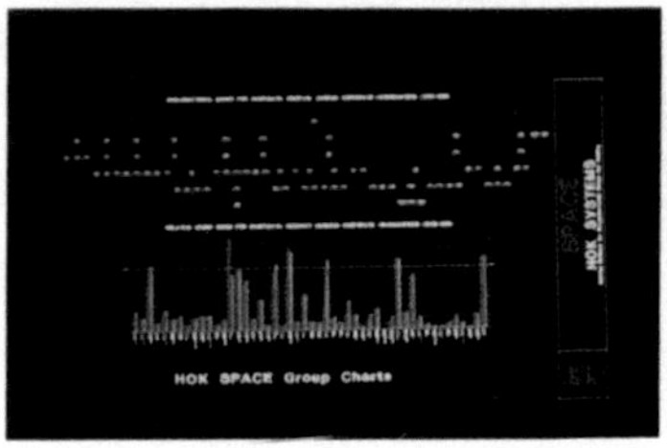

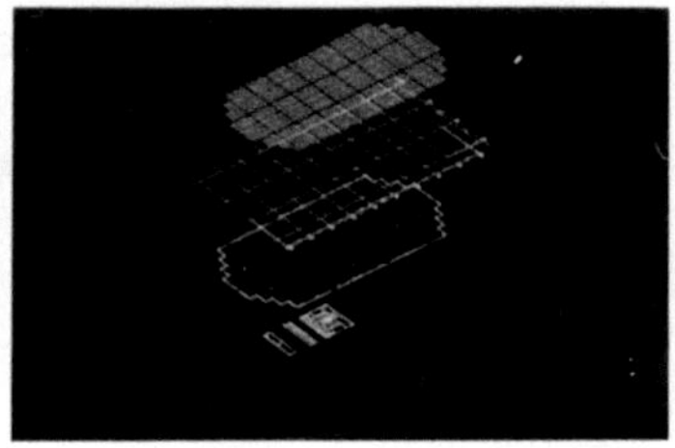

rvice a system, train users, and update soft-
ıre?

ɛwood: As architects, we are used to being
the service business. Our field service for
ırdware comes from DEC. We'll enhance
ır mature products such as HOK Draw and

Ihere's a question as
ɔ whether
ɾchitecture will
ventually become a
art of facility
ıanagement . . .'

ɔK Space once a year with updates and
wer products more often. HOK has de-
oped enhancements all along from recom-
endations by a users group representing
the firm's disciplines.

ɔ: How much does the system cost?

wood: The basic cost of a system ($35–
,000 per workstation) includes software,
rdware, and customer support over the
one. We've structured the cost of training
additional so that a person who needs only
ɔ days of training isn't charged the same
ıount as the person who needs two weeks.
th the release of the new MicroVAX this
ring, we'll be able to drive our prices down
low $30,000.

ɔ: What types of application software are
ı marketing?

ıcoff: We committed ourselves to design
ftware to encompass the entire design
ocess. HOK Draw, our 3-D graphics soft-
re, and HOK Space, our software for pro-
ımming, form the basis of our thinking.

wood: We're working on 20 systems in var-
g levels of detail. One of the major decisions last year was to develop our facility management applications.

Huebner: Currently, we are marketing HOK Draw, HOK Space, Plot, Database (report format), and Invest (lease analysis). By the end of the year, we will offer six more systems, from stacking and blocking to an interface between HOK Draw and other CAD software.

DD: How has CAD changed HOK?

Sincoff: There's much more communication and coordination between disciplines that promote a real team spirit.

Atwood: The quality of drawings and level of detail have changed. The computer is a limited resource, so in the St. Louis office, we are working two six-hour shifts.

Huebner: One of the complaints from designers is that the system isn't fast enough. For production, it's a cost and quality control.

DD: How do you think traditional vendors will react to architect-defined software such as yours?

Atwood: Software firms are doing well, but the large vendors aren't. One factor is the personal computer. It's cheap, and architects already have it for accounting and specs. The hottest seller right now is Autocad that runs on the IBM-PC. But, of course, unlike HOK's 3-D capabilities, it's fairly unsophisticated.

DD: How is CAD changing the architectural profession?

Atwood: There's a question as to whether architecture will eventually become a part of facility management as a design service within the life-cycle of a building. As a reflection of this trend, HOK's work these days is less than 50 percent architecture and more concentrated on related disciplines. Architectural firms are going to have to become more diversified and the computer is helping them to do that. ■

Deborah Dietsch is a freelance journalist in New York City who writes for design publications.

Perspective views (facing page and below) of an unbuilt mosque interior in Saudi Arabia demonstrate the 3-D capabilities of HOK Draw. The diagram (above) illustrates the multiple layers in which data—structural, mechanical, interior design, etc.—is stored. The charts (above left and middle) are developed on the HOK Space program, which forms the basis of the firm's facilities management software package: Using information from a client's present and future business operations, it formulates space layouts and forecasts costs.

How One Firm Broke into CAD Through Design, Not Production

By John Hughes

James Stewart Polshek and Partners used CAD from the first for 3-D modeling, but not without initial problems. Despite hardware upgrades in 1989 to '386/33MHz and '486/25MHz machines, JSPP's stand-alone PCs were isolated in a distant corner of the office. Anyone wanting to use them had to leave their desks and teammates. It was also difficult to track and protect CAD files. "Keeping track of and protecting drawings became a chore that could only be solved by networking," says Benedict Okoh, JSPP's systems manager. "The machines also were put on an automatic tape-backup system that runs every 24 hours to protect against data loss."

The decision to network all of the firm's PCs was made in 1990, allowing JSPP to develop its first complete set of construction documents with CAD. The project selected was Inventure Place, Home of the National Inventors Hall of Fame (photo above right), an 80,000-square-foot technology and science center in Akron, Ohio.

The project is three distinct blocks set on a landscaped plaza. A stainless-steel wing rises above the plaza and shelters a wall. Within, five tiers carry exhibits exalting innovation. Below the plaza is an underground exhibit "laboratory," where visitors explore invention concepts using a hands-on approach. A four-story service building contains a lobby, gift shop, cafe, classrooms, access to an underground large-screen theater, mechanical spaces, and a resource center. A 200-foot-high tower completes the composition.

JSPP first used CAD to build a 3-D model of downtown Akron and illustrate how the Hall of Fame would fit in. (The model has since become useful for another commission the firm secured about three blocks away from the Hall of Fame: the Akron Convention Center.) As the architects focused on the Hall of Fame itself, the project team continually updated its 3-D database, which now covers the entire building down to handrails and stair treads. "The Hall of Fame's 3-D model has been both a design and analytical tool for studying the character of spaces and details, and for showing how the building's functions relate," says Donald Weinreich, a JSPP senior partner.

Mr. Hughes is a freelance writer in Ft. Collins, Colorado.

Easier response to program changes

When JSPP began design development, the client asked the firm to produce documents for a building to be built in phases. So the architects produced documents for a 37,000-square-foot first phase. They came up with their own layer naming system and developed drawings with about 20 layers, which show column grids, structure, enclosure, glazing, furniture, dimensions, and ceiling systems. The layers would allow information to be easily transported to other drawings of similar areas in later phases. "On this first project, we placed great emphasis on the quality of the drawings," says Weinreich. "Using colored lines on the screen indicating seven pen widths, we were able to establish a drafting standard that mimics high-quality inked linework."

At the end of each project phase, JSPP filled a tape with all of the data as a record set. The architects continued to develop and embellish the data to complete the construction documents. CAD became invaluable when, toward the end of construction-documents, the client changed the scope of the project and gave the go-ahead to develop the entire 80,000-square-foot building as one package.

"This would be very inconvenient if you were drawing in a conventional manner," says Weinreich. "How do you transfer all the information from one drawing to another without going through the enormous expense of paying for mylar washoffs? CAD made it simple to change the size of sheets and add or extend all of the building components to create a much bigger project. An added bonus was that, in the end, our drawings still looked new. In this case, CAD benefitted the client and kept us from having to do a lot of drudge work."

Keeping use flexible

After JSPP's CAD success on the Hall of Fame, the technology sold itself. Now junior draftspeople and associates use it. They are encouraged to fit it to their own needs and to

National Inventors Hall of Fame.

consider it as one of many tools at their disposal. No one has had any formal CAD training; new users are trained on the job by those with more experience, although they must show enough interest to become competent fairly fast. According to Weinreich, JSPP can have people working productively after about 30 hours of learning time. "CAD has worked well for some of us and less well for others," says Weinreich. "The more general exposure one has had to computers before learning CAD, the better off one is. Computers demand a level of precise thinking that many people find constraining and annoying until they get used to it."

Now CAD covers the range of drafting tasks within JSPP's offices. The system is a comfortable tool for about 10 of the firm's architects, who do everything from developing perspectives and modeling complex buildings to working out details and generating door and window schedules.

Managing the system

JSPP's systems department is managed by Okoh, who is responsible for researching, developing, and integrating new software and hardware products into the office, as well as for supporting PC users, troubleshooting, and overseeing the daily operations of networks and systems.

Although DataCAD is still JSPP's CAD software of choice, the firm has expanded its automated arsenal significantly in the last few years. JSPP's primary CAD stations ar[e] '486/33MHz and '486/25MHz PCs, each wit[h] at least 16MB of RAM, a 200MB hard disk, high-resolution graphics card, and a 16-inch

While many offices first look at CAD for its production efficiencies, James Stewart Polshek and Partners looked at the creative possibilities first.

or-greater multifrequency monitor that meets the Swedish Board for Technical Accreditation's maximum recommended values for electric and magnetic fields. The firm's architects share a C-size Hewlett Packard 7550A pen plotter for in-house test plots, as well as a Versatec 8500 Series electrostatic plotter for large-format output. Moreover, JSPP has a high-speed modem (19,200 baud) for sending files to its plot bureau, and sharing files with consultants and others.

All CAD computers are networked via a central computer running Novell's SFT Netware with duplexed, external 650MB drives. According to Okoh, the duplexed drives provide tremendous fault tolerance as data on a primary drive are mirrored automatically to a secondary drive, thus virtually eliminating the possibility of data loss. Furthermore, since the drives are external, a failed drive can be replaced without disrupting people at work, which cuts costly down-times.

Complementing JSPP's CAD system are numerous "satellite" '486DX and '386DX-based computers (each of which also is CAD capable and ready) running Microsoft Excel for spreadsheets, schedules, management, and financial analysis and reporting; Aldus PageMaker for desktop publishing; WordPerfect for word processing; Micrografx Designer and Graph Plus, Alias Upfront, and Corel Draw, Deluxe Paint II, and Picture Publisher for graphics work other than drafting; and a Benelog Tracking System for logging shop drawings.

Printing is done on several networked Hewlett Packard Laserjet Series III, IID and II printers. Most Series IIs are outfitted with Postscript boards for faster and clearer text and graphics printing. The firm's "satellite" PCs are networked through a second server also running Novell's SFT Netware. This file server is seamlessly bridged to the CAD server, thus making it possible to access and share both CAD and non-CAD files across the network and to absorb sudden workload increases.

"In setting up and configuring a computer system, in addition to making it as simple as possible to use, there should be as much input as possible from those who will ultimately use it daily," says Okoh. "The idea is to provide our people with tools powerful enough to do their work without sacrificing safety, comfort, or efficiency."

CAD did substantially boost JSPP's productivity. "My advice to those interested in their own CAD system is to learn as much as they can about how PCs, networks, and software work," says Weinreich, "even if they will not be setting it up. This will help communicate unique needs to specialists who will. *And* a few basic computer management skills will help handle minor daily problems. ■

CAD's Evolution in Polshek's Office

• 1984. First use CAD by agreeing to be a beta tester for a manufacturer. Get 3-D/2-D software to run on one PC. Package proves slow, unsophisticated, and of little use.

• 1988. CAD permanently introduced with purchase of CADKEY's DataCAD package and two '386-20MHz workstations. Two architects are trained to use the program as a design tool for mainly 3-D modeling.

• 1989. Three additional architects are trained in 2-D and 3-D modeling. Hardware upgrades to '386-33MHz and '486-25MHz computers.

• 1990. Purchase of two additional workstations and the first set of construction documents done entirely with CAD. Installation of a dedicated CAD network with automated daily file backups.

• 1991. '486-33MHz PCs replace four slower units. Direct modem connection established to blueprinting service for all plotting. Two projects placed fully on CAD, and other projects partially.

• 1992. Firm up to six workstations. Develops screen-capture and image-painting techniques. Five projects on CAD and more expected.

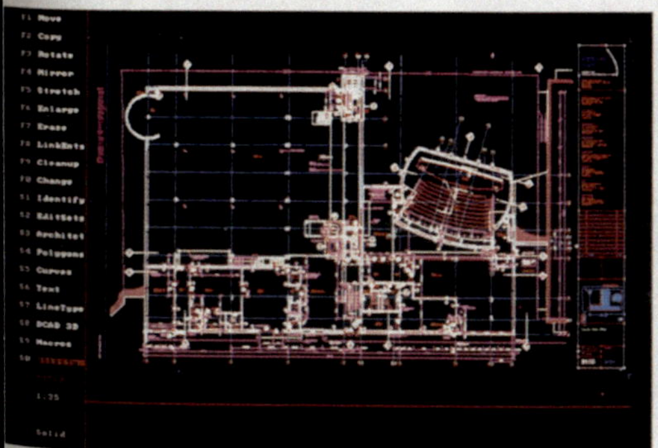

First floor plan showing colored lines that translate into varied line widths on prints.

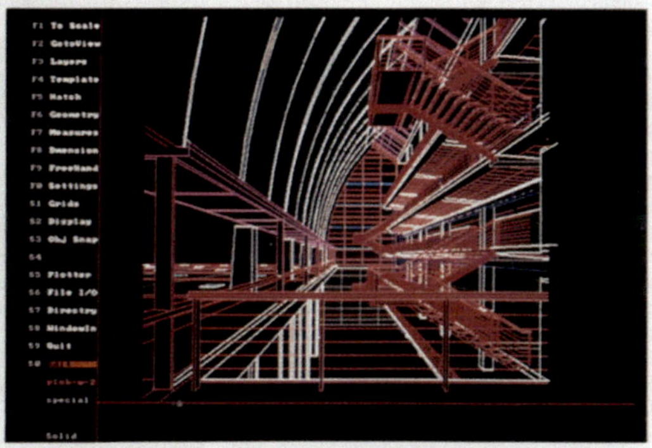

Interior perspective showing great wall and tiers.

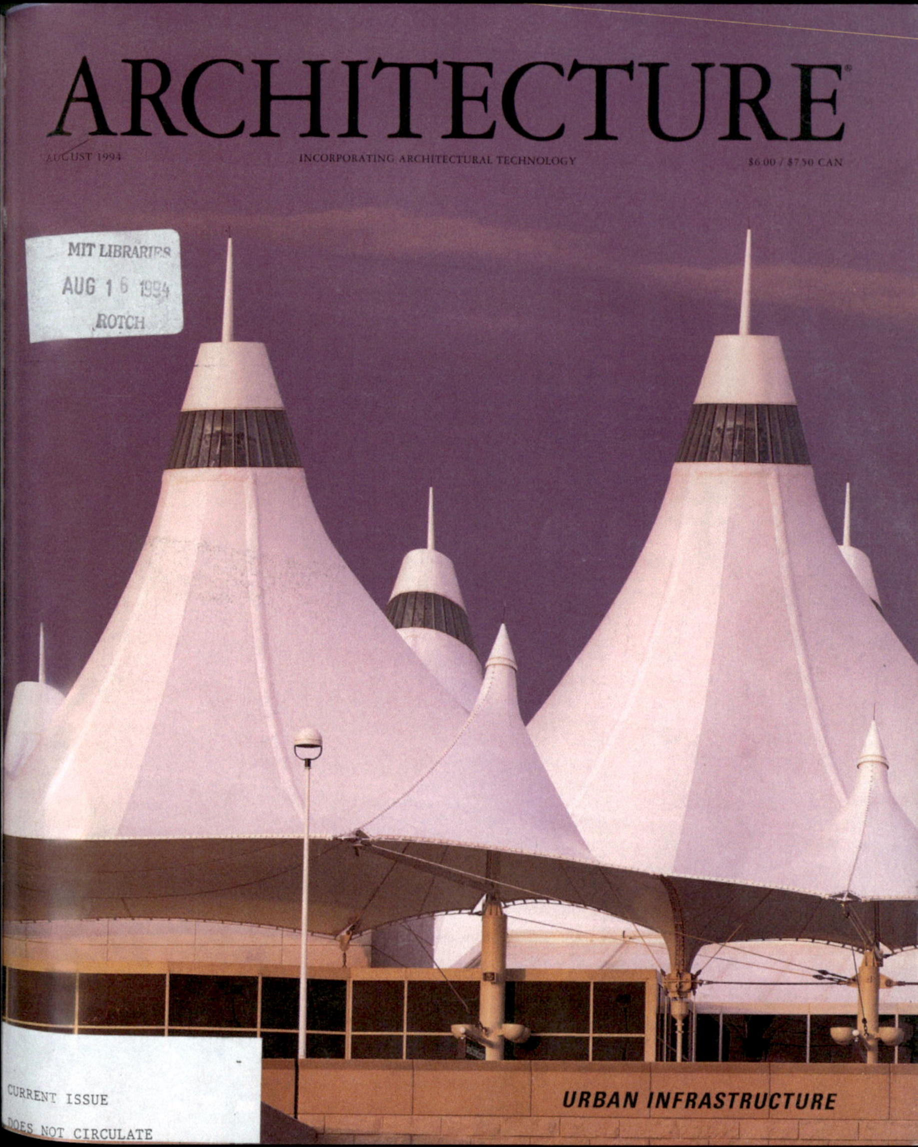
ARCHITECTURE
AUGUST 1994
INCORPORATING ARCHITECTURAL TECHNOLOGY
$6.00 / $7.50 CAN
MIT LIBRARIES
AUG 16 1994
ROTCH
URBAN INFRASTRUCTURE
CURRENT ISSUE
DOES NOT CIRCULATE

Freedom of Form

Advanced CAD programs enable architects to explore irregularly shaped geometries.

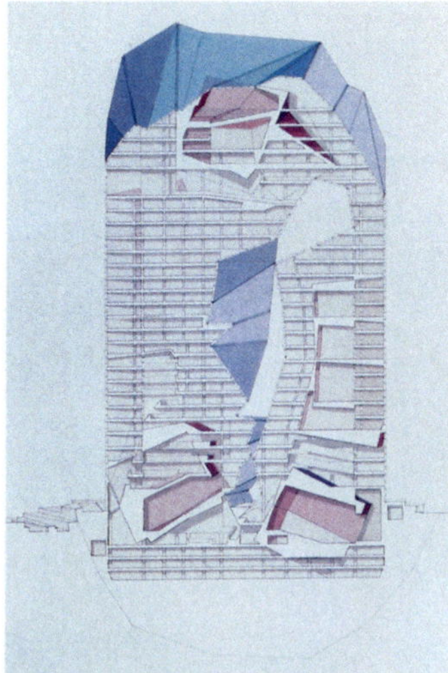

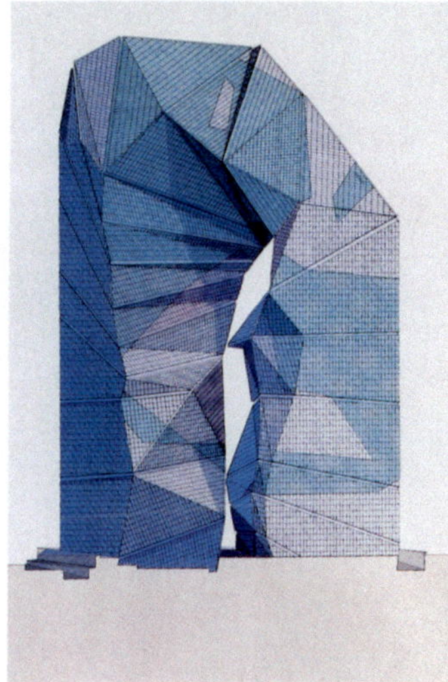

ABOVE LEFT AND RIGHT: For the Max Reinhardt Haus in Berlin, Eisenman Architects executed a sequence of computer modeling procedures to move a site-shaped element along a Mobius strip-shaped path, producing the high rise's irregular form.

Ever since computers established their role as menial drafters in architecture firms, some have wondered when this technology would make a visible mark on form making. But as long as the machines remained drafting tools, they only changed the process of production, not the appearance of buildings. Now, however, architectural design software has grown in sophistication, and some firms are beginning to create unusual or irregular geometries that would not have been possible to construct without the technology. With these new programs, buildings may be angled in any of three dimensions to respond to view, function, or irregular sites. Complex connections between nonrectilinear geometries can be detailed without figuring out how the disparate forms come together. And sharing the technology with the building trades enables these irregular forms to be constructed at reasonable costs.

Computer-assisted schematic design

For the past few years, New York architect Peter Eisenman has been applying computers to the earliest design phases. In contrast to those who exploit the "hands-on" sculptural capabilities of modeling software, Eisenman Architects begin with a philosophy, express it and transform it mathematically, then let the computer construct the three-dimensional result of that mathematical expression.

For the Max Reinhardt Haus, a cultural center and office building in Berlin, the architect drew on the idea of the Mobius strip. This geometry is defined as a continuous, one-sided surface formed by twisting one end of a rectangular strip 180 degrees and attaching it to the other end. Eisenman subjected the two-dimensional shape of the Berlin site to a series of transformations in response to contextual influences. Through mathematical manipulations within autodessys's modeling software form-Z, he rotated and further transformed the shape as it moved along a path defined by the Mobius strip. Principal George Kewin recalls: "We were trying to get a crystalline form, so we chose certain parameters that stopped it along the path to create planar surfaces." The architects subjected the strip to several hundred iterations, changing parameters each time to obtain new variations. "That shape was derived entirely from the mathematical formulas," explains Kewin. "We didn't obtain a shape and then modify it graphically."

When finally satisfied with the form and convinced that the high-rise building could be engineered, Eisenman Architects exported the computer model to AutoCAD where it was further tested to ensure it could be translated into physical form. The model was then sent electronically to a service bureau, where each surface was laser-cut from colored plastic. The pieces were then assembled into a physical presentation model. When the building permit review process is completed, the mathematical description inherent in the design model will be applied to the construction drawings. "The computer is now integral

ABOVE LEFT AND RIGHT: An angled, skylit gallery bisects a house designed by Samuel Mockbee and modeled by Charles Calvo. The gallery tilts in every dimension, resulting in complex intersections that would have been difficult to work out by hand.

with everything the office does," Kewin asserts. "If you want to represent a philosophy through geometrical relationships, you have to do it by computer."

Studying complex intersections

It is still rare for architects to rely on the computer so extensively in schematic design. More commonly, architects develop initial design ideas with traditional media and then move to computers later for design development. A case in point is the Nagoya (Japan) Station Building, by the New York firm Kohn Pedersen Fox (KPF). This 4.8 million-square-foot mixed-use complex will house a high-speed rail station, retail and cultural facilities, a cylindrical hotel tower, and a quarter-circle office tower.

Although schematic design was performed with paper drawings and clay models, KPF's director of computer services, Tomas Hernandez, insists that the design development and construction documents could not have been accomplished without a computer. Large-radius arcs, easy to construct in a CAD system, are tedious if not impossible to reproduce on a drawing board with conventional instruments. In addition, the junction of intersecting planes and cylinders proved geometrically complex. Hernandez explains the challenge: "When you have a sloping plane joining a sloping, curved surface, how do you treat the intersection? You can document some ideas loosely in schematics, but for design development and construction documents, these connections require accurate design decisions, and the computer allows you to be geometrically precise."

KPF Associate Partner John Koga, the building's senior designer, credits the firm's work with Intergraph CAD software for enabling them to study the complex geometric relationships between elements in a logical way. He explains: "We used the computer to zoom in on and study the intersections of the architectural volumes. We could read the resulting complex angles very accurately." In the past, he notes, KPF resolved such intersections by constructing the angles with an adjustable triangle. But that method was approximate, depending on how precisely the adjustable triangle was calibrated. Now, in addition to the technical assistance CAD has provided, Koga feels that the technology has also given the firm "a certain comfort level in knowing that the details can be worked out."

Knowing the computer would eventually come into play during design development also helped architect Samuel Mockbee, principal of Mockbee/Coker in Canton, Mississippi, and a professor at Alabama's Auburn University. For clients with an extensive art collection, Mockbee designed a house on a peninsula jutting into a lake. He envisioned the house as butterfly-shaped in plan, giving each wing a particular view and putting the central gallery on axis with two special trees and the lake. The gallery's skylight was angled to block direct sunlight but admit a certain amount of bounced and filtered light.

ABOVE LEFT AND RIGHT: Ellerbe Becket's design for a corporate headquarters in Jeddah depended on computer modeling to create the dramatically curved shape of the main tower (left) and its irregular connections to the second tower (right) of the project.

After Mockbee had sketched the house on paper, his colleague at Auburn, Charles Calvo, modeled it in form-Z. As difficult as the modeling was, Calvo claims it would have been nearly impossible to work out without a computer. He notes: "The skylight is tilted in plan, section, and elevation relative to the gallery. So the computer was essential to resolve the soffits, parapets, and roofing conditions needed to join the skylight to the gallery. I couldn't have done it without the solid modeling operations that enabled me to join and carve the rotated forms."

Complexity in section

The difficulty of figuring out the connections was further eased by Calvo's practice, impossible with a physical model, of continually changing scales as needed. After he completed the 3D model, Calvo cut sections through the house that became the basis of the working drawings. If, during construction, the contractor decides another section is needed, the architects will simply return to the computer model and cut another section at the point of interest.

Although Mockbee believes architects will always need pencil and paper to "plug into the muse," he credits the computer with helping to flesh out his design ideas and develop them into reality. "What's so wonderful about the computer is that you can go through several ideas in a couple of hours, where in the past it might have taken several days. And you might have gotten discouraged about trying to discover all the possibilities and maybe given up too easily."

Like Mockbee, the architects at Ellerbe Becket worked first with traditional media in designing a corporate office building on the Red Sea in Saudi Arabia. Design Principal Peter Pran developed a schematic form of two towers, one rectangular and one sail-shaped, connected by horizontal elements at several points throughout the building's height. The design was modeled first in foam, then with IBM's Architecture & Engineering Series (A&ES) software. Project designer Jeffrey Walden describes the process of generating the sail-like form:

In section, he sketched its general shape, then tried to fit a mathematically defined curve to key points along its height. Through repeated reshaping, Walden eventually arrived at a curve that matched the physical model. He then extruded the curved profile to create the seaward face of the building. Because every point on the curving face could be defined and analyzed mathematically, the architects could share precise data with structural engineers and curtain wall consultants. In the past, the architects would have tediously measured points on the physical model, and a structural engineer, constrained by uncertainties, might have erred on the side of caution in determining the building's structural viability. Now Ellerbe Becket can experiment with more daring options, and the entire design team works with more confidence in their data. The computer model

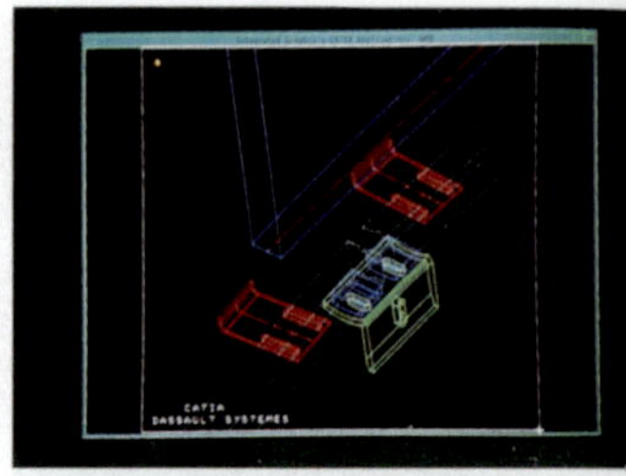

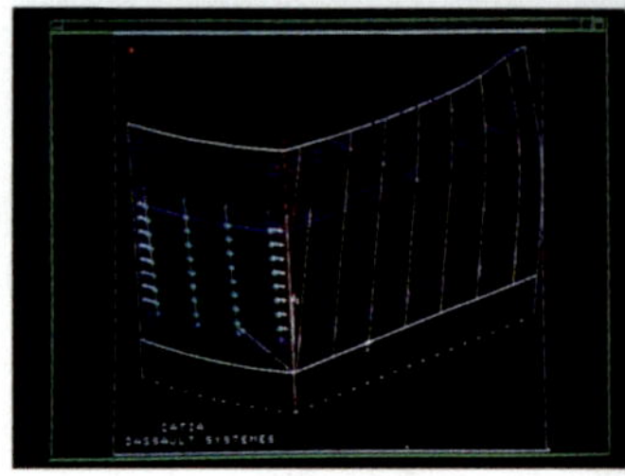

ABOVE RIGHT AND FAR RIGHT: Stonecutting subcontractors for Frank Gehry's Disney Concert Hall submitted samples of limestone walls cut with machines driven by data from the architects' CAD files.
FAR RIGHT, BELOW: Gehry's CAD data is also applied to formulate the design of the stone's support structure.

was also helpful in designing the irregular connections between the two towers and the sail-like foil that shades the central atrium.

In more recent projects, the firm has extended its study of geometry by exporting the A&ES models into Autodesk's 3D Studio rendering software and showing what the buildings look like when rendered with realistic colors, textures, reflectivity, and transparency. "It's one thing to study geometry in the abstract," observes designer Timothy Johnson, "but when you can give these forms the appearance of real materials, you get more valuable feedback from the model that can affect important design changes."

Complexity in plan

Pressing the computer into service for developing irregular forms is not restricted to high-profile, high-budget structures. In the Steamboat Point low-income housing development, San Francisco architect Backen Arrigoni & Ross took advantage of technology to bring a degree of amenity to a project with a restrictive budget. CAD enabled the firm to conform the housing's footprint to an irregularly curved site. This manipulation allowed the apartments to front the street like traditional town houses; the resulting triangular courtyard added character and created a false perspective that exaggerates the project's scale. The funneling effect of the pedestrian entries into the courtyard formed a sense of welcome often lacking in outdoor spaces around low-income housing.

To achieve these effects, each unit along the curved streets had to be slightly wedge-shaped. Instead of typical 90 degree angles, some rooms had corners with angles ranging from 75 to 105 degrees. According to architect Patrick Mays, Backen Arrigoni & Ross CAD administrator, this variation is barely noticeable for the occupants.

"It was like slicing pieces of a pie to mak it go together," Mays recalls. "CAD helped u figure out the center points, radial dimensions, and angles, which changed with every unit. If we had had to draw this manually, we would have constantly needed to readjus our triangles." More likely, he admits, the d sign would have been more rectangular, thu sacrificing the amenities afforded by the foo print conforming to the curved site.

Instead, the CAD drafters easily determined the angles for each unit and set the software to construct lines at those angles au tomatically. They also had the computer de velop presentation perspectives which, because of the curves, would have been very time-consuming to work out by hand. "Shif ing the tedious work to machines," Mays says, "is especially important in low-income housing because the budget for design is already so low." He notes that help from the computer in working with odd angles is also invaluable in renovating historic structures which old walls have shifted out of square.

While many architects today rely on com puters during construction management, fe apply the technology as directly as Los Angel

architect Frank Gehry. Although Gehry designed the Disney Concert Hall with traditional modeling methods, translating its dramatically and irregularly shaped stone walls into construction documents required sophisticated CAD software developed for the aerospace industry (ARCHITECTURE, August 1992, pages 105-110). Two years ago, Principal James Glymph explained that the design staff was "rationalizing" the curves into mathematically definable forms within Dassault's Catia software to reduce the number of unique stones, expecting this method to reduce stonecutting costs.

Now, the story is playing out in unexpected ways. As a requirement for bidding, four Italian stonecutting firms constructed sample walls from the architect's CAD files. The winning bidder, Furrer, has come in on budget, "lower than any us of expected," claims Glymph. The architects learned that, because the cutting machines are driven by electronic data, the degree of variation between stones does not affect cost as significantly as once believed. Nevertheless, Gehry will continue to rationalize the stone for other reasons, including seismic stability and to simplify the steel support system for the stone.

Harmon Contract W.S.A., the subcontractor responsible for coordinating the stonecutting and the fabrication of the steel supports, has also acquired Catia for modeling and engineering. Michael Budd, Harmon's director of sales and engineering of stone products, and his staff have developed computer subroutines to produce the stone fabrication documents. This mathematically defined information about the stones' shapes will be translated directly into the milling machines without the error-prone process of intermediary paper drawings and human interpretations. Harmon is now working with steel fabricators in developing the Catia files into numerically controlled data for constructing the structural steel tubes. "We'll provide a general blueprint showing the intent and visual representation of the pieces," Budd explains, "but the actual fabrication information will be in the computer file."

Liberation from tradition

Glymph acknowledges that the sharing of electronic data between architects and subcontractors has "run up against a lot of traditional relationships." But all the players have learned from the experience, and the architects are already planning their next challenge: modeling concrete forming methods.

As computer technology improves, and as the architecture profession acquires a collective understanding about how to apply it to design and construction, examples such as these pioneering efforts will become more common. They will demonstrate how freedom of form can liberate architects from traditional constraints and allow them to respond more creatively to the urban context and to their own artistic vision. As Mockbee notes: "With computers, you can stretch your imagination further."—*B.J. Novitski*

ABOVE LEFT: Gehry's Disney Concert Hall is now under construction in Los Angeles. Because the shape of each stone was precisely calculated by the milling equipment, there was little cost premium for the diversity of stone shapes within the walls.

ARCHITECTURAL RECORD

INNOVATION

CHAIN REACTION: How New Ideas Are Transforming Architecture

Building Design in 2030 Will Make a Brave New World

Radical Shift: Technology Transfer Is Altering the Way We Build

SUPPLEMENT TO ARCHITECTURAL RECORD

Technology Briefs

lew Gehry Technologies will enable many to boldly go where nly Frank has gone before

ank O. Gehry, FAIA, is taking his pertise to the masses. This fall arks the launch of the sidekick to architectural practice, Gehry chnologies (GT)—a business vene he hopes will raise the level of chnological fluency within architural practice, as well as cement legacy as one of the field's forest innovators.

Heading the new company as ef executive officer is senior part r James Glymph, who has worked ngside Gehry for more than a cade. Dennis Shelden, Gehry rtners' director of computing, will ve as GT's chief technical officer.

The vision for GT is to create a building ecosystem' tackling innoions in construction practices d associated technologies," cording to a press release. sentially, it will be a consulting actice, providing technologies and pertise to teams who are building specific projects as well as to the industry at large. "Manufacturing industries have completely transformed the way products are designed, built, and delivered," says Glymph, "but the building industry remains entrenched in a paper-based, two-dimensional world. We realized that substantial opportunities existed in bringing advances in practice that we have discovered to the rest of the industry." He adds that faster, cheaper computers make it feasible for firms of all sizes to use the digitally driven process that Gehry follows in his practice, and that the process is suitable for a variety of project types, not just the high-end cultural buildings for which Gehry is renowned.

GT may also serve as a software developer, creating specialized interfaces or additional capabilities for existing design software such as CATIA, the aerospace program the firm has used on many projects. Such tools could be developed on a project-specific basis—a common practice in manufacturing and other industries—and then licensed for a fee to the software maker for widespread use, or sold to the company paying for the project work.

The AIA, the Civil Engineering Research Foundation (CERF), and the Massachusetts Institute of Technology's Media Laboratory have already agreed to collaborate with GT; the projects they will take on together have yet to be fully scoped. In time, the company hopes to create partnerships with the entire range of organizations that have a stake in the design and construction of the built environment.

What Glymph wants to achieve is "a fundamental reshuffling of the roles, responsibilities, and compensation structures for participants across the industry as a consequence of the digital revolution," he says. This could mean, for instance, that all participants in a construction project share the liability for its completion on time and within budget, or that project deliverables be submitted in digital rather than paper form. Many technology enthusiasts believe that requiring architects and their collaborators to rely on digital design information is a necessary step toward reestablishing the architect as a master builder, as well as shortening the time needed to design and construct buildings.

Whether the business model for GT can succeed in a down-market for design and construction services has yet to be determined—firms aren't spending on training and technology like they once were. But like many innovators, Glymph and his staff aren't cowed. "We've been pretty lonely pioneers," he says. *Deborah Snoonian, P.E.*

The expertise that made buildings like the Disney Concert Hall possible, coming soon to a studio near you.

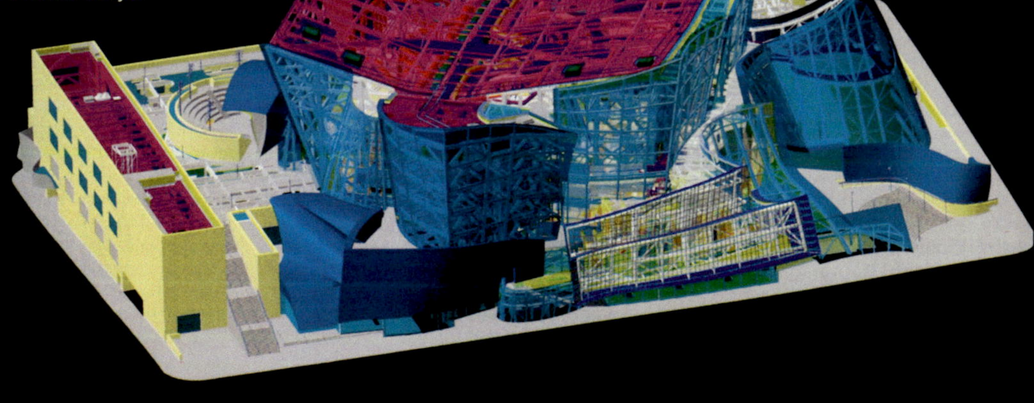

TOSHIKO MORI ARCHITECT

Toshiko Mori Architect

Headquarters
New York, NY

Founding Partner
Toshiko Mori

1981

Toshiko Mori Architect

Populous

Headquarters
Kansas City, MO

Other Locations
Boston, MA; London, UK; Brisbane, Australia; New York, NY; San Francisco, CA; Denver, CO; Knoxville, TN; Rio de Janeiro, Brazil; New Delhi, India; Hong Kong; Sydney, Australia; Melbourne, Australia; Singapore; Taipei, Taiwan; Norman, OK; Auckland, New Zealand

Founding Partners
Jerry Sincoff, Chris Carver, Ron Labinski, Joe Spear, Dennis Wellner

Current Partners
Rod Sheard, Christopher Lee, Nicholas Reynolds, Ben Vickery

Populous

Rafael Viñoly Architects

Headquarters
New York, NY

Other Locations
Tokyo, Japan; Buenos Aires, Argentina; London, UK; Abu Dhabi, United Arab Emirates

Founding Partner
Rafael Viñoly

Current Partners
Rafael Viñoly, Jay Bargmann, Charles Blomberg, James Herr, David Hodge, Andrea Lamberti, Chan-Li Lin, David Rolland

1983

Rafael Viñoly Architects

Rafael Viñoly, an Uruguayan architect with an enormously successful practice in Buenos Aires, Argentina, fled the country in 1979 during the height of the Argentine military dictatorship. He opened his New York office in 1983, four years after his arrival in the United States. Unable at first to practice as a licensed architect in the United States, Viñoly started as a developer in New York City. In 1988, as he was pushed out from a West Side development he had helped engineer, Viñoly was awarded his license to practice architecture through a special provision — originally created for the German émigré Ludwig Mies van der Rohe — for distinguished foreign practitioners.[1] Upon receiving his license, his office, Rafael Viñoly Architects, began to seek commissions in earnest. The firm's first major project, the John Jay College of Criminal Justice in New York, was completed in the same year.

In 1989, Rafael Viñoly Architects won the international competition to design the Tokyo International Forum. The project, featuring a dramatic 1.5 million square foot space with commercial, cultural and public services in the heart of Tokyo, immediately skyrocketed the firm to international acclaim. Soon after the commission, Viñoly opened a second office in Tokyo. The scale and complexity of the project also forced a significant restructuring of the office and led to a major expansion of personnel. By the time the building opened in 1996 to great critical praise, Rafael Viñoly Architects had over 100 employees, offices in New York, Tokyo, and a new office in Buenos Aires.

In the 1990s, the firm completed several major projects abroad and in the US, including the Samsung Jong-ro Tower (1994–1999) in Seoul, South Korea, the Princeton University Stadium (1998) in Princeton, New Jersey, and the University of San Andres Library (1999) in Buenos Aires, Argentina. In 2001, an increase in European commissions led the firm to open an additional office in London, soon to be followed by an office in Abu Dhabi to accommodate the firm's expanding work in the Middle East.

Rafael Viñoly Architects continues to develop a diverse portfolio of projects around the world from its five international offices. The firm has developed expertise across several building types, including convention and hospitality centers, academic institutions, commercial high-rise towers, healthcare facilities, mixed-use buildings, and research laboratories. Most recently, Rafael Viñoly Architects has completed work for several academic institutions in the United States, Argentina, and London, as well as a major addition and renovation to the Cleveland Museum of Art. — JJ

①
Rafael Viñoly, "Rafael Viñoly in Conversation," in *Rafael Viñoly* (New York: Princeton Architectural Press, 2002).

KieranTimberlake

Headquarters
Philadelphia, PA

Founding Partners
Stephan Kieran, James Timberlake

Current Partners
Stephan Kieran, James Timberlake,
Richard Maimon, David Riz

1984

Kieran Timberlake

Shortly after both independently winning the Rome Prize, Stephan Kieran and James Timberlake opened their Philadelphia office in 1984. Kieran and Timberlake had previously worked together in the office of Venturi, Scott Brown and Associates, and both had attended the University of Pennsylvania. Beginning with the design of the Student Activity Center at Chestnut Hill College (1987) in Philadelphia, KieranTimberlake gained prominence for its design methodology and its commitment to exploring innovative material and environmental technologies. The firm's technological focus, particularly on the development of "smart" wall systems, placed it at the forefront of a renewed interest in environmental design in architecture in the early 1990s. The firm's significant projects in this period included the Science and Technology Center at Rider University in Lawrenceville, New Jersey, the University Center at East Stroudsburg University of Pennsylvania (1993), and the Shipley Middle School (1993) in Bryn Mawr, Pennsylvania.

KieranTimberlake has gone on to develop a robust portfolio of educational and civic facilities, including several buildings for Yale University, the University of Pennsylvania, and other major academic institutions. The firm has also completed buildings for the Philadelphia Theater Company, the James A. Michener Art Museum, and the Sidwell Friends School.

KieranTimberlake has gained national attention with its proposals for mass-produced housing based on the development of new materials, including SmartWrap, as well as for its early adoption of new project delivery methods using Building Information Modeling, or BIM, systems. The firm has been among the leading proponents of prefabrication techniques in architecture and has developed several housing prototypes based on these techniques. KieranTimberlake also has a dedicated research group that focuses on the development of wireless sensor networks, environmental analysis and predictions tools, and assessment methods for building performance.[1] In 2008, the firm presented a portion of their design and fabrication research through their installation of the Cellophane House at the Museum of Modern Art (MoMA) in New York.

In 2008, through the Design Excellence Program run by the Bureau of Overseas Building Operations (OBO) of the US State Department, KieranTimberlake was invited to participate in the design competition for a new US Embassy in London, to replace the existing embassy by Eero Saarinen and Associates. The firm's entry was chosen over submissions by Pei Cobb Freed & Partners Architects, Morphosis Architects, and Richard Meier & Partners Architects, and the firm was awarded the commission in 2010. Once completed, the building, a ten-story glass cube screened by a façade made of high-performance ETFE plastic, will be the firms's first built project overseas.
— JJ

①
Stephen Kieran, James Timberlake and Karl Wallick, *KieranTimberlake: Inquiry* (New York: Rizzoli, 2011).

hplusf

1984–

Hodgetts + Fung

Headquarters
Culver City, CA

Founding Partners
Craig Hodgetts, Hsinming Fung

1984

Hodgetts + Fung

STUDIOS architecture

1985–

STUDIOS Architecture

Headquarters
San Francisco, CA

Other Locations
Los Angeles, CA; Washington, D.C.; New York, NY; Paris, France; Mumbai, India

Founding Partners
Erik Sueberkrop, Darryl Roberson, Gene Rae, Phil Olsen, Martin Yardley

Current Partners
Christopher Budd, David Burns, James Cowey, Todd DeGarmo, Melissa Duffy, Marnique Heath, Sophie Henley-Price, Tom Krizmanic, Rob McNamara, Nathan Minch, Pierre Pastellas, Marc Pfenninger, Brian Pilot, Darryl Roberson, David Sabalvaro, Erik Sueberkrop, Brian Tolman, Thomas Yee

STUDIOS Architecture

Gajah Madah Plaza
1981

Architect
Daniel, Mann, Johnson & Mendenhall

Location
Jakarta, Indonesia

Client
P.T. Harapan Motor Sakti Industri Company

Aviano School
1981

Architect
Mitchell/Giurgola Architects

Location
Aviano, Italy

Client
US Agency for International Development of Petroleum and Minerals

Ruwais New Town
1981

Architect
CRS Group

Location
Abu Dhabi, United Arab Emirates

Client
Abu Dhabi National Oil Company

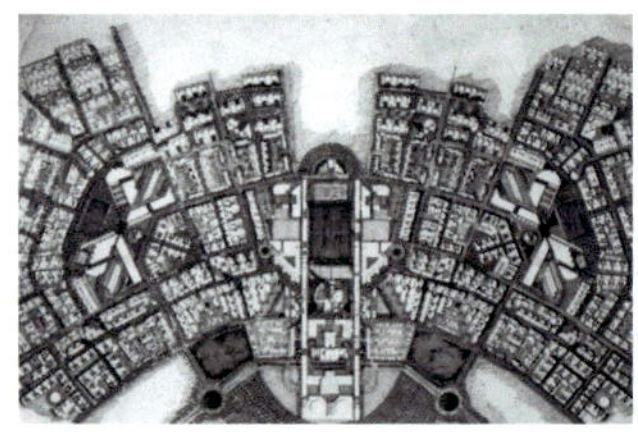

National Methanol Company Headquarters
1981

Architect
CRS Group

Location
Jubail, Saudi Arabia

Client
National Methanol Company

IBA Social Housing
1981–1985

EISENMAN ARCHITECTS

Architect
Eisenman Architects

Location
Berlin, Germany

Client
International Bauaustellung Berlin

11 Diagonal Street
1981–1985

Architect
JAHN

Location
Johannesburg, South Africa

Client
Anglo American Properties

Colonnade Condominiums
1981–1987

Architect
Paul Rudolph

Location
Singapore, Singapore

Client
Pontiac Land Private Ltd.

Tegel Harbor Phase I Housing
1981–1987

moore ruble yudell
architects & planners

Architect
Moore Ruble Yudell Architects & Planners

Location
Berlin, Germany

Client
Beta Siebente

Shanghai Centre
1981–1990

Architect
John Portman and Associates

Location
Shanghai, China

Concourse Complex
1981–1993

Architect
Paul Rudolph

Location
Singapore, Singapore

Client
Hong Fok Land

Royal Jordan Armed Command of Staff College
1982

LEO A DALY

Architect
Leo A Daly

Location
Hisban, Jordan

Client
Royal Jordan Armed Forces

Khulafa Street Building
1982

VSBA
VENTURI, SCOTT BROWN AND ASSOCIATES

Architect
Venturi, Scott Brown and Associates

Location
Baghdad, Iraq

Doha Sheraton Hotel
1982

Architect
William L. Pereira & Associates

Location
Doha, Qatar

Client
Sheraton Hotels and Resorts

PEI COBB FREED & PARTNERS Architects LLP

362 West Street
1982–1986

Architect
JAHN

Location
Durban, South Africa

Client
Anglo American Properties

JAHN

United Gulf Bank
1982–1987

Architect
Skidmore, Owings & Merrill

Location
Manama, Bahrain

Client
United Gulf Bank

SOM

Banco de Credito Headquarters
1982–1988

Architect
Arquitectonica

Location
Lima, Peru

Client
Banco de Credito de Peru

ARQUITECTONICA

US Embassy
1982–1988

Architect
Kallmann, McKinnell & Wood Architects

Location
Dhaka, Bangladesh

Client
US Department of State, Foreign Buildings Operations

KMW Architecture

UNITED STATES OF AMERICA EMBASSY

Dharmala Sakti Building
1982–1988

Architect
Paul Rudolph

Location
Jarkata, Indonesia

Client
Dharmala Corporation

Bank of China Tower
1982–1990

Architect
I.M. Pei & Parnters

Location
Hong Kong, Hong Kong

Associate Architect
Kung @ Lee Associate Architects

Client
Bank of China/Hong Kong

PEI COBB FREED & PARTNERS Architects LLP

US Embassy
1983

Architect
Perry Dean Rogers | Partners Architects

Location
Amman, Jordan

Client
US Department of State, Foreign Buildings Operations

PERRY DEAN ROGERS | PARTNERS ARCHITECTS

UNITED STATES OF AMERICA EMBASSY

Bouygues World Headquarters
1983–1988

Architect
Kevin Roche John Dinkeloo and Associates

Location
Paris, France

Client
Bouygues

KRJDA
KEVIN ROCHE JOHN DINKELOO AND ASSOCIATES LLC

Louvre Renovation
1983–1989

Architect
I.M. Pei & Partners

Location
Paris, France

Associate Architect
Michel Macary

Client
Établissement Public du Grand Louvre

PEI COBB FREED & PARTNERS Architects LLP

Siemens Headquarters and Research Facilities
1983–1989

Architect
Richard Meier and Partners Architects

Location
Munich, Germany

Client
Siemens Immobilien Management

Richard Meier & Partners
Architects LLP

GSIS Headquarters
1984

Architect
The Architects Collaborative

Location
Manila, Philippines

Client
Government Service Insurance System

TAC

Hotel Meridian
1984

Architect
Daniel, Mann, Johnson & Mendenhall

Location
Singapore, Singapore

Client
The Harapan Group

Citicorp Center
1984

Architect
Leo A Daly

Location
Hong Kong, Hong Kong

Client
Citicorp

Volvo Headquarters
1984

Architect
Mitchell/Giurgola Architects

Location
Göteborg, Sweden

Client
AB Volvo Holding Company

El Gezirah Sheraton Hotel
1984

Architect
CRS Sirrine Inc.

Location
Cairo, Egypt

Client
Sheraton Hotels and Resorts

Marina Square
1984–1987

Architect
John Portman and Associates

Location
Singapore, Singapore

Client
The Oriental Hotel,
Marina Mandarin Hotel,
Pan Pacific Hotel

Humboldt Bibliothek
1984–1988

Architect
Moore Ruble Yudell Architects & Planners

Location
Berlin, Germany

Client
Bezirkstamt Reinickendorf

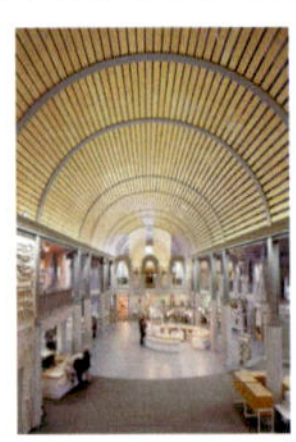

Bond Centre
1984–1988

Architect
Paul Rudolph

Location
Hong Kong, Hong Kong

Client
Lippo Group, Indonesia

King Faisal Military School
1985

PERKINS+WILL

Architect
Perkins + Will

Location
Khamis Mushayt, Saudi Arabia

Client
National College of Agriculture

Royal Dutch Shell Bank Headquarters
1985

SOM

Architect
Skidmore, Owings & Merrill

Location
The Hague, Netherlands

Client
Shell Onroerend Goed BV, Royal Dutch Shell Petroleum Co.

Ardmore Habitat Condominiums
1985

SafdieArchitects

Architect
Safdie Architects

Location
Singapore, Singapore

Client
Robin Loh Enterprises

Regent Hotel
1985–1986

JPA

Architect
John Portman and Associates

Location
Singapore, Singapore

Client
Regent International Hotels

Mexx International Headquarters
1985–1987

RAMSA
ROBERT A.M. STERN ARCHITECTS

Architect
Robert A.M. Stern Architects

Location
Voorschoten, The Netherlands

Client
Mexx International, B.V.

Profit Margin: Signature Developments In Europe and Japan

The expansion of US architectural firms in the 1980s was precipitated by the expansion of US real estate models for large-scale development abroad. By this time, the flows of finance capital had begun to coalesce into "financescapes" across the globe, with concomitant urbanisms ranging from finance districts and housing estates to industrial parks, call centers, and slums, all linked together through financial and architectural feedback loops operating at an unprecedented scale.[1] The most prosperous, post-industrial nodes of these new "multi-national cities" were located in the northern hemisphere and the Pacific Rim, particularly in formerly industrial or untapped urban areas in Europe and Japan. All instantiations of the contemporary "global financial imaginary," the largest such projects involving US architects—whether new office districts, fantasy resorts, or luxury housing showcases—were all orchestrated by developers.[2]

The London Docklands site of Canary Wharf was developed at the height of the building boom spurred by Margaret Thatcher's incentives for private development. Congregating the world's financial power to a degree matched only by New York's World Trade Center, Canary Wharf was first conceived in 1985 by American developer G. Ware Travelstead, but developed by the Canadian firm Olympia & York, the same entity that developed its Manhattan counterpart. Initially master-planned by Skidmore, Owings & Merrill (SOM) and subsequently by Koetter Kim & Associates, Canary Wharf includes tenants like Citigroup, HSBC, Barclays, J.P. Morgan Chase, and Merrill Lynch, and boasts the building that was London's tallest for two decades, One Canada Square (1986–1991), by Cesar Pelli & Associates. Other commissions to design offices and interiors went to Pei Cobb Freed & Partners, SOM, Kohn Pedersen Fox Associates (KPF), and Gensler, with many of these US firms establishing London outposts in this period. By 2007, certain buildings in this area were

① See Arjun Appadurai, "Disjuncture and Difference in the Global Cultural Economy," *Public Culture* 2.2 (Spring 1990): 1–24; Reinhold Martin and Kadambari Baxi, *Multi-National City: Architectural Itineraries* (Barcelona: Actar, 2007).

② Reinhold Martin, "Financial Imaginaries: Toward a Philosophy of the City," paper for Global Cities Conference at Max Plank Institute (July 2009).

1975

1979 • European Monetary System (EMS) and European Monetary Cooperation Fund (EMCF) established • Berlin establishes *Internationale Bauausstellung* building program

1981 London Docklands Development Corporation (LDDC) established

1982 • President François Mitterand of France launches building program of *Grands Projets* • London Docklands declared Enterprise Zone to spur commercial development

1983 Tokyo Disneyland opens

1986 Deregulation of London Stock Exchange

1987 • *Internationale Bauaustellung* (International Building Exhibition) opens in Berlin • Walt Disney signs agreement with French government to build European resort

1989 • Fall of the Berlin Wall • Asia-Pacific Exposition held in Fukuoka, Japan worth over $1 billion dollars, the Docklands now fully transformed from its previously derelict status into one of the key financial centers of the world. Canary Wharf Group has recently hired Gensler to re-envision the 39th floor of One Canada Square as "Europe's largest Fin/Tech accelerator," proposing that the space will offer tech startups "a chance to disrupt the financial sector."[3] Such new hopes for "disruption," structurally necessary to ensure the value of the properties in question, are simply the latest iteration of the same tax and profit speculation that has governed the history of the development.

At the same time a different development model was being propagated by Disney, which opened its first international theme park, Tokyo Disney, in 1983, followed by the Euro Disney Resort on the outskirts of Paris in 1992.[4] In the leisure urbanism of the Disney resorts, historic American environments were "filtered through the lens of Hollywood," as Robert A.M. Stern Architects (RAMSA) described the firm's design for the Cheyenne Hotel at Euro Disney, based on the scenography of a nineteenth-century Western town.[5] Other symbolic environments included the Newport Bay Club, also by RAMSA; Hotel New York, by Michael Graves and Associates, and Hotel Santa Fe, by Antoine Precook Architects PC. The resort currently includes financial stakes from Saudi Prince Al-Waleed bin Talal of Kingdom Holdings and the US money manager Invesco, and its shares are traded on the Paris Euronext exchange. Regarded as a poor offspring of its US cousins when it first opened, Euro Disney has since become one of the top performers in Disney's multinational network. Together, the eleven Disney parks worldwide account for nearly a third of the company's $45 billion revenue.[6]

Along with other developer-driven districts featuring international architects, like the Nexus World housing showcase built by Fukuoka Jisho Co. Ltd and Qaeda Corporation for the Asia-Pacific Exposition in Fukuoka, Japan in 1989, models like Canary Wharf and Euro Disney helped launch a global trend in which architecture came to serve as a temporary "spatial fix" for capital.[7] Its capacity to do so is linked to the perceived "specialty" of such developments as well as their usefulness. While the phenomenon of architects working with developers is hardly new, the ever-expanding circulation of capital, often literally conquering new geographical territory, now both requires and produces starchitecture worldwide. — AM

③ Max Smolaks, "FinTech Accelerator Space Level 39 to Open at Canary Wharf," *Tech Week Europe* (October 2, 2012), http://www.techweekeurope.co.uk/ (last accessed November 29, 2014).

④ Cesar Pelli, "Canary Wharf; The Mega-Building in Context," in Andreas C. Papadakis, ed., *New Directions in Current Architecture* (London and New York: Academy Editions, St. Martin's Press, 1988): 41.

⑤ Robert A.M. Stern Architects website, http://www.ramsa.com/en/projects-search/hotels/hotel-cheyenne.html (last accessed November 29, 2014).

⑥ Christian Sylt, "The Secrets Behind Disney's $2.2 Billion Theme Park Profits," *Forbes* (July 14, 2014), http://onforb.es/1mDwrRh (last accessed November 29, 2014).

⑦ David Harvey, "Globalization and the 'Spatial Fix'," *Geographische Revue* (2001): 23–29.

1985

2002

1990 • Fall of Communism in Central and Eastern Europe • Reunification of East and West Germany

1991 First Canary Wharf buildings completed at London Docklands

1992 • reaty of Maastricht formally establishes European Union (EU) • Euro Disney Resort opens outside Paris • Barcelona hosts Olympic Games • Universal Exposition of Seville (Expo '92) held

1998 Lisbon World Exposition (Expo '98) held

1999 Euro currency begins virtual circulation

2002 Euro coins and banknotes replace national European currencies

2005

–1991 First Persian Gulf War

2001 Afghanistan War

2003 Iraq War

Americans Abroad: Some Coming Attractions

Europe and Asia are fast becoming the leading importers of American architecture, as evidenced in the projects shown here. Some clearly transport the American urban esthetic overseas; others borrow from the host country's vernacular and traditions. All are intriguing.

By Nora Richter Greer

A 12 million-square-foot, mixed-use development ultimately will link two bends in the Thames River in London's Docklands district. For the 71-acre Canary Wharf site, offices, retail shops, two hotels, and parking are planned in symmetrical buildings flanking a formally landscaped boulevard and plaza. Left, the building in right foreground is by Skidmore, Owings & Merrill; the one in left foreground is by Kohn Pedersen Fox. Flanking the street on the right is a building by I.M. Pei & Partners, and on the left is one by SOM. At the complex's heart will be an 800-foot-tall, pyramid-topped skyscraper (right) designed by Cesar Pelli. Contrasting with London's mostly modernist towers, Pelli's is characterized by, in his words, "flair and dignity." Authors of the site's master plan are SOM, I.M. Pei & Partners, and YRM Associates. The landscape architect is Hanna Olin.

The Sainsbury Wing of London's National Gallery, designed by Venturi, Rauch & Scott Brown, relates to the 1838 original building by William Wilkins but also asserts its own identity. Cornice lines and materials are similar; new are large, square cutouts and small metal columns. Top photo, view from Trafalgar Square; above, elevation of entry lobby facing west; left, view of connecting galleries.

A new office retail complex that reflects traditional English architecture will grace the banks of the Thames. Designed by John Burgee Architects with D.Y. Davies Associates, the complex (London Bridge City Phase IIA, above) features two 14-story towers, which step down to nine- and six-story wings. The focus of the complex is the river, with views of the London and Tower bridges. Materials and detailing are to be compatible with those of existing buildings—light-colored limestone stringcourses that alternate with dark gray granite panels and stretch out the building's lines horizontally.

Joint ventures are common between American and foreign architects. For the Palasport Milano arena in Milan, Italy, HOK teamed up with Italian architect Aldo Rossi to design this 18,000-seat velodrome and multipurpose arena. In the center is HOK's contribution: the design of three levels of seating for sports and entertainment events. The perimeter spaces and towers were designed by Rossi for commercial and retail use. The building will be marble and granite.

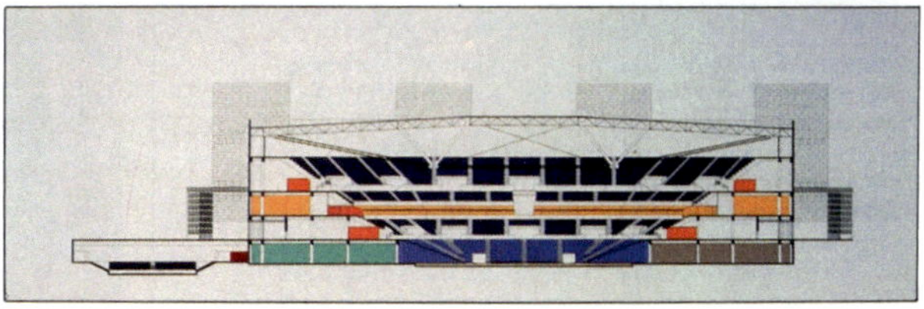

J. SCOTT SMITH

Administrative and Maritime Center
Antwerp, Belgium
Richard Meier & Partners

Meier's mixed-use project of offices, hotel, shops, and res aurants (below) is part of a major public/private redevelopment scheme within Antwerp's waterfront area. In additio to creating the master plan for the 1.2-million-square-foot site, Meier is working on a 16-story headquarters for a major Belgian shipping corporation. Circular in plan, the tower will be clad in glass and white metal panels. Construction is scheduled to begin early next year.

American Center
Paris, France
Frank O. Gehry & Associates

Scheduled to open in 1992, Frank Gehry's 175,000-square-foot cultural center (above) will house the American Center, a nonprofit institution founded in 1941 to assist emerging artists. The $40-million structure will be located on the southeastern bank of the Seine in a redeveloped cultural district, which will include L'Opéra Bastille, the Ministère des Finances, and the Bibliothèque de France. Facing the entrance to Bercy Park, Gehry's complex is broken into two separate masses, one for the programs of the American Center—galleries, theaters, studios, and a restaurant—and the other for a complex of 27 apartments for visiting artists.

JOCK POTTLE/ESTO

European Forecast

BY ANDREA OPPENHEIMER DEAN

AS THE ECONOMIC SUPREMACY OF THE UNITED STATES wanes and architects face a weak construction climate at home, Europe is reshaping itself into a powerful economic giant—a potentially rich source of new work for American architects. In the grip of the "Eurosclerosis" of the 1980s, European economies grew a scant 2 percent, well below Japan's 4.2 percent and America's 2.8 percent during the boom years of the Reagan era. Predictions for the 1990s, by contrast, forecast that Europe's economic growth will be 3 to 5 percent.

Three momentous events have interacted to decalcify and renew Europe: the decision to create a single European market in 1992, the reunification of Germany, and the breakup of Eastern Europe into sovereign, predominantly pro-Western, democratic nations.

For U.S. architects, entering the European market in 1992 w mean facing an entity composed of 12 nations: Belgium, Denmar France, Germany, Greece, Ireland, Italy, Luxembourg, t Netherlands, Portugal, Spain, and the United Kingdom. evidence of Europe's increasing power, Turkey and Austr have applied for associate European Community (EC) mer bership; Norway, Sweden, Cyprus, and Malta are debatir whether to join; and several former Soviet satellites, most notab Hungary and Poland, are also expected to apply soon.

In its present configuration, the EC will constitute an increa ingly barrier-free construction market worth $330 billion, or 2

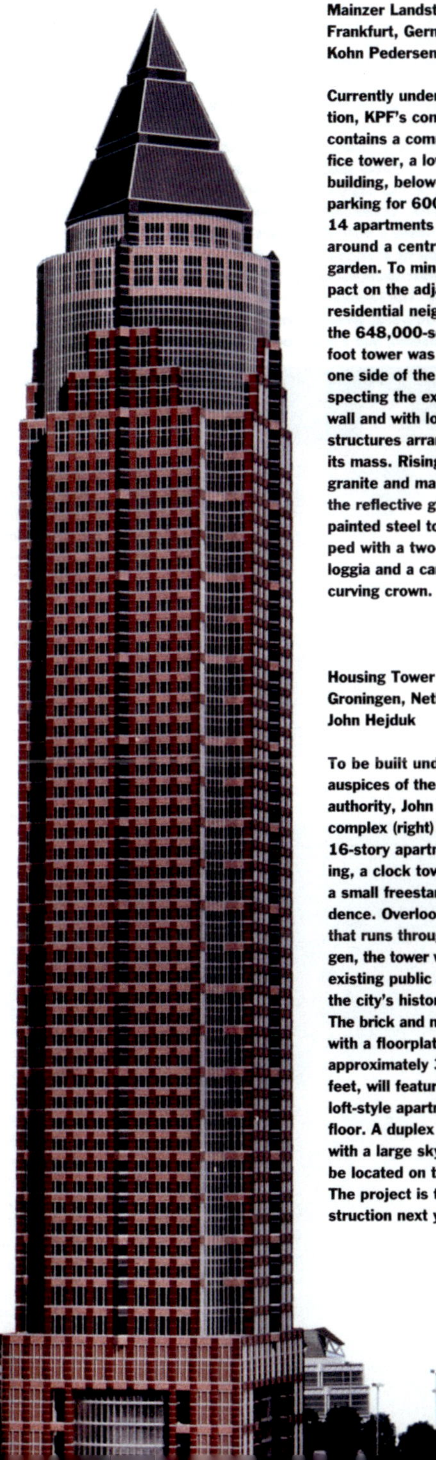

esse Frankfurt Complex
rankfurt, Germany
urphy/Jahn Architects

the heart of Frankfurt, a ajor expansion (right) of e city's existing exhibi-on complex is composed an office tower, cere-onial entrance pavilion, id a 750,000-square-ot exhibit hall. Designed resemble a campanile ithin a composition of low uildings, Helmut Jahn's eestanding, 825-foot-gh tower will be Europe's llest building when ompleted later this year. he building is constructed concrete and finished ith polished red granite olumns detailed with a riped pattern and profiled ith aluminum bands at very floor. The circular ntry pavilion (left in odel), recently completed, crowned with a glass yramid and houses a staurant and ticketing and gistration facilities for e complex.

Mainzer Landstrasse 58
Frankfurt, Germany
Kohn Pedersen Fox

Currently under construction, KPF's complex (right) contains a commercial office tower, a low-rise office building, below-grade parking for 600 cars, and 14 apartments located around a central winter garden. To minimize its impact on the adjacent residential neighborhood, the 648,000-square-foot tower was placed on one side of the site, respecting the existing street wall and with low-rise structures arranged around its mass. Rising from a granite and marble base, the reflective glass and painted steel tower is topped with a two-story loggia and a cantilevered, curving crown.

JOCK POTTLE/ESTO

Housing Tower
Groningen, Netherlands
John Hejduk

To be built under the auspices of the city housing authority, John Hejduk's complex (right) comprises a 16-story apartment building, a clock tower, and a small freestanding residence. Overlooking a canal that runs through Groningen, the tower will border an existing public square in the city's historic quarters. The brick and metal tower, with a floorplate measuring approximately 30 by 40 feet, will feature one large, loft-style apartment per floor. A duplex studio unit with a large skylight will be located on the top floor. The project is to begin construction next year.

Novoli Multi-Use Center
Florence, Italy
Gunnar Birkerts & Associates

Located within the 70-acre site of a former Fiat manufacturing facility, Birkerts's mixed-use project (below) is part of a major redevelopment master plan, developed through a workshop led by landscape architect Lawrence Halprin. The 850,000-square-foot building is designed with clustered masses and interconnecting pedestrian pathways to reduce its apparent bulk. The development will focus on a public park at its center surrounded by projects by 13 other architects, including Aldo Rossi and Richard Rogers.

Custom House Docks
Dublin, Ireland
Benjamin Thompson & Associates

Based on the firm's winning entry in an international competition, BTA's master plan for a 23-acre waterfront site (bottom) incorporates shops, offices, and housing within the city's historic fabric. The first phase, scheduled for completion in 1993, includes a 300,000-square-foot office building intended to bring four major corporate headquarters to Dublin's center city. The second phase will provide a 6,000-seat arena, a marina and maritime museum, and a major public park.

STEVE ROSENTHAL

percent of the world construction market By last year, in anticipation of the disman tling of trade barriers, Europe had becom the most profitable overseas architectura market, and the most lucrative foreign mar ket for Fortune-500-company clients. Be tween 1987 and 1988, total design billing in Europe tripled; U.S. A/E firm billings ros 28 percent from 1988 to 1989.

Most designers approach the new E 1992 with caution. "You have to analyz your firm and make sure you have specia skills and abilities to sell. Don't be lured b a gold rush mentality," counsels Harol Adams, FAIA, chairman of RTKL, a firn with projects in Amsterdam, Frankfurt, Lis bon, London, and several cities in France an Scotland. Robert Cooke, president of Perkin & Will International, which has work in th United Kingdom and the Netherlands adds, "This league is mainly for the large firms. The yellow lights are flashing al along the way for the weaker ones."

European clients look to American firm for prestigious design and managerial abil ity, and familiarity with large, mixed-us buildings. With land scarcer and pricier an rents higher than in the U.S., some develop ers gamble that a design by a renowne American architect will enhance a building' value and sell office space. European govern ments and institutions, meanwhile, appea more interested in, and willing to pay fo distinguished design than are their U.S counterparts, as evidenced by the wide spread use of competitions to select archi tects. Richard Meier, for instance, has bee commissioned to design 18 buildings in nin of the 12 EC countries.

Since most European architecture prac tices are small, offer few services, and are in experienced with high-rise design, Europea clients are receptive to U.S. firms that ca manage all phases of design and are familia with large-scale, complex, and fast-track construction. But, as David Syphard, senio vice president of Houston-based CRSS, In points out, while EC 1992 will give Ameri can firms access to a larger market and fu ther economies of scale in the beginning, th American advantage is likely to recede a European firms tool up to compete.

Many American firms entered th European market by following U.S. client to London during its recent constructio boom, and are using the British capital as springboard to the rest of the continen Some have opened European offices, other have formed joint ventures with local archi tects. Virtually all Americans working in Eu rope stress that success requires makin long-term financial commitments. Eugen Kohn of Kohn Pedersen Fox warns that hi firm spent $1.3 million opening a Londo office. RTKL's Adams points out that "mos rchitectural firms that fail abroad do so because they're oblivious to the cultural factors that shape business relationships. You have to be there. You have to be part of a foreign locale's social life and community." Ezra Ehrenkrantz, whose firm Ehrenkrantz, Ecktut & Whitelaw is working for Olympia & York at Canary Wharf in London, adds, "It's all networking, especially since our interest is not just working in London, where the boom has spent itself, but in getting work elsewhere through referrals." Kohn also recommends that U.S. architects align themselves with major engineering and construction companies and with local architectural colleagues who can help pave the way and interpret local codes and customs.

Alliances with local practitioners are all the more important because many European countries (Germany, France, the Netherlands, Spain, and the United Kingdom) protect their own practices through some form of subsidy, risk-sharing, or taxes on foreign firms or imports of goods and services. Additional difficulties for American designers include a diminished dollar that has pumped up the cost of commercial properties and of doing business in Europe. Also, accounting and legal procedures are different from those in the U.S., building densities tend to be lower, and zoning rules are less flexible. Working abroad can also place enormous strains on a firm's home office, since it often siphons off the "most senior, best, and most experienced persons," says Richard Roth, Jr., chairman of Emery Roth & Sons, New York. And it can mean missing work opportunities in the U.S., as Benjamin Thompson & Associates has discovered. The problems and benefits will vary from firm to firm and from one country to the next.

Which countries are the best bets? In England, London's Docklands have been a booming construction site, with huge new commercial buildings designed by Kohn Pedersen Fox, Cesar Pelli, SOM, and others. But the construction market "is only about six months behind ours," explains Richard Hayden of Swanke Hayden Connell Architects. London has become overbuilt, has high interest rates, and is the most expensive city in Europe. "If you're not over there now, forget it," adds Robert Cooke of Perkins & Will. There are design opportunities in other parts of England and in Scotland, especially for industrial and rehab construction, but the Organization for Economic Cooperation & Development estimates England's economic growth in 1990 at only 1.3 percent.

With reunification under way, Germany is emerging as the economic locomotive of Europe. The financial well-being of other European nations will, therefore, depend considerably on their relationship with Germany, especially since geography and wealth will impel Germany to take the lead in helping to rebuild and develop Eastern Europe. According to *Business Week*, "German reunification and the hint of an era of prosperity in the East are behind a new European investment boom by U.S. companies." According to David Hale, chief economist of Kemper Financial Services in Chicago, reunification will add 16 million to West Germany's population of 62 million, while its GNP of $1.2 trillion will rise to a possible $1.6 trillion, 30 percent greater than that of France, Europe's second-largest economy.

Ingeborg Flagge of the Bund Deutscher Architekten (West Germany's equivalent of the AIA) writes that even before reunification, West Germany needed about half a million new housing units for refugees. But the nation also has the largest number of architects per capita in the industrialized

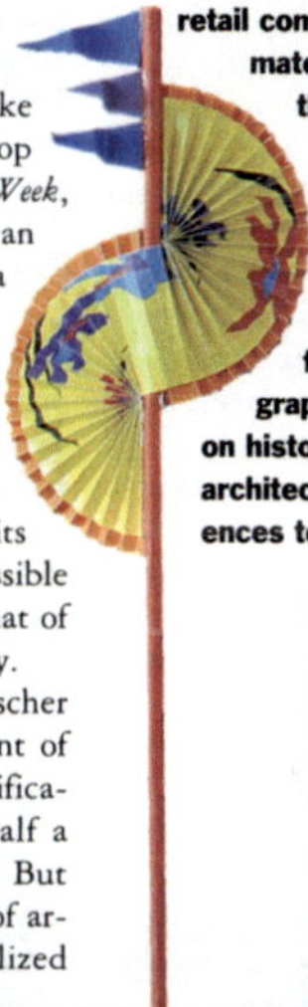

The Colombo
Lisbon, Portugal
RTKL Associates

Linked to the center of Lisbon with a new highway and served by subway and bus, the Colombo (bottom) will be Portugal's largest mixed-use development when completed in 1993. Designed by the Baltimore firm RTKL Associates, the 2-million-square-foot complex will contain a multilevel shopping center, offices, and a hotel. Three levels of underground parking for 6,000 cars encompass another 2 million square feet. An existing public plaza will be relandscaped to serve as the main entrance to the complex, with a rotunda and curving formal arcades connecting the pair of 17-story office towers, which will feature panoramic views of downtown Lisbon. Enlivened by interior arcades, the retail component will house approximately 500 specialty shops, movie theaters, health clubs, restaurants, an amusement area, and a landscaped roof garden. The hotel's public spaces will be located on a garden level facing a courtyard of pools and fountains. Building details and graphics (below and inset, left) draw on historic Portuguese and Moorish architecture and incorporate references to the country's nautical past.

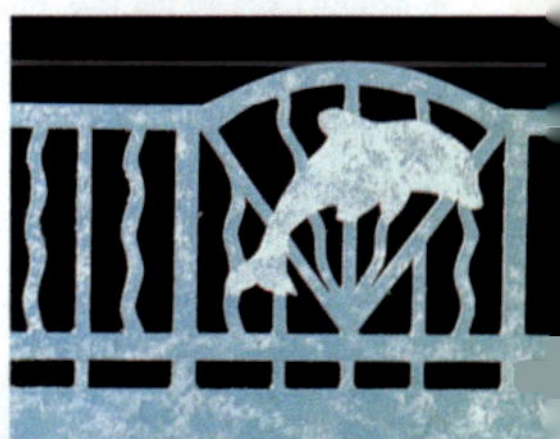

Sundsterrassen
Malmö, Sweden
Moore Ruble Yudell Architects

A large tract of undeveloped land along the sound that separates Sweden and Denmark is now the site of a 500-unit government-subsidized housing project (above). Moore Ruble Yudell arranged apartments within a large crescent-shaped structure facing the water and created a gently sloping lawn bounded by arcades and a series of eight-unit "villas." Simple landscaping takes advantage of mature trees on the site, while a new lawn creates an axis linking the waterfront to a church and neighborhoods beyond. The complex is scheduled for completion in 1993.

Banque de Luxembourg
Luxembourg
Arquitectonica

Arquitectonica's new headquarters for the Banque de Luxembourg (below) is located on a prominent corner site at the focus of Boulevard Royal in the city's downtown financial district. The Miami-based architects combined a glass- and stone-clad six-story structure with a cantilevered limestone block detailed with a grid of square punched windows. The 200,000-square-foot building will include eight levels below grade, which house a banking hall, support facilities, bank safes, and parking. Construction of the project is scheduled to begin early next year.

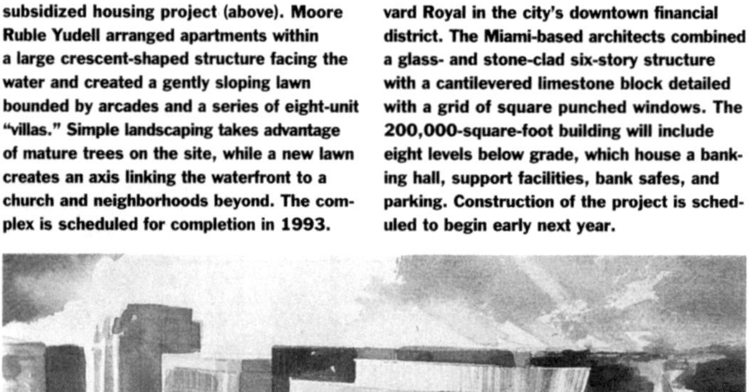

world, according to Flagge, and expects an influx of architects from other European countries. She warns that American architects would need to "have a good command of the native language, be willing to cooperate, adapt to different working conditions, and accept rules and regulations of the national professional bodies." RTKL's Adams warns, "Barriers in Germany are numerous, codes and regulations are tight, and it's very difficult to break in."

There may be other pitfalls awaiting those who want to enter the West German construction market. East Germany's huge appetite for new equipment and consumer goods may jack up West German growth to 5 or 6 percent, and the fear is that so much money changing hands will create a burst of inflation. To avoid pushing up prices, Germany will have to meet the surge in demand by importing more and exporting less, a boon for Germany's trading partners.

France, as Germany's largest trading partner, will benefit most as Germany draws in imports to meet demand. Because France has one of Europe's lowest inflation rates and a 15 percent annual-corporate-profits growth rate, foreign money is pouring into the French bourse. The rush to invest also stems from docile labor unions and rising productivity, with forecasts of 3.6 percent growth in 1990, according to *Business Week*. For architects, says Harold Adams, "there may be comparable opportunities in France to those in London four years ago." Also, as a result of François Mitterrand's *Grands Projets*, "there is scarcely a mayor who does not dream of erecting some building that will win him fame at home and abroad," writes French critic Jacques Lucan. For less glamorous commercial work, however, France may be less receptive to American architects than the British were.

As Germany's neighbors, Austria, Switzerland, and the Netherlands also stand to gain substantially from reunification and from the rebirth of Eastern Europe. About 22 percent of the Netherlands' exports go to Germany, as do 31 percent of Austria's, according to the *Economist*, which predicts that West Germany, Austria, and Switzerland, followed by the Netherlands and Ireland, would be the five strongest European markets. Ireland's unexpected strength derives from having Europe's largest capital-goods exports as a

Vila Olimpica
Barcelona, Spain
Skidmore, Owings & Merrill
and Frank O. Gehry & Associates

Responding to the master plan by Martorell, Bohigas & Mackay for the Olympic Village, SOM generated a variety of civic and public spaces for the regatta and sailing events of the 1992 summer games. With its exposed structural system, Bruce Graham's 45-story Hotel of the Arts comprises 600 rooms and 33 luxury apartments and will create a strong visual presence on the city's skyline. A variety of retail, commercial, and maritime elements, including one of Gehry's famous fish, provide points of activity along the waterfront promenades. Section (bottom, these pages) illustrates the diversity of scale.

percentage of GNP, and the fourth-lowest wages on the continent.

Low wages have also made Greece, Italy, Portugal, and Spain attractive for investment in labor-intensive industries that provide construction opportunities. But these countries will have to compete with newly liberated, low-wage, Eastern European countries, especially since the four southern European nations have high inflation and high import rates, and Germany accounts for only a small share of their total exports.

In fact, no southern European nation is a reliably promising market for U.S. architects. Italy showed marked entrepreneurial strength in the 1980s, but its chaotic and huge public sector, aging infrastructure, rising inflation and deficit rates, and its stillborn attempts to deregulate and privatize state-owned industries are bound to be damaging in the 1990s, according to *Business Week*. Both the Spanish and Portuguese economies have improved since the mid-1980s; Spain is the EC's fifth largest economy, Portugal its 10th largest. But American architectural opportunities in Portugal have not yet materialized, while those in Spain may peak once construction for the 1992 Olympics in Barcelona is complete. The control of design work by architectural colleges makes it difficult for Americans to work in Spain. The relatively few existing opportunities will probably focus on Madrid and favor large corporate firms.

Despite these problems, the benefits to American architects from EC 1992 and German reunification could be prodigious. But the results of reconstituting Eastern Europe into sovereign nations are still unclear. "Although the potential is tremendous, the only enthusiasm I get so far is in the press," says KPF's Eugene Kohn. The problems of working in Eastern Europe seem insurmountable. Currencies, except in Poland and Yugoslavia, are not convertible, which raises the question of how an architect is to be paid. For now, the best answer seems to be an alliance with a developer willing to be paid in bartered goods. Banking systems are crude, accounting systems and laws on repatriation of profits are generally unhelpful, and land ownership is unclear. Houston-based developer Gerald Hines, for one, is waiting until Westerners can own property before moving into Eastern Europe. ■

Americans in

London

Comprising 10 million square feet of office space, Canary Wharf in the Docklands (these pages) is the largest concentration of American design in London. The first phase of SOM's master plan (inset), which includes a 50-story office tower and retail building by Cesar Pelli & Associates, is scheduled for completion in 1991.

AMERICANS ABROAD

SPURRED BY THE DEREGULATION OF its stock exchange and Thatcherite incentives for private development, London is undergoing a building boom unprecedented in the city's history since the reconstruction following the Great Fire of 1666. To house increasing numbers of foreign investment banks and British financial institutions in the easternmost areas of the capital, developers have passed over local talent in favor of importing the design expertise of American architects. The reason is based on an immediate need for deep floor plates and efficient layouts—the kind of quality spec office buildings on which practices such as Swanke Hayden Connell Architects, Kohn Pedersen Fox Associates, and Skidmore, Owings & Merrill have built their reputations. Unlike their British counterparts, U.S. architects are accustomed to fast-track scheduling and the organizational and management skills practiced by their corporate clients, many of whom are also Americans. Top firms in the U.K., on the other hand, traditionally have turned their backs on "crass" speculative, commercial development, preferring to concentrate on custom-designed headquarters or public commissions (for more on British practices, turn to page 101).

Over the past five years, America's largest architectural firms have established permanent offices in London, affording them the opportunity to secure additional British and European commissions from these new locations. With a permanent, 305-person office, SOM is the most visible American presence in London, responsible for the city's most expansive projects—the master plan of Canary Wharf in the Docklands (facing and following pages) and Broadgate in the City of London (page 68). Swanke Hayden Connell, with a 64-person London office, has been commissioned to design 21 architectural and interiors projects in the capital, including a 13-acre mixed-use development (page 71), which was originally awarded to a pair of British firms. Other U.S. firms with major commissions in London include Kohn Pedersen Fox Associates; Hellmuth Obata and Kassabaum; Gensler and Associates; Cesar Pelli & Associates; and Pei Cobb Freed & Partners. The need for sophisticated interiors within the first wave of U.S.-designed buildings has also prompted smaller architectural and interior design firms, such as Studios, to join the American invasion, as well as top U.S. electrical and mechanical engineers, and construction managers.

Although confronted by Yankee-bashing critics in the approvals process and the press, the American presence in London has encouraged the local architectural community to become more involved in commercial development and its concomitant disciplines of space planning and facility management. Recently, several British and European firms have been invited to design buildings within American-authored master plans—collaborations which should benefit both sides of the Atlantic.

—DEBORAH K. DIETSCH

Canary Wharf

Docklands

THE LONDON DOCKLANDS WERE DESIGnated in 1981 as an 8.5-square-mile urban development area east of the city's financial district. Controlled by the London Docklands Development Corporation, the sprawling district of abandoned wharfs and warehouses is freed of traditional planning constraints to encourage private investment. This lack of planning controls, however, has resulted in a jumble of commercial and residential construction of little architectural merit. An exception is Canary Wharf, a 71-acre business complex originally conceived in 1985 by American developer G. Ware Travelstead. The Beaux-Arts inspired ensemble of office buildings, retail spaces, boulevards, and parks is masterplanned by SOM and Hanna/Olin with guidelines for building envelopes, continuity of massing, and ground-floor arcades. Now controlled by Olympia & York, which took over the project in 1987, Canary Wharf is setting new standards for future Docklands development. In addition to the participation of U.S. firms, several of the 27 building sites (plan below) have been designed by British and European firms. Olympia & York is also developing Heron Quays to the south as a residential enclave and an historic warehouse to the north as a retail marketplace.

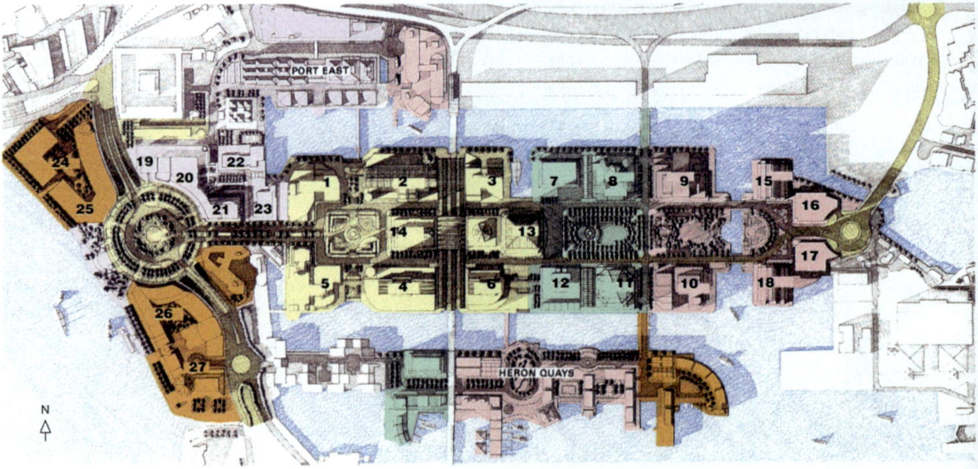

- PHASE I
- PHASE II
- PHASE III
- PHASE IV
- PHASE V

1	PEI COBB FREED & PARTNERS
2	SKIDMORE, OWINGS & MERRILL
3	TROUGHTON MCASLAN
4	KOHN PEDERSEN FOX ASSOCIATES
5	SKIDMORE, OWINGS & MERRILL
6	KOHN PEDERSEN FOX ASSOCIATES
7-11	NOT YET ANNOUNCED
12	ALLIES MORRISON
13	CESAR PELLI & ASSOCIATES
14	CESAR PELLI & ASSOCIATES
15-18	NOT YET ANNOUNCED
19	SKIDMORE, OWINGS & MERRILL
20-21	NOT YET ANNOUNCED
22	ALDO ROSSI
23	ALDO ROSSI
24-27	NOT YET ANNOUNCED

NIALL CLUTTON / ARCAID

Phase I centers on a 50-story tower (previous pages), retail building, and light railway station designed by Cesar Pelli (facing page), and includes office buildings by KPF (above) and SOM Chicago (right).

NIALL CLUTTON / ARCAID

Broadgate

City of London

THE FIRST COMPLETED EVIDENCE OF American design in London is a complex of office buildings grouped around Liverpool Street Station. After commissioning the British firm Arup Associates to design the first phase of the 29-acre project, British developers Rosehaugh Stanhope turned to SOM Chicago to add three more buildings, and ultimately commissioned the U.S. architects to design eight more. Compared with the three Arup-designed structures (lower left in site model, below), the SOM ensemble is more historicist in spirit, as exemplified by the entrance arch of the Bankers Trust headquarters (facing page, top right), and by the towers of Hamilton House (facing page, bottom) and Broadwalk House (facing page, top left). Designed by partner Bruce Graham, most of Broadgate's buildings share a palette of granite, limestone, and cast stone, yet each conveys an identity distinct from its neighbors. The most striking structure is Exchange House (right), an engineering tour de force that spans the railroad yard. (For technical details, turn to page 109.)

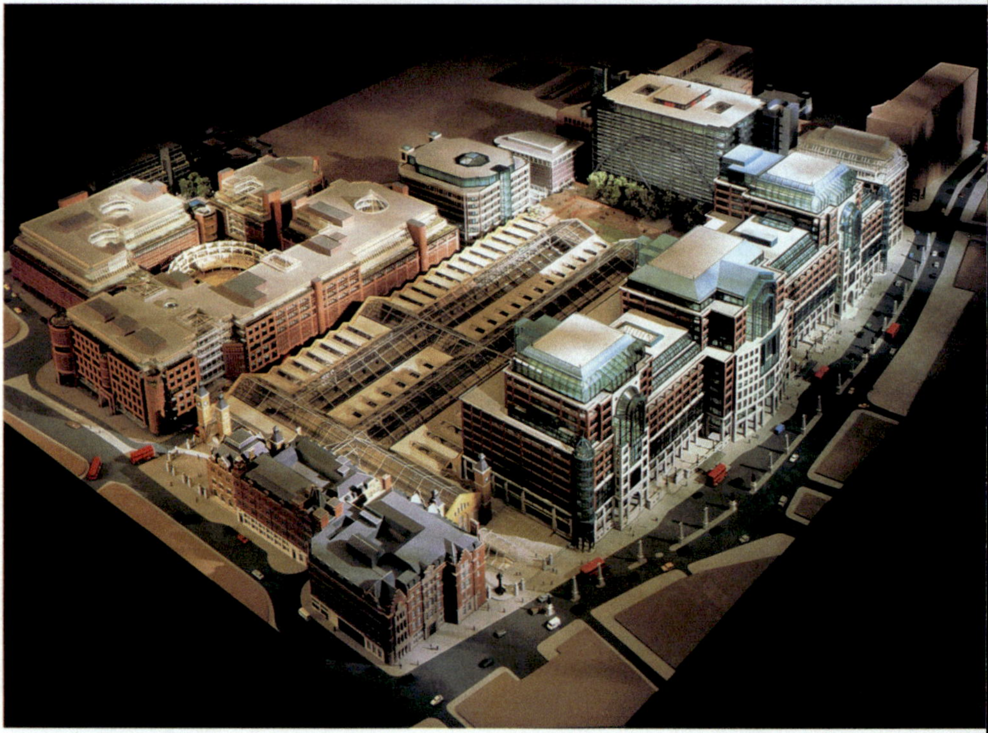

NIALL CLUTTON / ARCAID PHOTOS

NIALL CLUTTON / ARCAID PHOTOS

Bishopsgate

City of London

LOCATED AT THE EASTERN EDGE OF LIVERPOOL STREET STATION, the largest portion of the SOM-designed Broadgate complex is an ensemble of office buildings totaling 1.5 million square feet. Named Bishopsgate after the street bordering the site, the three buildings were designed in 1986 by Chicago partner Bruce Graham to convey the classically inspired cohesion of John Nash's Regent Street terraces. The 900-foot-long street facade (left) is punctuated by Chicago-style steel windows and granite cladding above a limestone base. A ground-floor arcade lined with mahogany-framed shopfronts (below) is elevated five feet above the street, and a passageway on the western side of the buildings connects Bishopsgate to the train station. The first structure at the southern end of the site opened last year, and is occupied by National Westminster Bank in offices also designed by SOM.

SOM's Bishopsgate complex of three office buildings (above) and shopping arcade (right) is located to the east of Liverpool Street Station (site plan below). Swanke Hayden Connell's Spitalfields development (facing page and site plan below) also borders Bishopsgate site.

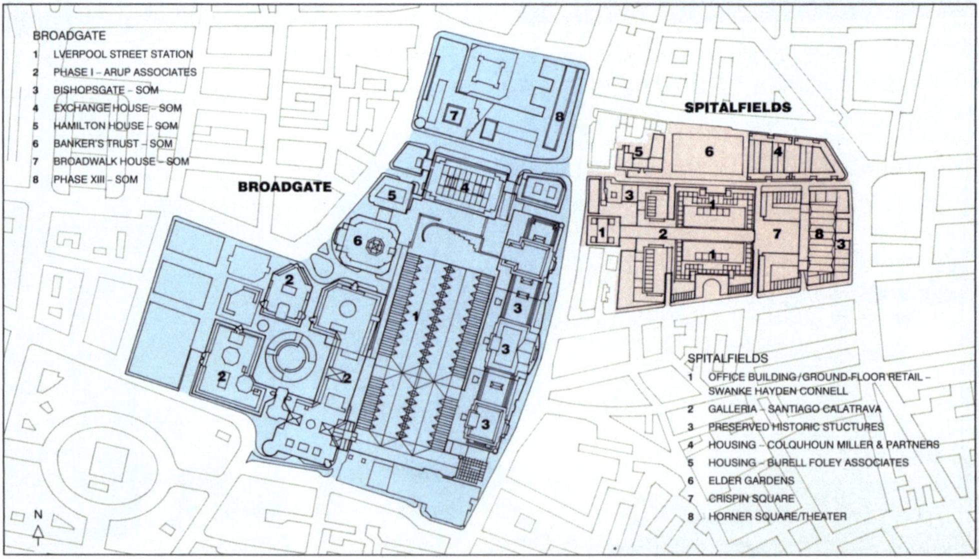

Spitalfields

Tower Hamlets

FORMERLY THE SITE OF A FOOD MARKET in London's East End, Spitalfields will be transformed by Swanke Hayden Connell Architects into a 13-acre mixed-use development when construction begins next year. The project is the result of a design competition held in 1986 that was won by the Spitalfields Development Group, which originally commissioned the British firms of Fitzroy Robinson and Richard MacCormac to conceive an urban design. After a lengthy approvals process, requiring the passage of a Parliamentary bill to relocate the market, the developer decided to replace Fitzroy Robinson with Swanke Hayden Connell (MacCormac subsequently resigned). The 2.5-million-square-foot redevelopment scheme includes office buildings, retail spaces, and housing grouped around traditional squares, as well as a galleria engineered by the Spanish architect Santiago Calatrava, and two apartment blocks designed by the U.K. firms of Burell Foley Associates and Colquhoun Miller & Partners. The 19th-century buildings of Spitalfields Market will be restored and integrated into the urban design. ■

Spitalfields' office buildings and housing flank public squares (top left). Restored historic townhouses and meeting hall enclose a theater within a glazed-over plaza (top right) that leads beneath apartments to another public square (right). Buildings are highest on the portion of the site nearest Bishopsgate (right in model, below) and step down to the east (bottom left).

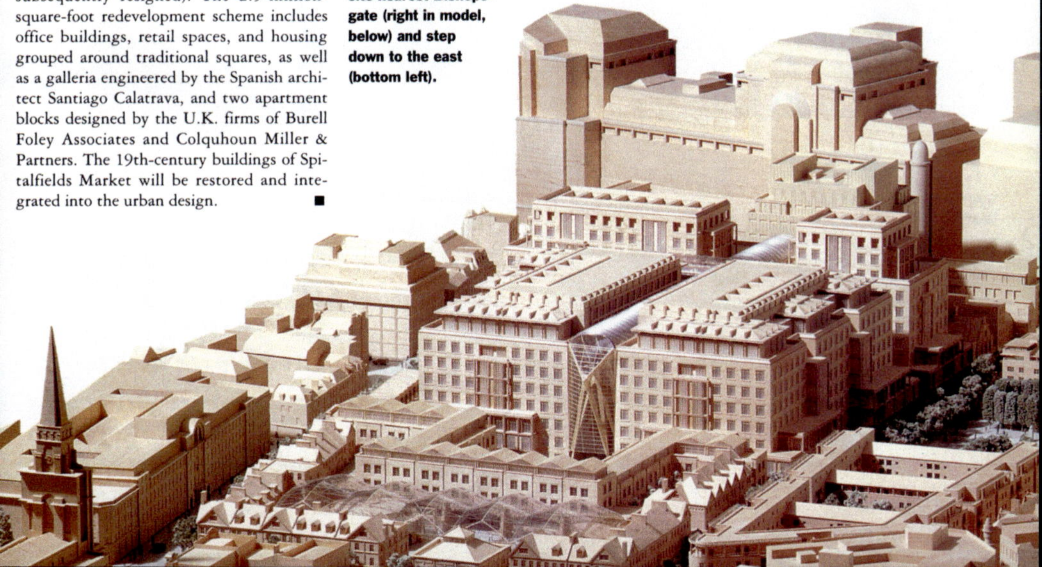

Japanese Imports

BY MILDRED F. SCHMERTZ

AMERICANS ABROAD

STIMULATED BY A BOOMING ECONOMY, THE JAPANESE have been on a global shopping spree over the past few years that has included vast acquisitions of Western artworks. Impressionist paintings have vanished from museum walls only to disappear into private Japanese hands, and America's architectural wonder of the world, Rockefeller Center, is controlled from Tokyo. The Japanese are now steadily acquiring another form of art, the best designs of the world's leading architects.

This trend has been a lifesaver for many American architectural firms unable to find enough work in the troubled U.S. construction market. Today, architectural and design/build firms with offices in Japan have more business than they can handle. Japanese office buildings of the early 1960s, now obsolete in their capacity for large computers, are being torn down and replaced. Other building types offer even more opportunities. The Japanese consumer's demand for better housing, retail, and recreational facilities is finally being met, as the nation recoups the benefits of its postwar dedication to the production of exports.

And there may finally be enough buildable land. Japan is undertaking vast waterfront landfill projects in Tokyo, Yokohama, Osaka, Kobe, and Fukuoka. The Tokyo Bay waterfront has 1,136 acres of landfill areas that will eventually support a population of 120,000 daytime workers. Plans call for 30 to 40 large office buildings and 63,000 new housing units. This single project is twice as large as all of Shinjuku—a rapidly developing Tokyo district of skyscrapers, hotels, department stores, the city's most chaotic railway station, and Kenzo Tange's nearly completed city hall complex. In addition to the waterfront landfills, Japan has its own rust belt of obsolete dockyards, abandoned textile mills, and metal factories.

Selecting U.S. architects is part of Japan's effort to redress the balance of trade, thereby reducing the tensions between the two nations. American architects, however, are only one component of this goodwill gesture. Other beneficiaries are U.S. building trades, product manufacturers, and suppliers. Because of the strong yen, American fee structures are very competitive, and Japanese developers have begun to respond to aggressive marketing on the part of U.S. firms.

R.H. Mori, deputy general manager in the real estate and development department of C. Itoh & Company, one of Japan's largest global trading companies, offers additional reasons for buying American architectural talent. "Japanese developers look toward giving their projects identity. Just as importantly, we believe that bringing in outside talent will improve our buildings. C. Itoh builds its own projects, including middle- to high-income housing, international hotels, and speculative office buildings." The company engages architectural expertise in the planning and design of shopping centers, housing, and new towns.

Most U.S. architects who fly to and from Tokyo work with one or more of Japan's "Big Six" construction firms: Takenaka, Shimizu, Kajima, Taisei, Obayashi-Gumi, and Kumagai-Gumi. The Kajima Corporation is the best known internationally, and very well connected in the world of American architectural leadership. The CEO of Kajima, Dr. Shoichi Kajima, is an alumnus of Harvard University's Department of Architecture and maintains a strong association with his school. He has been known to fly members of Harvard's design faculty to Tokyo to address Kajima's architectural staff—many of whom also studied at Harvard—on a variety of topics.

The Kajima Corporation's architectural design division has nearly 1,000 licensed architects, including some who are also structural and mechanical engineers. Half of the buildings Kajima erects are designed by inhouse architects. The company designs and constructs office buildings, factories, shopping centers, housing, and recreational facilities including golf clubs. Overseas, it is undertaking three hotels in East Berlin and Dresden, and Kajima International has had an office in Los Angeles for 20 years. It is currently building automobile factories in the U.S. for Matsuda and Subaru.

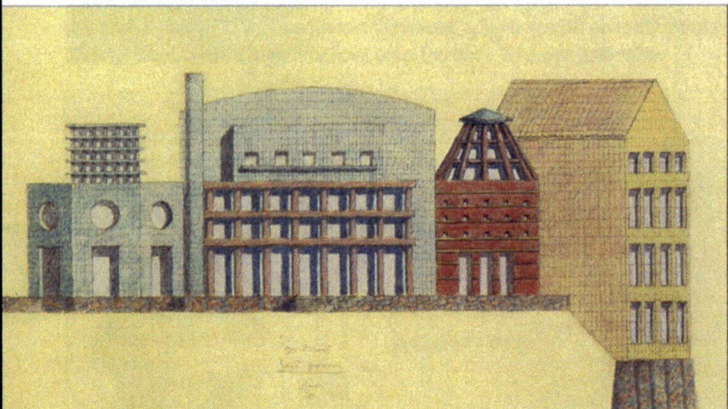

500 Forest
Susono City

Onjuku Town Hall
Onjuku

Among the first American architects to work in Japan, Michael Graves has completed four projects, and 12 others are in various stages of design and construction. They include the five projects shown on these pages: guest houses for a golf club (far left); a new government center for Onjuku (above); the Midousuji Minami, a 10-story office building; (facing page, left), and the nine-story Tajima headquarters (facing page). The 27-story Portside Tower (facing page, center), now under construction, is part of the vast Minato Mirai mixed-use development in Yokohama.

Midousuji Minami Building
Osaka

Tajima Building
Tokyo

Portside Tower
Yokohama

American architects working with Kajima or other Big Six firms find that since they have no counterparts in the U.S., architectural life there is not easily comparable to practice here. The Big Six and their close competitors in the design/build industry secure most of the major work in Japan. Most of the best young Japanese architects go to work for these firms to avoid the long hours and low salaries that prevail in the offices of Japanese star architects, where they must follow the master. It is also difficult to move from a master's atelier to a design/build firm that wants its employees to start upon graduation and stay for a lifetime, as do most Japanese corporations. Japanese star architects tend to come from aristocratic families that are powerfully connected with the upper reaches of government and business. Architects from the middle class lack the connections necessary to get major work, and they are fated to run small practices for even lower fees than similar practitioners earn in the United States.

For all these reasons, the big design/build firms tend to be able to hire all the local talent they need. According to architect Osamu Ebata, a young Harvard graduate on the Kajima staff, "Working in a big office like Kajima isn't all that bad. There is more freedom of expression than to be found in working for a star. Ten years ago, very few clients who wanted good design asked Kajima to design for them. Now they engage our total service from preliminary design studies to construction supervision."

Fortunately for the Big Six and other Japanese client and developer groups, American stars are available as needed. Japanese world-class architects such as Fumihiko Maki, Tadao Ando, and Arata Isozaki, for example, are often too busy working abroad or on major cultural or civic facilities at home to answer the construction firm's call. Not so for the rest of the world's leading designers, including the very best the U.S. has to offer. Getting to know Tokyo better and better are Michael Graves, Robert A.M. Stern, Peter Eisenman, Stanley Tigerman, Steven Holl, Frank Gehry, Michael Rotondi, Cesar Pelli, Kevin Roche, Benjamin and Jane Thompson, Herbert McLaughlin, Emilio Ambasz, Helmut Jahn, Arthur Gensler, Hugh Stubbins, Gyo Obata, Mark Mack, and more. The Architects Collaborative, RTKL, Skidmore, Owings & Merrill, and Kohn Pedersen Fox also have entered the Japanese scene with major planning projects.

Robert A.M. Stern Architects' first finished project in Tokyo is Bancho House, five floors of offices and a two-story penthouse in Ichiban-cho, near the Imperial Gardens and the British embassy (page 76). Stern has also designed a luxury apartment house in Cap d'Akiya, 60 kilometers south of Tokyo in the Hayama district. "I took my cue," he explains, "from the Western architects who have synthesized Classicism and the national traditions of Asia, such as Frank Lloyd Wright in Japan, and Edwin Lutyens and Herbert Baker in India." Now under construction, the building's classical vocabulary is intended to be enriched by traditional Japanese materials and details. Stern's other projects in Japan include two golf clubs on the Izu Peninsula, and other golf-related facilities in Tochigi prefecture.

Most of Stern's work in Japan is in collaboration with Kajima. According to the architect, it is an efficient process. "We do design and preliminary drawings. Working drawings and engineering are done in Tokyo. Fax machines and computers simplify everything. So does the difference in time. When our workday ends, we fax everything to them as their workday starts. In effect, work goes on for 24 hours." Stern reports that most of his firm's time is spent on design rather than on technology, materials, and costs. "We start out proposing how we would like to construct the building. Kajima then budgets for the whole project. We never go over the budget because we are outsiders to the budgeting process. We do not get into the negotiation of each detail. The Japanese do a lot of private caucusing and politely suggest revisions. They lack the American gift of shooting from the hip."

Eisenman Architects has just completed a 10-story, 50,000-square-foot headquarters for the Koizumi Sangyo Company in the Akihabara district in Tokyo (page 81). It

Dai Nippon
Tokyo
RTKL Associates

Located on a narrow street of low-rise buildings, the seven-story headquarters for a large Japanese construction company (above) will feature a massive stone base and a facade detailed with an overscaled, steel structural grid. A curtain wall composed of four types of glazing materials will interlace through the primary grid in a series of angles. Construction is scheduled to begin next year.

Higashi Azabu Building
Tokyo
Morphosis

Morphosis's slender tower on a corner site in Tokyo (two views, above) will house a restaurant, a two-story gallery space on the ground level, and office space on the upper six floors. The slenderness of the tower is exaggerated through shard-like volumes and a sheer wall bisecting the section, which contains the entrance. Construction of the project is expected to begin in 1991.

Tokyo International Forum
Tokyo
Rafael Vinoly Architects

The winning scheme in an international competition, Vinoly's $670-million cultural center (above) will be built on a 6.7-acre parcel in Tokyo's most prestigious business district. The design includes a 5,000-seat theater containing large screens for broadcasting and a curving, glass exhibition hall with an exposed structural-steel frame. The complex is scheduled for completion in 1994.

was built by Taisei Construction with the 10-person firm of Kojiro Kitayama as the local architect. Eisenman is also working on a similarly sized headquarters for Nunotani Corporation in Edogawa, with Zenitaka Construction Company. On the question of technology, materials, and costs, Peter Eisenman agrees with Stern: the construction company sets everything up, and it turns out fine. He adds, "The construction companies take pride in their work and like to do difficult things well. Technologically, the Japanese are more advanced in curtain walls, windows, handrails, elevator cabs, lighting systems, and mechanical equipment. As for costs, tax is a big problem. A value-added tax is taken off the architect's fee." Although Eisenman presently has only two projects in Japan, he hopes for more. "I enjoy working in Japan. They have respect for what you try to do. I was picked because I am a brand-name architect doing quality work. My Japanese clients want high visibility, they want to take design risks. They like my work because it is speculative. I am seen as working in the spirit of the Japanese. Michael Graves, on the other hand, is seen as an exotic."

"Exotic," in this case, means "ahead." Michael Graves discovered and was discovered by the Japanese at least 10 years ago. He has worked on 16 projects there, including two competition entries. Four Graves-designed projects are now complete. A $4.4-million, 14,000-square-foot health club for Shiseido, an international cosmetics company, opened in 1986. In 1988, the architect finished the designs for a collection of carpet tiles and vinyl floor tiles for Tajima, Inc. He completed an exterior mural for the IDC office tower in Yokohama in 1989. Graves, along with Stanley Tigerman, was also among a group of internationally noted architects invited by Arata Isozaki to work on the 193-acre model city project in the landfill Momochi district of Fukuoka City, on the island of Kyushu (page 90).

American architects Steven Holl and Mark Mack also designed apartment buildings for another portion of the Fukuoka project. Holl, who worked five months on his stucture, with Shimizu completing the working drawings and supervision, admits, "The building was a bit over budget. It was to be $7 million but became $8.5 million. We got it down to $7.8 million and Shimizu swallowed the $800,000. This would never have happened in America."

Morphosis is also at work in Japan. The Los Angeles firm was the only one from the U.S. to be selected by Arata Isozaki to join 13 other young firms, each engaged in the act of designing a folly. The program, precisely named "Thirteen Follies," called for the design of that number of objects to be located along the pathways of an exposition held this year on the grounds of the 1970 World's Fair in Osaka.

Morphosis's other client is the industrialist and art collector Fukusabura Maedo, for whom the firm is working on a nine-story office building in Tokyo and a golf club in the Chiba prefecture. On Nipponese golfing, Morphosis principal Michael Rotondi reports: "Japanese do their most serious business on the golf course and in bars. They are now being encouraged by their corporations to do more business on the course for the sake of their health. Because agricultural land is precious and therefore preserved from development, many of the new courses are

Continued on page 154

Harumi Waterfront
Tokyo
Benjamin Thompson & Associates

Due to the scarcity of land in Tokyo, developers looked to the surrounding bay for future growth. On an island reached by bridge from downtown, the Harumi project (above) is one of these enormous landfill developments, and construction is scheduled to begin next year. Master-planned by BTA, the 35-acre complex comprises a multilevel retail street, small hotels, and office space.

Minato Mirai
Yokohama
The Stubbins Associates

Stubbins's 75-story Landmark Tower (left), now under construction and scheduled for completion in 1993 and a 80,000-square-meter rounded tower (below right) are part of the massive "Waterfront for the 21st Century" landfill complex in Yokohama (which also includes Michael Graves's Portside Tower, previous page). The $1 billion complex is intended to serve as the gateway to Yokohama's redeveloped waterfront.

Japanese *from page 75*

being built in the mountains. Conveyor belts move the players up and down the steep terrains from hole to hole. Robots, moving along separate pathways, carry the clubs."

Japanese construction companies do most of the hiring of U.S. architects, and they are clearly attracted to the American vanguard. The work of Graves, Stern, Eisenman, Tigerman, Holl, and Rotondi is as exotic and wonderful to them as that of Maki, Ando, and Isozaki is to us. But *A+U* and *Process Architecture* publish the work of the more conservative American architects as well as that of the design radicals, and globe-trotting Japanese architects travel to the U.S. to learn from both, forming valuable associations with their American counterparts. For example, Takenaka Corporation, one of the Big Six, needed to find its way into the U.S. design community. Last year it formed a partnership with The Architects Collaborative, creating a jointly-owned firm called TAC International. Takenaka chose TAC because Walter Gropius continues to be widely revered in Japan, and because of TAC's broad experience in West Germany, Saudi Arabia, Iraq, Kuwait, Bahrain, and Algeria. The new company's first project is a high-rise office building in downtown Los Angeles, which is being developed by Takenaka and the Mitsubishi Trust Group.

Kevin Roche John Dinkeloo & Associates is working with Shimizu to complete an office tower addition to two adjoining venerable buildings in the heart of Tokyo, opposite the Imperial Palace Garden. Roche finds his Japanese clients to be similar to those he deals with at home. "Putting the cultural differences aside—formality of meetings, entertainment, customs and so on—working in Japan is much the same as working in the U.S. Some Americans get hung up on the cultural differences. They either ignore them completely—a big mistake—or they come super-armed with knowledge of local customs and folkways. Because most of my clients are corporate, I bring a decision-making process and a working relationship with which the Japanese are familiar."

Like all architectural compatriots fortunate enough to be working in Japan, Roche extols the virtues of Japanese construction. "Pride of workmanship induces the Japanese to spend money. Both the construction firm and the owner want to do a good building, and neither will take advantage of the other. Only fools would attempt to operate at this level of trust in the United States."

Cesar Pelli & Associates was engaged to build in Japan because the client group is directly familiar with the firm's work. Pelli is designing the 32-story, 900,000-square-foot headquarters for Nippon Telephone and Telegraph (NTT), the largest corporation in the world, to be constructed in Shinjuku. Yamashita Sekkei, a purely architectural firm of 500 employees, invited Pelli to submit a proposal with them because they admire the American embassy in Tokyo that he designed, as well as the World Financial Center in Battery Park City and the Pacific Center in Los Angeles. In the typical Japanese way, NTT would have had the building designed by its huge staff of 2,000 architects and built by one of the large contracting firms. Because of the importance, however, of opening Japanese construction markets to competition from foreign builders, NTT sought a collaboration between a foreign architect and a Japanese architectural firm. The construction contract will be open for foreign bidding, and American suppliers and contractors will be invited to participate.

Most foreign architects working in Japan are designing single buildings or planning for various mixes of building types on relatively small sites. Not many are yet planning on the scale demanded by Japan's vast waterfront landfill and rust-belt sites. Few Japanese architects are trained in land planning. Most have never dealt with large space problems, because until now they have lacked large spaces to consider. Realizing the need for expertise at megascale design, the Japanese architectural firm Nikken Sekkei invited Benjamin Thompson & Associates to collaborate on two projects with budgets in the billions. Both are large retail and residential projects that incorporate towers designed by Japanese firms, and both are on sites within commuting distance to downtown Tokyo. Ben and Jane Thompson and their team enjoy working with the Japanese, and echo other American architects in describing how BTA is treated by them. In the give and take of work, Jane Thompson finds that, for the Japanese, "personal opinion counts for very little. They caucus, talk it over among themselves, and decide what they like and don't like. They then present their conclusions to us." She finds them sensitive about requesting changes. "They don't make you feel that you have failed. You simply figure out the aspects that don't meet the requirements and fix them."

BTA is finding that work in Japan is challenging. "The Japanese are not interested in preservation or looking back," Jane Thompson adds. "They like novelty and ideas for their own sake. The work designed by the Japanese architects themselves is stimulating and contagious. We are learning from it. We are on a frontier there. It is a lot better than working in London and having your designs vetoed by Prince Charles." ■

Mildred F. Schmertz, FAIA, is a journalist and member of the New York City Landmarks Preservation Commission.

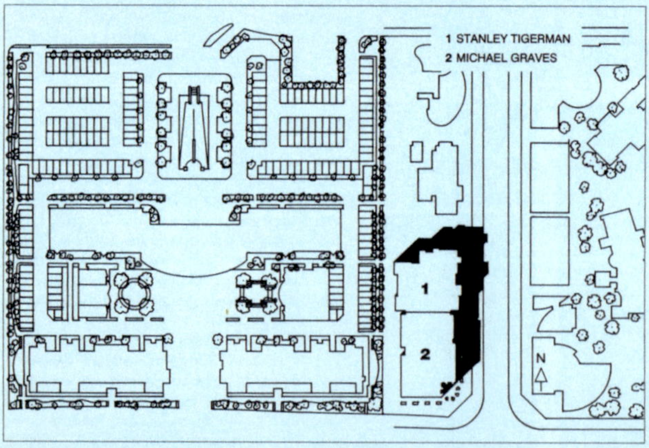

MOMOCHI HOUSING

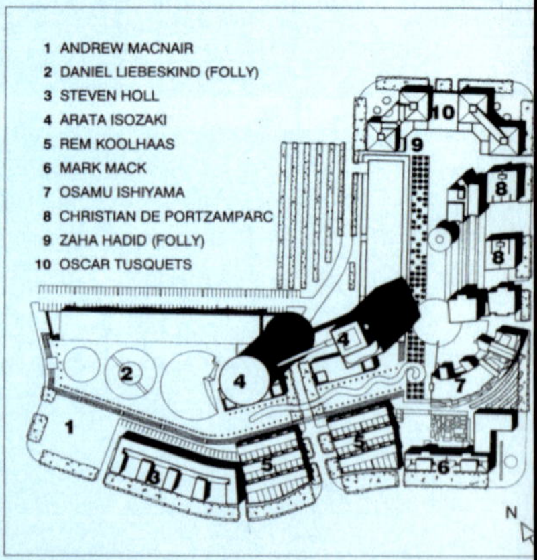

KASHII HOUSING

Model Homes

Tigerman's complex abstraction (facing page, right in photo) and Graves's quieter composition (facing page, left in photo) are the first completed components of Fukuoka's Momochi housing project (facing page, left site plan). The second phase in Kashii (facing page, right site plan) comprises Isozaki's two towers and a cluster of six low-rise structures. For the Kashii corner site, San Francisco architect Mark Mack created two interconnecting buildings (top). The smaller of the two encloses an urban plaza; the larger helps define the commercial street. New York architect Steven Holl's building has a linear spine (above center) with five projecting residential wings (above).

AMERICANS ABROAD

ONE OF THE MAJOR ISsues facing Japanese cities today, says Arata Isozaki, is whether "traditional Japanese housing with its intimate, private gardens can be replaced by urban housing in a form which offers a panorama instead." Isozaki posed the challenge last May at a highly publicized international conference in Fukuoka, a port city located on the island of Kyushu, at Japan's southwestern tip. Sponsored by Fukuoka Jisho, one of the city's major development companies, the conference brought together seven Western architects recommended by Isozaki to address urban issues and develop innovative housing solutions appropriate for Japan's changing cities.

Inspired in part by Berlin's lauded Internationale Bauausstellung (IBA) housing program established in 1979, Fukuoka Jisho, (which had already constructed 2,500 housing units throughout the city) also sought to build model housing projects by individuals in the forefront of architectural thinking. IBA's ambitious program involved approximately 200 architects from around the world for 3,000 new and 5,500 renovated housing units, on redeveloped land destroyed by war, insensitive urban renewal, and neglect. However in Fukuoka, the developers were charged with extending a cohesive urban fabric on two vast sites of reclaimed land along the waterfront, with the model housing designed by international "name" architects comprising only a small component of the two major developments.

The first completed demonstration housing projects in Fukuoka are mixed-use apartment buildings located adjacent to one another. Designed by Michael Graves and Stanley Tigerman, and built as components of a model city for the 1989 Asia-Pacific Exposition, the Nexus condominiums now serve as the gateway to the 193-acre Momochi development on the west bank of Hakata Harbor.

Kashii is a second waterfront urban development project equal in scope to Momochi, and likewise includes exhibition housing. On a 12-acre site, under the coordination of Arata Isozaki, 10 young architects, including Mark Mack, Steven Holl, Rem Koolhaas, Oscar Tusquets, Christian de Portzamparc, and Osamu Ishiyama, have clustered low structures around two towers by Isozaki. The first buildings are scheduled for completion next year. ■

—LYNN NESMITH

CRITICISM

That's Entertainment

The Walt Disney Company enlisted a roster of architectural luminaries—Michael Graves, Frank Gehry, Antoine Grumbach, Antoine Predock, and Robert Stern—to build hotels and an entertainment/shopping complex for its European debut at Marne-la-Vallée, a suburb of Paris. A multibillion-dollar venture, Euro Disneyland will be the largest theme park in Europe. Is Disney CEO Michael Eisner the current client of choice and will Disneytopia be the dystopia of the 1990s?
By Suzanne Stephens.

Michael Eisner is the client architects seem to fantasize about these days. Since the chairman and CEO of Walt Disney Company started enlisting high-profile architects such as Michael Graves, Robert A. M. Stern, Frank Gehry, Antoine Predock, Arata Isozaki, Charles Gwathmey, and Robert Siegel to design for Walt Disney World in Orlando or Euro Disneyland in Marne-la-Vallée, France, he has quickly become today's answer to the "enlightened developer."

Instead of granite-clad spec office buildings commissioned from Gerald Hines, we now hear about the colorfully stuccoed "entertainment architecture" of Disney's hotels and restaurants. Disney's architecture may not be quite as visible (or expensive) as Hines's urban high-rises, but it is seen by a *really* large audience—over 22 million people a year visit Walt Disney World in Orlando, according to its accounts. If one hears that the Disney company is tight-fisted, and Eisner's henchmen anxious to chisel away at the designs, the same holds true for developers. And Disney's architects are encouraged to get a little wilder and have more fun with the program. All they have to do is come up with a compelling and accessible "theme." It sounds so free, even creative. Or is it?

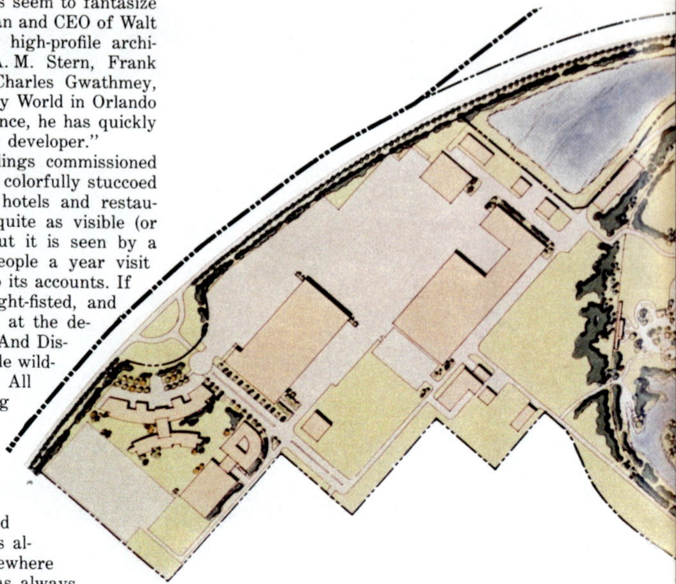

There are certain considerations with which the architects working for Disney must grapple. Disney's utopian environments have always been about fun and fantasy, where life is clean, the good guys always win, and the intellectual age is somewhere under 11. For its own part architecture has always been cast in a more problematic role. Its mission was to upgrade reality in a grittier, less morally clear-cut context. The pursuit of fantasy can easily lead to the frivolous and the kitschy—the nemesis of "good" architecture.

To be sure, these high-profile architects are not being solicited to create Disney's aggressively picturesque parks, such as the Magic Kingdom or Disney-MGM Studios. Main Street and Hollywood are still the province of the Imagineers, Disney's in-house designers. But whereas the Imagineers also used to "theme up" the surrounding Disney-operated hotels and entertainment complexes (in association with architectural firms of a less-defined design image), now Disney is hiring name-brand architects to come up with different resort treatments.

Of all the building types in which to try out fantasy settings, the resort hotel, where people go to get away from it all, seems the most appropriate. And the architect-designed hotels being built at Euro Disneyland or in Disney World at Orlando [RECORD, March 1988, page 59], are meant to be more abstract than the condensed and idealized Disneytopia of the Magic Kingdom.

But the architect must still tell a story simple enough for everyone to get, yet one no one will easily tire of. And in designing these imagined oases, the architect must create a setting that holds up under extended scrutiny. With film and stage sets, the audience may be more willing to pretend that an aluminum "plank" wall is actually wood, that pressed fiberboard is clapboard. But hotels aren't meant to be experienced for only two hours and at a comfortable distance. Thus craftsmanship and use of materials are still very much a part of the overall effect. Just how closely Disney's self-stated program of entertainment architecture can meet the expectations established by less-entertaining architecture will depend on how Disney and its designer-collection architects resolve these

Suzanne Stephens writes on architecture and design for Architectural Digest *and* The New York Times. *She is editor of* Oculus, *the newsletter of the New York City Chapter of the American Institute of Architects.*

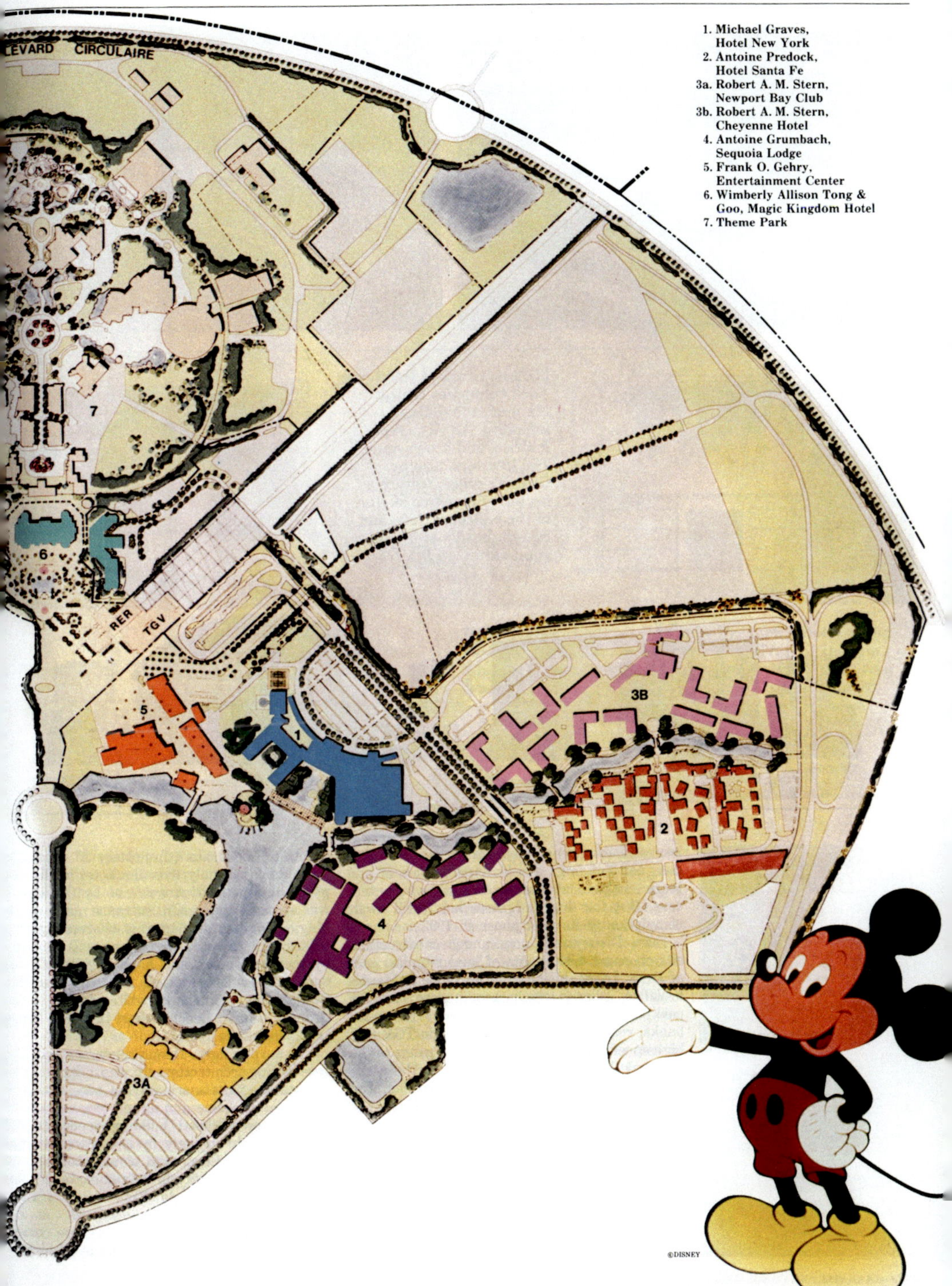

1. Michael Graves, Hotel New York
2. Antoine Predock, Hotel Santa Fe
3a. Robert A. M. Stern, Newport Bay Club
3b. Robert A. M. Stern, Cheyenne Hotel
4. Antoine Grumbach, Sequoia Lodge
5. Frank O. Gehry, Entertainment Center
6. Wimberly Allison Tong & Goo, Magic Kingdom Hotel
7. Theme Park

©DISNEY

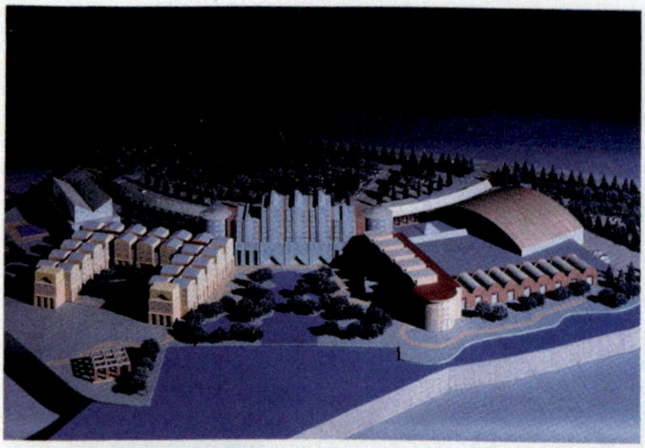

BALLROOM

Michael Graves's Hotel New York comprises typical Manhattan buildings, including the skyscraper, midrise, and brownstone. The interiors, also by Graves's office, feature a backlit silhouetted skyline in the ballroom (left) and custom headboards in the guest suites (right).

SECTION

******HOTEL NEW YORK**

Design architect: *Michael Graves, Architect—Patrick Burke, senior associate*
Production Architect: *McCary-Menu (SCAU)*
Interior Designers: *Michael Graves, Architect; Interart (production)*
Engineers: *Sechaud et Bossuyt & Cie (structural and mechanical)*
Landscape Architect: *EDAW, Inc.,*
Lighting Consultant: *Fisher-Marantz (exterior); The Lighting Design Partnership (interior)*
Construction Manager: *Cotéba*
Site Size: *21 acres*
Building Size: *480,000 sq ft (576 rooms), convention facilities, two restaurants, four shops*
Structure: *Poured-in-place concrete load-bearing walls, floor slabs*
Major Materials: *Colored metal roofing, stucco, brick and stone*
Illumination: *Fiber-optic grid of stars in lobby; ballroom has silhouetted skyline with "windows" of light*
Security: *Sprinklers, smoke detectors (both California and French codes being followed)*

issues. Euro Disneyland, where the architect-designed buildings are planned as part of one large enclave, should provide a superb test case. But the final judgment must still await completion of its first phase in 1992.

Euro Disneyland, now under construction, sits on some 4,800 acres of land 20 miles east of Paris. In establishing its presence in Marne-la-Vallée, Disney wisely arranged to have its park, heavily financed by several European banks, reached by a new stop on the TGV (the high-speed train), which connects France to the Channel Tunnel, Brussels, and northeastern Europe, and the long-distance metro line. The road to the international airport already goes right by the complex.

The work of the high-design architects shouldn't be too difficult to find, since the five hotels and entertainment center are arranged around the mandatory man-made lake situated by the entrance to the Magic Kingdom. While the hotels vary from budget accommodations (or what the French designate as a two-star hotel) to moderate (three-star) to "upsca[le] (four-star), the only five-star hotel in the fi[rst] phase of construction won't be by the lake[. It] will straddle the main entrance gate to [the] Magic Kingdom. In fact, this 450-room piec[e of] teased and turreted Victoriana was design[ed] by the Imagineers and hotel architects W[im]berly Allison Tong & Goo, the team that g[ave] Orlando the gleamingly white, floridly gr[and] Grand Floridian Beach Resort [RECORD, Feb[ru]ary 1990, pages 118-121].

Not surprisingly, Disney likes a strong [im]age for its architecture. It was decided ea[rly] on that the hotels around the lake would [be] American in theme and allude to geographi[c] locations or regional building types. It w[as] deemed highly unlikely by the powers-that [be] at Disney that Europeans would choose to [go] to Disneyland to stay in a faux-chateau w[hen] the real thing was in France's own Lo[ire] Valley.

Choosing the architects was a more com[pli]cated tale. Had it been a movie, it could ha[ve]

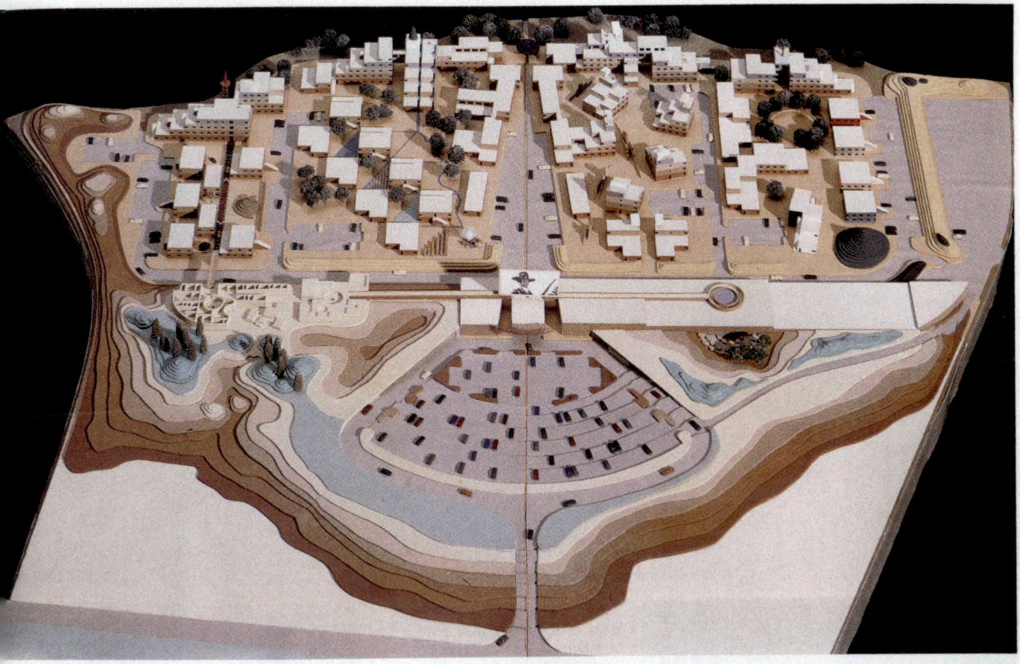

The terraced clusters of Antoine Predock's Hotel Santa Fe are arranged on both sides of his "Trail of Infinite Space." A drive-in movie screen (below left) stands as a "vanishing icon of the West," according to the architect.

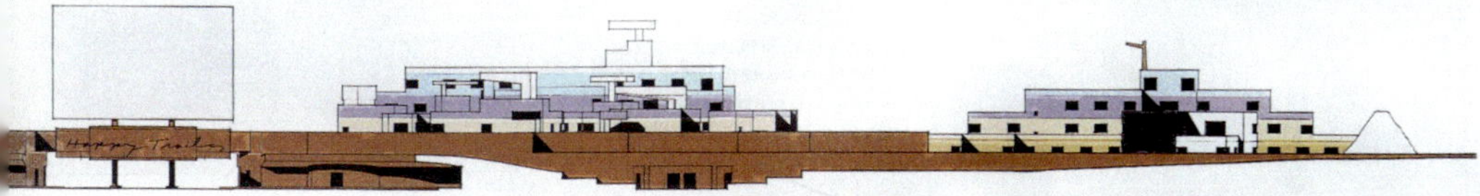

n called "Cinderfella." And a lot of architects nd the shoe didn't always fit. Graves, Stern, Gehry had been involved in early master-nning charrettes with Stanley Tigerman and turi, Rauch and Scott Brown (now VSB). But he end, Tigerman and VSB were put on hold, h VSB designing a hotel for Euro Disney-d's second phase. Predock was then brought and Antoine Grumbach hired as the sole nch architect working on the lake.

es Disnées, as they are (sometimes) affec-nately called—Eisner, Robert Fitzpatrick, irman of Euro Disneyland, Peter Rummell Wing Chao, president and senior vice-presi-t for master planning, architecture, and de-n, respectively, at Disney Development—l also looked over a group of high-profile ropean architects that included Rem Kool-s, Hans Hollein, Aldo Rossi, Jean Nouvel, ristian de Portzamparc, and Bernard humi. All these architects were given sites und the lake and then competed for the com-ssions with an assortment of schemes. In the end, however, the Europeans seemed too outré for Disney. (Rossi's New Orleans Hotel was selected, but he backed out, some say, because of too many threatened changes to his design.) Grumbach, who had originally designed a park at the lake's edge, came up with an idea for a hotel sitting among tall trees, like the mountain lodges he saw on holidays to the American West following his teaching stints on the East Coast. A theme was born and it became the Sequoia Lodge.

Occupying the central position on the lake is the only four-star hotel, the Hotel New York, designed by return Disney architect Michael Graves. Graves has created a "village" of discrete but attached units, each of which refers to different places or types of architecture in Manhattan. A midtown skyscraper motif dominates the eight-story central entrance block; one wing is meant to conjure up brownstones, another wing Gramercy Park. There is even a Rockefeller Center skating rink and a Rainbow Room-like restaurant

****HOTEL SANTA FE:**
Design Architect: *Antoine Predock, Architect—Jon Anderson, project architect*
Production Architect: *Fernier & Associates*
Interior Designers: *Wilson & Associates; Interart (production)*
Engineers: *BET Vilanova (structural); Gerba 7 (mechanical)*
Landscape Architect: *EDAW, Inc.*
Construction Manager: *Cotéba*
Lighting Consultant: *Fisher-Marantz*
Site Size: *29 acres*
Building Size: *1,000 rooms, one restaurant, 575 parking slots*
Structure: *Poured-in-place concrete, including roof and floor spans*
Major Materials: *Integrally painted stucco over walls*
Illumination: *Industrial galvanized "new" west reflectors, typical American street lights*

Dormers, striped awnings, and shingled gable roofs are some of the elements Robert Stern incorporated in his Newport Bay Club to recall turn-of-the-century estates along the East Coast of the United States. The interiors (right), designed by the Atlanta-based firm of Design Continuum, further elaborate the three-star hotel's nautical theme.

*****NEWPORT BAY CLUB**
DESIGN ARCHITECT: *Robert A. M. Stern, Architects—Paul Whelan, project architect*
PRODUCTION ARCHITECT: *Macary-Menu (SCAU)*
INTERIOR DESIGNERS: *Design Continuum; Pascal Desproz (production)*
ENGINEERS: *BET HAC (structural and mechanical)*
LANDSCAPE ARCHITECT: *EDAW, Inc.*
LIGHTING CONSULTANT: *Fisher-Marantz*
CONSTRUCTION MANAGER: *Cotéba*
SITE SIZE: *25 acres*
BUILDING SIZE: *581,250 sq ft (1,101 rooms), two restaurants, three shops, meeting facilities*
STRUCTURE: *Concrete frame*
MAJOR MATERIALS: *Pressed fiber-board for siding; composite shingle roof*
ILLUMINATION: *Lighting along portico colonnade, custom rotating lighting in lighthouse tower*

While each section has a different character and scale, the look is still very much more Graves's than it is New York's. This absence of literal mimicry holds true for the architecture inside as well. However, as if to make up for this more abstract narrative, Graves has deployed an artillery of signs and symbols of New York—its iconography—throughout the hotel. Armoires and beds in the guestrooms are decorated with big-apple patterns, the desk lamp is in the form of a skyscraper, and baseball and apple logos are embedded in the lobby floor. The playful motifs call attention to the make-believe aspect of this world, and could provide the right ironically corny touches that would appeal to European, as well as American, sensibilities. The New Yorkerish sophistication some visitors may expect, however, could well be lacking in the final product. But then again if you go to Disneyland expecting the Carlyle Hotel, you are a little *fou*.

In the Hotel Santa Fe, Antoine Predock, of Albuquerque, has bent over backwards to make his two-star (budget) accommodations a high poeticized, abstracted vision of the Southwe and Santa Fe, in particular. In the non-Disne parts of the U. S., a hotel where guests drive their rooms is usually called a motel, but Marne-la-Vallée it's different. "The great thi about a two-star hotel," says Predock, "is th it is not burdened by room service. The dece tralization made possible by the dispersal buildings allowed us to create an imagined se ting analogous to the landscape of the Sout west." The guest rooms are separated into va ous terraced clusters that resemble t configuration of mesas and buttes. Much of t landscaping and the earth-and-sky color schen of the stuccoed buildings refer to the Sout west's colors.

While Predock is not trying to be site specit to France in his imagery, he points out certa characteristics that address the problem of t hotel's actual location in a cold, often rai climate. The rooms with generous windows a adjoining courtyards face south; at the rear

Robert Stern's two-star Cheyenne Hotel is based on more modest American vernacular imagery than the lavish Newport Bay Club (opposite). Western films were the source of inspiration for this complex of small-scale lodgings—as is apparent in the design of facades (right), which will be constructed of pressed fiberboard, and the rustic interior (left).

ıe complex, the buildings form a wall ("like a :ountain range") to buffer the hotel against ıe wind.

The Commons building where guests check in actually two structures, connected by a cano-y on which a drive-in movie screen ("a vanish-g icon of the West," explains Predock) sits. In ıis manner two lobbies are created, one for ›ur groups, the other for individual guests, 'hich also connects to the restaurant and bar. redock calls the entry drive that bisects the ommons the "Trail of Infinite Space." This ıth, marked by a yellow stripe, continues be-ond the building, where it gradually is nar-›wed by the guest wings placed on an angle to 'eate a forced perspective.

Other trails abound to evoke the history and ıyths of the far-off place, but they are more onceptual. With names such as the "Trail of rtifacts," "Trail of Legends," "Trail of Wa-r," and "Trail of Monuments," these "trails" :e formulated in the mind, pieced together by ertain buildings and artifacts appearing and reappearing throughout the complex. "Here the site of the imagination expands into a cinematographic realm. This is a healthy form of escapism," Predock maintains.

Guests will probably notice that the interiors of the Santa Fe refer more explicitly to the decorative arts of the Southwest. Designed by Wilson & Associates, they include "banco" seating in the lobby, plus Navajo blanket patterned bedcovers, lamp bases adorned with cactus and galloping horse motifs, and distressed wood furniture. As James Flick of Wilson & Associates puts it, "We're trying to bridge the gap between Predock's metaphoric ideas and Disney's desire to be figurative." If Predock is thinking of the films of director Wim Wenders, Disney seems to be thinking of Clint Eastwood. How the two merge remains to be seen.

Robert Stern's interpretation of themes is much simpler and more in the tradition of an old-time Hollywood movie—sets in which the guests/actors should have no trouble figuring out their assigned roles. His Newport Bay

****CHEYENNE HOTEL**
Design Architect: *Robert A. M. Stern Architect—Alex Lamis, project architect*
Production Architect: *Viguier Jodry and Associates*
Interior Designers: *Wilson & Associates; Interart (production)*
Engineers: *Gerba 7 (structural and mechanical)*
Landscape Consultant: *EDAW, Inc.*
Construction Manager: *Cotéba*
Site Size: *29 acres*
Building Size: *351,000 sq ft (1,000 rooms), one restaurant, 900 sq ft of retail space*
Structure: *Concrete frame*
Major Materials: *Pressed fiberboard cladding*
Illumination: *Klieg lights*
Security: *Sprinkler, smoke alarm*

The design of the Sequoia Lodge by Paris-based Antoine Grumbach was inspired by such American vacation spots as Yellowstone National Park.

*****SEQUOIA LODGE**
DESIGN ARCHITECT: *Antoine Grumbach—Françoise Sogno, project architect*
PRODUCTION ARCHITECT/ENGINEER: *Alexandre et Sandoz*
INTERIOR DESIGNERS: *Hirsch/Bedner Associates; Wilson & Associates*
LANDSCAPE ARCHITECT: *EDAW, Inc.*
LIGHTING CONSULTANT: *Fisher-Marantz*
CONSTRUCTION MANAGER: *Cotéba*
SITE SIZE: *25 acres*
BUILDING SIZE: *513,1019 sq ft (1,011 rooms), two restaurants*
STRUCTURE: *Concrete columns and walls; timber roof framing*
MAJOR MATERIALS: *Stone base, wood, green aluminum roofing*
ILLUMINATION: *Exterior lighting on facades and under eaves*
SECURITY: *Smoke alarm, sprinklers*

Club, like the Disney Yacht Club and Beach Club currently under construction in Orlando, is conceived in the tradition of the rambling shingled and gabled summer retreats built at the turn of the century. You expect to see Ronald Coleman, spiffed up in a navy blazer and white slacks, strolling through the lobby.

Since this three-star inn charges moderate prices, however, one has to wonder if enough money will be put into the set to sustain the grand illusion. Moreover, because the hotel faces north, the architects and interior designers decided to make the interior finishes and furnishings light, airy, and summery. Wood, painted and stained in pale colors, along with large windows, are intended to make one think there is more direct sunlight than is actually possible. Stern is optimistic about the psychological effect, but it may be time to invest in some artificial "sun" lighting.

The Cheyenne Hotel suggests a back-lot version of a cowboy town, as portrayed in every shoot-'em-up film made in the last 60 years. With this two-star hotel, Stern designed the decentralized blocks of rooms as if they were scenic backdrops for various main streets in the wild and woolly west. The ironic metafantasy may be made more tongue-in-cheek by the kleig lighting to be used at night.

The movie-set imagery continues inside in a two-story lobby with massive wood trusses plus a two-story restaurant housed in a barn-like structure. A "scramble" (a.k.a. food court) contains more stagesetlike structures that evoke a farmhouse, stable, etc. The home-on-the-range look reaches a fevered pitch in the guest rooms, which actually seem more directly inspired by 1950s Western roadside motels than, say, John Wayne's celluloid bedroom. Covered-wagon friezes, gun and saddle motifs on headboards, cowboy-boot lampshades, and bunk beds faithfully serve up a thick pan-fried slice of kitsch (but authentic kitsch) Americana.

The Sequoia Lodge's theme is clearly more grownup. It is meant to evoke a Western retreat that might exist at Yellowstone National

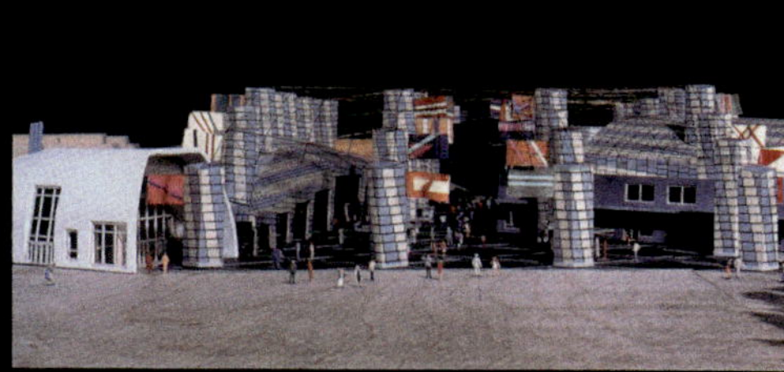

Frank Gehry's entertainment and shopping complex will include the Key West, Chicago, and California restaurants, and Rodeo, a combined dinner theater, disco, and saloon. Outdoor lighting will be provided by a steel grid of fixtures perched atop 40-foot-high columns, which will be wrapped in brightly colored metal.

. SCOTT SMITH PHOTOS

ark. In describing sources of inspiration, its rchitect, Antoine Grumbach, of Paris, talks of ie houses of Frank Lloyd Wright and Greene nd Greene. Actually, the statically constrained, lassical organization of the rectilinear wood nd stone forms suggests rather a large undorned Swiss chalet.

The rooms, also designed by Wilson & Assoates (incorporating suggestions from Grumach), use Stickleyish Arts and Crafts-style furishings to create the proper mood. "This is not ni-chi," says Grumbach of the moderate-price otel. "Nor is it a decorated barracks."

Of all the contributions to Disney's program f entertainment architecture, Frank Gehry's ntertainment Center is clearly the least conentional. Even if an interiors firm is actually esigning the dinner theater where one watches rodeo while eating barbecued ribs, Gehry's ersonal stamp is all over the outside. The unky geometric forms are wrapped in a colorıl metal skin. Forty columns, 65 feet high, ıpport a grid of reflectors bouncing light from fixtures concealed in the columns. The whole ensemble should provide a highly reverberant trill from the architect the French have dubbed "la diva Californienne."

But the Gehry commission did not come without suspense. According to unofficial reports, when Disney asked Gehry to design the complex, it also asked another firm to come up with a second scheme in case Gehry's was too abstract. Fortunately Gehry's submission appealed to Eisner and "won" the secret contest. "Fifty Disnoids say 'no,'" says one architect, about the approval process, "And then Eisner says 'yes.'" Eisner is surrounded by Disney Development staff members who willingly play the heavies (Wing Chao, 18 years with Disney, also has a Master of Architecture in Urban Design and Planning from Harvard's Graduate School of Design). But the architects quickly discover that in addition to the many levels of "clients" overseeing their work, they have many layers of consultants—even more than

Continued on page 121

ENTERTAINMENT CENTER

Design Architect: *Frank O. Gehry and Associates—Robert Hale and Bruce Simons, project architects*
Production Architect: *Saubot et Jullien*
Interior Designers: *Morris Nathanson Design (restaurants); Brand and Allen (retail)*
Engineers: *INEX Ingenierie (mechanical); O.T.E. Ingenierie (structural)*
Landscape Architect: *Frank O. Gehry and Associates*
Construction Manager: *Bovis Copra*
Site Size: *12.4 acres*
Building Size: *230,000 sq ft; five restaurants and retail space*
Structure: *Poured-in-place walls and floor slabs, with timber roof trusses; 40 steel columns on concrete pedestals; steel-framed lighting grid*
Major Materials: *Metal skin on walls, roof, columns; plaster over concrete or masonry on "out" buildings*
Illumination: *Grid of cables and reflectors*
Security: *Fire lanes for access*

Classified Advertising

To Advertise Call
212-512-2422
FAX 212-512-6800

POSITIONS VACANT

Department Chair Environmental Design

PARSONS SCHOOL OF DESIGN

Parsons School of Design, a division of New School for Social Research, invites applications and nominations for Chair of the Environmental Design Department.

The Department offers the BFA degree in Architecture and Interior Design, the MA in Architecture and Design Criticism, and the Master of Architecture degree (a new program to be inaugurated in 1990-91). Candidates should have records of leadership and achievement in relevant professional and academic fields. Starting date, after January 1, 1991. Salary negotiable. Nominations and applications should be sent by September 10, 1990 to: **DEAN CHARLES S. OLTON, PARSONS SCHOOL OF DESIGN, 66 FIFTH AVENUE, NEW YORK, N.Y. 10011.** Affirmative Action/Equal Opportunity Employer.

Architects — $25,000-95,000. The Shaddox/Csutora Group Executive Architectural Recruiters. Key positions nationwide at all levels with Regional & National firms. Experience in research/development, health care, commercial, criminal justice, educational, institutional, industrial and sports complexes. Confidential. No fee. Include salary requirements. The Shaddox/Csutora Group. Send resume to P.O. Box 460010, Denver, CO 80046. (303) 690-3440.

TO ANSWER BOX NUMBERED ADS:

Address separate envelopes (smaller than 11" x 5") for each reply to:

Key number from ad
Architectural Record
Post Office Box 900
NY NY 10108

MANUFACTURERS REPS

Protected territories! Introduce unique, imported roofing product to Architects and Specifiers. Seeking Rep organizations currently interfacing with architectural audience. Knowledge of roofing market or representation of non-conflicting lines helpful.

Contact: Dave Connor
(508) 852-4888

Michael Latas & Associates, Executive Search and Professional Recruiting Consultants, Specialists in the architectural and engineering fields. Operating nationally. Inquiries held in the strictest of confidence. 1311 Lindbergh Plaza Center, St. Louis, Missouri 63132; (314) 993-6500.

Assistant University Architects. Indiana University — University Architect's Office Two Positions. Assist the Associate University Architect's Office in the design renovation, and construction of facilities on all Indiana University campuses. Serve as liaison to users, contractors, and architects. Qualifications: Bachelor's degree in Architecture; Licensed by the State of Indiana; five years experience in the design and construction large academic/institutional buildings is desirable. Please send resume to Mr. Richard Macek, Indiana University, Personnel Division, Poplars 121, 400 E. 7th St., Bloomington, IN 47405.

Medical Renovation Architect. Indiana University — University Architects Office at the Indianapolis, Indiana campus. Provide Architectural services for the renovation of interior remodeling of minor University Medical Center Facilities projects. Work with the space users to determine and provide for their facilities requirements; prepare project budgets, specifications, blueprints, and documents necessary to bid and construct projects. Qualifications: Bachelor's degree in Architecture; Licensed by the State of Indiana; five years experience in the design and construction of medical facilities remodeling is desirable. Please send resume to Ms. Marcia Combs, Indiana University — Purdue University, Department of Human Resources, Union Building Room 358, 620 Union Drive, Indianapolis, IN 46202-5168.

Medical Architectural Design Assistant. Indiana University — University Architects Office at the Indianapolis, Indiana campus. Assist the Medical Renovation Architect by conceiving designs, preparing computer aided design (CAD) drawings, specifications, and project cost estimates for the renovation and remodeling of University Medical Facilities. Qualifications: Associate Degree in Architectural Drafting preferred, with proficiency in CAD. Two-three (2-3) years drafting experience with architectural firm preferred. Please send resume to Ms. Marcia Combs, Indiana University — Purdue University, Department of Human Resources, Union Building Room 358, 620 Union Drive, Indianapolis, IN 46202-5168.

Museum of Contemporary Art. Reque nominations of architects to design a n 100,000-125,000 square foot museum of c temporary art and sculpture garden on a pri two acre Chicago site between Michigan Ave and Lake Michigan. Architects may s nominate or be nominated by another party. nominees must have a bachelor's degree in Arc tecture and a minimum of five years professio experience in addition to having designed a completed at least one major public/commerc facility. Submit cover letter, brief resume or b graphy, short description of current firm affi tion, list of major projects designed and compl ed, and maximum of 10 slides showing one more projects, to Architect Nominations, M seum of Contemporary Art, 237 East Onta Street, Chicago, IL 60611. All nominations m be received by Monday, August 20, 1990.

POSITIONS WANTED

Denver Architect seeks emp. in com-i based firm. NCARB cert. Will relocate. Reply PW-6346, Architectural Record.

LEGAL SERVICES

HARTER, SECREST & EMERY
ATTORNEYS AT LAW

PROVIDING
LEGAL SERVICES to
the DESIGN PROFESSIONS
Mergers & Acquisitions

Contract/Specification Review
Environment
Litigation
Personnel
Real Estate

JAMES C. MOORE, Esq.
700 Midtown Tower
Rochester, New York 14604
716/232-6500
Albany, NY **Naples, FL**

SPECIAL SERVICES

COMPLETE PREPARATION FOR THE REGISTRATION EXAMS

Architectural License Seminars (213) 208-7112
Box 64188 Los Angeles California 90064

BOOKS FOR SALE

Old and rare books. Architecture a Decorative Arts. Send for free illustrated cata to: James Beattie, 105 North Wayne Ave., De R, Wayne, PA 19087 or call 1-800-441-6705.

Continued from page 79
is typical in the U. S.—working on their design. Because of contractual arrangements, the name architects generally carry the design through schematics and 50 percent of design development. After that, local French architects complete the latter phase and execute working drawings, although the design architects are allowed to review the documents. Everyone expects some changes to be made in the field, and supposedly the design architects will be consulted. Evidently, Gehry's arrangement is different, for it permits him closer supervision throughout construction.

With the parceling out of responsibilities over design and construction, architecture and interiors, it is understandable that the original concepts could lose their integrity on the way to realization. In many ways the schemes are like screenplays, and, not surprisingly, a movie-making approach permeates much of Disney's undertakings. Some of the architects have observed they feel as if they are screenwriters whose "treatments" are meant to be tampered with by the directors, producers, and anybody else who comes into the picture. "It's as if Disney commissioned five different screenplays and mushed them together to satisfy market tastes," notes one. One wonders if this process will create architecture or simply three-dimensional filmic attractions.

Certainly many treacherous pitfalls await the idealistic architect who embarks on a project for Disney, the most obvious being the theming itself. To be sure, each of the architects has approached this aspect of their commission with a distinct method, including the use of iconography, irony, narrative, and dream sequences. But "high concept" isn't everything.

Designing high-use low-maintenance accommodations on relatively modest budgets (which the *Disnées* have admitted are much tighter than the Imagineer's big money-making theme-park attractions) could diminish the effect. The architects also don't have the benefit of Florida's or California's dazzling sunshine and warm weather to sidetrack visitors' attention from a low-rent look.

If carried too far, the chosen themes can end up as cute and cloying, and there is nothing worse than a hollow theme that doesn't stop reverberating. What will be created at Euro Disneyland is not just a three-dimensional cinematic attraction, but, supposedly, architecture. Or something that simulates it, however fleetingly, however entertainingly. □

EXPORTING

NEW YORK ARCHITECTS ABROAD

New York architects have been exporting their expertise for decades, but in recent years, construction booms in Asia, relaxed trade barriers, and the fall of Communism in Eastern Europe have brought a new surge of work and with it the realization that there is much to learn from working around the world.

Cultural Exchange

"If one isn't culturally attuned to the way of life and the languages wherever one works, then one is at a disadvantage. It turns out that we can learn a lot from the way architecture is practiced in Russia," said **Ted Liebman** of the Liebman Melting Partnership, who is renovating and adding onto the Ducate Place office complex and commercial center in Moscow. "Russian architects initiate plans of neighborhood districts like a mini city planning office. They understand how buildings fit in the open space, how buildings relate to each other, and what facilities are needed. All of the issues about context that were discussed only recently in NYC have been done naturally in Moscow. Everything involves planning; that is why the cities look so uniform. We are hired to help the Russian architect understand the role of the developer-owner, which they don't really have."

Luca Vignelli

"Working in a foreign country really requires a certain type of person who is adaptable to other cultures," said **William Louie** of Kohn Pedersen Fox "The necessary presentation style varies from country to country. You have to be tolerant, to try to understand their point of view. You are always an outsider to them."

Luca Vignelli

"The frustrating thing about working in foreign countries is that architects like spontaneous dialogue," his partner **William Pedersen** added. "We can't have a spontaneous dialogue when it is filtered through a translator."

Abigail Scheuer

"One of the most useful things learned in these different countries," **Steven Holl** said, "is that there is a kind of balance and tension that is continuous in the process of architecture, but if you keep your hope during this process, often a bitter struggle turns into a cooperative action full of joy. So what starts out to look like it won't work, when it does, everyone is even more pleased."

Free (or Freer) Reign

New York architects are able to experiment more freely in other countries, but they face philosophical dilemmas about overdevelopment and how to include cultural traditions.

Pach Brothers, NY

"In Kowloon, Hong Kong, for our project, Plaza Hollywood," said **Yann Leroy** of Brennan Beer Gorman, "we have been able to expand our design vocabulary. In New York latel the taste is more conservative because we are finally concer trating on the conservation c historic archi tecture."

Pach Brothers, NY

Davi Beer added, "There is a reversal of what happened in the 1970s, when we worked in Saudi Arabia and Egypt, where the was a pride and an interest i their own culture, so we usec the local vernacular element But now, where we are working in Kuala Lumpur, they have torn down the tradition Colonial buildings because i wasn't their culture to begin with. What has been fun is that we have had to do much stronger contemporary build ings than our firm has done since the 1970s. But there ar places that need preservatio attention, such as Surabaya,

BY NINA RAPPAPORT

ARCHITECTURE

Indonesia, which has over 20 square blocks of fantastic Dutch Colonial architecture."

"The positive part for our firm in Shanghai," said **Bruce Fowle** of Fox & Fowle, "has been that they are interested in new and exciting architecture. Our clients don't know what they want until you present them something, so you have to define that for yourself. The construction managers aren't there to tell the owners to cut costs. They are not concerned with a relationship between the cost per square foot and rental fees, as in New York. The Chinese want to flex their muscles with each building, to stir up an identity, interest, and excitement, because they have been suppressed so long.

"But," he added, "I feel awful about the massive modern structures in China. Most are by Hong Kong hit-and-run architects who give the projects to local firms that do not execute them well. We can help with their planning process, which is now nonexistent, and teach the fundamentals. We can show them the mistakes that we made in the name of urban renewal in the USA. The culture of the people is disappearing. In Shanghai they are relocating people from the traditional two-story neighborhoods to remote high-rise towers that are beyond the average bicycle-commuting distance."

Jerry Davis from Hellmuth Obata & Kassabaum (HOK) said, "New York architects think a lot about context and respond to the context, but the Chinese are looking for object architecture. In some ways the new towers have no place in their cities from technological and design standpoints. They are not looking at all at the context, because where they are building there is no context. All the new buildings are in suburban office zones away from the city centers. This could be the best way, so if the buildings don't work, they haven't lost the city core."

H. Wang

The same pattern appears in Turkey and Venezuela, as **Richard Hayden** of Swanke Hayden Connell explained: "Our high-rise buildings for the Isbank in Istanbul are in a corporate suburban area outside of the center of Istanbul. Their image is to get out of where they are, to move into the twentieth century. Our goal is to integrate experience and stylistic thoughts with the local flavor and keep the individuality of and respect for the countries we are working in, and then help to bring the work in those countries up to another technological level."

John Ashworth

Robert A. M. Stern believes that Asia, in particular, wants to hire American architects because "it is fashionable, and we know more about how to put together large, complex mixed-use projects. We have invented many of the paradigms for these building types, so it is both the desire for the fashion and the function of American architecture."

Incorporating the Cultural Context

Working abroad, New York City architects strive to create a new contextual union between the cultural requirements of each site and new technology. "Even tall buildings," Pedersen said, "must be representative of the place where they are located. Whether in Chicago and New York or Jakarta, the proof of the translation of the work is the work. In our Mainzer Landstrasse office building in Frankfurt, the German building code requirements, such as the dimensions for high-rise buildings and the need for each office to have natural light, promoted the change in our design philosophy. We seek opportunities that reside in a place to inform the design."

from left to right:
Ducate Place, Moscow, Liebman Melting Partnership
Plaza Hollywood, Kowloon, Hong Kong, Brennan Beer Gorman
Jahwa Shanghai Tower, Shanghai, China, Fox & Fowle, Gluckman, Liu

rendering by Yann Leroy

"We had to incorporate cultural aspects into the Bank Niaga headquarters building in Jakarta," Louie said. "We included a mosque, ablution sinks in the bathrooms, and pantries for tea, so the entire core is different from a New York building. We had to take into consideration the frequent separation of men and women. We had to consider different climatic issues, such as ways to deal with the intensity of the sun. We looked to their 1950s buildings, which included screens over glass with small apertures, so we developed a new brise-soleil system to shield direct sunlight. We also used local materials and crafts and referenced the patterns of the native textile designs in the interior."

Hunter Tura

Describing the administrative building for Department of Haut Savoie in Chambéry, France, which Polshek and Partners won through a competition, **Richard Olcott** said, "we needed to provide a French office building. It was not like projects in Asia where they want an American building. The French locals thought it strange that outsiders were trying to figure out how the French do architecture. Thus elements such as the creation of one large, open floor space at the top story were eliminated because in France each worker requires a separate office. In the end, the offices for the architecture department did remain like an open studio, but it was a cultural issue, not an architectural one."

The snow removal equipment in the Museum of Contemporary Art in Helsinki "is a respected sacred cow," Steven Holl said. "It has to be lodged in the building, accessible 24 hours a day, and the edges of buildings have to be designed so the snow removal equipment can fit. The windows had to be triple-glazed. They are very conscious of the consequences of climate.

"The museum," Holl continued, "was made and conceived for that site and for Finland.... Each building and site concept are fused. I am not trying to import a style from another site. I am using a standing-seam metal roofing system on wooden sleepers, an almost traditional system, which they have the labor to build. It is the most economical."

Lee Meltzer

"In Asia they want flash, but the Middle East is very different," said **John Gerring** of HLW. "In Saudi Arabia, because of the climate they use concrete. We had to design for wind and sun. For the design of the Kuwait Chamber of Commerce, the client didn't want just International Style ideas. We did precedent studies analyzing the typical fortresses, the internal courtyards, and the intimate spaces that screen out the sun and wind. We suggested these elements in the building by using details such as splayed walls, deep penetrating windows for shade, and the image of energy with a flame shape on the top of the tower.

"Cultural issues had to be considered in the design for the Korean Army Pension Fund office tower in Seoul," Gerring continued. "We were required to have operable windows in a high-rise tower, which is not what we would do in NYC, but the client wanted them even though they are more expensive. It is just a different sense of priorities. We also included a traditional wedding banquet hall in the basement, something that we would never put in a commercial office building here. Even the sequence of how they arrive in the building is different; there are multiple entrances with halls separated from the public space."

"In Japan they hire Americans because they want American work," Stern said. "They don't want their own traditional motifs. For the Greenbrier Golf Club at West Village, I made a relationship between the new and old, so that depending on where your eyes have been it might look Italian or Japanese; it depends which blinders you wear. For Euro Disneyland in France, I designed the Newport Bay Club Hotel, a ver nacular American hotel, New England in style. The French thought I meant Newport Beach. They actually came to Newport to see what I was referring to. There is an educa tion process on both sides, tha is the fun of it."

"In Germany," Liebman said, "we have been hired to work on apartment planning and make projects marketable, because American apartment building planning is better in terms of the way amenities are organized and provided."

"In some countries safety code are nonexistent," Hayden said. "They don't have handicapped laws as we do, and they are cre ating world-class buildings. We tell our clients that if you want a building financed on the world market, you should put in handicapped access. Some countries only require one stai in a high-rise building. This is ludicrous. We are insisting that they should put in two, becaus for fire safety they will have to later. We also try to get them t spend a bit more now to have flexible building with capacity for adding air-conditioning in the future. As Americans, this is what we can bring to other countries."

rendering by CADD

CI & A Photography

from left to right:

Xin Zhao, mixed-use development, Shanghai, China, Hellmuth, Obata & Kassabaum

IS Bank, Istanbul, Turkey, Swanke Hayden Connell

Bank Niaga headquarters, Jakarta, Indonesia, Kohn Pedersen Fox

n what Hayden calls "Two-and- -Half-World" countries, rather han Third or First World, "they ave electricity, but it doesn't ork all the time. So we must lan a building around the ailties of the local services. In ne building we have installed aree water systems — piping r the city system, a stainless- eel water tank, and we actually ave a processing plant on the remises for gray water."

Architecture transcends cultur- differences," Holl observed, ike great music. When you can ake it, it is transcultural. specially today, why try to ationalize everything? Let's eak of a transcultural hope of chitecture that has the unique ower on each site and situa- on. I don't mean transporting particular style from site to te. I mean that the aspiration ad hope of the architecture is anscultural, but the individual chitecture is unique."

uts and Bolts (of Practice)

ne organization of work road is often unwieldy. New rk architects often affiliate th local firms because they e not locally registered or miliar with the local building rmit processes. Some firms ablish offices abroad or send associate over for the dura- n of a project. Many have ni exchange programs with reign architects. "We learn m the way they are taught d the techniques that they ," Richard Hayden said. But w, with fax and computer teleconferencing, it is possible make a few trips abroad a year and then do most of the work from New York.

Most architects working in China note difficulties in getting paid. "In Shanghai," Fowle said, "they pay us a large 20 percent retainer fee, but all that is prepayment for schematic design, and we are not paid again until design development. We are trying to change that system. Additional services and design changes are also difficult to charge for, besides the fact that the approval process is tedious, about 17 government agencies review the documents. If we had our druthers, we would work for Western clients in China."

The control of working drawings and the construction process is also challenging. Some offices complete the design development phase, and then the local architect or contractor takes on the project, while other firms follow the project through to completion with their own architect or construction manager on site.

Dick Frank

"In my project in Tokyo for the Nunotani Publishing Company," **Peter Eisenman** said, "we did the detailed design development, and then the construction company completed the construction documents, so that it was not possible to make change orders. It is a very smooth working process, and there is not the game being played by contractors to find mistakes to charge extras. But if you see a detail that you want to change, you can't correct it. This was a very distancing experience. I prefer doing the working drawings and site supervision. In Japan they produce quality buildings, but it removes you from the process."

"It was illuminating to deal with European manufacturers," **Charles Gwathmey** said, "and finally to be able to build a solid building in Switzerland. You feel that the house is forever and that it will also make a great ruin. But the construction was a bit problematic because the level of invention was a bit limited. I wanted to make the shutters integral to the facade, making them part of the windows, so it wasn't as if they were added. But the Swiss couldn't do it that way. They resisted reinventing technological elements because they had a standardized way of doing things and were not flexible."

The negotiation processes are also different in each country. "Our meetings in Singapore for the Nanyang Polytechnic were like a therapy session," Gwathmey said. "First you discuss all of the black things and then the white. It was a very unemotional and open way of communication. Their goal was design, flexibility, and a future consensus. When we work on another university in the USA, we can bring an alternative experience to the table and say, look, there is another possibility, in Singapore we did it this way."

Leroy said that to him a "surprising thing was that the developer of Plaza Hollywood in Hong Kong personally had power over the project day to day. We had to meet with him and show him sketches until he was satisfied. He took a personal interest in the project until it was approved."

Luca Vignelli

Part of working in Germany "was getting used to a new time-frame for a project," **Richard Meier** said. "I won the Frankfurt Museum project in 1979, but the construction schedule was to complete the building in six years, while the High Museum in Atlanta began a year later, and was designed and built in three years. Each was on schedule, but the schedules were just different. As an American I'm used to seeing things built quickly. The quality of work was excellent; you just have to relax a little bit."

Office dA

Headquarters
Boston, MA

Other Locations
New York, NY

Founding Partners
Nader Tehrani, Monica Ponce de Leon

1986

2010

Office dA

1986–

Sorg Architects

Headquarters
Washington, D.C.

Other Locations
New Delhi, India

Founding Partners
Suman Sorg

Current Partners
Suman Sorg, Rachel Chung

1986

Sorg Architects

Tod Williams Billie Tsien Architects

Headquarters
New York, NY

Founding Partners
Tod Williams, Billie Tsien

Current Partners
Tod Williams, Billie Tsien,
Paul Schulhof

Jason Fulford

RUR ARCHITECTURE PC

1986–

RUR Architecture PC

Headquarters
New York, NY

Founding Partners
Jesse Reiser, Nanako Umemoto

RUR Architecture PC

1986

BERNARD TSCHUMI ARCHITECTS
NEW YORK I PARIS

1988–

Bernard Tschumi Architects

Headquarters
New York, NY

Other Locations
Paris, France

Founding Partner
Bernard Tschumi

Current Partners and Directors
Bernard Tschumi, Véronique Descharrières (codirector and partner), Joel Rutten (codirector, BTA New York)

1988

Bernard Tschumi Architects

1988–

Acconci Studio

Headquarters
Brooklyn, NY

Founding Partner
Vito Acconci

Acconci Studio

Selldorf Architects

Headquarters
New York, NY

Founding Partner
Annabelle Selldorf

1988

Selldorf Architects

Asymptote Architecture

Headquarters
New York, NY

Founding Partners
Lise Ann Couture, Hani Rashid

Asymptote Architecture

US Embassy
1985–1989

Architect
James Stewart Polshek and Partners

Location
Muscat, Oman

Client
US Department of State, Foreign Buildings Operations

Messeturm
1985–1991

Architect
JAHN

Location
Frankfurt, Germany

Client
Messe Frankfurt GmbH

Canary Wharf
1985–2005

Master Plan
Skidmore, Owings & Merrill (SOM)

Location
London, UK

Architects
SOM, Cesar Pelli & Associates, KPF, Perkins+Will, HOK, Pei Cobb Freed & Partners

Client
Canary Wharf Group, PLC

US Embassy
1986

Architect
Integrus

Location
Bogotá, Colombia

Client
US Department of State, Foreign Buildings Operations

Fish Dance Restaurant
1986–1987

Architect
Frank O. Gehry And Associates

Location
Kobe, Japan

Associate Architect
Takenaka Komuten Co. Ltd.

Client
The World Company and the City of Kobe

Kachofugetsu-kan (SDC Corporate Headquarters)
1986–1988

Architect
Santos Prescott and Associates

Location
Tokyo, Japan

Client
SDC Corporation, Shingo Nomura, CEO

Sainsbury Wing
1986–1991

Architect
Venturi, Scott Brown and Associates

Location
London, England

Client
National Gallery, London

Broadgate Development
1986–1992

Architect
Skidmore, Owings & Merrill

Location
London, UK

Client
British Railways Board, Broadgate Estates Ltd., Broadgate Plaza Ltd., Rosehaugh Group PLC, British Land, Olympia & York Properties

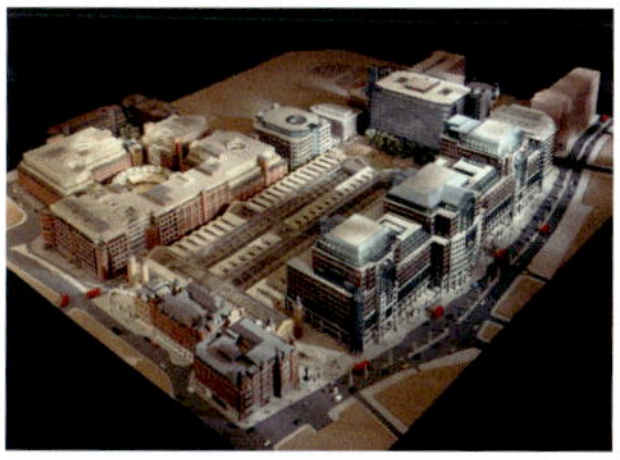

Westendstraße 1 (DZ Bank Headquarters)
1986–1993

Architect
Kohn Pedersen Fox Associates

Location
Frankfurt, Germany

Client
AGIMA/DG Immobillen Anlagegesellschaft

Stadthaus Ulm
1986–1993

Architect
Richard Meier and Partners Architects

Location
Ulm, Germany

Client
City of Ulm

City Hall and Library
1986–1995

Architect
Richard Meier and Partners Architects

Location
The Hague, Netherlands

Client
City of The Hague

Ring of Fire Aquarium and Tempozan Marketplace
1987–1990

Architect
Cambridge Seven Associates

Location
Osaka, Japan

Client
Osaka Waterfront Development Co. Ltd.

Goldman Sachs Headquarters
1987–1991

KPF

Architect
Kohn Pedersen Fox Associates

Location
London, United Kingdom

Client
LTD Partners

US Embassy
1987–1993

Architect
Eduardo Catalano

Location
Buenos Aires, Argentina

Client
US Department of State, Foreign Buildings Operations

US Embassy
1987–1994

Architect
The Leonard Parker Design Group

Location
Santiago, Chile

Client
US Department of State, Foreign Buildings Operations

Museum of Contemporary Art of Barcelona
1987–1995

Richard Meier & Partners Architects LLP

Architect
Richard Meier and Partners Architects

Location
Barcelona, Spain

Client
Consorci Museu d'Art Contemporani

Kreuzberg Tower and Wing
1988

Architect
John Hejduk

Location
Berlin, Germany

Client
Internationale Bauausstellung Berlin

Tegel Housing
1988

Architect
John Hejduk

Location
Berlin, Germany

Client
Internationale Bauausstellung Berlin

National Gallery of Canada
1988

Architect
Safdie Architects

Location
Ottawa, Canada

Client
National Gallery of Canada

SafdieArchitects

Koizumi Sangyo Corporation Headquarters
1988–1990

Architect
Eisenman Architects

Location
Tokyo, Japan

Client
Koizumi Sangyo Corporation

EISENMAN ARCHITECTS

Euro Disney Resort
1988–1992

Architect
Gehry Partners, Michael Graves and Associates, Gwathmey Siegel Kaufman Architects, Antoine Predock, Robert A.M. Stern Architects

Location
Marne-la-Vallee, France

Client
Walt Disney

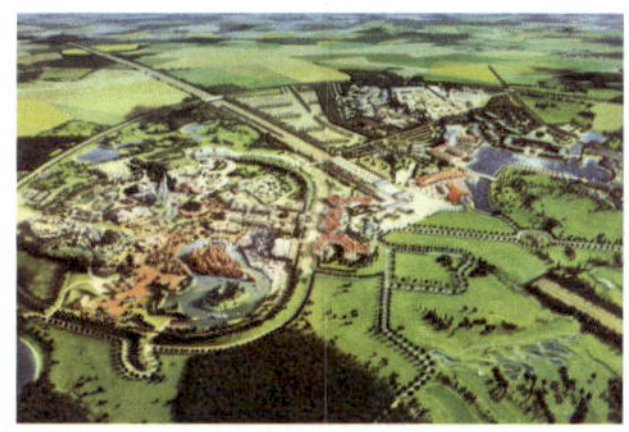

US Embassy
1988–1995

Architect
Arquitectonica

Location
Lima, Peru

Client
US Department of State, Foreign Buildings Operations

ARQUITECTONICA

Kobe Nishiokamato Housing
1988–1996

Architect
Moore Ruble Yudell Architects & Planners

Location
Kobe, Japan

Client
Mitsui Real Estate Development

moore ruble yudell
architects & planners

US Embassy
1988–1996

Architect
Kallman Archite, McKinnell & Wood Architects

Location
Bangkok, Thailand

Client
US Department of State, Foreign Buildings Operations

KMW Architecture

Getting Defensive: FBO Security Protocols After the Cold War

From 1960 onward, as Congress was asked to pick up the tab for the construction of US embassies, some of the already critical voices in Washington began to have more sway over the Foreign Buildings Operations (FBO) program beyond the narrow professional circle which had previously governed it. With a vigorous reshuffling of Congressional responsibilities in 1978 and the departure of one of the embassy program's harshest critics, Representative Wayne Hays, new FBO director William Slayton sought room to maneuver, appointing architects Hugh Stubbins, Donn Emmons, and O'Neil Ford to the Advisory Council. Yet despite this search for new talent, by 1980 the program had become "hostage to the Congressional oversight committees… chaired in several instances by Washington's most notorious power brokers." Shifts in global politics also made the process of constructing US embassies far more precarious. Articles warned that "The sudden emergence of a generalissimo or an ayatollah in a far-off land can deflect US foreign policy abruptly and stall or even collapse an FBO project without warning and at any stage of development."[1]

The explosion in 1968 of a hole through the fragile perimeter wall of the US Embassy in Saigon, killing 22 and wounding 188, had ushered in a new era for the program. As US involvement in Vietnam escalated, security became a pressing issue for the FBO. Symptomatic of the anger towards US foreign policy in the aftermath of the war, there were 243 attacks and attempted attacks on US diplomatic installations abroad between 1975 and 1984.[2] Architectural elements that had become hallmarks of the embassy program in its heyday, such as ornamental screens, buildings raised on stilts, and large openings were eliminated from new projects, rapidly ensuring that the FBO would churn out its first "fortress without apologies" by the 1980s.[3]

① Barclay F. Gordon, "America Turns a Fresh Face Overseas," *Architectural Record* (December 1980): 96–97.

② Jane Loeffler, "Diplomacy Doesn't Belong in Bunkers," *The Washington Post* (August 23, 1998): C4.

③ Karen D. Stein, "A Fortress With No Apologies," *Architectural Record* (October 1996): 78–87.

④ See Margaret Arbanas and Ana Miljački, "Embassies: Under Pressure," in Eva Franch i Gilabert, Amanda Lawrence, Ana Miljački, Ashley Schafer, ed., *OfficeUS Agenda* (Zurich: Lars Müller, 2014): 212–217.

⑤ Jane Loeffler, "The American Embassy: Design Excellence vs. Security?" *Architectural Record* (July 2004): 67–68.

1975

1983 Suicide bombing of the US Embassy In Beirut

1985 Inman Report
Sets new security regulations for the design of diplomatic posts.
- 100 ft setback
- Consolidate all facilities in one secure compound
- Purchase land for expansion within compound.
- 15% maximum glazed surface
- Isolated locations preferred to dense urban areas
- Controlled access to the compound
- No-climb walls and fences
- Anti-ram barriers
- Blast resistant construction

1989 Fall of the Berlin Wall

1990–1991 First Persian Gulf War

Following the 1983 suicide bombing of the US Embassy in Beirut, the State Department submitted a series of design recommendations and security upgrades for existing and new embassies to Congress, known as the Inman Report (1985), which set in motion a powerful architectural makeover of the US presence abroad.[4] The Inman Report called for the replacement of 126 diplomatic posts, requiring all facilities to be collected into single compounds built outside of city centers and surrounded by tall walls, with minimal glazing and certified blast-resistant materials where possible.[5] Following the adoption of these criteria, US diplomatic facilities overseas were attacked on more than 200 occasions in the decade after 1987.[6] By far the bloodiest of these attacks took place in 1998 with the simultaneous bombing of US embassies in Nairobi and Dar-es-Salaam, killing 224 people.

In 2001 retired General Charles Williams, newly appointed as director of the FBO (now renamed the Bureau of Overseas Building Operations), formed an Industry Advisory Panel and invited the engineering and construction conglomerate URS Corporation to advise on the production of a standard embassy prototype, intended to meet increasingly strict security requirements while reducing costs through common design features and integrated project delivery methods. Marginalizing the existing Architectural Advisory Board, three sizes of a "Standard Embassy Design" were developed, based on RTKL's US Embassy for Kampala, Uganda (1999).[7] At the time over 80% of primary US diplomatic facilities failed to meet the 100-foot setback required by the plan, resulting in the rapid construction of 160 new replacement facilities within a short time period. Projecting a more fearful version of "Americanness" than the one Pietro Belluschi had advocated for in 1954, the standard plan was decidedly unresponsive to locality, closed to any discussion of the aesthetic, symbolic, or even diplomatic value of its buildings from the outset.[8]

Criticism ensued, both of US foreign policy and of the new crop of US embassies. In response, the State Department launched the Design Excellence Program in early 2011.[9] Welcomed equally by designers and critics, the program has revived the architectural conversation about openness and security. Though it maintains some of the rigid guidelines inherited through decades of securitization, the program attempts to reconcile the inherent conflict between such stringent security standards and a desired message of openness by offering vague guidelines, including a "renewed preference for urban sites" and an advocacy for "cohesive design for site and structure." — AM

⑥ United States General Accounting Office (GAO), "Embassy Construction: The United States Has Implemented Management Reforms, But Challenges Remain," GAO 04–100 (November 2003).

⑦ The plan is publicly available in a variety of print and online publications. See "Adapting Standard Embassy Design to Specific Sites, Contributed by the U.S. Department of State and the U.S. General Services Administration" (revised May 2007), http://www.aia.org/aiaucmp/groups/ek_members/documents/pdf/aiap017590.pdf (last accessed February 9, 2014).

⑧ See "Architecture to Represent America Abroad," *Architectural Record* (May 1955): 237–242.

⑨ Jayne Merkel, "State Department Names Architects For Design Excellence Program," *Architectural Record* (December 17, 2012), http://archrecord.construction.com/news/2012/12/121217-State-Department-Names-Architects-for-Design-Excellence-Program.asp (last accessed November 20, 2014).

1989

1998 US Embassies in Nairobi and Dar Es Salam bombed

1999 Congress authorized the Secure Embassy Construction and Counterterrorism Act

2001 Foreign Buildings Operations office (FBO) restructured and renamed Bureau of Overseas Building Operations (OBO)

2005 Standard Embassy Plan Issued

2011 Design Excellency program Launched

2012 US Consulate in Benghazi, Libya attacked

2013 Design Excellency Program renamed Excellence in Diplomatic Facilities

2015

2011

2001 Afghanistan War

2003 Iraq War

Attacks on US Embassies

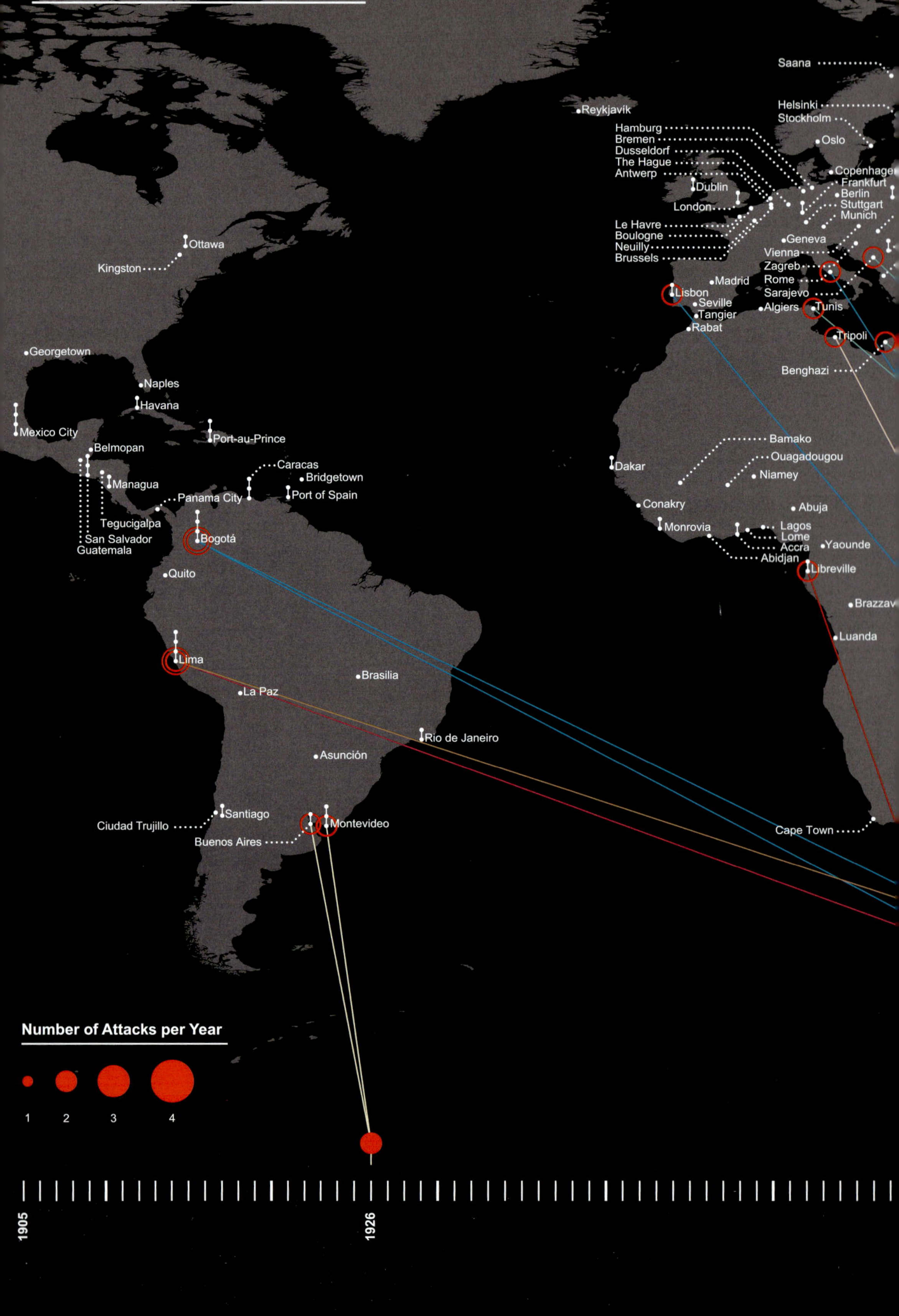

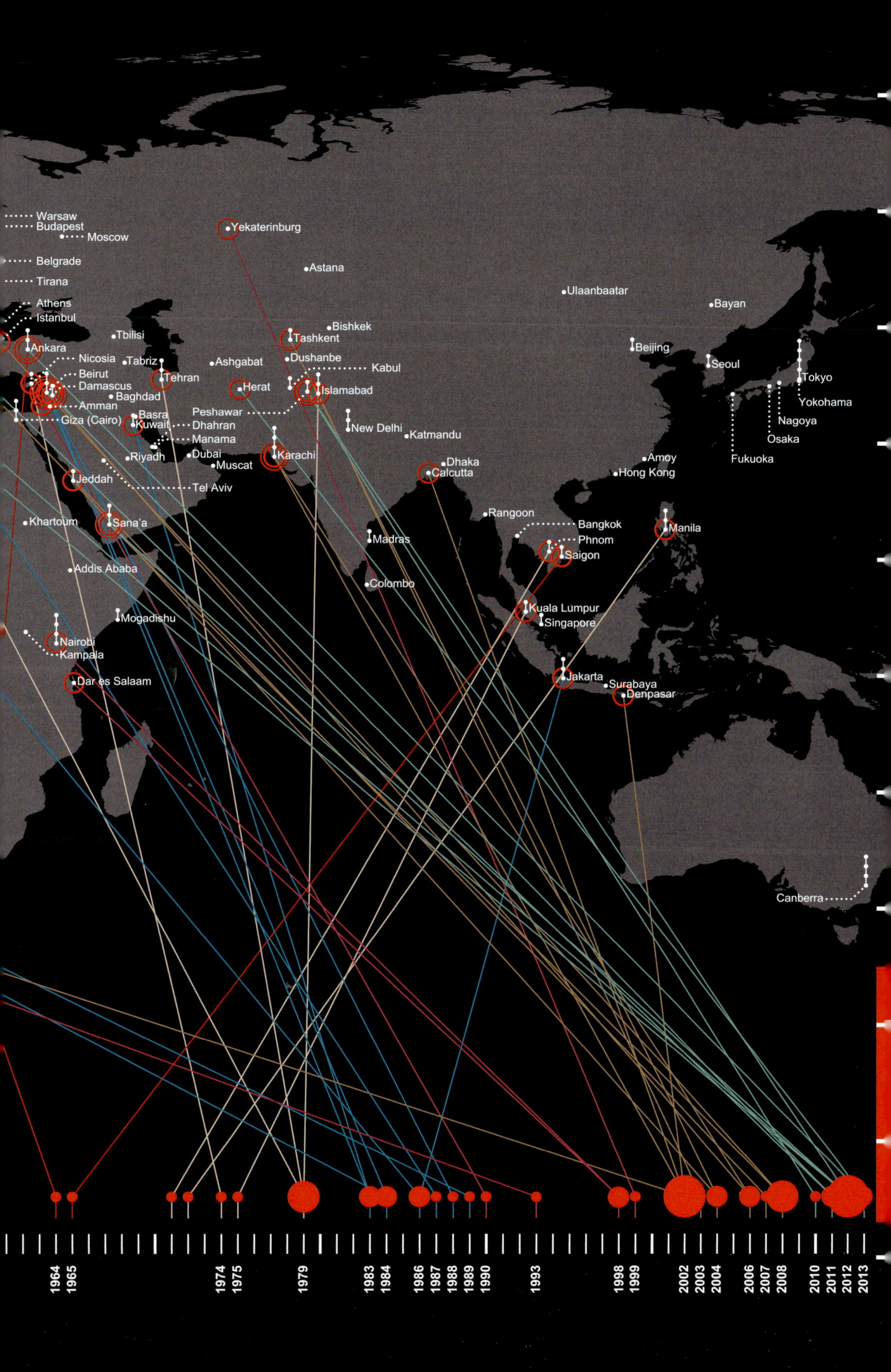

Warsaw
Budapest
Moscow
Yekaterinburg
Belgrade
Astana
Tirana
Ulaanbaatar
Athens
Bayan
Istanbul
Bishkek
Tbilisi
Tashkent
Ankara
Beijing
Nicosia
Tabriz
Ashgabat
Dushanbe
Seoul
Kabul
Beirut
Tehran
Tokyo
Damascus
Herat
Islamabad
Baghdad
Yokohama
Amman
Peshawar
Basra
New Delhi
Giza (Cairo)
Kuwait
Dhahran
Katmandu
Nagoya
Manama
Osaka
Riyadh
Dubai
Karachi
Muscat
Dhaka
Amoy
Fukuoka
Jeddah
Calcutta
Hong Kong
Tel Aviv
Rangoon
Khartoum
Sana'a
Bangkok
Manila
Madras
Phnom
Saigon
Addis Ababa
Colombo
Kuala Lumpur
Mogadishu
Singapore
Nairobi
Kampala
Jakarta
Dar es Salaam
Surabaya
Denpasar
Canberra
1964
1965
1974
1975
1979
1983
1984
1986
1987
1988
1989
1990
1993
1998
1999
2002
2003
2004
2006
2007
2008
2010
2011
2012
2013

The Current State Of State Dept. Building

Does security dictate a fortress image?

By Bill N. Lacy, FAIA

Not since Jefferson was in the White House has architecture received great priority in the federal consciousness. Few Presidents since then, with the exception of John F. Kennedy, who caused the brief but cogent "guiding principles of federal architecture" to be drafted, have understood the importance of architecture. Andrew Jackson sited the Treasury building by arrogantly sticking his cane in the ground, ruining forever the axial view from the White House to the Capitol. And Harry Truman suggested making all our embassies miniature White Houses.

The Foreign Buildings Operations of the U.S. Department of State are often the butt of Senate criticism and are regularly castigated in the press for cost overruns and security lapses in embassies and office buildings abroad. But they also have received recent Presidential awards for excellence in architectural design and frequent commendation for their enlightened approach to the execution of overseas commissions.

Much of the credit for the favorable part of this assessment of the FBO is due to a procedure set up under former Secretary of State John Foster Dulles back in 1954. Acting on the advice of Pietro Belluschi, FAIA, Ralph T. Walker, and Henry Shepley, Dulles established a three-member outside panel to select architects and oversee preliminary designs. That system resulted in immediate critical acclaim for the New Delhi Embassy designed by Edward Durell Stone (see page 76) and has been successful, with minor setbacks, down to the present. The current three-member Architectural Advisory Board, which I chair, includes Charles Graves, FAIA, of Lexington, Ky., and Charles Moore, FAIA, of Austin, Tex.

Under the current procedure, we are summoned to Washington, D.C., periodically to review qualifications submitted by architecture firms throughout the country in response to notices of projects in *Commerce Business Daily*. Projects can range from an office building annex in Budapest to an embassy in Singapore. During the past few years the volume of building activity has increased dramatically because of the need to upgrade security at foreign outposts.

When our board meets, we are presented with a dozen or so finalists whose technical qualifications have been reviewed and approved by a preselection board comprising FBO members and members from Sverdrup Corp., which has been retained to manage certain projects. Our board reserves the right to bring forth candidates from the prescreened pool of rejections if we feel that special design potential warrants such action.

When Belluschi set up the board he told Dulles emphatically, "You get the best architect, and you get the best architecture"—a simple maxim but one not always easy to implement. Basically, our recommendations are based on review of the somewhat tedious government forms called 254 and 255, which give a statistical portrait of a firm and its qualifications, supplemented by brochures containing photographic evidence of its skills. We review these materials and match up design talent and ability with projects that suit a particular firm's experience and potential. As architects increasingly are selected by the interview method, many architects welcome the FBO method because it doesn't require the persuasive theatrical skills called for in face-to-face client presentations.

Many of the more reputable firms, however, choose not to compete for any but the largest jobs, citing the problems of dealing with the federal bureaucracy as their reason. Another deterrent has been recent increased emphasis on security to the virtual exclusion of other criteria, mandated unfortunately by the Congress. Though well designed embassy projects such as Lisbon (Bassetti/Norton/Metler), Nicosia (Kohn Pedersen Fox), and Santiago (Leonard Parker Associates) have proved that security requirements need not dictate a fortress image abroad, nevertheless it is true the heavy emphasis on security has discouraged some architects with superior design talent from seeking consideration.

William Slayton, Hon. AIA, former executive vice president of AIA, served as deputy assistant secretary of FBO from 1978 to 1983. While he had his detractors within the State Department for the somewhat unorthodox management style he brought from the private sector, during his tenure some of the best architects in the country were engaged to design our embassies abroad. Harry Weese & Associates designed staff housing in Tokyo; Hartman-Cox designed the embassy in Kuala Lumpur; and even a small auxiliary facility in Brasilia, the Casa Thomas Jefferson, was designed by Mitchell/Giurgola for the USIA.

Mr. Lacy, former president of the Cooper Union in New York City and of the American Academy in Rome, now heads his own firm, Bill Lacy Design, in New York.

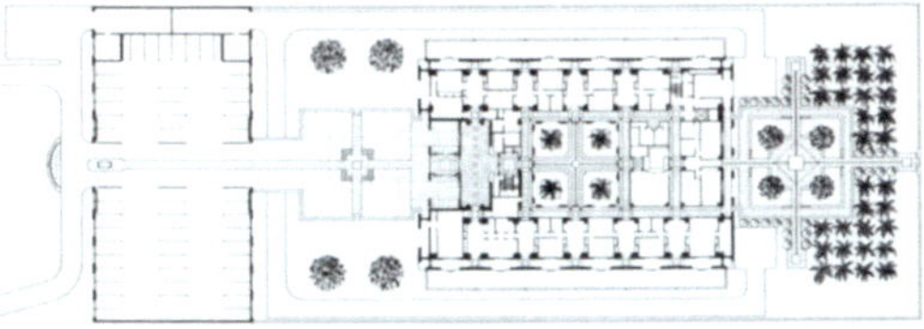

Below and left, U.S. Embassy in Muscat, Oman, by James Stewart Polshek & Partners. Organized around courtyards, the building is surrounded by a 10-foot-high fence. Bottom, U.S. Embassy complex in Lisbon, Portugal. Bassetti/Norton/Metler is architect.

Coinciding with Slayton's departure in 1983, embassy design was thrust into the spotlight abruptly and tragically with the terrorist attacks in Beirut in October 1983 and in Kuwait two months later. Suddenly, a President who thus far had managed to escape any direct blame for his Administration's actions was held personally accountable for the deaths of 241 Marines. As a consequence, Congress acted with unusual speed to authorize $2 billion for rebuilding our embassies to make them secure. Thick research documents were produced detailing how to ward off "pickup truck" bombers; high walls were erected at existing embassy sites; and new sites were procured with space separating them from the neighborhoods.

As the first high-security embassies were built, a furor erupted in Moscow over the $190 million U.S. chancery, housing, and school. Security in the chancery was breached by Soviet contractors who infested the structure with bugging devices, and the incident focused even more attention on security and further contributed to its position of overriding concern at FBO.

It is a tribute to the present administration of FBO under Richard Dertadian that the Architectural Advisory Board continues to fulfill its original mission as outside consultants as effectively as it does. Our decisions still are upheld in the selection process at the departmental level, but top choices and recommendations sometimes give way to lesser selections. The exclusive emphasis on security has put too much stress on engineers' and technocrats' "delivery systems" without enough regard to what is being delivered; moreover, there is too much involvement by Congress in architect selection where constituent satisfaction supercedes concern for the U.S. image abroad.

Not even today's White House is immune to the damage that can be done by imposing security measures without design consideration. The view of the White House from the south lawn is still a beautiful and moving experience, but the north facade on Pennsylvania Avenue, once equally grand, has been reduced to a "tank trap" by the insensitive placement of a bollard barricade. The same situation has been played out around the world as a result of terrorist attacks and our security-prompted responses. The once beautiful and serenely graceful embassy in New Delhi has been visually obliterated by heavy-handed efforts to make it secure without taking into account any other considerations.

The United States is coming to the end of a decade in which our pre-eminence as a world power has been seriously challenged and altered in economics, if not in the arts. For the present we still dominate architecture. Our image abroad is too important not to put that talent to its most effective use. □

Below, the U.S. Embassy in Abu Dhabi, United Arab Emirates, by Harry C. Wolf, FAIA. This project (on indefinite hold pending funding) is conceived as four large, stone-clad cubes sitting on a plinth, one cube rotated slightly. A court (shown in the line-drawing perspective) is a cubic space carved into the center of the building. Right, colored drawing of the U.S. Embassy in a suburb of Santiago, Chile, by Leonard Parker Associates, a project in construction drawings phase. The building is to be entered through a two-story rotunda. Below right, Kohn Pedersen Fox's U.S. Embassy in Nicosia, Cyprus, now in construction. Offices occupy the larger block fronting a major street; the ambassador's residence in foreground at right.

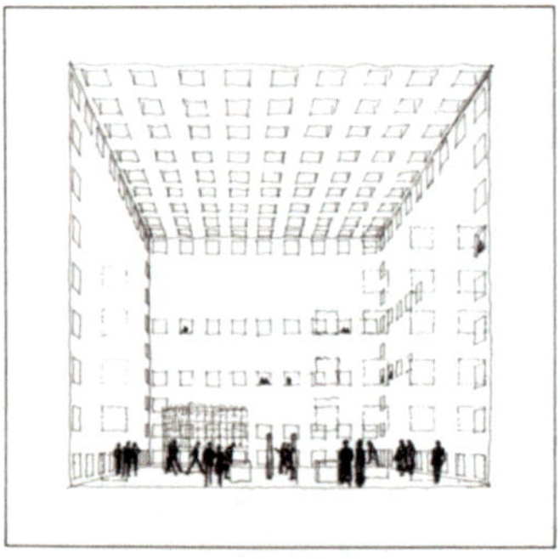

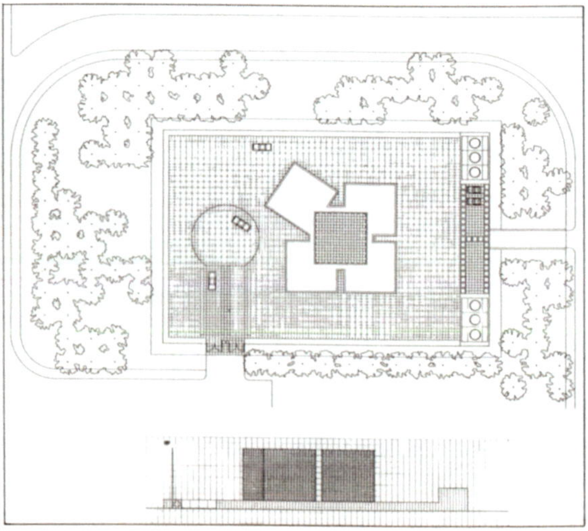

The Institute *from page 18*
among the three design associations is "to reach a consensus on an approach to state regulation of interior designers that will benefit the design profession and the public they serve." The agreement spells out seven areas that will be addressed in future negotiations among the associations:

- Title registration.
- Requirements for registration, including a four-year minimum professional degree, accredited by the Foundation for Interior Design Education Research or the equivalent; National Council for Interior Design Qualification testing or the equivalent; and a monitored internship, to be developed.
- No grandfathering without strict and equivalent education, training, and testing criteria.
- Joint regulatory boards.
- The development of a clear definition of interior designer.
- Voluntary continuing education.
- Recognition of the right of licensed architects to continue to perform interior design services.

The accord also states that "final agreement will require resolution of these and additional issues" and that the three associations have "agreed to appoint representatives to work toward resolution of these difficult issues."

The AIA board of directors supported the joint statement at its December meeting and accepted the recommendations of AIA's licensing law task force in its report on interior designer practice regulations and title registration.

According to the task force's report, the proposed policies will "accommodate the agreement between AIA, ASID, and IBD" while allowing "flexibility for AIA components to deal with licensing issues and initiatives in the state legislatures." The report also recognizes that AIA wishes "to reach an acceptable compromise with the interior design associations but continues to have reservations regarding the long-term implications of title registration of specialized disciplines as opposed to private certification."

In hailing the joint statement, AIA President Ted P. Pappas, FAIA, praised the "spirit of cooperation that has brought us to this important moment. The willingness of all of our organizations to put aside our differences and work to find common ground will ultimately benefit not only our professions but the public we serve."

Expressing hope that the agreement is the beginning of an era of successful collaboration, Charles Gandy, president of ASID, said, "We are all members of the team responsible for the built environment, and each of us in our own professional role adds to the quality of life of the people we work for and with."

Michael Bourque, president of IBD, said that the accord "signifies only the first agreement of a blossoming relationship between our closely allied design disciplines."—LYNN NESMITH

Government

State Department Calls for Razing Of Bugged Embassy in Moscow

The chancery building of the U.S. Embassy in Moscow was uninhabitable before it was completed. The seven-building embassy complex, designed by Skidmore, Owings & Merrill/San Francisco with Gruzen & Partners, was to be the State Department's largest and most elaborate embassy, reflecting the United States' wealth, power, and architectural prowess. However, in August 1985 work on the chancery (the office building component of the embassy complex) was stopped when American intelligence agents discovered the building's structure was infested with permanent, sophisticated eavesdropping and transmitting systems that had been installed during construction.

Last November, following numerous private engineering and government studies, President Reagan recommended that the $22 million chancery building be razed. The President's recommendation came after the State Department concluded that "dismantling and reconstructing the Moscow embassy office building offered the only solution which provides the degree of security required for use of the building as a chancery."

For more than three years, the eight-story chancery has stood empty, a stark reminder of the series of problems that have plagued the State Department and its Foreign Buildings Operations (see page 80) in the quest to build a monumental embassy complex in the Soviet Union's capital city. The tumultuous history of its construction began soon after the United States established diplomatic relations wit the Soviet Union in 1934. Within a year, William C. Bullitt, America's first amba sador to the U.S.S.R., reported that Stalin had promised him an embassy site high atop the Lenin Hills overlooking Mo cow. While negotiations were being held the embassy staff moved into temporary quarters downtown near Red Square.

Thirty years passed before an agreeme was reached on the location of the embassy. Rather than the hilltop site, th State Department chose a 10-acre down town parcel. In exchange, the Soviets wer given a site atop Mount Alto, one of the highest spots in Washington, D.C. (At th time the agreement was signed in 1969, U.S. officials did not know that a hilltop site would become crucial as new espio nage techniques became more dependen on microwave transmission.)

The agreement on the two sites was onl the first of many State Department concessions and blunders. Next came negot ations for the construction of the two compounds. Responding to the spirit of detente during the Nixon Administration the State Department agreed to allow sit work, structure, and facade to be completed by Soviet workers. William P. Ro ers, who was Secretary of State in 1972 when the agreement was signed, was quoted in a recent New York *Times* arti cle saying, "I didn't favor it because it wa a one-sided deal. But I was carrying out the orders of the [Nixon] White House."

While officials from the two governments were negotiating the constructio details, the architects were put on hold.

continued on page 2

The taller building in the background is the chancery, scheduled to be razed.

David Drapkin/Time Magazine

Government *from page 20*
SOM/Gruzen was awarded the embassy commission in 1968 but did not start active design until 1975. Ben Larson of SOM, who has worked on the project since the early '70s, recalled that the late John B. Rodgers, the SOM partner who signed the original agreement, reached mandatory retirement age before the design process was started. Larson said Rodgers later bemoaned the fact that "he had picked off one of the plums of the universe" and the firm never even started on the project during his tenure. (Edward C. Bassett, FAIA, was the senior design partner on the embassy project.)

Although working drawings were completed by 1976, construction did not begin until 1979 and was subject to numerous delays from the outset. State Department officials immediately were confronted with inferior Soviet construction standards and shoddy work habits and absenteeism of the Soviet workers. But the most serious problem resulted from the fact that precast structural components of the chancery were constructed at Soviet factories unsupervised by American inspectors.

Soon after construction commenced, security experts began to suspect that the Soviets were implanting spying devices. Rather than halt construction, the State Department moved ahead, confident that American security experts could neutralize the Soviet eavesdropping systems.

A U.S. Senate report in September 1985 charged that diplomatic objectives precluded full consideration of counterintelligence concerns during negotiations.

After construction was halted in August 1985, security specialists reported that it would be impossible to neutralize the sophisticated surveillance systems implanted within the steel and concrete structural elements and precast floor slabs, which the Senate report called "the most massive, sophisticated, and skillfully executed bugging operation in history."

Meanwhile, during the next three years, the other buildings of the embassy compound (four housing buildings, a school, Marine guard quarters, and a concourse with recreation and service facilities) were accepted and occupied, while the chancery building stood empty.

The Reagan Administration's recommendation that the chancery be demolished followed a study by the engineering firm BDM-MK Ferguson, under the auspices of the State Department, reporting that dismantling the building and constructing a new one would be more economical and less time-consuming than attempting to de-activate the surveillance systems in the existing structure.

The State Department hopes to develop a design scheme for a new chancery building as soon as possible. Joseph S. Hulings, head of a newly formed State Department office that oversees the embassy project in Moscow, said, "If the Congress decides to appropriate the money for the reconstruction it will be a totally new effort."

According to Hulings, SOM most lik will continue as architect. "SOM must come up with a totally new design that will incorporate many of the elements re ommended by the engineering study," sa Hulings. In addition, one American co tractor will be responsible for the entir chancery project, and all the constructi will be done by American workers usin American materials. Huling's estimated cost of the new chancery building is approximately $300 million.

The fiasco of the Moscow embassy i not so much an architecture or constru tion failure but rather, in the words of t Senate report, "a textbook example of bureaucratic inertia, turf warfare, and ina equate interagency coordination."

—Lynn Nesmi

Women's Vietnam Memorial Approved but Site Unspecified

In November President Reagan signed i law a bill authorizing construction of a memorial to honor women Vietnam ve erans. The memorial is to be built on a site as yet undetermined, somewhere o federal lands in or near the District of Columbia, but not necessarily on the si of the Vietnam Veterans Memorial.

Last June the Senate passed a bill (se Aug. '88, page 32, and May '88, page 4 that would have allowed a statue of a

Set into the side of a mountain overlooking the city of Caracas, the new chancery building will be clad with the indigenous granite of its hillside site. The large parcel of land allowed flexibility in siting the structure, but the mountains rising behind the chancery mandated additional security considerations. "On any embassy project, you determine the security requirements, then you design the building," claims Birkerts, "rather than starting with a concept and trying to fit in security." The chancery's carved facade (above) is detailed with structural posts and colonnades shading the entrances. The small apertures in the wall shield interiors from strong south sunlight, while admitting natural light within the mandated limitations for exterior windows. The building is scheduled to begin construction later this year; a future phase will include a new ambassador's residence and an American recreational center.

INVISIBLE ARCHITECTURE

SECURITY

Safe Diplomacy

New safeguards established by the U.S. State Department are changing the way American embassies are designed.

THE BERLIN WALL HAS COME tumbling down, but the State Department continues to build barriers around U.S. enclaves throughout the world. Despite *peristroika* and *glasnost,* security for our embassies across the globe is being maintained at unprecedented levels. While security remains a major consideration in the design of new embassies, the architects of these outposts of diplomacy are striving to enhance protection through vocabularies appropriate to foreign locales.

Approximately 10 embassies built under sweeping new security requirements mandated in 1986 are now in use and very successful, according to Richard Dertadian, who heads the State Department's Foreign Buildings Operations division. Commenting on the upgraded facilities, Paul Weidlinger, whose engineering firm helped develop the State Department's guidelines, says: "Our objective has always been to deter terrorism. Fortunately, there have been no bombings against any of the new facilities. In that regard, we have been successful."

The Foreign Buildings Operations, which oversees the construction of our country's embassies, changed drastically during the last decade. Follow-

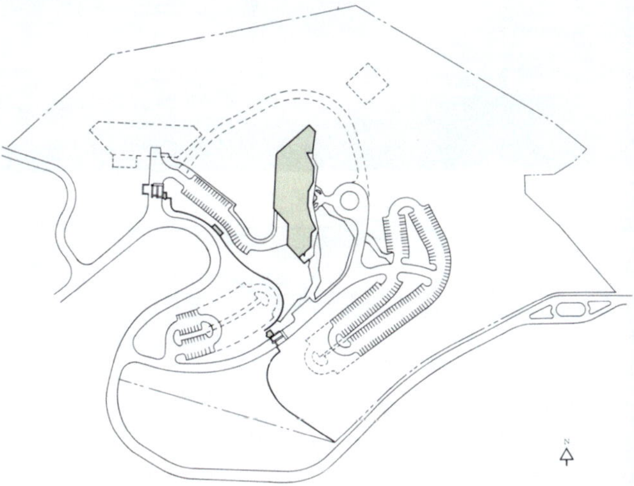

U.S. Embassy
San Salvador, El Salvador
CRSS, Architects
With J.A. Jones Construction Company

Following a limited design/build competition, the embassy complex, now under construction, will replace existing facilities seriously damaged in the 1986 earthquake. Located on a 26-acre site in a newly-developed suburban section of San Salvador, the project is comprised of 11 new buildings, including a chancery (left in photo below), Agency for International Development office building (center in photo below), and the ambassador's residence (far right in photo below). Responding to the suburban context, the architect clustered the buildings in a village-like setting and used simple forms and indigenous materials (above right). Although the large site allowed substantial setbacks, the entire building envelope will be constructed with a tall, anti-ram wall with high blast resistance.

ing numerous terrorist attacks on U.S. complexes during the 1970s and 1980s, the State Department charged an advisory panel with setting criteria for protecting Americans on diplomatic business overseas. The findings, released in 1985, recommended a massive program to renovate or replace our embassies and auxiliary structures in foreign countries. Shortly thereafter, Congress authorized billions of dollars and the State Department reorganized to meet the challenge.

In addition to expanding the Foreign Buildings Operations, a new Bureau of Diplomat Security Services was created to implement the tougher requirements, and the State Department hired Sverdrup Corporation as a program management consultant on 22 projects.

"We are searching for ways to create a safe environment to conduct foreign affairs," explains Greg Bujac, the State Department's deputy assistant secretary for countermeasures and physical security. "Embassies are in a sense public buildings and receive visitors, but we would be ill advised not to include security requirements." Yet the overambitious requirements of the report have gradually evolved over the past five years according to economics rather than changes in the international political climate. "We are looking at specific threat levels as an indicator of how much security is required to maximize a building's effectiveness while keeping costs down," says Bujac.

In determining security needs, the consensus is to protect people, information, and a building—in that order. Integration of security requirements early in the design stage is crucial. "Yet security in connection with architecture is a relatively new concept," notes Robert A. Taylor, vice president of System Planning Corporation.

"Prior to 1980, security was always an applique put onto a building after the construction was completed," Taylor claims. "About this time, people started taking advantage of the fact that the buildings themselves, and the way they were positioned in different environments, could really enhance the security of the whole facility." Incorporating security early in the process is much more efficient and cost-effective. "When you start from scratch, the security is not as obvious or obtrusive, and can become almost invisible," says Dertadian.

Most security experts agreed that siting is also important. The new requirements call for significantly larger sites, in some cases as large as 15 acres so the buildings can be set back 100 feet. Christopher Degenhardt, president of the landscape architectural firm EDAW, Inc., points out: "Although these requirements dictate huge sites, the distance comes from a very real relationship between what is a reasonable risk and the explosive potential of a car bomb." In tight urban sites, the relationship to the existing street pattern and threats from nearby buildings becomes especially critical.

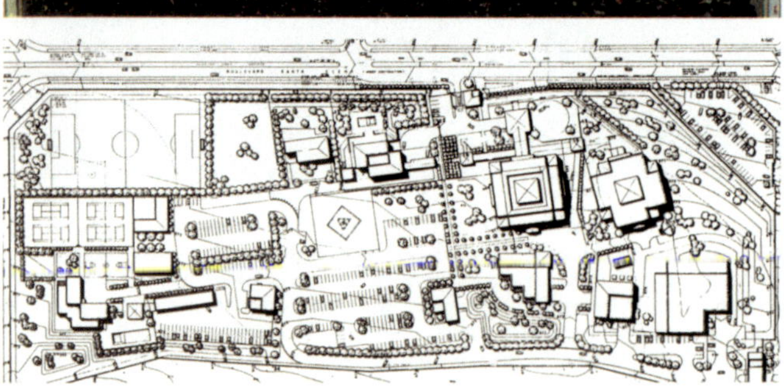

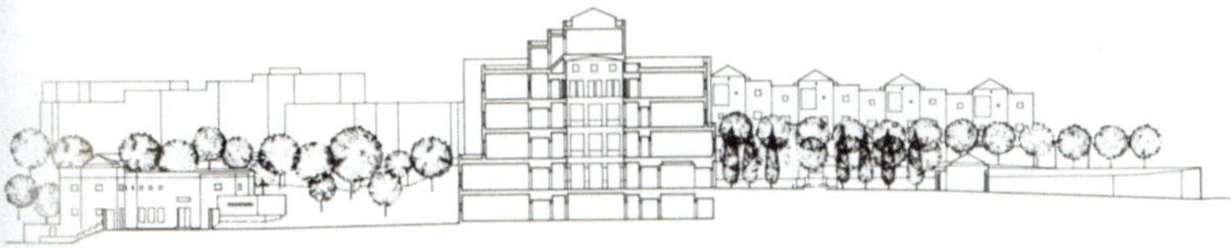

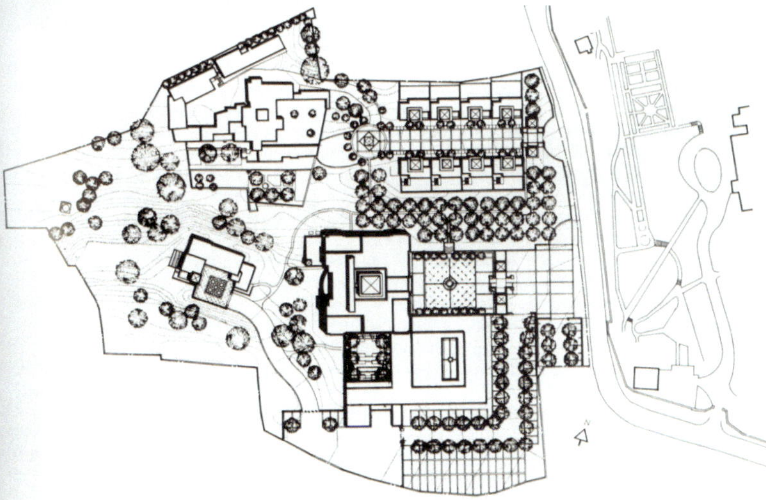

U.S. Embassy
Algiers, Algeria
Keyes Condon Florance, Architects

The new embassy's site plan (left) provides for the required 100-foot setbacks from a nine-foot-high perimeter wall, which complies with the State Department's anti-personnel design standards. A ceremonial entrance opens onto a landscaped courtyard on axis with the chancery (taller structure in model above); a secondary sally port provides vehicular and pedestrian access to staff housing (top right in site plan). The chancery is vertically organized and subdivided to provide a clear separation between public spaces and controlled access areas (section). Exterior openings are kept to a reasonable size to comply with requirements aimed at preventing bomb blasts and forced entry.

U.S. Embassy
Amman, Jordan
Perry Dean Rogers
& Partners, Architects

The architects emphasized bold geometric forms, stone detailing, and landscaping to meet the symbolic, programmatic, and security requirements of a new diplomatic enclave in Amman. The large drum (right and above), with an interior vehicular drive, serves as a secure sally port and provides a strong visual design element for the sharply angled corner of the site. Located on a 13-acre parcel, the 200,000-square-foot complex (above) scheduled for completion next year, will be constructed primarily of native white stone with decorative accents. Responding to demands for windows no larger than 15 percent per bay, the architects created a fenestration pattern reminiscent of traditional Middle Eastern architecture (top). A series of interconnected interior gardens will provide safe circulation throughout the compound, which includes a chancery, consular offices, ambassador's residence, Marine guard quarters, and an American community center.

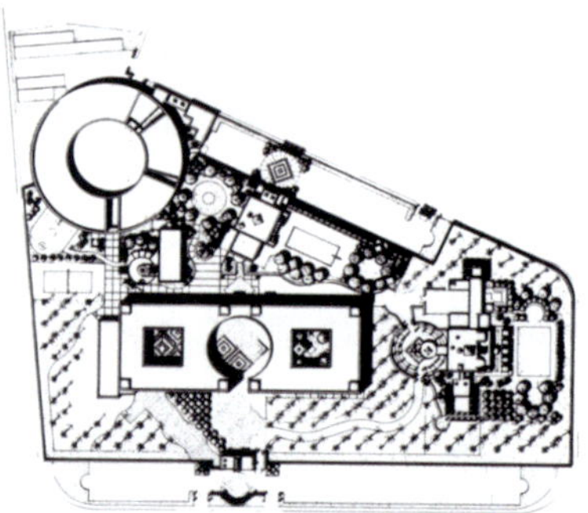

Protecting the perimeter wall of an embassy is also a major concern. One security specialist notes that as an ameliorative effect, a wall doesn't have to be a wall and suggests the use of earth berms or moats. But in any wall, the "weak link" is at the access point; the solution is fewer entries.

Dertadian confirms that the Foreign Buildings Operations is now considering threats according to specific sites instead of applying the same standards to all. "However, we will require that all new sites will allow us flexibility to respond with increased security if necessary," Dertadian added. Not all embassies will be relocated to large parcels outside the city. To insure our presence in major capitals, security has been upgraded at central embassies in Rome, Paris, and London.

The design of the facility is important but not the only factor in preventing terrorism. The architecture must be augmented with improved training for the operators of X-ray and metal detectors.

In 1986, the State Department brought in Sverdrup Corporation to help manage the multibillion-dollar design and construction effort. Sverdrup is also developing a unique system of technology transfer. "We have some rather sophisticated information management, scheduling, estimating, and project control systems," says Sverdrup's W. Donald Kingsley. "Our system will allow the State Department to incorporate these procedures in future projects."

Washington architect Stuart L. Knoop of Oudens & Knoop maintains: "The State Department is the vanguard in security planning. Ten years ago, architects would say architecture in a democratic society is supposed to be open and free. Now it is our responsibility to consider security as a part of every program."

Architects, however, are often caught in the middle. Lee Polisano, Kohn Pedersen Fox's partner in charge of the Nicosia embassy maintains: "A clear disparity exists between the various forces in Washington. Although it was a remarkable and unique experience working on the embassy, there is a belief that these buildings can be executed without the ongoing participation of their authors."

Since World War II, the State Department has maintained a rich tradition of hiring the best architects for embassy projects, credited in part to a three-member architectural review board founded in 1954. Bill Lacy, chairman of the board from 1985-1989, says: "It is a tribute to the present administration of Foreign Buildings Operations that the board continues to fulfill its original mission as effectively as it does." But he warns that "the exclusive emphasis on security has put too much stress on engineers' and technocrats' delivery systems without enough regard to what is being delivered." ■

—Lynn Nesmith

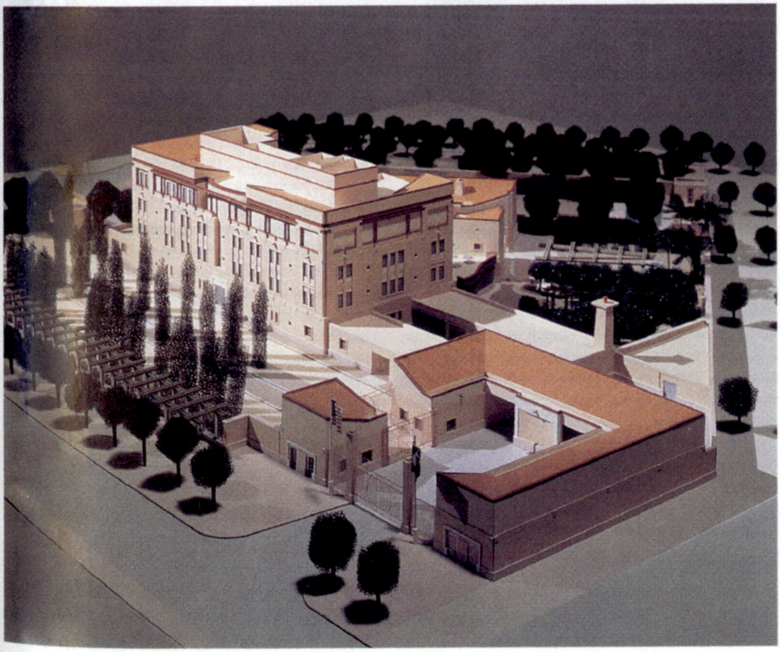

U.S. Embassy
Nicosia, Cyprus
Kohn Pedersen Fox Associates, Architects

KPF created a traditional embassy enclave within the confines of an oddly-shaped site, defined by the prescribed perimeter wall and a setback of 100 feet. The chancery's ceremonial entry fronts Nicosia's Embassy Row (top of photo above), while an entry pavilion with a protected courtyard (left) will ensure controlled access. The ambassador's residence (foreground in photo above) is oriented for privacy toward the rear of the site facing an existing olive grove and monastery. A circular component mediates between the chancery and residence. Landscaped outdoor spaces provide a transition from public processional courtyards to the ambassador's informal private garden. Totalling 71,000 square feet of space, the complex is scheduled for completion next year.

Ambivalent Symbol

With security concerns paramount, Perry Dean Rogers's embassy in Amman reflects an increasingly turbulent world.

United States Embassy
Amman, Jordan
Perry Dean Rogers & Partners Architects

It's hard to consider the architecture of U. S. embassies without reflecting on the 1983 destruction of the Marine barracks and embassy in Lebanon by a terrorist truck bombing. With hundreds of marines and staff killed, the catastrophe set off a soul-searching that produced strict new congressional mandates for the design of consular facilities. While the debate as to whether the elaborate security measures are worth their great expense continues, Amman's new embassy compound represents the difficulty of reconciling security with diplomatic welcome.

At the time of the bombing, Perry Dean Rogers was being considered as architect only for a new embassy residence in Jordan. The new security requirements caused the State Department to bring together facilities from several different locations, creating a new compound fortified with full perimeter walls, deep building setbacks, secured entrances monitored by Marine guards, and small external windows. [For more on embassy security, see RECORD, August 1992, pages 36-37]. To find a site large enough to meet these needs meant that the embassy had to move to the edge of the city from its center, a location both less convenient and less important symbolically.

Architects of other recent embassy projects have had some difficulty meeting antiterrorist guidelines while representing the building as an embassy rather than a bunker. Perry Dean Rogers drew on local building traditions: "We didn't have problems with the security directives because it's so hot you don't want large openings," comments partner Charles Rogers. The embassy is an architecture of walls: rough cut or honed (which reveals the delicate figuring of the Jordanian stone); uncoursed fieldstone and one-third running bond. The structures within the compound, built as primary geometric forms, pick up the sharp, powerful light. The chancery, the symbolic as well as administrative center of the compound, rises over the perimeter walls as a formidable masonry block, its tower-like corners evoking fortifications (previous pages). Public areas, such as offices for information and development, commercial attachés, and visa applications, are located in an annex (site plan).

Though the stone surfaces echo the monochromatic landscape, the severity of the architecture is tempered by grillwork drawn from local prototypes, tinted-concrete paving that abstracts traditional fabric patterns, and trellises and awnings painted bright colors inspired by Bedouin clothing. Though these elements are deployed in a consistent way throughout the compound's five buildings, connections between individual structures are much less clearly integrated. (The architects aligned buildings to the irregular site's edges.)

The project's contextual touches suggest that Americans want to learn from the Middle East's rich and ancient culture. In contrast, the embassy building boom of the '60s gave us an image of *pax Americana:* open, confident, forward-looking, but arguably indifferent to local conditions. Even in the skilled hands of Perry Dean Rogers, the Amman Embassy is defensive, inward-looking, its message about America ambivalent. It's an apt reflection of America's uncertain place in a radically altered world. *James S. Russell*

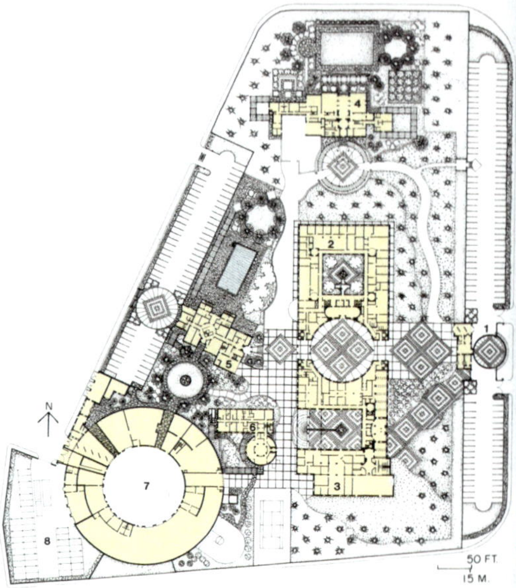

1. Main gate house
2. Chancery
3. Chancery annex
4. Ambassador's residence
5. American Club
6. Marine guard quarters
7. Service annex
8. Motor pool

© *Richard Mandelkorn photos*

Strict security requirements, which included deep building setbacks from adjacent streets ("standoffs" to dissipate terrorist-bomb explosions), meant that the new embassy compound needed a large site, one that could only be obtained on the developing edge of Amman. The 9-ft-high perimeter wall is interrupted at the entrance by a trellised metal fence, which invites the eye into the courtyard of the chancery (previous pages—a guarded sally port is just outside the photo). Grilled windows on this elevation are tempered triple-layered glass. Two massive piers and paired stone drums mark the central ceremonial entrance that leads to a circular courtyard, faced with yellow stucco, inside the chancery (opposite).

A Fortress With No Apologies

Designed in the wake of attacks on U.S. facilities, an embassy puts security first. Has it gone too far?

United States Embassy Chancery Building
Lima, Peru
Arquitectonica, Architect

"One of the most secure buildings in the entire world," is what the facility manager of the new United States Embassy in Lima, Peru, calls his charge. It certainly looks that way. It's longer than a football field by nearly a third (a typically American form of measurement), some 90-ft high, with few windows, and, like a Medieval fortress, surrounded by seemingly impenetrable walls. When the building was being designed in 1989, Lima was one of the most dangerous cities in the world. The activities of a terrorist group known as The Shining Path, participants in a civil war that, according to *The New York Times*, had cost 35,000 lives and $25 billion in damage, included frequent attacks on the former U.S. embassy, a more open, street-front structure in the city's downtown.

The embassy campus is located in the Monterrico section of Lima, east of downtown (opposite). It is in the foothills of the Andes mountains on land that was once used for polo fields. The Lima Polo club still maintains two playing fields behind the embassy.

A new world

At the time it seemed only prudent to design an embassy that would meet the strictest security standards. But the Peru that greeted the new embassy, dedicated with appropriate pomp and circumstance on July 4, 1995, is a changed place. With the capture of the leaders of the Shining Path in 1993, the era of widespread lawlessness and near economic dissolution is, if not over, then in remission. The Peruvian economy has been transformed under the leadership of President Alberto Fujimori, now in his sixth year and second administration. Inflation has dropped from 7,500 percent to 10 percent annually and economic growth has set a record in Latin America. Fujimori is getting high marks from his constituency for his war on crime and poverty, and his aggressive enticement of foreign investment. Currently, he enjoys an approval rating of over 60 percent.

The changes of the last half decade are evident throughout Lima. A new crop of strip shopping malls has been layered on top of the existing fabric that includes grand Spanish Colonial mansions and civic monuments, tree-lined plazas, and standouts of International Modernism. The once perilous drive from the airport through some of the city's poorest sections to more affluent downtown neighborhoods like San Isidro and Miraflores is now paved with outward signs of prosperity, American-style: new outposts of Kentucky Fried Chicken, Tony Roma's, and Blockbuster Video.

But, even as Fujimori's economic turn-around is touted in the foreign press and Peru has been repositioned as a tourist destination, holdouts of The Shining Path have been making very different news. The guerrilla group took credit for bombing the Lima home of Peru's chief military officer and a central police station in early August. A full-fledged comeback is deemed impossible by Fujimori and unlikely by international experts on terrorism, who argue that the Shining Path has splintered into irreconcilable factions.

There remains, however, a powerful monetary incentive for the group's activities since it offers protection to coca growers in the dense jungle of the Huallaga valley, the country's main coca-growing region, which is said to be responsible for the raw material for nearly half of the world's cocaine supply.

Visitors to the embassy must pass through a sally port (above). The majority are applying for entry visas to the U.S. and must proceed to the consular courtyard at the building's north end rather than queue out front as at the former embassy. A courtyard with palms is used for formal visits (top).

The new-generation embassy

While Peru is undergoing intense political and physical change, so is the very nature of U.S. embassies, not only in their role as emissaries of American culture, political and economic policies, and moral values, but also in their public appearance. "U.S. embassies were, until recently, designed to convey the image of a nation confident in its guiding principles and open to the world," stated Stuart L. Knoop, an expert in embassy design, in this magazine [RECORD, August 1992, pages 36-37]. But embassy design was irrevocably changed in 1983,

EMBASSY OF THE UNITED STATES OF AMERICA
LIMA, PERU

when the U.S. Embassy and marine barracks in Lebanon were attacked by truck bombs. America responded to the Beirut attack with the passage of the Omnibus Diplomatic Security Act of 1986 and the institution of new embassy design guidelines.

The front entrance, which is primarily for ceremonial use, is framed in alternating bands of American and Peruvian stone and metal (opposite). The bronze door was designed by Arquitectonica principal Laurinda Spear.

Finding the right site, right architect

An important early step for the U.S. Department of State's Office of Foreign Building Operations (FBO) in overseeing the design of a new-generation embassy is the selection of the site, one large enough to accommodate the new FBO preference for 100-ft setbacks from the street and parking separated from the building. Convenience for employees, visiting Americans, and the over 400 Peruvians who seek entry visas to the U.S. daily is sacrificed for safety. Amid the sprawl of Lima, the choices were limited, and the FBO eventually purchased 1 1/2 polo playing fields from the Lima Polo Club, a total land package of some 21 acres, in Monterrico, a growing residential and commercial neighborhood in the east edge of the city, near the foothills of the Andes.

The Miami-based firm Arquitectonica was selected as architect based on the qualifications of the team it assembled. Principal Bernardo Fort-Brescia's Peruvian heritage, an asset in the firm's capture of the $54-million Banco de Credito commission in Lima [RECORD, February, 1989, pages 90-99] was, the architect claims, a mixed blessing when it came to the U.S. embassy because of political tensions that then existed between the U.S. and the host country. His firm's previous experience with the bank, which was at a scale, structural complexity (the building is in an earthquake zone), and level of finish unusual for Lima at the time, outweighed any perceived risks of divided loyalties. What's more, he, like all members of his firm who worked on the project and all firms that do work for the FBO, was subject to background checks to obtain security clearance.

The facade was designed as a tapestry to cloak the five-story bulk and minimal fenestration, "a Modern architectural version of a pre-Columbian textile," according to Arquitectonica (above). Different materials give the illusion of depth. (Terrorists can't scale flat surfaces.) Reinforced perimeter walls are meant to resemble rock patterns of Inca structures.

The message is "keep out!"

Like many of the embassies built since 1986, (Bolivia, Chile, Columbia, Cyprus, El Salvador, Kuwait, Jordan [RECORD, May 1993, pages 66-73], Oman, Thailand, Venezuela), the Lima embassy puts a different face on foreign diplomacy. Forget architecture as goodwill ambassador. The message now is "keep out!" Following the adoption of the more stringent guidelines, which in addition to setback requirements, also limit the percentage of surface area that can be devoted to windows and the actual size of the openings (in this case, 15 percent of the structural bay of 32.5 ft wide by 13 ft high), virtually pre-determines a bunker-like appearance.

As with the Banco de Credito, Arquitectonica's brash style proved ideally suited to the task. The firm originally proposed three possible schemes within a masterplan that included an Ambassador's residence, Marine dormitories, and an annex office building (all of which remain unbuilt, for now), which is consistent with FBO requirements. A Z-shaped structure and a courtyard scheme were dismissed in favor of the single rectangular volume that was ultimately built because, says Fort-Brescia, the "corner is the weak point" for blast resistance. "The fewer corners, the better."

The program was big and complex—from offices for the Ambassador and a vast array of staff to consular services; accommodations for Drug Enforcement Agency personnel; information libraries; and medical, security, and housing services for members of the Foreign Service stationed in the host country. To accommodate these functions, the rectangular block had to be enormous: 200,000 sq ft in five stories. The architects studied the proportions of various rectangles, eventually accepting that the building would have no subtle manipulation of form, save for the ceremonial entry framed by alternating planes of stone and metal that give the appearance of a forced perspective. "There is a moment when you decide there are no apologies," says Fort-Brescia of attempts to disguise the building's bulk. "How do you give life to this coffer? You make it into a mural."

"Neo Andean" style

Arquitectonica quite literally took inspiration from Peruvian history, modeling the base of the building on the structures of the ancient cities of Cuzco and Machu Picchu. (For more contemporary, defensive purposes, the trapezoidal panels are welded to steel plates embedded in concrete.) Layered on top are more Modern references that commingle Peruvian and American cultures. A grid of gold squares is meant to refer to Peru's rich mining heritage. Sized to match the windows, they make the wall look less formidable. The bands of tinted glass suggest ashlar-patterned stone while recalling the strip windows of Modern office buildings.

Meant to create the illusion of depth along the top is a triangular pattern of two shades of limestone, anchored to the concrete structure, like all facade cladding, by steel bolts on support angles. Glenn Cameron, local FBO civil engineer and project director, calls the overall mixture of patterns and materials "Neo-Andean style." Patrick Collins, FBO's chief architect, calls it a "billboard building."

Inside, the building's footprint is highly flexible because it "allows for large chunks of contiguous, adjacent floor space," says Miguel Aparicio, FBO's project architect for Lima, who rates the overall plan of offices as "very successful," particularly since embassy staff is continuously growing and shrinking, affected by government cutbacks and the changing demands of the host country. A main corridor along the east wall provides views to the mountains and, says Aparicio, reduces the need for orienting graphics. A landscape plan that includes palm trees and lush lawns is proving costly to maintain, since it rarely rains in Lima and the local river that was to be diverted for irrigation does not meet American Food and Drug Administration health and safety standards. (A water-treatment facility is in the works since, as embassy workers concede, high water bills for the use of city water, which is a precious commodity, are not good for public relations.)

The dawn of yet another era

While the Lima embassy employs elaborate security techniques, recent events—the attack on barracks in Saudi Arabia and the destruction of the Murrah Federal Building in Oklahoma City—suggest that the notion of who "the enemy" is is subject to change. Are architects to design against a "war or a weirdo?" asks Fort-Brescia.

Whatever the defensive position, the overall public image of the ultra-secure embassy is uncomfortable to many, including those who work inside the walls. As FBO's Collins explained to RECORD regarding the design competition for the new U.S. embassy in Berlin [RECORD, March 1996, pages 36-43], diplomatic personnel are increasingly resistant to living behind walls. In fact, FBO relaxed building-setback requirements for embassies currently being designed, including Berlin and Ottawa, partly to avoid the effect of a fortified compound, partly to respond to the realities of an urban context, and partly due to the prohibitive cost of applying the 1986 standards around the world. These developments shed new light on the Lima embassy: is it, one year old, anachronistic already or, is it, in an ever-volatile world, harbinger of the future? Certainly it's one of a kind. *Karen D. Stein*

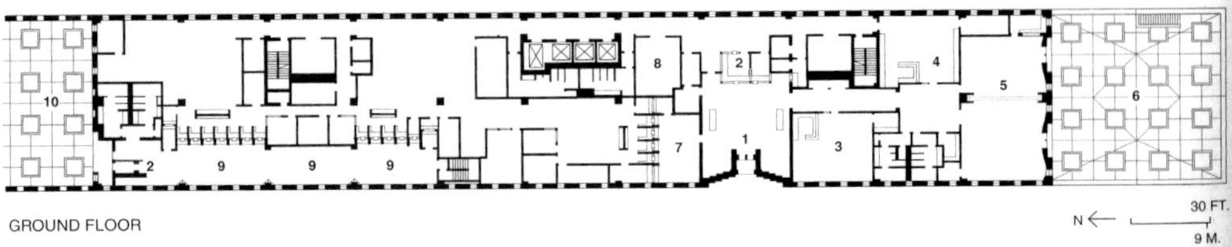

Due to U.S. Department of State security requirements, only a schematic floor plan can be shown.

1. *Ceremonial lobby*
2. *Security checkpoint*
3. *Business information center*
4. *Research center*
5. *Auditorium*
6. *Reception terrace*
7. *Library*
8. *Conference room*
9. *Consular services*
10. *Consular courtyard*

Arquitectonica's use of materials counters the impression of impenetrability. Gold-painted stainless-steel squares mimic windows (above middle) and, along with strips of tinted glass at the building's top, give the impression of more openings. The architects took advantage of a higher grade on the north side to create a protected forecourt for consular services (top), where Peruvians come to apply for visas to the U.S.

Inside the consular area, one of the most heavily-used sections of the embassy, is a waiting room with terrazzo floor patterns that are meant to recall Peruvian textiles (left). Consular officials review visa applications from behind protected booths.

EXIT

Credits
United States Embassy Chancery Building Lima, Peru
Architect: *Arquitectonica—Bernardo Fort-Brescia and Laurinda Spear, principals-in-charge; Armando Trujillo, Martin Wander, project managers; Sergio Bakas, project architect; Ailsa Simon, Eduardo Luaces, Dan Zabowski, Peter Alvarez, Janice Rauzin, Diana Farmer, Tony Moreno, team*
Engineers: *EDAW (civil); Lehr & Associates (mechanical/electrical/plumbing); Riva Klein & Partners (structural); Law Engineering (geotechnical)*
Consultants: *Arquitectonica with MBB Design (interiors); EDAW (landscape); Robert J. Laughlin & Associates (lighting); Cini Little International (kitchen)*
General Contractor: *J.A. Jones and Graña Montero*

Walls of the ceremonial lobby are lined with two wood species creating broad stripes, while the ceiling is covered in blue metal panels with gold stars (opposite and top). A security checkpoint is occupied by a receptionist and an on-duty Marine who direct visitors (above). Upstairs, corridors are lined with black granite columns. Their forms were derived from ancient Incan structures (top right).

LEESER Architecture

Headquarters
Brooklyn, NY

Founding Partner
Thomas Leeser

1989

LEESER Architecture

1989–

Preston Scott Cohen

Headquarters
Cambridge, MA

Founding Partner
Preston Scott Cohen

Preston Scott Cohen

1989

Studio Daniel Libeskind

Headquarters
New York, NY

Other Locations
Milan, Italy; Zurich, Switzerland

Founding Partner
Daniel Libeskind

Current Partners
Daniel Libeskind (founder and owner), Carla Swickerath (architect, principal and CEO), Stefan Blach (architect and principal), Yama Karim (architect and principal), Nina Libeskind (COO)

Lana Barkin

WEISS / MANFREDI
ARCHITECTURE / LANDSCAPE / URBANISM

1989–

WEISS/MANFREDI Architecture/Landscape/Urbanism

Headquarters
New York, NY

Founding Partners
Marion Weiss, Michael Manfredi

WEISS/MANFREDI Architecture/Landscape/Urbanism

1989

Potatisakern Housing and Villas Phases I, II and III
1988–2002

Architect
Moore Ruble Yudell Architects & Planners

Location
Malmo, Sweden

Client
MKB Fastighets AB

moore ruble yudell
architects & planners

Vitra Design Museum
1989

Architect
Frank O. Gehry and Associates

Location
Weil Am Rhein, Germany

Executive Architect
Frele Architekten Gunter Pfeifer & Assoziierte Roland Mayer

Client
Vitra International

Four Continents Bridge
1989

Architect
SITE

Location
Hiroshima, Japan

Client
Hiroshima City

Daimler-Benz Research Center
1989–1992

Architect
Richard Meier & Partners Architects

Location
Ulm, Germany

Client
Daimler-Benz

Richard Meier & Partners
Architects LLP

US Embassy
1989–1993

Architect
Gunnar Birkerts and Associates

Location
Caracas, Venezuela

Client
US Department of State, Foreign Buildings Operations

Nexus/Momochi International Housing Exhibition
1989–1993

Architect
Michael Graves and Associates, Tigerman McCurry Architects, Steven Holl Architects, MACK Architect(s)

Location
Fukuoka, Japan

Client
Fukuoka Jisho Co., Ltd and Maeda Corporation

Northwest Frontier Province Agricultural University
1989–1993

SOM

Architect
Skidmore, Owings & Merrill

Location
Peshawar, Pakistan

Client
US Agency for International Development Mission to Pakistan, U.S. AID

Tokyo International Forum
1989–1996

RAFAEL VIÑOLY ARCHITECTS

Architect
Rafael Viñoly Architects

Location
Tokyo, Japan

Client
Tokyo International Foundation

Jewish Museum
1989–1999

Architect
Studio Daniel Libeskind

Location
Berlin, Germany

Client
Stiftung Juedisches Museum Berlin

Arp Museum
1989–2007

Richard Meier & Partners Architects LLP

Architect
Richard Meier & Partners Architects

Location
Rolandseck, Germany

Client
Arp Museum Bahnhof Rolandseck and the Ministry of Finance

Latvian National Library
1989–2014

Architect
Gunnar Birkerts and Associates

Location
Riga, Latvia

Client
Ministry of Culture, Republic of Latvia

Nunotami Corporation Headquarters
1990–1992

EISENMAN ARCHITECTS

Architect
Eisenman Architects

Location
Tokyo, Japan

Client
Nunotani Corporation

Architecture, Engineering, Construction, Operations, Management: The Rise of the Multinational Office

When Caudill, Rowlett Scott (CRS) became a publicly traded architecture firm in 1971, initiating a series of acquisitions that transformed the firm into a vast global engineering and construction conglomerate over the next two decades, it was among the first of its kind.[1] While journalists noted that "Not every firm is willing to share ownership and control with a large number of mostly anonymous stockholders and to bare its financial soul to them and to the world," by 1978 at least 33 other large design and construction firms in the US had chosen to issue public stock and so become subject to the forms of expansion and diversification demanded by shareholders on the open market.[2]

The most dramatic example of such scope and mega-scale is AECOM, the largest architecture and engineering firm in the world. While its 1,370 architects alone make it the single biggest employer of designers in the world, with over 45,000 employees as of 2013 this number makes up a mere three percent of the firm's total staff.[3] The origins of AECOM lay in the decision by Ashland Oil, Inc. to expand its services in 1984 by acquiring five large architecture and engineering companies, including Daniel, Mann, Johnson & Mendenhall (DMJM). When Ashland decided to refocus on its petroleum refining business in 1990, an employee buyback program led by Richard G. Newman, the president of DMJM prior to its acquisition, spun off these companies into a new entity, AECOM Technology Corporation. The firm's acronym is emblematic of its anonymity as well as its scope, referring not to the initials of partners but to the range of services it provides: Architecture, Engineering, Construction, Operations, and Management. A sweeping program of acquisitions of over 40

① Paolo Tombesi, "Capital gains and architectural losses: the transformative journey of Caudill Rowlett Scott (1948-1994)," *Journal of Architectural Education*, vol. 11, no. 2 (2006): 145–168.

② Oliver W. Witte, "Learn from the Public Giants," *Building Design & Construction* (July 1978): 48.

③ Aaron Seward, "Making It Big," *Architects Newspaper*, June 16, 2010: 11–13.

1955

1959 The Architects Collaborative (TAC) opens Rome office

1967 Leo A Daly opens Hong Kong office

1971 CRS Inc. becomes first publicly traded US architecture firm

1975 Leo A Daly opens Tehran, Rome offices, forms joint venture with Saudi Consulting House

1979 Leo A Daly opens Riyadh office

1980 Leo A Daly opens Singapore office

1983 CRS Group merges with J.E. Sirrine engineers to become CRSS Inc.

1984 Ashland Oil Inc. acquires DMJM among five architecture and engineering firms

1985
- Lebanese conglomerate Dar Al-Handasah acquires Perkins + Will, forms The Dar Group
- Leo A Daly opens Tokyo office

1962 Cuban Missile Crisis

1950–1975 Vietnam War

companies since 1998 has allowed AECOM to diversify into an ever-increasing range of global geographies and services, from courthouses and civic design to sports facilities, healthcare, aviation, land surveying, economic research, environmental services, and infrastructural engineering. The firm became a publicly traded company in 2007, reorganizing two years later to consolidate all of these entities into a single brand under the name AECOM. The most recent of the firm's acquisitions, of the engineering conglomerate URS Corporation, will likely double the size of the company, putting it close the 100,000-employee mark.

Other firms pursued non-acquisition-based models for multinational expansion after the 1980s. The model of internal growth is perhaps best exemplified by Gensler, the second largest employer of architects in the world after AECOM, yet whose 1,346 architects make up close to half of the company's total size.[4] Gensler's growth came in part from clients who expanded internationally and brought the architecture firm with them. Gensler's London office opened in 1989 at the request of Goldman Sachs, with whom the office continues to work with on projects in the city.[5] Other US firms with permanent offices in London by 1990, largely due to work on the massive London Docklands development at Canary Wharf, included Skidmore, Owings & Merrill (SOM), HOK, Kohn Pedersen Fox (KPF), RTKL, Cesar Pelli & Associates, and Pei Cobb Freed & Partners.[6] Stephan Reinke, then director of HOK's London office, was clear about the shift in scope such practices entailed, claiming "We're not a US practice based in London, we're an international practice using London as a base."[7]

With over 3,100 total employees distributed among 43 offices in 14 countries as of 2008, Gensler exemplifies the productive demands of such globally distributed mega-firms, ones in which work runs around the clock.[8] The economic logic of this model relies on the circulation of capital as well as time among the international network of offices within a firm. Indeed, the Architects' Journal noted in 1997 that "the global nature of most of the US-owned firms [in London] should mean that local recessions can be offset by sharing workload peaks and troughs with offices elsewhere in the world."[9] As such entities have increased in size and complexity, they have become known less through their evaluation in the architectural press than by their market categorization in trade journals as "AEC" firms, providers of architecture, engineering, and construction as simply three among an immense array of building services. — MK

4. "WA100 2013, The World's Largest Architecture Practices," *World Architecture* (January 2013): 13.

5. David Taylor, "US practices find their feet in expanding London," *The Architects' Journal* (April 17, 1997): 22. See Peter Bill, "Goldman Sachs might be looking at boosting its city footprint," *The Evening Standard* (March 18, 2011), http://www.standard.co.uk/business/markets/goldman-sachs-might-be-looking-at-boosting-its-city-footprint-6579163.html (last accessed October 16, 2014).

6. Deborah K. Dietsch, "Americans in London," *Architecture* (September 1990): 64; in the same issue see Karin Tetlow, "Foreign Exchange," "Advice From the Experts," and "British Reaction": 101–105.

7. Taylor, "US practices find their feet in expanding London": 23.

8. Jacob Reidel, "Interview With Gensler," *Perspecta* 40 (2008): 186–193.

9. Taylor, "US practices find their feet in expanding London": 22.

1986 • Skidmore, Owings & Merrill opens London office • HOK opens Hong Kong office

1988 HOK opens London office

1989 Gensler opens London office

1990 • DMJM separates from Ashland to form AECOM Technology Corp. • RTKL opens London office

1991 • Leo A Daly acquires Lockheed, Andrews & Newnam engineers • HOK opens Tokyo office

1993 American Institute of Architects founds London chapter

1994 CRSS Inc. sells architecture group to HOK, engineering group to Jacobs Engineering Group

1995 Leo A Daly opens Dubai office

1998 • AECOM begins large-scale international acquisition program • Gensler opens Shanghai office

2007 Hillier Group merges with Scottish conglomerate RMJM

2011 KlingStubbins acquired by Jacobs Engineering Group

2014 AECOM acquires URS Corporation

2015

1990–1991 First Persian Gulf War

2001 Afghanistan War

2003 Iraq War

1990

2014

AECOM Family Tree

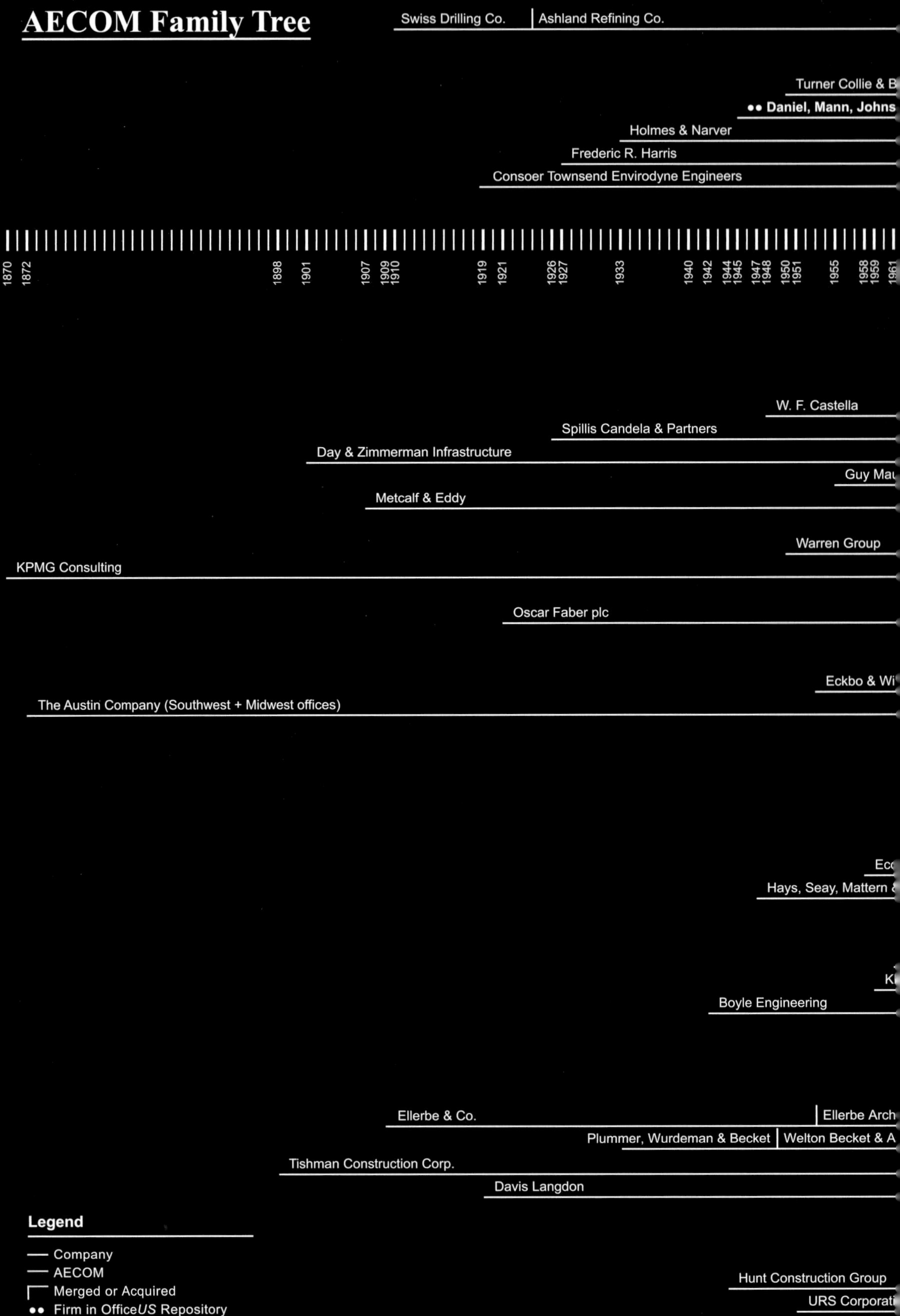

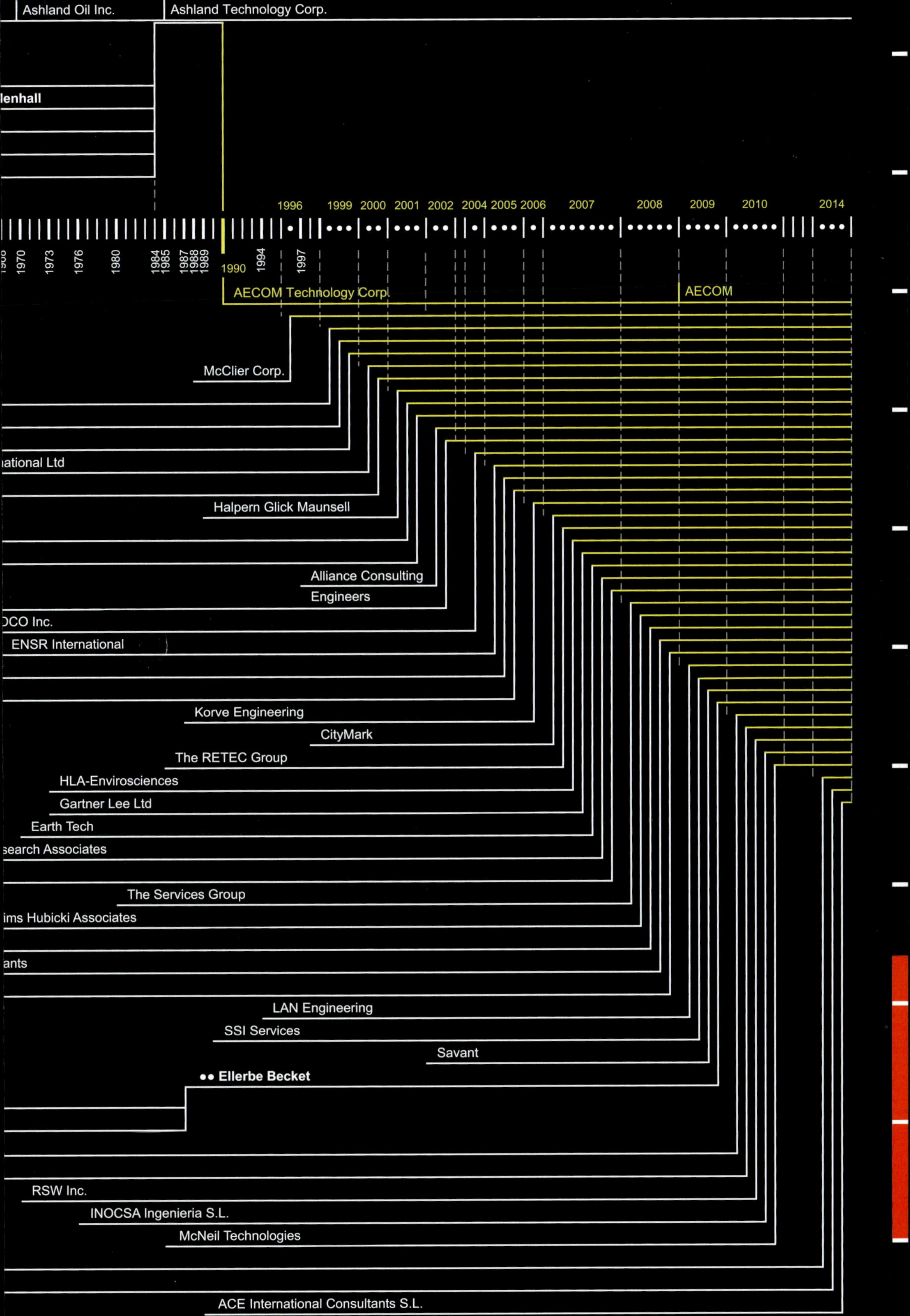

Ashland Oil Inc.
Ashland Technology Corp.
lenhall
1996
1999
2000
2001
2002
2004
2005
2006
2007
2008
2009
2010
2014
1970
1973
1976
1980
1984
1985
1987
1988
1989
1990
1994
1997
AECOM Technology Corp.
AECOM
McClier Corp.
ational Ltd
Halpern Glick Maunsell
Alliance Consulting
Engineers
DCO Inc.
ENSR International
Korve Engineering
CityMark
The RETEC Group
HLA-Envirosciences
Gartner Lee Ltd
Earth Tech
search Associates
The Services Group
ims Hubicki Associates
ants
LAN Engineering
SSI Services
Savant
Ellerbe Becket
RSW Inc.
INOCSA Ingenieria S.L.
McNeil Technologies
ACE International Consultants S.L.

Foreign Exchange: Advice From the Experts, British Reaction

SEPTEMBER 1990 • SIX DOLLARS

ARCHITECTURE

INCORPORATING ARCHITECTURAL TECHNOLOGY

AMERICAN
ARCHITECTS
ABROAD

TECHNOLOGY

& PRACTICE

Foreign Exchange

PRACTICE:
WORKING ABROAD

Architects from the United States offer tips on practicing overseas, while their British counterparts discuss the American presence in London.

In July, ARCHITECTURE invited British architects for breakfast at the Design Museum's Blueprint Cafe in London (above) to discuss the American "invasion" (page 104).

WHILE EACH AMERICAN FIRM HAS ITS own strategies for working abroad, practitioners agree on several basic factors, including the timely arrival of the fax machine. Expenditures of time and money are considerable, and so is the stress of global travel. Swanke Hayden Connell Architects, which established its London base in 1987, emphatically urges firms to commit themselves for the long term. "The challenge is to develop a sense of trust, because they're still looking at us with hesitation," notes Richard Carlson, design principal of Swanke Hayden Connell Architects.

Leaders of several U.S. firms working on overseas projects strongly recommend securing expert advice on matters ranging from compensation to national cultures. Diane Barnes of Barnes & Brandt, a New York-based international-marketing consultancy, has several clients anxious to set up practices and design-related businesses in the United Kingdom. For one client, a New York contractor considering expanding to the U.K., Barnes organized three days of conversations in London with experts on labor unions and construction practices; the client decided against the move.

Staffing problems can be avoided by accepting advice from consultants who are familiar with design schools and local firms. RTKL follows the practice of arranging seminars by experts on local culture and history. Forming associations with local architectural professionals is also a must. Local firms offer experience, vital information on local power structures and building codes, and, at the beginning, necessary credentials. They provide an essential operational base—especially in Japan, where clients may select the U.S. architect as lead designer, who then contracts with one of the huge design/build firms. Local firms can also be an invaluable source for understanding contracts. "A local association cures a lot of problems if the project goes bad," says Jeffrey Heller of Heller and Leake Architects of San Francisco, whose project in the Philippines was put on hold after a recently attempted political coup. Heller advises setting up an escrow account in Switzerland, staying current with billing, and limiting foreign work to a small percentage of the firm's business.

One strength that keeps U.S. firms in good stead in the global arena is their marketing know-how and willingness to set aside substantial budgets for the task. Many architects believe that connections are critical elements of successful marketing. They may be clients, employees and former students from abroad, or corporate associates.

Using the firm's own offices as a marketing tool, while a familiar strategy back home, is rare in the U.K. Richard Carlson and managing principal Richard Hayden, shocked at the state of British offices in general and architects' quarters in particular, determined that their storefront office in London should serve as an expression of creativity. Designating the ground floor as gallery space, Swanke Hayden Connell now controls its image from the moment a client walks in the door.

Communicating an understanding of foreign custom is vital everywhere. Recognizing the reserved approach of the British, Swanke Hayden Connell replaced its usual recorded slide presentations with conversations supported by portfolio. RTKL marketing vice president Laurin McCracken co-authored a handbook on doing business in Japan, in which he spells out the critical art of exchanging cards and the protocol of conducting business meetings (the average meeting lasts one hour; punctuality is imperative).

Diane Barnes recommends employing a European graphic designer to produce a brochure that does not look American. Country telephone codes and locations of projects should be included. Books containing illustrations of projects are often well received and help potential clients remember a firm's work. (More tips from architects follow on the next two pages.)

Clearly, global practice in all its variety is here to stay. The benefits are considerable, from improving profits to gaining insight on practice at home—all of which, in the long run, can lead to better buildings everywhere.

—KARIN TETLOW

Karin Tetlow is a New York-based writer.

Advice from the Experts

To understand the complexities of working abroad, ARCHITECTURE *interviewed principals of eight U.S. firms about their experiences practicing in Europe and Asia.*

Participants included **Harold L. Adams**, chairman of RTKL; **Richard Hayden**, managing principal of Swanke Hayden Connell; **Cesar Pelli**, principal of Cesar Pelli & Associates; **Charles Redmon**, managing principal of Cambridge Seven; **Erik Sueberkrop**, principal of Studios; **Benjamin and Jane Thompson**, partners of Benjamin Thompson & Associates; **Stanley Tigerman**, principal of Tigerman McCurry Architects; and **Carolina Woo**, partner of Skidmore, Owings & Merrill.

How easy was it to set up an overseas office and recruit foreign personnel? How did immigration laws affect your practice?

HAROLD L. ADAMS: Opening a new office anywhere, whether abroad or down the street, is no easy task. The secret of our success has been obtaining outstanding legal, financial, and other professional advice.

Immigration laws have not adversely affected our practice. Once we decided to move abroad, we knew there would be certain requirements and restrictions. British immigration laws state that you cannot be in the country while your work permit is being processed, something that takes a few weeks. Our office directors had to leave the country while the projects were just beginning. Fortunately, we were able to serve the client in the interim.

In our first office abroad—London—we decided to form a partnership with an existing U.K.-based firm. Though we've been working on many international projects, we felt the partnership would make our first step a little easier. One of the reasons for this is that it avoided what can be a very frustrating endeavor—recruiting foreign personnel. When we cannot supply the appropriate personnel from the U.S., we tap into our partner's resources.

ERIK SUEBERKROP: Immigration laws were not a critical issue for us in London, although they are for many firms. Our London office is managed on a day-to-day basis by a British citizen who had worked for Studios in the United States.

All of our London staff are legal residents. There is quite a large pool of American-trained interior designers and architects in London, and we have been fortunate to find new staff members from this group. Opening an office in Paris, on the other hand, is somewhat more restrictive.

BENJAMIN AND JANE THOMPSON: Our firm is currently working in nine foreign cities. We maintain a single, centralized design/production organization in the U.S., and we do not set up satellite offices, preferring to work in close association with an architect in each location. Nevertheless, we set up a four-man project office in Dublin, for coordination and supervision, due to the speed and complexity of our redevelopment project there. In transferring personnel, we obtained temporary work permits without difficulty. However, all salaries are subject to Irish income taxes and value-added taxes, and that amount is greater than what we pay in the U.S. There is also a corporate tax on fees for the work done there. In addition, there is a 25 percent tax on all supplies purchased in the country. It is certainly more expensive than working in the U.S.

RICHARD HAYDEN: We have found it no more difficult to establish an office in London than to establish an office in Chicago. Our offices are always set up with a major project as the impetus and are staffed by our own people. The immigration laws had a very modest impact on us since they recognize specialized and experienced talents and allow them to relocate. No one dictated the percentage of local people we needed to have, but we did not wish to have a "carpetbagger" presence and looked forward to building a permanent staff incorporating local practitioners. We recruited through acquaintances, agencies, and a modest use of local classified ads. At present, 10 percent of the staff is American.

Richard Hayden

CAROLINA WOO: Setting up an office in the U.K. was really no different from setting up any other office in a foreign country. The immigration laws in the U.K. are very similar to those of the U.S. It is important to seek legal advice to tackle such problems as immigration and taxation laws, which are very complex. At present, 15 percent of our employees in the U.K. are American.

CHARLES REDMON: In most cases, we did not set up an overseas office largely because of foreign taxes. We have entered associations with local design firms to facilitate getting the project done. We have also been sendi[ng] our own staff members abroad for extende[d] working periods, working out of our associ[ates'] offices.

What are the procedures for getting a project approved by planning commissions an[d] local authorities?

SUEBERKROP: In Switzerland, France, and Japan, there are specific codes; however, they are often subject to discussion and interpretation. As you might imagine in a ci[ty] with the long history of London, there are many and various codes. In the Docklands however, new codes being written for getti[ng] projects through aren't subject to borough approval. It is not as difficult a review proc[ess] as it is in the rest of London.

Erik Sueberkrop

Benjamin Thompso[n]

THOMPSON: In Britain there seem to be mo[re] layers of approval than in the U.S. The process is more systematic and appears mo[re] bureaucratic than political—except when royalty intervenes. In Ireland, the codes are more general, with less specific requirements of how life-safety issues (fire egress and access, for example) must be resolved. Architects tend to ignore the codes and reso[rt] to negotiation when there is a specific design. Because of our collaboration with resi[dent] architectural firms, most of the proce[ss] is handled and understood by designated technicians in those offices.

HAYDEN: The approval processes in the U.[K.] are very similar to the variance-procedure methods in New York and other major citi[es.] The major difference is derived from the philosophical difference between British co[m]mon law and American statute law. In Britain, there are no clearly stated administrative codes governing building-design issu[es,] but there are guidelines that are interprete[d] through agency staff with final decisions being made by the legislative body or elect council. The major difference is that in the U.S. there is always the opportunity to test out an "as-of-right" approach, which doesn't exist in the U.K. In England, the number of agencies involved in the process is never quantified. In addition to actual government agencies, special-interest groups, such as preservation societies, are consulted by local authorities.

CESAR PELLI: The review and approval process by British public authorities is more interactive and subjective in nature. For example, an inspector here in the U.S. reviews a set of drawings for compliance to a clearly defined set of standards mandated in the applicable building code, and then issues a building permit to allow construction to commence. In the U.K., however, a district surveyor (the equivalent of our building inspector) addresses specific health and safety issues as they are raised by the architect throughout both the design and construction process. Instead of referring to a building code, the district surveyor will render judgment based on his experience with similar issues on previous projects.

Harold L. Adams

Cesar Pelli

How do foreign construction methods differ from those in the U.S.?

ADAMS: In general, the architect abroad has far less control over the construction process than here in the U.S. The process is closer to the design/build format, where the contractor has broader responsibilities.

SUEBERKROP: In countries such as France, Switzerland, and Japan, a large proportion of the construction pricing and contractor selection is based on what would be considered a detailed design development set of drawings in the U.S. There is, however, a lot of maneuvering room for both the contractor and the architect in the final execution of the work. In Europe, the architect is frequently the construction manager. Contractors in the U.K are not as familiar as American firms with the concept of fast-track scheduling.

THOMPSON: The significant difference between the U.S. and U.K. is the presence of the quantity surveyor as a key player in the team process. Working directly for the client, the quantity surveyor estimates costs, controls the specifications and bid documents, receives and evaluates bids, selects subs, negotiates all contracts and extras, and seeks the best value for the price. This process provides the client with an independent view. But, because the quantity surveyor doesn't work for the architect, there is often little input on important issues like material quality, and substitutions can be made without the architect's approval or knowledge. The architects, nonetheless, are responsible for supervision.

HAYDEN: For large-scale projects the systems, methods and procedures are quite similar in the U.K., though more detail is expected from architects than from contractors and suppliers.

STANLEY TIGERMAN: Technological differentiation between the U.S. and other countries is minimal. What can be different is the level of craftsmanship. Having worked in Berlin, for example, the well-known German craftsmanship is a bit of a myth. On the other hand, my experience in Japan was extraordinary, producing the best building I have ever been part of.

PELLI: Construction methods and systems are similar to those in the U.S. However, builders in the U.K. support a systems approach to construction more than U.S. builders do. For example, bathrooms in high-rise buildings are prefabricated in modules and lifted, complete with accessories, into place by crane. However, there is less of a reliance on mass production—there is no such thing as a hollow metal or wood door-frame profile.

REDMON: Quantity surveyors and construction involvement in the U.K., and "director of works" roles in Italy, are quite different and have significant impact on fees.

Are you importing materials and furnishings from the U.S. for your projects abroad?

ADAMS: Work abroad carries with it certain restrictions and expectations, one of them being that you don't rely too heavily on the crutch of American materials. Why use an American curtain wall system for a project in Germany when a German curtain wall system is every bit as acceptable?

SUEBERKROP: Although we import some materials and furnishings from the U.S., we tend to use only manufacturers that also have outlets in Europe. We are intrigued by the materials that are available to us in Europe, and think it makes good sense to use those materials from the point of view of cost and service. We find, for instance, a much better selection of light fixtures in Europe.

HAYDEN: Within the European Community there is little need to import products except for highly specialized materials. Already a number of American contract furniture companies such as Knoll, Herman Miller, and Steelcase are manufacturing in Europe, and we have purchased from them for many years. We have always purchased our marble and stone from Europe for buildings both here and abroad, and of course continue to do so.

PELLI: Most of the materials and furnishings for our projects come out of Europe, not the United States.

WOO: We are importing some materials such as precast curtain walls, systems furniture, and carpet tiles.

How often do your principals travel abroad to supervise overseas operations?

ADAMS: The people we've positioned abroad are all competent professionals, each offering the skills necessary to make the venture a success. When our principals travel abroad, it is not to supervise operations, but to attend board meetings, deliver formal presentations, and explore other types of marketing opportunities.

THOMPSON: We find that travel abroad is required monthly or bimonthly during the planning and presentation phases of each project, which often extend for several years. This schedule continues during construction even though we make supervision arrangements with associated architects.

Overseas travel is a special cost of this long-distance work—not only travel time and jet lag, but planning, arranging, and accounting of such trips. We feel it justifies a 10 percent surcharge on our fees and are attempting to implement this increase.

HAYDEN: Travel is required on a biweekly basis. We have a principal and associates in charge of the London office; this arrangement is similar to the relationship between offices in the United States.

TIGERMAN: The fax machine has greatly reduced overseas travel. My associates and I traveled to Japan five or six times. Our Japanese associates and clients took two or three trips to Chicago. There were also thousands of faxes between us.

WOO: So far we have six full-time principals stationed in the U.K. Some principals travel abroad on specific projects all the time.

REDMON: Hardly a week passes without a principal traveling abroad.

British Reaction

In London, millions of square feet of office buildings and interiors are being designed by U.S. architects. How do local firms feel about this American invasion? To find out, ARCHITECTURE *invited a group of British architects to express their opinions at a roundtable held at the Design Museum in London.*

Participants included **Francis Duffy**, chairman of DEGW, a 100-person firm in London with offices in Glasgow, Paris, Milan, and Madrid; **Piers Gough**, partner in CZWG, a 40-person office that designs commercial, residential, and institutional buildings; **Eva Jiricna**, a Czech architect working in Britain for the past 22 years and principal of a 12-person firm that specializes in retail interiors and small-scale commercial work; **Rick Mather**, an American living in Britain for the past 25 years and principal of a 15-person firm known for university, residential, and commercial buildings; **Ian Ritchie**, principal of Ian Ritchie Architects, a 19-person firm specializing in both commercial and residential work with offices in London and Paris; **Julyan Wickham**, partner of Wickham & Associates, a six-person firm that specializes in residential and commercial buildings.

Millions of square feet of development have been taken from British architects by U.S. firms. Why are the Americans so successful?

JULYAN WICKHAM: It's not so much the American firms, but their size. The Americans are no better than big British firms: they are businesses doing architecture rather than architects being businesslike. I've nothing against them except the product. It's a cynical type of architecture.

RICK MATHER: The developers at Canary Wharf are North American. They're used to working with Americans, so they go to what they know. The British process is slower. Americans can come up with an image, a design package, in days. They know how to present very quickly, offering lots of variations. The British, on the other hand, want to be thoughtful and serious, not so fast or superficial.

IAN RITCHIE: Another reason is greed. The British are not so good at putting so many square feet on a site. That's why Stanhope Properties asked SOM to design the second phase of Broadgate [page 68]. They started with a gentlemanly British practice, Arup Associates, putting up sophisticated buildings, but because of their greed and time scale, they moved to Americans.

WICKHAM: Broadgate was just too big for most British firms. That's why SOM got the commission.

How are the British influenced by American developments in terms of work methods and esthetics?

FRANCIS DUFFY: Americans from the Beaux-Arts tradition find it possible to split off design from production. That's enormously attractive to developers. It looks decisive and clear. The British think small because of the Arts and Crafts tradition. We worry about every detail. It's limited our scale of operations and imagination.

PIERS GOUGH: There's a generosity of space at Broadgate which the Americans have taught us. They may design appalling Edwardian pastiche facades, but there is an incredible richness to their buildings.

Is it true that part of the American success is due to office interiors?

RITCHIE: Yes. One reason Stuart Lipton goes to SOM is because he gets the whole lot—right down to services, engineers, interiors.

DUFFY: Broadgate's office interiors cost at least as much as the shell, because sophisticated, international tenants have asked for them that way.

RITCHIE: But is architecture exportable in cultural terms? American architects think you can drop in the American product, maybe round off the corners.

DUFFY: I think the opposite. I think architecture is very site-dependent, very local. What has recently happened is the result of

DEGW conducts research on office environments, as well as designing interiors and buildings, such as the 9,000-square-foot Willow House in London.

Francis Duffy

CZWG's Cascades housing complex, completed last year, is located near Olympia & York's Canary Wharf development in London's Docklands.

Piers Gough

Jiricna Associates has built its reputation on precisely crafted office and retail interiors, such as those designed for Jardine's Insurance Services.

Eva Jiricna

PORTRAITS BY CHRIS GASCOIGNE / ARCAID

strong economic forces making the local product inadequate for the aspirations of the user. It's a failure of the profession in this country.

GOUGH: We should have the wit to learn from the Americans who are here. British commercial architecture is pretty dire.

EVA JIRICNA: But I don't think good architects could survive at SOM. I've interviewed people from there, and it's so commercial they kill the idea of good architecture. There's huge money spent on presentations that the client can see and understand. There are models worth £25,000 that they give to the client. No Briton can compete. I saw the SOM presentation for a development in London. They didn't understand the existing architecture.

RITCHIE: SOM flew in with 600 renderings and models to show to British Rail and Stanhope for the King's Cross presentation. A British Rail director asked, "Where's the railway?" SOM asked, "What railway?" Now an English architect would have caved in at that point. But they went into a huddle, came back and said, "We'll raise the whole thing a floor." That's the ability of the Americans.

DUFFY: SOM's presentation skills are formidable. They're skilled politically, intellectually, and graphically. Their ideas can be grasped by people who don't come from their background. I've worked with a dozen other American firms like that.

MATHER: Yes, they are much more professional in their communication skills.

JIRICNA: They are trained for it and take it very seriously.

MATHER: Norman Foster said the greatest thing he learned as a student at Yale was how to relate to other people, and he's supremely successful at communicating when he presents projects.

RITCHIE: British architects are not that keen to do commercial work. We need work to fund the projects on which we don't make a profit, but where we enjoy the architecture. We're happy to do a commercial project like we have for Stanhope at Stockley Park. But we don't want to be saturated with "skin" projects—empty shells with no feeling. We're arguing with Olympia & York because we think they shouldn't put in air-conditioning without knowing the tenant. We're concerned about the human context. We were asked to design a 250,000-square-foot building at Canary Wharf. We questioned it, and produced a master plan which we're about to show to the client. Meantime, recognizing they had a problem, they employed Fred Koetter [principal of Koetter, Kim & Associates, Boston].

How would you characterize the American sensibility?

DUFFY: Americans are eclectic. They use a dozen different styles.

RITCHIE: Yes, they ask a developer what style he wants—high-tech, modern, traditional.

WICKHAM: That's my point. They're not architects.

RITCHIE: American architects don't ask the same sort of questions we do. They accept the client's instructions more easily.

DUFFY: It's an architect's job to influence the processes that are going on.

JIRICNA: It's a problem of how much architects respect what they are asked to do. That applies to Americans, Italians, British. It doesn't matter what nationality you are.

What do Americans have to learn from British architects?

RITCHIE: It's important for them to understand about not having power.

DUFFY: There is a tradition of user research and public concern coming from the great social programs of the 1950s, which Americans tend to skip.

MATHER: Americans will learn from controls, planning restrictions, and local participation in England.

RITCHIE: Americans assume that having answered what they consider to be all the questions, they can draw a scheme, and that's it. The English mind carries on thinking and then makes the next series of comments.

JIRICNA: Americans tend to sweep aside things that get in their way.

RITCHIE: There's a difficulty in transferring architectural cultures. Americans assume you can embrace Englishness. ■

Jose Manser contributed to this article.

Rick Mather

Mather has moved from small-scale projects such as interiors to designing 2 Pennington Street, a 100,000-square-foot office complex in the City of London.

Ian Ritchie

Ritchie Architects' office facility in Stockley Park was commissioned by Stanhope Properties, a British developer known for patronage of high design.

Julyan Wickham

Horselydown, a housing block recently completed by Wickham & Associates, is located on a redeveloped wharf on the south bank of the River Thames.

How to get ahead and stay there

Arthur Gensler reveals the secret of Gensler's success

For the second year running, Gensler have emerged as the leader of *World Architecture*'s *World Survey*. Founded by Arthur Gensler, FAIA, in 1965, the firm now has a staff of over 900 in 14 offices across the USA, as well as in London, Tokyo and Hong Kong, with a turnover of US$ 100-120 million. They are, without a doubt, architecture's greatest corporate giant. Arthur Gensler speaks to *WA* about the importance of not just meeting but exceeding the client's expectations.

WA: What is the reason for your continuing success?
Arthur Gensler: Since Gensler was founded in 1965, the cornerstones of our success haven't changed: superior talent, solid finances and a passion for what we do. We are still finding opportunities that others cannot see.
Could you pick out two or three key projects that have contributed disproportionately to your workload?
Last year we worked with 700 clients on over 2,000 projects. No one client provides more than three percent of our revenue. We believe that is a unique feature of Gensler.
What structural changes are taking place in the architect-client relationship and in the construction market as a whole?
Architects are becoming much more involved in the project process and with pre-design and post-design services. They are repositioning their leadership role.

At Gensler, our work is based on the notion of the studio as the professional building block and basic unit of client service. We have fewer levels of authority and a more even distribution of responsibility which allows the next generation of leaders to develop.
With the increasing emphasis on technology and computer aided design etcetera – do you see any implications for the construction market or the way that architects work in the world-wide growth of the Internet? What is Gensler's involvement in this field?
Full use of the Internet may be a bit in the future, but Dodge Reports are already available as well as other critical pieces of information.

"Last year we worked with 700 clients on over 2,000 projects."

Architects can use the Internet for the bidding process, transmission of documents, client communications. Eventually the Request for Proposals (RFP) process will take place on the Internet.
So is there a place for the traditional skills of design are in the late twentieth-century? The emphasis seems to be on the architect as computer operater or the architect as businessman?
Design is the premise on which Gensler is built. We are not in the commodity business. Architecture properly undertaken has, for its end, the making of great places. We want to be a firm that is recognised for design excellence as defined, not by the profession, but by our customers. We are adamant about advocating the benefits of good design. We want our clients to understand the value they receive for the fee we charge.

"Design is the premise on which Gensler is built. We are not in the commodity business"

How much does your strategy focus on the client?
Exceeding clients' expectations is our main ambition. We focus on building client relationships, not doing projects, and 85 percent of our work is from repeat clients or referrals. Clients do not receive a Gensler "look": they are given a Gensler approach.
Most of your clients seem to be involved in business parks and commercial developments. Can you point to any significant trends in this area?
Most of our work is in urban centres, where there is a need for information and support spaces. We are intensively involved with developing centres for companies who wish to relocate certain functions outside the central facility. In the financial industry, we are focused on bank consolidations and mergers. The revitalisation of the urban centre is also leading to another strong facility type for us, retail and entertainment. In general, there is a repositioning of properties and functions. Last year, the US market grew in our areas of project work. Health care projects diminished; housing is up; institutional and government work is up. The number of build-to-suit architectural projects rose considerably, as did lease-to-suit.

Your work in Europe and Asia has grown substantially during the year. Is this a reflection of the underlying economic conditions or an increased marketing effort on your part?
The business climate in England is strong. A large portion of our client base are UK organisations. We have intensified marketing efforts in Asia, although we are also asked by numerous US clients to do additional work for them.

Growth in the Pacific Rim has slowed this year. Do you feel that this is only a temporary phenomenon, or does it have greater long-term significance?
Our growth in the Pacific Rim has speeded up. Besides corporate interiors, we are working on a number of retail and entertainment projects and airports.
What do you identify as the major growth sectors of the market, both geographically and in terms of building type?
The major growth areas in the US will be the south-east and the west coast. In general, however, all regions in the US are growing, with perhaps the exception of the north-east. As for facility type, we are seeing many purpose-built project but clients are requesting an exit strategy.

With respect to clients: we expect government work to continue to grow. Adaptive re-use is also strong. As manufacturing becomes more capital-focused, there will be a shift from other countries to the US. Airports continue to be a strong market. We are beginning to see quite a bit of work in South America.

The market for industrial warehouses and distributions is growing. There is a shift in the kind of retail work we are seeing, more and more department stores are being converted into office space, movie theatres etcetera. Retail companies are requesting an entertainment component. In the UK we are seeing more office construction. In Asia, there are more industrial and entertainment projects. **WA**

American practices in London are bullish about the future. Gensler, HOK, KPF, Swanke Hayden Connell, SOM and RTKL have told the AJ that they plan to increase staffing levels substantially over the next 12 months. Many reported that financial work in the capital was coming more readily because of the particular management structures and working methods they employ, and because of London's emergence as what they judge to be the dominant financial centre in Europe, signalled by the decision by many US and European banks to build headquarters here in recent years. The Americans believe the UK leisure market will expand due to an increase in public prosperity. Although some expressed a note of caution about trying to avoid the boom and bust cycles that could result from expanding offices too quickly, information technology and the global nature of most of the US-owned firms should mean that local recessions can be offset by sharing workload peaks and troughs with other offices elsewhere in the world.

US practices find their feet in expanding London

London's biggest US-owned practices reveal widespread ambitions to expand on the back of burgeoning workload

BY DAVID TAYLOR

Left: HOK's new St Petersburg rail terminal. Right: RTKL's Trocadero scheme

Swanke Hayden Connell

Swanke Hayden Connell's London office aims to expand from 55 staff to 80 within 12-18 months, according to its business development manager, Andrew Justice. He told the AJ that the end of the lease of its office in Finsbury Square presents the opportunity to expand into a new building, with a larger staff, to handle important new contracts. In particular, the firm has won the new Merrill Lynch headquarters building in the City and is hopeful of securing a plum job to fit out Foster and Partners' London Millennium Tower, if it eventually receives planning permission. The Midland Bank – part of the the Hong Kong and Shanghai Bank company, the headquarters of which Foster designed in Hong Kong – is said to be interested in a pre-let of a significant part of the controversial building. Swanke Hayden Connell is also working with Fosters on its Citibank headquarters. 'He [Foster] is very aware that to attract owner-occupiers he has to have people looking at buildings inside out,' said Justice.

The nature of the work undertaken by the firm is also changing. When it first established a UK presence in 1989 its ratio of architecture to interior work was 90:10. During the recession, said Justice, the ratio reversed, with the 10 per cent of its architecture work coming from restoration projects. Currently it's 50:50, but Justice hopes the office will settle on 40 per cent interiors, 40 per cent architecture and 20 per cent restoration work. The practice has developed restoration expertise in the US on such work – even on the Statue of Liberty – and intends to push the sector here. 'The reason we've been so successful recently is because of the recognition that the tenant is king,' said Justice. Like many of the US firms in London, its office is populated by a majority of British architects, including the managing director, David Hughes.

RTKL

Like Swanke Hayden Connell, RTKL plans to recruit and relocate from its cramped space above Heal's on Tottenham Court Road. The practice, which has had a London presence since 1990, has 38 staff – 26 architects, including eight Part Three students, seven administrative staff and five graphic designers – under managing director Paul Hanegraaf and director Candace Sheeley. It says it is looking for about five extra designers. RTKL, well-known for its work in the leisure market, reports an upturn there, shown in jobs such as its £6 million 3D IMAX project for the Trocadero Centre in central London, now on site. This will complement the 50,000m² overhaul of the centre for Burford's, which bought the Trocadero in 1994. The practice is also involved in 'confidential' work for Warner Brothers cinemas, having worked with them in Leicester, Dagenham, Leeds and Bolton. Also from its London office, RTKL is working on a project outside Cairo, which involves masterplanning a 32km² resort, called Sahl Hasheesh. 'We can offer a different perspective, because retail is so different in the States,' said a spokeswoman.

Gensler

Gensler aims to increase its staff from a total of 85 to around 100-120 people (ie, by 17-41 per cent) inside a year, according to the new director of its London practice, Peter Hoyt. At the moment there's a roughly even split between interior designers and architects, with 10 or so administration staff. 'We've grown tremendously,' said Hoyt, who puts the doubling in size of the practice in one year down to an improving market. He also attrib-utes it to the fact that Gensler is becomin[g] more 'visible', with buildings under constru-tion, including No 2 Gresham Street, next [to] Goldsmith's Hall, and No 1 Curzon Street [in] Mayfair. 'That's been a significant factor [–] more people are aware of us,' he said.

With its parent company quoted as th[e] largest US architectural firm, Gensler [is] known for its presence in designing studi[os] for the major entertainments firms, offic[es] and fit-outs. The office opened a London ou[t]post eight years ago at the invitation of Gold[-]man Sachs, for which it was working. It wa[s] recessionary London, and Hoyt points to th[e] networking powers of the UK-born managin[g] principal of the office, Tony Harbour, as bein[g] key to winning new work. 'He's got [a] Rollerdex to die for,' said Hoyt.

The practice in London is increasing[ly] mirroring Gensler in the US, with millions [of] square footage of trading space for financi[al] firms and lawyers offices on the go, and it [is] now also working in the entertainment sec-tor, with cinema design. Hoyt said it als[o] hopes to win masterplanning work with Lon-don City Airport, for which it made a presen-tation last week. He too says that IT has mad[e] a difference, with millions of pounds investe[d] in networks to enhance global working. 'Yo[u] get 1000 people when you hire Gensler,' h[e] said. This practice too employs few US staff [–] only five of 80-plus staff.

Kohn Pedersen Fox

Kohn Pedersen Fox 'absolutely' has plans t[o] expand from its 80 staff, even though it ha[s] already grown from 43 staff just four year[s] ago. Again the market is reported to be gener-ally on the mend, and KPF sets particula[r] store by the recent MIPIM property confere, which takes place annually in Cannes at which it always takes a stand to win k. The senior partner of the practice, Lee isano, told the AJ that workload is 'clearly cing up', with projects that the practice has n involved in for a long time going ough various planning processes. 'Clearly see a rise,' he said. 'I'd say that in six nths from now if our projections are right ll have a rise of great significance – maybe 35 per cent.' KPF will not, however, be uiting for the next three to four months. The majority of the workload is in end- buildings – financial services, institution- ork and transportation schemes – most of ch are outside the UK. One exception is the ctice's scheme for an Institute of American dies in Oxford. The firm chose London in 9, again in recession, because of its finan- centre and because KPF valued it as one of then three 'truly global cities' in the world, gside New York and Los Angeles. When UK was in a downturn, said Polisano, the ce was still busy, attracting staff from other practices and 'solid' UK firms.

There is now a 'resurgence in the office or' but the practice is not heavily reliant any one sector, even banks, which seem so cessful for US firms. 'Whether you like it or the US financial business globally is fairly ninated by US houses. I think they look at ry specific kind of expertise not necessari- om Americans – the expertise is more to with the way buildings work on the inside n on how they look on the outside.'

M

M director Roger Kallman said it too had ns to increase its London presence, but also cautious about giving the numbers wanted to add to the current 40 staff, ch is split between interiors, planning architecture groups. The office, which is uiting at the moment, was set up in 1986 he back of the job to masterplan Canary arf and work on the Broadgate develop- nt, but an important history of SOM k in the UK includes the Heinz building, d Grade II* last year, and the Boots dquarters in Nottingham.

There is no doubt that the market is com- back again from the depths of recession,' Kallman, 'but it is clearly not what it was ne 1980s, which was unbelievably frantic.' eign banks are making a significant act, he says, but not all the opportunities coming from clients abroad – a job for roders Bank is under construction on sham Street and there is also renewed rest in the leisure sector. Kallman says he no doubt that projects are benefiting from Lottery (although Lottery-funded pro- s are not undertaken by any of the US s the AJ spoke to) and he points to high-profile public projects as difficult for foreign firms to break into. The London office is also doing significant work outside the UK, including a hotel in Cairo, a world trade centre in Jordan and an arena for Expo 98. Closer to home, work is progressing on a building at 11-13 Holborn Viaduct as the gateway to the Ludgate development, a scheme on Queen Victoria Street, and work away from the traditional City sites in areas like Hackney. The firm is also working across diverse building types, such as airport projects, offices, and financial institution buildings, 'because it makes simple commercial sense', says Kallman, to cover for fluctuations in market sectors.

HOK International

Stephan Reinke is both a founding president of the American Institute of Architects' London chapter in 1993 and, latterly, the director of project development for HOK International. His firm has 150 staff in London, but, when pressed, he suggests that it may increase its staff numbers by as much as 20 per cent, year on year. It may also seek to consolidate its London office, currently split between Oxford Circus and Piccadilly Circus, into premises large enough to cope with the expansion.

HOK merged with Cecil Denny Highton last November. Then it had 40 staff, now it has 147 as a result and the practice has grown by 30 people in the last twelve months. With a worldwide staff of a mammoth 1700 people, the firm tends to open up offices abroad on the back of major projects. In the case of the London office, the job in question was the world headquarters of BP in Finsbury Circus. HOK also has a Portsmouth branch, a legacy of the merger with Cecil Denny Highton. The London office has a markedly international feel, with Australians, New Zealanders, British, Spanish and French in the office under British managing director Ralph Courtenay.

'We're not a US practice based in London, we're an international practice using London as a base,' said Reinke. HOK in London serves clients as far afield as the Far East and South Africa, and deals with its Birmingham Centenary plaza scheme alongside work from Portugal and Russia.

Reinke says the difference between US-owned practices in London and the Brits is difficult to pin down, but could be in attitudes toward the client. 'I've always felt that there's a sense of expediency in terms of delivery,' he said. 'There's also no question that US practices are more focused on customer service.' Certainly, if the fact that the AIA's London chapter is the original and fastest-growing of all of its 300 foreign divisions is anything to go by, US firms in London are here to stay.

business

Business plans more building activity . . .

Construction output will rise 2 per cent this year and 3 per cent in 1998, says the latest report from the National Council of Building Material Producers (BMP). The figures would be higher but for a 7 per cent fall in government investment in infrastructure and buildings. A growing housing market, and a 'flurry' of new office developments and entertainment projects, will account for much of the predicted 7 per cent construction output increase over three years. Public sector work is predicted to decline over the next two years, partly because of cuts in the Housing Corporation's home starts.

. . . as Tarmac agrees . . .

Following £65 million of exceptional charges due to restructuring, Tarmac nevertheless pleased the City last week with results implying a 29 per cent leap in operating profits to £124 million. Chief executive Neville Simms forecast strong recovery in the sector this year and next.

. . . and so do surveyors

Nearly 60 per cent of surveyors expect a workload increase this year, according to an RICS survey published this week. In the first quarter of this year workload was up 9.1 per cent on the 1996 equivalent. Forty per cent of respondents said that they already had difficulty in finding skilled employees, especially bricklayers.

Housing starts jump, contracts are stable

Housing starts in the quarter to the end of February were 20 per cent up on the 1996 equivalent, at 42,000 dwellings, according to latest DoE figures. In the month of February, 14,700 homes started, compared with 13,500 in 1996, though completions were down 400 at 13,100. Meanwhile, the volume of new construction orders for the period was 1 per cent up on a year earlier at constant 1990 prices. Total value of new orders in February was £1.98 billion.

German construction slump helps no one

Concrete producer RMC says that German construction output will fall for a second successive year – compared with a 3 to 5 per cent rise in the UK market. Ironically, the architectural market in Germany is doing well, and the government has pledged to help boost construction-sector jobs, partly by preventing employers paying foreign workers less than the high minimum wage. Meanwhile, British Steel is suffering as the strength of the pound against the D-mark affects sales in Germany, helping to cause a forecast pre-tax profit of £190 million against £400 million last time.

When BIGGER is better

LESSONS FROM AMERICA'S LARGEST FIRMS

DOES SIZE MATTER? A SURVEY OF "VERY LARGE" FIRMS INDICATES THAT ECONOMIES OF SCALE NEED TO BE BALANCED WITH CREATIVE MANAGEMENT PRACTICES.

by Philip Langdon

You can sense the discomfort in some circles whenever the subject comes up: big firms and their growing share of the profession's work. American architecture, as a segment of the arts, has always venerated resourceful, brilliant (and, when necessary, stubborn) individuals: Richardson, Sullivan, Wright. They, not their firms, are the heroes we revere. But American architecture is also a business, and an increasingly collaborative one. No matter how often critics may present the inspired individual as the source of lasting architectural achievement, the reality is that American architecture is increasingly the province of very large firms—those with 200 to more than 2,000 employees and billings in the tens or even hundreds of millions of dollars.

The AIA Firm Survey hints at the change. "The proportion of AIA member firms with 20 or more employees has almost doubled since 1990," says Kermit Baker, the AIA's chief economist. "In 1996, for the first time, we had enough firms of 50 or more employees to break them out as a separate category." Firms with 50 or more employees, which comprise 2.5 percent of the nation's architecture firms, now collect over 38 percent of the profession's billings. Billings per employee are much higher in big firms than in small ones. The average firm reports $65,000 of billings per employee; in firms of 50 or more, that figure shoots up to $95,000.

Though the AIA survey lacks a category for "very large" firms, it is these that seem to be expanding the fastest, and becoming an increasingly powerful segment of the profession. "Over the course of a century, large firms are getting larger, and there are more large firms," says Robert Gutman, Princeton University's longtime analyst of architectural practice. "McKim, Mead and White was a very big firm at the turn of the century, when it had about 100 people. Albert Kahn had 200 to 300 in the 1920s." Today, according to figures supplied by the firms themselves, Hillier Group, A. Epstein & Sons International, and HKS each have about 400 employees, DLR Group has about 500, RTKL has nearly 600, SmithGroup has over 600, NBBJ, Ellerbe Becket, and Leo A Daly over 700 each, SOM about 800, Gensler over 1,400, and HOK and HNTB over 2,000 employees each. The degree of concentration on architecture ranges widely. HNTB says 206 of its employees are architects, while Gensler has 410 architects; HOK employs the most architects of any U.S. firm: 842.

Philip Langdon is the author of A Better Place to Live: Reshaping the American Suburb, *among other books. He is writer/editor for the Connecticut Conference of Municipalities and associate editor of* The American Enterprise.

Fewer and larger practices

"Architecture still doesn't have a Microsoft equivalent or a General Motors equivalent," says Ed Friedrichs, president of Gensler, the San Francisco–based architecture and interiors firm. Nor has architecture achieved the concentration of a profession like accounting, with its "Big Six." But the design field is gravitating toward fewer and larger practices. "You could equate us more to law firms," offers Friedrichs, noting that "there's been a lot of consolidation in that profession." "The big firms are gobbling fast," says Herbert McLaughlin, a partner and director of design for Kaplan McLaughlin Diaz, a 190-person firm in San Francisco. When a firm's leaders or founding principals are in their 60s, he observes, it may be easy pickings for a bigger firm that has both the wherewithal to make an acquisition and a desire for the greater geographical reach or additional forms of expertise that an acquisition can bring.

Some, like DLR (founded in Omaha in 1966 as Dana Larson Roubal & Associates), have acquired firms in other cities and allowed those offices to operate as relatively autonomous enterprises. It was only last year that all 15 offices under the DLR Group umbrella changed their names to that of the holding company. Other firms have steered more in the direction of HOK's "one-firm philosophy," attempting to shape their acquisitions into a single, highly integrated organization.

Acquisitions and mergers are just one source of the profession's growing concentration. "Gensler has never acquired a firm," says chairman and CEO Art Gensler Jr., FAIA. "We've grown internally." Some

NBBJ: THE NEW PLAYER IN SPORTS

Four years ago NBBJ Architects had little involvement in one of the big growth areas of architecture: sports and entertainment facilities. Today the Seattle-based firm of more than 750 people ranks third nationally in that field, behind two longer-established leaders, HOK and Ellerbe Becket. The story of how NBBJ got to be a member of the sports-design elite illustrates some of the advantages of very large architecture firms.

NBBJ reassesses its goals every year, and had wanted for some time to expand into sports facilities. In 1995 it got the chance when a group of principals in Ellerbe Becket's sports group in Los Angeles decided to split from their Midwest parent and pursue a quintessentially 1990s concept: "sports as a subset of entertainment."

Michael Hallmark, one of the Los Angeles principals (and earlier a founder of Ellerbe Becket's sports practice in Kansas City), says his group considered establishing an independent new firm but decided that was impractical. To succeed at complicated, highly technical sports projects, which often take several years to come to fruition, it's advantageous to be part of a large firm, according to Hallmark. "For us, bigness was important," he says. "The scale of the projects meant we felt we needed to be big from day one. We needed the resources: a vertically integrated group of specialists."

By becoming part of the corporate network of NBBJ, Hallmark and his colleagues were able to assure themselves access to experts on matters such as project management, graphics, and foreign cultures, and to guarantee themselves the capacity to handle highly technical issues, such as retractable stadium domes.

NBBJ REASSESSES ITS GOALS EVERY YEAR, AND HAD WANTED FOR SOME TIME TO EXPAND INTO SPORTS FACILITIES. IN 1995 IT GOT THE CHANCE.

The members of NBBJ Architects sports group.

"We toyed with the idea of being a design firm and, when assistance was needed, having an associate architect," Hallmark says. "The problem is, the projects are very technical. You can't associate with just any architect, even a good one, and expect the follow-through to be there."

The addition of the sports group, which now employs nearly 90 architects, has helped NBBJ fulfill what its managing partner, James Jonassen, identifies as a vision of being "a multi-building-specialty firm—experts in a number of building types." The sports group has contributed in other ways, such as "opening our eyes to the ability to communicate with video." The group uses tools of Hollywood moviemakers, such as Silicon Graphics workstations, which aren't normally within the domain of architects. Of that particular tool, Jonassen says, "It was technology we would never have thought was worth the cost." To his delight, it enables the firm to "tell a very complex story in a way that satisfies very short attention spans."

NBBJ prides itself, Jonassen says, on being extremely "studio-focused. There are no layers of management. The unit of delivery of services is the studios. They are almost autonomous." The combination of having studios concentrate on projects and having firm-wide resources such as digital technology, economic analysis, and "experience with alternative delivery approaches, from fast-track to design/build, to bidder design," are key, in Jonassen's view, to how a big firm can prosper and continue to grow.

Total Number of Employees	Number of Architects	Number of Offices
750+	600	9

Locations: Columbus, Ohio; Los Angeles; New York City; Research Triangle Park, N.C.; San Francisco; Seattle; Oslo; Taipei; Tokyo.

GENSLER: "A LEARNING ORGANIZATION"

"In the past we focused on our clients' projects one at a time," says Ed Friedrichs, president of Gensler. "They each had a beginning and an end." Today the San Francisco–based firm, best known for its interiors work, finds that its assignments tend to flow together and stretch far into the future. The clients, many of them companies occupying buildings not only in the United States but throughout the world, are erecting, altering, and updating facilities continually; they want Gensler to help devise an overall strategy for handling their needs. The organization, Friedrichs explains, sees itself as a partner with the big businesses it serves. Its work, he adds, has gone from being "transaction-driven" to being "relationship-driven."

Since its start as a three-person practice in San Francisco in 1965, Gensler has grown into a 1,450-person firm with 13 offices in the United States (from Los Angeles to Boston), as well as offices in London, Hong Kong, and Tokyo. "Being diversified geographically means we don't have to bet the company on one city or one location," says chairman and CEO Art Gensler. "There have been times when one office went well and another office went in the tank. We share work."

Repeat work for big clients is a major source of Gensler's billings, which reached a record $170 million in 1997, up 30 percent from the year before. Sony, for example, has had Gensler work on a new studio in Culver City, California, an urban entertainment center in San Francisco, a 13-screen theater complex near New York's Lincoln Center, and small screening theaters (for Sony's corporate review of movies) in Tokyo. Gensler's work for the clothing retailer Gap, Inc., has gone on for three decades. "Our relationships," Friedrichs says, "have really facilitated our growth."

Projects are typically handled by "studios"—groups of as few as 12 to 15 staff members or as many as 30 to 50, who work together on a variety of projects. The premise of the studio system, Friedrichs explains, is that "people who know one another well are likely to produce better results for a client." Kevin Hart, a director of design in the San Francisco office, points out an additional advantage: "Studios are very helpful at making large firms easier to handle for young employees and new employees. If you came to Gensler, you would be joining an office of more than 200 but a studio of 20 to 30. That's your 'home room.'"

M. Arthur Gensler Jr., FAIA, chairman/CEO

Total Number of Employees	Number of Architects	Number of Offices
1,450	410	16

Locations: Atlanta; Boston; Chicago; Denver; Dallas; Detroit; Newport Beach, Calif.; Parsippany, N.J.; San Francisco; Washington, D.C.; Hong Kong; Tokyo.

growth is the result of opening multiple offices across the U.S. and overseas. More and more architecture firms have "not three or four offices" but "six or eight or ten," says Jerome Sincoff, FAIA, president and CEO of HOK. "That in itself makes firms larger." HOK now operates 15 offices in the United States and nine in other countries.

Firms establish multiple offices not only to get business in new territories but also because their clients have far-flung operations and want their architects close at hand. Larry Self, HOK's executive vice president, says, "Our clients want the comfort and confidence of knowing that their American architect is going to provide the same quality service in Prague or Shanghai—or any point on the globe—that they get in the U.S."

Going global

The globalization of trade, which has been official U.S. policy in Republican and Democratic administrations alike, has also spurred consolidation in the architectural profession. Most small firms cannot afford to pursue overseas work; this is mainly the big firms' turf. The AIA found in 1996 that international work, which had risen to $625 million annually, was being done by just under 10 percent of American firms. But international work was being carried out by more than 50 percent of firms that had 50 or more employees. Many businesses, in fields ranging from publishing to automaking, are evolving into "boundary-spanning" organizations that have enormous appetites for construction, renovation, and management of facilities—propelling the growth of big firms. "If you're any good at all at what you do and you work for large clients who are at the top of their businesses, it's almost inevitable you will grow," explains Paul Nakazawa, a management consultant with Pearson Egan Nakazawa in Wellesley, Massachusetts.

From a big-business perspective, it's easier to work with one very large architecture firm than with several smaller ones. Large firms tend to have a businesslike attitude, substantial liability coverage, and a high likelihood of remaining in existence from one decade to the next. Conversely, the smaller the firm, the greater the chance it will disappear. From 1990 to 1996 the number of AIA member firms declined to 15,000 from 17,000.

As a firm becomes large, it can afford state-of-the-art technology and experts, reinforcing its power to outdistance the majority of small to midsize competitors. Architectural information system managers, who run highly sophisticated, interlinked computers, command "very high salaries," says Robert Hillier, head of the 400-person Hillier Group in Princeton, New Jersey. So do top human resources directors. Money is available at big firms, and so are large-scale projects, which can make effective use of specialists. "You have people whose lifetime career is to research building materials and write about them," Hillier emphasizes. "In a large firm, that person has a real place and a real job."

LEO A DALY: BUILDING FROM TECHNICAL SKILLS

"We speak the language, we understand the language of the project type: the airport," LaVern Rollet says when asked to explain how the firm he works for, Omaha-based Leo A Daly, came to collaborate with Cesar Pelli & Associates on the new south terminal of Washington's Ronald Reagan National Airport. Earlier, Rollet had led a team from Leo A Daly working on an international arrivals building (unbuilt) at Honolulu's airport. He's been working on aviation projects since 1979, when the firm dispatched him to renovate terminals at Los Angeles International Airport.

Daly, the largest privately held architecture firm in the United States, with some 750 employees, about 230 of them architects, has based much of its success on an ability to carry out highly technical projects such as airports, laboratories, hospitals, and educational facilities. Leo A Daly III, FAIA, chairman and CEO of the firm his grandfather founded in 1915, says clients are drawn to the firm in large part because of their belief in the value of experience: "Hospitals want to talk to people who have done a number of hospitals before. They want someone who is coming off a very similar one."

Along with technical expertise, Daly is known for its willingness to open new offices—and on occasion buy established firms—that can broaden its geographic reach and technical skills. "When a bank comes to you and says, 'We want to build 1,000 offices spread throughout the U.S.,' you need to have offices in those areas," Leo Daly observes. The firm's 1991 acquisition of Lockwood Andrews Newnam, the largest civil engineering office in Texas, is part of a strategy aimed at expanding into Texas and Mexico while simultaneously gaining new expertise in environmental and civil engineering. Daly now has 15 offices, four of them in the Far East, the Middle East, and Europe.

The firm's reputation for design has not been as strong as its technical skills. This may help explain the enthusiasm voiced over the hiring, three years ago, of Richard Clark, formerly at Kohn Pedersen Fox, as corporate head of design and as director of design for Daly's 125-person Washington office. Clark, who reports being given "pretty much a free hand," has allowed design to stay with a project longer, as part of a team, instead of having designers quickly turn the project over to production.

Leo A Daly III, FAIA, chairman and president

DALY, THE LARGEST PRIVATELY HELD ARCHITECTURE FIRM IN THE U.S., HAS BASED MUCH OF ITS SUCCESS ON HIGHLY TECHNICAL PROJECTS.

Total Number of Employees	Number of Architects	Number of Offices
700+	230	15

Locations: Atlanta; Council Bluffs, Iowa; Dallas; Honolulu; Houston; Las Vegas; Los Angeles; Omaha; Phoenix; San Antonio; Washington, D.C.; Berlin; Dubai, U.A.E.; Hong Kong; Madrid.

Above: Generations of Dalys have worked in the firm. Left to right: Leo Daly Sr., William T. Daly, AIA, and Leo A Daly Jr., FAIA.

RTKL: Going International

"We're in a shift," says Lisbeth Quebe, the head of firm-wide marketing for Baltimore-based RTKL. With her health-care specialist husband Jerry Quebe and corporate practice specialist James C. Allen, Quebe left Perkins & Will to open a Chicago office for RTKL in 1996. She observes that in the past RTKL "had always expanded geographically. It was a way to be closer to our clients."

Today RTKL is expanding in a different fashion, concentrating not only on being physically near its clients but also on pursuing "a sector approach." That means building the firm's strength in its core markets of retail, entertainment, hospitality, health care, corporations, and government. Clients increasingly expect expertise from their architects, and RTKL believes that firms must deepen their knowledge of client issues in order to develop, rather than simply respond to, the next generation of ideas.

Disciplined, rational plotting of the firm's direction is one of the things that makes RTKL "a very strong company," according to Mark Zweig of Zweig White and Associates management consultants. In 1967 RTKL, with four principals and 45 employees, was one of the first architectural practices to decide it needed a leader who would concentrate on management.

The partners who reached that decision brought in a young manager, 28-year-old Harold Adams, who had gained high-level corporate and governmental exposure at John Carl Warnecke, working on projects with President Kennedy and his Cabinet, among others. Thirty-one years later Adams remains in charge, leading an organization that has grown to nearly 600 employees, with 309 architects, and has become increasingly international in its ambitions.

"We manage our affairs in a pretty conservative, businesslike way," Adams says. "While we take risks, it's all studied risk." Two of Adams's chief responsibilities are identifying market sectors where a major investment of money and personnel is likely to pay off in the long haul and going after international work, which now accounts for more than a third of RTKL's revenue.

Design and production, Adams says, is best done by "teams that have worked together repeatedly." He notes, "Over the years, we've broken our office down into studios. Those studios are concentrated on a specific project type." Studios allow RTKL to amass in-house expertise, which has become critical as the pace of decision-making has accelerated. Today, he says, "you need expertise *now*. If you don't have it, you will miss a market opportunity."

John Gosling, a vice president and urban designer in the Washington office, observes, "Once you get an expertise, you tend to attract the larger projects. You get 10- to 25-acre urban renewal properties, as opposed to one or two acres." A firm can also export the expertise and even "re-import" it later, as in the case of high-rise office building technology or housing.

In five decades RTKL has taken a local practice regional, then national, and finally global. Its most recent transformation, still in progress, involves going from being a large national practice doing business overseas to becoming a truly international practice. There was a time, Gosling says, when the firm "had some difficulty promoting people who did not grow up in the mother ship"—the Baltimore office. But now the firm has principals born in Britain, Argentina, China, and India. The direction is unmistakable.

Harold L. Adams, FAIA, chairman and CEO

TODAY, RTKL IS EXPANDING IN A DIFFERENT FASHION, BUILDING ITS STRENGTH IN ITS CORE MARKETS.

RTKL's board of directors. Back row, left to right: Kenneth V. Moreland, Paul F. Jacob III, AIA, Lance K. Josal, AIA, Paul G. Hanegraaf, AIA. Front row: Todd C. Lundgren, AIA, David I. Brotman, FAIA, Harold L. Adams, FAIA, David C. Hudson, AIA.

Total Number of Employees	Number of Architects	Number of Offices
574	309	8

Locations: Baltimore, Chicago, Dallas, Los Angeles, Washington, D.C., Hong Kong, London, Tokyo. Affiliates: Cologne, Guadalajara, Shanghai.

A firm that establishes expertise in rapidly expanding sectors, such as sports facilities or criminal justice facilities—two specialties in which HOK is strong—gathers tremendous momentum. At some point, the best such firms learn that the objective, as Nakazawa explains it, is not just to be "in a market," it is to "lead the market." That's what generates continuing rewards and keeps a staff excited. The leader of a market sector can ride its position to worldwide success.

Often, success in the United States leads to success overseas and then back again. RTKL used its decades of experience in designing American shopping centers to win big retail assignments overseas. And the foreign work, some of it on a larger scale than in the United States, has inspired the firm's designers. A retail specialist in RTKL's Baltimore office marveled at a Japanese mall with a ski slope in its core. International work has set the firm thinking about new ways for retail complexes to captivate the public. The "ID8" section of RTKL, with its eclectic mix of architects; interior, graphic, and industrial designers; and people from television, is dreaming up not just buildings but the entire shopping-cum-entertainment experience.

Every big-firm leader attributes some of the rise of the very large firms to changes in the nature of building design. "Projects have gotten larger and more complex, and clients want them done faster," Hillier observes. The first corporate headquarters Hillier produced, a 500,000-square-foot facility done 15 years ago for Beneficial Corporation, took four years from start to finish; by contrast, Hillier's latest headquarters, 890,000 square feet for Bristol-Myers Squibb, was done in 15 months. Big architecture firms typically understand alternative delivery methods, such as fast-track construction and design/build. Most big firms can also spread the work across more than one office. When RTKL's Dallas office landed a three-hotel commission in the Bahamas, the project was shared with the Chicago and Los Angeles offices because of the need for speed.

One of the motives for continually growing is the desire to attract and retain talented younger people. That's accomplished, in part, by providing opportunities for promotion. "A lot of it boils down to statistics," says Hillier. One principal per 10 to 30 employees is an economically reasonable ratio, he calculates; therefore, "a firm has to grow by another 30 people before it can add another principal." If growth stops, the best staff members on the way up may depart.

For the foreseeable future, bigness in architecture seems likely to keep ratcheting upward. The consolidation occurring among corporate clients shows no signs of abating, and those mergers and acquisitions will spur demand for more unified architectural services, Nakazawa believes. "If BankAmerica and Nationsbank merge, they're going to want fewer relationships—and more from the ones they deal with. How many people do you want to educate?"

"We're at a real turning point in the profession," says Harold Adams, chairman of RTKL and of the AIA's Large Firm Roundtable. (Twice a year the roundtable convenes the heads of big firms—those with at least 50 registered architects who are AIA members—to discuss concerns such as insurance, architecture education, and legal questions.) "With the globalization of architecture, we will see some big mergers," Adams predicts. Will those mergers be "within countries," he asks, or will they be "across borders"? He answers his own question: "Both."

Is this the death knell for small firms? Although AIA surveys indicate that from 1990 to 1996 many two- to four-person firms disappeared, everyone interviewed for this article agreed that there will always be a place for small firms, which have lower overhead and the ability to give each client a principal's full attention. There will also be room for smaller firms that focus on artistic innovation. "Design firms" like Cesar Pelli & Associates and Kohn Pedersen Fox also seem to have a tight grip on certain clients looking for distinctive design. Indeed, design firms with prestigious names coexist amicably with very large firms, teaming up with them to carry out big, complicated projects both here and abroad.

It's at some in-between size, where the principals' involvement diminishes but the economies of scale are not yet present, that the crunch will be felt, according to the apostles of bigness. "The firm that's really problematic," says Hillier, "is the 20- to 50-person firm that does midsize office buildings, firehouses, canned stuff you can take off the Internet and customize." Maybe. But Gutman notes, "There still are regional firms in many parts of the country that do pretty well because there's a preference in many quarters for local firms that can be contacted readily. The problem many big firms have is that they're regarded as impersonal and distant."

Does design suffer?

Another analyst of architectural practice, Dana Cuff at UCLA, says large firms are always confronted with the question, "How do you maintain design quality?" Currently the very large firms deal with that issue predominantly by breaking themselves down into "studios"—groups that are large enough to handle all the components of a project and small enough to operate as a team. This arrangement works best, says consultant Weld Coxe, when the studio is headed by a principal who brings in work and has the authority to commit the firm. If studio heads have to go higher in the hierarchy for decisions, clients quickly become dissatisfied, Coxe says.

With a studio-based organization, "the same people can follow the project all the way through," says Bruce Fowle, senior principal at New York's Fox & Fowle. Such follow-through has become more critical, Fowle adds, as "integration of plumbing, mechanical, fire control, communication wiring," and other elements of buildings has grown in complexity. The practice that some big firms used to employ—that of generating a design and then handing it off to the production department—is on the wane. This is welcome news both for design quality and for the morale of lower-echelon staff members, many of whom were once consigned to monotonously repetitive tasks. (Another reason for the rise of the studio-based structure is that corporations have shifted much decision-making downward, from the top executive to vice presidents or managers, who are more comfortable dealing with studio heads. To make the client comfortable, the organization of a big architecture firm must mirror the current fashion in corporate hierarchies.)

How well a firm with a slew of offices can deliver on design quality is subject to debate. A. Eugene Kohn, a senior partner at Kohn Pedersen Fox, says his firm's decision to "concentrate our design and technical skill in two places"—a Manhattan office with about 170 employees and a London office with about 80 employees—has enabled the firm to maintain a consistent level of quality. Bruce Fowle sees another hazard in bigness: "The larger it gets, the more it becomes a business, where there's a greater concern for the bottom line and all the things that go with it."

Bigness is good for clients, employees, and projects in some respects and bad for them in others. Those who run big firms are aware of the dangers, and many invest in abundant travel, conferences, educational programs, and other efforts aimed at keeping their organizations attractive to employees and to clients. They've heard E. F. Schumacher's memorable phrase, "Small is beautiful," and they know that misgivings about bigness run deep. Size cannot be safely touted in all quarters.

"When we go in to see a client, we don't talk about size," Hillier says. "Architecture is still a personal business. It's still a service that's delivered one-on-one. So many clients talk about 'their architect' and not about 'their architecture firm.'" ■

THE HOUSE OF

MORRISON

SCOTTISH BUSINESSMEN SIR FRASER AND PETER MORRISON, WHO JUST ACQUIRED HILLIER, HAVE TURNED THE LANGUISHING FIRM RMJM INTO A GLOBAL POWERHOUSE.

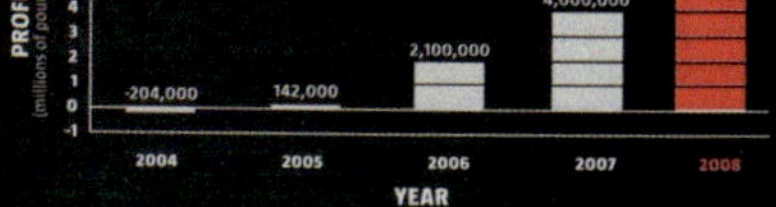

Text Amanda Kolson Hurley **Portrait** Art Streiber

PETER MORRISON IS NERVOUS. He has just taken the podium in the Piper Auditorium, at Harvard's GSD, before a crowd of architecture-firm CEOs—his peers. Wearing a navy suit and a blue-and-white checked shirt with cuff links, the 34-year-old CEO of the U.K.-based megafirm RMJM, a rugby enthusiast and former officer in the British army, would look more at home in London's banking district, talking global finance over a few pints in the pub. Instead, he's here at the GSD, announcing his firm's $1.5 million gift to the school for a new program in "integrated design." It is an unmistakable bid by RMJM for the attention of the American design elite.

Morrison delivers his speech, which he has memorized. After some polite praise of the school and its professors, he visibly relaxes as he warms to his theme: the architect of the future. "I believe the architect of the future will be much more than a stylist," he says. "Instead, he or she will be a leader ... The architect of the future must regain the status of master builder." He lauds RMJM's collective process as superior to "the media-created phenomenon" of the "starchitect" before moving on to some "hard truths" of the industry as a whole: first and foremost, that the financial reward for architects is "miniscule," so that the agent who sells a building will often earn a higher fee than the firm that designed it (a fact that Morrison will point out to me multiple times over two days in Cambridge). He wonders why a top-tier design firm can't command the same respect and compensation for its "intellectual capital" as McKinsey, the famed management consulting company, does.

This call to arms, albeit a rather mild one, seems to go over well with the audience. But one listener doesn't need any convincing. Sitting inconspicuously in the middle of the room, beside his wife, is Sir Fraser Morrison, Peter's father—and the CEO of RMJM Hillier, the American arm that RMJM gained last year when it acquired Hillier Architecture for $30 million. The story of how two non-architects came to run one of the world's biggest architecture firms—and now aspire to turn it into one of the world's most valued design brands—starts with him.

"I RECKONED I KNEW HOW TO SORT IT"

Fraser Morrison was born in Tain, a small town in the Scottish Highlands, in 1948, the same year his father established Morrison Construction. His father "built houses, he built factories, he built whatever there was to build," says Sir Fraser, whose soft burr and polite, almost diffident manner are at odds with the larger-than-life persona of many a business leader.

For its first two-and-a-half decades, the business remained small and local, its reach confined to the sparsely populated north of Scotland. But that changed in 1974, when it was bought by a mining conglomerate. A few years later, Fraser Morrison—who had joined Morrison Construction in 1970, after finishing a degree in civil engineering, and stayed on to run it under the new owners—moved the base of operations to Edinburgh, Scotland's capital. Thanks in part to the economic boost from the recent discovery of North Sea oil, Morrison's division expanded from a building contractor to "a very broadly spread construction business," involved in building homes, roads, and bridges, and in commercial development.

Despite his success running it, Morrison could see that the division "wasn't flavor of the month," as he puts it, inside the conglomerate. The owners weren't especially interested in its fortunes and didn't know how to manage the high risks inherent in construction. "The [construction] business in England had been losing a lot of money," he says. And then, an understatement that could be attributed to Scottish pragmatism or personal modesty, or a mix of both: "I reckoned I knew what needed to be done to sort it."

Sort it he did. In 1989, Fraser and Gordon Morrison, Fraser's brother, led a management buyout of the Scottish construction division as well as the underperforming English one. Over the next decade, the brothers grew the business into one of the largest construction firms in the U.K. Fraser Morrison was knighted in 1998. In 2000, the *Sunday Times* of London named him the second-richest person in Scotland—right behind J.K. Rowling of *Harry Potter* fame—with 1999 earnings of more than £23 million. The same year, the Morrison brothers sold their company to a British utility, AWG, for £263 million.

In 2003, with Morrison foundering under new ownership, AWG slapped Sir Fraser with a £130 million lawsuit, alleging that he had exaggerated his company's profit forecast. Sir Fraser called the claim "preposterous," blaming the decline on AWG's poor oversight. The lawsuit dragged on until 2006, when it was settled out of court, with Sir Fraser reportedly paying AWG £10 million.

STAGNATION AND BUYOUT

One of the biggest projects that Morrison Construction took on before the sale to AWG was the Falkirk Wheel, a massive rotating boat lift that connects two Scottish canals, one of which lies 115 feet below the other. Originally, Morrison "bid on that project on a design-and-construct basis," Sir Fraser recalls. "And the client came to us and said, 'We really want to do this with you, but we think your design's awful. Can you do something about it?'"

Morrison couldn't, but RMJM, a Scottish architecture firm founded in 1956, could. The firms had worked together on numerous projects over the years. With a consortium including Morrison handling the engineering side, RMJM designer Tony Kettle came up with a striking, playful scheme that resembles a row of giant bottle-openers. Finished in 2002, the Wheel is now one of Scotland's top tourist attractions and even appears on Scottish banknotes.

> "I TOOK [PETER MORRISON] TO OUR HOUSE FOR DINNER, WITH A FEW OF THE PRINCIPALS. THE NEXT MORNING, HE UPPED HIS OFFER. THEN WE WENT TO THE PHILADELPHIA OFFICE AND TOURED THE PRINCETON OFFICE. WE SAT DOWN TO LUNCH—HE UPPED IT SOME MORE. AT THE END, HE MATCHED THE [HIGHEST BIDS]." —BOB HILLIER, FOUNDER OF HILLIER ARCHITECTURE, ON THE MERGER WITH RMJM

One month before Queen Elizabeth II officially opened the Wheel as part of her Golden Jubilee, another event that was more momentous for RMJM occurred—this time without any fanfare. Sir Fraser backed a management buyout of RMJM. The firm had "stagnated," he says. Sixty percent of the shares were held by people who didn't have an active interest in the company: retired partners, the families of partners who had died. The working shareholders approached Sir Fraser and asked him to help.

"'We have this problem': That's how they put it," he recalls, summing up the rest of their pitch: "'We know you know us, we know you know the industry—are you interested in sitting down with us and trying to figure out a way forward?'" In the words of Bob Hillier, the founding principal of Hillier Architecture and now a "lifetime principal" of RMJM Hillier, "Fraser kind of backed into [architecture]. And then he got fascinated by it."

After an exploration period of nine months, beginning in late 2001, Sir Fraser bought out the nonworking shareholders and invested money in the company. The working directors also bought more shares, "so we had buy-in, a successful formula for making a management buyout work." With a 56-percent stake in RMJM, Sir Fraser and son Peter, then 28 and having just earned an MBA from Imperial College, London, joined the firm as non-executive directors. Peter took over as CEO in 2005 and, two years later, appointed his father to run RMJM Hillier. (The upside-down arrangement gives rise to some gentle joking between father and son: Asked whether he plans to stay in New York long-term, Sir Fraser deadpans, looking sidelong at Peter, "Depends what the boss says.")

To describe RMJM at that time as stagnated would, however, be charitable. Thirty miles from the Falkirk showpiece, in Edinburgh, the firm was grappling with a project that kept sprouting new heads, arms, legs—the new home for the Scottish Parliament, designed by Catalan architect Enric Miralles with RMJM acting as executive architect. Miralles had died shortly after completing the design, leaving the project without its visionary. By the time the building was finally finished in 2004, costs had reached a staggering £414 million—10 times the original estimate—and the Scottish government had conducted an inquiry into the delays and overruns.

According to British press reports, Brian Stewart, then chief executive of RMJM, broke down in tears while giving evidence. He left the firm in 2005, amid rumors that he had been forced out. The head of the inquiry, Lord Fraser of Carmyllie (no relation to Sir Fraser Morrison), concluded that most of the blame lay with the client for choosing a "fast track" procurement method while not understanding the risks and complexities involved. Still, in his final report, Lord Fraser observed that RMJM and EMBT, Miralles' firm, "had very different cultures and ways of working and found it difficult to adopt a cohesive approach ... whilst working in separate locations and communicating mainly via fax."

In the midst of the recriminations over the parliament—which won the Stirling Prize, Britain's most illustrious architecture award, in 2005—did the Morrisons regret their decision? Never, they claim. "Outside of Scotland, very few people related to the controversy over it," says Peter Morrison. "It was largely recognized as a fantastic design, an iconic building." Sir Fraser says that it's been a "springboard" for designing major projects around the world, and his son agrees: "We had the guys from Gazprom there for a day, and we could barely get them out of it. They ended up there for five or six hours, going around looking at the detailing."

On that day, an old controversy met one that was just brewing.

AFTER THE MERGER, LITTLE FALLOUT

Profits at RMJM have jumped exponentially since the Morrisons arrived—nearly 90 percent between 2006 and 2007 alone—and when they recount how they turned things around, you marvel not so much at their business acumen as at the state of the company they inherited. Back in 2003, when it was a firm of 350 people in four countries, RMJM did not have an attorney on staff, or an accountant.

"They had the architects doing everything," recalls Peter Morrison. "They were managing the finance systems, they were managing the HR, the marketing; for all we know, they were taking the board minutes." Morrison remembers asking a now-departed executive, in 2003 or 2004, where the conference phones were kept. "I was told there was one conference phone in the entire firm, and it was locked away in [a] cupboard."

The solution was simple: Get the designers back to designing by improving support systems, and make sure they're talking to each other. Peter Morrison put a finance management system in place and beefed up the firm's marketing and business development efforts. A corporate law firm was retained to help negotiate contracts. Architects in Hong Kong and Dubai were encouraged to talk to—and work with—their colleagues in Glasgow and London.

But the firm still had no presence in the United States. Meanwhile, in Princeton, N.J., Bob Hillier was phasing out a long career at the helm of his eponymous firm and on the lookout for a merger opportunity. Engineering companies were coming up with good offers: "But the problem is that architects don't want to work for an engineering company," Hillier says. Then an investment banker called him, he remembers, and said, "'I may have a firm that could be interested in you.' And that was RMJM."

Next Hillier got a call from Peter Morrison, who made an offer for the firm. It was too low. Morrison called back and upped it; Hillier again declined and suggested that "we ought to close this whole conversation down." So Morrison immediately got on a plane to New York.

Hillier describes the couple of days that followed as if they were an elaborate parlor game: "I took him to our house for dinner, with a few of the principals. The next morning, he upped his offer. Then we went to the Philadelphia office and toured the Princeton office. We sat down to lunch—he upped it some more. At the end, he matched the engineering offers." Hillier's impression of Morrison was that "he was charming and has a good backbone. He's very definitive when he wants to be."

With the acquisition of Hillier, RMJM swelled to nearly 1,200 people working in seven countries. It was a marriage between two well-matched building portfolios: RMJM did more office and residential design while Hillier brought healthcare expertise (the firms were equally strong in education). The Morrisons organized the firm into studios that span offices, even oceans—the Global Education Studio, headed by Gordon Hood, works out of Cambridge and Princeton—and shuffled up its workers, sending Brits to New York and Americans to Edinburgh and Dubai. Today there is "more rigor in the business side," Hillier says. With management paying closer attention to how work plans are

A MORRISON TIMELINE

- **1948:** Fraser Morrison born in Tain, Scotland • Morrison Construction founded by his father
- **1956:** RMJM founded in Edinburgh and London by Robert Matthew and Stirrat Johnson-Marshall
- **1966:** Hillier Architecture founded in Princeton, N.J., by J. Robert Hillier
- **1974:** Morrison Construction taken over by conglomerate • Peter Morrison born
- **1989:** Fraser and Gordon Morrison lead management buyout of Morrison Construction
- **1999:** Construction begins on Scottish Parliament building
- **2000:** Morrison Construction sold to AWG for £263 million
- **2002:** Falkirk Wheel opens • Sir Fraser and Peter Morrison back management buyout of RMJM
- **2003:** Sir Fraser Morrison sued by AWG for £130 million • Inquiry begins into Scottish Parliament delays and overruns
- **2004:** Scottish Parliament opens
- **2005:** Peter Morrison becomes CEO of RMJM • Scottish Parliament wins Stirling Prize
- **2006:** RMJM wins Gazprom competition
- **2007:** RMJM acquires Hillier Architecture for $30 million • Sir Fraser Morrison becomes CEO of RMJM Hillier

drawn up and fees are assessed, he says, "I think we're charging more realistic and [higher] fees than we were before."

What's more, "there's been very, very little fallout" from the merger in the U.S. offices, Hillier claims, citing two reasons: First, there were no layoffs; and second, an ESOP (employee stock ownership plan), which owned "40-some" percent of shares in Hillier Architecture, meant that every employee received a cash payout. "The mail guy got $65,000 because he'd been here for 15 years. Everybody got something in the merger." RMJM does not have an ESOP.

"WE DO A LOT OF DUE DILIGENCE ON THE PEOPLE WE WORK FOR. IF WE BELIEVED THERE WAS SOMETHING MORALLY DEFICIENT, WE WOULDN'T WORK FOR THESE CLIENTS. WHAT WE'RE NOT GOING TO DO IS SAY WE WON'T WORK FOR RUSSIA OR CHINA BECAUSE OF A HISTORY OF PROBLEMS IN THOSE COUNTRIES."

—PETER MORRISON

ARCHITECTURAL POLITICS RUN AMOK

On a March morning in RMJM Hillier's unassuming New York headquarters, which occupies the 24th floor of an Art Deco building on Seventh Avenue, designers hunch over their desks and the principals look out from their glass-walled offices. The staff is as cosmopolitan as you'd expect, but with a decidedly Celtic, and youthful, bent—even the principals.

"Early forties, late thirties, is where most of the senior people are," agrees Morrison. "And that's a fantastic advantage in an industry where there are a number of firms that have very senior management teams."

Chris Jones, who leads RMJM Hillier's new Jrban Studio, and Peter Schubert, the firm's U.S. lesign director, give me a demonstration of Glo, ın "international architectural visualization and ınimation studio" within the firm. A Scottish nember of the Glo team, Andrew Maxwell, still ooking a bit dazed several weeks after moving ıere from Glasgow, runs the demo on his com- ›uter. And there *it* is, gleaming and heroic in CGI as time-lapse clouds dart over a virtual St. Petersburg, to the strains of Camille Saint-Saëns: :he 1,300-foot-tall Gazprom tower.

In December 2006, RMJM won a competi- :ion to design the headquarters of Gazprom, Russia's state-controlled energy giant, beating ›ut the likes of Daniel Libeskind and Rem Kool- ıaas. Even at this early stage, the project, and RMJM's design, had kicked up storms of outrage. The St. Petersburg Union of Architects protested the notion of a tower that reached three times higher than the historic cityscape, boycotting the selection process. And RMJM's win was far from straightforward. The three architects on the jury—Norman Foster, Rafael Viñoly, and Kisho Kurokawa—had walked off (Kurokawa voiced his objection to all six of the designs being considered). The decision had been left to the rest of the jury and to the results of a public poll conducted by Gazprom through its website. *New York Times* critic Nicolai Ourous- soff inveighed against RMJM's proposed tower as "a bone-chilling expression of corporate ego run amok" on an "obscene scale." Since then, in 2007, 4,000 people, including the chess player Garry Kasparov, took to the streets in St. Peters- burg to demonstrate against the project—now

STRENGTH IN NUMBERS

TOP FIRMS WORLDWIDE BY TOTAL STAFF

Firm	Employees
1. GENSLER	3,100
2. HOK	2,788
3. SKIDMORE, OWINGS & MERRILL	1,525
4. PERKINS+WILL	1,400
5. HKS	1,300
6. LEO A DALY	1,200
7. RMJM	1,176
8. RTKL	1,159
9. SMITHGROUP	800
10. NBBJ	770
11. CALLISON	750

RMJM AROUND THE WORLD

ASIA
EMPLOYEES: 234
OFFICES: Hong Kong, Shanghai, Singapore
CEO, MIDDLE EAST AND ASIA: David Pringle
DESIGN DIRECTOR: Scott Findley

EUROPE
EMPLOYEES: 362
OFFICES: Cambridge, Edinburgh, Glasgow, London, Moscow, Warsaw
MANAGING DIRECTOR: Hugh Mullan
DESIGN DIRECTOR: Paul Stallan

MIDDLE EAST
EMPLOYEES: 314
OFFICE: Dubai
MANAGING DIRECTOR: Hazel Wong

NORTH AMERICA (RMJM HILLIER)
EMPLOYEES: 308
OFFICES: New York, Philadelphia, Princeton, Washington, D.C.
CEO: Sir Fraser Morrison
MANAGING DIRECTOR: Steven Gifford
DESIGN DIRECTOR: Peter Schubert

HUGH MULLAN
Managing director
• RMJM Europe

STEVEN GIFFORD
Managing director
• RMJM Hillier

PETER SCHUBERT
Design director
• RMJM Hillier

TONY KETTLE
Group design director
• RMJM

PAUL STALLAN
Design director
• RMJM Europe

DAVID PRINGLE
CEO • RMJM Middle East and RMJM Asia

renamed Okhta Center—and UNESCO may strip St. Petersburg of its World Heritage Site status; it will vote on the matter in July.

When asked about the project, both Morrisons are adamant that the design, by RMJM group design director and Falkirk Wheel alumnus Tony Kettle, is first-rate ("sensational," Peter says) and wholly appropriate for its urban context. They point out that there's already a 1,000-foot-high media tower in St. Petersburg and claim the impact of their tower on the skyline has been exaggerated by the media. "As far as Gazprom," says Peter Morrison, "they've been fantastic. Great clients. Very supportive—we communicate well."

What about the poor human-rights record of the Russian government, which has a controlling stake in Gazprom? And what about China, where RMJM is building the Olympic Green Convention Center for the Beijing Olympics—at the same time that China's treatment of Tibet is sparking demonstrations around the globe?

"We do a lot of due diligence on the people we work for," says Peter Morrison. "If we believed there was something morally deficient or something we didn't believe in, we wouldn't work for these particular clients. What we're not going to do is say we're not going to work for Russia or China because of a history of problems in those countries."

But political repression and human-rights abuses aren't just a problem of the past—aren't they a problem in the here and now?

"We're not in politics. We're about delivering fantastic buildings for people who are going to use that building and for our client. That's what our focus is on. We don't think it's a good enough reason to not build buildings for our clients and the people in these countries because the government in the past or at some stage has been involved in ...," he tapers off. In a follow-up e-mail, Morrison calls the Olympics protests "misguided," asserts that RMJM has embraced Chinese culture, and adds, "I very much look forward to being at the opening ceremony."

VALUE-ADDED

The thing about both Gazprom and RMJM's City Palace tower in Moscow, which takes the abstracted form of a lovers' embrace, is that they finesse, rather than jettison, the template of the "conventional corporate tower ... that can be found in abundance in Dubai, Singapore and Beijing," as the *Times*' Ouroussoff scoffs of Gazprom. And surely that's the point: Many clients, as U.S. managing director Steve Gifford told me in the New York office, are looking for "simple, big ideas." Architectural subtlety does not always fall under that umbrella.

At lunch the day after Peter Morrison's speech at the GSD, Tony Kettle, who has elfin features under a shock of brown hair and seems unfazed by UNESCO's threats, sketches in the air with his index finger to explain RMJM's client communication. Another firm, he says, even if the client is the focal point of its activity, might circle around that point endlessly without ever touching it; RMJM—he draws the petals of a flower—continually loops back to the client for an exchange of ideas.

Sitting at the table with us are Peter Morrison and Matthew Edgar, who was a commercial real estate broker for 20 years before joining RMJM in January. Edgar is the managing director of Futureplace, which he calls an "incubator" within the firm. If sponsoring a program at the GSD is the macro remedy for what frustrates the Morrisons about the construction process today—that the architect is seen as just another service provider, that he enters the conversation too late and departs with too little—Futureplace is their micro answer to the problem.

> **"WE WOULD LIKE TO WORK OURSELVES INTO THE SCHEME EARLIER, AND IF WE HAVE A RELATIONSHIP WITH THE LANDOWNER RATHER THAN THE DEVELOPER, IT GIVES US A GREATER DEGREE OF CONTROL."** —MATTHEW EDGAR, MANAGING DIRECTOR OF RMJM'S FUTUREPLACE DIVISION

"We would like to work ourselves into the scheme earlier, and the key player is the landowner: If we have a relationship with the landowner rather than the developer, it gives us a greater degree of control," explains Edgar. The idea, in short, is for RMJM to approach landowners—universities, financial institutions, and other bodies with more land than development expertise—and propose design and development options that would increase the value of the land. A few years down the line, when the site has been developed and money has been made, RMJM will then take a cut of the profits.

Although he and the Morrisons are still trying to figure out the precise role that RMJM will play relative to the developer and landowner, Edgar has secured two projects under the Futureplace model, with another 10 or so under consideration. Futureplace is expected to generate "a significant proportion" of the firm's profits within five years, Edgar says. And the margins on this type of work should be "quite a bit higher" than typical project fees, more in line with the 15 to 20 percent that developers make. Still, RMJM's initiative is not unique, Edgar adds: "We are not the only ones doing this."

The Futureplace model isn't applicable to the lion's share of the firm's work, of course, but the same entrepreneurial impulse drives RMJM's overall growth strategy. The firm is eager to establish a presence in Western Europe and on the West Coast and may keep its current project office in San Francisco long-term. Peter Morrison does not rule out more acquisitions, either, although he maintains that RMJM will be "very selective" about which firms it courts. Over the next five years, RMJM will set its sights on major-league clients who are active around the globe, such as U.S. universities opening satellite campuses in Asia and the Middle East (and academic medical centers doing the same). It will leverage its global portfolio: "We're starting to work for developers in one part of the world," says Peter Morrison, "who could easily be developing in other parts of the world." Projects are getting bigger, as the rising cost of land and materials creates an economy of scale for developers; Peter Morrison estimates that only five or six firms around the world, including RMJM, can currently deliver megaprojects. And even if the next decade sees an explosion of "superfirms" within the industry—as he predicts—RMJM will be ahead of the curve. Especially if RMJM succeeds in becoming an indispensable, trusted adviser to its clients, as he hopes it will.

Of course, RMJM is not alone in its ambitions. "We're seeing a lot of activity over the last four or five years in terms of strategic planning by firms, trying to position themselves differently," says Kermit Baker, chief economist for the AIA. Much of the time, that means consolidation. "There are a lot of advantages to being a large national or international firm in terms of scope of services [and] access to capital." Baker believes the industry is gravitating toward a "dual market," with big firms getting even bigger and more global and small and midsized firms meeting local and regional needs. But Futureplace—that's something different, he thinks. "I would say that's crossing over a line ... it's beyond the scope of where traditionally architecture firms have gone."

As Sir Fraser himself admits, though, you can't change an industry overnight. A few hours after our lunch, Peter Morrison is back in the Piper Auditorium, this time on a panel with other architects and an owner's rep. When the discussion turns to fees, Morrison—who uses the phrase "value-added" so often that it seems a kind of mantra—argues again that architects ought to be better rewarded for their efforts.

Another panelist, Joshua Prince-Ramus of REX, points out that, during fee negotiations, some clients will object, "'You don't pay interns anything, anyway'"—so well-versed are clients in the architectural culture of low pay and low expectations.

To which Morrison can only respond, with a slight lift of the shoulders, "It's chicken and egg, isn't it?"

KEY PROJECTS

1. PROJECT Falkirk Wheel
LOCATION Falkirk, Scotland
DATE 2002
DETAILS Inspired in part by Legos, Tony Kettle's design for the Falkirk Wheel, a rotating boat lift that links two canals, has also been compared to a Celtic two-headed axe. The Wheel has become one of Scotland's most popular tourist attractions.

2. PROJECT Beijing Olympic Green Convention Center
LOCATION Beijing, China
DATE 2008
DETAILS RMJM beat out OMA, Philip Cox Architects, and other firms to design one of the main venues of the Beijing Olympics. The 3-million-square-foot center will host events in fencing and pistol shooting and will serve as the media hub for the Games.

3. PROJECT University Town Library, Shenzhen
LOCATION Shenzhen, China
DATE 2007
DETAILS The winning design in an invited competition, RMJM's Shenzhen library serves the graduate schools of four Chinese universities. Its long, gently sloping form echoes the surrounding hills.

4. PROJECT Okhta Center (Gazprom tower)
LOCATION St. Petersburg, Russia
DATE Expected 2016
DETAILS This twisting, 1,300-foot-tall tower with a star-shaped floor plan will house the headquarters of Gazprom, the third-largest company in the world—if it survives fierce opposition to the project from inside Russia and abroad.

5. PROJECT Scottish Parliament
LOCATION Edinburgh, Scotland
DATE 2004
DETAILS Designed by Catalan architect Enric Miralles with RMJM acting as executive architect, the irregular volumes of the Scottish Parliament sit beside Edinburgh's Holyrood Palace in the city's Old Town. Miralles, who died in 2000, hoped the complex would look as if it were "almost surging out of the rock." The project won the Stirling Prize in 2005.

FRENCH KISSED continued from front page the Riverside Center and Carnegie 57, both for flourishing diamond-dealer-turned-developer Gary Barnett and his Extell Development.

"They're very reasonable, they're not prima donnas," Barnett said in an interview. "We give them all kinds of challenges to hit and they do. They're creative and also able to handle the challenges of building in New York and designing in New York and keeping the budget in mind while still coming up with something spectacular."

Both the Riverside Center and Carnegie 57 present considerable challenges. The former occupies the final site at Riverside South, an 8-acre space that was originally designated for a 2 million-square-foot TV studio. Instead, Barnett has proposed a 3 million-square-foot residential complex with six signature crystalline towers by de Portzamparc. The City Planning Commission certified the project on May 24, kicking off the seven-month public review process.

The following day, the announcement of Carnegie 57 made the front page of *The New York Times*, touting that it would become the tallest residential tower in the city at 1,005 feet, surpassing both Frank Gehry's Beekman Tower (867 feet) and the Trump World Plaza (861 feet). More noteworthy, perhaps, is the fact that the tower, which Barnett hopes will command the highest prices in the city, is coming along at a time when the economy is improving but far from the heights of architectural bombast just a few years ago.

And this was no spec rendering. Foundation work began on Carnegie 57 in April and steel girders should be rising above the sidewalk by the end of June. Barnett had been trying to make the site—near 7th Avenue, across from Carnegie Hall—larger but he wound up with an offset-L where the 57th Street frontage is 150 feet compared to 70 feet on 58th Street.

André Terzibachian, a de Portzamparc principal, said the greatest challenge for the designers was determining how to take this unusual lot, along with the strict setbacks mandated by the zoning code, and craft it into an elegant, cohesive tower. De Portzamparc decided to curve the setbacks,

Carnegie 57 is mid-block on the north side of 57th Street.

COURTESY EXTELL

creating a cascading effect to express "New York's vertical energy," according to Terzibachian.

The east and west are more like cuts than cascades—in part because the vertical reflections had to be masked in the crook of the L where a semi-abstracted "Klimt" pattern, in the architect's words, employs a third type of glass. The most difficult part of the design was making it all invisible from the inside. "Our client's concern is that it had to be as nice as possible, not too aggressive," Terzibachian said.

Barnett demurs at the suggestion that brand-name architecture is a new approach for a firm that has worked in the past with the likes of Costas Kondylis, Lucien Lagrange, Cetra/Ruddy, and Cook + Fox. "We seek out the right architect and the right aesthetic for each project," he said. Still, with more high-profile projects underway, such as SOM's Gem Tower in the Diamond District and KPF's World Product Centre on the Far West Side, Barnett said he will continue to work with good firms. Names? "You'll have to wait and see," he said. **MC**

AT DEADLINE

EAST SIDE'S ALL ABOARD

After years of planning, New York City is finally moving ahead with one of its more ambitious yet simple transportation projects: a bus rapid transit system serving eastern Manhattan. On June 7, city officials announced that starting in October, new dedicated bus lanes would be installed northbound on 1st Avenue and southbound on 2nd, serving much like an overland subway with stations every ten blocks or so, where passengers will pay before boarding. Signal prioritization, another time-saving maneuver, is planned for a future phase beginning next year. The project is meant to alleviate congestion, speed up buses that now take 90 minutes to cover the 8.5-mile route from Houston to 125th Street, and create a "complete streets" system, though a protected bike lane that was to have run the entire length of the route will now terminate at 34th Street. A similar system in the Bronx has sped up buses by 30 percent.

HUDSON YARDS DEAL FINALLY SEALED

Speaking of long-gestating projects, it took two years, but the Related Companies finally signed a contract for Hudson Yards with the MTA on May 26. It happened to be the same day *The Wall Street Journal* revealed that the developer received a major investment of $475 million from the Ontario Municipal Employees Retirement System toward the $15 million, 26-acre development on the Far West Side. Related put $21.7 million into escrow as art of its deal with the MTA, but will not begin paying the $1 billion it agreed to when it took over from Tishman Speyer—the initial winning bidder in 2008—until a series of triggers, agreed to in April, are met, such as Midtown commercial rents at 11 percent (around 14 percent in May) and AIA commercial billings above 50 (48.5 in April).

1

2

3

4

WITH 45,000 EMPLOYEES, OFFICES AROUND THE GLOBE, AND EXPERTISE IN NEARLY EVERY FEATURE OF THE BUILT AND NATURAL ENVIRONMENT, AECOM IS A GIANT IN THE FIELD. BUT WHAT IS IT? BY AARON SEWARD

MAKING IT BIG

Reconstruction work at the World Trade Center in New York has required a level of coordination and cooperation that would demoralize even the largest of integrated design firms. This is especially true of the transit hub, which reaches out to connect the various buildings on the site with multiple train lines traversing Lower Manhattan.

The way it is told in the halls of AECOM—the company in charge of the hub's engineering, site preparation, PATH facilities, security, wayfinding systems, and more—getting a handle on Santiago Calatrava's vision for the project proved to be a tall order for the transportation experts assigned to the job. The Spanish architect may be renowned for his clarity and eloquence, but his high-flown presentations proved to be Greek to these men and women who are more accustomed to planning circulation paths and calculating load patterns. Luckily, AECOM had a solution to this communication breakdown. It reached into the voluminous folds of its global network and pulled out a few architects—employees of a former DMJM office in Arlington, Virginia, to be specific—sending them north to act as emissaries and interpreters between the silver-tongued architect and his iron-eared collaborators. The result, reportedly, has been a smoother integration of the project's sculptural and functional design elements.

The past decade has seen a proliferation of large and complex projects that draw upon global resources both intellectual and material. The World Trade Center is but a small example. Entire cities are being built from scratch in the wilderness of China. Luxury developments stocked with the finest in convenience and culture are rising from the deserts of the Middle East. As the projects have gotten bigger, more all-encompassing in their scope, and located in what were once far-flung corners of the world, the firms that design and build them have followed suit. No one company has taken this impulse further than AECOM. With 45,000 employees and offices on every continent, this megalith has assembled expertise in every area necessary to design, build, and fuel a modern city. Its reason for being—"to make the world a better place"—is as magnanimous as it is grandiose; its purpose—"to enhance and sustain the world's built, natural, and social environments"—is as singular as it is vague.

If you have never heard of AECOM, or if you have only just recently become aware of the name but aren't certain what exactly it is or does, you are not alone. Up until last year, AECOM was little more than a holding company, a fairly abstract entity that held together a loose consortium of design, engineering, and project management firms operating in their own sectors and under their own names. Its genesis dates to the late 1980s, when Kentucky-based Ashland Oil, looking to diversify its business, purchased five large architecture and engineering companies, creating a design firm called Ashland. The oilmen, however, soon lost interest in this line and allowed the companies to buy themselves back. In 1990, those five firms, including architecture giants DMJM and Frederic R. Harris, established the AECOM name, which stands for architecture, engineering, construction, operations, and management. From that moment forth, the growth did not cease as more and more firms were acquired and more and more disciplines were incorporated. In 2007, AECOM became a publicly traded company, and today it is one of America's biggest firms with more than $6 billion in annual revenue.

This mushrooming to such gargantuan proportions was not conducted randomly, of course. Rather, AECOM leadership singled out companies for acquisition that filled a market or geographical niche not yet represented in the portfolio. To use architecture as an example, shortly after 1990, Spillis Candela of Miami was acquired for its expertise in civic and courthouse design. Hays Seay Mattern & Mattern of Virginia were brought aboard for their cultural experience. Chinese firm CityMark was purchased because, well, they were in China. EDAW was sought out and wooed for its highly developed global planning and landscape design practice. Most recently, Ellerbe Becket was merged for its strength in the Midwest and expertise in sports and healthcare typologies. That last acquisition more or less rounded out AECOM's portfolio, giving it influence everywhere on the planet and skill in everything imaginable, but that doesn't mean that it will stop its search. The company is always looking for smoothly operating integrated design firms, and would particularly like to increase its competence in airport design.

AECOM made its official debut in October 2009. "Two years ago it was decided to reorganize the company," explained Tom Fridstein, an AECOM executive vice president and head of global architecture. "It had grown to such a size and there were so many companies we wanted to rebrand to one identity." The company's many disciplines were organized into five main business lines: Planning Design and Development, which includes architecture, engineering, landscape design, project management, and economics; Transportation, with everything from airports to bridges and tunnels; Energy, both generation and transmission; Environmental, from brownfield restorations to carbon footprint assessments; and Water, with wastewater treatment facilities,

5

6

7

8

9

10

11

desalination plants, you name it. All of the business lines share a common financial structure, business development and marketing department, data systems, and, of course, human resources, as was shown in the example of the World Trade Center.

It is difficult to conceive of how such a many-limbed beast would even begin to function with one mind, but AECOM has devised a fairly simple matrix to help navigate its global business. On one axis of this matrix are geographical regions, and on the other are business lines. While local offices are largely in charge of developing and maintaining their own business—as with many firms, most of AECOM's clientele are repeat customers, legacy clients of the legacy firms—the company's top leadership, which is mostly made up of architects and engineers, is in charge of looking across geographical boundaries and market sectors to locate opportunities and assign resources as needed. This gives AECOM an edge over firms that may not have such a deep pool of talent to draw from, or a network of offices around the world. "If you're going to be global, your expertise is not going to exist in every location. That's where collaboration comes in," said Jon Miller, an AECOM senior vice president in the Arlington, Virginia, office. "If you have a project in Kuwait, but not the right people for it on the spot, you can draw from other regions and establish the right talent in the right location. The global market is changing," he added. "Today in Dubai they want people there on the ground. It used to be you could do it all from the U.S. and just send the drawings. Now clients want people who are committed to the region."

This global reach is also beneficial for AECOM clients that want to expand their business overseas. Rick Lincicome, an AECOM senior vice president who has come in from Ellerbe Becket, said that one of his old clients, a hospital based in South Dakota, wanted to expand its business outside of the U.S. They were thinking they would

12

13

20

14

15

16

17

21

18

19

1 Inner Northern Busway, Australia
2 Mercy Medical Center, Baltimore
3 Barclays Center, Brooklyn
4 Cedar Creek Windfarm, Colorado
5 Loyola Marymount University, LA
6 Judicial Center, Rockville, Maryland
7 Midtown Landscape Design, Tokyo
8 Giant Interactive, Shanghai
9 Samsung Cancer Center, Seoul
10 National Guard, Arlington, Virginia
11 RAND Headquarters, Santa Monica
12 207 Goode Office Building, Glendale
13 NASA New Town, Hampton, Virginia
14 University Hospital, Dubai
15 Yingze Streetscape, Taiyuan, China
16 Stafford Hospital, Stafford, Virginia
17 Van Nuys Flyaway, California
18 Dayton Air Traffic Tower, Ohio
19 Los Angeles Police Department, LA
20 2012 Olympic Masterplan, London
21 Heart of Doha Masterplan, Qatar

have to find another architect to do the job, one with more global experience. "We had to educate them that we actually had global reach," said Lincicome. "Joining AECOM is going to be great for that client."

Though enormous, AECOM tries to balance its portfolio with both large and small projects. "The challenge today is being able to operate locally and globally, to work on a small level and be able to scale up," said Fridstein. "We operate like any other firm. We have the benefit of having a huge amount of people, but we can put together a team of two people or 200 people depending on the size of the project." And though of its 45,000 employees only 4,000 are in the Planning Design and Development division, of which about 1,500 are architects, it wishes to be seen as a design firm. "There's a fear that these large firms put design as a subset to construction," said Miller. "Not so here. We are very much about design. The upper management is made up of designers. When I look up I see architects above me, and that's comforting." If these desires sound a bit contradictory, that's because they are. How can an entity be both large and small, both dedicated to design and composed mostly of management types? Scaling project teams down to meet the demands of a given project is one thing, but operating like a small business with all of the cultural trappings of a boutique design house, and perhaps the guiding force of a single genius, is something quite different.

What this boils down to is a bit of a personality crisis—if having multiple personalities is a crisis. The public launch of AECOM fused a multitude of businesses under one name, but it didn't create a single culture, at least not yet. For the time being, the firm seems happy to have those different voices all under the same roof. "When we merge with a company, it's because we think they're doing something very good," said Fridstein. "We don't want to lose what that is. I've seen other firms buy a company and dismantle it. Once they do that, they lose the value they've acquired." The large size and investment in a wide range of markets helps make the company stable, as when one sector is down, those that are up can carry things along. And the fact that it is publicly owned, without one defining principal at the top handing down the gift of their brilliance, provides for smooth changes of leadership. "When you're this large, you can't have one personality. Our very purpose is to be beyond one defining feature," said Lincicome. "We are AECOM, we can do anything."

AARON SEWARD IS AN ASSOCIATE EDITOR AT *AN*.

AECOM

Headquarters
Los Angeles, CA

Other Locations (Main Offices)
London, UK; Hong Kong, China; Brisbane, Australia; Moscow, Russia; New York, NY; Abu Dhabi, United Arab Emirates

Founding Partners
Richard G. Newman (founding principal), John M. Dionisio, Mike Burke, Joseph E. Brown

1990

AECOM

KVA matx

Headquarters
Boston, MA

Founding Partners
Sheila Kennedy, J. Frano Violich

KVA matx

SAA

1990–

Stan Allen Architect

Headquarters
New York, NY

Founding Partner
Stan Allen

1990

Stan Allen Architects

1991–

Louise Braverman, Architect

Headquarters
New York, NY

Founding Partner
Louise Braverman

Louise Braverman

1991

Zago Architecture

Headquarters
Los Angeles, CA

Founding Partner
Andrew Zago

Current Partners
Andrew Zago, Laura Bouwman

Zago Architecture

LOT-EK

1993–

Headquarters
New York, NY

Other Locations
Napoli, Italy

Founding Partners
Ada Tolla, Giuseppe Lignano

LOT-EK

1993

MICHAEL
MALTZAN
ARCHITECTURE

1995–

Michael Maltzan Architecture

Headquarters
Los Angeles, CA

Founding Partner
Michael Maltzan

Current Partners
Michael Maltzan, Betty Tanaka,
Tim Williams

1995

Michael Maltzan Architecture

VJAA

Headquarters
Minneapolis, MN

Founding Partner
Vincent James

Current Partners
Vincent James, Jennifer Yoos, Nathan Knutson

VJAA

C A R L O S
Z A P A T A
S T U D I O

1996–

Carlos Zapata Studio

Headquarters
New York, NY

Founding Partners
Carlos Zapata, Melissa Koff

1996

Carlos Zapata

sh p

1996–

SHoP

Headquarters
New York, NY

Founding Partners
Christopher Sharples, William Sharples, Coren Sharples, Gregg Pasquarelli, Kimberly Holden

Current Partners
Christopher Sharples, William Sharples, Coren Sharples, Gregg Pasquarelli, Kimberly Holden, Jonathan L. Mallie, Vishaan Chakrabarti

Jeremy Bitterman

The Palace of the Lost City
1990–1992

WATG

Architect
Wimberly Allison Tong & Goo

Location
Sun City, South Africa

Client
Kerzner International

Yokohama Landmark Tower
1990–1993

Architect
Hugh Stubbins and Associates

Location
Yokohama, Japan

Client
Mitsubishi Estate Company

Hong Kong Stadium
1990–1994

POPULOUS

Architect
HOK Sport

Location
Hong Kong, China

Client
Hong Kong Jockey Club;
Leisure and Cultural Services
Department

Tokyo Telecom Centre
1990–1995

Architect
Hellmuth, Obata + Kassabaum

Location
Tokyo, Japan

Local Architect
Nippon Sogo Architects

Client
Tokyo Telecom

The Greenbrier Golf Resort
1990–1995

RAMSA

Architect
Robert A.M. Stern Architects

Location
Fukushima Prefecture, Japan

Client
CYD Japan Company, Ltd.

Munich Airport Center
1990–1999

JAHN

Architect
JAHN

Location
Munich, Germany

Client
Bürozentrum Parkstadt
München-Schwabing

JR Central Towers and Nagoya Marriott Hotel
1990–2000

Architect
Kohn Pedersen Fox Associates

Location
Nagoya, Japan

Client
Central Japan Railway Co.

Scottish Equitable Headquarters
1991–1995

Architect
Koetter Kim & Associates

Location
Edinburgh, Scotland

Client
Pentland Estates Limited; Scottish Equitable Insurance Company

Puerta Europa Towers
1991–1995

Architect
Philip Johnson Alan Ritchie Architects

Location
Madrid, Spain

Client
Fernando Cid Garcia per Gestora, Immobiliari

Inanc Lisesi School for Gifted Children
1991–1995

Architect
Hillier Group

Location
Gebze, Turkey

Client
Inanç Vakfi

Le Fresnoy Art Center
1991–1997

Architect
Bernard Tschumi Architects

Location
Tourcoing, France

Client
French Ministry of Culture and Region Nord-Pas-de-Calais, France

Guggenheim Museum
1991–1997

Architect
Frank O. Gehry and Associates

Location
Bilbao, Spain

Client
Consorcio del Proyecto Guggenheim and Solomon R. Guggenheim Foundation

Miho Museum
1991–1997

Architect
I. M. Pei Architect

Location
Shiga, Japan

Associate Architect
Kibowkan International

Client
Shinji Shumeikai / Shumei Cultural Foundation

Olympic Fish
1992

Architect
Frank O. Gehry and Associates

Location
Barcelona, Spain

Avenue Number Five
1992

Architect
SITE

Location
Seville, Spain

Client
World Expo '92

Makuhari Bay New Town
1992–1996

STEVEN HOLL ARCHITECTS

Architect
Steven Holl Architects

Location
Chiba, Japan

Associate Architect
Kajima Design, K. Sone & Design Associates

Client
Mitsui Fudosan Group

Mielparque Nikko Kirifuri Hotel and Spa
1992–1997

VSBA VENTURI, SCOTT BROWN AND ASSOCIATES

Architect
Venturi, Scott Brown and Associates

Location
Nikko, Japan

Client
The Ministry of Posts and Telecommunications

Petronas Towers
1992–1998

Pelli Clarke Pelli Architects

Architect
Cesar Pelli & Associates

Location
Kuala Lumpur, Malaysia

Client
Kuala Lumpur City Centre Holdings Sdn. Bhd.

Kiasma Museum of Contemporary Art
1992–1998

STEVEN HOLL ARCHITECTS

Architect
Steven Holl Architects

Location
Helsinki, Finland

Local Architect
Juhani Pallasmaa Architects

Client
Finnish Ministry of Public Building

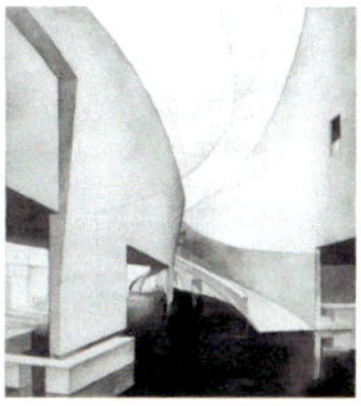

Provincial Capital Building
1992–1999

VSBA VENTURI, SCOTT BROWN AND ASSOCIATES

Architect
Venturi, Scott Brown and Associates

Location
Toulouse, France

Client
Département de la Haute-Garônne

US Embassy
1993

KPF

Architect
Kohn Pedersen Fox Associates

Location
Nicosia, Cyprus

Client
US Department of State, Foreign Buildings Operations

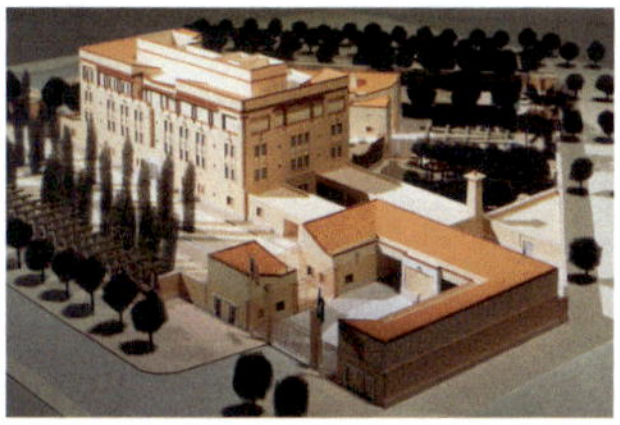

Mamilla District
1993

SafdieArchitects

Architect
Safdie Architects

Location
Jerusalem, Israel

Client
Ladbroke Group/Alrov

Hong Kong Convention and Exhibition Center
1993–1997

SOM

Architect
Skidmore, Owings & Merrill

Location
Hong Kong, Hong Kong

Client
HKCEC, Hong Kong Trade Development Council, Wong & Ouyang (HK) Ltd

Oceanario de Lisboa
1993–1998

C7A

Architect
Cambridge Seven Associates

Location
Lisbon, Portugal

Client
Parque Expo/IDEA

Castalia Ministry of Health, Welfare and Sport
1993–1998

Architect
Michael Graves and Associates

Location
The Hague, Netherlands

Client
MAB Groep bv (Building); Rijksgebouwdienst (Executive Office Interiors)

MICHAEL GRAVES & ASSOCIATES
MICHAEL GRAVES DESIGN GROUP

Jin Mao Tower
1993–1999

Architect
Skidmore, Owings & Merrill

Location
Shanghai, China

Client
China Jin Mao Group Co.Ltd., China Shanghai Foreign Trade Centre Co. Ltd (owner)

SOM

The Scientific Center of Kuwait
1993–2000

Architect
Cambridge Seven Associates

Location
Kuwait City, Kuwait

Client
Kuwait Foundation for the Advancement of Science

Sony Center Berlin
1993–2000

Architect
JAHN

Location
Berlin, Germany

Client
Sony, Tishman Speyer Properties, Kajima

JAHN

Darwin Centre Museum
1993–2002

Architect
Hellmuth, Obata + Kassabaum

Location
London, United Kingdom

Client
London Natural History Museum

Memorial Towers
1993–2003

Architect
John Hejduk

Location
Santiago de Compostela, Spain

Client
Fundacion Cidade da Cultura de Galicia, Xunta de Galicia

Cinémathèque Française (American Center)
1994

Architect
Frank O. Gehry and Associates

Location
Paris, France

Associate Architect
Sabout & Julian

Menara Multi-Purpose at Capital Square
1994

Architect
John Portman and Associates

Location
Kuala Lumpur, Malaysia

Client
Bandar Raya Developments Berhad

Ottawa City Hall
1994

SafdieArchitects

Architect
Safdie Architects

Location
Ottawa, Canada

Client
City of Ottawa

Suter Town Houses
1994–1996

Architect
MACK Architect(s)

Location
Buus, Switzerland

Kadota Housing
1994–1996

Santos Prescott and Associates

Architect
Santos Prescott and Associates

Location
Kitakrushu, Japan

Executive Architect
SAM Architect and Associates

Client
Kitakyushu Building Bureau

Dairi Nishi Housing
1994–1996

Santos Prescott and Associates

Architect
Santos Prescott and Associates

Location
Kitakrushu, Japan

Excutive Architect
SAM Architects

Client
Fukuoka Prefecture

Orchards Scott Hotel and Residences
1994–1998

Architect
Arquitectonica

Location
Singapore, Singapore

Client
Far East Hospitality Organization

Atlantico Pavilion
1994–1998

Architect
Skidmore, Owings & Merrill

Location
Lisbon, Portugal

Client
Parque Expo '98 S.A.

University of Marne-la-Vallée School of Architecture
1994–1999

Architect
Bernard Tschumi Architects

Location
Marne-la-Vallée, France

Client
University of Marne-la-Vallée

Samsung Jong-ro Tower
1994–1999

Architect
Rafael Viñoly Architects

Location
Seoul, South Korea

Client
Samsung Corporation

Slither Housing
1994–2000

Architect
Diller + Scofidio

Location
Gifu, Japan

Client
Government of Gifu Prefecture

Rothermere American Institute at Oxford University
1994–2000

Architect
Kohn Pedersen Fox Associates

Location
Oxford, United Kingdom

Client
Oxford University

Korea Development Bank Headquarters
1994–2001

Architect
AECOM

Location
Seoul, South Korea

Client
Korea Development Bank

Valeo Electricity
1994–2007

Architect
Davis Brody Bond Architects & Planners

Location
San Luis Potosi, Mexico

Client
Valeo

Shanghai World Financial Center
1994–2008

Architect
Kohn Pedersen Fox Associates

Location
Shanghai, China

Client
Mori Building Company

Dancing House
1995

Architect
Frank O. Gehry and Associates

Location
Prague, Czech Republic

Collaborative Architect
Vladimir Milunic, STUDIO V.M.

Client
ING Group

Vancouver Library Square
1995

Architect
Safdie Architects

Location
Vancouver, Canada

Client
City of Vancouver

Rodin Pavilion at Samsung Plaza
1995–1997

Architect
Kohn Pedersen Fox Associates

Location
Seoul, South Korea

Client
Samsung Corp.

Sun Tower
1995–1997

Architect
Morphosis Architects

Location
Seoul, South Korea

Client
Village Trading Company, Ltd.

morphosis

Organization for the Prohibition of Chemical Weapons
1995–1999

Architect
Kallman, McKinnell & Wood Architecture

Location
The Hague, Netherlands

Client
Organization for the Prohibition of Chemical Weapons

KMW Architecture

Cheung Kong Center
1995–1999

Architect
Leo A Daly, Cesar Pelli & Associates

Location
Hong Kong, Hong Kong

Client
Cheung Kong Holdings Ltd. (CKH), Hutchison Whampoa Ltd. (HWL)

LEO A DALY
Pelli Clarke Pelli Architects

Tour EDF at La Défense
1995–2001

Architect
Pei Cobb Freed & Partners

Location
La Défense, France

Associate Architect
Saubot-Rouit & Associés

Client
The Hines Corporation

PEI COBB FREED & PARTNERS Architects LLP

International School of Beijing
1995–2001

Architect
Perkins + Will

Location
Beijing, China

Client
International School of Beijing

PERKINS+WILL

Sabanci University New Campus
1995–2002

Architect
Cannon Design

Location
Istanbul, Turkey

Client
Sabanci University

CANNONDESIGN

Arcade at Cyberport
1995–2005

Architect
Jerde Partnership

Location
Hong Kong, China

Client
Pacific Century Premium Developments Limited (PCPD)

Suvarnabhumi International Airport
1995–2006

Architect
JAHN

Location
Bangkok, Thailand

Client
New Bangkok International Airport Co., Ltd.

Ara Pacis Museum
1995–2006

Architect
Richard Meier & Partners Architects

Location
Rome, Italy

Client
Comune di Roma

Orascom Red Sea Resorts
1995–2007

Architect
Michael Graves and Associates

Location
El Gouna, Egypt

Client
Orascom Touristic Establishments

US Embassy
1995–2008

Architect
Moore Ruble Yudell Architects & Planners

Location
Berlin, Germany

Client
US Department of State, Bureau of Overseas Building Operations

Canal City Hakata
1996

Architect
Jerde Partnership

Location
Fukuoka, Japan

Associate Architect
Fukuoka Jisho CO., Ltd. Urban Design and Development Co.

Client
Fukuoka Jisho Co., Ltd Urban Design and Development Co., Sumitomo Life Insurance

Felix Nussbaum Haus
1996–1998

Architect
Studio Daniel Libeskind

Location
Osnabrück, Germany

Client
Stadt Osnabrück

ANZ Stadium
1996–2000

Architect
HOK Sport

Location
Sydney, Australia

Client
Sydney Organising Committee for the Olympic Games; Stadium Australia Group

Hypo Alpe-Aldria Center
1996–2002

Architect
Morphosis Architects

Location
Klagenfurt, Austria

Client
Karntner Landes-und-Hypothekenbank

Mori Arts Center
1996–2003

Architect
Gluckman Mayner Architects

Location
Tokyo, Japan

Local Architect
Iris Miyaka Architects & Engineers

Client
Mori Arts Center

Roppongi Hills
1996–2003

Architect
Kohn Pedersen Fox Associates

Location
Tokyo, Japan

Architect of Record
Mori Biru

Client
Mori Building Co.

Jubilee Church
1996–2003

Architect
Richard Meier & Partners Architects

Location
Rome, Italy

Client
Vicariato of Rome

Roppongi Hills
1996–2003

Architect
Jerde Partnership

Location
Tokyo, Japan

Client
Mori Building Company

Exaltis Office Tower
1996–2004

Architect
Arquitectonica

Location
La Défense

Client
Bouygues Immobilier

Camana Bay
1996–2012

Architect
Moore Ruble Yudell Architects & Planners

Location
Grand Cayman, Cayman Islands

Client
Cayman Shores Development

Breitenleerstrasse Housing
1997

Architect
MACK Architect(s)

Location
Vienna, Austria

Client
Stadt Gemeinde Judenburg

Star City Hotel and Casino
1997

Architect
Studio Hillier

Location
Sydney, Australia

Client
Tabcorp, New South Wales Casino Control Authority

WestEnd City Centre
1997–1999

Architect
Jerde Partnership

Location
Budapest, Hungary

Architect of Record
Finta Studio

Client
TriGranit Development Corporation

Millennium Stadium
1997–1999

Architect
HOK Sport

Location
Cardiff, Wales

Client
Welsh Rugby Union; Cardiff County Council

POPULOUS

Shanghai Museum of Science and Technology
1997–2001

RTKL
AN ARCADIS COMPANY

Architect
RTKL

Location
Shanghai, China

Client
Shanghai Science Land

Imperial War Museum North
1997–2001

STUDIO DANIEL LIBESKIND

Architect
Studio Daniel Libeskind

Location
Manchester, UK

Client
Imperial War Museum North

Kingdom Centre
1997–2002

Architect
Ellerbe Becket

Location
Riyadh, Saudi Arabia

Local Architect
Omrania & Associates

Client
Kingdom Holding Company, LLC; Prince Alwaleed Bin Talal

AECOM

Bayer AG Headquarters
1997–2002

Architect
JAHN

Location
Leverkusen, Germany

Client
Bayer AG

JAHN

Dongbu Financial Center
1997–2002

Architect
Kohn Pedersen Fox Associates

Location
Seoul, South Korea

Client
Dongbu Corporation

KPF

De Hoftoren
1997–2003

Architect
Kohn Pedersen Fox Associates

Location
The Hague, Netherlands

Client
Rijksgebouwendienst (RGD), ING Vastgoed

KPF

International Vaccine Institute at Seoul National University
1997–2003

Architect
Payette

Location
Seoul, South Korea

Client
United Nations Development Program, Government of South Korea, Seoul National University Organization of Iran

PAYETTE

Two International Finance Centre
1997–2003

Architect
Cesar Pelli & Associates

Location
Hong Kong, Hong Kong

Local Architect
Rocco Design Architects

Client
IFC Development; Sun Hung Kai Properties

Pelli Clarke Pelli Architects

Cologne/Bonn Airport Terminal 2
1997–2004

Architect
JAHN

Location
Cologne, Germany

Client
Flughafen Köln/Bonn GmbH

JAHN

Memorial to the Murdered Jews of Europe
1997–2005

Architect
Eisenman Architects

Location
Berlin, Germany

Client
Stiftung Denkmal für die ermordeten Juden Europas

EISENMAN ARCHITECTS

Dreamworlds: Architectures of Conspicuous Consumption

In 1999, two years after the opening of the Guggenheim Bilbao gave a name to the notorious “Bilbao effect,” *World Architecture* reported that the “spirit of the age” was the reinvention of the museum.[1] Over the previous two decades, national and civic governments had embarked on ambitious museum-building campaigns as indicators of cultural maturity or to reify national and local identities, intended to lure a global tourist class with the promise of culture, consumption, and experience collapsed into a single destination. Such projects have often coupled new construction with the acquisition of art collections in competition with other locales, as with the Museum for Contemporary Art in Barcelona (MACBA) by Richard Meier and Partners, which at the time of its commissioning in 1985 had neither collection nor location. “I’d like to think the museum can do for this area what the Georges Pompidou Center in Paris did for the Marais,” Meier said, referring to the previous model of museum-led urban renewal following the opening of the Pompidou in 1977.[2]

Eager for opportunities to experiment with new forms and technologies on the world stage, US architects have often been at the center of this global expansion. Firms like Gehry Partners have specialized in museum types, while others have transitioned from conceptual practices to large-scale building through international museum commissions, as with Studio Daniel Libeskind’s Jewish Museum in Berlin (1989–1999) or Preston Scott Cohen’s Tel Aviv Museum in Israel (2003–2011). For their architects and clients, high-profile museums abroad promise both international recognition and potentially large financial rewards. *Museum News* reported that the city of Bilbao paid $12.1 million to Gehry Partners to design the Guggenheim Bilbao (1991–1997), while the Solomon R. Guggenheim Foundation itself received $24.7 million.[3] Financing by private patrons and local governments has allowed museums to undertake global building campaigns on the franchise model, an approach pursued most notably by Thomas Krens, the director responsible for the Guggenheim’s expansions into Berlin, Spain, Las Vegas,

① Nicola Turner, “Spirit of the age,” *World Architecture* (July 1999): 92–99.

② Alan Riding, “A Modern ‘Pearl’ Inside Old Barcelona,” *The New York Times* (May 10, 1995): C13.

③ Beatriz Plaza, “The Bilbao effect (Guggenheim Museum Bilbao),” *Museum News* (September-October, 2007), http://mpra.ub.uni-muenchen.de/12681/1/Bilbao_Effect.pdf (last accessed October 26, 2014).

④ Michael Kimmelman, “What on Earth is the Guggenheim Up To?” *The New York Times* (October 14, 1990): H1.

⑤ Karen Stein, “Canal City Hakata, Fukuoka, Japan,” *Architectural Record* (March 1997): 110–115.

1975

1979 Jebel Ali port and World Trade Center completed in Dubai, UAE

1985 UAE establishes first Free Trade Zone at Jebel Ali, Dubai

1988 Thomas Krens appointed Director of Solomon R. Guggenheim Foundation

1990–1991 First Persian Gulf War

1995 Qatar Foundation for Education, Science and Community Development established, announces plan for Education City

1997
- Guggenheim Bilbao opens
- Deutsche Guggenheim opens in Berlin

and Abu Dhabi. Critic Michael Kimmelman described Krens's method as "the cultural equivalent of a multinational conglomerate, with branches around the world…[where] real estate and international gamesmanship figure as prominently in Guggenheim's planning as scholarship."[4]

The scale of global museum construction has been paralleled by that of other venues for cultural consumption including shopping malls, hotels, casinos, and luxury resorts. A year prior to the opening of the Guggenheim Bilbao, Jerde Partnership's Canal City Hakata in Fukuoka, Japan (1996) heralded the impact of such retail-entertainment models, which like museums had become "standard fare for revitalizing urban centers and developing suburban brownfield sites in the last decade."[5] Gehry's mall at Euro Disney (1988–1992) and Libeskind's Westside Shopping and Leisure Center in Bern, Switzerland (2001–2008) attest to the involvement of the same architects across both cultural and commercial types.[6] Mike Davis has described extravagant architectural spectacles like the Dubai Mall, adjacent to the Burj Khalifa—"big enough to be seen from space and bursting with architectural steroids"—as the "dreamworlds of neoliberalism," fantasy environments in which "Speer meets Disney on the shores of Araby."[7] Central to this proliferation has been the development of new tax-free zones and trade ports, oases of free enterprise and havens for luxury consumption. Such dreamworlds crystallized the effects of the economic policies which followed the untethering of the US dollar from the Bretton Woods exchange system in 1971, encouraging flows of speculative capital no longer backed by the gold standard.

Nearly two decades after the opening of the Guggenheim Bilbao, there are currently two dozen new cultural centers focused on museums in progress around the world, at an estimated cost of $250 billion.[8] China alone plans to establish 1,000 museums in the next ten years, with a projected attendance of 1 billion by 2020.[9] In the meantime, recent projects for Guggenheims in Abu Dhabi and Helsinki have prompted protests based on the social and human consequences of this global proliferation.[10] The promise of revitalization from the construction of cultural commercial venues has increasingly given way to a striving for excess, requiring cities to "embrace the 'perfected' synthesis of shopping, entertainment and architectural spectacle' on the most pharaonic scale."[11] — IC

⑥ See C.J. Hughes, "Shopping malls not beneath Libeskind's 'dignity'," *Architectural Record* (November 2008): 41.

⑦ Mike Davis, "Fear and Money in Dubai," *New Left Review* 41 (September–October 2006): 68.

⑧ "Cultural centers: The Bilbao effect," *The Economist* (December 21, 2013), http://www.economist.com/news/special-report/21591708-if-you-build-it-will-they-come-bilbao-effect (last accessed October 6, 2014).

⑨ Gene Jeffers and Judith Rubin, ed., *TEA/AECOM 2013 Theme Index & Museum Index: The Global Attractions Attendance Report* (2013): 54.

⑩ Colin Moynihan, "Protesters Urge Guggenheim to Aid Abu Dhabi Workers," *The New York Times* (May 24, 2014), http://www.nytimes.com/2014/05/25/nyregion/protesters-urge-guggenheim-to-aid-abu-dhabi-workers.html (last accessed October 10, 2014).

⑪ Davis, "Fear and Money in Dubai": 54.

2001 • Construction of Palm Island, Dubai begins • Guggenheim Hermitage Museum and Guggenheim Las Vegas open

2003 Guggenheim Las Vegas closes

2004 • Abu Dhabi Tourism & Culture Authority announces Saadiyat Island master plan including Guggenheim and Louvre museums • Qatar approves foreign ownership of real estate for international investors

2005 Kingdom of Saudi Arabia announces construction of King Abdullah Economic City

2008 • World's largest mall opens in Dubai • Guggenheim Hermitage Museum closes

2009 Human Rights Watch issues report on labor conditions for Saadiyat Island construction

2013 Deutsche Guggenheim closes

2014 1,715 firms enter competition for Guggenheim in Helsinki

2015

2001 Afghanistan War

2003 Iraq War

1997

2014

Canal City Hakata Fukuoka, Japan

JON JERDE TAKES HIS BRAND OF "EXPERIENTIAL ENVIRONMENTS" ABROAD TO CREATE THE LARGEST PRIVATELY DEVELOPED PROJECT IN JAPAN.

by Karen Stein

Project: *Canal City Hakata, Fukuoka, Japan*
Owners: *Fukuoka Jisho Co., Sumitomo Life Insurance Co., Fukuoka Japan Urban Design & Development Co.*
Developers: *Fukuoka Jisho Co., Fukuoka Japan Urban Design & Development Co., Organization for Promoting Urban Development*
Design Architect: *The Jerde Partnership International—Jon Jerde, FAIA, principal/designer; Eddie Wong, AIA, principal/management; Brian Honda and David Moreno, project designers; John Leggitt, tenant design; Duncan Paterson, Mike Hong, Ed Borrego, Ralf Konietzko, senior designers; Kiharu Tsuge, Charles Pigg, Wasa Sakamoto, Bob Cloud, John Simones, Tammy McKerrow, David Green, Hank Hockenberger, project team*
Architect of Record: *Fukuoka Japan Urban Design & Development Co.*
Landscape Architect: *EDAW, Inc.*
Environmental Merchandise Designer: *Clifford Selbert Design Collaborative*
Water Features Designer: *WET Design*
Lighting Designer: *Joe Kaplan Architectural Lighting*
General Contractors: *The Zenitaka Corp., Shimizu Corp., Obayashi Corp., Fujita Corp.*

If there was any lingering doubt that the merging of entertainment and other commercial uses was a transnational trend, it is dispelled by the completion of Canal City Hakata, a 2.5-million sq ft, $1.4-billion megacomplex that fills nine acres of riverfront property in Fukuoka, Japan.

Canal City Hakata was designed by the Jerde Partnership International (JPI), the firm that invented the retail-office-entertainment behemoth that has become standard fare for revitalizing urban centers and developing suburban greenfield sites in the last decade. Or, at least, JPI *re*-invented the type in 1985, with the completion of Horton Plaza in downtown San Diego, a $40-million shopping district described variously as a "pastel-swathed, stucco-and-tile catalog of archetypal urban components and stylistic allusions" or "Post-modernism gone amok" [RECORD, March 1986, pages 128-135]. Jon Jerde, FAIA, himself described it as savior to the central city's previously desolate business district.

Success at home

"The regional shopping center is the last vestige of the communal scene in America," says Jerde of his attempt to create a sense of place for a failing community and, not incidentally, a source of profit for his clients. In his view, he does not just design shopping centers; he also, along with colleagues at his 140-person firm, practices a new architectural discipline, which JPI calls "experiential design and place-making."

The impressive 25 million annual visitors to San Diego's Horton Plaza (nearly three times initial predictions) made Jerde, in his words, America's "fair-haired boy of retail," attracting clients and inspiring projects across the United States. It even led to the country's largest theme park-like retail outlet, the $625-million Mall of America, located outside of Minneapolis in Bloomington, Minneapolis, in which JPI also played a role. It was only a matter of time before Jerde started exporting his expertise in retail design abroad.

1. *Naka River*
2. *Nakasu district*
3. *Grand hotel*
4. *Business hotel*
5. *Performing arts center*
6. *Office building*
7. *Cineplex*
8. *Parking (located above department store)*
9. *Pedestrian bridge (leading to metro station)*

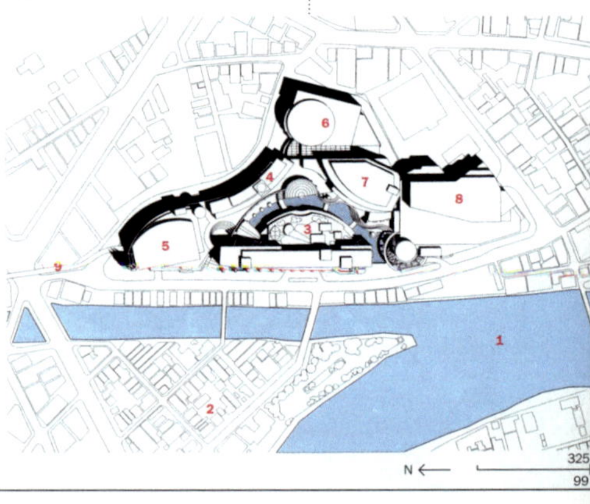

1. *Theater*
2. *Retail*
3. *Star Court*
4. *Moon Walk*
5. *Sun Plaza*
6. *Earth Walk*
7. *Sea Life Playground*
8. *Department store*
9. *Parking*

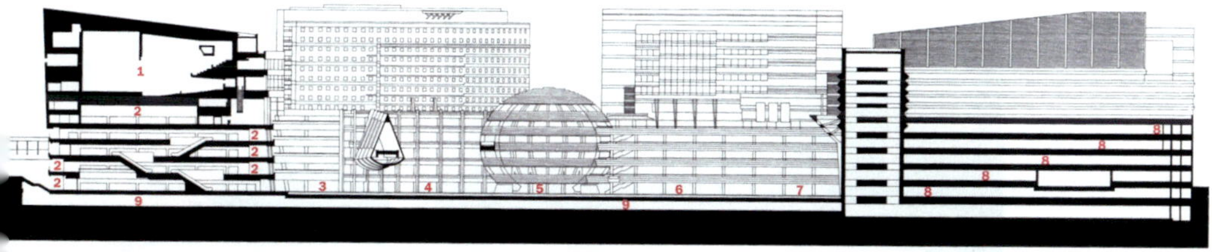

NORTH-SOUTH SECTION

An aerial view of Canal City Hakata shows the nine-acre development alongside Fukuoka's Naka River (above). Buildings, including the business hotel, are clad in contrasting stripes to resemble a family of zebras, according to Jon Jerde (right). A view from the Star Court toward the city of Fukuoka (left).

Identifying elements of the Jerde design include a tower and the vine-covered "wiggle wall" (near right), and the hollowed sphere of the red Sun Plaza (far right). A performance at the Sun Plaza amphitheater draws crowds; some 20 million people are expected to visit in the first year. Bridges connect to shops and hotels (below).

Taking it on the road

His first completed project outside American borders is Canal City Hakata. Thanks to a small but deep-pocketed group of enlightened developers, the bustling port city of Fukuoka in southern Japan already has had its share of international architectural star turns since the late 1980s, including Aldo Rossi's monumental Il Palazzo Hotel [Record, May 1990, pages 70-75].

JPI, however, was engaged on a much larger scale than Rossi or others like Rem Koolhaas, Michael Graves, and Steven Holl who have all completed projects in Fukuoka. JPI was to masterplan the largest privately-developed project in Japan's history. Work on the complex began in 1988 and the project survived several starts and seemingly complete stops—influenced by dramatic fluctuations in the Japanese economy—to open to the public some eight years later, on April 20, 1996.

The initial design concept, developed early in the process, also survived what JPI principal and one of Canal City Hakata's project designers, David Moreno recalls as "three major redesigns and 12 minor redesigns" along the way. According to the project's concept statement, written by Moreno, Canal City Hakata is "an environment of experience based on natural patterns, effects, mysteries, and life forms affecting our world."

Making it unique to Fukuoka

Toward that end, the architectural team conceived a masterplan around the central natural feature of the site, the Naka River, "diverting" its path so it would bisect the site and provide for a 700-ft long pedestrian promenade along its banks. (Ultimately, changing the course of the ocean-fed river proved too complicated and too costly, so a separate canal was made.)

The meandering arc of water is the armature of the design—the project's proverbial main street—connecting the five themed outdoor environments of the stars, moon, sun, earth, and sea, which are symbolically rendered in contrasting geometrical forms. Four destinations anchor the concept: the Fukuoka City Theater, Daiei's Mega Vandle department store, a Grand Hyatt Hotel, and the Canal City Business Center.

But JPI's simple environmental theme had to withstand major challenges over the years. The ordering and coherence of the spaces was threatened as prospective tenants made demands as conditions of signing on—then dropped out for a variety of reasons. The mix of retail, business, hotel, and entertainment components of the development program seemed perpetually in flux, explains JPI principal and one of Canal City Hakata project designers Brian Honda. Rather than specific buildings for specific tenants, during the first few years of the design process, "We were designing 'place holders.' It was about spirit rather than character," recalls Honda of the process.

Communal design process

Design development was also influenced by JPI's method of working, called "co-creativity." According to this premise, the Venice, Calif.-based

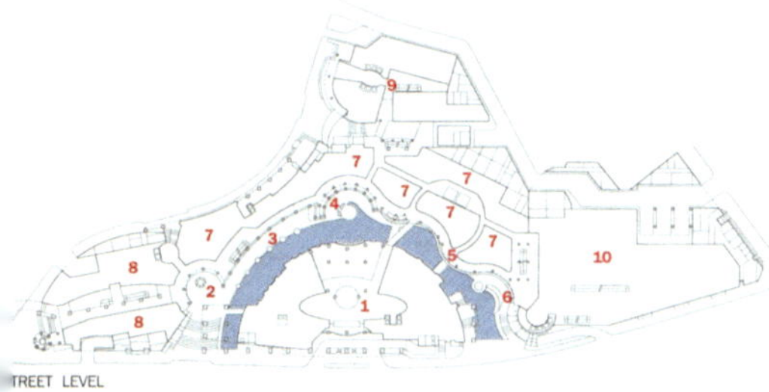

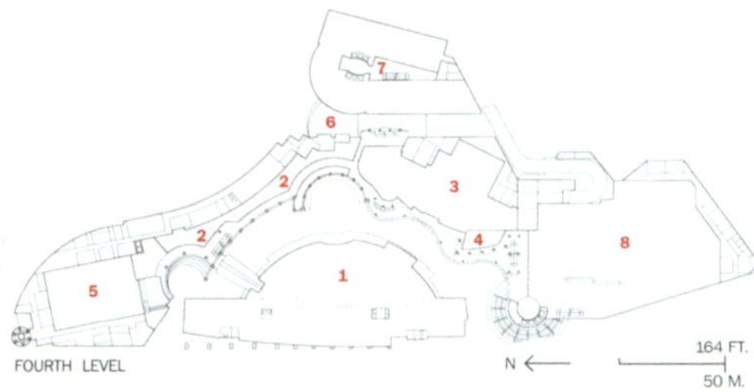

1. *Lobby*
2. *Star Court*
3. *Moon Walk*
4. *Sun Plaza*
5. *Earth Walk*
6. *Sea Life Playground*
7. *Retail*
8. *Restaurant*
9. *Showroom*
10. *Department store*

1. *Hotel banquet functions*
2. *Retail*
3. *Amusement center*
4. *Cinema*
5. *Restaurant*
6. *Office atrium*
7. *Showroom*
8. *Department store*

ignage, banners, and culpture are by the lifford Selbert Design ollaborative. estaurants overlook he Star Court (oppo- ite). Joe Kaplan rchitectural Lighting id neon curves to cho the canal's arc near right). Interior paces are brightly col- red to maintain xcitement levels, says erde (below).

PI team members worked closely vith outside designers and consul- ants—in this case landscape rchitects EDAW of Irvine, Calif.; nvironmental-merchandise lesigner Clifford Selbert Design ollaborative of Santa Monica; and vater features designer WET Design f Universal City— as if all were articipants in a seamless, virtual tudio. The result is that all the ele- nents—from signage to site culpture to lighting—reinforce the entral image.

herd of buildings

n order to distinguish the various uildings within the complex while naintaining a sense of unity, JPI nvisioned them as members of a amily of zebras, each with slightly ifferent stripes. The zebra-herd netaphor was also meant to echo he overall theme of the master- lan: nature. "The architecture nakes a reference to time and ature," writes Moreno in Hakata anal City's concept statement. The uilding bases are stone, and their ertical faces rise from a canal, a eference to how a river over cen- uries erodes the land, forming a anyon.

"In the process, layers of vary- ng stone are exposed, thus the esign of the horizontal banding. pper building layers become more efined, lighter and modern. Japan, ecause of its long appreciation and respect for nature, its ancient his- tory and far-reaching image of the future, is a prime location for this idea. Fukuoka specifically, with its history as an original gateway to civilization and its desire to become one of the world's great modern cities, would be an ideal place for this Biosphere of man's natural world."

While the theme of nature was intended to give some specificity to the project, to relate it to the exist- ing environment and the specific landscape features of Fukuoka, it also draws on universal themes of light, space, scale, and color— issues that Jerde is now exporting throughout Asia in new projects that he and his colleagues are currently developing for sites in Tokyo, Jakarta, Taipei, Manila, Shanghai, Beijing, and Seoul.

In Fukuoka, JPI discovered it knew more about retailing than its client consortium, providing the opportunity for a larger role for the firm. Says Honda: "We expanded our services. We could provide things beyond design, like market- ing, leasing strategies, promotion."

Jerde's Japanese clients came to rely on him as a guru of the retail industry, and Jerde is happy to fore- cast the future. His prognosis: "This [Canal City Hakata] is visionary stuff. Seventy-five years from now this is what Fifth Avenue [in New York City] will be like." ■

Manufacturers' Sources

Open mall area reinforced concrete with tiles: *Toto*

Mall area fire-control steel doors with security grilles: *Sanwa shutter*

Mall area lockets, hinges, pulls: *Miwa Lock*

Mall area aluminum chairs: *Nitiesu*

Mall area aluminum tables: *Yamazaki Sangyo*

Mall area exterior lighting pole: *Koizumi*

Business center concrete: *Toto*

Business center sheet glass: *Tanatyoh*

Business center aluminum, steel: *Okuju*

The Pharaoh's fantasy

MICHAEL GRAVES' LATEST HOTEL BRINGS A TOUCH OF DISNEY-STYLE KITSCH TO EGYPT'S RED SEA COAST. ELEANOR CURTIS CHECKS IN

PHOTOGRAPHS BY ELEANOR CURTIS

Row upon row of bland concrete blocks stretch down Egypt's Red Sea coast, clustering together in places like Hurghada to provide cheap accommodation for Western tourists without any pretence of offering an authentic Egyptian experience. In reaction to this decontextualised sprawl are new resorts such as El-Gouna, 22km north of Hurghada, which features the Miramar Hotel by Michael Graves as its centrepiece.

One catalyst of the area's current building boom is the sale by the Egyptian government of 300km of coastline sites to private investors. As a result the country is about to witness an assortment of resort experiments as developers rush to meet the government's imposed requirement of laying the first stones within three years of land purchase.

Passing under the gate to enter this amalgam of colours and shapes, you recognise Graves' playful classical references jumbled up with indigenous Egyptian forms

Michael Graves' experience in designing hotels for Disney World in Florida and Paris is clearly evident in the Miramar Hotel, part of the new resort of El-Gouna on Egypt's Red Sea coast. Guest rooms are arranged around artificial lagoons, left and above, in clusters of buildings which draw on ancient Egyptian architecture as well as more recent indigenous forms, right and opposite page below

Owned and developed by Orascom, one of Egypt's largest construction and engineering companies, El-Gouna challenges the established model of the no-context complex by exploiting its origins as a small fishing village. The site spans an area of seven square kilometres and carves up the desert, Disney World style, with artificial lagoons and clusters of buildings. Priority here is placed on the architectural experience rather than maximum lettable space. Plans include roads, an airport, village centre, post office, school, hospital, various cultural and sports amenities in addition to six tourist hotels, private villas and restaurants.

Designed by local architects Rami El-Dahan and Soheir Farid (both apprentices of the late and revered Hassan Fathy), the new village centre of Kafr El-Gouna has been created with reference to Egypt's rural architectural heritage, taking as its primary forms the vernacular domes and vaults to give that "authentic" Egyptian look.

By commissioning Michael Graves (famous for his fanciful Dolphin and Swan hotels in Disney World, Florida) to design a hotel for the resort, Samih Sawiris, president of the family-run Orascom, hoped to fulfil his vision of creating a distinctive building to dramatise the remote landscape and to deviate slightly from the more restrained and indigenous-looking domes and vaults of the village.

On Graves' first visit Sawiris took him on a tour of El-Gouna, around the clinical but efficient five-star Mövenpick hotel and the village of Kafr El-Gouna. The domed and vaulted skyline of the Kafr – the shopping arcade, the museum, villas and the two hotels (one of which is modelled on the Dawar El-Omda, the archetypal major's house found in Upper Egyptian villages) – then became Graves' point of departure. Sawiris' brief was to "modernise" the vernacular approach of Fathy, interpreting "old" ways of building and making the best use of local materials and craftsmen.

Graves' initial designs for the Miramar Hotel made extensive use of dome and vault forms but was too "rural" for Sawiris, with its tall bottle-shaped structures and references to slim African pigeon-houses. So it was modified to deviate more from the vernacular and to give Sawiris the Disney-style magic he wanted.

Miramar's site covers an area of practically 200,000 square metres, one sixth of which is filled with man-made lagoons, and has a water frontage of half a kilometre. The 284-room hotel with its numerous suites – including the "presidential suite" with its own extended terrace, pool and private access to the sea – boasts the unique design feature of having waterside views from every room, be they over the artificial lagoons or the sea.

By modifying the local vocabulary, Graves has combined indigenous forms with his inimitable set-building skills to bring life and movement to the vaults and domes. Adhering to the local two-storey height limit, he has built wide rather than in his usual soaring manner and the Miramar has developed into a series of shaped islands – resembling circular lagoons or seaside ovals – that are connected by wooden bridges across the water.

From the village the hotel appears Toy Town-ish with its series of bright blue, red and yellow forms. Approaching from the road, crossing the bridge and passing under the gate to enter this amalgam of colours and shapes, you recognise Graves' playful classical references jumbled up with indigenous Egyptian forms. The colours enrich the overall desert-sea relationship, reflecting the blues of the skies and the water, the reds of the distant mountains and the dust of the sand.

Inside the reception area, which is set high above the water, there are references to ancient pharaonic halls with their thick walls and giant columns. Guests catch a glimpse of the water through the narrow openings which reveal turquoise lagoons and palm

tree landscaped terraces. Beyond these is the small marina from which guests are transported to their rooms by boat.

Throughout the hotel an icing of ornament crudely covers a concrete structure, blue palisades fortify balconies, wavy handrails reflect the water rippling around individual terraces and great blue drums encircle yellow staircases. In form the bedrooms make reference to the pigeon-houses – an elongated cone structure punctuated with ledges – which are found throughout rural Egypt. In Graves' version they are decorated with the local brick pattern of "sevens and eights" (the shapes resemble the Arabic numbers seven and eight). The restaurant adjoining the lobby, with its expansive view over the front lagoon and the sea, is a series of vaults and arches leading into a tall rotunda which will house the "buffet-in-the-round". All the hotel's furniture is designed by Graves, though the variable standards in Egyptian manufacturing have resulted in interesting but slightly crude modifications.

With the Miramar almost complete, Sawiris has now commissioned Graves to design another hotel and club house for the 18-hole golf course as well as numerous private villas in El-Gouna. And for Orascom's latest project in Sinai (called Taba Heights and with a town centre also masterplanned by Dahan and Farid) he has commissioned the tireless architect to design two of the three new hotels. Looks like Mr Graves could be on another roll...

The Miramar Hotel, managed by ITT Sheraton, is scheduled to open this autumn

FEATURES

The Bilbao Effect

WHAT ARE THE IMPLICATIONS OF BILBAO'S SUCCESS BOTH FOR GEHRY'S PRACTICE AND FOR THE ARCHITECTURAL WORLD AT LARGE?

After Bilbao: The Weatherhead School of Management at Case Western Reserve University, Cleveland, Ohio.

by Suzanne Stephens

With the unprecedented success of the Guggenheim Museum in Bilbao, Frank Gehry, FAIA, has ascended from the ranks of being "America's most obscure great architect," as Martin Filler described him in 1986, to being a "genius," as reported in RECORD, October 1997. While Gehry has received any number of raves for previous work, Bilbao put him into a special category. It is the Big Whammy that every architect dreams about.

Not only did Bilbao open 20 months ago to ecstatic accolades from critics and architects, but also it has been an unparalleled success with the public. Tourism to Bilbao was galvanized by the museum, with 1.4 million visitors tallied in the first year. "Bilbao," observes Kurt Forster in *Frank O. Gehry, the Complete Works* (Monacelli Press), "will not only go down as one of the most complex formal inventions of our time, it will stand as a monument to the productive capacities at our disposal if an architect, such as Gehry, puts them to imaginative use." Clearly the world has been inexorably drawn to the gleaming effervescence of its exterior and to the high-powered oomph of the spaces inside.

In this light, Bilbao could be terrific for architecture. As part of the "Bilbao Effect," cities, regions, countries reportedly are looking now at arty architects to design innovative buildings to lure tourism. "Bilbao has brought back the significance of the real artifact to the public, not just as a structure, but as a spectacle," Peter Eisenman, FAIA, comments. "The sense of exaggeration, scale, and climax all come into consonance in Bilbao."

With all the carrying on, there are some nagging questions. First,

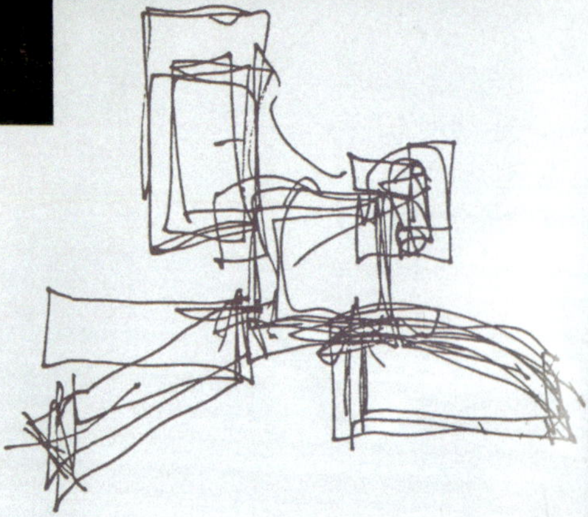

what does it mean to be a "creative genius" in architecture these days? Is not such a label just playing into the hands of the hyperventilating media, which inflate reputations of celebrities and architecture-as-spectacle to sell magazines? Will success spoil Gehry—especially when clients just want Bilbaoesque buildings that shimmy and gleam? And what happens when others knock off Bilbao? Will spectacle spoil architecture?

To examine the situation, let's go back 25 years. Louis Kahn was the last American architect described as a creative genius, on the level of Frank Lloyd Wright, Mies van der Rohe, and Le Corbusier. When Kahn died in 1974, the question "Who will be the next one?" was frequently answered with long disquisitions about the day of such heroes being over. The world of architecture needed to succumb to bottom-line budgets and restrictive construction schedules to stay competitive in the building industry.

Despite such prognostications, however, the individual creative architect was not entirely subsumed within the large corporate firm. Boutique operations continued to flourish. And at the time of Kahn's death, the "the next one" had been running his own office in Los Angeles for 12 years.

In those early days, in the 1960s, only local and regional papers and magazines paid attention to Gehry's work on concert pavilions, exhibition design, and projects for the Rouse Company. Gehry had designed the serenely cubiform Danziger House in Hollywood in 1964–65. But not until he produced the laminated-cardboard Easy Edges furniture (1969–73) did the national press discover Gehry and the professional journals start anticipating his next move. Still, in 1977 Gehry's earlier work was classified by historians David Gebhard and Deborah Nevins as "part of the vernacular-built architecture of Southern California," with exceptions made for the Danziger House (1964-65), Gemini G.E.L. Studios (1976–79), and the Ron Davis house (1968–72).

Then Frank Gehry finished his own controversial and groundbreaking home in Santa Monica in 1978. Suddenly eyes were riveted on him. Press coverage went international. His house, a 1920s cottage stripped down to stud walls and wrapped with a carapace of aluminum siding, chain-link fence, glass, and plywood was definitely avant-garde. Even the neighbors complained of its being an eyesore. But while the architectural community recognized the innovation and daring in its formal combustion of parts and pieces, the Santa Monica house came across as an experiment in challenging assumptions about art and architecture, rather than establishing the direction for the future. As Philip Johnson, FAIA, now recalls: "Even with his own house, who knew?"

After a string of dramatic projects, such as the evocative village of buildings of the Loyola University Law School (1978–85), the collaged assemblage of the California Aerospace Museum and Theater (1982–84), and the clustered, minimal forms of the Winton Guest House (1982–87), the architectural world recognized a new phase. Gehry was moving away from the earlier plywood and chain link, planar, two-dimensional layered architecture to more volumetric design. His swerve to distorted Platonic solids was suggestive of Aldo Rossi's explorations, Vincent Scully argues, except that Gehry began to push the solids out of shape. His capability to change and transform his art continued to surprise Gehry-watchers. He could still do "normal" Gehry, for example, using his industrial vocabulary

Left to right: Guggenheim Museum, Bilbao, Spain (1991–97); Winton Guest House, Wayzata, Minnesota (1982– 1987); Gehry's Santa Monica House (1977–78); Fritz Burns Building, Loyola University Law School, Los Angeles (1978–82).

to turn a scuzzy warehouse into the spatially modulated Temporary Contemporary exhibition space (now the Geffen Contemporary) in 1982.

Honors and awards and ample press became a matter of course in the late 1980s when Gehry finished the complexly configured Schnabel House (1986–89) or the more explosively dynamic Vitra Museum (1987–89). Gehry, trying to capture movement in his architecture, had already begun to "fiddle with fish forms," as he puts it. The fish became more abstracted and left its trace as a nongeometric shape in his succeeding projects. In the 1990s the colliding, exploding forms of metal cladding or stone of the Frederick R. Weisman Museum in Minneapolis (1990–93), the University of Toledo Center for the Visual Arts (1989), and the American Center in Paris (1988–94), all dynamically pointed the road to Bilbao.

Gehry's rational use of intuition

In many ways, Gehry has subverted the role model for the "creative" architect by not staying within the traditional patterns or expectations established by his illustrious predecessors. They came out of a Modernist age in which their architecture was based on a system of rational principles with construction, materials, and program determining interior spaces and the exterior envelope. "Gehry," as Scully notes, is "figural" in contrast to someone like Kahn, who was a "constructor." Architecture was codified in ways that could be transmitted to other architects. "This is not a judgment as to value," says Eisenman, "but you can't teach Bilbao to students. You could teach Le Corbusier because he was interested in typology, systems, and proportions. Corbu was aesthetic, didactic, and theoretical."

Le Corbusier's plans, sections, and elevations provided a syntax used by architects for years to come. When he made a radical break from that rational language with Notre-Dame-du-Haut at Ronchamp (1950–55), it caused some disquiet for the young, relatively unknown James Stirling. Stirling wrote about Ronchamp in 1956: "Remembering, however, that this is a product of Europe's greatest architect, it is important to consider whether this building should influence the course of modern architecture." Stirling concluded that Ronchamp's "sensational impact" would not last, since its emotional appeal took precedence over intellectual engagement. Ronchamp survived this critical attack. Gehry, in fact, claims that it is his favorite building.

Like Ronchamp, Bilbao's forms are expressionist rather than rational, and the structure is not explicitly revealed. Bilbao's titanium-clad surface-as-form is attached to, but does not call out the lineaments of the frame. Here, structure follows form, not the other way around, and the frame is distorted to allow those shapes and continuous surfaces to happen.

While Gehry's own design process appears intuitive, it is bolstered by advanced scientific resources. The computer technology used by his office for Bilbao subverts the notion he is a head-in-the-clouds sculptor. CATIA software, engineered by Dassault Systems, the French aerospace company, is an important computer-modeling building tool that Gehry began using with the fish form in the Vila Olimpica in Barcelona (1989–92). In Bilbao it enabled his artistically derived, manually rendered models to be quantified, digitized, and mapped as continuous surfaces. The data could be given to a contractor who, with another software program, BOCAD, would generate the brace-framed and secondary steel structures for the museum.

GEHRY'S WORKING METHOD BEGINS WITH FUNCTIONAL DECISIONS.

Those who have been associated with Gehry describe his design method beginning with functional decisions before the artist takes over. Michael Lehrer, a Los Angeles architect, teacher, and president of the Los Angeles chapter of the AIA who worked closely with Gehry in the early 1980s, observes: "Frank starts out by solving basic problems straightforwardly in the true Modernist manner. Then he begins to change the scheme and to incorporate the unknown into his method." Part of the unknown relates to Gehry's well-known absorption with contemporary art. His relationships and sometimes collaborations with artists Claes Oldenburg, Richard Serra, and Coosje Van Bruggen, among others, have

Right: Vitra Design Museum, Weil am Rhein, Germany (1987–89). Below: Schnabel House, Brentwood, California (1986–89). Far right: Center for Visual Arts, University of Toledo, Toledo, Ohio (1989).

been influential, as noted by Francesco Dal Co in *Frank O. Gehry*. The art idea is transformed in the process of being integrated with the architectural concept: It is not a matter of sticking windows and doors onto overblown sculptures.

A critical vs. nonverbal approach

The top creative architects of the century usually expounded systematic theories of design in rhetorical or polemical writing. Gehry feels no need to validate his work in this way. The contrast is all the more unusual in an era when theory, influenced by philosophy and literary criticism, has penetrated deeply into architectural consciousness. As Johnson puts it, "Gehry's work is nonverbal, noncommunicable. That's what art is about. I've always said 'The word kills art.'"

So, is Gehry's hybrid of art and architecture critical, self-consciously questioning the language and traditions of architecture in a way that advances it? "Gehry's Bilbao is singular and personal," Eisenman says. On the other hand, Stirling's Staatsgalerie in Stuttgart is a statement of critical architecture in which "Stuttgart says something about the museum as a type, and something about context." Gehry's architecture is more like the films of Steven Spielberg, Eisenman contends: "Spielberg is able to zero in on the collective unconscious of the audience. He produces films of incredible art, but they are not necessarily critical. They are totally emotional experiences. Gehry also has that unerring aim."

Spielberg comparisons aside, Gehry has brought the visceral and experiential element to architecture. And, like Spielberg, Gehry is known to watch finances and production. He has not been branded as a reckless artist-architect famous for leaky, overbudget, uncomfortable buildings. To be sure, the American Center in Paris did shut down, but the blame was placed on an insufficiently planned operating budget, rather than on cost overruns by the architect; and if the bids for Disney Concert Hall originally came in too high, the glitch was with the production drawings by an outside firm. If Bilbao's titanium has been stained by the roof's polyurethane, Gehry's defense is also convincing. His buildings are made of Teflon, as far as complaints are concerned.

Gehry's architecture never has been known for its high level of detail, something he has frequently admitted. The razzle-dazzle of his forms, however, increases with the precision of construction. With Bilbao, it does seem as if technique of construction was able to almost match the amazingly bold artistic concept. At least for now. Yet some visitors are complaining that the construction inside as well as outside Bilbao is not quite up to par. A "Bilbao Backlash" could be forming.

The Bilbao Effect, or the influence Bilbao's success is having in encouraging more and more private and public clients to go after the big whammy, was much scrutinized in a conference titled "Urban Spectacle," held in March at the Museum of Modern Art in New York City. Although Gehry was not one of the participants (among them Bernard Tschumi, AIA, Zaha Hadid, Daniel Libeskind, and Eisenman), his presence was palpable in the packed auditorium. The danger with a Bilbao, that is with an architecture that grips the public, Eisenman warned, is that architects won't be sufficiently critical of the society for which they design. They risk becoming "part of the system of spectacle." By this, Eisenman alludes to a fear that architects have with popular success. When the spectacle is

sought, the criteria for evaluating architecture shift: The adulation may not rely on thoughtful evaluation as much as it does thrill per square foot.

The question is, can an architect be consciously critical of his or her work, as well as create the "spectacular" work? Michelangelo was capable of both, argues Judith di Maio, an architect who teaches at Yale. His Sistine Chapel, she says, astonished the public with its vivid colors, its size and scale. "He challenged the conventions of painting a barrel-vault ceiling, reinterpreted the Biblical narrative, and transformed his style as he went along, thereby critiquing the style of the period and his own style at the same time," Di Maio notes.

One could argue that Gehry is critical on a more restricted level of his own architectural history and language. While it is not the same architecturally referential critique that Stirling made with Stuttgart, the trajectory of Gehry's work shows a transformation occurring every 5 to 10 years. During each period, he moves his architecture into a new area, enriching (and usually improving) it as he goes along.

Gehry himself now faces pressures to duplicate his success at Bilbao—with the same level of accomplishment. The Bilbao Effect has already affected Gehry's clients, many of whom want that shiny, curvy stuff: Bilbao's babies can be found among his current projects. Warren Schwartz, of Schwartz Silver in Boston, finds Bilbao successful because it engages in dialogue with the psyche of the Basque people and with the context of its culture and place. He fears other cities "may wrongly assume they can transpose the particularity of Bilbao and have it work elsewhere."

The problem goes further: Bilbao's success could generate too many frenzied efforts by lesser talents to come up with flashy sequels. Half-baked results of unquestioning, uncritical attempts by architects to imitate Bilbao would be disastrous for the significant gains to architecture made by Gehry. The Gehry example suggests that creativity still depends more on feeling than on verbalized design principles and more on innate talent than on the acquisition of a design language. But only a few can squeeze into this exclusive category.

"If a creator becomes astonishingly successful by his own criteria," states Howard Gardner, the Harvard psychologist who wrote *Creating Minds* (Basic Books), "he runs the risk of repeating himself. What typically happens is that the creator himself increases the challenge by veering off in a new direction." This Gehry has managed to do before. "But," warns Gardner, "the desire on the part of the artist to create and respond to new challenges does not always work."

Be that as it may, Gehry's achievements are nevertheless formidable. Unlike his predecessors, he has reaffirmed the possibility of the intuitive architect generating a major creative body of work in a day of increasingly technological and financial domination. Ten years ago Ada Louise Huxtable, a jury member for the Pritzker Prize, wondered if success with institutional clients would spoil Gehry's "nonformulaic art." A decade later Gehry's architecture still emerged as fresh and as transformative as ever. Success hasn't spoiled Gehry yet. And it's too soon to tell if the spectacle will spoil architecture. ■

Left and facing page: Jean-Marie Tjibaou Culture Centre, Nouméa, New Caledonia, South Pacific, by Renzo Piano. **Below:** North-east elevation

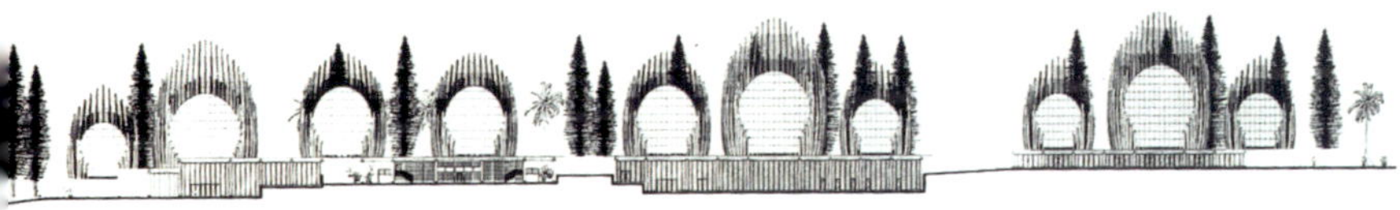

tween 1981 and 1995 France alone saw 400 museums created or renovated. The 1990s have tnessed the reinvention of the museum as a celebration of national culture and barometer of onomic wealth, as architects from Frank Gehry and Renzo Piano to Steven Holl and Daniel Libeskind ve been inspired to produce their best work. Nicola Turner reports.

Spirit of the age

"Painting and sculpture... are orphans," said Paul Valery in his 1925 essay "The Problem of Museums". "Their mother is dead, their mother, Architecture. As long as she was alive, she gave them their place, their function, their constraints."

Say what you like about the dumbing down of museums at the end of the millennium, the triumph of the tourist buck over the education ticket; there is one point on which we must all agree. Architecture has never been more alive, and painting and sculpture are its greatest benefactors, although some might argue that at the end of the 1990s mother architecture has come back to life and in the process killed her children.

As early as *WA*3 the issues facing national and private museum clients and their architects were subjected to scrutiny: "Is the museum building now more important than the art it contains? Well, yes – and sometimes this is because the art is not worthy of the buiding. More art has not meant more quality... fortunately there is much to show that is worthy of the architect's investment. Yet the architect should beware of hubris." (Foreword, page 35).

With the birth of Rem Koolhaas' Rotterdam Kunsthal, Frank Gehry's Bilbao Guggenheim and Daniel Libeskind's Jewish Museum in Berlin it would seem that architects have made dramatic strides forward and the envelope has been stretched to its outer limits, but the debates which preoccupy curators, academics and critics have remained the same.

The development in museum architecture, alongside the "museumification" of everything from art to cultural identity and music, has been a necessary move to maintain public interest. Given the short attention span of the museum-going public, and the competition for its attention in this age of multi-media, museums have had to revolutionise their approach to the built form and adjust to commercial realities in order to survive at all. That this process has resulted in a critical new chapter in the history of 20th century architecture is the happy consequence of inevitable evolution.

This issue of *World Architecture*, celebrating ten years of architecture, is dominated by museums, which garnered 25 per cent of the votes for the seminal buildings of the 1990s. Interviews and retrospectives of the two front runners at the end of the decade, Frank Gehry and Norman Foster, have centred on the architects' cultural designs. Richard Meier, during the anniversary jury session, asserted that "the museum is the public building experience of our time". The museum has provoked different ways of "thinking about ▸

v: Museum of Contemporary Art, Barcelona, by Richard Meier **Bottom left and right:** The Guggenheim Museum, Bilbao, Frank O Gehry and Associates **Facing page:** Museum of Modern Art, Niteroi, Brazil, by Oscar Niemeyer

Richard Bryant/Arcaid

▼▲ Erika Barahona Ede

▼▲Bitter + Bredt Fotographie

Left, above and below: The Jewish Museum, Berlin, by Daniel Libeskind

▸ architecture. They say something about our art and make us rethink the world of architecture as a result." (See page 83).

These designers, among others, have used architecture to re-connect the container with the contained. Marc Pachter, chief counsellor to the secretary of the Smithsonian Institution in Washington DC, believes that "there is a sense that modernism can create a more universal symbol" for the complex programme of diverse museums. The crucial role of museums at the turn of the century is to "impress on society a secular notion of culture".

Politics

Six hundred new art museums have opened across the US since 1970. The role of the museum in society has gone beyond that of the 20th century cathedral, to become an alternative "spiritual" meeting place. They are now crucial magnets for commerce – in the shape of tourism – and beacons of political confidence.

Although museums have been political since the 19th century, recently the nature of the politics has changed. They are now inextricably bound to a more complex representation of national identity where minority groups are celebrated within a larger culture; the Jews in Germany, or the American Indian in the USA and Canada. Their role, says Pachter, is to provide "discourse amid discord". The identity of individual countries is still disseminated through museums, but today – not unlike tall buildings – they are built as indicators of national economic wealth and prosperity, and as a way of positioning a country or city in the context of the wider world.

The re-shaping of Europe in the last decade has played a huge part in galvanising governments into full-time building programmes. In Germany, to show international corporations that Frankfurt am Main should be considered both a competitor to London for financial supremacy but also one of Europe's dominant cultural centres, Frankfurt's local government pioneered the construction of 13 museums within ten years.

Under President Mitterand France went into cultural overdrive in advance of post-1992 Europe, as Charlotte Ellis related in 1989, also in *WA*3 (pages 56-61): "The current interest in museums [in France] has been stimulated by the prospect of post-1992 Europe, [says Germain Viatte, in overall charge of major national and state-funded museums] which has made French towns and cities ever more anxious to assert their own identities. To that end, museums are now being encouraged to seek private funding and sponsorship, for new acquisitions, special exhibitions and the like. By becoming open to the present and attracting private patrons, says Viatte, museums are

▼▲John Edward Linden/Arcaid

Left, above and below: The Getty Center, Los Angeles, USA, by Richard Meier

becoming 'places of civic confluence'."

Over 400 new or renovated museums were designed in France 1981-95, for example the extensions to the Louvre – the pyramid completed in 1989 by I M Pei & Partners and the Richelieu Wing by Pei Cobb Freid & Partners in 1993.

In Italy, the world's largest living museum, the government has woken up to the fact that tourists are demanding more for their money. It has recently launched an impressive building programme which will surely reinvigorate both cultural life and architectural debate in the country. The Uffizi is to get an extension by Arata Isozaki, Gae Aulenti is refurbishing a museum near Turin, and Zaha Hadid has fought off competition from Rem Koolhaas, Steven Holl, Toyo Ito and Vittorio Gregotti to secure the commission for the Centre of Contemporary Arts in Rome.

In the special report on museums in 1997 (*WA*55 104-129) US museum consultant Arthur Rosenblat commended the British government for its "courageous and progressive attitude toward the celebration of a national culture" with its commission for Libeskind's spiral creation for the extension to London's Victoria and Albert Museum. The competition win was heralded as a break with English conservatism and a guiding light for the future.

Public space

Hadid's L-shaped linear scheme for the Rome museum addresses one of the most critical issues in museum design of the future, offering what she describes as "a quasi-urban field, a 'world' to dive into rather than a building as signature object. The campus is organised and navigated on the basis of directional drifts and the distribution of densities rather than key points. [the character will be] porous, immersive a field space".

Regardless of the noble pursuit of space over object, what she and the client both know is that with a Hadid project in the bag Rome is sure to get the attention it craves. There will be many who will still regard it a "signature" building, but the project is significant as the generator for a new cultural quarter in the capital, as was Richard Meier's Museum of Contemporary Art in Barcelona and the Guggenheim in Bilbao. What architects have little or no control over is the accessibility of their museum; whether or not it is a truly public, 24-hour space. Given that the collective footprint of museums in the world's cultural capitals tends to be greater than the open space around them, one of the foremost issues in the next millennium must be how to improve accessibility.

Architects have taken on the responsibility of making museums more culturally accessible and commercially viable, with the addition of ▸

Paul V

From left to right: ground, first and second floor plans

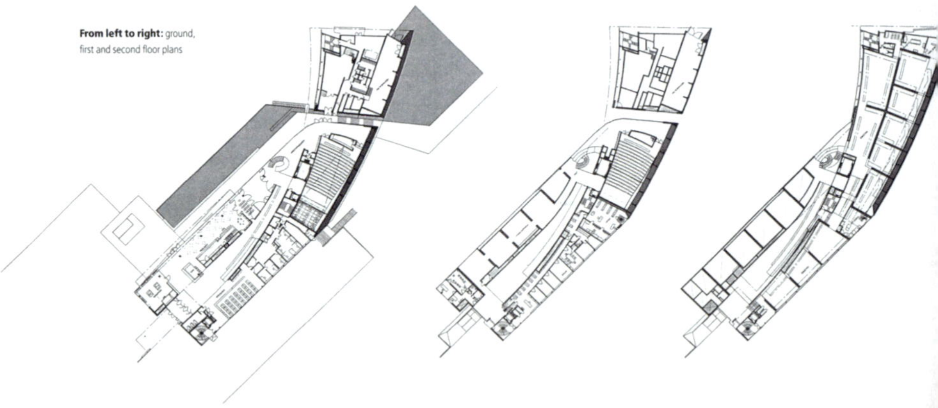

Shinkenchiku-sha

Hélène Binet

Above left: Miho Museum, Shiga, Japan, by I M Pei **Below left:** Kunsthaus Bregenz, Austria, by Peter Zumthor. **Facing page, above:** Kiasma Museum of Contemporary Art, Helsinki, Finland, by Stephen Holl Architects

► restaurants, retail outlets and entertainment facilities. Pachter asserts that "we need the grand spaces of museums, not as treasure houses of the 19th century, but as gathering places in a fractured world". He cites Richard Meier's Getty Center in Los Angeles as "truly a piazza for the city", a democratic space which has dispelled the notion of a museum or cultural centre as a place of snobbery or class. Interestingly, he claims that the only complaints have been to do with the facilities for parking and washrooms. The architecture works brilliantly as a tourist trap, but some feel it's not accessible enough. The impact of the complex would seem to have been underestimated.

Fast forward

Frances Morris, curator at London's Tate Gallery, and involved with the Herzog & de Meuron renovation at Bankside for the additional secondary gallery, sees the future of the museum not merely as an exhibition space, but as a carapace. A building which can be used inside and out, in a variety of formations, which encourages less conventional "contemporary interventions" and contributes to the community in a pro-active rigorous way.

Will museums survive the electronic age? On current form the answer must be yes. Museums of all kinds must communicate meaning implicitly, not necessarily through the objects on display. Herein lies the responsibility of the architect. The objects on display may well be accessible via the internet, television or the written word, but to register the intangible – akin to listening to a live musical performance rather than reading the score or listening to a recording – requires the physical experience of visiting the museum. Libeskind's Jewish Museum in Berlin is an extreme example of this – here the architecture *is* the programme. Even if visitors are unable to interpret the symbolism in every architectural gesture they can still be affected by the emotion they seduce. Museums provide a vital counterbalance to the electronic world.

The leap in the next decade will be in commercial initiatives, believes Marc Pachter. Museums will have to look beyond retail and entertainment – but to what, he cannot say. What he does know is that world class architecture is essential for raising the public consciousness and attracting top-dollar investment.

Gehry argues that "a lot of artists don't like neutral spaces for their art. They want their work to be shown in an important place, rather than a deferential one... [to build a museum which is itself a work of art] sends the message that the town must love artists". That, and the fact that the town is eager to get noticed. It's a small investment for an immeasurably huge return. WA

HSS

1998–

Hashim Sarkis Studios

Headquarters
Cambridge, MA

Other Locations
Beirut, Lebanon

Founding Partner
Hashim Sarkis

1998

Hashim Sarkis Studios

1998–

Slade Architecture

Headquarters
New York, NY

Founding Partners
James Slade, Hayes Slade

Slade Architecture

1998

Studio SUMO

Headquarters
Long Island City, NY

Founding Partners
Sunil Bald, Yolande Daniels

1998

Studio SUMO

OBRA Architects

Headquarters
New York, NY

Other Locations
Beijing, China; Seoul, South Korea; Rome, Italy

Founding Partners
Pablo Castro, Jennifer Lee

OBRA Architects

2001–

L.E.FT

Headquarters
New York, NY

Other Locations
Beirut, Lebanon

Founding Partners
Makram el Kadi, Ziad Jamaleddine, Naji Moujaes

Current Partners
Makram el Kadi, Ziad Jamaleddine

2001

L.E.FT

2003–

SsD

Headquarters
New York, NY

Other Locations
Cambridge, MA; Seoul, South Korea

Founding Partners
Jinhee Park, John Hong

SsD

Judenburg West Master Plan
1998

Architect
MACK Architect(s)

Location
Judenburg, Austria

Client
Stadtgemeinde Judenburg

MidCity Place
1998–2001

Architect
Kohn Pedersen Fox Associates

Location
London, UK

Client
Matsushita Investment and Development UK Ltd.

International American School of Warsaw
1998–2001

Architect
NELSON H2L2

Location
Warsaw, Poland

Client
American School of Warsaw

Xintiandi
1998–2001

Architect
Studio Shanghai

Location
Shanghai, China

Client
Shui On Land

Kyonggi University Master Plan and Teleconference Center
1998–2003

Architect
Cannon Design

Location
Suwon, South Korea

Client
Kyonggi University

US Embassy
1998–2003

Architect
Hellmuth, Obata + Kassabaum

Location
Dar-es-Salaam, Tanzania

Client
US Department of State, Bureau of Overseas Buildings Operations

Namba Parks
1998–2003

JERDE

Architect
Jerde Partnership

Location
Osaka, Japan

Project Architect
Obayashi Corporation

Client
Nankai Electric Railway Co., Ltd. Obayashi Corporation

Museo Picasso Malaga
1998–2004

GLUCKMAN MAYNER ARCHITECTS

Architect
Gluckman Mayner Architects

Location
Malaga, Spain

Client
Fundacion Museo Picasso Malaga

US Embassy
1998–2005

Architect
Hellmuth, Obata + Kassabaum

Location
Nairobi, Kenya

Client
US Department of State, Bureau of Overseas Buildings Operations

Atlantis and The Cove Atlantis at Paradise Island
1998–2007

WATG

Architect
Wimberly Allison Tong & Goo

Location
Paradise Island, Bahamas

Client
Kerzner

Housing for the Fishermen of Tyre
1998–2008

HSS

Architect
Hashim Sarkis Studios

Location
Tyre, Lebanon

Client
Al Baqaa Housing Cooperative and the Association for the Development of Rural Areas in Southern Lebanon, Yousif Khalil, Director

Ranger Pavilion
1998–2014

Architect
SITE

Location
Briosco, Italy

Client
Ranger Italia

Nanyang Polytechnic
1999

GWATHMEY SIEGEL KAUFMAN ARCHITECTS llc

Architect
Gwathmey Siegel Kaufman Architects

Location
Singapore

Client
Singapore Ministry of Education

Tango Bo01 Housing Exhibition
1999–2001

moore ruble yudell
architects & planners

Architect
Moore Ruble Yudell Architects & Planners

Location
Malmo, Sweden

Client
MKB Fastighets AB

Blur Building
1999–2002

DS+R

Architect
Diller + Scofidio

Location
Yverdone-les-Bains, Switzerland

Client
Swiss Expo 2002

Danube House and Nile House in River City
1999–2003

KPF

Architect
Kohn Pedersen Fox Associates

Location
Prague, Czech Republic

Client
AHI Development a.s., Europolis Real Estate Asset Management s.r.o.

Endesa Headquarters
1999–2003

KPF

Architect
Kohn Pedersen Fox Associates

Location
Madrid, Spain

Client
Grupo ENDESA SA

US Consulate Compound
1999–2003

ZGF
ZIMMER GUNSUL FRASCA ARCHITECTS LLP

Architect
Zimmer Gunsul Frasca Architects

Location
Istanbul, Turkey

Client
US Department of State, Bureau of Overseas Building Operations

Cyberport Hotel Office and University
1999–2004

Architect
Arquitectonica

Location
Hong Kong, China

Client
Pacific Century Cyberworks Ltd.

Salamanca Train Station
1999–2004

Architect
RTKL

Location
Salamanca, Spain

Client
Riofisa S.A

City of Culture of Galicia
1999–2011

Architect
Eisenman Architects

Location
Santiago de Compostela, Spain

Client
The Foundation for the City of Culture of Galicia

Heron Tower
1999–2011

Architect
Kohn Pedersen Fox Associates

Location
London, United Kingdom

Client
Schatunowski Brooks, Alexander Forbes, Allgood

DZ Bank Buliding
2000

Architect
Frank O. Gehry and Associates

Location
Berlin, Germany

Executive Architect
Palnungs AG Neufert Nuttman Graf

Client
DG Immobilien Management, Hines

Fine Venture Office Tower
2000–2002

Architect
Zago Architecture

Location
Seoul, South Korea

Executive Architect
eCO-MyA Korea

Client
Jay Park, President, Fine Toy Company Ltd.

Morgan Stanley Headquarters
2000–2003

Architect
Skidmore, Owings & Merrill

Location
London, England

Client
Canary Wharf Contractors HQ1 Ltd, Canary Wharf Group PLC

Ciudad Grupo Santander
2000–2005

Architect
Kevin Roche John Dinkeloo and Associates

Location
Madrid, Spain

Client
Banco Santander

Suzhou Museum
2000–2006

Architect
I. M. Pei Architect

Location
Suzhou, China

Local Architect
Suzhou Institute of Architectural Design Co. Ltd.

Client
Suzhou Municipal Administration of Culture, Radio & Television

Zlote Tarasy
2000–2006

Architect
Jerde Partnership

Location
Warsaw, Poland

Client
ING Real Estate, Rodamco Europe

Emirates Stadium
2000–2006

Architect
HOK Sport

Location
London, United Kingdom

Client
Arsenal Football Club

Beijing Finance Street
2000–2007

Architect
Skidmore, Owings & Merrill

Location
Beijing, China

Client
Financial Street Holding Co., Ltd.

Samsung Cancer Center
2000–2008

Architect
AECOM

Location
Seoul, South Korea

Local Architect
Samoo Architects Engineers

Client
Samsung Cancer Center

Museum of Islamic Art
2000–2008

Architect
I. M. Pei Architect

Location
Doha, Qatar

Associate Architect
Qatari Engineer & Associates

Client
Museum of Islamic Art

First International Bank of Israel
2000–2009

PEI COBB FREED & PARTNERS Architects LLP

Architect
Pei Cobb Freed & Partners

Location
Tel Aviv, Israel

Local Architect
Nir-Kutz Architects

Client
The First International Bank of Israel, Ltd.

International Commerce Centre
2000–2011

Architect
Kohn Pedersen Fox Associates

Location
Hong Kong, China

Client
Harbour Vantage Management Ltd., Sun Hung Kai Properties Ltd., Sun Hung Kai Real Estate Agency Ltd.

Open For Business: Developments in Asia

Following the rise of Deng Xiaoping to the position of China's "paramount leader" in 1978, experiments with trade, foreign investments, and market competition began to transform both living standards across the country's vast expanse and its global economic power.[1] The announcement of the Open Door Policy unleashed a "maelstrom of modernization," fundamentally altering existing conditions across China and Asia and producing "a completely new urban substance" in its wake.[2] Xiaoping advocated for the establishment of "experimental" enclaves, modeled in part on the economic success of Hong Kong and Macau, in order to test their urban and economic effects while allowing for only temporary commitment if the models proved unsuccessful. Guangdong and Fujian were the first cities granted the status of Special Economic Zone (SEZ), while in Sichuan, Jiangsu, and Zhejiang the experiment involved industrial management, and in Shekou, voting. Xiaoping had grand ideas for these enclaves as a calibrated opening to the outside world: "Through the zones, we can import technology, acquire knowledge, and learn about management, which is also a form of knowledge."[3]

Investments from Hong Kong, where labor-intensive industries had begun to lose their competitive edge, began flowing in; soon all of the "Four Asian Tigers" (South Korea, Hong Kong, Singapore, and Taiwan) became springboards for the flood of foreign investment into China. In the three decades after the opening of the SEZs, Chinese exports increased over a hundred-fold, ushering in the megalopolis of the Pearl River Delta (PRD). Between 1979 and 1995 the population of Shenzhen rose from 20,000 to 10 million, and the city's industrial output increased 1,256-fold. By 2004 China was spending nearly 16 percent of its GDP on construction, using an astonishing "54.7 percent of the world's production of concrete, 36.1 percent of the world's steel and 30.4 percent of the world's coal" in the process.[4]

① Ezra F. Vogel, *Deng Xiaoping and the Transformation of China* (Cambridge, MA: The Belknap Press of Harvard University Press, 2011); "Deng Xiaoping's legacy: the great stabiliser," *The Economist* (October 22, 2011), http://www.economist.com/node/21533354 (last accessed Novermber 21, 2014).

② Rem Koolhaas, "Introduction," in Chuihua Judy Chung, Jeffrey Inaba, Rem Koolhaas, Sze Tsung Leong, ed., *Great Leap Forward* (Cologne: Taschen, 2002): 27.

③ Quoted in Mihai Craciun, "Ideology: Shenzhen Special Economic Zone," *Great Leap Forward*: 87.

④ Clifford A. Pearson, "China: Moving Heaven and Earth, and Doing it Faster Than You Thought Possible,"

1958–1963 Mao Zedong's First-Five-Year Plan, *The Great Leap Forward*

1966–1976 *The Cultural Revolution* in China

1955

1976 Mao Zedong dies

1978 Chinese Premier Deng Xiaoping announces Open Door Policy to modernize China's economy

1979 China and the US announce opening of full diplomatic relations

1980 China inaugurates Special Economic Zones in Shenzen, Zhuhai, Shantou, Xiamen

1989 Protests in Tiananmen Square

1992 Kim Young-Sam elected first civilian President of South Korea in thirty years, announces *Segyehwa* (globalization) policy

1962 Cuban Missile Crisis

1950–1975 Vietnam War

Lacking the architects per capita to build at anywhere close to this unprecedented scale, the production of this new urbanism would have been impossible without the foreign architects who rushed to join the Chinese construction boom. These firms operated in a closely regulated system in which architects could act primarily as design consultants, while local institutes were charged with developing full drawing sets and supervising construction. In 1981 alone there were over 600 projects involving foreign architects in Shenzhen, 41 of which were high-rise buildings.[5] The wave of successively tallest towers in the region by US architects included the Bank of China in Hong Kong (1982–1990) by I. M. Pei & Partners, the Petronas Towers in Kuala Lumpur, Malaysia (1992–1998) by Cesar Pelli & Associates, Jin Mao Tower in Shanghai (1993–1999) by Skidmore, Owings & Merrill, and the Shanghai World Financial Center (1994–2008) by Kohn Pedersen Fox, construction of which was stalled by the Asian financial crisis of 1997 for nearly a decade. Though neither the Tiananmen Square protests in 1989 nor the short-lived financial crisis ultimately stopped the production of ever-greater architectural superlatives and experiments, the extravagant desires of investors and the freedom granted to foreign architects compelled some to ponder their responsibility in this context, worrying that "The preoccupation with Western-style architecture has resulted in an architectural Chernobyl—an uncontrolled fallout of conflicting building styles and contradictory land uses."[6]

The environmental consequences of rapid expansion and the strength of the Chinese economy, which by estimates of the International Monetary Fund has surpassed that of the US, have recently compelled China's current president, Xi Jinping, to call for the making of the "Chinese Dream," perhaps a greener, more self-sustainable version of its American counterpart.[7] Jinping made news in October 2014 at a literary symposium, surrounded by party veterans, in which one of his pronouncements immediately sent shivers through the global architectural media: "No more weird architecture."[8] While the prospect of a more regulated construction market has been interpreted as a form of undemocratic censorship or a nationalistic showing of teeth, it may also be a sign of China taking responsibility for its contribution to the global environmental crisis and a new dedication to prospective planning—a challenge (if poorly worded) to architects involved in the region to aim higher than they have thus far. — AM

Architectural Record (March 2004): 71.

⑤ According to Nancy Lin, in 1996 China had 10,000 times more people per architect than in the US. See Lin, "Architecture: Shenzhen," *Great Leap Forward*: 161.

⑥ "Asia Bound: What are American Architects' Responsibilities in Developing Countries?" *Progressive Architecture* (March 1995): 46.

⑦ Mike Bird, "China Just Overtook The US As The World's Largest Economy," *Business Insider* (October 8, 2014), http://www.businessinsider.com/china-overtakes-us-as-worlds-largest-economy-2014-10#ixzz3IQcDS71a (last accessed November 8, 2014).

⑧ Jia Jia, "Xi Has Had Enough of 'Weird' Architecture—And So Have I," *Huffington Post* (October 28, 2014), http://www.huffingtonpost.com/jia/xi-weird-architecture_b_6062750.html?utm_hp_ref=world (last accessed November 8, 2014).

1993 Jiang Zemin becomes President of China

1996 Korea becomes member of Organisation for Economic Co-operation and Development

1997
- Sovereignty over Hong Kong transferred from United Kingdom to China
- Deng Xiaoping dies
- Asian financial crisis

1999 China-U.S. Center for Sustainable Development established

2002
- China ends local monopoly control over gambling in Macau, plans Cotai Island for international casinos
- South Korea and Japan jointly host FIFA World Cup
- Hu Jintao becomes President of China

2007 The Venetian Macao first casino resort to open on Cotai Strip, Macau

2008 Beijing hosts Olympic Games with Xi Jinping in charge of the event

2013 Xi Jinping becomes President and announces the "Chinese Dream"

1990–1991 First Persian Gulf War

2001 Afghanistan War

2003 Iraq War

1980 **2015** **2014**

Currency Exchange Rates

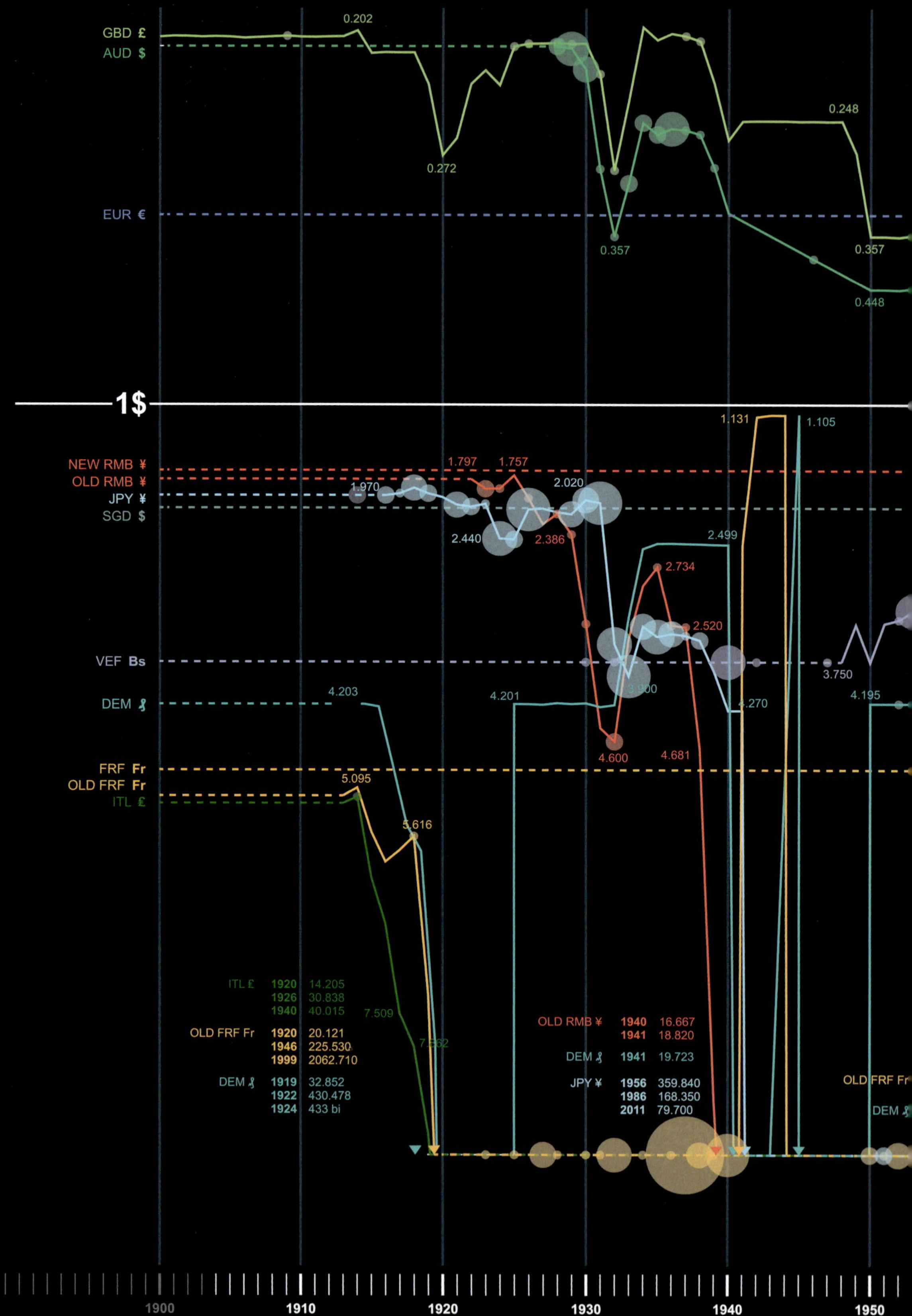

Number of Projects
1
3
8
14
Projects in:
England
Euro Countries
Australia
Singapore
Germany
Venezuela
China
France
Japan
Italy
0.417
0.573
0.771
0.566
0.499
0.623
0.695
0.899
0.870
1.277
1.490
1.703
1.834
1.881
1.171
1.934
1.454
1.257
2.140
2.084
2.517
2.942
3.350
3.992
3.767
4.450
4.297
4.290
4.905
5.529
5.779
6.769
6.947
7.017
8.083
8.276
8.639
8.980
79.700
1945 50.733
1959 490.677
1949 588.582
VEF Bs 1987 14.500
2007 2144.600
1960
1970
1980
1990
2000
2010

75TH ANNIVERSARY YEAR

PA

Progressive Architecture

A Penton Publication March 1995

Also in this issue

- Campus Museums
- Technics File: Security
- Process: Preassembled Public Building
- Critique: Guggenheim Museum

What are American Architects' Responsibilities in Developing Countries?

What are American Architects' Responsibilities in Developing Countries?

Asia Bound

In the modernizing countries of Asia, U.S. architects are creating buildings of often enormous size and exaggerated style, unconstrained by city planning. What should designers do when their clients want the wrong thing?

by Philip Langdon

China's future buildings include Kohn Pedersen Fox's Nanjing Xi Lu towers in Shanghai (below), S.O.M. Chicago's Jin Mao Tower in Shanghai (right), and Loebl Schlossman and Hackl's Luo-Hu Commercial Center in Shenzhen (far right).

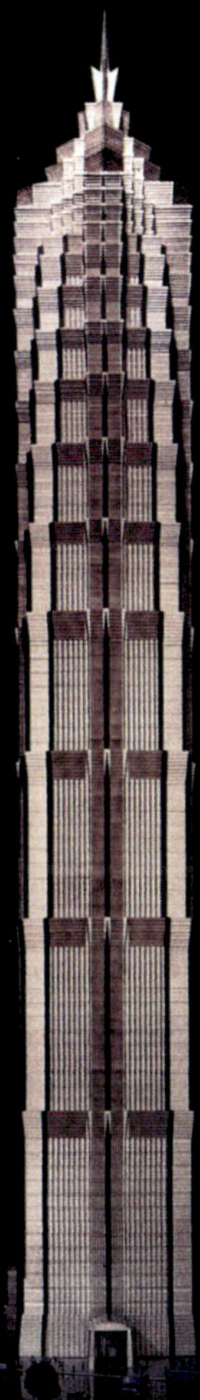

Jock Pottle/Esto (left); ©Steinkamp/Ballogg Chicago (center and right)

Across East and Southeast Asia, the conscience of the architectural profession faces a momentous challenge. Asia is riding a widespread economic boom, one so potent that *The Economist* says the modernization of Asia is likely to be the most earth-shaking public event in the lifetime of those living today. Countries such as Indonesia, Malaysia, and above all the People's Republic of China are hungry for monuments to their fast-rising prosperity. Galloping toward industrialization at a pace that makes Western economies look practically indolent, the modernizing nations of the East are providing plentiful work for American architects. But the buildings being produced raise nettlesome questions about the responsibilities architects should bear when they take their advanced technical skills into societies that have had little experience with the problems that big, Modern, Western-style development brings.

Even a cursory inspection suggests that something is going very wrong. A great many buildings planned or constructed in the emerging Asia are glaringly slick. The horizons of East Asia and Southeast Asia increasingly are punctuated by brightly lighted towers of reflective glass and shiny metal, in shapes that shout novelty above all else. Some Asian towers, especially in mainland China, are so flashy they make Houston seem a paragon of restraint.

The Sky's The Limit

Projects involving American architects frequently rank among the most ambitious things these countries have ever built. In Jakarta, the Sun Center designed by HOK's San Francisco office will have nine high-rise buildings containing more than 3,000 apartments and more than 4 million square feet of office space. In Kuala Lumpur, Malaysia, the Sogo Pernas Centre designed by HOK will combine a 75-story office tower, a 515-room hotel, a department store, an air terminal, a 3,000-car garage, and a cultural museum. In Shanghai, the largest and most cosmopolitan city in China, construction cranes are raising towers by numerous Western architects – behemoths that dwarf the treasured Neoclassical and Art Deco buildings erected by European banks and traders in the 1920s and 1930s. A frenetic contest has broken out for the title of tallest building in China. As of Autumn 1998, that distinction will be claimed by the 88-story Jin Mao tower, designed by Skidmore, Owings & Merrill's Chicago office and now going up in a vast redeveloping district of Shanghai called Pudong New Area (see report on p. 35). There is talk of towers that may rise higher still in the south China boomtown of Shenzhen (P/A, Sept. 1994, p. 49) and in the inland city of Chongqing, although in China it's never easy to know how seriously such proposals should be taken.

The highest building in the world is rising in Malaysia, a resource-rich country of 19 million that gained its independence 38 years ago. The structure of Cesar Pelli's Petronas Towers, two identical office structures 1,476 feet high on a former racetrack in the capital, Kuala Lumpur, is 35 percent complete. When the towers are finished, it will be the first time since at least 1891 that the tallest building on earth will be outside North America – indeed, outside the domain of what Americans are used to calling the "developed" world. A shift of historic proportions is taking place, and architecture is the premier symbol of that transformation.

It is silly, if not downright repugnant, to accuse American architects of "carpetbagging in Asia," as one American architectural editor did a few months ago. The economy is increasingly marked by global competition and global alliances, and architects have every right to hunt for jobs overseas, particularly at a time when opportunities in the United States have left some 15 to 20 percent of this country's architects unemployed or underemployed. Pursuing openings overseas is a way to grow during a

Among the towers coming to Asia are, from left, Grand Gateway Shanghai, by Callison Architecture; Union Square, Shanghai, by Daniel Dolan/HOK, New York; Shekou Harbor Building, Shekou, China, by Loebl, Schlossman & Hackl; Anhui International Trade Center, Anhui, China, by Stubbins Associates; and Sun Center, Jakarta, by HOK San Francisco.

period when the American market for offices, shopping centers, and hotels is still hobbled by overbuilding in the 1980s. RTKL reports that 30 percent of its work is outside the U.S., half of it in Asia. Kohn Pedersen Fox gets 35 percent of its commissions in Asia. Other firms busy in Asia also include Brennan Beer Gorman; Callison Architecture; Fox & Fowle; HLW; Kaplan McLaughlin Diaz; Loebl Schlossman and Hackl; John Portman & Associates; and the Stubbins Associates, to name a few. Jobs there are being pursued by individual practitioners as well. One example is Steven Lombardi of San Diego, a P/A Young Architect in 1987, who recently established a partnership in Hong Kong with Frank Desenyi to work on projects ranging from utilities buildings at the Hong Kong airport to transit facilities in Bangkok and Manila.

Opportunities Unavailable in the U.S.

"You can do things over there that you would never get to do back home," says Christopher Choa, who leads HLW's design work in Asia. "In the U.S., if you go after a research lab, you're asked how many research labs you've done in the past six months. In China, it's assumed that if you're an American firm, you're qualified to do all kinds of work." This is a powerful incentive, one that reinvigorates American firms and expands their skills. Carpetbagging indeed!

Large American firms are hired, in part, because they have a reputation for handling projects that the modernizing parts of Asia have had limited experience in producing. "The tall building is a specialty of ours," says Jon Pickard, a senior associate at Cesar Pelli & Associates. "Because we have so much experience with all the complex issues involved in tall buildings, we can design them efficiently and with an artistic intention."

Large mixed-use buildings, common in the U.S., are just beginning to be built in substantial numbers in some parts of Asia. RTKL plays on its mixed-use expertise to get such projects in the Far East. These in turn sometimes allow designers to try new things and master greater challenges. In Manila, for instance, RTKL is working on the Paramount retail center, a two-million-square-foot "entertainment-driven" project that will have a major attraction on each of its five levels to lure shoppers through the complex. The Paramount will incorporate a 12,000-seat cinema complex, a 2,000-seat food court, and an extraordinary array of amusements (including, if all goes well, "human pinball machines" – bumper cars that take their occupants on a ride across a tilted floor, bouncing from point to point while the activity is shown on a huge screen for the mall crowds to enjoy).

In East and Southeast Asia, a mixed-use project may contain a podium of three to seven stories devoted primarily to retailing, with one or more other uses, such as offices, hotels, or apartments, placed above. Where such mixed-use developments have been built in the U.S., they have contained 1.5 to 2.5 million square feet. In Asia, they swell to 2 to 4 million square feet, according to David Brotman, vice chairman of RTKL. Americans also make good candidates for Asian work because of expertise in resorts, theme parks, suburban housing and urban design, all of which will become more important as Asian prosperity grows. Golf course and waterfront projects are underway in countries such as Malaysia and Indonesia.

America's reputation for trendsetting further aids U.S. firms. "In China today, they're in love with everything Western, everything they see on TV," Brotman says. Don Hackl, president of Loebl Schlossman and Hackl in Chicago, observes, "The Chinese have the perception that Americans are at the leading edge of form-giving." This is an advantage for Americans in getting work, but it can also be an invitation to superficial design. *(continued on next page)*

What They Want in Asia

The way China is developing amazes American architects. The government has designated five coastal areas as "special economic zones," liberating them from many of the restrictions that apply elsewhere. Investment and entrepreneurial talent, not to mention good old capitalistic greed, have surged in, directed principally by ethnic Chinese developers based in Hong Kong and Taiwan. The peculiar partnership of an authoritarian Communist regime, non-national or inexperienced local capitalists, and passport-carrying designers has had the effect of inflating development plans and exaggerating their architectural expression. Government officials want as much development as they can get, and in the absence of the discipline imposed by a true market economy, they encourage capitalists to promise what seem, to outside observers, absurdly high concentrations of development. The architects then sketch giddy visions of these tomorrowlands of tall towers, complemented, in some cases, by enough searchlights to illuminate a football stadium.

"The preoccupation with Western-style architecture has resulted in an architectural Chernobyl – an uncontrolled fallout of conflicting building styles and contradictory land uses." – *Nelson Chen*

The city of Chongqing, not in a special economic zone but hungry for investment, told a developer he could acquire a site in the city's center, but only if he put up a building at least 100 stories high. HLW actually produced a design for a 114-story tower, which received a number of required approvals and then stalled, as many Chinese projects do. Guarantees of seeing a job completed, and of not being replaced by another firm, are elusive. "China," Hackl cautions, "is no place for the faint-hearted or the undercapitalized."

Notions of what a building will be used for can be surprisingly vague. Sometimes architects are asked to sketch a tower that might end up containing offices or apartments or hotel rooms or all three. The fact that some mainland-based developers have never built anything before (they've made their money in some unrelated field) exacerbates the uncertainty. "The dialogue we have with the client is more about the imagery: what looks good, what satisfies their egotistical and corporate requirements," says Bruce Fowle of New York's Fox & Fowle. "We don't discuss the net-and-gross issue. We have yet to have a dialogue on interior design. Space planning is all new to them."

Chinese clients do have preferences about form and style. With notable exceptions such as Beijing, which favors relatively low, monumental buildings, the Chinese, as well as many other Asians, tend to want buildings as tall as possible and in as ostentatiously Modern a style as can be found. "Why are these countries building?" A. Eugene Kohn, the marketing partner for Kohn Pedersen Fox, asks. "One reason is to catch up with the West. They don't think of themselves as Third World. They've chosen the tower for its skyline image, which immediately puts them in the First World." When American architects are hired, usually teaming up with a design institute based at a Chinese university, it's more or less expected that the Americans will be bold stylists. As Hackl puts it, "There are no quiet buildings in China." Yu-Heng Shang, an American-educated Taiwanese who works as a marketing specialist for HLW in China, is often told by potential clients: "Show me something I've never seen before." In such an environment, it should be no surprise that buildings sprout astonishing tops and arbitrary-looking walls.

The Question of Context

For China, which never seems to make its mistakes on a less than gargantuan scale, rampant development is the latest trouble in a tragic land. Nelson K. Chen, an American-born, Harvard-educated architect who is the design partner for Wong Chen Architects in Hong Kong, says, "It's amazing how quickly hundreds or even thousands of years of environmental compatibility can get wiped out." In Harvard's *GSD News*, Chen lamented, "The preoccupation with Western-style architecture has resulted in an architectural Chernobyl – an uncontrolled fallout of conflicting building styles and contradictory land uses." The problem is not just the buildings' looks; it's how they fit into the form of the city. Though many Asian clients want the newest architectural forms, they tend to combine them with flawed, older planning ideas. "The idea of a tall central tower on open land is an *idée fixe* in China right now," says Choa. The socialist planners of China, like their discredited mentors in Russia, have made a habit of erecting hulking apartment buildings on big stretches of land; it is a kind of bureaucratic reflex that leads naturally to the positioning of today' flamboyant towers on superblocks and megablocks. Because of Asian cities' tremendous densities, it's possible that some of the plazas surrounding the towers will be well-populated. But if Western experience teaches anything, it's that the tower-in-the-park concept ought to be used sparingly. It should not be the standard approach to city planning.

A second urbanistic problem is that some of these projects embrace the idea, increasingly resisted in the U.S., of separation of uses. Old Asian cities are lively and interesting because they mix offices, apartments, shops, and markets tightly together. Many new developments have apartment buildings in one area, office buildings in another area, and so on. This simplifies planning, financing, and management, but it may do a disservice to the inhabitants. Where housing, shops, and other aspects of living are not closely tied together, there is a danger that the new places will be dull – or worse.

A third problem is that Asian cities do not necessarily have systems of utilities, roads, and public transit satisfactorily linking the new projects to areas already built up. It remains to be seen whether big Asian projects now going forward will aggravate difficulties. Cities like Bangkok and Jakarta are notorious for their choking traffic. One compensation for bogged-down transportation systems is that mixed-use projects may stand a better chance of being built. They offer relief from an inadequate infrastructure, Brotman says, since "you can live, work, shop, and find entertainment in one place."

Searching for Responsible Design

If Asian cities are to be distinctive, coherent places, globally commuting designers – and the individuals and institutions they work for – will have to adopt a more *(continued on page 86)*

RENDERING

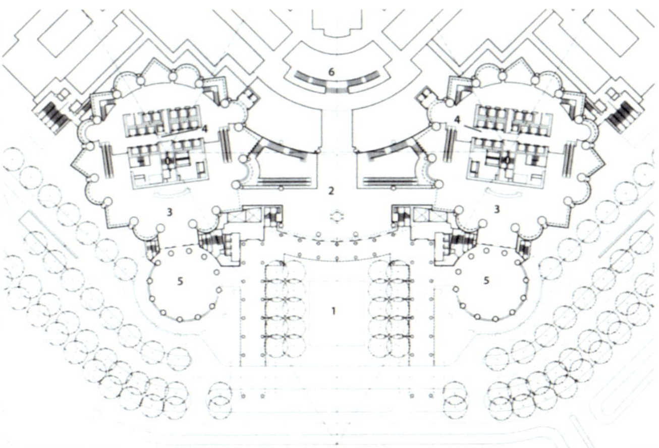

GROUND FLOOR PLAN 1 FORECOURT 2 RECEPTION HALL 3 LOBBY 4 ELEVATORS 5 ROTUNDA 6 RETAIL CENTER N 40'/12m

Mammoth, Modern, and Malaysian

Cesar Pelli's Petronas Towers for Kuala Lumpur brilliantly synthesize a number of remarkably divergent buildings. To those who have just the slightest familiarity with Malaysia, they suggest, with their faceted, tapered silhouettes, the graceful Kek Lok Si, the country's, and Southeast Asia's, largest Buddhist temple. To those who know of Pelli's consultations with the Petronas national petroleum company and Malaysian government officials, the buildings are Islamic in inspiration, taking the Moslem propensity for interlocking squares as a source of their geometry. Yet at the same time, the 88-story towers, with their stainless steel cladding, are resolutely Modern, befitting their function as super-high-profile office space for occupancy by mainly the oil company. In a tropical region where many recent buildings depend on mirror-glass to keep out the fierce sun, Pelli is using a more artful climate-control device, horizontal bars, teardrop-shaped in section, which will block 50 to 60 percent of the solar gain and at the same time give a sense of protection to workers stationed near the windows. At the 42nd story is a bridge that, together with its angled supports, forms what Pelli calls "a portal to the sky," a void he says is more important than the shapes of the buildings themselves. On the interior, geometrically patterned floors, wooden screens on the lobby windows, and a frieze pattern based on traditional songkets – handwoven silk fabrics with gold threads pulled through them – all accentuate the complex's imaginatively Malaysian character.

A Market in the Heart of Beijing

Redevelopment of the Dong An Market in Beijing is one of the many Asian mixed-use projects providing work for Americans – in this case the Los Angeles office of RTKL. A podium containing 1.5 million square feet of retailing, with six stories of offices above, is under construction on the site of what began in 1903 as an open-air market. Located where 200,000 to 500,000 people a day pass by, the retail center will include department stores, a night club, a bowling alley, and a food court in a five-story base and one of the floors below grade. David Brotman of RTKL says municipal officials and the client, a joint venture of the local Dong An Group and Sun Hung Kai Properties of Hong Kong, "felt it shouldn't be a copy of ancient Chinese architecture, but they also didn't want slick contemporary buildings, which would be out of context in this capital city. They felt it should be a contemporary interpretation of classic Chinese architecture." In designing the project, in association with Wong Tung & Partners of Hong Kong, the Americans studied photos of an early generation of the market, razed in the 1940s, and elements of classic Chinese architecture, particularly proportions, fenestration, hierarchy, and façade treatments. Brotman says the project satisfies such unusual requirements as having an air raid shelter, a pathway through the center of the building strong enough to carry a fire truck, and a huge area to accommodate an electrical substation for the Wang Fu Jing District.

MODEL

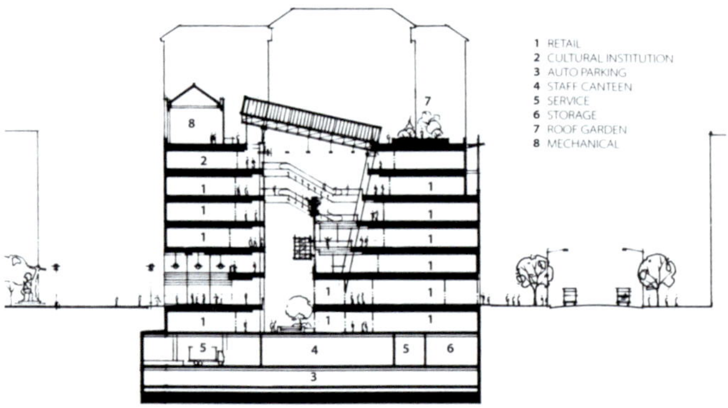

SECTION THROUGH CENTRAL ATRIUM

SECTION

RETAIL
OFFICE
RECREATION
PARKING
THEATER
MECHANICAL
FOOD COURT

100'/30m

MODEL OF TOWN

RENDERING OF ADMINISTRATIVE BUILDING (LEFT) AND OBSERVATION TOWER

A Chinese Town for Agricultural Technology

Some American firms are garnering large Asian master-planning jobs, one of the most striking of which is Kohn Pedersen Fox's design for Ceres, a new town south of Beijing, dedicated to agricultural research and technology. The irregular 519-acre site is tied together by a sweeping arc of a road, along which will be situated 24 factories and 18 research buildings. Other buildings, each of distinctive design, will sit in a patchwork of small fields; they will be assigned to exhibitors such as foreign agricultural companies, which can use their plots to demonstrate newly developed agricultural products or processes. The town's 8,000 inhabitants will live mainly in five-story apartment buildings arranged in U-shaped configurations, with generous light, air, and landscaping. What stands out most about the town, however, is the world's-fair-style architecture of its centerpiece buildings: a globe-shaped museum and four pyramidal structures containing administrative offices, a light-rail station, a greenhouse, and an observation tower. The town is envisioned as a kind of Chinese EPCOT where farmers, who account for well over half of China's population, will come to get an introduction to agricultural progress and a vision of what the developer, the Chinese company Sanju, intends as a representation of "a natural way of life in a new world." Money to build the town is now being raised.

Villas in a Historic Chinese City

Suzhou, a city 50 miles west of Shanghai, is renowned for the beauty of its gardens and canals, and for that reason development is treading more carefully there than in many other parts of China. In the Suzhou Garden Villas mixed-use development, Nelson K. Chen of Wong Chen Architects in Hong Kong designed 88 houses using the gray tile roofs, white walls, geometric openings, and other elements of traditional Suzhou houses. The houses, now under construction by a Hong Kong developer in a joint venture with the municipal government, contain 2,900 to 3,300 square feet and overlook a network of canals and gardens. Principal rooms face south, as Chinese tradition dictates.

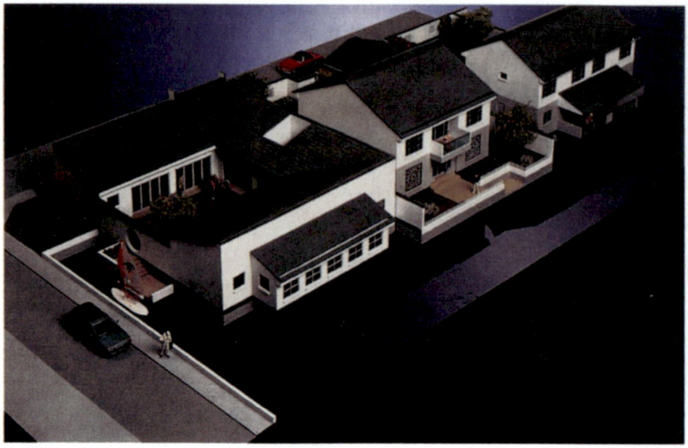

MODEL

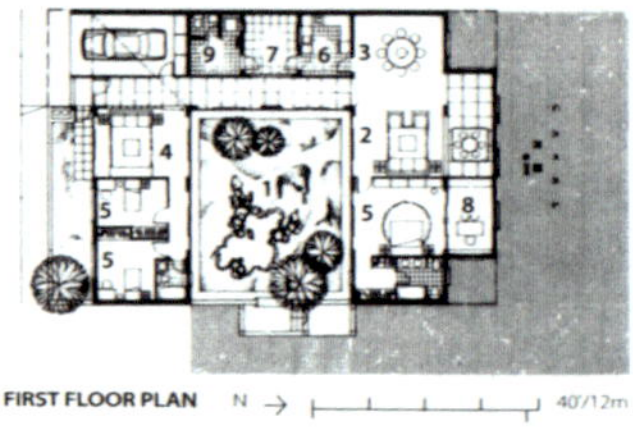

1 GARDEN
2 LIVING
3 DINING
4 FAMILY
5 BEDROOM
6 KITCHEN
7 SERVICE COURT
8 STUDY
9 UTILITY

FIRST FLOOR PLAN

An Ancient Form Adapted to Telecommunications

Late last year HLW of New York entered a competition to design the Asia Broadcast Center, a new satellite TV distribution facility in Kuala Lumpur, Malaysia. For its form, the designers, led by Christopher Choa, turned to the longhouse, which traditionally was used by Dayak tribes in East Malaysia to house entire villages. The abstracted longhouse they proposed has a curving steel truss-rib roof under which breezes can circulate. Air also passes beneath the building (where cars can park in the shade) and through other openings. There is a continuous sequence of open-air atriums, verandas, bridges, and stairs. Though HLW did not win the competition – in the end, the commission was awarded to a local entry – HLW demonstrated it was possible to fuse regional customs and Modern design.

1 VEHICULAR BRIDGE
2 VEHICULAR TERRACE
3 VEHICULAR DROP-OFF
4 ENTRANCE FOYER
5 VERANDA
6 VERTICAL CIRCULATION
7 STUDIO
8 APARTMENT
9 OFFICE

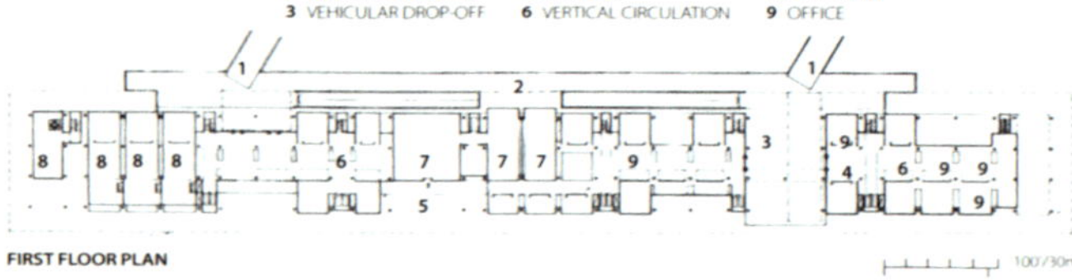

FIRST FLOOR PLAN

AERIAL PERSPECTIVE

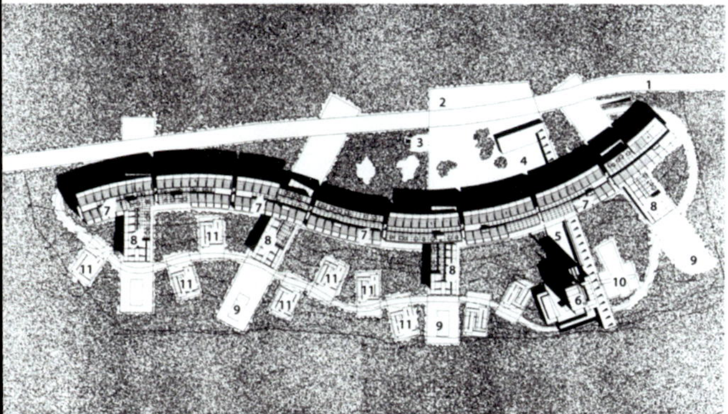

SITE PLAN

1 ACCESS ROAD
2 PUBLIC DROP-OFF AREA
3 PARKING ENTRY
4 ENTRY COURT
5 RETAIL ARCADE
6 HOTEL
7 DUPLEX CONDOMINIUMS
8 SINGLE-LEVEL CONDOMINIUMS
9 TENNIS/ATHLETIC COURTS
10 POOL
11 VILLAS

N 300'/100m

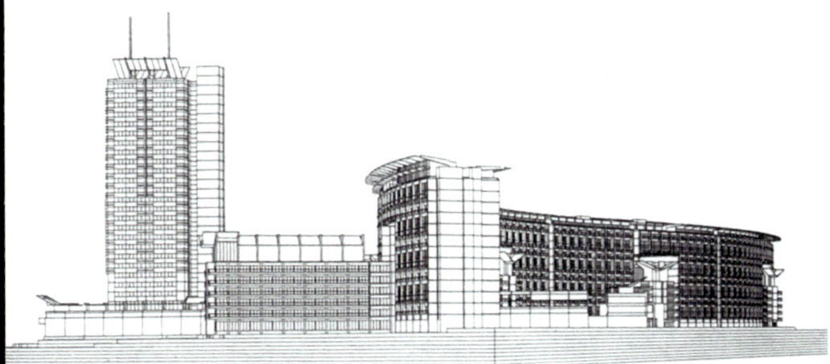

PARTIAL ELEVATION

Corbusian Resort on a Chinese Island

As China opens up to foreign investment, resort developments for the affluent are likely to proliferate. HLW of New York won a commission from the Asia Pacific Corporation of Hong Kong to design the Hainan Royal Garden Development, a 2-million-square-foot condominium and hotel complex on the southern island of Hainan. The condos are organized in a serpentine ten-story structure of concrete, each unit commanding a view of an adjoining golf course. Elevators stop at every third floor to serve an apartment layout based on Le Corbusier's Unité block section from the 1950s. All the apartments – simplexes, duplexes, and penthouses – extend clear though, giving them natural ventilation. At the southern bend of the complex, a monumental 79-foot-high gateway invites visitors to pass from the paved roads and walkway into the tranquil landscape on the golf course side. The complex is segmented into eight blocks for phased construction. HLW worked with Hsu & Partners of Taiwan and the Hainan branch of the Xan Xie Design Institute on the project, which calls for a high-rise hotel and an underground parking garage for 1,200 cars. HLW also designed three resort villas, called the Miami, the Dallas, and the Malibu, each of which would have an office suite including small conferencing facilities for business people. Prospects for building the villas are slim, but the first segment of condos is now under construction.

Asia Bound *(continued from page 46)*

disciplined approach, one that takes seriously the history, culture, or other defining characteristics of each locality. Pelli's work on Petronas Towers is an example of how an American architect can produce a building that responds to its setting. The sponsors of an international competition for the Kuala Lumpur City Centre invited entries from a small group of prominent architects around the world, emphasizing, Pelli says, that "they wanted a Malaysian building." Kuala Lumpur, a relatively young city, contains numerous flat-topped Modern office buildings of the sort that were built worldwide in the 1960s and 1970s, so it was not initially clear what a "Malaysian" building of the 1990s ought to be. Alison Horne and others in Pelli's New Haven office launched an extensive investigation into the history, design, and culture of Malaysia. That, along with many consultations with the clients, including the national petroleum company and high government officials, led to a design based on interlocking squares – an Islamic geometric motif meaningful to the Malays, who began converting to the Moslem faith around the 13th Century. "Geometric principles are more understood in Islamic countries than among us [Westerners]," Pelli notes. Pelli regards his design as the only competition entry that seriously strove for a Malaysian character. The towers taper in a fashion suggesting traditional Malay buildings, but they use modern materials (stainless steel on the exterior) and they refrain from copying the past. Because of this fusing of contemporary and traditional influences, it seems likely that Petronas Towers will feel Malaysian while accomplishing its other purpose: advertising the country's arrival as a modern industrial nation.

The Influence of *Feng Shui*

Many designers in Asia have responded to the local culture by applying *feng shui*, the Chinese art of placement, to the design and siting of buildings. *Feng shui* holds that some locations and shapes are auspicious while others are likely to bring misfortune. Buildings influenced by *feng shui* are usually laid out with their most important spaces facing south. Symmetry is considered desirable. Often buildings are constructed as pairs – not slipping past each other, like New York's World Trade Center towers, but closely aligned. Certain shapes, such as a fish profile, appear frequently. The five-story atrium of Kohn Pedersen Fox's big Nanjing Xi Lu mixed-use project on the main commercial street in Shanghai has a fish-shaped plan. Certain numbers, such as eight, are considered lucky; many Chinese highrises are articulated in eight-story increments.

Symbolism plays an important role. For instance, the Shekou Harbor Building near Shenzhen, designed by Chicago's Loebl Schlossman and Hackl, will display a sail-like shape across much of its 40-story curtain wall and will have a plan like that of a ship, to recall the countless junks that have sailed past its site in the Pearl River basin. Sometimes a gesture of this sort can be effective. Many attempts at symbolic expression, however, seem slick and superficial. If large numbers of oversize symbolic buildings join an all-out competition for conspicuousness, as is currently the trend, *(continued on page 88)*

Asia Bound *(continued from page 86)*

"Chinese junk" may take on a whole new meaning.

Asia has come to a crucial point. Its countries and its cities need to decide what path to follow, because the future character of these lands lies in the balance. American firms would do Asian cities a service if they questioned the obsession with towers and superblocks insensitive to human scale. A number of American designers have tried to do that. For instance, Fox & Fowle has worked to educate clients, design professionals, and planners in China about current thinking on urban design. Americans know from experience that urban environments are usually more comfortable when the buildings – whether tall or medium-height – rest on bases that have pedestrian-oriented enterprises along their perimeter. Choa says HLW typically submits varied schemes to a client but incorporates certain fundamental principles of urban design into all of them; whichever concept the client decides to pursue, it provides a decent relationship between the buildings, on the one hand, and the streets and the pedestrians, on the other.

Learning from the West's Experience

A final illustration of the difficulty of doing what, from an American perspective, seems the right thing is a competition held in 1993 for the Jin Mao tower in Shanghai. Chinese officials wanted a landmark building as the centerpiece of the Pudong New Area, so they conducted a competition that six firms from the U.S., Japan, China, and Hong Kong were invited to enter. SOM's Chicago office, under design partner Adrian Smith, submitted a design that suggested, in a gracefully abstracted way, a Chinese pagoda; it promised to be distinctively Chinese while avoiding clichés such as a pagoda roof on top of a skyscraper. Had the decision been left up solely to the Chinese, SOM's design would not have been chosen. It triumphed because of the support of non-Chinese on a jury most of whose members were American, Japanese, and English. This suggests that the modernizing nations need to ask Western architects for guidance on what kind of design and planning is appropriate. Westerners have traveled the road of modernization longer than anyone else in the world. They have learned, from harsh experience, where the dangers and the dead ends lurk. Countries in the early stages of modernization are naturally exhilarated by the prospect of obtaining the gloriously new. But as modernization proceeds, they will inevitably find that continuity matters, and that a city's distinctiveness is an important asset.

The fact that some clients and countries are indifferent to their own traditions right now does not excuse American architects from their responsibilities. Rather, it makes it all the more incumbent on Americans to fulfill their professional obligations to developing societies – to argue for what's right in the long run. Thomas V. Czarnowski of Fox & Fowle observes, "The reason they [Asians] went to the trouble of hiring Western architects is that they're open. They want to hear what you have to say." American architects will be letting down their clients, and themselves, if this flashpoint in Asia's history is treated as nothing more than business as usual. □

ARCHITECTURAL
RECORD
CURRENT ISSUE
DOES NOT CIRCULATE
CHINA Builds with
Superhuman Speed,
Reinventing Its Cities
from the Ground Up
MIT LIBRARIES
MAR 1 0 2004
ROTCH
ALSO Lighting and new
Architectural Technology Section

China

Moving heaven and earth, and doing it faster than you thought possible

By Clifford A. Pearson

Cars are replacing bicycles on major streets in Shanghai (above right), as skyscrapers rise all over town. The city, which has a population of about 20 million, now has more than 2,800 buildings taller than 18 stories and another 2,000 being planned.

In scale and pace, the building boom currently sweeping over China has no precedent in human history. From the Three Gorges Dam in Hubei Province (price tag: \$24.65 billion) to the 1,625-foot-tall World Financial Center under construction in Shanghai (price tag: \$825 million), the physical and financial dimensions of what's going up boggles the mind. China is spending about \$375 billion each year on construction, nearly 16 percent of its gross domestic product. In the process, it is using 54.7 percent of the world's production of concrete, 36.1 percent of the world's steel, and 30.4 percent of the world's coal. Funded by an ocean of foreign investments and encouraged by local and national governments intent on shaping a new future, building activity is racing forward. The spiky new skylines of Shanghai and Beijing signal a historic transformation affecting the country's social, political, cultural, and economic spheres. But buildings aren't the only things going skyward; in October 2003, China sent its first man into space. What had been a closed, mostly rural country with a malfunctioning, centrally controlled economy just 25 years ago has emerged as one of the world's fastest-growing, most dynamic nations.

With lofty ambitions come down-to-earth consequences. During the first two decades of the 21st century, 200 million people will migrate from rural China to its cities, states the *United Nations World Population Prospects* of 2002. This monumental shift in population will transform the nation's urban areas, burdening physical and social infrastructures but also fueling an array of building and economic opportunities. Finding jobs for all the rural workers moving to the cities, as well as the people being laid off as giant state-operated enterprises are privatized, will be one of the great tests of the Chinese experiment. While some economists say China cannot continue growing at its current pace (an 11 percent to 13 percent jump in GDP in the second half of last year), others warn that any slowdown would imperil the country's efforts to find jobs for the millions of people looking for work.

For architects, whether foreign or Chinese, most of the action is happening in the cities. As Beijing, Shanghai, Tianjin, Wuhan, Chongqing, Guangzhou, and Shenzhen balloon in size, architects and planners must balance a host of competing demands—for massive amounts of new buildings, modern infrastructure, improved environmental design, and historic preservation. Change one element and you affect all of the others. Build new highways and upgrade city roads, as has been done in

Note: The Chinese usually place a person's family name before the given name, but we have followed Western custom in this issue and put the family name at the end.

For additional coverage of architecture in China, go to **www.architecturalrecord.com**.

Shanghai, and you create the opportunity for municipal authorities to ban bicycles on major streets (as they did recently). Design a spectacular new high-rise and a finely knit neighborhood of old courtyard houses may be razed (as is happening in Beijing at an alarming rate).

During the past few years, a chorus of observers has predicted dire consequences from China's remarkably rapid changes. The economic bubble will soon burst. Construction will bring environmental degradation. Rapid development imperils the rich social and historic fabric of city neighborhoods. The drive to make a quick profit allows little room for architectural quality. Certainly, all of these dangers are real. But recently, some of the experts who might be expected to sound the alarms are expressing a new sense of optimism.

William McDonough, FAIA, who has made green design an essential element in all of his work, speaks excitedly about China. In 1999, he helped establish the China-U.S. Center for Sustainable Development, whose cochair is Deng Nan, China's vice minister of science and technology and the daughter of Deng Xiaoping, the country's paramount leader from 1978 until his death in 1997. "The Chinese are practical people and they understand that sustainable development is the way to grow," says McDonough. He and his Chinese organization are currently working on four urban design projects, including a sustainable village in Liaoning Province northwest of North Korea, a pedestrian- and transit-oriented new town near Wenling south of Shanghai, and a mixed-use, high-density district in the northeast part of Beijing. McDonough also sees China as an essential element in developing economical solar-energy cells for the entire world. "China is the world's lowest-cost producer," says McDonough, "so once you get the Chinese working on solar cells, you can make solar energy cheaper than coal."

Anyone who has visited China recently after being away for even just a few years notices the large pieces of urban fabric unraveling in major cities. Anthony M. Tung, an architect and former member of New York City's Landmarks Preservation Commission, investigated the situation in Beijing while working on his book *Preserving the World's Great Cities* (Clarkson Potter, 2001). When the Communists took power in China in 1949, imperial Beijing—whose plan dates back thousands of years and most of whose extant buildings and fortified city walls survived from the 16th century—remained largely intact. During the following three decades, however, Soviet-educated planners tore down almost all of the city's imposing walls, moats, and entry portals, while building highways and erecting factories in residential areas.

Today, many of the factories remain in operation, spewing pollution and contributing to acid rain that is eroding the magnificent stone carvings of the Forbidden City. But the Beijing authorities gave Soviet planning strategies the boot and adopted laws in the early 1980s that established 187 developmental control zones around important historic monuments. In theory, these designations limit the height and scale of new developments so they do not impinge on the character of historic landmarks. In practice, enforcement of these control zones has been lax.

While alarmed by the pace of change in Beijing, Tung believes that the regulatory system needed to protect the city's historic fabric is in place. The most important landmarks, such as the Forbidden City and the Temple of Heaven—which account for about 10 percent of imperial Beijing—have long been protected. "If development in the control zones were properly limited, the city could protect another 20 percent" of historic Beijing, explains Tung. When asked what are the chances of that happening, Tung expresses cautious optimism. Because the Communist government owns most of the city's land, it can control development in a way that is impossible in most other countries. Foreign pressure, especially when linked to the 2008 Olympics, can push the Chinese to enforce the developmental control-zone regulations, he says.

Other strategies to relieve developmental pressures in historic Beijing have been proposed by people involved with the Harvard Design School's Project on the City, the studio taught by Rem Koolhaas and others. After examining hypergrowth in the Pearl River Delta (Hong Kong-Shenzhen-Guangzhou) in the book *Great Leap Forward* (Taschen, 2001), the studio turned its attention to Beijing this past fall. Participants in the studio recommended "land-banking" certain districts, which would restrict development for a designated period, giving residents and planners a key resource in short supply: time to carefully consider what gets built, says Jeffrey Inaba, a principal of AMO who also teaches at Harvard and SCI-Arc. The studio also developed a scheme to build a "massive green belt" outside of Beijing, which would be a megastructure incorporating stacked highways and green, mixed-use buildings.

Although the quality of buildings going up can still be very low, Benjamin Wood, AIA, a partner of Wood + Zapata, says the Chinese have made huge progress since he started working in China in 1998. "In the past, even when Norman Foster did a building, it would look cheap because they used local products," says Wood. "But now Pilkington has a factory in China and you can get top-quality curtain wall and glass." He also marvels at the rapidly improving skills of Chinese architects. "Some of the younger architects worked for world-class architects abroad. Now they've set up their own firms back home and they're starting to do great architecture." Behind all the changes, Wood sees a remarkable, driving force. "They're creating a modern Chinese culture and they're doing it in real time." Westerners accustomed to incremental change need to switch gears to understand what's happening in China. Blink for a moment and you're liable to miss something important. ■

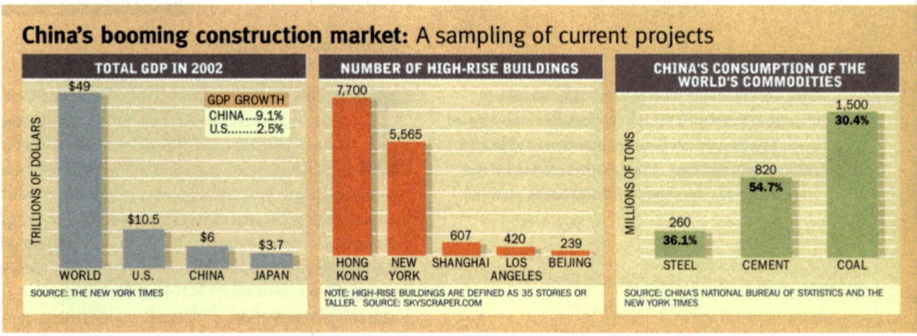

China's booming construction market: A sampling of current projects

The Pearl of the Orient tower (opposite, top) has become a symbol of the hypergrowth in Shanghai's Pudong district. All over the country, building cranes and giant billboards announce further massive change (opposite, bottom left and right).

BEIJING
TIANJIN
XI'AN
NANJING
CHENGDU
SHANGHAI
CHONGQING
KUNMING
NANNING
GUANGZHOU
HONG KONG

Projects Taking Shape in China

1. Project: *Beijing Books Building*
Location: *Beijing*
Architect: *Rem Koolhaas, Office of Metropolitan Architecture (OMA)*
Program: *The $77 million project will be a phased redevelopment and enlargement of an existing bookstore in Beijing. The new building will be composed predominantly of reinforced concrete with a deep, glazed "bookshelf" facade. The store will also serve as a business center for publishing, film, television, Internet, and cultural exchange.*
Schedule: *Construction will begin near the end of 2004 and progress for 24 to 30 months.*

2. Project: *ZhongGuanCun West Office Complex*
Location: *Beijing*
Architect: *Kohn Pedersen Fox Asssociates with China Architecture Design and Research Institute (CADRI).*
Program: *A 1-million-square-foot office complex that will include a 500-foot-tall office tower, an office podium, and an exhibition bridge structure. A series of curved planes and volumes are clad with glass and metal and are designed to unfold like the petals of a plant or the feathers of a bird. An important element of the Beijing Science and Technology Park.*
Schedule: *Project completion date December 2004.*

1

2

More firms are entering the Chinese market each day. Their many designs will further transform the landscape of a country already changing beyond recognition. Below is a list of just a few of the projects being designed by foreign practices in China, often collaborating with local Chinese design institutes. The roster features some of the most prominent architects in the world.

Many designs will make you dizzy with their sheer size, in a land where bigger seems to be better. Others will amaze with their originality. Encouraged by their clients to express the notion of progress, many foreign firms are using China as a testing ground for new ideas in technology, engineering, and design.

"In the United States, we are quite constrained in what we can do," says Steve Weindel, a principal at Gensler. "In China, people are a lot more tolerant and expectant of innovative design and architecture that has an impact on its surroundings and its environment."

Some of the designs may never be built. This occurs regularly in a country where so much is happening so quickly. But those that do will likely take form quickly, with construction progressing under the hands of massive crews working at all hours of the day.

Like it or not, a new China is rising very fast. *Sam Lubell*

3

4

5

ZAHA HADID ARCHITECTS (5)

3. Project: *Nanjing Jinling Hotel Phase II*
Location: *Nanjing*
Architect: *Skidmore, Owings & Merrill (San Francisco)*
Program: *1,050 feet tall, the building is sited in the heart of Nanjing's commercial center. The building's skin forms a rigid, diagonal grid that functions like a twisting tube. The project will feature offices, apartments, and a luxury hotel.*
Schedule: *Construction set to begin in 2005, with completion in 2008.*

4. Project: *Looped Hybrid Housing*
Location: *Beijing*
Architect: *Steven Holl Architects*
Program: *Mixed-use building complex with more than 700 apartments sited adjacent to the old city wall of Beijing. Composed mainly of towers linked by a ring of cafés and services and meant to be a "city within a city." The 1.7-million-square-foot project will be able to support more than 2,500 occupants.*
Schedule: *Construction begins October 2004 and ends in 2006.*

5. Project: *Guangzhou Opera House*
Location: *Guangzhou*
Architect: *Zaha Hadid Architects*
Program: *A fluid, rigorously contoured design will provide open river access and create a new "dialogue" with the town. Standing at the foot of a major boulevard, the opera house is meant to furnish a focal point for civic and cultural buildings in the city.*
Schedule: *Not determined yet.*

6. Project: *Boan Residential Development*
Location: *Shenzhen*
Architect: *T.R. Hamzah & Yeang Architects*
Program: *2.1-million-square-foot complex will include residential, retail, sports center, schools, plazas, an ecopark, and a central park. Apartment towers are located along the periphery, overlooking vehicle-free landscaping.*
Schedule: *Construction began January 2003.*

6

7. Project: *Suzhou Museum*
Location: *Suzhou*
Architect: *Pei Partnership with Suzhou Institute of Architectural Design*
Program: *A 1.6-million-square-foot museum of history. Located in the city's historic quarter, the concrete and glass-and-steel building is organized around a series of gardens and courts that mediate between the building and its surroundings.*
Schedule: *Construction set to begin summer 2004 and to finish in 2006.*

7

8. Project: *Hangzhou Lakeshore Redevelopment*
Location: *Hangzhou*
Architect: *Jerde Partnership with Zhejiang Building Design Research Institute*
Program: *A mixed-use district combining urban and natural components. One block is designed around a central canal that extends west into the city. The landscaped side of the canal contains a mixture of restaurants and cafés. The urban side, a three-block pedestrian street, contains retail, restaurants, and a cinema. The two sides are connected by a series of multilevel bridges.*
Schedule: *Projected opening is set for 2006.*

8

9

10

11

9. Project: *Anting, New Town Residential Towers*
Location: *Anting*
Architect: *Behnisch, Behnisch & Partner*
Program: *Six floors of apartment units with an attic community room and terrace. An alternative to conventional mid-rise housing, the design has the look of full units stacked above each other in an uneven fashion.*
Schedule: *No timeline set.*

10. Project: *Shanghai-Pudong Museum (Archives and Exhibition Hall)*
Location: *Shanghai*
Architect: *von Gerkan, Marg and Partner Architects with Shanghai Institute of Architectural Design & Research (SIADR)*
Program: *The building will contain historic archives and document Pudong's history with ongoing exhibitions. The 441,000-square-foot space is lifted above the street on a "pedestal," stressing its importance. The clear cube has a semitransparent glass exterior on which movies and text will be projected via projectors mounted in wall recesses.*
Schedule: *Construction period set for 2003 through 2004.*

11. Project: *Lujiazui Financial Center*
Location: *Shanghai*
Architect: *Gensler*
Program: *An 800,000-square-foot, 246-foot-high office building with a transparent, double-skin exterior. The office space is organized in two wings around a central atrium. Transparent "wrapper" creates a clear cube that will be a distinct landmark along the city's river.*
Schedule: *Not determined yet.*

Shanghai World Financial Center RISES AGAIN

COLIN GALLOWAY

Shanghai's tallest building will open its doors next year, more than ten years after breaking ground. But the path to the top has been fraught with challenges.

IT IS NOT OFTEN THAT office buildings take more than ten years to put up, even very tall ones in all-action locations like Shanghai, where local land policy requires developers to "use it or lose it," and where a round-the-clock work ethic has seen forests of new towers sprout like mushrooms in the morning rain. But by the time the Shanghai World Financial Center (WFC) in Shanghai's Pudong district is finally completed—sometime around the beginning of 2008—more than ten years will have passed since workers first broke ground on the project back in 1997. The 1,614-foot (492-m) tower, which comprises some 2.4 million square feet (227,000 sq m) of office space and a 180-room Hyatt hotel, is being developed by Mori Building Corporation of Japan, designed by Bill Pedersen of New York–based Kohn Pedersen Fox Architects (KPF).

Some might say that the long delay to completion of a building once set to be easily the tallest on the planet has allowed others to steal its thunder. Taiwan's Taipei 101, a 1,669-foot (509-m) office block completed in 2004 that is currently the world's tallest, will retain its mantle according to the most commonly

©COLIN GALLOWAY

The Shanghai World Financial Center (WFC), in Shanghai's Pudong district, is rising at the rate of one floor every four days and will be completed sometime around the beginning of 2008.

ccepted measure (i.e., highest architectural op). The WFC's flat-top design may give it omething of a moral victory over its spire-nhanced rival, allowing Mori at least to claim ne title for the world's highest roof. In the neantime, though, another super-tall build-ng, known as the Burj Dubai, is currently nder construction in the Middle East. lthough Mori's 101-floor tower is barreling pward at the rate of one floor every four ays, the completion of the Burj, which ulti-nately will top out at a dizzying 2,624 feet 800 m) or possibly more, will ensure that the Mori project's reign in the record books re-nains short lived.

For many, however, the matter of honors or the world's tallest building is perhaps sec-ndary to the fact that, for several years after Mori halted work in the wake of the Asian nancial crisis in 1997, many doubted that the uilding, with its award-winning design of weeping curves, would be finished at all. The conomics of constructing one of the most xpensive office towers ever built—it was lated originally to come in at some $850 mil-on—were precarious even in the best of mes. But with demand for office space in hanghai's notoriously volatile property sector ncertain and developers around the region oing belly up, the project remained on life upport until the local market picked up again ix years after construction started. During the nterim, the hopes of the building taking hape languished in the shape of a large hole n the ground.

But while its start may have been inaus-icious, the elegance of the WFC's abstract, nderstated design, standing in stark contrast o its often flamboyant local counterparts, uickly became apparent once the structure egan rising from that hole. The disparity was o coincidence. According to Gene Kohn, hairman of KPF, "From the start, we felt that building that was elegant, quiet, powerful—omething that was really one great statement hat rose bottom to top—would be the most ppropriate." Describing the concept as a ombination of function, efficiency, and esign aesthetic, Kohn compares it to an air-lane, where sleek beauty is a byproduct of erodynamics.

In this case, the building's tapered, contin-ously changing shape that rises to a chiseled top is functional in various ways. First, says Kohn, it is adapted for different types of users who may want offices of varying dimensions. In addition, the design works well for the Hyatt hotel set to open on the highest floors because "if you build a hotel straight up, the same size as the office part, it becomes very inefficient at the top."

Another aspect of functional design is the by-now iconic hole set into the building's crest. On the one hand, the hole plays an aesthetic role. Reflecting a balance of yin and yang, earth and sky, it also serves to differentiate the tower from some of the more outlandish pyramids, spires, and pylons that make up the Shanghai skyline. At the same time, though, it plays a crucial part in the building's design, helping to relieve wind pressures that increase dramatically as the structure rises, with two-thirds of the wind forces acting on the highest one-third of the building. While countering wind is always the main design issue of a super-tall building—the WFC is designed to withstand a 200-year wind—it is especially important in Shanghai, which is subject to typhoons sweeping in from the Pacific Ocean at least every few years.

While punching a hole in the top has reduced the design costs of incorporating other wind-shedding properties into the structure, the building's very sleekness has created problems of its own. According to Paul Katz, KPF principal in charge of Asia, "On a tall building, you don't want to be too aerodynamic because that could increase the negative load. And curved structures are very hard to predict—they could actually become like aircraft wings." As that would not be a good thing, notches were carved into the tower's corners, creating turbulence that acts to decelerate winds on the facing side.

KOHN PEDERSEN FOX ASSOCIATES

Not only will it be the tallest structure in Shanghai when completed, and one of the tallest buildings in the world, the elegance of the WFC's abstract, understated design will stand in stark contrast to its often flamboyant local counterparts.

Planning for wind may have been KPF's most important design issue, but it was by no means the only one. In fact, building tall in Shanghai presents architects with a laundry list of challenges. Unlike New York, where builders find rock within a few feet of the surface, Shanghai sits in a river delta on top of almost 1,000 feet (305 m) of silt and mud. Reaching bedrock is impossible, so engineers had to construct an elaborate and expensive system of friction piles stretching 230 to 262 feet (70 to 80 m) underground. The fact that silt is relatively unstable in the event of an earthquake presents other design challenges, and the design must also deal with the possibility of a waterlogged subsurface. As Kohn says, "You have the problem of the building overturning because of water pushing it out, you have wind, you have earthquakes. This is the toughest place to put a tall building."

Working with Chinese officials, meanwhile, creates problems of another kind—in particular, bureaucracy. To a certain extent, dealing with red tape is simply an on-the-ground reality in the mainland, but in this case it is also a function of the fact that the property sector historically has been dominated by small fly-by-night operators with ready access to deals when government land was offered for sale. That has begun to change in recent years, but the result, says Katz, is that while other markets with cultures of good construction are almost self-regulating, "In China, it is all about regulations and approvals, because otherwise people will build anything." That makes life hard for those involved in long, complex projects, because inevitable changes, big or small, involve long—and therefore costly—approval processes.

One such change that was forced on Mori, though it occurred while the project was still in hibernation, was the need to introduce new safety features in the wake of the destruction of New York City's World Trade Center on 9/11. The extent of these changes was minimized by the fact that China's earthquake code (which mandates, for example, steel refuge floors every 12 stories) already required a far higher degree of redundancy compared with standards in force in the United States. This meant that many features not commonly incorporated in American buildings before 2001 already operated to shield the building's core, where three of its four stairways are located, and to protect against progressive collapse. Still, another $200 million was spent on a redesign to further strengthen the structure and improve safety, allowing the building's expected 20,000 inhabitants to exit within a maximum of 90 minutes, according to Takayuki Kubo, a Mori architect.

Political problems also have plagued the project, a result of China's often fractious political relationship with Japan. In particular, the tower's trademark hole in its peak, originally intended as a 150-foot (45.7-m) circle that would mirror the Chinese cosmological representation of the sky, bore an uncomfortable—for the Chinese—resemblance to the rising sun emblazoned on the Japanese flag. After several years of sometimes hysterical debate, the hole eventually was also redesigned, emerging in a new plan as a trapezoidal square. "I like it," says Katz. More recently, when Mori decided to change the name of the project, ostensibly because another planned building bore a confusingly similar name, to "Shanghai Hills" (an echo of Mori's landmark development in Japan known as Roppongi Hills), the local government nixed the plan, claiming it had not been consulted on the change. Shanghai Hills, which

An Accessible Top

©COLIN GALLOWAY

In contrast to many tall buildings around the world where access to the top floors is denied, the builders of the World Financial Center were eager to create a space that would be publicly accessible. As a result, at least eight of the highest floors will be generally accessible, including facilities ranging from a hotel lobby to shops and restaurants and an exhibition space able to display large exhibits such as cars, which will be hauled up the building by placing them upright in specially strengthened cargo lifts. In addition, an observation deck cut across the top of the trapezoidal opening on the 100th floor will be the world's highest, at some 1,548 feet (472 m).

Kohn Pedersen Fox Architects' original plan had also called for a Ferris wheel to be incorporated into the hole at the summit. However, the scheme was complicated by the move away from a circular opening and shelved altogether as a result of objections from the city fire authority. Concerns centered on how fast the cars could be evacuated. "It's not that they didn't take it seriously," says Katz, "it's just that nobody felt qualified to approve it."

The 79th through 93rd floors will feature a 180-room hotel, variously described as a five- or six-star facility, to be managed by the Park Hyatt brand.

Building elevators include 16 "super double-deckers" supplied by Otis and 42 built by ThyssenKrupp, four of which will also be double-deckers that have been touted by the company as the fastest such machines in the world, capable of speeds of 33 feet (10 m) per second.

Tuned-mass dampers (basically large metal pendulums that can absorb sway created by high winds) will serve to offset the impact of high winds, swaying independently so that the building does not experience excessive acceleration. These are especially important given that hotel guests will be residing at the top.—C.G.

not descriptive of Shanghai's pancake-flat environment, has therefore been demoted to an "unofficial" title.

While the WFC's agonizingly slow gestation over a span of almost 15 years must have seemed like torture for many of those involved since the project's inception, it has also offered some instructive lessons. One of these has been the astonishingly fast pace of change in the Chinese construction and construction materials industry. When design work commenced back in 1994, the standard of construction in China lagged far behind that in Japan and the West, and all important materials were imported.

Since then, says Katz, "China has made massive strides in quality of construction and in the sourcing of materials," with most products now manufactured locally and generally to a high standard. Not only has that improved the quality and lowered the cost of construction in China, but it has also had repercussions on property development worldwide. In particular, the huge amount of construction going on in Asia generally, and China in particular, has meant that many building products, finishes, and materials are now being exported back to the United States and Europe. "A lot of people in the U.S. and Europe don't realize this," says Katz, "but I think that looking forward, one of the lessons of the whole process of the last 15 years in Asia is that more and more buildings in the West are looking more and more like the buildings you see here. There's a convergence of standards, a convergence of materials, and a convergence of product."

©COLIN GALLOWAY

A worker welds a girder on the 77th floor of the WFC. The Jin Mao tower, currently China's tallest building and the world's fifth highest, rises in the background.

©COLIN GALLOWAY

Building tall in Shanghai is particularly challenging because the city sits in a river delta on top of almost 1,000 feet (305 m) of silt and mud, making it impossible to reach bedrock. Engineers had to construct an elaborate and expensive system of friction piles stretching 230 to 262 feet (70 to 80 m) underground.

Not only that, but the fact that China has been able to offer so much work to the West's tall-building architects and engineers has effectively saved the practice from becoming something of a dying art. According to Kohn, "For us as a firm, all through the 1990s there were no tall buildings built in the States or in Europe. It was due to the economy; there just wasn't the demand for the space. Even after 9/11 there were not a lot of new buildings built until just about now." It was only because KPF and other big firms were able to keep groups of architects working on challenging projects in Asia that they could continue to experiment and develop new ideas. "We would never have had a chance to do this building in the States—it just wouldn't have happened," adds Kohn. "If we hadn't been out here, the tradition in the U.S. would have been lost." UL

COLIN GALLOWAY is a Hong Kong–based freelance journalist who writes frequently on Asian topics for *Urban Land*.

2002–

Studio Shanghai

Headquarters
Shanghai, China

Founding Partner
Benjamin T. Wood

2002

Studio Shanghai

2002–

Utile

Headquarters
Boston, MA

Founding Partner
Timothy Love

Current Partners
Michael LeBlanc, Matthew Littell,
Mimi Love, Timothy Love

2002

Utile

M●S

2003–

MOS Architects

Headquarters
New Heaven, CT (2005-2011);
New York, NY (2011-present)

Founding Partners
Michael Meredith, Hilary Sample

2003

MOS Architects

Wodiczko + Bonder

Headquarters
Boston, MA

Founding Partners
Julian Bonder, Krzysztof Wodiczko

Wodiczko + Bonder

Diagonal Mar Entertainment and Retail Center
2001

Architect
Robert A.M. Stern Architects

Location
Barcelona, Spain

Client
Hines

Torre Almirante
2001

Architect
Robert A.M. Stern Architects

Location
Rio de Janeiro, Brazil

Client
Hines

Indian School Of Business Academic Center
2001

Architect
John Portman and Associates

Location
Hyderabad, India

Client
Indian School of Business

Mangrove West Coast
2001–2005

Architect
Arquitectonica

Location
Shenzhen, China

Client
Shenzhen Sinolink Enterprises Co. Lit.

Highlight Munich Business Towers
2001–2005

Architect
JAHN

Location
Munich, Germany

Client
Bürozentrum Parkstadt München-Schwabing

Langham Place
2001–2005

Architect
Jerde Partnership

Location
Hong Kong, China

Architect of Record
Wong & Quyang (HK) Ltd, Architects & Engineers

Client
Great Eagle Holdings LTD

Chinese Museum of Film
2001–2005

Architect
RTKL

Location
Beijing, China

Client
China Film Museum Committee

The Wohl Centre
2001–2005

Architect
Studio Daniel Libeskind

Location
Ramat-Gan, Israel

Client
Bar-Ilan University Maurice Wohl Foundation

Emirates Palace
2001–2005

Architect
Wimberly Allison Tong & Goo

Location
Abu Dhabi, United Arab Emirates

Client
Government of Abu Dhabi, Kempinski Hotels S.A.

Kanyon
2001–2006

Architect
Jerde Partnership

Location
Istanbul, Turkey

Client
Eczacibasi, Is Real Estate and Investment

Torre Espacio
2001–2008

Architect
Pei Cobb Freed & Partners

Location
Madrid, Spain

Client
Torre Espacio, Castellana S.A., Grupo Villar Mir

US Embassy
2001–2008

Architect
Skidmore, Owings & Merrill

Location
Beijing, China

Client
US Department of State, Bureau of Overseas Buildings Operations

Westside Shopping and Leisure Centre
2001–2008

Architect
Studio Daniel Libeskind

Location
Bern, Switzerland

Client
Neue Brünnen AG, Migros Aare

Acropolis Museum
2001–2009

Architect
Bernard Tschumi Architects

Location
Athens, Greece

Associated Architect
Michael Photliadis

Client
Organization for the Construction of the New Acropolis Museum (OANMA)

China World Trade Center
2001–2010

Architect
Skidmore, Owings & Merrill

Location
Beijing, China

Client
China World Trade Center Co. Ltd., Shangri-La Hotels & Resorts

Asia Society Hong Kong Center
2001–2012

Architect
Tod Williams Billie Tsien Architects

Location
Hong Kong, China

Local Architect
AGC Design Ltd. Hong Kong, Associated Architects Ltd.

Client
Asia Society Hong Kong

American University of Beirut Master Plan
2002

Architect
Machado and Silvetti Associates

Location
Beirut, Lebanon

Client
American University of Beirut

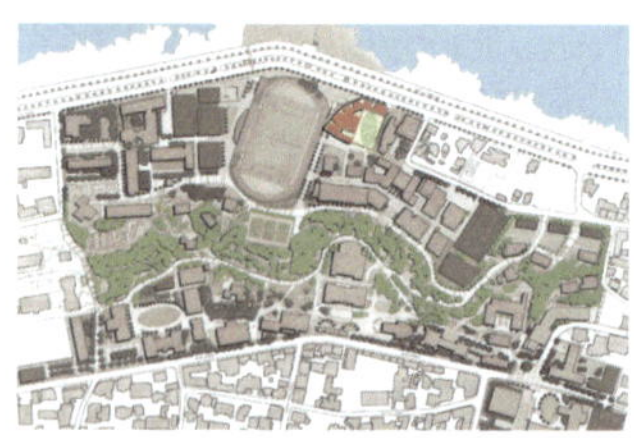

Telenor Headquarters
2002

Architect
NBBJ

Location
Oslo, Norway

Client
Telenor Group

Apple Store Ginza
2002–2003

Architect
Bohlin Cywinski Jackson

Location
Tokyo, Japan

Client
Apple, Inc.

Bohlin Cywinski Jackson
Architecture Planning Interior Design

Dalki Theme Park
2002–2004

Architect
Slade Architecture

Location
Gyeonggido, South Korea

Client
Hokyun Chun

Associated Architects
Mass Studies, Ga.A Architects

SLADE ARCHITECTURE

Edificio Portico
2002–2005

Architect
Skidmore, Owings & Merrill

Location
Madrid, Spain

Client
Hines Europe

SOM

US Embassy
2002–2005

Architect
Sorg Architects

Location
Kabul, Afghanistan

Client
US Department of State, Bureau of Overseas Building Operations

SORG ARCHITECTS

Knowledge and Innovation Community
2002–2006

Architect
Skidmore, Owings & Merrill

Location
Shanghai, China

Client
Shui On Property Development Co., Ltd.

SOM

The Gate Building
2002–2006

Architect
Gensler

Location
United Arab Emirates, Dubai

Client
Dubai International Financial Centre

Gensler

US Embassy
2002–2006

Architect
Integrus

Location
Conakry, Guinea

Client
US Department of State, Bureau of Overseas Building Operations

Madrid Public Housing
2002–2006

Architect
Morphosis Architects

Location
Madrid, Spain

Associate Architect
B+DU Estudio

Client
Empresa Municipal De La Viviende-City of Madrid

US Embassy
2002–2006

Architect
Sorg Architects

Location
Bridgetown, Barbados

Client
US Department of State, Bureau of Overseas Building Operations

Beijing Yintai Centre
2002–2007

Architect
John Portman and Associates

Location
Beijing, China

Client
Hyatt International, China Yin Tai Holdings, Merrill Lynch

Poly Corporate Headquarters
2002–2007

Architect
Skidmore, Owings & Merrill

Location
Beijing, China

Client
Beijing New Poly Plaza Real Estate Company, China Poly Group Corporation

Normandy American Cemetery New Visitor Center
2002–2007

Architect
SmithGroupJJR

Location
Colleville-sur-Mer, France

Client
American Battle Monuments Commission

Royal Ontario Museum
2002–2007

Architect
Studio Daniel Libeskind

Location
Toronto, Canada

Client
Royal Ontario Museum

Beijing Olympics Master Plan
2002–2008

Architect
Sasaki Associates

Location
Beijing, China

Client
Beijing Municipal Planning Commission

Yamano Gakuen Complex
2002–2009

Architect
Hodgetts + Fung

Location
Tokyo, Japan

Client
Michael Yamano, Yamano Gakuen Beauty School

Kipco Tower
2002–2011

Architect
Kohn Pedersen Fox Associates

Location
Kuwait City, Kuwait

Client
The United Real Estate Co.

Universidade Agostinho Neto
2002–2011

Architect
Perkins + Will

Location
Luanda, Angola

Client
Universidade Agostinho Neto

Biomuseo
2002–2014

Architect
Gehry Partners

Location
Panama City, Panama

Executive Architect
Ensitu, S. A.

Zaitunay Bay
2002–2014

Architect
Steven Holl Architects, L.E.FT

Location
Beirut, Lebanon

Associate Architect
Nabil Gholam Architecture

Client
Solidere

University of Balamand Female Residence Hall, Library Learning Center, School of Engineering and Master Plan
2002–2016

Architect
Sasaki Associates

Location
El Khoura, Lebanon

Client
University of Balamand

International School
2003

Architect
Studio Hillier

Location
Chennai, India

Mur Island
2003

Architect
Acconci Studio

Location
Graz, Austria

Client
Graz 2003 Kulturhaupstadt
Europasa Organisations GbmH

Tongxian Gatehouse
2003

Architect
Office dA

Location
Tongxian, China

Client
Tongxian Artist Community

Hotel Puerta America
2003–2005

Architect
Gluckman Mayner Architects

Location
Madrid, Spain

Client
Group Urvasco S.A.

Josai School of Management
2003–2006

studioSUMO

Architect
studio SUMO

Location
Sakado, Japan

Client
Josai University

Shanghai Traditional Chinese Medical University Shuguang Hospital Replacement
2003–2006

SMITHGROUPJJR

Architect
SmithGroupJJR

Location
Shanghai, China

Local Architect
CNA Group

Client
Shanghai Traditional Chinese Medical University

Valeo Security Systems
2003–2006

Davis Brody Bond

Architect
Davis Brody Bond Architects & Planners

Location
Sao Paulo, Brazil

Client
Valeo

Limoges Concert Hall
2003–2007

BERNARD TSCHUMI ARCHITECTS
NEW YORK I PARIS

Architect
Bernard Tschumi Architects

Location
Limoges, France

Local Architect
Atelier 4

Client
Communauté d'Agglomération Limoges Métropole

Shenzhen Meteorological Tower
2003–2007

AECOM

Architect
AECOM

Location
Shenzhen, China

Client
Meteorological Bureau of Shenzhen Municipality

American University of Beirut Suliman S. Olayan School of Business
2003–2009

Machado and Silvetti Associates

Architect
Machado and Silvetti Associates

Location
Beirut, Lebanon

Local Architect
Builders Design Consultants

Client
American University of Beirut

Beirut Exhibition Centre
2003–2009

Architect
L.E.FT

Location
Beirut, Lebanon

Client
Solidere

L.E.FT ARCHITECTS

Linked Hybrid
2003–2009

Architect
Steven Holl Architects

Location
Beijing, China

Associate Architect
Beijing Capital Engineering Architecture Design Co. Ltd

Client
Modern Green Development Co., Ltd. Beijing

STEVEN HOLL ARCHITECTS

Burj Khalifa
2003–2010

Architect
Skidmore, Owings & Merrill

Location
Dubai, United Arab Emirates

Client
EMAAR Properties

SOM

Louwman Museum
2003–2010

Architect
Michael Graves and Associates

Location
The Hague, Netherlands

Client
Louwman Group; HET National Automobile Museum

MICHAEL GRAVES & ASSOCIATES
MICHAEL GRAVES DESIGN GROUP

Memorial to the Abolition of Slavery
2003–2011

Architect
Wodiczko + Bonder

Location
Nantes, France

Local Architects
Maitre D'Oeuvre, Arcadis,Agence, Roulieau

Tel Aviv Museum
2003–2011

Architect
Preston Scott Cohen

Location
Tel Aviv, Israel

Client
Tel Aviv Museum of Art

Alésia Museum and Archaeological Park
2003–2012

BERNARD TSCHUMI ARCHITECTS
NEW YORK I PARIS

Architect
Bernard Tschumi Architects

Location
Alésia, France

Client
Bourgogne Region, France

Nanjing Sifang Art Museum
2003–2013

STEVEN HOLL ARCHITECTS

Architect
Steven Holl Architects, Architectural Design Institute, Nanjing University

Location
Nanjing, China

Client
Nanjing Foshou Lake Architecture and Art Developments Ltd

Canadian Museum for Human Rights
2003–2014

ANTOINE PREDOCK ARCHITECT PC

Architect
Antoine Predock Architect PC

Location
Winnipeg, Canada

Client
Canadian Museum for Human Rights

London 2012 Olympic Legacy Communities Scheme
2003–

AECOM

Architect
AECOM

Location
London, United Kingdom

Client
London Development Agency

Loreto Bay Resort Village
2003–

DPZ
DUANY PLATER-ZYBERK & COMPANY
ARCHITECTS AND TOWN PLANNERS

Architect
Duany Plater-Zyberk & Company

Location
Loreto, Mexico

Client
David Butterfield, FONATUR

Balloon Landing Park
2004

HSS

Architect
Hashim Sarkis Studios

Location
Beirut, Lebanon

Client
Round Concepts, Etc

Architectural Playgrounds: Emerging Practices, Global Platforms

A confluence of financial crises in the West, developing economies abroad, and networked technologies have enabled smaller, boutique architecture practices to compete for the first time with large firms in the roster of US architects working internationally. The post-bubble US economy after 2008 left a generation of young architects with newly-opened offices suddenly adrift. Having already had the opportunity to build before the crash, many of these firms were not content to pursue "paper" practices, as previous generations had in responding to the recessions of the 1970s and 1990s, taking the downturn as a challenge to create their own opportunities.[1] Many of these small offices became developers for their own projects, while others turned to design-build installations and interiors for clients on tight budgets. Such non-traditional opportunities were often found abroad as easily as at home. Since 2008 these commissions have significantly included hospitals, educational facilities, and other social services for NGOs and governmental institutions in Botswana, Kenya, Rwanda, Senegal, and other African countries, often built through new models of non-profit architectural practice such as those of MASS Design Group and ATOPIA.

Prior to the crash, a very different platform for small architecture firms abroad was provided by high-profile, developer-sponsored architectural showcases for international architects. The economic conditions which enabled these commissions combined with changes in architecture culture, particularly the rise of digital technologies which enabled emerging firms to leap from designing small installations and interiors to building projects in an international context. Networked file-sharing and software platforms shared by architects and builders reduced the need for large field offices and enabled machine files to be sent directly to fabricators thousands of miles away. At the same, the global circulation of digital images heightened the visibility of emerging practices abroad and prompted the desire for their work, whether

(1) See Michael Meredith, Amanda Lawrence, Ashley Schafer, ed., *PRAXIS* 11/12 (2010); Sebastian Schmaling, "The New Small Architectural Practices," *Harvard Design Magazine* 32 (Spring-Summer 2010): 114–121.

1985

1987 Partners in Health (PIH) established

1990–1991 First Persian Gulf War

1997 Land purchased for Paju Book City, Korea

1999 Architecture for Humanity network established

2000 Young Architects Program (YAP) established at PS1 in New York as necessity or commodity. The previous terms of expertise through which US architects had sought to gain international commissions were replaced increasingly by ones of branding and consumption.

South Korea was one of the earliest countries in which young, international architects were invited to participate in high-profile developments following the election in 1992 of Kim Young-Sam, the country's first non-military President in thirty years. In 1997, art-book publisher Kim Eun-ho purchased land for a "book village," Paju Book City, along the underdeveloped edge of the country's demilitarized zone with North Korea. By the time construction began in 2001 the development, renamed Heyri Art Valley, had expanded to include 400 lots of studios, workshops, cultural buildings, and artists' housing. With over 120 buildings by 2008, Heyri includes Cho Slade's Dalki Theme Park (2000-2004), SHoP's Hangil Book House (2004), and Slade Architecture's White Block Gallery (2011), all small US firms at the time of commission.[2]

In China, regulations for Creative Business Districts (CBDs) and Special Creative Zones (SCZs) combined economic stimulus with urban planning, often including developments with a programmatic emphasis on architectural consumption. Jinhua Architecture Park, organized by artist Ai Wei Wei and opening in 2005, features seventeen architectural follies including Toshiko Mori Architect's Newspaper Cafe (2004–2007) and Michael Maltzan Architecture's Ministructure No. 16 (2004–2006).[3] The most notorious of these urban playgrounds was Ordos 100, launched in 2008 as a luxury gated community by Cai Jaing, a Chinese billionaire who made his fortune in coal and milk. Ai Wei Wei developed the master plan and architects Herzog & de Meuron selected 100 emerging architects from across the globe, each to design a 1000 m^2 (10,764 sf) private villa for the Cultural Creative Industry Park in the new city of Ordos. According to Ai Wei Wei, the project was an experiment in "how to bring in the world contemporary architectural knowledge into Chinese practice."[4] Designed remotely (Jaing paid the invited architects to travel twice to the city), its architects were given creative freedom, but accepted a loss of control over construction beyond the submission of drawings. As of late 2013, only five building shells stood as ruins, never inhabited, empty and deteriorating in the inner Mongolian desert landscape. Referring to the development of the city, *Forbes* has called Ordos "one of the most egregious examples of Chinese Late Stage Growth Obesity."[5] — AS

② See "Architectural Heterogenity in Korean Society," dialogue between Kyong Park and Minsuk Cho, http://www.massstudies.com/texts/hetero_EN.html (last accessed October 21, 2014).

③ Toshiko Mori, "Jinhua Architecture Park: organized by Ai Weiwei," *32 Beijing/New York* No. 5-6 (December 2005): 32–35.

④ Bert de Muynck, "How Foreign Architects became International Architects: A Case Study of China's Creative Construction Agenda," http://orgnets.net/urban_china/demuynck (last accessed September 20, 2014).

⑤ Vitaliy Katsenelson, "Why China is in Really Big Trouble," *Forbes* (October 18, 2010), http://www. forbes.com/sites/greatspeculations/2010/10/18/why-china-is-really-in-big-trouble/?partner=relatedstoriesbox (last accessed September 20, 2014).

2001 • Construction begins on Heyri Art Valley (formerly Paju Book City) • Clinton Foundation established

2005 • Jinhua Architecture Park opens in China • Clinton Global Initiative launched

2006 Kenya Vision 2030 includes plan for Konza Technology City

2008 • Ordos 100 development launched, Mongolia • Botswana Excellence Strategy includes plan for Botswana Innovation Hub (BIH) • Global financial crisis

2010 CONSTRUCTO program in Santiago, Chile joins MoMA PS1 YAP

2011 MAXXI in Rome joins MoMA PS1 YAP

2012 Istanbul Modern joins MoMA PS1 YAP

2014 Korean National Museum of Modern and Contemporary Art (MMCA) joins MoMA PS1 YAP

Afghanistan War **2003** Iraq War

borderline personality

A themed venue sends mixed messages from a cultural enclave on the border of North and South Korea.

BY IRIS MOON | PHOTOGRAPHS BY YONG KWAN KIM

The 14,000-square-foot theme park, which was cited in the 2003 P/A Awards, sits next to an art warehouse in Heyri Art Valley, an unusual arts community located north of Seoul, South Korea, close to the border with North Korea.

Visiting Paju City, in South Korea's Gyeonggi province, can be an unnerving experience. Barbed-wire fences and armed soldiers on constant guard for possible North Korean infiltrators are inherent to the scenery. Daily North Korean propaganda broadcasts ceased only in June. But despite these glaring reminders that the two Koreas are still technically at war with each other, a little cultural oasis has managed to spring up just down the street from the Unification Observation Tower, a structure built on Mt. Udosan in the demilitarized border zone so that displaced North Koreans can view their former homeland.

Dubbed the "City of Romantics" by *Hankook Ilbo*, a Korean newspaper, Heyri Art Valley is a well-planned, 122-acre residential community located about an hour north of Seoul. Meant to spur creative production and thought, Heyri was started by cultured city slickers who wanted to escape the urban chaos of Seoul. Here, fences are banned; architectural harmony, neighborly values, and the arts are encouraged. At least 40 percent of each of the mostly small multifamily buildings must house a public, cultural activity.

Dalki Theme Park, officially known as "I Like Dalki," and the Ssamzie Art Warehouse next door, are perhaps the only two buildings that don't lay claim to heavy-handed messages of peace and culture. With more of an interest in play than politics, the architects—Moongyu Choi of Seoul's Ga.A Architects, Minsuk Cho of Seoul's Mass Studies, and James Slade of New York City's Slade Architects—say that their plan was to create a dynamic, visually stimulating place where low and high culture, and reality and fantasy, would mix.

BLURRING THE *BAPSANG*

Two years ago, Hokyun Chun, the bohemian-spirited president of the Korean clothing and accessories company (and sponsor of the arts) Ssamzie, was inspired to create "some kind of commercial space" in Heyri. On the western side of I Like Dalki, a warehouse was constructed where leftover space on the lot allowed room for another building. Low-budget innovation is the defining characteristic of the three-story warehouse, which playfully serves the double function of storing and exhibiting the company's art holdings. The 17-

A sod roof and walls holding bags of earth and grass seed suggest the garden home of the venue's namesake character and offer counterpoint to its whimsical artifice: metal orbs, translucent mesh, and bright acrylics.

foot-by-130-foot building is built of exposed concrete; stored art pieces are visible from the outside through standard-sized (about 8 feet by 11 feet) sheets of ready-made insulated glass, while the interior walls are lined with plywood.

The theme park and the warehouse opened June 12 to a modest crowd of mostly elementary-school students and teenage girls. These two groups form the central fan base for Dalki—which means "strawberry" in Korean—a redheaded cartoon character that serves as a branding icon for a whole line of Ssamzie merchandise.

The central idea behind I Like Dalki is the blurring of boundaries between multiple programs and open areas, between structural and visual elements. Visitors are guided by the architects' newly coined concept of a "*bapsang* sequence," named for the traditional table setting in Korea. Instead of serving the meal through courses, diners choose from a variety of *banchan*, or side dishes, simultaneously. Choi said that while this process of picking and choosing activities is often used in theme parks, the architects chose to implant that sequence within a singular structure.

VIDEO-GAME COCOON

The 27,000-square-foot Dalki Theme Park building changes in appearance depending upon the visitor's viewing angle. The slanted roof is carpeted with a thick turf of grass that extends to the northern façade. Large panels of floor-to-ceiling reinforced glass, fixed at sharp angles, offer views of the art valley to the south and the art warehouse to the west.

Chung-woo Lee, a critic who reviewed Dalki for the Korean architecture magazine *Space*, said that walking through the photogenic interior is comparable to being immersed in a PlayStation 2 video game. On the exterior ground-level area where an "artificial garden" is located, visitors can choose between two entrances. One leads into the theme park's exhibition area and the other into "Dalki's bedroom," an activity space for kids to draw and play. Inside, pink, purple, and green paint seem to be the only things dividing program areas. The transitional areas between floors vary from tunnels and ramps to spiral staircases. The raised interior ground-level section contains a large, open shopping area. Oblong shelves display purses, toys, and

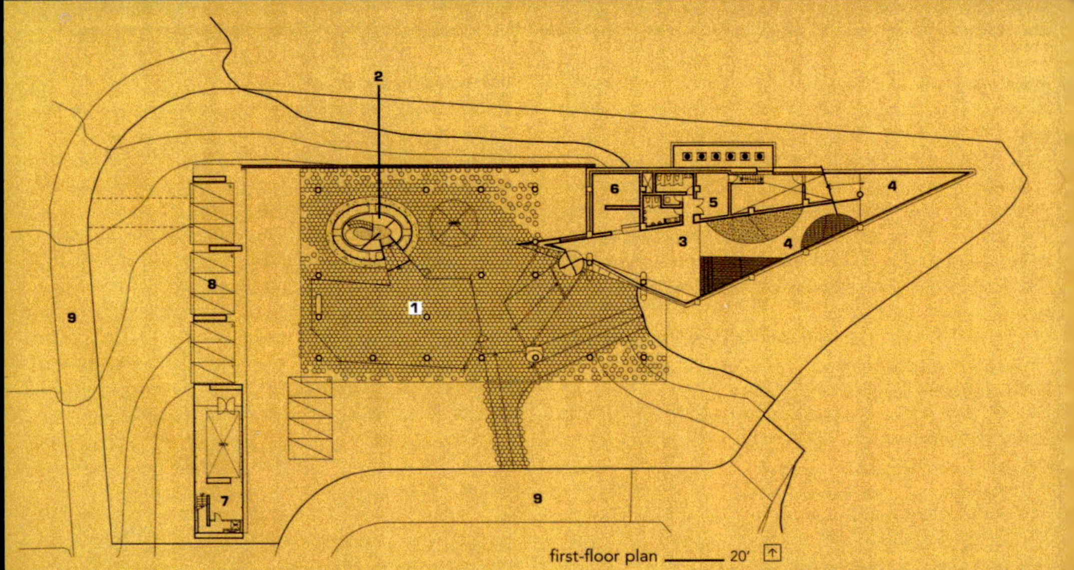

first-floor plan 20'

Multiple, blurred circulation routes bridge fantasy and prosaic domains, including "Dalki Room" (above), retail displays, a children's book café, and performance and play areas like the bowl-shaped amphitheater with cheese-wedge cushions (opposite), surrounded by merchandise. Like the traditional Korean *bapsang* meal, there is no prescribed sequence. As is also customary in Korea, the interiors were delivered as a design-build package.

1 terrace
2 exhibit space
3 theme-park entry/display
4 ramp and "Dalki room"
5 mechanical
6 coat check
7 art-warehouse entry
8 parking
9 road
10 art storage and display
11 retail display
12 amphitheater
13 open to below
14 gift shop

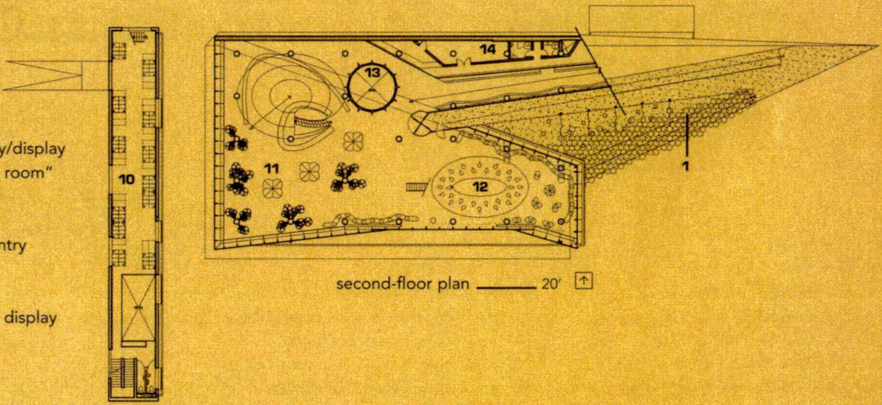

second-floor plan

The complicated concrete formwork (top left) and unusual details, such as the green plastic-coated metal mesh (abo right) punctuated by misters, light fixtures, and heating elements, presented some risk for the builder. The proje took about 18 months to construct, 50 percent longer than anticipated.

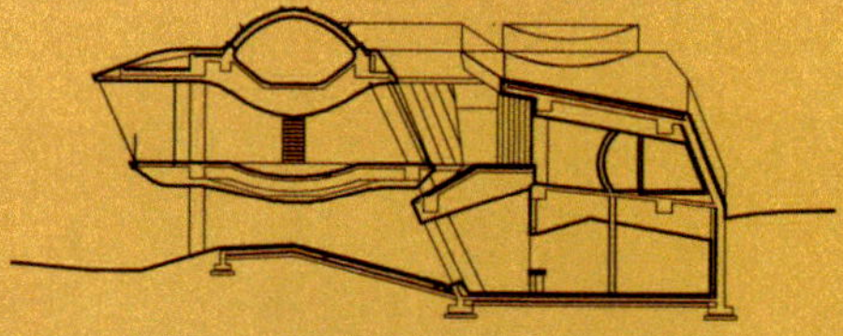

north-south section 12'

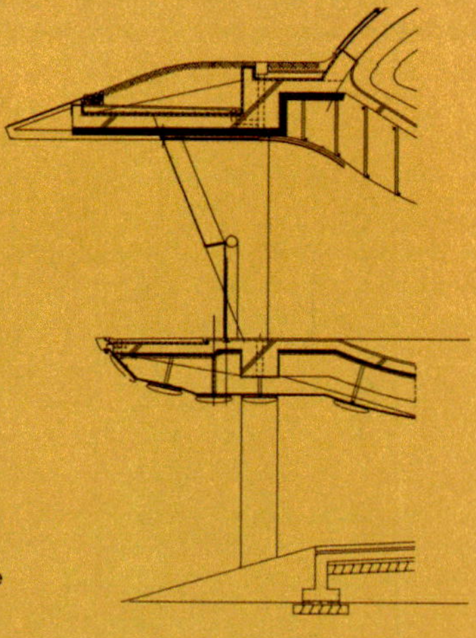

section detail 4'

1 steel plate
2 steel angle
3 galvanized steel sheet
4 clear double-glazed panel
5 PVC mesh and burlap bags of earth with grass seed
6 asphalt membrane over mortar
7 insulation
8 painted gypsum board
9 concrete slab
10 steel channel and tube
11 gravel and urethane on steel plate
12 grass over porous plastic pad
13 stainless-steel drain in volcanic stone
14 tempered glass with safety film
15 lamps, heaters, and misters

cks filled with earth and grass seed—used commonly in landscaping and building projects in the hills around Seoul camouflage structures—were set inside a steel frame resting on a poured-concrete wall. (The original design con-pt called for a steel truss wall.) Detailing was kept simple to control costs and match local materials and standards.

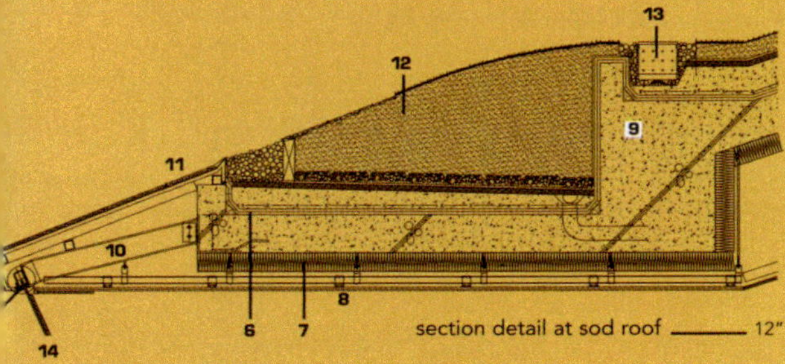

section detail at sod roof ——— 12″

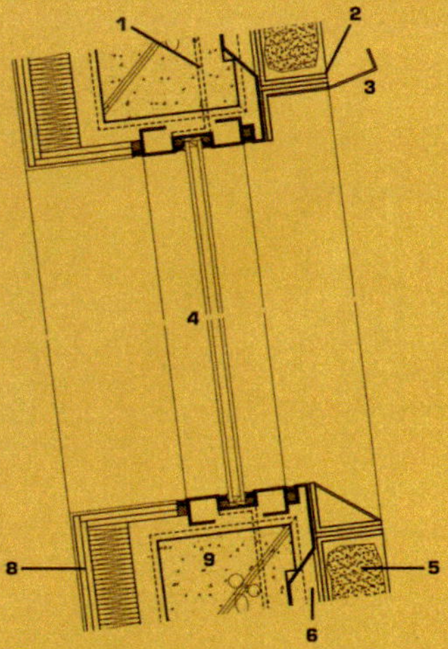

detail at window in grass wall ——— 4″

A lounge space with built-in wood seating is sheltered by a steel-and-polycarbonate space frame, with brightly colored, decorative disks to help limit direct sunlight.

1 retail
2 cantilevered shelving
3 terrace
4 lounge
5 amphitheater
6 ramp and "Dalki Room"
7 art storage and display
8 entry

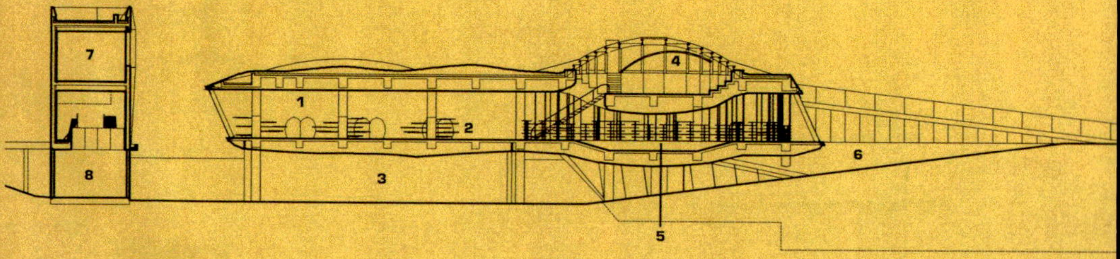

east-west section 12'

Bubbles, blisters, and tubes intersecting the main spaces offer shortcuts between levels and activities. Originally planned to contain a slide, a light shaft (above) instead offers visual connections between spaces.

other Ssamzie products. The merchandise takes on a decorative effect around a seating area comprising a concavity in the floor, where visitors can sink into cheese-wedge–shaped cushions; architect Cho calls it a "cocoonlike autonomous space."

While others have timidly stepped into cultural-commercial enterprises elsewhere by setting up adjoining galleries and cafés, Ssamzie's Chun knows that his roughly $2.4 million building is not about the merchandise on sale. "In the case of 'I Like Dalki,' the space is more important than the contents," he says; it's the building itself that is the selling point. But according to Lee, Dalki is also "the worst kind of experiment, [one] that combines the narcissism of Frank Gehry's greedy commercialism while taking orders from Rem Koolhaas with weak logic." Yet, he said, it's a success, "because people like it. I've heard they have to wait in line to get inside."

It would be nice to imagine Heyri and its buildings as representative of South Korea's flourishing capitalist and cultural future, the panacea to its war-scarred past. But if anything, this strange little valley where a nexus of geopolitical tension, commercial fantasy, and utopian dreams coexist is just a part of the reality of present-day Korea.

Based in Seoul, Iris Moon reports on art and architecture for *The Korea Herald*.

I Like Dalki Theme Park, Heyri Art Valley, Paju City, Republic of Korea

client: Ssamzie Corporation—Hokyun Chun (president) **architects:** Ga.A Architects, Seoul, Korea—Moongyu Choi (principal), Jeonghui Kim, Kwangho Cha, Inchul Kang, Taekwon Yun, Bongki Song, Daegon Koh, Jeyong Kang (project team); Mass Studies, Seoul, Korea, and New York City—Minsuk Cho (principal), Kisu Park, Hyungjoo Lee, Joungwon Lee, Sunbok Choi, Soon Pyo Lee, Byulnam Yoo (project team); Slade Architecture, New York City—James Slade (principal), Hayes Slade, Ilya Korolev, Francisco Pardo (project team) **interior designer and interior architect:** Ga.A Architects; Mass (Interior) Studies **engineers:** Shin Structural Engineering (structural); Han On Eng., Dong-Ho Eng. (M/E/P); Kyoung-In Eng. (civil) **consultants:** Jun Sung Kim, Jong Kyu Kim (master plan); Hyungjoo Lee (artistic collaboration); 44 (Sasa)... (mural design) **general contractor:** Hanool Construction, Seoul—Daeshik Kim (CEO), Sang Yong Choi (construction manager) **area:** 12,000 square feet **cost:** $2.4 million

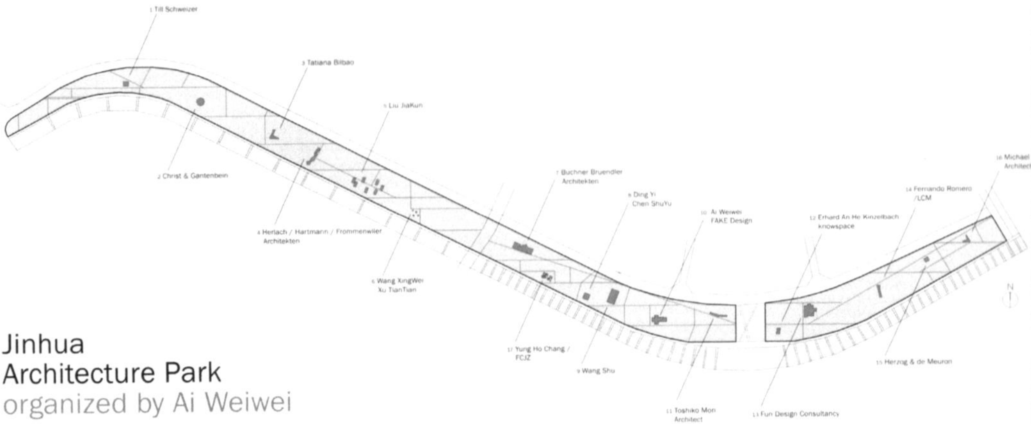

Jinhua Architecture Park organized by Ai Weiwei

text by Toshiko Mori

The Jinhua Urban Park project is a unique and ambitious project, not only for China, but also for other parts of the world. Rather than a high profile structure by a star architect concerned with the bottom line, the park will be a collection of small structures by diverse architects with a public objective.

The city of Jinhua commissioned seventeen architects to design seventeen structures for the park. The park itself and the museum are being designed by Ai Weiwei. The mixture of architects includes different nationalities and a wide range of backgrounds, from international stars to young, emerging architects. Individual structures were not assigned or won; rather all of the architects literally picked a project out of a box—a red Chinese ballot box with 17 numbered slips of paper. This democratic atmosphere has created an easy dialogue and wonderful rapport among those of us involved. Michael Maltzan used the word "constellation" in describing this heterogeneous group of architects and projects. We all share the vision of this universe orchestrated by Ai Weiwei.

Jinhua is an old city, and its leaders are determined to maintain its ancient traditions, even as it industrializes. They are especially proud of its literary heritage. Ai Qing, who was a greatly admired 20th century poet and novelist, and the father of Ai Weiwei, was born in Jinhua. The city has commissioned the Swiss architects Herzog and de Meuron to prepare an urban center master plan, but in an unusual and ambitious move, the city has decided to go ahead with the park before the other urban components.

The park will face the memorial to Ai Qing across the river, creating a transition zone between the existing city and the new proposed city. The sole purpose of the park will be to provide a place of rest and relaxation for the local community. This is a highly unusual, and, for the high-powered Shanghai developers, an almost unfathomable proposition. The most intriguing technical aspect of the project is the size and the multiplicity of its parts. In fact, the project is a pointed critique of the extra large projects being constructed in China today. Each structure is small, under 1,000 square feet, and each will be built simultaneously. While it appears to be ambitious in scale, it is far more economical and effective than building a giant office tower or theatre by a single architect. It is economical because the buildings are to be small and simple in design, using local techniques and materials, where the relative investment is not astronomical. It is effective because the architects involved act as ambassadors, telling others of this exciting project in Jinhua.

It seems not often enough that architects can participate in a collective statement and process that so directly involves designing for the everyday life of ordinary people. In contrast to architecture that is often exploited as propaganda to promote the agendas of business or media, this project promotes the value of the microeconomy which exists behind the megastructure of capitalist development in China today. Just walk around the other side of a highrise in Shanghai or Beijing, and you will observe a traditional microeconomy composed of multiple elements that mutually support each other. One is forced to ask—if this economic structure is displaced, where would these people with their micro enterprises go? Jinhua's city planners realize that the foundation for development of a vibrant city must start with this structure and the lives of its citizens.

This project has broken ground and the park is scheduled to open to the public in March of 2005.

1 Till Schweizer, Heidelberg, Germany

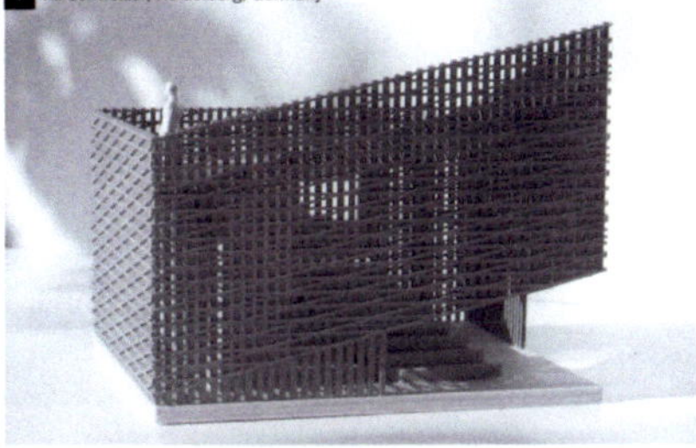

2 Christ & Gantenbein, Basel, Switzerland

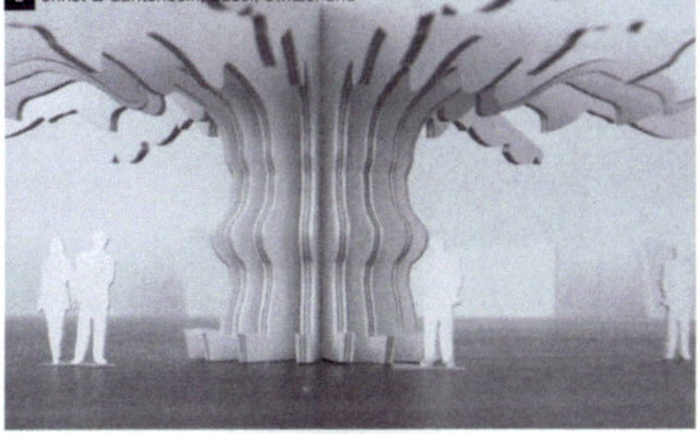

3 Tatiana Bilbao, mx.a, Mexico City, Mexico

4 Herlach/Hartmann/Frommenwiler Architekten
Basel, Switzerland

5 Liu JiaKun Architect, Chengdu, China

Jinhua Architecture Park
projects

6 Wang XingWei, Xu TianTiàn, Shanghai/Beijing, China

7 Buchner Bruendler Architekten, Basel, Switzerland

8 Ding Yi / Chen ShuYu, Beijing, China

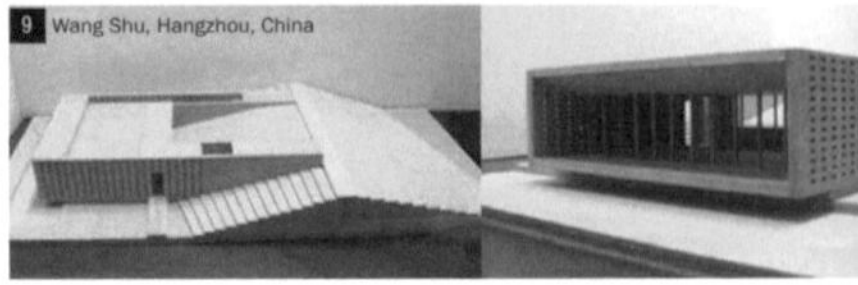

9 Wang Shu, Hangzhou, China

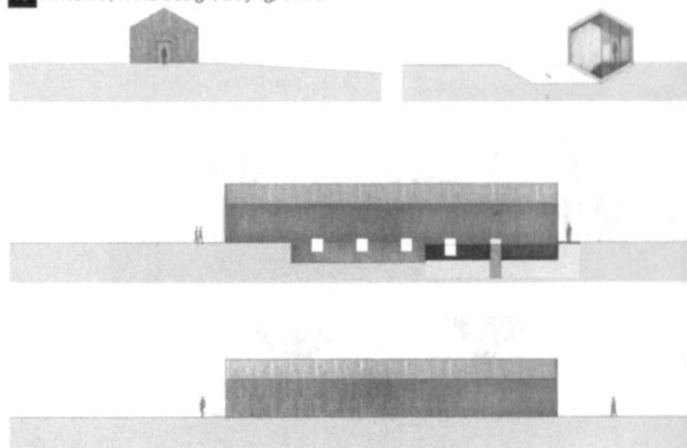

10 Ai Weiwei/FAKE Design, Beijing, China

11 Toshiko Mori Architect, New York, USA

ard An-He Kinzelbach, knowspace, New York, USA

Design Consultancy
erdam, Netherlands

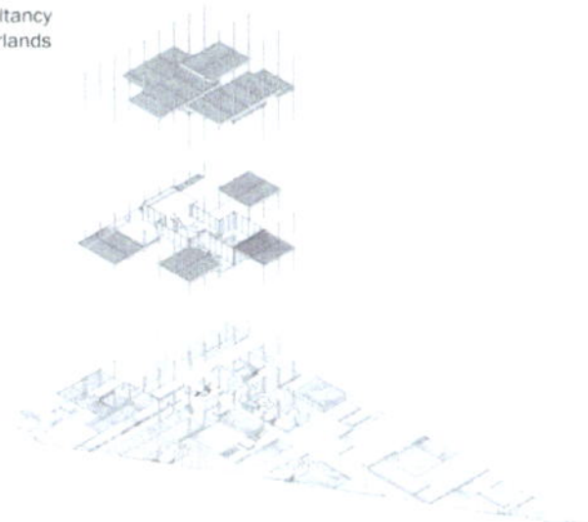

ando Romero/LCM, Mexico City, Mexico

15 Herzog & de Meuron, Basel, Switzerland

16 Michael Maltzan Architecture, Los Angeles, USA

17 Yung Ho Chang / FCJZ (Beijing, China)

Sebastian Schmaling

THE NEW SMALL ARCHITECTURAL PRACTICES

CREATIVITY INCUBATORS OR CO-OPTED BRANDERS?

In a society with an insatiable appetite for newness and obsessed with youth and instant celebrity, it is perhaps not surprising that young designers and small design offices are *en vogue* these days. Programs targeted at progressive design talent—Emerging Voices, the Next Generation Design Prize, the Prize for Young Architects + Designers, the Ordos Prize, *Architectural Review*'s Emerging Architecture Awards, *Architectural Record*'s annual Design Vanguard issue and its monthly archrecord2 feature, as well as invited design competitions for emerging architects such as the MoMA/P.S.1 Young Architects Program—give participants a tremendous degree of public exposure and often jump-start their professional ascent. Organized by foundations, museums, and savvy editors eager to prove their cultural street cred and their relevance as public tastemakers, these awards seek to create an instant elite of designers whose practices, overwhelmingly small in size and noncorporate in structure, operate outside the confines of architectural orthodoxy.

Despite the irony that today's avant-garde is usually being hand-selected and coronated by stalwarts of the status quo itself—cultural bastions like the Museum of Modern Art, or docile publications like the 119-year-old *Architectural Record*—the newfound and heavily mediated interest in nonestablished designers and innovative practices may be seen as an encouraging sign for the future of a profession now dominated by large corporate players: It signals the reemergence of the small office as a critical part in the mechanics of architectural production, suggesting an organizational upheaval with profound consequences, a structural shift within the architectural profession that is bound to recalibrate the balance of power between large firms and their smaller and often younger counterparts and to redefine their respective roles in the making of architecture. More important, the new prominence of smaller offices on the architectural firmament and a renewed interest in experimental creativity indicates a dramatic rise in the currency of artistic design, clearly challenging Jeffrey Kipnis's doomsdayist prophesy that architecture "will become a science," a lifeless, quantitative profession ultimately purified from those practitioners who cling to a life in "a world of doxologies."[1]

In recent years, and at a perhaps unprecedented rate, emerging practices have been able to secure notable commissions from clients seeking to benefit from "the unique, fresh approach they can bring to a project."[2] Examples abound: In 2000, Vitra, the prestigious and image-conscious maker of high-end furniture, interviewed a handful of architects for the design of the company's New York showroom. Vitra's CEO, who had emphasized the importance to find "a new voice, a new promise"—as if the company were in need of messianic salvation—hired Lindy Roy, known at the time mostly for her competition-

winning P.S.1 courtyard installation, consciously choosing her over her more prominent competitors to take advantage of Roy's unconventional design sensitivities. Harvard University, not known in recent memory for architectural adventurousness, skipped the usual large firm suspects and instead commissioned a twelve-person Los Angeles-based office led by Gehry alumnus Kevin Daly and his partner, Chris Genik, for one of its most visible projects, a new art center anchoring the University's ambitious (and now stalled) campus expansion across the river in Allston. wHY Architecture, a young and, until recently, virtually unknown office in Culver City, California, was hired to design the *Grand Rapids Art Museum*, a sizable job that would have been a prized commission for any of the protagonists in today's brand-name starchitecture establishment relentlessly jet-setting the globe in search for similar projects. The new waterfront home for Boston's Institute of Contemporary Art was designed by Diller Scofidio + Renfro, gave them an unusual jump in scale for an experimental office with a portfolio largely based on clever installations and conceptual art. Like the ICA, which had assembled a short list of four small offices before making its choice, the board of the Museum of Arts and Design in Manhattan focused its search for an architect to spearhead the redesign of Edward Durell Stone's *2 Columbus Circle* almost exclusively on emerging firms. In 2002, the institution selected Allied Works Architecture from Portland, Oregon, then still a relatively obscure studio headed by Brad Cloepfil, who remarked that "[a] lot of the next generation of architects are getting opportunities now that, say thirty years ago, I am not sure a small ten- to fifteen-person firm would have gotten."[3]

What is significant about the new prominence of small practices is that it appears to indicate a reversal of architecture's century-old metamorphosis from fuzzy art nurtured by divine inspiration to a corporate service industry, a development that can be traced back to Daniel Burnham's implementation of Fordist principles in his professional practice, which replaced the architect as generalist with the architect as specialist.[4] With the methodical introduction of division of labor into architectural production, Burnham created the prototype for the large corporate architecture office, establishing an organizational paradigm that may very well be one of America's most enduring contributions to the design profession.[5] The evolving perception that there was a direct relationship between size, efficiency, and embodied expertise eventually made the large office the industry's preferred business model, giving corporate design sweatshops, for almost a century, a virtual stranglehold on large commissions thought too complex for the limited resources of a small practice: "Large clients expect an organizational model similar to their own," as a principal at a Chicago firm explained.[6]

Over time, the profession's gradual adoption of an inherently risk-adverse corporate model changed its attitude toward freewheeling design experimentation whose innate unpredictability seemed irreconcilable with the ubiquitous brand control vital to any corporation: Once the atelier became an *office*, its internal culture shifted "from craftsmanship to draftsmanship."[7] The rise of the big firm and the organizational homogenization of practice institutionalized an increasingly compartmentalized corporate profession and transformed it into an unapologetic service provider with a shrinking commitment to aesthetic innovation.

THE NEW PROMINENCE OF SMALL EXPERIMENTAL PRACTICES SEEMS TO INDICATE A REVERSAL OF ARCHITECTURE'S CENTURY-OLD METAMORPHOSIS FROM FUZZY ART NURTURED BY DIVINE INSPIRATION TO A CORPORATE SERVICE INDUSTRY.

The renaissance of the small practice as a viable professional player can be attributed to a variety of factors. For one, the increasingly affordable access to technology and information has leveled the playing field among architects, allowing smaller firms (and even students) to produce graphic material virtually undistinguishable in quality and quantity from that of larger offices, which traditionally had the necessary manpower and financial resources to outdo smaller competitors. Furthermore, technological advances triggered the emergence of a new type of academic practitioner who recognized early on the significance of the digital revolution and its potential to democratize architectural production. Their facility in experimenting with the newest technologies installed at their schools as soon as they were available and their

Page 115: Roy Co. design, *Vitra Showroom*, view of display tongue from lower level, New York City, 2002. Photo: Richard Barnes. Courtesy Roy Co.
Above: wHY Architecture, Grand Rapids Art Museum, Michigan, 2007.
Photo: Grand Rapids Art Museum. Courtesy wHY Architecture

bility to harvest the technological skills of their students ave catapulted many of them into the forefront of archiectural creativity. The dual role of practitioner and academician affords many of them a position of ideological ndependence and some aloofness from commerce—omething arguably not seen since the demise of the ge of the independently wealthy gentleman architect—llowing them to conduct meaningful research and to xperiment with innovative design methodologies in irect competition with the well-funded engineering epartments of corporate heavyweights such as kidmore, Owings & Merrill.[8] As a result, studios with lose ties to academia—Office dA, Kennedy & Violich, Ain|Day, nARCHITECTS, MOS, and ewis.Tsurumaki.Lewis, ust to name a few—are increasingly setting the agenda or today's architectural discourse, in both theory and ractice.

In this context, Office dA and its principals, Monica Ponce de Leon and Nader Tehrani, may be regarded as leaders of the pack. Perennial winners of the annual P/A Awards, the ur-prize for innovative design in America, Ponce de Leon and Tehrani both have had distinguished teaching careers, but "the intensity of [their] desire ... for the 'real' of building," has set them apart from many of their academic peers, as Graham Owen pointed out in an early monograph of Office dA's work.[9] Dedicated to the idea of praxis, they entered the perpetual academic debate about the validity of surface and decoration as legitimate architectural themes not by delivering another theoretical manifesto arguing for one side or the other but by presenting a series of earnest and rigorously researched design proposals exploiting the physical attributes and tectonic characteristics of cladding materials, transforming them into tantalizing wrappers of building

Office dA, *Casa la Roca*, model, Caracas, Venezuela, 1995

volumes. Although mostly unbuilt, Office dA's early work introduced a new paradigm for aspiring practices by fusing bold aesthetic experimentations with a sincere commitment to buildability, providing a tangible alternative to colleagues such as Greg Lynn, whose algorithmic formalism, alluring as it may be, only seldom enters the realm of constructability. Projects such as Office dA's *Zahedi House* and, perhaps even more important, *Casa la Roca* are significant because they represent a courageous inversion of Louis Kahn's proverbial and inherently submissive dialogue with "brick" (in which "brick" tells the architect how to use it properly): Suddenly the architects reclaim control, liberating themselves from formulaic preconceptions about material properties and confidently submitting brick, metal, and wood to materialize autonomous aesthetic objectives. New fabrication techniques such as CNC milling and digital design tools facilitating the proper documentation of complex geometries and folding or warped surfaces allowed Office dA to test its ideas in practice. An early example is the extensive

Office dA, *GSD Offices*, Gund Hall, Harvard Graduate School of Design, Cambridge, Massachusetts, 2001. Photo: John Horner

casework installed in the administrative offices at Harvard's GSD, where Tehrani and Ponce de León, with the help of Shane Williamson, one of their technically well-versed students, milled cabinet surfaces into sensually undulating and seemingly liquefied surfaces, radically redefining the aesthetic boundaries of plywood by revealing its sculptural potential.[10]

It is work like that of Office dA and its like-minded peers that have inspired an energetic generation of emerging architects, sparking a renewed interest among designers in serious material research, innovative fabrication and production methods, and, ultimately, the art of *building*, their work a reminder that profound architecture based on aesthetic, programmatic, and behavioral innovation is possible after all, even in a professional arena largely controlled by corporate firms apathetic to change. For those of us with a genuine distaste for the uninspired architectural junk produced by a vast majority of profit-driven corporate design offices, the narrative of an imminent cultural counterrevolution is compelling: Small practices and innovative designers armed with an unprecedented arsenal of new and multidisciplinary design techniques are finally repossessing their profession.

And yet I wonder—conflicted as I am in my dual role as critical observer of the architectural world and as purveyor of small-practice architecture myself—if there is another, perhaps less benevolent and self-adulatory reading of the current development, one in which small practitioners emerge not as the profession's saviors but as willing foot soldiers in architecture's ongoing and inexorable commodification. After all and perhaps counterintuitively, the current reempowerment of the small practice coincided with the recent gilded age in which cheap money fueled construction projects at an unprecedented pace and is being propelled by the same cultural and macroeconomic forces that, over the last two decades, have also triggered stunning mergers between already sizable design firms into even larger corporate behemoths with multiple offices around the world.[11] In a globalized age shaped by transcontinental flows of capital creating internationally operating conglomerates, *small* has become again a virtue, a quality synonymous with integrity—not only in architecture but also in the economy at large, as the recent emergence of niche and specialty players in other industries shows. Microbreweries, local coffee roasters, boutique tailors, independent cinemas, and farmers' markets all cater to a clientele that feels increasingly disenfranchised by globally operating mega-corporations deemed too impersonal, too formulaic, too ruthless, or simply too detached from regional particularities or individual tastes. The laws of post-Fordism require commodities to be "continually tweaked and markets constantly niched"[12] in order to give mass products an individualized, au courant appearance, and this appearance has pushed slow-moving giants like General Motors to the brink of bankruptcy. The same laws apply in the world of professional design, where large architectural firms find it progressively difficult to stay in touch with an ever-changing aesthetic Zeitgeist whose half-life is decreasing exponentially. The inflexibility to react to new aesthetic sensibilities is rooted in a systemic flaw in the traditional organization of the corporate firm: The principals in charge of design, an area still viewed as the most prestigious in an architecture office, usually reach that position of power only after years of rising through the ranks, at which point they might be hopelessly out of touch with innovative architectural currents, a real liability at a time when up-to-dateness is considered a necessity.

THE ATELIER ACTS AS A PROVOCATEUR ON A LEASH, PACKAGING OTHERWISE MUNDANE PRODUCTS IN A VEIL OF HIPNESS AND CHEERFULLY PIMPING THE CORPORATE RIDE.

To better understand the new role that small practices play within the machinery of architectural production, it is instructive to look beyond the sizable signature projects single-handedly authored by them and instead consider the proliferation of design teams spearheaded by traditional corporate architecture firms working hand in hand with their noncorporate and often young counterparts on substantial and ambitious commissions. In some cases this type of collaboration between offices at the opposite end of the professional spectrum is instigated by governmental requirements stipulating the involvement of minority consultants, local contractors, or disadvantaged businesses in the design of publicly financed projects.[13] More often, though, the engagement of small studios as team members for large-scale commissions is a voluntary strategy pursued by clever clients looking to hedge their bets and seeking to harvest the aesthetic dexterity of a younger generation while simultaneously benefiting from the assumed competence of an established design corporation leading the project.[14]

This strategy highlights the growing symbiosis between seemingly incompatible professional models, suggesting that the newfound interest in noncorporate practices may not be a reversal of the profession's basic evolutionary trajectory after all, but rather a logical step in architecture's ongoing segmentation into fiefdoms of proficiency, creating a poly-nuclear profession that relies on an ever-expanding circle of expert consultants and specialists to cope with the complexities of contemporary building, and in which aesthetic design is only one of many commodifiable segments of the overall building process that can be easily outsourced.[15] The perceived advantage of smaller firms is their unlimited access, real or imagined, to boundless creativity—creativity not as an ephemeral cultural concept but as the ultimate commodity in today's mediatic world of commerce where image trumps substance, and where finding the "Buzz," as John Seabrook calls it, is key to the survival in a marketplace perpetually seeking the "next big thing."[16]

There is perhaps no recent example that better illustrates the triangular codependence of small offices, large firms, and a clientele in constant need for the "Buzz" than developer Bruce Ratner's Atlantic Yards project in Brooklyn, New York, envisioned as the epicenter of the borough's urban transformation. The twenty-two-acre development's master plan by Frank Gehry included *Barclays Center*, a new arena for the to-be-relocated New Jersey Nets, whose design was widely celebrated as a visionary interpretation of a generally drab typology but that quickly became too expensive to build. Ratner swiftly replaced Gehry's plans with a $200 million less expensive version designed by Ellerbe Becket, a large corporate player whose portfolio includes dozens of generic stadiums for major-league teams and universities. When it became clear that the uninspired new arena design was turning into a public relations nightmare, Ratner paired up Ellerbe Becket with SHoP Architects, a prolific young office (and, incidently, another previous winner of the MoMA/P.S.1 Young Architects Program) considered by many to be one of the most innovative design firms in the country. The transparent move to add glamour to a stale proposal by adding a well-reputed emerging studio to the team provoked *New York* magazine's Justin Davidson to title an article "Bruce Ratner SHoPs for respectability."[17]

SHoP, *Barclays Center*, Atlantic Avenue looking South, New York City, 2009. Courtesy, SHoP Architects.

By all measures, SHoP's design of perforated weathering steel ribbons provocatively wrapping Ellerbe Becket's formulaic core is an elegant and daring aesthetic proposition, one that pushes the envelope, figuratively and literally, of stadium design in America. At the same time, SHoP Architects, whose principals pride themselves as "neither ivory-tower elitists nor superficial stylists"[18] risk to be dismissed as just that: mere window dressers who "gussy up a degraded project with architectural flimflam." [19]

If anything, the case of *Barclays Center* serves as a reminder of how quickly the collaboration between emerging and established offices can turn into corroboration of the status quo. Viewed against the backdrop of the branding that permeates all sectors of culture, small practices suddenly function not as authentic design innovators or as harbingers of a libratory movement freeing architecture from the shackles of aesthetic timidity but as facilitators of a system that shamelessly commercializes subcultural trends and exploits cliché notions of independence, authenticity, and individuality. In this context, the atelier acts as a provocateur on a leash, packaging otherwise mundane products in a veil of hipness and cheerfully pimping the corporate ride.[20]

The ultimate victim of the profession's ongoing transformation, then, is the idealistic concept of design as a holistic exercise in which a building's form, function, and overall appearance are conceived simultaneously by one overarching ingenious authority. Instead, small practices will have to embrace their role as providers of compelling imagery in the making of large-scale and technically complex commissions: This may be the price that must be paid to secure a sustained future in the increasingly fragmented field of architecture. ◆

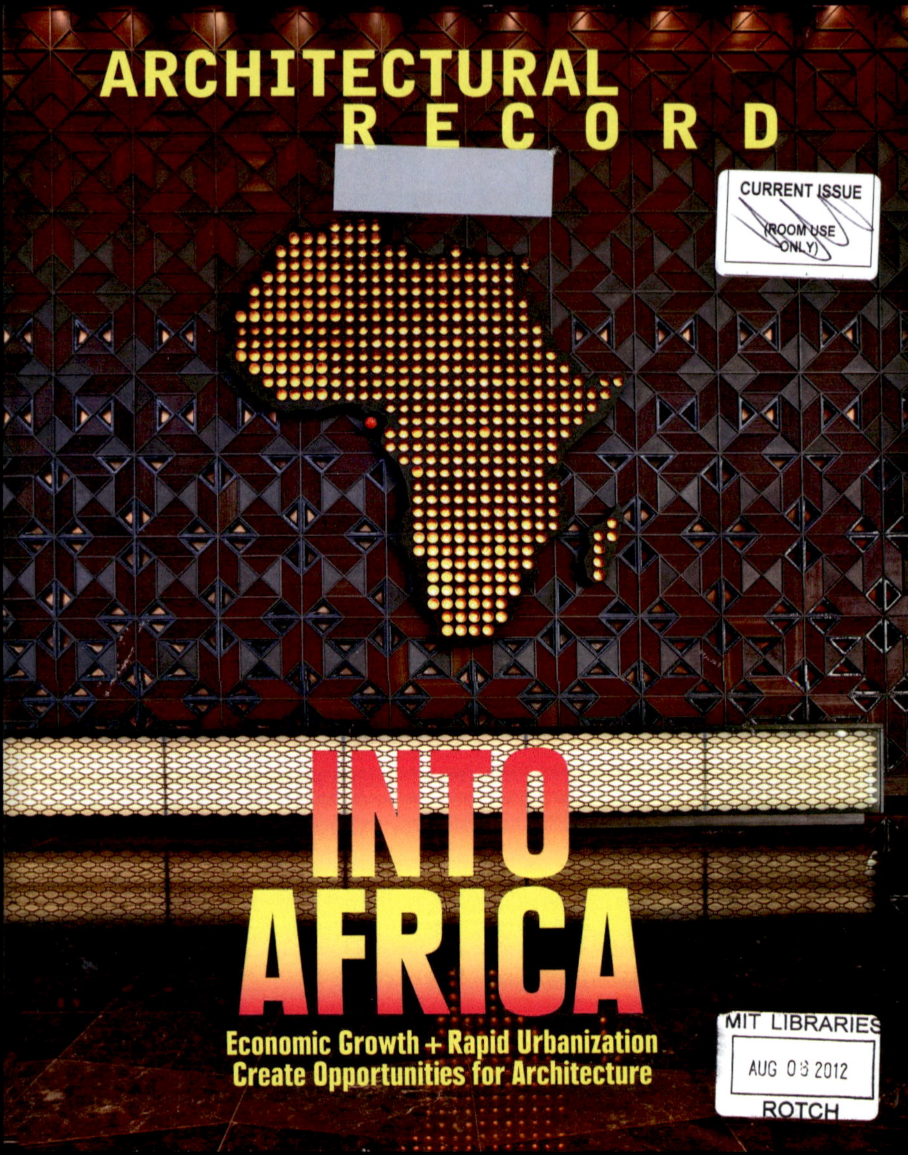
ARCHITECTURAL
RECORD
CURRENT ISSUE
(ROOM USE ONLY)
INTO
AFRICA
Economic Growth + Rapid Urbanization
Create Opportunities for Architecture
MIT LIBRARIES
AUG 08 2012
ROTCH

INTO AFRICA

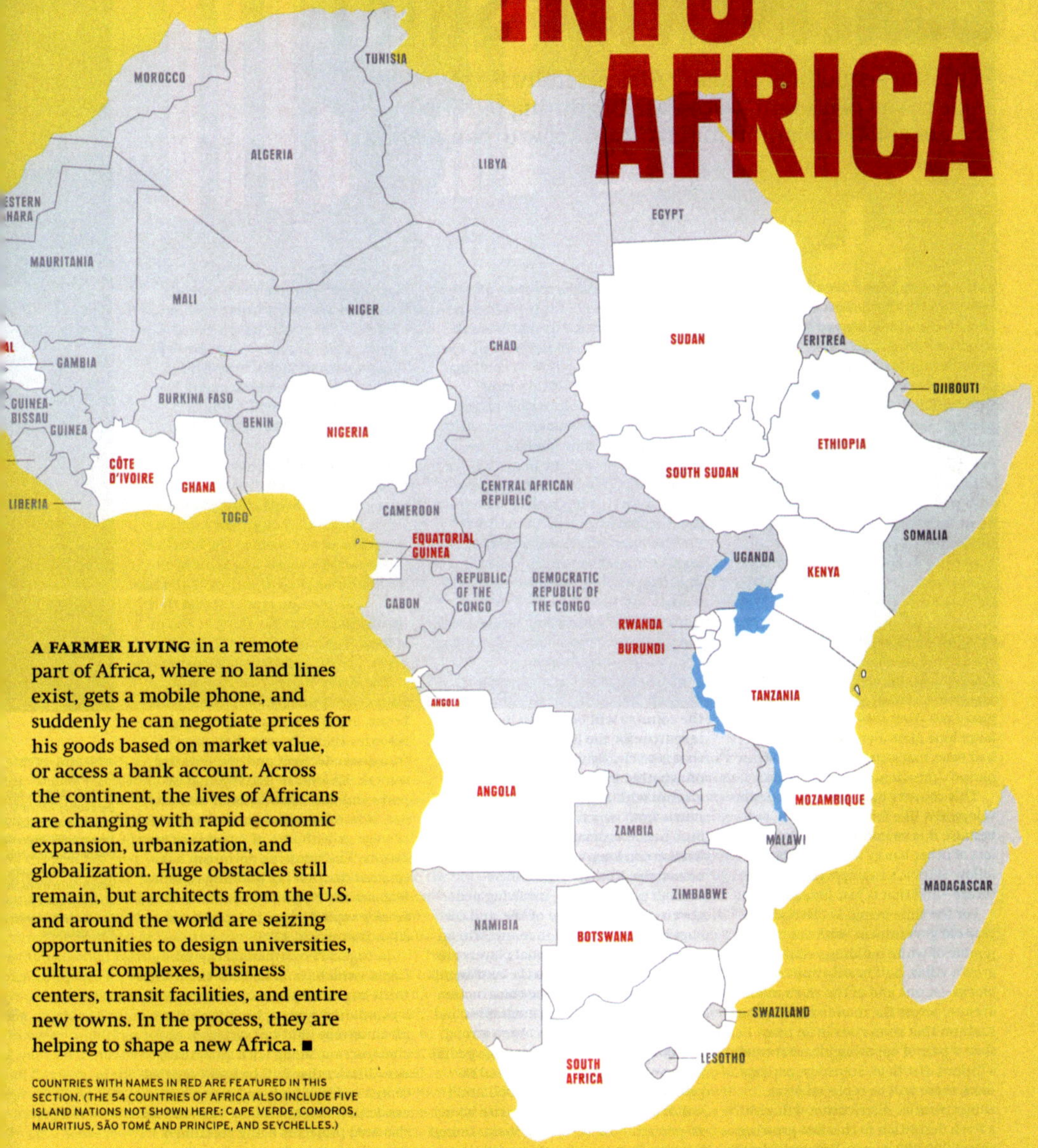

A FARMER LIVING in a remote part of Africa, where no land lines exist, gets a mobile phone, and suddenly he can negotiate prices for his goods based on market value, or access a bank account. Across the continent, the lives of Africans are changing with rapid economic expansion, urbanization, and globalization. Huge obstacles still remain, but architects from the U.S. and around the world are seizing opportunities to design universities, cultural complexes, business centers, transit facilities, and entire new towns. In the process, they are helping to shape a new Africa. ■

COUNTRIES WITH NAMES IN RED ARE FEATURED IN THIS SECTION. (THE 54 COUNTRIES OF AFRICA ALSO INCLUDE FIVE ISLAND NATIONS NOT SHOWN HERE: CAPE VERDE, COMOROS, MAURITIUS, SÃO TOMÉ AND PRINCIPE, AND SEYCHELLES.)

CONTINENTAL SHIFT

With the economies of many African countries growing rapidly, the continent's cities are beginning to reflect the enormous potential for creating a new urban realm.

BY HOWARD W. FRENCH

ABIDJAN, CÔTE D'IVOIRE
By mid-century, 60 percent of Africa's booming and relativ young population wi live in cities like this modern metropolis, which, with more th 5 million people, is n the second largest c the continent.

FROM THE AIR, Juba, South Sudan, the capital of Africa's newest country, looks like nothing so much as a giant village, sprawling brown, flat, and ragged from the banks of the White Nile. At first glance this might seem a most unlikely frontier for architects seeking new markets, but the closer one looks, the more this city begins to resemble a vast construction project waiting to happen.

I had been warned to carry a lot of cash with me here, because there were no international banks, much less functioning ATMs, from which to access funds. But wandering by foot "downtown" my first evening in the city, on a dusty side street I stumbled upon the gleaming local headquarters of Stanbic Bank, a subsidiary of South Africa's Standard Bank and a major presence around the continent. When I inquired, the watchmen standing guard out front informed me that the large blue glass-and-metal structure had been inaugurated by the new nation's president that very week.

This country may embody underdevelopment like few other places, but because it is swimming in oil wealth, lots of other banks will undoubtedly follow Stanbic's example in the near future—and that is just for starters.

For the time being, South Sudan's year-old government works out of a jumble of white buildings—half overgrown villas, half hastily built concrete blocks—at one end of the city's main avenue, across the road from a national stadium that comprises little more than a pair of opposing bleachers and a forlorn dirt field. Someday, perhaps soon, these will be replaced by an administrative district that will give a fresh definition to this fast-growing city of 300,000 people. Who will design and build it remains an open question.

In large part because of its newness, South Sudan is an extreme example of a phenomenon taking place all over sub-Saharan Africa. Here, a combination of some of the world's most vigorous economic growth—at least a dozen African economies have grown by 6 percent or more a year for six straight years—and the planet's fastest urbanization rates are creating new cities and reshaping existing ones on a scale exceeded only by China. This phenomenon, which is likely to last at least until mid-century, is underpinned in equal parts by strong international demand for the continent's immense mineral and hydrocarbon riches and by the rapid rise of new middle classes in one country after another.

But South Sudan is an extreme example in another sense, too. Whether the country will be able to harness its resources for the huge building boom that is so clearly needed will depend on whether it can reach a modus vivendi with Sudan, the country to the north from which it recently seceded—and, just as crucially, whether its leaders can keep corruption within reasonable limits.

High political risk—involving poor governance, weak rule of law, and corruption—is a problem in many African countries. Yet international players are increasingly attracted to the continent's markets, including in the construction industry, because the demographic and economic fundamentals are so strong. By 2050, one in four working-age people in the world will be African, and 60 percent of the continent's population will live in cities, compared with about 40 percent now, according to the United Nations. Because Africa's overall population rate is zooming, there will be three times as many urban dwellers as there are today. Like people everywhere, a great many of them will demand to shop in modern malls, to stay in international-style hotels, and to live and work in modern buildings.

In the last two years, traveling widely around the continent while researching a book about China's booming relations with Africa, I have seen glimpses of this emerging urban realm in city after city. New expressways deliver motorists to the hearts of fast-growing capitals like Windhoek, Namibia; Dakar, Senegal; and Bamako, Mali. Construction cranes crowd the skyline in cities as far-flung as Dar es Salaam, Tanzania; Lusaka, Zambia; Accra, Ghana; and Maputo, Mozambique.

The last of these countries, and places like Guinea, Liberia, and Sierra Leone, are now embarking on huge, resource-fueled booms that stand to transform decrepit and overcrowded capitals. Thanks to massive coal exports and vast discoveries of natural gas, Mozambique has enjoyed an annual average growth rate of 7.2 percent for a decade. The resulting optimism has spurred the first big building push in Maputo, the elegant but hitherto sleepy seaside capital, since independence from Portugal in 1975.

In Nigeria's commercial capital, Lagos—which could become the world's third-largest city by mid-century, with a population approaching 40 million—an ambitious light-rail system is under construction, along with an entirely new district that will be half financial center and half high-end oceanfront residential neighborhood. The land for this bold project is being reclaimed from the sea.

⁄leanwhile, south along the Atlantic st, Angola has seen some of the :est economic growth in the world, ‹raging over 17 percent per year ween 2004 and 2008, with 9 percent wth expected next year. Large ıths of the capital, Luanda, are being ıpletely rebuilt, with modern new ırters rising to replace blighted atter settlements. At the same time, city's colonial Portuguese seafront, ich compares for scenic value with ‹ana's more famous Malecón, is ıg lavishly restored and refurbished. łowever ambitious, ongoing build- spurts like these represent only a ıll foretaste of the construction and perty boom that is likely in store much of sub-Saharan Africa.

'o get a sense of what is to come, it ps to consider the not-so-distant past. Tanzania, Côte d'Ivoire, and especially Nigeria all stand out as exemplars of a kind of boldness of urban development that few outsiders associate with Africa. In each of these countries, new capitals were decreed and built, each more ambitious than the last—beginning with Dodoma, Tanzania, in the 1970s and followed by Yamoussoukro, Côte d'Ivoire, in the 1980s and Abuja, Nigeria, in the early 1990s.

Yamoussoukro's international claim to fame ever since has been the largest church in the world, the Basilica of Our Lady of Peace, built by the country's late founding father, Félix Houphouët-Boigny, and finished in 1989 at a reported cost of $300 million. The city contains other monumental structures, such as a presidential palace made famous in the writings of V.S. Naipaul, a large five-star hotel complex, and, most recently, a National Assembly building. But Yamoussoukro has never drawn large-scale migration from other parts of the country, and its avenues, some as broad as Paris's Champs-Élysées, remain eerily free of traffic.

By contrast, Abuja, the capital that Nigeria began to build in 1991, has quickly become one of the biggest cities in Africa's most populous country. When I first visited there, in 1994, the neighborhoods meant to house newly arrived civil servants emerged from an uninspiring grid and still had a rough and unfinished feel to them. Back then, the streets were also largely deserted. The city's two big international hotels were the main focus of life and housed senior officials—and sometimes even their domestic staffs, who cooked their meals in the rooms—for long-term stays.

Although the official census puts Abuja's population at just over a million, Nigerian demographers say that the true number today approaches 5 million, and the city has quickly established itself as one of the biggest and busiest construction markets on the continent, with office buildings, modern housing complexes, and shopping centers rising everywhere.

Unless they do more to join the ongoing building fray, students of African urbanism may look back someday at Yamoussoukro and Abuja as the high-water mark for Western architecture and city design in Africa. With the end of the Cold War, the West's engagement with the continent faded sharply, leaving a void that China has moved energetically to fill since the turn of the century.

Nowadays, there are few major African cities without significant Chinese building projects underway, and the Chinese construction firms plying these markets have moved well beyond their initial penchant for large stadiums to sleek airports, government ministries, hospitals, national theaters, and new central-business-district complexes.

Perhaps the best measure of China's ambition can be found in oil-rich Angola, where the China International Trust and Investment Corporation (CITIC) is completing work on an entire satellite city at Kilamba, 18 miles from Luanda. This new urban development, comprising 750 eight-story apartment buildings, a dozen schools, and more than 100 retail spaces, was built at a cost of $3.5 billion in a mere three years.

With their own economy now slowing, Chinese builders are looking to Africa to pick up the slack, pushing plans for similar satellite cities in numerous markets including Nigeria, Kenya, and Mozambique. Although China has drawn controversy and criticism for employing large numbers of its own workers in the construction of projects like these, its biggest advantage probably lies in the low financing costs its companies can offer because of support from China's state-owned banks.

In most of their big projects in Africa, Chinese companies have used designs that convey an off-the-shelf feel. Their building costs are low, but it is the lack of originality and the rapid execution that have fed a widespread perception among Africans of cheap quality and even poor durability.

Though China is aggressively pursuing development, certain competing players are undaunted, seeing huge, untapped possibilities. Here South Africa is the best example, with its architecture and building firms ranging ever farther in new markets, notably Nigeria.

The opportunities for international architecture and construction firms are potentially enormous. If, as more and more experts are beginning to predict, Africa can sustain its recent strong economic growth, what has long been discounted as the world's poorest continent will instead become the scene for globalization's next big act. ■

Howard W. French, an associate professor at the Columbia University Graduate School of Journalism, is the author of A Continent for the Taking: The Tragedy and Hope of Africa.

JUBA, SOUTH SUD
A road near the dust capital, a few months before South Sudan became the world's newest nation last y Chinese investors ha a jump-start here, as they do in much of Africa.

FORWARD THINKING

Western-trained architects are designing housing, schools, and buildings for social services in Africa's expanding cities and its rural areas. Here's a look at a number of projects currently on the boards. **BY ASAD SYRKETT**

RCHITECTS HAVE long traveled to far-flung corners of the orld in search of inspiration, information, and work. ut few places remain as unfamiliar to most architects as frica—a continent with an area equal to the United States us Europe and half of Asia. According to the World Bank, frica's rural populations are moving into urban centers at ıch a rate that 60 percent of the people will live in cities the middle of the century. Urban areas are booming, ong with opportunity to build.

But many Western architects fail to see the potential. 'eople have very strong notions of Africa based on ecific, singular images like famine and war," says Bjarne astenbroek, whose Amsterdam-based firm, SeARCH, ımpleted the Dutch embassy in Ethiopia in 2005 (RECORD, ecember 2006). Increasingly, however, American architects 'e ignoring these misconceptions, working with not-for-profit undations and government agencies to get commissions.

The most successful designs are those that don't just import ale Western ideas but respond to the local topography and ılture. That's how New York–based design-build practice IoP Architects landed the job to design the graphic, 320,000-uare-foot Botswana Innovation Hub, a new center for chnological and scientific research. Botswana's dry, hot imate and local basket-weaving tradition inspired aspects of IoP's design, explains founding principal William Sharples.

SHoP ARCHITECTS

GABORONE, BOTSWANA The Botswana Innovation Hub (BIH), top and above, will be a 320,000-square-foot center for research in technology and science. SHoP snagged the $100 million commission through a competition sponsored by Bostwana's government, with its plan for a sustainable series of interconnected offices and laboratories; the BIH is designed to be the country's first LEED-certified structure. Government officials, who are still raising construction funds, hope the building will spur growth in the country's tech sector, decreasing the nation's economic dependence on diamond mining by providing a place for local and foreign entrepreneurs to incubate ideas and interact.

View additional images at architecturalrecord.com.

KÉRÉ ARCHITECTURE

LAONGO, BURKINA FASO The late German film and theater director Christoph Schlingensief convinced Berlin-based architect and Burkina Faso native Diébédo Francis Kéré to build the Opera House for Africa, a music-education complex, in the landlocked country known as a center of African f and music. The first phase, which opened in October 2011, is a school for up t 500 local children. The 30-acre master plan includes several clay-and-ceme pavilions that will house a theater, guesthouses, and a health center.

FREDERIC SCHWARTZ ARCHITECTS

DIAMNIADIO, SENEGAL Former Senegalese president Abdoulaye Wade commissioned Nev York-based architect Fred Schwartz to design One Family, One Home, an 800-acre town plan with 3,600 units of affordable housing north of the capital city, Dakar. The new town wi also provide parks, shopping, schools, and other services for a working-class population. Ground was broken for phase one in October 2011, and construction is under way.

EHRLICH ARCHITECTS

ABUJA, NIGERIA In the 1960s, California architect Steven Ehrlich was a Peace Corps volunteer in Africa, working for Morocco's Department of Urban Planning. After his service, Ehrlich traveled around the continent, living in Mali for a time and finally arriving in Zaria, Nigeria, to teach architecture at Ahmadu Bello University. In the mid-1970s he completed his first work on the continent, for the university, a clay-and-mud amphitheater that features bas-relief carvings in a traditional pattern (left). In 2009 Ehrlich won a competition to build the New Abuja Gate City, a 98-acre complex and symbolic entryway into the new Nigerian capital, Abuja. Commissioned by the government and designed to resemble a traditional bow harp, the gateway is meant to symbolize national unity. Its packed program includes a reception hall, children's zoo, gymnasium, and marketplace. It's not clear when construction will begin on the project.

ARON DAVIS DESIGN

KAYONZA, RWANDA The nonprofit Women for Women International (WFW) commissioned New York architect Sharon Davis, who had worked with WFW in Kosovo, to design the Women's Opportunity Center. The 5-acre "mini-village," with classrooms, dormitories, and communal spaces, is meant for women survivors of the war in Rwanda. Canopies of corrugated metal sit atop circular bases of handmade brick, fired and produced by local women. WFW hopes to open the center on March 8, 2013, International Women's Day.

DeBARTOLO ARCHITECTS

SHEBRABER, ETHIOPIA Phoenix-based architect Jack DeBartolo partnered with the nonprofit Engineer Ministries International to design the Shebraber School, a K-12 facility in this rural town near the Ethiopian capital, Addis Ababa. DeBartolo developed both a master plan and construction documents with a group of Arizona State University students of architecture and design. Now under construction, the library, community spaces, and school building are slated for completion in late 2013.

This project and a host of others—including a master plan for affordable housing in Senegal by New York–based Frederic Schwartz Architects and an opera "village" in Burkina Faso by native architect Diébédo Francis Kéré, who practices in Berlin—reflect the ambition of clients across the continent. One prolific client, the Aga Khan Development Network, which has raised the profile of Muslim architecture in Africa with a triennial award, has begun commissioning its own projects, including a university in development in Tanzania, with a master plan by Beyer Blinder Belle of New York and design by Weiss/Manfredi, also of New York, and Mexican firm Legorreta + Legorreta. Smaller but no less significant pro bono work for social initiatives—like Phoenix architect Jack DeBartolo's Shebraber School in Ethiopia or New York–based Sharon Davis's Women's Opportunity Center in Rwanda—points to an ethos of forward-thinking, inventive architecture on a variety of scales.

Such adventurous approaches don't mean there aren't serious challenges for architects who build in Africa. Simply transporting materials to a site can be a major stumbling block. Just ask Louise Braverman, who had rebar and other industrial goods unavailable in the small central African nation of Burundi shipped to the site of a new health complex from "as far afield as Dubai and Israel," she reports. That's one reason why local design and building traditions often figure prominently in the work of Western architects in Africa. Increasingly, this is a way to meet the challenges posed by difficult climates and poor transportation infrastructure. In the years to come, the best of contemporary architecture on the continent is likely to be this hybrid of Western design and local construction methods, rather than an imposition of Western styles in the vein of the colonial era. The goal is "to break the gaps between the Western world and Africa," says Mastenbroek of SeARCH. "We can create a dialogue through architecture." ■

LOUISE BRAVERMAN ARCHITECT

KIGUTU, BURUNDI Louise Braverman's plan for this 40-acre medical campus in Burundi, contracted by the nonprofit organization Village Health Works, includes a 29,000-square-foot women's health center, staff residences, and several other facilities. Though operating rooms require HVAC, the New York-based architect designed most of the buildings on site to be naturally ventilated, and the complex will produce its own electricity with photovoltaics and other energy sources. Phase one of construction—the staff residences—is scheduled for completion this fall.

ADJAYE ASSOCIATES

ELMINA, GHANA London- and New York-based architect David Adjaye is currently developing a number of projects in Africa, including at least two in Ghana. Elmina College, a private international boarding school (left) on 116 acres, is modeled on a Maghreb military fortification, elevated and centered on a quad within its forested site.

PRINCES TOWN, GHANA Adjaye's design for a 52,000-square-foot five-star resort, commissioned by British-Ghanaian developer Soroma Capital, sits along Ghana's southern coast (below). It, too, draws on the country's history, incorporating a former German fort, built in 1683, that is now a World Heritage site.

2003–

WORKac

Headquarters
New York, NY

Founding Partners
Amale Andraos, Dan Wood

2003

WORKac

Höweler + Yoon Architecture

Headquarters
Boston, MA

Founding Partners
J. Meejin Yoon, Eric Höweler

Höweler Yoon Architecture

2006–

over,under

Headquarters
Boston, MA

Founding Partners
Roberto de Oliveira Castro, Rami el Samahy, Chris Grimley, Mark Pasnik

2006

over,under

REX Architecture

Headquarters
New York, NY

Founding Partners
Joshua Prince-Ramus, Erez Ella

Current Partners
Joshua Prince-Ramus

REX Architecture

Hangil Book House
2004

Architect
SHoP

Location
Seoul, South Korea

Client
Hangil Publishing Co.

Ben Gurion International Airport
2004

Architect
Safdie Architects

Location
Tel Aviv, Israel

Client
Israel Airport Authority

New Jiang Wan Cultural Center
2004–2005

Architect
RTKL

Location
China, Beijing

Client
Shanghai Oriental International

Ministructure No. 16 (BookBar)
2004–2006

Architect
Michael Maltzan Architecture

Location
Jinhua Architecture Park, Jinhua, China

Client
Ai Weiwei

Shanghai American School
2004–2006

Architect
Studio Shanghai

Location
Shanghai, China

Client
Shanghai American School

Menara Karya Tower
2004–2007

Architect
Arquitectonica

Location
Indonesia, Jarkata

Client
PT Karyadeka Pancamurni

Newspaper Cafe
2004–2007

TOSHIKO MORI ARCHITECT

Architect
Toshiko Mori

Location
Jinhua Architecture Park, Jinhua City, China

Client
Jindong New District Architecture Park

Almaty Financial District–Kazkommertsbank Headquarters
2004–2008

SOM

Architect
Skidmore, Owings & Merrill

Location
Almaty, Kazakhstan

Client
Capital Partners LLP

Esentai Tower
2004–2008

SOM

Architect
Skidmore, Owings & Merrill

Location
Almaty, Kazakhstan

Client
Capital Partners LLP

Microsoft European Headquarters
2004–2009

ARQUITECTONICA

Architect
Arquitectonica

Location
Paris, France

Client
Microsoft Corporation, Generali Immobilier / Groupe Generali

Zifeng Tower
2004–2009

SOM

Architect
Skidmore, Owings & Merrill

Location
Nanjing, China

Client
Greenland Group, Nanjing Guozi Greenland Financial Center Co. Ltd. / Nanjing Greenland International Commercial Center Co. Ltd.

Wuhan Tiandi
2004–2009

STUDIO SHANGHAI

Architect
Studio Shanghai

Location
Wuhan, China

Client
Shui On Land

Chongqing Tiandi
2004–2009

Architect
Studio Shanghai

Location
Chongqing, China

Client
Shui On Land

Cambridge Water Town
2004–2009

Architect
Studio Shanghai

Location
Shanghai, China

Client
SPG

Abdul Aziz Al-Babtain Cultural Waqf Tower
2004–2010

Architect
NBBJ

Location
Kuwait City, Kuwait

Client
Abdul Aziz Al Babtain

International Finance Centre
2004–2011

Architect
Arquitectonica

Location
Seoul, South Korea

Client
American International Group, AIG Global Real Estate Development

Torre de Cristal
2004–2011

Architect
Pelli Clarke Pelli Architects

Location
Madrid, Spain

Local Architect
Ortiz Leon Arquitectos

Client
Mutua Madrileña Automovilista

Tianjin Global Financial Center
2004–2011

Architect
Skidmore, Owings & Merrill

Location
Tianjin, China

Client
Finance Street Jinta (Tianjin) Real Estate Co., LTD

Reflections at Keppel Bay
2004–2011

Architect
Studio Daniel Libeskind

Location
Singapore, Singapre

Client
Keppel Land International

STUDIO DANIEL LIBESKIND

Palazzo Lombardia
2004–2013

Architect
Pei Cobb Freed & Partners Architects

Location
Milan, Italy

Client
Regione Lombardia

PEI COBB FREED & PARTNERS Architects LLP

Atlantis at The Palms
2005–2008

Architect
Wimberly Allison Tong & Goo

Location
Dubai, United Arab Emirates

Client
Kerzner International

WATG

Mahler 4
2005

Architect
Rafael Viñoly Architects

Location
Amsterdam, Netherlands

Client
Mahler 4 Consortium; G&S Vastgoed, Fortis Vastgoed Ontwikkeling, ING Vastgoed

RAFAEL VIÑOLY ARCHITECTS

Yad Vashem Holocaust History Museum
2005

Architect
Safdie Architects

Location
Jerusalem, Israel

Client
Holocaust Martyrs' and Heroes' Remembrance Authority

SafdieArchitects

MegaBox
2005

Architect
Jerde Partnership

Location
Hong Kong, China

Architect of Record
Wong Tung & Partners Ltd.

Client
Kerry Properties

JERDE

Sanlitun North
2005–2006

Architect
LOT-EK

Location
Beijing, China

Client
Guo Feng Development

Wellcome Trust Sanger Institute
2005

Architect
NBBJ

Location
Cambridgeshire, UK

Client
Wellcome Trust

Songdo International Business District
2005–2008

Architect
Kohn Pedersen Fox Associates

Location
Incheon, South Korea

Client
Gale International

The Sail at Marina Bay
2005–2008

Architect
NBBJ

Location
Singapore, Singapore

Associate Architect
Team Design Architects Private Limited

Client
City Developments Limited & AIG Asian Real Estate Partners, L.P.

City of Dreams
2005–2009

Architect
Arquitectonica

Location
Macau, China

Client
Melco Crown Entertainment

Xi'an City Gateway
2005–2009

Architect
Goettsch Partners

Location
Xi'an, China

Client
Shanghai Greenland Xi'an Property Co.

Arcapita Bank Headquarters
2005–2009

Architect
Skidmore, Owings & Merrill

Location
Manama, Bahrain

Client
Arcapita Bank, Arcapita Ltd

Herning Museum of Contemporary Art
2005–2009

Architect
Steven Holl Architects

Location
Herning, Denmark

Local Architect
Kjaer and Richter A/S

Client
Herning Center of the Arts

The Gate Towers, Sun Tower and Sky Tower
2005–2010

Architect
Arquitectonica

Location
Abu Dhabi, United Arab Emirates

Client
Aldar Properties PJSC

Bitexco Financial Tower
2005–2010

Architect
Carlos Zapata Studio

Location
Ho Chi Minh City, Vietnam

Client
Bitexco Group

China Huaneng Group Headquarters
2005–2010

Architect
Kohn Pedersen Fox Associates

Location
Beijing, China

Client
China Huaneng Group

Kerry Parkside Towers
2005–2010

Architect
Kohn Pedersen Fox Associates

Location
Shanghai, China

Client
Shanghai Pudong Kerry City Properties Co. Ltd.

City of Capitals
2005–2010

Architect
NBBJ

Location
Moscow, Russia

Client
Capital Group

Giant Interactive Group Corporate Headquarters
2005–2010

Architect
Morphosis Architects

Location
Shanghai, China

Local Architect
SURV

Client
Giant Interactive Group

Al Hamra Tower
2005–2011

Architect
Skidmore, Owings & Merrill

Location
Kuwait City, Kuwait

Client
Ajial Real Estate and Entertainment; Al Hamra Real Estate

Hysan Place
2005–2012

Architect
Kohn Pedersen Fox Associates

Location
Hong Kong, China

Client
Hysan Development Co. Ltd.

Win Sing AIT Residential Towers
2005–2013

Architect
Moore Ruble Yudell Architects & Planners

Location
Taipei, Taiwan

Client
Win Sing Development

Cayan Tower
2005–2013

Architect
Skidmore, Owings & Merrill

Location
Dubai, United Arab Emirates

Client
Cayan Investment and Development, JADE Development Co.

Tata Consultancy Services
2005–

Architect
Tod Williams Billie Tsien Architects

Location
Mumbai, India

Local Architect
Somaya & Kalappa Consultants Pvt Ltd.

Client
TATA Consultancy Services, LTD.

798 Arts District Vision Plan
2006

SASAKI

Architect
Sasaki Associates

Location
Beijing, China

Client
Urbis Development

Singapore Changi International Airport Terminal 2
2006

Gensler

Architect
Gensler

Location
Changi, Singapore

Client
RSP Architects, Inc.

Pan-Gyo Housing
2006

MACK ARCH

Architect
MACK Architect(s)

Location
Seongnam, South Korea

Client
Korea National Housing Corporation

China Science and Technology Museum
2006–2009

RTKL
AN ARCADIS COMPANY

Architect
RTKL1

Location
Beijing, China

Client
China Science and Technology Museum

Dolce Vita Tejo Mall
2006–2009

RTKL
AN ARCADIS COMPANY

Architect
RTKL

Location
Lisbon, Portugal

Client
Chamartin Immobiliaria and ING Real Estate

Soccer City (FNB Stadium)
2006–2009

Architect
Populous

Location
Johannesburg, South Africa

Client
Johannesburg Development Agency

Vanke Center (Horizontal Skyscraper)
2006–2009

Architect
Steven Holl Architects

Location
Shenzhen, China

Associate Architect
CCDI

Client
Vanke Real Estate Co.

Cultural Center
2006–2010

Architect
Bernard Tschumi Architects

Location
Bordeaux Cenon, France

Client
Town of Cenon

Agricultural Bank of China and Construction Bank of China
2006–2011

Architect
Arquitectonica

Location
Shanghai, China

Client
CITIC Pacific Group

Jack Nicklaus Golf Club of Korea
2006–2011

Architect
Cannon Design

Location
New Songdo City, South Korea

Client
The Gale Company

O-14 Tower
2006–2011

Architect
RUR Architecture PC

Location
Dubai, United Arab Emirates

Client
Creekside Development Corporation

Tata Medical Centre Cancer Hospital
2006–2011

Architect
Cannon Design

Location
Kolkata, India

Client
Tata Trust

CANNONDESIGN

VanDusen Botanical Garden Visitor Centre
2006–2011

Architect
Perkins + Will

Location
Vancouver, Canada

Client
City of Vancouver

PERKINS+WILL

London Olympic Stadium
2006–2012

Architect
Populous

Location
London, UK

Client
Olympic Delivery Authority

POPULOUS

US Embassy
2006–2012

Architect
Sorg Architects

Location
Libreville, Gabon

Client
US Department of State, Bureau of Overseas Building Operations

SORG ARCHITECTS

UNITED STATES OF AMERICA EMBASSY

Zhengzhou Greenland Plaza
2006–2012

Architect
Skidmore, Owings & Merrill

Location
Zhengzhou, China

Client
Greenland Group

SOM

JW Marriott Hotel
2006–2013

Architect
Carlos Zapata Studio

Location
Hanoi, Vietnam

Client
Bitexco Group

CARLOS ZAPATA STUDIO

Leatop Plaza
2006–2013

Architect
JAHN

Location
Guangzhou, China

Client
Guangdong Leatop Real Estate Investment Co. Ltd.

Lingnan Tiandi
2006–2013

Architect
Studio Shanghai

Location
Foshan, China

Client
Shui On Land

Pearl River Tower
2006–2013

Architect
Skidmore, Owings & Merrill

Location
Guangzhou, China

Client
The Guangzhou Pearl River Tower Properties Co., Ltd

SIP Hengyu International Center
2006–2013

Architect
Goettsch Partners

Location
Suzhou, China

Client
Suzhou Industrial Park Hengyu Real Estate Co. Ltd.

The Nile Corniche
2006–

Architect
Michael Graves & Associates

Location
Cairo, Egypt

Client
Qatari Diar Real Estate and Tourism Investment Company - Egypt

Shanghai Tower
2006–

Architect
Gensler

Location
Shanghai, China

Client
Shanghai City Construction Investment Development Company

Phare Tower
2006–

Architect
Morphosis Architects

Location
La Défense, France

Consulting Architect
SRA ARchitectes

Client
SCI CNIT Development

morphosis

Al Waab City
2006–

Architect
AECOM

Location
Doha, Qatar

Client
Msheireb Properties

AECOM

Princess Nora Bint Abdulrahman University
2009–2013

Architect
Perkins + Will

Location
Riyadh, Saudi Arabia

Client
Kingdom of Saudi Arabia - Ministry of Finance; Ministry of Higher Education

PERKINS+WILL

Beyond Mega-: Sustaining Superlatives

The biggest, tallest, and most advanced technological emblems produced by US architects have long been objects of fetishization and emulation abroad. In 1965, describing the other-worldly impression upon European visitors of "machine-absolute" buildings like Skidmore, Owings & Merrill's Chase Manhattan Bank in New York, Peter Smithson wrote that they "arouse the strongest cargo-cult feelings in foreigners, and are truly hints of *une architecture autre*."[1] His term referred to the shock of Melanesian islanders at the sight of US warplanes and their cargo during World War II, and to the elaborate cult ceremonies they invented to copy the forms of these planes in bamboo and paint, hoping that such mimicry would bring the same abundance from the gods. Smithson interpreted the "rash of black towers" in the United Kingdom as signs of just such a cargo-cult mentality, intended to signify a "nearness to the fountain of technological culture." Henry-Russell Hitchcock linked the fetish character of such products with the professionalization of the firms that produced them, predicting that in the future it would be "not only the American skyscraper that has come to be adopted abroad but, up to a point at least, the methods of its design and production."[2]

In its migration from the US outward first to Asia and now to the Middle East, the evolution of the extreme building type known as the "supertall" tower has thus far resulted less conspicuously in the adoption of US office models, as Hitchcock predicted, than in the proliferation of buildings abroad by US architects. Following a resumption of the competition for the world's tallest building between the World Trade Center in New York City and the Sears (today Willis) Tower in Chicago in the 1970s, dormant since the completion of the Empire State Building four decades earlier, five of the six successors as the world's tallest building—all of them abroad—have been by US architects. Such firms figure among the handful of offices globally which specialize in the supertall type, a short list that includes Adrian Smith + Gordon Gill (AS+GG), Skidmore, Owings & Merrill (SOM), Pelli Clarke

① Peter Smithson, "The fine and the folk: An essay on McKim, Mead and White and the American tradition," *Architectural Design* (August 1965): 394.

② Henry-Russell Hitchcock, "The Rise to World Prominence of American Architecture," *Zodiac 8: America*, ed. Bruno Alfieri (Milan: 1961): 2.

1980

1984 King Khaled Airport in Riyadh (HOK) world's largest airport

1985 King Saud University in Riyadh (HOK+4 Consortium) world's largest university

1990–1991 First Persian Gulf War

1993 US Green Building Council established

1996 Shun Hing Square in Shenzhen first supertall tower outside the US

1998 Petronas Towers in Kuala Lumpur (Cesar Pelli & Associates) first world's tallest tower outside the US

Pelli Architects, Kohn Pedersen Fox (KPF), and Gensler. All of these firms competed in 2009 to design the world's tallest tower in Jeddah, Saudi Arabia; won by AS+GG, the Kingdom Tower, scheduled for completion in 2019, will usher in the era of towers occupiable above the 600-meter height, which constitute the wholly new category of "megatall" buildings.

Significantly, the desire for the biggest and tallest is increasingly bound to the rhetoric of expertise in "sustainable" energy technologies, achieved through similarly capital-intensive means. This fusion of mega-scale with "advanced" environmental performance is clear in AS+GG's proposals for Tianfu Ecological City in China (2011–) and the headquarters of Masdar in Abu Dhabi (2008–), the centerpiece of the company's planned ecological showpiece, Masdar City. KPF's ongoing Songdo City in Seoul, an area within the Incheon Free Economic Zone intended to lure international investment and commerce, is currently being touted as the pilot candidate for a new LEED rating system at the urban scale, LEED-ND (for Neighborhood Development).[3] Responding to criticism that the resources required for such mega-scale projects are by definition unsustainable, Adrian Smith has argued for the connection between scale and environmental performance, claiming that while some feel that "any building over 60 stories is an inefficient ego trip if you create a city more compact, that is far more sustainable than a suburban model."[4]

The emergence of such regulatory categories reflects the growing expectation of global firms to engineer large-scale systems through extreme technological means, whether by means of the megatall tower or the sustainable urban sector. The arenas for such territorial systems-planning abroad have shifted from the industrial cities and military complexes of the postwar period to the consumer landscapes of mega-airports and shopping malls, free trade zones, and prototype eco-cities.[5] Smithson's concluding remarks on US architects in 1965 might be taken to refer just as well to this shift in technological cargo-cult to the mega-scale and its increasingly territorial ambitions: "American architects almost have it made: if they could only stop worrying about architecture."[6] — MK

③ Kelly DiNardo, "South Korea's Aerotropolis Blueprint Is No Flight of Fancy," *The Guardian* (January 15, 2013), http://www.theguardian.com/world/2013/jan/15/songdo-south-korea-aerotropolis (last accessed October 22, 2014); Elizabeth Woyke, "Very Smart Cities," *Forbes*, September 9, 2009, *http://www.forbes.com/2009/09/03/korea-gale-meixi-technology-21-century-cities-09-songdo.html* (last accessed October 22, 2014).

④ "The Foundation of Supertalls," interview with Adrian Smith, *Discovery Channel Magazine* (April 2012): 73.

⑤ Keller Easterling, *Extrastatecraft: The Power of Infrastructure Space* (London and New York: Verso, 2014).

⑥ Smithson, "The fine and the folk: An essay on McKim, Mead and White and the American tradition": 397.

2000 LEED (Leadership in Energy and Environmental Design) green building certification system established

2004 Taipei 101 in Taiwan world's tallest tower

2006 Abu Dhabi announces plan for Masdar, world's first zero-carbon, zero-waste city

2008 World's largest mall opens in Dubai

2009 AS+GG wins competition to design world's tallest tower in Jeddah, Saudi Arabia

2010 Burj Khalifa in Dubai (Skidmore, Owings & Merrill) world's tallest tower

2012 AS+GG announces master plan for Tianfu Ecological City

1998

2020

1 Afghanistan War

2003 Iraq War

2014

World's Tallest Buildings

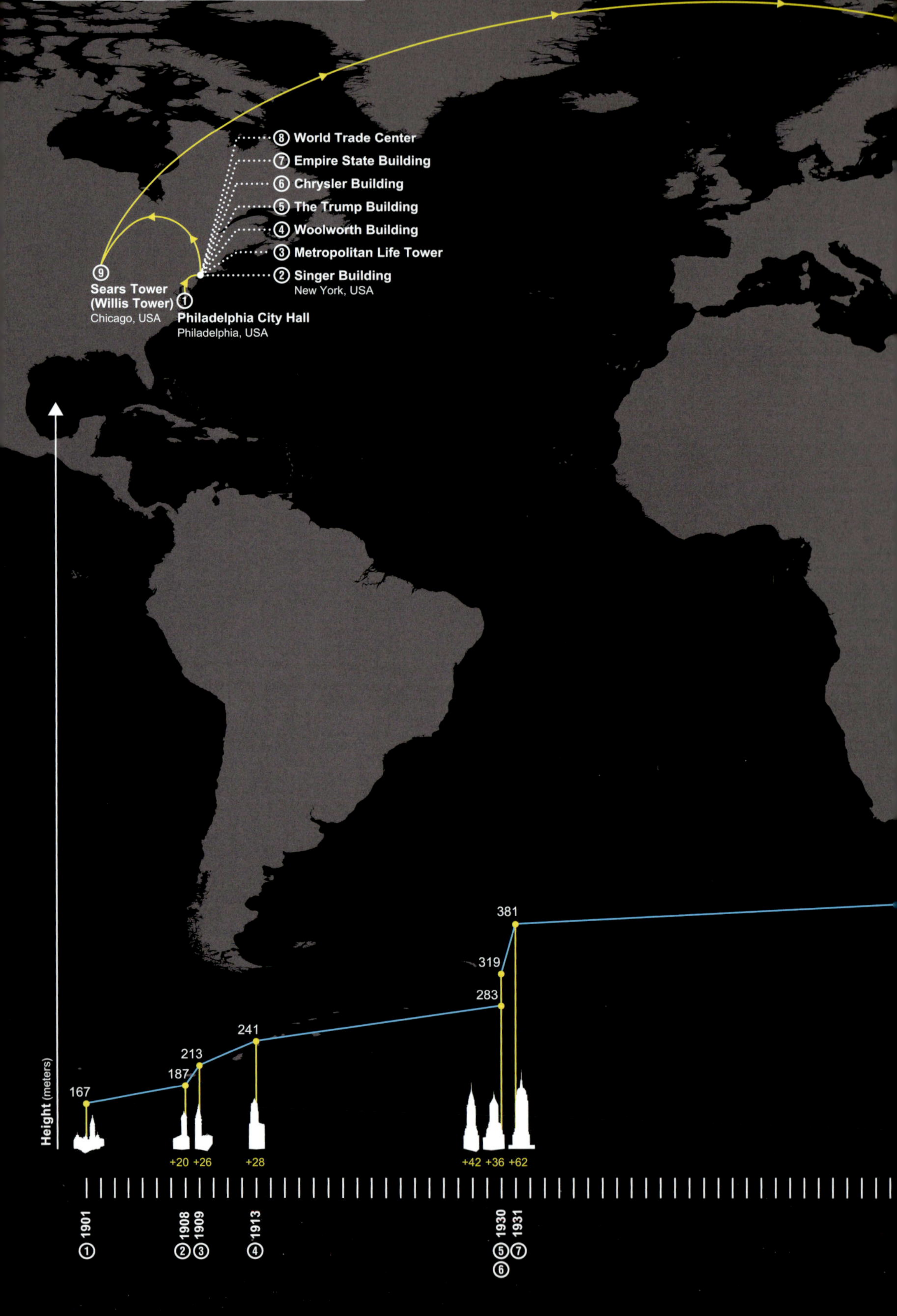

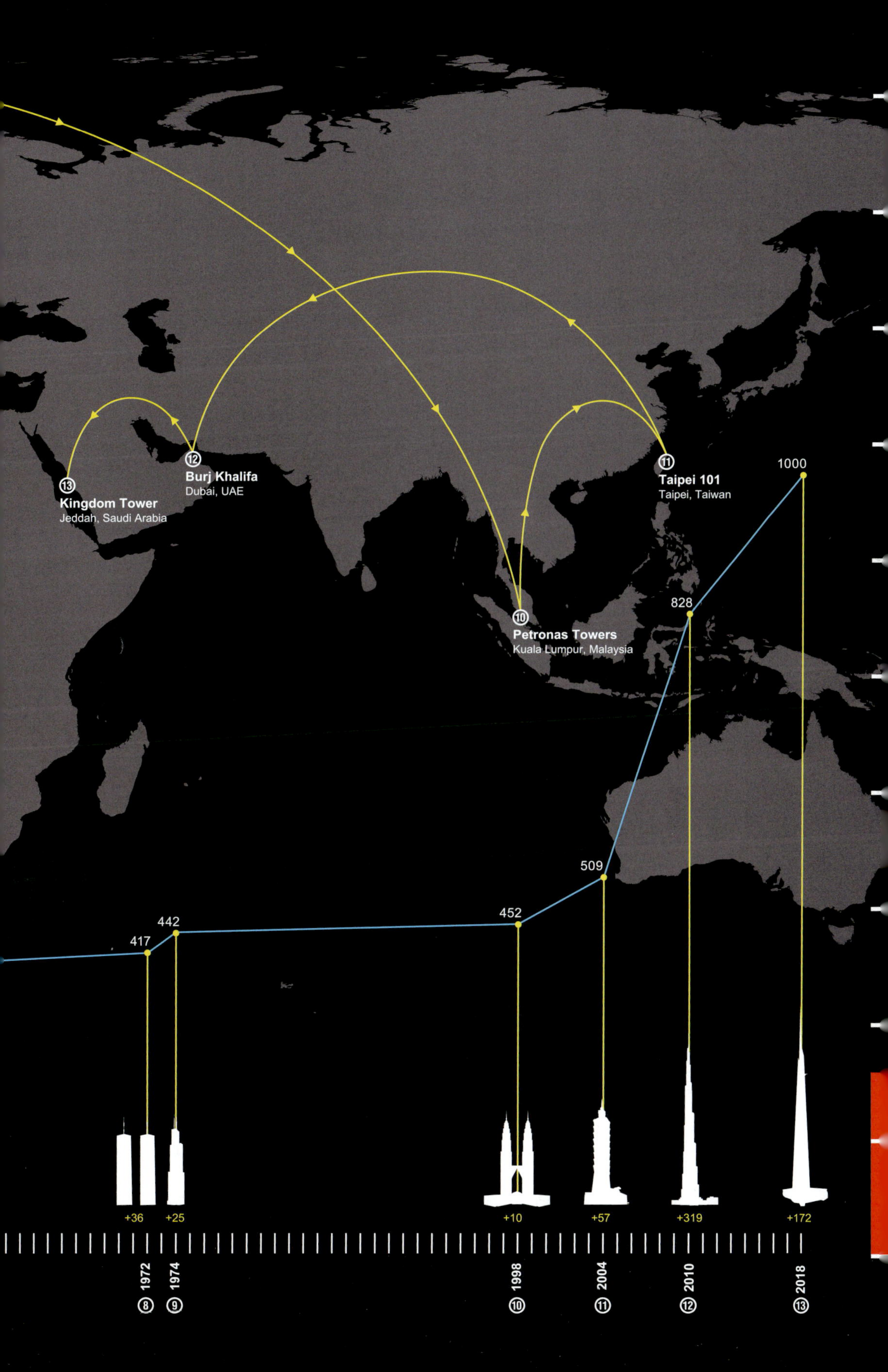

⑬ Kingdom Tower
Jeddah, Saudi Arabia
⑫ Burj Khalifa
Dubai, UAE
⑪ Taipei 101
Taipei, Taiwan
⑩ Petronas Towers
Kuala Lumpur, Malaysia
417
442
452
509
828
1000
+36
+25
+10
+57
+319
+172
1972 ⑧
1974 ⑨
1998 ⑩
2004 ⑪
2010 ⑫
2018 ⑬

ARCHITECTURE

SEPTEMBER 1996

$8.95 US / $11.00 CAN

IN THIS ISSUE:
Vancouver's Hidden Talents
Asia's Tallest Towers
Europe's Single-Artist Museums

INTERNATIONAL ARCHITECTURE

High-strength concrete is enabling American architects to design the highest structures in the world.

ASIA'S TALLEST TOWERS

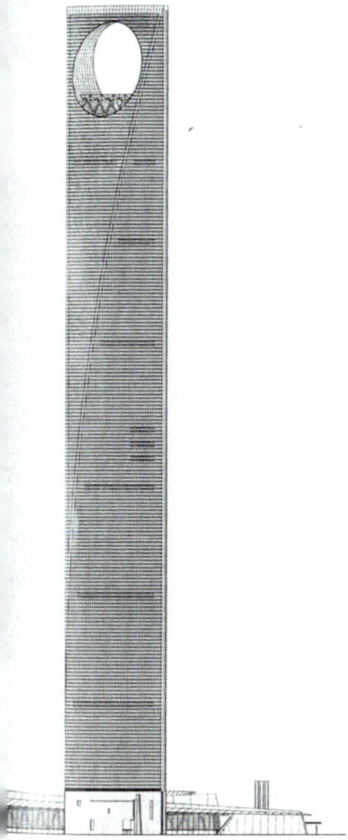

E: Kohn Pedersen Fox Associates' meter-tall Shanghai World Finan- Center relies on concrete core and reinforced perimeter frame.

Asian cities with surging economies and ambitious urban plans are now hosts to the tallest buildings in the world. Previous record-breaking towers depended on steel frames, including Chicago's Sears Tower (1974) designed by Skidmore, Owings & Merrill (SOM) and New York's World Trade Center (1974) designed by Minoru Yamasaki and Emery Roth and Sons. Today, high-strength concrete is the material of choice for super-tall buildings. Cesar Pelli & Associates' Petronas Towers in Kuala Lumpur, Malaysia, and two skyscrapers by SOM and Kohn Pedersen Fox (KPF) Associates in Shanghai, China, will be constructed of concrete boasting strengths of as much as 12,000 pounds per square inch.

Loosely defined as concrete with compressive strength that exceeds 6,000 pounds per square inch, high-strength concrete carries loads more efficiently, requiring smaller, lighter structural members than conventional concrete. At the same time, high-strength concrete has greater damping characteristics, which enable it to absorb more external forces—reducing sway and improving occupant comfort—than a steel structure of equal strength. As Raymond Crane, managing principal at Ove Arup & Partners, explains, "The main criterion in the design of a super-tall building is acceleration control under wind loading"—an especially important consideration when designing high-rises in typhoon-prone regions such as Shanghai.

Greater access to high-strength concrete, improved methods of pumping concrete up to high elevations, and refined formwork have propelled high-strength concrete's application over the last 10 years. These technological advances, however, are less earth-shattering than the cultural implications of the towers—they are the first skyscrapers with record-breaking heights to be built on foreign shores. Cesar Pelli's 452-meter Petronas Towers in Kuala Lumpur captured the title of world's tallest in April, following a controversial decision by the Council on Tall Buildings and Urban Habitat to include the towers' stainless steel masts in calculating their height. The masts gave the Petronas Towers the boost needed to surpass the Sears Tower—despite the fact that their highest occupied floors are 45 meters lower than the Chicago skyscraper's. The council ruled that the 66-meter masts are integral to the buildings' design, while the Sears Tower's radio antennas are not.

While Chicagoans lament the loss of their city's 22-year-old record, residents of Kuala Lumpur may not have much time to gloat. Foundation work is beginning in Shanghai for KPF's 460-meter Shanghai World Financial Center. And in Hong Kong, Arthur C.S. Kwok Architects & Associates is waiting for final approval from the civil aviation authority to proceed with plans for the 468-meter-tall Nina Tower, which is projected to reach more than 500 meters with the assistance of a mast. Engineered by Ove Arup & Partners, the Nina Tower will incorporate a reinforced concrete core and high-strength concrete columns with external steel bracing.

In light of the Petronas controversy, the Council on Tall Buildings decided to expand its record keeping on super towers. While the distance to the top of the tower or mast will remain the standard for determining height, data on the heights of the highest occupied floor and the roof will also be collected. For now, Chicagoans can console themselves with the world's highest observation deck atop the Sears Tower.—*Ann C. Sullivan*

Petronas Towers
Kuala Lumpur, Malaysia
Cesar Pelli & Associates, Architect

Cesar Pelli & Associates' 88-story twin towers for Petronas, the Malaysian national oil company, were topped off in March at 452 meters. Designed with Adamson Associates of Toronto, Ontario, the Petronas headquarters building is part of the first phase of Kuala Lumpur City Centre, an 18 million-square-foot commercial and retail development on the 100-acre urban site of a former racetrack.

Scheduled to open early next year, the two towers are identical: slender cylinders measuring 46 meters in diameter are connected by a two-story pedestrian bridge at levels 41 and 42 and flanked by narrower, 44-story towers, called "bustles," that attach to their north face. Clad in stainless steel and glass panels, the main towers are set back at levels 60, 73, 82, 85, and 88, and culminate in steel spires.

New York City-based Thornton-Tomasetti Engineers, with Malaysian engineers Ranhill Bersekutu, designed the structure so that a central concrete core and concrete perimeter columns carry the vertical loads. At the setbacks at floors 60, 73, and 82, the columns slope over three stories to eliminate the need for transfer girders, which would not fit within the towers' standard 4-meter floor heights.

Lateral strength is bolstered by concrete ring beams that link the columns to frame the main towers and bustles. Unlike the deep spandrel beams typical of concrete high-rises, the ring beams feature a haunched shape to provide clearance for mechanical components within the ceiling plenum. To balance vertical loads, concrete outrigger beams connect the central core and perimeter frame between levels 38 and 40.

Structural steel is limited to areas requiring longer spans and smaller, easy-to-install members. On each level, wide-flange steel beams carry concrete-filled metal-deck floor

FRED BYFIELD

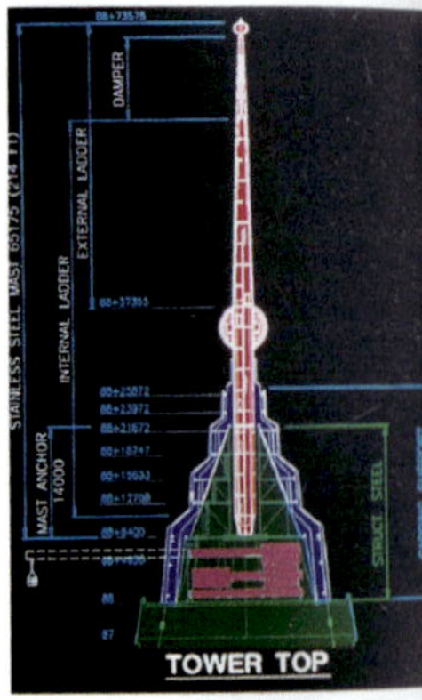

TOP LEFT: Petronas Towers surpass Sea Tower's height by 10 meters.
TOP RIGHT AND ABOVE: Pinnacle and ma are framed in steel.
AXONOMETRIC: Shorter towers enlarge floor plates of lower stories.
FACING PAGE, TOP LEFT: Hinged bridge supports extend 51 meters.
FACING PAGE, CENTER LEFT: Bridge's preassembled central section was raised i tact with hydraulic jacks.
FACING PAGE, BOTTOM LEFT: Twin steel girders support bridge's bolted steel frame and glazing.
FACING PAGE, TOP RIGHT: Perimeter columns slope to accommodate setbacks without transfer girders.
FACING PAGE, CENTER RIGHT: Haunched beams accommodate lights and ducts in ceilings.
FACING PAGE, BOTTOM RIGHT: Triangular and semicircular extensions cantilever beyond stepped column.

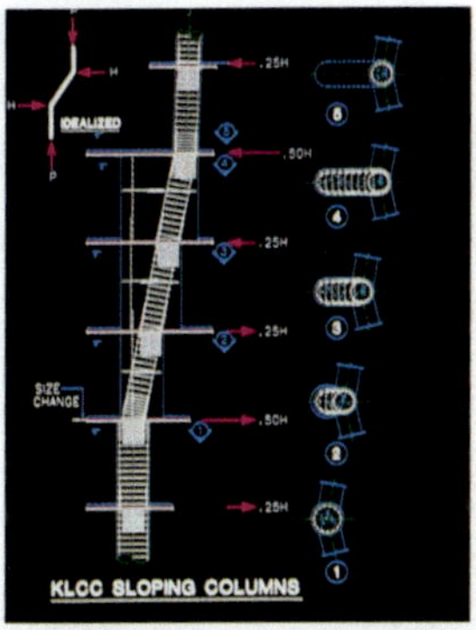

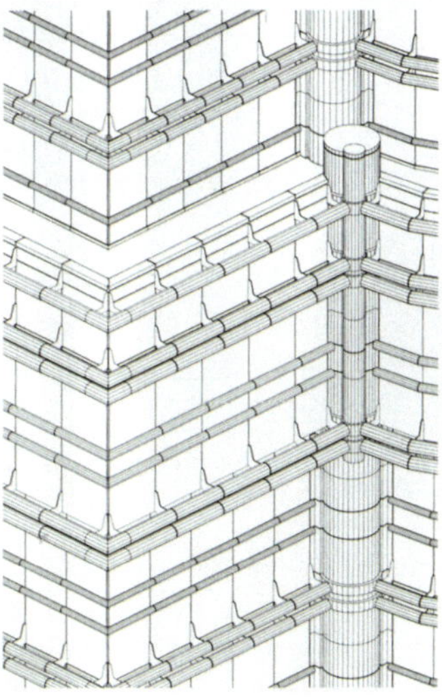

slabs; prefabricated steel trusses support semicircular and triangular floor extensions that cantilever outside the column ring. Above level 84, columns and ring beams are fabricated of steel, as are the towers' pinnacle and 66-meter mast.

Steel is also the primary structural material of the two-level, 58-meter-long skybridge, which is supported on twin parallel steel girders. The secondary framing consists of steel beams bolted to steel columns that bear on the two main girders. Like wishbones, pairs of steel pipes diagonally extend from spring points at level 29 to prop the bridge at midspan. Spherical bearings at these spring points accommodate the towers' torsional movement.

Fortunately, wind loads are not high in Kuala Lumpur. Expansion joints allow the bridge to tolerate building movement up to 800 millimeters, reducing the impact of deflection on bridge glazing; a box girder in the center of the bridge helps resist twisting. The inherent damping characteristics and stiffness of the towers' large concrete sections will keep occupant perception of building movement and acceleration to a minimum, predicts wind consultant Rowan Williams Davies & Irwin of Guelph, Ontario.

Soil conditions also did not pose formidable problems. Kuala Lumpur is built up on stiff, silty sand with limestone bedrock buried 60 to 180 meters below grade. The distance to bedrock made it impractical to extend bearing piles. Instead, 208 concrete friction elements called Barrette piles distribute the towers' loads. Cast through slurry-wall techniques, the rectangular barrettes measure 2.8 by 1.2 meters and extend 60 to 115 meters. Twin 4.5-meter-thick, cast-concrete raft foundations mediate between foundation piles and tower columns, and an 800-millimeter-thick perimeter diaphragm wall encircles the site.

Shanghai World Financial Center
Shanghai, China
Kohn Pedersen Fox Associates, Architect

If construction begins next year and proceeds on schedule, Kohn Pedersen Fox (KPF) Associates' Shanghai World Financial Center will capture the title of world's tallest building from the Petronas Towers and replace its neighbor, the Jin Mao Building, as China's tallest. The chiseled profile of this latest contender, to be completed in 2001, will stand 460 meters tall and overshadow Malaysia's twin towers by 8 meters, without resorting to spires, masts, or antennas.

Instead, the office and hotel tower terminates in a giant aperture carved out of a tapered stainless steel- and glass-clad shaft. Inspired by a Chinese moongate, a motif often found in Chinese gardens as an opening inserted in walls or partitions, the aperture is intended to reduce wind load at the top of the tower.

This sculptural, abstract terminus contrasts dramatically with the Jin Mao Building's pagoda-inspired pinnacle to the west. Commissioned by a division of the Tokyo-based Mori Building Company, the World Financial Center will be the second of three high-rises to be built as part of a new financial center in the Pudong district.

Instead of designing a lateral system based on a central structural core, engineer Ove Arup & Partners specified a perimeter tube system which comprises steel columns encased in reinforced concrete for resisting lateral loads and internal steel columns for carrying gravity loads. The perimeter columns are spaced 3.6 meters on center and connected at each floor by concrete-encased steel spandrel beams.

"The steel allowed us to make the columns' sections quite small; encasing them in concrete gave us the advantage of high damping characteristics," explains Raymond Crane, managing principal at Ove Arup & Partners. "The perimeter tube is a very efficient structural form, be-

LEFT: Tower terminates in circular aperture inspired by moongate.
BELOW: Pedestrian bridge will span tower's 54-meter-diameter aperture.
BELOW LEFT AND CENTER: Square base tapers to 78-by-3-meter apex.
SECTION: Floors above mid-height hotel lobby shift to oblong plan.
FACING PAGE, TOP: Bridgeless preliminary scheme shows exposed steel framing.
FACING PAGE, BOTTOM: Stainless steel and reflective glass panels clad perimeter structures.

EDGE MEDIA RENDERINGS

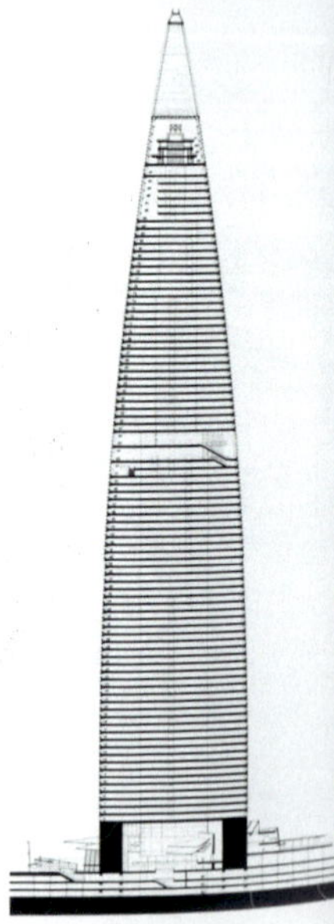

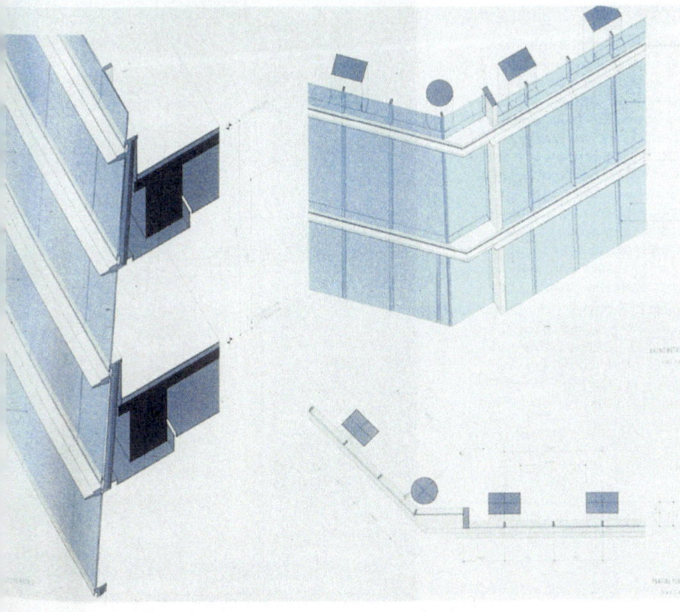

cause the entire width of the building is utilized to resist lateral loads, rather than more conventional systems that rely on cores only, or cores with outriggers."

Economics, however, have altered the design. Under the control of Tokyo-based Shimizu Corporation, the architect and engineer of record who won the construction bid, Arup's preliminary scheme has evolved into a hybrid double-tube structure. Shimizu essentially reversed the ratio of steel to concrete: The perimeter columns will remain the same size and spaced at 3.6-meter centers, but are now specified as steel-reinforced concrete. To supplement the slender perimeter columns, Shimizu added a second concrete tube around the core. The core and perimeter are tied together approximately every 15 levels to increase lateral resistance.

KPF and project architect Forest Overseas encountered the same soil conditions that challenged Skidmore, Owings & Merrill in designing the Jin Mao Building. KPF's tower relies on friction piles extending 50 to 70 meters below a 4-meter-thick concrete foundation mat.

Chinese building codes impose notoriously strict drift limitations to protect against the typhoons and earthquakes that plague the region. While the irregular geometry of the Jin Mao Building tends to break the wind and reduce exterior pressure, the World Financial Center stands like a solid block, 78 meters wide at the top. To reduce drift and increase occupant comfort, Shimizu specified "super-sloshing," tuned-mass dampers: eight 7.5-meter-diameter, 5-meter-tall tanks of water will be mounted in groups of four on the northeast and southwest ends of the tower's apex. Their volume and position are calculated so that, in a wind storm, the movement of the water in the tanks will counterbalance the motion of the building.

Jin Mao Building Shanghai, China Skidmore, Owings & Merrill, Architect

Difficult site conditions influenced Skidmore, Owings & Merrill's structural design of the Jin Mao Building in Shanghai. The region is prone to typhoons, susceptible to earthquakes, and situated on a delta of clay and sand with no bedrock within 100 meters. Despite the harsh environment, the 88-story tower—which will be the tallest in China—is now under construction and scheduled for completion in late 1998. Designed for the China Shanghai Foreign Trade Centre Company, it is part of a 3 million-square-foot, mixed-use development in the nation's developing Pudong district.

SOM designed the 421-meter-high office and hotel tower to withstand natural forces through a combination of high-strength concrete and structural steel. Above grade, a reinforced-concrete core and eight perimeter supercolumns are linked by outrigger trusses to resist lateral and vertical loads. Beneath the frame is a 4-meter-thick concrete mat and a grid of 429 hollow steel piles extending 65 meters. Stiff sand below the piles provides some bearing capacity, but the foundation primarily depends on friction for support.

The concrete core measures 850 millimeters thick at the base and 450 millimeters thick at the top. On the first 52 floors of office space, the core is filled with elevators and mechanical rooms; for additional strength and stiffness, it is spanned by concrete web walls. In the hotel above level 53, the core is open, creating a 34-story atrium with glazed elevator shafts at its center. Corridors are cantilevered off the core.

Fabricated from structural steel sections encased in reinforced concrete, the eight supercolumns are positioned in pairs and centered on four sides of the tower. The rectangular composites measure 1.5 by 5 meters at the bottom and taper toward the top. The floor plates

STEINKAMP/BALLOGG

ABOVE: SOM's 88-story Jin Mao Building tapers to structural steel spire inspired by pagoda.
TOP RIGHT: Granite, stainless steel, and aluminum curtain-wall mock-up was tested for wind resistance.
CENTER RIGHT: Octagon-shaped core and set of eight columns invoke Chinese lucky number eight.
RIGHT: Solid core opens to atrium at level 53. Steel outrigger trusses divide tower into three segments.
FACING PAGE, TOP LEFT: 429 steel piles reach 65 meters below surface.
FACING PAGE, TOP RIGHT: Outrigger trusses combined with core improve tower's wind resistance.
FACING PAGE, CENTER: Pairs of supercolumns are aligned on each face; steel columns anchor diagonals.
FACING PAGE, BOTTOM: Pin connections at outrigger trusses reconcile structural members' movement.

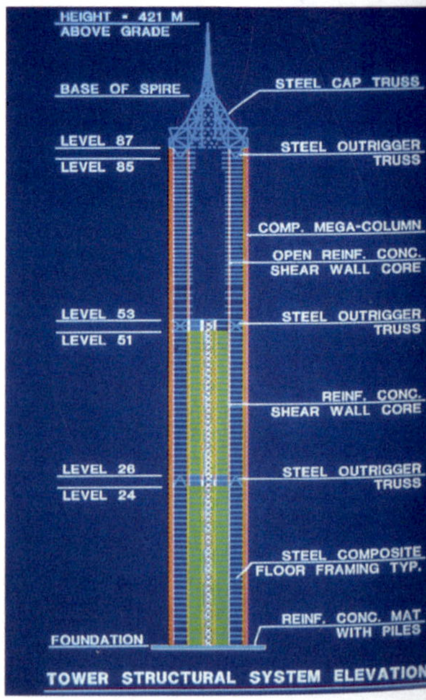

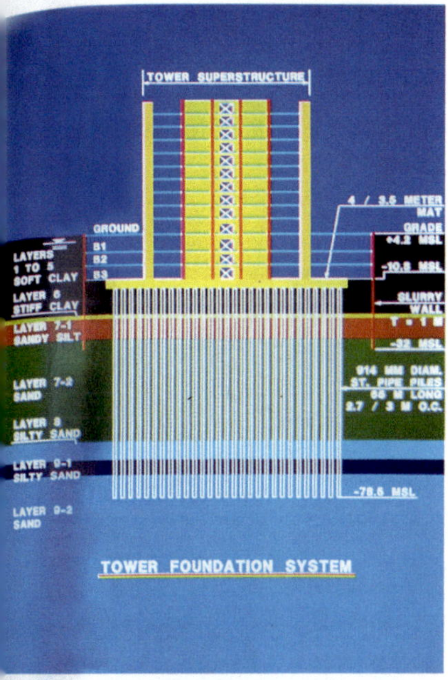

TOWER FOUNDATION SYSTEM

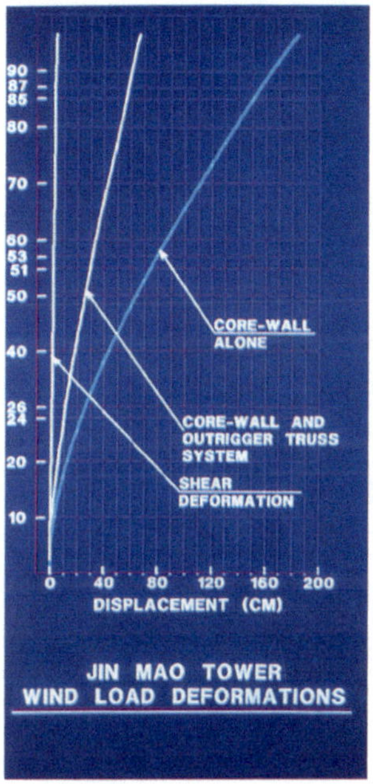

JIN MAO TOWER
WIND LOAD DEFORMATIONS

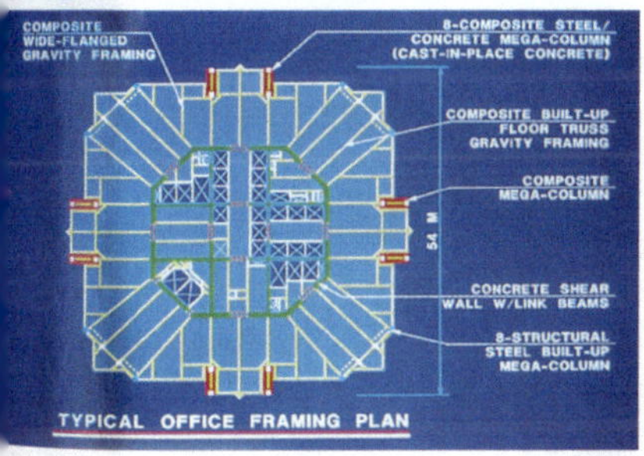

TYPICAL OFFICE FRAMING PLAN

narrow as they approach the pagoda-shaped steel spire, but the eight supercolumns remain essentially vertical to maximize the building's structural depth—a deeper section is more resistant to lateral forces.

Three sets of eight outrigger trusses, each two stories high, connect the columns to the core at floors 24 and 26; 51 and 53; and 85 and 87. These monumental steel-and-concrete trusses "act like levers or struts between the central core and the outside columns," explains Mark Sarkisian, SOM associate partner and senior project structural engineer. "As the core tries to bend in a typhoon or seismic event, it is restrained by the trusses on four sides."

To accommodate the relative movements of the core and columns during construction, the engineering team devised a way of temporarily fastening the outrigger trusses. For example, the trusses between levels 24 and 26 are being erected this month and temporarily stabilized with pin connections that allow the concrete core and composite columns to move freely. After the construction team installs the second set of trusses, the bolts and pins will be locked on the lower set.

The tower includes structural steel components designed to assume only gravity loads. Eight steel columns are interspersed among the perimeter supercolumns to provide a column-free interior on the office levels. The floor framing, too, consists of steel members with a composite metal deck slab.

Wind-tunnel testing validated SOM's choice of high-strength concrete and steel. No supplemental dampers are necessary, as was revealed by drift analyses performed by the University of Western Ontario. And despite the tower's exposure to Shanghai's strong winds, occupants' perception of building movement will be minimal, falling below internationally accepted levels.

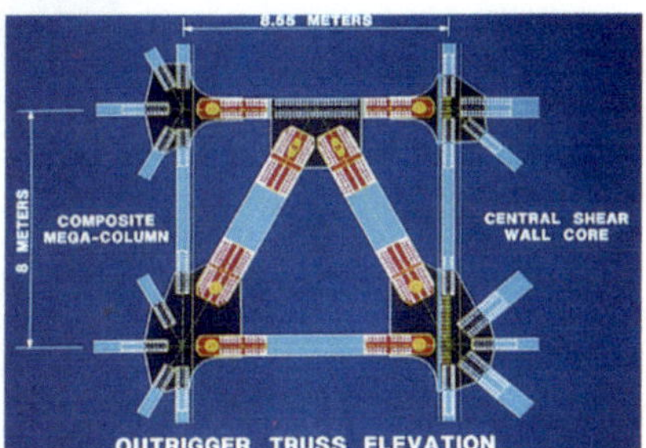

OUTRIGGER TRUSS ELEVATION

Text Vernon Mays

positive energy

Abu Dhabi's Masdar City promises to set a standard for sustainable urbanism. Its proposed centerpiece—a high-performance complex by Adrian Smith + Gordon Gill Architecture—could do the same for sustainable building.

IF THINGS GO ACCORDING TO PLAN, it won't be long before Masdar City in Abu Dhabi is the undisputed pacesetter for sustainable design practices. The desert city—with its highly publicized master plan by Foster + Partners of London—broke ground on Feb. 9. Developed by the Masdar Initiative, a government program for "energy security, climate change and truly sustainable human development," the project boasts a $22 billion budget and the goal of being zero-carbon, zero-waste, and zero-energy.

Near the city center, the Masdar Initiative plans to build itself a headquarters that will be the world's first large-scale, mixed-use, "positive-energy" building. In other words, the 1.5-million-square-foot complex will aim to produce more energy than it consumes. The schematic design emerged from a two-stage international competition conducted at breakneck speed (about six weeks from start to finish) and won by Adrian Smith + Gordon Gill Architecture (AS+GG)—a Chicago architecture firm launched just 19 months ago by seasoned SOM alumni Smith, Gill, and partner Robert Forest.

The project brief laid out square footage requirements, a mix of office and residential uses, and an ambitious sustainability mandate. Beyond that, the competitors were given a height limitation of eight stories, an outline of infrastructure and mass transit concepts, and a site plan indicating where surrounding open space is planned. Gill maintains that the headquarters will change the way buildings are designed, constructed, and inhabited. "Philosophically," he says, "we are seeking to absorb the environment and use it to its best advantage."

building section

environmental systems

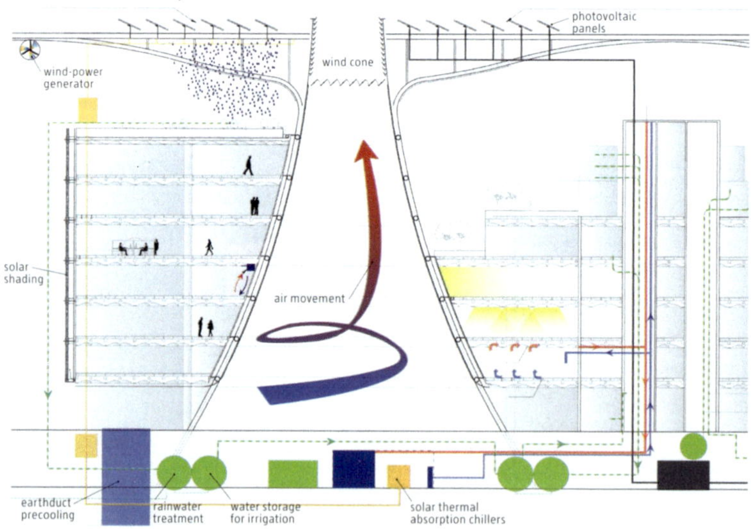

office spaces

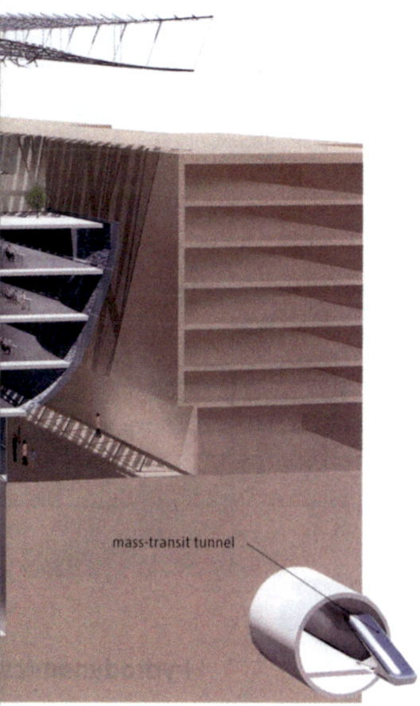

ytime effect

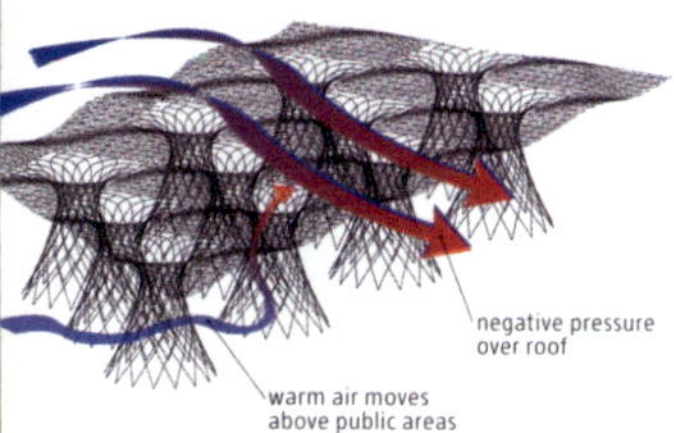

ghttime effect

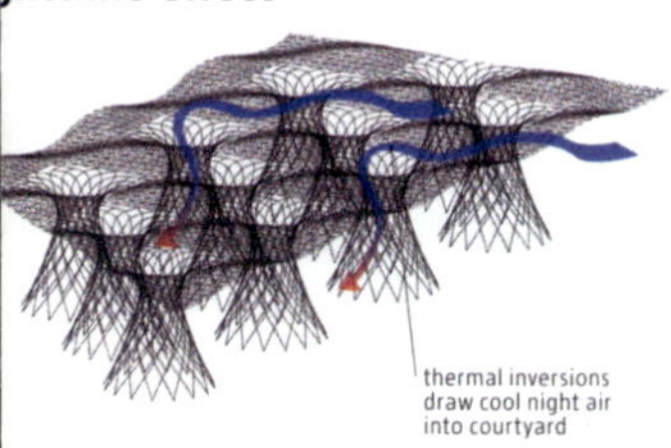

wind cones

ELEVEN TOWERING, glass-enclosed wind cones perform many critical functions. At the top, they provide the structural support for the building's curvilinear roof. At the ground plane, they delineate courtyards that serve as entrances, orientation points, and giant intakes to bring ground-source cool air into the building. In between, they siphon warm air up and out of the building and allow diffused daylight from the rooftop into the office floors below.

To aid pedestrian movement, the cones are placed at strategic locations connecting with paths penetrating the site. Some cones serve as entries or gardens on the grand plaza to the west. Others are cut into the building, forming negative space on the east façade. Interior courtyards vary—some are landscaped, some have water features, others have suspended artwork or pedestrian bridges overhead. "We want to make each one memorable, to not be confusing or disorienting as one moves through," says Gill. The overall layout is regularized to move people efficiently through the building.

While the exact number of cones may vary in the final design, the choice of 11 during the competition phase was based on pragmatic concerns, such as spacing, structure, and projected volume of air movement. The geometry resembles that of a nuclear plant cooling tower, promoting wind movement while preventing sunlight from shining directly on the interior glass surfaces below the narrow neck of the cone. Cones are organized in the core to optimize the penetration of diffused daylight into the office interiors. Workers adjacent to a cone will enjoy views into the courtyard, and operable windows would allow for cross-ventilation.

The design team is exploring the use of operable louvers at the top of the cones to close off the neck during dust storms. Caps on the top of the cones could also help in balancing horizontal air movement through the office space, says Gill, because one cone could be closed off and the next one opened to shift the pattern of air flow. Engineers tested different orientations and forms for the tops of the cones, settling on a chamfered top with the high point facing toward the prevailing wind. This resulted in the most negative pressure at the top of the cone, promoting the greatest draw.

roof and garden

AS+GG COLLABORATED CLOSELY with its consulting engineers from the early stages of the competition. Gill says the fundamental idea of wind cones supporting a broad roof was no more than "a simple little section drawn on a piece of paper about three inches square" before the M/E/P and structural engineers were brought in to react. "With the idea of the cones and the roof, the structural engineers were important," says Gill. "And that curve in the roof provides structural integrity."

Gill likens the project to an oasis—a fragile microclimate in which a pool of water provides nourishment to palm trees, which in turn shade the water and keep it from evaporating too quickly. "So you end up with a canopy structure there that's protecting the very source that allows the canopy to exist in the first place," he muses. "It's totally symbiotic—they coexist in this kind of equilibrium."

Likewise, Masdar's floating roof literally translates that idea by shading the building and creating a cool environment beneath, reducing the demand for air conditioning. Plans call for the roof to be covered with a 290,000-square-foot photovoltaic array that will harvest the intense solar energy in the Abu Dhabi desert and convert it to power for the building. Beneath the curving roof, which articulates and promotes the pattern of air movement, is a vast garden space—what Gill refers to as "a displaced ground plane." Residential units with human-scale massing are organized around the perimeter of the garden. Residents will enjoy views of the shaded courtyard or the city, which is limited to a height of six stories (two less than the Masdar headquarters). "It gives one a very unique perspective," Gill says.

In keeping with its desire to build humane environments, AS+GG has already asked the client to consider the possibility of building the roof and cones first, which would allow the photovoltaics to provide energy for constructing the rest of the building while at the same time shading the construction site so that the workers aren't toiling in the hot sun. The proposal's practicality is still being evaluated.

energy generation systems

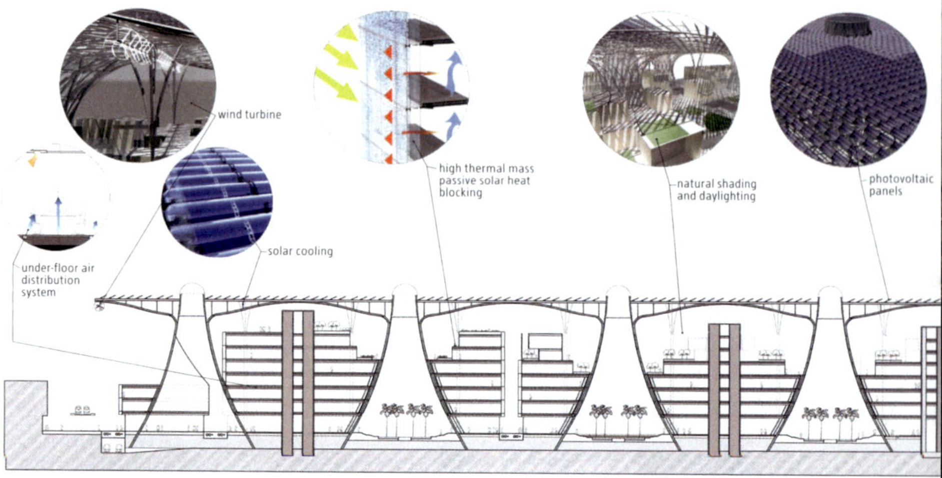

sustainable systems and materials

THE BIG IDEAS AT WORK in the building won't succeed without a nexus of sustainable systems and materials. "It's a tightly woven relationship between environmental systems, building performance, and usability," says Gill. If properly implemented, the latent systems and new technologies should produce 3 percent more energy than the building will use. And because of Masdar's central political control, excess energy can be transferred to the grid.

In addition to generating its own power with photovoltaics—envisioned now as polycrystalline cells on the roof surface—the building uses solar vacuum tubes for air conditioning. Plus a geothermal system is being explored for additional cooling.

The architects also are proposing the use of wind turbines for power generation, a technology they used in a Chicago high-rise. Gill says the inclusion of wind turbines is conjectural at this point, awaiting further analysis of economic feasibility. But if the turbines become a demonstration project, they may be justifiable simply for data collection, he adds.

As the project moves forward, a key area for research and development will be the exterior wall, a critical component in minimizing the building's thermal load. "During the competition, we were thinking in terms of a masonry wall, eight stories tall and solid, with maybe 30 percent open," Gill recalls. The ultimate goal is to thermally shield the building while allowing controlled daylight in to reduce the lighting load, and the design team is working with a manufacturer to develop a high-performance wall system.

Building materials will be evaluated with respect to what Gill calls "global environmental contextualism"—a phrase he uses to describe how a building should relate to its local environmental context while respecting its global context in terms of developing and available technologies. "What we are finding in terms of the sustainable performance of buildings is there can be a much greater global influence on the building," he asserts. "It can be winds. It can be solar patterns. But, especially in today's market, it can also be materials. One can look at a bigger pattern of access to material or at sustainable processes and bring those to the project in order to increase performance." In the case of Masdar, the client is demanding cradle-to-cradle office interiors. But Gill says that seemingly simple performance standard raises a host of other questions. Where do the products and raw materials come from? What manufacturing processes are involved? And how do those factors impact zero-carbon and zero-waste goals?

hydrodynamics

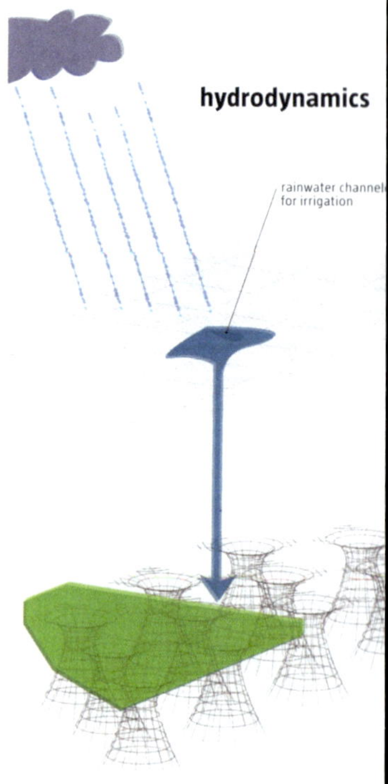

rst floor

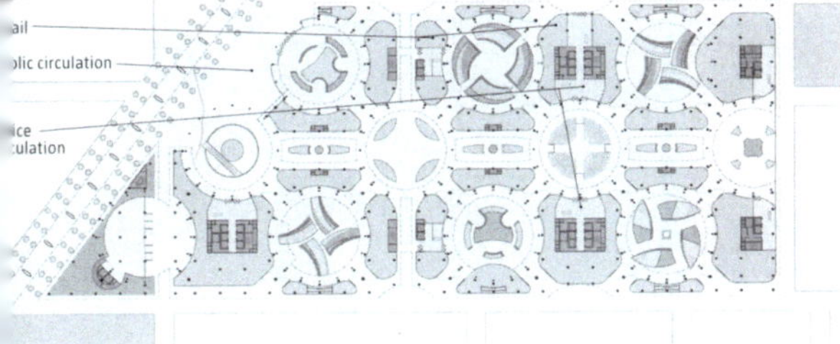

cond floor

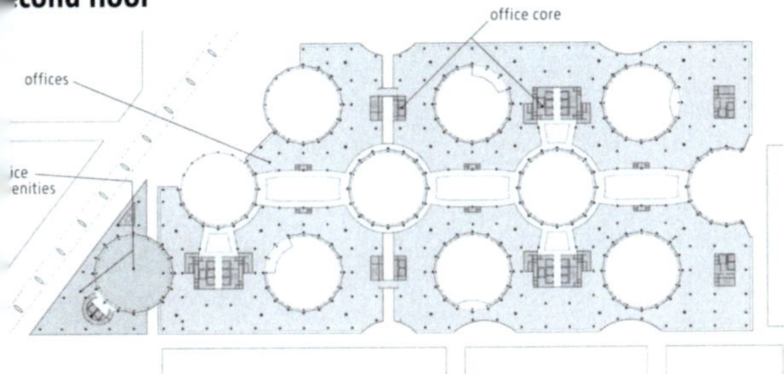

ection

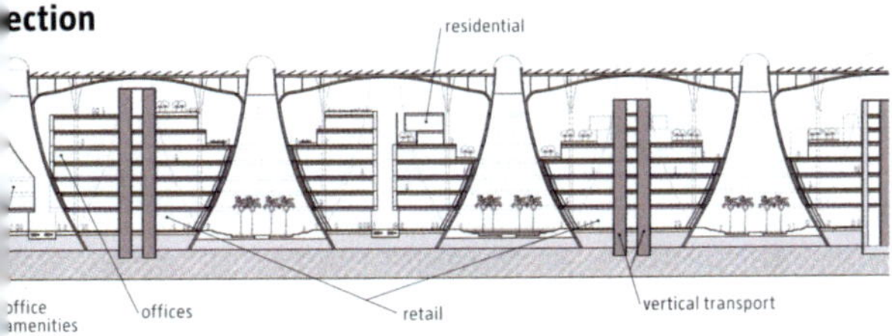

solar dynamics

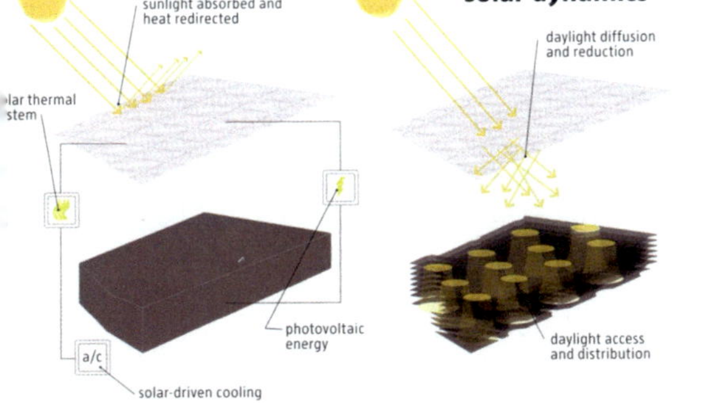

toolbox

design and presentation

Adrian Smith + Gordon Gill Architecture designed the Masdar headquarters using **AutoCAD**, **3DS Max**, and **Rhino 3D**. This software combination allowed the architects to analyze the building in three dimensions.

design concept

In the competition process, AS+GG also created 3-D fly-through simulations for the jury to consider. Most of the modeling was done in-house before being turned over to an outside consultant for material-specific rendering. Gordon Gill explains: "The final product is out-of-house; the process is in-house." Renderings are available for viewing on AS+GG's website, smithgill.com.

solar studies

Once the basic design was in place, the architects uploaded the information into **Ecotect** (squ1.com/products/ecotect), a building-design and environmental-analysis tool developed by Square One Research. Gill recalls that this particular program was very useful in planning the energy-generation tactics that will make the Masdar headquarters a positive-energy building. "We use Ecotect to run radiosity performance diagrams," he says. "In other words, you could run a solar study on it, which allows you to see where the greatest heat is occurring on your wall surfaces. You can begin to see where it protects it and where it does not."

wind studies

The architects used other types of models, such as CFD or **computational fluid dynamic models,** to analyze the effect and performance of the wind cones. The engineers also used these models in more directed and specific tests on the wind cones. "They ran wind speeds of 3.5 meters per second to see what kind of negative draw they were getting on the cone vertically," Gill says. "So they knew what kind of wind they were creating."

PROJECT Masdar Headquarters, Masdar City, Abu Dhabi, United Arab Emirates
CLIENT The Masdar Initiative, Abu Dhabi, United Arab Emirates
ARCHITECT Adrian Smith + Gordon Gill Architecture, Chicago—Gordon Gill, Adrian Smith (design partners); Robert Forest (management partner); Les Ventsch (director of design); Gail Borthwick, Ying Liu (senior designers)
STRUCTURAL ENGINEERING CONSULTANT Thornton Tomasetti
M/E/P ENGINEERING CONSULTANT Environmental Systems Design
SIZE 1.5 million square feet

ARCHITECTURAL
RECORD
CURRENT ISSUE
(ROOM USE ONLY)
SAND CASTLES
BURJ KHALIFA, DUBAI
CITYCENTER, LAS VEGAS
MIT LIBRARIES
August 3, 2010
ROTCH

Beyond Limits

The Burj Khalifa's designers tackle extreme height and extreme climate to create a landmark for the 21st century.

By Josephine Minutillo

Continuing Education

Use the following learning objectives to focus your study while reading "Burj Khalifa, Dubai" (page 78) and this month's ARCHITECTURAL RECORD/AIA Continuing Education article "Beyond Limits." To earn one AIA learning unit, including one hour of health, safety, and welfare (HSW) credit, turn to page 94 and follow the instructions.

Learning Objectives

1. Identify the various challenges involved in designing a supertall structure.
2. Describe the structural system utilized in the design of the Burj Khalifa.
3. Discuss the various m/e/p and life-safety systems used in the Burj Khalifa.
4. Discuss how the Burj Khalifa differs from other supertall structures.

SKEPTICS QUESTION THE LOGIC behind building a supertall skyscraper in the middle of the desert. Others are less interested in why the Burj Khalifa exists than how it was built. The secrets to its construction might surprise you. While the Dubai landmark dwarfs its closest rival in the competition for world's tallest building by more than 1,000 feet, it doesn't flaunt its architectural muscle. Rather, its design is as straightforward and logical as it gets.

At the heart of that logic is the building's triaxial geometry. "The Y-shaped plan is ideal for a residential building because it gives plenty of surface area per unit, and structurally, it is much better than a cruciform or linear tower," explains Adrian Smith, FAIA, former design partner at Skidmore, Owings & Merrill (SOM) in charge of the project through the completion of construction documents. And though SOM's competition-winning design for the Burj far exceeded the approximately 550-meter (1,800 foot) height called for in the brief to make it the world's tallest, the scheme – originally at about 700 meters, or 2,300 feet – was selected based on its appearance and construction feasibility, according to Smith.

The center of the structural-concrete tower features a hexagonal core that surrounds the elevators. Since the core is not big enough to rise to such extreme heights on its own, it is buttressed by the three wings. While the core functions as an axle to keep the building from twisting, 2-foot-thick corridor walls on either side of each wing act like the web of an I-beam; cross walls like the flanges. Round columns are located at the pointed end of each wing between ordinary flat plate slabs. The result is a tower that is extremely stiff laterally and torsionally.

"These are very conventional systems, just arranged in a unique manner," says William Baker, structural engineer partner at SOM. The driving force behind the structural design was wind. "Tall building design is dominated by wind forces, even in most seismic areas where earthquakes are a major concern," Baker says. Since wind velocities increase with height, it was an even greater concern here. Consulting engineers Rowan Williams Davies and Irwin (RWDI) carried out extensive wind-tunnel testing over the course of two years in its renowned facilities in Ontario, Canada. First, balsa wood models of the slender tower were subjected to force balance tests. Later, more sophisticated aeroelastic tests were conducted. RWDI studied the building's six important wind directions – the pointed end, or nose, of each of the three wings, and the areas between two wings, called tails.

The Burj Khalifa's organic form has a triaxial geometry. The Y-shaped building's three wings are connected to a central core. As the tower rises, one wing at each tier sets back in a spiraling pattern.

The most significant change to come from RWDI's analysis did not significantly affect the building's design but rather its orientation. Since analysis indicated less excitation in wind patterns blowing at the nose, the tower was rotated 120 degrees from its original position so that the noses faced into the wind. RWDI also suggested that the Burj's different tiers be made more regular. "Initially, the building spiraled much more dramatically," says Smith. "But each time it steps back, it changes how the wind reacts. To keep the wind from organizing into vortices, we evened out the setbacks."

While changes to the design were being made, so too were changes to the building's use. Originally meant to be all residential, the client, Dubai-based Emaar Properties, added offices to the program. Corporate suites were located at the top of the tower, which, with floor areas as low as 5,000 square feet, is more ideally suited for apartments, the original intent for those floors.

But the program was not the only element to be in flux. The tower's final height remained a question mark until rather late in the game. It wasn't until after the foundation was in place and construction of the superstructure began that the magic number – 828 meters, or 2,717 feet – was finally determined. "I hated the proportions of the shorter tower and kept pushing for it to be taller," recalls Smith. The economy was on Smith's side at that point, and the client agreed it looked better taller.

The tower's strategic design allowed flexibility in terms of changes in program and height. The addition of offices required an extra set of elevators, which were accommodated in one of the wings. The other two wings would then house elevators for the apartments and hotel, respectively. Issues of proportion and scale were paramount in the Burj Khalifa's design. Unlike the Willis (formerly Sears) Tower, which scales by the cube, the Burj scales by the square. So whereas doubling the height of the Willis Tower would increase its area eightfold, doubling the height of the Burj only increases its area fourfold; its wings would get longer but not wider.

Nevertheless, most of the extra height was in the spire, which Baker calls "a nest of steel triangles that sits on the hexagonal walls." At the opposite end, at the very bottom of the building, a 12-foot-thick concrete mat, or raft, foundation rests on the surface of a calcisiltite rock mass. It was constructed in four separate pours – one for each of the three wings and the center core. Then, 194 5-foot-diameter piles were driven 140 feet below the mat. Most of the piles are located toward the edge of the mat, with very few at the center. "It's all about decreasing wind forces and managing gravity," says Baker. "By the time you get to the bottom, everything is in compression, so you don't need much reinforcing. The reinforcing there is similar to what you'd see in an average 20-story building. We're very proud of that."

None of this would have been possible without recent material advancements. "We discovered this new material called concrete," Baker jokes. "It is so different from the stuff we used to call concrete." While in the past, slump tests were used to measure how hard and consistent a sample of concrete was, the chemicals in the ultra-high-performance concrete used for the Burj make it so flowable that it forms a puddle. (Silica fume and fly ash are its main ingredients.) The quality control comes in measuring the diameter of the puddle.

Regardless of the concrete's 100 MPa (14,500 psi) strength, all concrete changes dimension over time. Fifteen separate three-dimensional finite-element analysis models predicted the effects of creep, shrinkage, and foundation settlement. "We made precise calculations with data that is very rough," says Baker. "It's all going to shrink. The problem comes when one part moves differently from another."

The key to minimizing that kind of differential movement was to use the same concrete in every vertical element, and to ensure that columns and walls had similar volume-to-surface ratios so that they dried at the same rate. There are virtually no transfers within the concrete structure. Designers adhered to a strict 9-meter (29.5 foot) module. Where a wing sets back and the columns at its nose drop off, the next set of columns appears directly over the walls beneath it.

"You verify as much as possible through computer programs and calculations, but it's not an easy thing," Baker admits. "In the end, you walk the building and look for cracks." So far, the building has settled about 2 inches.

Samsung Corporation was responsible for making the design a reality. The Seoul-based contractor used an automated self-climbing formwork system to build the concrete structure. Specially developed pumps brought the concrete to heights of 600 meters (1,970 feet). The structural steel spire was constructed from inside the building and jacked to its full height of over 200 meters, or approximately 700 feet, using a hydraulic pump.

Seven two- to three-story-high mechanical floors are distributed throughout the building, about every 30 floors or so. "It's really a series of 30-story buildings stacked on top of one another," Baker says. "There would be too much pressure in the pipes, and ducts would get too big, if you try to move things too far."

The mechanical floors house various equipment, including water tanks and pumps, air-handling units, and electrical substations. Track-mounted building-maintenance units, used for window washing, are stored in garages within the structure. "We were very aware of the sand

Structural concrete gives way to steel at the tower's top section, where a structural-steel spire utilizes a diagonally braced lateral system.

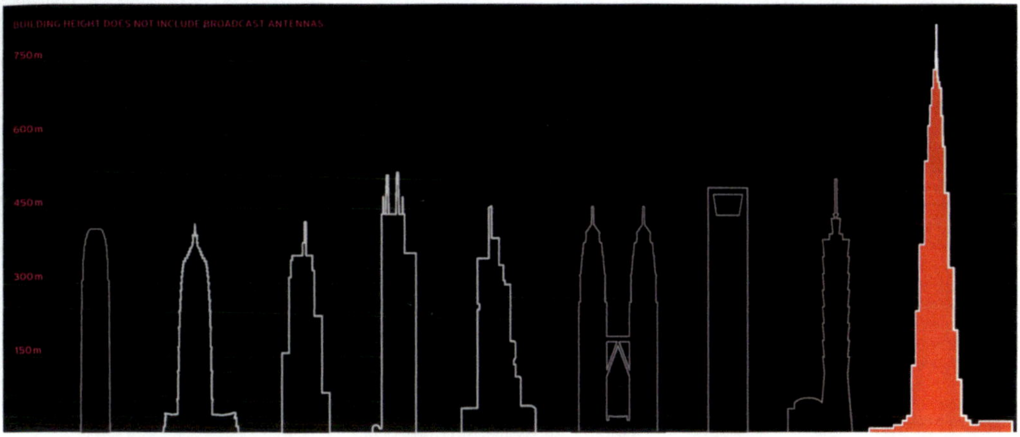

TWO INTERNATIONAL FINANCE CENTER	JIN MAO BUILDING	TRUMP INTERNATIONAL HOTEL AND TOWER	WILLIS TOWER (FORMERLY SEARS TOWER)	NANJING GREENLAND FINANCIAL CENTER	PETRONAS TOWER 1 & 2	SHANGHAI WORLD FINANCIAL CENTER	TAIPEI 101	BURJ KHALIFA
HONG KONG	SHANGHAI	CHICAGO	CHICAGO	NANJING	KUALA LUMPUR	SHANGHAI	TAIPEI	DUBAI
2003	1999	2009	1974	2010	1998	2008	2004	2010
412 m	421 m	423 m	442 m	450 m	452 m	492 m	508 m	828 m
1,352 ft	1,381 ft	1,387 ft	1,450 ft	1,476 ft	1,483 ft	1,614 ft	1,667 ft	2,717 ft

problem," Smith says. "The consistency of the sand in Dubai is more like talcum powder. It sticks to everything." The building was kept as flush as possible, and ledges were kept to a minimum to reduce the number of areas where sand could settle. Window washing is expected to take place every few months.

Over 26,000 low-E, antiglare glass panels were used in the exterior cladding of Burj Khalifa, which features more than 1.8 million square feet of glass. Eight-inch-long wing-shaped, stainless-steel mullions occur at every glass joint. "We originally designed the exterior wall with steel tubes, but it looked too industrial," recalls Smith. "The sheen of the vertical stainless steel, especially in the horizontal sun of morning and evening, makes the building sing."

While the building's structure and its exterior, including the cladding, were designed to resist a variety of forces, forces of a different kind needed to be addressed inside the tower. According to SOM's Luke Leung, "There is a tremendous amount of pressure in a building of this height, both on the water side and on the air side."

The typical system pressure for water is 300 psi. The Burj has one of the highest water pressures in the world at up to 460 psi. "Imagine a water pipe that is 800 meters tall," says Leung. "You don't want to be standing under that."

Pressure breaks are typically added in high-rise

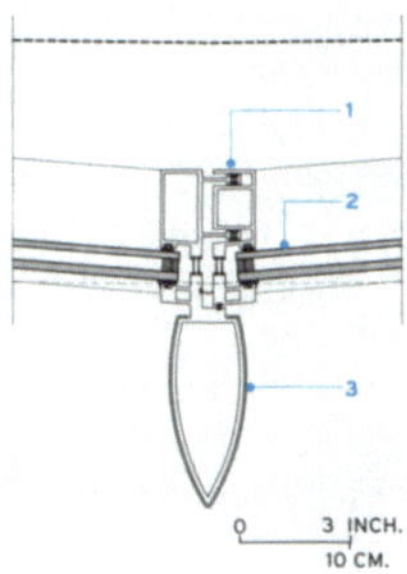

CURTAIN-WALL DETAIL

1. ALUMINUM VERTICAL MULLION
2. CLEAR REFLECTIVE INSULATING VISION GLASS
3. STAINLESS-STEEL VERTICAL FIN
4. HORIZONTAL SPANDREL PANEL
5. CONCRETE SLAB

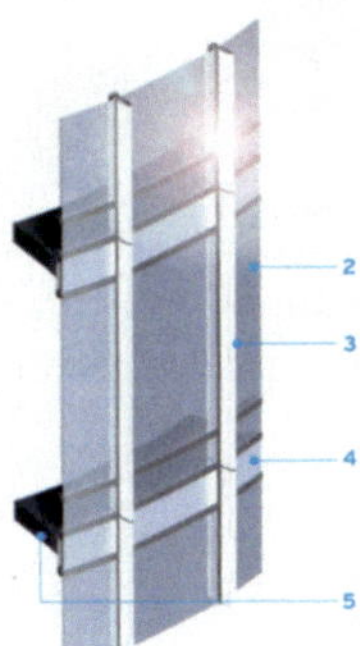

CURTAIN-WALL DETAIL

The tower used over 430,000 cubic yards of concrete and 43,000 tons of steel rebar. To help determine the concrete-to-rebar ratio, three-dimensional finite-element analysis models were used to predict the effects of creep and shrinkage.

buildings to alleviate the forces. In the Burj, SOM created some of the highest pressure breaks ever in a building, consisting mainly of heat exchangers to isolate one riser from another. The tower's water system supplies an average of 250,000 gallons of water daily.

Cooling the water presented another challenge for SOM's engineers. "When we first started coming to Dubai, we noticed that the hot water in our hotels was very hot, and that the cold water was also very hot," says Leung. "Imagine getting hot water out of the cold faucet at the Armani Hotel!"

Since Dubai has limited fresh water and relies on the sea, the water had to travel through the very hot ground during the salt evaporation process. Instead of following that scenario, SOM took advantage of the area's high humidity and the large amount of condensation that results. "The moisture is so high that if you collect condensate in the air during a cooling period, you get a significant amount of water in the 55–65 degree Fahrenheit range," explains Leung. This water is collected and drained in a separate piping system to a holding tank. The system provides about 15 million gallons of supplemental water per year. A sitewide graywater collection system collects water for use in landscape irrigation.

The effects of air pressure are more noticeable to the average visitor to the Burj. There is an enormous amount of air movement going through the building. Due to Dubai's high temperatures, reaching 115 degrees Fahrenheit and higher in the summers, the stack effect is reversed. Instead of hot air rising, it is sucked in from the top of the building and directed downward because the inside of the building is cooler than the outside.

Stack effect is a function of both the building's height and the temperature difference between the inside and the outside. Both are extreme in this case. When you enter the building in the heat of summer, the air will feel like it is trying to push you out. "In Chicago, for instance, it is 75 degrees inside and as high as 95 degrees outside on a summer day," Leung explains. "In Dubai, the temperature difference in summer can be more than 40 degrees Fahrenheit."

What is not so apparent from the building's height is the amount of power it consumes. As electricity travels through the building, which in essence is a stack of five 30-story buildings, it loses voltage similar to the way water loses pressure flowing through a small pipe. To supply these massive loads efficiently, the Burj's electrical mains are supplied with 11 kV, 23 times higher than the 480V typically used in the U.S. Transformers located at each of the mechanical levels reduce the voltage to intermediate levels for heavy equipment and to 220V, the normal voltage used in the U.A.E., for office equipment and appliances.

Fire- and life-safety issues are a vital concern in high-rise buildings, particularly one of unprecedented height such as this. The Burj contains 57 elevators, some of the fastest in the world, serving different building zones, though no one elevator travels more than 500 meters (1,640 feet). According to Baker, the longest elevator ride takes under two minutes – with the express elevator to the observation deck on level 124 taking much less time. Baker also admits to walking down the full height of the building (at a leisurely pace) in about 45 minutes. A typical floor contains three sets of concrete-encased fire stairs, one in each wing.

In case of fire emergency, the building deploys a "defend in place" strategy. Fire-rated, air-conditioned refuge areas accommodate building occupants until further instruction. Some elevators are equipped with cameras so that elevator shafts can be inspected remotely.

Despite the challenges involved in designing the Burj Khalifa, and the criticisms leveled against it in the wake of Dubai's subsequent financial meltdown, Adrian Smith staunchly defends it. "The Burj was an important piece for Dubai at the time it was built," says Smith. "Dubai wanted to be recognized as an international player on par with other major world cities, and it needed an international landmark to do that." ■

ARCHITECTURAL RECORD

THE SHORT AND THE TALL OF IT

American Design Ingenuity at Every Scale

plus: Good Design is Good Business

SIZE MATTERS. But small can be as challenging for an architect as big, presenting its own set of design problems in terms of context, materials, structure, and budget. The projects featured in this issue range in size from a 70-square-foot water-research station hovering above a river in Nebraska to supertall towers rising more than 1,300 feet and containing millions of square feet of space. What links them all is American ingenuity, a can-do attitude that practitioners are applying to all scales of building. Whether the job is to convert a trio of rooftop sheds into a light-filled "project space" for an art foundation or to create the world's tallest building, American architects continue to push the boundaries of design. Sometimes they do that in places like Hennessey, Oklahoma, and other times they export their skills to Asia and the Middle East. Looking at extremes in size offers us the chance to examine how architects use similar sets of skills to solve problems of vastly different dimensions. Fasten your seat belts as we take you on a ride from tiny to towering. *Clifford A. Pearson*

the Short *and the* Tall *of it*

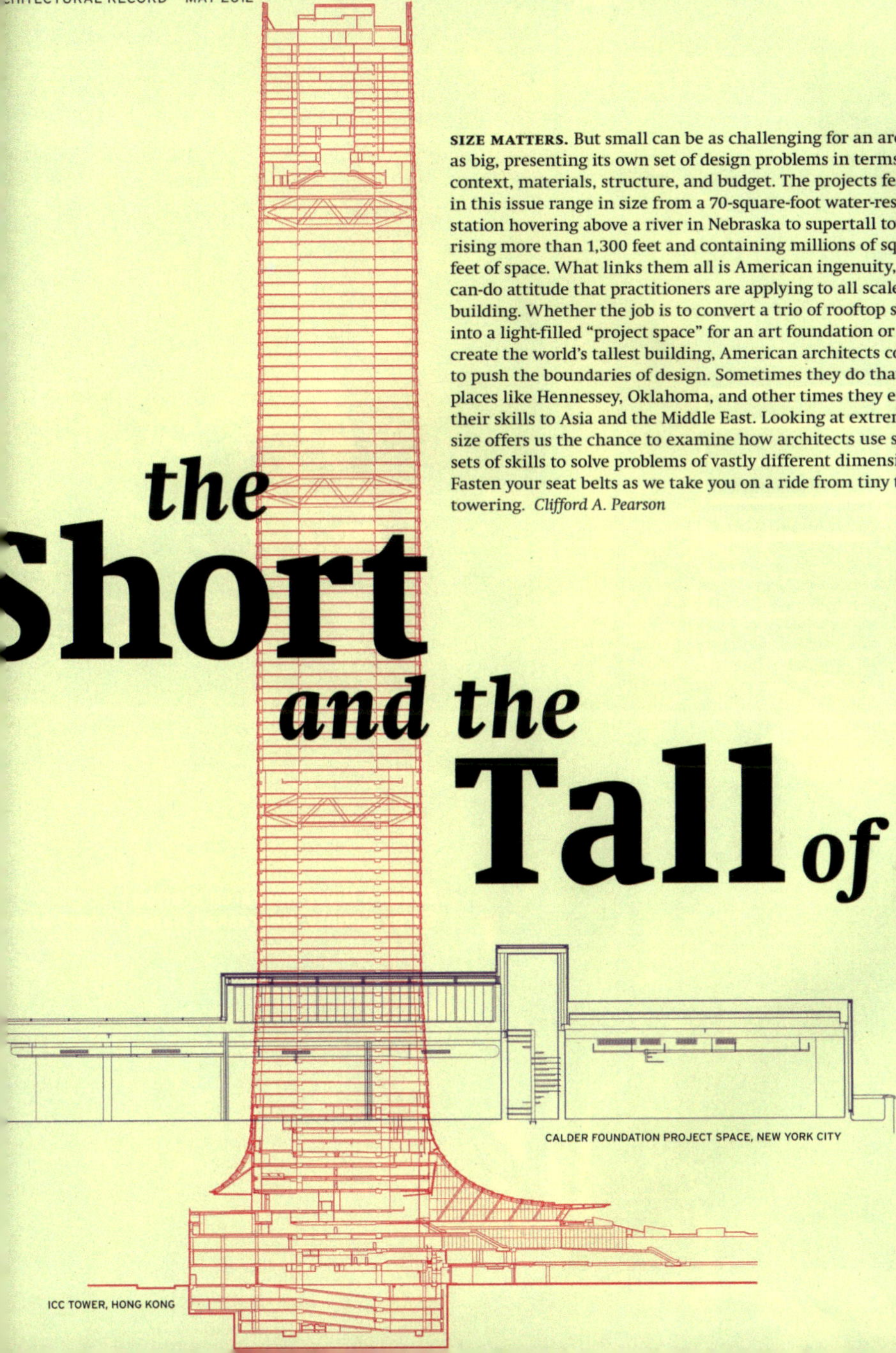

CALDER FOUNDATION PROJECT SPACE, NEW YORK CITY

ICC TOWER, HONG KONG

International Commerce Centre | Hong Kong | Kohn Pedersen Fox Architects

Enter the Dragon

In the Kowloon district of Hong Kong, across the harbor from the main part of the city, looms a trimly tapered mixed-use tower.

BY SUZANNE STEPHENS

HARBOR VIEW The ICC looms above the West Kowloon Station's levels of retail and mass transit. Views from within the shaft overlooking Victoria Harbor are expansive, especially from the Ritz-Carlton Hotel rooms at the top.

AMERICAN ARCHITECTS are exporting a luxury product of a dimension and scale few clients in the United States can afford at home: the supertall skyscraper—that is, a skyscraper over 1,250 feet tall (page 160). Kohn Pedersen Fox (KPF), the architect for the 1,588-foot-high International Commerce Centre (ICC) in Hong Kong, opened in 2011, ventured into Asia in the 1990s, and soon made its mark with towers in Shanghai and Tokyo. By the time the firm completed the tallest building in China in 2008—the 1,614-foot-tall Shanghai World Financial Center—it was at the center of an inner circle of (mostly American) architects designing supertall skyscrapers. Now KPF's roster of higher-than-high-rises in the works include five in China—in Shenzhen, Chongqing, Guangzhou, Shenyang, and Suzhou—one in Seoul, and another in Doha, Qatar.

William Pedersen, KPF design partner, credits America's

View additional images at architecturalrecord.com.

TAILORED TOWER
The ICC's elongated, glass-paneled shaft tapers gently toward the roof. Floors in the tower are typically 32,000 square feet, gradually shrinking to 29,000 square feet above the 78th floor. As the tower inclines inward 1 degree toward the top, the four glass facades seem to lift away from the shaft. In the crevasses, the reentrant corners gradually widen to mitigate wind turbulence, one of the major challenges for the supertall structure. When the four facades reach the top, they form parapet walls at the roof level. At the base, angular glass-paneled canopies for offices and the hotel shelter visitors arriving by car (below right) on the top of the station roof. On the north side, the glass forms a scooped canopy (opposite, bottom) over the atrium connecting the tower to retail and mass transit below.

edge in the global skyscraper boom to its historic role in inventing and advancing the tall-building type. And American architectural firms, says managing partner Pau Katz, are less hierarchical and more heterogeneous in their organization than many firms abroad. A "flatter" management structure allows U.S. architects to be "more inventive and motivated," he says.

In 2000, KPF won the commission to design the 2.8 million-square-foot ICC that would loom up over the Wes Kowloon Station on the other side of Victoria Harbor fron Hong Kong Island. The invited competition, which includ Skidmore, Owings & Merrill (SOM), Pelli Clarke Pelli, and Kenzo Tange Associates, was initiated by developers Sun Hung Kai Properties, who had joined up with the Mass Transit Railway Corporation (MTR) to create an urban complex on 825 acres of reclaimed land. Residential high-rises, a W Hotel, restaurants, and cafés surround the signature tower planted atop a retail and mass-transit hu In addition to spec office space, the ICC contains the supe luxe Ritz-Carlton Hotel within its upper reaches–for now the highest hotel in the world.

On the waterfront side of the tower to the east, constru tion of the Express Rail Link (ERL), a high-speed train to mainland China, is under way, and soon the much-toutec West Kowloon Cultural District, planned by Foster + Part as a series of low-rise museums and parks, will take shap the south. Across the harbor rises the 1,335-foot-high Two International Finance Centre (2 IFC) in the Central Distri also developed by Sun Hung Kai, and designed by Pelli Cl Pelli in 2003. 2 IFC and ICC now form a totemic, monume gateway to the city, each shooting up among an asparagu patch of Hong Kong's skyscrapers. If ICC's gleaming shaft lacks the instant recognition of Foster's much shorter HS (1986), its quiet comportment serves as a welcome antido to the hurly-burly of most Hong Kong high-rises. Overlapp glass panels articulate the tapering elongated shaft, whic terminates at the ground in a curved glass shed over the atrium. ICC's glass shingles and scooping canopy allude obliquely to the scales and tail of a dragon. " 'Kowloon' means 'nine dragons,' " says Pedersen of the place name refers to the dragonlike form of Hong Kong's hills.

You arrive at the ICC by metro from the airport or Hor

1 HOTEL LOBBY
2 ATRIUM/RETAIL
3 PARKING
4 TRADING FLOOR
5 MECHANICAL
6 OFFICES
7 MECHANICAL AND REFUGE
8 OBSERVATION DECK
9 HOTEL RECEPTION/BAR
10 GUEST ROOMS
11 RESTAURANT

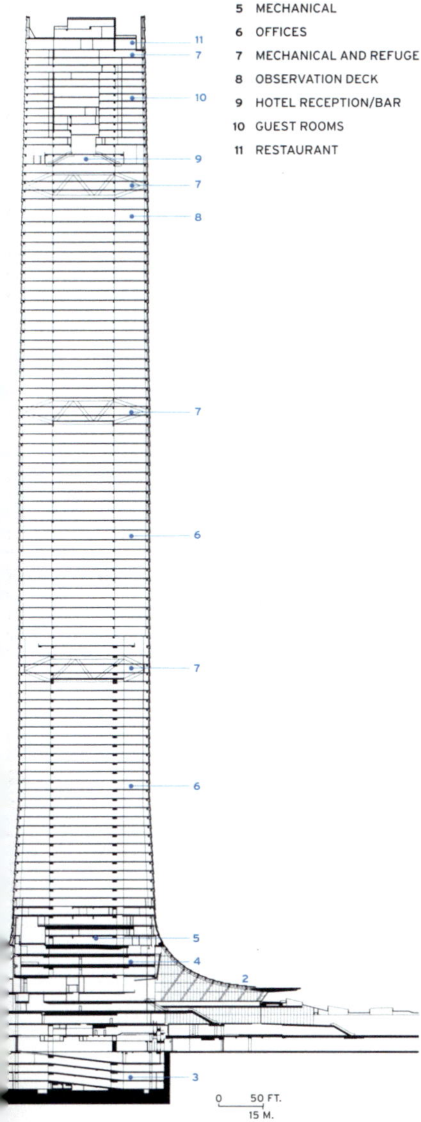

Kong Island—or by car on a curving road that leads to the hotel and office lobbies atop the station roof. From the car drop-off at Level 9, local and express elevators with requisite sky lobbies shoot up the tower: One stop away is the Ritz-Carlton reception area on the 103rd floor, where double-height restaurants overlook the city. On the uppermost (118th) floor you find the gym and pool, plus the over-the-top pulsating Ozone bar. It's all about the view, which sometimes the interior designers of the restaurants (Tokyo-based SPIN Design Studio) and the bar (the Japanese firm Wonderwall) forget in drowning the spaces in cocktail concoctions of splashy colors and frenetic motifs. LTW Design Works of Singapore gave the guest rooms a rich Buddhist-boudoir look.

The ICC tower relies on a reinforced-concrete central core and an eight-mega-column structure for its square-donut plan, proposed by the structural engineer for the conceptual design, Leslie E. Robertson. An outrigger system of tubular steel columns just over 6 inches in diameter helps transfer loads to the mega-columns. To deal with the soil and, below that, a clifflike bedrock, structural engineers for the execution of ICC, ARUP, turned to shaft-grouted friction barrettes for the foundation. As ARUP director Philip Lai explains, the barrettes—rectangular concrete piles, with an average depth of 230 feet—transfer loads on four sides to adjacent soil for stability (for more details see architecturalrecord.com).

Since the major problem confronting supertall towers is wind loads, Pedersen designed a reentrant (notched) corner to mitigate vortex shedding. Overlapping glass panels, each one-story high, spill down the facade, articulating the skin and creating canopies for the offices and hotel entrances. The flat, shingled panels lift up horizontally 5 degrees from the sloping wall; at the base, where the tower meets the atrium, the panels seem to slide into a catenary curve formed by three tangential arc segments.

The silver-coated, low-E glass shingles come in two types—one, a 10-foot-wide-by-5-foot-high glass-spandrel panel covering the slab edge and perimeter beam; the other, a 5-foot-wide and 10-foot-high vision panel. (At the reentrant corners, a striped, ceramic-frit spandrel panel helps cut glare.) The high-performance glass—and a system of sensors and monitors for HVAC use, which was developed with Hong Kong Polytechnic University—should reduce energy consumption by 15 percent, compared with an average office building.

Clearly, the cost of the supertall is not cheap. According to the architects, ICC's total budget was not made known even to the team. Katz maintains that the developers supervised costs and construction time quite closely on a need-to-know basis as the different parts of the building went out to bid.

Now, a year after this vast, vertical city opened, it is possible to stay in the Ritz-Carlton, do business with financial firms, such as Credit Suisse, Morgan Stanley, and Deutsche Bank ensconced below, shop in the mall, and take the metro to 2 IFC, where you can repeat this experience—without going outside. Soon you will be able to go directly from the ICC to Shenzhen or Guanzhou. Most of the time you'll occupy American export architecture, a fitting ambience for a monocultural luxury retail environment dominated by Armani, Chanel, and the like. It's almost like being in New York, but unlike Manhattan, it's a lot taller, denser, and harder to go outside and just take a walk around the block. ■

1 HOTEL LOBBY
2 OFFICE LOBBY
3 ATRIUM
4 OFFICES
5 GUEST ROOMS

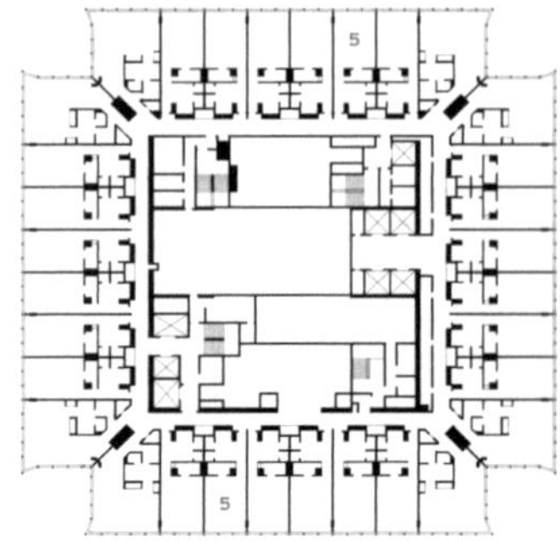

TYPICAL HOTEL FLOOR

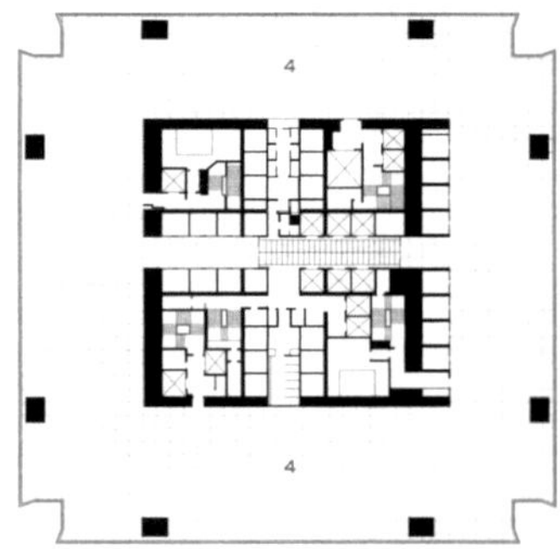

TYPICAL OFFICE FLOOR

0 30 FT. 9 M.

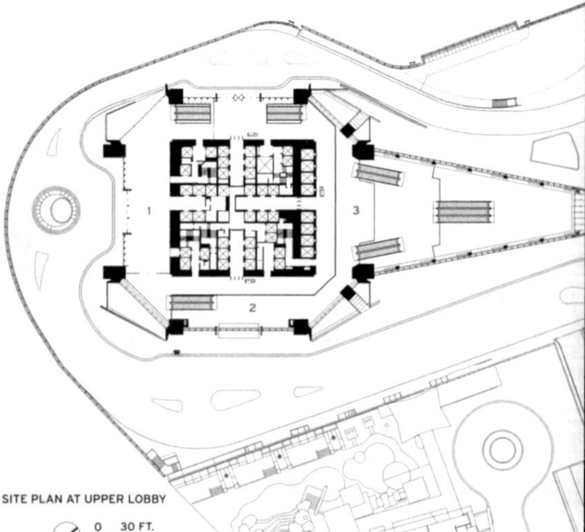

SITE PLAN AT UPPER LOBBY

0 30 FT. 9 M.

SLEEK SURROUND
KPF designed the public lobbies and circulation spaces for the tower's offices (left), using a corporate-posh palette. Cove lighting articulates the horizontal strips of travertine marble cladding the walls. The Ritz-Carlton Hotel has two lobbies, with the main one on the 103rd floor. A smaller "street" lobby (left, bottom) at "Level 9" is reached by driving up a curving road to the hotel entrance atop the station roof. The Singapore-based LTW Design Works designed the rectangular hotel lobby, which includes a pastry café, in a softly hued contemporary-luxe manner.

CREDITS

ARCHITECT: Kohn Pedersen Fox Associates – William Pedersen, design principal; Paul Katz, managing principal; Shawn Duffy, project manager; David Malott, Trent Tesch, senior designers; Kar-hwa Ho, senior designer, interiors

ASSOCIATE ARCHITECT: Wong & Ouyang

CLIENT: Sun Hung Kai Properties

ENGINEERS: ARUP (structural, civil, fire safety); J. Roger Preston (m/e/p)

CONSULTANTS: Lerch Bates (vertical transport); ALT Cladding & Design Philippines (exterior wall)

SIZE: 2,822,136 square feet

COMPLETION DATE: May 2011

SOURCES

METAL PANELS AND METAL AND GLASS CURTAIN WALL: Permasteelisa

GLASS: Shanghai Yaohua Pilkington

ELEVATOR: Schindler

View additional images at architecturalrecord.com.

-lamra Firdous Tower | Kuwait City
dmore, Owings & Merrill

:culpting he Skyline

:hitects, engineers, and ıtractors tackle a challenging ɔmetry to build a supertall ver with a striking silhouette a desert city.

JOANN GONCHAR, AIA

IN THE NATURE of tall buildings that rankings are t-lived, but at least for the moment, the 1,354-foot-tall, ory Al Hamra Firdous Tower, by Skidmore, Owings & :ill (SOM), is the tallest building in Kuwait City. It is :allest all-office building and the tallest skyscraper with ıcrete structure in the region.

ther tall buildings now sprout from the sand in Kuwait, ıding the lipsticklike NBK Tower, by Foster + Partners, ıe early stages of construction just across the street, the hourglass-shaped United Towers by Kohn Pedersen almost complete on a site a few blocks away. At 984 and feet tall, these are shorter than SOM's tower and don't ify as "supertall" (see page 160). But if, or when, Al ıra's height is superseded, its contribution to the city's ine shouldn't be diminished. It possesses both a geomet- igor and a graceful asymmetry since it is mostly glass- ned and rectilinear, but seemingly wears a flowing k of concrete.

supertall tower was not the original plan for the site, :h sits at the center of a promontory jutting out into the ɔian Gulf (also known as the Persian Gulf). The consor- ı that owns the land, Al Hamra Real Estate, initially ıned a 50-story office building and an adjoining 4-story ɔping mall—both designed by a local firm, Al Jazera sultants. But in 2005, soon after starting construction he mall and beginning excavation for the tower, Kuwaiti :ials changed the zoning regulations to allow for a much ɾ structure. The clients decided to move forward with retail portion of the project. For the architecture and ineering of the tower, however, they called in SOM, ɔse tall-building experience stretches back at least as far

VING FORM The mostly rectilinear Al Hamra has three glazed facades allow occupants to take advantage of views of the Gulf to the north, and west. However, a pair of ribbonlike reinforced-concrete walls on its ı side make the tower appear as though it wears a billowing cloak.

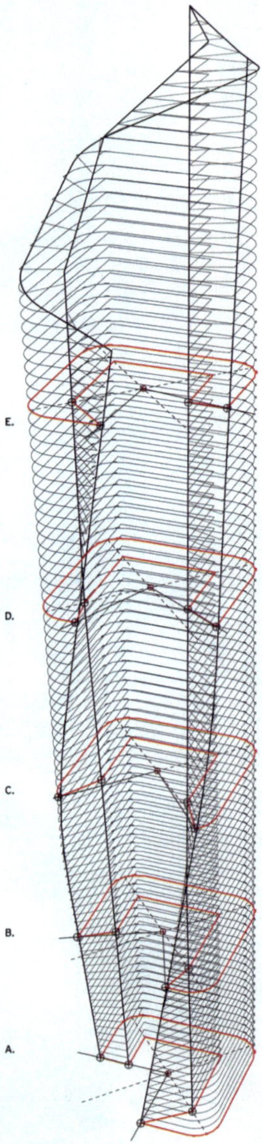

TOWER GEOMETRY AND STRUCTURE

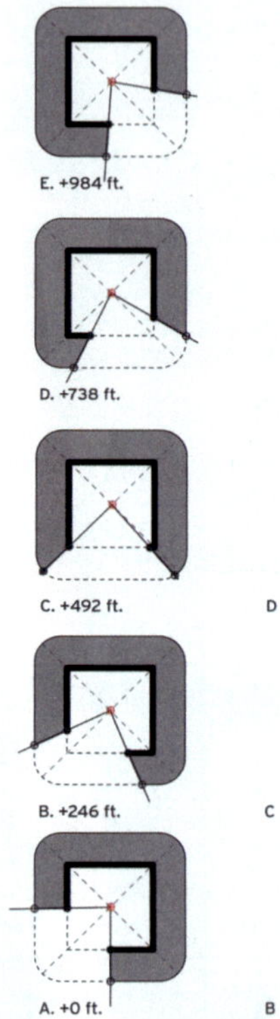

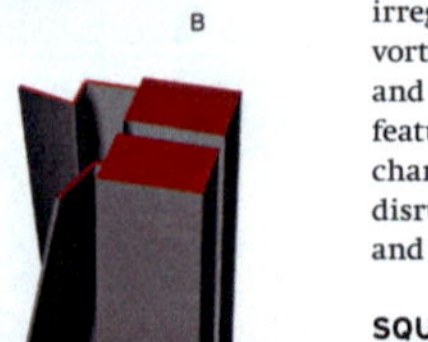

as the 60-story One Chase Manhattan Plaza, completed in Lower Manhattan in 1961, and now includes Dubai's Burj Khalifa, the world's tallest skyscraper.

FORM FOLLOWS PROGRAM

The tower was completed late last year, though work on tenant spaces and some of the public areas continues. But even before completion, some observers compared its striking silhouette to a figure wrapped in a cloak or a *dish sha*—the floor-length robe worn by Kuwaiti men. The towe project team, however, says any such associations are pur coincidental. "It's the product of parametric study," says G Haney, SOM design partner, referring to the computationa process used to generate Al Hamra's form. The tower's geo etry is based on a set of criteria that took into account the clients' leasing strategy as well as environmental factors s as solar exposure and wind loading. "The tower responds to its context and cannot be repeated elsewhere," confirm Farid Abou Arraj, projects development manager for Ajial Real Estate & Entertainment, the owner's representative.

Among the clients' programmatic needs was office spa of a certain size and configuration: The developers wante floor plates each with a gross area of about 25,000 square feet—a size they decided would appeal to tenants intereste in leasing a single floor. They also desired a narrow core-t curtain wall span of no more than 40 feet and office spac oriented to take advantage of views of the gulf to the nort east, and west.

To meet these requirements, SOM found it would have t reduce the maximum-allowable floor plate by about 25 percent on every floor. The desire to make the most of the views of the water suggested a floor plan without south-facing office space. However, solar analyses conducted wit the aim of reducing heat gain from the brutal desert sun supported the removal of the quadrant at the southwest corner of every floor. Meanwhile, computational fluid dynamic (CFD) studies and the subsequent wind-tunnel testi of physical models demonstrated that a tower with a sligh irregular profile would be the most effective in mitigatin vortex shedding—a phenomenon that creates wind eddies and induces side-to-side movement—an obviously undesira feature in a supertall building. "If the shape of the tower changes as it rises, the formation of organized vortices is disrupted," explains Mark Sarkisian, SOM director of seisn and structural engineering.

SQUARE BUT SINUOUS

From the process of balancing the various criteria, a tower with a nearly conventional plan emerged: It has a central shear wall core surrounded by a perimeter moment-resisti frame. However, the building appears to have been vertica sliced, with a chiseled-out section equal to about a quarter every floor plate that gradually travels from the southwest corner near the building's base, where it meets the retail podium, to the southeast corner at the tower's apex. A pai

SUBTRACTIVE GEOMETRY Like many tall buildings, the Al Hamra has a central shear wall core and a perimeter moment frame. However, about o quarter of its otherwise square floor plate has been removed. The remov portion incrementally shifts at each level. The edges of the resulting cut defined by a pair of hyperbolic paraboloid walls.

yperbolic paraboloid, reinforced-concrete "flare walls" ineate the edges of the incrementally shifting void. And within the resulting recess is an almost 5-foot-thick nforced-concrete wall with punched openings angled to trol penetration of the sun. On every office floor behind hefty facade is a circulation corridor that provides a tage point for occupants to take in framed views of the 's developing skyline.

he building is divided vertically into three stacked office- or zones. Visitors and tenants reach the upper two by ing express elevators to sky lobbies that offer meeting ce and other amenities, and then travel to intervening ors via local elevators. Eventually, by way of a set of VIP ators, they will be able to travel from the lobby directly he crown, where developers plan a restaurant or sky nge. It is not yet leased or fitted out, but has a dramatic ing ceiling, almost 100 feet tall at its highest point, and rds sweeping views over the gulf. SOM wisely preserved potentially valuable real estate as habitable space by osing to locate Al Hamra's cooling towers on top of the il podium instead of the tower roof.

DERNEATH IT ALL

andem with the development of the scheme for the er's superstructure, Sarkisian's team worked on the design he foundation, starting with the assumption that the ding would be around 70 stories tall and built of cast-in- e concrete. But as the tower concept took shape, it ame evident that the spiraling form would concentrate vity loads on the west side of the building footprint below southwest flare wall, while very little load would be lied to the north and southeast edges. In response to this d differential, engineers devised a 13-foot-thick reinforced- crete raft supported on 289 piles, each between 66 and 89 long, with the deeper piles located densely around the as of greatest stress.

he roughly 200-by-230-foot raft, which required almost 00 cubic yards of concrete, was poured in 15 separate ions over a period of four months. This segmented roach was dictated largely by local production capacity, it also helped contractors control the heat generated ing concrete hydration—the chemical reaction that urs when cement is mixed with water. If the material gets hot—a particular concern given the desert environment— trength can be compromised. Performing the work at nt, along with the use of a concrete mix containing a percentage of fly ash (a byproduct of coal combustion) helped keep temperatures in check, says Ali Asfour, struction manager for Ahmadiah Contracting & Trading. company is part of the client consortium and is the ject's general contractor.

onstruction of the beefy south-facing wall and the onlike flare walls, which play an integral role in the ding's lateral- and gravity-load-resisting systems, was tricky. As part of a so-called "construction correction gram" devised by SOM, the contractors adjusted the climbing formwork with each pour to compensate for lacement caused by the counterclockwise-torqued metry. The process accounted for the elastic movement of concrete under its own weight during construction and long-term movement from shrinkage and creep. "Loaded

SOLID AND SHAPED The tower's almost 5-foot-thick south-facing wall has deeply set windows for solar protection. This punched wall is clad in limestone panels, both inside (top) and out (bottom). The sculptural walls that flare from this facade are clad in the same stone, but with *trencadís*—a mosaic of shardlike pieces.

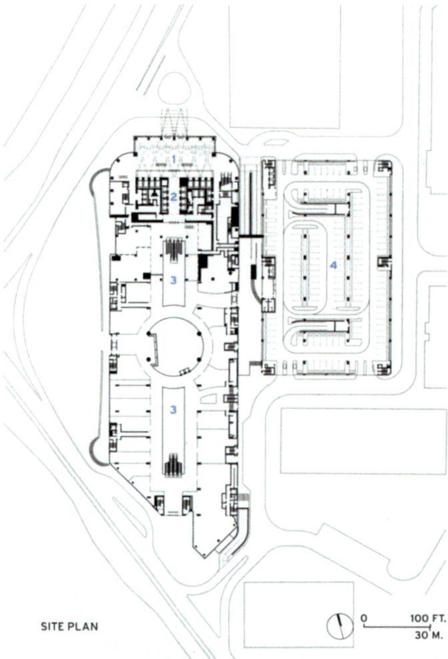

SITE PLAN

1 LOBBY
2 CORE
3 SHOPPING MALL
4 PARKING
5 OFFICE SPACE
6 VIP OFFICES
7 SPA
8 MECHANICAL
9 REFUGE
10 SKY LOBBY
11 SKY LOUNGE

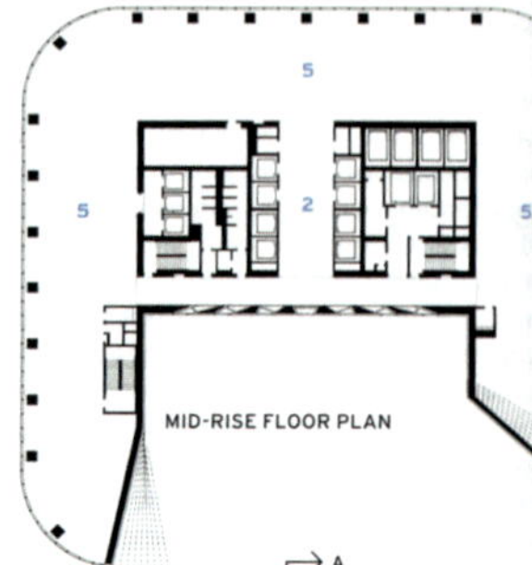

MID-RISE FLOOR PLAN

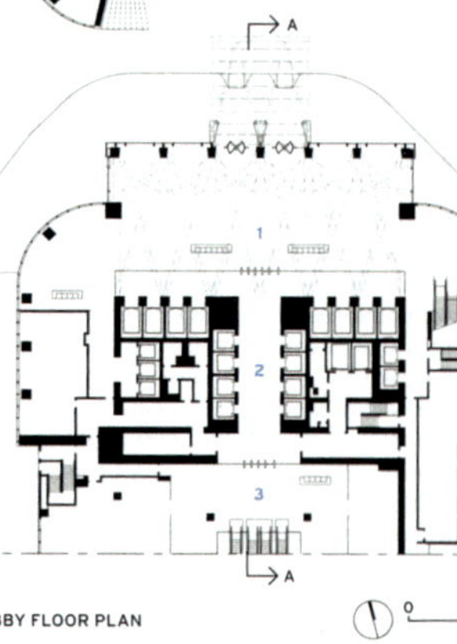

LOBBY FLOOR PLAN

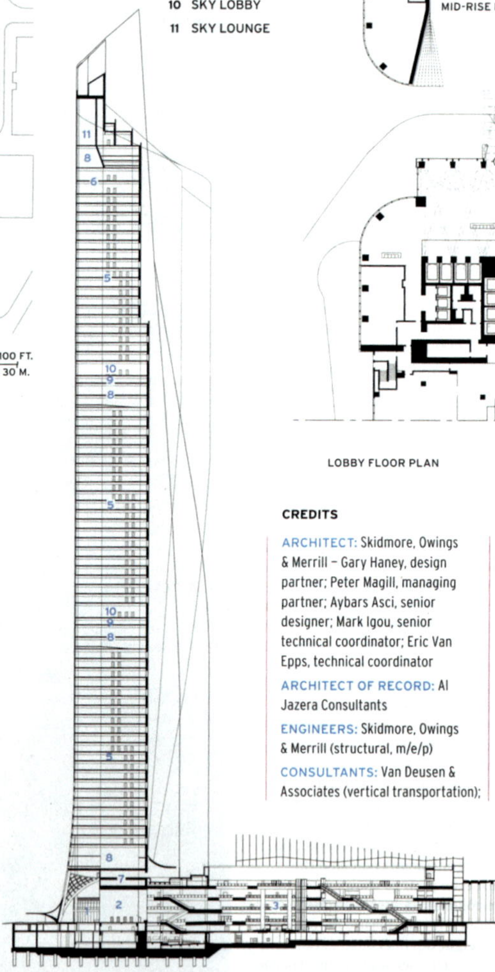

SECTION A-A

CREDITS

ARCHITECT: Skidmore, Owings & Merrill – Gary Haney, design partner; Peter Magill, managing partner; Aybars Asci, senior designer; Mark Igou, senior technical coordinator; Eric Van Epps, technical coordinator

ARCHITECT OF RECORD: Al Jazera Consultants

ENGINEERS: Skidmore, Owings & Merrill (structural, m/e/p)

CONSULTANTS: Van Deusen & Associates (vertical transportation); Office for Visual Interactio (lighting), Consultancy Gro Company (geotechnical)

CLIENT: Al Hamra Real Est

SIZE: 1.9 million square fee

COST: withheld

COMPLETION DATE: Dece

SOURCES

STONE: Jura Limestone S

GLAZING: Guardian, Pilkin

CURTAIN WALL: Wuhan L

Continuing Education

To earn one AIA/CES continuing education hour (CEH), including one hour of health, safety, and welfare (HSW) credit, read "Sculpting the Skyline" and complete the test online at no charge at ce.construction.com. Upon passing the test, you will receive a certificate of completion and your credit will automatically be reported to the AIA. Additional information regarding credit-reporting and continuing-education requirements can be found at ce.construction .com, under "resources and requirements."

Learning Objectives

1 Explain how evaluation of programmatic requirements and environmental conditions helped designers generate the form of Kuwait City's Al Hamra Firdous Tower.

2 Describe the key structural elements of the tower and its foundations.

3 Explain the structural and construction challenges presented by the tower's geometry.

4 Describe how construction methods were adapted for the harsh desert environment.

AIA/CES Course #K1205A

ıncrete can hydrate for up to 10 years," says Sarkisian, plaining the latter phenomenon. "Its properties can ntinue to change during that period," he says.

Arguably, the tower's base presented an even tougher sign and construction challenge than its sculpted superucture. "How a supertall building meets the ground is ways problematic," says Aybars Asci, an SOM director. mpared to a lower-rise building, a supertall tower has a uch smaller footprint relative to its height, but with any more people coming and going, he explains. It is also iere gravity loads are greatest and where the structural ements tend to be the largest, he points out.

At Al Hamra, the architects created ground-floor space at could handle the tower's anticipated foot traffic by canting the perimeter columns on the building's north face, increasing the lobby's depth. Designers also made Al Hamra's nearly 80-foot-tall entry hall almost Gothic by devising a system of lamellae—a series of reinforced-concrete weblike vaults—that transfer the tower's gravity load to the foundations. Developed through nonlinear buckling analysis, the system works by reducing the unbraced length of the lobby columns and by decreasing the structural demand on each of them through load sharing with parallel members, explains Sarkisian. The lamellae's primary members are about 4 feet square where they meet the lobby floor. But without use of the bracing technique, the space would have required perimeter columns almost three times as large, he estimates.

The lamellae, which Asci describes as "structurally

FORCES AND FORM
On the building's north face, perimeter columns cant outwards to increase the lobby depth and create an impressive entrance. The columns form part of a system of weblike reinforced-concrete vaults called lamellae.

LOBBY LAMELLA BUCKLING ANALYSIS

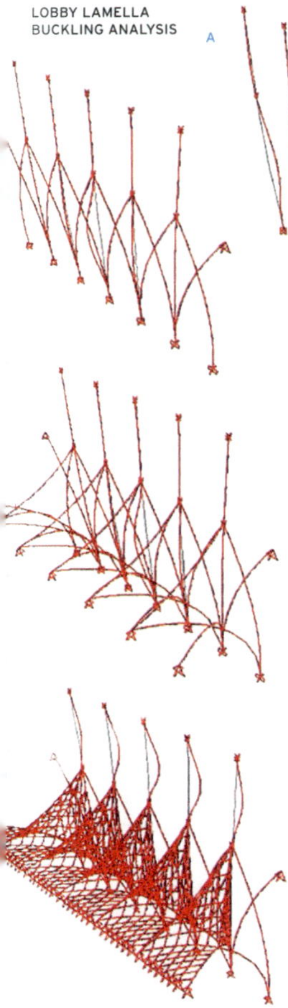

A BUCKLING CAPACITY: 25,000 KN

B BUCKLING CAPACITY: 48,500 KN

C BUCKLING CAPACITY: 49,500 KN

D BUCKLING CAPACITY: 189,000 KN

LACY BUT STRONG
Developed through nonlinear buckling analysis, the lamella system reduces the unbraced length of structural elements. It increases load-carrying capacity almost eightfold but allows designers to keep columns slender.

sensible but spatially interesting" were built with fibergla formwork fabricated from shop drawings generated from SOM's 3-D model. Even so, constructing the lamellae was slow process, requiring nearly 100 days to complete. In the meantime, work advanced on the rest of the tower, with floor framing on the north side catching up to the other sections of the building at the 52nd floor, according to Asfo

White paint covers the lamellae, enhancing their filigr quality, but somewhat diminishing the brute power evide in construction photographs. "No one likes exposed concr other than architects," says Asci. Aesthetic concerns aside however, exposed concrete was never a practical option, especially on the exterior, due to Kuwait City's salty gulf a and its tendency to corrode rebar. In part to prevent such deterioration, the architects chose an especially durable t of limestone cladding, covering the south-facing planar w in 2.5-foot-by-4.5-foot panels. They clad the serpentine fla walls in the same stone, but with *trencadis*—a mosaic of shardlike pieces.

The treatment of the flare walls lends them a handcraf character, especially evident up close. Their texture contras with the silvery smoothness of the insulated glazing units (IGUs) cladding the east, north, and west facades. The IGUs include a low-E coating that imparts just enough reflectiv to catch the sky, points out Haney. This coating proved to one of the key curtain wall challenges, since the architect needed to make sure it would be compatible with the heat ing and bending process required to fabricate the glass th wraps the corners. These curved units make up 30 percen of the building's glazing.

The reflectivity that Haney is so fond of was evident on sunny day in mid-March, even though the curtain wall wa still covered with construction grime, as well as a coating of dust from the region's frequent sand storms. After an initial cleaning, the glazing will be cleaned once every thr months by workers suspended from a maintenance unit t encircles the building on a track cleverly concealed withi the steeply sloping parapet.

The owners are in the process of completing their own 26th-floor offices. However, it isn't clear how many other office tenants have committed to taking space in the Al Hamra. The retail anchor tenant, Hermes, opened in December, and as of early this spring, about 86 percent of the shopping mall had been leased—information that Abo Arraj readily volunteers. However, of the tower office floo he says only that there is "considerable interest." Despite t evasiveness, and an undisclosed budget—even the architec say they don't know the building's total cost—it would be inappropriate to gauge the success of the tower from the vantage point of American developers, who are generally focused on quick financial returns. The tower is undeniab an iconic addition to Kuwait City's skyline, and Abou Arra seems confident that tenants will materialize—eventually. "We are building for the future," he says. ■

ALMOST GOTHIC Al Hamra has a soaring, 80-foot-tall entry hall, with a floor and core walls finished in the same limestone that clads the sculptural south-facing elevation. The entry hall's vaulted, reinforced-concrete lamellae are painted white, enhancing their lacelike quality.

Kingdom Come

At a time when American architects are designing ever-soaring skyscrapers in far-flung places, **CAROL WILLIS**, the director of the Skycraper Museum in New York, talks to RECORD's deputy editor, Suzanne Stephens, about the highs and whys of tall buildings.

What is your definition of a "supertall" building?

In the *Supertall!* exhibition at the Skyscraper Museum in Lower Manhattan [on view July 27–February 19, 2011], we set a benchmark higher than the standard 300 meters used by the Council on Tall Buildings and Urban Habitat (CTBUH). To be included in the show, the building had to be at least 380 meters (1,250 feet)—the height of the Empire State Building—and likely to be topped out by 2016. (It takes an average of five years to complete a supertall.) Forty-eight projects met these criteria for the show.

With design of the Kingdom Tower in Jedda, Saudi Arabia, by Adrian Smith + Gordon Gill Architecture at more than 3,280 feet, we are seeing the bar raised so much higher. Why are so many supertall buildings springing up in Asia and the Middle East? Besides the money being there?

The context is important with regard to tall buildings. In a place like Hong Kong, which encourages skyscrapers, the government owns the land and can gain high bids from developers by allowing what I call "vertical-density" development. Projects such as International Commerce Centre by Kohn Pedersen Fox [page 142] are part of a centralized urban-planning and development scheme that includes transit hubs, offices, housing, and retail.

In other cities with less sophisticated infrastructure and technology, supertalls are used to create an autonomous urban place with complementary uses for business people—offices, hotel, apartments, and shopping. This is a fully acclimatized environment with reliable electricity and other services—even if the local grid is not reliable. These buildings are advanced machines of efficiency that serve a lot of people in a small space.

Urbanization in China is so explosive that many cities have populations as large or larger than New York City's 8 million. Chinese cities offer a huge, growing demand for new buildings. Yet in the Middle East—for example, Dubai—developers try to create demand by designing tall buildings that will attract affluent buyers and investors in real estate. The idea is that glamorous buildings can create demand.

Is the role of the private developer the same as in the United States?

Governments often play an important role in Asia and the Middle East, either selecting developers or investing and building themselves. For example, with the Shanghai Tower [page 156], Gensler is working with a state-run construction and investment company. I think the tower will make money, but it's hard to compare Shanghai Tower to one developed by a purely private market.

How have American architectural firms gotten into the supertall inner circle of skyscraper designers? Obviously we can claim having been there first with our skyscrapers built in the late 19th century in New York and Chicago. But on our home turf we haven't been doing towers at this scale.

American architects and engineers had an edge when the global embrace of skyscraper design began about 20 years ago. Experience clearly matters in doing a supertall. Designers lead a team, and its members know each other and often work together in problem solving to build a better skyscraper machine. Understanding

ON A CLEAR DAY On the 157th floor of the future Kingdom Tower in Jeddah, Adrian Smith + Gordon Gill Architecture has designed a 5,800-square-foot projecting, outdoor terrace (above), part of which will have a glass bottom. An observation deck also is planned for the 123rd floor. The reinforced-concrete tower, sheathed in high-performance glass (opposite), will taper to a height over 3,280 feet.

View additional images at architecturalrecord.com.

uper Supertall:
ingdom Tower

TALLEST supertall in the world, Kingdom Tower,
ddah, Saudi Arabia, is expected to zoom upward of
0 feet (over 1000 meters) when completed in 2017.
Adrian Smith + Gordon Gill Architecture won't say
much "over" that height it will soar. It could be the
petition thing. Ever since the first tall buildings
ed breaking height records in New York in the late
century, architects and their clients have vied for
allest-in-the-world title. If technology and money
provide the wherewithal, the adventurous will want
ever higher, wrapping desire within rationales
solving population density, saving energy).
ngdom Tower, the ultra-seductive crown of a new
lopment—the 1,312-acre Kingdom City, in north
ah—got its final building approval in February.
ently it is undergoing load testing for soil condi-
s and has completed its test pile program.
nith, who was the lead designer of the world's tall-
ower—the 2,717-foot-high Burj Khalifa in Dubai
)—while he was a partner at Skidmore, Owings &
ill (SOM)'s Chicago office, left in 2006. He joined up
Gill, an SOM colleague, and soon the new firm was
ed by Prince Alwaleed bin Talal of the Kingdom
ing Company (KHC) to compete for the reportedly
billion tower overlooking the Red Sea. In 2011,
h and Gill won the coveted commission over high-
s SOM, Foster + Partners, Kohn Pedersen Fox, Pelli
ke Pelli, as well as Pickard Chilton, Atkins, and
ning Larsen Architects. And while HOK is master-
ning Kingdom City, Smith and Gill are in charge
e 57-acre waterfront district around the tower.
nith maintains the scheme—a reinforced-concrete
e-legged structure, designed with engineers
nton Tomasetti—won the day because "it was cost-
tive, efficient in the floor plan, and dynamic to
at from all vantage points." Like Burj Khalifa,
dom Tower uses a basic tripodlike form to spread
oad. But this tower's tapering slope, Smith notes,
s reduce wind load more effectively than the Burj
ifa's stepped profile. "The slope mitigates vortex
ding," says Smith, pointing out that every floor sets
from 4 to 8 inches as it inclines upward.
ne tower, clad in high-performance glazing, will
ain a mix of offices, hotels, condominium units,
"service" condos maintained by the hotel, not to
tion retail and observation decks. Currently Smith
Gill have a supertall just beginning construction in
a—the Wuhan Greenland Center, at 1,988 feet
—with another, the 1,476-feet-high Yongsan tower,
ned for Seoul. "It's exciting to design a building that
ing to be a landmark," Smith says. "I look for a form
will function well and represent the country's
th and cultural leadership." *Suzanne Stephens*

the challenges of designing a curtain wall, elevators, floor plans, and rentable floor area takes experience.

So how would Gensler get the commission to design the supertall Shanghai Tower since it had never designed anything higher than 54 stories (the L.A. LIVE, 2010)? Gensler might be the second-largest architecture firm in the U.S. in terms of revenue [RECORD, July 2011, page 24] and it has over 3,000 employees, but, as we know, a small coterie of American architects—along with Foster + Partners and others—gets these jobs. So far Gensler hasn't been part of the cloud club. Also whether the firm likes it or not, Gensler is better known for its commercial interior design work than for tall buildings.

As I understand it, Gensler builds relationships and trust, starting with interior design work for corporate clients, and then it pushes the boundaries from the office to the whole building. It builds trust with clients by coming in at the ground floor, so to speak. Gensler also has hired people and has assembled a team who had worked on supertalls elsewhere, such as SOM. Also it worked with Thornton Tomasetti and Cosentini Associates for the engineering of Shanghai Tower. I heard Arthur Gensler represented the firm for official meetings and ceremonies—which makes a strong impression with the clients.

Does it make sense to keep going higher, as we see with the Kingdom Tower? The architects involved in supertalls talk about sustainability values of such density and agglomerating various forms of transit within the project.

A lot of conditions are cultural. I was just in Frankfurt, a city that likes skyscrapers, but where retrofitting and recladding towers built in the 1960s to 1980s for energy-efficiency is an important trend. In terms of the supertall sustainable skyscraper, the next step is toward net-zero energy—that is, towers producing as much energy as they consume. This idea is already starting to happen with shorter towers.

Isn't there a point when a supertall is just too tall? Even if it is energy-efficient?

A lot of people believe supertalls are irrational acts. I think they are fundamentally rational, but also aspirational. To build a supertall you are taking a risk, more than if you were building a conventional structure, but you are trying to do something that gets extra attention. These bigger-than-life skyscrapers are beautiful. Supertalls are the celebrities of the skyscraper world. ■

Carol Willis is the founder and director of the Skyscraper Museum in New York City, and a professor of Urban Studies at Columbia University's Graduate School of Architecture, Preservation and Planning.

VIEW FROM THE TOP The three-legged massing of the reinforced-concrete Kingdom Tower provides stability, while the large notches in the tower help shade terraces from the sun. No facade faces the sun directly, and the outdoor air temperature at the top of the tower is expected to be lower than that at ground level. The 5.7 million-square-foot tower, with 59 elevators and three sky lobbies, overlooks a waterfront district, which Smith and Gill are master-planning as a part of the new development of Kingdom City on the Red Sea.

A | S
G | G

2006–

Adrian Smith + Gordon Gill Architecture

Headquarters
Chicago, IL

Other Locations
Beijing, China

Founding Partners
Adrian Smith, Gordon Gill, Robert Forest

Adrian Smith + Gordon Gill Architecture

2006

2007–

ATOPIA

Headquarters
Princeton, NJ

Other Locations
London, UK; Nairobi, Kenya

Founding Partners
Jane Harrison, David Turnbull

2007

ATOPIA

ORG

ORGANIZATION FOR PERMANENT MODERNITY

2007–

ORG Organization for Permanent Modernity

Headquarters
Boston, MA

Other Locations
Brussels, Belgium

Founding Partners
Alexander D'Hooghe, Natalie Seys, Luk Peeters

ORG Organization for Permanent Modernity

2007

2008–

MASS Design Group

Headquarters
Boston, MA

Other Locations
Kigali, Rwanda; Port-au-Prince, Haiti

Founding Partners
Michael Murphy, Alan Ricks

2008

MASS Design Group

SO–IL

Headquarters
Brooklyn, NY

Founding Partners
Florian Idenburg, Jing Liu

Current Partners
Florian Idenburg, Jiang Liu (principals),
Ilias Papageorgiou (associate principal)

SO-IL

LEONG LEONG ARCHITECTURE

NEW YORK

Leong Leong

Headquarters
New York, NY

Founding Partners
Dominic Leong, Chris Leong

2009

Leong Leong

NADAAA

Headquarters
Boston, MA

Other Locations
New York, NY

Founding Partners
Nader Tehrani, Daniel Gallagher, Katherine Faulkner

NADAAA

Dubai Festival Waterfront Centre
2007

JERDE

Architect
Jerde Partnership

Location
Dubai, United Arab Emirates

Architect of Record
Wakefield Beasley

Client
Al Futtaim Group/Al Futtaim Investments

Dubai Marina
2007

Architect
Hellmuth, Obata + Kassabaum

Location
Dubai, United Arab Emirates

Client
Emaar Properties

Rohm and Haas China
2007

Architect
RMJM Hillier

Location
Pudong, China

Client
Rohm and Haas Company

Abercrombie and Fitch Flagship Store
2007–2009

SELLDORF ARCHITECTS

Architect
Selldorf Architects

Location
Tokyo, Japan

Client
Abercrombie & Fitch

Barbie Shanghai Flagship Store
2007–2009

SLADE ARCHITECTURE

Architect
Slade Architecture

Location
Shanghai, China

Client
Mattel, Inc.

Yas Viceroy Abu Dhabi Hotel
2007–2009

Architect
Asymptote Architecture

Location
Abu Dhabi, United Arab Emirates

Client
Viceroy Hotel Group

Apple Store Covent Garden
2007–2010

Architect
Bohlin Cywinski Jackson

Location
London, England

Client
Apple, Inc.

Bohlin Cywinski Jackson
Architecture Planning Interior Design

Apple Store Opéra
2007–2010

Architect
Bohlin Cywinski Jackson

Location
Paris, France

Client
Apple, Inc.

Bohlin Cywinski Jackson
Architecture Planning Interior Design

Aviva Stadium
2007–2010

Architect
Populous

Location
Dublin, Ireland

Local Architect
Scott Tallon

Client
Aviva

POPULOUS

Convention Centre Dublin
2007–2010

Architect
Kevin Roche John Dinkeloo and Associates

Location
Dublin, Ireland

Client
Treasury Holdings

KRJDA
KEVIN ROCHE JOHN DINKELOO AND ASSOCIATES LLC

US Embassy
2007–2010

Architect
Integrus

Location
Sarajevo, Bosnia & Herzegovina

Client
Bureau of Overseas Building Operations

integrus ARCHITECTURE

UNITED STATES OF AMERICA EMBASSY

Torre Iberdrola
2007–2011

Architect
Pelli Clarke Pelli Architects

Location
Bilbao, Spain

Local Architect
Ortiz Leon Arquitectos

Pelli Clarke Pelli Architects

2007

2014

Shanghai International Finance Center
2007–2011

Architect
Pelli Clarke Pelli Architects

Location
Shanghai, China

Client
IFC Development,
Sun Hung Kai Properties

Pelli Clarke Pelli Architects

Capitaland Raffles City (Sliced Porosity Block)
2007–2012

Architect
Steven Holl Architects

Location
Chengdu, China

Client
CapitaLand Development

STEVEN HOLL ARCHITECTS

Taiyuan Museum of Art
2007–2013

Architect
Preston Scott Cohen

Location
Taiyuan, China

Client
Taiyuan City Government

The Avenues—Phase III
2007–2013

Architect
Gensler

Location
Kuwait City, Kuwait

Client
Mabanee Company S.A.K.

Gensler

Torre Begonias (HSBC Headquarters)
2007–2013

Architect
Arquitectonica

Location
Lima, Peru

Client
Urbanizadora Jardin S.A.

ARQUITECTONICA

Tour Carpe Diem
2007–2013

Architect
Robert A.M. Stern Architects

Location
La Défense, France

Client
Aviva France, Crédit Agricol,
Hines

RAMSA
ROBERT A.M. STERN ARCHITECTS

Baku Flame Towers
2007–2013

Architect
Hellmuth, Obata + Kassabaum

Location
Baku, Azerbaijan

Client
DIA Holding, Azinko Development MMC

Chennai International Airport Domestic and International Terminals
2007–

Architect
Gensler, Frederick Schwartz Architects

Location
Chennai, India

Client
Airports Authority of India

Guggenheim Museum
2007–

Architect
Frank O. Gehry and Associates

Location
Abu Dhabi, United Arab Emirates

Client
Tourism Development & Investment Company, Abu Dhabi

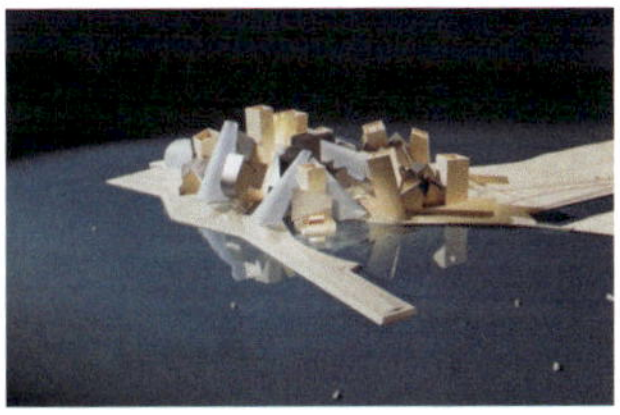

American University in Cairo New Campus
2008

Architect
Sasaki Associates Inc.

Location
Cairo, Egypt

Client
The American University in Cairo

Art Gallery of Ontario
2008

Architect
Gehry Partners

Location
Toronto, Canada

Client
Art Gallery of Ontario

Charles Hostler Student Center
2008

Architect
VJAA

Location
Beirut, Lebanon

Client
American University of Beirut

Louis Dreyfus Grande Armée
2008

STUDIOS architecture

Architect
STUDIOS Architecture

Location
Paris, France

Client
The Louis Dreyfus Group

Sanlitun
2008

sh p

Architect
SHoP

Location
Beijing, China

Client
Swire Properties

Salim Publishing House
2008–2009

KPF

Architect
Kohn Pedersen Fox Associates

Location
Rio de Janeiro, Brazil

Client
Tishman Speyer, Carmargo Correa Group

Butaro District Hospital
2008–2011

SAA

Architect
Stan Allen Architect

Location
Paju Book City, Korea

Client
Salim Publishing Company

Salim Publishing House
2008–2009

MASS

Architect
MASS Design Group

Location
Butaro, Burera District, Rwanda

Client
Rwanda Ministry of Health, Partners In Health

Chengdu Skycourts
2008–2011

Höweler + Yoon Architecture

Architect
Höweler + Yoon Architecture

Location
Chendu China

Client
Chengdu Qingyang SCD, Ltd

Antilia House
2008-2011

Architect
Perkins + Will

Location
Mumbai, India

Client
Mukesh Ambani

PERKINS+WILL

OCT Shenzhen Clubhouse
2008–2012

Architect
Richard Meier & Partners Architects

Location
Shenzhen, China

Client
OCT Urban Entertainment Investment Company Of Shenzhen

Richard Meier & Partners Architects LLP

Campus for Research Excellence and Technological Enterprise University Centre
2008–2013

Architect
Perkins + Will

Location
Singapore, Singapore

Client
Singapore National Research Foundation

PERKINS+WILL

Centro de Artes Nadir Afonso Museum
2008–2013

Architect
Louise Braverman, Architect

Location
Boticas, Portugal

Client
Municipio de Boticas

LOUISE BRAVERMAN ARCHITECT

Taekwondo Park
2008–2013

Architect
WEISS/MANFREDI Architecture/Landscape/Urbanism

Location
Muju, Korea

Client
Taekwondo Promotion Foundation

WEISS / MANFREDI
ARCHITECTURE / LANDSCAPE / URBANISM

Lotte World Tower
2008–2015

Architect
Kohn Pedersen Fox Associates

Location
Chongqing, China

Client
Shui On Land Ltd.

KPF

NATO Headquarters
2008–

Architect
Skidmore, Owings & Merrill

Location
Brussels, Belgium

Client
North Atlantic Treaty Organization

SOM

Chongqing International Trade and Commerce Center
2008–

Architect
Kohn Pedersen Fox Associates

Location
Chongqing, China

Client
Shui On Land Ltd.

KPF

Datong Library
2008–

Architect
Preston Scott Cohen

Location
Datong, China

Client
Datong Planning Bureau

Masdar Headquarters
2008–

Architect
Adrian Smith + Gordon Gill Architecture

Location
Abu Dhabi, United Arab Emirates

Client
Masdar

AS
GG

Carrasco International Airport
2009

Architect
Rafael Viñoly Architects

Location
Montevideo, Uruguay

Client
Puerta del Sur, S.A.

RAFAEL VIÑOLY ARCHITECTS

Fortabat Collection
2009

Architect
Rafael Viñoly Architects

Location
Buenos Aires, Argentina

Client
Amalia Lacroze de Fortabat

RAFAEL VIÑOLY ARCHITECTS

Novartis Pharma A.G. Campus
2009

Architect
Gehry Partners

Location
Basel, Switzerland

Client
Novartis Pharma AG

Philip Lim Store
2009

LEONG LEONG ARCHITECTURE
NEW YORK

Architect
Leong Leong

Location
Seoul, Korea

Client
3.1 Philip Lim

Apple Store IFC Pudong
2009–2010

Bohlin Cywinski Jackson
Architecture Planning Interior Design

Architect
Bohlin Cywinski Jackson

Location
Shanghai, China

Client
Apple, Inc.

Vakko Fashion Center and Power Media Center
2009–2010

REX

Architect
REX Architecture

Location
Istanbul, Turkey

Client
Vakko Power and Media

Naked Stables
2009–2011

STUDIO SHANGHAI

Architect
Studio Shanghai

Location
Hangzhou, China

Client
Naked Stables Private Reserve

Umubano School
2009–2011

MASS

Architect
MASS Design Group

Location
Kigali, Rwanda

Client
A Partner In Education (APIE)

White Block Gallery
2009–2011

Architect
SsD

Location
Heyri, South Korea

Client
Lee Soo Moon

Mizuta Museum Of Art
2009–2012

Architect
Studio SUMO

Location
Sakado, Japan

Client
Josai University

National University of Ireland, Galway Research Bundle
2009–2014

Architect
Payette

Location
Galway, Ireland

Client
National University of Ireland

Sochi Olympic Stadium
2009–2014

Architect
Populous

Location
Sochi, Russia

Local Architect
Mosproject-4

Client
Olympstroy; Engeocom

University of Melbourne Faculty of Architecture, Building and Planning
2009–2014

Architect
John Wardle Architects, NADAAA

Location
Melbourne, Australia

Client
University of Melbourne

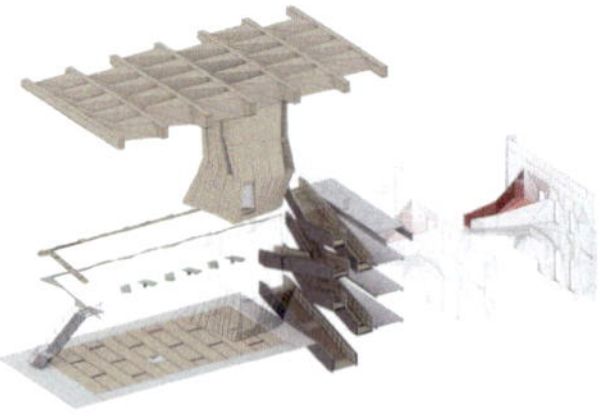

Heart of Lake
2009–2014

Architect
Robert A.M. Stern Architects

Location
Xiamen, China

Client
Xiamen Vanke Real Estate Enterprise Co. Ltd

Firestation and Youth Center (ASCO)
2009–2014

Architect
ORG Organization For Permanent Modernity

Location
Asse, Belgium

Client
Town of Asse

Museum of Image and Sound
2009–

Architect
Diller Scofidio + Renfro

Location
Rio de Janeiro, Brazil

Client
Fundação Roberto Marinho

Guangzhou CTF Finance Centre
2009–

Architect
Kohn Pedersen Fox Associates

Location
Guangzhou, China

Client
New World Development Company Ltd.

Abu Dhabi National Oil Company Headquarters
2009–

Architect
Hellmuth, Obata + Kassabaum

Location
Abu Dhabi, United Arab Emirates

Client
Abu Dhabi National Oil Company

Capital Market Authority Tower
2009–

Architect
Hellmuth, Obata + Kassabaum

Location
Riyadh, Saudi Arabia

Local Architect
Omrania & Associates

Client
Alraidah Investment Company, KSA.

King Abdullah Financial District
2009–

Architect
FXFOWLE Architects

Location
Riyadh, Saudi Arabia

Client
Rayadah Investment Company

Lali Gurans Orphanage and Learning Centre
2009–

Architect
MOS Architects

Location
Kathmandu, Nepal

Client
Seeds of Change Foundation

Singapore University of Technology and Design Master Plan
2010

Architect
Sasaki Associates

Location
Singapore, Singapore

Client
Singapore Government Ministry of Education

APAP Open School
2010–2011

Architect
LOT-EK

Location
Seoul, South Korea

Client
Anyang Public Arts Program

Krabbesholm Højskole Studios
2010–2012

Architect
MOS Architects

Location
Skive, Denmark

Client
Kurt Finsten, Krabbesholm Højskole

Kukje Art Center
2010–2012

Architect
SO-IL

Location
Seoul, South Korea

Client
Modern Media Group/Get it Louder

Samsung Model Home Gallery
2010–2012

Architect
NADAAA

Location
Seoul, South Korea

Local Architect
aandd

Client
Samsung

Al Maryah Island Vision Plan
2010–2013

Architect
over,under, Utile

Location
Abu Dhabi, United Arab Emirates

Client
Mubadala Real Estate and Infrastructure

Soft House
2010–2013

Architect
KVA matx

Location
Hamburg, Germany

Client
PATRIZIA Projektentwicklung GmbH; Internationale Bauausstellung (IBA) Hamburg

MIDEA VIP and Golf Clubhouse
2010–2013

Architect
RTKL

Location
Foshan, China

Client
Midea Group

Jaipur Residential Development
2010–

Architect
STUDIOS Architecture

Location
Jaipur, India

Client
Jaipur Development Authority Foundation

Worldmark Development at Indira Ghandi International Airport
2010–

Architect
Kohn Pedersen Fox Associates

Location
Delhi, India

Client
Aspen Buildtech Ltd

Kingdom Tower
2010–

Architect
Adrian Smith + Gordon Gill Architecture

Location
Jeddah, Saudi Arabia

Client
Jeddah Economic Company

US Embassy Office Annex
2010–

Architect
Hellmuth, Obata + Kassabaum

Location
Moscow, Russia

Client
US Department of State, Bureau of Overseas Buildings Operations

Botswana Innovation Hub
2010–

Architect
SHoP

Location
Gabarone, Botswana

Client
National Government of Botswana

Kempegowda Airport Terminal 1 Expansion
2010–

Architect
Hellmuth, Obata + Kassabaum

Location
Bangalore, India

Client
GVK Group

Tri-Climatic Biosphere
2010–

Architect
LEESER Architecture

Location
Abu Dhabi, United Arab Emirates

Client
Confidential

US Embassy
2010–

Architect
KieranTimberlake

Location
London, England

Client
US Department of State, Bureau of Overseas Buildings Operations

50 Connaught Road Central
2011

Architect
Robert A.M. Stern Architects

Location
Hong Kong, China

Client
Century Land Limited; Apollo Global Real Estate Management; National Properties Holdings, Ltd

Khalsa Heritage Centre
2011

Architect
Safdie Architects

Location
Anandpur Sahib, India

Client
Anandpur Sahib Foundation

Konoha Eco-Mall
2011

Architect
Jerde Partnership

Location
Fukuoka, Japan

Architect of Record
Fukuoka Jisho Co., Ltd

Client
Fukuoka Jisho Co., Ltd., Urban Design and Development Co.

Marina Bay Sands Integrated Resort
2011

Architect
Safdie Architects

Location
Singapore, Singapore

Client
Las Vegas Sands Corporation

Butaro Doctors' Housing
2011–2012

Architect
MASS Design Group

Location
Butaro, Burera District, Rwanda

Client
Rwanda Ministry of Health, Partners In Health

Village Health Works Staff Housing
2011–2013

Architect
Louise Braverman, Architect

Location
Kigutu, Burundi

Client
Village Health Works

Tianfu Ecological City
2011–

Architect
Adrian Smith + Gordon Gill Architecture

Location
Chengdu, China

Client
Beijing Vantone Citylogic Investment Company

Byblos Town Hall
2011–

Architect
Hashim Sarkis Studios

Location
Byblos, Lebanon

Client
Byblos Municipality

Konza Technology Pavilion
2011–

Architect
SHoP

Location
Nairobi, Kenya

Local Architects
Zed Architects

Client
Kenyan Ministry of Information and Communication (MoIC)

New Holland Island Master Plan and Cultural Center
2011–

Architect
WORKac

Location
St. Petersburg, Russia

Client
Millhouse

World One
2011–

Architect
Pei Cobb Freed & Partners

Location
Mumbai, India

Client
Lodha Developers

Tsing Tao Pearl Visitor Center
2012

Architect
Bohlin Cywinski Jackson

Location
Qingdao, China

Client
Qingdao Vanke Real Estate Co., Ltd.

WATERBANKSchool
2012

Architect
ATOPIA

Location
Nanyuki, Kenya

Donor
Guernsey Overseas Aid, Ellen Rihoy Trust

GHESKIO Cholera Treament Center
2012–

Architect
MASS Design Group

Location
Port-au-Prince, Haiti

Client
Les Centres GHESKIO

L'Assemblée Radiuese Conference Center
2012–

Architect
WORKac

Location
Liberville, Gabon

Client
ANGT, Gabon

Sanhe School
2012

Architect
OBRA Architects

Location
Beijing, China

Client
Sanhe Bai Jia Real Estate Co., Ltd.

Songpa Micro-Housing
2012–

Architect
SsD

Location
Seoul, South Korea

Client
Lee Chanill

Songzhuang Arts and Agriculture City
2012–

Architect
Sasaki Associates

Location
Beijing, China

Client
Tongzhou District Government

Sowwah Square
2012

Architect
Goettsch Partners

Location
Abu Dhabi, United Arab Emirates

Client
Mubadala Real Estate & Infrastructure

WATERBANKCanteen
2013–2014

Architect
ATOPIA

Location
Nanyuki, Kenya

Donor
O'Reilly Family

WATERBANKDormitory
2013–2014

Architect
ATOPIA

Location
Nanyuki, Kenya

Client
Guernsey Overseas Aid, Ellen Rihoy Trust

PITCHKenya Stadium
2013–2014

Architect
ATOPIA

Location
Nanyuki, Kenya

Donor
Samuel Eto'o Foundation, O'Reilly Family, Zeitz Foundation

Sinthian Cultural Center
2013–

TOSHIKO MORI ARCHITECT

Architect
Toshiko Mori Architect

Location
Sinthian, Senegal

Client
Josef and Anni Albers Foundation, The American Friends of Le Korsa

One Horizon Center
2013–

RAMSA
ROBERT A.M. STERN ARCHITECTS

Architect
Robert A.M. Stern Architects

Location
Gurgaon, India

Client
Hines and DLF Limited

Chhatrapati Shivaji International Airport Terminal 2
2014

SOM

Architect
Skidmore, Owings & Merrill

Location
Mumbai, India

Client
Mumbai International Airport, Ltd.

College of Media and Communication at Education City
2014–

Architect
Antoine Predock Architect PC

Location
Doha, Qatar

Executive Architect
Burns & McDonnell

Client
Qatar Foundation for Education, Science and Community Development

Repository Office Articles

Offices Established 1853–1895

SmithGroupJJR

"Death of prominent citizen of Detroit Railroad Schemes Marine Disaster," *The Chicago Tribune* (June 2, 1869).

"Two Virginia developments rate honor housing exhibit," *The Washington Post* (August 23, 1953).

"Organization For Efficient Practice: Smith, Hinchman, and Grylls Associates, Inc. Architects and Engineers," *Architectural Record* (July 1960): 165–170.

"Smith, Hinchman and Grylls headquarters: Staying downtown with style," *Architectural Record* (April 1974): 120–121.

Robert A. Benson, "Detroit's Smith, Hinchman and Grylls, America's oldest corporate architectural firm, confidently positions itself for the 21st century," *Inland Architect* (March–April 1993): 32–41.

Norman Kanderlan, "It's still a design firm or is it not?," *Architectural Record* (March 1994): 28–31.

"Smith Group: a proud history, a vibrant future," *Building Design and Construction* (May 2007): 25–27.

D. H. Burnham & Company

"The Organization of an Architects Office," *The Engineering and Building Record* (December 7, 1889): 83–84.

"Daniel H. Burnham, Famous Architect, Dies in Germany," *The Chicago Journal* (June 1, 1912).

"Death Takes Greatest of Architects," *The Pittsburgh Dispatch* (June 2, 1912).

Peter B. Wight, "Daniel Hudson Burnham and his Associates," *Architectural Record* (July 1915): 1–31.

"Firm of Graham, Burnham and Co. Dissolves," *The Western Architect* (August 1917): 12–14.

"Dissolution and Reconstruction of the Burnham Firm," *The Western Architect* (September 1917): 17–18.

Thomas S. Hines, "The Imperial Facade: Daniel H. Burnham and American Architectural Planning in the Philippines," *Pacific Historical Review* (February 1972): 33–53.

Thomas S. Hines, "American Modernism in the Philippines: The Forgotten Architecture of William E. Parsons," *Journal of the Society of Architectural Historians* (December 1973): 316–326.

Jay Wickersham, "Learning From Burnham: The Origins of Modern Architectural Practice," *Harvard Design Magazine* 32 (Spring/Summer 2010): 18–27.

The Austin Company

"Building in one package," *Architectural Forum* (January 1945): 93–113.

Richard Korman, "Survivors still dealing with poor conditions," *Engineering News Record* (January 2, 2006): 12–13.

McKim, Mead & White

D. Everett Waid, "The Business Side of an Architect's Office," *The Brickbuilder* (December 1913): 179–181.

Peter Smithson, "The fine and the folk: An essay on McKim, Mead and White and the American tradition," *Architectural Design* (August 1965): 394–397.

Holabird & Root

John Wellborn Root, "John Augur Holabird—An Appreciation," *Journal of The American Institute of Architects* (November 1945): 213–220.

"Holabird & Root," *Architectural Forum* (April 1937): 10–11.

"Hotels," *Architectural Forum* (June 1950): 90–101.

"Intercontinental Hotels: Design for Tourism," *Architectural Record* (October 1953): 14–15.

Lisa Pfueller Davidson, "Early Twentieth-Century Hotel Architects and the Origins of Standarization," *The Journal of Decorative and Propaganda Arts*, Vol 25 (2005): 73–103.

George A. Fuller Company

"Great building firm organized," *The Chicago Tribune* (March 30, 1901): 4.

David B. Carlson, "Building's No. 1 contractor," *Architectural Forum* (April 1961): 112–123, 168, 172, 176.

Jeffrey W. Cody, "Erecting Monuments to the God of Business and Trade," *The Construction History* (1996): 67–81.

Cass Gilbert

Francis S. Swales, "The Work of Cass Gilbert," *The Architectural Review* (January–June 1912): 3–16.

Jonas Lie, "Cass Gilbert 1859–1934," *Architectural Forum* (June 1934): 6

Geoffrey Blodgett, "Cass Gilbert, Architect: Conservative at Bay," *Journal of American History* (December 1985): 615–636.

Shepley Bulfinch

J.D. Forbes, "Shepley, Bulfinch, Richardson & Abbott, Architects: An Introduction," *Journal of the Society of Architectural Historians* (Fall 1958): 19–31.

"Recent work of Shepley, Bulfinch, Richardson and Abbott," *Architectural Record* (February 1959): 153–168.

"Regional Focus," *World Architecture* (June 1997): 47–59.

Helmle & Corbett

Harvey Wiley Corbett, "Design in Office Buildings," *Architectural Forum* (May 1930): 779.

"F.J. Helmle dead; retired architect," *The New York Times* (July 16, 1939): 30.

"Architect Harvey Corbett dies at 81," *Architectural Forum* (May 1954): 45.

Frank Lloyd Wright

"Mosaics," *The Inland Architect and News Record* (March 1901): 16.

"In the cause of architecture," *The Architectural Record* (March 1908): 208–209.

"The studio home of Frank Lloyd Wright," *The Architectural Record* (January 1930): 5–10.

Harry Seckel, "Frank Lloyd Wright," *The North American Review* (September 1938): 48–64.

"Usonian Architect," *Time* (January 17, 1938): 29–32.

"'Taliesin West,' Arizona," *The Architects' Journal* (March 1941): 177–178.

Ulrich Middeldorf, "Architecture as an art: Prologue to a lecture by Frank Lloyd Wright," *College Art Journal* (Autumn 1946): 37–42.

Samuel Cauman, "The Science of Art History," *College Art Journal* (Autumn 1946): 43.

Henry-Russell Hitchcock, "The Architecture of Bureaucracy and the Architecture of Genius," *The Architectural Review* (January 1947): 3–6.

"Taliesin West," *Byggmasteren* (January 1948): 8–12.

Elizabeth B. Mock, "Taliesin West," *House and Garden* (August 1948): 52–55.

"Frank Lloyd Wright dies; faned architect was 89," *The New York Times* (April 10, 1959): 1, 26.

"Architect Wright dies at age of 89," *The Washington Post* (April 10, 1959): 1.

Jean White, "Frank Wright's legacy to mankind: 700 buildings all around the world," *The Washington Post* (April 10, 1959). D2.

Frederick Gutheim, "Critic describes Wright's style as his passion for originality," *The Washington Post* (April 10, 1961): D2.
Vincent Scully, "The Heritage of Wright," *Zodiac 8: America* (1961): 9–13.
Robert Kostka, "Frank Lloyd Wright in Japan," *The Prairie School Review* (1966): 5–23.
Dimitri Tselos, "Frank Lloyd Wright and World Architecture," *Journal of the Society of Architectural Historians* (March 1969): 59–72.
Paul Sprague, "Frank Lloyd Wright Home and Studio: Homeward Bound," *Historic Preservation* (September 1976): 4–8.
Bernard M. Boyle, "Taliesin, Then and Now," *Architecture* (March 1984): 129–133.
Arthur Dennis Stevens, "Classes at Taliesin Not in the Collegiate Mold," *The Journal of the Taliesin Fellows* (January 1990): 6–7.
Paul Kruty, "Art work in the Oak Park Studio," *Arris* (2003): 17–31.
Marsha L. Fader, "Historic Structure Report: Drafting Studio," *The Journal of the Taliesin Fellows* (Summer 2009): 27–28.
Cornelia Brierly, "Taliesin West: The Early Years," *Frank Lloyd Wright Quarterly* (March 2012): 18–21.
Hannele Jaameri-Pallasmaa, "Learning through the skin," *Frank Lloyd Wright Quarterly* (Summer 2013): 38–41.

Perkins, Fellows and Hamilton
"The New Office Building of Perkins, Fellows & Hamilton, Chicago," *Architectural Record* (December 1917): 559–568.

Albert Kahn Associates
George C. Baldwin, "The Offices of Albert Kahn, Architect, Detroit, Michigan," *Architectural Forum* (October 1918): 125–130.
"Industrial Buildings: Albert Kahn Inc," *Architectural Forum* (August 1938): 87–96.
"Producer of Production Lines," *Architectural Record* (June 1942): 39–42.
Henry-Russell Hitchcock, "The Architecture of Bureaucracy and the Architecture of Genius," *The Architectural Review* (January 1947): 3–6.
Henry Jonas Magaziner, "Working for a Genius: My Time with Albert Kahn," *APT Bulletin* (February/March 2001): 59–63.

Offices Established 1853–1895

William Welles Bosworth
"Social Centre Planned," *The New York Times* (April 1933): L23.
"Welles Bosworth Active in Paris Cultural Life," *The Chicago Daily Tribune* (November 1935): VIII5.
"Architect was 97 Wm. Welles Bosworth Designed MIT Campus," *The Boston Sunday Globe* (June 5, 1966): 91.
"W.W. Bosworth Dies in France," *The New York Times* (June 5, 1966): 8J.

Delano & Aldrich
William Lawrence Bottomley, "A Selection from the Works of Delano & Aldrich," *Architectural Record* (July 1923): 3–9.
"Architects in Washington," *Time* (June 2, 1930): 24–28.
Christopher Gray, "How an Upper-Class Firm Tweaked Classical Forms," *The New York Times* (April 27, 2003): RE7.

John Russell Pope
"John Russell Pope, architect, passes," *The Constitution* (August 28, 1937).
"Dean of architects dies in New York," *The Boston Globe* (August 28, 1937): 11.
"J. R. Pope dies; architect for Mellon Gallery," *The Chicago Daily Tribune* (August 28, 1937): 18.
"Operation fatal to John R. Pope," *The Los Angeles Times* (August 28, 1937): I5.
"John Russell Pope, architect, 63, dead," *The New York Times* (August 28, 1937): L15.
"J. R. Pope's will is filed," *The New York Times* (September 2, 1937): L44.
Thomas S. Hines, "Bringing B.C. to D.C.," *The New York Times* (November 15, 1998): BR60.
"Master Draftsman VIII," *Pencil Points* (December 1924): 65–80.
Parker Morse Hooper, "Office Procedure, I: Office Manual of John Russell Pope, Architect," *Architectural Record* (January 1931): 177–182.
Parker Morse Hooper, "Office Procedure, 2: Office Manual of John Russell Pope, Architect," *Architectural Record* (June 1931): 261–272.

Henry Killam Murphy
"Henry Killam Murphy will draw plans for rebuilding of Nanking," *The China Weekly Review* (December 22, 1928): 159.
"Declares China's problem biggest," The *Boston Globe* (November 20, 1930): 21.
"N.Y Architect joins realty company here," *The China Press* (June 4, 1933): 14.
"Mr. H.K. Murphy in new coneection," *The North China Herald* (June 7, 1933): 372.
"H.K. Murphy leaves China for U.S. today," *The China Press* (July 16, 1936): 1.
"Picturesque 'Madarin-type' Residence," *The Los Angeles Times* (July 11, 1937): V5.
"Henry K. Murphy, Architect, Dead," *The New York Times* (October 15, 1954): 29.
Jeffrey W. Cody, "American Planning in Republican China, 1911–1937," *Planning Perspectives* (November 1996): 339–377.

Walter Burley Griffin & Marion Mahony
Robin Boyd, "Griffin in Melbourne," *The Architectural Review* (January 1965): 133–136.

Leo A Daly
"American Designers in Arabia," *Middle East Construction* (August 1985): 37–43.
Philip Langdon, "When Bigger is Better: Lessons from America's Largest Firms," *Architectural Record* (August 1998): 58–63.

Offices Established 1921–1926

Epstein
Nora Richter Greer, "The Theme is Architecture," *Architecture* (April 1986): 50–51.

Raymond & Rado
"Raymond, Antonin, "Concrete for New Designs," *Architectural Record* (January 1936): 3, 8, 14.
"A Portfolio of Recent Work by Antonin Raymond, Architect," *Architectural Forum* (November 1941): 341–352.
"Antonin Raymond," *Kenchiku Bunka* (July 1989): 155–161.
Junichi Ishizaki, "Tracing the geneaology of modernism and materiality in the works of Raymond, Yoshimura and Masuzawa," *Japan Architect* (Summer 1996): 13–15.
"Raymond Farm/ New Hope," *Japan Architect* (April 1999): 34–35.
"Raymond House and Studio in Azabu," *Japan Architect* (April 2000): 30–31.
"Antonin Raymond," *Kenchiku Bunka* (January 2000): 90–93.

Schultze & Weaver
Jose A. Gelabert-Navia, "American Architects in Cuba: 1900–1930," *The Journal of Decorative and Propaganda Arts 22* (1996): 133–150.

Andrew S. Dolkart, "Millionaires' Elysiums: The Luxury Apartment Hotels of Schultze and Weaver," *The Journal of Decorative and Propaganda Arts 25* (2005): 11–45.

Lisa Pfueller Davidson, "Early Twentieth-Century Hotel Architects and the Origins of Standardization," *The Journal of Decorative and Propaganda Arts 25* (2005): 72–103.

Paul R. Williams Architects

"A Forgotten Black Architect Who Designed Mansions for Movie Stars," *The Los Angeles Times* (July 23, 1989): VIII1, 16.

"He Was (and Is) The Architect To the Stars," *The New York Times* (July 26, 1990): L, C1, C6.

Perry Dean Rogers | Partners Architects

Antonio DiMambro, "Perry Dean Rogers & Partners: Progetti Recenti," *Spazio e Societa* (July–September 1992): 22–35.

Shreve, Lamb & Harmon

"L. P. Hollander Company Building," *Architectural Record* (January–June 1931): 367.

"Architect's Fee in Getting Business," *Architectural Record* (January–June 1931): 423–424.

"A Corporation's Office," *Architectural Forum* (October 1933): 247–259.

Henry H. Saylor, "The Firm of Shreve, Lamb and Harmon," *Architectural Record* (August 1941): 73–77.

Richard J. Neutra

"Architect Richard Neutra," *Time* (August 1949): 58–66.

"Machine Made America—Syntax," *The Architectural Review* (May 1957): 336–341.

Thomas S. Hines, "Richard Neutra, AIA's 1977 Gold Medalist," *AIA Journal* (March 1977): 53–61.

Thomas S. Hines, "Knowing Neutra," *Dwell* (July–August 2006): 148–157.

Harrison & Abramovitz

"Building Types—Office Buildings," *Architectural Record* (April 1955): 199–217.

Charles Thomsen, "The Making of an Architect," *AIA Journal* (August 1967): 73–80.

"Wallace K. Harrison: 1895–1981," *Progressive Architecture* (January 1982): 44

Offices Established 1928–1936

Adrian Wilson Associates

"L.A Architect to Design NATO Defense Projects," *The Los Angeles Times* (March 27, 1955): V17.

"L.A. Firm to Design Greek Defense Works," *The Los Angeles Times* (April 21, 1966): I26.

"L.A. Architectural Firm Cited by Navy," *The Los Angeles Times* (June 25, 1961): J4.

"Firm to Plan Hospitals in Vietnam and Korea," *The Los Angeles Times* (November 12, 1967): J9.

"Higher Educational Standards Urged in Realty Field," *The Los Angeles Times* (January 14, 1968): J1.

"L.A. Firm Picked for Asian Transport Study," *The Los Angeles Times* (August 9, 1970): K20.

"Adrian Wilson View Oriental Air Scene," *The Los Angeles Times* (July 30, 1972): K27.

"Adrian Wilson Firm in Saudi Arabian Venture," *The Los Angeles Times* (November 30, 1975): VIII7.

William L Pereira & Associates

"Old Empire, New Prince," *Time* (June 10, 1946): 79–87.

"Tax Bill Would Help Architects, Engineers," *Architectural Record* (March 1952): 18.

"The Man With the Plan," *Time* (September 6, 1963): 68–72.

Ruth Ryon, "Los Angeles Companies Create Worldwide Impact," *The Los Angeles Times* (June 4, 1978): VI1.

Payette

"Payette Associates," *Ideal Architecture* (June 2003): 70–71.

"The Many Faces of IDP," *Architect* (April 2010): 20–21.

James H. Collins, "Practical Science," *ArchitectureBoston* (Fall 2011): 21–24.

Edward Durell Stone & Associates

"Meet Edward Stone," *House Beautiful* (September 1945): 66–67.

"Machine Made America—Syntax," *The Architectural Review* (May 1957): 298.

"Genetrix: Personal Contributions to American Architecture," *The Architectural Review* (May 1957): 346–347.

"The Record Reports," *Architectural Record* (July 1957): 53.

"An architecture of space and grace," *Architectural Record* (July 1957): 154–177.

"More than modern," *Time* (March 1958): 56–64.

Giulia Veronesi, "Some Tendencies in American Architecture: Yamasaki and Stone," *Zodiac 8: America* (1961): 129–139.

"New work in the office of Ed Stone," *Architectural Forum* (October 1961): 113, 121–131.

"GSA presents 10 design awards," *Progressive Architecture* (October 1978): 21–23.

Ellerbe Becket

"L.A. Architectural Firm Opens New Egyptian Office," *The Los Angeles Times* (May 1, 1955): V10.

"Welton Becket, Noted Architect," *The New York Times* (January 18, 1969): L31.

"Welton Becket & Associates Acquires Firm," *The Los Angeles Times* (April 23, 1972): K11.

"Welton Becket Acquires Firm," *The Los Angeles Times* (July 16, 1972): K16.

Ruth Ryon, "Los Angeles Companies Create Worldwide Impact," *The Los Angeles Times* (June 4, 1978): VIII1.

Evelyn De Wolfe, "Becket: Firm's 50th Anniversary Near," *The Los Angeles Times* (December 19, 1982): VIII1, 5.

E. K., "Classical spirit," *Architecture Minnesota* (November–December 1988): 38–41.

Leon Whiteson, "Merger Boosts Firm's Size, Status and Creative Energies," *The Los Angeles Times* (May 24, 1990): E10.

"Projects Ellerbe Becket," *Progressive Architecture* (October 1991): 102–103.

"Ellerbe Becket," *World Architecture* (December 1998): 160–161.

Bradford Mckee, "AECOM Acquires Ellerbe Becket," *Architect* (November 2009): 1.

Louis I. Kahn

"Machine Made America—Syntax," *The Architectural Review* (May 1957): 298–336.

"Introduction," *Zodiac 8* (1961): 10–11.

"The Mind of Louis Kahn," *Architectural Forum* (July–August 1972): 42–91.

Perkins + Will

Ronald Litke, "Perkins + Will: the first 50 years," *Inland Architect* (October 1985): 11–15.

Stephen Leucking, "Cultural Accommodations: art in the New State of Illinois building," *Inland Architect* (October 1985): 15–18.

Thomas D. Sullivan, "Cultural Evolution: Building a Practice in China," *Oculus* (Fall 2003).

"Revealing creativity from within, Perkins and Will promotes Innovation within the firm by staging its own internal competitions," *Competitions* (Fall 2009): 3–6, 37–39.
Tim McKeough, "Perkins + Will Expands Again," *Architectural Record* (February 2010): 30.
Kriston Capps, Jason Fulford, "Perkins + Will," *Architect* (March 2012): 64–65.

Alfred L. Aydelott and Associates
"The architect and his community," *Progressive Architecture* (April 1955): 80–81.

Skidmore, Owings & Merrill
"$2 Billion Worth of Design by Conference," *Business Week* (December 4, 1954): 96–97, 100–104.
Sigfried Giedion, "The Experiment of S.O.M.," *Bauen + Wohnen* (August 1957): 109–114.
William E. Hartmann, "S.O.M. Organization," *Bauen + Wohnen* (August 1957): 115–116.
"The Architects from 'Skid's Row'," *Fortune* (January 1958): 137–140, 210–212, 215.
"Designers For a Busy World: Mood for Working," *Newsweek* (May 4, 1959): 97–100.
Peter Smithson, "The fine and the folk: An essay on McKim, Mead and White and the American tradition," *Architectural Design* (August 1965): 394–397.
"To Cherish Rather Than Destroy," *TIME* (August 2, 1968): 39–50.
"The Chicago office of Skidmore, Owings & Merrill," *Interiors* (January 1959): 90–95, 102–103.
Sam Davis, "The Architect as Product Designer," *Architectural Record* (October 1974): 18–19.
"SOM's computer approach," *Architectural Record* (Mid-August 1980): 84–91.
Suzanne Stephens, "SOM at midlife," *Progressive Architecture* (May 1981): 138–149.
Cynthia Davidson-Powers, "SOM 50 and counting," *Inland Architecture* (March–April 1987): 28–54.
Andrea Oppenheimer Dean, "SOM, a Legend in transition," *Architecture* (February 1989): 52–59, 144–145.
John Pastier, "Richard Keating and the varieties of Modernism," *Architecture + Urbanism* (October 1990): 58–59, 62–71.
Bradford McKee, "SOM Retrenches," *Architecture* (May 1996): 231–237.
Ken Tadashi Oshima, "Interview with Wilfried Wang about the SOM Journal," *Architecture + Urbanism* (November 2002): 31–46, 94–99, 138–143.
Vishaan Chakrabarti, "Letter from the front line: the radical potential of urban corporate practice," *Architectural Design* (September 2002): 46–47.
Kristin Richards, "So Says... Marilyn Jordan Taylor," *Oculus* (June 2003): 20–21.
Fred A. Bernstein, "Not Your Daddy's SOM," *Metropolis* (December 2003): 118–123, 162–163.
Nicholas Adams, "Skidmore, Owings & Merrill. SOM dal 1936," *Casabella* (September 2006): 86–89.
Nicholas Adams, "Skidmore, Owings & Merrill: SOM since 1936," *Journal of the Society of Architectural Historians* (September 2007): 409–411.
Roger Duffy, "SOM in Numbers," *Domus* (May 2008): 117–121.
Carl Galioto, "SOM loses top architects to HOK," *Architectural Record* (November 2009): 33.

Offices Established 1937–1943

Marcel Breuer Associates
"Genetrix: Personal Contributions to American Architecture," *The Architectural Review* (May 1957): 348.
Paolo Portoghesi, "Marcel Breuer," *Zodiac 8: America* (1961): 55–57.
Tician Papachristou, "MBA Today," *PROCESS:Architecture* 32 (1982): 106–109, 152–159.

The Office of Mies van der Rohe
A. James Speyer, "Mies van der Rohe," *Art News* (September 1947): 20–23, 42.
"Mies van der Rohe, 83, Architect of 'Glass House' Fame, is Dead," *The Chicago Tribune* (August 19, 1969): I7.
Walter Segal, "Mies Van Der Rohe 1886–1969," *The Architect's Journal* (August 27, 1969): 472–475.
Peter Blake, "Mies van der Rohe," *Architectural Forum* (October 1969): 35–39.

The Eggers Group
"Organization For Efficient Practice," *Architectural Record* (April 1960): 206–212.

Arthur B. Froehlich and Associates
"Happy Crowds," *The New Yorker* (October 8, 1955): 38–39.
James Murray, "Dreamland for the $2 Bettor," *Sports Illustrated* (August 1959): 44–45.
Audax Minor, "The race track," *The New Yorker* (September 12, 1959): 120–123.

Victor Gruen International
"Genetrix: Personal Contributions to American Architecture," *The Architectural Review* (May 1957): 348–350.
"Firm Appoints 3 Associates," *The Los Angeles Times* (January 12, 1958): VI21.
"Moscow Exhibit to Show Work of L.A. Architects," *The Los Angeles Times* (June 15, 1958): VI9.
"Architectural Firm Moves N.Y. Office," *The Los Angeles Times* (February 15, 1959): VI12.
"Firm Enlarges Chicago Office," *The Los Angeles Times* (June 12, 1960): J4.
"Victor Gruen Associates," *Interiors* (July 1960): 2–5.
Victor Gruen, "Architecture and Urban Development," *Zodiac 8: America* (1961): 90–95.
"American Architects Honor Victor Gruen," *The Boston Sunday Globe* (May 7, 1961): A40.
"Organization For Efficient Practice," *Architectural Record* (October 1961): 133–135.
"Gruen Firm Gets French Projects," *The Los Angeles Times* (April 1, 1962): J6.
Bob Boich, "Victor Gruen Exports Ideas," *The Los Angeles Times* (August 26, 1962): J1.
Esther McCoy, "Victor Gruen," *Arts & Architecture* (October 1964): 26–30.
Joyce Haber, "Victor Gruen: Architect, Dreamer and Doer," *The Los Angeles Times* (September 18, 1966).
Maggie Savoy, "The Sky-High Outlook of Victor Gruen Foundation," *The Los Angeles Times* (June 2, 1969): IV1, 7.
Art Seidenbaum, "Gruen Critiques 'Old Hometown'," *The Los Angeles Times* (June 20, 1976): VII1.
Ruth Ryon, "Los Angeles Companies Create Worldwide Impact," *The Los Angeles Times* (June 4, 1978): VI1.
"Architect, Environmentalist Gruen Dies," *The Los Angeles Times* (February 15, 1980): II2.
"Victor Gruen, 76, Architect, Is Dead," *The New York Times* (February 16, 1980): L26.
"Gruen Associates, at 40, Still Busy With Major Commissions," *The Los Angeles Times* (July 19, 1987): VIII1, 6.

Eero Saarinen and Associates
"The maturing modern," *Time* (July 2, 1956): 50–57.
"Genetrix: Personal Contributions to American Architecture," *The Architectural Review* (May 1957): 360–361.

Gillo Dorfles, "Eero Saarinen: The TWA Terminal and the Embassy," *Zodiac 8: America* (1961): 84–89
Walter McQuade, "The New Saarinen Office," *Architectural Forum* (April 1963): 113–119.
"Eero Saarinen's firm changes its name," *Architectural Record* (September 1966): 36.
"Saarinen firm changes name," *Progressive Architecture* (September 1966): 51.
"Saarinen fest at Cranbrook," *Progressive Architecture* (October 1995): 37–38.
"Lessons from Eero," *Metropolis* (November 2008): 18.
Paul Makovsky, "Iconic workplace," *Metropolis* (November 2008): 69–79.

Morris Lapidus Associates
John S. Margolies, "Morris Lapidus: Now, Once and or All, Know Why I Did It," *Progressive Architecture* (September 1970): 118–123.
"Lapidus laughs last," *Architectural Record* (September 1996): 92–97.
"Lapidus cuts loose," *Architecture* (February 1997): 41–43.
Jonathan Ringen, "Lapidus of luxury," *Metropolis* (January 2001): 58–62.
Alice T. Friedman, "Merchandising Miami Beach: Morris Lapidus and the architecture of Abundance," *The Journal of Decorative and Propaganda Arts Vol. 25* (2005): 217–253.
Gabrielle Esperdy, "'I Am a Modernist': Morris Lapidus and His Critics," *Journal of the Society of Architectural Historians* (December 2007): 494–517.

Philip Johnson / Alan Ritchie Architects
"New Directions: Phillip Johnson," *Perspecta* 1 (1952): 26–27.
"Genetrix: Personal Contributions to American Architecture," *The Architectural Review* (May 1957): 354–355.
Henry-Russell Hitchcock, "The Current Work of Phillip Johnson," *Zodiac 8: America* (1961): 65–81.
Robin Middelton, "Dear Phillip," *Architectural Design* (March 1967).
Nora Richter Greer, "Americans Abroad: Some Coming Attractions," *AIA Journal* (December 1989): 64–71.
Paul Goldberger, "Phillip Johnson is dead at 98; Architecture's restless intellect," *The New York Times* (January 27, 2005): C18.

Ralph Rapson
"Genetrix: Personal Contributions to American Architecture," *Architectural Review* (May 1957): 42–43.
Peter A. Rand, "Rapson unwrapped," *Architecture Minnesota* (March 1999): 32–33, 46, 48, 54.
Ralph Rapson, "Rapson abroad," *Architecture Minnesota* (November 2001): 50–53.
Aaron Britt, "Bohemian Rapson," *Dwell* (October 2007): 119–126.
Bette Hammel, "Ralph Rapson, 93, a modernist who drew to the end," *Architectural Record* (May 2008): 68

Town Planning Associates
"Aids City Plans in South America," *The New York Times* (February 18, 1951): 4R.
"Harvard Planning Aide Named," *The New York Times* (February 24, 1957): 62.
"Paul Schulz," *The New York Times* (June 16, 1959): 35.
"Paul Lester Wiener, Architect and City Planner, is Dead at 72," *The New York Times* (November 18, 1967): 37.

NBBJ
Douglas Brenner, "Scaling the office landscape," *Architectural Record* (May 1984): 163–167.
"Building the studio system," *Interiors* (February 1992): 38–39.
Justin Henderson, "Regional Renaissance," *Interiors* (February 1992): 37, 53.
Justin Henderson, "Classical Neon," *Interiors* (February 1992): 52.
"NBBJ, Interviews with partners," *World Architecture* (1995): 23–25.
"Region and identitiy in America," *World Architecture* (1995): 26–29.
Philip Langdon, "When Bigger is Better: Lessons from America's Largest Firms," *Architectural Record* (August 1998): 58–63.
Ned Cramer, "Timothy Johnson, the company man," *Architecture* (May 1999): 112–115.
"NBBJ," *World Architecture* (July 1999): 4.
Stanley Collyer, "NBBJ's Dan Meis and Peter Pran, Raising the profile of a large firm by competing," *Competitions* (Summer 2002): 42–51.
Ian Chodikoff, "Design for change," *Canadian Architect* (October 2006): 48–50.
Lisa Delgado, "Inner Space," *Oculus* (Fall 2008): 32–33.
Bradford McKee, "NBBK and Chan Krieger Sieniewicz to Merge," *Architect* (April 2010): 14.
Brian Libby, "Under the Hood," *Architect* (April 2012): 50–52.

Offices Established 1945–1948

The Architects Collaborative
"The Architects' Collaborative: Statement of Aims," *Arts & Architecture* (August 1946): 28–29.
Helen Henley, "Two Girls Share as Equal Partners in Modern Architects' Collaborative," *The Christian Science Monitor* (January 13, 1947): 10.
Barbara Brooks, "No Woman Should Stay Home: Two Cambridge Wives Solve Career Problem," *The Boston Sunday Globe* (March 2, 1947): A9.
"Gropius Appraises Today's Architect," *Architectural Forum* (May 1952): 111–113, 166.
"Genetrix: Personal Contributions to American Architecture," *The Architectural Review* (May 1957): 370–371.
"The Architects' Collaborative," *Baukust und Werkform* (December 1957): 681–683.
"Walter Gropius," *Baunen + Wohnen* (December 1959): 409–417.
Gillo Dorfles, "Walter Gropius Today," *Zodiac 8: America* (1961): 35–53.
"U.S. Firm Radiates from Rome," *Progressive Architecture* (October 1964): 239–246.
Jane Holtz Kay, "Would you have hired these men to design you a building? The story of The Architects Collaborative," *The Boston Sunday Globe* (August 18, 1971): 126–131.
John C. Harkness, "Thirty Five Years of TAC," *PROCESS:Architecture* 19 (1980): 11–15.
Leonard J. Currie, Virginia M. Currie, "TAC: Principles, Process and Product," *PROCESS:Architecture* 19 (1981): 40–45.
"TAC Office Organization System," *PROCESS:Architecture* 19: 156–159.
"TAC's demise," *Architecture* (December 1995): 117–119.

Cannon Design
"Cannon—Build to last," *World Architecture* (May 1997): 66–105.
"Cannon + OWP/P," *Architect* (June 2009): 20.

Wimberly Allison Tong & Goo
"Architectural Firm Specializes in Exotic Hotels," *The Los Angeles Times* (November 12, 1985): IV5D.
Michael Flagg, "Hawaiian Architects Win Contract for $700 Million Australian Project," *The Los Angeles Times* (February 29, 1988): IV9.
"Architect George J. 'Pete' Wimberly died December 30," *Planning* (June 1996): 33.

Mads Gaardboe, "Urban Tourism: Global Projects of Architectural Excellence," *Built Environment* (2000): 130–141.
Sandi Cain, "Wimberly Allison Buys Singapore Design Firm," *The Orange County Business Journal* (April 23, 2001): 19.
Amanda Kolson Hurley, "WATG before after," *Architect* (March 2008): 74–77.
Randle Pollock, "A Conversation with Howard J. Wolff, Senior Vice President and Worldwide Director of Marketing, WATG," *Marketer* (April 2011): 18–21.

CRSS Inc.
"Organization For Efficient Practice," *Architectural Record* (November 1960): 179–184.
"People Involvement, Research, Planning Teams, Economy, and Regionalism Dictate the Design of Caudill, Rowlett and Scott," *Architectural Record* (January 1965): 111–112.
"Out on Buffalo Bayou," *Progressive Architecture* (September 1970): 105–107.
"CRS invests in computer-aided drafting to streamline production," *Architectural Record* (April 1978): 65–69.
Charles E. Estes, "Gaming at CRS," *Journal of Architectural Education* (September 1979): 35.
"Design in a process-oriented firm," *Space Design* (March 1980): 22–29.
"Editorials—Caudill, Rowlett, Scott," *Architectural Record* (September 1994): 9.

Daniel, Mann, Johnson & Mendenhall
"Architects move to new quarters," *The Los Angeles Times* (February 17, 1952): V8.
"Architects get Thailand job," *The Los Angeles Times* (March 7, 1954): V5.
"Architect firm plans addition," *Los Angeles Times* (August 29, 1954): V5.
"Architect to give far East report," *The Los Angeles Times* (September 19, 1954): V8.
"Architects and Engineers consolidate offices here," *The Los Angeles Times* (October 7, 1956): VI4.
"Organization For Efficient Practice," *Architectural Record* (June 1960): 189–194.
Norris Leap, "Engineer manages team of five talented architects to success," *The Los Angeles Times* (October 9, 1960): E2.
Tom Cameron, "Firm creates wide variety of projects," *The Los Angeles Times* (July 26, 1964): J26.
"Design director named by architectural firm," *The Los Angeles Times* (August 30, 1964): J21.
"Names: Daniel, Mann, Johnson and Mendenhall," *Architecture and Engineering news* (June 1967): 104–105."Korean contract goes to L.A. firm," *The Los Angeles Times* (May 30, 1968): III15.
"Architecture for big business has become big business," *The Los Angeles Times* (April 6, 1972): II7.
"Local firms awarded Indonesian contracts," *The Los Angeles Times* (July 2, 1972): H11.
"Architect, civic leader Phillip J. Daniel dies," *The Los Angeles Times* (November 22, 1972): III4.
"Services held for architect S. K. Johnson," *The Los Angeles Times* (November 10, 1974): V16.
John Pastier, "Nongravitational architecture: works of Anthony Lumsden," *Architecture + Urbanism* (March 1975): 63–159.
Michael Franklin Ross, "The development of an aesthetic system at DJMJ," *Architectural Record* (May 1975): 111–117.
"Phillipine, African projects for DMJM," *The Los Angeles Times* (November 30, 1975): VIII8.
"A tug-of-war in Architecture," *The Los Angeles Times* (November 21, 1977): IV11.
Ruth Ryon, "Los Angeles Companies Create Worldwide Impact," *The Los Angeles Times* (June 4, 1978): VI1.
"State architects elected to AIA College of Fellows," *The Los Angeles Times* (April 8, 1979): IX1, IX4.
"Speaker," *The Los Angeles Times* (July 8, 1980): VIII27.
"American Designers in Arabia," *Middle East Construction* (August 1985): 37–43.
Andrea Adelson, "A new field for a firm of architects," *The New York Times* (June 5, 1993): L39.

Joseph Allen Stein and Associates
"Low Cost House," *Architectural Forum* (October 1940): 264–265.
"Joseph Allen Stein," *Arts and Architecture* (November 1946): 42–43
Stein, Doshi, Bhalia "Atelier Doshi A Ahmedabad, Inde," *L' Architecture d'Aujourd'hui* (September 1983): 80–83.
Stein, Doshi, Bhalia "Atelier D' Architecture Sangath Ahmedabad," *Techniques and Architecture* (September 1985): 122–123.
"French Cultural Center, New Delhi," *The Architectural Review* (August 1987): 44–47.
"Sangath, Architect's Studio," *Architecture + Urbanism* (July 1997): 80–87.
Paul Lewis, "Joseph Stein, 89, Architect noted for work in India, is dead," *The New York Times* (October 14, 2001).
Achyut P. Kanvinde, "Joseph Stein in India," *Journal of Landscape Architecture* (Winter 2001–2002): 10–12.
Ravindra Bhan, "A Deep Personal Loss...," *Journal of Landscape Architecture* (Winter 2001–2003): 13.
Adit Pal, "Nature in the city," *Journal of Landscape Architecture* (Winter 2001–2004): 14–15.
"A global man in the true sense in conversation with Anuraag Chowfla," *Journal of Landscape Architecture* (Winter 2001–2005): 16–19.
Vikram Lall, "Holistic Accounting," *Architecture and Design* (May–June 2002): 89–92.

RTKL
David Vachon, "Names: Rogers, Taliaferro, Kostritsky, Lamb," *Architecture and Engineering News* (December 1968): 70–71.
Philip Langdon, "When Bigger is Better: Lessons from America's Largest Firms," *Architectural Record* (August 1998): 58–63.
Kira L. Gould, "Your firm is your people. Are they happy?," *Architectural Record* (Jan 2000): 66–70.
Ray Peloquin, "A New Urban Heart for Dubai," *Urban Land* (June 2000): 30.
Daun St. Amand, "Crossing Design Borders," *Urban Land* (May 2006): 82–85.

Vincent G. Kling Associates
"Valuable service to the client," *Progressive Architecture* (November 1964): 156–167.
John Anderson, "Design Firm Case Study: Vincent G. Kling and partners," *Contract Interiors* (February 1972): 58–61.
Robert Morrison, "Project management: organization, communication, and keeping the client plugged in," *Architectural Record* (November 1982): 48–49.

Bassetti Architects
William Marlin, "Federal Architecture: Why Not The Best?," *Architectural Record* (December 1978): 83–121.

Lathrop Douglass
Lathrop Douglass, "New Departures in Office Building Design," *Architectural Record* (October 1947): 119–121.

Lathrop Douglass, "Perhaps the Best is Actually the Cheapest," *Architectural Record* (October 1947): 122–123.

Max Abramovitz, "Fenestration," *Architectural Record* (April 1955): 199–216.

Harry Weese & Associates

"Genetrix: Personal Contributions to American Architecture," *The Architectural Review* (May 1957): 373–374.

"The first Chicago school—and the second," *Architectural Forum* (May 1962): 90–107.

"Weese (Ben) versus Mies (Tigerman): two buildings, two architects, two points of view," *Architectural Record* (April 1975): 83–90.

"Harry Weese of Chicago," *AIA Journal* (May 1978): 56–65.

Eve M. Kahn, "The complexities of a pioneer," *Architect* (January 2011): 104–106.

John M. Johansen

"Genetrix: Personal Contributions to American Architecture," *The Architectural Review* (May 1957): 337, 374–375.

John M. Johansen, "Architecture: Three Imperatives," *AIA Journal* (March 1984): 156–164.

Offices Established 1948–1949

Oficina Don Hatch

Don Hatch, "the architect and his community: Oficina Don Hatch," *Progressive Architecture* (March 1954): 100–109.

"Venezuela," *L'Architecture d'Aujourd'hui* (October 1956): 129–134.

Yamasaki and Associates

"Genetrix: Personal Contributions to American Architecture," *The Architectural Review* (May 1957): 337, 366–369.

Giulia Veronesi, "Some Tendencies in American Architecture: Yamasaki and Stone," *Zodiac 8: America* (1961): 129–139.

Minoru Yamasaki, "A Humanist Architecture For America & Its Relation to the Traditional Architecture of Japan," *Zodiac* (1961): 129–145.

"Minoru Yamasaki Designs His Own Office," *Architectural Record* (September 1968): 137–142.

"The road to Xanadu," *TIME* (January 18, 1963): 54–64.

Edward Larrabee Barnes Associates

Jonathan Barnett, "Speaking of Architecture," *Architectural Record* (August 1961): 10, 194.

"Genetrix: Personal Contributions to American Architecture," *The Architectural Review* (May 1957): 336–337.

"Architecture of Edward Barnes," *Architectural Forum* (August 1963): 74–79.

"Edward L. Barnes," *Space Design* (July 1985): 6–11.

Hugh Stubbins and Associates

"Genetrix: Personal Contributions to American Architecture," *The Architectural Review* (May 1957). 364–366.

"Architecture in the Spirit of the Times," *PROCESS:Architecture* 10 (1979): 5–15, 158–161.

Roger Kimball, "Hugh Stubbins and the life of architecture," *Architectural Record* (April 1987): 61–64.

"The Stubbins Associates: in touch with the times," *World Architecture* (November 1997): 56–61.

Offices Established 1951–1953

Eduardo Catalano

"A new way to span space," *Architectural Forum* (November 1955): 171–177.

"Structures of warped surfaces by Eduardo F. Catalano," *Arts and Architecture* (December 1963): 22–24.

Paul Rudolph

"Paul Rudolph," *The Architectural Review* (May 1957): 378–381.

Giulia Veronesi, "Paul Rudolph," *Zodiac 8: America* (1961): 149–162.

Paul Rudolph, "Architectural Education in U.S.A," *Zodiac 8: America* (1961): 163–165.

Von Paul R. Krammer, "Paul Rudolph oder, <Die Formulierung der Bedeutung eines Bauwerks>," *Werk* (April 1973): 446–457.

"Nineteen Questions to Paul Rudolph," *Architecture + Urbanism* (January 1973): 133–136,138, 139–140.

Paul Rudolph, "Enigmas of architecture," *Architecture + Urbanism* (July 1977): 317–320.

Herbert Muschamp, "Paul Rudolph is dead at 78; Modernist architect of the 60's," *The New York Times* (August 1997): 50.

Davis Brody Bond Architects & Planners

Susan Braybrooke, "Two old hands talk about housing," *Architectural Record* (February 1988): 122–127.

David W. Dunlap, "Minority firm joins Davis, Brody architects," *The New York Times* (October 21, 1990): R13.

Anna Dietzche, "Elegancia e eficiencia," *Dome* (January 2006): 100–111.

Sert, Jackson and Associates

Emilio Donato, "Sert 1929–1953," *Cuadernos de Arquitectura y Urbanismo* (December 1972): 2–7.

Jaume Freixa, "1953–1968," "1968–1973," *Cuadernos de Arquitectura y Urbanismo* (December 1972): 8–17, 22–43.

Paul Goldberger, "Josep L. Sert, 80, Architect, Was Harvard Dean of Design," *The New York Times* (March 1983): D20.

Leonard Greenwood, "Architect Josep Sert dies in Spain at 80, had international reputation for works reflecting love of arts," *The Los Angeles Times* (March 1983): 11.

Benjamin Forgey, "The art of planning for the ages," *The Washington Post* (March 1983): C1.

Integrus

Rocky Wilson, "Integrus designs embassies—High security structures under way in Guinea, Mali, Sierre Leone, Algeria," *Spokane Journal of Business* (February 26, 1997), n.p.

Mike McLean, "Integrus architecture designs embassy compound to be built in northern Africa," *Spokane Journal of Business* (January 30, 2014), n.p.

John Portman and Associates

"John Portman: Atlanta's One-Man Urban Renewal Program," *Architectural Record* (January 1966): 133–140.

Walter McQuade, "Atlanta, the Hopeful City," *Fortune* (August 1996): 155–160.

Gurney Breckenfeld, "The Architects Want a Voice in Redesigning America," *Fortune* (November 1971): 144–147.

John Portman, "An Architecture for People and not for Things," *Architectural Record* (January 1977): 134–140.

"Architect/Developer John Portman Interviewed by the RIBAJ Editors in Atlanta," *RIBA* (December 1977): 504–513.

Maeve Slavin, "Portmania," *Interiors* (October 1984): 118–127.

Robert Guenther, "U.S. Developers Sign Contracts To Put Up Projects in China," *The Wall Street Journal* (November 12, 1984): II.

John C. Portman, "An Architecture for Contemporary China," *Building in China* (December 1990): 34–38.

Mitchell Pacelle, "U.S. Architects in Asia: Only Way to Go Is Up," *The Wall Street Journal* (March 21, 1996): B1.

Aric Chen, "The Kubla Khan of Hotels," *The New York Times* (June 25, 2006): 5.

Charlie Qiuli Xue, Yingchun Li, "Importing American Architecture to China: the Practice of John Portman & Associates in Shanghai," *The Journal of Architecture* (March 2008): 317–333.

Sasaki Associates

"Harvard Designer Appointed," *The Washington Post* (August 1962): C2.

"19 Selected by Kennedys as Advisers," *The Boston Globe* (April 1964): 5.

"Hideo Sasaki, 80, Influential Landscape Architect, Dies," *The New York Times* (September 2000): B9.

Peter Walker, "In Memoriam," *Land Forum* (2001): 26–29.

Offices Established 1954–1955

John Hejduk

Kenneth Frampton, "John Hejduk and the cult of humanism," *Architecture + Urbanism* (May 1975): 134–143.

Martin Filler, "John Hejduk: The Practice of Theory," *Art in America* (February 1980): 84–89.

"Ricostruire A Berlino, Berlin Renewal," *Domus* (April 1982): 22–25.

Victor A. Lundy

"New ideas of Victor A. Lundy," *Architectural Record* (February 1962): 105–120.

Esther McCoy, "Young Architects in the United States," *Zodiac 8: America* (November 1968): 168–185.

"Victor Lundy in Marfa: a show records when architects could draw," *Cite* (August 2006): 10.

HOK

Gyo Obata, George E. Kassabaum, George F. Hellmuth, "Organization For Efficient Practice," *Architectural Record* (February 1961): 137–145.

"Architect Firms Agree on Merger," *The New York Times* (December 19, 1972): 74.

Stephen Trombley "HOK: an American Recipe for Success," *RIBA Journal* (March 1982) .

William Remmington, "HOK marketing effort pays off," *RIBA Journal* (March 1982).

"Architect George Kassabaum dies," *The Chicago Tribune* (August 17, 1982): IV3.

"George Kassabaum, Leading Architect; Headed Large Firm," *The New York Times* (August 17, 1982): B4.

Susan Doubilet, Thomas Fisher, "Computers: The Profession Adjusts," *Progressive Architecture* (June 1985): 137–138.

Susan Doubilet, Thomas Fisher, "The Traditional Office is Transformed," *Progressive Architecture* (June 1985): 139.

"American Designers in Arabia," *Middle East Construction* (August 1985): 37–43.

Nora Richter Greer, "Americans Abroad: Some Coming Attractions," *Architecture the AIA Journal* (January 1989): 64–71.

Karin Tetlow, "Business Tactics," *Interiors* (January 1991): 30–33.

Jeremy Myerson, "Into Europe," *World Architecture* (October 1991): 69–79.

"Riding the Shock of the New," *World Architecture* (October 1995): 37–41.

David Taylor, "US Practices find their feet in expanding London," *The Architects Journal* (April 1997): 22–23.

"HOK London—the first ten years," *The Architects Journal* (October 1997): 43–50.

Bay Brown, "When the going gets tough... the tough consolidate," *World Architecture* (December 1998): 128–131.

"HOK cap sur l'europe," *Architecture Interieure cree* (September 1998): 159–162.

"The new space race," *World Architecture* (December 1999): 92, 135–136.

Roger Yee, "The New york Architects Abroad," *Oculus* (Fall 2003): 50–51.

Dhaval Barbhaya, Jeff Davis, "Coming of Age," *Urban Land* (June 2009): 62–66.

Pei Cobb Freed & Partners Architects

Arthur Herzog, "He loves things to be beautiful," *The New York Times Magazine* (March 1965): 34–35.

Arthur Herzog, "He loves beautiful things," *The New York Times Magazine* (March 1965): 98–100.

Lee Mitgang, "I.M. Pei: Changing city faces," *The Washington Post* (April 1997): E19.

Paul Goldberger, "Winning ways of I. M. Pei," *The New York Times Magazine* (May 1970): 24–27, 116–124.

"Special Feature, I. M. Pei & Partners," *Space Design* (June 1982): 3–5.

Andrea Oppenheimer Dean, "Changes for survival," *Architecture* (February 1990): 56–61.

Andrea Oppenheimer Dean, "Henry N. Cobb," *Architecture* (February 1990): 62–64.

Andrea Oppenheimer Dean, "James I. Freed," *Architecture* (February 1990): 65–67.

Stephanie Williams, "I. M. Pei, Adventurer In Geometry and Light," *World Architecture* (December 1991): 36–41.

Janet Abrams, "Classic Outsider," *World Architecture* (December 1991): 42–48.

Russell Johnson, "Sound with vision," *World Architecture* (December 1991): 49–53.

"Lo studio e L'architetto: I. M. Pei Partnership," *Ottagono* (September 1996).

James S. Russell, "Architect James Ingo Freed, partner at Pei Cobb Freed dies," *Architectural Record* (February 2006): 30.

Wiliam B. Tabler Architects

"Hilton plus Statler: A big client gets bigger," *Architectural Record* (October 1954): 154–155.

"Perspectives," *Architectural Record* (May 1957): 9.

"Building Types Study Number 246–Hotels," *Architectural Record* (May 1957): 213–240.

"Bill Tabler's hotel boom," *Architectural Forum* (July 1957): 115–121.

"Building Types Study 257: Motor Hotels," *Architectural Record* (April 1958): 203–205.

"Building Types Study 298: Hotels–Motels," *Architectural Record* (September 1961): 131–139.

"Hotels," *Architectural Record* (October 1964): 165–176.

Offices Established 1957–1962

Brown Daltas and Associates

"Americans abroad: Brown and Daltas in Iran," *Architectural Forum* (October 1962): 126–133.

"American Designers in Arabia," *Middle East Construction* (August 1985): 37–43.

Richard Chin, "St. Paul architect Spero Daltas, 89, built globally and mentored locally," *The National Herald* (November 21–27, 2009): 8.

Dale Mulfinger, "Pasta, piazzas and the Pantheon: a Minessota architect reflects on his working years abroad," *Architecture Minnesota* (November–December 1989): 13, 78–79.

Mitchell/Giurgola Architects

Andrea O. Dean, "Profile of the firm award recipient: Mitchell/Giurgola," *AIA Journal* (April 1976): 58–61.

Christopher Vernon, "Lines that speak," *Architecture Australia* (March–April 2011): 25–26.

Parker Design Group

Leonard S. Parker, "Collaboration: Same Bed, Different Dream?," *Architecture Minnesota* (November 1991): 13, 52.

Heather Beal, "Like Father, Like Son," *Architecture Minnesota* (March–April 2007): 21, 61.

Venturi, Scott Brown and Associates

"Introduction by Editor," *Architecture + Urbanism* (August 1982): 4–5, 220–223.

Stanisiaus von Moos, "Venturi, Scott Brown and Associates" *Architecture + Urbanism* (June 1990): 39–41.

Corrado Gavinelli, "Lo studio e L'architetto," *Ottagono* (September–November 1996): 81–83.

Barbara Flanagan, "Born to be Bad," *Metropolis* (October 2001): 82–87.

Gunnar Birkerts and Associates

"A search for architectural principles," *Progressive Architecture* (September 1964): 72–91.

Gunnar Birkerts, "Design: the critical years," *The Canadian Architect* (July 1974): 48–53.

"Defining a design methodology," *Architectural Record* (February 1977): 91–95.

"The agony and the ecstasy," *World Architecture* (December 1995): 23–45.

"Prodigious prodigals," *World Architecture* (September 1999): 38–39.

"Iconic Workplace," *Metropolis* (November 2008): 70–79.

Zimmer Gunsul Frasca Architects

Deborah K. Dietsch, "Learning from Portland," *AIA Journal* (March 1991): 82–85.

Eva Hagberg, "Twelve West," *Metropolis* (February 2010): 60–63, 78–79.

Tigerman McCurry Architects

Alan Turner, "A possible strategy for the US," *AIA Journal* (November 1970): 32.

Cy Paumier Jr., "The case of a new town," *AIA Journal* (November 1970): 33–36.

Jack Fraser, "Small firm with a big stake in housing," *AIA Journal* (November 1970): 37.

Stanley Tigerman and Margaret McCurry, "Interiors initiative: the new office greenscape," *Interiors* (May 1981): 152–157.

David A. Greenspan, "The elliptical architecture of Stanley Tigerman," *Inland Architect* (March–April 1990): 12,15,16.

"Roundtable discussion on designer's power and influence: Boston roundtable," *Harvard University Graduate School of Design News* (August 1993): 3.

Wes Jones, "Architecture in the land of Silicon and Snow White," *Harvard University Graduate School of Design News* (August 1993): 28–29.

Margaret McCurry, "A voice," *Harvard University Graduate School of Design News* (August 1993): 29–30.

Jane C. Loeffler, "Invisible Architects," *Harvard University Graduate School of Design News* (August 1993): 30.

Mark C. Taylor, "Criticism: Unsettling Architecture," *Architecture + Urbanism* (May 1994): 8–15, 122–123.

Stanley Tigerman, "The Constituent of an Architectural Hippocratic Oath," *Architecture + Urbanism* (May 1994): 144.

Stanley Tigerman, "writing IN architecture," *Architecture + Urbanism* (May 1994): 146–147.

"Biography," *Architecture + Urbanism* (May 1994): 150.

Eric Fredericksen, "How Stanley Tigerman became an ethicist, and other stories," *Architecture* (July 2001): 81–87.

Blair Kamin, "Architects do no harm," *Metropolis* (August 2002): 78–80.

Sebastian Howard, "Drawing as process, drawing as practice," *Architectural Record* (May 2008): 348.

"Stanley Tigerman," *Metropolis* (November 2011): 75.

Cambridge Seven Associates

Charles Redmon, "Principal's Statement," *PROCESS:Architecture* 119 (1994): 6–7.

Mildred F. Schmertz, "Works of Cambridge Seven Associates," *PROCESS:Architecture* 119 (1994): 8–11.

Peter Chermayeff, "The Ongoing Work," *PROCESS:Architecture* 119 (1994): 12–16.

Gehry Partners

"Firm Profile: Frank O.Gehry & Associates," *Progressive Architecture* (March 1980): 69–85.

Judith Davidson, "Light Hearted Models for Serious Results," *Architectural Record* (July 1992): 30–33.

Michael Webb, "Realizing Frank O. Gehry's Vision and Challenging Contemporary Artists," *Architecture + Urbanism* (July 1998): 130–137.

Robert Ivy, "Frank Gehry: Plain Talk with a Master," *Architectural Record* (May 1999): 185–192.

Nicola Turner, "Living his dream," *World Architecture* (July 1999): 100–105.

Michael Cannel, "Frank Gehry: The Master," *Architecture* (May 2000): 128–129.

Paolo Tombesi, "Involving the Industry: Gehry's use of 'Request for Proposals' packages," *Arq* (January 2002): 77–87.

Deborah Snoonian, "New Gehry Technologies will enable many to boldly go where only Frank has gone before," *Architectural Record* (October 2003): 12.

Laur E. Manfra, "Rick Smith Joins Frank Gehry," *Metropolis* (April 2006): 179.

Nicolai Ouroussoff, "Let the 'Starchitects' Work All the Angles," *The New York Times* (December 16, 2007): 9–12.

Heather Roberge, "Plastic Realities: How Technology Alters Materiality," *Architecture + Urbanism* (August 2008): 58–63.

KMW Architecture

Robert Campbell, "Kallmann, McKinnell & Wood Receives AIA's Firm Award," *AIA Journal* (March 1984): 21–27

Offices Established 1963–1972

Polshek Partnership

Michael J. Crosbie, "Polshek and partners named firm of the year," *Architecture* (February 1992): 23.

"Architectural ethics," *Architecture* (March 1992): 68–79.

John Hughes, "How one firm broke into CAD through design, not production," *Architectural Record* (February 1993): 34–35.

Marisa Bartlucci, "Citizen architect," *Metropolis* (June 1995): 62–67, 74–79.

"Polshek and partners: a firm and its universe," *Architectural Record* (August 2000): 88–95.

David Sokol, "On the drawing board: Jim Polshek on 'The ethical architect,'" *Oculus* (December 2001): 7.

"An architect who adopts an earnest approach to fulfilling one's social responsability as an architect," *Space* (December 2007): 103–119.

Fred A. Bernstein, "Polshek Partnership's new identity: Ennead architects," *Architect* (July 2010): 12.

Phillip Nobel, "Succession Story," *Metropolis* (October 2011): 89–98.

C. J. Hughes, "A surprising name change for Polshek Partnership," *Architectural Record* (August 2010): 30.

Richard Meier & Partners Architects

"Distinguished Neighbor," *Progressive Architecture* (September 1966): 88–95.

"Richard Meier & Partners," *Architecture + Urbanism* (March 1988): 113–119.

Edie Lee Cohen, "Richard Meier & Partners," *Interior Design* (May 1988): 278–285.
Kenneth Frampton, "Progetti in Europa di Richard Meier & Partners," *Casabella* (December 1990): 4–5.
Joseph Giovannini, "Is Richard Meier Really Modern?," *Architecture* (February 1996): 65–69.
Raul A. Barreneche, "Meier's White Turns Green," *Architecture* (February 1997): 131.
"Richard Meier & Partners Architects LLP," *Architecture + Urbanism* (February 2006): 25–27.
Roger Yee, "A Tale of Two Manhattans," *Oculus* (Fall 2008): 24–29.
Luigi Prestinenza Puglisi, "New York Meier's Models Museum," *Arca* (January 2010): 92–95.
Suzanne Stephens, "Richard Meier," *Architectural Record* (September 2013): 28.

<u>Michael Graves and Associates</u>
Martin Filler, "Michael Graves: Before and After," *Art in America* (September 1980): 99–105.
John Morris Dixon, "Case Study: Michael Graves—Introduction," *Progressive Architecture* (March 1990): 73.
Sylvia Lavin, "Case Study: Michael Graves—Critique," *Progressive Architecture* (March 1990): 74–75.
"A Grave approach to Egypt," *World Architecture* (April 1999): 64–65.

<u>Eisenman Architects</u>
Frédéric Levrat, "Peter Eisenman," *L'Architecture d'Aujourd'hui* (Februray 1992): 98–104.
Matthew Barhydt, "Tools of the Stars," *Progressive Architecture* (November 1992): 110–111.
Ole Bouman, "Salt Peter in my wounds, The Eisenman Excess," *Archis* (Februray 1994): 57–63.
B.J. Novitski, "Freedom of form," *Architecture* (August 1994): 107–111.
Ignasi de Sola-Morales, "Forma, memoria, acontecimiento (form, memory, event)," *AV Monografias* (May–June 1995): 20–26.
Peter Eisenman, "El 'zeitgeist' y el problema de la inmanencia (Architecture ans the 'zeitgeist': the problem of Immanence)," *AV Monografias* (May–June 1995): 27.
Luis Fernandez-Galiano, "Construcciones craqueladas," *AV Monografias* (May–June 1995): 2.
Nina Rappaport, "Architecture," *Oculus* (October 1995): 11–13.
Susana Gil, "Peter the mad," *World Architecture* (April 1996): 60–61.
Von Rudolf Kammerl, "Theorie + Praxis," *Architektur, Innenarchitektur, Technischer Ausbau* (July–August 1997): 28–29.

<u>Gwathmey Siegel Kaufman Architects</u>
William Marin, "A section through the thinking of Gwathmey Siegel Architects," *Architectural Record* (September 1979): 91–102.
Stanley Abercrombie, "Gwathmey Siegel: winner of AIA's 1982 Firm Award," *AIA Journal* (February 1982): 70–79.
Sanford Kwinter, "What's Eating Charles Gwathmey?," *Any* 11 (August 1995): 50–51.
"Energizing Urban Infill," *Oculus* (January 1998): 3.
Nina Rappaport, "Architects on the Web," *Oculus* (January 1998): 12.
Martin Filler, "Fame: a fickle mistress," *Architectural Record* (December 2009): 33–34.

<u>Bohlin Cywinski Jackson</u>
Rita Reif, "The architect knew the needs of both clients—his parents," *The New York Times* (May 25, 1971): 32L.
Paul Goldberger, "At once a rugged cabin and a glass box," *The New York Times Magazine* (September 26, 1976): 23, 68–69.
Gerald Allen, "Profile: In search of the high quality," *Architecture + Urbanism* (September 1988): 115–119.
Alexandra Lange, "The Visceralist," *Metropolis* (May 2010): 86–93, 136–137.

<u>Hartman-Cox Architects</u>
Andrea Oppenheimer Dean, "Firm of the year: Hartman Cox very much of Washington, D.C.," *Architecture* (February 1988): 44–55.

<u>Gensler</u>
Thomas Fisher, Jim Murphy, Darlice D. Boles, "The Big Sell," *Progressive Architecture* (July 1988): 84–93.
Michael Wagner, "Gensler and Associates/architects," *Interiors* (December 1988): 91–111.
Douglas E. Gordon, M. Stephanie Stubbs, "Practice in the '80s," *Architecture* (December 1980): 81.
"More work up front," *Architecture* (December 1980): 86.
George Heery, Laura Heery, "How do they get those commissions?," *Architectural Record* (February 1990): 48–49.
George Heery, Laura Heery, "Bill Lacy," *Architectural Record* (February 1990): 49–50.
Jean Gorman, "Business as usual?," *Interiors* (February 1994): 35.
Beverly Russell, "Gensler goes International," *Interiors* (February 1994): 36–53.
Virginia Kent Dorris, "Greening the firm," *Architecture* (July 1995): 121–127.
"How to get ahead and stay there," *World Architecture* (January 1997): 8–9.
"Gensler...Architecture, design and planning worldwide," *World Architecture* (January 1997): 54.
David Taylor, "US practices find their feet in expanding London," *The Architects' Journal* (April 1997): 22–23.
Philip Langdon, "When Bigger is Better: Lessons from America's Largest Firms," *Architectural Record* (August 1998): 58–63.
"The secret of success," *Architecture* (September 1998): 67, 69–70.
"Ch-ch-ch-ch-changes," *World Architecture* (July-August 1999).
Elizabeth Kubany Harrison, "Gensler named Firm of the year," *Architectural Record* (May 2000): 166–177.
Bradford McKee, "Art Gensler: The Boss," *Architecture* (May 2000): 127.
Mickey O'Connor, "What has your firm done for you lately?," *Architecture* (October 2000): 137–138.
"View from the top," *World Architecture* (September 2001): 64–67.
Karen Eisenberg, "Art Gensler on Strategic Design," *Blueprints* (Summer 2001): 13,18.
"Gensler predicts upturn," *Building Design* (October 2002).
Ian Chodikoff, "Measuring for success," *Canadian Architect* (June 2007): 26–32.
George Anders, "Secrets of the Talent Scouts," *The New York Times* (March 2009): 6–7.
Ben Ikenson, "Gensler's Secret Sauce," *Metropolis* (June 2013): 108–110.

<u>Kevin Roche John Dinkeloo and Associates</u>
"Review of Books: Architecture," *Art in America* (June 1986): 11,13.
"Prodigious prodigals," *World Architecture* (October 1999): 38–39.
Sangleem Lee, "Leading architects of the 20th century: Kevin Roche," *Space* (July 2006): 159–181.
Jeffrey Inaba, "Maturing Ambition," *Volume* 3 (2007): 60–65.
Paul Makovsky, "Iconic Workplace," *Metropolis* (November 2008): 70–79.

<u>Studio Hillier</u>
Elizabeth M. Fowler, "Prospects better for architects," *The New York Times* (March 1985): 22.

Thomas Fisher, "Architectural Urbanity," *Progressive Architecture* (October 1994): 70–77.
Bradford McKee, "The tricks to fast track," *Architecture* (March 1995): 135–137
Thomas Vonier, "Importing new design talent," *Architecture* (July 1996): 125–129.
Charles D. Linn, Clifford A. Pearson, "Lessons from America's best-managed firms," *Architectural Record* (January 1997): 106–117.
Roger Yee, "Heads up!," *Oculus* (Summer 2003): 48–50.
C.C. Sullivan, "Mature Firms, New Talent," *Architecture* (January 2004): 23–24.
Andrew S. West, "Hillier Architect and RMJM Group Unite," *Architect* (July 2007).
Amanda Hurley Kolson, "The house of Morrison," *Architect* (May 2008): 96–102.
Ralph Steinglass, "What makes a merger work?," *Oculus* (October 2008): 44–45.

BTA Architects
Dennis J. De Witt, "BTA in the 1990's: the place, the people, the culture," *PROCESS:Architecture* 89 (1990): 6–13.
"The 'Design Research' Prophesy," "The Studio Design Process Reconsidered," "Visualizing Environments," *PROCESS:Architecture* 89 (1990): 14–35.
Mass Cambridge, "Thompson opens his own office," *Progressive Architecture* (February 1966): 49.
Scott Simpson, "Live, Work, Play," *ArchitectureBoston* (Spring 2011): 40–45.

Antoine Predock Architect PC
"Antoine Predock," *Architecture + Urbanism* (November 1988): 75–79.
David Dillon, "Border Crossings," *Architecture* (August 1991): 58–63.
Stanley Collyer, "Antoine Predock," *Competitions* (Winter 1992): 50–61.
Deborah K. Dietsch, "Predock's Example," *Architecture* (March 1995): 15.
David Dillon, "American Visionary," *Architecture* (March 1995): 55–57.
Kriston Capp, Timothy Hursley, "Antoine Predock Architect," *Architect* (March 2011): 78–79.
Clifford A. Pearson, "Antoine Predock rides high with the gold medal," *Architectural Record* (June 2006): 212–223.

Center for Environmental Structure
"Christopher Alexander's Timeless Way of Building," *Architecture + Urbanism, Volume 3* (1975): 49–53.
Dorit Fromm, "An Approach to Wholeness," *The Architectural Review* (February 1986): 24–27.
Ismet Khambatta, "Making a Building," *Crit* (Winter 1987): 16–19.
Christopher Alexander, "Perspectives: Manifiesto 1991," *Progressive Architecture* (July 1991): 108–112.
Kenneth Powell "The Alexander Technique," *The Architect's Journal* (August 1995): 14–15.

JAHN
"Xerox Center," *Architecture + Urbanism* (April 1981): 9–33.
Heinrich Klotz, "Revision of the modern: Helmut Jahn," *Architectural Design* (March–April 1985): 26–27.
Jim Murphy, "To be continued," *Progressive Architecture* (March 1990): 102–112.
Michael J. P. Smith, "Murphy Jahn," *Inland Architect* (May–June 1992): 28–36.
Von Robert Specht, "Passion," *Architektur, Innenarchitektur, Technischer Ausbau* (May 1998): 38–39.
James S. Russell, "It's Helmut Jahn's moment," *Architectural Record* (May 2004): 96–102.
Von Friedrich H. Dassler, "Ein Gesprach mit Helmut Jahn in Chicago: von munchen uber mannheim nach Bangkok," *Intelligente Architektur* (October–December 2006): 24–29.
"Werner Sobek—Enginering," *Intelligente Architektur* (July–September 2009): 23–33.

Goettsch Partners
Nick Poulos, "Mies' Associates Spread Architect's Philosophy," *The Chicago Tribune* (June 24, 1970): III7.
Wolf Von Eckardt, "Mies van der Rohe's Firm Moves in New Direction," *The Los Angeles Times* (June 24, 1979): X34.
Paul Gapp, "Life after Mies: The disciples of the master go their separate ways," *The Chicago Tribune* (February 27, 1983): VI20.
"Mies' old firm is now Lohan," *The Chicago Tribune* (December 12, 1985): II3.
"Former Murphy/Jahn, SOM execs form new design firm," *Building Design & Construction* (September 1989): 28.
Deborah Wilk, "Corporate Transparency," *Interior Design* (November 2012): 88–92.

Robert A.M. Stern Architects
Vincent Scully, "Robert A.M. Stern Perspecta to Post-Modernism," *Architectural Design* 51 (December 1981): 98–99.
Charles Jencks, "On the edge of content," *Skyline* (June 1992): 28–29.
Carol Vogel, "The Trend-Setting Traditionalism of Architect Robert A.M. Stern," *The New York Times* (January 13, 1985): 41–49.
"Pencil Points," *Progressive Architecture* (March 1986): 21–23.
"Robert Stern und der moderne Traditionalismus," *Baumeister* (July 1986): 44–61.
"Robert A.M. Stern Architects," *Architecture + Urbanism* (May 1998): 62–123.
Thomas Fisher, Jim Murphy, Daralice D. Boles, "The Big Sell," *Progressive Architecture* (July 1988): 84–93.
Nora Richter Greer, "Americans Abroad: Some Coming Attractions," *AIA Journal* (December 1989): 64–71.
"Robert A.M. Stern," *Perspecta* 37 (2005): 50–57.
Joseph Giovannini, "Miracle on 34th Street," *Architectural Digest* (July 2007): 32–40.

SITE
Pilar Viladas, "Insights on site: Pilar Viladas takes a look at a maverick architectural group," *Interiors* (August 1980): 78–80.
Martin Filler, "Harbingers: Ten Architects," *Art in America* (Summer 1981): 114–123.
Herbert. L. Smith Jr., "A new site for SITE," *Architectural Record* (September 1984): 152–154.
Tim McKeough, "Vintage wines," *Azure* (May 2008): 92–96.
"Lo studio e l'architecto, Studio James Wines," *Ottagono* (September 2009).
Sam Jacob, "James Wines: the 'outsider' who thinks real culture occurs in car parks," *The Architectural Review* (December 2009): 25–26.

Morphosis Architects
Michael Rotundi, "Morphosis," *Skala* (September 1988): 12–17.
"The making of mega Morphosis," *Interiors* (October 1989): 99–107.
Aaron Betsky, "Morphosis: The Landscape of Tension and Risk," *Modulus* (January 1991): 140–145.
"Thomas Mayne, Morphosis," *Dimensions* (March 1991): 78–83.
"Morphosis: The Chiba Project," *Architectural Design* (January 1992): 46–61.
Jeffrey Kipnis, "El Ultimo Reloj De La Arquitectura," *El Croquis* (January 1993): 6–16.

Francisco Spadoni, "Forma e representacao na arquitetura de Thom Mayne," *Projeto* (October 1998): 79–81.

Ami Ran, "The Abstract Context of 'Morphosis': Interview with Thom Mayne," *Architecture of Israel* (June 2000): 2–15.

Bradford Mckee, ".../q+a," *I.D.* (June 2005): 28–29.

Rachel Pulfer, "Q & A: Thom Mayne," *Azure* (July 2005).

Yoshio Futagawa, "Interview with Thom Mayne," *GA Document* (August 2005): 8–17.

Olivier Touraine, "L'emulation plutot que le code," *Le Moniteur Architecture* (March 2006): 40–44.

"Morphosis," *GA Document (*November 2006): 62–67.

Jeffrey Inaba, "Ambition then and now," *Volume* (January 2007): 112–116.

Herman Diaz Alonso, Thom Mayne, "Generation(s) and The Generative," *Log* (September 2009): 127–135.

Ann Gray, "The Mayne Idea," *Form* (January 2011): 31–33.

Gwen Webber, "Profile: Thom Mayne," *Blueprint* (July 2011): 42–46.

Peter Cook, "On being Thom Mayne: reminding cynics of the beauty of serious design," *The Architectural Review* (August 2011): 27.

Min Zhao, "Thom Mayne: Beyond the Form, It Is Urban and Globalization," *Journal of Circulation Research* (January 2012): 100–105.

Michael Webb, "Morphosis Realizes its Vision," *The Plan* (May 2012): 20–35.

"Morphosis," *GA Document* (September 2012): 112–127.

Offices Established 1974–1980

Machado and Silvetti Associates

"Architettura," *Controspazio* (January–February 1978): 9–21.

Werner Oechslin, "New Possibilities of distinction," *Lotus International* (January 1980): 117–125.

Claudio d'Amato, "Il Projetto—Machado & Silvetti," *Eupalino* (March 1984): 28–32.

Roberto Machado, Jorge Silvetti, "Statement," *Architecture + Urbanism* (April 1990): 67–70

Michael Hays, "The Material Force of the Architectural Imagination," *Architecture + Urbanism* (April 1990): 71–79.

Edmund White, "Visionaries at Home," *House and Garden* (July 1991): 172–175,194–196.

Elizabeth Bennet, "Machado & Silvetti Associates Inc.," *Arq* (December 1992): 31–37.

Roberto Machado, Jorge Silvetti, "Get Real," *Architecture* (April 1997): 80–83.

Paolo Bercah, C. Tito, "Machado, Silvetti and the Battery," *Zodiac* (September 1999): 64–85.

Kohn Pedersen Fox Associates

Nora Klebow, "Contextual Functionalism—The Work of Kohn Pedersen Fox," *CRIT* (Fall 1983): 14–17.

Eugene Kohn, "Statement," *PROCESS:Architecture* 86 (1990): 6–9.

Joseph Giovannini, "Kohn Pedersen Fox," *PROCESS:Architecture* 86 (1990): 10–13.

William Pedersen, "Method & Intentions 1976–1989," *PROCESS:Architecture* 86 (1990): 14–18.

Koos Boosma, "Books—KPF Kohn Pedersen Fox. Architecture + Urbanism 1986–1992; Kohn Pedersen Fox DG Bank—Frankfurt am Main," *Archis* (March 1995): 86–89.

Eugene Kohn, "Japan: Key to KPF's Global View," *Architecture + Urbanism* (June 1996): 82–83.

William Pedersen, "Strategies for the Design of Tall Buildings," *Architecture + Urbanism* (June 1996): 84–90.

Tim McKeough, "Five Partners split from KPF London," *Architectural Record* (November 2009): 33.

Fred A. Bernstein, "Software Guru," *Architect* (December 2012): 31.

Steven Holl Architects

Cathy Curtis, "Details Is the Key to Architecture, Steven Holl Tells UCI Forum," *The Los Angeles Times* (March 21, 1990): F2.

Herbert Muschamp, "Designing in the Dark Workshop of the Soul," *The New York Times* (September 8, 2002): 90.

"Holl on Hybrids," *Architectural Design* (September–October 2005): 79–83.

Steven Holl, "Office Process," *Architecture + Urbanism* (January 2006): 156.

Julie V. Iovine, "Steven Holl's Dark Year Gets Brighter," *The New York Times* (December 31, 2006): 32.

Cathy Lang Ho, "Steven Holl Architects," *Blueprint* (June 2007): 44–49.

Silver Silber, "Celebrity Architects," *The New York Times* (December 22, 2007): A24.

Li Hu, Hideki Hirahara, Matthias Michael Schuler, "Steven Holl Architects," *Architecture + Urbanism* (February 2008): 36–53.

Emmanuel Petit, "Interview—Steven Holl," *The Architectural Review (*March 2013): 20–22.

Martin C. Pederson, "Morning Rituals," *Metropolis* (March 2013): 62–65.

Gluckman Mayner Architects

Suzanne Stephens, "Rem Koolhaas' and Richard Gluckman's Bank renovation for Second Stage Theater grabs the spotlight with economy, efficiency, and a bit of flash," *Architectural Record* (August 1999): 93–95.

David Hay, "The Artists' Architect, Building For Art's Sake," *The New York Times* (November 14, 2004): 36.

Richard Staub, "2nd Act," *Oculus* (Summer 2005): 30–31.

Tim McKeough, "Gluckman Mayner tapped for Beijing gallery," *Architectural Record* (July 2008): 36.

Arquitectonica

"Arquitectonica," *Architectural Design* (August 1979): 186–187.

"Portfolio of Recent Works," *Perspecta* 18 (1982): 169–181.

"Building in AD," *Architectural Record* (August 1982): 188–189.

Charles K. Gandee, "Making it in Miami," *Architectural Record* (August 1982): 112–121.

Toshiro Sato, "Conversation with Women Architects," *Space Design* (June 1990): 6–9, 62–63.

Kira L. Gould, "Urban Legend," *Interiors* (September 1999): 66–71.

Moore Ruble Yudell Architects & Planners

Andrea Truppin, "Cover story," *Interiors* (September 1987): 192–208.

Stanley Collyer, "Buzz Yudell," *Competitions* (Fall 1996): 50–61.

Stanley Collyer, "Playing the China Card: The Middle Kingdom Beckons Western Architects," *Competitions* (Summer 2006): 30–37, 40–41.

"Moore Ruble Yudell Architects & Planers," *Architecture + Urbanism* (March 2008): 24.

James Mary O'Connor, Neal Matsumo, "Building a 'Bridge' Firm," *Architecture + Urbanism* (March 2008): 25–35.

Pelli Clarke Pelli Architects

"Design Director Named by Architectural Firm," *The Los Angeles Times* (August 30, 1964): J22.

Paul Gapp, "No tall order for this architect," *The Chicago Tribune* (May 25, 1969): 2–3.

"Pelli Named Dean of School at Yale," *The New York Times* (June 18, 1976): A11.

"Yale appoints Pelli as Dean of Architecture," *The Los Angeles Times* (June 20, 1976): 10.

John Dreyfuss, "Cesar Pelli: Architect Soon to Depart for Yale University Post; Professional Skill, Imagination Will Be Missed Here," *The Los Angeles Times* (December 19, 1976): VII19.

John Dreyfuss, “An Architect of the Select, and Common, People,” *The Washington Post* (December 21, 1976): B5.
Paul Goldberger, “An Argentine for the Modern,” *The New York Times* (February 4, 1977): C19.
John Dreyfuss, “The L.A. 12: A Good Idea Which has Gone Nowhere,” *The Los Angeles Times* (August 14, 1977): VII1.
Paul Goldberger, “Architects Discuss Future of the Art,” *The New York Times* (May 19, 1978): C11.
Craig R. Whitney, “Prince Attacks Modern Architects Once More,” *The New York Times* (October 30, 1988): L16.
Nora Richter Greer, “Americans Abroad: Some Coming Attractions,” *The AIA Journal* (January 1989): 64–65.
“Tokyo Project for Cesar Pelli,” *The Wall Street Journal* (April 12, 1990): A10.
Thomas Hine, “A Builder of Our Time,” *The New York Times* (June 16, 1991): 23.
Patricia Dane Rogers, “Architectural Digest’s Top Architects,” *Washington Home* (August 1, 1991).
Naomi B. Pollock, “Foreign Architects are Building Bridges to Japan,” *The New York Times* (March 8, 1992): 36.
Cesar Pelli, “Architects Working in Countries Other Than Their Own,” *Architecture + Urbanism* (January 1993): 133–134.
Jayne Merkel, “Practice profile—Pelli Clarke Pelli,” *Architectural Design* (November 2008): 106–113.
Martin C. Pedersen, “Office Space,” *Metropolis* (November 2011): 92–97.

Jerde Partnership
“Jon Jerde: Instant City,” *Arch+* (December 1992): 117.
Christoph Korne, Lars Kruckeberd, Wolfram Putz, “Jon Jerde and the architecture of pleasure,” *Stadt Bauwelt* (December 2000): 46–51.
“Up close: Architect Jon Jerde,” *Planning* (December 2000): 39.
David Moreno, “Design Lyrics,” *Urban Land* (July 2001): 55–59.
Frederic Nantois, “Jon Jerde: le marketing au coeur des villes,” *L’Architecture d’Aujourd’hui* (September 2003): 54–61.
Kriston Capps, “The Jerde Partnership,” *Los Angeles Architect* (October 2011): 80–83.

FXFOWLE Architects
Ralph Steinglass, “What Makes a Merger Work?,” *Oculus* (Fall 2008): 44–45.
Richard Staub, “Outward Bound,” *Oculus* (Winter 2010/2011): 24–25.
Kriston Capps, “Office Space,” *Architect* (August 2011): 44–45.

Koetter Kim & Associates
“Fred Koetter and Susie Kim, Fred Koetter & Associates,” *Progressive Architecture* (January 1980): 112–113.
Philip Arcidi, “Urban Ethics,” *Progressive Architecture* (February 1992): 92–93.

MACK Architect(s)
Mark Mack, “Domesticity and Experiment,” *GA Houses* (October 1988): 6–39.
“An interview with Mark Mack,” *University of Tennessee Journal of Architecture* (January 1991): 4–9.
“Mark Mack Architects,” *GA Houses* (March 1993): 82–87.
Marco Biagi, “Estro e panorama,” *Ville giardini* (December 1995). 10–17.

Safdie Architects
James Geoffrey, “Triumph of an outcast,” *Maclean’s* (May 1988): 31–38.
Vivek Sabherwal, “I have been blessed to work on difficult and complicated sites,” *Architecture + Design* (June 2012): 20–28.

Diller Scofidio + Renfro
Nancy Princenthal, “Architecture’s Iconoclasts,” *Sculpture* (December 1989): 18–23.
David Cohn, “Visiones trastocadas,” *Architectura Viva* (January 1992): 70–73.
Gillian Horn, “Cross-border architecture,” *Blueprint* (March 1996): 24–26.
Gonzalo Casals, “Ladrillos + pixels,” *Summa+* (April 2001)
Jayne Merkel, “Word of Mouth,” *Architectural Design* (November 2001): 58–63.
Kate Zarnet, “Clarity Refreshes the Parts,” *Blueprint* (May 2003): 117.
Peter Stegner, “Von der Choreographie der Raüme und Menschen,” *Baumeister* (August 2003): 60–65.
Patricia C. Phillips, “A Parallax Pratice: A Conversation with Elizabeth Diller and Ricardo Scofidio,” *Art Journal* (Fall 2004): 62–77.
Dana Lixenberg, “Mind Over Matter,” *Blueprint* (March 2005): 46–49.
Benedict Clouette, Jeffrey Inaba, “Elizabeth Diller,” *Volume* 3 (2007): 120–121.
Philip Nobel, “Die Another Day,” *Metropolis* (May 2007): 98–99.
Dirk Meyhofer, “Wir Bauen Nur One Ever Buildings,” *Archithese* (September 2007): 74–75.
Joseph Giovannini, “In her own words,” *Interior Design* (January 2011): 45–48.

Santos Prescott and Associates
Peter Papademetriou, “Habitat as a means to architecture,” *Progressive Architecture* (February 1978): 62–69.
Peter Popham, “Japan: Superpatron of Daring Design,” *Metropolitan Home* (December 1988): 53–60, 126.
Philip Arcidi, “Adèle Naudé Santos in Tokyo,” *Progressive Architecture* (November 1990): 102–104.
Naude Santos, “Excerpts from a conversation: thoughts on light, landscape, and human experience; a personal statement,” *Perspecta* 28 (1997): 78–93.
Ruggero Lenci, “Adèle Naudé Santos: Architectural itinerary in two hemispheres,” *L’architecttura* (May 2003): 172–173.

Duany Plater-Zyberk and Company
Toshiro Sato, “Conversations with Women Architects—Elizabeth Plater-Zyberk,” *Space Design* (June 1990): 60–62.

Offices Established 1981–1985

Toshiko Mori Architect
Toshiko Mori, “Design and Fabrication,” *Harvard Design Magazine* (Summer 1998): 51–53.
“Toshiko Mori,” *Architectural Design* (January 2003): 23–33.
Alexandra Lange, “Stepping Out,” *Metropolis* (August–September 2003): 98–102.

Populous
Kriston Capps, “Office Space,” *Architect* (August 2011): 44–45.

Rafael Viñoly Architects
John Morris Dixon, “Projects: Rafael Vinoly Architects,” *Progressive Architecture* (May 1991): 120–122.

KieranTimberlake
Thomas Fisher, “Serious About Systems,” *Progressive Architecture* (March 1994): 64–69.
Sara Hart, “New ways to build better, faster, cheaper,” *Architectural Record* (January 2002): 131–138.
Sara Hart, “Seeking innovative alternatives, KieranTimberlake Associates pumps research into architecture,” *Architectural Record* (October 2003): 43–45.
Sara Hart, “Prefabrication, the speculative builder’s tool has been discovered by modernist designers,” *Architectural Record* (December 2003): 123–126.

James Woudhuysen, "Mass costumization and the manufactured module," *Architectural Design* (March 2006): 49–51.
Jayne Merkel, "Practice Profile—KieranTimberlake Associates," *Architectural Design* (January 2008): 114–119.

Hodgetts + Fung
"The ephemerality of a cinema architecture," *The Architectural Review* (December 1987): 59–60.
"Hodgetts and Fung," *Architecture + Urbanism* (March 1991): 68–71.
Kurt W. Forster, "Beauty (and the beast) in the Parlor: Hodgetts+Fung's Architecture in the (C) Age of Media Culture," *Architecture + Urbanism* (March 1991): 72–75.
Denise Bratton, "Hodgetts+Fung the art of the remix," *Architectural Design* (September 2005): 107–114.
Stanley Collyer, "Hodgetts+Fung," *Competitions* (June 2006): 42–51.

STUDIOS Architecture
Laura Fisher Kaiser, "The Studios Secret," *Interior Design* (November 2002): S4–S46.

Offices Established 1986–1988

Office dA
Ned Cramer, "Portfolio Office dA," *Architecture* (September 2001): 116–127.
"Monica Ponce de Leon, Figuring Configurations," *Dimensions* (2006): 116–123.
Beth Broome, "Office dA puts it down on paper," *Architectural Record* (July 2007): 248.
Ron Nyren, "Emerging Designers," Urban Land (November 2008): 62–67.
Sebastian Schmaling, "The New Small Architectural Practices," *Harvard Design Magazine* (Spring/Summer 2010): 114–121.
Conrad Bercah, "Office dA—Nader Tehrani in USA," *The Plan* (July 2011): 28–42.

Sorg Architects
"Representing the U.S. and Staying Secure," *Bloomberg Business Week* (October 16, 2006).
Jennifer Sergent, "Designing Women," *DC Magazine* (May 2013): 50.

Tod Williams Billie Tsien Architects
"Rites of Passage," *Metropolis* (January–February 1984): 14–19.
Christine Pittel, "Serene Pursuits," *Elle Decor* (March 1990): 129–133.
"Interview: Tod Williams & Billie Tsien," *Progressive Architecture* (May 1990): 119–123.
Philippe Barriere, "Tod Williams et Billie Tsien," *L'Architecture d'Aujourd'hui* (October 1990): 127–131.
"Slowness," *Arcade* (Winter 1996): 35.
Tod Williams, "The way we work," *Practices* (1996): 195–197.
"Tod Williams & Billie Tsien," *GA Document* (January 1997): 42–45.
"The World Upside Down: Stage and Costume Design," *Architectural Design* (May–June 1997): VIVIII.
Raymund Ryan, "nature : fabric : beauty," *Architecture + Urbanism* (June 1997): 54–58.
"The Tension of Not Being Specific: Billie Tsien and Tod Williams in conversation with Peter Zumthor," *2G* (February 1999): 8–29.
Tod Williams, Billie Tsien, "Slowness," "Slowly (improving) Vision," *2G* (February 1999): 130–143.
"Family of Work," *Dimensions* 13 (1999): 170–177.
Clifford A. Pearson, "Material Affairs," *Architectural Record* (March 2001): 68–72.
Kriston Capps, "Tod Williams Billie Tsien Architects," *Architect* (June 2011): 80–81.
Josephine Minutillo, "Tod Williams and Billie Tsien," *Architectural Digest* (June 2012): 62–64.
Martin C. Pedersen, Paul Makovsky, "Living in a Material World," *Metropolis* (December 2012): 50–59.
Karrie Jacobs, "We Two," *Architect* (June 2013): 182–187.

RUR Architecture PC
"Kansai-Kan of the National Diet Library," *Architectural Design* (May 1997): 92–94.
Antoine Picon, "Toward a Well-Tempered Digital Design: The Architecture of Reiser+Umemoto," *Harvard Design Magazine* (Fall 2006/ Winter 2007): 77–83.

Bernard Tschumi Architects
Victoria Geibel, "Carrying Columbia into the 21st Century," *Metropolis* (May 1988): 38.
Anthony Vidler, "The Pleasure of the Architect," *Architecture + Urbanism* (September 1988): 11–23.
Marta Cervelló, "It's time for Change," *Quaderns* (January 1990): 13–22.
Bernard Tschumi, "Photograms," *Ottagono* (March 1991): 73–88.
Matthew Barhydt, "Tools of the Stars," *Progressive Architecture* (Nov 1992): 110–111.
Francesco Bonami, "Bernard Tschumi, The schizophrenic side of Architecture," *Flash Art* (October 1995): 83–86.
"Conversation: Zaha M. Hadid, Wolf Prix, and Bernard Tschumi," *Architecture + Urbanism* (July 1998): 4–11.
Andrew MacNair, "Letter to Bernard Tschumi," *Architecture + Urbanism* (July 2003): 148–151.
Renata Hedjuk, "Death Becomes Her: transgression, decay, and eROTicism in Bernard Tschumi's early writings and projects," *The Journal of Architecture* (September 2007): 393–411.

Acconci Studio
Cathy Lang Ho, "Curriculum Vito," *Architecture* (January 2001): 51–53
Cecilia Anderson, "Worth a Thousand Words," *Blueprint* (July 2005): 91.

Selldorf Architects
Nicholas von Hoffman, "Annabelle Selldorf—cultivating an architectural calling," *Architectural Digest* (December 2001): 102–103.
Philip Nobel, "Annabelle Selldorf—Her Father's Influence Sparked a Sensibility Entrenched in Midcentury Modernism," *Architectural Digest* (January 2002): 214–217.
Stephen Drucker, "The Right Proportions," *Architectural Digest* (May 2005): 128–131.

Offices Established 1989–1990

Asymptote Architecture
"Designing the Unpredictable," *World Architecture* (March 1997): 72–75.
Bonnie Evans, "Tangent to an infinite curve," *Architecture of Israel* (September 2007): 77–89.
Hani Rashid, Eunju Han, "Hani Rashid: The Position of Architects For The Future," *Space* (November 2012): 40–47.

LEESER Architecture
Thomas Fisher, "Against Beauty," *Progressive Architecture* (September 1988): 114–115.
"Theory and Practice: Thomas Leeser," *Oculus* (November 1990): 10.
Holger Beisitzer, "Schlaflos in NY," *Architekur Innen Tech* (September 2004): 36–37.
Jacqueline Pezzillo, "Launch Pad to Success," *Oculus* (Spring 2012): 34–35.

Preston Scott Cohen
Michael Weinstock, "Preston Scott Cohen: Stereotomic Permutations," *AA Files* 31 (June 1996): 94–95.

Ingeborg M. Rocker, "On Distortions: An Interview with Preston Scott Cohen," *Log* 24 (Winter/Spring 2012): 116–125.

Studio Daniel Libeskind

"Daniel Libeskind: An Architectural Design Interview," *Architectural Design* (September–October 1990): 14–19.

Leslie Van Duzer, "A conversation with Nina Libeskind," *Dimensions* 10 (1996): 20–27.

Philip Nobel, "Of Lindenstrasse," *Metropolis* (January 1999): 74–93.

Victoria Newhouse, "Designs that reach out and grab," *The New York Times* (June 2000).

"Foundations of memory," *Landscape Design* (July–August 2003): 12–15.

Layla Dawson, "Daniel Libeskind, master of memorials, on the healing power of architecture," *The Achitectural Review* (April 2010): 32–33.

William J. R. Curtis, "Reputations: Daniel Libeskind," *The Architectural Review* (October 2011): 116–117.

WEISS/MANFREDI Architecture/ Landscape/ Urbanism

Donald Albrecht, "Weiss/Manfredi," *Architecture* (January 1996): 92–99.

Abby Bussel, "Interview: Marion Weiss & Michael Manfredi," *Practices* (January 1997): 122–125.

Susana Torre, "Rediscovering context in the work of Weiss/Manfredi Architects," *Oculus* (November 2000): 15.

Alastair Gordon, "Site Specific," *Metropolis* (February 2004): 82–87, 106–107.

Jayne Merkel, "Practice Profile: Weiss/ Manfredi Architects," *Architectural Design* (January 2007): 104–111.

Offices Established 1990–1996

AECOM

Bradford McKee, "AECOM Acquires Ellerbe Becket," *Architect* (November 2009): 17.

Joe Brown, "AECOM, Los Angeles, New York, et al," *Harvard Design Magazine* (Fall/Winter 2010–2011): 124–125.

KVA matx

Thomas Fisher, "Emerging Talent: Kennedy & Violich Architecture," *Progressive Architecture* (May 1993): 84–91.

Javier Mozas, "What to do? Three attitudes toward cost reduction," *A+T* (January 1996): 8–31.

Raul A. Barreneche, "Mind and Matter," *Architecture* (July 2007): 41–44.

Sheila Kennedy, "Electrical Effects (A) Material Media," *PRAXIS 6* (2004): 84–93.

"Give Back Curtain," *Arch+* (December 2004): 67–68.

Julie Sinclair Eakin, "Portable Light," *Architecture* (April 2006): 54–61.

Beth Broome, "Joint Venture," *Architectural Record* (February 2010): 79–83.

Uli Hellweg, Nikolaus Kuhnert, Anh-Linh Ngo, "Haus der Zukunft Bausteine Post-Oil City," *Arch+* (May 2010): 10–19.

J. Frano Violich, "KVA," *ArchitectureBoston* (September 2011): 24.

Stan Allen Architect

Stan Allen, "Practice vs. Project," *PRAXIS* 0 (1999): 112–123.

Stan Allen, "Article by Stan Allen," *Assemblage* 41 (April 2000): 8.

Louise Braverman, Architect

Walters, "Emerging Voices: Louise Braverman," *Oculus* (October 1996): 15.

Claire Wilson, "When Small Firms Venture Abroad," *Oculus* (Winter 2010/2011): 26–27.

Zago Architecture

"Andrew Zago: Olypmic West Office Towers, Site 2/ Berlin Spreebogen International Design Competition," *Space Design* (September 1994): 8–17.

"Spotlight," *Architectural Design* (September 2012): 8–13.

LOT-EK

Maurizio Vitta, "Il design del rifiuto," *L'Arca* (April 1996): 82–83.

Jayne Merkel, "LOT/EK," *Architectural Design* (November 1999): 105–109.

Zoe Ryan, "Container culture," *Blueprint* (May 2002): 96–99.

Michael Maltzan Architecture

Martin Filler, "Michael Maltzan," *House Beautiful* (February 2001): 56–58.

Brian Cavanaugh, "Movement in Architecture—A conversation with Michael Maltzan," *LA Architect* (September 2005): 41–47.

"Michael Maltzan Architecture," *Architecture + Urbanism* (March 2011).

VJAA

Thomas Fisher, "Best Practice," *Architecture Minnesota* (November 2009): 25.

Carlos Zapata Studio

Suzanne Stephens, "Design Credits," *Oculus* (March 1994): 12–13.

Ann C. Sullivan, Raul A. Barreneche, "Architects' Favorite Toys," *Architecture* (June 1997): 122–127.

SHoP

Sara Moss, "Calculated Risk," *Architectural Design* (January–February 2004): 16–19.

Philip Nobel, "Model Shop," *Metropolis* (September 2007): 88–92.

Edie Cohen, "The fav five," *Interior Design* (November 2007): 172.

Linda G. Miller, "Out of Africa," *Oculus* (Winter 2010/2011): 32–33.

Lisa Delgado, "Redesigned Practice," *Oculus* (Fall 2011): 24–27.

Philip Nobel, "Perspective: Vishaansanity," *Metropolis* (May 2012): 60–64.

Offices Established 1998–2000

Hashim Sarkis Studios

Jessica Dheere, "You Can Go Home Again," *Architectural Record* (October 2008): 108–113.

Hashim Sarkis, "Op Arch: Alternative A," *Journal of Architectural Education* (May 2009): 93–94.

Slade Architecture

Sarah Ameiar, "Cho Slade Architecture combines nature and building in collagelike designs," *Architectural Record* (December 2000): 88–93.

Heather Hodson, "Beyond the velvet rope," *Interior Design* (April 2010): 145–148.

Bill Millard, "Public Projects, Small Firms, Targeted Tactics," *Oculus* (September 2012): 24–27.

Studio SUMO

David Sokol, " Studio SUMO eschews signatures by approaching every project inquisitively," *Architectural Record* (December 2006): 92–95.

Masha Panteleyeva, "Studio Visit: Studio Sumo," *The Architects Newspaper* (February 2008): 12–13.

"A Conversation with Sunil Bald," *Perspecta* 43 (2010): 160–163.

Marisa Bartolucci, "Building Boomers," *House and Garden* (November 2011): 68–70.

OBRA Architects

Wendy Ordemann, "Small Firm Workplace: The Whole Wide World," *Oculus* (January 2012): 28–29.

L.E.FT

"Datahome," *L'Architecture d'Aujourd'hui* (April 2002): 78–79.

Carlos Santana, "L.E.FT," *Architecture e Vida* (August 2005): 64–67.

Markus Miessen, "Constructive Cynicism," *Build* (February 2006): 25–27.

Laura Raskin, "L.E.FT," *Architectural Record* (December 2010): 70–71.

SsD
Ingrid Spencer, "The Acceleration of Single Speed Design," *Architectural Record* (September 2006): 53–54.
Asad Syrkett, "SsD Cambridge, MA/ New York City/Seoul," *Architectural Record* (December 2012): 68–71.

Offices Established 2002–2003

Studio Shanghai
Blair Kamin, "Architect Do No Harm," *Metropolis* (August–September 2002).
Ned Kelly, "Benjamin Wood—the man who made Xintiandi," *www. urbanatomy.com* (June 2011).

Utile
Anne Holtzman, "Who's the boss," *Architecture* (July 2005): 31–34.
Hubert Murray, "The New Establishment Meets the Next Wave," *Architectural Record* (March 2008): 106–112.

MOS Architects
Mimi Zeiger "Pattern Language," *Form* (July/August 2007): 35–39.
"Discussion: Idea-Driven Practices," *Harvard Design Magazine* 32 (Spring/ Summer 2010): 106–113.
Amanda Reeser Lawrence, Ashley Schafer, "Editorial conversation between Michael Meredith and Praxis," *PRAXIS* 11+12 (2010): 4–7.
"PATTERNS interviews MOS," *PRAXIS* 11+12 (2010): 8–13.

Wodiczko + Bonder
Maureen P. Sherlock, "Krzysztof Wodiczko and the Architecture of Signs," *Chicago Architectural Journal* (April 1989): 46–49.
Edith Ackermann, "Edith Ackermann & Krzysztof Wodiczko in conversation," *Thresholds* (January 1999): 57–63.
"Dean & DeLuca coffee shop conversation with Krzysztof Wodiczko," *Perspecta* 34 (2003): 70–79.
Ginger Nolan, "Disruptive Agency: A Conversation with Krzysztof Wodiczko," *Thresholds* (December 2005): 81–85.

Offices Established 2003–2006

WORKac
Randi Greenberg, "Generating form through program," *Architectural Record* (April 2005): 95–96.
Eva Hagberg, "The Long Approach," *Metropolis* (July 2005): 131, 156–157.
Clifford A. Pearson, "Design Vanguard 2006," *Architectural Record* (December 2006): 73.
Clifford A. Pearson, "WORK Architecture Company draws strength from diverse perspectives," *Architectural Record* (December 2006): 116–119.
Eva Hagberg, "On the Cusp," *Metropolis* (July 2007): 90–99.
Marisa Bartolucci, "Building Boomer," *House and Garden* (November 2007): 68–70.
"Text Message: Amale Andraos," *Metropolis* (September 2009): 116.
Edie Cohen, "Quite an outfit," *Interior Design* (April 2011): 63–66.
Wonne Ickx, Ashley Schafer, "Interview: WORKac," *PRAXIS* 11+12 (2010): 54–64.

Höweler + Yoon Architecture
"The Living Interviews Höweler + Yoon," *PRAXIS* 11+12 (2010): 108–119.

over,under
Elizabeth Padjen, "Imagine That!," *ArchitectureBoston* (September–October 2007): 27–29.
Hubert Murray, "The New Establishment Meets the Next Wave," *Architectural Record* (March 2008): 106–112.

REX Architecture
Tim Abrahams, "American Evolution," *Blueprint* (August 2006): 36–40.
Earnest Beck, "BIM Well with Others," *Architecture* (January 2011): 158–161.
"Joshua Prince-Ramus: the lost art of productivity losing control," *Monitor* (January 2011): 61–75.
James Gaddy, "Joshua Prince-Ramus," *Details* (August 2011): 86.

Offices Established 2006–2011

Adrian Smith + Gordon Gill Architecture
"Parting Company," *Metropolis* (January 2007): 30–32.
Gordon Gill, "Signing sustainable buildings," *Urban Land* (June 2007): 55–59.
Herbert Wright, "When Adrian Smith was forced to consider retirement, he set up a new practice with a zero-energy approach," *Blueprint* (October 2007): 47.

ATOPIA
Richard Francis, "Room," *AA Files* (September 1992): 47–54.
"Hybrid," *Architectural Design* (July 1997): 80–84.
Y-Jean Mun-Delsalle, "Beyond Education," *FuturArc* (January 2014): 15–25.

ORG Organization For Permanent Modernity
Alexander D'Hooghe, "The Case For the Big Box: Joys of a non-expressionist architecture," *Volume* 19 (January 2009): 32–39.
Amanda Kelsen Hurley, "Don't forget the burbs," *Architect* (May 2013): 84–88.

MASS Design Group
Ken Shulman, "Straight Out of School," *Metropolis* (January 2011): 62–66.
Holly Jacobsen, Michael Murphy, Alan Ricks, "An Update from MASS Design Group," *Contract* (January 2013): 126–127.
Thomas de Monchaux, "South-To-North Thinking," *Metropolis* (February 2013): 71–74.
Michael Webb ,"Michael Murphy and Alan Ricks of MASS Design Group improve healthcare with little means," *MARK* (April 2013): 118–125.
"Interview: MASS Design Group," *Architecture + Urbanism* (August 2013).

SO – IL
Katya Tylevich, "Flexible, small, and scrappy," *MARK* (August 2012): 130–141.
Kennie Jacobs, "The Art of Business," *Architect* (March 2013): 56–60.

Leong Leong
Jessica Sheridan, "Emerging Architects Synthesize Southpoint," *Oculus* (March 2006): 40–41.
Linda G. Miller, "New Faces, New York," *Oculus* (March 2010): 28–31.
"Ten Questions," *PIN UP Magazine* (May 2011).
Lisa Delgado, "Studio Visit: Leong Leong Architecture," *Architect's Newspaper* (July 2011): 8.
Kelsey Keith, "The rising stars," *Dwell* (January 2012): 14.

NADAAA
Michael Hensel, "Practices Abroad—Today's Diaspora Tomorrow's Architecture," *Architectural Design* (May 2012): 104–113.
Nader Tehrani, "Three Schools of Architecture," *Perspecta* 45 (2012): 17–26.

Project Image Credits

1898 – 1918

Master Plan for Manila • D. H. Burnham & Company • *Architectural Record, April 1917* | **Master Plan for Baguio** • D. H. Burnham & Company • *Architectural Record, April 1917* | **Master Plan for Canberra Federal Capital** • Walter Burley Griffin and Marion Mahony • *Mati Maldre, National Library of Australia* | **American Academy in Rome** • McKim, Mead and White • *Architectural Record, February 1916* | **Leeton Town Centre Plan** • Walter Burley Griffin and Marion Mahony • *Mati Maldre, National Library of Australia* | **Nanjing University** • Perkins, Fellows and Hamilton • *Special Collections, Yale Divinity School Library* | **Newman College, University of Melbourne** • Walter Burley Griffin and Marion Mahony • *Mati Maldre, National Library of Australia* | **Imperial Hotel** • Frank Lloyd Wright • Frank Lloyd Wright Foundation Archives, Avery Architectural & Fine Arts Library, Columbia University | **Peking Union Medical College** • Shepley Bulfinch | **Master Plan for Castlecrag Residential Community** • Walter Burley Griffin and Marion Mahony • *Evening News, May 1925*

1918 – 1928

Nippon Oil Company Building • George A. Fuller Company • *Far Eastern Review, October 1922* | **Yenching University** • Henry Killiam Murphy • *Journal of the Society of Architectural Historians, March 2004* | **Jiyu Gakuen School** • Frank Lloyd Wright • *Flickr User: Patrick Collins* | **Marunouchi Building** • George A. Fuller Company • *Far Eastern Review, December 1921* | **Hotel Sevilla-Biltmore** • Schultze & Weaver • *Jose Gelabert-Navia* | **Austin Standard Factory** • The Austin Company • *Courtesy of the Ohio Historical Society* | **Leonard House Office Building** • Walter Burley Griffin and Mariont Mahony | **Bush House** • Helmle & Corbett | **Tokyo Women's Christian College** • Raymond & Rado • *Tuttle Publishing* | **Hoshi University Main Building** • Raymond & Rado • *Tuttle Publishing* | **Capital Theatre** • Walter Burley Griffin and Marion Mahony • *National Library of Australia, Mati Maldre* | **Restoration of the Palace at Versailles** • William Welles Bosworth • *The New York Times, September 1926* | **US Embassy** • Raymond & Rado • *US Department of State* | **Incinerators for Reverberatory Incinerator and Engineering Company (REICo)** • Walter Burley Griffin and Marion Mahony • *National Library of Australia Archive* | **Oriental Park Racetrack** • Schultze & Weaver • *Narcisco Menocal Collection* | **Restoration of the Palace at Versailles** • William Welles Bosworth • *The New York Times, September 1926* | **Casino Nacional** • Schultze & Weaver | **Housing and Offices for Rising Sun Petroleum Company** • Raymond & Rado • *Tuttle Publishing* | **US Embassy** • Cass Gilbert • *The Canadian Press* | **YMCA Jerusalem** • Shreve, Lamb and Harmon • *Flickr User: A30 YoYo* | **Automobile Plant and Industrial City** • The Austin Company • *New Industrial Landscape, 1978* | **Stalingrad Tractor and Tank Factory** • Albert Kahn Associates • *Chelyabinsk Tractor Plant Museum*

1928 – 1937

US Pavilion, Giardini della Biennale • Delano and Aldrich • *The Architect, 1930* | **US Embassy** • Delano and Aldrich | **Nanjing Revolutionists Memorial** • Henry Killam Murphy • *The China Press, Sunday, April 1, 1934* | **Hotel Nacional de Cuba** • McKim, Mead and White • *Joe Abraham* | **Gasoline Stations for Rising Sun Petroleum Company** • Raymond & Rado • *Tuttle Publishing* | **Tokyo Golf Club** • Raymond & Rado • *Japan Architect, November 1961. Photographer: Akio Kawasumi* | **Chelyabinsk Tractor and Tank Factory** • Albert Kahn Associates | **Elgin Marble WIng, British Museum** • John Russell Pope | **Overseas Chinese Home** • Henry Killam Murphy • *The China Press, May 13, 1932* | **Lucknow University Library** • Walter Burley Griffin and Marion Mahony | **Golconde Dormitory** • Raymond & Rado • *Tuttle Publishing* | **Avila Hotel** • Harrison and Abramovitz • *Wallace K. Harrison Archives, Avery Architectural & Fine Arts Library, Columbia University.*

1937 – 1945

Jai Alai Auditorium • Ellerbe Becket | **Hotel Granada** • Paul R. Williams Architects • *Maynard L. Parker, photographer. Courtesy of The Huntington Library, San Marino,CA* | **Prototype for Open-Air Schools** • Richard J. Neutra • *Architectural Forum, March 1945* | **Prototype for Rural Health Centers** • Richard J. Neutra • *Architectural Forum, March 1945* | **Prototype for District Hospitals** • Richard J. Neutra • *Architectural Forum, March 1945* | **Hotel Nutibara** • Paul R. Williams Architects • *Maynard L. Parker, photographer. Courtesy of The Huntington Library, San Marino,CA*

1948 – 1949

Creole Petroleum Town Plan • Skidmore, Owings & Merrill • *MIT Libraries, Rotch Visual Collections* | **El Panama Hotel** • Edward Durell Stone and Associates • *Ezra Stoller, ESTO* | **US Embassy** • The Eggers Group • *US Department of State* | **Club Ariston** • Marcel Breuer Associates • *Architectural Record, June 1948. Photographer: L. Souessia* | **US Embassy** • Harrison and Abramovitz • *Wallace K. Harrison Archives, Avery Architectural & Fine Arts Library, Columbia University* | **General Motors Assembly Plant** • SmithGroupJJR • *Architecture Forum, January 1955* | **Reader's Digest Building** • Raymond & Rado • t*Collection of Kitazawa Kōichi* | **Creole Petroleum Corporation Offices** • Lathrop Douglass • *Architectural Record, June 1955* | **US Embassy** • Harrison and Abramovitz • *Wallace K. Harrison Archives, Avery Architectural & Fine Arts Library, Columbia University* | **Hotel Tamanaco** • Holabird & Root • *Neal A. Prince Special Collection & Archives, New York School of Interior Design* | **Hotel del Lago** • Holabird & Root • *Neal A. Prince Special Collection & Archives, New York School of Interior Design* | **Hotel Tequendama** • Holabird & Root • *Neal A. Prince Special Collection & Archives, New York School of Interior Design*

1949 – 1954

US Embassy Staff Housing • Raymond & Rado • *David Leavitt Collection, The Architectural Archives, University of Pennsylvania* | **Standard Oil Vacuum Company Facilities and Housing** • Skidmore, Owings & Merrill | **Ciudad Piar and Puerto Ordaz New Towns** • Town Planning Associates • *The Josep Lluis Sert Collection, Courtesy of the Frances Loeb Library, Harvard University Graduate School of Design* | **Neighborhood Unit in Pomona** • Town Planning Associates • *The Josep Lluis Sert Collection, Courtesy of the Frances Loeb Library, Harvard University Graduate School of Design* | **US Embassy** • Ralph Rapson • *The Architectural Review, October 1955* | **Hospital of Social Security for Employees** • Edward Durell Stone and

Associates, Alfred L. Aydelott Associates • *Progressive Architecture, June 1962* | **Istanbul Hilton Hotel •** Skidmore, Owings & Merrill • *Ezra Stoller, Esto* | **Centro Commercial Las Mercedes •** Oficina Don Hatch • *Progressive Architecture, October 1955* | **US Embassy Staff Housing •** Ralph Rapsonh • *The Architectural Review, October 1955* | **US Embassy •** Ralph Rapson • *Ralph Rapson Archives* | **US Consulate and Staff Housing •** Skidmore, Owings & Merrill • *US Department of State* | **US Consulate •** Skidmore, Owings & Merrill • *Ezra Stoller, Esto* | **US Consulate •** Skidmore, Owings & Merrill | **St. Anselm Church •** Raymond & Rado • *Tuttle Publishing* | **Amerika Haus •** Skidmore, Owings & Merrill • *Ezra Stoller, Esto* | **UNESCO Headquarters •** Marcel Breuer Associates • *Marcel Breuer Papers, Special Collections Research Center, Syracuse University Libraries* | **US Embassy •** Raymond & Rado • *E.Gill Lui, 2005*

1954–1956

Phoenicia Intercontinental Hotel • Edward Durell Stone and Associates • *Neal A. Prince Special Collection & Archives, New York School of Interior Design* | **US Embassy •** Edward Durell Stone and Associates • *E.Gill Lui, 2005* | **Master Plan for Canberra Federal Capital •** Walter Burley Griffin and Marion Mahony • *National Library of Australia* | **Esso Building •** Lathrop Douglass • *Architectural Record, March 1958. Photographer: Paul Beer* | **Tire and Footwear Plant •** Oficina Don Hatch • *L'Architecture d'Aujourd'hui, October 1956* | **Joan Miro Studio •** Sert, Jackson and Associates • *The Josep Lluis Sert Collection, Courtesy of the Frances Loeb Library, Harvard University Graduate School of Design* | **Quinta Palatino •** Town Planning Associates • *The Josep Lluis Sert Collection, Courtesy of the Frances Loeb Library, Harvard University Graduate School of Design* | **US Consulate •** Yamasaki, Hellmuth and Leinweber • *Architectural Forum, February 1958. Photographer: John Launois* | **US Embassy •** Eero Saarinen and Associates • *E.Gill Lui, 2005* | **Luce Memorial Chapel •** Pei Cobb Freed & Partners Architects • *Pei Cobb Freed & Partners* | **US Pavilion, Indian Industries Fair •** United States Information Agency • *USIA: Courtesy Jack Masey* | **Aruba Caribbean Hotel •** Morris Lapidus Associates • *Interiors, November 1959. Photographer: Victor Gelberg* | **US Embassy •** Richard J. Neutra • *Domus, June 1962* | **Congress Hall •** Hugh Stubbins and Associates • *Baukunst und Werkform 1, 1958* | **Interbau Housing Block •** The Architects Collaborative • *The Architects Collaborative, 1966* | **Hipódromo La Rinconada •** Arthur B. Froehlich and Associates • *Archivos de la Fundacion de la Memoria Urbana* | **US Embassy •** Hugh Stubbins and Associates • *Architectural Forum, July 1955* | **US Embassy •** Eero Saarinen and Associates • *Courtesy Yale University Manuscripts and Archives* | **Gunma Music Center •** Raymond & Rado • *Tuttle Publishing* | **US Embassy Baghdad •** Sert, Jackson and Associates • *The Josep Lluis Sert Collection, Courtesy of the Frances Loeb Library, Harvard University Graduate School of Design* | **US Pavilion, Jeshyn International Fair •** United States Information Agency • *The Cudney Collection* | **US Embassy •** Alfred L. Aydelott and Associates • *Progressive Architecture, June 1962*

1956–1962

US Embassy • Harry Weese Associates • *US Department of State* | **Soreq Nuclear Research Center •** Philip Johnson / Alan Ritchie Architects • *Zodiac, Volume 8 1961* | **US Embassy •** The Architects Collaborative • *E. Gill Lui, 2005* | **US Embassy •** Vincent G. Kling Associates • *Progressive Architecture, June 1962. Photographer: Estudio Wuth* | **Place Ville-Marie •** Pei Cobb Freed & Partners Architects • *Joseph Molitor* | **US Pavilion, International Trade Fairs •** Office of International Trade Fairs • *Industrial Design, February 1957; Photographer: Jack Masey* | **US Embassy •** John M. Johansen • *Wayne Andrews, ESTO* | **Banque Lambert •** Skidmore, Owings & Merrill • *Ezra Stoller, ESTO* | **George C. Marshall House, "America Builds Exhibition" •** United States Information Agency • *Peter Blake, NARAA* | **Arawak Hotel •** Morris Lapidus Associates • *Architectural Record, July 1960. Photographer: Gottscho-Schleiser* **US Embassy •** Marcel Breuer Associates • *Marcel Breuer Papers, Special Collections Research Center, Syracuse University Libraries* | **US Consulate •** ROMA Design Group | **Hotel Ponce Intercontinental •** Wiliam B. Tabler Architects • *Neal A. Prince Special Collection & Archives, New York School of Interior Design* | **Ron Bacardi y Compania Building •** The Office of Mies van der Rohe • *Bauen + Wohnen, October 1962* | **University of Baghdad •** The Architects Collaborative • *The Architects Collaborative, 1966* | **US Pavilion, Universal and International Exposition •** United States Information Agency • *Architectural Record, July 1958. Photographer: Louis Checkman* | **Habana Hilton Hotel •** Ellerbe Becket • *Hospitality Industry Archives (Hilton Archive)* | **Berlin Hilton Hotel •** William L. Pereira & Associates • *F.C. Gundlach* | **El Monte Renewal Project •** Edward Larrabee Barnes Associates • *Alexandre Georges* | **Civil Air Terminal •** Yamasaki and Associates • *Architectural Record, March 1963* | **Fondation Maeght •** Sert, Jackson and Associates • *The Josep Lluis Sert Collection, Courtesy of the Frances Loeb Library, Harvard University Graduate School of Design* | **US Consulate •** Edward Larrabee Barnes Associates • *The Edward Larrabee Barnes Collection, Courtesy of the Frances Loeb Library, Harvard University Graduate School of Design* | **American National Exhibition •** United States Information Agency • *Collection: Dr. Shelly Weinig* | **Nile Hilton Hotel •** Ellerbe Becket • *Welton Becket, Total Design* | **Britz-Buckow-Rudow Master Plan (Gropiusstadt) •** The Architects Collaborative • *The Architects Collaborative, 1966* | **San Juan Intercontinental Hotel •** Morris Lapidus Associates • *Neal A. Prince Special Collection & Archives, New York School of Interior Design* | **India International Centre •** Joseph Allen Stein and Associates • *MIT Libraries, Rotch Visual Collections. Photographer; Peter Serenyi* | **IBM Research Center •** Marcel Breuer Associates • *Japan Architect, March 1963* | **BEWO-Bau Development I + II •** Richard J. Neutra • *Teutsch Bauzeitung, July 1966* | **US Embassy •** Adrian Wilson Associates • *U.S. Army Military History Institute* | **Ellinikon International Airport •** Eero Saarinen and Associates • *Architectural Record, August 1962* | **US Embassy •** Pei Cobb Freed & Partners Architects • *E.Gill Lui, 2005* | **American International School •** Joseph Allen Stein and Associates • *MIT Libraries, Rotch Visual Collections. Photographer; Peter Serenyi* | **University of Tunis School of Law •** The Architects Collaborative • *Aga Khan Visual Archive, Aga Khan Documentation Center at MIT* | **Nanzan University Campus •** Raymond & Rado • *Tuttle Publishing* | **American Traveling Exhibitions •** United States Information Agency • *USIA, Courtesy Jack Masey* | **Hotel La Flaine •** Marcel Breuer Associates • *Marcel Breuer Papers, Special Collections Research Center, Syracuse University Libraries* | **US**

Embassy • Victor A. Lundy • *Victor Lundy* | **Palace of Princess Fatemah** • Brown Daltas and Associates • *Architectural Forum, October 1962* | **Coca-Cola Plant** • Brown Daltas and Associates • *Architectural Forum, October 1962* | **Office Tower and Shopping Center** • Brown Daltas and Associates • *Architectural Forum, October 1962* | **Teijin Institute for Biomedical Research** • Polshek Partnership • *James Polshek* | **Dublin Intercontinental Hotel** • Wiliam B. Tabler Architects • *Neal A. Prince Special Collection & Archives, New York School of Interior Design* | **Society Verbi Divini Seminary Chapel** • Raymond & Rado • *Tuttle Publishing* | **Parly II Shopping Center** • Lathrop Douglass • *Architectural Record, March 1973* | **Neue Nationalgalerie** • The Office of Mies van der Rohe • *Roland Halbe* | **Indian Institute of Management** • Louis I. Kahn • *James Ewing, OTTO* | **National Capital of Bangladesh** • Louis I. Kahn • *Jatiyo Sangsad Bhaban*

1962–1972

US Embassy • Ellerbe Becket • *Architectural Record, August 1961* | **Teijin Applied Textile Science Center** • Polshek Partnership • *James Polshek* | **National College of Agriculture** • Perkins + Will • *Perkins + Will* | **Toronto-Dominion Centre** • The Office of Mies van der Rohe • *John Vetterli* | **University of Guelph Long Range Development Plan and Buildings** • Sert, Jackson and Associates • *The Josep Lluis Sert Collection, Courtesy of the Frances Loeb Library, Harvard University Graduate School of Design* | **Westmount Square** • The Office of Mies van der Rohe • *Chicago History Museum* | **Carlton Centre** • Skidmore, Owings & Merrill • *Ezra Stoller, ESTO* | **King Fahd University of Petroleum and Minerals** • CRSS Inc. • *Architectural Record, April 1976* | **USAID and United Nations Building** • Leo A Daly • *Leo A Daly* | **USAID General Services Building** • Leo A Daly • *Leo A Daly* | **Heinz Headquarters** • Skidmore, Owings & Merrill • *Ezra Stoller, ESTO* | **Jeddah International Airport** • Edward Durell Stone and Associates • *Edward Durell Stone Papers, University of Arkansas Libraries Special Collections* | **Pakistan Institute of Nuclear Science and Technology** • Edward Durell Stone and Associates • *Edward Durell Stone Papers, University of Arkansas Libraries Special Collections* | **Master Plan for Baguio** • D. H. Burnham & Company • *Architectural Record, April 1917* | **Ford Foundation Headquarters** • Joseph Allen Stein and Associates • *MIT Libraries, Rotch Visual Collections. Photographer; Peter Serenyi* | **Master Plan of Tehran** • Victor Gruen International • *Tehran Comprehensive Plan, 1968* | **Kuwait Fund for Arab Economic Development** • The Architects Collaborative • *Pace* | **US Embassy** • Robert P. Madison International • *Robert P. Madison International* | **Presidential Palace and Governmental Complex** • Edward Durell Stone and Associates • *Edward Durell Stone Papers, University of Arkansas Libraries Special Collections* | **Cummins Engine Company Component Plant** • Kevin Roche John Dinkeloo and Associates • *Architectural Design, August 1967* | **Master Plan for East Pakistan Agricultural University** • Paul Rudolph • *Architecture + Urbanism, July 1977* | **US Pavilion, Canadian World Exhibition** • United States Information Agency • *Courtesy: Chermayeff & Geismar* | **Carmel de la Paix Convent** • Sert, Jackson and Associates • *The Josep Lluis Sert Collection, Courtesy of the Frances Loeb Library, Harvard University Graduate School of Design* | **Ecole des Beaux-Arts et des Arts Appliquées** • Sert, Jackson and Associates • *The Josep Lluis Sert Collection, Courtesy of the Frances Loeb Library, Harvard University Graduate School of Design* | **University of Islamabad** • Edward Durell Stone and Associates • *Edward Durell Stone Papers, University of Arkansas Libraries Special Collections* | **Canadian Imperial Bank of Commerce** • Pei Cobb Freed & Partners Architects • *Ezra Stoller, ESTO* | **Bielefeld Kunsthalle** • Philip Johnson / Alan Ritchie Architects • *Philip Johnson / Alan Ritchie Architects* | **Manila Hilton Hotel** • Ellerbe Becket • *Welton Becket, Total Design* | **Boots Pure Drug Company Headquarters** • Skidmore, Owings & Merrill • *Ezra Stoller, ESTO* | **Cap 3000 Shopping Center** • Victor Gruen International • *Techniques et Architecture, February 1970. Photographer: Traphot* | **Louvain la Neuve Master Plan** • Victor Gruen International • *Victor Gruen* | **Baldegg Convent** • Marcel Breuer Associates • *Werk, 1973* | **Wolfson Center for Mechanical and Transportation Engineering** • Louis I. Kahn • *Josep Maria Torra* | **Fundació Joan Miró** • Sert, Jackson and Associates • *Process, 1982* | **Costa Smeralda Resort Master Plan** • Sasaki Associates • *Sasaki Associates* | **US Embassy** • Skidmore, Owings & Merrill • *US Department of State* | **Chase Manhattan Bank** • Skidmore, Owings & Merrill • *Skidmore, Owings & Merrill Archives* | **Pacific Centre** • Victor Gruen International • *Architectural Record, January 1975. Photographer: James K.M. Cheng* | **PREVI Lima Proyecto Experimental de Vivienda** • Center for Environmental Structure • *Center for Environmental Structure* | **US Pavilion, Japan World Exposition** • United States Information Agency • *USIA, Courtesy Jack Masey* | **US Embassy** • Eduardo Catalano • *E.Gill Lui, 2005* | **Rosenthal Glass Factory** • The Architects Collaborative • *PROCESS: Architecture No. 19, 1980* | **Family Planning Center and Maternal Health Center** • Louis I. Kahn | **Oversea-Chinese Banking Corporation Centre** • Pei Cobb Freed & Partners Architects • *W. Thom* | **Union Oil New Town** • Leo A Daly • *Leo A Daly* | **Daiei Building** • Paul Rudolph • *Architecture + Urbanism, 1973. Photographer: Taisuke Ogawa* | **Tour FIAT** • Skidmore, Owings & Merrill • *Ezra Stoller, ESTO* | **The Aga Khan University Hospital, Medical College and School of Nursing** • Payette • *Payette Associates*

1972–1973

Hotel Babin Kuk • Edward Durell Stone and Associates • *Architectural Record, September 1978* | **Express Towers** • Joseph Allen Stein and Associates • *MIT Libraries, Rotch Visual Collections. Photographer; Peter Serenyi* | **Tour Gan** • Harrison and Abramovitz • *Flickr User: Guillame oMeChaNiCal* | **US Embassy** • Victor Gruen International • *Japan Architect, March 1977* | **Torin Corporation** • Marcel Breuer Associates • *Marcel Breuer Papers, Special Collections Research Center, Syracuse University Libraries* | **Polimex-Cekop Food Plant** • Epstein • *Epstein* | **Souk Al Safat** • The Architects Collaborative • *Aga Khan Visual Archive, Aga Khan Documentation Center at MIT* | **Souk Al Manakh** • The Architects Collaborative • *Aga Khan* SmithGroupJJR • *Architectural Record, October 1976. Photographer: Balthazar Korab* | **National Library** • The Architects Collaborative • *Aga Khan Visual Archive, Aga Khan Documentation Center at MIT*

1973–1980

Raffles City • Pei Cobb Freed & Partners Architects • *Shang Wei Kouo* | **Dow Chemical Executive Housing** • Leo A Daly • *Leo A Daly* | **SABIC Headquarters** • Leo A Daly • *Leo A Daly* | **Montego Bay Hospital** • The

Architects Collaborative • *Architectural Record, August 1974* | **Imperial Medical Center of Iran** • William L. Pereira & Associates • *William L. Pereira & Associates* | **Centro Banaven** • Philip Johnson / Alan Ritchie Architects • *Flickr User: Heisia* | **National Center for the Performing Arts** • Philip Johnson / Alan Ritchie Architects • *Progressive Architecture, March 1981* | **Hajj Terminal, Jeddah International Airport** • Skidmore, Owings & Merrill • *Jay Langlois Owens Corning* | **King Khalid Military City** • Brown Daltas and Associates • *Google Earth* | **Torre Picasso** • Yamasaki and Associates • *Xauxa Håkan Svensson* | **Al-Jubail Petrochemical Co. Headquarters Building** • Leo A Daly • *Leo A Daly* | **Union Carbide Cellulose Casings Plant** • Epstein • *Epstein* | **Sharjah Intercontinental Hotel** • The Architects Collaborative • *Michael Kubo* | **Arabian-American Oil Company Workers' Housing** • CRSS Inc. • *Aramco and its World, 1980* | **King Khaled Airport** • HOK • *MIMAR 40, 1991. Photographer: Robert Azzi and Gregory Murphey* | **King Saud University** • HOK+4 Consortium • *HOK* | **University of Blida Teaching Hospital and Housing Communities** • Skidmore, Owings & Merrill • *Skidmore, Owings & Merrill Archives* | **King Abdulaziz Military Academy** • CRSS Inc. • *CRSS, Saudi Search* | **Hotel Bernardin Resort** • The Architects Collaborative • *Architectural Record, October 1977* | **Moscow World Trade Center** • Ellerbe Becket • *Los Angeles Times, September 12, 1976* | **Abu Dhabi Intercontinental Hotel** • Benjamin Thompson Associates • *Architecture Intérieure, December 1975* | **Joint Banking Centre** • Skidmore, Owings & Merrill • *PACE* | **Yanbu New Community Master Plan** • Skidmore, Owings & Merrill • *Skidmore, Owings & Merrill Archives* | **Yanbu Industrial City Residential District** • Leo A Daly • *Leo A Daly* | **Yanbu Industrial City Residential District** • CRSS Inc. • *CRSS, Saudi Search* | **Yanbu Industrial City Residential District** • The Architects Collaborative • *TAC, The Architects Collaborative, Inc., 1984, Courtesy of the MIT Libraries, Aga Khan Visual Archives* | **Shiraz Technical Institute** • Hugh Stubbins and Associates • *Architecture, December 1976* | **Jubail Industrial City Master Plan** • The Architects Collaborative • *Sam Sweezy* | **US Embassy** • Bassetti Architects • *Architecture: AIA Journal, January 1989* | **National Commercial Bank** • Skidmore, Owings & Merrill • *Wolfgang Hoyt* | **Tnuva Dairy Processing Plant** • Epstein • *Epstein* | **Monetary Agency Head Office** • Yamasaki and Associates | **Ministry of Foreign Affairs Housing** • CRSS Inc. • *CRSS, Saudi Search* | **US Embassy** • Hartman-Cox Architects • *Peter Aaron* | **Australian Parliament House** • Mitchell/Giurgola Architects • *Mitchell/Giurgola Architects* | **Sheraton Miyako Hotel** • Yamasaki and Associates • *Architectural Digest, January 2004. Photographer: Erhard Pfeiffer* | **Porto Carras Resort** • The Architects Collaborative • *PROCESS: Architecture No. 19, 1980* | **Israeli Air Force Bases** • Epstein • *Epstein* | **US Embassy Staff Housing** • Harry Weese Associates • *The Japan Architect, September 1983* | **Khulafa Street Development** • The Architects Collaborative • *Sam Sweezy* | **Kuwait Institute for Scientific Research** • The Architects Collaborative • *Pace* | **Founders Hall (Meishusama Hall)** • Yamasaki and Associates • *Japan Architect, September 1983. Photographer: Masao Arai* | **Frankfurt Museum for the Decorative Arts** • Richard Meier and Partners Architects • *Ezra Stoller, ESTO* | **Al-Ahli Bank** • Skidmore, Owings & Merrill • *PACE* | **Institute for Public Administration** • The Architects Collaborative • *Aga Khan Visual Archive, MIT* | **US Embassy** • CRSS Inc. • *E.Gill Lui, 2005* | **Tanjong Jara Beach Hotel** • Wimberly Allison Tong & Goo • *Architecture in Continuity, 1985* | **Basrah Sheraton Hotel** • The Architects Collaborative • *Aga Khan Visual Archive, MIT*

1980 – 1985

Gajah Madah Plaza • Daniel, Mann, Johnson & Mendenhall • *Anthony J. Lumsden* | **Aviano School** • Mitchell/Giurgola Architects • *Mitchell/Giurgola Architects* | **Ruwais New Town** • CRSS Inc. • *Space Design, March 1980* | **National Methanol Company Headquarters** • Jubail • *Middle East Construction, August 1985* | **IBA Social Housing** • Eisenman Architects • *Eisenman Architects* | **11 Diagonal Street** • JAHN • *JAHN* | **Colonnade Condominiums** • Paul Rudolph • *Peter Aaron* | **Tegel Harbor Phase I Housing** • Moore Ruble Yudell • *Moore Ruble Yudell* | **Shanghai Centre** • John Portman and Associates • *John Portman and Associates: Michael Portman* | **Concourse Complex** • Paul Rudolph • *l'Arca, 1988* | **Royal Jordanian Armed Command of Staff College** • Leo A Daly • *Leo A Daly* | **Khulafa Street Building** • Venturi, Scott Brown and Associates • *Process, Volume 58, May 1985* | **Doha Sheraton Hotel** • William L. Pereira & Associates • *Architecture + Urbanism, October 1982* | **362 West Street** • JAHN • *JAHN* | **United Gulf Bank Building** • Skidmore, Owings & Merrill • *Hedrich Blessing* | **Banco de Credito Headquarters** • Arquitectonica • *Arquitectonica* | **US Embassy** • KMW Architecture • *KMW Architecture* | **Dharmala Sakti Building** • Paul Rudolph • *Peter Aaron, OTTO* | **Bank of China Tower** • Pei Cobb Freed & Partners Architects • *John Nye* | **US Embassy** • Perry Dean Rogers | Partners Architects • *Richard Mandelkorn* | **Bouygues World Headquarters** • Kevin Roche John Dinkeloo and Associates • *Architecture & Urbanism, April 1988* | **Louvre Renovation** • Pei Cobb Freed & Partners Architects • *Koji Horiuchi* | **Siemens Headquarters and Research Facilities** • Richard Meier and Partners Architects • *Baumeister, April 1991* | **GSIS Headquarters** • The Architects Collaborative • *Sam Sweezy* | **Hotel Meridian** • Daniel, Mann, Johnson & Mendenhall • *Anthony J. Lumsden* | **Citicorp Center** • Leo A Daly • *Leo A Daly* | **Volvo Headquarters** • Mitchell/Giurgola Architects • *Mitchell/Giurgola Architects* | **El Gezirah Sheraton Hotel** • CRSS Inc. • *Magnus Manske* | **Marina Square** • John Portman and Associates • *John Portman and Associates: Michael Portman* | **Humboldt Bibliothek** • Moore Ruble Yudell • *Moore Ruble Yudell* | **Bond Centre** • Paul Rudolph • *Peter Aaron* | **King Faisal Military School** • Perkins + Will • *Perkins + Will* | **Royal Dutch Shell Bank Headquarters** • Skidmore, Owings & Merrill • *Peter Aaron* | **Ardmore Habitat Condominiums** • Safdie Architects • *Cyrnie Payne* | **Regent Hotel** • John Portman and Associates • *John Portman and Associates Photographer: Bernard Mexx* | **International Headquarters** • Robert A.M. Stern Architects • *Robert A.M. Stern Architects*

1985 – 1989

US Embassy • Polshek Partnership • *Jeff Goldberg, Esto* | **Messeturm** • JAHN • *JAHN* | **Canary Wharf** • Skidmore, Owings & Merrill, Pelli Clarke Pelli Architects, Kohn Pedersen Fox Associates, Perkins + Will, HOK, Pei Cobb Freed and Partners • *SOM Archives* | **US Embassy** • Integrus • *Integrus* | **Fish Dance Restaurant** • Gehry Partners • *Japan Architect, September 1987* | Sainsbury Wing • Venturi, Scott Brown and Associates • *Venturi, Scott Brown and Associates* |

Broadgate Development • Skidmore, Owings & Merrill • *SOM Archives* | **Westendstraße 1 (DZ Bank Headquarters)** • Kohn Pedersen Fox Associates • *Kohn Pedersen Fox Associates* | **Stadthaus Ulm** • Richard Meier and Partners Architects • *Scott Frances, OTTO* | **City Hall and Library** • Richard Meier and Partners Architects • *AV Monografias, May-June 1996* | **Kachofugetsu-kan (SDC Corporate Headquarters)** • Santos Prescott and Associates • *Santos Prescott and Associates* | **Ring of Fire Aquarium and Tempozan Marketplace** • Cambridge Seven Associates • *Peter Aaron, OTTO* | **Goldman Sachs Headquarters** • Kohn Pedersen Fox Associates • *Process, No. 86, 1990* | **US Embassy** • Eduardo Catalano • *E. Gill Lui, 2005* | **US Embassy** • Parker Design Group • E. Gill Lui, 2005 | **Museum of Contemporary Art of Barcelona** • Richard Meier and Partners Architects • *Scott Frances, OTTO* | **Kreuzberg Tower and Wing** • John Hejduk • *Architettura, February 1990* | **Tegel Housing** • John Hejduk • *Architectural Record, July 1989* | **National Gallery of Canada** • Safdie Architects | **Koizumi Sangyo Corporation Headquarters** • Eisenman Architects • *Peter Aaron, OTTO* | **Euro Disney Resort** • Gehry Partners, Michael Graves and Associates, Gwathmey Siegel Kaufman Architects, Antoine Predock Architect, Robert A.M. Stern Architects • *Google Earth* | **US Embassy** • Arquitectonica • *Peter Aaron, OTTO* | **Kobe Nishiokamato Housing** • Moore Ruble Yudell • *Moore Ruble Yudell* | **US Embassy (Bangkok)** • KMW Architecture • *KMW Architecture*

1989–1990

Potatisakern Housing and Villas Phases I, II and III • Moore Ruble Yudell • *Moore Ruble Yudell* | **Vitra Design Museum** • Gehry Partners • *Markus Keuter* | **Four Continents Bridge** • SITE • *SITE* | **Daimler-Benz Research Center** • Richard Meier and Partners Architects • *AV Monografias, May-June 1996* | **US Embassy** • Gunnar Birkerts and Associates • *Gunnar Birkerts* | **Nexus/Momochi International Housing Exhibition** • Michael Graves and Associates, Tigerman McCurry Architects, Steven Holl Architects, Mack Architect(s) • *Peter Aaron, OTTO* | **Northwest Frontier Province Agricultural University** • Skidmore, Owings & Merrill • *Wolfgang Hoyt* | **Tokyo International Forum** • Rafael Viñoly Architects • *Rafael Viñoly Architects* | **Jewish Museum** • Studio Daniel Libeskind • *Guenter Schneider* | **Arp Museum** • Richard Meier and Partners Architects • *Roland Halbe Fotografie* | **Latvian National Library** • Gunnar Birkerts and Associates • *Gunnar Birkerts* | **Nunotami Corporation Headquarters** • Eisenman Architects • *Kenchiku Bunka, September 1990*

1990–1997

The Palace of the Lost City • Wimberly Allison Tong & Goo • *Wimberly Allison Tong & Goo* | *Yokohama Landmark Tower* • *Hugh Stubbins and Associates* • *World Architecture, November 1997* | **Hong Kong Stadium** • Populous • *Populous* | **Tokyo Telecom Centre** • HOK • *HOK* | **The Greenbrier at West Village Golf Resort** • Robert A.M. Stern Architects • *Robert A.M. Stern Architects* | **Munich Airport Center** • JAHN • *JAHN* | **JR Central Towers and Nagoya Marriott Hotel** • Kohn Pedersen Fox Associates • *Kohn Pedersen Fox Associates* | **Scottish Equitable Headquarters** • Koetter Kim & Associates • *Koetter Kim & Associates* | **Puerta Europa Towers** • Philip Johnson / Alan Ritchie Architects • Philip Johnson / Alan Ritchie Architects | **Inanc Lisesi School for Gifted Children** • Studio Hillier • *Studio Hillier* | **Le Fresnoy Art Center** • Bernard Tschumi Architects • *Bernard Tschumi Architects* | **Guggenheim Museum** • Gehry Partners • *Archis, Volume 1, 1998* | **Miho Museum** • I. M. Pei Architect • *Timothy Hursley* | **Makuhari Bay New Town** • Steven Holl Architects • *Steven Holl Architects* | **Mielparque Nikko Kirifuri Hotel and Spa** • Venturi, Scott Brown and Associates • *Venturi, Scott Brown and Associates* | **Petronas Towers** • Pelli Clarke Pelli Architects • *Jeff Goldberg, Esto* | **Kiasma Museum of Contemporary Art** • Steven Holl Architects • *Steven Holl Architects* | **Provincial Capital Building** • Venturi, Scott Brown and Associates • *Venturi, Scott Brown and Associates* | **Olympic Fish** • Gehry Partners • *Domus, November 1992* | **Avenue Number Five** • SITE • *SITE* | **US Embassy** • Kohn Pedersen Fox Associates • *Process, No. 86, 1990* | **Mamilla District** • Safdie Architects • *Timothy Hurley* | **Hong Kong Convention and Exhibition Center** • Skidmore, Owings & Merrill • *James Steinkamp* | **Oceanario de Lisboa** • Cambridge Seven Associates • *Cambridge Seven Associates* | **Castalia Ministry of Health, Welfare and Sport** • Michael Graves and Associates • *Michael Graves and Associates* | **Jin Mao Tower** • Skidmore, Owings & Merrill • *Nick Merrick, Hedrich Blessing* | **The Scientific Center of Kuwait** • Cambridge Seven Associates • *Cambridge Seven Associates* | **Sony Center Berlin** • JAHN • *JAHN* | **Darwin Centre Museum** • HOK • *HOK* | **Memorial Towers** • John Hejduk • *Architecture + Urbanism, January 2005* | **Cinémathèque Française [American Center]** • Gehry Partners • *Scott Frances, OTTO* | **Menara Multi-Purpose At Capital Square** • John Portman and Associates • *John Portman and Associates. Photographer: Michael Portman* | **Ottawa City Hall** • Safdie Architects • *Canadian Architect, February 1995* | **Suter Townhouses** • MACK Architect(s) • MACK Architect(s) | **Kadota Housing** • Santos Prescott and Associates • *Santos Prescott and Associates* | **Dairi Nishi Housing** • Santos Prescott and Associates • *Santos Prescott and Associates* | **Orchards Scott Hotel and Residences** • Arquitectonica • *Arquitectonica* | **Atlantico Pavilion** • Skidmore, Owings & Merrill • *SOM Archives* | **University of Marne-la-Vallée School of Architecture** • Bernard Tschumi Architects • *Bernard Tschumi Architects* | **Samsung Jong-ro Tower** • Rafael Viñoly Architects • *Rafael Viñoly Architects* | **Slither Housing** • Diller Scofidio + Renfro • *Diller Scofidio + Renfro* | **Rothermere American Institute at Oxford University** • Kohn Pedersen Fox Associates • *Kohn Pedersen Fox Associates* | **Korea Development Bank Headquarters** • AECOM • *AECOM* | **Valeo Electricity** • Davis Brody Bond Architects & Planners • *Davis Brody Bond Architects & Planners* | **Shanghai World Financial Center** • Kohn Pedersen Fox Associates • *Kohn Pedersen Fox Associates* | **Dancing House** • Gehry Partners • *Pedro Szekely* | **Vancouver Library Square** • Safdie Architects • *Timothy Hursley* | **Rodin Pavilion at Samsung Plaza** • Kohn Pedersen Fox Associates • *Kohn Pedersen Fox Associates* | **Sun Tower** • Morphosis Architects • *Domus, November 1999* | **Organisation for the Prohibition of Chemical Weapons (OPCW World Headquarters)** • KMW Architecture • *KMW Architecture* | **Cheung Kong Center** • Leo A Daly, Cesar Pelli & Associates • *Leo A Daly* | **Tour EDF at La Défense** • Pei Cobb Freed & Partners Architects • *Geraid Morand* | **International School of Beijing** • Perkins + Will • *Perkins + Will* | **Sabanci University** • Cannon Design • *Cannon Design* | **Arcade at Cyberport** • Jerde Partnership • *Jerde Partnership* | **Suvarnabhumi International Airport** •

JAHN • *JAHN* | **Ara Pacis Museum •** Richard Meier and Partners Architects • *Roland Halbe Fotografie* | **Orascom Red Sea Resorts** • Michael Graves and Associates • *Michael Graves and Associates* | **US Embassy** • Moore Ruble Yudell • *Moore Ruble Yudell* | **Canal City Hakata** • Jerde Partnership • *Jerde Partnership* | **Felix Nussbaum Haus** • Studio Daniel Libeskind • *BitterBredt* | **ANZ Stadium** • Populous • *Populous* | **Hypo Alpe-Adria Center •** Morphosis Architects • *Chop Suey Photo* | **Mori Arts Center** • Gluckman Mayner Architects • *Gluckman Mayner Architects* | **Roppongi Hills** • Kohn Pedersen Fox Associates • *Kohn Pedersen Fox Associates* | **Jubilee Church** • Richard Meier and Partners Architects • *Alan Karchmer, Esto* | **Roppongi Hills •** Jerde Partnership • *Jerde Partnership* | **Exaltis Office Tower** • Arquitectonica • *Arquitectonica* | **Camana Bay** • Moore Ruble Yudell • *Moore Ruble Yudell* | **Breitenleerstrasse Housing** • MACK Architect(s) • *MACK Architect(s): Manfred Seidl* | **Star City Hotel and Casino** • Studio Hillier • *Studio Hillier* | **WestEnd City Centre** • Jerde Partnership • *Jerde Partnership* | **Millenium Stadium** • Populous • *Populous* | **Shanghai Museum of Science and Technology** • RTKL • *Tim Griffith, Esto* | **Imperial War Museum North** • Studio Daniel Libeskind • *BitterBredt* | **Kingdom Centre** • AECOM • *AECOM* | **Bayer AG Headquarters •** JAHN • *JAHN* | **Dongbu Financial Center** • Kohn Pedersen Fox Associates • *Kohn Pedersen Fox Associates* | **De Hoftoren** • Kohn Pedersen Fox Associates • *Kohn Pedersen Fox Associates* | **Seoul National University International Vaccine Institute** • Payette • *Payette Associates* | **Two International Finance Centre** • Pelli Clarke Pelli Architects • *Pelli Clarke Pelli Architects* | **Cologne/Bonn Airport Terminal 2 •** JAHN • *JAHN* | **Memorial to the Murdered Jews of Europe** • Eisenman Architects • *Eisenman Architects*

1997–2002

Judenburg West Master Plan • MACK Architect(s) • *MACK Architect(s). Photographer: Manfred Seidl* | **MidCity Place** • Kohn Pedersen Fox Associates • Kohn Pedersen Fox Associates | **International American School of Warsaw** • NELSON H2L2 • *NELSON H2L2* | **Xintiandi** • Studio Shanghai • *Studio Shanghai* | **Kyonggi University Master Plan and Teleconference Center** • Cannon Design • Cannon Design | **US Embassy** • HOK • *E. Gill Lui, 2005* | **Namba Parks** • Jerde Partnership • *Jerde Partnership: Hiroyuki Kawano* | **Museuo Picasso Malaga •** Gluckman Mayner Architects • *Gluckman Mayner Architects* | **US Embassy** • HOK • *E. Gill Lui, 2005* | **Atlantis and The Cove Atlantis at Paradise Island** • Wimberly Allison Tong & Goo • *Wimberly Allison Tong & Goo* | **Housing for the Fishermen of Tyre •** Hashim Sarkis Studios • *Hashim Sarkis Studios* | **Ranger Pavilion** • SITE • *SITE* | **Nanyang Polytechnic** • Gwathmey Siegel Kaufman Architects • *Gwathmey Siegel Kaufman Architects* | **Tango Bo01 Housing Exhibition** • Moore Ruble Yudell • *Moore Ruble Yudell* | **Blur Building** • Diller Scofidio + Renfro • *Diller Scofidio + Renfro* | **Danube House and Nile House in River City** • Kohn Pedersen Fox Associates • *Kohn Pedersen Fox Associates* | **Endesa Headquarters • Kohn Pedersen Fox Associates • Kohn Pedersen Fox Associates | US Consulate Compound** • Zimmer Gunsul Frasca Architects • *Zimmer Gunsul Frasca Architects* | **Cyberport Hotel Office and University** • Arquitectonica • *Arquitectonica* | **Salamanca Train Station** • RTKL • *RTKL* | **City of Culture of Galicia** • Eisenman Architects • *Eisenman Architects* | **Heron Tower •** Kohn Pedersen Fox Associates • *Kohn Pedersen Fox Associates* | **DZ Bank Buliding** • Gehry Partners • *Roland Halbe Fotografie* | **Fine Venture Office Tower** • Zago Architecture • *Zago Architecture* | **Morgan Stanley Headquarters** • Skidmore, Owings & Merrill • *H.G. Esch Photography* | **Ciudad Grupo Santander** • Kevin Roche John Dinkeloo and Associates • *Kevin Roche John Dinkeloo and Associates* | **Suzhou Museum** • I. M. Pei Architect • *Kerun Ip* | **Zlote Tarasy •** Jerde Partnership • *Jerde Partnership* | **Emirates Stadium** • Populous • *Simon Warren* | **Beijing Finance Street •** Skidmore, Owings & Merrill • *Tim Griffith, Esto* | **Samsung Cancer Center •** AECOM • *AECOM* | **Museum of Islamic Art** • I. M. Pei Architect • *Iwan Baan* | **First International Bank of Israel** • Pei Cobb Freed & Partners Architects • *Amit Geron* | **International Commerce Centre** • Kohn Pedersen Fox Associates • *Kohn Pedersen Fox Associates*

2002–2004

Diagonal Mar Entertainment and Retail Center • Robert A.M. Stern Architects • *Abitare, September 2008* | **Torre Almirante** • Robert A.M. Stern Architects • *Projects, March 2005* | **Indian School Of Business Academic Center** • John Portman and Associates • *John Portman and Associates, Michael Portman* | **Mangrove West Coast •** Arquitectonica • *Arquitectonica* | **Highlight Munich Business Towers •** JAHN • *JAHN* | **Langham Place** • Jerde Partnership • *Jerde Partnership: Hiroyuki Kawano* | **Chinese Museum of Film •** RTKL • *RTKL* | **The Wohl Centre •** Studio Daniel Libeskind • *BitterBredt* | **Emirates Palace** • Wimberly Allison Tong & Goo • WATG | **Kanyon** • Jerde Partnership • *Jerde Partnership* | **Torre Espacio** • Pei Cobb Freed & Partners Architects • *Foto Felix* | **US Embassy •** Skidmore, Owings & Merrill • *Tim Hursley* | **Westside Shopping and Leisure Centre** • Studio Daniel Libeskind • *BitterBredt* | **Acropolis Museum** • Bernard Tschumi Architects • *Peter Mauss, Esto* | **China World Trade Center** • Skidmore, Owings & Merrill • *Tim Griffith, Esto* | **Asia Society Hong Kong Center** • Tod Williams Billie Tsien Architects • *Michael Moran, OTTO* | **Knowledge and Innovation Community** • Skidmore, Owings & Merrill • *Tim Griffith* | **American University of Beirut Master Plan •** Machado and Silvetti Associates • *Machado and Silvetti Associates* | **Telenor Headquarters** • NBBJ • *Tim Griffith* | **Apple Store Ginza** • Bohlin Cywinski Jackson • *Koji Okamura* | **Dalki Theme Park** • Slade Architecture • *Slade Architecture* | **Edificio Portico •** Skidmore, Owings & Merrill • *Joe Aker* | **US Embassy Compound** • Sorg Architects • *Sorg Architects* | **The Gate Building** • Gensler • *Gensler* | **US Embassy** • Integrus • *Integrus* | **Madrid Housing** • Morphosis Architects • *Roland Halbe Fotografie* | **US Embassy •** Sorg Architects • *Sorg Architects* | **Beijing Yintai Centre** • John Portman and Associates • *John Portman and Associates, Courtesy of Beijing Yintai Property Company* | **Poly Corporate Headquarters** • Skidmore, Owings & Merrill • *Tim Griffith* | **Normandy American Cemetery New Visitor Center** • SmithGroupJJR • *SmithGroupJJR* | **Royal Ontario Museum** • Studio Daniel Libeskind • *l'Arca, July 2009* | **Beijing Olympics Master Plan** • Sasaki Associates • *Sasaki Associates* | **Yamano Gakuen Complex** • Hodgetts + Fung • *Hodgetts + Fung* | **Kipco Tower** • Kohn Pedersen Fox Associates • *Kohn Pedersen Fox Associates* | **Universidade Agostinho Neto Phase I New Campus** • Perkins + Will • *Perkins + Will* | **Biomuseo** • Gehry Partners • *Monica Mora* | **Zaitunay Bay •** Steven Holl Architects, L.E.FT • *Steven Holl Architects, L.E.FT* | **University of Balamand Female Residence Hall,**

Library Learning Center, School of Engineering and Master Plan • Sasaki Associates • *Sasaki Associates* | **International School** • Studio Hillier • *Studio Hillier* | **Mur Island** • Acconci Studio • *Acconci Studio* | **Tongxian Gatehouse** • Office dA • *NADAAA* | **Hotel Puerta America** • Gluckman Mayner Architects • *Gluckman Mayner Architects* | **Josai School of Management** • studio SUMO • *studio SUMO* | **Shanghai Traditional Chinese Medical University Shuguang Hospital Replacement** • SmithGroupJJR • *SmithGroupJJR* | **Valeo Security Systems** • Davis Brody Bond Architects & Planners • *Davis Brody Bond Architects & Planners* | **Limoges Concert Hall** • Bernard Tschumi Architects • *Peter Mauss, Esto* | **Shenzhen Meteorological Tower** • AECOM • *AECOM* | **American University of Beirut Suliman S. Olayan School of Business** • Machado and Silvetti Associates • *Machado and Silvetti Associates* | **Beirut Exhibition Centre** • L.E.FT • *L.E.FT* | **Linked Hybrid** • Steven Holl Architects • *David Sundberg, Esto* | **Burj Khalifa** • Skidmore, Owings & Merrill • *Francis Dzikowski, Esto* | **Louwman Museum** • Michael Graves and Associates • *Michael Graves and Associates* | **Memorial to the Abolition of Slavery** • Wodiczko + Bonder • *Wodiczko + Bonder* | **Tel Aviv Museum** • Preston Scott Cohen • *Amit Geron* | **Alésia Museum and Archaeological Park** • Bernard Tschumi Architects • *Peter Mauss, Esto* | **Nanjing Sifang Art Museum** • Steven Holl Architects • *Iwan Baan* | **Canadian Museum for Human Rights** • Antoine Predock Architect PC • *Aaron Cohen/CMHR* | **London 2012 Olympic Legacy Communities Scheme** • AECOM • *AECOM* | **Loreto Bay Resort Village** • Duany Plater-Zyberk & Company • *James Hawley* | **Balloon Landing Park** • Hashim Sarkis Studios • *Hashim Sarkis Studios*

2004–2006

Hangil Book House • SHoP • *SHoP* | **Ben Gurion International Airport** • Safdie Architects • *Alan Karchmer, ESTO* | **New Jiang Wan Cultural Center** • RTKL • *RTKL* | **Ministructure No. 16 (BookBar)** • Michael Maltzan Architecture • *Michael Maltzan Architecture* | **Shanghai American School** • Studio Shanghai • *Studio Shanghai* | **Menara Karya Tower** • Arquitectonica • Arquitectonica | **Newspaper Cafe, Jinhua Architecture Park** • Toshiko Mori Architect • *Toshiko Mori Architect* | **International Finance Centre** • Arquitectonica • *Arquitectonica* | **Almaty Financial District–Kazkommertsbank Headquarters** • Skidmore, Owings & Merrill • *Timothy Soar Valency* Archive | **Esentai Tower** • Skidmore, Owings & Merrill • *Timothy Soar Valency Archive* | **Microsoft European Headquarters** • Arquitectonica • *Arquitectonica* | **Zifeng Tower** • Skidmore, Owings & Merrill • *Liu Qihua* | **Wuhan Tiandi** • Studio Shanghai • *Studio Shanghai* | **Chongqing Tiandi** • Studio Shanghai • *Studio Shanghai* | **Cambridge Water Town** • Studio Shanghai • *Studio Shanghai* | **Abdul Aziz Al-Babtain Cultural Waqf Tower** • NBBJ • *Christian Richters* | **Torre de Cristal** • Pelli Clarke Pelli Architects • *Pelli Clarke Pelli Architects* | **Tianjin Global Financial Center** • Skidmore, Owings & Merrill • *Tim Griffith* | **Reflections at Keppel Bay** • Studio Daniel Libeskind • *Courtesy of Keppel Bay Pte Ltd.* | **Palazzo Lombardia** • Pei Cobb Freed & Partners Architects • *Fernando Guerra* | **Atlantis at The Palms** • Wimberly Allison Tong & Goo • *WATG* | **Wellcome Trust Sanger Institute** • NBBJ • *Matt Milios/NBBJ* | **Mahler 4** • Rafael Viñoly Architects • *Rafael Vinoly* | **Yad Vashem Holocaust History Museum** • Safdie Architects • *Timothy Harley* | **MegaBox** • Jerde Partnership • *Jerde Partnership* | **Sanlitun North** • LOT-EK • *LOT-EK* | **Songdo International Business District and Convensia Convention Center** • Kohn Pedersen Fox Associates • *Kohn Pedersen Fox Associates* | **The Sail at Marina Bay** • NBBJ • *Tim Griffith* | **City of Dreams** • Arquitectonica • *Arquitectonica* | **Xi'an City Gateway** • Goettsch Partners • *Goettsch Partners* | **Herning Museum of Contemporary Art** • Steven Holl Architects • *Iwan Baan* | **The Gate Towers, Sun Tower and Sky Tower** • Arquitectonica • *Arquitectonica* | **Bitexco Financial Tower** • Carlos Zapata Studio • *Carlos Zapata Studio* | **China Huaneng Group Headquarters** • Kohn Pedersen Fox Associates • *Kohn Pedersen Fox Associates* | **Kerry Parkside Towers** • Kohn Pedersen Fox Associates • *Kohn Pedersen Fox Associates* | **City of Capitals** • NBBJ • *Tim Griffith* | **Arcapita Bank Headquarters** • Skidmore, Owings & Merrill • *SOM Archives* | **Giant Interactive Group Corporate Headquarters** • Morphosis Architects • *Iwan Baan* | **Al Hamra Tower** • Skidmore, Owings & Merrill • *Hedrick Blessing* | **Hysan Place** • Kohn Pedersen Fox Associates • *Kohn Pedersen Fox Associates* | **Win Sing AIT Residential Towers** • Moore Ruble Yudell • *Moore Ruble Yudell* | **Cayan [Infinity] Tower** • Skidmore, Owings & Merrill • *SOM Archives* | **Tata Consultancy Services** • Tod Williams Billie Tsien Architects • *Michael Moran, OTTO* | **798 Arts District Vision Plan** • Sasaki Associates • *Sasaki Associates* | **Changi International Airport Terminal 2** • Gensler • *Gensler* | **Pan-Gyo Housing** • MACK Architect(s) • *MACK Architect(s)* | **China Science and Technology Museum** • RTKL • *RTKL* | **Dolce Vita Tejo Mall** • RTKL • *RTKL* | **Soccer City (FNB Stadium)** • Populous • *Mike Schumker* | **Vanke Center (Horizontal Skyscraper)** • Steven Holl Architects • *Iwan Baan* | **Cultural Center** • Bernard Tschumi Architects • Mark, April 2011 | **Agricultural Bank of China + Construction Bank of China** • Arquitectonica • Arquitectonica | **Jack Nicklaus Golf Club of Korea** • Cannon Design (Yazdani Studio) • *Cannon Design (Yazdani Studio)* | **O-14 Tower** • RUR Architecture PC • *RUR Architecture PC* | **Tata Medical Centre Cancer Hospital** • Cannon Design • *Cannon Design* | **VanDusen Botanical Garden Visitor Centre** • Perkins + Will • *Perkins + Will* | **Princess Nora Bint Abdulrahman University** • Perkins + Will • *Perkins + Will* | **London Olympic Stadium** • Populous • *Getty Images* | **US Embassy** • Sorg Architects • *Sorg Architects* | **Zhengzhou Greenland Plaza** • Skidmore, Owings & Merrill • *Si-ye Zhang* | **JW Marriott Hotel** • Carlos Zapata Studio • *Carlos Zapata Studio* | **Leatop Plaza** • JAHN • *JAHN* | **Lingnan Tiandi** • Studio Shanghai • *Studio Shanghai* | **Pearl River Tower** • Skidmore, Owings & Merrill • *Tim Griffith* | **SIP Hengyu International Center** • Goettsch Partners • *Goettsch Partners* | **The Nile Corniche** • Michael Graves and Associates • *Michael Graves and Associates* | **Shanghai Tower** • Gensler • *Gensler* | **Phare Tower** • Morphosis Architects • *Morphosis Architects* | **Al Waab City** • AECOM • *AECOM*

2006–2014

Dubai Festival Waterfront Centre • Jerde Partnership • *Jerde Partnership* | **Dubai Marina** • HOK • *HOK* | **Rohm and Haas China** • Studio Hillier • *Studio Hillier* | **Abercrombie and Fitch Flagship Store** • Selldorf Architects • *Selldorf Architects* | **Barbie Shanghai Flagship Store** • Slade Architecture • *Slade Architecture* | **Yas Viceroy Abu Dhabi Hotel** • Asymptote Architecture • *Asymptote Architecture* | **Apple Store Covent Garden** • Bohlin Cywinski Jackson • *Peter Aaron, OTTO* | **Apple Store Opéra** • Bohlin Cywinski Jackson •

Roy Zipstein | **Aviva Stadium** • Populous • *Chris Gascoigne, Walker Photography* | **Convention Centre Dublin** • Kevin Roche John Dinkeloo and Associates • *Kevin Roche John Dinkeloo and Associates* | **US Embassy** • Integrus • *Integrus* | **Iberdrola Tower** • Pelli Clarke Pelli Architects • *Jeff Goldberg, ESTO* | **Shanghai International Finance Center** • Pelli Clarke Pelli Architects • *Pelli Clarke Pelli Architects* | **Capitaland Raffles City (Sliced Porosity Block)** • Steven Holl Architects • *Iwan Baan* | **Taiyuan Museum** • Preston Scott Cohen • *Iwan Baan* | **The Avenues—Phase III** • Gensler • *Nick Merrick Hedrich Blessing, PACE* | **Torre Begonias** • Arquitectonica • *Arquitectonica* | **Tour Carpe Diem** • Robert A.M. Stern Architects • *Peter Aaron, OTTO* | **Baku Flame Towers** • HOK • *HOK* | **Chennai International Airport Domestic and International Terminals** • Gensler • *Gensler* | **Guggenheim Museum** • Gehry Partners • *The Architectural Review, March 2007* | **American University in Cairo New Campus** • Sasaki Associates • *Metropolis, August/September 2003* | **Art Gallery of Ontario** • Gehry Partners • *Iwan Baan* | **Charles Hostler Student Center** • VJAA • *VJAA* | **Louis Dreyfus Grande Armée** • STUDIOS Architecture • *STUDIOS Architecture* | **Sanlitun** • SHoP • *SHoP* | **Ventura Corporate Towers** • Kohn Pedersen Fox Associates • *Projecto, August 2009* | **Salim Publishing House** • Stan Allen Architect • *Stan Allen Architect* | **Butaro District Hospital** • MASS Design Group • *Iwan Baan* | **Chengdu Skycourts** • Höweler + Yoon Architecture • *Höweler + Yoon Architecture* | **Antilia House** • Perkins + Will • *Fram Petit* | **OCT Shenzhen Clubhouse** • Richard Meier and Partners Architects • *Roland Halbe Fotografie* | **Campus for Research Excellence and Technological Enterprise University Centre** • Perkins + Will • *Perkins + Will* | **Centro de Artes Nadir Afonso Museum** • Louise Braverman, Architect • *Louise Braverman, Architect* | **Taekwondo Park** • WEISS/MANFREDI Architecture/Landscape/Urbanism • *WEISS/MANFREDI Architecture/Landscape/Urbanism* | **Lotte World Tower** • Kohn Pedersen Fox Associates • *Kohn Pedersen Fox Associates* | **NATO Headquarters** • Skidmore, Owings & Merrill • *SOM* | **Chongqing International Trade and Commerce Center** • Kohn Pedersen Fox Associates • *Kohn Pedersen Fox Associates* | **Datong Library** • Preston Scott Cohen • *Preston Scott Cohen* | **Masdar Headquarters** • Adrian Smith + Gordon Gill Architecture • *Adrian Smith + Gordon Gill Architecture* | **Carrasco International Airport** • Rafael Viñoly Architects • *Rafael Vinoly* | **Fortabat Collection** • Rafael Viñoly Architects • *Rafael Vinoly* | **Novartis Pharma A.G. Campus** • Gehry Partners • *clauss markisen projekt GmbH* | **Philip Lim Store** • Leong Leong • *Leong Leong* | **Apple Store IFC Pudong** • Bohlin Cywinski Jackson • *Roy Zipstein* | **Vakko Headquarters and Power Media Center** • REX Architecture • *REX Architecture* | **Naked Stables** • Studio Shanghai • *Studio Shanghai* | **Umubano School** • MASS Design Group • *Iwan Baan* | **White Block Gallery** • SsD • *SsD* | **Mizuta Museum Of Art** • studio SUMO • *studio SUMO* | **National University of Ireland, Galway Research Bundle** • Payette • *Payette Associates* | **Sochi Olympic Stadium** • Populous • *Populous* | **University of Melbourne Faculty of Architecture, Building and Planning** • John Wardle Architects, NADAAA • *John Wardle Architects, NADAAA* | **Heart of Lake** • Robert A.M. Stern Architects • *Robert A.M. Stern Architects* | **Firestation and Youth Center (ASCO)** • ORG Organization For Permanent Modernity • *ORG Organization For Permanent Modernity* | **Museum of Image and Sound** • Diller Scofidio + Renfro • *Diller Scofidio + Renfro* | **Guangzhou CTF Finance Centre** • Kohn Pedersen Fox Associates • *Kohn Pedersen Fox Associates* | **Abu Dhabi National Oil Company Headquarters** • HOK • *HOK* | **Capital Market Authority Tower** • HOK • *HOK* | **King Abdullah Financial District** • FXFOWLE Architects • *FXFOWLE Architects* | **Lali Gurans Orphanage and Learning Centre** • MOS Architects • *MOS Architects* | **Singapore University of Technology and Design Master Plan** • Sasaki Associates • *Sasaki Associates* | **APAP Open School** • LOT-EK • *Kim Myoung-Sik* | **Krabbesholm Hojskole Studios** • MOS Architects • *MOS Architects* | **Kukje Art Center** • SO-IL • *SO-IL* | **Samsung Model Home Gallery** • NADAAA • *NADAAA* | **Al Maryah Island Vision Plan** • over,under, Utile • *over,under* | **IBA Soft House** • KVA matx • *KVA matx* | **MIDEA VIP and Golf Clubhouse** • RTKL • *RTKL* | **Jaipur Residential Development** • STUDIOS Architecture • *STUDIOS Architecture* | **Worldmark Development at Indira Ghandi International Airport** • Kohn Pedersen Fox Associates • *Kohn Pedersen Fox Associates* | Kingdom Tower • Adrian Smith + Gordon Gill Architecture • *Adrian Smith + Gordon Gill Architecture* | **US Embassy Office Annex** • HOK • *Alan Karchmer, ESTO* | **Botswana Innovation Hub** • SHoP • *SHoP* | Kempegowda International Airport • HOK • *HOK* | **Tri-Climatic Biosphere** • LEESER Architecture • *LEESER Architecture* | **US Embassy** • KieranTimberlake • *KieranTimberlake* | **50 Connaught Road Central** • Robert A.M. Stern Architects • *Robert A.M. Stern Architects* | **Khalsa Heritage Centre** • Safdie Architects • *Ram Rahman* | **Konoha Eco-Mall** • Jerde Partnership • *Jerde Partnership* | **Marina Bay Sands Integrated Resort** • Safdie Architects • *Timothy Hurley* | **Butaro Doctors' Housing** • MASS Design Group • *Iwan Baan* | **Village Housing Works Staff Residence** • Louise Braverman, Architect • *Iwan Baan* | **Tianfu Ecological City** • Adrian Smith + Gordon Gill Architecture • *Adrian Smith + Gordon Gill Architecture* | **Byblos Town Hall** • Hashim Sarkis Studios • *Hashim Sarkis Studios* | **Konza Technology Pavilion** • SHoP • *SHoP* | **New Holland Island Master Plan and Cultural Center** • WORKac • *WORKac* | **World One** • Pei Cobb Freed & Partners Architects • *Pei Cobb Freed & Partners Architects* | **GHESKIO Cholera Treament Center** • MASS Design Group • *MASS Design Group* | **L'Assemblée Radiuese Conference Center** • WORKac • *WORKac* | **Sanhe School** • OBRA Architects • *OBRA Architects* | **Songpa Micro-Housing** • SsD • *SsD* | **Songzhuang Arts and Agriculture City** • Sasaki Associates • *Sasaki Associates* | **Sowwah Square** • Goettsch Partners • *Goettsch Partners* | **Tsing Tao Pearl Visitor Center** • Bohlin Cywinski Jackson • *Bohlin Cywinski Jackson* | **WATERBANKSchool** • ATOPIA • ATOPIA | **WATERBANK Canteen** • ATOPIA • ATOPIA | **WATERBANKDormitory** • ATOPIA • ATOPIA | **PITCHKenya Stadium** • ATOPIA • ATOPIA | **Sinthian Cultural Center** • Toshiko Mori Architect • Toshiko Mori Architect | **One Horizon Center** • Robert A.M. Stern Architects • Architecture and Design, December 2012 | **Education City** • Antoine Predock Architect PC • *Antoine Predock Architect PC* | **Chhatrapati Shivaji International Airport Terminal 2** • Skidmore, Owings & Merrill • *Robert Polidori*

OFFICE*US*
US Pavilion, 14th International Architecture Exhibition – la Biennale di Venezia

Commissioner
Storefront for Art and Architecture

Curators
Eva Franch i Gilabert, Ana Miljački, Ashley Schafer

Associate Curator
Michael Kubo

Assistant Curators
Carlos Mínguez Carrasco, Jacob Reidel

Co-Organizer
PRAXIS

Exhibition Design
LEONG LEONG: Dominic Leong, Chris Leong, Gabriel Burkett; Jackie Woon Bae, Clare Johnston, Yu-Hsiang Lin, Jane Jonghyun Yi

Graphic Design
Pentagram: Natasha Jen, Jeffrey Waldman; Justin Chen, Jang Hyun Han, Oeun Kwon, Yenwei Liu, Lucia del Zotto

Technology Architecture
CASE

Office*US* Partners
Arielle Assouline-Lichten, Cooking Sections: Daniel Fernández Pasqual, Alon Schwabe, Matteo Ghidoni, M-A-U-S-E-R: Mona Mahall, Asli Serbest, Curtis Roth, Manuel Shvarzberg Carió

Global Network Strategy
Therrien-Barley

Media Producer
Andrew Fierberg

Web Design
M-A-U-S-E-R; Partner & Partners

Publishing Partner
Lars Müller Publishers

Media Partner
Architizer

Project Coordinator
Irina Chernyakova

Research Coordinator
Juan Jofre

Development, External Relations and Special Events
Kara L. Meyer

Technology and Production Coordinator
Piotr Chizinski

Outreach and Communications Manager
Zeynep Göksel

Project Assistants
Natalie Snyder, Melissa Weisberg

Austin E. Knowlton School at The Ohio State University
Laila Ammar, Levi Bedall, Tyler Brozovich, Joe Carifa, Nicholas Castillo, Luke Dougal, Clay Ellerbrook, Abdelrahman Elzamly, Talia Friedman, Chris Mannella, Nicholas Miller, Dustin Page, Darren Spensiero, Alexander Stagge, Jacqueline Stern, Jianning Zhong, Michael Zumpano

MIT Department of Architecture
Kyle Barker, Christianna Bonin, Kyle Coburn, Nathan Friedman, Sam Ghantous, Anastasia Hiller, Jessica Jorge, Karen Kitayama, Gabriel Kozlowski, Jasmine Kwak, Patrick Evan Little, Ann Lok Lui, Moojin Park, Austin Smith, Tyler Stevermer, Evelyn Ting, Michael Waldrep, Sarah Weir, Natthida Wiwatwicha, Rixt Woudstra, Wenfei Xu *Support:* Daniel Chang, Kristina Eldrenkamp, Nicolo Guida, Lee Moreau, David Oliver, Chiranit Prateepasen, Claire Shafer, Trygve Wastvedt

PRAXIS
Amanda Reeser Lawrence, Margaret Arbanas, Andrew Colopy, Megan Miller, Fred Tang, Irina Verona

Storefront for Art and Architecture
Silvia Callegari, Tyrene Calvesbert, Maria Castro, Diandra Cohen, Ian Costello, Erica Angel Fernandez de Soto, Ashely Kuto, Francesca Lantieri, Itzel Lavanderos, Charlene Liang, Anu Lill, Yuma Shinohara, Michael Signorile, Zaina Soueid, Melody Stein, Elise Stella, Mario Torres

Project Advisors
Laurie Beckleman, Aaron Betsky, Holly Block, Beatriz Colomina, Keller Easterling, Campbell Hyers, Cathy Lang Ho, James von Klemperer, Marc Kushner, Lars Müller, Douglass Rice, Bob Rubin, Sylvia J. Smith, Lisa Phillips, Artur Walther, Sarah Whiting, Karen Wong

Special Thanks
Peter Aaron, Zahra Ali Baba, Dana Aljoud`er, Jordan Anderson, Alan I. Appel, Iwan Baan, Chiara Barbieri, Cecil Barnes, Roberta Bartalone, Cameron Blaylock, Barry Beagan, Brett Beyer, Gary Boyd, Roy Brand, Beth Broome, Bryan Cave LLP: Alan Appel, Greg Galvin, Nicole Gates, Robert Lancaster, Margery Perlmutter, Stefan Skulesch; Michael Cadwell, Rebecca Chamberlain, Alan Cross, Nicholas de Moncheaux, Giacomo DiThiene, Patricia Driscoll, Ignacio Peydro Duclos, Ellen Finnie Duranceau, Nazareth Ekmakijan, Igor Ekštajn, Rami el Samahy, Britt Eversole, Alia Farid, Enrico Fontanari, Christine Foushee, Frener & Reifer: Thomas Geissler, Michael Purzer; Miles Fujiki, Curt Gambetta, Emil Rodriguez Garabot, Roland Halbe, Jim Harrington, Sarah Herda, Dessen Hillman, Adam Himes, Margaret Ho, Yasmina Khan, Duncan Kincaid, Ryan John King, Arianne Kouri, Naho Kubota, Ricardo Leon, Neil Levine, Nicolò Lewanski, Rungu Lin, Rob Livesey, Hannah Loomis, George Louras, Elizabeth Gill Lui, Sebastian Lux, Richard Mandelkorn, Mark Jarzombek, Sandro Marpillero, Melissa Marsh, Jack Masey, Lorrie A. McAllister, Brendan McGetrick, Cathleen McGuigan, John McLaughlin, Franco Micucci, Antoni Muntadas, Hansrobyn van Oosten, Saverio Panata & Silvia Zini, Janet Parks, Partner & Partners: Greg Mihalko, Zach Mihalko, David Liss; Beverly Payeff-Masey, Ivan Rašković, Bika Rebek, Karl Roarty, Julian Rose, Marco Ariso Rota, Ryan Rothman, Joel Sanders, Adèle Naudé Santos, Kelly Schein, Ori Scialom, Neslihan Sen, Karin Šerman, Douglas Sershen, Sarah Sherman, Tarek Shuaib, Amber Sinicrope, Monica Socorro, Erica Stoller, Hicks Stone, Sam Sweezy, Nader Tehrani, Wayne Thom, Dicle Uzunyayla, Gary Van Zante, Ana Cristina Vargas, Davi Weber, Ann Whiteside, Mark Wigley, Jaren Wilcoxson, Mark Young, Ines Zalduendo

Office*US* Sponsors
Austin E. Knowlton School of Architecture
at the Ohio State University
Autodesk *Creative Partner*
Bureau of Educational and Cultural Affairs,
US Department of State
Herman Miller *Creative Partner*
Peggy Guggenheim Collection, Venice
(Solomon R. Guggenheim Foundation, New York)
The Massachusetts Institute of Technology,
Department of Architecture

Office*US* Supporter
AECOM
Arup
Esto
Graham Foundation for Advanced Studies in the Fine Arts
Hewlett Packard | AMD
Kohn Pedersen Fox Associates (KPF)
Reggiani S.p.A. Illuminazione

Office*US* Benefactor
American Apparel
Elise Jaffe and Jeffrey Brown
Frederick Iseman
FXFOWLE Architects
MakerBot
Oldcastle BuildingEnvelope
Robert Melvin Rubin and Stéphane Samuel
Skidmore, Owings & Merrill LLP
Walther Family Foundation

Office*US* Leader
Arthur H. Schein Memorial Fund
JAHN

Office*US* Contributor
Cornell University
Dreamair
Lanny and Sharon Martin
OTTO Archive
RTKL
The University of San Diego

Office*US* Patron
Charles Renfro
Control Group
Harman
Iwan Baan
Michael A. Manfredi and Marion Weiss
Peter Aaron
Prolitec
RD RICE Construction Inc.
The American Institute of Architects

Office*US* Circle
Acción Cultural Española
Adrian Smith + Gordon Gill Architecture
Barbara Jakobson
Beth Rudin DeWoody
David and Jane Walentas
Daniel and Estrellita Brodsky
Elizabeth Gill Lui
Eva Ching and Jeff Small
Frederieke Taylor
Knowlton School Alumni Society
Lauren Kogod and David Smiley
Richard Mishaan Design
Roland Halbe
Todd DeGarmo
Toshiko Mori Architect PLLC

Office*US* Friends
American Printing Company
Belmont Freeman
Carlos Brillembourg and Karin Waisman
Claudia Gould
C & M Shade Corporation
Glenn Horowitz
Holly Block
Illy
Jinhee Park + John Hong, SsD
Karen Wong
Linda and Harry Macklowe
Mabel Wilson
Margery Perlmutter
NRI (National Reprographics Inc.)
Sara P. Meltzer
Soho Art Materials
Steven T. Incontro and David Joselit
The Henry Ford
Vram Malek

This project is commissioned by Storefront for Art and Architecture, on behalf of the U.S. Department of State's Bureau of Educational and Cultural Affairs

Storefront for Art and Architecture

Founded in 1982, Storefront for Art and Architecture is a nonprofit organization committed to the advancement of innovative positions in architecture, art and design. Our program of exhibitions, artists talks, film screenings, conferences and publications is intended to generate dialogue and collaboration across geographic, ideological and disciplinary boundaries. As a public forum for emerging voices, Storefront explores vital issues in art and architecture with the intent of increasing awareness of and interest in contemporary design.
www.storefrontnews.org